THE
COLLECTED
JACK
LONDON

THE COLLECTED JACK LONDON

Thirty-Six Stories
Four Complete Novels
A Memoir

EDITED BY STEVEN J. KASDIN

BARNES & NOBLE BOOKS
NEW YORK

This edition published by Barnes & Noble, Inc.

1992 Barnes & Noble Books

ISBN 0-88029-596-1 *casebound*
ISBN 1-56619-602-7 *leatherbound*

Printed and bound in the United States of America

MC 9 8
ML 9 8 7 6 5 4 3 2 1

A Note on This Edition

FROM his first story-collection in 1900, until his death in 1916, Jack London published fifty books, including novels, stories, essays, social criticism, memoirs, letters and a play; an average of three books a year. Not only was he the most popular writer of his day—the first millionaire writer in history—he is still one of the bestselling American authors in the world. Yet less than half—twenty-one—of his books are still in print.

While there is no single complete collection of his works, anthologies abound. Most, unfortunately, are severely limited, generally concentrating on but a single aspect of London's prolific career.

In this edition, we are attempting to present not a complete view, but rather a well-rounded one: who Jack London was, his concerns, what he wrote about, what he thought, what he believed in. These stories have been exciting and delighting readers for nearly a century and will continue to do so as long as people crave great adventure.

Introduction

A MAN of fierce contradictions, Jack London was a believer in both Socialism and Social Darwinism. He followed both Marx and Nietzche, but held one philosophy above all others: Live life to the fullest! His life and work belong to that uniquely American tradition of the artist as a man of action. Like Melville and Twain before him, and Hemingway and Kerouac who followed, London was never content to write about the adventures of others—to him, firsthand experience was the only basis for art. One simply cannot picture him as a parlor sophisticate or boulevard dandy like his European contemporaries; the search for new experiences, adventures, and sensations was what drove him.

A sailor, laborer, oyster pirate, fish and game warden, tramp, gold prospector, soap-box orator, war correspondent, rancher, bohemian—all these hats he wore and more—yet still he wrote a thousand words a day for sixteen years, his entire professional life. The hardships of his early years, it seems, had instilled in him both discipline and a strong work ethic.

The story of his life is, of course, legend: a childhood of hopeless poverty, a spectacular and controversial rise, wealth and international fame, disillusion and an early death. It was a mirror of other success stories of the time, yet unique. London was a man of intense contradictions that could never be reconciled. For all his democratic and socialist ideals about the equality of man, he embraced Nietzsche's writings on the "Superman," and, in fact, considered himself one. For all his anti-capitalist rhetoric, he sought and achieved great personal wealth, spent it all, and was often broke. For all his uncompromising artistic vision, he would sometimes send substandard works to the popular magazines for extra money. London was more than aware of these glaring inconsistencies in his character; he believed they made him a better, more-rounded writer.

He grew up in a family that was always poor, often destitute. His stepfather, John London, tried his hand at farming, ranching, selling groceries, and failed at everything he tried. Jack quit school at thirteen to work, spending two years in a cannery, fourteen hours a day, for ten cents an hour. At fifteen he borrowed enough money to buy a small boat, the "Razzle Dazzle," and became an oyster pirate, raiding privately owned oyster beds on lower San Francisco Bay with a young female first-mate named Mamie who apparently came with the price of the boat. He soon joined the California Fish and Game Patrol, pursuing his former cohorts around the Bay as he had once been chased. Drinking and fighting through the waterfront saloons, he listened to the sailors' stories of ocean voyages, and at seventeen he shipped out on a sealing vessel. A year later he was back, hopping trains across the country, living the road-life of a hobo.

Up to this time he seemed no different from most young men of his class, destined to hard labor and poverty. What happened to London to set him apart was a discovery: a discovery of knowledge and ideas, a discovery of his own insatiable curiosity. With the help of a local librarian he began reading, finding a world he had never known existed: that of the mind. He finished high school, began college at Berkeley, became politically aware, and joined the Socialist Party. He was beginning to understand that it was better to make a living with his mind than from manual labor.

However, he needed one last reminder. In 1897 he joined the gold rush to the Klondike. He found no gold, but returned with a determination to tell others what he had seen, heard, and lived. He became a writer. In less than a decade he was as famous as anyone in the world.

The period in which Jack London lived and wrote was a transitional one for America: post Victorian, post "Gilded Age," yet pre "Modernist." It was the time between the Spanish-American War and World War I, when America was leaving its childhood behind, flexing its muscles, building its empire and stepping to the forefront of world affairs. Anything, it seemed, was possible. It was the age of Teddy Roosevelt and Emma Goldman, Rockefeller and the Wobblies, "Little Women" and . . . *Call of the Wild.*

Perhaps most importantly, it was the age of William Hearst and D.W. Griffith, the dawn of mass media and the shared experience—and Jack London was one of its stars. He was, as stated, the first millionaire writer (or artist of any kind, for that matter), and his popularity with the masses eclipsed even that of Twain. Not only his work, but his travels, exploits, politics, and divorce were national news. London went from being a pure product of his generation to a representative of its beliefs, values, and possibilites.

This opening-up of America was not, however, represented in its popular literature. When London began writing, most readers were middle-class women who wanted uplifting stories that reflected their own lifestyles of picnics and parlor courting. Anethema was the harsh, brutal underside of life that was commonplace in many American lives. Or so it was decreed by that great arbiter of literary taste, the *Atlantic Monthly* magazine. For a whole generation *Little Women* was as literature should be. At least until London's stories began appearing.

Through public education the masses were beginning to read, and Jack London belonged to them. He wrote of their lives and their dreams. His brauny tales reflected not only their reality, but their fantasies as well. By contrasting life's harshness with its beauty, violence with love, individual determination with overwhelming adversity, the stories touched readers in a way only truth-in-art can.

In order to best understand the range of London's experiences and the way in which he incorporated them into his fiction, we are including into each section a sample of non-fiction; reminiscences of his own true adventures within the environments he made famous in his stories and novels. To see the way he used factual events as a starting point for creative interpretation, we are allowed a unique glimpse of both London's artistic process and the man himself.

CONTENTS

THE SEA

THE NORTH

The North

The Klondike tales, both stories and novels, were what brought London his initial literary fame. The people he wrote about—mountain men, prospectors, the Indians and Eskimos—had rarely been portrayed accurately in fiction before. London took a remote, foreign environment, infused it with his own energy, and presented honestly its harshness and brutality. The violence and beauty brought an immediacy that continues to grip readers the world over.

London spent only eight months along the Yukon river during the great gold rush, between the fall of 1897 and spring of 1898. Most of that time was spent snowbound in a remote cabin and in the saloons of Dawson, not digging for gold. But London was a good listener and persuaded those he met to open up to him. He listened to the legends the Indians told, the drunken tales and bragging of the old-timers, and the dreams of the newcomers who were hoping to strike it rich. Many of his stories were true, or were at least claimed to be when relayed to him. And, too, many of his fictional characters were directly based on people he knew; often he didn't even change their names.

But most of his stories came directly from his own imagination; secondhand stories, rumors, and the environment itself served merely as a backdrop. His great characters as well—Malamute Kid, Sitka Charley the Indian, the wandering priest Father Roubeau—were composites of people he had known and heard about. The Malamute Kid, in particular, seems to have embodied for London all the attributes of the Great Northern Man. He is skilled, adventuresome, intelligent, honest, a good friend and partner.

Perhaps London's greatest accomplishment, a talent he was to nurture and draw upon throughout his career, was his genius for bringing a landscape to life. The "white silence," as he termed the northland with its endless snow fields, was as much a state of mind as a physical environment. It was a place where man is humbled in the face of nature, where ". . . man becomes timid, affrighted at the sound of his own voice." Nature to London, is enveloping, awesome, and stubbornly resistant to man's attempts to dominate.

To Build a Fire

Day had broken cold and gray, exceedingly cold and gray, when the man turned aside from the main Yukon trail and climbed the high earth-bank, where a dim and little-travelled trail led eastward through the fat spruce timberland. It was a steep bank, and he paused for breath at the top, excusing the act to himself by looking at his watch. It was nine o'clock. There was no sun nor hint of sun, though there was not a cloud in the sky. It was a clear day, and yet there seemed an intangible pall over the face of things, a subtle gloom that made the day dark, and that was due to the absence of sun. This fact did not worry the man. He was used to the lack of sun. It had been days since he had seen the sun, and he knew that a few more days must pass before that cheerful orb, due south, would just peep above the sky line and dip immediately from view.

The man flung a look back along the way he had come. The Yukon lay a mile wide and hidden under three feet of ice. On top of this ice were as many feet of snow. It was all pure white, rolling in gentle undulations where the ice jams of the freeze-up had formed. North and south, as far as his eye could see, it was unbroken white, save for a dark hairline that curved and twisted from around the spruce-covered island to the south, and that curved and twisted away into the north, where it disappeared behind another spruce-covered island. This dark hairline was the trail—the main trail—that led south five hundred miles to the Chilcoot Pass, Dyea, and salt water; and that led north seventy miles to Dawson, and still on to the north a thousand miles to Nulato, and finally to St. Michael, on Bering Sea, a thousand miles and half a thousand more.

But all this—this mysterious, far-reaching hairline trail, the absence of sun from the sky, the tremendous cold, and the strangeness and weirdness of it all—made no impression on the man. It was not because he was long used to it. He was a newcomer in the land, a *chechaquo,* and this was his first winter. The trouble with him was that he was without imagination. He was quick and alert in the things of life, but only in the things, and not in the significances. Fifty degrees below zero meant eighty-odd degrees of frost. Such fact impressed him as being cold and uncomfortable, and that was all. It did not lead him to meditate upon his frailty as a creature of temperature, and upon man's frailty in general, able only to live within certain narrow limits of heat and cold; and from there on it did not lead him to the conjectural field of immortality and man's place in the universe. Fifty degrees below zero stood for a bite of frost that hurt and that must be guarded against by the use of mittens, ear flaps, warm moccasins, and thick socks. Fifty degrees below zero was to him just precisely fifty degrees below zero. That there should be anything more to it than that was a thought that never entered his head.

As he turned to go, he spat speculatively. There was a sharp, explosive crackle that startled him. He spat again. And again, in the air, before it could fall to the snow, the spittle crackled. He knew that at fifty below spittle crackled on the snow, but this spittle had crackled in the air. Undoubtedly it was colder than fifty below—how much colder he did not know. But the temperature did not matter. He was bound for the old claim on the left fork of Henderson Creek, where the boys were already. They had come over across the divide from the Indian Creek country, while he had come the roundabout way to take a look at the possibilities of getting out logs in the spring from the islands in the Yukon. He would be in to camp by six o'clock; a bit after dark, it was true, but the boys would be there, a fire would be going, and a hot supper would be ready. As for lunch, he pressed his hand against the protruding bundle under his jacket. It was also under his shirt, wrapped up in a handkerchief and lying against the naked skin. It was the only way to keep the biscuits from freezing. He smiled agreeably to himself as he thought of those biscuits, each cut open and sopped in bacon grease, and each enclosing a generous slice of fried bacon.

He plunged in among the big spruce trees. The trail was faint. A foot of snow had fallen since the last sled had passed over, and he was glad he was without a sled, travelling light. In fact, he carried nothing but the lunch wrapped in the handkerchief. He was surprised, however, at the cold. It certainly was cold, he concluded, as he rubbed his numb nose and cheekbones with his mittened hand. He was a warm-whiskered man, but the hair on his face did not protect the high cheek-bones and the eager nose that thrust itself aggressively into the frosty air.

At the man's heels trotted a dog, a big native husky, the proper wolf dog, gray-coated and without any visible or temperamental difference from its brother, the wild wolf. The animal was depressed by the tremendous cold. It knew that it was no time for travelling. Its instinct told it a truer tale than was told to the man by the man's judgment. In reality, it was not merely colder than fifty below zero; it was colder than sixty below, than seventy below. It was seventy-five below zero. Since the freezing point is thirty-two above zero, it meant that one hundred and seven degrees of frost obtained. The dog did not know anything about thermometers. Possibly in its brain there was no sharp consciousness of a condition of very cold such as was in the man's brain. But the brute had its instinct. It experienced a vague but menacing apprehension that subdued it and made it slink along at the man's heels, and that made it question eagerly every unwonted movement of the man as if expecting him to go into camp or to seek shelter somewhere and build a fire. The dog had learned fire, and it wanted fire, or else to burrow under the snow and cuddle its warmth away from the air.

The frozen moisture of its breathing had settled on its fur in a fine powder of frost, and especially were its jowls, muzzle and eyelashes whitened by its crystalled breath. The man's red beard and mustache were likewise frosted, but more solidly, the deposit taking the form of ice and increasing with every warm, moist breath he exhaled. Also, the man was chewing tobacco, and the muzzle of ice held his lips so rigidly that he was unable to clear his chin when he expelled the juice. The result was that a crystal beard of the color and solidity of amber was increasing its length on his chin. If he fell down it would shattter itself, like glass, into brittle fragments. But he did not mind the appendage. It was the penalty all tobacco chewers paid in that country, and he had been out before in two cold snaps. They had not been so cold as this, but by the spirit thermometer at Sixty Mile he knew that they had been registered at fifty below and at fifty-five.

He held on through the level stretch of woods for several miles, crossed a wide flat of nigger heads, and dropped down a bank to the frozen bed of a small stream. This was Henderson Creek, and he knew he was ten miles from the forks. He looked at his watch. It was ten o'clock. He was making four miles an hour, and he calculated that he would arrive at the forks at half-past twelve. He decided to celebrate that event by eating his lunch there.

The dog dropped in again at his heels, with a tail drooping discouragement, as the man swung along the creek bed. The furrow of the old sled trail was plainly visible, but a dozen inches of snow covered the marks of the last runners. In a month no man had come up or down that silent creek. The man held steadily on. He was not much given to thinking, and just then particularly he had nothing to think about save that he would eat lunch at the forks and that at six o'clock he would be in camp with the boys. There was nobody to talk to; and, had there been, speech would have been impossible because of the ice muzzle on his mouth. So he continued monotonously to chew tobacco and to increase the length of his amber beard.

Once in a while the thought reiterated itself that it was very cold and that he had never experienced such cold. As he walked along he rubbed his cheekbones and nose with the back of his mittened hand. He did this automatically, now and again changing hands. But, rub as he would, the instant he stopped his cheekbones went numb, and the following instant the end of his nose went numb. He was sure to frost his cheeks; he knew that, and experienced a pang of regret that he had not devised a nose strap of the sort Bud wore in cold snaps. Such a strap passed across the cheeks, as well, and saved them. But it didn't matter much, after all. What were frosted cheeks? A bit painful, that was all; they were never serious.

Empty as the man's mind was of thoughts, he was keenly observant, and he noticed the changes in the creek, the curves and bends and timber jams, and always he sharply noted where he placed his feet. Once, coming around a bend he shied abruptly, like a startled horse, curved away from the place where he had been walking, and retreated several paces back along the trail. The creek he knew was frozen clear to the bottom—no creek could contain water in that arctic winter—but he knew also that there were springs that bubbled out from the hillsides and ran along under the snow and on top the ice of the creek. He knew that the coldest snaps never froze these springs, and he knew likewise their danger. They were traps. They hid pools of water under the snow that might be three inches deep, or three feet. Sometimes a skin of ice half an inch thick covered them, and in turn was covered by the snow. Sometimes there were alternate layers of water and ice skin, so that when one broke through he kept on breaking through for a while, sometimes wetting himself to the waist.

That was why he had shied in such panic. He had felt the give under his feet and heard the crackle of a snow-hidden ice skin. And to get his feet wet in such a temperature meant trouble and danger. At the very least it meant delay, for he would be forced to stop and build a fire, and under its protection to bare his feet while he dried his socks and mocassins. He stood and studied the creek bed and its banks, and decided that the flow of water came from his right. He reflected awhile, rubbing his nose and cheeks, then skirted to the left, stepping gingerly and testing the footing for each step. Once clear of the danger, he took a fresh chew of tobacco and swung along at his four-mile gait.

In the course of the next two hours he came upon several similar traps. Usually the snow above the hidden pools had a sunken, candied appearance that advertised the danger. Once again, however, he had a close call; and once, suspecting danger, he compelled the dog to go on in front. The dog did not want to go. It hung back until the man shoved it forward, and then it went quickly across the white, unbroken surface. Suddenly it broke through, floundered to one side, and got away to firmer footing. It had wet its forefeet and legs, and almost immediately the water that clung to it turned to ice. It made quick efforts to lick the ice off its legs, then dropped down in the snow and began to bite out the ice that had formed between the toes. This was a matter of instinct. To permit the ice to remain would mean sore feet. It did not know this. It merely obeyed the mysterious prompting that arose from the deep crypts of its being.

But the man knew, having achieved a judgment on the subject, and he removed the mitten from his right hand and helped tear out the ice particles. He did not expose his fingers more than a minute, and was astonished at the swift numbness that smote them. It certainly was cold. He pulled on the mitten hastily, and beat the hand savagely across his chest.

At twelve o'clock the day was at its brightest. Yet the sun was too far south on its winter journey to clear the horizon. The bulge of the earth intervened between it and Henderson Creek, where the man walked under a clear sky at noon and cast no shadow. At half-past twelve, to the minute, he arrived at the forks of the creek. He was pleased at the speed he had made. If he kept it up, he would certainly be with the boys by six. He unbuttoned his jacket and shirt and drew forth his lunch. The action consumed no more than a quarter of a minute, yet in that brief moment the numbness laid hold of the exposed fingers. He did not put the mitten on, but, instead, struck the fingers a dozen sharp smashes against his leg. Then he sat down on a snow-covered log to eat. The sting that followed upon the striking of his fingers against his leg ceased so quickly that he was startled. He had had no chance to take a bite of biscuit. He struck the fingers repeatedly and returned them to the mitten, baring the other hand for the purpose of eating. He tried to take a mouthful, but the ice muzzle prevented. He had forgotten to build a fire and thaw out. He chuckled at his foolishness, and as he chuckled he noted the numbness creeping into the exposed fingers. Also, he noted that the stinging which had first come to his toes when he sat down was already passing away. He wondered whether the toes were warm or numb. He moved them inside the moccasins and decided that they were numb.

He pulled the mitten on hurriedly and stood up. He was a bit frightened. He stamped up and down until the stinging returned into the feet. It certainly was cold, was his thought. That man from Sulphur Creek had spoken the truth when telling how cold it sometimes got in the country. And he had laughed at him at the time! That showed one must not be too sure of things. There was no mistake about it, it *was* cold. He strode up and down, stamping his feet and threshing his arms, until reassured by the returning warmth. Then he got out matches and proceeded to make a fire. From the undergrowth, where high water of the previous spring had lodged a supply of seasoned twigs, he got his firewood. Working carefully from a small beginning, he soon had a roaring fire, over which he thawed the ice from his face and in the protection of which he ate his biscuits. For the moment the cold of space was outwitted. The dog took satisfaction in the fire, stretching out close enough for warmth and far enough away to escape being singed.

When the man had finished, he filled his pipe and took his comfortable time over a smoke, then he pulled on his mittens, settled the ear flaps of his cap firmly about his ears, and took the creek trail up the left fork. The dog was disappointed and yearned back towards the fire. This man did not know cold. Possibly all the generations of his ancestry had been ignorant of cold, of real cold, of cold one hundred and seven degrees below freezing point. But the dog knew; all its ancestry knew, and it had inherited the knowledge. And it knew that it was not good to walk abroad in such fearful cold. It was the time to lie snug in a hole in the snow and wait for a curtain of cloud to be drawn across the face of outer space whence this cold came. On the other hand, there was no keen intimacy between the dog and the man. The one was the toil slave of the other, and the only caresses it had ever received were the caresses of the whip lash and of harsh and menacing throat sounds that threatened the whip lash. So the dog made no effort to communicate its apprehension to the man. It was not concerned in the welfare of the man; it was for its own sake that it yearned back toward the fire. But the man whistled, and spoke to it with the sound of whip lashes, and the dog swung in at the man's heels and followed after.

The man took a chew of tobacco and proceeded to start a new amber beard. Also, his moist breath quickly powdered with white his mustache, eyebrows, and lashes. There did not seem to be so many springs on the left fork of the Henderson, and for half an hour the man saw no signs of any. And then it happened. At a place where there were no signs, where the soft, unbroken snow seemed to advertise solidity beneath, the man broke through. It was not deep. He wet himself halfway to the knees before he floundered out to the firm crust.

He was angry, and cursed his luck aloud. He had hoped to get into camp with the boys at six o'clock, and this would delay him an hour, for he would have to build a fire and dry out his footgear. This was imperative at that low temperature—he knew that much; and he turned aside to the bank, which he climbed. On top, tangled in the underbrush about the trunks of several small spruce trees, was a high-water deposit of dry firewood—sticks and twigs, principally, but also larger portions of seasoned branches and fine, dry, last year's grasses. He threw down several large pieces on top of the snow. This served for a foundation and prevented the young flame from drowning itself in the snow it otherwise would melt. The flame he got by touching a match to a small shred of birch bark that he took from his pocket. This burned even more readily than paper. Placing it on the foundation, he fed the young flame with wisps of dry grass and with the tiniest dry twigs.

He worked slowly and carefully, keenly aware of his danger. Gradually, as the flame grew stronger, he increased the size of the twigs with which he fed it. He squatted in the snow, pulling the twigs out from their entanglement in the brush and feeding directly to the flame. He knew there must be no failure. When it is seventy-five below zero, a man must not fail in his first attempt to build a fire—that is, if his feet are wet. If his feet are dry, and he fails, he can run along the trail for half a mile and restore his circulation. But the circulation of wet and freezing feet cannot be restored by running when it is seventy-five below. No matter how fast he runs, the wet feet will freeze the harder.

All this the man knew. The old-timer on Sulphur Creek had told him about it the previous fall, and now he was appreciating the advice. Already all sensation had gone out of his feet. To build the fire he had been forced to remove his mittens, and the fingers had quickly gone numb. His pace of four miles an hour had kept his heart pumping blood to the surface of his body and to all the extremities. But the instant he stopped, the action of the pump eased down. The cold of space smote the unprotected tip of the planet, and he, being on that unprotected tip, received the full force of the blow. The blood of his body recoiled before it. The blood was alive, like the dog, and like the dog it wanted to hide away and cover itself up from the fearful cold. So long as he walked four miles an hour, he pumped the blood, willy-nilly, to the surface; but now it ebbed away and sank down into the recesses of his body. The extremities were the first to feel its absence. His wet feet froze the faster, and his exposed fingers numbed the faster, though they had not yet begun to freeze. Nose and cheeks were already freezing, while the skin of all his body chilled as it lost its blood.

But he was safe. Toes and nose and cheeks would be only touched by the frost, for the fire was beginning to burn with strength. He was feeding it with twigs the size of his finger. In another minute he would be able to feed it with branches the size of his wrist, and then he could remove his wet footgear, and, while it dried, he could keep his naked feet warm by the fire, rubbing them at first, of course, with snow. The fire was a success. He was safe. He remembered the advice of the old-timer on Sulphur Creek, and smiled. The old-timer had been very serious in laying down the law that no man must travel alone in the Klondike after fifty below. Well, here he was; he had had the accident; he was alone; and he had saved himself. Those old-timers were rather womanish, some of them, he thought. All a man had to do was to keep his head, and he was all right. Any man who was a man could travel alone. But it was surprising, the rapidity with which his cheeks and nose were freezing. And he had not thought his fingers could go lifeless in so short a time. Lifeless they were, for he could scarcely make them move together to grip a twig, and they seemed remote from his body and from him. When he touched a twig, he had to look and see whether or not he had hold of it. The wires were pretty well down between him and his finger ends.

All of which counted for little. There was the fire, snapping and crackling and promising life with every dancing flame. He started to untie his moccasins. They were coated with ice; the thick German socks were like sheaths of iron halfway to the knees; and the moccasin strings were like rods of steel all twisted and knotted as by some conflagration. For a moment he tugged with his numb fingers, then, realizing the folly of it, he drew his sheath knife.

But before he could cut the strings, it happened. It was his own fault or, rather, his mistake. He should not have built the fire under the spruce tree. He should have built it in the open. But it had been easier to pull the twigs from the brush and drop them directly on the fire. Now the tree under which he had done this carried a weight of snow on its boughs. No wind had blown for weeks, and each bough was full freighted. Each time he had pulled a twig he had communicated a slight agitation to the tree—an imperceptible agitation, so far as he was concerned, but an agitation sufficient to bring about the disaster. High up in the tree one bough capsized its load of snow. This fell on the boughs beneath, capsizing them. This process continued, spreading out and involving the whole tree. It grew like an avalanche, and it descended upon the man and the fire, and the fire was blotted out! Where it had burned was a mantle of fresh and disordered snow.

The man was shocked. It was as though he had just heard his own sentence of death. For a moment he sat and stared at the spot where the fire had been. Then he grew very calm. Perhaps the old-timer on Sulphur Creek was right. If he had only had a trail mate he would have been in no danger now. The trail mate could have built the fire. Well, it was up to him to build the fire over again, and this second time there must be no failure. Even if he succeeded, he would most likely lose some toes. His feet must be badly frozen by now, and there would be some time before the second fire was ready.

Such were his thoughts, but he did not sit and think them. He was busy all the time they were passing through his mind. He made a new foundation for a fire, this time in the open, where no treacherous tree could blot it out. Next he gathered dry grasses and tiny twigs from the high-water flotsam. He could not bring his fingers together to pull them out, but he was able to gather them by the handful. In this way he got many rotten twigs and bits of green moss that were undesirable, but it was the best he could do. He worked methodically, even collecting an armful of the larger branches to be used later when the fire gathered strength. And all the while the dog sat and watched him, a certain wistfullness in its eyes, for it looked upon him as the fire provider, and the fire was slow in coming.

When all was ready, the man reached in his pocket for a second piece of birch bark. He knew the bark was there, and though he could not feel it with his fingers, he could hear its crisp rustling as he fumbled for it. Try as he would, he could not clutch hold of it. And all the time, in his consciousness, was the knowledge that each instant his feet were freezing. This thought tended to put him in a panic, but he fought against it and kept calm. He pulled on his mittens with his teeth, and threshed his arms back and forth, beating his hands with all his might against his sides. He did this sitting down, and he stood up to do it; and all the while the dog sat in the snow, its wolf brush of a tail curled around warmly over its forefeet, its sharp wolf ears pricked forward intently as it watched the man. And the man, as he beat and threshed with his arms and hands, felt a great surge of envy as he regarded the creature that was warm and secure in its natural covering.

After a time he was aware of the first faraway signals of sensations in his beaten fingers. The faint tingling grew stronger till it evolved into a stinging ache that was excruciating, but which the man hailed with satisfaction. He stripped the mitten from his right hand and fetched forth the birch bark. The exposed fingers were quickly going numb again. Next he brought out his bunch of sulphur matches. But the tremendous cold had already driven the life out of his fingers. In his effort to separate one match from the others, the whole bunch fell into the snow. He tried to pick it out of the snow, but failed. The dead fingers could neither clutch nor touch. He was very careful. He drove the thought of his freezing feet, and nose, and cheeks, out of his mind, devoting his whole soul to the matches. He watched, using the sense of vision in place of that of touch, and when he saw his fingers on each side the bunch, he closed them—that is, he willed to close them, for the wires were down, and the fingers did not obey. He pulled the mitten on the right hand, and beat it fiercely against his knee. Then, with both mittened hands, he scooped the bunch of matches, along with much snow, into his lap. Yet he was no better off.

After some manipulation he managed to get the bunch between the heels of his mittened hands. In this fashion he carried it to his mouth. The ice crackled and snapped when by a violent effort he opened his mouth. He drew the lower jaw in, curled the upper lip out of the way and scraped the bunch with his upper teeth in order to separate a match. He succeeded in getting one, which he dropped on his lap. He was no better off. He could not pick it up. Then he devised a way. He picked it up in his teeth and scratched it on his leg. Twenty times he scratched before he succeeded in lighting it. As it flamed he held it with his teeth to the birch bark. But the burning brimstone went up his nostrils and into his lungs, causing him to cough spasmodically. The match fell into the snow and went out.

The old-timer on Sulphur Creek was right, he thought in the moment of controlled despair that ensued: after fifty below, a man should travel with a partner. He beat his hands, but failed in exciting any sensation. Suddenly he bared both hands, removing the mittens with his teeth. He caught the whole bunch between the heels of his hands. His arm muscles not being frozen enabled him to press the hand heels tightly against the matches. Then he scratched the bunch along his leg. It flared into flame, seventy sulphur matches at once! There was no wind to blow them out. He kept his head to one side to escape the strangling fumes, and held the blazing bunch to the birch bark. As he so held it, he became aware of sensation in his hand. His flesh was burning. He could smell it. Deep down below the surface he could feel it. The sensation developed into pain that grew acute. And still he endured it, holding the flame of the matches clumsily to the bark that would not light readily because his own burning hands were in the way, absorbing most of the flame.

At last, when he could endure no more, he jerked his hands apart. The blazing matches fell sizzling into the snow, but the birch bark was alight. He began laying dry grasses and the tiniest twigs on the flame. He could not pick and choose, for he had to lift the fuel between the heels of his hands. Small pieces of rotten wood and green moss clung to the twigs, and he bit them off as well as he could with his teeth. He cherished the flame carefully and awkwardly. It meant life, and it must not perish. The withdrawal of blood from the surface of his body now made him begin to shiver, and he grew more awkward. A large piece of green moss fell squarely on the little fire. He tried to poke it out with his fingers, but his shivering frame made him poke too far, and he disrupted the nucleus of the little fire, the burning grasses and the tiny twigs separating and scattering. He tried to poke them together again, but in spite of the tenseness of the effort, his shivering got away with him, and the twigs were hopelessly scattered. Each twig gushed a puff of smoke and went out. The fire provider had failed. As he looked apathetically about him, his eyes chanced on the dog, sitting across the ruins of the fire from him, in the snow, making restless, hunching movements, slightly lifting one forefoot and then the other, shifting its weight back and forth on them with wistful eagerness.

The sight of the dog put a wild idea into his head. He remembered the tale of the man, caught in a blizzard, who killed a steer and crawled inside the carcass, and so was saved. He would kill the dog and bury his hands in the warm body until the numbness went out of them. Then he could build another fire. He spoke to the dog, calling it to him; but in his voice was a strange note of fear that frightened the animal, who had never known the man to speak in such a way before. Something was the matter, and its suspicious nature sensed danger—it knew not what danger, but somewhere, somehow, in its brain arose an apprehension of the man. It flattened its ears down at the sound of the man's voice, and its restless, hunching movements and the liftings and shiftings of its forefeet became more pronounced; but it would not come to the man. He got on his hands and knees and crawled toward the dog. This unusual posture again excited suspicion, and the animal sidled mincingly away.

The man sat up in the snow for a moment and struggled for calmness. Then he pulled on his mittens, by means of his teeth, and got upon his feet. He glanced down at first in order to assure himself that he was really standing up, for the absence of sensation in his feet left him unrelated to the earth. His erect position in itself started to drive the webs of suspicion from the dog's mind; and when he spoke peremptorily, with the sound of whip lashes in his voice, the dog rendered its customary allegiance and came to him. As it came within reaching distance, the man lost his control. His arms flashed out to the dog, and he experienced genuine surprise when he discovered that his hands could not clutch, that there was neither bend nor feeling in his fingers. He had forgotten for the moment that they were frozen and that they were freezing more and more. All this happened quickly, and before the animal could get away, he encircled its body with his arms. He sat down in the snow, and in this fashion held the dog, while it snarled and whined and struggled.

But it was all he could do, hold its body encircled in his arms and sit there. He realized that he could not kill the dog. There was no way to do it. With his helpless hands he could neither draw nor hold his sheath knife nor throttle the animal. He released it, and it plunged wildly away, with tail between its legs, and still snarling. It halted forty feet away and surveyed him curiously, with ears sharply pricked forward.

The man looked down at his hands in order to locate them, and found them hanging on the ends of his arms. It struck him as curious that one should have to use his eyes in order to find out where his hands were. He began threshing his arms back and forth, beating the mittened hands against his sides. He did this for five minutes, violently, and his heart pumped enough blood up to the surface to put a stop to his shivering. But no sensation was aroused in the hands. He had an impression that they hung like weights on the ends of his arms, but when he tried to run the impression down, he could not find it.

A certain fear of death, dull and oppressive, came to him. This fear quickly became poignant as he realized that it was no longer a mere matter of freezing his fingers and toes, or of losing his hands and feet, but that it was a matter of life and death with the chances against him. This threw him into a panic, and he turned and ran along the old, dim trail. The dog joined in behind and kept up with him. He ran blindly, without intention, in fear such as he had never known in his life. Slowly, as he plowed and floundered through the snow, he began to see things again—the banks of the creek, the old timber jams, the leafless aspens, and the sky. The running made him feel better. He did not shiver. Maybe, if he ran on, his feet would thaw out; and, anyway, if he ran far enough, he would reach camp and the boys. Without doubt he would lose some fingers and toes and some of his face; but the boys would take care of him, and save the rest of him when he got there. And at the same time there was another thought in his mind that said he would never get to the camp and the boys; that he would soon be stiff and dead. This thought he kept in the background and refused to consider. Sometimes it pushed itself forward and demanded to be heard, but he thrust it back and strove to think of other things.

It struck him as curious that he could run at all on feet so frozen that he could not feel them when they struck the earth and took the weight of his body. He seemed to himself to skim along above the surface, and to have no connection with the earth. Somewhere he had once seen a winged Mercury, and he wondered if Mercury felt as he felt when skimming over the earth.

His theory of running until he reached camp and the boys had one flaw in it: he lacked the endurance. Several times he stumbled, and finally he tottered, crumpled up, and fell. When he tried to rise, he failed. He must sit and rest, he decided, and next time he would merely walk and keep on going. As he sat and regained his breath, he noted that he was feeling quite warm and comfortable. He was not shivering, and it even seemed that a warm glow had come to his chest and trunk. And yet, when he touched his nose or cheeks, there was no sensation. Running would not thaw them out. Nor would it thaw out his hands and feet. Then the thought came to him that the frozen portions of his body must be extending. He tried to keep this thought down, to forget it, to think of something else; he was aware of the panicky feeling that it caused, and he was afraid of the panic. But the thought asserted itself, and persisted, until it produced a vision of his body totally frozen. This was too much, and he made another wild run along the trail. Once he slowed down to a walk, but the thought of the freezing extending itself made him run again.

And all the time the dog ran with him, at his heels. When he fell down a second time, it curled its tail over its forefeet and sat in front of him, facing him, curiously eager and intent. The warmth and security of the animal angered him, and he cursed it till it flattened down its ears appeasingly. This time the shivering came more quickly upon the man. He was losing in his battle with the frost. It was creeping into his body from all sides. The thought of it drove him on, but he ran no more than a hundred feet, when he staggered and pitched headlong. It was his last panic. When he had recovered his breath and control, he sat up and entertained in his mind the conception of meeting death with dignity. However, the conception did not come to him in such terms. His idea of it was that he had been making a fool of himself, running around like a chicken with its head cut off—such was the simile that occured to him. Well, he was bound to freeze anyway, and he might as well take it decently. With this newfound peace of mind came the first glimmerings of drowsiness. A good idea, he thought, to sleep off to death. It was like taking an anesthetic. Freezing was not so bad as people thought. There were lots worse ways to die.

He pictured the boys finding his body the next day. Suddenly he found himself with them, coming along the trail and looking for himself. And, still with them, he came around a turn in the trail and found himself lying in the snow. He did not belong with himself any more, for even then he was out of himself, standing with the boys and looking at himself in the snow. It certainly was cold, was his thought. When he got back to the States he could tell the folks what real cold was. He drifted on from this to a vision of the old-timer on Sulphur Creek. He could see him quite clearly, warm and comfortable, and smoking a pipe.

"You were right, old hoss; you were right," the man mumbled to the old-timer of Sulphur Creek.

Then the man drowsed off into what seemed to him the most comfortable and satisfying sleep he had ever known. The dog sat facing him and waiting. The brief day drew to a close in a long, slow twilight. There were no signs of a fire to be made, and, besides, never in the dog's experience had it known a man to sit like that in the snow and make no fire. As the twilight drew on, its eager yearning for the fire mastered it, and with a great lifting and shifting of forefeet, it whined softly, then flattened its ears down in anticipation of being chidden by the man. But the man remained silent. Later the dog whined loudly. And still later it crept close to the man and caught the scent of death. This made the animal bristle and back away. A little longer it delayed, howling under the stars that leaped and danced and shone brightly in the cold sky. Then it turned and trotted up the trail in the direction of the camp it knew, where there were other food providers and fire providers.

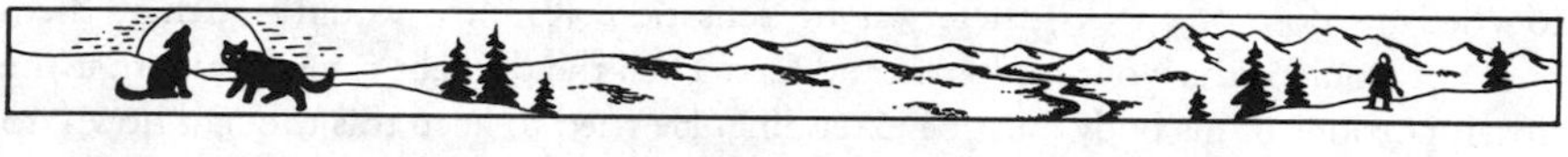

AN ODYSSEY OF THE NORTH

I

THE sleds were singing their eternal lament to the creaking of the harness and the tinkling bells of the leaders; but the men and dogs were tired and made no sound. The trail was heavy with new-fallen snow, and they had come far, and the runners, burdened with flintlike quarters of frozen moose, clung tenaciously to the unpacked surface and held back with a stubbornness almost human. Darkness was coming on, but there was no camp to pitch that night. The snow fell gently through the pulseless air, not in flakes, but in tiny frost crystals of delicate design. It was very warm—barely ten below zero—and the men did not mind. Meyers and Bettles had raised their ear flaps, while Malemute Kid had even taken off his mittens.

The dogs had been fagged out early in the afternoon, but they now began to show new vigor. Among the more astute there was a certain restlessness—an impatience at the restraint of the traces, an indecisive quickness of movement, a sniffing of snouts and pricking of ears. These became incensed at their more phlegmatic brothers, urging them on with numerous sly nips on their hinder quarters. Those, thus chidden, also contracted and helped spread the contagion. At last the leader of the foremost sled uttered a sharp whine of satisfaction, crouching lower in the snow and throwing himself against the collar. The rest followed suit. There was an ingathering of back hands, a tightening of traces; the sleds leaped forward, and the men clung to the gee poles, violently accelerating the uplift of their feet that they might escape going under the runners. The weariness of the day fell from them, and they whooped encouragement to the dogs. The animals responded with joyous yelps. They were swinging through the gathering darkness at a rattling gallop.

"Gee! Gee!" the men cried, each in turn, as their sleds abruptly left the main trail, heeling over on single runners like luggers on the wind.

Then came a hundred yards' dash to the lighted parchment window, which told its own story of the home cabin, the roaring Yukon stove, and the steaming pots of tea. But the home cabin had been invaded. Threescore huskies chorused defiance, and as many furry forms precipitated themselves upon the dogs which drew the first sled. The door was flung open, and a man, clad in the scarlet tunic of the Northwest Police, waded knee-deep among the furious brutes, calmly and impartially dispensing soothing justice with the butt end of a dog whip. After that the men shook hands; and in this wise was Malemute Kid welcomed to his own cabin by a stranger.

Stanley Prince, who should have welcomed him, and who was responsible for the Yukon stove and hot tea aforementioned, was busy with his guests. There were a dozen or so of them, as nondescript a crowd as ever served the Queen in the enforcement of her laws or the delivery of her mails. They were of many breeds, but their common life had formed of them a certain type—a lean and wiry type, with trail-hardened muscles, and sun-browned faces, and untroubled souls which gazed frankly forth, clear-eyed and steady. They drove the dogs of the Queen, wrought fear in the hearts of her enemies, ate of her meager fare, and were happy. They had seen life, and done deeds, and lived romances; but they did not know it.

And they were very much at home. Two of them were sprawled upon Malemute Kid's bunk, singing chansons which their French forebears sang in the days when first they entered the Northwest land and mated with its Indian women. Bettles' bunk had suffered a similar invasion, and three or four lusty *voyageurs* worked their toes among its blankets as they listened to the tale of one who had served on the boat brigade with Wolseley when he fought his way to Khartoum. And when he tired, a cowboy told of courts and kings and lords and ladies he had seen when Buffalo Bill toured the capitals of Europe. In a corner two half-breeds, ancient comrades in a lost campaign, mended harnesses and talked of the days when the Northwest flamed with insurrection and Louis Riel was king.

Rough jests and rougher jokes went up and down, and great hazards by trail and river were spoken of in the light of commonplaces, only to be recalled by virtue of some grain of humor or ludicrous happening. Prince was led away by these uncrowned heroes who had seen history made, who regarded the great and the romantic as but the ordinary and the incidental in the routine of life. He passed his precious tobacco among them with lavish disregard, and rusty chains of reminiscence were loosened, and forgotten odysseys resurrected for his especial benefit.

When conversation dropped and the travelers filled the last pipes and lashed their tight-rolled sleeping furs, Prince fell back upon his comrade for further information.

"Well, you know what the cowboy is," Malemute Kid answered, beginning to unlace his moccasins; "and it's not hard to guess the British blood in his bed partner. As for the rest, they're all children of the *coureurs du bois,* mingled with God knows how many other bloods. The two turning in by the door are the regulation 'breeds' of *Boisbrûles.* That lad with the worsted breech scarf—notice his eyebrows and the turn of his jaw—shows a Scotchman wept in his mother's smoky tepee. And that handsome looking fellow putting the capote under his head is a French half-breed—you heard him talking; he doesn't like the two Indians turning in next to him. You see, when the 'breeds' rose under the Riel the full-bloods kept the peace, and they've not lost much love for one another since."

"But I say, what's that glum-looking fellow by the stove? I'll swear he can't talk English. He hasn't opened his mouth all night."

"You're wrong. He knows English well enough. Did you follow his eyes when he listened? I did. But he's neither kith nor kin to the others. When they talked their own patios you could see he didn't understand. I've been wondering myself what he is. Let's find out."

"Fire a couple of sticks into the stove!" Malemute Kid commanded, raising his voice and looking squarely at the man in question.

He obeyed at once.

"Had discipline knocked into him somewhere," Prince commented in a low tone.

Malemute Kid nodded, took off his socks, and picked his way among recumbent men to the stove. There he hung his damp footgear among a score or so of mates.

"When do you expect to get to Dawson?" he asked tentatively.

The man studied him a moment before replying. "They say seventy-five mile. So? Maybe two days."

The very slightest accent was perceptible, while there was no awkward hesitancy or groping for words.

"Been in the country before?"

"No."

"Northwest Territory?"

"Yes."

"Born there?"

"No."

"Well, where the devil were you born? You're none of these." Malemute Kid swept his hand over the dog drivers, even including the two policemen who had turned into Prince's bunk. "Where did you come from? I've seen faces like yours before, though I can't remember just where."

"I know you," he irrelevantly replied, at once turning the drift of Malemute Kid's questions.

"Where? Ever see me?"

"No; your partner, him priest, Pastilik, long time ago. Him ask me if I see you, Malemute Kid. Him give me grub. I no stop long. You hear him speak 'bout me?"

"Oh! you're the fellow that traded the otter skins for the dogs?"

The man nodded, knocked out his pipe, and signified his disinclination for conversation by rolling up in his furs. Malemute Kid blew out the slush lamp and crawled under the blankets with Prince.

"Well, what is he?"

"Don't know—turned me off, somehow, and then shut up like a clam. But he's a fellow to whet your curiosity. I've heard of him. All the coast wondered about him eight years ago. Sort of mysterious, you know. He came down out of the North, in the dead of winter, many a thousand miles from here, skirting Bering Sea and traveling as though the devil were after him. No one ever learned where he came from, but he must have come far. He was badly travel-worn when he got food from the Swedish missionary on Golovin Bay and asked the way south. We heard of all this afterward. Then he abandoned the shore line, heading right across Norton Sound. Terrible weather, snowstorms and high winds, but he pulled through where a thousand other men would have died, missing St. Michaels and making the land at Pastilik. He'd lost all but two dogs, and was nearly gone with starvation.

"He was so anxious to go on that Father Roubeau fitted him out with grub; but he couldn't let him have any dogs, for he was only waiting my arrival, to go on a trip himself. Mr. Ulysses knew too much to start on without animals, and fretted around for several days. He had on his sled a bunch of beautifully cured otter skins, sea otters, you know, worth their weight in gold. There was also at Pastilik an old Shylock of a Russian trader, who had dogs to kill. Well, they didn't dicker very long, but when the Strange One headed south again, it was in the rear of a spanking dog team. Mr. Shylock, by the way, had the otter skins. I saw them, and they were magnificent. We figured it up and found the dogs brought him at least five hundred apiece. And it wasn't as if the Strange One didn't know the value of sea otter; he was an Indian of some sort, and what little he talked showed he'd been among white men.

"After the ice passed out of the sea, word came up from Nunivak Island that he'd gone in there for grub. Then he dropped from sight, and this is the first heard of him in eight years. Now where did he come from? and what was he doing there? and why did he come from there? He's Indian, he's been nobody knows where, and he's had discipline, which is unusual for an Indian. Another mystery of the North for you to solve, Prince."

"Thanks awfully, but I've got too many on hand as it is," he replied.

Malemute Kid was already breathing heavily; but the young mining engineer gazed straight up through the thick darkness, waiting for the strange orgasm which stirred his blood to die away. And when he did sleep, his brain worked on, and for the nonce he, too, wandered through the white unknown, struggled with the dogs on endless trails, and saw men live, and toil, and die like men.

The next morning, hours before daylight, the dog drivers and policemen pulled out for Dawson. But the powers that saw to Her Majesty's interests and ruled the destinies of her lesser creatures gave the mailmen little rest, for a week later they appeared at Stuart River, heavily burdened with letters for Salt Water. However, their dogs had been replaced by fresh ones; but, then, they were dogs.

The men had expected some sort of a layover in which to rest up; besides, this Klondike was a new section of the Northland, and they had wished to see a little something of the Golden City where dust flowed like water and dance halls rang with never-ending revelry. But they dried their socks and smoked their evening pipes with much the same gusto as on their former visit, though one or two bold spirits speculated on desertion and the possibility of crossing the unexplored Rockies to the east, and thence, by the Mackenzie Valley, of gaining their old stamping grounds in the Chippewyan country. Two or three even decided to return to their homes by that route when their terms of service had expired, and they began to lay plans forthwith, looking forward to the hazardous undertaking in much the same way a city-bred man would to a day's holiday in the woods.

He of the Otter Skins seemed very restless, though he took little interest in the discussion, and at last he drew Malemute Kid to one side and talked for some time in low tones. Prince cast curious eyes in their direction, and the mystery deepened when they put on caps and mittens and went outside. When they returned, Malemute Kid placed his gold scales on the table, weighed out the matter of sixty ounces, and transferred them to the Strange One's sack. Then the chief of the dog drivers joined the conclave, and certain business was transacted with him. The next day the gang went on upriver, but He of the Otter Skins took several pounds of grub and turned his steps back toward Dawson.

"Didn't know what to make of it," said Malemute Kid in response to Prince's queries: "but the poor beggar wanted to be quit of the service for some reason or other —at least it seemed a most important one to him, though he wouldn't let on what. You see, it's just like the army: he signed for two years, and the only way to get free was to buy himself out. He couldn't desert and then stay here, and he was just wild to remain in the country. Made up his mind when he got to Dawson, he said; but no one knew him, hadn't a cent, and I was the only one he'd spoken two words with. So he talked it over with the lieutenant-governor, and made arrangements in case he could get the money from me—loan, you know. Said he'd pay back in the year, and, if I wanted, would put me onto something rich. Never'd seen it, but he knew it was rich.

"And talk! why, when he got me outside he was ready to weep. Begged and pleaded; got down in the snow to me till I hauled him out of it. Palavered around like a crazy man. Swore he's worked to this very end for years and years, and couldn't bear to be disappointed now. Asked him what end, but he wouldn't say. Said they might keep him on the other half of the trail and he wouldn't get to Dawson in two years, and then it would be too late. Never saw a man take on so in my life. And when I said I'd let him have it, had to yank him out of the snow again. Told him to consider it in the light of a grubstake. Think he'd have it? No sir! Swore he'd give me all he found, make me rich beyond the dreams of avarice, and all such stuff. Now a man who puts his life and time against a grubstake ordinarily finds it hard enough to turn over half of what he finds. Something behind all this, Prince; just you make a note of it. We'll hear of him if he stays in the country—"

"And if he doesn't?"

"Then my good nature gets a shock, and I'm sixty some odd ounces out."

The cold weather had come on with the long nights, and the sun had begun to play his ancient game of peekaboo along the southern snow line ere aught was heard of Malemute Kid's grub-stake. And then, one bleak morning in early January, a heavily laden dog train pulled into his cabin below Stuart River. He of the Otter Skins was there, and with him walked a man such as the gods have almost forgotten how to fashion. Men never talked of luck and pluck and five-hundred-dollar dirt without bringing in the name of Axel Gunderson; nor could tales of nerve or strength or daring pass up and down the campfire without the summoning of his presence. And when the conversation flagged, it blazed anew at mention of the woman who shared his fortunes.

As has been noted, in the making of Axel Gunderson the gods had remembered their old-time cunning and cast him after the manner of men who were born when the world was young. Full seven feet he towered in his picturesque costume which marked a king of Eldorado. His chest, neck, and limbs were those of a giant. To bear his three hundred pounds of bone and muscle, his snowshoes were greater by a generous yard than those of other men. Rough-hewn, with rugged brow and massive jaw and unflinching eyes of palest blue, his face told the tale of one who knew but the law of might. Of the yellow of ripe corn silk, his frost-incrusted hair swept like day across the night and fell far down his coat of bearskin. A vague tradition of the sea seemed to cling about him as he swung down the narrow trail in advance of the dogs; and he brought the butt of his dog whip against Malemute Kid's door as a Norse sea rover, on southern foray, might thunder for admittance at the castle gate.

Prince bared his womanly arms and kneaded sour-dough bread, casting, as he did so, many a glance at the three guests—three guests the like of which might never come under a man's roof in a lifetime. The Strange One, whom Malemute Kid had surnamed Ulysses, still fascinated him; but his interest chiefly gravitated between Axel Gunderson and Axel Gunderson's wife. She felt the day's journey, for she had softened in comfortable cabins during the many days since her husband mastered the wealth of frozen pay streaks, and she was tired. She rested against his great breast like a slender flower against a wall, replying lazily to Malemute Kid's good-natured banter, and stirring Prince's blood strangely with an occasional sweep of her deep, dark eyes. For Prince was a man, and healthy, and had seen few women in many months. And she was older than he, and an Indian besides. But she was different from all native wives he had met; she had traveled—had been in his country among others, he gathered from the conversation; and she knew most of the things the women of his own race knew, and much more that it was not in the nature of things for them to know. She could make a meal of sun-dried fish or a bed in the snow; yet she teased them with tantalizing details of many-course dinners, and caused strange internal dissensions to arise at the mention of various quondam dishes which they had well-nigh forgotten. She knew the ways of the moose, the bear, and the little blue fox, and of the wild amphibians of the Northern seas; she was skilled in the lore of the woods, and the streams, and the tale writ by man and bird and beast upon the delicate snow crust was to her an open book; yet Prince caught the appreciative twinkle in her eye as she read the Rules of the Camp. These rules had been fathered by the Unquenchable Bettles at a time when his blood ran high, and were remarkable for the terse simplicity of their humor. Prince always turned them to the wall before the arrival of ladies; but who could suspect that this native wife——Well, it was too late now.

This, then, was the wife of Axel Gunderson, a woman whose name and fame had traveled with her husband's, hand in hand, through all the Northland. At table, Malemute Kid baited her with the assurance of an old friend, and Prince shook off the shyness of first acquaintance and joined in. But she held her own in the unequal contest, while her husband, slower in wit, ventured naught but applause. And he was very proud of her; his every look and action revealed the magnitude of the place she occupied in his life. He of the Otter Skins ate in silence, forgotten in the merry battle; and long ere the others were done he pushed back from the table and went out among the dogs. Yet all too soon his fellow travelers drew on their mittens and parkas and followed him.

There had been no snow for many days, and the sleds slipped along the hard-packed Yukon trail as easily as if it had been glare ice. Ulysses led the first sled; with the second came Prince and Axel Gunderson's wife; while Malemute Kid and the yellow-haired giant brought up the third.

"It's only a hunch, Kid," he said, "but I think it's straight. He's never been there, but he tells a good story, and shows a map I heard of when I was in the Kootenay country years ago. I'd like to have you go along; but he's a strange one, and swore point-blank to throw it up if anyone was brought in. But when I come back you'll get first tip, and I'll stake you next to me, and give you a half share in the town site besides.

"No! no!" he cried, as the other strove to interrupt. "I'm running this, and before I'm done it'll need two heads. If it's all right, why, it'll be a second Cripple Creek, man; do you hear?—a second Cripple Creek! It's quartz, you know, not placer; and if we work it right we'll corral the whole thing—millions upon millions. I've heard of the place before, and so have you. We'll build a town—thousands of workmen—good waterways—steamship lines—big carrying trade—light-draught steamers for head reaches—survey a railroad, perhaps—sawmills—electric-light plant—do your own banking—commercial company—syndicate—— Say! just you hold your hush till I get back!"

The sleds came to a halt where the trail crossed the mouth of Stuart River. An unbroken sea of frost, its wide expanse stretched away into the unknown east. The snowshoes were withdrawn from the lashings of the sleds. Axel Gunderson shook hands and stepped to the fore, his great webbed shoes sinking a fair half yard into the feathery surface and packing the snow so the dogs should not wallow. His wife fell in behind the last sled, betraying long practice in the art of handling the awkward foot-gear. The stillness was broken with cheery farewells; the dogs whined; and He of the Otter Skins talked with his whip to a recalcitrant wheeler.

An hour later the train had taken on the likeness of a black pencil crawling in a long, straight line across a mighty sheet of foolscap.

II

ONE night, many weeks later, Malemute Kid and Prince fell to solving chess problems from the torn page of an ancient magazine. The Kid had just returned from his Bonanza properties and was resting up preparatory to a long moose hunt. Prince, too, had been on creek and trail nearly all winter, and had grown hungry for a blissful week of cabin life.

"Interpose the black knight, and force the king. No, that won't do. See, the next move——"

"Why advance the pawn two squares? Bound to take it in transit, and with the bishop out of the way——"

"But hold on! That leaves a hole, and——"

"No; it's protected. Go ahead! You'll see it works."

It was very interesting. Somebody knocked at the door a second time before Malemute Kid said, "Come in." The door swung open. Something staggered in. Prince caught one square look and sprang to his feet. The horror in his eyes caused Malemute Kid to whirl about; and he, too, was startled, though he had seen bad things before.

The thing tottered blindly toward them. Prince edged away till he reached the nail from which hung his Smith & Wesson.

"My God! what is it?" he whispered to Malemute Kid.

"Don't know. Looks like a case of freezing and no grub," replied the Kid, sliding away in the opposite direction. "Watch out! It may be mad," he warned, coming back from closing the door.

The thing advanced to the table. The bright flame of the slush lamp caught its eye. It was amused, and gave voice to eldritch cackles which betokened mirth. Then, suddenly, he—for it was a man—swayed back, with a hitch to his skin trousers, and began to sing a chantey, such as men lift when they swing around the capstan circle and the sea snorts in their ears:

Yan-kee ship come down de ri-ib-er,
Pull! my bully boys! Pull!
D'yeh want—to know de captain ru-uns her?
Pull! my bully boys! Pull!
Jon-a-than Jones ob South Caho-li-in-a,
Pull! my bully—

He broke off abruptly, tottered with a wolfish snarl to the meat shelf, and before they could intercept was tearing with his teeth at a chunk of raw bacon. The struggle was fierce between him and Malemute Kid; but his mad strength left him as suddenly as it had come, and he weakly surrendered the spoil. Between them they got him upon a stool, where he sprawled with half his body across the table. A small dose of whiskey strengthened him, so that he could dip a spoon into the sugar caddy which Malemute Kid placed before him. After his appetite had been somewhat cloyed, Prince, shuddering as he did so, passed him a mug of weak beef tea.

The creature's eyes were alight with a somber frenzy, which blazed and waned with every mouthful. There was very little skin to the face. The face, for that matter, sunken and emaciated, bore little likeness to human countenance. Frost after frost had bitten deeply, each depositing its stratum of scab upon the half-healed scar that went before. This dry, hard surface was of a bloody-black color, serrated by grievous cracks wherein the raw red flesh peeped forth. His skin garments were dirty and in tatters, and the fur of one side was singed and burned away, showing where he had lain upon his fire.

Malemute Kid pointed to where the sun-tanned hide had been cut away, strip by strip—the grim signature of famine.

"Who—are—you?" slowly and distinctly enunciated the Kid.

The man paid no heed.

"Where do you come from?"

"Yan-kee ship come down de ri-ib-er," was the quavering response.

"Don't doubt the beggar came down the river," the Kid said, shaking him in an endeavor to start a more lucid flow of talk.

But the man shrieked at the contact, clapping a hand to his side in evident pain. He rose slowly to his feet, half leaning on the table.

"She laughed at me—so—with the hate in her eye; and she—would—not—come."

His voice died away, and he was sinking back when Malemute Kid gripped him by the wrist and shouted, "Who? Who would not come?"

"She, Unga. She laughed, and struck at me, so, and so. And then——"

"Yes?"

"And then——"

"And then what?"

"And then he lay very still in the snow a long time. He is—still in—the—snow."

The two men looked at each other helplessly.

"Who is in the snow?"

"She, Unga. She looked at me with the hate in her eye, and then—"

"Yes, yes."

"And then she took the knife, so; and once, twice—she was weak. I traveled very slow. And there is much gold in that place, very much gold."

"Where is Unga?" For all Malemute Kid knew, she might be dying a mile away. He shook the man savagely, repeating again and again, "Where is Unga? Who is Unga?"

"She—is—in—the—snow."

"Go on!" The Kid was pressing his wrist cruelly.

"So—I—would—be—in—the—snow—but—I—had—a—debt—to—pay. It—was—heavy—I—had—a—debt—to—pay—a—debt—to—pay I—had——" The faltering monosyllables ceased as he fumbled in his pouch and drew forth a buckskin sack. "A—debt—to—pay—five—pounds —of—gold—grub—stake—Mal—e—mute—Kid—I——" The exhausted head dropped upon the table; nor could Malemute Kid rouse it again.

"It's Ulysses," he said quietly, tossing the bag of dust on the table. "Guess it's all day with Axel Gunderson and the woman. Come on, let's get him between the blankets. He's Indian; he'll pull through and tell a tale besides."

As they cut his garments from him, near his right breast could be seen two unhealed, hard-lipped knife thrusts.

III

"I will talk of the things which were in my own way; but you will understand. I will begin at the beginning, and tell of myself and the woman, and, after that, of the man."

He of the Otter Skins drew over to the stove as do men who have been deprived of fire and are afraid the Promethean gift may vanish at any moment. Malemute Kid picked up the slush lamp and placed it so its light might fall upon the face of the narrator. Prince slid his body over the edge of the bunk and joined them.

"I am Naass, a chief, and the son of a chief, born between a sunset and a rising, on the dark seas, in my father's oomiak. All of a night the men toiled at the paddles, and the women cast out the waves which threw in upon us, and we fought with the storm. The salt spray froze upon my mother's breast till her breath passed with the passing of the tide. But I—I raised my voice with the wind and the storm, and lived.

"We dwelt in Akatan——"

"Where?" asked Malemute Kid.

"Akatan, which is in the Aleutians; Akatan, beyond Chignik, beyond Kardalak, beyond Unimak. As I say, we dwelt in Akatan, which lies in the midst of the sea on the edge of the world. We farmed the salt seas for the fish, the seal, and the otter; and our homes shouldered about one another on the rocky strip between the rim of the forest and the yellow beach where our kayaks lay. We were not many, and the world was very small. There were strange lands to the east—islands like Akatan; so we thought all the world was islands and did not mind.

"I was different from my people. In the sands of the beach were the crooked timbers and wave-warped planks of a boat such as my people built; and I remember on the point of the island which overlooked the ocean three ways there stood a pine tree which never grew there, smooth and straight and tall. It is said the two men came to that spot, turn about, through many days, and watched with the passing of the light. These two men came from out of the sea in the boat which lay in pieces on the beach. And they were white like you, and weak as the little children when the seal have gone away and the hunters come home empty. I know of these things from the old men and the old women, who got them from their fathers and mothers before them. These strange white men did not take kindly to our ways at first, but they grew strong, what of the fish and the oil, and fierce. And they built them each his own house, and took the pick of our women, and in time children came. Thus he was born who was to become the father of my father's father.

"As I said, I was different from my people, for I carried the strong, strange blood of this white man who came out of the sea. It is said we had other laws in the days before these men; but they were fierce and quarrelsome, and fought with out men till there were no more left who dared to fight. Then they made themselves chiefs, and took away our old laws, and gave us new ones, insomuch that the man was the son of his father, and not his mother, as our way had been. They also ruled that the son, first-born, should have all things which were his father's before him, and that the brothers and sisters should shift for themselves. And they gave us other laws. They showed us new ways in the catching of fish and the killing of bear which were thick in the woods; and they taught us to lay by bigger stores for the time of famine. And these things were good.

"But when they had become chiefs, and there were no more men to face their anger, they fought, these strange white men, each with the other. And the one whose blood I carry drove his seal spear the length of an arm through the other's body. Their children took up the fight, and their children's children; and there was great hatred between them, and black doings, even to my time, so that in each family but one lived to pass down the blood of them that went before. Of my blood I was alone; of the other man's there was but a girl. Unga, who lived with her mother. Her father and my father did not come back from the fishing one night; but afterward they washed up to the beach on the big tides, and they held very close to each other.

"The people wondered, because of the hatred between the houses, and the old men shook their heads and said the fight would go on when children were born to her and children to me. They told me this as a boy, till I came to believe, and to look upon Unga as a foe, who was to be the mother of children which were to fight with mine. I thought of these things day by day, and when I grew to a stripling I came to ask why this should be so. And they answered, 'We do not know, but that in such way your fathers did.' And I marveled that those which were to come should fight the battles of those that were gone, and in it I could see no right. But the people said it must be, and I was only a stripling.

"And they said I must hurry, that my blood might be the older and grow strong before hers. This was easy, for I was head man, and the people looked up to me because of the deeds and the laws of my fathers, and the wealth which was mine. Any maiden would come to me, but I found none to my liking. And the old men and the mothers of maidens told me to hurry, for even then were the hunters bidding high to the mother of Unga; and should her children grow strong before mine, mine would surely die.

"Nor did I find a maiden till one night coming back from the fishing. The sunlight was lying, so, low and full in the eyes, the wind free, and the kayacks racing with the white seas. Of a sudden the kayak of Unga came driving past me, and she looked upon me, so, with her black hair flying like a cloud of night and the spray wet on her cheek. As I say, the sunlight was full in the eyes, and I was a stripling; but somehow it was all clear, and I knew it to be the call of kind to kind. As she whipped ahead she looked back within the space of two strokes—looked as only the woman Unga could look—and again I knew it as the call of kind. The people shouted as we ripped past the lazy oomiaks and left them far behind. But she was quick at the paddle, and my heart was like the belly of a sail, and, I did not gain. The wind freshened, the sea whitened, and, leaping like the seals on the windward breech, we roared down the golden pathway of the sun."

Naass was crouched half out of his stool, in the attitude of one driving a paddle, as he ran the race anew. Somewhere across the stove he beheld the tossing kayak and the flying hair of Unga. The voice of the wind was in his ears, and its salt beat fresh upon his nostrils.

"But she made the shore, and ran up the sand, laughing, to the house of her mother. And a great thought came to me that night—a thought worthy of him that was chief over all the people of Akatan. So, when the moon was up, I went down to the house of her mother, and looked upon the goods of Yash-Noosh, which were piled by the door —the goods of Yash-Noosh, a strong hunter who had it in mind to be the father of the children of Unga. Other young men had piled their goods there and taken them away again; and each young man had made a pile greater than the one before.

"And I laughed to the moon and the stars, and went to my own house where my wealth was stored. And many trips I made, till my pile was greater by the fingers of one hand than the pile of Yash-Noosh. There were fish, dried in the sun and smoked; and forty hides of the hair seal, and half as many of the fur, and each hide was tied at the mouth and big bellied with oil; and ten skins of bear which I killed in the woods when they came out in the spring. And there were beads and blankets and scarlet cloths, such as I got in trade from the people who lived to the east, and who got them in trade from the people who lived still beyond in the east. And I looked upon the pile of Yash-Noosh and laughed, for I was head man in Akatan, and my wealth was greater than the wealth of all my young men, and my fathers had done deeds, and given laws, and put their names for all time in the mouths of the people.

"So, when the morning came, I went down to the beach, casting out of the corner of my eye at the house of the mother of Unga. My offer yet stood untouched. And the women smiled, and said sly things one to the other. I wondered, for never had such a price been offered; and that night I added more to the pile, and put beside it a kayak of well-tanned skins which never yet had swam in the sea. But in the day it was yet there, open to the laughter of all men. The mother of Unga was crafty, and I grew angry at the shame in which I stood before my people. So that night I added till it became a great pile, and I hauled up my oomiak, which was of the value of twenty kayaks. And in the morning there was no pile.

"Then made I preparation for the wedding, and the people that lived even to the east came for the food of the feast and the potlatch token. Unga was older than I by the age of four suns in the way we reckoned the years. I was only a stripling; but then I was a chief, and the son of a chief, and it did not matter.

"But a ship shoved her sails above the floor of the ocean, and grew larger with the breath of the wind. From her scuppers she ran clear water, and the men were in haste and worked hard at the pumps. On the bow stood a mighty man, watching the depth of the water and giving commands with a voice of thunder. His eyes were of the pale blue of the deep waters, and his head was maned like that of a sea lion. And his hair was yellow, like the straw of a southern harvest or the manila rope yarns which sailormen plait.

"Of late years we had seen ships from afar, but this was the first to come to the beach of Akatan. The feast was broken, and the women and children fled to the houses, while we men strung our bows and waited with spears in hand. But when the ship's forefoot smelled the beach the strange men took no notice of us, being busy with their own work. With the falling of the tide they careened the schooner and patched a great hole in her bottom. So the women crept back, and the feast went on.

"When the tide rose, the sea wanderers kedged the schooner to deep water and then came among us. They bore presents and were friendly; so I made room for them, and out of the largeness of my heart gave them tokens such as I gave all the guests, for it was my wedding day, and I was head man in Akatan. And he with the mane of the sea lion was there, so tall and strong that one looked to see the earth shake with the fall of his feet. He looked much and straight at Unga, with his arms folded, so, and stayed till the sun went away and the stars came out. Then he went down to his ship. After that I took Unga by the hand and led her to my own house. And there was singing and great laughter, and the women said sly things, after the manner of women at such times. But we did not care. Then the people left us alone and went home.

"The last noise had not died away when the chief of the sea wanderers came in by the door. And he had with him black bottles, from which we drank and made merry. You see, I was only a stripling, and had lived all my days on the edge of the world. So my blood became as fire, and my heart as light as the froth that flies from the surf to the cliff. Unga sat silent among the skins in the corner, her eyes wide, for she seemed to fear. And he with the mane of the sea lion looked upon her straight and long. Then his men came in with bundles of goods, and he piled before me wealth such as was not in all Akatan. There were guns, both large and small, and powder and shot and shell, and bright axes and knives of steel, and cunning tools, and strange things the like of which I had never seen. When he showed me by sign that it was all mine, I thought him a great man to be so free; but he showed me also that Unga was to go away with him in his ship. Do you understand?—that Unga was to go away with him in his ship. The blood of my fathers flamed hot on the sudden, and I made to drive him through with my spear. But the spirit of the bottles had stolen the life from my arm, and took me by the neck, so, and knocked my head against the wall of the house. And I was made weak like a newborn child, and my legs would no more stand under me. Unga screamed, and she laid hold of the things of the house with her hands, till they fell all about us as he dragged her to the door. Then he took her in his great arms, and when she tore at his yellow hair laughed with a sound like that of the big bull seal in the rut.

"I crawled to the beach and called upon my people, but they were afraid. Only Yash-Noosh was a man, and they struck him on the head with an oar, till he lay with his face in the sand and did not move. And they raised the sails to the sound of their songs, and the ship went away on the wind.

"The people said it was good, for there would be no more war of the bloods in Akatan; but I said never a word, waiting till the time of the full moon, when I put fish and oil in my kayak and went away to the east. I saw many islands and many people, and I, who had lived on the edge, saw that the world was very large. I talked by signs; but they had not seen a schooner nor a man with the mane of a sea lion, and they pointed always to the east. And I slept in queer places, and ate odd things, and met strange faces. Many laughed, for they thought me light of head; but sometimes old men turned my face to the light and blessed me, and the eyes of the young women grew soft as they asked me of the strange ship, and Unga, and the men of the sea.

"And in this manner, through rough seas and great storms, I came to Unalaska. There were two schooners there, but neither was the one I sought. So I passed on to the east, with the world growing ever larger, and in the island of Unamok there was no word of the ship, nor in Kadiak, nor in Atognak. And so I came one day to a rocky land, where men dug great holes in the mountain. And there was a schooner, but not my schooner, and men loaded upon it the rocks which they dug. This I thought childish, for all the world was made of rocks; but they gave me food and set me to work. When the schooner was deep in the water, the captain gave me money and told me to go; but I asked which way he went, and he pointed south. I made signs that I would go with him, and he laughed at first, but then, being short of men, took me to help work the ship. So I came to talk after their manner, and to heave on ropes, and to reef the stiff sails in sudden squalls, and to take my turn at the wheel. But it was not strange, for the blood of my fathers was the blood of the men of the sea.

"I had thought it an easy task to find him I sought, once I got among his own people; and when we raised the land one day, and passed between a gateway of the sea to a port, I looked for perhaps as many schooners as there were fingers to my hands. But the ships lay against the wharves for miles, packed like so many little fish; and when I went among them to ask for a man with the mane of a sea lion, they laughed, and answered me in the tongues of many peoples. And I found that they hailed from the uttermost parts of the earth.

"And I went into the city to look upon the face of every man. But they were like the cod when they run thick on the banks, and I could not count them. And the noise smote upon me till I could not hear, and my head was dizzy with much movement. So I went on and on, through the lands which sang in the warm sunshine; where the harvests lay rich on the plains; and where great cities were fat with men that lived like women, with false words in their mouths and their hearts black with the lust of gold. And all the while my people of Akatan hunted and fished, and were happy in the thought that the world was small.

"But the look in the eyes of Unga coming home from the fishing was with me always, and I knew I would find her when the time was met. She walked down quiet lanes in the dusk of the evening, or led me chases across the thick fields wet with the morning dew, and there was a promise in her eyes such as only the woman Unga could give.

"So I wandered through a thousand cities. Some were gentle and gave me food, and others laughed, and still others cursed; but I kept my tongue between my teeth, and went strange ways and saw strange sights. Sometimes I, who was a chief and the son of a chief, toiled for men—men rough of speech and hard as iron, who wrung gold from the sweat and sorrow of their fellow men. Yet no word did I get of my quest till I came back to the sea like a homing seal to the rookeries. But this was at another port, in another country which lay to the north. And there I heard dim tales of the yellow-haired sea wanderer, and I learned that he was a hunter of seals, and that even then he was abroad on the ocean.

"So I shipped on a seal schooner with the lazy Siwashes, and followed his trackless trail to the north where the hunt was then warm. And we were away weary months, and spoke many of the fleet, and heard much of the wild doings of him I sought; but never once did we raise him above the sea. We went north, even to the Pribilofs, and killed the seals in herds on the beach, and brought their warm bodies aboard till our scuppers ran grease and blood and no man could stand upon the deck. Then were we chased by a ship of slow steam, which fired upon us with great guns. But we put on sail till the sea was over our decks and washed them clean, and lost ourselves in a fog.

"It is said, at this time, while we fled with fear at our hearts, that the yellow-haired sea wanderer put in to the Pribilofs, right to the factory, and while the part of his men held the servants of the company, the rest loaded ten thousand green skins from the salt houses. I say it is said, but I believe; for in the voyages I made on the coast with never a meeting the northern seas rang with his wildness and daring, till the three nations which have lands there sought him with their ships. And I heard of Unga, for the captains sang loud in her praise, and she was always with him. She had learned the ways of his people, they said, and was happy. But I knew better—knew that her heart harked back to her own people by the yellow beach of Akatan.

"So, after a long time, I went back to the port which is by a gateway of the sea, and there I learned that he had gone across the girth of the great ocean to hunt for the seal to the east of the warm land which runs south from the Russian seas. And I, who was become a sailorman, shipped with men of his own race, and went after him in the hunt of the seal. And there were few ships off that new land; but we hung on the flank of the seal pack and harried it north through all the spring of the year. And when the cows were heavy with pup and crossed the Russian line, our men grumbled and were afraid. For there was much fog, and every day men were lost in the boats. They would not work, so the captain turned the ship back toward the way it came. But I knew the yellow-haired sea wanderer was unafraid, and would hang by the pack, even to the Russian Isles, where few men go. So I took a boat, in the black of night, when the lookout dozed on the fo'c'slehead, and went alone to the warm, long land. And I journeyed south to meet the men by Yeddo Bay, who are wild and unafraid. And the Yoshiwara girls were small, and bright like steel, and good to look upon; but I could not stop, for I knew that Unga rolled on the tossing floor by the rookeries of the north.

"The men by Yeddo Bay had met from the ends of the earth, and had neither gods nor homes, sailing under the flag of the Japanese. And with them I went to the rich beaches of Copper Island, where our salt piles became high with skins. And in that silent sea we saw no man till we were ready to come away. Then one day the fog lifted on the edge of a heavy wind, and there jammed down upon us a schooner, with close in her wake the cloudy funnels of a Russian man-of-war. We fled away on the beam of the wind, with the schooner jamming still closer and plunging ahead three feet to our two. And upon her poop was the man with the mane of the sea lion, pressing the rails under with the canvas and laughing in his strength of life. And Unga was there—I knew her on the moment—but he sent her below when the cannons began to talk across the sea. As I say, with three feet to our two, till we saw the rudder lift green at every jump—and I swinging on to the wheel and cursing, with my back to the Russian shot. For we knew he had it in mind to run before us, that he might get away while we were caught. And they knocked our masts out of us till we dragged into the wind like a wounded gull; but he went on over the edge of the sky line—he and Unga.

"What could we? The fresh hides spoke for themselves. So they took us to a Russian port, and after that to a lone country, where they set us to work in the mines to dig salt. And some died, and—and some did not die."

Naass swept the blanket from his shoulders, disclosing the gnarled and twisted flesh, marked with the unmistakable striations of the knout. Prince hastily covered him, for it was not nice to look upon.

"We were there a weary time and sometimes men got away to the south, but they always came back. So, when we who hailed from Yeddo Bay rose in the night and took the guns from the guards, we went to the north. And the land was very large, with plains, soggy with water, and great forests. And the cold came, with much snow on the ground, and no man knew the way. Weary months we journeyed through the endless forest—I do not remember, now, for there was little food and often we lay down to die. But at last we came to the cold sea, and but three were left to look upon it. One had shipped from Yeddo as captain, and he knew in his head the lay of the great lands, and of the place where men may cross from one to the other on the ice. And he led us—I do not know, it was so long—till there were but two. When we came to that place we found five of the strange people which live in that country, and they had dogs and skins, and we were very poor. We fought in the snow till they died, and the captain died, and the dogs and skins were mine. Then I crossed on the ice, which was broken, and once I drifted till a gale from the west put me upon the shore. And after that, Golovin Bay, Pastilik, and the priest. Then south, south, to the warm sunlands where first I wandered.

"But the sea was no longer fruitful, and those who went upon it after the seal went to little profit and great risk. The fleets scattered, and the captains and the men had no word of those I sought. So I turned away from the ocean which never rests, and went among the lands, where the trees, the houses, and the mountains sit always in one place and do not move. I journeyed far, and came to learn many things, even to the way of reading and writing from books. It was well I should do this, for it came upon me that Unga must know these things, and that someday, when the time was met—we —you understand, when the time was met.

"So I drifted, like those little fish which raise a sail to the wind but cannot steer. But my eyes and my ears were open always, and I went among men who traveled much, for I knew they had but to see those I sought to remember. At last there came a man, fresh from the mountains, with pieces of rock in which the free gold stood to the size of peas, and he had heard, he had met, he knew them. They were rich, he said, and lived in the place where they drew the gold from the ground.

"It was in a wild country, and very far away; but in time I came to the camp, hidden between the mountains, where men worked night and day, out of the sight of the sun. Yet the time was not come. I listened to the talk of the people. He had gone away—they had gone away—to England, it was said, in the matter of bringing men with much money together to form companies. I saw the house they had lived in; more like a palace, such as one sees in the old countries. In the nighttime I crept in through a window that I might see in what manner he treated her. I went from room to room, and in such way thought kings and queens must live, it was all so very good. And they all said he treated her like a queen, and many marveled as to what breed of woman she was for there was other blood in her veins, and she was different from the women of Akatan, and no one knew her for what she was. Aye, she was a queen; but I was a chief, and the son of a chief, and I had paid for her an untold price of skin and boat and bead.

"But why so many words? I was a sailorman, and knew the way of the ships on the seas. I followed to England, and then to other countries. Sometimes I heard of them by word of mouth, sometimes I read of them in the papers; yet never once could I come by them, for they had much money, and traveled fast, while I was a poor man. Then came trouble upon them, and their wealth slipped away one day like a curl of smoke. The papers were full of it at the time; but after that nothing was said, and I knew they had gone back where more gold could be got from the ground.

"They had dropped out of the world, being now poor, and so I wandered from camp to camp, even north to the Kootenay country, where I picked up the cold scent. They had come and gone, some said this way, and some that, and still others that they had gone to the country of the Yukon. And I went this way, and I went that, ever journeying from place to place, till it seemed I must grow weary of the world which was so large. But in the Kootenay I traveled a bad trail, and a long trail, with a breed of the Northwest, who saw fit to die when the famine pinched. He had been to the Yukon by an unknown way over the mountains, and when he knew his time was near gave me the map and the secret of a place where he swore by his gods there was much gold.

"After that all the world began to flock into the north. I was a poor man; I sold myself to be a driver of dogs. The rest you know. I met him and her in Dawson. She did not know me, for I was only a stripling, and her life had been large, so she had no time to remember the one who had paid for her an untold price.

"So? You bought me from my term of service. I went back to bring things about in my own way, for I had waited long, and now that I had my hand upon him was in no hurry. As I say, I had it in mind to do my own way, for I ready back in my life, through all I had seen and suffered, and remembered the cold and hunger of the endless forest by the Russian seas. As you know, I led him into the east—him and Unga—into the east where many have gone and few returned. I led them to the spot where the bones and the curses of men lie with the gold which they may not have.

"The way was long and the trail unpacked. Our dogs were many and ate much; nor could our sleds carry till the break of spring. We must come back before the river ran free. So here and there we cached grub, that our sleds might be lightened and there be no chance of famine on the back trip. At the McQuestion there were three men, and near them we built a cache, as also did we at the Mayo, where was a hunting camp of a dozen Pellys which had crossed the divide from the south. After that, as we went on into the east, we saw no men; only the sleeping river, the moveless forest, and the White Silence of the North. As I say, the way was long and the trail unpacked. Sometimes, in a day's toil, we made no more than eight miles, or ten, and at night we slept like dead men. And never once did they dream that I was Naass, head man of Akatan, the righter of wrongs.

"We now made smaller caches, and in the nighttime it was a small matter to go back on the trial we had broken and change them in such way that one might deem the wolverines the thieves. Again there be places where there is a fall to the river, and the water is unruly, and the ice makes above and is eaten away beneath. In such a spot the sled I drove broke through, and the dogs; and to him and Unga it was ill luck, but no more. And there was much grub on that sled, and the dogs the strongest. But he laughed, for he was strong of life, and gave the dogs that were left little grub till we cut them from the harnesses one by one and fed them to their mates. We would go home light, he said, traveling and eating from cache to cache, with neither dogs nor sleds; which was true, for our grub was very short, and the last dog died in the traces the night we came to the gold and the bones and the curses of men.

"To reach that place—and the map spoke true—in the heart of the great mountains, we cut ice steps against the wall of a divide. One looked for a valley beyond, but there was no valley; the snow spread away, level as the great harvest plains, and here and there about us mighty mountains shoved their white heads among the stars. And midway on that strange plain which should have been a valley the earth and the snow fell away, straight down toward the heart of the world. Had we not been sailormen our heads would have swung round with the sight, but we stood on the dizzy edge that we might see a way to get down. And on one side, and one side only, the wall had fallen away till it was like the slope of the decks in a topsail breeze. I do not know why this thing should be so, but it was so. 'It is the mouth of hell,' he said; 'let us go down.' And we went down.

"And on the bottom there was a cabin, built by some man, of logs which he had cast down from above. It was a very old cabin, for men had died there alone at different times, and on pieces of birch bark which were there we read their last words and their curses. One had died of scurvy; another's partner had robbed him of his last grub and powder and stolen away; a third had been mauled by a baldface grizzly; a fourth had hunted for game and starved—and so it went, and they had been loath to leave the gold, and had died by the side of it in one way or another. And the worthless gold they had gathered yellowed the floor of the cabin like in a dream.

"But his soul was steady, and his head clear, this man I had led thus far. 'We have nothing to eat,' he said, 'and we will only look upon this gold, and see whence it comes and how much there be. Then we will go away quick, before it gets into our eyes and steals away our judgment. And in this way we may return in the end, with more grub, and possess it all.' So we looked upon the great vein, which cut the wall of the pit as a true vein should, and we measured it, and traced it from above and below, and drove the stakes of the claims and blazed the trees in token of our rights. Then, our knees shaking with lack of food, and a sickness in our bellies, and our hearts chugging close to our mouths, we climbed the mighty wall for the last time and turned our faces to the back trip.

"The last stretch we dragged Unga between us, and we fell often, but in the end we made the cache. And lo, there was no grub. It was well done, for he thought it the wolverines, and damned them and his gods in one breath. But Unga was brave, and smiled, and put her hand in his, till I turned away that I might hold myself. 'We will rest by the fire,' she said, 'till morning, and we will gather strength from our moccasins.' So we cut the tops of our moccasins in strips, and boiled them half of the night, that we might chew them and swallow them. And in the morning we talked of our chance. The next cache was five days' journey; we could not make it. We must find game.

" 'We will go forth and hunt,' he said.

" 'Yes,' said I, 'we will go forth and hunt.'

"And he ruled that Unga stay by the fire and save her strength. And we went forth, he in quest of the moose and I to the cache I had changed. But I ate little, so they might not see in me much strength. And in the night he fell many times as he drew into camp. And I, too, made to suffer great weakness, stumbling over my snowshoes as though each step might be my last. And we gathered strength from our moccasins.

"He was a great man. His soul lifted his body to the last; nor did he cry aloud, save for the sake of Unga. On the second day I followed him, that I might not miss the end. And he lay down to rest often. That night he was near gone; but in the morning he swore weakly and went forth again. He was like a drunken man, and I looked many times for him to give up, but his was the strength of the strong, and his soul the soul of a giant, for he lifted his body through all the weary day. And he shot two ptarmigan, but would not eat them. He needed no fire; they meant life; but his thought was for Unga, and he turned toward camp. He no longer walked, but crawled on hand and knee through the snow. I came to him, and read death in his eyes. Even then it was not too late to eat of the ptarmigan. He cast away his rifle and carried the birds in his mouth like a dog. I walked by his side, upright. And he looked at me during the moments he rested, and wondered that I was so strong. I could see it, though he no longer spoke; and when his lips moved, they moved without sound. As I say, he was a great man, and my heart spoke for softness; but I read back in my life, and remembered the cold and hunger of the endless forest by the Russian seas. Besides, Unga was mine, and I had paid for her an untold price of skin and boat and bead.

"And in this manner we came through the white forest, with the silence heavy upon us like a damp sea mist. And the ghosts of the past were in the air and all about us; and I saw the yellow beach of Akatan, and the kayaks racing home from the fishing, and the houses on the rim of the forest. And the men who had made themselves chiefs were there, the lawgivers whose blood I bore and whose blood I had wedded in Unga. Aye, and Yash-Noosh walked with me, the wet sand in his hair, and his war spear, broken as he fell upon it, still in his hand. And I knew the time was met, and saw in the eyes of Unga the promise.

"As I say, we came thus through the forest, till the smell of the camp smoke was in our nostrils. And I bent above him, and tore the ptarmigan from his teeth. He turned on his side and rested, the wonder mounting in his eyes, and the hand which was under slipping slow toward the knife at his hip. But I took it from him, smiling close in his face. Even then he did not understand. So I made to drink from black bottles, and to build high upon the snow a pile of goods, and to live again the things which had happened on the night of my marriage. I spoke no word, but he understood. Yet was he unafraid. There was a sneer to his lips, and cold anger, and he gathered new strength with the knowledge. It was not far, but the snow was deep, and he dragged himself very slow. Once he lay so long I turned him over and gazed into his eyes. And sometimes he looked forth, and sometimes death. And when I loosed him he struggled on again. In this way we came to the fire. Unga was at his side on the instant. His lips moved without sound; then he pointed at me, that Unga might understand. And after that he lay in the snow, very still, for a long while. Even now is he there in the snow.

"I said no word till I had cooked the ptarmigan. Then I spoke to her, in her own tongue, which she had not heard in many years. She straightened herself, so, and her eyes were wonder-wide, and she asked who I was, and where I had learned that speech.

" 'I am Naass,' I said.

" 'You?' she said. 'You?' And she crept close that she might look upon me.

" 'Yes,' I answered; 'I am Naass, head man of Akatan, the last of the blood, as you are the last of the blood.'

"And she laughed. By all the things I have seen and the deeds I have done may I never hear such a laugh again. It put the chill to my soul, sitting there in the White Silence, alone with death and this woman who laughed.

" 'Come!' I said, for I thought she wandered. 'Eat of the food and let us be gone. It is a far fetch from here to Akatan.'

"But she shoved her face in his yellow mane, and laughed till it seemed the heavens must fall about our ears. I had thought she would be overjoyed at the sight of me, and eager to go back to the memory of old times, but this seemed a strange form to take.

" 'Come!' I cried, taking her strong by the hand. 'The way is long and dark. Let us hurry!'

" 'Where?' she asked, sitting up, and ceasing from her strange mirth.

" 'To Akatan,' I answered, intent on the light to grow on her face at the thought. But it became like his, with a sneer to the lips, and cold anger.

" 'Yes,' she said; 'we will go, hand in hand, to Akatan, you and I. And we will live in the dirty huts, and eat of the fish and oil, and bring forth a spawn—a spawn to be proud of all the days of our life. We will forget the world and be happy, very happy. It is good, most good. Come! Let us hurry. Let us go back to Akatan.'

"And she ran her hand through his yellow hair, and smiled in a way which was not good. And there was no promise in her eyes.

"I sat silent, and marveled at the strangeness of woman. I went back to the night when he dragged her from me and she screamed and tore at his hair—at his hair which now she played with and would not leave. Then I remembered the price and the long years of waiting; and I gripped her close, and dragged her away as he had done. And she held back, even as on that night, and fought like a she-cat for its whelp. And when the fire was between us and the man, I loosed her, and she sat and listened. And I told her of all that lay between, of all that had happened to me on strange seas, of all that I had done in strange lands; of my weary quest, and the hungry years, and the promise which had been mine from the first. Aye, I told all, even to what had passed that day between the man and me, and in the days yet young. And as I spoke I saw the promise grow in her eyes, full and large like the break of dawn. And I read pity there, the tenderness of woman, the love, the heart and the soul of Unga. And I was a stripling again, for the look was the look of Unga as she ran up the beach, laughing, to the home of her mother. The stern unrest was gone, and the hunger, and the weary waiting. The time was met. I felt the call of her breast, and it seemed there I must pillow my head and forget. She opened her arms to me, and I came against her. Then, sudden, the hate flamed in her eye, her hand was at my hip. And once, twice, she passed the knife.

" 'Dog!' she sneered, as she flung me into the snow. 'Swine!' And then she laughed till the silence cracked, and went back to her dead.

"As I say, once she passed the knife, and twice; but she was weak with hunger, and it was not meant that I should die. Yet was I minded to stay in that place, and to close my eyes in the last long sleep with those whose lives had crossed with mine and led my feet on unknown trails. But there lay a debt upon me which would not let me rest.

"And the way was long, the cold bitter, and there was little grub. The Pellys had found no moose, and had robbed my cache. And so had the three white men, but they lay thin and dead in their cabins as I passed. After that I do not remember, till I came here, and found food and fire—much fire."

As he finished, he crouched closely, even jealously, over the stove. For a long while the slush-lamp shadows played tragedies upon the wall.

"But Unga!" cried Prince, the vision still strong upon him.

"Unga? She would not eat of the ptarmigan. She lay with her arms about his neck, her face deep in his yellow hair. I drew the fire close, that she might not feel the frost, but she crept to the other side. And I built a fire there; yet it was little good, for she would not eat. And in this manner they still lie up there in the snow."

"And you?" asked Malemute Kid.

"I do not know; but Akatan is small, and I have little wish to go back and live on the edge of the world. Yet is there small use in life. I can go to Constantine, and he will put irons upon me, and one day they will tie a piece of rope, so, and I will sleep good. Yet—no; I do not know."

"But, Kid," protested Prince, "this is murder!"

"Hush!" commanded Malemute Kid. "There be things greater than our wisdom, beyond our justice. The right and the wrong of this we cannot say, and it is not for us to judge."

Naass drew yet closer to the fire. There was a great silence, and in each man's eyes many pictures came and went.

The White Silence

"Carmen won't last more than a couple of days." Mason spat out a chunk of ice and surveyed the poor animal ruefully, then put her foot in his mouth and proceeded to bite out the ice which clustered cruelly between the toes.

"I never saw a dog with a highfalutin' name that ever was worth a rap," he said, as he concluded his task and shoved her aside. "They just fade away and die under the responsibility. Did ye ever see one go wrong with a sensible name like Cassiar, Siwash, or Husky? No, sir! Take a look at Shookum here, he's—"

Snap! The lean brute flashed up, the white teeth just missing Mason's throat.

"Ye will, will ye?" A shrewd clout behind the ear with the butt of the dog whip stretched the animal in the snow, quivering softly, a yellow slaver dripping from its fangs.

"As I was saying, just look at Shookum here—he's got the spirit. Bet ye he eats Carmen before the week's out."

"I'll bank another proposition against that," replied Malemute Kid, reversing the frozen bread placed before the fire to thaw. "We'll eat Shookum before the trip is over. What d'ye say, Ruth?"

The Indian woman settled the coffee with a piece of ice, glanced from Malemute Kid to her husband, then at the dogs, but vouchsafed no reply. It was such a palpable truism that none was necessary. Two hundred miles of unbroken trail in prospect, with a scant six days' grub for themselves and none for the dogs, could admit no other alternative. The two men and the woman grouped about the fire and began their meager meal. The dogs lay in their harnesses, for it was a midday halt, and watched each mouthful enviously.

"No more lunches after today," said Malemute Kid. "And we've got to keep a close eye on the dogs—they're getting vicious. They'd just as soon pull a fellow down as not, if they get a chance."

"And I was president of an Epworth once, and taught in the Sunday school." Having irrelevantly delivered himself of this, Mason fell into a dreamy contemplation of his steaming moccasins, but was aroused by Ruth filling his cup. "Thank God, we've got slathers of tea! I've seen it growing, down in Tennessee. What wouldn't I give for a hot corn pone just now! Never mind, Ruth; you won't starve much longer, nor wear moccasins either."

The woman threw off her gloom at this, and in her eyes welled up a great love for her white lord—the first white man she had ever seen—the first man whom she had known to treat a woman as something better than a mere animal or beast of burden.

"Yes, Ruth," continued her husband, having recourse to the macaronic jargon in which it was alone possible for them to understand each other; "wait till we clean up and pull for the Outside. We'll take the White Man's canoe and go to the Salt Water. Yes, bad water, rough water—great mountains dance up and down all the time. And so big, so far, so far away—you travel ten sleep, twenty sleep, forty sleep"—he graphically enumerated the days on his fingers—"all the time water, bad water. Then you come to great village, plenty people, just the same mosquitoes next summer. Wigwams oh, so high—ten, twenty pines. Hi-yu skookum!"

He paused impotently, cast an appealing glance at Malemute Kid, then laboriously placed the twenty pines, end on end, by sign language. Malemute Kid smiled with cheery cynicism; but Ruth's eyes were wide with wonder, and with pleasure; for she half believed he was joking, and such condescension pleased her poor woman's heart.

"And then you step into a—a box, and pouf! up you go." He tossed his empty cup in the air by way of illustration and, as he deftly caught it, cried: "And biff! down you come. Oh, great medicine men! You go Fort Yukon, I go Arctic City—twenty-five sleep—big string, all the time—I catch him string—I say, 'Hello, Ruth! How are ye?'—and you say, 'Is that my good husband?'—and I say, 'Yes'—and you say, 'No can bake good bread, no more soda'—then I say, 'Look in cache, under flour; good-by.' You look and catch plenty soda. All the time you Fort Yukon, me Arctic City. Hi-yu medicine man!"

Ruth smiled so ingenuously at the fairy story that both men burst into laughter. A row among the dogs cut short the wonders of the Outside, and by the time the snarling combatants were separated, she had lashed the sleds and all was ready for the trail.

"Mush! Baldy! Hi! Mush on!" Mason worked his whip smartly and, as the dogs whined low in the traces, broke out the sled with the gee pole. Ruth followed with the second team, leaving Malemute Kid, who had helped her start, to bring up the rear. Strong man, brute that he was, capable of felling an ox at a blow, he could not bear to beat the poor animals, but humored them as a dog driver rarely does—nay, almost wept with them in their misery.

"Come, mush on there, you poor sore-footed brutes!" he murmured, after several ineffectual attempts to start the load. But his patience was at last rewarded, and though whimpering with pain, they hastened to join their fellows.

No more conversation; the toil of the trail will not permit such extravagance. And of all deadening labors, that of the Northland trail is the worst. Happy is the man who can weather a day's travel at the price of silence, and that on a beaten track.

And of all heartbreaking labors, that of breaking trail is the worst. At every step the great webbed shoe sinks till the snow is level with the knee. Then up, straight up, the deviation of a fraction of an inch being a certain precursor of disaster, the snowshoe must be lifted till the surface is cleared; then forward, down, and the other foot is raised perpendicularly for the matter of half a yard. He who tries this for the first time, if haply he avoids bringing his shoes in dangerous propinquity and measures not his length on the treacherous footing, will give up exhausted at the end of a hundred yards; he who can keep out of the way of the dogs for a whole day may well crawl into his sleeping bag with a clear conscience and a pride which passeth all understanding; and he who travels twenty sleeps on the Long Trail is a man whom the gods may envy.

The afternoon wore on, and with the awe, born of the White Silence, the voiceless travelers bent to their work. Nature has many tricks wherewith she convinces man of his finity—the ceaseless flow of the tides, the fury of the storm, the shock of the earthquake, the long roll of heaven's artillery—but the most tremendous, the most stupefying of all, is the passive phase of the White Silence. All movement ceases, the sky clears, the heavens are as brass; the slightest whisper seems sacrilege, and man becomes timid, affrighted at the sound of his own voice. Sole speck of life journeying across the ghostly wastes of a dead world, he trembles at his audacity, realizes that his is a maggot's life, nothing more. Strange thoughts arise unsummoned, and the mystery of all things strives for utterance. And the fear of death, of God, of the universe, comes over him—the hope of the Resurrection and the Life, the yearning for immortality, the vain striving of the imprisoned essence—it is then, if ever, man walks alone with God.

So wore the day away. The river took a great bend, and Mason headed his team for the cutoff across the narrow neck of land. But the dogs balked at the high bank. Again and again, though Ruth and Malemute Kid were shoving on the sled, they slipped back. Then came the concerted effort. The miserable creatures, weak from hunger, exerted their last strength. Up—up—the sled poised on the top of the bank; but the leader swung the string of dogs behind him to the right, fouling Mason's snowshoes. The result was grievous. Mason was whipped off his feet; one of the dogs fell in the traces; and the sled toppled back, dragging everything to the bottom again.

Slash! the whip fell among the dogs savagely, especially upon the one which had fallen.

"Don't, Mason," entreated Malemute Kid; "the poor devil's on its last legs. Wait and we'll put my team on."

Mason deliberately withheld the whip till the last word had fallen, then out flashed the long lash, completely curling about the offending creature's body. Carmen—for it was Carmen—cowered in the snow, cried piteously, then rolled over on her side.

It was a tragic moment, a pitiful incident of the trail—a dying dog, two comrades in anger. Ruth glanced solicitously from man to man. But Malemute Kid restrained himself, though there was a world of reproach in his eyes, and, bending over the dog, cut the traces. No word was spoken. The teams were double-spanned and the difficulty overcome; the sleds were under way again, the dying dog dragging herself along in the rear. As long as an animal can travel, it is not shot, and this last chance is accorded it—the crawling into camp, if it can, in the hope of a moose being killed.

Already penitent for his angry action, but too stubborn to make amends, Mason toiled on at the head of the cavalcade, little dreaming that danger hovered in the air. The timber clustered thick in the sheltered bottom, and through this they threaded their way. Fifty feet or more from the trail towered a lofty pine. For generations it had stood there, and for generations destiny had had this one end in view—perhaps the same had been decreed of Mason.

He stooped to fasten the loosened thong of his moccasin. The sleds came to a halt, and the dogs lay down in the snow without a whimper. The stillness was weird; not a breath rustled the frost-encrusted forest; the cold and silence of outer space had chilled the heart and smote the trembling lips of nature. A sigh pulsed through the air—they did not seem to actually hear it, but rather felt it, like the premonition of movement in a motionless void. Then the great tree, burdened with its weight of years and snow, played its last part in the tragedy of life. He heard the warning crash and attempted to spring up but, almost erect, caught the blow squarely on the shoulder.

The sudden danger, the quick death—how often had Malemute Kid faced it! The pine needles were still quivering as he gave his commands and sprang into action. Nor did the Indian girl faint or raise her voice in idle wailing, as might many of her white sisters. At his order, she threw her weight on the end of a quickly extemporized handspike, easing the pressure and listening to her husband's groans, while Malemute Kid attacked the tree with his ax. The steel rang merrily as it bit into the frozen trunk, each stroke being accompanied by a forced, audible respiration, the "Huh!" "Huh!" of the woodsman.

At last the Kid laid the pitiable thing that was once a man in the snow. But worse than his comrade's pain was the dumb anguish in the woman's face, the blended look of hopeful, hopeless query. Little was said; those of the Northland are early taught the futility of words and the inestimable value of deeds. With the temperature at sixty-five below zero, a man cannot lie many minutes in the snow and live. So the sled lashings were cut, and the sufferer, rolled in furs, laid on a couch of boughs. Before him roared a fire, built of the very wood which wrought the mishap. Behind and partially over him was stretched the primitive fly—a piece of canvas, which caught the radiating heat and threw it back and down upon him—a trick which men may know who study physics at the fount.

And men who have shared their bed with death know when the call is sounded. Mason was terribly crushed. The most cursory examination revealed it. His right arm, leg, and back were broken; his limbs were paralyzed from the hips; and the likelihood of internal injuries was large. An occasional moan was his only sign of life.

No hope; nothing to be done. The pitiless night crept slowly by—Ruth's portion, the despairing stoicism of her race, and Malemute Kid adding new lines to his face of bronze. In fact, Mason suffered least of all, for he spent his time in eastern Tennessee, in the Great Smoky Mountains, living over the scenes of his childhood. And most pathetic was the melody of his long-forgotten Southern vernacular, as he raved of swimming holes and coon hunts and watermelon raids. It was as Greek to Ruth, but the Kid understood and felt—felt as only one can feel who has been shut out for years from all that civilization means.

Morning brought consciousness to the stricken man, and Malemute Kid bent closer to catch his whispers.

"You remember when we foregathered on the Tanana, four years come next ice run? I didn't care so much for her then. It was more like she was pretty, and there was a smack of excitement about it, I think. But d'ye know, I've come to think a heap of her. She's been a good wife to me, always at my shoulder in the pinch. And when it comes to trading, you know there isn't her equal. D'ye recollect the time she shot the Moosehorn Rapids to pull you and me off that rock, the bullets whipping the water like hailstones?—and the time of the famine at Nuklukyeto?—or when she raced the ice run to bring the news? Yes, she's been a good wife to me, better'n that other one. Didn't know I'd been there? Never told you, eh? Well, I tried it once, down in the States. That's why I'm here. Been raised together, too. I came away to give her a chance for divorce. She got it.

"But that's got nothing to do with Ruth. I had thought of cleaning up and pulling for the Outside next year—her and I—but it's too late. Don't send her back to her people, Kid. It's beastly hard for a woman to go back. Think of it!—nearly four years on our bacon and beans and flour and dried fruit, and then to go back to her fish and caribou. It's not good for her to have tried our ways, to come to know they're better'n her people's, and then return to them. Take care of her, Kid—why don't you—but no, you always fought shy of them—and you never told me why you came to this country.

Be kind to her, and send her back to the States as soon as you can. But fix it so she can come back—liable to get homesick, you know.

"And the youngster—it's drawn us closer, Kid. I only hope it is a boy. Think of it!—flesh of my flesh, Kid. He mustn't stop in this country. And if it's a girl, why, she can't. Sell my furs; they'll fetch at least five thousand, and I've got as much more with the company. And handle my interests with yours. I think that bench claim will show up. See that he gets a good schooling; and, Kid, above all, don't let him come back. This country was not made for white men.

"I'm a gone man, Kid. Three or four sleeps at the best. You've got to go on. You must go on! Remember, it's my wife, it's my boy—O God! I hope it's a boy! You can't stay by me—and I charge you, a dying man, to pull on."

"Give me three days," pleaded Malemute Kid. "You may change for the better; something may turn up."

"No."

"Just three days."

"You must pull on."

"Two days."

"It's my wife and my boy, Kid. You would not ask it."

"One day."

"No, no! I charge—"

"Only one day. We can shave it through on the grub, and I might knock over a moose."

"No—all right; one day, but not a minute more. And, Kid, don't—don't leave me to face it alone. Just a shot, one pull on the trigger. You understand. Think of it! Think of it! Flesh of my flesh, and I'll never live to see him!

"Send Ruth here. I want to say good-by and tell her that she must think of the boy and not wait till I'm dead. She might refuse to go with you if I didn't. Good-by, old man; good-by.

"Kid! I say—a—sink a hole above the pup, next to the slide. I panned out forty cents on my shovel there.

"And, Kid!" He stooped lower to catch the last faint words, the dying man's surrender of his pride. "I'm sorry—for—you know—Carmen."

Leaving the girl crying softly over her man, Malemute Kid slipped into his parka and snowshoes, tucked his rifle under his arm, and crept away into the forest. He was no tyro in the stern sorrows of the Northland, but never had he faced so stiff a problem as this. In the abstract, it was a plain, mathematical proposition—three possible lives as against one doomed one. But now he hesitated. For five years, shoulder to shoulder, on the rivers and trails, in the camps and mines, facing death by field and flood and famine, had they knitted the bonds of their comradeship. So close was the tie that he had often been conscious of a vague jealousy of Ruth, from the first time she had come between. And now it must be severed by his own hand.

Though he prayed for a moose, just one moose, all game seemed to have deserted the land, and nightfall found the exhausted man crawling into camp, lighthanded, heavy-hearted. An uproar from the dogs and shrill cries from Ruth hastened him.

Bursting into the camp, he saw the girl in the midst of the snarling pack, laying about her with an ax. The dogs had broken the iron rule of their masters and were rushing the grub. He joined the issue with his rifle reversed, and the hoary game of natural selection was played out with all the ruthlessness of its primeval environment. Rifle and ax went up and down, hit or missed with monotonous regularity; lithe bodies flashed, with wild eyes and dripping fangs; and man and beast fought for supremacy to the bitterest conclusion. Then the beaten brutes crept to the edge of the firelight, licking their wounds, voicing their misery to the stars.

The whole stock of dried salmon had been devoured, and perhaps five pounds of flour remained to tide them over two hundred miles of wilderness. Ruth returned to her husband, while Malemute Kid cut up the warm body of one of the dogs, the skull of which had been crushed by the ax. Every portion was carefully put away, save the hide and offal, which were cast to his fellows of the moment before.

Morning brought fresh trouble. The animals were turning on each other. Carmen, who still clung to her slender thread of life, was downed by the pack. The lash fell among them unheeded. They cringed and cried under the blows, but refused to scatter till the last wretched bit had disappeared—bones, hide, hair, everything.

Malemute Kid went about his work, listening to Mason, who was back in Tennessee, delivering tangled discourses and wild exhortations to his brethren of other days.

Taking advantage of neighboring pines, he worked rapidly, and Ruth watched him make a cache similar to those sometimes used by hunters to preserve their meat from the wolverines and dogs. One after the other, he bent the tops of two small pines toward each other and nearly to the ground, making them fast with thongs of moosehide. Then he beat the dogs into submission and harnessed them to two of the sleds, loading the same with everything but the furs which enveloped Mason. These he wrapped and lashed tightly about him, fastening either end of the robes to the bent pines. A single stroke of his hunting knife would release them and send the body high in the air.

Ruth had received her husband's last wishes and made no struggle. Poor girl, she had learned the lesson of obedience well. From a child, she had bowed, and seen all women bow, to the lords of creation, and it did not seem in the nature of things for woman to resist. The Kid permitted her one outburst of grief, as she kissed her husband—her own people had no such custom—then led her to the foremost sled and helped her into her snowshoes. Blindly, instinctively, she took the gee pole and whip, and "mushed" the dogs out on the trail. Then he returned to Mason, who had fallen into a coma, and long after she was out of sight crouched by the fire, waiting, hoping, praying for his comrade to die.

It is not pleasant to be alone with painful thoughts in the White Silence. The silence of gloom is merciful, shrouding one as with protection and breathing a thousand intangible sympathies; but the bright White Silence, clear and cold, under steely skies, is pitiless.

An hour passed—two hours—but the man would not die. At high noon the sun, without raising its rim above the southern horizon, threw a suggestion of fire athwart the heavens, then quickly drew it back. Malemute Kid roused and dragged himself to his comrade's side. He cast one glance about him. The White Silence seemed to sneer and a great fear came upon him. There was a sharp report; Mason swung into his aerial sepulcher, and Malemute Kid lashed the dogs into a wild gallop as he fled across the snow.

The Son of the Wolf

MAN rarely places a proper valuation upon his womankind, at least not until deprived of them. He has no conception of the subtle atmosphere exhaled by the sex feminine, so long as he bathes in it; but let it be withdrawn, and an ever-growing void begins to manifest itself in his existence, and he becomes hungry, in a vague sort of way, for a something so indefinite that he cannot characterize it. If his comrades have no more experience than himself, they will shake their heads dubiously and dose him with strong physic. But the hunger will continue and become stronger; he will lose interest in the things of his everyday life and wax morbid; and one day, when the emptiness has become unbearable, a revelation will dawn upon him.

In the Yukon country, when this come to pass, the man usually provisions a poling boat, if it is summer, and if winter, harnesses his dogs, and heads for the Southland. A few months later, supposing him to be possessed of a faith in the country, he returns with a wife to share with him in that faith, and incidentally in his hardships. This but serves to show the innate selfishness of man. It also brings us to the trouble of "Scruff" Mackenzie, which occurred in the old days, before the country was stampeded and staked by a tidal-wave of *che-cha-quas,* and when the Klondike's only claim to notice was its salmon fisheries.

"Scruff" Mackenzie bore the earmarks of a frontier birth and frontier life. His face was stamped with twenty-five years of incessant struggle with Nature in her wildest moods,—the last two, the wildest and hardest of all, having been spent in groping for the gold which lies in the shadow of the Arctic Circle. When the yearning sickness came upon him, he was not surprised, for he was a practical man and had seen other men thus stricken. But he showed no sign of his malady, save that he worked harder. All summer he fought mosquitoes and washed the sure-thing bars of the Stuart River for a double grubstake. Then he floated a raft of houselogs down the Yukon to Forty Mile, and put together as comfortable a cabin as any the camp could boast of. In fact, it showed such cozy promise that many men elected to be his partner and to come and live with him. But he crushed their aspirations with rough speech, peculiar for its strength and brevity, and bought a double supply of grub from the tradingpost.

As has been noted, "Scruff" Mackenzie was a practical man. If he wanted a thing he usually got it, but in doing so, went no farther out of his way than was necessary. Though a son of toil and hardship, he was averse to a journey of six hundred miles on the ice, a second of two thousand miles on the ocean, and still a third thousand miles or so to his last stamping-grounds,—all in the mere quest of a wife. Life was too short. So he rounded up his dogs, lashed a curious freight to his sled, and faced across the divide whose westward slopes were drained by the head-reaches of the Tanana.

He was a sturdy traveler, and his wolf-dogs could work harder and travel farther on less grub than any other team in the Yukon. Three weeks later he strode into a hunting-camp of the Upper Tanana Sticks. They marveled at his temerity; for they had a bad name and had been known to kill white men for as trifling a thing as a sharp ax or a broken rifle. But he went among them single-handed, his bearing being a delicious composite of humility, familiarity, *sangfroid*, and insolence. It required a deft hand and deep knowledge of the barbaric mind effectually to handle such diverse weapons; but he was a past-master in the art, knowing when to conciliate and when to threaten with Jove-like wrath.

He first made obeisance to the Chief Thling-Tinneh, presenting him with a couple of pounds of black tea and tobacco, and thereby winning his most cordial regard. Then he mingled with the men and maidens, and that night gave a *potlach*. The snow was beaten down in the form of an oblong, perhaps a hundred feet in length and quarter as many across. Down the center a long fire was built, while either side was carpeted with spruce boughs. The lodges were forsaken, and the fivescore or so members of the tribe gave tongue to their folk-chants in honor of their guest.

"Scruff" Mackenzie's two years had taught him the not many hundred words of their vocabulary, and he had likewise conquered their deep gutturals, their Japanese idioms, constructions, and honorific and agglutinative particles. So he made oration after their manner, satisfying their instinctive poetry-love with crude flights of eloquence and metaphorical contortions. After Thling-Tinneh and the Shaman had responded in kind, he made trifling presents to the menfolk, joined in their singing, and proved an expert in their fifty-two-stick gambling game.

And they smoked his tobacco and were pleased. But among the younger men there was a defiant attitude, a spirit of braggadocio, easily understood by the raw insinuations of the toothless squaws and the giggling of the maidens. They had known few white men, "Sons of the Wolf," but from those few they had learned strange lessons.

Nor had "Scruff" Mackenzie, for all his seeming carelessness, failed to note these phenomena. In truth, rolled in his sleeping-furs, he thought it all over, thought seriously, and emptied many pipes in mapping out a campaign. One maiden only had caught his fancy,—none other than Zarinska, daughter to the chief. In features, form, and poise, answering more nearly to the white man's type of beauty, she was almost an anomaly among her tribal sisters. He would possess her, make her his wife, and name her—ah, he would name her Gertrude! Having thus decided, he rolled over on his side and dropped off to sleep, a true son of his all-conquering race, a Samson among the Philistines.

It was slow work and a stiff game; but "Scruff" Mackenzie maneuvered cunningly, with an unconcern which served to puzzle the Sticks. He took great care to impress the men that he was a sure shot and a mighty hunter, and the camp rang with his plaudits when he brought down a moose at six hundred yards. Of a night he visited in Chief Thling-Tinneh's lodge of moose and cariboo skins, talking big and dispensing tobacco with a lavish hand. Nor did he fail to likewise honor the Shaman; for he realized the medicine-man's influence with his people, and was anxious to make of him an ally. But that worthy was high and mighty, refused to be propitiated, and was unerringly marked down as a prospective enemy.

Though no opening presented for an interview with Zarinska, Mackenzie stole many a glance to her, giving fair warning of his intent. And well she knew, yet coquettishly surrounded herself with a ring of women whenever the men were away and he had a chance. But he was in no hurry; besides, he knew she could not help but think of him, and a few days of such thought would only better his suit.

At last, one night, when he deemed the time to be ripe, he abruptly left the chief's smoky dwelling and hastened to a neighboring lodge. As usual, she sat with squaws and maidens about her, all engaged in sewing moccasins and beadwork. They laughed at his entrance, and badinage, which linked Zarinska to him, ran high. But one after the other they were unceremoniously bundled into the outer snow, whence they hurried to spread the tale through all the camp.

His cause was well pleaded, in her tongue, for she did not know his, and at the end of two hours he rose to go.

"So Zarinska will come to the White Man's lodge? Good! I go now to have talk with thy father, for he may not be so minded. And I will give him many tokens; but he must not ask too much. If he say no? Good! Zarinska shall yet come to the White Man's lodge."

He had already lifted the skin flap to depart, when a low exclamation brought him back to the girl's side. She brought herself to her knees on the bearskin mat, her face aglow with true Eve-light, and shyly unbuckled his heavy belt. He looked down, perplexed, suspicious, his ears alert for the slightest sound without. But her next move disarmed his doubt, and he smiled with pleasure. She took from her sewing bag a moosehide sheath, brave with bright beadwork, fantastically designed. She drew his great hunting-knife, gazed reverently along the keen edge, half tempted to try it with her thumb, and shot it into place in its new home. Then she slipped the sheath along the belt to its customary resting-place, just above the hip.

For all the world, it was like a scene of olden time—a lady and her knight, Mackenzie drew her up full height and swept her red lips with his moustache,—the, to her, foreign caress of the Wolf. It was a meeting of the stone age and the steel; but she was none the less a woman, as her crimson cheeks and the luminous softness of her eyes attested.

There was a thrill of excitement in the air as "Scruff" Mackenzie, a bulky bundle under his arm, threw open the flap of Thling-Tinneh's tent. Children were running about in the open, dragging dry wood to the scene of the *potlach,* a babble of women's voices was growing in intensity, the young men were consulting in sullen groups, while from the Shaman's lodge rose the eerie sounds of an incantation.

The chief was alone with his blear-eyed wife, but a glance sufficed to tell Mackenzie that the news was already told. So he plunged at once into the business, shifting the beaded sheath prominently to the fore as advertisement of the betrothal.

"O Thling-Tinneh, mighty chief of the Sticks and the land of the Tanana, ruler of the salmon and the bear, the moose and the cariboo! The White Man is before thee with a great purpose. Many moons has his lodge been empty, and he is lonely. And his heart has eaten itself in silence, and grown hungry for a woman to sit beside him in his lodge, to meet him from the hunt with warm fire and good food. He has heard strange things, the patter of baby moccasins and the sound of children's voices. And one night a vision came upon him, and he beheld the Raven, who is thy father, the great Raven, who is the father of all the Sticks. And the Raven spake to the lonely White Man, saying: 'Bind thou thy moccasins upon thee, and gird thy snowshoes on, and lash thy sled with food for many sleeps and fine tokens for the Chief Thling-Tinneh. For thou shalt turn thy face to where the midspring sun is wont to sink below the land and journey to this great chief's hunting-grounds. There thou shalt make big presents, and Thling-Tinneh, who is my son, shall become to thee as a father. In his lodge there is a maiden into whom I breathed the breath of life for thee. This maiden shalt thou take to wife.'

"O Chief, thus spake the great Raven; thus do I lay many presents at thy feet; thus am I come to take thy daughter!"

The old man drew his furs about him with crude consciousness of royalty, but delayed reply while a youngster crept in, delivered a quick message to appear before the council, and was gone.

"O White Man, whom we have named Moose-Killer, also known as the Wolf, and the Son of the Wolf! We know thou comest of a mighty race; we are proud to have thee our *potlach-* guest; but the king-salmon does not mate with the dog-salmon, nor the Raven with the Wolf."

"Not so!" cried Mackenzie. "The daughters of the Raven have I met in the camps of the Wolf,—the squaw of Mortimer, the squaw of Tregidgo, the squaw of Barnaby, who came two ice-runs back, and I have heard of other squaws, though my eyes beheld them not."

"Son, your words are true; but it were evil mating, like the water with the sand, like the snow-flake with the sun. But met you one Mason and his squaw? No? He came ten ice-runs ago,—the first of all the Wolves. And with him there was a mighty man, straight as a willow-shoot, and tall; strong as the bald-faced grizzly, with a heart like the full summer moon; his—"

"Oh!" interrupted Mackenzie, recognizing the well-known Northland figure,—"Malemute Kid!"

"The same,—a mighty man. But saw you aught of the squaw? She was full sister to Zarinska."

"Nay, Chief; but I have heard. Mason—far, far to the north, a spruce-tree, heavy with years, crushed out his life beneath. But his love was great, and he had much gold. With this, and her boy, she journeyed countless sleeps toward the winter's noonday sun, and there she yet lives,—no biting frost, no snow, no summer's midnight sun, no winter's noonday night."

A second messenger interrupted with imperative summons from the council. As Mackenzie threw him into the snow, he caught a glimpse of the swaying forms before the council-fire, heard the deep basses of the men in rhythmic chant, and knew the Shaman was fanning the anger of his people. Time pressed. He turned upon the chief.

"Come! I wish thy child. And now, see! Here are tobacco, tea, many cups of sugar, warm blankets, handkerchiefs, both good and large; and here, a true rifle, with many bullets and much powder."

"Nay," replied the old man, struggling against the great wealth spread before him. "Even now are my people come together. They will not have this marriage."

"But thou art chief."

"Yet do my young men rage because the Wolves have taken their maidens so that they may not marry."

"Listen, O Thling-Tinneh! Ere the night has passed into the day, the Wolf shall face his dogs to the Mountains of the East and fare forth to the Country of the Yukon. And Zarinska shall break trail for his dogs."

"And ere the night has gained its middle, my young men may fling to the dogs the flesh of the Wolf, and his bones be scattered in the snow till the springtime lay them bare."

It was threat and counter-threat. Mackenzie's bronzed face flushed darkly. He raised his voice. The old squaw, who till now had sat an impassive spectator, made to creep by him for the door. The song of the men broke suddenly and there was a hubbub of many voices as he whirled the old woman roughly to her couch of skins.

"Again I cry—listen, O Thling-Tinneh! The Wolf dies with teeth fast-locked, and with him there shall sleep ten of thy strongest men,—men who are needed, for the hunting is but begun, and the fishing is not many moons away. And again, of what profit should I die? I know the custom of thy people; thy share of my wealth shall be very small. Grant me thy child, and it shall all be thine. And yet again, my brothers will come, and they are many, and their maws are never filled; and the daughters of the Raven shall bear children in the lodges of the Wolf. My people are greater than thy people. It is destiny. Grant, and all this wealth is thine."

Moccasins were crunching the snow without. Mackenzie threw his rifle to cock, and loosened the twin Colts in his belt.

"Grant, O Chief!"

"And yet will my people say no."

"Grant, and the wealth is thine. Then shall I deal with thy people after."

"The Wolf will have it so. I will take his tokens,—but I would warn him."

Mackenzie passed over the goods, taking care to clog the rifle's ejector, and capping the bargain with a kaleidoscopic silk kerchief. The Shaman and half a dozen young braves entered, but he shouldered boldly among them and passed out.

"Pack!" was his laconic greeting to Zarinska as he passed her lodge and hurried to harness his dogs. A few minutes later he swept into the council at the head of the team, the woman by his side. He took his place at the upper end of the oblong, by the side of the chief. To his left, a step to the rear, he stationed Zarinska,—her proper place. Besides, the time was ripe for mischief, and there was need to guard his back.

On either side, the men crouched to the fire, their voices lifted in a folk-chant out of the forgotten past. Full of strange, halting cadences and haunting recurrences, it was not beautiful. "Fearful" may inadequately express it. At the lower end, under the eye of the Shaman, danced half a score of women. Stern were his reproofs of those who did not wholly abandon themselves to the ecstasy of the rite. Half hidden in their heavy masses of raven hair, all dishevelled and falling to their waists, they slowly swayed to and fro, their forms rippling to an ever-changing rhythm.

It was a weird scene; an anachronism. To the south, the nineteenth century was reeling off the few years of its last decade; here flourished man primeval, a shade removed from the prehistoric cave-dweller, a forgotten fragment of the Elder World. The tawny wolf-dogs sat between their skin-clad masters or fought for room, the fire-light cast backward from their red eyes and dripping fangs. The woods, in ghostly shroud, slept on unheeding. The White Silence, for the moment driven to the rimming forest, seemed ever crushing inward; the stars danced with great leaps, as is their wont in the time of the Great Cold; while the Spirits of the Pole trailed their robes of glory athwart the heavens.

"Scruff" Mackenzie dimly realized the wild grandeur of the setting as his eyes ranged down the fur-fringed sides in quest of missing faces. They rested for a moment on a newborn babe, suckling at its mother's naked breast. It was forty below,—seven and odd degrees of frost. He thought of the tender women of his own race and smiled grimly. Yet from the loins of some such tender woman had he sprung with a kingly inheritance,—an inheritance which gave to him and his dominance over the land and sea, over the animals and the peoples of all the zones. Single-handed against fivescore, girt by the Arctic winter, far from his own, he felt the prompting of his heritage, the desire to possess, the wild danger-love, the thrill of battle, the power to conquer or to die.

The singing and the dancing ceased, and the Shaman flared up in rude eloquence. Through the sinuosities of their vast mythology, he worked cunningly upon the credulity of his people. The case was strong. Opposing the creative principles as embodied in the Crow and the Raven, he stigmatized Mackenzie as the Wolf, the fighting and the destructive principle. Not only was the combat of these forces spiritual, but men fought, each to his totem. They were the children of Jelchs, the Raven, the Promethean fire-bringer; Mackenzie was the child of the Wolf, or in other words, the Devil. For them to bring a truce to this perpetual warfare, to marry their daughters to the arch-enemy, were treason and blasphemy of the highest order. No phrase was harsh nor figure vile enough in branding Mackenzie as a sneaking interloper and emissary of Satan. There was a subdued, savage roar in the deep chests of his listeners as he took the swing of his peroration.

"Aye, my brothers, Jelchs is all-powerful! Did he not bring heaven-born fire that we might be warm? Did he not draw the sun, moon, and stars, from their holes that we might see? Did he not teach us that we might fight the Spirits of Famine and of Frost? But now Jelchs is angry with his children, and they are grown to a handful, and he will not help. For they have forgotten him, and done evil things, and trod bad trails, and taken his enemies into their lodges to sit by their fires. And the Raven is sorrowful at the wickedness of his children; but when they shall rise up and show they have come back, he will come out of the darkness to aid them. O brothers! the Fire-Bringer has whispered messages to thy Shaman; the same shall ye hear. Let the young men take the young women to their lodges; let them fly at the throat of the Wolf; let them be undying in their enmity! Then shall their women become fruitful and they shall multiply into a mighty people! And the Raven shall lead great tribes of their fathers and their fathers' fathers from out of the North; and they shall beat back the Wolves till they are as last year's campfires; and they shall again come to rule over all the land! 'T is the message of Jelchs, the Raven."

This foreshadowing of the Messiah's coming brought a hoarse howl from the Sticks as they leaped to their feet. Mackenzie slipped the thumbs of his mittens and waited. There was a clamor for the "Fox," not to be stilled till one of the young men stepped forward to speak.

"Brothers! The Shaman has spoken wisely. The Wolves have taken our women, and our men are childless. We are grown to a handful. The Wolves have taken our warm furs and given for them evil spirits which dwell in bottles, and clothes which come not from the beaver or the lynx, but are made from the grass. And they are not warm, and our men die of strange sicknesses. I, the Fox, have taken no woman to wife; and why? Twice have the maidens which pleased me gone to the camps of the Wolf. Even now have I laid by skins of the beaver, of the moose, of the cariboo, that I might win favor in the eyes of Thling-Tinneh, that I might marry Zarinska, his daughter. Even now are her snowshoes bound to her feet, ready to break trail for the dogs of the Wolf. Nor do I speak for myself alone. As I have done, so has the Bear. He, too, had fain been the father of her children, and many skins has he cured thereto. I speak for all the young men who know not wives. The Wolves are ever hungry. Always do they take the choice meat at the killing. To the Ravens are left the leavings.

"There is Gugkla," he cried, brutally pointing out one of the women, who was a cripple. "Her legs are bent like the ribs of a birch canoe. She cannot gather wood nor carry the meat of the hunters. Did the Wolves choose her?"

"Ai! ai!" vociferated his tribesmen.

"There is Moyri, whose eyes are crossed by the Evil Spirit. Even the babes are affrighted when they gaze upon her, and it is said the bald-face gives her the trail. Was she chosen?"

Again the cruel applause rang out.

"And there sits Pischet. She does not hearken to my words. Never has she heard the cry of the chit-chat, the voice of her husband, the babble of her child. She lives in the White Silence. Cared the Wolves aught for her? No! Theirs is the choice of the kill; ours is the leavings.

"Brothers, it shall not be! No more shall the Wolves slink among our campfires. The time is come."

A great streamer of fire, the aurora borealis, purple, green, and yellow, shot across the zenith, bridging horizon to horizon. With head thrown back and arms extended, he swayed to his climax.

"Behold! The spirits of our fathers have arisen and great deeds are afoot this night!"

He stepped back, and another young man somewhat diffidently came forward, pushed on by his comrades. He towered a full head above them, his broad chest defiantly bared to the frost. He swung tentatively from one foot to the other. Words halted upon his tongue, and he was ill at ease. His face was horrible to look upon, for it had at one time been half torn away by some terrific blow. At last he struck his breast with his clenched fist, drawing sound as from a drum, and his voice rumbled forth as does the surf from an ocean cavern.

"I am the Bear,—the Silver-Tip and the Son of the Silver-Tip! When my voice was yet as a girl's, I slew the lynx, the moose, and the cariboo; when it whistled like the wolverines from under a cache, I crossed the Mountains of the South and slew three of the White Rivers; when it became as the roar of the Chinook, I met the bald-faced grizzly, but gave no trail."

At this he paused, his hand significantly sweeping across his hideous scars.

"I am not as the Fox. My tongue is frozen like the river. I cannot make great talk. My words are few. The Fox says great deeds are afoot this night. Good! Talk flows from his tongue like the freshets of the spring, but he is chary of deeds. This night shall I do battle with the Wolf. I shall slay him, and Zarinska shall sit by my fire. The Bear has spoken."

Though pandemonium raged about him, "Scruff" Mackenzie held his ground. Aware how useless was the rifle at close quarters, he slipped both holsters to the fore, ready for action, and drew his mittens till his hands were barely shielded by the elbow gauntlets. He knew there was no hope in attack *en masse*, but true to his boast, was prepared to die with teeth fast-locked. But the Bear restrained his comrades, beating back the more impetuous with his terrible fist. As the tumult began to die away, Mackenzie shot a glance in the direction of Zarinska. It was a superb picture. She was leaning forward on her snow-shoes, lips apart and nostrils quivering, like a tigress to spring. Her great black eyes were fixed upon her tribesmen, in fear and defiance. So extreme the tension, she had forgotten to breathe. With one hand pressed spasmodically against her breast and the other as tightly gripped about the dog-whip, she was as turned to stone. Even as he looked, relief came to her. Her muscles loosened; with a heavy sigh she settled back, giving him a look of more than love—of worship.

Thling-Tinneh was trying to speak, but his people drowned his voice. Then Mackenzie strode forward. The Fox opened his mouth to a piercing yell, but so savagely did Mackenzie whirl upon him that he shrank back, his larynx all a-gurgle with suppressed sound. His discomfiture was greeted with roars of laughter, and served to soothe his fellows to a listening mood.

"Brothers! The White Man, whom ye have chosen to call the Wolf, came among you with fair words. He was not like the Innuit; he spoke not lies. He came as a friend, as one who would be a brother. But your men have had their say, and the time for soft words is past. First, I will tell you that the Shaman has an evil tongue and is a false prophet, that the messages he spake are not those of the Fire-Bringer. His ears are locked to the voice of the Raven, and out of his own head he weaves cunning fancies, and he has made fools of you. He has no power. When the dogs were killed and eaten, and your stomachs were heavy with untanned hide and strips of moccasins; when the old men died, and the old women died, and the babes at the dry dugs of the mothers died; when the land was dark, and ye perished as do the salmon in the fall; aye, when the famine was upon you, did the Shaman bring reward to your hunters? did the Shaman put meat in your bellies? Again I say, the Shaman is without power. Thus I spit upon his face!"

Though taken aback by the sacrilege, there was no uproar. Some of the women were even frightened, but among the men there was an uplifting, as though in preparation or anticipation of the miracle. All eyes were turned upon the two central figures. The priest realized the crucial moment, felt his power tottering, opened his mouth in denunciation, but fled backward before the truculent advance, upraised fist, and flashing eyes, of Mackenzie. He sneered and resumed.

"Was I stricken dead? Did the lightning burn me? Did the stars fall from the sky and crush me? Pish! I have done with the dog. Now will I tell you of my people, who are the mightiest of all the peoples, who rule in all the lands. At first we hunt as I hunt, alone. After that we hunt in packs; and at last, like the cariboo-run, we sweep across all the land. Those whom we take into our lodges live; those who will not come die. Zarinska is a comely maiden, full and strong, fit to become the mother of Wolves. Though I die, such shall she become; for my brothers are many, and they will follow the scent of my dogs. Listen to the Law of the Wolf: *Whoso taketh the life of one Wolf, the forfeit shall ten of his people pay.* In many lands has the price been paid; in many lands shall it yet be paid.

"Now will I deal with the Fox and the Bear. It seems they have cast eyes upon the maiden. So? Behold, I have bought her! Thling-Tinneh leans upon the rifle; the goods of purchase are by his fire. Yet will I be fair to the young men. To the Fox, whose tongue is dry with many words, will I give of tobacco five long plugs. Thus will his mouth be wetted that he may make much noise in the council. But to the Bear, of whom I am well proud, will I give of blankets two; of flour, twenty cups; of tobacco, double that of the Fox; and if he fare with me over the Mountains of the East, then will I give him a rifle, mate to Thling-Tinneh's. If not? Good! The Wolf is weary of speech. Yet once again will he say the Law: *Whoso taketh the life of one Wolf, the forfeit shall ten of his people pay.*"

Mackenzie smiled as he stepped back to his old position, but at heart he was full of trouble. The night was yet dark. The girl came to his side, and he listened closely as she told of the Bear's battletricks with the knife.

The decision was for war. In a trice, scores of moccasins were widening the space of beaten snow by the fire. There was much chatter about the seeming defeat of the Shaman; some averred he had but withheld his power, while others conned past events and agreed with the Wolf. The Bear came to the center of the battleground, a long naked hunting-knife of Russian make in his hand. The Fox called attention to Mackenzie's revolvers; so he stripped his belt, buckling it about Zarinska, into whose hands he also intrusted his rifle. She shook her head that she could not shoot,—small chance had a woman to handle such precious things.

"Then, if danger come by my back, cry aloud, 'My husband!' No; thus, 'My husband!'"

He laughed as she repeated it, pinched her cheek, and reentered the circle. Not only in reach and stature had the Bear the advantage of him, but his blade was longer by a good two inches. "Scruff" Mackenzie had looked into the eyes of men before, and he knew it was a man who stood against him; yet he quickened to the glint of light on the steel, to the dominant pulse of his race.

Time and again he was forced to the edge of the fire or the deep snow, and time and again, with the foot tactics of the pugilist, he worked back to the center. Not a voice was lifted in encouragement, while his antagonist was heartened with applause, suggestions, and warnings. But his teeth only shut the tighter as the knives clashed together, and he thrust or eluded with a coolness born of conscious strength. At first he felt compassion for his enemy; but this fled before the primal instinct of life, which in turn gave way to the lust of slaughter. The ten thousand years of culture fell from him, and he was a cave-dweller, doing battle for his female.

Twice he pricked the Bear, getting away unscathed; but the third time caught, and to save himself, free hands closed on fighting hands, and they came together. Then did he realize the tremendous strength of his opponent. His muscles were knotted in painful lumps, and cords and tendons threatened to snap with the strain; yet nearer and nearer came the Russian steel. He tried to break away, but only weakened himself. The furclad circle closed in, certain of and anxious to see the final stroke. But with wrestler's trick, swinging partly to the side, he struck at his adversary with his head. Involuntarily the Bear leaned back, disturbing his center of gravity. Simultaneous with this, Mackenzie tripped properly and threw his whole weight forward, hurling him clear through the circle into the deep snow. The Bear floundered out and came back full tilt.

"O my husband!" Zarinska's voice rang out, vibrant with danger.

To the twang of a bow-string, Mackenzie swept low to the ground, and a bonebarbed arrow passed over him into the breast of the Bear, whose momentum carried him over his crouching foe. The next instant Mackenzie was up and about. The Bear lay motionless, but across the fire was the Shaman, drawing a second arrow.

Mackenzie's knife leaped short in the air. He caught the heavy blade by the point. There was a flash of light as it spanned the fire. Then the Shaman, the hilt alone appearing without his throat, swayed a moment and pitched forward into the glowing embers.

Click! Click!—the Fox had possessed himself of Thling-Tinneh's rifle and was vainly trying to throw a shell into place. But he dropped it at the sound of Mackenzie's laughter.

"So the Fox has not learned the way of the plaything? He is yet a woman. Come! Bring it, that I may show thee!"

The Fox hesitated.

"Come, I say!"

He slouched forward like a beaten cur.

"Thus, and thus; so the thing is done." A shell flew into place and the trigger was at cock as Mackenzie brought it to shoulder.

"The Fox has said great deeds were afoot this night, and he spoke true. There have been great deeds, yet least among them were those of the Fox. Is he still intent to take Zarinska to his lodge? Is he minded to tread the trail already broken by the Shaman and the Bear? No? Good!"

Mackenzie turned contemptuously and drew his knife from the priest's throat.

"Are any of the young men so minded? If so, the Wolf will take them by two and three till none are left. No? Good! Thling-Tinneh, I now give thee this rifle a second time. If, in the days to come, thou shouldst journey to the Country of the Yukon, know thou that there shall always be a place and much food by the fire of the Wolf. The night is now passing into the day. I go, but I may come again. And for the last time, remember the Law of the Wolf!"

He was supernatural in their sight as he rejoined Zarinska. She took her place at the head of the team, and the dogs swung into motion. A few moments later they were swallowed up by the ghostly forest. Till now Mackenzie had waited; he slipped into his snowshoes to follow.

"Has the Wolf forgotten the five long plugs?"

Mackenzie turned upon the Fox angrily; then the humor of it struck him.

"I will give thee one short plug."

"As the Wolf sees fit," meekly responded the Fox, stretching out his hand.

TO THE MAN ON TRAIL

"DUMP it in."

"But I say, Kid, isn't that going it a little too strong? Whisky and alcohol's bad enough; but when it comes to brandy and pepper sauce and—"

"Dump it in. Who's making this punch, anyway?" And Malemute Kid smiled benignantly through the clouds of steam. "By the time you've been in this country as long as I have, my son, and lived on rabbit tracks and salmon belly, you'll learn that Christmas comes only once per annum. And a Christmas without punch is sinking a hole to bedrock with nary a pay streak."

"Stack up on that fer a high cyard," approved Big Jim Beldon, who had come down from his claim on Mazy May to spend Christmas, and who, as everyone knew, had been living the two months past on straight moose meat. "Hain't fergot the hooch we-uns made on the Tanana, hev yeh?"

"Well, I guess yes. Boys, it would have done your hearts good to see that whole tribe fighting drunk—and all because of a glorious ferment of sugar and sour dough. That was before your time," Malemute Kid said as he turned to Stanley Prince, a young mining expert who had been in two years. "No white women in the country then, and Mason wanted to get married. Ruth's father was chief of the Tananas, and objected, like the rest of the tribe. Stiff? Why, I used my last pound of sugar; finest work in that line I ever did in my life. You should have seen the chase, down the river and across the portage."

"But the squaw?" asked Louis Savoy, the tall French Canadian, becoming interested; for he had heard of this wild deed when at Forty Mile the preceding winter.

Then Malemute Kid, who was a born raconteur, told the unvarnished tale of the Northland Lochinvar. More than one rough adventurer of the North felt his heartstrings draw closer and experienced vague yearnings for the sunnier pastures of the Southland, where life promised something more than a barren struggle with cold and death.

"We struck the Yukon just behind the first ice run," he concluded, "and the tribe only a quarter of an hour behind. But that saved us; for the second run broke the jam above and shut them out. When they finally got into Nuklukyeto, the whole post was ready for them. And as to the forgathering, ask Father Roubeau here: he performed the ceremony."

The Jesuit took the pipe from his lips but could only express his gratification with patriarchal smiles, while Protestant and Catholic vigorously applauded.

"By gar!" ejaculated Louis Savoy, who seemed overcome by the romance of it. "*La petite* squaw; *mon* Mason *brav.* By gar!"

Then, as the first tin cups of punch went round, Bettles the Unquenchable sprang to his feet and struck up his favorite drinking song:

"There's Henry Ward Beecher
And Sunday-school teachers,
All drink of the sassafras root;
But you bet all the same,
If it had its right name,
It's the juice of the forbidden fruit."

"Oh, the juice of the forbidden fruit,"

roared out the bacchanalian chorus,

"Oh, the juice of the forbidden fruit;
But you bet all the same,
If it had its right name,
It's the juice of the forbidden fruit."

Malemute Kid's frightful concoction did its work; the men of the camps and trails unbent in its genial glow, and jest and song and tales of past adventure went round the board. Aliens from a dozen lands, they toasted each and all. It was the Englishman, Prince, who pledged "Uncle Sam, the precocious infant of the New World"; the Yankee, Bettles, who drank to "The Queen, God bless her"; and together, Savoy and Meyers, the German trader, clanged their cups to Alsace and Lorraine.

Then Malemute Kid arose, cup in hand, and glanced at the greased-paper window, where the frost stood full three inches thick. "A health to the man on trail this night; may his grub hold out; may his dogs keep their legs; may his matches never miss fire."

Crack! Crack! They heard the familiar music of the dog whip, the whining howl of the Malemutes, and the crunch of a sled as it drew up to the cabin. Conversation languished while they waited the issue.

"An old-timer; cares for his dogs and then himself," whispered Malemute Kid to Prince as they listened to the snapping jaws and the wolfish snarls and yelps of pain which proclaimed to their practiced ears that the stranger was beating back their dogs while he fed his own.

Then came the expected knock, sharp and confident, and the stranger entered. Dazzled by the light, he hesitated a moment at the door, giving to all a chance for scrutiny. He was a striking personage, and a most picturesque one, in his Arctic dress of wool and fur. Standing six foot two or three, with proportionate breadth of shoulders and depth of chest, his smooth-shaven face nipped by the cold to a gleaming pink, his long lashes and eyebrows white with ice, and the ear and neck flaps of his great wolfskin cap loosely raised, he seemed, of a verity, the Frost King, just stepped in out of the night. Clasped outside his Mackinaw jacket, a beaded belt held two large Colt's revolvers and a hunting knife, while he carried, in addition to the inevitable dog whip, a smokeless rifle of the largest bore and latest pattern. As he came forward, for all his step was firm and elastic, they could see that fatigue bore heavily upon him.

An awkward silence had fallen, but his hearty "What cheer, my lads?" put them quickly at ease, and the next instant Malemute Kid and he had gripped hands. Though they had never met, each had heard of the other, and the recognition was mutual. A sweeping introduction and a mug of punch were forced upon him before he could explain his errand.

"How long since that basket sled, with three men and eight dogs, passed?" he asked.

"An even two days ahead. Are you after them?"

"Yes; my team. Run them off under my very nose, the cusses. I've gained two days on them already—pick them up on the next run."

"Reckon they'll show spunk?" asked Belden, in order to keep up the conversation, for Malemute Kid already had the coffeepot on and was busily frying bacon and moose meat.

The stranger significantly tapped his revolvers.

"When'd yeh leave Dawson?"

"Twelve o'clock."

"Last night?"—as a matter of course.

"Today."

A murmur of surprise passed round the circle. And well it might; for it was just midnight, and seventy-five miles of rough river trail was not to be sneered at for a twelve hours' run.

The talk soon became impersonal, however, harking back to the trails of childhood. As the young stranger ate of the rude fare Malemute Kid attentively studied his face. Nor was he long in deciding that it was fair, honest, and open, and that he liked it. Still youthful, the lines had been firmly traced by toil and hardship. Though genial in conversation, and mild when at rest, the blue eyes gave promise of the hard steel-glitter which comes when called into action, especially against odds. The heavy jaw and square-cut chin demonstrated rugged pertinacity and indomitability. Nor, though the attributes of the lion were there, was there wanting the certain softness, the hint of womanliness, which bespoke the emotional nature.

"So thet's how me an' the ol' woman got spliced," said Belden, concluding the exciting tale of his courtship. " 'Here we be, Dad,' sez she. 'An' may yeh be damned,' sez he to her, an' then to me, 'Jim, yeh—yeh git outen them good duds o' yourn; I want a right peart slice o' thet forty acre plowed 'fore dinner.' An' then he sort o' sniffled an' kissed her. An' I was thet happy—but he seen me an' roars out, 'Yeh, Jim!' An' yeh bet I dusted fer the barn."

"Any kids waiting for you back in the States?" asked the stranger.

"Nope; Sal died 'fore any come. Thet's why I'm here." Belden abstractedly began to light his pipe, which had failed to go out, and then brightened up with, "How 'bout yerself, stranger—married man?"

For reply, he opened his watch, slipped it from the thong which served for a chain, and passed it over. Belden picked up the slush lamp, surveyed the inside of the case critically, and, swearing admiringly to himself, handed it over to Louis Savoy. With numerous "By gars!" he finally surrendered it to Prince, and they noticed that his hands trembled and his eyes took on a peculiar softness. And so it passed from horny hand to horny hand—the pasted photograph of a woman, the clinging kind that such men fancy, with a babe at the breast. Those who had not yet seen the wonder were keen with curiosity; those who had became silent and retrospective. They could face the pinch of famine, the grip of scurvy, or the quick death by field or flood; but the pictured semblance of a stranger woman and child made women and children of them all.

"Never have seen the youngster yet—he's a boy, she says, and two years old," said the stranger as he received the treasure back. A lingering moment he gazed upon it, then snapped the case and turned away, but not quick enough to hide the restrained rush of tears.

Malemute Kid led him to a bunk and bade him turn in.

"Call me at four sharp. Don't fail me," were his last words, and a moment later he was breathing in the heaviness of exhausted sleep.

"By Jove! He's a plucky chap," commented Prince. "Three hours' sleep after seventy-five miles with the dogs, and then the trail again. Who is he, Kid?"

"Jack Westondale. Been in going on three years, with nothing but the name of working like a horse, and any amount of bad luck to his credit. I never knew him, but Sitka Charley told me about him."

"It seems hard that a man with a sweet young wife like his should be putting in his years in this Godforsaken hole, where every year counts two on the outside."

"The trouble with him is clean grit and stubborness.He's cleaned up twice with a stake, but lost it both times."

Here the conversation was broken off by an uproar from Bettles, for the effect had begun to wear away. And soon the bleak years of monotonous grub and deadening toil were being forgotten in rough merriment. Malemute Kid alone seemed unable to lose himself, and cast many an anxious look at his watch. Once he put on his mittens and beaver-skin cap, and, leaving the cabin, fell to rummaging about in the cache.

Nor could he wait the hour designated; for he was fifteen minutes ahead of time in rousing his guest. The young giant had stiffened badly, and brisk rubbing was necessary to bring him to his feet. He tottered painfully out of the cabin, to find his dogs harnessed and everything ready for the start. The company wished him good luck and a short chase, while Father Roubeau, hurriedly blessing him, led the stampede for the cabin; and small wonder, for it is not good to face seventy-four degrees below zero with naked ears and hands.

Malemute Kid saw him to the main trail, and there, gripping his hand heartily, gave him advice.

"You'll find a hundred pounds of salmon eggs on the sled," he said. "The dogs will go as far on that as with one hundred and fifty of fish, and you can't get dog food at Pelly, as you probably expected." The stranger started, and his eyes flashed, but he did not interrupt. "You can't get an ounce of food for dog or man till you reach Five Fingers, and that's a stiff two hundred miles. Watch out for open water on the Thirty Mile River, and be sure you take the big cutoff above Le Barge."

"How did you know it? Surely the news can't be ahead of me already?"

"I don't know it; and what's more, I don't want to know it. But you never owned that team you're chasing. Sitka Charley sold it to them last spring. But he sized you up to me as square once, and I believe him. I've seen your face; I like it. And I've seen—why, damn you, hit the high places for salt water and that wife of yours, and—" Here the Kid unmittened and jerked out his sack.

"No; I don't need it," and tears froze on his cheeks as he convulsively gripped Malemute Kid's hand.

"Then don't spare the dogs; cut them out of the traces as fast as they drop; buy them, and think they're cheap at ten dollars a pound. You can get them at Five Fingers, Little Salmon, and Hootalinqua. And watch out for wet feet," was his parting advice. "Keep a-traveling up to twenty-five, but if it gets below that, build a fire and change your socks."

Fifteen minutes had barely elapsed when the jingle of bells announced new arrivals. The door opened, and a mounted policeman of the Northwest Territory entered, followed by two half-breed dog drivers. Like Westondale, they were heavily armed and showed signs of fatigue. The half-breeds had been borne to the trail and bore it easily; but the young policeman was badly exhausted. Still, the dogged obstinacy of his race held him to the pace he had set, and would hold him till he dropped in his tracks.

"When did Westondale pull put?" he asked. "He stopped here, didn't he?" This was supererogatory, for the tracks told their own tale too well.

Malemute Kid had caught Belden's eye, and he, scenting the wind, replied evasively, "A right peart while back."

"Come, my man; speak up," the policeman admonished.

"Yeh seem to want him right smart. Hez he ben gittin' cantankerous down Dawson way?"

"Held up Harry McFarland's for forty thousand; exchanged it at the P. C. store for a check on Seattle; and who's to stop the cashing of it if we don't overtake him? When did he pull out?"

Every eye suppressed its excitement, for Malemute Kid had given the cue, and the young officer encountered wooden faces on every hand.

Striding over to Prince, he put the question to him. Though it hurt him, gazing into the frank, earnest face of his fellow countryman, he replied inconsequentially on the state of the trail.

Then he espied Father Roubeau, who could not lie. "A quarter of an hour ago," the priest answered; "but he had four hours' rest for himself and dogs."

"Fifteen minutes' start, and he's fresh! My God!" The poor fellow staggered back, half fainting from exhaustion and disappointment, murmuring something about the run from Dawson in ten hours and the dogs being played out.

Malemute Kid forced a mug of punch upon him; then he turned for the door, ordering the dog drivers to follow. But the warmth and promise of rest were too tempting, and they objected strenuously. The Kid was conversant with their French patois, and followed it anxiously.

They swore that the dogs were gone up; that Siwash and Babette would have to be shot before the first mile was covered; that the rest were almost as bad; and that it would be better for all hands to rest up.

"Lend me five dogs?" he asked, turning to Malemute Kid.

But the Kid shook his head.

"I'll sign a check on Captain Constantine for five thousand—here's my papers—I'm authorized to draw at my own discretion."

Again the silent refusal.

"Then I'll requisition them in the name of the Queen."

Smiling incredulously, the Kid glanced at his well-stocked arsenal, and the Englishman, realizing his impotency, turned for the door. But the dog drivers still objecting, he whirled upon them fiercely, calling them women and curs. The swart face of the older half-breed flushed angrily as he drew himself up and promised in good, round terms that he would travel his leader off his legs, and would then be delighted to plant him in the snow.

The young officer—and it required his whole will—walked steadily to the door, exhibiting a freshness he did not possess. But they all knew and appreciated his proud effort; nor could he veil the twinges of agony that shot across his face. Covered with frost, the dogs were curled up in the snow, and it was almost impossible to get them to their feet. The poor brutes whined under the stinging lash, for the dog drivers were angry and cruel; nor till Babette, the leader, was cut from the traces, could they break out the sled and get under way.

"A dirty scoundrel and a liar!" "By gar! Him no good!" "A thief!" "Worse than an Indian!" It was evident that they were angry—first at the way they had been deceived; and second at the outraged ethics of the Northland, where honesty, above all, was man's prime jewel. "An' we gave the cuss a hand, after knowin' what he'd did." All eyes turned accusingly upon MalmuteKid, who rose from the corner where he had been making Babette comfortable, and silently emptied the bowl for a final round of punch.

"It's a cold night, boys—a bitter cold night," was the irrelevant commencement of his defense. "You've all traveled trail, and know what that stands for. Don't jump a dog when he's down. You've only heard one side. A whiter man than Jack Westondale never ate from the same pot nor stretched blanket with you or me. Last fall he gave his whole clean-up, forty thousand, to Joe Castrell, to buy in on Dominion. Today he'd be a millionaire. But while he stayed behind at Circle City, taking care of his partner with the scurvy, what does Castell do? Goes into McFarland's, jumps the limit, and drops the whole sack. Found him dead in the snow the next day. And poor Jack laying his plans to go out this winter to his wife and the boy he's never seen. You'll notice he took exactly what his partner lost—forty thousand. Well, he's gone out; and what are you going to do about it?"

The Kid glanced round the circle of his judges, noted the softening of their faces, then raised his mug aloft. "So a health to the man on trail this night; may his grub hold out; may his dogs keep their legs; may his matches never miss fire. God prosper him; good luck go with him; and—"

"Confusion to the Mounted Police!" cried Bettles, to the crash of the empty cups.

THE WISDOM OF THE TRAIL

SITKA Charley had achieved the impossible. Other Indians might have known as much of the wisdom of the trail as he did; but he alone knew the white man's wisdom, the honor of the trail, and the law. But these things had not come to him in a day. The aboriginal mind is slow to generalize, and many facts, repeated often, are required to compass an understanding. Sitka Charley, from boyhood, had been thrown continually with white men, and as a man he had elected to cast his fortunes with them, expatriating himself, once and for all, from his own people. Even then, respecting, almost venerating their power, and pondering over it, he had yet to divine its secret essence—the honor and the law. And it was only by the cumulative evidence of years that he had finally come to understand. Being an alien, when he did know, he knew it better than the white man himself; being an Indian, he had achieved the impossible.

And of these things had been bred a certain contempt for his own people—a contempt which he had made it a custom to conceal, but which now burst forth in a polygot whirlwind of curses upon the heads of Kah-Chucte and Gowhee. They cringed before him like a brace of snarling wolf dogs, too cowardly to spring, too wolfish to cover their fangs. They were not handsome creatures. Neither was Sitka Charley. All three were frightful-looking. There was no flesh to their faces; their cheekbones were massed with hideous scabs which had cracked and frozen alternately under the intense frost; while their eyes burned luridly with the light which is born of desperation and hunger. Men so situated, beyond the pale of the honor and the law, are not to be trusted. Sitka Charley knew this; and this was why he had forced them to abandon their rifles with the rest of the camp outfit ten days before. His rifle and Captain Eppingwell's were the only ones that remained.

"Come, get a fire started," he commanded, drawing out the precious matchbox with its attendant strips of dry birchbark.

The two Indians fell sullenly to the task of gathering dead branches and underwood. They were weak and paused often, catching themselves, in the act of stooping, with giddy motions, or staggering to the center of operations with their knees shaking like castanets. After each trip they rested for a moment, as though sick and deadly weary. At times their eyes took on the patient stoicism of dumb suffering; and again the ego seemed almost bursting forth with its wild cry, "I, I, I want to exist!"—the cominant note of the whole living universe.

A light breath of air blew from the south, nipping the exposed portions of their bodies and driving the frost, in needles of fire, through fur and flesh to the bones. So, when the fire had grown lusty and thawed a damp circle in the snow about it, Sitka Charley forced his reluctant comrades to lend a hand in pitching a fly. It was a primitive affair, merely a blanket stretched parallel with the fire and to windward of it, at an angle of perhaps forty-five degrees. This shut out the chill wind and threw the heat backward and down upon those who were to huddle in its shelter. Then a layer of green spruce boughs were spread, that their bodies might not come in contact with the snow. When this task was completed, Kah-Chucte and Gowhee proceeded to take care of their feet. Their icebound moccasins were saldy worn by much travel, and the sharp ice of the river jams had cut them to rags. Their Siwash socks were similarly conditioned, and when these had been thawed and removed, the dead-white tips of the toes, in the various stages of mortification, told their simple tale of the trail.

Leaving the two to the drying of their footgear, Sitka Charley turned back over the course he had come. He, too, had a mighty longing to sit by the fire and tend his complaining flesh, but the honor and the law forbade. He toiled painfully over the frozen field, each step a protest, every muscle in revolt. Several times, where the open water between the jams had recently crusted, he was forced to miserably accelerate his movements as the fragile footing swayed and threatened beneath him. In such places death was quick and easy; but it was not his desire to endure no more.

His deepening anxiety vanished as two Indians dragged into view round a bend in the river. They staggered and panted like men under heavy burdens; yet the packs on their backs were a matter of but a few pounds. He questioned them eagerly, and their replies seemed to relieve him. He hurried on. Next came two white men, supporting between them a woman. They also behaved as though drunken, and their limbs shook with weakness. But the woman leaned lightly upon them, choosing to carry herself forward with her own strength. At the sight of her a flash of joy cast its fleeting light across Sitka Charley's face. He cherished a very great regard for Mrs. Eppingwell. He had seen many white women, but this was the first to travel the trail with him. When Captain Eppingwell proposed the hazardous undertaking and made him an offer for his services, he had shaken his head gravely; for it was an unknown journey through the dismal vastnesses of the Northland, and he knew it to be of the kind that try to the uttermost the souls of men. But when he learned that the captain's wife was to accompany them, he had refused flatly to have anything further to do with it. Had it been a woman of his own race he would have harbored no objections; but these women of the Southland—no, no, they were too soft, too tender, for such enterprises.

Sitka Charley did not know this kind of woman. Five minutes before, he did not even dream of taking charge of the expedition; but when she came to him with her wonderful smile and her straight clean English, and talked to the point, without pleading or persuading, he had incontinently yielded. Had there been a softness and appeal to mercy in the eyes, a tremble to the voice, a taking advantage of sex, he would have stiffened to steel; instead her clear-searching eyes and clear-ringing voice, her utter frankness and tacit assumption of equality, had robbed him of his reason. He felt, then, that this was a new breed of woman; and ere they had been trail mates for many days he knew why the sons of such women mastered the land and the sea, and why the sons of his own womankind could not prevail against them. *Tender and soft!* Day after day he watched her, muscle-weary, exhausted, indomitable, and the words beat in upon him in a perennial refrain. *Tender and soft!* He knew her feet had been born to easy paths and sunny lands, strangers to the moccasined pain of the North, unkissed by the chill lips of the frost, and he watched and marveled at them twinkling ever through the weary day.

She had always a smile and a word of cheer, from which not even the meanest packer was excluded. As the way grew darker she seemed to stiffen and gather greater strength, and when Kah-Chucte and Gowhee, who had bragged that they knew every landmark of the way as a child did the skin bails of the tepee, acknowledged that they knew not where they were, it was she who raised a forgiving voice amid the curses of the men. She had sung to them that night till they felt the weariness fall from them and were ready to face the future with fresh hope. And when the food failed and each scant stint was measured jealously, she it was who rebelled against the machinations of her husband and Sitka Charley, and demanded and received a share neither greater nor less than that of the others.

Sitka Charley was proud to know this woman. A new richness, a greater breadth, had come into his life with her presence. Hitherto he had been his own mentor, had turned to right or left at no man's beck; he had moulded himself according to his own dictates, nourished his manhood regardless of all save his own opinion. For the first time he had felt a call from without for the best that was in him. Just a glance of appreciation from the clear-searching eyes, a word of thanks from the clear-ringing voice, just a slight wreathing of the lips in the wonderful smile, and he walked with the gods for hours to come. It was a new stimulant to his manhood; for the first time he thrilled with a conscious pride in his wisdom of the trail; and between the twain they ever lifted the sinking hearts of their comrades.

The faces of the two men and the woman brightened as they saw him, for after all he was the staff they leaned upon. But Sitka Charley, rigid as was his wont, concealing pain and pleasure impartially beneath an iron exterior, asked them the welfare of the rest, told the distance to the fire, and continued on the backtrip. Next he met a single Indian, unburdened, limping, lips compressed, and eyes set with the pain of a foot in which the quick fought a losing battle with the dead. All possible care had been taken of him, but in the last extremity the weak and unfortunate must perish, and Sitka Charley deemed his days to be few. The man could not keep up for long, so he gave him rough cheering words. After that came two more Indians, to whom he had allotted the task of helping along Joe, the third white man of the party. They had deserted him. Sitka Charley saw at a glance the lurking spring in their bodies, and knew they had at last cast off his mastery. So he was not taken unawares when he ordered them back in quest of their abandoned charge, and saw the gleam of the hunting knives that they drew from the sheaths. A pitiful spectacle, three weak men lifting their puny strength in the face of the mighty vastness; but the two recoiled under the fierce rifle blows of the one and returned like beaten dogs to the leash. Two hours later, with Joe reeling between them and Sitka Charley bringing up the rear, they came to the fire, where the remainder of the expedition crouched in the shelter of the fly.

"A few words, my comrades, before we sleep," Sitka Charley said after they had devoured their slim rations of unleavened bread. He was speaking to the Indians in their own tongue, having already given the import to the whites. "A few words, my comrades, for your own good, that ye may yet perchance live. I shall give you the law; on his own head by the death of him that breaks it. We have passed the Hills of Silence, and we now travel the head reaches of the Stuart. It may be one sleep, it may be several, it may be many sleeps, but in time we shall come among the men of the Yukon, who have much grub. It were well that we look to the law. Today Kah-Chucte and Gowhee, whom I commanded to break trail, forgot they were men, and like frightened children ran away. True, they forgot; so let us forget. But hereafter let them remember. If it should happen they do not . . ." He touched his rifle carelessly, grimly. "Tomorrow they shall carry the flour and see that the white man Joe lies not down by the trail. The cups of flour are counted; should so much as an ounce be wanting at nightfall . . . Do ye understand? Today there were others that forgot. Moose Head and Three Salmon left the white man Joe to lie in the snow. Let them forget no more. With the light of day shall they go forth and break trail. Ye have heard the law. Look well, lest ye break it."

Sitka Charley found it beyond him to keep the line close up. From Moose Head and Three Salmon, who broke trail in advance, to Kah-Chucte, Gowhee, and Joe, it straggled out over a mile. Each staggered, fell or rested as he saw fit. The line of march was a progression through a chain of irregular halts. Each drew upon the last remnant of his strength and stumbled onward till it was expended, but in some miraculous way there was always another last remnant. Each time a man fell it was with the firm belief that he would rise no more; yet he did rise, and again, and again. The flesh yielded, the will conquered; but each triumph was a tragedy. The Indian with the frozen foot, no longer erect, crawled forward on hand and knee. He rarely rested, for he knew the penalty exacted by the frost. Even Mrs. Eppingwell's lips were at last set in a stony smile, and her eyes, seeing, saw not. Often she stopped, pressing a mittened hand to her heart, gasping and dizzy.

Joe, the white man, had passed beyond the stage of suffering. He no longer begged to be let alone, prayed to die; but was soothed and content under the anodyne of delirium. Kah-Chucte and Gowhee dragged him on roughly, venting upon him many a savage glance or blow. To them it was the acme of injustice. Their hearts were bitter with hate, heavy with fear. Why should they cumber their strength with his weakness? To do so meant death; not to do so—and they remembered the law of Sitka Charley, and the rifle.

Joe fell with greater frequency as the daylight waned, and so hard was he to raise that they dropped farther and farther behind. Sometimes all three pitched into the snow, so weak had the Indians become. Yet on their backs was life, and strength, and warmth. Within the flour sacks were all the potentialities of existence. They could not but think of this, and it was not strange, that which came to pass. They had fallen by the side of a great timber jam where a thousand cords of firewood waited the match. Near by was an air hole through the ice. Kah-Chucte looked on the wood and the water, as did Gowhee; then they looked on each other. Never a word was spoken. Gowhee struck a fire; Kah-Chucte filled a tin cup with water and heated it; Joe babbled of things in another land, in a tongue they did not understand. They mixed flour with the warm water till it was a thin paste, and of this they drank many cups. They did not offer any to Joe; but he did not mind. He did not mind anything, not even his moccasins, which scorched and smoked among the coals.

A crystal mist of snow fell about them, softly, caressingly, wrapping them in clinging robes of white. And their feet would have yet trod many trails had not destiny brushed the clouds aside and cleared the air. Nay, ten minutes' delay would have been salvation. Sitka Charley, looking back, saw the pillared smoke of their fire, and guessed. And he looked ahead at those who were faithful, and at Mrs. Eppingwell.

* * *

"So, my good comrades, ye have again forgotten that you were men? Good! Very good. There will be fewer bellies to feed."

Sitka Charley retied the flour as he spoke, strapping the pack to the one on his own back. He kicked Joe till the pain broke through the poor devil's bliss and brought him doddering to his feet. Then he shoved him out upon the trail and started him on his way. The two Indians attempted to slip off.

"Hold, Gowhee! And thou, too, Kah-Chucte! Hath the flour given such strength to thy legs that they may outrun the swift-winged lead? Think not to cheat the law. Be men for the last time, and be content that ye die full-stomached. Come, step up, back to the timber, shoulder to shoulder. Come!"

The two men obeyed, quietly, without fear; for it is the future which pressed upon the man, not the present.

"Thou, Gowhee, hast a wife and children and a deerskin lodge in the Chipewyan. What is thy will in the matter?"

"Give thou her of the goods which are mine by the word of the captain—the blankets, the beads, the tobacco, the box which makes strange sounds after the manner of the white men. Say that I did die on the trail, but say not how."

"And thou, Kah-Chucte, who hast nor wife nor child?"

"Mine is a sister, the wife of the factor at Koshim. He beats her, and she is not happy. Give thou her the goods which are mine by the contract, and tell her it were well she go back to her own people. Shouldst thou meet the man, and be so minded, it were a good deed that he should die. He beats her, and she is afraid."

"Are ye content to die by the law?"

"We are."

"Then good-bye, my good comrades. May ye sit by the well-filled pot, in warm lodges, ere the day is done."

As he spoke he raised his rifle, and many echoes broke the silence. Hardly had they died away when other rifles spoke in the distance. Sitka Charley started. There had been more than one shot, yet there was but one other rifle in the party. He gave a fleeting glance at the men who lay so quietly, smiled viciously at the wisdom of the trail, and hurried on to meet the men of the Yukon.

IN A FAR COUNTRY

WHEN a man journeys into a far country, he must be prepared to forget many of the things he has learned, and to acquire such customs as are inherent with existence in the new land; he must abandon the old ideals and the old gods, and oftentimes he must reverse the very codes by which his conduct has hitherto been shaped. To those who have the protean faculty of adaptability, the novelty of such change may even be a source of pleasure; but to those who happen to be hardened to the ruts in which they were created, the pressure of the altered environment is unbearable, and they chafe in body and in spirit under the new restrictions which they do not understand. This chafing is bound to act and react, producing divers evils and leading to various misfortunes. It were better for the man who cannot fit himself to the new groove to return to his own country; if he delay too long, he will surely die.

The man who turns his back upon the comforts of an elder civilization, to face the savage youth, the primordial simplicity of the North, may estimate success at an inverse ratio to the quantity and quality of his hopelessly fixed habits. He will soon discover, if he be a fit candidate, that the material habits are the less important. The exchange of such things as a dainty menu for rough fare, of the stiff leather shoe for the soft, shapeless moccasin, of the feather bed for a couch in the snow, is after all a very easy matter. But his pinch will come in learning properly to shape his mind's attitude toward all things, and especially toward his fellow man. For the courtesies of ordinary life, he must substitute unselfishness, forbearance, and tolerance. Thus, and thus only, can he gain that pearl of great price—true comradeship. He must not say "Thank you"; he must mean it without opening his mouth, and prove it by responding in kind. In short, he must substitute the deed for the word, the spirit for the letter.

When the world rang with the tale of Arctic gold, and the lure of the North gripped the heartstrings of men, Carter Weatherbee threw up his snug clerkship, turned the half of his savings over to his wife, and with the remainder bought an outfit. There was no romance in his nature—the bondage of commerce had crushed all that; he was simply tired of the ceaseless grind, and wished to risk great hazards in view of corresponding returns. Like many another fool, disdaining the old trails used by the Northland pioneers for a score of years, he hurried to Edmonton in the spring of the year; and there, unluckily for his soul's welfare, he allied himself with a party of men.

There was nothing unusual about this party, except its plans. Even its goal, like that of all the other parties, was the Klondike. But the route it had mapped out to attain that goal took away the breath of the hardiest native, born and bred to the vicissitudes of the Northwest. Even Jacques Baptiste, born of a Chippewa woman and a renegade *voyageur* (having raised his first whimpers in a deerskin lodge north of the sixty-fifth parallel, and had the same hushed by blissful sucks of raw tallow), was surprised. Though he sold his services to them and agreed to travel even to the never-opening ice, he shook his head ominously whenever his advice was asked.

Percy Cuthfert's evil star must have been in the ascendant, for he, too, joined this company of argonauts. He was an ordinary man, with a bank account as deep as his culture, which is saying a good deal. He had no reason to embark on such a venture—

no reason in the world, save that he suffered from an abnormal development of sentimentality. He mistook this for the true spirit of romance and adventure. Many another man has done the like, and made as fatal a mistake.

The first break-up of spring found the party following the ice-run of Elk River. It was an imposing fleet, for the outfit was large, and they were accompanied by a disreputable contingent of half-breed *voyageurs* with their women and children. Day in and day out, they labored with the bateaux and canoes, fought mosquitoes and other kindred pests, or sweated and swore at the portages. Severe toil like this lays a man naked to the very roots of his soul, and ere Lake Athabasca was lost in the south, each member of the party had hoisted his true colors.

The two shirks and chronic grumblers were Carter Weatherbee and Percy Cuthfert. The whole party complained less of its aches and pains that did either of them. Not once did they volunteer for the thousand and one petty duties of the camp. A bucket of water to be brought, an extra armful of wood to be chopped, the dishes to be washed and wiped, a search to be made through the outfit for some suddenly indispensable article—and these two effete scions of civilization discovered sprains or blisters requiring instant attention. They were the first to turn in at night, with score of tasks yet undone; the last to turn out in the morning, when the start should be in readiness before the breakfast was begun. They were the first to fall to at mealtime, the last to have a hand in the cooking; the first to dive for a slim delicacy, the last to discover they had added to their own another man's share. If they toiled at the oars, the slyly cut the water at each stroke and allowed the boat's momentum to float up the blade. They thought nobody noticed; but their comrades swore under their breaths and grew to hate them, while Jacques Baptiste sneered openly and damned them from morning till night. But Jacques Baptiste was no gentleman.

At the Great Slave, Hudson Bay dogs were purchased, and the fleet sank to the guards with its added burden of dried fish and pemican. Then canoe and bateau answered to the swift current of the Mackenzie, and they plunged into the Great Barren Ground. Every likely-looking "feeder" was prospected, but the elusive "paydirt" danced ever to the north. At the Great Bear, overcome by the common dread of the Unknown Lands, their *voyageurs* began to desert, and Fort of Good Hope saw the last and bravest bending to the towlines as they bucked the current down which they had so treacherously glided. Jacques Baptiste alone remained. Had he not sworn to travel even to the never-opening ice?

The lying charts, compiled in main from hearsay, were now constantly consulted. And they felt the need of hurry, for the sun had already passed its northern solstice and was leading the winter south again. Skirting the shores of the bay, where the Mackenzie disembogues into the Arctic Ocean, they entered the mouth of the Little Peel River. Then began the arduous upstream toil, and the two Incapables fared worse than ever. Towline and pole, paddle and tumpline, rapids and portages—such tortures served to give the one a deep disgust for great hazards, and printed for the other a fiery text on the true romance of adventure. One day they waxed mutinous, and being vilely cursed by Jacques Baptiste, turned, as worms sometimes will. But the half-breed thrashed the twain, and sent them, bruised and bleeding, about their work. It was the first time either had been manhandled.

Abandoning their river craft at the headwaters of the Little Peel, they consumed the rest of the summer in the great portage over the Mackenzie watershed to the West Rat. This little stream fed the Porcupine, which in turn joined the Yukon where that mighty highway of the North countermarches on the Arctic Circle. But they had lost in the race with winter, and one day they tied their rafts to the thick eddy-ice and hurried their goods ashore. That night the river jammed and broke several times; the following morning it had fallen asleep for good.

"We can't be more'n four hundred miles from the Yukon," concluded Sloper, multiplying his thumb nails by the scale of the map. The council, in which the two Incapables had whined to excellent disadvantage, was drawing to a close.

"Hudson Bay Post, long time ago. No use um now." Jacques Baptiste's father had made the trip for the Fur Company in the old days, incidentally marking the trail with a couple of frozen toes.

"Sufferin' cracky!" cried another of the party. "No whites?"

"Nary white," Sloper sententiously affirmed; "but it's only five hundred more up the Yukon to Dawson. Call it a rough thousand from here."

Weatherbee and Cuthfert groaned in chorus.

"How long'll that take, Baptiste?"

The half-breed figured for a moment. "Workum like hell, no man play out, ten—twenty—forty—fifty days. Um babies come" (designating the Incapables), "no can tell. Mebbe when hell freeze over; mebbe not then."

The manufacture of snowshoes and moccasins ceased. Somebody called the name of an absent member, who came out of an ancient cabin at the edge of the campfire and joined them. The cabin was one of the many mysteries which lurk in the vast recesses of the North. Built when and by whom, no man could tell. Two graves in the open, piled high with stones, perhaps contained the secret of those early wanderers. But whose hand had piled the stones?

The moment had come. Jacques Baptiste paused in the fitting of a harness and pinned the struggling dog in the snow. The cook made mute protest for delay, threw a handful of bacon into a noisy pot of beans, then came to attention. Sloper rose to his feet. His body was a ludicrous contrast to the healthy physiques of the Incapables. Yellow and weak, fleeing from a South American fever-hole, he had not broken his flight across the zones, and was still able to toil with men. His weight was probably ninety pounds, with the heavy hunting knife thrown in, and his grizzled hair told of a prime which had ceased to be. The fresh young muscles of either Weatherbee or Cuthfert were equal to ten times the endeavor of his; yet he could walk them into the earth in a day's journey. And all this day he had whipped his stronger comrades into venturing a thousand miles of the stiffest hardship man can conceive. He was the incarnation of the unrest of his race, and the old Teutonic stubbornness, dashed with the quick grasp and action of the Yankee, held the flesh in the bondage of the spirit.

"All those in favor of going on with the dogs as soon as the ice sets, say ay."

"Ay!" rang out eight voices—voices destined to string a trail of oaths along many a hundred miles of pain.

"Contrary minded?"

"No!" For the first time the Incapables were united without some compromise of personal interests.

"And what are you going to do about it?" Weatherbee added belligerently.

"Majority rule! Majority rule!" clamored the rest of the party.

"I know the expedition is liable to fall through if you don't come," Sloper replied sweetly; "but I guess, if we try real hard, we can manage to do without you. What do you say, boys?"

The sentiment was cheered to the echo.

"But I say, you know," Cuthfert ventured apprehensively; "what's a chap like me to do?"

"Ain't you coming with us."

"No-o."

"Then do as you damn well please. We won't have nothing to say."

"Kind o' calkilate yuh might settle it with that canoodlin' pardner of yourn," suggested a heavy-going Westerner from the Dakotas, at the same time pointing out Weatherbee. "He'll be shore to ask yuh what yur a-goin' to do when it comes to cookin' an' gatherin' the wood."

"Then we'll consider it all arranged," concluded Sloper. "We'll pull out tomorrow, if we camp within five miles—just to get everything in running order and remember if we've forgotten anything."

The sleds groaned by on their steel-shod runners, and the dogs strained low in the harnesses in which they were born to die. Jacques Baptiste paused by the side of Sloper to get a last glimpse of the cabin. The smoke curled up pathetically from the Yukon stovepipe. The two Incapables were watching them from the doorway.

Sloper laid his hand on the other's shoulder.

"Jacques Baptiste, did you ever hear of the Kilkenny cats?"

The half-breed shook his head.

"Well, my friend and good comrade, the Kilkenny cats fought till nether hide, nor hair, nor yowl, was left. You understand?—till nothing was left. Very good. Now, these two men don't like work. They'll be all alone in that cabin all winter—a mighty long, dark winter. Kilkenny cats—well?"

The Frenchman in Baptiste shrugged his shoulders, but the Indian in him was silent. Nevertheless, it was an eloquent shrug, pregnant with prophecy.

Things prospered in the little cabin at first. The rough badinage of their comrades had made Weatherbee and Cuthfert conscious of the mutual responsibility which had devolved upon them; besides, there was not so much work after all for two healthy men. And the removal of the cruel whiphand, or in other words the bulldozing half-breed, had brought with it a joyous reaction. At first, each strove to outdo the other, and they performed petty tasks with an unction which would have opened the eyes of their comrades who were now wearing out bodies and souls on the Long Trail.

All care was banished. The forest, which shouldered in upon them from three sides, was an inexhaustible woodyard. A few yards from their door slept the Porcupine, and a hole through its winter robe formed a bubbling spring of water, crystal clear and painfully cold. But they soon grew to find fault with even that. The hole would persist in freezing up, and thus gave them many a miserable hour of ice-chopping. The unknown builders of the cabin had extended the sidelogs so as to support a cache at the rear. In this was stored the bulk of the party's provisions. Food there was, without stint, for three times the men who were fated to live upon it. But the most of it was the kind which built up brawn and sinew, but did not tickle the palate. True, there was sugar in plenty for two ordinary men; but these two were little else than children. They early discovered the virtues of hot water judiciously saturated with sugar, and they prodigally swam their flapjacks and soaked their crusts in the rich, white syrup. Then coffee and tea, and especially the dried fruits, made disastrous inroads upon it. The first words they had were over the sugar question. And it is a really serious thing when two men, wholly dependent upon each other for company, begin to quarrel.

Weatherbee loved to discourse blatantly on politics, while Cuthfert, who had been prone to clip his coupons and let the commonwealth jog on as best it might, either ignored the subject or delivered himself of startling epigrams. But the clerk was too obtuse to appreciate the clever shaping of thought, and this waste of ammunition irritated Cuthfert. He had been used to blinding people by his brilliancy, and it worked him quite a hardship, this loss of an audience. He felt personally aggrieved and unconsciously held his muttonhead companion responsible for it.

Save existence, they had nothing in common—came in touch on no single point. Weatherbee was a clerk who had known naught but clerking all his life; Cuthfert was a master of arts, a dabbler in oils, and had written not a little. The one was a lower-class man who considered himself a gentleman, and the other was a gentleman who knew himself to be such. From this it may be remarked that a man can be a gentleman without possessing the first instinct of true comradeship. The clerk was as sensuous as the other was aesthetic, and his love adventures, told at great length and chiefly coined from his imagination, affected the supersensitive master of arts in the same way as so many whiffs of sewer gas. He deemed the clerk a filthy, uncultured brute, whose place was in the muck with the swine, and told him so; and he was reciprocally informed that he was a milk-and-water sissy and a cad. Weatherbee could not have defined "cad" for his life; but it satisfied its purpose, which after all seems the main point in life.

Weatherbee flatted every third note and sang such songs as "The Boston Burglar" and "The Handsome Cabin Boy," for hours at a time, while Cuthfert wept with rage, till he could stand it no longer and fled into the outer cold. But there was no escape. The intense frost could not be endured for long at a time, and the little cabin crowded them—beds, stove, table, and all—into a space of ten by twelve. The very presence of either became a personal affront to the other, and they lapsed into sullen silences which increased in length and strength as the days went by. Occasionally, the flash of an eye or the curl of a lip got the better of them, though they strove to wholly ignore each other during these mute periods. And a great wonder sprang up in the breast of each, as to how God had ever come to create the other.

With little to do, time because an intolerable burden to them. This naturally made them still lazier. They sank into a physical lethargy which there was no escaping, and which made them rebel at the performance of the smallest chore. One morning when it was his turn to cook the common breakfast, Weatherbee rolled out of his blankets, and to the snoring of his companion, lighted first the slush-lamp and then the fire. The kettles were frozen hard, and there was no water in the cabin with which to wash. But he did not mind that. Waiting for it to thaw, he sliced the bacon and plunged into the hateful task of bread-making. Cuthfert had been slyly watching through his half-closed lids. Consequently there was a scene, in which they fervently blessed each other, and agreed, henceforth, that each do his own cooking. A week later, Cuthfert neglected his morning ablutions, but none the less complacently ate the meal which he had cooked. Weatherbee grinned. After that the foolish custom of washing passed out of their lives.

As the sugar-pile and other little luxuries dwindled, they began to be afraid they were not getting their proper shares, and in order that they might not be robbed, they fell to gorging themselves. The luxuries suffered in this gluttonous contest, and did also the men. In the absence of fresh vegetables and exercise, their blood became impoverished, and a loathsome, purplish rash crept over their bodies. Yet they refused to heed the warning. Next, their muscles and joints began to swell, the flesh turning black, while their mouths, gums, and lips took on the color of rich cream. Instead of being drawn together by their misery, each gloated over the other's symptoms as the scurvy took its course.

They lost all regard for personal appearance, and for that matter, common decency. The cabin became a pigpen, and never once were the beds made or fresh pine boughs laid underneath. Yet they could not keep to their blankets, as they would have wished; for the frost was inexorable, and the fire box consumed much fuel. The hair of their heads and faces grew long and shaggy, while their garments would have disgusted a ragpicker. But they did not care. They were sick, and there was no one to see; besides, it was very painful to move about.

To all this was added a new trouble—the Fear of the North. This fear was the joint child of the Great Cold and the Great Silence, and was born in the darkness of December, when the sun dipped below the horizon for good. It affected them according to their natures. Weatherbee fell prey to the grosser superstitions, and did his best to resurrect the spirits which slept in the forgotten graves. It was a fascinating thing, and in his dreams they came to him from out of the cold, and snuggled into his blankets, and told him of their toils and troubles ere they died. He shrank away from the clammy contact as they drew closer and twined their frozen limbs about him, and when they whispered in his ear of things to come, the cabin rang with his frightened shrieks. Cuthfert did not understand—for they no longer spoke—and when thus awakened he invariably grabbed for his revolver. Then he would sit up in bed, shivering nervously, with the weapon trained on the unconscious dreamer. Cuthfert deemed the man going mad, and so came to fear for his life.

His own malady assumed a less concrete form. The mysterious artisan who had laid the cabin, log by log, had pegged a wind-vane to the ridgepole. Cuthfert noticed it always pointed south, and one day, irritated by its steadfastness of purpose, he turned it toward the east. He watched eagerly, but never a breath came by to disturb it. Then he turned the vane to the north swearing never again to touch it till the wind did blow. But the air frightened him with its unearthly calm, and he often rose in the middle of the night to see if the vane had veered—ten degrees would have satisfied him. But no, it poised above him as unchangeable as fate. His imagination ran riot, till it became to him a fetish. Sometimes he followed the path it pointed across the dismal dominions, and allowed his soul to become saturated with the Fear. He dwelt upon the unseen and the unknown till the burden of eternity appeared to be crushing him. Everything in the Northland had that crushing effect—the absence of life and motion; the darkness; the infinite peace of the brooding land; the ghastly silence, which made the echo of each heartbeat a sacrilege; the solemn forest which seemed to guard an awful, inexpressible something, which neither word nor thought could compass.

The world he had so recently left, with its busy nations and great enterprises, seemed very far away. Recollections occasionally obtruded—recollections of marts and galleries and crowded thoroughfares, of evening dress and social functions, of good men and dear women he had known—but they were dim memories of a life he had lived long centuries agone, on some other planet. This phantasm was the Reality. Standing beneath the wind-vane, his eyes fixed on the polar skies, he could not bring himself to realize that the Southland really existed, that at that very moment it was a-roar with life and action. There was no Southland, no men being born of women, no giving and taking in marriage. Beyond his bleak skyline there stretched vast solitudes, and beyond these still vaster solitudes. There were no lands of sunshine, heavy with the perfume of flowers. Such things were only old dreams of paradise. The sunlands of the West and the spicelands of the East, the smiling Arcadias and blissful Islands of the Blest—ha!

ha! His laughter split the void and shocked him with its unwonted sound. There was no sun. This was the Universe, dead and cold and dark, and he its only citizen. Weatherbee? At such moments Weatherbee did not count. He was a Caliban, a monstrous phantom, fettered to him for untold ages, the penalty of some forgotten crime.

He lived with Death among the dead, emasculated by the sense of his own insignificance, crushed by the passive mastery of the slumbering ages. The magnitude of all things appalled him. Everything partook of the superlative save himself—the perfect cessation of wind and motion, the immensity of the snow-covered wildness, the height of the sky and the depth of the silence. That wind-vane—if it would only move. If a thunderbolt would fall, or the forest flare up in flame. The rolling up of the heavens as a scroll, the crash of Doom—anything, anything! But no, nothing moved; the Silence crowded in, and the Fear of the North laid icy fingers on his heart.

Once, like another Crusoe, by the edge of the river he came upon a track—the faint tracery of a snowshoe rabbit on the delicate snow-crust. It was a revelation. There was life in the Northland. He would follow it, look upon it, gloat over it. He forgot his swollen muscles, plunging through the deep snow in an ecstasy of anticipation. The forest swallowed him up, and the brief midday twilight vanished; but he pursued his quest till exhausted nature asserted itself and laid him helpless in the snow. There he groaned and cursed his folly, and knew the track to be the fancy of his brain; and late that night he dragged himself into the cabin on hands and knees, his cheeks frozen and a strange numbness about his feet. Weatherbee grinned malevolently, but made no offer to help him. He thrust needles into his toes and thawed them out by the stove. A week later mortification set in.

But the clerk had his own troubles. The dead men came out of their graves more frequently now, and rarely left him, waking or sleeping. He grew to wait and dread their coming, never passing the twin cairns without a shudder. One night they came to him in his sleep and led him forth to an appointed task. Frightened into inarticulate horror, he awoke between the heaps of stones and fled wildly to the cabin. But he had lain there for some time, for his feet and cheeks were also frozen.

Sometimes he became frantic at their insistent presence, and danced about the cabin, cutting the empty air with an axe, and smashing everything within reach. During these ghostly encounters, Cuthfert huddled into his blankets and followed the madman about with a cocked revolver, ready to shoot him if he came too near. But, recovering from one of these spells, the clerk noticed the weapon trained upon him. His suspicions were aroused, and thenceforth he, too, lived in fear of his life. They watched each other closely after that, and faced about in startled fright whenever either passed behind the other's back. The apprehensiveness became a mania which controlled them even in their sleep. Through mutual fear they tacitly let the slush-lamp burn all night, and saw to a plentiful supply of bacon-grease before retiring. The slightest movement on the part of one was sufficient to arouse the other, and many a still watch their gazes countered as they shook beneath their blankets with fingers on the trigger-guards.

What with the Fear of the North, the mental strain, and the ravages of the disease, they lost all semblance of humanity, taking on the appearance of wild beats, hunted and desperate. Their cheeks and noses, as an aftermath of the freezing, had turned black. Their frozen toes had begun to drop away at the first and second joints. Every movement brought pain, but the fire box was insatiable, wringing a ransom of torture from their miserable bodies. Day in, day out, it demanded its food—a veritable pound of flesh—and they dragged themselves into the forest to chop wood on their knees.

Once, crawling thus in search of dry sticks, unknown to each other they entered a thicket from opposite sides. Suddenly, without warning, two peering death's-heads confronted each other. Suffering had so transformed them that recognition was impossible. They sprang to their feet, shrieking with terror, and dashed away on their mangled stumps; and falling at the cabin's door, they clawed and scratched like demons till they discovered their mistake.

Occasionally they lapsed normal, and during one of these sane intervals, the chief bone of contention, the sugar, had been divided equally between them. They guarded their separate sacks, stored up in the cache, with jealous eyes; for there were but a few cupfuls left, and they were totally devoid of faith in each other. But one day Cuthfert made a mistake. Hardly able to move, sick with pain, with his head swimming and eyes blinded, he crept into the cache, sugar canister in hand, and mistook Weatherbee's sack for his own.

January had been born but a few days when this occurred. The sun had some time since passed its lowest southern declination, and at meridian now threw flaunting streaks of yellow light upon the northern sky. On the day following his mistake with the sugarbag, Cuthfert found himself feeling better, both in body and in spirit. As noontime drew near and the day brightened, he dragged himself outside to feast on the evanescent glow, which was to him an earnest of the sun's future intentions. Weatherbee was also feeling somewhat better, and crawled out beside him. They propped themselves in the snow beneath the moveless wind-vane, and waited.

The stillness of death was about them. In other climes, when nature falls into such moods, there is a subdued air of expectancy, a waiting for some small voice to take up the broken strain. Not so in the North. The two men had lived seeming eons in this ghostly peace. They could remember no song of the past; they could conjure no song of the future. This unearthly calm had always been—the tranquil silence of eternity.

Their eyes were fixed upon the north. Unseen, behind their backs, behind the towering mountains to the south, the sun swept toward the zenith of another sky than theirs. Sole spectators of the mighty canvas, they watched the false dawn slowly grow. A faint flame began to glow and smoulder. It deepened in intensity, ringing the changes of reddish-yellow, purple, and saffron. So bright did it become that Cuthfert thought the sun must surely be behind it—a miracle, the sun rising in the north! Suddenly, without warning and without fading, the canvas was swept clean. There was no color in the sky. The light had gone out of the day. They caught their breaths in half-sobs. But lo! the air was aglint with particles of scintillating frost, and there, to the north, the wind-vane lay in vague outline of the snow. A shadow! A shadow! It was exactly midday. They jerked their heads hurriedly to the south. A golden rim peeped over the mountain's snowy shoulder, smiled upon them an instant, then dipped from sight again.

There were tears in their eyes as they sought each other. A strange softening came over them. They felt irresistibly drawn toward each other. The sun was coming back again. It would be with them tomorrow, and the next day, and the next. And it would stay longer every visit, and a time would come when it would ride their heaven day and night, never once dropping below the skyline. There would be no night. The ice-locked winter would be broken; the winds would blow and the forests answer; the land would bathe in the blessed sunshine, and life renew. Hand in hand, they would quit this horrid dream and journey back to the Southland. They lurched blindly forward, and their hands met—their poor maimed hands, swollen and distorted beneath their mittens.

But the promise was destined to remain unfulfilled. The Northland is the Northland, and men work out their souls by strange rules, which other men, who have not journeyed into far countries, cannot come to understand.

An hour later, Cuthfert put a pan of bread into the oven, and fell to speculating on what the surgeons could do with his feet when he got back. Home did not seem so very far away now. Weatherbee was rummaging in the cache. Of a sudden, he raised a whirlwind of blasphemy, which in turn ceased with startling abruptness. The other man had robbed his sugar-sack. Still, things might have happened differently, had not the two dead men come out from under the stones and hushed the hot words in his throat. They led him quite gently from the cache, which he forgot to close. That consummation was reached; that something they had whispered to him in his dreams was about to happen. They guided him gently, very gently, to the woodpile, where they put the axe in his hands. Then they helped him shove open the cabin door, and he felt sure they shut it after him—at least he heard it slam and the latch fall sharply into place. And he knew they were waiting just without, waiting for him to do his task.

"Carter! I say, Carter!"

Percy Cuthfert was frightened at the look on the clerk's face, and he made haste to put the table between them.

Carter Weatherbee followed, without haste and without enthusiasm. There was neither pity nor passion in his face, but rather the patient, stolid look of one who has certain work to do and goes about it methodically.

"I say, what's the matter?"

The clerk dodged back, cutting off his retreat to the door, but never opening his mouth.

"I say, Carter, I say; let's talk. There's a good chap."

The master of arts was thinking rapidly, now, shaping a skillful flank movement on the bed where his Smith & Wesson lay. Keeping his eyes on the madman, he rolled backward on the bunk, at the same time clutching the pistol.

"Carter!"

The powder flashed full in Weatherbee's face, but he swung his weapon and leaped forward. The axe bit deeply at the base of the spine, and Percy Cuthfert felt all consciousness of his lower limbs leave him. Then the clerk fell heavily upon him, clutching him by the throat with feeble fingers. The sharp bite of the axe has caused Cuthfert to drop the pistol, and as his lungs panted for release, he fumbled aimlessly for it among the blankets. Then he remembered. He slid a hand up the clerk's belt to the sheath-knife; and they drew very close to each other in that last clinch.

Percy Cuthfert felt his strength leave him. The lower portion of his body was useless. The inert weight of Weatherbee crushed him—crushed him and pinned him there like a bear under a trap. The cabin became filled with a familiar odor, and he knew the bread to be burning. Yet what did it matter? He would never need it. And there were all of six cupfuls of sugar in the cache—if he had forseen this he would not have been so saving the last several days. Would the wind-vane ever move? Why not? Had he not seen the sun today? He would go and see. No; it was impossible to move. He had not thought the clerk so heavy a man.

How quickly the cabin cooled! The fire must be out. The cold was forcing in. It must be below zero already, and the ice creeping up the inside of the door. He could not see it, but his past experience enabled him to gauge its progress by the cabin's temperature. The lower hinge must be white ere now. Would the tale of this ever reach the world? How would his friends take it? They would read it over their coffee, most likely, and talk it over at the clubs. He could see them very clearly. "Poor Old Cuthfert," they murmured; "not such a bad sort of a chap, after all." He smiled at their eulogies, and passed on in search of a Turkish bath. It was the same old crowd upon the streets. Strange, they did not notice his moosehide moccasins and tattered German socks! He would take a cab. And after the bath a shave would not be bad. No; he would eat first. Steak, and potatoes, and green things how fresh it all was! And what was that? Squares of honey, streaming liquid amber! But why did they bring so much? Ha! ha! he could never eat it all. Shine! Why certainly. He put his foot on the box. The bootblack looked curiously up at him, and he remembered his moosehide moccasins and went away hastily.

Hark! The wind-vane must be surely spinning. No; a mere singing in his ears. That was all—a mere singing. The ice must have passed the latch by now. More likely the upper hinge was covered. Between the moss-chinked roof-poles, little points of frost began to appear. How slowly they grew! No; not so slowly. There was a new one, and there another. Two—three—four; they were coming too fast to count. There were two growing together. And there, a third had joined them. Why, there were no more spots. They had run together and formed a sheet.

Well, he would have company. If Gabriel ever broke the silence of the North, they would stand together, hand in hand, before the great White Throne. And God would judge them, God would judge them!

Then Percy Cuthfert closed his eyes and dropped off to sleep.

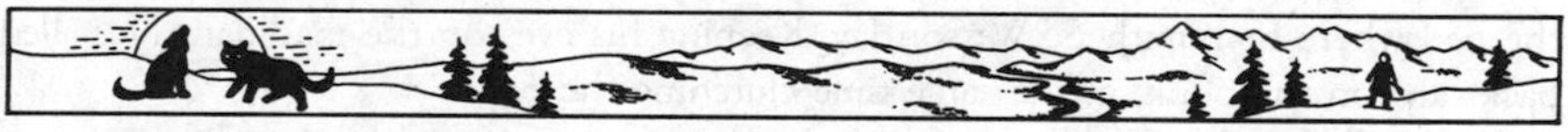

SIWASH

"If I was a man—" Her words were in themselves indecisive, but the withering contempt which flashed from her black eyes was not lost upon the men-folk in the tent.

Tommy, the English sailor, squirmed, but chivalrous old Dick Humphries, Cornish fisherman and erstwhile American salmon capitalist, beamed upon her benevolently as ever. He bore women too large a portion of his rough heart to mind them, as he said, when they were in the doldrums, or when their limited vision would not permit them to see all around a thing. So they said nothing, these two men who had taken the half-frozen woman into their tent three days back, and who had warmed her, and fed her, and rescued her goods from the Indian packers. This latter had necessitated the payment of numerous dollars, to say nothing of a demonstration in force—Dick Humphries squinting along the sights of a Winchester while Tommy apportioned their wages among them at his own appraisement. It had been a little thing in itself, but it meant much to a woman playing a desperate single-hand in the equally desperate Klondike rush of '97. Men were occupied with their own pressing needs, nor did they approve of women playing, single-handed, the odds of the arctic winter.

"If I was a man, I know what I would do." Thus reiterated Molly, she of the flashing eyes, and therein spoke the cumulative grit of five American-born generations.

In the succeeding silence, Tommy thrust a pan of biscuits into the Yukon stove and piled on fresh fuel. A reddish flood pounded along under his suntanned skin, and as he stooped, the skin of his neck was scarlet. Dick palmed a three-cornered sail needle through a set of broken pack straps, his good nature in nowise disturbed by the feminine cataclysm which was threatening to burst in the storm-beaten tent.

"And if you was a man?" he asked, his voice vibrant with kindness. The three-cornered needle jammed in the damp leather, and he suspended work for the moment.

"I'd be a man. I'd put the straps on my back and light out. I wouldn't lay in camp here, with the Yukon like to freeze most any day, and the goods not half over the portage. And you—you are men, and you sit here, holding your hands, afraid of a little wind and wet. I tell you straight, Yankee-men are made of different stuff. They'd be hitting the trail for Dawson if they had to wade through hell-fire. And you, you—I wish I was a man."

"I'm very glad, my dear, that you're not." Dick Humphries threw the bight of the sail twine over the point of the needle and drew it clear with a couple of deft turns and a jerk.

A snort of the gale dealt the tent a broad-handed slap as it hurtled past, and the sleet rat-tat-tatted with snappy spite against the thin canvas. The smoke, smothered in its exit, drove back through the fire-box door, carrying with it the pungent odor of green spruce.

"Good Gawd! Why can't a woman listen to reason?" Tommy lifted his head from the denser depths and turned upon her a pair of smoke-outraged eyes.

"And why can't a man show his manhood?"

Tommy sprang to his feet with an oath which would have shocked a woman of lesser heart, ripped loose the sturdy reef-knots and flung back the flaps of the tent.

The trio peered out. It was not a heartening spectacle. A few water-soaked tents formed the miserable foreground, from which the streaming ground sloped to a foaming gorge. Down this ramped a mountain torrent. Here and there, dwarf spruce, rooting and groveling in the shallow alluvium, marked the proximity of the timber line. Beyond, on the opposing slope, the vague outlines of a glacier loomed dead-white through the driving rain. Even as they looked, its massive front crumbled into the valley, on the breast of some subterranean vomit, and it lifted its hoarse thunder above the screeching voice of the storm. Involuntarily, Molly shrank back.

"Look, woman! Look with all your eyes! Three miles in the teeth of the gale to Crater Lake, across two glaciers, along the slippery rimmock, knee-deep in a howling river! Look, I say, you Yankee woman! Look! There's your Yankeemen!" Tommy pointed a passionate hand in the direction of the struggling tents. "Yankees, the last mother's son of them. Are they on trail? Is there one of them with the straps to his back? And you would teach us men our work? Look, I say!"

Another tremendous section of the glacier rumbled earthward. The wind whipped in at the open doorway, bulging out the sides of the tent till it swayed like a huge bladder at its guy ropes. The smoke swirled about them, and the sleet drove sharply into their flesh. Tommy pulled the flaps together hastily, and returned to his tearful task at the fire-box. Dick Humphries threw the mended pack straps into a corner and lighted his pipe. Even Molly was for the moment persuaded.

"There's my clothes," she half-whimpered, the feminine for the moment prevailing. "They're right at the top of the cache, and they'll be ruined! I tell you, ruined!"

"There, there," Dick interposed, when the last quavering syllable had wailed itself out. "Don't let that worry you, little woman. I'm old enough to be your father's brother, and I've a daughter older than you, and I'll tog you out in fripperies when we get to Dawson if it takes my last dollar."

"When we get to Dawson!" The scorn had come back to her throat with a sudden surge. "You'll rot on the way, first. You'll drown in a mudhole. You—you—Britishers!"

The last word, explosive, intensive, had strained the limits of her vituperation. If that would not stir these men, what could? Tommy's neck ran red again, but he kept his tongue between his teeth. Dick's eyes mellowed. He had the advantage over Tommy, for he had once had a white woman for a wife.

The blood of five American-born generations is, under certain circumstances, an uncomfortable heritage; and among these circumstances might be enumerated that of being quartered with next of kin. These men were Britons. On sea and land her ancestry and the generations thereof had thrashed them and theirs. On sea and land they would continue to do so. The traditions of her race clamored for vindication. She was but a woman of the present, but in her bubbled the whole mighty past. It was not alone Molly Travis who pulled on gum boots, mackintosh, and straps; for the phantom hands of ten thousand forbears drew tight the buckles, just so as they squared her jaw and set her eyes with determination. She, Molly Travis, intended to shame these Britishers; they, the innumerable shades, were asserting the dominance of the common race.

The men-folk did not interfere. Once Dick suggested that she take his oilskins, as her mackintosh was worth no more than paper in such a storm. But she sniffed her independence so sharply that he communed with his pipe till she tied the flaps on the outside and slushed away on the flooded trail.

"Think she'll make it?" Dick's face belied the indifference of his voice.

"Make it? If she stands the pressure till she gets to the cache, what of the cold and misery, she'll be stark, raving mad. Stand it? She'll be dumb-crazed. You know it yourself, Dick. You've wind-jammed round the Horn. You know what it is to lay out on a topsail yard in the thick of it, bucking sleet and snow and frozen canvas till you're ready to just let go and cry like a baby. Clothes? She won't be able to tell a bundle of skirts from a gold pan or a teakettle."

"Kind of think we were wrong in letting her go, then?"

"Not a bit of it. So help me, Dick, she'd'a' made this tent a hell for the rest of the trip if we hadn't. Trouble with her she's got too much spirit. This'll tone it down a bit."

"Yes," Dick admitted, "she's too ambitious. But then Molly's all right. A cussed little fool to tackle a trip like this, but a plucky sight better than those pick-me-up-and-carry-me kind of women. She's the stock that carried you and me, Tommy, and you've got to make allowance for the spirit. Takes a woman to breed a man. You can't suck manhood from the dugs of a creature whose only claim to womanhood is her petticoats. Takes a she-cat, not a cow, to mother a tiger."

"And when they're unreasonable we've got to put up with it, eh?"

"The proposition. A sharp sheath-knife cuts deeper on a slip than a dull one; but that's no reason for to hack the edge off over a capstan bar."

"All right, if you say so, but when it comes to woman, I guess I'll take mine with a little less edge."

"What do you know about it?" Dick demanded.

"Some." Tommy reached over for a pair of Molly's wet stockings and stretched them across his knees to dry.

Dick, eyeing him querulously, went fishing in her hand satchel, then hitched up to the front of the stove with divers articles of damp clothing spread likewise to the heat.

"Thought you said you never were married?" he asked.

"Did I? No more was I—that is—yes, by Gawd! I was. And as good a woman as ever cooked grub for a man."

"Slipped her moorings?" Dick symbolized infinity with a wave of his hand.

"Ay."

"Childbirth," he added, after a moment's pause.

The beans bubbled rowdily on the front lid, and he pushed the pot back to a cooler surface. After that he investigated the biscuits, tested them with a splinter of wood, and placed them aside under cover of a damp cloth. Dick, after the manner of his kind, stifled his interest and waited silently.

"A different woman to Molly. Siwash."

Dick nodded his understanding.

"Not so proud and wilful, but stick by a fellow through thick and thin. Sling a paddle with the next and starve as contentedly as Job. Go for'ard when the sloop's nose was more often under than not, and take in sail like a man. Went prospecting once, up Teslin way, past Surprise Lake and the Little Yellow-Head. Grub gave out, and we ate the dogs. Dogs gave out, and we ate harnesses, moccasins, and furs. Never a whimper; never a pick-me-up-and-carry-me. Before we went she said look out for grub, but when it happened, never a I-told-you-so. 'Never mind, Tommy,' she'd say, day after day, that weak she could bare lift a snowshoe and her feet raw with the work. 'Never mind. I'd sooner be flat-bellied of hunger and be your woman, Tommy, than have a *potlach* every day and be Chief George's *klooch.*' George was chief of the Chilcoots, you know, and wanted her bad.

"Great days, those. Was a likely chap myself when I struck the coast. Jumped a whaler, the *Pole Star,* at Unalaska, and worked my way down to Sitka on an otter hunter. Picked up with Happy Jack there—know him?"

"Had charge of my traps for me," Dick answered, "down on the Columbia. Pretty wild, wasn't he, with a warm place in his heart for whiskey and women?"

"The very chap. Went trading with him for a couple of seasons—*hooch,* and blankets, and such stuff. Then got a sloop of my own, and not to cut him out, came down Juneau way. That's where I met Killisnoo; I called her Tilly for short. Met her at a squaw dance down on the beach. Chief George had finished the year's trade with the Sticks over the Passes, and was down from Dyea with half his tribe. No end of Siwashes at the dance, and I the only white. No one knew me, barring a few of the bucks I'd met over Sitka way, but I'd got most of their histories from Happy Jack.

"Everybody talking Chinook, not guessing that I could spit it better than most; and principally two girls who'd run away from Haine's Mission up the Lynn Canal. They were trim creatures, good to the eye, and I kind of thought of casting that way; but they were fresh as fresh-caught cod. Too much edge, you see. Being a newcomer, they started to twist me, not knowing I gathered in every word of Chinook they uttered.

"I never let on, but set to dancing with Tilly, and the more we danced the more our hearts warmed to each other. 'Looking for a woman,' one of the girls says, and the other tosses her head and answers, 'Small chance he'll get one when the women are looking for men.' And the bucks and squaws standing around began to grin and giggle and repeat what had been said. 'Quite a pretty boy,' says the first one. I'll not deny I was rather smooth-faced and youngish, but I'd been a man amongst men many's the day, and it rankled me. 'Dancing with Chief George's girl,' pipes the second. 'First thing George'll give him the flat of a paddle and send him about his business.' Chief George had been looking pretty black up to now, but at this he laughed and slapped his knees. He was a husky beggar and would have used the paddle too.

"Who's the girls?' I asked Tilly, as we went ripping down the center in a reel. And as soon as she told me their names I remembered all about them from Happy Jack. Had their pedigree down fine—several things he'd told me that not even their own tribe knew. But I held my hush, and went on courting Tilly, they a-casting sharp remarks and everybody roaring. 'Bide a wee, Tommy,' I says to myself; 'bide a wee.'

"And bide I did, till the dance was ripe to break up, and Chief George had brought a paddle all ready for me. Everybody was on the lookout for mischief when we stopped; but I marched, easy as you please, slap into the thick of them. The Mission girls cut me up something clever, and for all I was angry I had to set my teeth to keep from laughing. I turned upon them suddenly.

" 'Are you done?' I asked.

"You should have seen them when they heard me spitting Chinook. Then I broke loose. I told them all about themselves, and their people before them; their fathers, mothers, sisters, brothers—everybody, everything. Each mean trick they'd played; every scrape they'd got into; every shame that'd fallen them. And I burned them without fear or favor. All hands crowded round. Never had they heard a white man sling their lingo as I did. Everybody was laughing save the Mission girls. Even Chief George forgot the paddle, or at least he was swallowing too much respect to dare to use it.

"But the girls. 'Oh, don't, Tommy,' they cried, the tears running down their cheeks. 'Please don't. We'll be good. Sure, Tommy, sure.' But I knew them well, and I scorched them on every tender spot. Nor did I slack away till they came down on their knees, begging and pleading with me to keep quiet. Then I shot a glance at Chief George; but he did not know whether to have at me or not, and passed it off by laughing hollowly.

"So be. When I passed the parting with Tilly that night I gave her word that I was going to be around for a week or so, and that I wanted to see more of her. Not thick-skinned, her kind, when it came to showing like and dislike, and she looked her pleasure for the honest girl she was. Ay, a striking lass, and I didn't wonder that Chief George was taken with her.

"Everything my way. Took the wind from his sails on the first leg. I was for getting her aboard and sailing down Wrangel way till it blew over, leaving him to whistle; but I wasn't to get her that easy. Seems she was living with an uncle of hers—guardian, the way such things go—and seems he was nigh to shuffling off with consumption or some sort of lung trouble. He was good and bad by turns, and she wouldn't leave him till it was over with. Went up to the tepee just before I left, to speculate on how long it'd be; but the old beggar had promised her to Chief George, and when he clapped eyes on me his anger brought on a hemorrhage.

" 'Come and take me, Tommy,' she says when we bid good-by on the beach. 'Ay,' I answers; 'when you give the word.' And I kissed her, white-man-fashion and lover-fashion, till she was all of a tremble like a quaking aspen, and I was so beside myself I'd half a mind to go up and give the uncle a lift over the divide.

"So I went down Wrangel way, past St. Mary's and even to the Queen Charlottes, trading, running whiskey, turning the sloop to most anything. Winter was on, stiff and crisp, and I was back to Juneau, when the word came. 'Come,' the beggar says who brought the news. 'Killisnoo say, "Come now," ' 'What's the row?' I asks. 'Chief George,' says he, '*Potlach.* Killisnoo, makum *klooch.*'

"Ay, it was bitter—the Taku howling down out of the north, the salt water freezing quick as it struck the deck, and the old sloop and I hammering into the teeth of it for a hundred miles to Dyea. Had a Douglass Islander for crew when I started, but midway up he was washed over from the bows. Jibed all over and crossed the course three times, but never a sign of him."

"Doubled up with the cold most likely," Dick suggested, putting a pause into the narrative while he hung one of Molly's skirts up to dry, "and went down like a pot of lead."

"My idea. So I finished the course alone, half-dead when I made Dyea in the dark of the evening. The tide favored, and I ran the sloop plump to the bank, in the shelter of the river. Couldn't go an inch further, for the fresh water was frozen solid. Halyards and blocks were that iced up I didn't dare lower mainsail or jib. First I broached a pinto of the cargo raw, and then, leaving all standing, ready for the start, and with a blanket around me, headed across the flat to the camp. No mistaking, it was a grand layout. The Chilcats had come in a body—dogs, babies, and canoes—to say nothing of the Dog-Ears, the Little Salmons, and the Missions. Full half a thousand of them to celebrate Tilly's wedding, and never a white man in a score of miles.

"Nobody took note of me, the blanket over my head and hiding my face, and I waded knee deep through the dogs and youngsters till I was well up to the front. The show was being pulled off in a big open place among the trees, with great fires burning and the snow moccasin-packed as hard as Portland cement. Next me was Tilly, beaded and scarlet-clothed galore, and against her Chief George and his head men. The shaman was being helped out by the big medicines from the other tribes, and it shivered my spine up and down, the deviltries they cut. I caught myself wondering if the folks in Liverpool could only see me now; and I thought of yellow-haired Gussie, whose brother I licked after my first voyage, just because he was not for having a sailor-man courting his sister. And with Gussie in my eyes I looked at Tilly. A rum old world, thinks I, with a man a-stepping in trails the mother little dreamed of when he lay at suck.

"So be. When the noise was loudest, walrus hides booming and priests a-singing, I says, 'Are you ready?' Gawd! Not a start, not a shot of the eyes my way, not the twitch of a muscle. 'I knew,' she answers, slow and steady as a calm spring tide. 'Where?' 'The high bank at the edge of the ice,' I whispers back. 'Jump out when I give the word.'

"Did I say there was no end of huskies? Well, there was no end. Here, there, everywhere, they were scattered about,—tame wolves and nothing less. When the strain runs thin they breed them in the bush with the wild, and they're bitter fighters. Right at the toe of my moccasin lay a big brute, and by the heel another. I doubled the first one's tail, quick, till it snapped in my grip. As his jaws clipped together where my hand should have been, I threw the second one by the scruff straight into his mouth. 'Go!' I cried to Tilly.

"You know how they fight. In the wink of an eye there was a raging hundred of them, top and bottom, ripping and tearing each other, kids and squaws tumbling which way, and the camp gone wild. Tilly'd slipped away, so I followed. But when I looked over my shoulder at the skirt of the crowd, the devil laid me by the heart, and I dropped the blanket and went back.

"By then the dogs'd been knocked apart and the crowd was untangling itself. Nobody was in proper place, so they didn't note that Tilly'd gone. 'Hello,' I says, gripping Chief George by the hand. 'May your potlach-smoke rise often, and the Sticks bring many furs with the spring.'

"Lord love me, Dick, but he was joyed to see me,—him with the upper hand and wedding Tilly. Chance to puff big over me. The tale that I was hot after her had spread through the camps, and my presence did him proud. All hands knew me, without my blanket, and set to grinning and giggling. It was rich, but I made it richer by playing unbeknowing.

" 'What's the row?' I asks. 'Who's getting married now?'

" 'Chief George,' the shaman says, ducking his reverence to him.

" 'Thought he had two *klooches.*'

" 'Him takum more,—three,' with another duck.

" 'Oh!' And I turned away as though it didn't interest me.

"But this wouldn't do, and everybody begins singing out, 'Killisnoo! Killisnoo!'

" 'Killisnoo what?' I asked.

" 'Killisnoo, *klooch,* Chief George,' they blathered. 'Killisnoo, *klooch.*'

"I jumped and looked at Chief George. He nodded his head and threw out his chest.

" 'She'll be no *klooch* of yours,' I says solemnly. 'No *klooch* of yours,' I repeats, while his face went black and his hand began dropping to his hunting-knife.

" 'Look!' I cries, striking an attitude. 'Big medicine. You watch my smoke.'

"I pulled off my mittens, rolled back my sleeves, and made half-a-dozen passes in the air.

" 'Killisnoo!' I shouts. 'Killisnoo! Killisnoo!'

"I was making medicine, and they began to scare. Every eye was on me, no time to find out that Tilly wasn't there. Then I called Killisnoo three times again, and waited; and three times more. All for mystery and to make them nervous. Chief George couldn't guess what I was up to, and wanted to put a stop to the foolery, but the shamans said to wait, and that they'd see me and go me one better, or words to that effect. Besides, he was a superstitious cuss, and I fancy a bit afraid of the white man's magic.

"Then I called Killisnoo, long and soft like the howl of a wolf, till the women were all a-tremble and the bucks looking serious.

" 'Look!' I sprang for'ard, pointing my finger into a bunch of squaws—easier to deceive women than men, you know. 'Look!' And I raised it aloft as though following the flight of a bird. Up, up, straight overhead, making to follow it with my eyes till it disappeared in the sky.

" 'Killisnoo,' I said, looking at Chief George and pointing upward again. 'Killisnoo.'

"So help me, Dick, the gammon worked. Half of them, at least, saw Tilly disappear in the air. They'd drunk my whiskey at Juneau and seen stranger sights, I'll warrant. Why should I not do this thing, I, who sold bad spirits corked in bottles? Some of the women shrieked. Everybody fell to whispering in bunches. I folded my arms and held my head high, and then they drew further away from me. The time was ripe to go. 'Grab him,' Chief George cries. Three or four of them came at me, but I whirled, quick, made a couple of passes like to send them after Tilly, and pointed up. Touch me? Not for the kingdoms of the earth. Chief George harangued them, but he couldn't get them to lift a leg. Then he made to take me himself; but I repeated the mummery and his grit went out through his fingers.

" 'Let your shamans work wonders the like of which I have done this night,' I says. 'Let them call Killisnoo down out of the sky whither I have sent her.' But the priests knew their limits. 'May your *klooches* bear you sons as the spawn of the salmon,' I says, turning to go, 'and may your totem pole stand long in the land, and the smoke of your camp rise always.'

"But if the beggars could have seen me hitting the high places for the sloop as soon as I was clear of them, they'd thought my own medicine had got after me. Tilly'd kept warm by chopping the ice away, and was all ready to cast off. Gawd! how we ran before it, the Taku howling after us and the freezing seas sweeping over at every clip. With everything battened down, me a-steering and Tilly chopping ice, we held on half the night, till I plumped the sloop ashore on Porcupine Island, and we shivered it out on the beach; blankets wet, and Tilly drying the matches on her breast.

"So I think I know something about it. Seven years, Dick, man and wife, in rough sailing and smooth. And then she died, in the heart of the winter, died in childbirth, up there on the Chilcat Station. She held my hand to the last, the ice creeping up inside the door and spreading thick on the gut of the window. Outside, the lone howl of the wolf and the Silence; inside, death and the Silence. You've never heard the Silence yet, Dick, and Gawd grant you don't ever have to hear it when you sit by the side of death. Hear it? Ay, till the breath whistles like a siren, and the heart booms, booms, booms, like the surf on the shore.

"Siwash, Dick, but a woman. White, Dick, white, clear through. Towards the last she says, 'Keep my feather bed, Tommy, keep it always.' And I agreed. Then she opened her eyes, full with the pain. 'I've been a good woman to you, Tommy, and because of that I want you to promise—to promise'—the words seemed to stick in her throat—'that when you marry, the woman be white. No more Siwash, Tommy. I know. Plenty white women down to Juneau now. I know. Your people call you "squaw-man," your women turn their heads to the one side on the street, and you do not go to their cabins like other men. Why? Your wife Siwash. Is it not so? And this is not good. Wherefore I die. Promise me. Kiss me in token of your promise.'

"I kissed her, and she dozed off, whispering, 'It is good.' At the end, that near gone my ear was at her lips, she roused for the last time. 'Remember, Tommy, remember my feather bed.' Then she died, in childbirth, up there on the Chilcat Station."

The tent heeled over and half flattened before the gale. Dick refilled his pipe, while Tommy drew the tea and set it aside against Molly's return.

And she of the flashing eyes and Yankee blood? Blinded, falling, crawling on hand and knee, the wind thrust back in her throat by the wind, she was heading for the tent. On her shoulders a bulky pack caught the full fury of the storm. She plucked feebly at the knotted flaps, but it was Tommy and Dick who cast them loose. Then she set her soul for the last effort, staggered in, and fell exhausted on the floor.

Tommy unbuckled the straps and took the pack from her. As he lifted it there was a clanging of pots and pans. Dick, pouring out a mug of whiskey, paused long enough to pass the wink across her body. Tommy winked back. His lips pursed the monosyllable, "clothes," but Dick shook his head reprovingly.

"Here, little woman," he said, after she had drunk the whiskey and straightened up a bit. "Here's some dry togs. Climb into them. We're going out to extra-peg the tent. After that, give us the call, and we'll come in and have dinner. Sing out when you're ready."

"So help me, Dick, that's knocked the edge off her for the rest of this trip," Tommy spluttered as they crouched to the lee of the tent.

"But it's the edge is her saving grace," Dick replied, ducking his head to a volley of sleet that drove around a corner of the canvas. "The edge that you and I've got, Tommy, and the edge of our mothers before us."

The God of His Fathers

I

On every hand stretched the forest primeval,—the home of noisy comedy and silent tragedy. Here the struggle for survival continued to wage with all its ancient brutality. Briton and Russian were still to overlap in the Land of the Rainbow's End—and this was the very heart of it—nor had Yankee gold yet purchased its vast domain. The wolf-pack still clung to the flank of the caribou herd, singling out the weak and the big with calf, and pulling them down as remorselessly as were it a thousand, thousand generations into the past. The sparse aborigines still acknowledged the rule of their chiefs and medicine men, drove out bad spirits, burned their witches, fought their neighbors, and ate their enemies with a relish which spoke well of their bellies. But it was at the moment when the stone age was drawing to a close. Already, over unknown trails and chartless wildernesses, were the harbingers of the steel arriving,—fair-faced, blue-eyed, indomitable men, incarnations of the unrest of their race. By accident or design, single-handed and in twos and threes, they came from no one knew whither, and fought, or died, or passed on, no one knew whence. The priests raged against them, the chiefs called forth their fighting men, and stone clashed with steel, but to little purpose. Like water seeping from some mighty reservoir, they trickled through the dark forests and mountain passes, threading the highways in bark canoes, or with their moccasined feet breaking trail for the wolf-dogs. They came of a great breed, and their mothers were many; but the fur-clad denizens of the Northland had this yet to learn. So many an unsung wanderer fought his last and died under the cold fire of the aurora, as did his brothers in burning sands and reeking jungles, and as they shall continue to do till in the fullness of time the destiny of their race be achieved.

It was near twelve. Along the northern horizon a rosy glow, fading to the west and deepening to the east, marked the unseen dip of the midnight sun. The gloaming and the dawn were so commingled that there was no night,—simply a wedding of day with day, a scarcely perceptible blending of two circles of the sun. A kildee timidly chirped good-night; the full, rich throat of a robin proclaimed good-morrow. From an island on the breast of the Yukon a colony of wild fowl voiced its interminable wrongs, while a loon laughed mockingly back across a still stretch of river.

In the foreground, against the bank of a lazy eddy, birch-bark canoes were lined two and three deep. Ivory-bladed spears, bone-barbed arrows, buckskin-thonged bows, and simple basket-woven traps bespoke the fact that in the muddy current of the river the salmon-run was on. In the background, from the tangle of skin tents and drying frames, rose the voices of the fisher folk. Bucks skylarked with bucks or flirted with the maidens, while the older squaws, shut out from this virtue of having fulfilled the end of their existence in reproduction, gossiped as they braided rope from the green roots of trailing vines. At their feet their naked progeny played and squabbled, or rolled in the muck with the tawny wolf-dogs.

To one side of the encampment, and conspicuously apart from it, stood a second camp of two tents. But it was a white man's camp. If nothing else, the choice of position at least bore convincing evidence of this. In case of offense, it commanded the Indian quarters a hundred yards away; of defense, a rise to the ground and the cleared intervening space; and last, of defeat, the swift slope of a score of yards to the canoes below. From one of the tents came the petulant cry of a sick child and the crooning song of a mother. In the open, over the smoldering embers of a fire, two men held talk.

"Eh? I love the church like a good son. *Bien!* So great a love that my days have been spent in fleeing away from her, and my nights in dreaming dreams of reckoning. Look you!" The half-breed's voice rose to an angry snarl. "I am Red River born. My father was white—as white as you. But you are Yankee, and he was British bred, and a gentleman's son. And my mother was the daughter of a chief, and I was a man. Ay, and one had to look the second time to see what manner of blood ran in my veins; for I lived with the whites, and was one of them, and my father's heart beat in me. It happened there was a maiden—white—who looked on me with kind eyes. Her father had much land and many horses; also he was a big man among his people, and his blood was the blood of the French. He said the girl knew not her own mind, and talked overmuch with her, and became wroth that such things should be.

"But she knew her mind, for we came quick before the priest. And quicker had come her father, with lying words, false promises, I know not what; so that the priest stiffened his neck and would not make us that we might live one with the other. As at the beginning it was the church which would not bless my birth, so now it was the church which refused me marriage and put the blood of men upon my hands. *Bien!* Thus have I Cause to love the church. So I struck the priest on his woman's mouth, and we took swift horses, the girl and I, to Fort Pierre, where was a minister of good heart. But hot on our trail was her father, and brothers, and other men he had gathered to him. And we fought, our horses on the run, till I emptied three saddles and the rest drew off and went on to Fort Pierre. Then we took east, the girl and I, to the hills and forests, and we lived one with the other, and we were not married,—the work of the good church which I love like a son.

"But mark you, for this is the strangeness of woman, the way of which no man may understand. One of the saddles I emptied was that of her father's, and the hoofs of those who came behind had pounded him into the earth. This we saw, the girl and I, and this I had forgot had she not remembered. And in the quiet of the evening, after the day's hunt were done, it came between us, and in the silence of the night when we lay beneath the stars and should have been one. It was there always. She never spoke, but it sat by our fire and held us ever apart. She tried to put it aside, but at such times it would rise up till I could read it in the look of her eyes, in the very intake of her breath.

"So in the end she bore me a child, a woman-child, and died. Then I went among my mother's people, that it might nurse at a warm breast and live. But my hands were wet with the blood of men, look you, because of the church, wet with the blood of men. And the Riders of the North came for me, but my mother's brother, who was then chief in his own right, hid me and gave me horses and food. And we went away, my woman-child and I, even to the Hudson Bay Country, where white men were few and the questions they asked not many. And I worked for the company as a hunter, as a guide, as a driver of dogs, till my woman-child was become a woman, tall, and slender, and fair to the eye.

"You know the winter, long and lonely, breeding evil thoughts and bad deeds. The Chief Factor was a hard man, and bold. And he was not such that a woman would delight in looking upon. But he cast eyes upon my woman-child who was become a woman. Mother of God! He sent me away on a long trip with the dogs, that he might—you understand, he was a hard man and without heart. She was most white, and her soul was white, and a good woman, and—well, she died.

"It was bitter cold the night of my return, and I had been away months, and the dogs were limping sore when I came to the fort. The Indians and breeds looked on me in silence, and I felt the fear of I knew not what, but I said nothing till the dogs were fed and I had eaten as a man with work before him should. Then I spoke up, demanding the word, and they shrank from me, afraid of my anger and what I should do, but the story came out, the pitiful story, word for word and act for act, and they marveled that I should be so quiet.

"When they had done I went to the Factor's house, calmer than now in the telling of it. He had been afraid and called upon the breeds to help him; but they were not pleased with the deed, and had left him to lie on the bed he had made. So he had fled to the house of the priest. Thither I followed. But when I was come to that place, the priest stood in my way, and spoke soft words, and said a man in anger should go neither to the right nor left, but straight to God. I asked by the right of a father's wrath that he give me past, but he said only over his body, and besought with me to pray. Look you, it was the church, always the church; for I passed over his body and sent the Factor to meet my woman-child before his god, which is a bad god, and the god of the white men.

"Then was there hue and cry, for word was sent to the station below, and I came away. Through the Land of the Great Slave, down the Valley of the Mackenzie to the never-opening ice over the White Rockies, past the Great Curve of the Yukon, even to this place did I come. And from that day to this, yours is the first face of my father's people I have looked upon. May it be the last! These people, which are my people, are a simple folk, and I have been raised to honor among them. My word is their law, and their priests but do my bidding, else would I not suffer them. When I speak for them I speak for myself. We ask to be let alone. We do not want your kind. If we permit you to sit by our fires, after you will come your church, your priests, and your gods. And know this, for each white man who comes to my village, him will I make deny his god. You are the first, and I give you grace. So it were well you go, and go quickly."

"I am not responsible for my brothers," the second man spoke up, filling his pipe in a meditative manner. Hay Stockard was at times as thoughtful of speech as he was wanton of action; but only at times.

"But I know your breed," responded the other.

"Your brothers are many, and it is you and yours who break the trail for them to follow. In time they shall come to possess the land, but not in my time. Already, have I heard, are they on the head-reaches of the Great River, and far away below are the Russians."

Hay Stockard lifted his head with a quick start. This was startling geographical information. The Hudson Bay post at Fort Yukon had other notions concerning the course of the river, believing it to flow into the Arctic.

"Then the Yukon empties into Bering Sea?" he asked.

"I do not know, but below there are Russians, many Russians. Which is neither here nor there. You may go on and see for yourself; you may go back to your brothers; but up the Koyukuk you shall not go while the priests and fighting men do my bidding. Thus do I command, I, Baptiste the Red, whose word is law and who am head man over this people."

"And should I not go down to the Russians, or back to my brothers?"

"Then shall you go swift-footed before your god, which is a bad god, and the god of the white men."

The red sun shot up above the northern skyline, dripping and bloody. Baptiste the Red came to his feet, nodded curtly, and went back to his camp amid the crimson shadows and the singing of the robins.

Hay Stockard finished his pipe by the fire, picturing in smoke and coal the unknown upper reaches of the Koyukuk, the strange stream which ended here its arctic travels and merged its waters with the muddy Yukon flood. Somewhere up there, if the dying words of a shipwrecked sailorman who had made the fearful overland journey were to be believed, and if the vial of golden grains in his pouch attested anything,—somewhere up there, in that home of winter, stood the Treasure House of the North. And as keeper of the gate, Baptiste the Red, English half-breed and renegade, barred the way.

"Bah!" He kicked the embers apart and rose to his full height, arms lazily outstretched, facing the flushing north with careless soul.

II

HAY Stockard swore, harshly, in the rugged monosyllables of his mother tongue. His wife lifted her gaze from the pots and pans, and followed his in a keen scutiny of the river. She was a woman of the Teslin Country, wise in the ways of her husband's vernacular when it grew intensive. From the slipping of a snowshoe thong to the forefront of sudden death, she could gauge occasion by the pitch and volume of his blasphemy. So she knew the present occasion merited attention. A long canoe, with paddles flashing back the rays of the westering sun, was crossing the current from above and urging in for the eddy. Hay Stockard watched it intently. Three men rose and dipped, rose and dipped, in rhythmical precision; but a red bandanna, wrapped about the head of one, caught and held his eye.

"Bill!" he called. "Oh, Bill!"

A shambling, loose-jointed giant rolled out of one of the tents, yawning and rubbing the sleep from his eyes. Then he sighted the strange canoe and was wide awake on the instant.

"By the jumping Methuselah! That damned sky-pilot!"

Hay Stockard nodded his head bitterly, half-reached for his rifle, then shrugged his shoulders.

"Pot-shot him," Bill suggested, "and settle the thing out of hand. He'll spoil us sure if we don't." But the other declined this drastic measure and turned away, at the same time bidding the woman return to her work, and calling Bill back from the bank. The two Indians in the canoe moored it on the edge of the eddy, while its white occupant, conspicuous by his gorgeous headgear, came up the bank.

"Like Paul of Tarsus, I give you greeting. Peace be unto you and grace before the Lord." His advances were met sullenly, and without speech.

"To you, Hay Stockard, blasphemer and Philistine, greeting. In your heart is the lust of Mammon, in your mind cunning devils, in your tent this woman whom you live with in adultery; yet of these divers sins, even here in the wilderness, I, Sturges Owen, apostle to the Lord, bid you to repent and cast from you your iniquities."

"Save your cant! Save your cant!" Hay Stockard broke in testily. "You'll need all you've got, and more, for Red Baptiste over yonder."

He waved his hand toward the Indian camp, where the half-breed was looking steadily across, striving to make out the newcomers. Sturges Owen, disseminator of light and apostle to the Lord, stepped to the edge of the steep and commanded his men to bring up the camp outfit. Stockard followed him.

"Look here," he demanded, plucking the missionary by the shoulder and twirling him about. "Do you value your hide?"

"My life is in the Lord's keeping, and I do but work in His vineyard," he replied solemnly.

"Oh, stow that! Are you looking for a job of martyrship?"

"If He so wills."

"Well, you'll find it right here, but I'm going to give you some advice first. Take it or leave it. If you stop here, you'll be cut off in the midst of your labors. And not you alone, but your men, Bill, my wife—"

"Who is a daughter of Belial and hearkeneth not to the true Gospel."

"And myself. Not only do you bring trouble upon yourself, but upon us. I was frozen in with you last winter, as you will well recollect, and I know you for a good man and a fool. If you think it is your duty to strive with the heathen, well and good; but do exercise some wit in the way you go about it. This man, Red Baptiste, is no Indian. He comes of our common stock, is as bull-necked as I ever dared be, and as wild a fanatic the one way as you are the other. When you two come together, hell'll be to pay, and I don't care to be mixed up in it. Understand? So take my advice and go away. If you go downstream, you'll fall in with the Russians. There's bound to be Greek priests among them, and they'll see you safe through to Bering Sea,—that's where the Yukon empties,—and from there it won't be hard to get back to civilization. Take my word for it and get out of here as fast as God'll let you."

"He who carries the Lord in his heart and the Gospel in his hand hath no fear of the machinations of man or devil," the missionary answered stoutly. "I will see this man and wrestle with him. One backslider returned to the fold is a greater victory than a thousand heathen. He who is strong for evil can be as mighty for good, witness Saul when he journeyed up to Damascus to bring Christian captives to Jerusalem. And the voice of the Saviour came to him, crying, 'Saul, Saul, why persecutest thou me?' And therewith Paul arrayed himself on the side of the Lord, and thereafter was most mighty in the saving of souls. And even as thou, Paul of Tarsus, even so do I work in the vineyard of the Lord, bearing trials and tribulations, scoffs and sneers, stripes and punishments, for His dear sake."

"Bring up the little bag with the tea and a kettle of water," he called the next instant to his boatmen; "not forgetting the haunch of caribou and the mixing-pan."

When his men, converts by his own hand, had gained the bank, the trio fell to their knees, hands and backs burdened with camp equipage, and offered up thanks for their passage through the wilderness and their safe arrival. Hay Stockard looked upon the function with sneering disapproval, the romance and solemnity of it lost to his matter-of-fact soul. Baptiste the Red, still gazing across, recognized the familiar postures, and remembered the girl who had shared his star-roofed couch in the hills and forests, and the woman-child who lay somewhere by bleak Hudson's Bay.

III

"CONFOUND it, Baptiste, couldn't think of it. Not for a moment. Grant that this man is a fool and of small use in the nature of things, but still, you know, I can't give him up."

Hay Stockard paused, striving to put into speech the rude ethics of his heart.

"He's worried me, Baptiste, in the past and now, and caused me all manner of troubles; but can't you see, he's my own breed—white—and—and—why, I couldn't buy my life with his, not if he was a nigger."

"So be it," Baptiste the Red made answer. "I have given you grace and choice. I shall come presently, with my priests and fighting men, and either shall I kill you, or you deny your god. Give up the priest to my pleasure, and you shall depart in peace. Otherwise your trail ends here. My people are against you to the babies. Even now have the children stolen away your canoes." He pointed down to the river. Naked boys had slipped down the water from the point above, cast loose the canoes, and by then had worked them into the current. When they had drifted out of rifle-shot they clambered over the sides and paddled ashore.

"Give me the priest, and you may have them back again. Come! Speak your mind, but without haste."

Stockard shook his head. His glance dropped to the woman of the Teslin Country with his boy at her breast, and he would have wavered had he not lifted his eyes to the men before him.

"I am not afraid," Sturges Owen spoke up. "The Lord bears me in his right hand, and alone am I ready to go into the camp of the unbeliever. It is not too late. Faith may move mountains. Even in the eleventh hour may I win his soul to the true righteousness."

"Trip the beggar up and make him fast," Bill whispered hoarsely in the ear of his leader, while the missionary kept the floor and wrestled with the heathen. "Make him hostage, and bore him if they get ugly."

"No," Stockard answered. "I gave him my word that he could speak with us unmolested. Rules of warfare, Bill; rules of warfare. He's been on the square, given us warning, and all that, and—why, damn it, man, I can't break my word!"

"He'll keep his, never fear."

"Don't doubt it, but I won't let a half-breed outdo me in fair dealing. Why not do what he wants,—give him the missionary and be done with it?"

"N-no," Bill hesitated doubtfully.

"Shoe pinches, eh?"

Bill flushed a little and dropped the discussion. Baptiste the Red was still waiting the final decision. Stockard went up to him.

"It's this way, Baptiste. I came to your village minded to go up the Koyukuk. I intended no wrong. My heart was clean of evil. It is still clean. Along comes this priest, as you call him. I didn't bring him here. He'd have come whether I was here or not. But now that he is here, being of my people, I've got to stand by him. And I'm going to. Further, it will be no child's play. When you have done, your village will be silent and empty, your people wasted as after a famine. True, we will be gone; likewise the pick of your fighting men—"

"But those who remain shall be in peace, nor shall the word of strange gods and the tongues of strange priests be buzzing in their ears."

Both men shrugged their shoulders and turned away, the half-breed going back to his own camp. The missionary called his two men to him, and they fell into prayer. Stockard and Bill attacked the few standing pines with their axes, felling them into convenient breastworks. The child had fallen asleep, so the woman placed it on a heap of furs and lent a hand in fortifying the camp. Three sides were thus defended, the steep declivity at the rear precluding attack from that direction. When these arrangements had been completed, the two men stalked into the open, clearing away, here and there, the scattered underbrush. From the opposing camp came the booming of war-drums and the voices of the priests stirring the people to anger.

"Worst of it is they'll come in rushes," Bill complained as they walked back with shouldered axes.

"And wait till midnight, when the light gets dim for shooting."

"Can't start the ball a-rolling too early, then." Bill exchanged the axe for a rifle, and took a careful rest. One of the medicine-men, towering above his tribesmen, stood out distinctly. Bill drew a bead on him.

"All ready?" he asked.

Stockard opened the ammunition box, placed the woman where she could reload in safety, and gave the word. The medicine-man dropped. For a moment there was silence, then a wild howl went up and a flight of bone arrows fell short.

"I'd like to take a look at the beggar," Bill remarked, throwing a fresh shell into place. "I'll swear I drilled him clean between the eyes."

"Didn't work." Stockard shook his head gloomily. Baptiste had evidently quelled the more warlike of his followers, and instead of precipitating an attack in the bright light of day, the shot had caused a hasty exodus, the Indians drawing out of the village beyond the zone of fire.

In the full tide of his proselyting fervor, borne along by the hand of God, Sturges Owen would have ventured alone into the camp of the unbeliever, equally prepared for miracle or martyrdom; but in the waiting which ensued, the fever of conviction died away gradually, as the natural man asserted itself. Physical fear replaced spiritual hope, the love of life, the love of God. It was no new experience. He could feel his weakness coming on, and knew it of old time. He had struggled against it and been overcome by it before.

He remembered when the other men had driven their paddles like mad in the van of a roaring ice-flood, how, at the critical moment, in a panic of worldly terror, he had dropped his paddle and besought wildly with his God for pity. And there were other times. The recollection was not pleasant. It brought shame to him that his spirit should be so weak and his flesh so strong. But the love of life! the love of life! He could not strip it from him. Because of it had his dim ancestors perpetuated their line; because of it was he destined to perpetuate his. His courage, if courage it might be called, was bred of fanaticism. The courage of Stockard and Bill was the adherence to deep-rooted ideals. Not that the love of life was less, but the love of race tradition more; not that they were unafraid to die, but that they were brave enough not to live at the price of shame.

The missionary rose, for the moment swayed by the mood of sacrifice. He half crawled over the barricade to proceed on the other camp, but sank back, a trembling mass, wailing: "As the spirit moves! As the spirit moves! Who am I that I should set aside the judgments of God? Before the foundations of the world were all things written in the book of life. Worm that I am, shall I erase the page or any portion thereof? As God wills, so shall the spirit move!"

Bill reached over, plucked him to his feet, and shook him, fiercely, silently. Then he dropped the bundle of quivering nerves and turned his attention to the two converts. But they showed little fright and a cheerful alacrity in preparing for the coming passage at arms.

Stockard, who had been talking in undertones with the Teslin woman, now turned to the missionary.

"Fetch him over here," he commanded of Bill.

"Now," he ordered, when Sturges Owen had been duly deposited before him, "make us man and wife, and be lively about it." Then he added apologetically to Bill: "No telling how it's to end, so I just thought I'd get my affairs straightened up."

The woman obeyed the behest of her white lord. To her the ceremony was meaningless. By her lights she was his wife, and had been from the day they first foregathered. The converts served as witnesses. Bill stood over the missionary, prompting him when he stumbled. Stockard put the responses in the woman's mouth, and when the time came, for want of better, ringed her finger with thumb and forefinger of his own.

"Kiss the bride!" Bill thundered, and Sturges Owen was too weak to disobey.

"Now baptize the child!"

"Neat and tidy," Bill commented.

"Gathering the proper outfit for a new trail," the father explained, taking the boy from the mother's arms. "I was grub-staked, once, into the Cascades, and had everything in the kit except salt. Never shall forget it. And if the woman and the kid cross the divide tonight they might as well be prepared for potluck. A long shot, Bill, between ourselves, but nothing lost if it misses."

A cup of water served the purpose, and the child was laid away in a secure corner of the barricade. The men built the fire, and the evening meal was cooked.

The sun hurried round to the north, sinking closer to the horizon. The heavens in that quarter grew red and bloody. The shadows lengthened, the light dimmed, and in the sombre recesses of the forest life slowly died away. Even the wild fowl in the river softened their raucus chatter and feigned the nightly farce of going to bed. Only the tribesmen increased their clamor, war-drums booming and voices raised in savage folk songs. But as the sun dipped they ceased their tumult. The rounded hush of midnight was complete. Stockard rose to his knees and peered over the logs. Once the child wailed in pain and disconcerted him. The mother bent over it, but it slept again. The silence was interminable, profound. Then, of a sudden, the robins burst into full-throated song. The night had passed.

A flood of dark figures boiled across the open. Arrows whistled and bowthongs sang. The shrill-tongued rifles answered back. A spear, and a mighty cast, transfixed the

Teslin woman as she hovered above the child. A spent arrow, diving between the logs, lodged in the missionary's arm.

There was no stopping the rush. The middle distance was cumbered with bodies, but the rest surged on, breaking against and over the barricade like an ocean wave. Sturges Owen fled to the tent, while the men were swept from their feet, buried beneath the human tide. Hay Stockard alone regained the surface, flinging the tribesmen aside like yelping curs. He had managed to seize an axe. A dark hand grasped the child by a naked foot, and drew it from beneath its mother. At arm's length its puny body circled through the air, dashing to death against the logs. Stockard clove the man to the chin and fell to clearing space. The ring of savage faces closed in, raining upon him spear-thrusts and bone-barbed arrows. The sun shot up, and they swayed back and forth in the crimson shadows. Twice, with his axe blocked by too deep a blow, they rushed him; but each time he flung them clear. They fell underfoot and he trampled dead and dying, the way slippery with blood. And still the day brightened and the robins sang. Then they drew back from him in awe, and he leaned breathless upon his axe.

"Blood of my soul!" cried Baptiste the Red. "But thou art a man. Deny the god, and thou shalt yet live."

Stockard swore his refusal, feebly but with grace.

"Behold! A woman!" Sturges Owen had been brought before the half-breed.

Beyond a scratch on the arm, he was uninjured, but his eyes roved about him in an ecstasy of fear. The heroic figure of the blasphemer, bristling with wounds and arrows, leaning defiantly upon his axe, indifferent, indomitable, superb, caught his wavering vision. And he felt a great envy of the man who could go down serenely to the dark gates of death. Surely Christ, and not he, Sturges Owen, had been molded in such manner. And why not he? He felt dimly the curse of ancestry, the feebleness of spirit which had come down to him out of the past, and he felt an anger at the creative force, symbolize it as he would, which had formed him, its servant, so weakly. For even a stronger man, this anger and the stress of circumstance were sufficient to breed apostasy, and for Sturges Owen it was inevitable. In the fear of man's anger he would dare the wrath of God. He had been raised up to serve the Lord only that he might be cast down. He had been given faith without the strength of faith; he had been given spirit without the power of spirit. It was unjust.

"Where now is thy god?" the half-breed demanded.

"I do not know." He stood straight and rigid, like a child repeating a catechism.

"Hast thou then a god at all?"

"I had."

"And now?"

"No."

Hay Stockard swept the blood from his eyes and laughed. The missionary looked at him curiously, as in a dream. A feeling of infinite distance came over him, as though of a great remove. In that which had transpired, and which was to transpire, he had no part. He was a spectator—at a distance, yes, at a distance. The words of Baptiste came to him faintly:—

"Very good. See that this man go free, and that no harm befall him. Let him depart in peace. Give him a canoe and food. Set his face toward the Russians, that he may tell their priests of Baptiste the Red, in whose country there is no god."

They led him to the edge of the steep, where they paused to witness the final tragedy. The half-breed turned to Hay Stockard.

"There is no god," he prompted.

The man laughed in reply. One of the young men poised a war-spear for the cast.

"Hast thou a god?"

"Ay, the God of my fathers."

He shifted the axe for a better grip. Baptiste the Red gave the sign, and the spear hurtled full against his breast. Sturges Owen saw the ivory head stand out beyond his back, saw the man sway, laughing, and snap the shaft short as he fell upon it. Then he went down to the river, that he might carry to the Russians the message of Baptiste the Red, in whose country there was no god.

Where the Trail Forks

Must I, then, must I, then, now leave this town—
And you, my love, stay here?

Schwabian Folk-song

The singer, clean-faced and cheery-eyed, bent over and added water to a pot of simmering beans, and then, rising, a stick of firewood in hand, drove back the circling dogs from the grub-box and cooking gear. He was blue of eye, and his long hair was golden, and it was a pleasure to look upon his lusty freshness. A new moon was thrusting a dim horn above the white line of close-packed snow-capped pines which ringed the camp and segregated it from all the world. Overhead, so clear it was and cold, the stars danced with quick, pulsating movements. To the southeast an evanescent greenish glow heralded the opening revels of the aurora borealis. Two men, in the immediate foreground, lay upon the bearskin which was their bed. Between the skin and naked snow was a six-inch layer of pine boughs. The blankets were rolled back. For shelter, there was a fly at their backs,—a sheet of canvas stretched between two trees and angling at forty-five degrees. This caught the radiating heat from the fire and flung it down upon the skin. Another man sat on a sled, drawn close to the blaze, mending moccasins. To the right, a heap of frozen gravel and a rude windlass denoted where they toiled each day in dismal groping for the paystreak. To the left, four pairs of snowshoes stood erect, showing the mode of travel which obtained when the stamped snow of the camp was left behind.

That Schwabian folk-song sounded strangely pathetic under the cold northern stars, and did not do the men good who lounged about the fire after the toil of the day. It put a dull ache into their hearts, and a yearning which was akin to belly-hunger, and sent their souls questing southward across the divides to the sunlands.

"For the love of God, Sigmund, shut up!" expostulated one of the men. His hands were clenched painfully, but he hid them from sight in the folds of the bearskin upon which he lay.

"And what for, Dave Wertz?" Sigmund demanded. "Why shall I not sing when the heart is glad?"

"Because you've got no call to, that's why. Look about you, man, and think of the grub we've been defiling our bodies with for the last twelvemonth, and the way we've lived and worked like beasts!"

Thus abjured, Sigmund, the golden-haired, surveyed it all, and the frost-rimmed wolf-dogs and the vapor breaths of the men. "And why shall not the heart be glad?" he laughed. "It is good; it is all good. As for the grub—" He doubled up his arm and caressed the swelling biceps. "And if we have lived and worked like beasts, have we not been paid like kings? Twenty dollars to the pan the streak is running, and we know it to be eight feet thick. It is another Klondike—and we know it—Jim Hawes there, by your elbow, knows it and complains not. And there's Hitchcock! He sews moccasins like an old woman, and waits against the time. Only you can't wait and work until the wash-up in the spring. Then we shall all be rich, rich as kings, only you cannot wait. You want to go back to the States. So do I, and I was born there, but I can wait, when each day the gold in the pan shows up yellow as butter in the churning. But you want your good time, and, like a child, you cry for it now. Bah! Why shall I not sing:

In a year, in a year, when the grapes are ripe,
I shall stay no more away.
Then if you still are true, my love,
It will be our wedding day.
In a year, in a year, when my time is past,
Then I'll live in your love for aye.
Then if you still are true, my love,
It will be our wedding day.

The dogs, bristling and growling, drew in closer to the firelight. There was a monotonous crunch-crunch of webbed shoes, and between each crunch the dragging forward of the heel of the shoe like the sound of sifting sugar. Sigmund broke off from his song to hurl oaths and firewood at the animals. Then the light was parted by a fur-clad figure, and an Indian girl slipped out of the webs, threw back the hood of her squirrel-skin *parka,* and stood in their midst. Sigmund and the men on the bearskin greeted her as "Sipsu," with the customary "Hello," but Hitchcock made room on the sled that she might sit beside him.

"And how goes it, Sipsu?" he asked, talking, after her fashion, in broken English and bastard Chinook. "Is the hunger still mighty in the camp? and has the witch doctor yet found the cause wherefore game is scarce and no moose in the land?"

"Yes; even so. There is little game, and we prepare to eat the dogs. Also has the witch doctor found the cause of all this evil, and tomorrow will he make sacrifice and cleanse the camp."

"And what does the sacrifice chance to be?—a newborn babe or some poor devil of a squaw, old and shaky, who is a care to the tribe and better out of the way?"

"It chanced not that wise; for the need was great, and he chose none other than the chief's daughter; none other than I, Sipsu."

"Hell!" The word rose slowly to Hitchcock's lips, and brimmed over full and deep, in a way which bespoke wonder and consideration.

"Wherefore we stand by a forking of the trail, you and I," she went on calmly, "and I have come that we may look once more upon each other, and once more only."

She was born of primitive stock, and primitive had been her traditions and her days;

so she regarded life stoically, and human sacrifice as part of the natural order. The powers which ruled the daylight and the dark, the flood and the frost, the bursting of the bud and the withering of the leaf, were angry and in need of propitiation. This they exacted in many ways,—death in the bad water, through the treacherous ice-crust, by the grip of the grizzly, or a wasting sickness which fell upon a man in his own lodge till he coughed, and the life of his lungs went out through his mouth and nostrils. Likewise did the powers receive sacrifice. It was all one. And the witch doctor was versed in the thoughts of the powers and chose unerringly. It was very natural. Death came by many ways, yet was it all one after all,—a manifestation of the all-powerful and inscrutable.

But Hitchcock came of a later world-breed. His traditions were less concrete and without reverence, and he said, "Not so, Sipsu. You are young, and yet in the full joy of life. The witch doctor is a fool, and his choice is evil. This thing shall not be."

She smiled and answered, "Life is not kind, and for many reasons. First, it made of us twain the one white and the other red, which is bad. Then it crossed our trails, and now it parts them again; and we can do nothing. Once before, when the gods were angry, did your brothers come to the camp. They were three, big men and white, and they said the thing shall not be. But they died quickly, and the thing was."

Hitchcock nodded that he heard, half-turned, and lifted his voice. "Look here, you fellows! There's a lot of foolery going on over to the camp, and they're getting ready to murder Sipsu. What d'ye say?"

Wertz looked at Hawes, and Hawes looked back, but neither spoke. Sigmund dropped his head, and petted the shepherd dog between his knees. He had brought Shep in with him from the outside, and thought a great deal of the animal. In fact, a certain girl, who was much in his thoughts, and whose picture in the little locket on his breast often inspired him to sing, had given him the dog and her blessing when they kissed good-by and he started on his Northland quest.

"What d'ye say?" Hitchcock repeated.

"Mebbe it's not so serious," Hawes answered with deliberation. "Most likely it's only a girl's story."

"That isn't the point!" Hitchcock felt a hot flush of anger sweep over him at their evident reluctance. "The question is, if it is so, are we going to stand it? What are we going to do?"

"I don't see any call to interfere," spoke up Wertz. "If it is so, it is so, and that's all there is about it. It's a way these people have of doing. It's their religion, and it's no concern of ours. Our concern is to get the dust and then get out of this God-forsaken land. 'T isn't fit for naught else but beasts? And what are these black devils but beasts? Besides, it'd be damn poor policy."

"That's what I say," chimed in Hawes.

"Here we are, four of us, three hundred miles from the Yukon or a white face. And what can we do against half-a-hundred Indians? If we quarrel with them, we have to vamose; if we fight, we are wiped out. Further, we've struck pay, and by God! I, for one, am going to stick by it!"

"Ditto here," supplemented Wertz.

Hitchcock turned impatiently to Sigmund, who was softly singing,—

In a year, in a year, when the grapes are ripe,
I shall stay no more away.

"Well, it's this way, Hitchcock," he finally said, "I'm in the same boat with the rest. It threescore bucks have made up their mind to kill the girl, why, we can't help it. One rush, and we'd be wiped off the landscape. And what' good'd that be? They'd still have the girl. There's no use in going against the customs of a people except you're in force."

"But we are in force!" Hitchcock broke in. "Four whites are a match for a hundred times as many reds. And think of the girl!"

Sigmund stroked the dog meditatively. "But I do think of the girl. And her eyes are blue like summer skies, and laughing like summer seas, and her hair is yellow, like mine, and braided in ropes the size of a big man's arms. She's waiting for me, out there, in a better land. And she's waited long, and now my pile's in sight I'm not going to throw it away."

"And shamed I would be to look into the girl's blue eyes and remember the black ones of the girl whose blood was on my hands," Hitchcock sneered, for he was born to honor and championship, and to do the thing for the thing's sake, nor stop to weigh or measure.

Sigmund shook his head. "You can't make me mad, Hitchcock, nor do mad things because of your madness. It's a cold business proposition and a question of facts. I didn't come to this country for my health, and, further, it's impossible for us to raise a hand. If it is so, it is too bad for the girl, that's all. It's a way of her people, and it just happens we're on the spot this one time. They've done the same for a thousand-thousand years, and they're going to do it now, and they'll go on doing it for all time to come. Besides, they're not our kind. Nor's the girl. No, I take my stand with Wertz and Hawes, and—"

But the dogs snarled and drew in, and he broke off, listening to the crunch-crunch of many snowshoes. Indian after Indian stalked into the firelight, tall and grim, fur-clad and silent, their shadows dancing grotesquely on the snow. One, the witch doctor, spoke gutturally to Sipsu. His face was daubed with savage paint blotches, and over his shoulders was drawn a wolfskin, the gleaming teeth and cruel snout surmounting his head. No other word was spoken. The prospectors held the peace. Sipsu arose and slipped into her snowshoes.

"Good-by, O my man," she said to Hitchcock.

But the man who had sat beside her on the sled gave no sign, nor lifted his head as they filed away into the white forest.

Unlike many men, his faculty of adaptation, while large, had never suggested the expediency of an alliance with the women of the Northland. His broad cosmopolitanism had never impelled toward covenanting in marriage with the daughters of the soil. If it had, his philosophy of life would not have stood between. But it simply had not. Sipsu? He had pleasured in camp-fire chats with her, not as a man who knew himself to be a man and she woman, but as a man might with a child, and as a man of his make certainly would if for no other reason than to vary the tedium of a bleak existence. That was all. But there was a certain chivalric thrill of warm blood in him, despite his Yankee ancestry and New England upbringing, and he was so made that the commercial aspect of life often seemed meaningless and bore contradiction to his deeper impulses.

So he sat silent, with head bowed forward, an organic force, greater than himself, as great as his race, at work within him. Wertz and Hawes looked askance at him from time to time, a faint but perceptible trepidation in their manner. Sigmund also felt this. Hitchcock was strong, and his strength had been impressed upon them in the course of many an event in their precarious life. So they stood in a certain definite awe and curiosity as to what his conduct would be when he moved to action.

But his silence was long, and the fire nigh out, when Wertz stretched his arms and yawned, and thought he'd go to bed. Then Hitchcock stood up his full height.

"May God damn your souls to the deepest hells, you chicken-hearted cowards! I'm done with you!" He said it calmly enough, but his strength spoke in every syllable, and every intonation was advertisement of intention. "Come on," he continued, "whack up, and in whatever way suits you best. I own a quarter-interest in the claims; our contracts show that. There're twenty-five or thirty ounces in the sack from the test pans. Fetch out the scales. We'll divide that now. And you, Sigmund, measure me my quarter-share of the grub and set it apart. Four of the dogs are mine, and I want four more. I'll trade you my share in the camp outfit and mining-gear for the dogs. And I'll throw in my six or seven ounces and the spare 45-90 with the ammunition. What d'ye say?"

The three men drew apart and conferred. When they returned, Sigmund acted as spokesman. "We'll whack up fair with you, Hitchcock. In everything you'll get your quarter-share, neither more nor less; and you can take it or leave it. But we want the dogs as bad as you do, so you get four, and that's all. If you don't want to take your share of the outfit and gear, why, that's your lookout. If you want it, you can have it; if you don't, leave it."

"The letter of the law," Hitchcock sneered. "But go ahead. I'm willing. And hurry up. I can't get out of this camp and away from its vermin any too quick."

The division was effected without further comment. He lashed his meager belongings upon one of the sleds, rounded in his four dogs, and harnessed up. His portion of outfit and gear he did not touch, though he threw onto the sled half a dozen dog harnesses, and challenged them with his eyes to interfere. But they shrugged their shoulders and watched him disappear in the forest.

A man crawled upon his belly through the snow. On every hand loomed the moosehide lodges of the camp. Here and there a miserable dog howled or snarled abuse upon his neighbor. Once, one of them approached the creeping man, but the man became motionless. The dog came closer and sniffed, and came yet closer, till its nose touched the strange object which had not been there when darkness fell. Then Hitchcock, for it was Hitchcock, upreared suddenly, shooting an unmittened hand out to the brute's shaggy throat. And the dog knew its death in that clutch, and when the man moved on, was left broken-necked under the stars. In this manner Hitchcock made the chief's lodge. For long he lay in the snow without, listening to the voices of the occupants and striving to locate Sipsu. Evidently there were many in the tent, and from the sounds they were in high excitement.

At last he heard the girl's voice, and crawled around so that only the moosehide divided them. Then burrowing in the snow, he slowly wormed his head and shoulders underneath. When the warm inner air smote his face, he stopped and waited, his legs and the greater part of his body still on the outside. He could see nothing, nor did he dare lift his head. On one side of him was a skin bale. He could smell it, though he carefully felt to be certain. On the other side his face barely touched a furry garment which he knew clothed a body. This must be Sipsu. Though he wished she would speak again, he resolved to risk it.

He could hear the chief and the witch doctor talking high, and in a far corner some hungry child whimpering to sleep. Squirming over on his side, he carefully raised his head, still just touching the furry garment. He listened to the breathing. It was a woman's breathing; he would chance it.

He pressed against her side softly but firmly, and felt her start at the contact. Again he waited, till a questioning hand slipped down upon his head and paused among the curls. The next instant the hand turned his face gently upward, and he was gazing into Sipsu's eyes.

She was quite collected. Changing her position casually, she threw an elbow well over on the skin bale, rested her body upon it, and arranged her *parka.* In this way he was completely concealed. Then, and still most casually, she reclined across him, so that he could breathe between her arm and breast, and when she lowered her head her ear pressed lightly against his lips.

"When the time suits, go thou," he whispered, "out of the lodge and across the snow, down the wind to the bunch of jack-pine in the curve of the creek. There wilt thou find my dogs and my sled, packed for the trail. This night we go down to the Yukon; and since we go fast, lay thou hands upon what dogs come nigh thee, by the scruff of the neck, and drag them to the sled in the curve of the creek."

Sipsu shook her head in dissent; but her eyes glistened with gladness, and she was proud that this man had shown toward her such favor. But she, like the women of all her race, was born to obey the will masculine, and when Hitchcock repeated "Go!" he did it with authority, and though she made no answer he knew that his will was law.

"And never mind harness for the dogs," he added, preparing to go. "I shall wait. But waste no time. The day chaseth the night away, nor does it linger for man's pleasure."

Half an hour later, stamping his feet and swinging his arms by the sled, he saw her coming, a surly dog in either hand. At the approach of these his own animals waxed truculent, and he favored them with the butt of his whip till they quieted. He had approached the camp up the wind, and sound was the thing to be most feared in making his presence known.

"Put them into the sled," he ordered when she had got the harness on the two dogs. "I want my leaders to the fore."

But when she had done this, the displaced animals pitched upon the aliens. Though Hitchcock plunged among them with clubbed rifle, a riot of sound went up and across the sleeping camp.

"Now we shall have dogs, and in plenty," he remarked grimly, slipping an axe from the sled lashings. "Do thou harness whichever I fling thee, and betweenwhiles protect the team."

He stepped a space in advance and waited between two pines. The dogs of the camp were disturbing the night with their jangle, and he watched for their coming. A dark spot, growing rapidly, took form upon the dim white expanse of snow. It was a forerunner of the pack, leaping cleanly, and, after the wolf fashion, singing direction to its brothers. Hitchcock stood in the shadow. As it sprang past, he reached out, gripped its forelegs in mid-career, and sent it whirling earthward. Then he struck it a well-judged blow beneath the ear, and flung it to Sipsu. And while she clapped on the harness, he, with his axe, held the passage between the trees, till a shaggy flood of white teeth and glistening eyes surged and crested just beyond reach. Sipsu worked rapidly. When she had finished, he leaped forward, seized and stunned a second, and flung it to her. This he repeated thrice again, and when the sled team stood snarling in a string of ten, he called, "Enough!"

But at this instant a young buck, the forerunner of the tribe, and swift of limb, wading through the dogs and cuffing right and left, attempted the passage. The butt of Hitchcock's rifle drove him to his knees, whence he toppled over sideways. The witch doctor, running lustily, saw the blow fall.

Hitchcock called to Sipsu to pull out. At her shrill "Chook!" the maddened brutes shot straight ahead, and the sled, bounding mightily, just missed unseating her. The powers were evidently angry with the witch doctor, for at this moment they plunged him upon the trail. The lead-dog fouled his snowshoes and tripped him up, and the nine succeeding dogs trod him under foot and the sled bumped over him. But he was quick to his feet, and the night might have turned out differently had not Sipsu struck backward with the long dog-whip and smitten him a blinding blow across the eyes. Hitchcock, hurrying to overtake her, collided against him as he swayed with pain in the middle of the trail. Thus it was, when this primitive theologian got back to the chief's lodge, that his wisdom had been increased in so far as concerns the efficacy of the white man's fist. So, when he orated then and there in the council, he was wroth against all white men.

"Tumble out, you loafers! Tumble out! Grub'll be ready before you get into your footgear!"

David Wertz threw off the bearskin, sat up, and yawned.

Hawes stretched, discovered a lame muscle in his arm, and rubbed it sleepily. "Wonder where Hitchcock bunked last night?" he queried, reaching for his moccasins. They were stiff, and he walked gingerly in his socks to the fire to thaw them out. "It's a blessing he's gone," he added, "though he was a mighty good worker."

"Yep. Too masterful. That was his trouble. Too bad for Sipsu. Think he cared for her much?"

"Don't think so. Just principle. That's all. He thought it wasn't right—and, of course, it wasn't,—but that was no reason for us to interfere and get hustled over the divide before our time."

"Principle is principle, and it's good in its place, but it's best left to home when you go to Alaska. Eh?" Wertz had joined his mate, and both were working pliability into their frozen moccasins. "Think we ought to have taken a hand?"

Sigmund shook his head. He was very busy. A scud of chocolate-colored foam was rising in the coffee-pot, and the bacon needed turning. Also, he was thinking about the girl with laughing eyes like summer seas, and he was humming softly.

His mates chuckled to each other and ceased talking. Though it was past seven, daybreak was still three hours distant. The aurora borealis had passed out of the sky, and the camp was an oasis of light in the midst of deep darkness. And in this light the forms of the three men were sharply defined. Emboldened by the silence, Sigmund raised his voice and opened the last stanza of the old song:—

In a year, in a year
When the grapes are ripe—

Then the night was split with a rattling volley of rifle shots. Hawes sighed, made an effort to straighten himself, and collapsed. Wertz went over on an elbow with drooping head. He chocked a little, and a dark stream flowed from his mouth. And Sigmund, the Golden-Haired, his throat a-gurgle with the song, threw up his arms and pitched across the fire.

The witch doctor's eyes were well blackened, and his temper none of the best; for he quarreled with the chief over the possession of Wertz's rifle, and took more than his share of the part-sack of beans. Also he appropriated the bearskin, and caused grumbling among the tribesmen. And finally, he tried to kill Sigmund's dog, which the girl had given him, but the dog ran away, while he fell into the shaft and dislocated his shoulder on the bucket. When the camp was well looted they went back to their own lodges, and there was a great rejoicing among the women. Further, a band of moose strayed over the south divide and fell before the hunters, so the witch doctor attained yet greater honor, and the people whispered among themselves that he spoke in council with the gods.

But later, when all were gone, the shepherd dog crept back to the deserted camp, and all the night long and a day it wailed the dead. After that it disappeared, though the years were not many before the Indian hunters noted a change in the breed of timber wolves, and there were dashes of bright color and variegated markings such as no wolf bore before.

HOUSEKEEPING IN THE KLONDIKE

HOUSEKEEPING in the Klondike—that's bad! And by *men*—worse. Reverse the proposition, if you will, yet you will fail to mitigate, even by a hair's breadth, the woe of it. It is bad, unutterably bad, for a man to keep house, and it is equally bad to keep house in the Klondike. That's the sum and substance of it. Of course men will be men, and especially is this true of the kind who wander off to the frozen rim of the world. The glitter of gold is in their eyes, they are borne along by uplifting ambition, and in their hearts is a great disdain for everything in the culinary department save "grub." "Just so long as it's grub" they say, coming in off trail, gaunt and ravenous, "grub and piping hot." Nor do they manifest the slightest regard for the genesis of the same: they prefer to begin at "revelations."

Yes, it would seem a pleasant task to cook for such men; but just let them lie around cabin to rest up for a week, and see with what celerity they grow high-stomached and make sarcastic comments on the way you fry the bacon or boil the coffee. And behold how each will spring his own strange and marvelous theory as to how sourdough bread should be mixed and baked. Each has his own recipe (formulated, mark you, from personal experience only), and to him it is an idol of brass, like unto no other man's, and he'll fight for it—ay, down to the last wee pinch of soda—and if need be, die for it. If you should happen to catch him on trail, completely exhausted, you may blacken his character, his flag, and his ancestral tree with impunity; but breathe the slightest whisper against his sourdough bread, and he will turn upon and rend you.

From this it may be gathered what an unstable thing sourdough is. Never was coquette so fickle. You cannot depend upon it. Still, it is the simplest thing in the world. Make a batter and place it near the stove (that it may not freeze) till it ferments or sours. Then mix the dough with it, and sweeten with soda to taste—of course replenishing the batter for next time. There it is. Was there ever anything simpler? But, oh, the tribulations of the cook! It is never twice the same. If the batter could only be placed away in an equable temperature, all well and good. If one's comrades did not interfere, much vexation of spirit might be avoided. But this cannot be; for Tom fires up the stove till the cabin is become like the hot-room of a Turkish bath; Dick forgets all about the fire till the place is a refrigerator; then along comes Harry and shoves the sourdough bucket right against the stove to make way for the drying of his mittens. Now heat is a most potent factor in accelerating the fermentation of flour and water, and hence the unfortunate cook is constantly in disgrace with Tom, Dick, and Harry. Last week his bread was yellow from a plethora of soda; this week it is sour from a prudent lack of the same; and next week—ah, who can tell save the god of the fire-box?

Some cooks aver they have so cultivated their olfactory organs that they can tell to the fraction of a degree just how sour the batter is. Nevertheless they have never been known to bake two batches of bread which were at all alike. But this fact casts not the slightest shadow upon the infallibility of their theory. One and all, they take advantage of circumstances, and meanly crawl out by laying the blame upon the soda, which was dampened "the time the canoe overturned", or upon the flour, which they got in trade from "that half-breed fellow with the dog."

The pride of the Klondike cook in his bread is something which passes understanding. The highest commendatory degree which can be passed upon a man in that country, and the one which distinguishes him from the tenderfoot, is that of being a "sourdough boy." Never was a college graduate prouder of his "sheepskin" than the old-timer of this appelation. There is a certain distinction about it, from which the newcomer is invidiously excluded. A tenderfoot with his baking powder is an inferior creature, a freshman; but a "sourdough boy" is a man of stability, a post-graduate in that art of arts—bread-making.

Next to bread a Klondike cook strives to achieve distinction by his doughnuts. This may appear frivolous at first glance, and at second, considering the materials with which he works, an impossible feat. But doughnuts are all-important to the man who goes on trail for a journey of any length. Bread freezes easily, and there is less grease and sugar, and hence less heat in it, than in doughnuts. The latter do not solidify except at extremely low temperatures, and they are very handy to carry in the pockets of a Mackinaw jacket and munch as one travels along. They are made much after the manner of their brethren in warmer climes, with the exception that they are cooked in bacon grease—the more grease, the better they are. Sugar is the cook's chief stumbling block; if it is very scarce, why, add more grease. The men never mind—on trail. In the cabin?—well, that's another matter; besides, bread is good enough for them then.

The cold, the silence, and the darkness somehow seem to be considered the chief woes of the Klondiker. But this is all wrong. There is one woe which overshadows all others—the lack of sugar. Every party which goes north signifies a manly intention to do without sugar, and after it gets there bemoans itself upon its lack of foresight. Man can endure hardship and horror with equanimity, but take from him his sugar, and he raises his lamentations to the stars. And the worst of it is that it all falls back upon the long-suffering cook. Naturally coffee, and mush, and dried fruit, and rice, eaten without sugar, do not taste exactly as they should. A certain appeal to the palate is missing. Then the cook is blamed for his vile concoctions. Yet, if he be a man of wisdom, he may judiciously escape the major part of this injustice. When he places a pot of mush upon the table, let him see to it that it is accompanied by a pot of stewed dried apples or peaches. This propinquity will suggest the combination to the men, and the flatness of the one will be neutralized by the sharpness of the other. In the distress of a sugar famine, if he be a cook of parts, he will boil rice and fruit together in one pot; and if he cook a dish of rice and prunes properly, of a verity he will cheer up the most melancholy member of the party, and extract from him great gratitude.

Such a cook must indeed be a man of resources. Should his comrades cry out that vinegar be placed upon the beans, and there is no vinegar, he must know how to make it out of water, dried apples, and brown paper. He obtains the last from the bacon-wrappings, and it is usually saturated with grease. But that does not matter. He will early learn that in a land of low temperatures it is impossible for bacon grease to spoil anything. It is to the white man what blubber and seal oil are to the Eskimo. Soul-winning gravies may be made from it by the addition of water and browned flour over the fire. Some cooks base far-reaching fame solely upon their gravy, and their names come to be on the lips of men wherever they foregather at the feast. When the candles give out, the cook fills a sardine can with bacon grease, manufactures a wick out of the carpenter's sail-twine, and behold! the slush-lamp stands complete. It goes by another and less complimentary name in the vernacular, and, next to sourdough bread, is responsible for more men's souls than any other single cause of degeneracy in the Klondike.

The ideal cook should also possess a Semitic incline to his soul. Initiative in his art is not the only requisite; he must keep an eye upon the variety of his larder. He must "swap" grub with the gentile understandingly; and woe upon him should the balance of trade be against him. His comrades will thrust it into his teeth every time the bacon is done over the turn, and they will even rouse him from his sleep to remind him of it. For instance, previous to the men going out for a trip on trail, he cooks several gallons of beans in the company of numerous chunks of salt pork and much bacon grease. This mess must then be moulded into blocks of convenient size and placed on the roof, where it freezes into bricks in a couple of hours. Thus the men, after a weary day's travel, have but to chop off chunks with an axe and thaw it out in a frying-pan. Now the chances preponderate against more than one party in ten having chilli-peppers in their outfits. But the cook, supposing him to be fitted for his position, will ferret out that one party, discover some particular shortage in its grub-supply of which he has plenty, and swap the same for chilli-peppers. These in turn he will incorporate in the mess aforementioned, and behold a dish which even the hungry arctic god may envy. Variety in the grub is as welcome to the men as nuggets. When, after eating dried peaches for months, the cook trades a few cupfuls of the same for apricots, the future at once takes on a more roseate hue. Even a change in the brand of bacon will revivify blasted faith in the country.

It is no sinecure, being cook in the Klondike. Often he must do his work in a cabin measuring ten by twelve on the inside, and occupied by three other men besides himself. When it is considered that these men eat, sleep, lounge, smoke, play cards, and entertain visitors there, and also in that small space house the bulk of their possessions, the size of the cook's orbit may be readily computed. In the morning he sits up in bed, reaches out and strikes the fire, then proceeds to dress. After that the centre of his orbit is the front of the stove, the diameter of the length of his arms. Even then his comrades are continually encroaching upon his domain, and he is at constant warfare to prevent territorial grabs.

If the men are working hard on the claim, the cook is also expected to find his own wood and water. The former he chops up and sleds into camp, the latter he brings home in a sack—unless he is unusually diligent, in which case he has a ton or so of water piled up before the door. Whenever he is not cooking, he is thawing out ice, and betweenwhiles running out and hoisting on the windlass for his comrades in the shaft. The care of the dogs also devolves upon him, and he carries his life and a long club in his hand every time he feeds them.

But there is one thing the cook does not have to do, nor any man in the Klondike—and that is, make another man's bed. In fact, the beds are never made except when the blankets become unfolded, or when the pine needles have all fallen off the boughs which form the mattress. When the cabin has a dirt floor and the men do their carpenter-work inside, the cook never sweeps it. It is much warmer to let the chips and shavings remain. Whenever he kindles a fire he uses a couple of handfuls of the floor. However, when the deposit becomes so deep that his head is knocking against the roof, he seizes a shovel and removes a foot or so of it.

Nor does he have any windows to wash; but if the carpenter is busy he must make his own windows. This is simple. He saws a hole out of the side of the cabin, inserts a home-made sash, and for panes falls back upon the treasured writing-tablet. A sheet of this paper, rubbed thoroughly with bacon grease, becomes transparent, sheds water when it thaws, and keeps the cold out and the heat in. In cold weather the ice will form upon the inside of it to the thickness of sometimes two or three inches. When the bulb of the mercurial thermometer has frozen solid, the cook turns to his window, and by the thickness of the icy coating infallibly gauges the outer cold within a couple of degrees.

A certain knowledge of astronomy is required of the Klondike cook, for another task of his is to keep track of the time. Before going to bed he wanders outside and studies the heavens. Having located the Pole Star by means of the Great Bear, he inserts two slender wands in the snow, a couple of yards apart and in line with the North Star. The next day, when the sun on the southern horizon casts the shadows of the wands to the northward and in line, he knows it to be twelve o'clock, noon, and sets his watch and those of his partners accordingly. As stray dogs are constantly knocking his wands out of line with the North Star, it becomes his habit to verify them regularly every night, and thus another burden is laid upon him.

But, after all, while the woes of the man who keeps house and cooks food in the northland are innumerable, there is one redeeming feature in his lot which does not fall to the women housewives of other lands. When things come to a pass with his feminine prototype, she throws her apron over her head and has a good cry. Not so with him, being a man and a Klondiker. He merely cooks a little more atrociously, raises a storm of grumbling, and resigns. After that he takes up his free outdoor life again, and exerts himself mightily in making life miserable for the unlucky comrade who takes his place in the management of destinies.

A Daughter of the Aurora

"You—what you call—lazy mans, you lazy mans would desire me to haf for wife. It is not good. Nevaire, no, nevaire, will lazy mans my hoosband be."

Thus Joy Molineau spoke her mind to Jack Harrington, even as she had spoken it, but more tritely and in his own tongue, to Louis Savoy the previous night.

"Listen, Joy—"

"No, no; why moos' I listen to lazy mans? It is vaire bad, you hang rount, make visitation to my cabin, and do nothing. How you get grub for the famille? Why haf not you the dust? Odder mans haf plentee."

"But I work hard, Joy. Never a day am I not on trail or up creek. Even now have I just come off. My dogs are yet tired. Other men have luck and find plenty of gold; but I—I have no luck."

"Ah! But when this mans with the wife which is Indian, this mans McCormack, when him discovaire the Klondike, you go not. Odder mans go; odder mans now rich."

"You know I was prospecting over on the headreaches of the Tanana," Harrington protested, "and knew nothing of the Eldorado or Bonanza until it was too late."

"That is deeferent; only you are—what you call way off."

"What?"

"Way off. In the—yes—in the dark. It is nevaire too late. One vaire rich mine is there, on the creek which is Eldorado. The mans drive the stake and him go 'way. No odder mans know what of him become. The mans, him which drive the stake, is nevaire no more. Sixty days no mans on that claim file the papaire. Then odder mans, plentee odder mans—what you call—jump that claim. Then they race, O so queek, like the wind, to file the papaire. Him be vaire rich. Him get grub for famille."

Harrington hid the major portion of his interest.

"When's the time up?" he asked. "What claim is it?"

"So I speak Louis Savoy last night," she continued, ignoring him. "Him I think the winnaire."

"Hang Louis Savoy!"

"So Louis Savoy speak in my cabin last night. Him say, 'Joy, I am strong mans. I haf good dogs. I haf long wind. I will be winnaire. Then you will haf me for hoosband?' And I say to him, I say—"

"What'd you say?"

"I say, 'If Louis Savoy is winnaire, then will he haf me for wife.' "

"And if he don't win?"

"Then Louis Savoy, him will not be—what you call—the father of my children."

"And if I win?"

"You winnaire? Ha! ha! Nevaire!"

Exasperating as it was, Joy Molineau's laughter was pretty to hear. Harrington did not mind it. He had long since been broken in. Besides, he was no exception. She had forced all her lovers to suffer in kind. And very enticing she was just then, her lips parted, her color heightened by the sharp kiss of the frost, her eyes vibrant with the lure which is the greatest of all lures and which may be seen nowhere save in woman's eyes. Her sled-dogs clustered about her in hirsute masses, and the leader, Wolf Fang, laid his long snout softly in her lap.

"If I do win?" Harrington pressed.

She looked from dog to lover and back again.

"What you say, Wolf Fang? If him strong mans and file the papaire, shall we his wife become? Eh? What you say?"

Wolf Fang picked up his ears and growled at Harrington.

"It is vaire cold," she suddenly added with feminine irrelevance, rising to her feet and straightening out the team.

Her lover looked on stolidly. She had kept him guessing from the first time they met, and patience had been joined unto his virtues.

"Hi! Wolf Fang!" she cried, springing upon the sled as it leaped into sudden motion. "Ai! Ya! Mush-on!"

From the corner of his eye Harrington watched her swinging down the trail to Forty Mile. Where the road forked and crossed the river to Fort Cudahy, she halted the dogs and turned about.

"O Mistaire Lazy Mans!" she called back. "Wolf Fang, him say yes—if you winnaire!"

But somehow, as such things will, it leaked out, and all Forty Mile, which had hitherto speculated on Joy Molineau's choice between her two latest lovers, now hazarded bets and guesses as to which would win in the forthcoming race. The camp divided itself into two factions, and every effort was put forth in order that their respective favorites might be the first in at the finish. There was a scramble for the best dogs the country could afford, for dogs, and good ones, were essential, above all, to success. And it meant much to the victor. Besides the possession of a wife, the like of which had yet to be created, it stood for a mine worth a million at least.

That fall, when news came down of McCormack's discovery on Bonanza, all the Lower Country, Circle City and Forty Mile included, had stampeded up the Yukon,—at least all save those who, like Jack Harrington and Louis Savoy, were away prospecting in the west. Moose pastures and creeks were staked indiscriminately and promiscuously; and incidentally, one of the unlikeliest of creeks, Eldorado. Olaf Nelson laid claim to five hundred of its linear feet, duly posted his notice, and as duly disappeared. At that time the nearest recording office was in the police barracks at Fort Cudahy, just across the river from Forty Mile; but when it became bruited abroad that Eldorado Creek was a treasure-house, it was quickly discovered that Olaf Nelson had failed to make the down-Yukon trip to file upon his property. Men cast hungry eyes upon the ownerless claim, where they knew a thousand-thousand dollars waited but shovel and sluice-box. Yet they dared not touch it; for there was a law which permitted sixty days to lapse between the staking and the filing, during which time a claim was immune. The whole country knew of Olaf Nelson's disappearance, and scores of men made preparation for the jumping and for the consequent race to Fort Cudahy.

But competition at Forty Mile was limited. With the camp devoting its energies to the equipping either of Jack Harrington or Louis Savoy, no man was unwise enough to enter the contest single-handed. It was a stretch of a hundred miles to the Recorder's office, and it was planned that the two favorites should have four relays of dogs stationed along the trail. Naturally, the last relay was to be the crucial one, and for these twenty-five miles their respective partisans strove to obtain the strongest possible animals. So bitter did the factions wax, and so high did they bid, that dogs brought stiffer prices than ever before in the annals of the country. And, as it chanced, this scramble for dogs turned the public eye still more searchingly upon Joy Molineau. Not only was she the cause of it all, but she possessed the finest sled-dog from Chilkoot to Bering Sea. As wheel or leader, Wolf Fang had no equal. The man whose sled he led down the last stretch was bound to win. There could be no doubt of it. But the community had an innate sense of the fitness of things, and not once was Joy vexed by overtures for his use. And the factions drew consolation from the fact that if one man did not profit by him, neither should the other.

However, since man, in the individual or in the aggregate, has been so fashioned that he goes through life blissfully obtuse to the deeper subtleties of his womenkind, so the men of Forty Mile failed to divine the inner deviltry of Joy Molineau. They confessed, afterward, that they had failed to appreciate this dark-eyed daughter of the aurora, whose father had traded furs in the country before ever they dreamed of invading it, and who had herself first opened eyes on the scintillant northern lights. Nay, accident of birth had not rendered her less the woman, nor had it limited her woman's understanding of men. They knew she played with them, but they did not know the wisdom of her play, its deepness and its deftness. They failed to see more than the exposed card, so that to the very last Forty Mile was in a state of pleasant obfuscation, and it was not until she cast her final trump that it came to reckon up the score.

Early in the week the camp turned out to start Jack Harrington and Louis Savoy on their way. They had taken a shrewd margin of time, for it was their wish to arrive at Olaf Nelson's claim some days previous to the expiration of its immunity, that they might rest themselves, and their dogs be fresh for the first relay. On the way up they found the men of Dawson already stationing spare dog teams along the trail, and it was manifest that little expense had been spared in view of the millions at stake.

A couple of days after the departure of their champions, Forty Mile began sending up their relays,—first to the seventy-five station, then to the fifty, and last to the twenty-five. The teams for the last stretch were magnificent, and so equally matched that the camp discussed their relative merits for a full hour at fifty below, before they were permitted to pull out. At the last moment Joy Molineau dashed in among them on her sled. She drew Lon McFane, who had charge of Harrington's team, to one side, and hardly had the first words left her lips when it was noticed that his lower jaw dropped with a celerity and emphasis suggestive of great things. He unhitched Wolf Fang from her sled, put him at the head of Harrington's team, and mushed the string of animals into the Yukon trail.

"Poor Louis Savoy!" men said; but Joy Molineau flashed her black eyes defiantly and drove back to her father's cabin.

Midnight drew near on Olaf Nelson's claim. A few hundred fur-clad men had preferred sixty below and the jumping, to the inducements of warm cabins and comfortable bunks. Several score of them had their notices prepared for posting and their dogs at hand. A bunch of Captain Constantine's mounted police had been ordered on duty that fair play might rule. The command had gone forth that no man should place a stake till the last second of the day had ticked itself into the past. In the northland such commands are equal to Jehovah's in the matter of potency; the dum-dum as rapid and effective as the thunderbolt. It was clear and cold. The aurora borealis painted palpitating color revels on the sky. Rosy waves of cold brilliancy swept across the zenith, while great coruscating bars of greenish white blotted out the stars, or a Titan's hand reared mighty arches above the Pole. And at this mighty display the wolf-dogs howled as had their ancestors of old time.

A bearskin-coated policeman stepped prominently to the fore, watch in hand. Men hurried among the dogs, rousing them to their feet, untangling their traces, straightening them out. The entries came to the mark, firmly gripping stakes and notices. They had gone over the boundaries of the claim so often that they could now have done it blindfolded. The policeman raised his hand. Casting off their superfluous furs and blankets, and with a final cinching of belts, they came to attention.

"Time!"

Sixty pairs of hands unmitted; as many pairs of moccasins gripped hard upon the snow.

"Go!"

They shot across the wide expanse, round the four sides, sticking notices at every corner, and down the middle where the two center stakes were to be planted. Then they sprang for the sleds on the frozen bed of the creek. An anarchy of sound and motion broke out. Sled collided with sled, and dog-team fastened upon dog-team with bristling manes and screaming fangs. The narrow creek was glutted with the struggling mass. Lashes and butts of dog-whips were distributed impartially among men and brutes. And to make it of greater moment, each participant had a bunch of comrades intent on breaking him out of jam. But one by one, and by sheer strength, the sleds crept out and shot from sight in the darkness of the overhanging banks.

Jack Harrington had anticipated this crush and waited by his sled until it untangled. Louis Savoy, aware of his rival's greater wisdom in the matter of dog-driving, had followed his lead and also waited. The rout had passed beyond earshot when they took the trail, and it was not till they had traveled the ten miles or so down to Bonanza that they came upon it, speeding along in single file, but well bunched. There was little noise, and less chance of one passing another at that stage. The sleds, from runner to runner, measured sixteen inches, the trail eighteen; but the trail, packed down fully a foot by the traffic, was like a gutter. On either side spread the blanket of soft snow crystals. If a man turned into this in an endeavor to pass, his dogs would wallow perforce to their bellies and slow down to a snail's pace. So the men lay close to their leaping sleds and waited. No alteration in position occurred down the fifteen miles of Bonanza and Klondike to Dawson, where the Yukon was encountered. Here the first relays waited. But here, intent to kill their first teams, if necessary, Harrington and Savoy had had their fresh teams placed a couple of miles beyond those of the others. In the confusion of changing sleds they passed full half the bunch. Perhaps thirty men were still leading them when they shot on to the broad breast of the Yukon. Here was the tug. When the river froze in the fall, a mile of open water had been left between two mighty jams. This had but recently crusted, the current being swift, and now it was as level, hard, and slippery as a dance floor. The instant they struck this glare ice Harrington came to his knees, holding precariously on with one hand, his whip singing fiercely among his dogs and fearsome abjurations hurtling about their ears. The teams spread out on the smooth surface, each straining to the uttermost. But few men in the North could lift their dogs as did Jack Harrington. At once he began to pull ahead, and Louis Savoy, taking the pace, hung on desperately, his leaders running even with the tail of his rival's sled.

Midway on the glassy stretch their relays shot out from the bank. But Harrington did not slacken. Watching his chance when the new sled swung in close, he leaped across, shouting as he did so and jumping up the pace of his fresh dogs. The other driver fell off somehow. Savoy did likewise with his relay, and the abandoned teams, swerving to right and left, collided with the others and piled the ice with confusion. Harrington cut out the pace; Savoy hung on. As they neared the end of the glare ice, they swept abreast of the leading sled. When they shot into the narrow trail between the soft snowbanks, they led the race; and Dawson, watching by the light of the aurora, swore that it was neatly done.

When the frost grows lusty at sixty below, men cannot long remain without fire or excessive exercise, and live. So Harrington and Savoy now fell to the ancient custom of "ride and run." Leaping from their sleds, tow-thongs in hand, they ran behind till the blood resumed its wonted channels and expelled the frost, then back to the sleds till the heat again ebbed away. Thus, riding and running, they covered the second and third relays. Several times, on smooth ice, Savoy spurted his dogs, and as often failed to gain past. Strung along for five miles in the rear, the remainder of the race strove to overtake them, but vainly, for to Louis Savoy alone was the glory given of keeping Jack Harrington's killing pace.

As they swung into the seventy-five-mile station, Lon McFane dashed alongside; Wolf Fang in the lead caught Harrington's eye, and he knew that the race was his. No team in the North could pass him on those last twenty-five miles. And when Savoy saw Wolf Fang heading his rival's team, he knew that he was out of the running, and he cursed softly to himself, in the way woman is most frequently cursed. But he still clung to the other's smoking trail, gambling on chance to the last. And as they churned along, the day breaking in the southeast, they marveled in joy and sorrow at that which Joy Molineau had done.

Forty Mile had early crawled out of its sleeping furs and congregated near the edge of the trail. From this point it could view the up-Yukon course to its first bend several miles away. Here it could also see across the river to the finish at Fort Cudahy, where the Gold Recorder nervously awaited. Joy Molineau had taken her position several rods back from the trail, and under the circumstances, the rest of Forty Mile forbore interposing itself. So the space was clear between her and the slender line of the course. Fires had been built, and around these men wagered dust and dogs, the long odds on Wolf Fang.

"Here they come!" shrilled an Indian boy from the top of a pine.

Up the Yukon a black speck appeared against the snow, closely followed by a second. As these grew larger, more black specks manifested themselves, but at a goodly distance to the rear. Gradually they resolved themselves into dogs and sleds, and men lying flat upon them.

"Wolf Fang leads," a lieutenant of police whispered to Joy. She smiled her interest back.

"Ten to one on Harrington!" cried a Birch Creek King, dragging out his sack.

"The Queen, her pay you not mooch?" queried Joy.

The lieutenant shook his head.

"You have some dust, ah, how mooch?" she continued.

He exposed his sack. She gauged it with a rapid eye.

"Mebbe—say—two hundred, eh? Good. Now I give—what you call—the tip. Covaire the bet." Joy smiled inscrutably. The lieutenant pondered. He glanced up the trail. The two men had risen to their knees and were lashing their dogs furiously, Harrington in the lead.

"Ten to one on Harrington!" bawled the Birch Creek King, flourishing his sack in the lieutenant's face.

"Covaire the bet," Joy prompted.

He obeyed, shrugging his shoulders in token that he yielded, not to the dictate of his reason, but to her charm. Joy nodded to reassure him.

All noise ceased. Men paused in the placing of bets.

Yawing and reeling and plunging, like luggers before the wind, the sleds swept wildly upon them. Though he still kept his leader up to the tail of Harrington's sled, Louis Savoy's face was without hope. Harrington's mouth was set. He looked neither to the right nor to the left. His dogs were leaping in perfect rhythm, firm-footed, close to the trail, and Wolf Fang, head low and unseeing, whining softly, was leading his comrades magnificently.

Forty Mile stood breathless. Not a sound, save the roar of the runners and the voice of the whips.

Then the clear voice of Joy Molineau rose on the air. "Ai! Ya! Wolf Fang! Wolf Fang!"

Wolf Fang heard. He left the trail sharply, heading directly for his mistress. The team dashed after him, and the sled poised an instant on a single runner, then shot Harrington into the snow. Savoy was by like a flash. Harrington pulled to his feet and watched him skimming across the river to the Gold Recorder's. He could not help hearing what was said.

"Ah, him do vaire well," Joy Molineau was explaining to the lieutenant. "Him—what you call—set the pace. Yes, him set the pace vaire well."

The Law of Life

Old Koskoosh listened greedily. Though his sight had long since faded, his hearing was still acute, and the slightest sound penetrated to the glimmering intelligence which yet abode behind the withered forehead, but which no longer gazed forth upon the things of the world. Ah! That was Sit-cum-to-ha, shrilly anathematizing the dogs as she cuffed and beat them into the harnesses. Sit-cum-to-ha was his daughter's daughter, but she was too busy to waste a thought upon her broken grandfather, sitting alone there in the snow, forlorn and helpless. Camp must be broken. The long trail waited while the short day refused to linger. Life called her, and the duties of life, not death. And he was very close to death now.

The thought made the old man panicky for the moment, and he stretched forth a palsied hand which wandered tremblingly over the small heap of dry wood beside him. Reassured that it was indeed there, his hand returned to the shelter of his mangy furs, and he again fell to listening. The sukly crackling of half-frozen hides to that the chief's moose-skin lodge had been struck, and even then was being rammed and jammed into portable compass. The chief was his son, stalwart and strong, head-man of the tribesmen, and a mighty hunter. As the women toiled with the camp luggage, his voice rose, chiding them for their slowness. Old Koskoosh strained his ears. It was the last time he would hear that voice. There went Geehow's lodge! And Tusken's! Seven, eight, nine; only the shaman's could still be standing. There! They were at work upon it now. He could hear the shaman grunt as he piled it on the sled. A child whimpered, and a woman soothed it with soft, crooning gutterals. Little Koo-tee, the old man thought, a fretful child, and not over-strong. It would die soon, perhaps, and they would burn a hole through the frozen tundra and pile rocks above to keep the wolverines away. Well, what did it matter? A few years at best, and as many an empty belly as a full one. And in the end, Death waited, ever-hungry and hungriest of them all.

What was that? Oh, the men lashing the sleds and drawing tight the thongs. He listened, who would listen no more. The whiplashes snarled and bit among the dogs. Hear them whine! How they hated the work and the trail! They were off! Sled after sled churned slowly away into the silence. They were gone. They had passed out of his life, and he faced the last bitter hour alone. No. The snow crunched beneath a moccasin; a man stood beside him; upon his head a hand rested gently. His son was good to do this thing. He remembered other old men whose sons had not waited after the tribe. But his son had. He wandered away into the past, till the young man's voice brought him back.

"It is well with you?" he asked.

And the old man answered, "It is well."

"There be wood beside you," the younger man continued, "and the fire burns bright. The morning is gray, and the cold has broken. It will snow presently. Even now it is snowing."

"Aye, even now it is snowing."

"The tribesmen hurry. Their bales are heavy and their bellies flat with lack of feasting. The trail is long and they travel fast. I go now. It is well?"

"It is well. I am as a last year's leaf, clinging lightly to the stem. The first breath that blows, and I fall. My voice is become like an old woman's. My eyes no longer show me the way of my feet, and my feet are heavy, and I am tired. It is well."

He bowed his head in content till the last noise of the complaining snow had died away, and he knew his son was beyond recall. Then his hand crept out in haste to the wood. It alone stood between him and the eternity that yawned in upon him. At last the measure of his life was a handful of faggots. One by one they would go to feed the fire, and just so, step by step, death would creep upon him. When the last stick had surrendered up its heat, the frost would begin to gather strength. First his feet would yield, then his hands; and the numbness would travel, slowly, from the extremities to the body. His head would fall forward upon his knees, and he would rest. It was easy. All men must die.

He did not complain. It was the way of life, and it was just. He had been born close to the earth, close to the earth he had lived, and the law thereof was not new to him. It was the law of all flesh. Nature was not kindly to the flesh. She had no concern for that concrete thing called the individual. Her interest lay in the species, the race. This was the deepest abstraction old Koskoosh's barbaric mind was capable of, but he grasped it firmly. He saw it exemplified in all life. The rise of the sap, the bursting greenness of the willow bud, the fall of the yellow leaf—in this alone was told the whole history. But one task did Nature set the individual. Did he not perform it, he died. Did he perform it, it was all the same, he died. Nature did not care; there were plenty who were obedient, and it was only the obedience in this matter, not the obedient, which lived and lived always. The tribe of Koskoosh was very old. The old men he had known when a boy had known old men before them. Therefore it was true that the tribe lived, that it stood for the obedience of all its members, way down into the forgotten past, whose very resting places were unremembered. They did not count; they were episodes. They had passed away like clouds from a summer sky. He also was an episode and would pass away. Nature did not care. To life she set one task, gave one law. To perpetuate was the task of life, its law was death. A maiden was a good creature to look upon, full-breasted and strong, with spring to her step and light in her eyes. But her task was yet before her. The light in her eyes brightened, her step quickened, she was now bold with the young men, now timid, and she gave them of her own unrest. And ever she grew fairer and yet fairer to look upon, till some hunter, able no longer to withhold himself, took her to his lodge to cook and toil for him and to become the mother of his children. And with the coming of her offspring her looks left her. Her limbs dragged and shuffled, her eyes dimmed and bleared, and only the little children found joy against the withered cheek of the old squaw by the fire. Her task was done. But a little while, on the first pinch of famine or the first long trail, and she would be left, even as he had been left, in the snow, with a little pile of wood. Such was the law.

He placed a stick carefully upon the fire and resumed his meditations. It was the same everywhere, with all things. The mosquitoes vanished with the first frost. The little tree squirrel crawled away to die. When age settled upon the rabbit it became slow and heavy and could no longer outfoot its enemies. Even the big bald-face grew clumsy and blind and quarrelsome, in the end to be dragged down by a handful of yelping huskies. He remembered how he had abandoned his own father on an upper reach of the Klondike one winter, the winter before the missionary came with his talk books and his box of medicines. Many a time had Koskoosh smacked his lips over the recollection of that box, though now his mouth refused to moisten. The "painkiller" had been especially good. But the missionary was a bother after all, for he brought no meat into the camp, and he ate heartily, and the hunters grumbled. But he chilled his lungs on the divide by the Mayo, and the dogs afterward nosed the stones away and fought over his bones.

Koskoosh placed another stick on the fire and harked back deeper into the past. There was the time of the great famine, when the old men crouched empty-bellied to the fire and let fall from their lips dim traditions of the ancient day when the Yukon ran wide open for three winters, and then lay frozen for three summers. He had lost his mother in that famine. In the summer the salmon run had failed, and the tribe looked forward to the winter and the coming of the caribou. Then the winter came, but with it there were no caribou. Never had the like been known, not even in the lives of the old men. But the caribou did not come, and it was the seventh year, and the rabbits had not replenished, and the dogs were naught but bundles of bones. And through the long darkness the children wailed and died, and the women, and the old men; and not one in ten of the tribe lived to meet the sun when it came back in the spring. That *was* a famine!

But he had seen times of plenty, too, when the meat spoiled on their hands, and the dogs were fat and worthless with overeating—times when they let the game go unkilled, and the women were fertile, and the lodges were cluttered with sprawling menren and women-children. Then it was the men became high-stomached, and revived ancient quarrels, and crossed the divides to the south to kill the Pellys, and to the west that they might sit by the dead fires of the Tananas. He remembered, when a boy, during a time of plenty, when he saw a moose pulled down by the wolves. Zing-ha lay with him in the snow and watched—Zing-ha, who later became the craftiest of hunters, and who, in the end, fell through an air hole in the Yukon. They found him, a month afterward, just as he had crawled halfway out and frozen stiff to the ice.

But the moose. Zing-ha and he had gone out that day to play at hunting after the manner of their fathers. On the bed of the creek they struck the fresh track of a moose, and with it the tracks of many wolves. "An old one," Zing-ha, who was quicker at reading the sign, said, "an old one who cannot keep up with the herd. The wolves have cut him out from his brothers, and they will never leave him." And it was so. It was their way. By day and night, never resting, snarling on his heels, snapping at his nose, they would stay by him to the end. How Zing-ha and he felt the blood lust quicken! The finish would be a sight to see!

Eager-footed, they took the trail, and even he, Koskoosh, slow of sight and an unversed tracker, could have followed it blind, it was so wide. Hot were they on the heels of the chase, reading the grim tragedy, fresh-written, at every step. Now they came to where the moose had made a stand. Thrice the length of a grown man's body, in every direction, had the snow been stamped about and uptossed. In the midst were the deep impressions of the splay-hoofed game, and all about, everywhere, were the lighter footmarks of the wolves. Some, while their brothers harried the kill, had lain to one side and rested. The full-stretched impress of their bodies in the snow was as perfect as though made the moment before. One wolf had been caught in a wild lunge of the maddened victim and trampled to death. A few bones, well picked, bore witness.

Again, they ceased the uplift of their snowshoes at a second stand. Here the great animal had fought desperately. Twice had he been dragged down, as the snow attested, and twice had he shaken his assailants clear and gained footing once more. He had done his task long since, but none the less was life dear to him. Zing-ha said it was a strange thing, a moose once down to get free again; but this one certainly had. The shaman would see signs and wonders in this when they told him.

And yet again, they came to where the moose had made to mount the bank and gain the timber. But his foes had laid on from behind, till he reared and fell back upon them, crushing two deep into the snow. It was plain the kill was at hand, for their brothers had left them untouched. Two more stands were hurried past, brief in time length and very close together. The trail was red now, and the clean stride of the great beast had grown short and slovenly. Then they heard the first sounds of the battle—not the full-throated chorus of the chase, but the short, snappy bark which spoke of close quarters and teeth to flesh. Crawling up the wind, Zing-ha bellied it through the snow, and with him crept he, Koskoosh, who was to be chief of the tribesmen in the years to come. Together they shoved aside the underbranches of a young spruce and peered forth. It was the end they saw.

The picture, like all of youth's impressions, was still strong with him, and his dim eyes watched the end played out as vividly as in that far-off time. Koskoosh marveled at this, for in the days which followed, when he was a leader of men and a head of councilors, he had done great deeds and made his name a curse in the mouths of the Pellys, to say naught of the strange white man he had killed, knife to knife, in open fight.

For long he pondered on the days of his youth, till the fire died down and the frost bit deeper. He replenished it with two sticks this time, and gauged his grip on life by what remained. If Sit-cum-to-ha had only remembered her grandfather, and gathered a larger armful, his hours would have been longer. It would have been easy. But she was ever a careless child, and honored not her ancestors from the time the Beaver, son of the son of Zing-ha, first cast eyes upon her. Well, what mattered it? Had he not done likewise in his own quick youth? For a while he listened to the silence. Perhaps the heart of his son might soften, and he would come back with the dogs to take his old father on with the tribe to where the caribou ran thick and the fat hung heavy upon them.

He strained his ears, his restless brain for the moment stilled. Not a stir, nothing. He alone took breath in the midst of the great silence. It was very lonely. Hark! What was that? A chill passed over his body. The familiar, long-drawn howl broke the void, and it was close at hand. Then on his darkened eyes was projected the vision of the moose—the old bull moose—the torn flanks and bloody sides, the riddled mane, and the great branching horns, down low and tossing to the last. He saw the flashing forms of gray, the gleaming eyes, the lolling tongues, the slavered fangs. And he saw the inexorable circle close in till it became a dark point in the midst of the stamped snow.

A cold muzzle thrust against his cheek, and at its touch his soul leaped back to the present. His hand shot into the fire and dragged out a burning faggot. Overcome for the nonce by his hereditary fear of man, the brute retreated, raising a prolonged call to his brothers; and greedily they answered, till a ring of crouching, jaw-slobbered gray was stretched around about. The old man listened to the drawing in of this circle. He waved his brand wildly, and sniffs turned to snarls; but the panting brutes refused to scatter. Now one wormed his chest forward, dragging his haunches after, now a second, now a third; but never a one drew back. Why should he cling to life? he asked, and dropped the blazing stick into the snow. It sizzled and went out. The circle grunted uneasily but held its own. Again he saw the last stand of the old bull moose, and Koskoosh dropped his head wearily upon his knees. What did it matter after all? Was it not the law of life?

THE SICKNESS OF LONE CHIEF

THIS is a tale that was told to me by two old men. We sat in the smoke of a mosquito-smudge, in the cool of the day, which was midnight; and ever and anon, throughout the telling, we smote lustily and with purpose at such of the winged pests as braved the smoke for a snack at our hides. To the right, beneath us, twenty feet down the crumbling bank, the Yukon gurgled lazily. To the left, on the rose-leaf rim of the low-lying hills, smoldered the sleepy sun, which saw no sleep that night nor was destined to see sleep for many nights to come.

The old men who sat with me and valorously slew mosquitos were Lone Chief and Mutsak, erstwhile comrades in arms, and now withered repositories of tradition and ancient happening. They were the last of their generation and without honor among the younger set which had grown up on the farthest fringe of a mining civilization. Who cared for tradition in these days, when spirits could be evoked from black bottles, and black bottles could be evoked from the complacent white men for a few hours' sweat or a mangy fur? Of what potency the fearful rites and masked mysteries of shamanism, when daily that living wonder, the steamboat, coughed and spluttered up and down the Yukon in defiance of all law, a veritable fire-breathing monster? And of what value was hereditary prestige, when he who now chopped the most wood, or best conned a stern-wheeler through the island mazes, attained the chiefest consideration of his fellows?

Of a truth, having lived too long, they had fallen on evil days, these two old men, Lone Chief and Mutsak, and in the new order they were without honor or place. So they waited drearily for death, and while their hearts warmed to the strange white man who shared with them the torments of the mosquito-smudge and lent ready ear to their tales of old time before the steamboat came.

"So a girl was chosen for me," Lone Chief was saying. His voice, shrill and piping, ever and again dropped plummet-like into a hoarse and rattling bass, and, just as one became accustomed to it, soaring upward into the thin treble—alternate cricket chirpings and bullfrog croakings, as it were.

"So a girl was chosen for me," he was saying. "For my father, who was Kask-ta-ka, the Otter, was angered because I looked not with a needful eye upon women. He was an old man, and chief of his tribe. I was the last of his sons to be alive, and through me, only, could he look to see his blood go down among those to come after and as yet unborn. But know, O White Man, that I was very sick; and when neither the hunting nor the fishing delighted me, and by meat my belly was not made warm, how should I look with favor upon women? or prepare for the feast of marriage? or look forward to the prattle and troubles of little children?"

"Ay," Mutsak interrupted. "For had not Lone Chief fought in the arms of a great bear till his head was cracked and blood ran from out his ears?"

Lone Chief nodded vigorously. "Mutsak speaks true. In the time that followed, my head was well, and it was not well. For though the flesh healed and the sore went away, yet was I sick inside. When I walked, my legs shook under me, and when I looked at the light, my eyes became filled with tears. And when I opened my eyes, the world outside went around and around, and when I closed my eyes, my head inside went around and around, and all the things I had ever seen went around and around inside my head. And above my eyes there was a great pain, as though something heavy rested always upon me, or like a band that is drawn tight and gives much hurt. And speech was slow to me, and I waited long for each right word to come to my tongue. And when I waited not long, all manner of words crowded in, and my tongue spoke foolishness. I was very sick, and when my father, the Otter, brought the girl Kasaan before me—"

"Who was a young girl, and strong, my sister's child," Mutsak broke in. "Strong-hipped for children was Kasaan, and straight-legged and quick of foot. She made better moccasins than any of all the young girls, and the bark-rope she braided was the stoutest. And she had a smile in her eyes, and a laugh on her lips; and her temper was not hasty, nor was she unmindful that men give the law and women ever obey."

"As I say, I was very sick," Lone Chief went on. "And when my father, the Otter, brought the girl Kasaan before me, I said rather should they make me ready for burial than for marriage. Whereat the face of my father went black with anger, and he said that I should be served according to my wish, and that I who was yet alive should be made ready for death as one already dead—"

"Which be not the way of our people, O White Man," spoke up Mutsak. "For know that these things that were done to Lone Chief it was our custom to do only to dead men. But the Otter was very angry."

"Ay," said Lone Chief. "My father, the Otter, was a man short of speech and swift of deed. And he commanded the people to gather before the lodge wherein I lay. And when they were gathered, he commanded them to mourn for his son who was dead—"

"And before the lodge they sang the death-song—*O-o-o-o-o-a-haa-ha-a-ick-klu-kuk-ich-klu-kuk,*" wailed Mutsak, in so excellent an imitation that all the tendrils of my spine crawled and curved in sympathy.

"And inside the lodge," continued Lone Chief, "my mother blackened her face with soot, and flung ashes upon her head, and mourned for me as one already dead; for so had my father commanded. So Okiakuta, my mother, mourned with much noise, and beat her breasts and tore her hair; and likewise Hooniak, my sister, and Seenatah, my mother's sister; and the noise they made caused a great ache in my head, and I felt that I would surely and immediately die.

"And the elders of the tribe gathered about me where I lay and discussed the journey my soul must take. One spoke of the thick and endless forests where lost souls wandered crying, and where I, too, might chance to wander and never see the end. And another spoke of the big rivers, rapid with bad water, where evil spirits shrieked and lifted up their formless arms to drag one down by the hair. For these rivers, all said together, a canoe must be provided me. And yet another spoke of the storms, such as no live man ever saw, when the stars rained down out of the sky, and the earth gaped wide in many cracks, and all the rivers in the heart of the earth rushed out and in. Whereupon they that sat by me flung up their arms and wailed loudly; and those outside heard, and wailed more loudly. And as to them I was as dead, so was I to my own mind dead. I did not know when, or how, yet did I know that I had surely died.

"And Okiakuta, my mother, laid beside me my squirrel-skin parka. Also she laid beside me my parka of caribou hide, and my rain coat of seal gut, and my wet-weather muclucs, that my soul should be warm and dry on its long journey. Further, there was mention made of a steep hill, thick with briers and devil's-club, and she fetched heavy moccasins to make the way easy for my feet.

"And when the elders spoke of the great beasts I should have to slay, the young men laid beside me my strongest bow and straightest arrows, my throwing-stick, my spear and knife. And when the elders spoke of the darkness and silence of the great spaces my soul must wander through, my mother wailed yet more loudly and flung yet more ashes upon her head.

"And the girl, Kasaan, crept in, very timid and quiet, and dropped a little bag upon the things for my journey. And in the little bag, I knew, were the flint and steel and the well-dried tinder for the fires my soul must build. And the blankets were chosen which were to be wrapped around me. Also were the slaves selected that were to be killed that my soul might have company. There were seven of these slaves, for my father was rich and powerful, and it was fit that I, his son, should have proper burial. These slaves we had got in war from the Mukumuks, who live down the Yukon. On the morrow, Skolka, the shaman, would kill them, one by one, so that their souls should go questing with mine through the Unknown. Among other things, they would carry my canoe till we came to the big river, rapid with bad water. And there being no room, and their work being done, they would come no farther, but remain and howl forever in the dark and endless forest.

"And as I looked on my fine warm clothes, and my blankets and weapons of war, and as I thought of the seven slaves to be slain, I felt proud of my burial and knew that I must be the envy of many men. And all the while my father, the Otter, sat silent and black. And all that day and night the people sang my death-song and beat the drums, till it seemed that I had surely died a thousand times.

"But in the morning my father arose and made talk. He had been a fighting man all his days, he said, as the people knew. Also the people knew that it were a greater honor to die fighting in battle than on the soft skins by the fire. And since I was to die anyway, it were well that I should go against the Mukumuks and be slain. Thus would I attain honor and chieftainship in the final abode of the dead, and thus would honor remain to my father, who was the Otter. Wherefore he gave command that a war party be made ready to go down the river. And that when we came upon the Mukumuks I was to go forth alone from my party, giving semblance of battle, and so be slain."

"Nay, but hear, O White Man!" cried Mutsak, unable longer to contain himself. "Skolka, the shaman, whispered long that night in the ear of the Otter, and it was his doing that Lone Chief should be sent forth to die. For the Otter being old, and Lone Chief the last of his sons, Skolka had it in mind to become chief himself over the people. And when the people had made great noise for a day and a night and Lone Chief was yet alive, Skolka was become afraid that he would not die. So it was the counsel of Skolka, with fine words of honor and deeds, that spoke through the mouth of the Otter."

"Ay," replied Lone Chief. "Well did I know it was the doing of Skolka, but I was unmindful, being very sick. I had no heart for anger, nor belly for stout words, and I cared little, one way or the other, only I cared to die and have done with it all. So, O White Man, the war party was made ready. No tired fighters were there, nor elders, crafty and wise—naught but five score of young men who had seen little fighting. And all the village gathered together above the bank of the river to see us depart. And we departed amid great rejoicing and the singing of my praises. Even thou, O White Man, wouldst rejoice at sight of a young man going forth to battle, even though doomed to die.

"So we went forth, the five score young men, and Mutsak came also, for he was likewise young and untried. And by command of my father, the Otter, my canoe was lashed on either side to the canoe of Mutsak and the canoe of Kannakut. Thus was my strength saved me from the work of the paddles, so that, for all of my sickness, I might make a brave show at the end. And thus we went down the river.

"Nor will I weary thee with the tale of the journey, which was not long. And not far above the village of the Mukumuks we came upon two of their fighting men in canoes, that fled at the sight of us. And then, according to the command of my father, my canoe was cast loose and I was left to drift down all alone. Also, according to his command, were the young men to see me die, so that they might return and tell the manner of my death. Upon this, my father, the Otter, and Skolka, the shaman, had been very clear, with stern promises of punishment in case they were not obeyed.

"I dipped my paddle and shouted words of scorn after the fleeing warriors. And the vile things I shouted made them turn their heads in anger, when they beheld that the young men held back, and that I came on alone. Whereupon, when they had made a safe distance, the two warriors drew their canoes somewhat apart and waited side by side for me to come between. And I came between, spear in hand, and singing the war-song of my people. Each flung a spear, but I bent my body, and the spears whistled over me, and I was unhurt. Then, and we were all together, we three, I cast my spear at the one to the right, and it drove into his throat and he pitched backward into the water.

"Great was my surprise thereat, for I had killed a man. I turned to the one on the left and drove strong with my paddle, to meet Death face to face; but the man's second spear, which was his last, but bit into the flesh of my shoulder. Then was I upon him, making no cast, but pressing the point into his breast and working it through him with both of my hands. And while I worked, pressing with all my strength, he smote me upon my head, once and twice, with the broad of his paddle.

"Even as the point of the spear sprang out beyond his back, he smote me upon the head. There was a flash, as of bright light, and inside my head I felt something give, with a snap—just like that, with a snap. And the weight that pressed above my eyes so long was lifted, and the band that bound my brows so tight was broken. And a great gladness came upon me, and my heart sang with joy.

"This be death, I thought; wherefore I thought that death was very good. And then I saw the two empty canoes, and I knew that I was not dead, but well again. The blows of the man upon my head had made me well. I knew that I had killed, and the taste of the blood made me fierce, and I drove my paddle into the breast of the Yukon and urged my canoe toward the village of the Mukumuks. The young men behind me gave a great cry. I looked over my shoulder and saw the water foaming white from their paddles—"

"Ay, it foamed white from our paddles," said Mutsak. "For we remembered the command of the Otter, and of Skolka, that we behold with our own eyes the manner of Lone Chief's death. A young man of the Mukumuks, on his way to a salmon trap, beheld the coming of Lone Chief, and of the five score men behind him. And the young man fled in his canoe, straight for the village, that alarm might be given and preparation made. But Lone Chief hurried after him, and we hurried after Lone Chief to behold the manner of his death. Only, in the face of the village, as the young man leaped to the shore, Lone Chief rose up in his canoe and made a mighty cast. And the spear entered the body of the young man above the hips, and the young man fell upon his face.

"Whereupon Lone Chief leaped up the bank war-club in hand and a great war cry on his lips, and dashed into the village. The first man he met was Itwilie, chief over the Mukumuks, and him Lone Chief smote upon the head with his war-club, so that he fell dead upon the ground. And for fear we might not behold the manner of his death, we too, the five score young men, leaped to the shore and followed Lone Chief into the village. Only the Mukumuks did not understand, and thought we had come to fight; so their bow-thongs sang and their arrows whistled among us. Whereat we forgot our errand, and fell upon them with our spears and clubs; and they being unprepared, there was great slaughter—"

"With my own hands I slew their shaman," proclaimed Lone Chief, his withered face a-work with memory of that old-time day. "With my own hands I slew him, who was a greater shaman than Skolka, our own shaman. And each time I faced a man I thought, 'Now cometh Death'; and each time I slew the man, and Death came not. It seemed the breath of life was strong in my nostrils and I could not die—"

"And we followed Lone Chief the length of the village and back again," continued Mutsak. "Like a pack of wolves we followed him, back and forth, and here and there, till there were no more Mukumuks left to fight. Then we gathered together five score men-slaves, and double as many women, and countless children, and we set fire and burned all the houses and lodges, and departed. And that was the last of the Mukumuks."

"And that was the last of the Mukumuks," Lone Chief repeated exultantly. "And when we came to our own village, the people were amazed at our burden of wealth and slaves, and in that I was still alive they were more amazed. And my father, the Otter, came trembling with gladness at the things I had done. For he was an old man, and I the last of his sons. And all the tired fighting men came, and the crafty and wise, till all the people were gathered together. And then I arose, and with a voice like thunder, commanded Skolka, the shaman, to stand forth—"

"Ay, O White Man," exclaimed Mutsak. "With a voice like thunder, that made the people shake at the knees and become afraid."

"And when Skolka had stood forth," Lone Chief went on, "I said that I was not minded to die. Also, I said it were not well that disappointment come to the evil spirits that wait beyond the grave. Wherefore I deemed it fit that the soul of Skolka fare forth into the Unknown, where doubtless it would howl forever in the dark and endless forest. And then I slew him, as he stood there, in the face of all the people. And when a murmuring arose, I cried aloud—"

"With a voice like thunder," prompted Mutsak.

"Ay, with a voice like thunder I cried aloud: 'Behold, O ye people! I am Lone Chief, slayer of Skolka, the false shaman! Alone among men, have I passed down through the gateway of Death and returned again. Mine eyes have looked upon the unseen things. Mine ears have heard the unspoken words. Greater am I than Skolka, the shaman. Greater than all the shamans am I. Likewise am I a greater chief than my father, the Otter. All his days did he fight with the Mukumuks, and lo, in one day I have destroyed them all. As with the breathing of a breath have I destroyed them. Wherefore, my father, the Otter, being old, and Skolka, the shaman, being dead, I shall be both chief and shaman. Henceforth I shall be both chief and shaman to you, O my people. And if any man dispute my word, let that man stand forth!'

"I waited, but no man stood forth. Then I cried: 'Hoh! I have tasted blood! Now bring meat, for I am hungry. Break open the caches, tear down the fish-racks, and let the feast be big. Let there be merriment, and songs, not of burial, but marriage. And last of all, let the girl Kasaan be brought. The girl Kasaan, who is to be the mother of the children of Lone Chief!'

"And at my words, and because that he was very old, my father, the Otter, wept like a woman, and put his arms about my knees. And from that day I was both chief and shaman. And great honor was mine, and all men yielded me obedience."

"Until the steamboat came," Mutsak prompted.

"Ay," said Lone Chief. "Until the steamboat came."

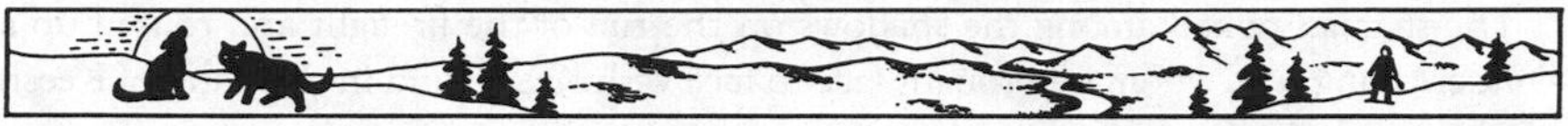

Keesh, the Son of Keesh

"Thus will I give six blankets, warm and double; six files, large and hard; six Hudson Bay knives, keen-edged and long; two canoes, the work of Mogum, The Maker of Things; ten dogs, heavy-shouldered and strong in the harness; and three guns—the trigger of one be broken, but it is a good gun and can doubtless be mended."

Keesh paused and swept his eyes over the circle of intent faces. It was the time of the Great Fishing, and he was bidding to Gnob for Su-Su his daughter. The place was the St. George Mission by the Yukon, and the tribes had gathered for many a hundred miles. From north, south, east, and west, they had come, even from Tozikakat, and far Tana-naw.

"And further, O Gnob, thou art the chief of the Tana-naw; and I, Keesh, the son of Keesh, am chief of the Thlunget. Wherefore, when my seed springs from the loins of thy daughter, there shall be a friendship between the tribes, a great friendship, and Tana-naw and Thlunget shall be brothers of the blood in the time to come. What I have said I will do, that will I do. And how is it with you, O Gnob, in this matter?"

Gnob nodded his head gravely, his gnarled and age-twisted face inscrutably masking the soul that dwelt behind. His narrow eyes burned like twin coals through their narrow slits, as he piped in a high-cracked voice, "But that is not all."

"What more?" Keesh demanded. "Have I not offered full measure? Was there ever yet a Tana-naw maiden who fetched so great a price? Then name her!"

An open snicker passed round the circle, and Keesh knew that he stood in shame before these people.

"Nay, nay, good Keesh, thou dost not understand." Gnob made a soft, stroking gesture. "The price is fair. It is a good price. Nor do I question the broken trigger. But that is not all. What of the man?"

"Ay, what of the man?" the circle snarled.

"It is said," Gnob's shrill voice piped, "it is said that Keesh does not walk in the way of his fathers. It is said that he has wandered into the dark, after strange gods, and that he is become afraid."

The face of Keesh went dark. "It is a lie," he thundered. "Keesh is afraid of no man!"

"It is said," old Gnob piped on, "that he has harkened to the speech of the white man up at the Big House, and that he bends head to the white man's god, and, moreover, that blood is displeasing to the white man's god."

Keesh dropped his eyes, and his hand clenched passionately. The savage circle laughed derisively, and in the ear of Gnob whispered Madwan, the shaman, high-priest of the tribe and maker of medicine.

The shaman poked among the shadows on the rim of the firelight and roused up a slender young boy, whom he brought face to face with Keesh; and in the hand of Keesh he thrust a knife.

Gnob leaned forward. "Keesh! O Keesh! Darest thou to kill a man? Behold! This be Kitz-noo, a slave. Strike, O Keesh, strike with the strength of thy arm!"

The boy trembled and waited the stroke. Keesh looked at him, and thoughts of Mr. Brown's higher morality floated through his mind, and strong upon him was a vision of the leaping flames of Mr. Brown's particular brand of hell-fire. The knife fell to the ground, and the boy sighed and went out beyond the firelight with shaking knees. At the feet of Gnob sprawled a wolf-dog, which bared its gleaming teeth and prepared to spring after the boy. But the shaman ground his foot into the brute's body, and so doing, gave Gnob an idea.

"And then, O Keesh, what wouldst thou do, should a man do this thing to you?"—as he spoke, Gnob held a ribbon of salmon to White Fang, and when the animal attempted to take it, smote him sharply on the nose with a stick. "And afterwards, O Keesh, wouldst thou do thus?"—White Fang was cringing back on his belly and fawning to the hand of Gnob.

"Listen!"—leaning on the arm of Madwan, Gnob had risen to his feet. "I am very old, and because I am very old I will tell thee things. Thy father, Keesh, was a mighty man. And he did love the song of the bowstring in battle, and these eyes have beheld him cast a spear till the head stood out beyond a man's body. But thou art unlike. Since thou left the Raven to worship the Wolf, thou art become afraid of blood, and thou makest thy people afraid. This is not good. For behold when I was a boy, even as Kitz-noo there, there was no white man in all the land. But they came, one by one, these white men, till now they are many. And they are a restless breed, never content to rest by the fire with a full belly and let the morrow bring its own meat. A curse was laid upon them, it would seem, and they must work it out in toil and hardship."

Keesh was startled. A recollection of a hazy story told by Mr. Brown of one Adam, of old time, came to him, and it seemed that Mr. Brown had spoken true.

"So they lay hands upon all they behold, these white men, and they go everywhere and behold all things. And ever do more follow in their steps, so that if nothing be done they will come to possess all the land and there will be no room for the tribes of the Raven. Wherefore it is meet that we fight with them till none are left. Then will we hold the passes and the land, and perhaps our children and our children's children shall flourish and grow fat. There is a great struggle to come, when Wolf and Raven shall grapple; but Keesh will not fight, nor will he let his people fight. So it is not well that he should take to him my daughter. Thus have I spoken, I, Gnob, chief of the Tana-naw."

"But the white men are good and great," Keesh made answer. "The white men have taught us many things. The white men have given us blankets and knives and guns, such as we have never made and never could make. I remember in what manner we lived before they came. I was unborn then, but I have it from my father. When we went on the hunt we must creep so close to the moose that a spear-cast would cover the distance. Today we use the white man's rifle, and farther away than can a child's cry be heard. We ate fish and meat and berries—there was nothing else to eat—and we ate without salt. How many be there among you who care to go back to the fish and meat without salt?"

It would have sunk home, had not Madwan leaped to his feet ere the silence could come. "And first a question to thee, Keesh. The white man up at the Big House tells you that it is wrong to kill. Yet do we not know that the white men kill? Have we forgotten the great fight on the Koyokuk? or the great fight at Nuklukyeto, where three white men killed twenty of the Tozikakats? Do you think we no longer remember the three men of the Tana-naw that the white man Macklewrath killed? Tell me, O Keesh, why does the Shaman Brown teach you that it is wrong to fight, when all his brothers fight?"

"Nay, nay, there is no need to answer," Gnob piped, while Keesh struggled with the paradox. "It is very simple. The Good Man Brown would hold the Raven tight whilst his brothers pluck the feathers." He raised his voice. "But so long as there is one Tana-naw to strike a blow, or one maiden to bear a manchild, the Raven shall not be plucked!"

Gnob turned to a husky young man across the fire. "And what sayest thou, Makamuk, who are brother to Su-Su?"

Makamuk came to his feet. A long face-scar lifted his upper lip into a perpetual grin which belied the glowing ferocity of his eyes. "This day," he began with cunning irrelevance, "I came by the Trader Macklewrath's cabin. And in the door I saw a child laughing at the sun. And the child looked at me with the Trader Macklewrath's eyes, and it was frightened. The mother ran to it and quieted it. The mother was Ziska, the Thlunget woman."

A snarl of rage rose up and drowned his voice, which he stilled by turning dramatically upon Keesh with outstretched arm and accusing finger.

"So? You give your women away, you Thlunget, and come to the Tana-naw for more? But we have need of our women, Keesh; for we must breed men, many men, against the day when the Raven grapples with the Wolf."

Through the storm of applause, Gnob's voice shrilled clear. "And thou, Nossabok, who art her favorite brother?"

The young fellow was slender and graceful, with the strong aquiline nose and high brows of his type; but from some nervous affliction the lid of one eye drooped at odd times in a suggestive wink. Even as he arose it so drooped and rested a moment against his cheek. But it was not greeted with the accustomed laughter. Every face was grave. "I, too, passed by the Trader Macklewrath's cabin," he rippled in soft girlish tones, wherein there was much of youth and much of his sister. "And I saw Indians with the sweat running into their eyes and their knees shaking with weariness—I say, I saw Indians groaning under the logs for the store which the Trader Macklewrath is to build. And with my eyes I saw them chopping wood to keep the Shaman Brown's Big House warm through the frost of the long nights. This be squaw work. Never shall the Tana-naw do the like. We shall be blood brothers to men, not squaws; and the Thlunget be squaws."

A deep silence fell, and all eyes centered on Keesh. He looked about him carefully, deliberately, full into the face of each grown man. "So," he said passionlessly. And

"So," he repeated. Then turned on his heel without further word and passed out into the darkness.

Wading among sprawling babies and bristling wolf-dogs, he threaded the great camp, and on its outskirts came upon a woman at work by the light of a fire. With strings of bark stripped from the long roots of creeping vines, she was braiding rope for the Fishing. For some time, without speech, he watched her deft hands bringing law and order out of the unruly mass of curling fibers. She was good to look upon, swaying there to her task, strong-limbed, deep-chested, and with hips made for motherhood. And the bronze of her face was golden in the flickering light, her hair blue-black, her eyes jet.

"Oh Su-Su," he spoke finally, "thou hast looked upon me kindly in the days that have gone and in the days yet young—"

"I looked kindly upon thee for that thou wert chief of the Thlunget," she answered quickly, "and because thou wert big and strong."

"Ay—"

"But that was in the old days of the Fishing," she hastened to add, "before the Shaman Brown came and taught the ill things and led thy feet on strange trails."

"But I would tell thee the—"

She held up one hand in a gesture which reminded him of her father. "Nay, I know already the speech that stirs in thy throat, O Keesh, and I make answer now. It so happeneth that the fish of the water and the beasts of the forest bring forth after their kind. And this is good. Likewise it happeneth to women. It is for them to bring forth their kind, and even the maiden, while she is yet a maiden, feels the pang of birth, and the pain of the breast, and the small hands at the neck. And when such feeling is strong, then does each maiden look about her with secret eyes for the man—for the man who shall be fit to father her kind. So have I felt. So did I feel when I looked upon thee and found thee big and strong, a hunter and fighter of beasts and men, well able to win meat when I should eat for two, well able to keep danger afar off when my helplessness drew nigh. But that was before the day the Shaman Brown came into the land and taught thee—"

"But it is not right, Su-Su. I have it on good word—"

"It is not right to kill. I know what thou wouldst say. Then breed thou after thy kind, the kind that does not kill; but come not on such quest among the Tana-naw. For it is said in the time to come, that the Raven shall grapple with the Wolf. I do not know, for this be the affair of men; but I do know that it is for me to bring forth men against that time."

"Su-Su," Keesh broke in, "thou must hear me—"

"A *man* would beat me with a stick and make me hear," she sneered. "But thou . . . here!" She thrust a bunch of bark into his hand. "I cannot give thee myself, but this, yes. It looks fittest in thy hands. It is squaw work, so braid away."

He flung it from him, the angry blood pounding a muddy path under his bronze.

"One more thing," she went on. "There be an old custom which thy father and mine were not strangers to. When a man falls in battle, his scalp is carried away in token. Very good. But thou, who hast forsworn the Raven, must do more. Thou must bring me, not scalps, but heads, two heads, and then will I give thee, not bark, but a brave-beaded belt, and sheath, and long Russian knife. Then will I look kindly upon thee once again, and all will be well."

"So," the man pondered. "So." Then he turned and passed out through the light.

"Nay, O Keesh!" she called after him. "Not two heads, but three at least!"

* * *

But Keesh remained true to his conversion, lived uprightly, and made his tribespeople obey the gospel as propounded by the Rev. Jackson Brown. Through all the time of the Fishing he gave no heed to the Tana-naw, nor took notice of the sly things which were said, nor the laughter of the women of the many tribes. After the Fishing, Gnob and his people, with great store of salmon, sun-dried and smoke-cured, departed for the Hunting on the head reaches of the Tana-naw. Keesh watched them go, but did not fail in his attendance at Mission service, where he prayed regularly and led the singing with his deep bass voice.

The Rev. Jackson Brown delighted in that deep bass voice, and because of his sterling qualities deemed him the most promising convert. Macklewrath doubted this. He did not believe in the efficacy of the conversion of the heathen, and he was not slow in speaking his mind. But Mr. Brown was a large man, in his way, and he argued it out with such convincingness, all of one long fall night, that the trader, driven from position after position, finally announced in desperation, "Knock out my brains with apples, Brown, if I don't become a convert myself, if Keesh holds fast, true blue, for two years!" Mr. Brown never lost an opportunity, so he clinched the matter on the spot with a virile handgrip, and thenceforth the conduct of Keesh was to determine the ultimate abiding-place of Macklewrath's soul.

But there came news one day, after the winter's rime had settled down over the land sufficiently for travel. A Tana-naw man arrived at the St. George Mission in quest of ammunition and bringing information that Su-Su had set eyes on Nee-Koo, a nervy young hunter who had bid brilliantly for her by old Gnob's fire. It was at about this time that the Rev. Jackson Brown came upon Keesh by the wood-trail which leads down to the river. Keesh had his best dogs in the harness, and shoved under sled-lashings was his largest and finest pair of snow-shoes.

"Where goest thou, O Keesh? Hunting?" Mr. Brown asked, falling into the Indian manner.

Keesh looked him steadily in the eyes for a full minute, then started up his dogs. Then again, turning his deliberate gaze upon the missionary, he answered, "No; I go to hell."

In an open space, striving to burrow into the snow as though for shelter from the appalling desolateness, huddled three dreary lodges. Ringed all about, a dozen paces away, was the somber forest. Overhead there was no keen, blue sky of naked space, but a vague, misty curtain, pregnant with snow, which had drawn between. There was no wind, no sound, nothing but the snow and silence. Nor was there even the general stir of life about the camp; for the hunting party had run upon the flank of the caribou herd and the kill had been large. Thus, after the period of fasting had come the plenitude of feasting, and thus, in broad daylight, they slept heavily under their roofs of moose-hide.

By a fire, before one of the lodges, five pairs of snowshoes stood on end in their element, and by the fire sat Su-Su. The hood of her squirrel-skin parka was about her hair, and well drawn up around her throat; but her hands were unmittened and nimbly at work with needle and sinew, completing the last fantastic design on a belt of leather faced with bright scarlet cloth. A dog, somewhere at the rear of one of the lodges, raised a short, sharp bark, then ceased as abruptly as it had begun. Once, her father, in the lodge at her back, gurgled and grunted in his sleep. "Bad dreams," she smiled to herself. "He grows old, and that last joint was too much."

She placed the last bead, knotted the sinew, and replenished the fire. Then, after gazing long into the flames, she lifted her head to the harsh *crunch-crunch* of a moccasined foot against the flinty snow granules. Keesh was at her side, bending slightly forward to a load which he bore upon his back. This was wrapped loosely in a soft-tanned moosehide, and he dropped it carelessly into the snow and sat down. They looked at each other long and without speech.

"It is a far fetch, O Keesh," she said at last, "a far fetch from St. George Mission by the Yukon."

"Ay," he made answer, absently, his eyes fixed keenly upon the belt and taking note of its girth. "But where is the knife?" he demanded.

"Here." She drew it from inside her parka and flashed its naked length in the firelight. "It is a good knife."

"Give it me," he commanded.

"Nay, O Keesh," she laughed. "It may be that thou wast not born to wear it."

"Give it me!" he reiterated, without change of tone. "I was so born."

But her eyes, glancing coquettishly past him to the moosehide, saw the snow about it slowly reddening. "It is blood, Keesh?" she asked.

"Ay, it is blood. But give me the belt and the long Russian knife."

She felt suddenly afraid, but thrilled when he took the belt roughly from her, thrilled to the roughness. She looked at him softly, and was aware of a pain at the breast and of small hands clutching her throat.

"It was made for a smaller man," he remarked grimly, drawing in his abdomen and clasping the buckle at the first hole.

Su-Su smiled, and her eyes were yet softer. Again she felt the soft hands at her throat. He was good to look upon, and the belt was indeed small, made for a smaller man; but what did it matter? She could make many belts.

"But the blood?" she asked, urged on by a hope newborn and growing. "The blood, Keesh? Is it . . . are they . . . heads?"

"Ay."

"They must be very fresh, else would the blood be frozen."

"Ay, it is not cold, and they be fresh, quite fresh."

"Oh, Keesh!" Her face was warm and bright. "And for me?"

"Ay; for thee."

He took hold of a corner of the hide, flirted it open, and rolled the heads out before her.

"Three," he whispered savagely; "nay, four at least."

But she sat transfixed. There they lay—the soft-featured Nee-Koo; the gnarled old face of Gnob; Makamuk, grinning at her with his lifted upper lip; and lastly, Nossabok, his eyelid, up to its old trick, drooped on his girlish cheek in a suggestive wink. There they lay, the firelight flashing upon and playing over them, and from each of them a widening circle dyed the snow to scarlet.

Thawed by the fire, the white crust gave way beneath the head of Gnob, which rolled over like a thing alive, spun around, and came to rest at her feet. But she did not move. Keesh, too, sat motionless, his eyes unblinking, centered steadfastly upon her.

Once, in the forest, an overburdened pine dropped its load of snow, and the echoes reverberated hollowly down the gorge; but neither stirred. The short day had been waning fast, and darkness was wrapping round the camp when White Fang trotted up toward the fire. He paused to reconoiter, but not being driven back, came closer. His nose shot swiftly to the side, nostrils a-tremble and bristles rising along the spine; and straight and true, he followed the sudden scent to his master's head. He sniffed it gingerly at first and licked the forehead with his red lolling tongue. Then he sat abruptly down, pointed his nose up at the first faint star, and raised the long wolf-howl.

This brought Su-Su to herself. She glanced across at Keesh, who had unsheathed the Russian knife and was watching her intently. His face was firm and set, and in it she read the law. Slipping back and hood of her parka, she bared her neck and rose to her feet. There she paused and took a long look about her, at the rimming forest, at the faint stars in the sky, at the camp, at the snow-shoes in the snow—a last long comprehensive look at life. A light breeze stirred her hair from the side, and for the space of one deep breath she turned her head and followed it around until she met it full-faced.

Then she thought of her children, ever to be unborn, and she walked over to Keesh and said, "I am ready."

The League of the Old Men

At the barracks a man was being tried for his life. He was an old man, a native from the Whitefish River, which empties into the Yukon below Lake Le Barge. All Dawson was wrought up over the affair, and likewise the Yukon dwellers for a thousand miles up and down. It has been the custom of the land-robbing and sea-robbing Anglo Saxon to give the law to conquered peoples, and ofttimes this law is harsh. But in the case of Imber the law for once seemed inadequate and weak. In the mathematical nature of things, equity did not reside in the punishment to be accorded him. The punishment was a foregone conclusion, there could be no doubt of that; and though it was capital, Imber had but one life, while the tale against him was one of scores.

In fact the blood of so many was upon his hands that the killings attributed to him did not permit of precise enumeration. Smoking a pipe by the trailside or lounging around the stove, men made rough estimates of the numbers that had perished at his hand. They had been whites, all of them, these poor murdered people, and they had been slain singly, in pairs, and in parties. And so purposeless and wanton had been these killings that they had long been a mystery to the mounted police, even in the time of the captains, and later, when the creeks realized and a governor came from the Dominion to make the land pay for its prosperity.

But more mysterious still was the coming of Imber to Dawson to give himself up. It was in the late spring, when the Yukon was growling and writhing under its ice, that the old Indian climbed painfully up the bank from the river trail and stood blinking on the main street. Men who had witnessed his advent noted that he was weak and tottery, and that he had staggered over to a heap of cabin logs and sat down. He sat there a full day, staring straight before him at the unceasing tide of white men that flooded past. Many a head jerked curiously to the side to meet his stare, and more than one remark was dropped anent to the old Siwash with so strange a look upon his face. No end of men remembered afterward that they had been struck by his extraordinary figure, and forever afterward prided themselves upon their swift discernment of the unusual.

But it remained for Dickensen, Little Dickensen, to be the hero of the occasion. Little Dickensen had come into the land with great dreams and a pocketful of cash; but with the cash the dreams vanished, and to earn his passage back to the States he had accepted a clerical position with the brokerage firm of Holbrook and Mason. Across the street from the office of Holbrook and Mason was the heap of cabin logs upon which Imber sat. Dickensen looked out of the window at him before he went to lunch; and when he came back from lunch he looked out of the window, and the old Siwash was still there.

Dickensen continued to look out of the window, and he, too, forever afterward prided himself upon his swiftness of discernment. He was a romantic little chap, and he likened the immobile old heathen to the genius of the Siwash race, gazing calm-eyed upon the hosts of the invading Saxon. The hours swept along, but Imber did not vary his posture, did not by a hairsbreadth move a muscle; and Dickensen remembered the man who once sat upright on a sled in the main street where men passed to and fro. They thought the man was resting, but later, when they touched him, they found him stiff and cold, frozen to death in the midst of the busy street. To undouble him, that he might fit into a coffin, they had been forced to lug him to a fire and thaw him out a bit. Dickensen shivered at the recollection.

Later on Dickensen went out on the sidewalk to smoke a cigar and cool off; and a little later Emily Travis happened along. Emily Travis was dainty and delicate and rare, whether in London or Klondike she gowned herself as befitted the daughter of a millionaire mining engineer. Little Dickensen deposited his cigar on an outside window ledge where he could find it again, and lifted his hat.

They chatted for ten minutes or so, when Emily Travis, glancing past Dickensen's shoulder, gave a startled little scream. Dickensen turned about to see, and was startled too. Imber had crossed the street and was standing there, a gaunt and hungry-looking shadow, his gaze riveted upon the girl.

"What do you want?" Little Dickensen demanded, tremulously plucky.

Imber grunted and stalked up to Emily Travis. He looked her over, keenly and carefully, every square inch of her. Especially did he appear interested in her silky brown hair and in the color of her cheek, faintly sprayed and soft, like the downy bloom of a butterfly wing. He walked around her, surveying her with the calculating eye of a man who studies the lines upon which a horse or a boat is builded. In the course of his circuit the pink shell of her ear came between his eye and the westering sun, and he stopped to contemplate its rosy transparency. Then he returned to her face and looked long and intently into her blue eyes. He grunted and laid a hand on her arm midway between the shoulder and elbow. With his other hand he lifted her forearm and doubled it back. Disgust and wonder showed in his face, and he dropped her arm with a contemptuous grunt. Then he muttered a few guttural syllables, turned his back upon her, and addressed himself to Dickensen.

Dickensen could not understand his speech, and Emily Travis laughed. Imber turned from one to the other, frowning, but both shook their heads. He was about to go away, when she called out:

"Oh, Jimmy! Come here!"

Jimmy came from the other side of the street. He was a big, hulking Indian clad in approved white-man style, with an Eldorado king's sombrero on his head. He talked with Imber, haltingly, with throaty spasms. Jimmy was a Sitkan, possessed of no more than a passing knowledge of the interior dialects.

"Him Whitefish man," he said to Emily Travis. "Me savve um talk no very much. He want to look see chief white man."

"The governor," suggested Dickensen.

Jimmy talked some more with the Whitefish man, and his face went grave and puzzled.

"I t'ink um want Cap'n Alexander," he explained. "Him say um kill white man, white woman, white boy, plenty kill um white people. Him want to die."

"Insane, I guess," said Dickensen.

"What you call dat?" queried Jimmy.

Dickensen thrust a finger figuratively inside his head and imparted a rotary motion thereto.

"Mebbe so, mebbe so," said Jimmy, returning to Imber, who still demanded the chief man of the white men.

A mounted policeman (unmounted for Klondike service) joined the group and heard Imber's wish repeated. He was a stalwart young fellow, broad-shouldered, deep-chested, legs cleanly built and stretched wide apart, and tall though Imber was, he towered above him by half a head. His eyes were cool and gray and steady, and he carried himself with the peculiar confidence of power that is bred of blood and tradition. His splendid masculinity was emphasized by his excessive boyishness—he was a mere lad—and his smooth cheek promised a blush as willingly as the cheek of a maid.

Imber was drawn to him at once. The fire leaped into his eyes at sight of a saber slash that scarred his cheek. He ran a withered hand down the young fellow's leg and caressed the swelling thew. He smote the broad chest with his knuckles, and pressed and prodded the thick muscle pads that covered the shoulders like a cuirass. The group had been added to by curious passersby—husky miners, mountaineers, and frontiersmen, sons of the long-legged and broad-shouldered generations. Imber glanced from one to another, then he spoke aloud in the Whitefish tongue.

"What did he say?" asked Dickensen.

"Him say um all the same one man, dat p'liceman," Jimmy interpreted.

Little Dickensen was little, and what of Miss Travis? He felt sorry for having asked the question.

The policeman was sorry for him and stepped into the breach. "I fancy there may be something in his story. I'll take him up to the captain for examination. Tell him to come along with me, Jimmy."

Jimmy indulged in more throaty spasms, and Imber grunted and looked satisfied.

"But ask him what he said, Jimmy, and what he meant when he took hold of my arm."

So spoke Emily Travis, and Jimmy put the question and received the answer.

"Him say you no afraid," said Jimmy.

Emily Travis looked pleased.

"Him say you no *skookum*, no strong, all the same very soft like little baby. Him break you, in um two hands, to little pieces. Him t'ink much funny, very strange, how you can be mother of men so big, so strong, like dat p'liceman."

Emily Travis kept her eyes up and unfaltering, but her cheeks were sprayed with scarlet. Little Dickensen blushed and was quite embarrassed. The policeman's face blazed with his boy's blood.

"Come along, you," he said gruffly, setting his shoulder to the crowd and forcing a way.

Thus it was that Imber found his way to the barracks, where he made full and voluntary confession, and from the precincts of which he never emerged.

Imber looked very tired. The fatigue of hopelessness and age was in his face. His shoulders drooped depressingly, and his eyes were lackluster. His mop of hair should have been white, but sun and weather had burned and bitten it so that it hung limp and lifeless and colorless. He took no interest in what went on around him. The courtroom was jammed with the men of the creeks and trails, and there was an ominous note in the rumble and grumble of their low-pitched voices, which came to his ears like the growl of the sea from deep caverns.

He sat close by a window, and his apathetic eyes rested now and again on the dreary scene without. The sky was overcast, and a gray drizzle was falling. It was floodtime on the Yukon. The ice was gone, and the river was up in the town. Back and forth on the main street, in canoes and poling boats, passed the people that never rested. Often he saw these boats turn aside from the street and enter the flooded square that marked the barracks' parade ground. Sometimes they disappeared beneath him, and he heard them jar against the house logs and their occupants scramble in through the window. After that came the slush of water against men's legs as they waded across the lower room and mounted the stairs. Then they appeared in the doorway, with doffed hats and dripping sea boots, and added themselves to the waiting crowd.

And while they centered their looks on him, and in grim anticipation enjoyed the penalty he was to pay, Imber looked at them and mused on their ways, and on their law that never slept, but went on unceasing in good times and bad, in flood and famine, through trouble and terror and death, and which would go on unceasing, it seemed to him, to the end of time.

A man rapped sharply on a table, and the conversation droned away into silence. Imber looked at the man. He seemed one in authority, yet Imber divined the square-browed man who sat by a desk farther back to be the one chief over them all and over the man who had rapped. Another man by the same table uprose and began to read aloud from many fine sheets of paper. At the top of each sheet he cleared his throat, at the bottom moistened his fingers. Imber did not understand his speech, but the others did, and he knew that it made them angry. Sometimes it made them very angry, and once a man cursed him, in single syllables, stinging and tense, till a man at the table rapped him to silence.

For an interminable period the man read. His monotonous, sing-song utterance lured Imber to dreaming, and he was dreaming deeply when the man ceased. A voice spoke to him in his own Whitefish tongue, and he roused up, without surprise, to look upon the face of his sister's son, a young man who had wandered away years agone to make his dwelling with the whites.

"Thou dost not remember me," he said by way of greeting.

"Nay," Imber answered. "Thou art Howkan who went away. Thy mother be dead."

"She was an old woman," said Howkan.

But Imber did not hear, and Howkan, with hand upon his shoulder, roused him again.

"I shall speak to thee what the man has spoken, which is the tale of the troubles thou hast done and which thou hast told, O fool, to the Captain Alexander. And thou shalt understand and say if it be true talk or talk not true. It is so commanded."

Howkan had fallen among the mission folk and been taught by them to read and write. In his hands he held the many fine sheets from which the white man had read aloud, and which had been taken down by a clerk when Imber first made confession, through the mouth of Jimmy, to Captain Alexander. Howkan began to read. Imber listened for a space, when a wonderment rose up in his face and he broke in abruptly.

"That be my talk, Howkan. Yet from thy lips it comes when thy ears have not heard."

Howkan smirked with self-appreciation. His hair was parted in the middle. "Nay, from the paper it comes, O Imber. Never have my ears heard. From the paper it comes, through my eyes, into my head, and out of my mouth to thee. Thus it comes."

"Thus it comes? It be there in the paper?" Imber's voice sank in whisperful awe as he crackled the sheets 'twixt thumb and finger and stared at the charactery scrawled thereon. "It be a great medicine, Howkan, and thou art a worker of wonders."

"It be nothing, it be nothing," the young man responded carelessly and pridefully. He read at hazard from the document: "In that year, before the break of the ice, came an old man, and a boy who was lame of one foot. These also did I kill, and the old man made much noise—"

"It be true," Imber interrupted breathlessly. "He made much noise and would not die for a long time. But how dost thou know, Howkan? The chief man of the white men told thee, mayhap? No one beheld me, and him alone have I told."

Howkan shook his head with impatience. "Have I not told thee it be there in the paper, O fool?"

Imber stared hard at the ink-scrawled surface. "As the hunter looks upon the snow and says, 'Here but yesterday there passed a rabbit; and here by the willow scrub it stood and listened, and heard, and was afraid; and here it turned upon its trail; and here it went with great swiftness, leaping wide; and here, with greater swiftness and wider leapings, came a lynx; and here, where the claws cut deep into the snow, the lynx made a very great leap; and here it struck, with the rabbit under and rolling belly up; and here leads off the trail of the lynx alone, and there is no more rabbit'—as the hunter looks upon the markings of the snow and says thus and so and here, dost thou, too, look upon the paper and say thus and so and here be the things old Imber hath done?"

"Even so," said Howkan. "And now do thou listen, and keep thy woman's tongue between thy teeth till thou art called upon for speech."

Thereafter, and for a long time, Howkan read to him the confession, and Howkan remained musing and silent. At the end he said:

"It be my talk, and true talk, but I am grown old, Howkan, and forgotten things come back to me which were well for the head man there to know. First, there was the man who came over the Ice Mountains, with cunning traps made of iron, who sought the beaver of the Whitefish. Him I slew. And there were three men seeking gold on the Whitefish long ago. Them also I slew, and left them to the wolverines. And at the Five Fingers there was a man with a raft and much meat."

At the moments when Imber paused to remember, Howkan translated and a clerk reduced to writing. The courtroom listened stolidly to each unadorned little tragedy, till Imber told of a red-haired man whose eyes were crossed and whom he had killed with a remarkably long shot.

"Hell," said a man in the forefront of the onlookers. He said it soulfully and sorrowfully. He was red-haired. "Hell," he repeated. "That was my brother Bill." And at regular intervals throughout the session, his solemn "Hell" was heard in the courtroom; nor did his comrades check him, nor did the man at the table rap him to order.

Imber's head drooped once more, and his eyes went dull, as though a film rose up and covered them from the world. And he dreamed as only age can dream upon the colossal futility of youth.

Later Howkan roused him again, saying: "Stand up, O Imber. It be commanded that thou tellest why you did these troubles, and slew these people, and at the end journeyed here seeking the law."

Imber rose feebly to his feet and swayed back and forth. He began to speak in a low and faintly rumbling voice, but Howkan interrupted him.

"This old man, he is damn crazy," he said in English to the square-browed man. "His talk is foolish and like that of a child."

"We will hear his talk which is like that of a child," said the square-browed man. "And we will hear it, word for word, as he speaks it. Do you understand?"

Howkan understood, and Imber's eyes flashed, for he had witnessed the play between his sister's son and the man in authority. And then began the story, the epic of a bronze patriot which might well itself be wrought into bronze for the generations unborn. The crowd fell strangely silent, and the square-browed judge leaned head on hand and pondered his soul and the soul of his race. Only was heard the deep tones of Imber, rhythmically alternating with the shrill voice of the interpreter, and now and again, like the bell of the Lord, the wondering and meditative "Hell" of the red-haired man.

"I am Imber of the Whitefish people." So ran the interpretation of Howkan, whose inherent barbarism gripped hold of him, and who lost his mission culture and veneered civilization as he caught the savage ring and rhythm of old Imber's tale. "My father was Otsbaok, a strong man. The land was warm with sunshine and gladness when I was a boy. The people did not hunger after strange things, nor hearken to new voices, and the ways of their fathers were their ways. The women found favor in the eyes of the young men, and the young men looked upon them with content. Babes hung at the breasts of the women, and they were heavy-hipped with increase of the tribe. Men were men in those days. In peace and plenty, and in war and famine, they were men.

"At that time there was more fish in the water than now, and more meat in the forest. Our dogs were wolves, warm with thick hides and hard to the frost and storm. And as with our dogs so with us, for we were likewise hard to the frost and storm. And when the Pellys came into our land we slew them and were slain. For we were men, we Whitefish, and our fathers and our fathers' fathers had fought against the Pellys and determined the bounds of the land.

"As I say, with our dogs so with us. And one day came the first white man. He dragged himself, so, on hand and knee, in the snow. And his skin was stretched tight, and his bones were sharp beneath. Never was such a man, we thought, and we wondered of what strange tribe he was, and of its land. And he was weak, most weak, like a little child, so that we gave him a place by the fire, and warm furs to lie upon, and we gave him food as little children are given food.

"And with him was a dog, large as three of our dogs, and very weak. The hair of this dog was short, and not warm, and the tail was frozen so that the end fell off. And this strange dog we fed, and bedded by him, and fought from it our dogs, which else would have killed him. And what of the moose meat and the sun-dried salmon, the man and dog took strength to themselves; and what of the strength they became big and unafraid. And the man spoke loud words and laughed at the old men and young men, and looked boldly upon the maidens. And the dog fought with our dogs, and for all of his short hair and softness slew three of them in one day.

"When we asked the man concerning his people, he said, 'I have many brothers,' and laughed in a way that was not good. And when he was in his full strength he went away, and with him went Noda, daughter to the chief. First, after that, was one of our bitches brought to pup. And never was there such a breed of dogs—big-headed, thick-jawed, and short-haired and helpless. Well do I remember my father, Otsbaok, a strong man. His face was black with anger at such helplessness, and he took a stone, so, and so, and there was no more helplessness. And two summers after that came Noda back to us with a manchild in the hollow of her arm.

"And that was the beginning. Came a second white man, with short-haired dogs, which he left behind him when he went. And with him went six of our strongest dogs, for which, in trade, he had given Koo-So-Tee, my mother's brother, a wonderful pistol that fired with great swiftness six times. And Koo-So-Tee was very big, what of the pistol, and laughed at our bows and arrows. 'Women's things,' he called them, and went forth against the bald-face grizzly, with the pistol in his hand. Now it be known that it is not good to hunt the bald-face with a pistol, but how were we to know? And how was Koo-So-Tee to know? So he went against the bald-face, very brave, and fired the pistol with great swiftness six times; and the bald-face but grunted and broke in his breast like it were an egg, and like honey from a bee's nest dripped the brains of Koo-So-Tee upon the ground. He was a good hunter, and there was no one to bring meat to his squaw and children. And we were bitter, and we said, 'That which for the white man is well, is for us not well.' And this be true. There be many white men and fat, but their ways have made us few and lean.

"Came the third white man, with great wealth of all manner of wonderful foods and things. And twenty of our strongest dogs he took from us in trade. Also, what of presents and great promises, ten of our young hunters did he take with him on a journey which fared no man knew where. It is said they died in the snow of the Ice Mountains where man has never been, or in the Hills of Silence which are beyond the edge of the earth. Be that as it may, dogs and young hunters were never seen again by the Whitefish people.

"And more white men came with the years, and ever, with pay and presents, they led the young men away with them. And sometimes the young men came back with strange tales of dangers and toils in the lands beyond the Pellys, and sometimes they did not come back. And we said: 'If they be unafraid of life, these white men, it is because they have many lives; but we be few by the Whitefish, and the young men shall go away no more.' But the young men did go away; and the young women went also; and we were very wroth.

"It be true, we ate flour, and salt pork, and drank tea which was a great delight; only, when we could not get tea, it was very bad and we became short of speech and quick of anger. So we grew to hunger for the things the white men brought in trade. Trade! Trade! All the time it was trade! One winter we sold our meat for clocks that would not go, and watches with broken guts, and files worn smooth, and pistols without cartridges and worthless. And then came famine, and we were without meat, and twoscore died ere the break of spring.

" 'Now we are grown weak,' we said; 'and the Pellys will fall upon us, and our bounds be overthrown.' But as it fared with us, so had it fared with the Pellys, and they were too weak to come against us.

"My father, Otsbaok, a strong man, was now old and very wise. And he spoke to the chief, saying: 'Behold, our dogs be worthless. No longer are they thick-furred and strong, and they die in the frost and harness. Let us go into the village and kill them, saving only the wolf ones, and these let us tie out in the night that they may mate with the wild wolves of the forest. Thus shall we have dogs warm and strong again.'

"And his word was harkened to, and we Whitefish became known for our dogs, which were the best in the land. But known we were not for ourselves. The best of our young men and women had gone away with the white men to wander on trail and river to far places. And the young women came back old and broken, as Nada had come, or they came not at all. And the young men came back to sit by our fires for a time, full of ill speech and rough ways, drinking evil drinks and gambling through long nights and days, with a great unrest always in their hearts, till the call of the white men came to them and they went away again to the unknown places. And they were without honor and respect, jeering the old-time customs and laughing in the faces of chief and shamans.

"As I say, we were become a week breed, we Whitefish. We sold our warm skins and furs for tobacco and whisky and thin cotton things that left us shivering in the cold. And the coughing sickness came upon us, and men and women coughed and sweated through the long nights, and the hunters on trail spat blood upon the snow. And now one and now another bled swiftly from the mouth and died. And the women bore few children, and those they bore were weak and given to sickness. And other sicknesses came to us from the white men, the like of which we had never known and could not understand. Smallpox, likewise measles, have I heard these sicknesses named, and we died of them as die the salmon in the still eddies when in the fall their eggs are spawned and there is no longer need for them to live.

"And yet—and here be the strangeness of it—the white men come as the breath of death; all their ways lead to death, their nostrils are filled with it; and yet they do not die. Theirs, the whisky and tobacco and short-haired dogs; theirs the many sicknesses, the smallpox and measles, the coughing and mouth-bleeding; theirs the white skin, and softness to the frost and storm; and theirs the pistols that shoot six times very swift and are worthless. And yet they grow fat on their many ills, and prosper, and lay a heavy hand over all the world and tread mightily upon its peoples. And their women, too, are soft as little babes, most breakable and never broken, the mothers of men. And out of all this softness and sickness and weakness come strength and power and authority. They be gods or devils, as the case may be. I do not know. What do I know—I, old Imber of the Whitefish? Only do I know that they are past understanding, these white men, far-wanderers and fighters over the earth that they be.

"As I say, the meat in the forest became less and less. It be true, the white man's gun is most excellent and kills a long way off; but of what worth the gun, when there is no meat to kill? When I was a boy on the Whitefish there was moose every hill, and each year came the caribou uncountable. But now the hunter may take the trail ten days and not one moose gladden his eyes, while the caribou uncountable come no more at all. Small worth the gun, I say, killing a long way off, when there be nothing to kill.

"And I, Imber, pondered upon these things, watching the while the Whitefish, and the Pellys, and all the tribes of land, perishing as perished the meat of the forest. Long I pondered. I talked with the shamans and the old men who were wise. I went apart that the sounds of the village might not disturb me, and I ate no meat so that my belly should not press upon me and make me slow of eye and ear. I sat long and sleepless in the forest-wide-eyed for the sign, my ears patient and keen for the word that was to come. And I wandered alone in the blackness of night to the river bank, where was wind-moaning and sobbing of water, and where I sought wisdom from the ghosts of old shamans in the trees and dead and gone.

"And in the end, as in a vision, came to me the short-haired and detestable dogs, and the way seemed plain. By the wisdom of Otsbaok, my father and a strong man, had the blood of our own wolf dogs been kept clean, wherefore had they remained warm of hide and strong in the harness. So I returned to my village and made oration to the men. 'This be a tribe, these white men,' I said. 'A very large tribe, and doubtless there is no longer meat in their land, and they are come among us to make a new land for themselves. But they weaken us, and we die. They are a very hungry folk. Already has our meat gone from us, and it were well, if we would live, that we deal by them as we have dealt by their dogs.'

"And further oration I made, counseling fight. And the men of the Whitefish listened, and some said one thing, and some another, and some spoke of other and worthless things, and no man made brave talk of deeds and war. But while the young men were weak as water and afraid, I watched that the old men sat silent, and that in their eyes fire came and went. And later, when the village slept and no one knew, I drew the old men away into the forest and made more talk. And now we were agreed, and we remembered the good young days, and the free land, and the times of plenty, and the gladness and sunshine; and we called ourselves brothers, and swore great secrecy, and a mighty oath to cleanse the land of the evil breed that had come upon it. It be plain we were fools, but how were we to know, we old men of the Whitefish?

"And to hearten the others, I did the first deed. I kept guard upon the Yukon till the first canoe came down. In it were two white men, and when I stood upright on the bank and raised my hand they changed their course and drove in to me. And as the man in the bow lifted his head, so, that he might know wherefore I wanted him, my arrow sang through the air straight to his throat, and he knew. The second man, who held paddle in the stern, had his rifle half to his shoulder when the first of my three spear casts smote him.

" 'These be the first,' I said when the old men had gathered to me. 'Later we will bind together all the old men of all the tribes, and after that the young men who remain strong, and the work will become easy.'

"And then the two dead white men we cast into the river. And of the canoe, which was a very good canoe, we made a fire, and a fire, also, of the things within the canoe. But first we looked at the things, and they were pouches of leather which we cut open with our knives. And inside these pouches were many papers, like that from which thou hast read, O Howkan, with markings on them which we marveled at and could not understand. Now I am become wise, and I know them for the speech of men as thou hast told me."

A whisper and buzz went around the courtroom when Howkan finished interpreting the affair of the canoe, and one man's voice spoke up: "That was the lost '91 mail, Peter James and Delaney bringing it in and last spoken at Le Barge by Matthews going out." The clerk scratched steadily away, and another paragraph was added to the history of the North.

"There be little more," Imber went on slowly. "It be there on the paper, the things we did. We were old men, and we did not understand. Even I, Imber, do not now understand. Secretly we slew, and continued to slay, for with our years we were crafty and we had learned the swiftness of going without haste. When white men came among us with black looks and rough words and took away six of the young men with irons binding them helpless, we knew we must slay wider and farther. And one by one we old men departed upriver and down to the unknown lands. It was a brave thing. Old we were, and unafraid, but the fear of far places is a terrible fear to men who are old.

"So we slew, without haste and craftily. On the Chilcoot and in the Delta we slew, from the passes to the sea, wherever the white men camped or broke their trails. It be true, they died, but it was without worth. Ever did they come over the mountains, ever did they grow and grow, while we, being old, became less and less. I remember, by the Caribou Crossing, the camp of a white man. He was a very little white man, and three of the old men came upon him in his sleep. And the next day I came upon the four of them. The white man alone still breathed, and there was breath in him to curse me once and well before he died.

"And so it went, now one old man, and now another. Sometimes the word reached us long after of how they died, and sometimes it did not reach us. And the old men of the other tribes were weak and afraid, and would not join with us. As I say, one by one, till I alone was left. I am Imber, of the Whitefish people. My father was Otsbaok, a strong man. There are no Whitefish now. Of the old men I am the last. The young men and young women are gone away, some to live with the Pellys, some with the Salmons, and more with the white men. I am very old and very tired, and it being vain fighting the law, as thou sayest, Howkan, I am come seeking the law."

"O Imber, thou art indeed a fool," said Howkan.

But Imber was dreaming. The square-browed judge likewise dreamed, and all his race rose up before him in a mighty phantasmagoria—his steel-shod, mail-clad race, and lawgiver and workmaker among the families of men. He saw it dawn red-flickering across the dark forests and sullen seas; he saw it blaze, bloody and red, to full and triumphant noon; and down the shaded slope he saw the blood-red sands dropping into night. And through it all he observed the law, pitiless and potent, ever unswerving and ever ordaining, greater than the motes of men who fulfilled it or were crushed by it, even as it was greater than he, his heart speaking for softness.

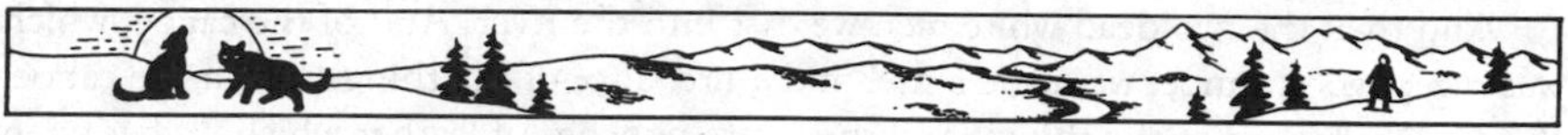

Bâtard

Bâtard was a devil. This was recognized throughout the Northland. "Hell's Spawn" he was called by many men, but his master, Black Leclère, chose for him the shameful name "Bâtard." Now Black Leclère was also a devil, and the twain were well matched. There is a saying that when two devils come together, hell is to pay. This is to be expected, and this certainly was to be expected when Bâtard and Black Leclère came together. The first time they met, Bâtard was a part-grown puppy, lean and hungry, with bitter eyes; and they met with snap and snarl, and wicked looks, for Leclère's upper lip had a wolfish way of lifting and showing the white, cruel teeth. And it lifted then, and his eyes glinted viciously, as he reached for Bâtard and dragged him out from the squirming litter. It was certain that they divined each other, for on the instant Bâtard had buried his puppy fangs in Leclère's hand, and Leclère, thumb and finger, was coolly choking his young life out of him.

"*Sacredam,*" the Frenchman said softly, flirting the quick blood from his bitten hand and gazing down on the little puppy choking and gasping in the snow.

Leclère turned to John Hamlin, storekeeper of the Sixty Mile Post. "Dat fo' w'at Ah lak heem. 'Ow moch, eh, you, *M'sieu'*? 'Ow moch? Ah buy heem, now; Ah buy heem queek."

And because he hated him with an exceeding bitter hate, Leclère bought Bâtard and gave him his shameful name. And for five years the twain adventured across the Northland, from St. Michael's and the Yukon delta to the head-reaches of the Pelly and even so far as the Peace River, Athabasca, and the Great Slave. And they acquired a reputation for uncompromising wickedness, the like of which never before attached itself to man and dog.

Bâtard did not know his father,—hence his name,—but, as John Hamlin knew, his father was a great gray timber wolf. But the mother of Bâtard, as he dimly remembered her, was snarling, bickering, obscene, husky, full-fronted and heavy-chested, with a malign eye, a cat-like grip on life, and a genius for trickery and evil. There was neither faith nor trust in her. Her treachery alone could be relied upon, and her wild-wood amours attested her general depravity. Much of evil and much of strength were there in these, Bâtard's progenitors, and, bone and flesh of their bone and flesh, he had inherited it all. And then came Black Leclère, to lay his heavy hand on the bit of pulsating puppy life, to press and prod and mould till it became a big bristling beast, acute in knavery, overspilling with hate, sinister, malignant, diabolical. With a proper master Bâtard might have made an ordinary, fairly efficient sled-dog. He never got the chance: Leclère but confirmed him in his congenital iniquity.

The history of Bâtard and Leclère is a history of war—of five cruel, relentless years, of which their first meeting is fit summary. To begin with, it was Leclère's fault, for he hated with understanding and intelligence, while the long-legged, ungainly puppy hated only blindly, instinctively, without reason or method. At first there were no refinements of cruelty (these were to come later), but simple beatings and crude brutalities. In one of these Bâtard had an ear injured. He never regained control of the riven muscles, and ever after the ear drooped limply down to keep keen the memory of his tormentor. And he never forgot.

His puppyhood was a period of foolish rebellion. He was always worsted, but he fought back because it was his nature to fight back. And he was unconquerable. Yelping shrilly from the pain of lash and club, he none the less contrived always to throw in the defiant snarl, the bitter vindictive menace of his soul which fetched without fail more blows and beatings. But his was his mother's tenacious grip on life. Nothing could kill him. He flourished under misfortune, grew fat with famine, and out of his terrible struggle for life developed a preternatural intelligence. His were the stealth and cunning of the husky, his mother, and the fierceness and valor of the wolf, his father.

Possibly it was because of his father that he never wailed. His puppy yelps passed with his lanky legs, so that he became grim and taciturn, quick to strike, slow to warn. He answered curse with snarl, and blow with snap, grinning the while his implacable hatred; but never again, under the extremest agony, did Leclère bring from him the cry of fear nor of pain. This unconquerableness but fanned Leclère's wrath and stirred him to greater deviltries.

Did Leclère give Bâtard half a fish and to his mates whole ones, Bâtard went forth to rob other dogs of their fish. Also he robbed cachés and expressed himself in a thousand rogueries, till he became a terror to all dogs and masters of dogs. Did Leclère beat Bâtard and fondle Babette,—Babette who was not half the worker he was,—why, Bâtard threw her down in the snow and broke her hind leg in his heavy jaws, so that Leclère was forced to shoot her. Likewise, in bloody battles, Bâtard mastered all his team-mates, set them the law of trail and forage, and made them live to the law he set.

In five years he heard but one kind word, received but one soft stroke of a hand, and then he did not know what manner of things they were. He leaped like the untamed thing he was, and his jaws were together in a flash. It was the missionary at Sunrise, a newcomer in the country, who spoke the kind word and gave the soft stroke of the hand. And for six months after, he wrote no letters home to the States, and the surgeon at McQuestion travelled two hundred miles on the ice to save him from blood-poisoning.

Men and dogs looked askance at Bâtard when he drifted into their camps and posts. The men greeted him with feet threateningly lifted for the kick, the dogs with bristling manes and bared fangs. Once a man did kick Bâtard, and Bâtard, with quick wolf snap, closed his jaws like a steel trap on the man's calf and crunched down to the bone. Whereat the man was determined to have his life, only Black Leclère, with ominous eyes and naked hunting-knife, stepped in between. The killing of Bâtard—ah, *sacredam, that* was a pleasure Leclère reserved for himself. Some day it would happen, or else—bah! who was to know? Anyway, the problem would be solved.

For they had become problems to each other. The very breath each drew was a challenge and a menace to the other. Their hate bound them together as love could never bind. Leclère was bent on the coming of the day when Bâtard should wilt in spirit and cringe and whimper at his feet. And Bâtard—Leclère knew what was in Bâtard's mind, and more than once had read it in Bâtard's eyes. And so clearly had he read, that when Bâtard was at his back, he made it a point to glance often over his shoulder.

Men marvelled when Leclere refused large money for the dog. "Some day you'll kill him and be out his price," said John Hamlin once, when Bâtard lay panting in the snow where Leclère had kicked him, and no one knew whether his ribs were broken, and no one dared look to see.

"Dat," said Leclère, dryly, "dat is my biz'ness, *M'sieu'*."

And the men marvelled that Bâtard did not run away. They did not understand. But Leclère understood. He was a man who lived much in the open, beyond the sound of human tongue, and he had learned the voices of wind and storm, the sigh of night, the whisper of dawn, the clash of day. In a dim way he could hear the green things growing, the running of the sap, the bursting of the bud. And he knew the subtle speech of the things that moved, of the rabbit in the snare, the moody raven beating the air with hollow wing, the baldface shuffling under the moon, the wolf like a gray shadow gliding betwixt the twilight and the dark. And to him Bâtard spoke clear and direct. Full well he understood why Bâtard did not run away, and he looked more often over his shoulder.

When in anger, Bâtard was not nice to look upon, and more than once had he leapt for Leclère's throat, to be stretched quivering and senseless in the snow, by the butt of the ever ready dogwhip. And so Bâtard learned to bide his time. When he reached his full strength and prime of youth, he thought the time had come. He was broad-chested, powerfully muscled, of far more than ordinary size, and his neck from head to shoulders was a mass of bristling hair—to all appearances a full-blooded wolf. Leclère was lying asleep in his furs when Bâtard deemed the time to be ripe. He crept upon him stealthily, head low to earth and lone ear laid back, with a feline softness of tread. Bâtard breathed gently, very gently, and not till he was close at hand did he raise his head. He paused for a moment, and looked at the bronzed bull throat, naked and knotty, and swelling to a deep and steady pulse. The slaver dipped down his fangs and slid off his tongue at the sight, and in that moment he remembered his drooping ear, his uncounted blows and prodigious wrongs, and without a sound sprang on the sleeping man.

Leclère awoke to the pang of fangs in his throat, and, perfect animal that he was, he awoke clear-headed and with full comprehension. He closed on Bâtard's windpipe with both his hands, and rolled out of his furs to get his weight uppermost. But the thousands of Bâtard's ancestors had clung at the throats of unnumbered moose and caribou and dragged them down, and the wisdom of those ancestors was his. When Leclère's weight came on top of him, he drove his hind legs upward and in, and clawed down chest and abdomen, ripping and tearing through skin and muscle. And when he felt the man's body wince above him and lift, he worried and shook at the man's throat. His team-mates closed around in a snarling circle, and Bâtard, with failing breath and fading sense, knew that their jaws were hungry for him. But that did not matter—it was the man, the man above him, and he ripped and clawed, and shook and worried, to the last ounce of his strength. But Leclère choked him with both his hands, till Bâtard's chest heaved and writhed for the air denied, and his eyes glazed and set, and his jaws slowly loosened, and his tongue protruded black and swollen.

"Eh? *Bon*, you devil!" Leclère gurgled, mouth and throat clogged with his own blood, as he shoved the dizzy dog from him.

And then Leclère cursed the other dogs off as they fell upon Bâtard. They drew back into a wider circle, squatting alertly on their haunches and licking their chops, the hair on every neck bristling and erect.

Bâtard recovered quickly, and at sound of Leclère's voice, tottered to his feet and swayed weakly back and forth.

"A-h-ah! You beeg devil!" Leclère spluttered. "Ah fix you; Ah fix you plentee, by *Gar!*"

Bâtard, the air biting into his exhausted lungs like wine, flashed full into the man's face, his jaws missing and coming together with a metallic clip. They rolled over and over on the snow, Leclère striking madly with his fists. Then they separated, face to face, and circled back and forth before each other. Leclère could have drawn his knife. His rifle was at his feet. But the beast in him was up and raging. He would do the thing with his hands—and his teeth. Bâtard sprang in, but Leclère knocked him over with a blow of the fist, fell upon him, and buried his teeth to the bone in the dog's shoulder.

It was a primordial setting and a primordial scene, such as might have been in the savage youth of the world. An open space in a dark forest, a ring of grinning wolf-dogs, and in the centre two beasts, locked in combat, snapping and snarling, raging madly about, panting, sobbing, cursing, straining, wild with passion, in a fury of murder, ripping and tearing and clawing in elemental brutishness.

But Leclère caught Bâtard behind the ear, with a blow from his fist, knocking him over, and, for the instant, stunning him. Then Leclère leaped upon him with his feet, and sprang up and down, striving to grind him into the earth. Both Bâtard's hind legs were broken ere Leclère ceased that he might catch breath.

"A-a-ah! A-a-ah!" he screamed, incapable of speech, shaking his fist, through sheer impotence of throat and larynx.

But Bâtard was indomitable. He lay there in a helpless welter, his lip feebly lifting and writhing to the snarl he had not the strength to utter. Leclère kicked him, and the tired jaws closed on the ankle, but could not the break the skin.

Then Leclère picked up the whip and proceeded almost to cut him to pieces, at each stroke of the lash crying: "Dis taim Ah break you! Eh? By *Gar!* Ah break you!"

In the end, exhausted, fainting from loss of blood, he crumpled up and fell by his victim, and when the wolf-dogs closed in to take their vengeance, with his last consciousness dragged his body on top Bâtard to shield him from their fangs.

This occured not far from Sunrise, and the missionary, opening the door to Leclère a few hours later, was surprised to note the absence of Bâtard from the team. Nor did his surprise lessen when Leclère threw back the robes from the sled, gathered Bâtard into his arms, and staggered across the threshold. It happened that the surgeon of McQuestion, who was something of a gadabout, was up on a gossip, and between them they proceeded to repair Leclère.

"*Merci, non,*" said he. "Do you fix firs' de dog. To die? *Non.* Eet is not good. Becos' heem Ah mus' yet break. Dat fo' w'at he mus' not die."

The surgeon called it a marvel, the missionary a miracle, that Leclère pulled through at all; and so weakened was he, that in the spring the fever got him, and he went on his back again. Bâtard had been in even worse plight, but his grip on life prevailed, and the bones of his hind legs knit, and his organs righted themselves, during the several weeks he lay strapped to the floor. And by the time Leclère, finally convalescent, sallow and shaky, took the sun by the cabin door, Bâtard had reasserted his supremacy among his kind, and brought not only his own team-mates but the missionary's dogs into subjection.

He moved never a muscle, nor twitched a hair, when, for the first time, Leclère tottered out on the missionary's arm, and sank down slowly and with infinite caution on the three-legged stool.

"*Bon!*" he said. "*Bon!* De good sun!" And he stretched out his wasted hands and washed them in the warmth.

Then his gaze fell on the dog, and the old light blazed back in his eyes. He touched the missionary lightly on the arm. "*Mon père,* dat is one beeg devil, dat Bâtard. You will bring me one pistol, so, dat Ah drink de sun in peace."

And thenceforth for many days he sat in the sun before the cabin door. He never dozed, and the pistol lay always across his knees. Bâtard had a way, the first thing each day, of looking for the weapon in its wonted place. At sight of it he would lift his lip faintly in token that he understood, and Leclère would lift his own lip in an answering grin. One day the missionary took note of the trick.

"Bless me!" he said. "I really believe the brute comprehends."

Leclère laughed softly. "Look you, *mon père.* Dat w'at Ah now spik, to dat does he lissen."

As if in confirmation, Bâtard just perceptibly wriggled his lone ear up to catch the sound.

"Ah say 'keel.' "

Bâtard growled deep down in his throat, the hair bristled along his neck, and every muscle went tense and expectant.

"Ah lift de gun, so, like dat." And suiting action to word, he sighted the pistol at Bâtard.

Bâtard, with a single leap, sideways, landed around the corner of the cabin out of sight.

"Bless me!" he repeated at intervals.

Leclère grinned proudly.

"But why does he not run away?"

The Frenchman's shoulders went up in the racial shrug that means all things from total ignorance to infinite understanding.

"Then why do you not kill him?"

Again the shoulders went up.

"*Mon père,*" he said after a pause, "de taim is not yet. He is one beeg devil. Some taim Ah break heem, so, an' so, all to leetle bits. Hey? Some taim. *Bon!*"

A day came when Leclère gathered his dogs together and floated down in a bateau to Forty Mile, and on to the Porcupine, where he took a commission from the P. C. Company, and went exploring for the better part of a year. After that he poled up the Koyokuk to deserted Arctic City, and later came drifting back, from camp to camp, along the Yukon. And during the long months Bâtard was well lessoned. He learned many tortures, and, notably, the torture of hunger, the torture of thirst, the torture of fire, and, worst of all, the torture of music.

Like the rest of his kind, he did not enjoy music. It gave him exquisite anguish, racking him nerve by nerve, and ripping apart every fibre of his being. It made him howl, long and wolf-like, as when the wolves bay the stars on frosty nights. He could not help howling. It was his one weakness in the contest with Leclère, and it was his shame. Leclère, on the other hand, passionately loved music—as passionately as he loved strong drink. And when his soul clamored for expression, it usually uttered itself in one or the other of the two ways, and more usually in both ways. And when he had drunk, his brain a-lilt with unsung song and the devil in him aroused and rampant, his soul found its supreme utterance in torturing Bâtard.

"Now we will haf a leetle museek," he would say. "Eh? W'at you t'ink, Bâtard?"

It was only an old and battered harmonica, tenderly treasured and patiently repaired; but it was the best that money could buy, and out of its silver reeds he drew weird vagrant airs that men had never heard before. Then Bâtard, dumb of throat, with teeth tight clenched, would back away, inch by inch, to the farthest cabin corner. And Leclère, playing, playing, a stout club tucked under his arm, followed the animal up, inch by inch, step by step, till there was no further retreat.

At first Bâtard would crowd himself into the smallest possible space, grovelling close to the floor; but as the music came nearer and nearer, he was forced to uprear, his back jammed into the logs, his fore legs fanning the air as though to beat off the rippling waves of sound. He still kept his teeth together, but severe muscular contractions attacked his body, strange twitchings and jerkings, till he was all a-quiver and writhing in silent torment. As he lost control, his jaws spasmodically wrenched apart, and deep throaty vibrations issued forth, too low in the register of sound for human ear to catch. And then, nostrils distended, eyes dilated, hair bristling in helpless rage, arose the long wolf howl. It came with a slurring rush upward, swelling to a great heart-breaking burst of sound, and dying away in sadly cadenced woe—then the next rush upward, octave upon octave; the bursting heart; and the infinite sorrow and misery, fainting, fading, falling, and dying slowly away.

It was fit for hell. And Leclère, with fiendish ken, seemed to divine each particular nerve and heartstring, and with long wails and tremblings and sobbing minors to make it yield up its last shred of grief. It was frightful, and for twenty-four hours after, Bâtard was nervous and unstrung, starting at common sounds, tripping over his own shadow, but, withal, vicious and masterful with his team-mates. Nor did he show signs of a breaking spirit. Rather did he grow more grim and taciturn, biding his time with an inscrutable patience that began to puzzle and weigh upon Leclère. The dog would lie in the firelight, motionless, for hours, gazing straight before him at Leclère, and hating him with his bitter eyes.

Often the man felt that he had bucked against the very essence of life—the unconquerable essence that swept the hawk down out of the sky like a feathered thunderbolt, that drove the great gray goose across the zones, that hurled the spawning salmon through two thousand miles of boiling Yukon flood. At such times he felt impelled to express his own unconquerable essence; and with strong drink, wild music, and Bâtard, he indulged in vast orgies, wherein he pitted his puny strength in the face of things, and challenged all that was, and had been, and was yet to be.

"Dere is somet'ing dere," he affirmed, when the rhythmed vagaries of his mind touched the secret chords of Bâtard's being and brought forth the long lugubrious howl. "Ah pool eet out wid bot' my han's, so, an' so. Ha! Ha! Eet is fonee! Eet is ver' fonee! De priest chant, de womans pray, de mans swear, de leetle bird go *peep-peep*, Bâtard, heem go *yow-yow*—an' eet is all de ver' same t'ing. Ha! Ha!"

Father Gautier, a worthy priest, once reproved him with instances of concrete perdition. He never reproved him again.

"Eet may be so, *mon père,* he made answer. "An' t'ink A go troo hell a-snappin', tak de hemlock troo de fire. Eh, *mon père?*"

But all bad things come to an end as well as good, and so with Black Leclère. On the summer low water, in a poling boat, he left McDougall for Sunrise. He left McDougall in company with Timothy Brown, and arrived at Sunrise by himself. Further, it was known that they had quarreled just previous to pulling out; for the *Lizzie,* a wheezy ten-ton sternwheeler, twenty-four hours behind, beat Leclère in by three days. And when he did get in, it was with a clean-drilled bullet-hole through his shoulder muscle, and a tale of ambush and murder.

A strike had been made at Sunrise, and things had changed considerably. With the infusion of several hundred gold-seekers, a deal of whiskey, and half a dozen equipped gamblers, the missionary had seen the page of his years of labor with the Indians wiped clean. When the squaws became preoccupied with cooking beans and keeping the fire going for the wifeless miners, and the bucks with swapping their warm furs for black bottles and broken timepieces, he took to his bed, said "bless me" several times, and departed to his final accounting in a rough-hewn, oblong box. Whereupon the gamblers moved their roulette and faro tables into the mission house, and the click of chips and clink of glasses went up from dawn till dark and to dawn again.

Now Timothy Brown was well beloved among these adventurers of the north. The one thing against him was his quick temper and ready fist,—a little thing, for which his kind heart and forgiving hand more than atoned. On the other hand, there was nothing to atone for Black Leclère. He was "black," as more than one remembered deed bore witness, while he was as well hated as the other was beloved. So the men of Sunrise put an antiseptic dressing on his shoulder and hauled him before Judge Lynch.

It was a simple affair. He had quarrelled with Timothy Brown at McDougall. With Timothy Brown he had left McDougall. Without Timothy Brown he had arrived at Sunrise. Considered in the light of his evilness, the unanimous conclusion was that he had killed Timothy Brown. On the other hand, Leclère acknowledged their facts, but challenged their conclusion, and gave his own explanation. Twenty miles out of Sunrise he and Timothy Brown were poling the boat along the rocky shore. From that shore two rifle-shots rang out. Timothy Brown pitched out of the boat and went down bubbling red, and that was the last of Timothy Brown. He, Leclère, pitched into the bottom of the boat with a stinging shoulder. He lay very quiet, peeping at the shore. After a time two Indians stuck up their heads and came out to the water's edge, carrying between them a birch-bark canoe. As they launched it, Leclère let fly. He potted one, who went over the side after the manner of Timothy Brown. The other dropped into the bottom of the canoe, and then canoe and poling boat went down the stream in a drifting battle. After that they hung up on a split current, and the canoe passed on one side of an island, the poling boat on the other. That was the last of the canoe, and he came on into Sunrise. Yes, from the way the Indian in the canoe jumped, he was sure he had potted him. That was all.

This explanation was not deemed adequate. They gave him ten hours' grace while the *Lizzie* steamed down to investigate. Ten hours later she came wheezing back to Sunrise. There had been nothing to investigate. No evidence had been found to back up his statements. They told him to make his will, for he possessed a fifty-thousand-dollar Sunrise claim, and they were a law-abiding as well as a law-giving breed.

Leclère shrugged his shoulders. "Bot one t'ing," he said; "a leetle, w'at you call, favor—a leetle favor, dat is eet. I gif my feefty t'ousan' dollair to de church. I gif my husky dog, Bâtard, to de devil. De leetle favor? Firs' you hang heem, an' den you hang me. Eet is good, eh?"

Good it was, they agreed, that Hell's Spawn should break trail for his master across the last divide, and the court was adjourned down to the river bank, where a big spruce tree stood by itself. Slackwater Charley put a hangman's knot in the end of a hauling-line, and the noose was slipped over Leclère's head and pulled tight around his neck. His hands were tied behind his back, and he was assisted to the top of a cracker box. Then the running end of the line was passed over an overhanging branch, drawn taut, and made fast. To kick the box out from under would leave him dancing on the air.

"Now for the dog," said Webster Shaw, sometime mining engineer. "You'll have to rope him, Slackwater."

Leclère grinned. Slackwater took a chew of tobacco, rove a running noose, and proceeded leisurely to coil a few turns in his hand. He paused once or twice to brush particularly offensive mosquitoes from off his face. Everybody was brushing mosquitoes, except Leclère, about whose head a small cloud was visible. Even Bâtard, lying full-stretched on the ground, with his fore paws rubbed the pests away from eyes and mouth.

But while Slackwater waited for Bâtard to lift his head, a faint call came down the quiet air, and a man was seen waving his arms and running across the flat from Sunrise. It was the storekeeper.

"C-call 'er off, boys," he panted, as he came in among them.

"Little Sandy and Bernadotte's jes' got in," he explained with returning breath. "Landed down below an' come up by the short cut. Got the Beaver with 'm. Picked 'm up in his canoe, stuck in a back channel, with a couple of bullet holes in 'm. Other buck was Klok-Kutz, the one that knocked spots out of his squaw and dusted."

"Eh? W'at Ah say? Eh?" Leclère cried exultantly. "Dat de one fo' sure! Ah know. Ah spik true."

"The thing to do is teach these damned Siwashes a little manners," spoke Webster Shaw. "They're getting fat and sassy, and we'll have to bring them down a peg. Round in all the bucks and string up the Beaver for an object lesson. That's the programme. Come on and let's see what he's got to say for himself."

"Heh, M'sieu'!" Leclère called, as the crowd began to melt away through the twilight in the direction of Sunrise. "Ah lak ver' moch to see de fon."

"Oh, we'll turn you loose when we come back," Webster Shaw shouted over his shoulder. "In the meantime meditate on your sins and the ways of providence. It will do you good, so be grateful."

As is the way with men who are accustomed to great hazards, whose nerves are healthy and trained to patience, so it was with Leclère, who settled himself to the long wait—which is to say that he reconciled his mind to it. There was no settling of the body, for the taut rope forced him to stand rigidly erect. The least relaxation of the leg muscles pressed the rough-fibred noose into his neck, while the upright position caused him much pain in his wounded shoulder. He projected his under lip and expelled his breath upward along his face to blow the mosquitoes away from his eyes. But the situation had its compensation. To be snatched from the maw of death was well worth a little bodily suffering, only it was unfortunate that he should miss the hanging of the Beaver.

And so he mused, till his eyes chanced to fall upon Bâtard, head between fore paws and stretched on the ground asleep. And then Leclère ceased to muse. He studied the animal closely, striving to sense if the sleep were real or feigned. Bâtard's sides were heaving regularly, but Leclère felt that the breath came and went a shade too quickly; also he felt that there was a vigilance or alertness to every hair that belied unshackling sleep. He would have given his Sunrise claim to be assured that the dog was not awake, and once, when one of his joints cracked, he looked quickly and guiltily at Bâtard to see if he roused. He did not rouse then, but a few minutes later he got up slowly and lazily, stretched, and looked carefully about him.

"*Sacredam,*" said Leclère, under his breath.

Assured that no one was in sight or hearing, Bâtard sat down, curled his upper lip almost into a smile, looked up at Leclère, and licked his chops.

"Ah see my feenish," the man said, and laughed sardonically aloud.

Bâtard came nearer, the useless ear wabbling, the good ear cocked forward with devilish comprehension. He thrust his head on one side quizzically, and advanced with mincing, playful steps. He rubbed his body gently against the box till it shook and shook again. Leclère teetered carefully to maintain his equilibrium.

"Bâtard," he said calmly, "look out. Ah keel you."

Bâtard snarled at the word, and shook the box with greater force. Then he upreared, and with his fore paws threw his weight against it higher up. Leclère kicked out with one foot, but the rope bit into his neck and checked so abruptly as nearly to overbalance him.

"Hi, ya! *Chook! Mush-on!*" he screamed.

Bâtard retreated, for twenty feet or so, with a fiendish levity in his bearing that Leclère could not mistake. He remembered the dog often breaking the scum of ice on the water hole, by lifting up and throwing his weight upon it; and, remembering, he understood what he now had in mind. Bâtard faced about and paused. He showed his white teeth in a grin, which Leclère answered; and then hurled his body through the air, in full charge, straight for the box.

Fifteen minutes later, Slackwater Charley and Webster Shaw, returning, caught a glimpse of a ghostly pendulum swinging back and forth in the dim light. As they hurriedly drew in closer, they made out the man's inert body, and a live thing that clung to it, and shook and worried, and gave to it the swaying motion.

"Hi, ya! *Chook!* you Spawn of Hell," yelled Webster Shaw.

But Bâtard glared at him, and snarled threateningly, without loosing his jaws.

Slackwater Charley got out his revolver, but his hand was shaking, as with a chill, and he fumbled.

"Here, you take it," he said, passing the weapon over.

Webster Shaw laughed shortly, drew a sight between the gleaming eyes, and pressed the trigger. Bâtard's body twitched with the shock, threshed the ground spasmodically for a moment, and went suddenly limp. But his teeth still held fast locked.

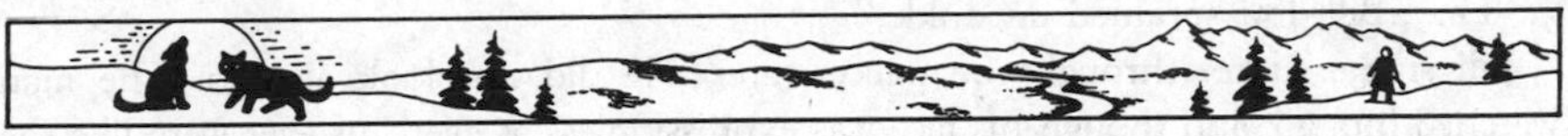

LOVE OF LIFE

THEY limped painfully down the bank, and once the foremost of the two men staggered among the rough-strewn rocks. They were tired and weak, and their faces had the drawn expression of patience which comes of hardship long endured. They were heavily burdened with blanket packs which were strapped to their shoulders. Head-straps, passing across the forehead, helped support these packs. Each man carried a rifle. They walked in a stooped posture, the shoulders well forward, the head still farther forward, the eyes bent upon the ground.

"I wish we had just about two of them cartridges that's layin' in that cache of ourn," said the second man.

His voice was utterly and drearily expressionless. He spoke without enthusiasm; but the first man, limping into the milky stream that foamed over the rocks, vouchsafed no reply.

The other man followed at his heels. They did not remove their foot-gear, though the water was icy cold—so cold that their ankles ached and their feet went numb. In places the water dashed against their knees, and both men staggered for footing.

The man who followed slipped on a smooth boulder, nearly fell, but recovered himself with a violent effort, at the same time uttering a sharp exclamation of pain. He seemed faint and dizzy, and put out his free hand while he reeled, as though seeking support against the air. When he had steadied himself he stepped forward, but reeled again and nearly fell. Then he stood still and looked at the other man, who had never turned his head.

The man stood still for fully a minute, as though debating with himself. Then he called out:

"I say, Bill, I've sprained my ankle."

Bill staggered on through the milky water. He did not look around. The man watched him go, and though his face was expressionless as ever, his eyes were like the eyes of a wounded deer.

The other man limped up the farther bank and continued straight on without looking back. The man in the stream watched him. His lips trembled a little, so that the rough thatch of brown hair which covered them was visibly agitated. His tongue even strayed out to moisten them.

"Bill!" he cried out.

It was the pleading cry of a strong man in distress, but Bill's head did not turn. The man watched him go, limping grotesquely and lurching forward with stammering gait up the slow slope toward the soft sky-line of the low-lying hill. He watched him go till he passed over the crest and disappeared. Then he turned his gaze and slowly took in the circle of the world that remained to him now that Bill was gone.

Near the horizon the sun was smoldering dimly, almost obscured by formless mists and vapors, which gave an impression of mass and density without outline or tangibility. The man pulled out his watch, the while resting his weight on one leg. It was four o'clock, and as the season was near the last of July or first of August—he did not know the precise date within a week or two—he knew that the sun roughly marked the northwest. He looked to the south and knew that somewhere beyond those bleak hills lay the Great Bear Lake; also, he knew that in that direction the Arctic Circle cut its forbidding way across the Canadian Barrens. This stream in which he stood was a feeder to the Coppermine River, which in turn flowed north and emptied into Coronation Gulf and the Arctic Ocean. He had never been there, but he had seen it, once, on a Hudson Bay Company chart.

Again his gaze completed the circle of the world about him. It was not a heartening spectacle. Everywhere was soft sky-line. The hills were all low-lying. There were no trees, no shrubs, no grasses—naught but a tremendous and terrible desolation that sent fear swiftly dawning into his eyes.

"Bill!" he whispered, once and twice; "Bill!"

He cowered in the midst of the milky water, as though the vastness were pressing in upon him with overwhelming force, brutally crushing him with its complacent awfulness. He began to shake as with an ague-fit, till the gun fell from his hand with a splash. This served to rouse him. He fought with his fear and pulled himself together, groping in the water and recovering the weapon. He hitched his pack farther over his left shoulder, so as to take a portion of its weight from off the injured ankle. Then he proceeded, slowly and carefully, wincing with pain, to the bank.

He did not stop. With a desperation that was madness, unmindful of the pain, he hurried up the slope to the crest of the hill over which his comrade had disappeared—more grotesque and comical by far than that limping, jerking comrade. But at the crest he saw a shallow valley, empty of life. He fought with his fear again, overcame it, hitched the pack still farther over on his left shoulder, and lurched on down the slope.

The bottom of the valley was soggy with water, which the thick moss held, sponge-like, close to the surface. This water squirted out from under his feet at every step, and each time he lifted a foot the action culminated in a sucking sound as the wet moss reluctantly released its grip. He picked his way from muskeg to muskeg, and followed the other man's footsteps along and across the rocky ledges which thrust like islets through the sea of moss.

Though alone he was not lost. Farther on he knew he would come to where dead spruce and fir, very small and weazened, bordered the shore of a little lake, the *tit-chin-nichile*— in the tongue of the country, the "land of little sticks." And into that lake flowed a small stream, the water of which was not milky. There was rushgrass on that stream—this he remembered well—but no timber, and he would follow it till its first trickle ceased at a divide. He would cross this divide to the first trickle of another stream, flowing to the west, which he would follow until it emptied into the River Dease, and here he would find a cache under an upturned canoe and piled over with many rocks. And in this cache would be ammunition for his empty gun, fish-hooks and lines, a small net—all the utilities for the killing and snaring of food. Also, he would find flour—not much—a piece of bacon and some beans.

Bill would be waiting for him there, and they would paddle away south down the Dease to the Great Bear Lake. And south across the lake they would go, ever south, till they gained the Mackenzie. And south, still south, they would go, while the winter raced vainly after them, and the ice formed in the eddies, and the days grew chill and crisp, south to some warm Hudson Bay Company post, where timber grew tall and generous and there was grub without end.

These were the thoughts of the man as he strove onward. But hard as he strove with his body, he strove equally hard with his mind, trying to think that Bill had not deserted him, that Bill would surely wait for him at the cache. He was compelled to think this thought, or else there would not be any use to strive, and he would have lain down and died. And as the dim ball of the sun sank slowly into the northwest he covered every inch, and many times, of his and Bill's flight south before the downcoming winter. And he conned the grub of the cache and the grub of the Hudson Bay Company post over and over again. He had not eaten for two days; for a far longer time he had not had all he wanted to eat. Often he stooped and picked pale muskeg berries, put them into his mouth and chewed and swallowed them. A muskeg berry is a bit of seed enclosed in a bit of water. In the mouth the water melts away and the seed chews sharp and bitter. The man knew there was no nourishment in the berries, but he chewed them patiently with a hope greater than knowledge and defying experience.

At nine o'clock he stubbed his toe on a rocky ledge, and from sheer weariness and weakness staggered and fell. He lay for some time, without movement, on his side. Then he slipped out of the pack straps and clumsily dragged himself into a sitting posture. It was not yet dark, and in the lingering twilight he groped about among the rocks for shreds of dry moss. When he had gathered a heap he built a fire—a smoldering, smudgy fire—and put a tin pot of water on to boil.

He unwrapped his pack and the first thing he did was to count his matches. There were sixty-seven. He counted them three times to make sure. He divided them into several portions, wrapping them in oil paper, disposing of one bunch in his empty tobacco pouch, of another bunch in the inside band of his battered hat, of a third bunch under his shirt on the chest. This accomplished, a panic came upon him and he unwrapped them all and counted them again. There were still sixty-seven.

He dried his wet foot-gear by the fire. The moccasins were in soggy shreds. The blanket socks were worn through in places and his feet were raw and bleeding. His ankle was throbbing and he gave it an examination. It had swollen to the size of his knee. He tore a long strip from one of his two blankets and bound the ankle tightly. He tore other strips and bound them about his feet to serve for both moccasins and socks. Then he drank the pot of water, steaming hot, wound his watch, and crawled between his blankets.

He slept like a dead man. The brief darkness around midnight came and went. The sun arose in the northeast—at least the day dawned in that quarter, for the sun was hidden by gray clouds.

At six o'clock he awoke, quietly lying on his back. He gazed straight up into the gray sky and knew that he was hungry. As he rolled over on his elbow he was startled by a loud snort, and saw a bull caribou regarding him with alert curiosity. The animal was not more than fifty feet away, and instantly into the man's mind leaped the vision and the savor of a caribou steak sizzling and frying over a fire. Mechanically he reached for the empty gun, drew a bead, and pulled the trigger. The bull snorted and leaped away, his hoofs rattling and clattering as he fled across the ledges.

The man cursed and flung the empty gun from him. He groaned aloud as he started to drag himself to his feet. It was a slow and arduous task. His joints were like rusty hinges. They worked harshly in their sockets, with much friction, and each bending or unbending was accomplished only through a sheer exertion of will. When he finally gained his feet another minute or so was consumed in straightening up, so that he could stand erect as a man should stand.

He crawled up a small knoll and surveyed the prospect. There were no trees, no bushes, nothing but a gray sea of moss scarcely diversified by gray rocks, gray-colored lakelets, and gray streamlets. The sky was gray. There was no sun or hint of sun. He had no idea of north, and he had forgotten the way he had come to this spot the night before. But he was not lost. He knew that. Soon he would come to the land of the little sticks. He felt that it lay off to the left somewhere, not far—possibly just over the next low hill.

He went back to put his pack into shape for travelling. He assured himself of the existence of his three separate parcels of matches, though he did not stop to count them. But he did linger, debating over a squat moose-hide sack. It was not large. He could hide it under his two hands. He knew that it weighed fifteen pounds—as much as all the rest of the pack—and it worried him. He finally set it to one side and proceeded to roll the pack. He paused to gaze at the squat moose-hide sack. He picked it up hastily with a defiant glance about him, as though the desolation were trying to rob him of it; and when he rose to his feet to stagger on into the day, it was included in the pack on his back.

He bore away to the left, stopping now and again to eat muskeg berries. His ankle had stiffened, his limp was more pronounced, but the pain of it was as nothing compared with the pain of his stomach. The hunger pangs were sharp. They gnawed and gnawed until he could not keep his mind steady on the course he must pursue to gain the land of little sticks. The muskeg berries did not allay this gnawing, while they made his tongue and the roof of his mouth sore with their irritating bite.

He came upon a valley where rock ptarmigan rose on whirring wings from the ledges and muskegs. Ker—ker—ker was the cry they made. He threw stones at them but could not hit them. He placed his pack on the ground and stalked them as a cat stalks a sparrow. The sharp rocks cut through his pant's legs till his knees left a trail of blood; but the hurt was lost in the hurt of his hunger. He squirmed over the wet moss, saturating his clothes and chilling his body; but he was not aware of it, so great was his fever for food. And always the ptarmigan rose, whirring, before him, till their ker—ker—ker became a mock to him, and he cursed them and cried aloud at them with their own cry.

Once he crawled upon one that must have been asleep. He did not see it till it shot up in his face from its rocky nook. He made a clutch as startled as was the rise of the ptarmigan, and there remained in his hand three tail-feathers. As he watched its flight he hated it, as though it had done him some terrible wrong. Then he returned and shouldered his pack.

As the day wore along he came into valleys or swales where game was more plentiful. A band of caribou passed by, twenty and odd animals, tantalizingly within rifle range. He felt a wild desire to run after them, a certitude that he could run them down. A black fox came towards him, carrying a ptarmigan in his mouth. The man shouted. It was a fearful cry, but the fox leaping away in fright did not drop the ptarmigan.

Late in the afternoon he followed a stream, milky with lime, which ran through sparse patches of rushgrass. Grasping these rushes firmly near the root, he pulled up what resembled a young onion-sprout no larger than a shingle-nail. It was tender and his teeth sank into it with a crunch that promised deliciously of food. But its fibers were tough. It was composed of stringy filaments saturated with water, like the berries, and devoid of nourishment. But he threw off his pack and went into the rush-grass on hands and knees, crunching and munching like some bovine creature.

He was very weary and often wished to rest—to lie down and sleep; but he was continually driven on—not so much by his desire to gain the land of little sticks but by his hunger. He searched little ponds for frogs and dug up the earth with his nails for worms, though he knew in spite that neither frogs nor worms existed so far north.

He looked into every pool of water vainly, until, as the long twilight came on, he discovered a solitary fish, the size of a minnow, in such a pool. He plunged his arm in up to the shoulder, but it eluded him. He reached for it with both hands and stirred up the milky mud at the bottom. In his excitement he fell in, wetting himself to the waist. Then the water was too muddy to admit of his seeing the fish and he was compelled to wait until the sediment had settled.

The pursuit was renewed, until the water was again muddied. But he could not wait. He unstrapped the tin bucket and began to bale the pool. He baled wildly at first, splashing himself and flinging the water so short a distance that it ran back into the pool. He worked more carefully, striving to be cool, though his heart was pounding against his chest and his hands were trembling. At the end of half an hour the pool was nearly dry. Not a cupful of water remained. And there was no fish. He found a hidden crevice among the stones through which it had escaped to the adjoining and larger pool—a pool which he could not empty in a night and a day. Had he known of the crevice, he could have closed it with a rock at the beginning and the fish would have been his.

Thus he thought, and crumpled up and sank down upon the wet earth. At first he cried softly to himself, then he cried loudly to the pitiless desolation that ringed him around; and for a long time after he was shaken by great dry sobs.

He built a fire and warmed himself by drinking quarts of hot water, and made camp on a rocky ledge in the same fashion he had the night before. The last thing he did was to see that his matches were dry and to wind his watch. The blankets were wet and clammy. His ankle pulsed with pain. But he knew only that he was hungry, and through his restless sleep he dreamed of feasts and banquets and of food served and spread in all imaginable ways.

He awoke chilled and sick. There was no sun. The gray of earth and sky had become deeper, more profound. A raw wind was blowing, and the first flurries of snow were whitening the hilltops. The air about him thickened and grew white while he made a fire and boiled more water. It was wet snow, half rain, and the flakes were large and soggy. At first they melted as soon as they came in contact with the earth, but ever more fell, covering the ground, putting out the fire, spoiling his supply of moss-fuel.

This was the signal for him to strap on his pack and stumble onward he knew not where. He was not concerned with the land of little sticks, nor with Bill and the cache under the upturned canoe by the River Dease. He was mastered by the verb, "to eat." He was hunger-mad. He took no heed of the course he pursued, so long as that course led him through the swale bottoms. He felt his way through the wet snow to the watery muskeg berries, and went by feel as he pulled up the rush-grass by the roots. But it was tasteless stuff and did not satisfy. He found a weed that tasted sour and he ate all he could find of it, which was not much, for it was a creeping growth, easily hidden under the several inches of snow.

He had no fire that night nor hot water, and crawled under his blanket to sleep the broken hunger-sleep. The snow turned into a cold rain. He awakened many times to feel it falling on his upturned face. Day came—a gray day and no sun. It had ceased raining. The keenness of his hunger had departed. Sensibility, so far as concerned the yearning for food, had been exhausted. There was a dull, heavy ache in his stomach, but it did not bother him so much. He was more rational, and once more he was chiefly interested in the land of little sticks and the cache by the River Dease.

He ripped the remnant of one of his blankets into strips and bound his bleeding feet. Also, he recinched the injured ankle and prepared himself for a day of travel. When he came to his pack he paused long over the squat moose-hide sack, but in the end it went with him.

The snow had melted under the rain and only the hilltops showed white. The sun came out and he succeeded in locating the points of the compass, though he knew now that he was lost. Perhaps, in his previous days' wanderings, he had edged away too far to the left. He now bore off to the right to counteract the possible deviation from his true course.

Though the hunger pangs were no longer so exquisite, he realized that he was weak. He was compelled to pause for frequent rests when he attacked the muskeg berries and rush-grass patches. His tongue felt dry and large, as though covered with a fine hairy growth, and it tasted bitter in his mouth. His heart gave him a great deal of trouble. When he had traveled a few minutes it would begin a remorseless thump, thump, thump, and then leap up and away in a painful flutter of beats that choked him and made him go faint and dizzy.

In the middle of the day he found two minnows in a large pool. It was impossible to bale it, but he was calmer now and managed to catch them in his tin bucket. They were no longer than his little finger, but he was not particularly hungry. The dull ache in his stomach had been growing duller and fainter. It seemed almost that his stomach was dozing. He ate the fish raw, masticating with painstaking care, for the eating was an act of pure reason. While he had no desire to eat he knew that he must eat to live.

In the evening he caught three more minnows, eating two and saving the third for breakfast. The sun had dried stray shreds of moss, and he was able to warm himself with hot water. He had not covered more than ten miles that day, and the next day, traveling whenever his heart permitted him, he covered no more than five miles. But his stomach did not give him the slightest uneasiness. It had gone to sleep. He was in a strange country, too, and the caribou were growing more plentiful, also the wolves. Often their yelps drifted across the desolation, and once he saw three of them slinking away before his path.

Another night, and in the morning, being more rational, he untied the leather string that fastened the squat moose-hide sack. From its open mouth poured a yellow stream of coarse gold-dust and nuggets. He roughly divided the gold in halves, caching one half on a prominent ledge, wrapped in a piece of blanket, and returning the other half to the sack. He also began to use strips of the one remaining blanket for his feet. He still clung to his gun, for there were cartridges in that cache by the River Dease.

This was a day of fog, and this day hunger woke in him again. He was very weak and was afflicted with a giddiness which at times blinded him. It was no uncommon thing now for him to stumble and fall; and stumbling once, he fell squarely into a ptarmigan nest. There were four newly hatched chicks a day old—little specks of pulsating life no more than a mouthful; and he ate them ravenously, thrusting them alive into his mouth and crunching them like egg-shells between his teeth. The mother ptarmigan beat about him with great out-cry. He used his gun as a club with which to knock her over, but she dodged out of reach. He threw stones at her and with one chance shot broke a wing. Then she fluttered away, running, trailing the broken wing, with him in pursuit.

The little chicks had no more than whetted his appetite. He hopped and bobbed clumsily along on his injured ankle, throwing stones and screaming hoarsely at times; at other times hopping and bobbing silently along, picking himself up grimly and patiently when he fell, or rubbing his eyes with his hand when the giddiness threatened to overpower him.

The chase led him across swampy ground in the bottom of the valley, and he came upon footprints in the soggy moss. They were not his own—he could see that. They must be Bill's. But he could not stop, for the mother ptarmigan was running on. He would catch her first, then he would return and investigate.

He exhausted the mother ptarmigan; but he exhausted himself. She lay panting on her side. He lay panting on his side, a dozen feet away, unable to crawl to her. And as he recovered she recovered, fluttering out of reach as his hungry hand went out to her. The chase was resumed. Night settled down and she escaped. He stumbled from weakness and pitched head-foremost on his face, cutting his cheek, his pack upon his back. He did not move for a long while; then he rolled over on his side, wound his watch, and lay there until morning.

Another day of fog. Half of his last blanket had gone into foot-wrappings. He failed to pick up Bill's trail. It did not matter. His hunger was driving him too compellingly—only—only he wondered if Bill too were lost. By midday the irk of his pack became too oppressive. Again he divided the gold, this time merely spilling half of it on the ground. In the afternoon he threw the rest of it away, there remaining to him only the half-blanket, the tin bucket, and the rifle.

An hallucination began to trouble him. He felt confident that one cartridge remained to him. It was in the chamber of the rifle and he had overlooked it. On the other hand, he knew all the time that the chamber was empty. But the hallucination persisted. He fought it for hours, then threw his rifle open and was confronted with emptiness. The disappointment was as bitter as though he had really expected to find the cartridge.

He plodded on for half an hour, when the hallucination arose again. Again he fought it and still it persisted, till for very relief he opened the rifle to unconvince himself. At times his mind wandered farther afield, and he plodded on, a mere automaton, strange conceits and whimsicalities gnawing at his brain like worms. But these excursions out of the real were of brief duration, for ever the pangs of the hunger-bite called him back. He was jerked back abruptly once from such an excursion by a sight that caused him nearly to faint. He reeled and swayed, doddering like a drunken man to keep from falling. Before him stood a horse. A horse! He could not believe his eyes. A thick mist was in them, intershot with sparkling points of light. He rubbed his eyes savagely to clear his vision, and beheld not a horse but a great brown bear. The animal was studying him with bellicose curiosity.

The man had brought his gun halfway to his shoulder before he realized. He lowered it and drew his hunting-knife from its beaded sheath at his hip. Before him was meat and life. He ran his thumb along the edge of his knife. It was sharp. The point was sharp. He would fling himself upon the bear and kill it. But his heart began its warning thump, thump, thump. Then followed the wild upward leap and tattoo of flutters, the pressing as of an iron band across his forehead, the creeping of the dizziness into his brain.

His desperate courage was evicted by a great surge of fear. In his weakness, what if the animal attacked him! He drew himself up to his most imposing stature, gripping the knife and staring hard at the bear. The bear advanced clumsily a couple of steps, reared up and gave vent to a tentative growl. If the man ran he would run after him; but the man did not run. He was animated now with the courage of fear. He too, growled savagely, terribly, voicing the fear that is to life germane and that lies twisted about life's deepest roots.

The bear edged away to one side, growling menacingly, himself appalled by this mysterious creature that appeared upright and unafraid. But the man did not move. He stood like a statue till the danger was past, when he yielded to a fit of trembling and sank down into the wet moss.

He pulled himself together and went on, afraid now in a new way. It was not the fear that he should die passively from lack of food, but that he should be destroyed violently before starvation had exhausted the last particle of the endeavor in him that made toward surviving. There were the wolves. Back and forth across the desolation drifted their howls, weaving the very air into a fabric of menace that was so tangible that he found himself, arms in the air, pressing it back from him as it might be the walls of a wind-blown tent.

Now and again the wolves in packs of two or three crossed his path. But they sheered clear of him. They were not in sufficient numbers, and besides they were hunting the caribou which did not battle; while this strange creature that walked erect might scratch and bite.

In the late afternoon he came upon scattered bones where the wolves had made a kill. The debris had been a caribou calf an hour before, squawking and running and very much alive. He contemplated the bones, clean-picked and polished, pink with the cell-life in them which had not yet died.

Could it possibly be that he might be that ere the day was done! Such was life, eh? A vain and fleeting thing. It was only life that pained. There was no hurt in death. To die was to sleep. It meant cessation, rest. Then why was he not content to die?

But he did not moralize long. He was squatting in the moss, a bone in his mouth, sucking at the shreds of life that still dyed it faintly pink. The sweet meaty taste, thin and elusive almost as a memory, maddened him. He closed his jaws on the bone and crunched. Sometimes it was the bone that broke, sometimes his teeth. Then he crushed the bones between rocks, pounded them to a pulp and swallowed them. He pounded his fingers, too, in his haste, and yet found a moment in which to feel surprise at the fact that his fingers did not hurt when caught under the descending rock.

Came frightful days of snow and rain. He did not know when he made camp, when he broke camp. He traveled in the night as much as in the day. He rested whenever he fell, crawled on whenever the dying life in him flickered up and burned less dimly. He as a man no longer strove. It was the life in him, unwilling to die, that drove him on. He did not suffer. His nerves had become blunted, numb, while his mind was filled with weird visions and delicious dreams.

But ever he sucked and chewed on the crushed bones of the caribou calf, the least remnants of which he had gathered up and carried with him. He crossed no more hills or divides, but automatically followed a large stream which flowed through a wide and shallow valley. He saw nothing save visions. Soul and body walked or crawled side by side, yet apart, so slender was the thread that bound them.

He awoke in his right mind, lying on his back on a rocky ledge. The sun was shining bright and warm. Afar off he heard the squawking of caribou calves. He was aware of vague memories of rain and wind and snow, but whether he had been beaten by the storm for two days or two weeks he did not know.

For some time he lay without movement, the genial sunshine pouring upon him and saturating his miserable body with warmth. A fine day, he thought. Perhaps he could manage to locate himself. By a painful effort he rolled over on his side. Below him flowed a wide and sluggish river. Its unfamiliarity puzzled him. Slowly he followed it with his eyes, winding in wide sweeps among the bleak bare hills, bleaker and barer and lower-lying than any hills he had yet encountered. Slowly, deliberately, without excitement or more than the most casual interest, he followed the course of the strange stream toward the sky-line and saw it emptying into a bright and shining sea. He was still unexcited. Most unusual, he thought, a vision or a mirage—more likely a vision, a trick of his disordered mind. He was confirmed in this by sight of a ship lying at anchor in the midst of the shining sea. He closed his eyes for a while, then opened them. Strange how the vision persisted! Yet not strange. He knew there were no seas or ships in the heart of the barren lands, just as he had known there was no cartridge in the empty rifle.

He heard a snuffle behind him—a half-choking gasp or cough. Very slowly, because of his exceeding weakness and stiffness, he rolled over on his other side. He could see nothing near at hand, but he waited patiently. Again came the snuffle and cough, and outlined between two jagged rocks not a score of feet away he made out the gray head of a wolf. The sharp ears were not pricked so sharply as he had seen them on other wolves; the eyes were bleared and blood-shot, the head seemed to droop limply and forlornly. The animal blinked continually in the sunshine. It seemed sick. As he looked it snuffled and coughed again.

This, at least, was real, he thought, and turned on the other side so that he might see the reality of the world which had been veiled from him before by the vision. But the sea still shone in the distance and the ship's spars were plainly discernible. Was it reality after all? He closed his eyes for a long while and thought, and then it came to him. He had been making north by east, away from the Dease Divide and into the Coppermine Valley. This wide and sluggish river was the Coppermine. That shining sea was the Arctic Ocean. That ship was a whaler, strayed east, far east, from the mouth of the Mackenzie, and it was lying at anchor at Coronation Gulf. He remembered the Hudson Bay Company chart he had seen long ago, and it was all clear and reasonable to him.

He sat up and turned his attention to immediate affairs. He had worn through the blanket-wrappings, and his feet were like shapeless lumps of raw meat. His last blanket was gone. Rifle and knife were both missing. He had lost his hat somewhere, with the bunch of matches in the band, but the matches against his chest were safe and dry inside the tobacco pouch and oil-paper. He looked at his watch. It marked eleven o'clock and was still running. Evidently he had kept it wound.

He was calm and collected. Though extremely weak he had no sensation of pain. He was not hungry. The thought of food was not even pleasant to him, and whatever he did was done by his reason alone. He ripped off his pant's legs to the knees and bound them about his feet. Somehow he had succeeded in retaining the tin bucket. He would have some hot water before he began what he foresaw was to be a terrible journey to the ship.

His movements were slow. He shook as with a palsy. When he started to collect dry moss he found he could not rise to his feet. He tried again and again, then contented himself with crawling about on hands and knees. Once he crawled near to the sick wolf. The animal dragged itself reluctantly out of his way, licking its chops with a tongue which seemed hardly to have the strength to curl. The man noticed that the tongue was not the customarily healthful red. It was a yellowish brown and seemed coated with a rough and half-dry mucus.

After he had drunk a quart of hot water the man found he was able to stand, and even to walk as well as a dying man might be supposed to walk. Every minute or so he was compelled to rest. His steps were feeble and uncertain, just as the wolf's that trailed him were feeble and uncertain; and that night, when the shining sea was blotted out by blackness, he knew he was nearer to it by no more than four miles.

Throughout the night he heard the cough of the sick wolf, and now and then the squawking of the caribou calves. There was life all around him, but it was strong life, very much alive and well, and he knew the sick wolf clung to the sick man's trail in the hope that the man would die first. In the morning, on opening his eyes, he beheld it regarding him with a wistful and hungry stare. It stood crouched, with tail between its legs, like a miserable and woebegone dog. It shivered in the chill morning wind, and grinned dispiritedly when the man spoke to it in a voice which achieved no more than a hoarse whisper.

The sun rose brightly, and all morning the man tottered and fell toward the ship on the shining sea. The weather was perfect. It was the brief Indian Summer of the high latitudes. It might last a week. To-morrow or next day it might be gone.

In the afternoon the man came upon a trail. It was of another man, who did not walk, but who dragged himself on all fours. The man thought it might be Bill, but he thought it in a dull, uninterested way. He had no curiosity. In fact sensation and emotion had left him. He was no longer susceptible to pain. Stomach and nerves had gone to sleep. Yet the life that was in him drove him on. He was very weary, but it refused to die. It was because it refused to die that he still ate muskeg berries and minnows, drank his hot water, and kept a wary eye on the sick wolf.

He followed the trail of the other man who dragged himself along, and soon came to the end of it—a few fresh-picked bones where the soggy moss was marked by the foot-pads of many wolves. He saw a squat moose-hide sack, mate to his own, which had been torn by sharp teeth. He picked it up, though its weight was almost too much for his feeble fingers. Bill had carried it to the last. Ha! Ha! He would have the laugh on Bill. He would survive and carry it to the ship in the shining sea. His mirth was hoarse and ghastly, like a raven's croak, and the sick wolf joined him, howling lugubriously. The man ceased suddenly. How could he have the laugh on Bill if that were Bill; if those bones, so pinky-white and clean, were Bill!

He turned away. Well, Bill had deserted him; but he would not take the gold, nor would he suck Bill's bones. Bill would have, though, had it been the other way around, he mused as he staggered on.

He came to a pool of water. Stooping over in quest of minnows, he jerked his head back as though he had been stung. He had caught sight of his reflected face. So horrible was it that sensibility awoke long enough to be shocked. There were three minnows in the pool, which was too large to drain; and after several ineffectual attempts to catch them in the tin bucket he forbore. He was afraid, because of his great weakness, that he might fall in and drown. It was for this reason that he did not trust himself to the river astride one of the many drift-logs that lined its sand-pits.

That day he decreased the distance between him and the ship by three miles; the next day by two—for he was crawling now as Bill had crawled; and at the end of the fifth day found the ship still seven miles away and him unable to make even a mile a day. Still the Indian Summer held on, and he continued to crawl and faint, turn and turn about; and ever the sick wolf coughed and wheezed at his heels. His knees had become raw meat like his feet, and though he padded them with the shirt from his back it was a red track he left behind him on the moss and stones. Once glancing back he saw the wolf licking hungrily his bleeding trail, and he saw sharply what his own end might be—unless—unless he could get the wolf. Then began as grim a tragedy of existence as was ever played—a sick man that crawled, a sick wolf that limped, two creatures dragging their dying carcasses across the desolation and hunting each other's lives.

Had it been a well wolf, it would not have mattered so much to the man; but the thought of going to feed the maw of that loathsome and all but dead thing was repugnant to him. He was finicky. His mind had begun to wander again, and to be perplexed by hallucinations, while his lucid intervals grew rarer and shorter.

He was awakened once from a faint by a wheeze close in his ear. The wolf leaped lamely back, losing its footing and falling in its weakness. It was ludicrous, but he was not amused. Nor was he even afraid. He was far too gone for that. But his mind was for the moment clear, and he lay and considered. The ship was no more than four miles away. He could see it quite distinctly when he rubbed the mists out of his eyes, and he could see the white sail of a small boat cutting the water of the shining sea. But he could never crawl those four miles. He knew that, and was very calm in the knowledge. He knew that he could not crawl half a mile. And yet he wanted to live. It was unreasonable that he should die after all he had undergone. Fate asked too much of him. And, dying, he declined to die. It was stark madness, perhaps, but in the very grip of Death he defied Death and refused to die.

He closed his eyes and composed himself with infinite precaution. He steeled himself to keep above the suffocating languor that lapped like a rising tide through all the wells of his being. It was very like a sea, this deadly languor, that rose and rose and drowned his consciousness bit by bit. Sometimes he was all but submerged, swimming through oblivion with a faltering stroke; and again, by some strange alchemy of soul, he would find another shred of will and strike out more strongly.

Without movement he lay on his back, and he could hear slowly drawing near and nearer the wheezing intake and output of the sick wolf's breath. It drew closer, ever closer, through an infinitude of time, and he did not move. It was at his ear. The harsh dry tongue grated like sandpaper against his cheek. His hands shot out—or at least he willed them to shoot out. The fingers were curved like talons, but they closed on empty air. Swiftness and certitude require strength, and the man had not this strength.

The patience of the wolf was terrible. The man's patience was no less terrible. For half a day he lay motionless, fighting off unconsciousness and waiting for the thing that was to feed upon him and upon which he wished to feed. Sometimes the languid sea rose over him and he dreamed long dreams; but ever through it all waking and dreaming, he waited for the wheezing breath and the harsh caress of the tongue.

He did not hear the breath, and he slipped slowly from some dream to the feel of the tongue along his hand. He waited. The fangs pressed softly; the pressure increased; the wolf was exerting its last strength in an effort to sink teeth in the food for which it had waited so long. But the man had waited long, and the lacerated hand closed on the jaw. Slowly, while the wolf struggled feebly and the hand clutched feebly, the other hand crept across to a grip. Five mintues later the whole weight of the man's body was on top of the wolf. The hands had not sufficient strength to choke the animal, but the face of the man was pressed close to the throat of the wolf and the mouth was full of hair. At the end of a half hour the man was aware of a warm trickle in his throat. It was not pleasant. It was like molten lead being forced into his stomach, but it was forced by his will alone. Later the man rolled over on his back and slept.

* * *

There were some members of a scientific expedition on the whaleship *Bedford.* From the deck they remarked a strange object on the shore. It was moving down the beach toward the water. They were unable to classify it, and, being scientific men, they climbed into the whaleboat alongside and went ashore to see it. And they saw something that was alive but that could hardly be called a man. It was blind, unconscious. It squirmed along the ground like some monstrous worm. Most of its efforts were ineffectual, but it was persistent, and it writhed and twisted and went ahead perhaps a score of feet an hour.

Three weeks afterward the man lay in a bunk on the whaleship *Bedford,* and with tears streaming down his wasted cheeks told who he was and what he had undergone. He also babbled incoherently of his mother, of sunny Southern California, and a home among the orange groves and flowers.

The days were not many after that when he sat at table with the scientific men and ship's officers. He gloated over the spectacle of so much food, watching it anxiously as it went into the mouths of others. With the disappearance of each mouthful an expression of deep regret came into his eyes. He was quite sane, yet he hated those men at meal-time because they ate so much food. He was haunted by a fear that it would not last. He inquired of the cook, the cabin boy, the captain, concerning the food stores. They reassured him countless times; but he could not believe them, and pried cunningly about the lazarette to see with his own eyes.

It was noticed that the man was getting fat. He grew stouter with each day. The scientific men shook their heads and theorized. They limited the man at his meals, but still his girth increased and his body swelled prodigiously under his shirt.

The sailors grinned. They knew. And when the scientific men set a watch on the man, they knew too. They saw him slouch for'ard after breakfast, and like a mendicant, with outstretched palm, accost a sailor. The sailor grinned and passed him a fragment of sea biscuit. He clutched it avariciously, looked at it as a miser looks at gold, and thrust it into his shirt bosom. Similar were the donations from other grinning sailors.

The scientific men were discreet. They left him alone. But they privily examined his bunk. It was lined with hardtack; every nook and cranny was filled with hardtack. Yet he was sane. He was taking precautions against another possible famine—that was all. He would recover from it, the scientific men said, and he did, ere the *Bedford's* anchor rumbled down in San Francisco Bay.

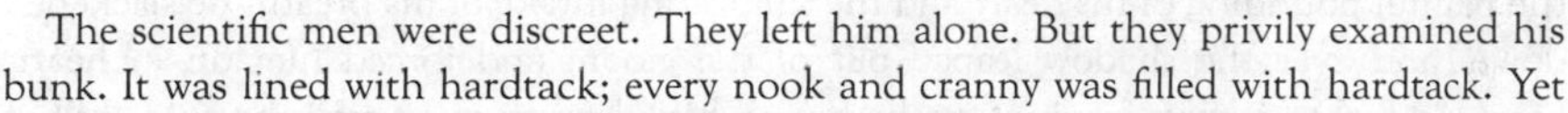

WHICH MAKE MEN REMEMBER

FORTUNE La Pearle crushed his way through the snow, sobbing, straining, cursing his luck, Alaska, Nome, the cards, and the man who had felt his knife. The hot blood was freezing on his hands, and the scene yet bright in his eyes,—the man, clutching the table and sinking slowly to the floor; the rolling counters and the scattered deck; the swift shiver throughout the room, and the pause; the game-keepers no longer calling, and the clatter of the chips dying away; the startled faces; the infinite instant of silence; and then the great blood-roar and the tide of vengeance which lapped his heels and turned the town mad behind him.

"All hell's broke loose," he sneered, turning aside in the darkness and heading for the beach. Lights were flashing from open doors, and tent, cabin, and dance-hall let slip their denizens upon the chase. The clamor of men and howling of dogs smote his ears and quickened his feet. He ran on and on. The sounds grew dim, and the pursuit dissipated itself in vain rage and aimless groping. But a flitting shadow clung to him. Head thrust over shoulder, he caught glimpses of it, now taking vague shape on an open expanse of snow, now merging into the deeper shadows of some darkened cabin or beach-listed craft.

Fortune La Pearle swore like a woman, weakly, with the hint of tears that comes of exhaustion, and plunged deeper into the maze of heaped ice, tents, and prospect holes. He stumbled over taut hawsers and piles of dunnage, tripped on crazy guy-ropes and insanely planted pegs, and fell again and again upon frozen dumps and mounds of hoarded driftwood. At times, when he deemed he had drawn clear, his head dizzy with the painful pounding of his heart and the suffocating intake of his breath, he slackened down; and ever the shadow leaped out of the gloom and forced him on in heart-breaking flight. A swift intuition flashed upon him, leaving in its trail the cold chill of superstition. The persistence of the shadow he invested with his gambler's symbolism. Silent, inexorable, not to be shaken off, he took it as the fate which waited at the last turn when chips were cashed in and gains and losses counted up. Fortune La Pearle believed in those rare, illuminating moments, when the intelligence flung from it time and space, to rise naked through eternity and read the facts of life from the open book of chance. That this was such a moment he had no doubt; and when he turned inland and sped across the snow-covered tundra he was not startled because the shadow took upon it greater definiteness and drew in closer. Oppressed with his own impotence, he halted in the midst of the white waste and whirled about. His right hand slipped from its mitten, and a revolver, at level, glistened in the pale light of the stars.

"Don't shoot. I haven't a gun."

The shadow had assumed tangible shape, and at the sound of its human voice a trepidation affected Fortune La Pearle's knees, and his stomach was stricken with the qualms of sudden relief.

Perhaps things fell out differently because Uri Bram had no gun that night when he sat on the hard benches of the El Dorado and saw murder done. To that fact also might be attributed the trip on the Long Trail which he took subsequently with a most unlikely comrade. But be it as it may, he repeated a second time, "Don't shoot. Can't you see I haven't a gun?"

"Then what the flaming hell did you take after me for?" demanded the gambler, lowering his revolver.

Uri Bram shrugged his shoulders. "It don't matter much, anyhow. I want you to come with me."

"Where?"

"To my shack, over on the edge of the camp."

But Fortune La Pearle drove the heel of his moccasin into the snow and attested by his various deities to the madness of Uri Bram. "Who are you," he perorated, "and what am I, that I should put my neck into the rope at your bidding?"

"I am Uri Bram," the other said simply, "and my shack is over there on the edge of camp. I don't know who you are, but you've thrust the soul from a living man's body,—there's the blood red on your sleeve,—and, like a second Cain, the hand of all mankind is against you, and there is no place you may lay your head. Now, I have a shack—"

"For the love of your mother, hold your say, man," interrupted Fortune La Pearle, "or I'll make you a second Abel for the joy of it. So help me, I will! With a thousand men to lay me by the heels, looking high and low, what do I want with your shack? I want to get out of here—away! away! away! Cursed swine! I've half a mind to go back and run amuck, and settle for a few of them, the pigs! One gorgeous, glorious fight, and end the whole damn business! It's a skin game, that's what life is, and I'm sick of it!"

He stopped, appalled, crushed by his great desolation, and Uri Bram seized the moment. He was not given to speech, this man, and that which followed was the longest in his life, save one long afterward in another place.

"That's why I told you about my shack. I can stow you there so they'll never find you, and I've got grub in plenty. Elsewise you can't get away. No dogs, no nothing, the sea closed, St. Michael the nearest post, runners to carry the news before you, the same over the portage to Anvik—not a chance in the world for you! Now wait with me till it blows over. They'll forget all about you in a month or less, what of stampeding to York and what not, and you can hit the trail under their noses and they won't bother. I've got my own ideas of justice. When I ran after you, out of the El Dorado and along the beach, it wasn't to catch you or give you up. My ideas are my own, and that's not one of them."

He ceased as the murderer drew a prayer-book from his pocket. With the aurora borealis glimmering yellow in the northeast, heads bared to the frost and naked hands grasping the sacred book, Fortune La Pearle swore him to the words he had spoken—an oath which Uri Bram never intended breaking, and never broke.

At the door of the shack the gambler hesitated for an instant, marveling at the strangeness of this man who had befriended him, and doubting. But by the candlelight he found the cabin comfortable and without occupants, and he was quickly rolling a cigarette while the other man made coffee. His muscles relaxed in the warmth and he lay back with half-assumed indolence, intently studying Uri's face through the curling wisps of smoke. It was a powerful face, but its strength was of that peculiar sort which stands girt in and unrelated. The seams were deep-graven, more like scars, while the stern features were in no way softened by hints of sympathy or humor. Under prominent bushy brows the eyes shone cold and gray. The cheekbones, high and forbidding, were undermined by deep hollows. The chin and jaw displayed a steadiness of purpose which the narrow forehead advertised as single, and, if needs be, pitiless. Everything was harsh, the nose, the lips, the voice, the lines about the mouth. It was the face of one who communed much with himself, unused to seeking counsel from the world; the face of one who wrestled oft of nights with angels, and rose to face the day with shut lips that no man might know. He was narrow but deep; and Fortune, his own humanity broad and shallow, could make nothing of him. Did Uri sing when merry and sigh when sad, he could have understood; but as it was, the cryptic features were undecipherable; he could not measure the soul they concealed.

"Lend a hand, Mister Man," Uri ordered when the cups had been emptied. "We've got to fix up for visitors."

Fortune purred his name for the other's benefit, and assisted understandingly. The bunk was built against a side and end of the cabin. It was a rude affair, the bottom being composed of driftwood logs overlaid with moss. At the foot the rough ends of these timbers projected in an uneven row. From the side next the wall Uri ripped back the moss and removed three of the logs. The jagged ends he sawed off and replaced so that the projecting row remained unbroken. Fortune carried in sacks of flour from the cache and piled them on the floor beneath the aperture. On these Uri laid a pair of long sea-bags, and over all spread several thicknesses of moss and blankets. Upon this Fortune could lie, with the sleeping furs stretching over him from one side of the bunk to the other, and all men could look upon it and declare it empty.

In the weeks which followed, several domiciliary visits were paid, not a shack or tent in Nome escaping, but Fortune lay in his cranny undisturbed. In fact, little attention was given to Uri Bram's cabin; for it was the last place under the sun to expect to find the murderer of John Randolph. Except during such interruptions, Fortune lolled about the cabin, playing long games of solitaire and smoking endless cigarettes. Though his volatile nature loved geniality and play of words and laughter, he quickly accommodated himself to Uri's taciturnity. Beyond the actions and plans of his pursuers, the state of the trails, and the price of dogs, they never talked; and these things were only discussed at rare intervals and briefly. But Fortune fell to working out a system, and hour after hour, and day after day, he shuffled and dealt, shuffled and dealt, noted the combinations of the cards in long columns, and shuffled and dealt again. Toward the end even this absorption failed him, and, head bowed upon the table, he visioned the lively all-night houses of Nome, where the gamekeepers and lookouts worked in shifts and the clattering roulette ball never slept. At such times his loneliness and bankruptcy stunned him till he sat for hours in the same unblinking, unchanging position. At other times, his long-pent bitterness found voice in passionate outbursts; for he had rubbed the world the wrong way and did not like the feel of it.

"Life's a skin-game," he was fond of repeating, and on this one note he rang the changes. "I never had half a chance," he complained. "I was faked in my birth and flim-flammed with my mother's mils. The dice were loaded when she tossed the box, and I was born to prove the loss. But that was no reason she should blame me for it, and look on me as a cold deck; but she did—ay, she did. Why didn't she give me a show? Why didn't the world? Why did I go broke in Seattle? Why did I take the steerage, and live like a hog to Nome? Why did I go to the El Dorado? I was heading for Big Pete's and only went for matches. Why didn't I have matches? Why did I want to smoke? Don't you see? All worked out, every bit of it, all parts fitting snug. Before I was born, like as not. I'll put the sack I never hope to get on it, before I was born. That's why! That's why John Randolph passed the word and his checks in at the same time. Damn him! It served him well right! Why didn't he keep his tongue between his teeth and give me a chance! He knew I was next to broke. Why didn't I hold my hand? Oh, why? Why? Why?"

And Fortune La Pearle would roll upon the floor, vainly interrogating the scheme of things. At such outbreaks Uri said no word, gave no sign, save that his gray eyes seemed to turn dull and muddy, as though from lack of interest. There was nothing in common between these two men, and this fact Fortune grasped sufficiently to wonder sometimes why Uri had stood by him.

But the time of waiting came to an end. Even a community's blood lust cannot stand before its gold lust. The murder of John Randolph had already passed into the annals of the camp, and there it rested. Had the murderer appeared, the men of Nome would certainly have stopped stampeding long enough to see justice done, whereas the whereabouts of Fortune La Pearle was no longer an insistent problem. There was gold in the creek beds and ruby beaches, and when the sea opened, the men with healthy sacks would sail away to where the good things of life were sold absurdly cheap.

So, one night, Fortune helped Uri Bram harness the dogs and lash the sled, and the twain took the winter trail south on the ice. But it was not all south; for they left the sea east from St. Michael's, crossed the divide, and struck the Yukon at Anvik, many hundred miles from its mouth. Then on, into the northeast, past Koyokuk, Tanana, and Minook, till they rounded the Great Curve at Fort Yukon, crossed and recrossed the Arctic Circle, and headed south through the Flats. It was a weary journey, and Fortune would have wondered why the man went with him, had not Uri told him that he owned claims and had men working at Eagle. Eagle lay on the edge of the line; a few miles farther on, the British flag waved over the barracks at Fort Cudahy. Then came Dawson, Pelly, the Five Fingers, Windy Arm, Caribou Crossing, Linderman, the Chilcoot and Dyea.

On the morning after passing Eagle, they rose early. This was their last camp, and they were now to part. Fortune's heart was light. There was a promise of spring in the land, and the days were growing longer. The way was passing into Canadian territory. Liberty was at hand, the sun was returning, and each day saw him nearer to the Great Outside. The world was big, and he could once again paint his future in royal red. He whistled about the breakfast and hummed snatches of light song while Uri put the dogs in harness and packed up. But when all was ready, Fortune's feet itching to be off, Uri pulled an unused backlog to the fire and sat down.

"Ever hear of the Dead Horse Trail?"

He glanced up meditatively and Fortune shook his head, inwardly chafing at the delay.

"Sometimes there are meetings under circumstances which make men remember," Uri continued, speaking in a low voice and very slowly, "and I met a man under such circumstances on the Dead Horse Trail. Freighting an outfit over the White Pass in '97 broke many a man's heart, for there was a world of reason when they gave that trail its name. The horses died like mosquitoes in the first frost, and from Skaguay to the Bennett they rotted in heaps. They died at the Rocks, they were poisoned at the Summit, and they starved at the Lakes; they fell off the trail, what there was of it, or they went through it; in the river they drowned under their loads, or were smashed to pieces against the boulders; they snapped their legs in the crevices and broke their backs falling backwards with their packs; in the sloughs they sank from sight or smothered in the slime, and they were disemboweled in the bogs where the corduroy logs turned end up in the mud; men shot them, worked them to death, and when they were gone, went back to the beach and bought more. Some did not bother to shoot them,—

stripping the saddles off and the shoes and leaving them where they fell. Their hearts turned to stone—those which did not break—and they became beasts, the men on Dead Horse Trail.

"It was there I met a man with the heart of a Christ and the patience. And he was honest. When he rested at midday he took the packs from the horses so that they, too, might rest. He paid $50 a hundred-weight for their fodder, and more. He used his own bed to blanket their backs when they rubbed raw. Other men let the saddles eat holes the size of water-buckets. Other men, when the shoes gave out, let them wear their hoofs down to the bleeding stumps. He spent his last dollar for horseshoe nails. I know this because we slept in the one bed and ate from the one pot, and became blood brothers where men lost their grip of things and died blaspheming God. He was never too tired to ease a strap or tighten a cinch, and often there were tears in his eyes when he looked on all that waste of misery. At a passage in the rocks, where the brutes upreared hindlegged and stretched their forelegs upward like cats to clear the wall, the way was piled with carcasses where they had toppled back. And here he stood, in the stench of hell, with a cheery word and a hand on the rump at the right time, till the string passed by. And when one bogged he blocked the trail till it was clear again; nor did the man live who crowded him at such time.

"At the end of the trail a man who had killed fifty horses wanted to buy, but we looked at him and at our own,—mountain cayuses from eastern Oregon. Five thousand he offered, and we were broke, but we remembered the poison grass of the Summit and the passage in the Rocks, and the man who was my brother spoke no word, but divided the cayuses into two bunches,—his in the one and mine in the other,—and he looked at me and we understood each other. So he drove mine to the one side and I drove his to the other, and we took with us our rifles and shot them to the last one, while the man who had killed fifty horses cursed us till his throat cracked. But that man, with whom I welded blood-brothership on the Dead Horse Trail—"

"Why, that man was John Randolph," Fortune, sneering the while, completed the climax for him.

Uri nodded, and said, "I am glad you understand."

"I am ready," Fortune answered, the old weary bitterness strong in his face again. "Go ahead, but hurry."

Uri Bram rose to his feet.

"I have had faith in God all the days of my life. I believe He loves justice. I believe He is looking down upon us now, choosing between us. I believe He waits to work His will through my own right arm. And such is my belief, that we will take equal chance and let Him speak His own judgment."

Fortune's heart leaped at the words. He did not know much concerning Uri's God, but he believed in Chance, and Chance had been coming his way ever since the night he ran down the beach and across the snow. "But there is only one gun," he objected.

"We will fire turn about," Uri replied, at the same time throwing out the cylinder of the other man's Colt and examining it.

"And the cards to decide! One hand of seven up!"

Fortune's blood was warming to the game, and he drew the deck from his pocket as Uri nodded. Surely Chance would not desert him now! He thought of the returning sun as he cut for deal, and he thrilled when he found the deal was his. He shuffled and dealt, and Uri cut him the Jack of Spades. They laid down their hands. Uri's was bare of trumps, while he held ace, deuce. The outside seemed very near to him as they stepped off the fifty paces.

"If God withholds His hand and you drop me, the dogs and outfit are yours. You'll find a bill of sale, already made out, in my pocket," Uri explained, facing the path of the bullet, straight and broad-breasted.

Fortune shook a vision of the sun shining on the ocean from his eyes and took aim. He was very careful. Twice he lowered as the spring breeze shook the pines. But the third time he dropped on one knee, gripped the revolver steadily in both hands, and fired. Uri whirled half about, threw up his arms, swayed wildly for a moment, and sank into the snow. But Fortune knew he had fired too far to one side, else the man would not have whirled.

When Uri, mastering the flesh and struggling to his feet, beckoned for the weapon, Fortune was minded to fire again. But he thrust the idea from him. Chance had been very good to him already, he felt, and if he tricked now he would have to pay for it afterward. No, he would play fair. Besides Uri was hard hit and could not possibly hold the heavy Colt long enough to draw a bead.

"And where is your God now?" he taunted, as he gave the wounded man the revolver.

And Uri answered: "God has not yet spoken. Prepare that He may speak."

Fortune faced him, but twisted his chest sideways in order to present less surface. Uri tottered about drunkenly, but waited, too, for the moment's calm between the cat-spaws. The revolver was very heavy, and he doubted, like Fortune, because of its weight. But he held it, arm extended, above his head, and then let it slowly drop forward and down. At the instant Fortune's left breast and the sight flashed into line with his eye, he pulled the trigger. Fortune did not whirl, but gay San Francisco dimmed and faded, and as the sunbright snow turned black and blacker, he breathed his last malediction on the Chance he had misplayed.

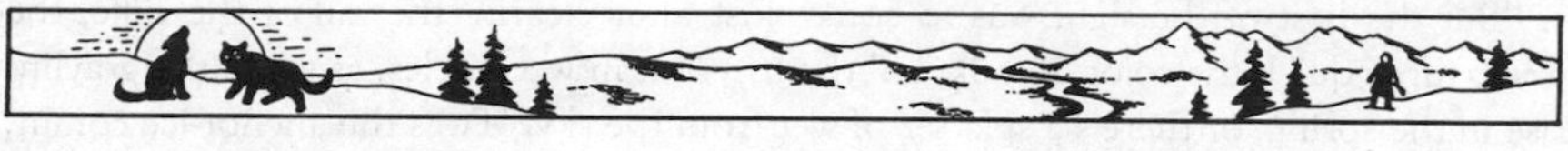

The Men of Forty-Mile

When Big Jim Belden ventured the apparently innocuous proposition that mush-ice was "rather pecooliar," he little dreamed of what it would lead to. Neither did Lon McFane, when he affirmed that anchor-ice was even more so; nor did Bettles, as he instantly disagreed, declaring the very existence of such a form to be a bugaboo.

"An' ye'd be tellin' me this," cried Lon, "after the years ye've spint in the land! An' we atin' out the same pot this many's the day!"

"But the thing's agin reasin," insisted Bettles. "Look you, water's warmer than ice—"

"An' little the difference, once ye break through."

"Still it's warmer, because it ain't froze. An' you say it freezes on the bottom?"

"Only the anchor-ice, David, only the anchor-ice. An' have ye niver drifted along, the water clear as glass, whin suddin, belike a cloud over the sun, the mushy-ice comes bubblin' up an' up, till from bank to bank an' bind to bind it's drapin' the river like a first snowfall?"

"Unh, hunh! more'n once when I took a doze at the steering-oar. But it allus come out the nighest side-channel, an' not bubblin' up an' up."

"But with niver a wink at the helm?"

"No; nor you. It's agin reason. I'll leave it to any man!"

Bettles appealed to the circle about the stove, but the fight was on between himself and Lon McFane.

"Reason or no reason, it's the truth I'm tellin' ye. Last fall, a year gone, 'twas Sitka Charley and meself saw the sight, droppin' down the riffle ye'll remember below Fort Reliance. An' regular fall weather it was—the glint o' the sun on the golden larch an' the quakin' aspens; an' the glister of light on ivery ripple; an' beyand, the winter an' the blue haze of the North comin' down hand in hand. It's well ye know the same, with a fringe to the river an' the ice formin' thick in the eddies—an' a snap an' sparkle to the air, an' ye a-feelin' it through all yer blood, a-takin' new lease of life with ivery suck of it. 'Tis then, me boy, the world grows small an' the wandtherlust lays ye by the heels.

"But it's meself as wandthers. As I was sayin', we a-paddlin', with niver a sign of ice, barrin' that by the eddies, when the Injin lifts his paddle an' sings out, 'Lon McFane! Look ye below! So have I heard, but niver thought to see!' As ye know, Sitka Charley, like meself, niver drew first breath in the land; so the sight was new. Then we drifted, with a head over ayther side, peerin' down through the sparkly water. For the world like the days I spint with the pearlers, watchin' the coral banks a-growin' the same as so many gardens under the sea. There it was, the anchor-ice, clingin' an' clusterin' to ivery rock, after the manner of the white coral.

"But the best of the sight was to come. Just after clearin' the tail of the riffle, the water turns quick the color of milk, an' the top of it in wee circles, as when the graylin' rise in the spring, or there's a splatter of wet from the sky. 'Twas the anchor-ice comin' up. To the right, to the lift, as far as iver a man cud see, the water was covered with the same. An' like so much porridge it was, slickin' along the bark of the canoe, stickin' like glue to the paddles. It's many's the time I shot the self-same riffle before, and it's many's the time after, but niver a wink of the same have I seen. 'Twas the sight of a lifetime."

"Do tell!" dryly commented Bettles. "D'ye think I'd b'lieve such a yarn? I'd ruther say the glister of light'd gone to your eyes, and the snap of the air to your tongue."

" 'Twas me own eyes that beheld it, an' if Sitka Charley was here, he'd be the lad to back me."

"But facts is facts, an' they ain't no gettin' round 'em. It ain't in the nature of things for the water furtherest away from the air to freeze first."

"But me own eyes—"

"Don't git het up over it," admonished Bettles, as the quick Celtic anger began to mount.

"Then yer not after belavin' me?"

"Sence you're so blamed forehanded about it, no; I'd b'lieve nature first, and facts."

"Is it the lie ye'd be givin' me?" threatened Lon. "Ye'd beter be askin' that Siwash wife of yours. I'll lave it to her, for the truth I spake."

Bettles flared up in sudden wrath. The Irishman had unwittingly wounded him; for his wife was the half-breed daughter of a Russian fur-trader, married to him in the Greek Mission of Nulato, a thousand miles or so down the Yukon, thus being of much higher caste than the common Siwash, or native, wife. It was a mere Northland nuance, which none but the Northland adventurer may understand.

"I reckon you kin take it that way," was his deliberate affirmation.

The next instant Lon McFane had stretched him on the floor, the circle was broken up, and half a dozen men had stepped between.

Bettles came to his feet, wiping the blood from his mouth. "It hain't new, this takin' and payin' of blows, and don't you never think but that this will be squared."

"An' niver in me life did I take the lie from mortal man," was the retort courteous. "An' it's an avil day I'll not be to hand, waitin' an' willin' to help ye lift yer debts, barrin' no manner of way."

"Still got that 38-55?"

Lon nodded.

"But you'd better git a more likely caliber. Mine'll rip holes through you the size of walnuts."

"Niver fear; it's me own slugs smell their way with soft noses, an' they'll spread like flapjacks against the coming out beyand. An' when'll I have the pleasure of waitin' on ye? The waterhole's a strikin' locality."

" 'Tain't bad. Jest be there in an hour, and you won't set long on my coming."

Both men mittened and left the Post, their ears closed to the remonstrances of their comrades. It was such a little thing; yet with such men, little things, nourished by quick tempers and stubborn natures, soon blossomed into big things. Besides, the art of burning of bedrock still lay in the womb of the future, and the men of Forty-Mile, shut in by the long Arctic winter, grew high-stomached with overeating and enforced idleness, and became as irritable as do the bees in the fall of the year when the hives are overstocked with honey.

There was no law in the land. The mounted police was also a thing of the future. Each man measured an offense, and meted out the punishment inasmuch as it affected himself. Rarely had combined action been necessary, and never in all the dreary history of the camp had the eighth article of the Decalogue been violated.

Big Jim Belden called an impromptu meeting. Scruff Mackenzie was placed as temporary chairman, and a messenger dispatched to solicit Father Roubeau's good offices. Their position was paradoxical, and they knew it. By the right of might could they interfere to prevent the duel; yet such action, while in direct line with their wishes, went counter to their opinions. While their rough-hewn, obsolete ethics recognized the individual prerogative of wiping out blow with blow, they could not bear to think of two good comrades, such as Bettles and McFane, meeting in deadly battle. Deeming the man who would not fight on provocation a dastard, when brought to the test it seemed wrong that he should fight.

But a scurry of moccasins and loud cries, rounded off with a pistol-shot, interrupted the discussion. Then the storm-doors opened and Malemute Kid entered, a smoking Colt's in his hand, and a merry light in his eye.

"I got him." He replaced the empty shell, and added, "Your dog, Scruff."

"Yellow Fang?" Mackenzie asked.

"No; the lop-eared one."

"The devil! Nothing the matter with him."

"Come out and take a look."

"That's all right after all. Buess he's got 'em, too. Yellow Fang came back this morning and took a chunk out of him, and came near to making a widower of me. Made a rush for Zarinska, but she whisked her skirts in his face and escaped with the loss of the same and a good roll in the snow. Then he took to the woods again. Hope he don't come back. Lost any yourself?"

"One—the best one of the pack—Shookum. Started amuck this morning, but didn't get very far. Ran foul of Sitka Charley's team, and they scattered him all over the street. And now two of them are loose, and raging mad; so you see he got his work in. The dog census will be small in the spring if we don't do something."

"And the man census, too."

"How's that? Who's in trouble now?"

"Oh, Bettles and Lon McFane had an argument, and they'll be down by the waterhole in a few minutes to settle it."

The incident was repeated for his benefit, and Malemute Kid, accustomed to an obedience which his fellow men never failed to render, took charge of the affair. His quickly formulated plan was explained, and they promised to follow his lead implicitly.

"So you see," he concluded, "we do not actually take away their priviledge of fighting; and yet I don't believe they'll fight when they see the beauty of the scheme. Life's a game and men the gamblers. They'll stake their whole pile on the one chance in a thousand. Take away that one chance, and—they won't play."

He turned to the man in charge of the Post. "Storekeeper, weight out three fathoms of your best half-inch manila.

"We'll establish a precedent which will last the men of Forty-Mile to the end of time," he prophesied. Then he coiled the rope about his arm and led his followers out of doors, just in time to meet the principals.

"What danged right'd he to fetch my wife in?" thundered Bettles to the soothing overtures of a friend. " 'Twa'n't called for," he concluded decisively. " 'Twa'n't called for," he reiterated again and again, pacing up and down and waiting for Lon McFane.

And Lon McFane—his face was hot and tongue rapid as he flaunted insurrection in the face of the Church. "Then, father," he cried, "it's with an aisy heart I'll roll in me flamy blankets, the broad of me back on a bed of coals. Niver shall it be said that Lon McFane took a lie 'twixt the teeth without iver liftin' a hand! An' I'll not ask a blessin'. The years have been wild, but it's the heart was in the right place."

"But it's not the heart, Lon," interposed Father Roubeau; "It's pride that bids you forth to slay your fellow man."

"Yer Frinch," Lon replied. And then, turning to leave him, "An' will ye say a mass if the luck is against me?"

But the priest smiled, thrust his moccasined feet to the fore, and went out upon the white breast of the silent river. A packed trail, the width of a sixteen-inch sled, led out to the waterhole. On either side lay the deep, soft snow. The men trod in single file, without conversation; and the black-stoled priest in their midst gave to the function the solemn aspect of a funeral. It was a warm winter's day for Forty-Mile—a day in which the sky, filled with heaviness, drew closer to the earth, and the mercury sought the unwonted level of twenty below. But there was no cheer in the warmth. There was little air in the upper strata, and the clouds hung motionless, giving sullen promise of an early snowfall. And the earth, unresponsive, made no preparation, content in its hibernation.

When the waterhole was reached, Bettles, having evidently reviewed the quarrel during the silent walk, burst out in a final " 'Twa'n't called for," while Lon McFane kept grim silence. Indignation so choked him that he could not speak.

Yet deep down, whenever their own wrongs were not uppermost, both men wondered at their comrades. They had expected opposition, and this tacit acquiescence hurt them. It seemed more was due them from the men they had been so close with, and they felt a vague sense of wrong, rebelling at the thought of so many of their brothers coming out, as on a gala occasion, without one word of protest, to see them shoot each other down. It appeared their worth had diminished in the eyes of the community. The proceedings puzzled them.

"Back to back, David. An' will it be fifty paces to the man, or double the quantity?"

"Fifty," was the sanguinary reply, grunted out, yet sharply cut.

But the new manila, not prominently displayed, but casually coiled about Malemute Kid's arm, caught the quick eye of the Irishman, and thrilled him with a suspicious fear.

"An' what are ye doin' with the rope?"

"Hurry up!" Malemute Kid glanced at his watch. "I've a batch of bread in the cabin, and I don't want it to fall. Besides, my feet are getting cold."

The rest of the men manifested their impatience in various suggestive ways.

"But the rope, Kid? It's bran' new, an' sure yer bread's not that heavy it needs raisin' with the like of that?"

Bettles by this time had faced around. Father Roubeau, the humor of the situation just dawning on him, hid a smile behind his mittened hand.

"No, Lon; this rope was made for a man." Malemute Kid could be very impressive on occasion.

"What man?" Bettles was becoming aware of a personal interest.

"The other man."

"An' which is the one ye'd mane by that?"

"Listen, Lon—and you, too, Bettles! We've been talking this little trouble of yours over, and we've come to one conclusion. We know we have no right to stop your fighting—"

"True for ye, me lad!"

"And we're not going to. But this much we can do, and shall do—make this the only duel in the history of Forty-Mile, set an example for every *che-cha-qua* that comes up or down the Yukon. The man who escapes killing shall be hanged to the nearest tree. Now, go ahead!"

Lon smiled dubiously, then his face lighted up. "Pace her off, David—fifty paces, wheel, an' niver a cease firin' till a lad's down for good. 'Tis their hearts'll niver let them do the deed, an' it's well ye should know it for a true Yankee bluff."

He started off with a pleased grin on his face, but Malemute Kid halted him.

"Lon! It's a long while since you first knew me?"

"Many's the day."

"And you, Bettles?"

"Five year next June high water."

"And have you once, in all that time, known me to break my word? Or heard of me breaking it?"

Both men shook their heads, striving to fathom what lay beyond.

"Well, then, what do you think of a promise made by me?"

"As good as your bond," from Bettles.

"The thing to safely sling yer hopes of heaven by," promptly endorsed Lon McFane.

"Listen! I, Malemute Kid, give you my word—and you know what that means—that the man who is not shot stretches rope within ten minutes after the shooting." He stepped back as Pilate might have done after washing his hands.

A pause and a silence came over the men of Forty-Mile. The sky drew still closer, sending down a crystal flight of frost—little geometric designs, perfect, envanescent as a breath, yet destined to exist till the returning sun had covered half its northern journey. Both men had led forlorn hopes in their time—led, with a curse or a jest on their tongues, and in their souls an unswerving faith in the God of Chance. But that merciful deity had been shut out from the present deal. They studied the face of Malemute Kid, but they studied as one might the Sphinx. As the quiet minutes passed, a feeling that speech was incumbent on them began to grow. At last the howl of a wolf-dog cracked the silence from the direction of Forty-Mile. The weird sound swelled with all the pathos of a breaking heart, then died away in a long-drawn sob.

"Well I be danged!" Bettles turned up the collar of his mackinaw jacket and stared about him helplessly.

"It's a gloryus game yer running', Kid," cried Lon McFane. "All the percentage to the house an' niver a bit to the man that's buckin'. The Devil himself'd niver tackle such a cinch—and damned if I do."

There were chuckles, throttled in gurgling throats, and winks brushed away with the frost which rimed the eyelashes, as the men climbed the ice-notched bank and started across the street to the Post. But the long howl had drawn nearer, invested with a new note of menace. A woman screamed round the corner. There was a cry of, "Here he comes!" Then an Indian boy, at the head of half a dozen frightened dogs, racing with death, dashed into the crowd. And behind came Yellow Fang, a bristle of hair and a flash of gray. Everybody but the Yankee fled. The Indian boy had tripped and fallen. Bettles stopped long enough to grip him by the slack of his furs, then headed for a pile of cordwood already occupied by a number of his comrades. Yellow Fang, doubling after one of the dogs, came leaping back. The fleeing animal, free of the rabies, but crazed with fright, whipped Bettles off his feet and flashed on up the street. Malemute Kid took a flying shot at Yellow Fang. The mad dog whirled a half airspring, came down on his back, then, with a single leap, covered half the distance between himself and Bettles.

But the fatal spring was intercepted. Lon McFane leaped from the woodpile, countering him in midair. Over they rolled, Lon holding him by the throat at arm's length, blinking under the fetid slaver which sprayed his face. Then Bettles, revolver in hand and coolly waiting a chance, settled the combat.

" 'Twas a square game, Kid," Lon remarked, rising to his feet and shaking the snow from out of his sleeves; "with a fair percentage to meself that bucked it."

That night, while Lon McFane sought the forgiving arms of the Church in the direction of Father Roubeau's cabin, Malemute Kid talked long to little purpose.

"But would you," persisted Mackenzie, "supposing they had fought?"

"Have I ever broken my word?"

"No; but that isn't the point. Answer the question. Would you?"

Malemute Kid straightened up. "Scruff, I've been asking myself that question ever since, and—"

"Well?"

"Well, as yet, I haven't found the answer."

At the Rainbow's End

I

It was for two reasons that Montana Kid discarded his "chaps" and Mexican spurs, and shook the dust of the Idaho ranges from his feet. In the first place, the encroachments of a steady, sober, and sternly moral civilization had destroyed the primeval status of the western cattle ranges, and refined society turned the cold eye of disfavor upon him and his ilk. In the second place, in one of its cyclopean moments the race had arisen and shoved back its frontier several thousand miles. Thus, with unconscious foresight, did mature society make room for its adolescent members. True, the new territory was mostly barren; but its several hundred thousand square miles of frigidity at least gave breathing space to those who else would have suffocated at home.

Montana Kid was such a one. Heading for the seacoast, with a haste several sheriff's posses might possibly have explained, and with more nerve than coin of the realm, he succeeded in shipping from a Puget Sound port, and managed to survive the contingent miseries of steerage seasickness and steerage grub. He was rather sallow and drawn, but still his own indomitable self, when he landed on the Dyea beach one day in the spring of the year. Between the cost of dogs, grub, and outfits, and the customs exactions of the two clashing governments, it speedily penetrated to his understanding that the Northland was anything save a poor man's Mecca. So he cast about him in search of quick harvests. Between the beach and the passes were scattered many thousands of passionate pilgrims. These pilgrims Montana Kid proceeded to farm. At first he dealt faro in a pineboard gambling shack; but disagreeable necessity forced him to drop a sudden period into a man's life, and to move on up trail. Then he effected a corner in horseshoe nails, and they circulated at par with legal tender, four to the dollar, till an unexpected consignment of a hundred barrels or so broke the market and forced him to disgorge his stock at a loss. After that he located at Sheep Camp, organized the professional packers, and jumped the freight ten cents a pound in a single day. In token of their gratitude, the packers patronized his faro and roulette layouts and were mulcted cheerfully of their earnings. But his commercialism was of too lusty a growth to be long endured; so they rushed him one night, burned his shanty, divided the bank, and headed him up the trail with empty pockets.

Ill-luck was his running mate. He engaged with responsible parties to run whisky across the line by way of precarious and unknown trails, lost his Indian guides, and had the very first outfit confiscated by the Mounted Police. Numerous other misfortunes tended to make him bitter of heart and wanton of action, and he celebrated his arrival at Lake Bennett by terrorizing the camp for twenty straight hours. Then a miners' meeting took him in hand, and commanded him to make himself scarce. He had a wholesome respect for such assemblages, and he obeyed in such haste that he inadvertently removed himself at the tail-end of another man's dog team. This was equivalent to horse-stealing in a more mellow clime, so he hit only the high places across Bennett and down Tagish, and made his first camp a full hundred miles to the north.

Now it happened that the break of spring was at hand, and many of the principal citizens of Dawson were traveling south on the last ice. These he met and talked with, noted their names and possessions, and passed on. He had a good memory, also a fair imagination; nor was veracity one of his virtues.

II

DAWSON, always eager for news, beheld Montana Kid's sled heading down the Yukon, and went out on the ice to meet him. No, he hadn't any newspapers; didn't know whether Durrant was hanged yet, nor who had won the Thanksgiving game; hadn't heard whether the United States and Spain had gone to fighting; didn't know who Dreyfus was; but O'Brien? Hadn't they heard? O'Brien, why, he was drowned in the White Horse; Sitka Charley the only one of the party who escaped. Joe Ladue? Both legs frozen and amputated at the Five Fingers. And Jack Dalton? Blown up on the "Sea Lion" with all hands. And Bettles? Wrecked on the "Carthagina," in Seymour Narrows,—twenty survivors out of three hundred. And Swiftwater Bill? Gone through the rotten ice of Lake LeBarge with six female members of the opera troupe he was convoying. Governor Walsh? Lost with all hands and eight sleds on the Thirty Mile. Devereaux? Who was Devereaux? Oh, the courier! Shot by Indians on Lake Marsh.

So it went. The word was passed along. Men shouldered in to ask after friends and partners, and in turn were shouldered out, too stunned for blasphemy. By the time Montana Kid gained the bank he was surrounded by several hundred fur-clad miners. When he passed the Barracks he was the center of a procession. At the Opera House he was the nucleus of an excited mob, each member struggling for a chance to ask after some absent comrade. On every side he was being invited to drink. Never before had the Klondike thus opened its arms to a che-cha-qua. All Dawson was humming. Such a series of catastrophes had never occurred in its history. Every man of note who had gone south in the spring had been wiped out. The cabins vomited forth their occupants. Wild-eyed men hurried down from the creeks and gulches to seek out this man who had told a tale of such disaster. The Russian half-breed wife of Bettles sought the fireplace, inconsolable, and rocked back and forth, and ever and anon flung white wood-ashes upon her raven hair. The flag at the Barracks flopped dismally at half-mast. Dawson mourned its dead.

Why Montana Kid did this thing no man may know. Nor beyond the fact that the truth was not in him, can explanation be hazarded. But for five whole days he plunged the land in wailing and sorrow, and for five whole days he was the only man in the Klondike. The country gave him its best of bed and board. The saloons granted him the freedom of their bars. Men sought him continuously. The high officials bowed down to him for further information, and he was feasted at the Barracks by Constantine and his brother officers. And then, one day, Devereaux, the government courier, halted his tired dogs before the gold commissioner's office. Dead! Who said so? Give him a moose streak and he'd show them how dead he was. Why, Governor Walsh was in camp on the Little Salmon, and O'Brien coming in on the first water. Dead? Give him a moose streak and he'd show them.

And forthwith Dawson hummed. The Barracks' flag rose to the masthead, and

Bettle's wife washed herself and put on clean raiment. The community subtly signified its desire that Montana Kid obliterate himself from the landscape. And Montana Kid obliterated; as usual, at the tail-end of someone else's dog team. Dawson rejoiced when he headed down the Yukon, and wished him godspeed to the ultimate destination of the case-hardened sinner. After that the owner of the dogs bestirred himself, made complaint to Constantine, and from him received the loan of a policeman.

III

WITH Circle City in prospect and the last ice crumbling under his runners, Montana Kid took advantage of the lengthening days and traveled his dogs late and early. Further, he had but little doubt that the owner of the dogs in question had taken his trail, and he wished to make American territory before the river broke. But by the afternoon of the third day it became evident that he had lost in his race with spring. The Yukon was growling and straining at its fetters. Long detours became necessary, for the trail had begun to fall through into the swift current beneath, while the ice, in constant unrest, was thundering apart in great gaping fissures. Through these and through countless airholes, the water began to sweep across the surface of the ice, and by the time he pulled into a woodchopper's cabin on the point of an island, the dogs were being rushed off their feet and were swimming more often than not. He was greeted sourly by the two residents, but he unharnessed and proceeded to cook up.

Donald and Davy were fair specimens of frontier inefficients. Canadian-born, city-bred Scots, in a foolish moment they had resigned their counting-house desks, drawn upon their savings, and gone Klondiking. And now they were feeling the rough edge of the country. Grubless, spiritless, with a lust for home in their hearts, they had been staked by the P. C. Company to cut wood for its steamers, with the promise at the end of a passage home. Disregarding the possibilities of the ice-run, they had fittingly demonstrated their inefficiency by their choice of the island on which they located. Montana Kid, though possessing little knowledge of the break-up of a great river, looked about him dubiously, and cast yearning glances at the distant bank where the towering bluffs promised immunity from all the ice of the Northland.

After feeding himself and dogs, he lighted his pipe and strolled out to get a better idea of the situation. The island, like all its river brethren, stood higher at the upper end, and it was here that Donald and Davy had built their cabin and piled many cords of wood. The far shore was a full mile away, while between the island and the near shore lay a back-channel perhaps a hundred yards across. At first sight of this, Montana Kid was tempted to take his dogs and escape to the mainland, but on closer inspection he discovered a rapid current flooding on top. Below, the river twisted sharply to the west, and in this turn its breast was studded by a maze of tiny islands.

"That's where she'll jam," he remarked to himself.

Half a dozen sleds, evidently bound up-stream to Dawson, were splashing through the chill water to the tail of the island. Travel on the river was passing from the precarious to the impossible, and it was nip and tuck with them till they gained the island and came up the path of the wood-choppers toward the cabin. One of them, snow-blind, towed helplessly at the rear of a sled. Husky young fellows they were, rough-garmented and trail-worn, yet Montana Kid had met the breed before and knew at once that it was not his kind.

"Hello! How's things up Dawson-way?" queried the foremost, passing his eye over Donald and Davy and settling it upon the Kid.

A first meeting in the wilderness is not characterized by formality. The talk quickly became general, and the news of the Upper and Lower Countries was swapped equitably back and forth. But the little the new-comers had was soon over with, for they had wintered at Minook, a thousand miles below, where nothing was doing. Montana Kid, however, was fresh from Salt Water, and they annexed him while they pitched camp, swamping him with questions concerning the outside, from which they had been cut off for a twelvemonth.

A shrieking split, suddenly lifting itself above the general uproar on the river, drew everybody to the bank. The surface water had increased in depth, and the ice, assailed from above and below, was struggling to tear itself from the grip of the shores. Fissures reverberated into life before their eyes, and the air was filled with multitudinous crackling, crisp and sharp, like the sound that goes up on a clear day from the firing line.

From up the river two men were racing a dog team toward them on an uncovered stretch of ice. But even as they looked, the pair struck the water and began to flounder through. Behind, where their feet had sped the moment before, the ice broke up and turned turtle. Through this opening the river rushed out upon them to their waists, burying the sled and swinging the dogs off at right angles in a drowning tangle. But the men stopped their flight to give the animals a fighting chance, and they groped hurriedly in the cold confusion, slashing at the detaining traces with their sheath-knives. Then they fought their way to the bank through swirling water and grinding ice, where, foremost in leaping to the rescue among the jarring fragments, was the Kid.

"Why, blime me, if it ain't Montana Kid!" exclaimed one of the men whom the Kid was just placing upon his feet at the top of the bank. He wore the scarlet tunic of the Mounted Police and jocularly raised his right hand in salute.

"Got a warrant for you, Kid," he continued, drawing a bedraggled paper from his breast pocket, "an' I 'ope as you'll come along peaceable."

Montana Kid looked at the chaotic river and shrugged his shoulders, and the policeman, following his glance, smiled.

"Where are the dogs?" his companion asked.

"Gentlemen," interrupted the policeman, "this 'ere mate o' mine is Jack Sutherland, owner of Twenty-Two Eldorado—"

"Not Sutherland of '92?" broke in the snow-blinded Minook man, groping feebly toward him.

"The same." Sutherland gripped his hand.

"And you?"

"Oh, I'm after your time, but I remember you in my freshman year,—you were doing P. G. work then. Boys," he called, turning half about, "this is Sutherland, Jack Sutherland, erstwhile fullback on the 'Varsity. Come up, you gold-chasers, and fall upon him! Sutherland, this is Greenwich,—played quarter two seasons back."

"Yes, I read of the game," Sutherland said, shaking hands. "And I remember that big run of yours for the first touchdown."

Greenwich flushed darkly under his tanned skin and awkwardly made room for another.

"And here's Matthews,—Berkeley man. And we've got some Eastern cracks knocking about, too. Come up, you Princeton men! Come up! This is Sutherland, Jack Sutherland!"

Then they fell upon him heavily, carried him into camp, and supplied him with dry clothes and numerous mugs of black tea.

Donald and Davy, overlooked, had retired to their nightly game of crib. Montana Kid followed them with the policeman.

"Here, get into some dry togs," he said, pulling them from out his scanty kid. "Guess you'll have to bunk with me, too."

"Well, I say, you're a good 'un," the policeman remarked as he pulled on the other man's socks. "Sorry I've got to take you back to Dawson, but I only 'ope they won't be 'ard on you."

"Not so fast." The Kid smiled curiously. "We ain't under way yet. When I go I'm going down river, and I guess the chances are you'll go along."

"Not if I know myself—"

"Come on outside, and I'll show you, then. These damn fools," thrusting a thumb over his shoulder at the two Scots, "played smash when they located here. Fill your pipe, first—this is pretty good plug—and enjoy yourself while you can. You haven't many smokes before you."

The policeman went with him wonderingly, while Donald and Davy dropped their cards and followed. The Minook men noticed Montana Kid pointing now up the river, now down, and came over.

"What's up?" Sutherland demanded.

"Nothing much." Nonchalance sat well upon the Kid. "Just a case of raising hell and putting a chunk under. See that bend down there? That's where she'll jam millions of tons of ice. Then she'll jam in the bends up above, millions of tons. Upper jam breaks first, lower jam holds, pouf!" He dramatically swept the island with his hand. "Millions of tons," he added reflectively.

"And what of the woodpiles?" Davy questioned.

The Kid repeated his sweeping gesture, and Davy wailed, "The labor of months! It canna be! Na, na, lad, it canna be. I doot not it's a jowk. Ay, say that it is," he appealed.

But when the Kid laughed harshly and turned on his heel, Davy flung himself upon the piles and began frantically to toss the cordwood back from the bank.

"Lend a hand, Donald!" he cried. "Can ye no lend a hand? 'Tis the labor of months and the passage home!"

Donald caught him by the arm and shook him, but he tore free. "Did ye no hear, man? Millions of tons, and the island shall be sweepit clean."

"Straighten yersel' up, man," said Donald. "It's a bit fashed ye are."

But Davy fell upon the cordwood. Donald stalked back to the cabin, buckled on his money belt and Davy's, and went out to the point of the island where the ground was highest and where a huge pine towered above its fellows.

The men before the cabin heard the ringing of his axe and smiled. Greenwich returned from across the island with the word that they were penned in. It was impossible to cross the back-channel. The blind Minook man began to sing, and the rest joined in with—

Wonder if it's true?
Does it seem so to you?
Seems to me he's lying—
Oh, I wonder if it's true?

"It's ay sinfu'," Davy moaned, lifting his head and watching them dance in the slanting rays of the sun. "And my guid wood a'going to waste."

Oh, I wonder if it's true,

was flaunted back.

The noise of the river ceased suddenly. A strange calm wrapped about them. The ice had ripped from the shores and was floating higher on the surface of the river, which was rising. Up it came, swift and silent, for twenty feet, till the huge cakes rubbed softly against the crest of the bank. The tail of the island, being lower, was overrun. Then, without effort, the white flood started downstream. But the sound increased with the momentum, and soon the whole island was shaking and quivering with the shock of the grinding bergs. Under pressure, the mighty cakes, weighing hundreds of tons, were shot into the air like peas. The frigid anarchy increased its riot, and the men had to shout into one another's ears to be heard. Occasionally the racket from the back channel could be heard above the tumult. The island shuddered with the impact of an enormous cake which drove in squarely upon its point. It ripped a score of pines out by the roots, then swinging around and over, lifted its muddy base from the bottom of the river and bore down upon the cabin, slicing the bank and trees away like a gigantic knife. It seemed barely to graze the corner of the cabin, but the cribbed logs tilted up like matches, and the structure, like a toy house, fell backward in ruin.

"The labor of months! The labor of months, and the passage home!" Davy wailed, while Montana Kid and the policeman dragged him backward from the woodpiles.

"You'll 'ave plenty o' hoppertunity all in good time for yer passage 'ome," the policeman growled, clouting him alongside the head and sending him flying into safety.

Donald, from the top of the pine, saw the devastating berg sweep away the cordwood and disappear downstream. As though satisfied with this damage, the ice-flood quickly dropped to its old level and began to slacken its pace. The noise likewise eased down, and the others could hear Donald shouting from his eyrie to look downstream. As forecast, the jam had come among the islands in the bend, and the ice was piling up in a great barrier which stretched from shore to shore. The river came to a standstill, and the water finding no outlet began to rise. It rushed up till the island was awash, the men splashing around up to their knees, and the dogs swimming to the ruins of the cabin. At this stage it abruptly became stationary, with no perceptible rise or fall.

Montana Kid shook his head. "It's jammed above, and no more's coming down."

"And the gamble is, which jam will break first," Sutherland added.

"Exactly," the Kid affirmed. "If the upper jam breaks first, we haven't a chance. Nothing will stand before it."

The Minook men turned away in silence, but soon "Rumsky Ho" floated upon the quiet air, followed by "The Orange and the Black." Room was made in the circle for Montana Kid and the policeman, and they quickly caught the ringing rhythm of the choruses as they drifted on from song to song.

"Oh, Donald, will ye no lend a hand?" Davy sobbed at the foot of the tree into which his comrade had climbed. "Oh, Donald, man, will ye no lend a hand?" he sobbed again, his hands bleeding from vain attempts to scale the slippery trunk.

But Donald had fixed his gaze upriver, and now his voice rang out, vibrant with fear:—

"God Almichty, here she comes!"

Standing knee-deep in the icy water, the Minook men, with Montana Kid and the policeman, gripped hands and raised their voices in the terrible "Battle Hymn of the Republic." But the words were drowned in the advancing roar.

And to Donald was vouchsafed a sight such as no man may see and live. A great wall of white flung itself upon the island. Trees, dogs, men, were blotted out, as though the hand of God had wiped the face of nature clean. This much he saw, then swayed an instant longer in his lofty perch and hurtled far out into the frozen hell.

THE CALL OF THE WILD

I

Into the Primitive

"Old longings nomadic leap,
Chafing at custom's chain;
Again from its brumal sleep
Wakens the ferine strain."

Buck did not read the newspapers, or he would have known that trouble was brewing, not alone for himself, but for every tide-water dog, strong of muscle and with warm, long hair, from Puget Sound to San Diego. Because men, groping in the Arctic darkness, had found a yellow metal, and because steamship and transportation companies were booming the find, thousands of men were rushing into the Northland. These men wanted dogs, and the dogs they wanted were heavy dogs, with strong muscles by which to toil, and furry coats to protect them from the frost.

Buck lived at a big house in the sun-kissed Santa Clara Valley. Judge Miller's place, it was called. It stood back from the road, half hidden among the trees, through which glimpses could be caught of the wide cool veranda that ran around its four sides. The house was approached by gravelled driveways which wound about through wide-spreading lawns and under the interlacing boughs of tall poplars. At the rear things were on even a more spacious scale than at the front. There were great stables, where a dozen grooms and boys held forth, rows of vine-clad servants' cottages, an endless and orderly array of outhouses, long grape arbors, green pastures, orchards, and berry patches. Then there was the pumping plant for the artesian well, and the big cement tank where Judge Miller's boys took their morning plunge and kept cool in the hot afternoon.

And over this great demesne Buck ruled. Here he was born, and here he had lived the four years of his life. It was true, there were other dogs. There could not but be other dogs on so vast a place, but they did not count. They came and went, resided in the populous kennels, or lived obscurely in the recesses of the house after the fashion of Toots, the Japanese pug, or Ysabel, the Mexican hairless,—strange creatures that rarely put nose out of doors or set foot to ground. On the other hand, there were the fox terriers, a score of them at least, who yelped fearful promises at Toots and Ysabel looking out of the windows at them and protected by a legion of housemaids armed with brooms and mops.

But Buck was neither house-dog nor kennel-dog. The whole realm was his. He plunged into the swimming tank or went hunting with the Judge's sons; he escorted Mollie and Alice, the Judge's daughters, on long twilight or early morning rambles; on wintry nights he lay at the Judge's feet before the roaring library fire; he carried the Judge's grandsons on his back, or rolled them in the grass, and guarded their footsteps through wild adventures down to the fountain in the stable yard, and even beyond, where the paddocks were, and the berry patches. Among the terriers he stalked imperiously, and Toots and Ysabel he utterly ignored, for he was king,—king over all creeping, crawling, flying things of Judge Miller's place, humans included.

His father, Elmo, a huge St. Bernard, had been the Judge's inseparable companion, and Buck bid fair to follow in the way of his father. He was not so large,—he weighed only one hundred and forty pounds,—for his mother, Shep, had been a Scotch shepherd dog. Nevertheless, one hundred and forty pounds, to which was added the dignity that comes of good living and universal respect, enabled him to carry himself in right royal fashion. During the four years since his puppyhood he had lived the life of a sated aristocrat; he had a fine pride in himself, was even a trifle egotistical, as country gentlemen sometimes become because of their insular situation. But he had saved himself by not becoming a mere pampered house-dog. Hunting and kindred outdoor delights had kept down the fat and hardened his muscles; and to him, as to the cold-tubbing races, the love of water had been a tonic and a health preserver.

And this was the manner of dog Buck was in the fall of 1897, when the Klondike strike dragged men from all the world into the frozen North. But Buck did not read the newspapers, and he did not know that Manuel, one of the gardener's helpers, was an undesirable acquaintance. Manuel had one besetting sin. He loved to play Chinese lottery. Also, in his gambling, he had one besetting weakness—faith in a system; and this made his damnation certain. For to play a system requires money, while the wages of a gardener's helper do not lap over the needs of a wife and numerous progeny.

The Judge was at a meeting of the Raisin Growers' Association, and the boys were busy organizing an athletic club, on the memorable night of Manuel's treachery. No one saw him and Buck go off through the orchard on what Buck imagined was merely a stroll. And with the exception of a solitary man, no one saw them arrive at the little flag station known as College Park. This man talked with Manuel, and money chinked between them.

"You might wrap up the goods before you deliver 'm," the stranger said gruffly, and Manuel doubled a piece of stout rope around Buck's neck under the collar.

"Twist it, an' you'll choke 'm plentee," said Manuel, and the stranger grunted a ready affirmative.

Buck had accepted the rope with quiet dignity. To be sure, it was an unwonted performance: but he had learned to trust in men he knew, and to give them credit for a wisdom that outreached his own. But when the ends of the rope were placed in the stranger's hands, he growled menacingly. He had merely intimated his displeasure, in his pride believing that to intimate was to command. But to his surprise the rope tightened around his neck, shutting off his breath. In quick rage he sprang at the man, who met him halfway, grappled him close by the throat, and with a deft twist threw him over on his back. Then the rope tightened mercilessly, while Buck struggled in a fury, his tongue lolling out of his mouth and his great chest panting futilely. Never in all his life had he been so vilely treated, and never in all his life had he been so angry. But his strength ebbed, his eyes glazed, and he knew nothing when the train was flagged and the two men threw him into the baggage car.

The next he knew, he was dimly aware that his tongue was hurting and that he was being jolted along in some kind of a conveyance. The hoarse shriek of a locomotive whistling a crossing told him where he was. He had travelled too often with the Judge not to know the sensation of riding in a baggage car. He opened his eyes, and into them came the unbridled anger of a kidnapped king. The man sprang for his throat, but Buck was too quick for him. His jaws closed on the hand, nor did they relax till his senses were choked out of him once more.

"Yep, has fits," the man said, hiding his mangled hand from the baggageman, who had been attracted by the sounds of struggle. "I'm takin' 'm up for the boss to 'Frisco. A crack dog-doctor there thinks that he can cure 'm."

Concerning that night's ride, the man spoke most eloquently for himself, in a little shed back of a saloon on the San Francisco water front.

"All I get is fifty for it," he grumbled; "an' I wouldn't do it over for a thousand, cold cash."

His hand was wrapped in a bloody handkerchief, and the right trouser leg was ripped from knee to ankle.

"How much did the other mug get?" the saloon-keeper demanded.

"A hundred," was the reply. "Wouldn't take a sou less, so help me."

"That makes a hundred and fifty," the saloon-keeper calculated; "and he's worth it, or I'm a squarehead."

The kidnapper undid the bloody wrappings and looked at his lacerated hand. "If I don't get the hydrophoby—"

"It'll be because you was born to hang," laughed the saloon-keeper. "Here, lend me a hand before you pull your freight," he added.

Dazed, suffering intolerable pain from throat and tongue, with the life half throttled out of him, Buck attempted to face his tormentors. But he was thrown down and choked repeatedly, till they succeeded in filing the heavy brass collar from off his neck. Then the rope was removed, and he was flung into a cagelike crate.

There he lay for the remainder of the weary night, nursing his wrath and wounded pride. He could not understand what it all meant. What did they want with him, these strange men? Why were they keeping him pent up in this narrow crate? He did not know why, but he felt oppressed by the vague sense of impending calamity. Several times during the night he sprang to his feet when the shed door rattled open, expecting to see the Judge, or the boys at least. But each time it was the bulging face of the saloon-keeper that peered in at him by the sickly light of a tallow candle. And each time the joyful bark that trembled in Buck's throat was twisted into a savage growl.

But the saloon-keeper let him alone, and in the morning four men entered and picked up the crate. More tormentors, Buck decided, for they were evil-looking creatures, ragged and unkempt; and he stormed and raged at them through the bars. They only laughed and poked sticks at him, which he promptly assailed with his teeth till he realized that that was what they wanted. Whereupon he lay down sullenly and allowed the crate to be lifted into a wagon. Then he, and the crate in which he was imprisoned, began a passage through many hands. Clerks in the express office took charge of him; he was carted about in another wagon; a truck carried him, with an assortment of boxes and parcels, upon a ferry steamer; he was trucked off the steamer into a great railway depot, and finally he was deposited in an express car.

For two days and nights this express car was dragged along at the tail of shrieking locomotives; and for two days and nights Buck neither ate nor drank. In his anger he had met the first advances of the express messengers with growls, and they had retaliated by teasing him. When he flung himself against the bars, quivering and frothing, they laughed at him and taunted him. They growled and barked like detestable dogs, mewed, and flapped their arms and crowed. It was all very silly, he knew; but therefore the more outrage to his dignity, and his anger waxed and waxed. He did not mind the hunger so much, but the lack of water caused him severe suffering and fanned his wrath to fever-pitch. For that matter, high-strung and finely sensitive, the ill treatment had flung him into a fever, which was fed by the inflammation of his parched and swollen throat and tongue.

He was glad for one thing: the rope was off his neck. That had given them an unfair advantage; but now that it was off, he would show them. They would never get another rope around his neck. Upon that he was resolved. For two days and nights he neither ate nor drank, and during those days and nights of torment, he accumulated a fund of wrath that boded ill for whoever first fell foul of him. His eyes turned blood-shot, and he was metamorphosed into a raging fiend. So changed was he that the Judge himself would not have recognized him; and the express messengers breathed with relief when they bundled him off the train at Seattle.

Four men gingerly carried the crate from the wagon into a small, high-walled back yard. A stout man, with a red sweater that sagged generously at the neck, came out and signed the book for the driver. That was the man, Buck divined, the next tormentor, and he hurled himself savagely against the bars. The man smiled grimly, and brought a hatchet and a club.

"You ain't going to take him out now?" the driver asked.

"Sure," the man replied, driving the hatchet into the crate for a pry.

There was an instantaneous scattering of the four men who had carried it in, and from safe perches on top the wall they prepared to watch the performance.

Buck rushed at the splintering wood, sinking his teeth into it, surging and wrestling with it. Wherever the hatchet fell on the outside, he was there on the inside, snarling and growling, as furiously anxious to get out as the man in the red sweater was calmly intent on getting him out.

"Now, you red-eyed devil," he said, when he had made an opening sufficient for the passage of Buck's body. At the same time he dropped the hatchet and shifted the club to his right hand.

And Buck was truly a red-eyed devil, as he drew himself together for the spring, hair bristling, mouth foaming, a mad glitter in his blood-shot eyes. Straight at the man he launched his one hundred and forty pounds of fury, surcharged with the pent passion of two days and nights. In mid air, just as his jaws were about to close on the man, he received a shock that checked his body and brought his teeth together with an agonizing clip. He whirled over, fetching the ground on his back and side. He had never been struck by a club in his life, and did not understand. With a snarl that was part bark and more scream he was again on his feet and launched into the air. And again the shock came and he was brought crushingly to the ground. This time he was aware that it was the club, but his madness knew no caution. A dozen times he charged, and as often the club broke the charge and smashed him down.

After a particularly fierce blow, he crawled to his feet, too dazed to rush. He staggered limply about, the blood flowing from nose and mouth and ears, his beautiful coat sprayed and flecked with bloody slaver. Then the man advanced and deliberately dealt him a frightful blow on the nose. All the pain he had endured was as nothing compared with the exquisite agony of this. With a roar that was almost lionlike in its ferocity, he again hurled himself at the man. But the man, shifting the club from right to left, coolly caught him by the under jaw, at the same time wrenching downward and backward. Buck described a complete circle in the air, and half of another, then crashed to the ground on his head and chest.

For the last time he rushed. The man struck the shrewd blow he had purposely withheld for so long, and Buck crumpled up and went down, knocked utterly senseless.

"He's no slouch at dog-breakin', that's wot I say," one of the men on the wall cried enthusiastically.

"Druther break cayuses any day, and twice on Sundays," was the reply of the driver, as he climbed on the wagon and started the horses.

Buck's senses came back to him, but not his strength. He lay where he had fallen, and from there he watched the man in the red sweater.

" 'Answers to the name of Buck,' " the man soliloquized, quoting from the saloon-keeper's letter which had announced the consignment of the crate and contents. "Well, Buck, my boy," he went on in a genial voice, "we've had our little ruction, and the best thing we can do is to let it go at that. You've learned your place, and I know mine. Be a good dog and all 'll go well and the goose hang high. Be a bad dog, and I'll whale the stuffin' outa you. Understand?"

As he spoke he fearlessly patted the head he had so mercilessly pounded, and though Buck's hair involuntarily bristled at the touch of the hand, he endured it without protest. When the man brought him water he drank eagerly, and later bolted a generous meal of raw meat, chunk by chunk, from the man's hand.

He was beaten (he knew that); but he was not broken. He saw, once for all, that he stood no chance against a man with a club. He had learned the lesson, and in all his after life he never forgot it. That club was a revelation. It was his introduction to the reign of primitive law, and he met the introduction halfway. The facts of life took on a fiercer aspect; and while he faced that aspect uncowed, he faced it with all the latent cunning of his nature aroused. As the days went by, other dogs came, in crates and at the ends of ropes, some docilely, and some raging and roaring as he had come; and, one and all, he watched them pass under the dominion of the man in the red sweater. Again and again, as he looked at each brutal performance, the lesson was driven home to Buck: a man with a club was a lawgiver, a master to be obeyed, though not necessarily conciliated. Of this last Buck was never guilty, though he did see beaten dogs that fawned upon the man, and wagged their tails, and licked his hand. Also he saw one dog, that would neither conciliate nor obey, finally killed in the struggle for mastery.

Now and again men came, strangers, who talked excitedly, wheedlingly, and in all kinds of fashions to the man in the red sweater. And at such times that money passed between them the strangers took one or more of the dogs away with them. Buck wondered where they went, for they never came back; but the fear of the future was strong upon him, and he was glad each time when he was not selected.

Yet his time came, in the end, in the form of a little weazened man who spat broken English and many strange and uncouth exclamations which Buck could not understand.

"Sacredam!" he cried, when his eyes lit upon Buck. "Dat one dam bully dog! Eh? How moch?"

"Three hundred, and a present at that," was the prompt reply of the man in the red sweater. "And seein' it's government money, you ain't got no kick coming, eh, Perrault?"

Perrault grinned. Considering that the price of dogs had been boomed skyward by the unwonted demand, it was not an unfair sum for so fine an animal. The Canadian Government would be no loser, nor would its despatches travel the slower. Perrault knew dogs, and when he looked at Buck he knew that he was one in a thousand—"One in ten t'ousand," he commented mentally.

Buck saw money pass between them, and was not surprised when Curly, a good-natured Newfoundland, and he were led away by the little weazened man. That was the last he saw of the man in the red sweater, and as Curly and he looked at receding Seattle from the deck of the *Narwhal*, it was the last he saw of the warm Southland. Curly and he were taken below by Perrault and turned over to a black-faced giant called François. Perrault was a French-Canadian, and swarthy; but François was a French-Canadian half-breed, and twice as swarthy. They were a new kind of men to Buck (of which he was destined to see many more), and while he developed no affection for them, he none the less grew honestly to respect them. He speedily learned that Perrault and François were fair men, calm and impartial in administering justice, and too wise in the way of dogs to be fooled by dogs.

In the 'tween-decks of the *Narwhal*, Buck and Curly joined two other dogs. One of them was a big, snow-white fellow from Spitzbergen who had been brought away by a whaling captain, and who had later accompanied a Geological Survey into the Barrens. He was friendly, in a treacherous sort of way, smiling into one's face the while he meditated some underhand trick, as, for instance, when he stole from Buck's food at the first meal. As Buck sprang to punish him, the lash of François's whip sang through the air, reaching the culprit first; and nothing remained to Buck but to recover the bone. That was fair of François, he decided, and the half-breed began his rise in Buck's estimation.

The other dog made no advances, nor received any; also, he did not attempt to steal from the newcomers. He was a gloomy, morose fellow, and he showed Curly plainly that all he desired was to be left alone, and further, that there would be trouble if he were not left alone. "Dave" he was called, and he ate and slept, or yawned between times, and took interest in nothing, not even when the *Narwhal* crossed Queen Charlotte Sound and rolled and pitched and bucked like a thing possessed. When Buck and Curly grew excited, half wild with fear, he raised his head as though annoyed, favored them with an incurious glance, yawned, and went to sleep again.

Day and night the ship throbbed to the tireless pulse of the propeller, and though one day was very like another, it was apparent to Buck that the weather was steadily growing colder. At last, one morning, the propeller was quiet, and the *Narwhal* was pervaded with an atmosphere of excitement. He felt it, as did the other dogs, and knew that a change was at hand. François leashed them and brought them on deck. At the first step upon the cold surface, Buck's feet sank into a white mushy something very like mud. He sprang back with a snort. More of this white stuff was falling through the air. He shook himself, but more of it fell upon him. He sniffed it curiously, then licked some up on his tongue. It bit like fire, and the next instant was gone. This puzzled him. He tried it again, with the same result. The onlookers laughed uproariously, and he felt ashamed, he knew not why, for it was his first snow.

II

The Law of Club and Fang

BUCK'S first day on the Dyea beach was like a nightmare. Every hour was filled with shock and surprise. He had been suddenly jerked from the heart of civilization and flung into the heart of things primordial. No lazy, sun-kissed life was this, with nothing to do but loaf and be bored. Here was neither peace, nor rest, nor a moment's safety. All was confusion and action, and every moment life and limb were in peril. There was imperative need to be constantly alert; for these dogs and men were not town dogs and men. They were savages, all of them, who knew no law but the law of club and fang.

He had never seen dogs fight as these wolfish creatures fought, and his first experience taught him an unforgetable lesson. It is true, it was a vicarious experience, else he would not have lived to profit by it. Curly was the victim. They were camped near the log store, where she, in her friendly way, made advances to a husky dog the size of a full-grown wolf, though not half so large as she. There was no warning, only a leap in like a flash, a metallic clip of teeth, a leap out equally swift, and Curly's face was ripped open from eye to jaw.

It was the wolf manner of fighting, to strike and leap away; but there was more to it than this. Thirty or forty huskies ran to the spot and surrounded the combatants in an intent and silent circle. Buck did not comprehend that silent intentness, nor the eager way with which they were licking their chops. Curly rushed her antagonist, who struck again and leaped aside. He met her next rush with his chest, in a peculiar fashion that tumbled her off her feet. She never regained them. This was what the on-looking huskies had waited for. They closed in upon her, snarling and yelping, and she was buried, screaming with agony, beneath the bristling mass of bodies.

So sudden was it, and so unexpected, that Buck was taken aback. He saw Spitz run out his scarlet tongue in a way he had of laughing; and he saw François, swinging an axe, spring into the mess of dogs. Three men with clubs were helping him to scatter them. It did not take long. Two minutes from the time Curly went down, the last of her assailants were clubbed off. But she lay there limp and lifeless in the bloody, trampled snow, almost literally torn to pieces, the swart half-breed standing over her and cursing horribly. The scene often came back to Buck to trouble him in his sleep. So that was the way. No fair play. Once down, that was the end of you. Well, he would see to it that he never went down. Spitz ran out his tongue and laughed again, and from that moment Buck hated him with a bitter and deathless hatred.

Before he had recovered from the shock caused by the tragic passing of Curly, he received another shock. François fastened upon him an arrangement of straps and buckles. It was a harness, such as he had seen the grooms put on the horses at home. And as he had seen horses work, so he was set to work, hauling François on a sled to the forest that fringed the valley, and returning with a load of firewood. Though his dignity was sorely hurt by thus being made a draught animal, he was too wise to rebel. He buckled down with a will and did his best, though it was all new and strange. François was stern, demanding instant obedience, and by virtue of his whip receiving instant obedience; while Dave, who was an experienced wheeler, nipped Buck's hind quarters whenever he was in error. Spitz was the leader, likewise experienced, and while he could not always get at Buck, he growled sharp reproof now and again, or cunningly threw his weight in the traces to jerk Buck into the way he should go. Buck learned easily, and under the combined tuition of his two mates and François made remarkable progress. Ere they returned to camp he knew enough to stop at "ho," to go ahead at "mush," to swing wide on the bends, and to keep clear of the wheeler when the loaded sled shot downhill at their heels.

"T'ree vair' good dogs," François told Perrault. "Dat Buck, heem pool lak hell. I tich heem queek as anyt'ing."

By afternoon, Perrault, who was in a hurry to be on the trail with his despatches, returned with two more dogs. "Billee" and "Joe" he called them, two brothers, and true huskies both. Sons of the one mother though they were, they were as different as day and night. Billee's one fault was his excessive good nature, while Joe was the very opposite, sour and introspective, with a perpetual snarl and a malignant eye. Buck received them in comradely fashion, Dave ignored them, while Spitz proceeded to thrash first one and then the other. Billee wagged his tail appeasingly, turned to run when he saw that appeasement was of no avail, and cried (still appeasingly) when Spitz's sharp teeth scored his flank. But no matter how Spitz circled, Joe whirled around on his heels to face him, mane bristling, ears laid back, lips writhing and snarling, jaws clipping together as fast as he could snap, and eyes diabolically gleaming —the incarnation of belligerent fear. So terrible was his appearance that Spitz was forced to forego disciplining him; but to cover his own discomfiture he turned upon the inoffensive and wailing Billee and drove him to the confines of the camp.

By evening Perrault secured another dog, an old husky, long and lean and gaunt, with a battle-scarred face and a single eye which flashed a warning of prowess that commanded respect. He was called Sol-leks, which means the Angry One. Like Dave, he asked nothing, gave nothing, expected nothing; and when he marched slowly and deliberately into their midst, even Spitz left him alone. He had one peculiarity which Buck was unlucky enough to discover. He did not like to be approached on his blind side. Of this offence Buck was unwittingly guilty, and the first knowledge he had of his indiscretion was when Sol-leks whirled upon him and slashed his shoulder to the bone for three inches up and down. Forever after Buck avoided his blind side, and to the last of their comradeship had no more trouble. His only apparent ambition, like Dave's, was to be left alone; though, as Buck was afterward to learn, each of them possessed one other and even more vital ambition.

That night Buck faced the great problem of sleeping. The tent, illumined by a candle, glowed warmly in the midst of the white plain; and when he, as a matter of course, entered it, both Perrault and François bombarded him with curses and cooking utensils, till he recovered from his consternation and fled ignominiously into the outer cold. A chill wind was blowing that nipped him sharply and bit with especial venom into his wounded shoulder. He lay down on the snow and attempted to sleep, but the frost soon drove him shivering to his feet. Miserable and disconsolate, he wandered about among the many tents, only to find that one place was as cold as another. Here and there savage dogs rushed upon him, but he bristled his neck-hair and snarled (for he was learning fast), and they let him go his way unmolested.

Finally an idea came to him. He would return and see how his own team-mates were making out. To his astonishment, they had disappeared. Again he wandered about through the great camp, looking for them, and again he returned. Were they in the tent? No, that could not be, else he would not have been driven out. Then where could they possibly be? With drooping tail and shivering body, very forlorn indeed, he aimlessly circled the tent. Suddenly the snow gave way beneath his fore legs and he sank down. Something wriggled under his feet. He sprang back, bristling and snarling, fearful of the unseen and unknown. But a friendly little yelp reassured him, and he went back to investigate. A whiff of warm air ascended to his nostrils, and there, curled up under the snow in a snug ball, lay Billee. He whined placatingly, squirmed and wriggled to show his good will and intentions, and even ventured, as a bribe for peace, to lick Buck's face with his warm wet tongue.

Another lesson. So that was the way they did it, eh? Buck confidently selected a spot, and with much fuss and waste effort proceeded to dig a hole for himself. In a trice the heat from his body filled the confined space and he was asleep. The day had been long and arduous, and he slept soundly and comfortably, though he growled and barked and wrestled with bad dreams.

Nor did he open his eyes till roused by the noises of the waking camp. At first he did not know where he was. It had snowed during the night and he was completely buried. The snow walls pressed him on every side, and a great surge of fear swept through him —the fear of the wild thing for the trap. It was a token that he was harking back through his own life to the lives of his forebears; for he was a civilized dog, an unduly civilized dog, and of his own experience knew no trap and so could not of himself fear it. The muscles of his whole body contracted spasmodically and instinctively, the hair on his neck and shoulders stood on end, and with a ferocious snarl he bounded straight up into the blinding day, the snow flying about him in a flashing cloud. Ere he landed on his feet, he saw the white camp spread out before him and knew where he was and remembered all that had passed from the time he went for a stroll with Manuel to the hole he had dug for himself the night before.

A shout from François hailed his appearance. "Wot I say?" the dog-driver cried to Perrault. "Dat Buck for sure learn queek as anyt'ing."

Perrault nodded gravely. As courier for the Canadian Government, bearing important despatches, he was anxious to secure the best dogs, and he was particularly gladdened by the possession of Buck.

Three more huskies were added to the team inside an hour, making a total of nine, and before another quarter of an hour had passed they were in harness and swinging up the trail toward the Dyea Cañon. Buck was glad to be gone, and though the work was hard he found he did not particularly despise it. He was surprised at the eagerness which animated the whole team and which was communicated to him; but still more surprising was the change wrought in Dave and Sol-leks. They were new dogs, utterly transformed by the harness. All passiveness and unconcern had dropped from them. They were alert and active, anxious that the work should go well, and fiercely irritable with whatever, by delay or confusion, retarded that work. The toil of the traces seemed the supreme expression of their being, and all that they lived for and the only thing in which they took delight.

Dave was wheeler or sled dog, pulling in front of him was Buck, then came Sol-leks; the rest of the team was strung out ahead, single file, to the leader, which position was filled by Spitz.

Buck had been purposely placed between Dave and Sol-leks so that he might receive instruction. Apt scholar that he was, they were equally apt teachers, never allowing him to linger long in error, and enforcing their teaching with their sharp teeth. Dave was fair and very wise. He never nipped Buck without cause, and he never failed to nip him when he stood in need of it. As François's whip backed him up, Buck found it to be cheaper to mend his ways than to retaliate. Once, during a brief halt, when he got tangled in the traces and delayed the start, both Dave and Sol-leks flew at him and administered a sound trouncing. The resulting tangle was even worse, but Buck took good care to keep the traces clear thereafter; and ere the day was done, so well had he mastered his work, his mates about ceased nagging him. François's whip snapped less frequently, and Perrault even honored Buck by lifting up his feet and carefully examining them.

It was a hard day's run, up the Cañon, through Sheep Camp, past the Scales and the timber line, across glaciers and snow-drifts hundreds of feet deep, and over the great Chilcoot Divide, which stands between the salt water and the fresh and guards forbiddingly the sad and lonely North. They made good time down the chain of lakes which fills the craters of extinct volcanoes, and late that night pulled into the huge camp at the head of Lake Bennett, where thousands of gold-seekers were building boats against the break-up of the ice in the spring. Buck made his hole in the snow and slept the sleep of the exhausted just, but all too early was routed out in the cold darkness and harnessed with his mates to the sled.

That day they made forty miles, the trail being packed; but the next day, and for many days to follow, they broke their own trail, worked harder, and made poorer time. As a rule, Perrault travelled ahead of the team, packing the snow with webbed shoes to make it easier for them. François, guiding the sled at the gee-pole, sometimes exchanged places with him, but not often. Perrault was in a hurry, and he prided himself on his knowledge of ice, which knowledge was indispensable, for the fall ice was very thin, and where there was swift water, there was no ice at all.

Day after day, for days unending, Buck toiled in the traces. Always, they broke camp in the dark, and the first gray of dawn found them hitting the trail with fresh miles reeled off behind them. And always they pitched camp after dark, eating their bit of fish, and crawling to sleep into the snow. Buck was ravenous. The pound and a half of sun-dried salmon, which was his ration for each day, seemed to go nowhere. He never had enough, and suffered from perpetual hunger pangs. Yet the other dogs, because they weighed less and were born to the life, received a pound only of the fish and managed to keep in good condition.

He swiftly lost the fastidiousness which had characterized his old life. A dainty eater, he found that his mates, finishing first, robbed him of his unfinished ration. There was no defending it. While he was fighting off two or three, it was disappearing down the throats of the others. To remedy this, he ate as fast as they; and, so greatly did hunger compel him, he was not above taking what did not belong to him. He watched and learned. When he saw Pike, one of the new dogs, a clever malingerer and thief, slyly steal a slice of bacon when Perrault's back was turned, he duplicated the performance the following day, getting away with the whole chunk. A great uproar was raised, but he was unsuspected; while Dub, an awkward blunderer who was always getting caught, was punished for Buck's misdeed.

This first theft marked Buck as fit to survive in the hostile Northland environment. It marked his adaptability, his capacity to adjust himself to changing conditions, the lack of which would have meant swift and terrible death. It marked, further, the decay or going to pieces of his moral nature, a vain thing and a handicap in the ruthless struggle for existence. It was all well enough in the Southland, under the law of love and fellowship, to respect private property and personal feelings; but in the Northland, under the law of club and fang, whoso took such things into account was a fool, and in so far as he observed them he would fail to prosper.

Not that Buck reasoned it out. He was fit, that was all, and unconsciously he accommodated himself to the new mode of life. All his days, no matter what the odds, he had never run from a fight. But the club of the man in the red sweater had beaten into him a more fundamental and primitive code. Civilized, he could have died for a moral consideration, say the defence of Judge Miller's riding-whip; but the completeness of his decivilization was now evidenced by his ability to flee from the defence of a moral consideration and so save his hide. He did not steal for joy of it, but because of the clamor of his stomach. He did not rob openly, but stole secretly and cunningly, out of respect for club and fang. In short, the things he did were done because it was easier to do them than not to do them.

His development (or retrogression) was rapid. His muscles became hard as iron, and he grew callous to all ordinary pain. He achieved an internal as well as external economy. He could eat anything, no matter how loathsome or indigestible; and, once eaten, the juices of his stomach extracted the last least particle of nutriment; and his blood carried it to the farthest reaches of his body, building it into the toughest and stoutest of tissues. Sight and scent became remarkably keen, while his hearing developed such acuteness that in his sleep he heard the faintest sound and knew whether it heralded peace or peril. He learned to bite the ice out with his teeth when it collected between his toes; and when he was thirsty and there was a thick scum of ice over the water hole, he would break it by rearing and striking it with stiff fore legs. His most conspicuous trait was an ability to scent the wind and forecast it a night in advance. No matter how breathless the air when he dug his nest by a tree or bank, the wind that later blew inevitably found him to leeward, sheltered and snug.

And not only did he learn by experience, but instincts long dead became alive again. The domesticated generations fell from him. In vague ways he remembered back to the youth of the breed, to the time the wild dogs ranged in packs through the primeval forest and killed their meat as they ran it down. It was no task for him to learn to fight with cut and slash and the quick wolf snap. In this manner had fought forgotten ancestors. They quickened the old life within him, and the old tricks which they had stamped into the heredity of the breed were his tricks. They came to him without effort or discovery, as though they had been his always. And when, on the still cold nights, he pointed his nose at a star and howled long and wolflike, it was his ancestors, dead and dust, pointing nose at star and howling down through the centuries and through him. And his cadences were their cadences, the cadences which voiced their woe and what to them was the meaning of the stillness, and the cold, and dark.

Thus, as token of what a puppet thing life is, the ancient song surged through him and he came into his own again; and he came because men had found a yellow metal in the North, and because Manuel was a gardener's helper whose wages did not lap over the needs of his wife and divers small copies of himself.

III

The Dominant Primordial Beast

THE dominant primordial beast was strong in Buck, and under the fierce conditions of trail life it grew and grew. Yet it was a secret growth. His new-born cunning gave him poise and control. He was too busy adjusting himself to the new life to feel at ease, and not only did he not pick fights, but he avoided them whenever possible. A certain deliberateness characterized his attitude. He was not prone to rashness and precipitate action; and in the bitter hatred between him and Spitz he betrayed no impatience, shunned all offensive acts.

On the other hand, possibly because he divined in Buck a dangerous rival, Spitz never lost an opportunity of showing his teeth. He even went out of his way to bully Buck, striving constantly to start the fight which could end only in the death of one or the other. Early in the trip this might have taken place had it not been for an unwonted accident. At the end of this day they made a bleak and miserable camp on the shore of Lake Le Barge. Driving snow, a wind that cut like a white-hot knife, and darkness had forced them to grope for a camping place. They could hardly have fared worse. At their backs rose a perpendicular wall of rock, and Perrault and François were compelled to make their fire and spread their sleeping robes on the ice of the lake itself.

The tent they had discarded at Dyea in order to travel light. A few sticks of driftwood furnished them with a fire that thawed down through the ice and left them to eat supper in the dark.

Close in under the sheltering rock Buck made his nest. So snug and warm was it, that he was loath to leave it when François distributed the fish which he had first thawed over the fire. But when Buck finished his ration and returned, he found his nest occupied. A warning snarl told him that the trespasser was Spitz. Till now Buck had avoided trouble with his enemy, but this was too much. The beast in him roared. He sprang upon Spitz with a fury which surprised them both, and Spitz particularly, for his whole experience with Buck had gone to teach him that his rival was an unusually timid dog, who managed to hold his own only because of his great weight and size.

François was surprised, too, when they shot out in a tangle from the disrupted nest and he divined the cause of the trouble. "A-a-ah!" he cried to Buck. "Gif it to heem, by Gar! Gif it to heem, the dirty t'eef!"

Spitz was equally willing. He was crying with sheer rage and eagerness as he circled back and forth for a chance to spring in. Buck was no less eager, and no less cautious, as he likewise circled back and forth for the advantage. But it was then that the unexpected happened, the thing which projected their struggle for supremacy far into the future, past many a weary mile of trail and toil.

An oath from Perrault, the resounding impact of a club upon a bony frame, and a shrill yelp of pain, heralded the breaking forth of pandemonium. The camp was suddenly discovered to be alive with skulking furry forms,—starving huskies, four or five score of them, who had scented the camp from some Indian village. They had crept in while Buck and Spitz were fighting, and when the two men sprang among them with stout clubs they showed their teeth and fought back. They were crazed by the smell of food. Perrault found one with head buried in the grub-box. His club landed heavily on the gaunt ribs, and the grub-box was capsized on the ground. On the instant a score of the famished brutes were scrambling for the bread and bacon. The clubs fell upon them unheeded. They yelped and howled under the rain of blows, but struggled none the less madly till the last crumb had been devoured.

In the meantime the astonished team-dogs had burst out of their nests only to be set upon by the fierce invaders. Never had Buck seen such dogs. It seemed as though their bones would burst through their skins. They were mere skeletons, draped loosely in draggled hides, with blazing eyes and slavered fangs. But the hunger-madness made them terrifying, irresistible. There was no opposing them. The team-dogs were swept back against the cliff at the first onset. Buck was beset by three huskies, and in a trice his head and shoulders were ripped and slashed. The din was frightful. Billee was crying as usual. Dave and Sol-leks, dripping blood from a score of wounds, were fighting bravely side by side. Joe was snapping like a demon. Once, his teeth closed on the fore leg of a husky, and he crunched down through the bone. Pike, the malingerer, leaped upon the crippled animal, breaking its neck with a quick flash of teeth and a jerk. Buck got a frothing adversary by the throat, and was sprayed with blood when his teeth sank through the jugular. The warm taste of it in his mouth goaded him to greater fierceness. He flung himself upon another, and at the same time felt teeth sink into his own throat. It was Spitz, treacherously attacking from the side.

Perrault and François, having cleaned out their part of the camp, hurried to save their sled-dogs. The wild wave of famished beasts rolled back before them, and Buck shook himself free. But it was only for a moment. The two men were compelled to run back to save the grub, upon which the huskies returned to the attack on the team. Billee, terrified into bravery, sprang through the savage circle and fled away over the ice. Pike and Dub followed on his heels, with the rest of the team behind. As Buck drew himself together to spring after them, out of the tail of his eye he saw Spitz rush upon him with the evident intention of overthrowing him. Once off his feet and under that mass of huskies, there was no hope for him. But he braced himself to the shock of Spitz's charge, then joined the flight out on the lake.

Later, the nine team-dogs gathered together and sought shelter in the forest. Though unpursued, they were in a sorry plight. There was not one who was not wounded in four or five places, while some were wounded grievously. Dub was badly injured in a hind leg; Dolly, the last husky added to the team at Dyea, had a badly torn throat; Joe had lost an eye; while Billee, the good-natured, with an ear chewed and rent to ribbons, cried and whimpered throughout the night. At day-break they limped warily back to camp, to find the marauders gone and the two men in bad tempers. Fully half their grub supply was gone. The huskies had chewed through the sled lashings and canvas coverings. In fact, nothing, no matter how remotely eatable, had escaped them. They had eaten a pair of Perrault's moose-hide moccasins, chunks out of the leather traces, and even two feet of lash from the end of François's whip. He broke from a mournful contemplation of it to look over his wounded dogs.

"Ah, my frien's," he said softly, "mebbe it mek you mad dog, dose many bites. Mebbe all mad dog, sacredam! Wot you t'ink, eh, Perrault?"

The courier shook his head dubiously. With four hundred miles of trail still between him and Dawson, he could ill afford to have madness break out among his dogs. Two hours of cursing and exertion got the harnesses into shape, and the wound-stiffened team was under way, struggling painfully over the hardest part of the trail they had yet encountered, and for that matter, the hardest between them and Dawson.

The Thirty Mile River was wide open. Its wild water defied the frost, and it was in the eddies only and in the quiet places that the ice held at all. Six days of exhausting toil were required to cover those thirty terrible miles. And terrible they were, for every foot of them was accomplished at the risk of life to dog and man. A dozen times, Perrault, nosing the way, broke through the ice bridges, being saved by the long pole he carried, which he so held that it fell each time across the hole made by his body. But a cold snap was on, the thermometer registering fifty below zero, and each time he broke through he was compelled for very life to build a fire and dry his garments.

Nothing daunted him. It was because nothing daunted him that he had been chosen for government courier. He took all manner of risks, resolutely thrusting his little weazened face into the frost and struggling on from dim dawn to dark. He skirted the frowning shores on rim ice that bent and crackled under foot and upon which they dared not halt. Once, the sled broke through, with Dave and Buck, and they were half-frozen and all but drowned by the time they were dragged out. The usual fire was necessary to save them. They were coated solidly with ice, and the two men kept them on the run around the fire, sweating and thawing, so close that they were singed by the flames.

At another time Spitz went through, dragging the whole team after him up to Buck, who strained backward with all his strength, his fore paws on the slippery edge and the ice quivering and snapping all around. But behind him was Dave, likewise straining backward, and behind the sled was François, pulling till his tendons cracked.

Again, the rim ice broke away before and behind, and there was no escape except up the cliff. Perrault scaled it by a miracle, while François prayed for just that miracle; and with every thong and sled lashing and the last bit of harness rove into a long rope, the dogs were hoisted, one by one, to the cliff crest. François came up last, after the sled and load. Then came the search for a place to descend, which descent was ultimately made by the aid of the rope, and night found them back on the river with a quarter of a mile to the day's credit.

By the time they made the Hootalinqua and good ice, Buck was played out. The rest of the dogs were in like condition; but Perrault, to make up lost time, pushed them late and early. The first day they covered thirty-five miles to the Big Salmon; the next day thirty-five more to the Little Salmon; the third day forty miles, which brought them well up toward the Five Fingers.

Buck's feet were not so compact and hard as the feet of the huskies. His had softened during the many generations since the day his last wild ancestor was tamed by a cave-dweller or river man. All day long he limped in agony, and camp once made, lay down like a dead dog. Hungry as he was, he would not move to receive his ration of fish, which François had to bring to him. Also, the dog-driver rubbed Buck's feet for half an hour each night after supper, and sacrificed the tops of his own moccasins to make four moccasins for Buck. This was a great relief, and Buck caused even the weazened face of Perrault to twist itself into a grin one morning, when François forgot the moccasins and Buck lay on his back, his four feet waving appealingly in the air, and refused to budge without them. Later his feet grew hard to the trail, and the worn-out foot-gear was thrown away.

At the Pelly one morning, as they were harnessing up, Dolly, who had never been conspicuous for anything, went suddenly mad. She announced her condition by a long, heart-breaking wolf howl that sent every dog bristling with fear, then sprang straight for Buck. He had never seen a dog go mad, nor did he have any reason to fear madness; yet he knew that here was horror, and fled away from it in a panic. Straight away he raced, with Dolly, panting and frothing, one leap behind; nor could she gain on him, so great was his terror, nor could he leave her, so great was her madness. He plunged through the wooded breast of the island, flew down to the lower end, crossed a back channel filled with rough ice to another island, gained a third island, curved back to the main river, and in desperation started to cross it. And all the time, though he did not look, he could hear her snarling just one leap behind. François called to him a quarter of a mile away and he doubled back, still one leap ahead, gasping painfully for air and putting all his faith in that François would save him. The dog-driver held the axe poised in his hand, and as Buck shot past him the axe crashed down upon mad Dolly's head.

Buck staggered over against the sled, exhausted, sobbing for breath, helpless. This was Spitz's opportunity. He sprang upon Buck, and twice his teeth sank into his unresisting foe and ripped and tore the flesh to the bone. Then François's lash descended, and Buck had the satisfaction of watching Spitz receive the worst whipping as yet administered to any of the teams.

"One devil, dat Spitz," remarked Perrault. "Some dam day heem keel dat Buck."

"Dat Buck two devils," was François's rejoinder. "All de tam I watch dat Buck I know for sure. Lissen: some dam fine day heem get mad lak hell an' den heem chew dat Spitz all up an' spit heem out on de snow. Sure. I know."

From then on it was war between them. Spitz, as lead-dog and acknowledged master of the team, felt his supremacy threatened by this strange Southland dog. And strange Buck was to him, for of the many Southland dogs he had known, not one had shown up worthily in camp and on trail. They were all too soft, dying under the toil, the frost, and starvation. Buck was the exception. He alone endured and prospered, matching the husky in strength, savagery, and cunning. Then he was a masterful dog, and what made him dangerous was the fact that the club of the man in the red sweater had knocked all blind pluck and rashness out of his desire for mastery. He was preeminently cunning, and could bide his time with a patience that was nothing less than primitive.

It was inevitable that the clash for leadership should come. Buck wanted it. He wanted it because it was his nature, because he had been gripped tight by that nameless, incomprehensible pride of the trail and trace—that pride which holds dogs in the toil to the last gasp, which lures them to die joyfully in the harness, and breaks their hearts if they are cut out of the harness. This was the pride of Dave as wheel-dog, of Sol-leks as he pulled with all his strength; the pride that laid hold of them at break of camp, transforming them from sour and sullen brutes into straining, eager, ambitious creatures; the pride that spurred them on all day and dropped them at pitch of camp at night, letting them fall back into gloomy unrest and uncontent. This was the pride that bore up Spitz and made him thrash the sled-dogs who blundered and shirked in the traces or hid away at harness-up time in the morning. Likewise it was this pride that made him fear Buck as a possible lead-dog. And this was Buck's pride, too.

He openly threatened the other's leadership. He came between him and the shirks he should have punished. And he did it deliberately. One night there was a heavy snowfall, and in the morning Pike, the malingerer, did not appear. He was securely hidden in his nest under a foot of snow. François called him and sought him in vain. Spitz was wild with wrath. He raged through the camp, smelling and digging in every likely place, snarling so frightfully that Pike heard and shivered in his hiding-place.

But when he was at last unearthed, and Spitz flew at him to punish him, Buck flew, with equal rage, in between. So unexpected was it, and so shrewdly managed, that Spitz was hurled backward and off his feet. Pike, who had been trembling abjectly, took heart at this open mutiny, and sprang upon his overthrown leader. Buck, to whom fair play was a forgotten code, likewise sprang upon Spitz. But François, chuckling at the incident while unswerving in the administration of justice, brought his lash down upon Buck with all his might. This failed to drive Buck from his prostrate rival, and the butt of the whip was brought into play. Half-stunned by the blow, Buck was knocked backward and the lash laid upon him again and again, while Spitz soundly punished the many times offending Pike.

In the days that followed, as Dawson grew closer and closer, Buck still continued to interfere between Spitz and the culprits; but he did it craftily, when François was not around. With the covert mutiny of Buck, a general insubordination sprang up and increased. Dave and Sol-leks were unaffected, but the rest of the team went from bad to worse. Things no longer went right. There was continual bickering and jangling. Trouble was always afoot, and at the bottom of it was Buck. He kept François busy, for the dog-driver was in constant apprehension of the life-and-death struggle between the two which he knew must take place sooner or later; and on more than one night the sounds of quarrelling and strife among the other dogs turned him out of his sleeping robe, fearful that Buck and Spitz were at it.

But the opportunity did not present itself, and they pulled into Dawson one dreary afternoon with the great fight still to come. Here were many men, and countless dogs, and Buck found them all at work. It seemed the ordained order of things that dogs should work. All day they swung up and down the main street in long teams, and in the night their jingling bells still went by. They hauled cabin logs and firewood, freighted up to the mines, and did all manner of work that horses did in the Santa Clara Valley. Here and there Buck met Southland dogs, but in the main they were the wild wolf husky breed. Every night, regularly, at nine, at twelve, at three, they lifted a nocturnal song, a weird and eerie chant, in which it was Buck's delight to join.

With the aurora borealis flaming coldly overhead, or the stars leaping in the frost dance, and the land numb and frozen under its pall of snow, this song of the huskies might have been the defiance of life, only it was pitched in minor key, with long-drawn wailings and half-sobs, and was more the pleading of life, the articulate travail of existence. It was an old song, old as the breed itself—one of the first songs of the younger world in a day when songs were sad. It was invested with the woe of unnumbered generations, this plaint by which Buck was so strangely stirred. When he moaned and sobbed, it was with the pain of living that was of old the pain of his wild fathers, and the fear and mystery of the cold and dark that was to them fear and mystery. And that he should be stirred by it marked the completeness with which he harked back through the ages of fire and roof to the raw beginnings of life in the howling ages.

Seven days from the time they pulled into Dawson, they dropped down the steep bank by the Barracks to the Yukon Trail, and pulled for Dyea and Salt Water. Perrault was carrying despatches if anything more urgent than those he had brought in; also, the travel pride had gripped him, and he purposed to make the record trip of the year. Several things favored him in this. The week's rest had recuperated the dogs and put them in thorough trim. The trail they had broken into the country was packed hard by later journeyers. And further, the police had arranged in two or three places deposits of grub for dog and man, and he was travelling light.

They made Sixty Mile, which is a fifty-mile run, on the first day; and the second day saw them booming up the Yukon well on their way to Pelly. But such splendid running was achieved not without great trouble and vexation on the part of François. The insidious revolt led by Buck had destroyed the solidarity of the team. It no longer was as one dog leaping in the traces. The encouragement Buck gave the rebels led them into all kinds of petty misdemeanors. No more was Spitz a leader greatly to be feared. The old awe departed, and they grew equal to challenging his authority. Pike robbed him of half a fish one night, and gulped it down under the protection of Buck. Another night Dub and Joe fought Spitz and made him forego the punishment they deserved. And even Billee, the good-natured, was less good-natured, and whined not half so placatingly as in former days. Buck never came near Spitz without snarling and bristling menacingly. In fact, his conduct approached that of a bully, and he was given to swaggering up and down before Spitz's very nose.

The breaking down of discipline likewise affected the dogs in their relations with one another. They quarrelled and bickered more than ever among themselves, till at times the camp was a howling bedlam. Dave and Sol-leks alone were unaltered, though they were made irritable by the unending squabbling. François swore strange barbarous oaths, and stamped the snow in futile rage, and tore his hair. His lash was always singing among the dogs, but it was of small avail. Directly his back was turned they were at it again. He backed up Spitz with his whip, while Buck backed up the remainder of the team. François knew he was behind all the trouble, and Buck knew he knew; but Buck was too clever ever again to be caught red-handed. He worked faithfully in the harness, for the toil had become a delight to him; yet it was a greater delight slyly to precipitate a fight amongst his mates and tangle the traces.

At the mouth of the Tahkeena, one night after supper, Dub turned up a snowshoe rabbit, blundered it, and missed. In a second the whole team was in full cry. A hundred yards away was a camp of the Northwest Police, with fifty dogs, huskies all, who joined the chase. The rabbit sped down the river, turned off into a small creek, up the frozen bed of which it held steadily. It ran lightly on the surface of the snow, while the dogs ploughed through by main strength. Buck led the pack, sixty strong, around bend after bend, but he could not gain. He lay down low to the race, whining eagerly, his splendid body flashing forward, leap by leap, in the wan white moonlight. And leap by leap, like some pale frost wraith, the snowshoe rabbit flashed on ahead.

All that stirring of old instincts which at stated periods drives men out from the sounding cities to forest and plain to kill things by chemically propelled leaden pellets, the blood lust, the joy to kill—all this was Buck's, only it was infinitely more intimate. He was ranging at the head of the pack, running the wild thing down, the living meat, to kill with his own teeth and wash his muzzle to the eyes in warm blood.

There is an ecstasy that marks the summit of life, and beyond which life cannot rise. And such is the paradox of living, this ecstasy comes when one is most alive, and it comes as a complete forgetfulness that one is alive. This ecstasy, this forgetfulness of living, comes to the artist, caught up and out of himself in a sheet of flame; it comes to the soldier, war-mad on a stricken field and refusing quarter; and it came to Buck, leading the pack, sounding the old wolf-cry, straining after the food that was alive and that fled swiftly before him through the moon-light. He was sounding the deeps of his nature, and of the parts of his nature that were deeper than he, going back into the womb of Time. He was mastered by the sheer surging of life, the tidal wave of being, the perfect joy of each separate muscle, joint, and sinew in that it was everything that was not death, that it was aglow and rampant, expressing itself in movement, flying exultantly under the stars and over the face of dead matter that did not move.

But Spitz, cold and calculating even in his supreme moods, left the pack and cut across a narrow neck of land where the creek made a long bend around. Buck did not know of this, and as he rounded the bend, the frost wraith of a rabbit still flitting before him, he saw another and larger frost wraith leap from the overhanging bank into the immediate path of the rabbit. It was Spitz. The rabbit could not turn, and as the white teeth broke its back in mid air it shrieked as loudly as a stricken man may shriek. At sound of this, the cry of Life plunging down from Life's apex in the grip of Death, the full pack at Buck's heels raised a hell's chorus of delight.

Buck did not cry out. He did not check himself, but drove in upon Spitz, shoulder to shoulder, so hard that he missed the throat. They rolled over and over in the powdery snow. Spitz gained his feet almost as though he had not been overthrown, slashing Buck down the shoulder and leaping clear. Twice his teeth clipped together, like the steel jaws of a trap, as he backed away for better footing, with lean and lifting lips that writhed and snarled.

In a flash Buck knew it. The time had come. It was to the death. As they circled about, snarling, ears laid back, keenly watchful for the advantage, the scene came to Buck with a sense of familiarity. He seemed to remember it all,—the white woods, and earth, and moonlight, and the thrill of battle. Over the whiteness and silence brooded a ghostly calm. There was not the faintest whisper of air—nothing moved, not a leaf quivered, the visible breaths of the dogs rising slowly and lingering in the frosty air. They had made short work of the snowshoe rabbit, these dogs that were ill-tamed wolves; and they were now drawn up in an expectant circle. They, too, were silent, their eyes only gleaming and their breaths drifting slowly upward. To Buck it was nothing new or strange, this scene of old time. It was as though it had always been the wonted way of things.

Spitz was a practised fighter. From Spitzbergen through the Arctic, and across Canada and the Barrens, he had held his own with all manner of dogs and achieved to mastery over them. Bitter rage was his, but never blind rage. In passion to rend and destroy, he never forgot that his enemy was in like passion to rend and destroy. He never rushed till he was prepared to receive a rush; never attacked till he had first defended that attack.

In vain Buck strove to sink his teeth in the neck of the big white dog. Wherever his fangs struck for the softer flesh, they were countered by the fangs of Spitz. Fang clashed fang, and lips were cut and bleeding, but Buck could not penetrate his enemy's guard. Then he warmed up and enveloped Spitz in a whirlwind of rushes. Time and time again he tried for the snow-white throat, where life bubbled near to the surface, and each time and every time Spitz slashed him and got away. Then Buck took to rushing, as though for the throat, when, suddenly drawing back his head and curving in from the side, he would drive his shoulder at the shoulder of Spitz, as a ram by which to overthrow him. But instead, Buck's shoulder was slashed down each time as Spitz leaped lightly away.

Spitz was untouched, while Buck was streaming with blood and panting hard. The fight was growing desperate. And all the while the silent and wolfish circle waited to finish off whichever dog went down. As Buck grew winded, Spitz took to rushing, and he kept him staggering for footing. Once Buck went over, and the whole circle of sixty dogs started up; but he recovered himself, almost in mid air, and the circle sank down again and waited.

But Buck possessed a quality that made for greatness—imagination. He fought by instinct, but he could fight by head as well. He rushed, as though attempting the old shoulder trick, but at the last instant swept low to the snow and in. His teeth closed on Spitz's left fore leg. There was a crunch of breaking bone, and the white dog faced him on three legs. Thrice he tried to knock him over, then repeated the trick and broke the right fore leg.

Despite the pain and helplessness, Spitz struggled madly to keep up. He saw the silent circle, with gleaming eyes, lolling tongues, and silvery breaths drifting upward, closing in upon him as he had seen similar circles close in upon beaten antagonists in the past. Only this time he was the one who was beaten.

There was no hope for him. Buck was inexorable. Mercy was a thing reserved for gentler climes. He manoeuvred for the final rush. The circle had tightened till he could feel the breaths of the huskies on his flanks. He could see them, beyond Spitz and to either side, half crouching for the spring, their eyes fixed upon him. A pause seemed to fall. Every animal was motionless as though turned to stone. Only Spitz quivered and bristled as he staggered back and forth, snarling with horrible menace, as though to frighten off impending death. Then Buck sprang in and out; but while he was in, shoulder had at last squarely met shoulder. The dark circle became a dot on the moon-flooded snow as Spitz disappeared from view. Buck stood and looked on, the successful champion, the dominant primordial beast who had made his kill and found it good.

IV

Who Has Won to Mastership

"Eh? Wot I say? I spik true w'en I say dat Buck two devils."

This was François's speech next morning when he discovered Spitz missing and Buck covered with wounds. He drew him to the fire and by its light pointed them out.

"Dat Spitz fight lak hell," said Perrault, as he surveyed the gaping rips and cuts.

"An' dat Buck fight lak two hells," was François's answer. "An' now we make good time. No more Spitz, no more trouble, sure."

While Perrault packed the camp outfit and loaded the sled, the dog-driver proceeded to harness the dogs. Buck trotted up to the place Spitz would have occupied as leader; but François, not noticing him, brought Sol-leks to the coveted position. In his judgment, Sol-leks was the best lead-dog left. Buck sprang upon Sol-leks in a fury, driving him back and standing in his place.

"Eh? eh?" François cried, slapping his thighs gleefully. "Look at dat Buck. Heem keel dat Spitz, heem t'ink to take de job."

"Go 'way, Chook!" he cried, but Buck refused to budge.

He took Buck by the scruff of the neck, and though the dog growled threateningly, dragged him to one side and replaced Sol-leks. The old dog did not like it, and showed plainly that he was afraid of Buck. François was obdurate, but when he turned his back Buck again displaced Sol-leks, who was not at all unwilling to go.

François was angry. "Now, by Gar, I feex you!" he cried, coming back with a heavy club in his hand.

Buck remembered the man in the red sweater, and retreated slowly; nor did he attempt to charge in when Sol-leks was once more brought forward. But he circled just beyond the range of the club, snarling with bitterness and rage; and while he circled he watched the club so as to dodge it if thrown by François, for he was become wise in the way of clubs.

The driver went about his work, and he called to Buck when he was ready to put him in his old place in front of Dave. Buck retreated two or three steps. François followed him up, whereupon he again retreated. After some time of this, François threw down the club, thinking that Buck feared a thrashing. But Buck was in open revolt. He wanted, not to escape a clubbing, but to have the leadership. It was his by right. He had earned it, and he would not be content with less.

Perrault took a hand. Between them they ran him about for the better part of an hour. They threw clubs at him. He dodged. They cursed him, and his fathers and mothers before him, and all his seed to come after him down to the remotest generation, and every hair on his body and drop of blood in his veins; and he answered curse with snarl and kept out of their reach. He did not try to run away, but retreated around and around the camp, advertising plainly that when his desire was met, he would come in and be good.

François sat down and scratched his head. Perrault looked at his watch and swore. Time was flying, and they should have been on the trail an hour gone. François scratched his head again. He shook it and grinned sheepishly at the courier, who shrugged his shoulders in sign that they were beaten. Then François went up to where Sol-leks stood and called to Buck. Buck laughed, as dogs laugh, yet kept his distance. François unfastened Sol-lek's traces and put him back in his old place. The team stood harnessed to the sled in an unbroken line, ready for the trail. There was no place for Buck save at the front. Once more François called, and once more Buck laughed and kept away.

"T'row down de club," Perrault commanded.

François complied, whereupon Buck trotted in, laughing triumphantly, and swung around into position at the head of the team. His traces were fastened, the sled broken out, and with both men running they dashed out on to the river trail.

Highly as the dog-driver had forevalued Buck, with his two devils, he found, while the day was yet young, that he had undervalued. At a bound Buck took up the duties of leadership; and where judgment was required, and quick thinking and quick acting, he showed himself the superior even of Spitz, of whom François had never seen an equal.

But it was in giving the law and making his mates live up to it, that Buck excelled. Dave and Sol-leks did not mind the change in leadership. It was none of their business. Their business was to toil, and toil mightily, in the traces. So long as that were not interfered with, they did not care what happened. Billee, the good-natured, could lead for all they cared, so long as he kept order. The rest of the team, however, had grown unruly during the last days of Spitz, and their surprise was great now that Buck proceeded to lick them into shape.

Pike, who pulled at Buck's heels, and who never put an ounce more of his weight against the breast-band than he was compelled to do, was swiftly and repeatedly shaken for loafing; and ere the first day was done he was pulling more than ever before in his life. The first night in camp, Joe, the sour one, was punished roundly—a thing that Spitz had never succeeded in doing. Buck simply smothered him by virtue of superior weight, and cut him up till he ceased snapping and began to whine for mercy.

The general tone of the team picked up immediately. It recovered its old-time solidarity, and once more the dogs leaped as one dog in the traces. At the Rink Rapids two native huskies, Teek and Koona, were added; and the celerity with which Buck broke them in took away François's breath.

"Nevaire such a dog as dat Buck!" he cried. "No, nevaire! Heem worth one t'ousan' dollair, by Gar! Eh? Wot you say, Perrault?"

And Perrault nodded. He was ahead of the record then, and gaining day by day. The trail was in excellent condition, well packed and hard, and there was no new-fallen snow with which to contend. It was not too cold. The temperature dropped to fifty below zero and remained there the whole trip. The men rode and ran by turn, and the dogs were kept on the jump, with but infrequent stoppages.

The Thirty Mile River was comparatively coated with ice, and they covered in one day going out what had taken them ten days coming in. In one run they made a sixty-mile dash from the foot of Lake Le Barge to the White Horse Rapids. Across Marsh, Tagish, and Bennett (seventy miles of lakes), they flew so fast that the man whose turn it was to run towed behind the sled at the end of a rope. And on the last night of the second week they topped White Pass and dropped down the sea slope with the lights of Skaguay and of the shipping at their feet.

It was a record run. Each day for fourteen days they had averaged forty miles. For three days Perrault and Francois threw chests up and down the main street of Skaguay and were deluged with invitations to drink, while the team was the constant centre of a worshipful crowd of dog-busters and mushers. Then three or four western bad men aspired to clean out the town, were riddled like pepper-boxes for their pains, and public interest turned to other idols. Next came official orders. François called Buck to him, threw his arms around him, wept over him. And that was the last of François and Perrault. Like other men, they passed out of Buck's life for good.

A Scotch half-breed took charge of him and his mates, and in company with a dozen other dog-teams he started back over the weary trail to Dawson. It was no light running now, nor record time, but heavy toil each day, with a heavy load behind; for this was the mail train, carrying word from the world to the men who sought gold under the shadow of the Pole.

Buck did not like it, but he bore up well to the work, taking pride in it after the manner of Dave and Sol-leks, and seeing that his mates, whether they prided in it or not, did their fair share. It was a monotonous life, operating with machine-like regularity. One day was very like another. At a certain time each morning the cooks turned out, fires were built, and breakfast was eaten. Then, while some broke camp, others harnessed the dogs, and they were under way an hour or so before darkness fell which gave warning of dawn. At night, camp was made. Some pitched the flies, others cut firewood and pine boughs for the beds, and still others carried water or ice for the cooks. Also, the dogs were fed. To them, this was the one feature of the day, though it was good to loaf around, after the fish was eaten, for an hour or so with the other dogs, of which there were fivescore and odd. There were fierce fighters among them, but three battles with the fiercest brought Buck to mastery, so that when he bristled and showed his teeth they got out of his way.

Best of all, perhaps, he loved to lie near the fire, hind legs crouched under him, fore legs stretched out in front, head raised, and eyes blinking dreamily at the flames. Sometimes he thought of Judge Miller's big house in the sun-kissed Santa Clara Valley, and of the cement swimming-tank, and Ysabel, the Mexican hairless, and Toots, the Japanese pug; but oftener he remembered the man in the red sweater, the death of Curly, the great fight with Spitz, and the good things he had eaten or would like to eat. He was not homesick. The Sunland was very dim and distant, and such memories had no power over him. Far more potent were the memories of his heredity that gave things he had never seen before a seeming familiarity; the instincts (which were but the memories of his ancestors become habits) which had lapsed in later days, and still later, in him, quickened and become alive again.

Sometimes as he crouched there, blinking dreamily at the flames, it seemed that the flames were of another fire, and that as he crouched by this other fire he saw another and different man from the half-breed cook before him. This other man was shorter of leg and longer of arm, with muscles that were stringy and knotty rather than rounded and swelling. The hair of this man was long and matted, and his head slanted back under it from the eyes. He uttered strange sounds, and seemed very much afraid of the darkness, into which he peered continually, clutching in his hand, which hung midway between knee and foot, a stick with a heavy stone made fast to the end. He was all but naked, a ragged and fire-scorched skin hanging part way down his back, but on his body there was much hair. In some places, across the chest and shoulders and down the outside of the arms and thighs, it was matted into almost a thick fur. He did not stand erect, but with trunk inclined forward from the hips, on legs that bent at the knees. About his body there was a peculiar springiness, or resiliency, almost catlike, and a quick alertness as of one who lived in perpetual fear of things seen and unseen.

At other times this hairy man squatted by the fire with head between his legs and slept. On such occasions his elbows were on his knees, his hands clasped above his head as though to shed rain by the hairy arms. And beyond that fire, in the circling darkness, Buck could see many gleaming coals, two by two, always two by two, which he knew to be the eyes of great beasts of prey. And he could hear the crashing of their bodies through the undergrowth, and the noises they made in the night. And dreaming there by the Yukon bank, with lazy eyes blinking at the fire, these sounds and sights of another world would make the hair to rise along his back and stand on end across his shoulders and up his neck, till he whimpered low and suppressedly, or growled softly, and the half-breed cook shouted at him, "Hey, you Buck, wake up!" Whereupon the other world would vanish and the real world come into his eyes, and he would get up and yawn and stretch as though he had been asleep.

It was a hard trip, with the mail behind them, and the heavy work wore them down. They were short of weight and in poor condition when they made Dawson, and should have had a ten days' or a week's rest at least. But in two days' time they dropped down the Yukon bank from the Barracks, loaded with letters for the outside. The dogs were tired, the drivers grumbling, and to make matters worse, it snowed every day. This meant a soft trail, greater friction on the runners, and heavier pulling for the dogs; yet the drivers were fair through it all, and did their best for the animals.

Each night the dogs were attended to first. They ate before the drivers ate, and no man sought his sleeping-robe till he had seen to the feet of the dogs he drove. Still, their strength went down. Since the beginning of the winter they had travelled eighteen hundred miles, dragging sleds the whole weary distance; and eighteen hundred miles will tell upon life of the toughest. Buck stood it, keeping his mates up to their work and maintaining discipline, though he, too, was very tired. Billee cried and whimpered regularly in his sleep each night. Joe was sourer than ever, and Sol-leks was unapproachable, blind side or other side.

But it was Dave who suffered most of all. Something had gone wrong with him. He became more morose and irritable, and when camp was pitched at once made his nest, where his driver fed him. Once out of the harness and down, he did not get on his feet again till harness-up time in the morning. Sometimes, in the traces, when jerked by a sudden stoppage of the sled, or by straining to start it, he would cry out with pain. The driver examined him, but could find nothing. All the drivers became interested in his case. They talked it over at meal-time, and over their last pipes before going to bed, and one night they held a consultation. He was brought from his nest to the fire and was pressed and prodded till he cried out many times. Something was wrong inside, but they could locate no broken bones, could not make it out.

By the time Cassiar Bar was reached, he was so weak that he was falling repeatedly in the traces. The Scotch half-breed called a halt and took him out of the team, making the next dog, Sol-leks, fast to the sled. His intention was to rest Dave, letting him run free behind the sled. Sick as he was, Dave resented being taken out, grunting and growling while the traces were unfastened, and whimpering broken-heartedly when he saw Sol-leks in the position he had held and served so long. For the pride of trace and trail was his, and, sick unto death, he could not bear that another dog should do his work.

When the sled started, he floundered in the soft snow alongside the beaten trail, attacking Sol-leks with his teeth, rushing against him and trying to thrust him off into the soft snow on the other side, striving to leap inside his traces and get between him and the sled, and all the while whining and yelping and crying with grief and pain. The half-breed tried to drive him away with the whip; but he paid no heed to the stinging lash, and the man had not the heart to strike harder. Dave refused to run quietly on the trail behind the sled, where the going was easy, but continued to flounder alongside in the soft snow, where the going was most difficult, till exhausted. Then he fell, and lay where he fell, howling lugubriously as the long train of sleds churned by.

With the last remnant of his strength he managed to stagger along behind till the train made another stop, when he floundered past the sleds to his own, where he stood alongside Sol-leks. His driver lingered a moment to get a light for his pipe from the man behind. Then he returned and started his dogs. They swung out on the trail with remarkable lack of exertion, turned their heads uneasily, and stopped in surprise. The driver was surprised, too; the sled had not moved. He called his comrades to witness the sight. Dave had bitten through both of Sol-lek's traces, and was standing directly in front of the sled in his proper place.

He pleaded with his eyes to remain there. The driver was perplexed. His comrades talked of how a dog could break its heart through being denied the work that killed it, and recalled instances they had known, where dogs, too old for the toil, or injured, had died because they were cut out of the traces. Also, they held it a mercy, since Dave was to die anyway, that he should die in the traces, heart-easy and content. So he was harnessed in again, and proudly he pulled as of old, though more than once he cried out involuntarily from the bite of his inward hurt. Several times he fell down and was dragged in the traces, and once the sled ran upon him so that he limped thereafter on one of his hind legs.

But he held out till camp was reached, when his driver made a place for him by the fire. Morning found him too weak to travel. At harness-up time he tried to crawl to his driver. By convulsive efforts he got on his feet, staggered, and fell. Then he wormed his way forward slowly toward where the harnesses were being put on his mates. He would advance his fore legs and drag up his body with a sort of hitching movement, when he would advance his fore legs and hitch ahead again for a few more inches. His strength left him, and the last his mates saw of him he lay gasping in the snow and yearning toward them. But they could hear him mournfully howling till they passed out of sight behind a belt of river timber.

Here the train was halted. The Scotch half-breed slowly retraced his steps to the camp they had left. The men ceased talking. A revolver-shot rang out. The man came back hurriedly. The whips snapped, the bells tinkled merrily, the sleds churned along the trail; but Buck knew, and every dog knew, what had taken place behind the belt of river trees.

V

The Toil of Trace and Trail

THIRTY days from the time it left Dawson, the Salt Water Mail, with Buck and his mates at the fore, arrived at Skaguay. They were in a wretched state, worn out and worn down. Buck's one hundred and forty pounds had dwindled to one hundred and fifteen. The rest of his mates, though lighter dogs, had relatively lost more weight than he. Pike, the malingerer, who, in his lifetime of deceit, had often successfully feigned a hurt leg, was now limping in earnest. Sol-leks was limping, and Dub was suffering from a wrenched shoulder-blade.

They were all terribly footsore. No spring or rebound was left in them. Their feet fell heavily on the trail, jarring their bodies and doubling the fatigue of a day's travel.

There was nothing the matter with them except that they were dead tired. It was not the dead-tiredness that comes through brief and excessive effort, from which recovery is a matter of hours; but it was the dead-tiredness that comes through the slow and prolonged strength drainage of months of toil. There was no power of recuperation left, no reserve strength to call upon. It had been all used, the last least bit of it. Every muscle, every fibre, every cell, was tired, dead tired. And there was reason for it. In less than five months they had travelled twenty-five hundred miles, during the last eighteen hundred of which they had had but five days' rest. When they arrived at Skaguay they were apparently on their last legs. They could barely keep the traces taut, and on the down grades just managed to keep out of the way of the sled.

"Mush on, poor sore feets," the driver encouraged them as they tottered down the main street of Skaguay. "Dis is de las'. Den we get one long res'. Eh? For sure. One bully long res'."

The drivers confidently expected a long stopover. Themselves, they had covered twelve hundred miles with two days' rest, and in the nature of reason and common justice they deserved an interval of loafing. But so many were the men who had rushed into the Klondike, and so many were the sweethearts, wives, and kin that had not rushed in, that the congested mail was taking on Alpine proportions; also, there were official orders. Fresh batches of Hudson Bay dogs were to take the places of those worthless for the trail. The worthless ones were to be got rid of, and, since dogs count for little against dollars, they were to be sold.

Three days passed, by which time Buck and his mates found how really tired and weak they were. Then, on the morning of the fourth day, two men from the States came along and bought them, harness and all, for a song. The men addressed each other as "Hal" and "Charles." Charles was a middle-aged, lightish-colored man, with weak and watery eyes and a mustache that twisted fiercely and vigorously up, giving the lie to the limply drooping lip it concealed. Hal was a youngster of nineteen or twenty, with a big Colt's revolver and a hunting-knife strapped about him on a belt that fairly bristled with cartridges. This belt was the most salient thing about him. It advertised his callowness—a callowness sheer and unutterable. Both men were manifestly out of place, and why such as they should adventure the North is part of the mystery of things that passes understanding.

Buck heard the chaffering, saw the money pass between the man and the Government agent, and knew that the Scotch half-breed and the mail-train drivers were passing out of his life on the heels of Perrault and François and the others who had gone before. When driven with his mates to the new owners' camp, Buck saw a slipshod and slovenly affair, tent half stretched, dishes unwashed, everything in disorder; also, he saw a woman. "Mercedes" the men called her. She was Charles's wife and Hal's sister—a nice family party.

Buck watched them apprehensively as they proceeded to take down the tent and load the sled. There was a great deal of effort about their manner, but no businesslike method. The tent was rolled into an awkward bundle three times as large as it should have been. The tin dishes were packed away unwashed. Mercedes continually fluttered in the way of her men and kept up an unbroken chattering of remonstrance and advice. When they put a clothes-sack on the front of the sled, she suggested it should go on the back; and when they had put it on the back, and covered it over with a couple of other bundles, she discovered overlooked articles which could abide nowhere else but in that very sack, and they unloaded again.

Three men from a neighboring tent came out and looked on, grinning winking at one another.

"You've got a right smart load as it is," said one of them; "and it's not me should tell you your business, but I wouldn't tote that tent along if I was you."

"Undreamed of!" cried Mercedes, throwing up her hands in dainty dismay. "However in the world could I manage without a tent?"

"It's springtime, and you won't get any more cold weather," the man replied.

She shook her head decidedly, and Charles and Hal put the last odds and ends on top the mountainous load.

"Think it'll ride?" one of the men asked.

"Why shouldn't it?" Charles demanded rather shortly.

"Oh, that's all right, that's all right," the man hastened meekly to say. "I was just a-wonderin', that is all. It seemed a mite top-heavy."

Charles turned his back and drew the lashings down as well as he could, which was not in the least well.

"An' of course the dogs can hike along all day with that contraption behind them," affirmed a second of the men.

"Certainly," said Hal, with freezing politeness, taking hold of the gee-pole with one hand and swinging his whip from the other. "Mush!" he shouted. "Mush on there!"

The dogs sprang against the breast-bands, strained hard for a few moments, then relaxed. They were unable to move the sled.

"The lazy brutes, I'll show them," he cried, preparing to lash out at them with the whip.

But Mercedes interfered, crying, "Oh, Hal, you mustn't," as she caught hold of the whip and wrenched it from him. "The poor dears! Now you must promise you won't be harsh with them for the rest of the trip, or I won't go a step."

"Precious lot you know about dogs," her brother sneered; "and I wish you'd leave me alone. They're lazy, I tell you, and you've got to whip them to get anything out of them. That's their way. You ask any one. Ask one of those men."

Mercedes looked at them imploringly, untold repugnance at sight of pain written in her pretty face.

"They're weak as water, if you want to know," came the reply from one of the men. "Plum tuckered out, that's what's the matter. They need a rest."

"Rest be blanked," said Hal, with his beardless lips; and Mercedes said, "Oh!" in pain and sorrow at the oath.

But she was a clannish creature, and rushed at once to the defence of her brother. "Never mind that man," she said pointedly. "You're driving our dogs, and you do what you think best with them."

Again Hal's whip fell upon the dogs. They threw themselves against the breast-bands, dug their feet into the packed snow, got down low to it, and put forth all their strength. The sled held as though it were an anchor. After two efforts, they stood still, panting. The whip was whistling savagely, when once more Mercedes interfered. She dropped on her knees before Buck, with tears in her eyes, and put her arms around his neck.

"You poor, poor dears," she cried sympathetically, "why don't you pull hard?—then you wouldn't be whipped." Buck did not like her, but he was feeling too miserable to resist her, taking it as part of the day's miserable work.

One of the onlookers, who had been clenching his teeth to suppress hot speech, now spoke up:—

"It's not that I care a whoop what becomes of you, but for the dogs' sakes I just want to tell you, you can help them a mighty lot by breaking out that sled. The runners are froze fast. Throw your weight against the gee-pole, right and left, and break it out."

A third time the attempt was made, but this time, following the advice, Hal broke out the runners which had been frozen to the snow. The overloaded and unwieldy sled forged ahead, Buck and his mates struggling frantically under the rain of blows. A hundred yards ahead the path turned and sloped steeply into the main street. It would have required an experienced man to keep the top-heavy sled upright, and Hal was not such a man. As they swung on the turn the sled went over, spilling half its load through the loose lashings. The dogs never stopped. The lightened sled bounded on its side behind them. They were angry because of the ill treatment they had received and the unjust load. Buck was raging. He broke into a run, the team following his lead. Hal cried "Whoa! whoa!" but they gave no heed. He tripped and was pulled off his feet. The capsized sled ground over him, and the dogs dashed on up the street, adding to the gayety of Skaguay as they scattered the remainder of the outfit along its chief thoroughfare.

Kind-hearted citizens caught the dogs and gathered up the scattered belongings. Also, they gave advice. Half the load and twice the dogs, if they ever expected to reach Dawson, was what was said. Hal and his sister and brother-in-law listened unwillingly, pitched tent, and overhauled the outfit. Canned goods were turned out that made men laugh, for canned goods on the Long Trail is a thing to dream about. "Blankets for a hotel," quoth one of the men who laughed and helped. "Half as many is too much; get rid of them. Throw away that tent, and all those dishes,—who's going to wash them, anyway? Good Lord, do you think you're travelling on a Pullman?"

And so it went, the inexorable elimination of the superfluous. Mercedes cried when her clothes-bags were dumped on the ground and article after article was thrown out. She cried in general, and she cried in particular over each discarded thing. She clasped hands about knees, rocking back and forth broken-heartedly. She averred she would not go an inch, not for a dozen Charleses. She appealed to everybody and to everything, finally wiping her eyes and proceeding to cast out even articles of apparel that were imperative necessaries. And in her zeal, when she had finished with her own, she attacked the belongings of her men and went through them like a tornado.

This accomplished, the outfit, though cut in half, was still a formidable bulk. Charles and Hal went out in the evening and bought six Outside dogs. These, added to the six of the original team, and Teek and Koona, the huskies obtained at the Rink Rapids on the record trip, brought the team up to fourteen. But the Outside dogs, though practically broken in since their landing, did not amount to much. Three were short-haired pointers, one was a Newfoundland, and the other two were mongrels of indeterminate breed. They did not seem to know anything, these newcomers. Buck and his comrades looked upon them with disgust, and though he speedily taught them their places and what not to do, he could not teach them what to do. They did not take kindly to trace and trail. With the exception of the two mongrels, they were bewildered and spirit-broken by the strange savage environment in which they found themselves and by the ill treatment they had received. The two mongrels were without spirit at all; bones were the only things breakable about them.

With the newcomers hopeless and forlorn, and the old team worn out by twenty-five hundred miles of continuous trail, the outlook was anything but bright. The two men, however, were quite cheerful. And they were proud, too. They were doing the thing in style, with fourteen dogs. They had seen other sleds depart over the Pass for Dawson, or come in from Dawson, but never had they seen a sled with so many as fourteen dogs. In the nature of Arctic travel there was a reason why fourteen dogs should not drag one sled, and that was that one sled could not carry the food for fourteen dogs. But Charles and Hal did not know this. They had worked the trip out with a pencil, so much to a dog, so many dogs, so many days, Q.E.D. Mercedes looked over their shoulders and nodded comprehensively, it was all so very simple.

Late next morning Buck led the long team up the street. There was nothing lively about it, no snap or go in him and his fellows. They were starting dead weary. Four times he had covered the distance between Salt Water and Dawson, and the knowledge that, jaded and tired, he was facing the same trail once more, made him bitter. His heart was not in the work, nor was the heart of any dog. The Outsides were timid and frightened, the Insides without confidence in their masters.

Buck felt vaguely that there was no depending upon these two men and the woman. They did not know how to do anything, and as the days went by it became apparent that they could not learn. They were slack in all things, without order or discipline. It took them half the night to pitch a slovenly camp, and half the morning to break that camp and get the sled loaded in fashion so slovenly that for the rest of the day they were occupied in stopping and rearranging the load. Some days they did not make ten miles. On other days they were unable to get started at all. And on no day did they succeed in making more than half the distance used by the men as a basis in their dog-food computation.

It was inevitable that they should go short on dog-food. But they hastened it by overfeeding, bringing the day nearer when underfeeding would commence. The Outside dogs, whose digestions had not been trained by chronic famine to make the most of little, had voracious appetities. And when, in addition to this, the worn-out huskies pulled weakly, Hall decided that the orthodox ration was too small. He doubled it. And to cap it all, when Mercedes, with tears in her pretty eyes and a quaver in her throat, could not cajole him into giving the dogs still more, she stole from the fish-sacks and fed them slyly. But it was not food that Buck and the huskies needed, but rest. And though they were making poor time, the heavy load they dragged sapped their strength severely.

Then came the underfeeding. Hal awoke one day to the fact that his dog-food was half gone and the distance only quarter covered; further, that for love or money no additional dog-food was to be obtained. So he cut down even the orthodox ration and tried to increase the day's travel. His sister and brother-in-law seconded him; but they were frustrated by their heavy outfit and their own incompetence. It was a simple matter to give the dogs less food; but it was impossible to make the dogs travel faster, while their own inability to get under way earlier in the morning prevented them from travelling longer hours. Not only did they not know how to work dogs, but they did not know how to work themselves.

The first to go was Dub. Poor blundering thief that he was, always getting caught and punished, he had none the less been a faithful worker. His wrenched shoulder-blade, untreated and unrested, went from bad to worse, till finally Hal shot him with the big Colt's revolver. It is a saying of the country that an Outside dog starves to death on the ration of the husky, so the six Outside dogs under Buck could do no less than die on half the ration of the husky. The Newfoundland went first, followed by the three short-haired pointers, the two mongrels hanging more grittily on to life, but going in the end.

By this time all the amenities and gentlenesses of the Southland had fallen away from the three people. Shorn of its glamour and romance, Arctic travel became to them a reality too harsh for their manhood and womanhood. Mercedes ceased weeping over the dogs, being too occupied with weeping over herself and with quarrelling with her husband and brother. To quarrel was the one thing they were never too weary to do. Their irritability arose out of their misery, increased with it, doubled upon it, outdistanced it. The wonderful patience of the trail which comes to men who toil hard and suffer sore, and remain sweet of speech and kindly, did not come to these two men and the woman. They had no inkling of such a patience. They were stiff and in pain; their muscles ached, their bones ached, their very hearts ached; and because of this they became sharp of speech, and hard words were first on their lips in the morning and last at night.

Charles and Hal wrangled whenever Mercedes gave them a chance. It was the cherished belief of each that he did more than his share of the work, and neither forbore to speak this belief at every opportunity. Sometimes Mercedes sided with her husband, sometimes with her brother. The result was a beautiful and unending family quarrel. Starting from a dispute as to which should chop a few sticks for the fire (a dispute which concerned only Charles and Hal), presently would be lugged in the rest of the family, fathers, mothers, uncles, cousins, people thousands of miles away, and some of them dead. That Hal's views on art, or the sort of society plays his mother's brother wrote, should have anything to do with the chopping of a few sticks of firewood, passes comprehension; nevertheless the quarrel was as likely to tend in that direction as in the direction of Charles's political prejudices. And that Charles's sister's tale-bearing tongue should be relevant to the building of a Yukon fire, was apparent only to Mercedes, who disburdened herself of copious opinions upon that topic, and incidentally upon a few other traits unpleasantly peculiar to her husband's family. In the meantime the fire remained unbuilt, the camp half pitched, and the dogs unfed.

Mercedes nursed a special grievance—the grievance of sex. She was pretty and soft, and had been chivalrously treated all her days. But the present treatment by her husband and brother was everything save chivalrous. It was her custom to be helpless. They complained. Upon which impeachment of what to her was her most essential sex-prerogative, she made their lives unendurable. She no longer considered the dogs, and because she was sore and tired, she persisted in riding on the sled. She was pretty and soft, but she weighed one hundred and twenty pounds—a lusty last straw to the load dragged by the weak and starving animals. She rode for days, till they fell in the traces and the sled stood still. Charles and Hal begged her to get off and walk, pleaded with her, entreated, the while she wept and importuned Heaven with a recital of their brutality.

On one occasion they took her off the sled by main strength. They never did it again. She let her legs go limp like a spoiled child, and sat down on the trail. They went on their way, but she did not move. After they had travelled three miles they unloaded the sled, came back for her, and by main strength put her on the sled again.

In the excess of their own misery they were callous to the suffering of their animals. Hal's theory, which he practised on others, was that one must get hardened. He had started out preaching it to his sister and brother-in-law. Failing there, he hammered it into the dogs with a club. At the Five Fingers the dog-food gave out, and a toothless old squaw offered to trade them a few pounds of frozen horse-hide for the Colt's revolver that kept the big hunting-knife company at Hal's hip. A poor substitute for food was this hide, just as it had been stripped from the starved horses of the cattlemen six months back. In its frozen state it was more like strips of galvanized iron, and when a dog wrestled it into his stomach it thawed into thin and innutritious leathery strings and into a mass of short hair, irritating and indigestible.

And through it all Buck staggered along at the head of the team as in a nightmare. He pulled when he could; when he could no longer pull, he fell down and remained down till blows from whip or club drove him to his feet again. All the stiffness and gloss had gone out of his beautiful furry coat. The hair hung down, limp and draggled, or matted with dried blood where Hal's club had bruised him. His muscles had wasted away to knotty strings, and the flesh pads had disappeared, so that each rib and every bone in his frame were outlined cleanly through the loose hide that was wrinkled in folds of emptiness. It was heartbreaking, only Buck's heart was unbreakable. The man in the red sweater had proved that.

As it was with Buck, so was it with his mates. They were perambulating skeletons. There were seven all together, including him. In their very great misery they had become insensible to the bite of the lash or the bruise of the club. The pain of the beating was dull and distant, just as the things their eyes saw and their ears heard seemed dull and distant. They were not half living, or quarter living. They were simply so many bags of bones in which sparks of life fluttered faintly. When a halt was made, they dropped down in the traces like dead dogs, and the spark dimmed and paled and seemed to go out. And when the club or whip fell upon them, the spark fluttered feebly up, and they tottered to their feet and staggered on.

There came a day when Billee, the good-natured, fell and could not rise. Hal had traded off his revolver, so he took the axe and knocked Billee on the head as he lay in the traces, then cut the carcass out of the harness and dragged it to one side. Buck saw, and his mates saw, and they knew that this thing was very close to them. On the next day Koona went, and but five of them remained: Joe, too far gone to be malignant; Pike, crippled and limping, only half conscious and not conscious enough longer to malinger; Sol-leks, the one-eyed, still faithful to the toil of trace and trail, and mournful in that he had so little strength with which to pull; Teek, who had not travelled so far that winter and who was now beaten more than the others because he was fresher; and Buck, still at the head of the team, but no longer enforcing discipline or striving to enforce it, blind with weakness half the time and keeping the trail by the loom of it and by the dim feel of his feet.

It was beautiful spring weather, but neither dogs nor humans were aware of it. Each day the sun rose earlier and set later. It was dawn by three in the morning, and twilight lingered till nine at night. The whole long day was a blaze of sunshine. The ghostly winter silence had given way to the great spring murmur of awakening life. This murmur arose from all the land, fraught with the joy of living. It came from the things that lived and moved again, things which had been as dead and which had not moved during the long months of frost. The sap was rising in the pines. The willows and aspens were bursting out in young buds. Shrubs and vines were putting on fresh garbs of green. Crickets sang in the nights, and in the days all manner of creeping, crawling things rustled forth into the sun. Partridges and woodpeckers were booming and knocking in the forest. Squirrels were chattering, birds singing, and overhead honked the wild-fowl driving up from the south in cunning wedges that split the air.

From every hill slope came the trickle of running water, the music of unseen fountains. All things were thawing, bending, snapping. The Yukon was straining to break loose the ice that bound it down. It ate away from beneath; the sun ate from above. Air-holes formed, fissures sprang and spread apart, while thin sections of ice fell through bodily into the river. And amid all this bursting, rending, throbbing of awakening life, under the blazing sun and through the soft-sighing breezes, like wayfarers to death, staggered the two men, the woman, and the huskies.

With the dogs falling, Mercedes weeping and riding, Hal swearing innocuously, and Charles's eyes wistfully watering, they staggered into John Thornton's camp at the mouth of White River. When they halted, the dogs dropped down as though they had all been struck dead. Mercedes dried her eyes and looked at John Thornton. Charles sat down on a log to rest. He sat down very slowly and painstakingly what of his great stiffness. Hal did the talking. John Thornton was whittling the last touches on an axe-handle he had made from a stick of birch. He whittled and listened, gave monosyllabic replies, and, when it was asked, terse advice. He knew the breed, and he gave his advice in the certainty that it would not be followed.

"They told us up above that the bottom was dropping out of the trail and that the best thing for us to do was to lay over," Hal said in response to Thornton's warning to take no more chances on the rotten ice. "They told us we couldn't make White River, and here we are." This last with a sneering ring of triumph in it.

"And they told you true," John Thornton answered. "The bottom's likely to drop out at any moment. Only fools, with the blind luck of fools, could have made it. I tell you straight, I wouldn't risk my carcass on that ice for all the gold in Alaska."

"That's because you're not a fool, I suppose," said Hal. "All the same, we'll go on to Dawson." He uncoiled his whip. "Get up there, Buck! Hi! Get up there! Mush on!"

Thornton went on whittling. It was idle, he knew, to get between a fool and his folly; while two or three fools more or less would not alter the scheme of things.

But the team did not get up at the command. It had long since passed into the stage where blows were required to rouse it. The whip flashed out, here and there, on its merciless errands. John Thornton compressed his lips. Sol-leks was the first to crawl to his feet. Teek followed. Joe came next, yelping with pain. Pike made painful efforts. Twice he fell over, when half up, and on the third attempt managed to rise. Buck made no effort. He lay quietly where he had fallen. The last bit into him again and again, but he neither whined nor struggled. Several times Thornton started, as though to speak, but changed his mind. A moisture came into his eyes, and, as the whipping continued, he arose and walked irresolutely up and down.

This was the first time Buck had failed, in itself a sufficient reason to drive Hal into a rage. He exchanged the whip for the customary club. Buck refused to move under the rain of heavier blows which now fell upon him. Like his mates, he was barely able to get up, but, unlike them, he had made up his mind not to get up. He had a vague feeling of impending doom. This had been strong upon him when he pulled in to the bank, and it had not departed from him. What of the thin and rotten ice he had felt under his feet all day, it seemed that he sensed disaster close at hand, out there ahead on the ice where his master was trying to drive him. He refused to stir. So greatly had he suffered, and so far gone was he, that the blows did not hurt much. And as they continued to fall upon him, the spark of life within flickered and went down. It was nearly out. He felt strangely numb. As though from a great distance, he was aware that he was being beaten. The last sensations of pain left him. He no longer felt anything, though very faintly he could hear the impact of the club upon his body. But it was no longer his body, it seemed so far away.

And then, suddenly, without warning, uttering a cry that was inarticulate and more like the cry of an animal, John Thornton sprang upon the man who wielded the club. Hal was hurled backward, as though struck by a falling tree. Mercedes screamed.

Charles looked on wistfully, wiped his watery eyes, but did not get up because of his stiffness.

John Thornton stood over Buck, struggling to control himself, too convulsed with rage to speak.

"If you strike that dog again, I'll kill you," he at last managed to say in a choking voice.

"It's my dog," Hal replied, wiping the blood from his mouth as he came back. "Get out of my way, or I'll fix you. I'm going to Dawson."

Thornton stood between him and Buck, and evinced no intention of getting out of the way. Hal drew his long hunting-knife. Mercedes screamed, cried, laughed, and manifested the chaotic abandonment of hysteria. Thornton rapped Hal's knuckles with the axe-handle, knocking the knife to the ground. He rapped his knuckles again as he tried to pick it up. Then he stooped, picked it up himself, and with two strokes cut Buck's traces.

Hal had no fight left in him. Besides, his hands were full with his sister, or his arms, rather; while Buck was too near dead to be of further use in hauling the sled. A few minutes later they pulled out from the bank and down the river. Buck heard them go and raised his head to see. Pike was leading, Sol-leks was at the wheel, and between were Joe and Teek. They were limping and staggering. Mercedes was riding the loaded sled. Hal guided at the gee-pole, and Charles stumbled along in the rear.

As Buck watched them, Thornton knelt beside him and with rough, kindly hands searched for broken bones. By the time his search had disclosed nothing more than many bruises and a state of terrible starvation, the sled was a quarter of a mile away. Dog and man watched it crawling along over the ice. Suddenly, they saw its back end drop down, as into a rut, and the gee-pole, with Hal clinging to it, jerk into the air. Mercedes's scream came to their ears. They saw Charles turn and make one step to run back, and then a whole section of ice give way and dogs and humans disappear. A yawning hole was all that was to be seen. The bottom had dropped out of the trail.

John Thornton and Buck looked at each other.

"You poor devil," said John Thornton, and Buck licked his hand.

VI

For the Love of a Man

When John Thornton froze his feet in the previous December, his partners had made him comfortable and left him to get well, going on themselves up the river to get out a raft of saw-logs for Dawson. He was still limping slightly at the time he rescued Buck, but with the continued warm weather even the slight limp left him. And here, lying by the river bank through the long spring days, watching the running water, listening lazily to the songs of birds and the hum of nature, Buck slowly won back his strength.

A rest comes very good after one has travelled three thousand miles, and it must be confessed that Buck waxed lazy as his wounds healed, his muscles swelled out, and the flesh came back to cover his bones. For that matter, they were all loafing,—Buck, John Thornton, and Skeet and Nig,—waiting for the raft to come that was to carry them down to Dawson. Skeet was a little Irish setter who early made friends with Buck, who, in a dying condition, was unable to resent her first advances. She had the doctor trait which some dogs possess; and as a mother cat washes her kittens, so she washed and cleansed Buck's wounds. Regularly, each morning after he had finished his breakfast, she performed her self-appointed task, till he came to look for her ministrations as much as he did for Thornton's. Nig, equally friendly, though less demonstrative, was a huge black dog, half bloodhound and half deerhound, with eyes that laughed and a boundless good nature.

To Buck's surprise these dogs manifested no jealousy toward him. They seemed to share the kindliness and largeness of John Thornton. As Buck grew stronger they enticed him into all sorts of ridiculous games, in which Thornton himself could not forbear to join; and in this fashion Buck romped through his convalescence and into a new existence. Love, genuine passionate love, was his for the first time. This he had never experienced at Judge Miller's down in the sun-kissed Santa Clara Valley. With the Judge's sons, hunting and tramping, it had been a working partnership; with the Judge's grandsons, a sort of pompous guardianship; and with the Judge himself, a stately and dignified friendship. But love that was feverish and burning, that was adoration, that was madness, it had taken John Thornton to arouse.

This man had saved his life, which was something; but, further, he was the ideal master. Other men saw to the welfare of their dogs from a sense of duty and business expediency; he saw to the welfare of his as if they were his own children, because he could not help it. And he saw further. He never forgot a kindly greeting or a cheering word, and to sit down for a long talk with them ("gas" he called it) was as much his delight as theirs. He had a way of taking Buck's head roughly between his hands, and resting his own head upon Buck's, of shaking him back and forth, the while calling him ill names that to Buck were love names. Buck knew no greater joy than that rough embrace and the sound of murmured oaths, and at each jerk back and forth it seemed that his heart would be shaken out of his body so great was its ecstasy. And when, released, he sprang to his feet, his mouth laughing, his eyes eloquent, his throat vibrant with unuttered sound, and in that fashion remained without movement, John Thornton would reverently exclaim, "God! you can all but speak!"

Buck had a trick of love expression that was akin to hurt. He would often seize Thornton's hand in his mouth and close so fiercely that the flesh bore the impress of his teeth for some time afterward. And as Buck understood the oaths to be love words, so the man understood this feigned bite for a caress.

For the most part, however, Buck's love was expressed in adoration. While he went wild with happiness when Thornton touched him or spoke to him, he did not seek these tokens. Unlike Skeet, who was wont to shove her nose under Thornton's hand and nudge and nudge till petted, or Nig, who would stalk up and rest his great head on Thornton's knee, Buck was content to adore at a distance. He would lie by the hour, eager, alert, at Thornton's feet, looking up into his face, dwelling upon it, studying it, following with keenest interest each fleeting expression, every movement or change of feature. Or, as chance might have it, he would lie farther away, to the side or rear, watching the outlines of the man and the occasional movements of his body. And often, such was the communion in which they lived, the strength of Buck's gaze would draw John Thornton's head around, and he would return the gaze, without speech, his heart shining out of his eyes as Buck's heart shone out.

For a long time after his rescue, Buck did not like Thornton to get out of his sight. From the moment he left the tent to when he entered it again, Buck would follow at his heels. His transient masters since he had come into the Northland had bred in him a fear that no master could be permanent. He was afraid that Thornton would pass out of his life as Perrault and François and the Scotch half-breed had passed out. Even in the night, in his dreams, he was haunted by this fear. At such times he would shake off sleep and creep through the chill to the flap of the tent, where he would stand and listen to the sound of his master's breathing.

But in spite of this great love he bore John Thornton, which seemed to bespeak the soft civilizing influence, the strain of the primitive, which the Northland had aroused in him, remained alive and active. Faithfulness and devotion, things born of fire and roof, were his; yet he retained his wildness and wiliness. He was a thing of the wild, come in from the wild to sit by John Thornton's fire, rather than a dog of the soft Southland stamped with the marks of generations of civilization. Because of his very great love, he could not steal from this man, but from any other man, in any other camp, he did not hesitate an instant; while the cunning with which he stole enabled him to escape detection.

His face and body were scored by the teeth of many dogs, and he fought as fiercely as ever and more shrewdly. Skeet and Nig were too good-natured for quarrelling,—besides, they belonged to John Thornton; but the strange dog, no matter what the breed or valor, swiftly acknowledged Buck's supremacy or found himself struggling for life with a terrible antagonist. And Buck was merciless. He had learned well the law of club and fang, and he never forewent an advantage or drew back from a foe he had started on the way to Death. He had lessoned from Spitz, and from the chief fighting dogs of the police and mail, and knew there was no middle course. He must master or be mastered; while to show mercy was a weakness. Mercy did not exist in the primordial life. It was misunderstood for fear, and such misunderstandings made for death. Kill or be killed, eat or be eaten, was the law; and this mandate, down out of the depths of Time, he obeyed.

He was older than the days he had seen and the breaths he had drawn. He linked the past with the present, and the eternity behind him throbbed through him in a mighty rhythm to which he swayed as the tides and seasons swayed. He sat by John Thornton's fire, a broad-breasted dog, white-fanged and long-furred; but behind him were the shades of all manner of dogs, half-wolves and wild wolves, urgent and prompting, tasting the savor of the meat he ate, thirsting for the water he drank, scenting the wind with him, listening with him and telling him the sounds made by the wild life in the forest, dictating his moods, directing his actions, lying down to sleep with him when he lay down, and dreaming with him and beyond him and becoming themselves the stuff of his dreams.

So peremptorily did these shades beckon him, that each day mankind and the claims of mankind slipped farther from him. Deep in the forest a call was sounding, and as often as he heard this call, mysteriously thrilling and luring, he felt compelled to turn his back upon the fire and the beaten earth around it, and to plunge into the forest, and on and on, he knew not where or why; nor did he wonder where or why, the call sounding imperiously, deep in the forest. But as often as he gained the soft unbroken earth and the green shade, the love for John Thornton drew him back to the fire again.

Thornton alone held him. The rest of mankind was as nothing. Chance travellers might praise or pet him; but he was cold under it all, and from a too demonstrative man he would get up and walk away. When Thornton's partners, Hans and Pete, arrived on the long-expected raft, Buck refused to notice them till he learned they were close to Thornton; after that he tolerated them in a passive sort of way, accepting favors from them as though he favored them by accepting. They were of the same large type as Thornton, living close to the earth, thinking simply and seeing clearly; and ere they swung the raft into the big eddy by the saw-mill at Dawson, they understood Buck and his ways, and did not insist upon an intimacy such as obtained with Skeet and Nig.

For Thornton, however, his love seemed to grow and grow. He, alone among men, could put a pack upon Buck's back in the summer travelling. Nothing was too great for Buck to do, when Thornton commanded. One day (they had grub-staked themselves from the proceeds of the raft and left Dawson for the head-waters of the Tanana) the men and dogs were sitting on the crest of a cliff which fell away, straight down, to naked bed-rock three hundred feet below. John Thornton was sitting near the edge, Buck at his shoulder. A thoughtless whim seized Thornton, and he drew the attention of Hans and Pete to the experiment he had in mind. "Jump, Buck!" he commanded, sweeping his arm out and over the chasm. The next instant he was grappling with Buck on the extreme edge, while Hans and Pete were dragging them back into safety.

"It's uncanny," Pete said, after it was over and they had caught their speech.

Thornton shook his head. "No, it is splendid, and it is terrible, too. Do you know, it sometimes makes me afraid."

"I'm not hankering to be the man that lays hands on you while he's around," Pete announced conclusively, nodding his head toward Buck.

"Py Jingo!" was Hans's contribution. "Not mineself either."

It was at Circle City, ere the year was out, that Pete's apprehensions were realized. "Black" Burton, a man evil-tempered and malicious, and been picking a quarrel with a tenderfoot at the bar, when Thornton stepped good-naturedly between. Buck, as was his custom, was lying in a corner, head on paws, watching his master's every action. Burton struck out, without warning, straight from the shoulder. Thornton was sent spinning, and saved himself from falling only by clutching the rail of the bar.

Those who were looking on heard what was neither bark nor yelp, but a something which is best described as a roar, and they saw Buck's body rise up in the air as he left the floor for Burton's throat. The man saved his life by instinctively throwing out his arm, but was hurled backward to the floor with Buck on top of him. Buck loosed his teeth from the flesh of the arm and drove in again for the throat. This time the man succeeded only in partly blocking, and his throat was torn open. Then the crowd was upon Buck, and he was driven off; but while a surgeon checked the bleeding, he prowled up and down, growling furiously, attempting to rush in, and being forced back by an array of hostile clubs. A "miners' meeting," called on the spot, decided that the dog had sufficient provocation, and Buck was discharged. But his reputation was made, and from that day his name spread through every camp in Alaska.

Later on, in the fall of the year, he saved John Thornton's life in quite another fashion. The three partners were lining a long and narrow poling-boat down a bad stretch of rapids on the Forty-Mile Creek. Hans and Pete moved along the bank, snubbing with a thin Manila rope from tree to tree, while Thornton remained in the boat, helping its descent by means of a pole, and shouting directions to the shore. Buck, on the bank, worried and anxious, kept abreast of the boat, his eyes never off his master.

At a particularly bad spot, where a ledge of barely submerged rocks jutted out into the river, Hans cast off the rope, and, while Thornton poled the boat out into the stream, ran down the bank with the end in his hand to snub the boat when it had cleared the ledge. This it did, and was flying down-stream in a current as swift as a mill-race, when Hans checked it with the rope and checked too suddenly. The boat flirted over and snubbed in to the bank bottom up, while Thornton, flung sheer out of it, was carried down-stream toward the worst part of the rapids, a stretch of wild water in which no swimmer could live.

Buck had sprung in on the instant; and at the end of three hundred yards, amid a mad swirl of water, he overhauled Thornton. When he felt him grasp his tail, Buck headed for the bank, swimming with all his splendid strength. But the progress shoreward was slow; the progress down-stream amazingly rapid. From below came the fatal roaring where the wild current went wilder and was rent in shreds and spray by the rocks which thrust through like the teeth of an enormous comb. The suck of the water as it took the beginning of the last steep pitch was frightful, and Thornton knew that the shore was impossible. He scraped furiously over a rock, bruised across a second, and struck a third with crushing force. He clutched its slippery top with both hands, releasing Buck, and above the roar of the churning water shouted: "Go, Buck! Go!"

Buck could not hold his own, and swept on down-stream, struggling desperately, but unable to win back. When he heard Thornton's command repeated, he partly reared out of the water, throwing his head high, as though for a last look, then turned obediently toward the bank. He swam powerfully and was dragged ashore by Pete and Hans at the very point where swimming ceased to be possible and destruction began.

They knew that the time a man could cling to a slippery rock in the face of that driving current was a matter of minutes, and they ran as fast as they could up the bank to a point far above where Thornton was hanging on. They attached the line with which they had been snubbing the boat to Buck's neck and shoulders, being careful that it should neither strangle him nor impede his swimming, and launched him into the stream. He struck out boldly, but not straight enough into the stream. He discovered the mistake too late, when Thornton was abreast of him and a bare half-dozen strokes away while he was being carried helplessly past.

Hans promptly snubbed with the rope, as though Buck were a boat. The rope thus tightening on him in the sweep of the current, he was jerked under the surface, and under the surface he remained till his body struck against the bank and he was hauled out. He was half drowned, and Hans and Pete threw themselves upon him, pounding the breath into him and the water out of him. He staggered to his feet and fell down. The faint sound of Thornton's voice came to them, and though they could not make out the words of it, they knew that he was in his extremity. His master's voice acted on Buck like an electric shock. He sprang to his feet and ran up the bank ahead of the men to the point of his previous departure.

Again the rope was attached and he was launched, and again he struck out, but this time straight into the stream. He had miscalculated once, but he would not be guilty of it a second time. Hans paid out the rope, permitting no slack, while Pete kept it clear of coils. Buck held on till he was on a line straight above Thornton; then he turned, and with the speed of an express train headed down upon him. Thornton saw him coming, and, as Buck struck him like a battering ram, with the whole force of the current behind him, he reached up and closed with both arms around the shaggy neck. Hans snubbed the rope around the tree, and Buck and Thornton were jerked under the water. Strangling, suffocating, sometimes one uppermost and sometimes the other, dragging over the jagged bottom, smashing against rocks and snags, they veered in to the bank.

Thornton came to, belly downward and being violently propelled back and forth across a drift log by Hans and Pete. His first glance was for Buck, over whose limp and apparently lifeless body Nig was setting up a howl, while Skeet was licking the wet face and closed eyes. Thornton was himself bruised and battered, and he went carefully over Buck's body, when he had been brought around, finding three broken ribs.

"That settles it," he announced. "We camp right here." And camp they did, till Buck's ribs knitted and he was able to travel.

That winter, at Dawson, Buck performed another exploit, not so heroic, perhaps, but one that put his name many notches higher on the totem-pole of Alaskan fame. This exploit was particularly gratifying to the three men; for they stood in need of the outfit which it furnished, and were enabled to make a long-desired trip into the virgin East, where miners had not yet appeared. It was brought about by a conversation in the Eldorado Saloon, in which men waxed boastful of their favorite dogs. Buck, because of his record, was the target for these men, and Thornton was driven stoutly to defend him. At the end of half an hour one man stated that his dog could start a sled with five hundred pounds and walk off with it; a second bragged six hundred for his dog; and a third, seven hundred.

"Pooh! pooh!" said John Thornton; "Buck can start a thousand pounds."

"And break it out? and walk off with it for a hundred yards?" demanded Matthewson, a Bonanza King, he of the seven hundred vaunt.

"And break it out, and walk off with it for a hundred yards," John Thornton said coolly.

"Well," Matthewson said, slowly and deliberately, so that all could hear, "I've got a thousand dollars that says he can't. And there it is." So saying, he slammed a sack of gold dust the size of a bologna sausage down upon the bar.

Nobody spoke. Thornton's bluff, if bluff it was, had been called. He could feel a flush of warm blood creeping up his face. His tongue had tricked him. He did not know whether Buck could start a thousand pounds. Half a ton! The enormousness of it appalled him. He had great faith in Buck's strength and had often thought him capable of starting such a load; but never, as now, had he faced the possibility of it, the eyes of a dozen men fixed upon him, silent and waiting. Further, he had no thousand dollars; nor had Hans or Pete.

"I've got a sled standing outside now, with twenty fifty-pound sacks of flour on it," Matthewson went on with brutal directness; "so don't let that hinder you."

Thornton did not reply. He did not know what to say. He glanced from face to face in the absent way of a man who has lost the power of thought and is seeking somewhere to find the thing that will start it going again. The face of Jim O'Brien, a Mastodon King and old-time comrade, caught his eyes. It was a cue to him, seeming to rouse him to do what he would never have dreamed of doing.

"Can you lend me a thousand?" he asked, almost in a whisper.

"Sure," answered O'Brien, thumping down a plethoric sack by the side of Matthewson's. "Though it's little faith I'm having, John, that the beast can do the trick."

The Eldorado emptied its occupants into the street to see the test. The tables were deserted, and the dealers and gamekeepers came forth to see the outcome of the wager and to lay odds. Several hundred men, furred and mittened, banked around the sled within easy distance. Matthewson's sled, loaded with a thousand pounds of flour, had been standing for a couple of hours, and in the intense cold (it was sixty below zero) the runners had frozen fast to the hard-packed snow. Men offered odds of two to one that Buck could not budge the sled. A quibble arose concerning the phrase "break out." O'Brien contended it was Thornton's privilege to knock the runners loose, leaving Buck to "break it out" from a dead standstill. Matthewson insisted that the phrase included breaking the runners from the frozen grip of the snow. A majority of the men who had witnessed the making of the bet decided in his favor, whereat the odds went up to three to one against Buck.

There were no takers. Not a man believed him capable of the feat. Thornton had been hurried into the wager, heavy with doubt; and now that he looked at the sled itself, the concrete fact, with the regular team of ten dogs curled up in the snow before it, the more impossible the task appeared. Matthewson waxed jubilant.

"Three to one!" he proclaimed. "I'll lay you another thousand at that figure, Thornton. What d'ye say?"

Thornton's doubt was strong in his face, but his fighting spirit was aroused—the fighting spirit that soars above odds, fails to recognize the impossible, and is deaf to all save the clamor for battle. He called Hans and Pete to him. Their sacks were slim, and with his own the three partners could rake together only two hundred dollars. In the ebb of their fortunes, this sum was their total capital; yet they laid it unhesitatingly against Matthewson's six hundred.

The team of ten dogs was unhitched, and Buck, with his own harness, was put into the sled. He had caught the contagion of the excitement, and he felt that in some way he must do a great thing for John Thornton. Murmurs of admiration at his splendid appearance went up. He was in perfect condition, without an ounce of superfluous flesh, and the one hundred and fifty pounds that he weighed were so many pounds of grit and virility. His furry coat shone with the sheen of silk. Down the neck and across the shoulders, his mane, in repose as it was, half bristled and seemed to lift with every movement, as though excess of vigor made each particular hair alive and active. The great breast and heavy fore legs were no more than in proportion with the rest of the body, where the muscles showed in tight rolls underneath the skin. Men felt these muscles and proclaimed them hard as iron, and the odds went down to two to one.

"Gad, sir! Gad, sir!" stuttered a member of the latest dynasty, a king of the Skookum Benches. "I offer you eight hundred for him, sir, before the test, sir; eight hundred just as he stands."

Thornton shook his head and stepped to Buck's side.

"You must stand off from him," Matthewson protested. "Free play and plenty of room."

The crowd fell silent; only could be heard the voices of the gamblers vainly offering two to one. Everybody acknowledged Buck a magnificent animal, but twenty fifty-pound sacks of flour bulked too large in their eyes for them to loosen their pouch-strings.

Thornton knelt down by Buck's side. He took his head in his two hands and rested cheek on cheek. He did not playfully shake him, as was his wont, or murmur soft love curses; but he whispered in his ear. "As you love me, Buck. As you love me," was what he whispered. Buck whined with suppressed eagerness.

The crowd was watching curiously. The affair was growing mysterious. It seemed like a conjuration. As Thornton got to his feet, Buck seized his mittened hand between his jaws, pressing in with his teeth and releasing slowly, half-reluctantly. It was the answer, in terms, not of speech, but of love. Thornton stepped well back.

"Now, Buck," he said.

Buck tightened the traces, then slacked them for a matter of several inches. It was the way he had learned.

"Gee!" Thornton's voice rang out, sharp in the tense silence.

Buck swung to the right, ending the movement in a plunge that took up the slack and with a sudden jerk arrested his one hundred and fifty pounds. The load quivered, and from under the runners arose a crisp crackling.

"Haw!" Thornton commanded.

Buck duplicated the manoeuvre, this time to the left. The crackling turned into a snapping, the sled pivoting and the runners slipping and grating several inches to the side. The sled was broken out. Men were holding their breaths, intensely unconscious of the fact.

"Now, MUSH!"

Thornton's command cracked out like a pistol-shot. Buck threw himself forward, tightening the traces with a jarring lunge. His whole body was gathered compactly together in the tremendous effort, the muscles writhing and knotting like live things under the silky fur. His great chest was low to the ground, his head forward and down, while his feet were flying like mad, the claws scarring the hard-packed snow in parallel grooves. The sled swayed and trembled, half-started forward. One of his feet slipped, and one man groaned aloud. Then the sled lurched ahead in what appeared a rapid succession of jerks, though it never really came to a dead stop again . . . half an inch . . . an inch . . . two inches. . . . The jerks perceptibly diminished; as the sled gained momentum, he caught them up, till it was moving steadily along.

Men gasped and began to breathe again, unaware that for a moment they had ceased to breathe. Thornton was running behind, encouraging Buck with short, cheery words. The distance had been measured off, and as he neared the pile of firewood which marked the end of the hundred yards, a cheer began to grow and grow, which burst into a roar as he passed the firewood and halted at command. Every man was tearing himself loose, even Matthewson. Hats and mittens were flying in the air. Men were shaking hands, it did not matter with whom, and bubbling over in a general incoherent babel.

But Thornton fell on his knees beside Buck. Head was against head, and he was shaking him back and forth. Those who hurried up heard him cursing Buck, and he cursed him long and fervently, and softly and lovingly.

"Gad, sir! Gad, sir!" spluttered the Skookum Bench king. "I'll give you a thousand for him, sir, a thousand, sir—twelve hundred, sir."

Thornton rose to his feet. His eyes were wet. The tears were streaming frankly down his cheeks. "Sir," he said to the Skookum Bench king, "no, sir. You can go to hell, sir. It's the best I can do for you, sir."

Buck seized Thornton's hand in his teeth. Thornton shook him back and forth. As though animated by a common impulse, the onlookers drew back a respectful distance; nor were they again indiscreet enough to interrupt.

VII

The Sounding of the Call

WHEN Buck earned sixteen hundred dollars in five minutes for John Thornton, he made it possible for his master to pay off certain debts and to journey with his partners into the East after a fabled lost mine, the history of which was as old as the history of the country. Many men had sought it; few had found it; and more than a few there were who had never returned from the quest. This lost mine was steeped in tragedy and shrouded in mystery. No one knew of the first man. The oldest tradition stopped before it got back to him. From the beginning there had been an ancient and ramshackle cabin. Dying men had sworn to it, and to the mine the site of which it marked, clinching their testimony with nuggets that were unlike any known grade of gold in the Northland.

But no living man had looted this treasure house, and the dead were dead; wherefore John Thornton and Pete and Hans, with Buck and half a dozen other dogs, faced into the East on an unknown trail to achieve where men and dogs as good as themselves had failed. They sledded seventy miles up the Yukon, swung to the left into the Stewart River, passed the Mayo and the McQuestion, and held on until the Stewart itself became a streamlet, threading the upstanding peaks which marked the backbone of the continent.

John Thornton asked little of man or nature. He was unafraid of the wild. With a handful of salt and a rifle he could plunge into the wilderness and fare wherever he pleased and as long as he pleased. Being in no haste, Indian fashion, he hunted his dinner in the course of the day's travel; and if he failed to find it, like the Indian, he kept on travelling, secure in the knowledge that sooner or later he would come to it. So, on this great journey into the East, straight meat was the bill of fare, ammunition and tools principally made up the load on the sled, and the time-card was drawn upon the limitless future.

To Buck it was boundless delight, this hunting, fishing, and indefinite wandering through strange places. For weeks at a time they would hold on steadily, day after day; and for weeks upon end they would camp, here and there, the dogs loafing and the men burning holes through frozen muck and gravel and washing countless pans of dirt by the heat of the fire. Sometimes they went hungry, sometimes they feasted riotously, all according to the abundance of game and the fortune of hunting. Summer arrived, and dogs and men packed on their backs, rafted across blue mountain lakes, and descended or ascended unknown rivers in slender boats whipsawed from the standing forest.

The months came and went, and back and forth they twisted through the uncharted vastness, where no men were and yet where men had been if the Lost Cabin were true. They went across divides in summer blizzards, shivered under the midnight sun on naked mountains between the timber line and the eternal snows, dropped into summer valleys amid swarming gnats and flies, and in the shadows of glaciers picked strawberries and flowers as ripe and fair as any the Southland could boast. In the fall of the year they penetrated a weird lake country, sad and silent, where wild-fowl had been, but where then there was no sign of life—only the blowing of chill winds, the forming of ice in sheltered places, and the melancholy rippling of waves on lonely beaches.

And through another winter they wandered on the obliterated trails of men who had gone before. Once, they came upon a path blazed through the forest, an ancient path, and the Lost Cabin seemed very near. But the path began nowhere and ended nowhere, and it remained mystery, as the man who made it and the reason he made it remained mystery. Another time they chanced upon the time-graven wreckage of a hunting lodge, and amid the shreds of rotted blankets John Thornton found a long-barrelled flint-lock. He knew it for a Hudson Bay Company gun of the young days in the Northwest, when such a gun was worth its height in beaver skins packed flat. And that was all—no hint as to the man who in an early day had reared the lodge and left the gun among the blankets.

Spring came on once more, and at the end of all their wandering they found, not the

Lost Cabin, but a shallow placer in a broad valley where the gold showed like yellow butter across the bottom of the washing-pan. They sought no farther. Each day they worked earned them thousands of dollars in clean dust and nuggets, and they worked every day. The gold was sacked in moose-hide bags, fifty pounds to the bag, and piled like so much firewood outside the spruce-bough lodge. Like giants they toiled, days flashing on the heels of days like dreams as they heaped the treasure up.

There was nothing for the dogs to do, save the hauling in of meat now and again that Thornton killed, and Buck spent long hours musing by the fire. The vision of the short-legged hairy man came to him more frequently, now that there was little work to be done; and often, blinking by the fire, Buck wandered with him in that other world which he remembered.

The salient thing of this other world seemed fear. When he watched the hairy man sleeping by the fire, head between his knees and hands clasped above, Buck saw that he slept restlessly, with many starts and awakenings, at which times he would peer fearfully into the darkness and fling more wood upon the fire. Did they walk by the beach of a sea, where the hairy man gathered shell-fish and ate them as he gathered, it was with eyes that roved everywhere for hidden danger and with legs prepared to run like the wind at its first appearance. Through the forest they crept noiselessly, Buck at the hairy man's heels; and they were alert and vigilant, the pair of them, ears twitching and moving and nostrils quivering, for the man heard and smelled as keenly as Buck. The hairy man could spring up into the trees and travel ahead as fast as on the ground, swinging by the arms from limb to limb, sometimes a dozen feet apart, letting go and catching, never falling, never missing his grip. In fact, he seemed as much at home among the trees as on the ground; and Buck had memories of nights of vigil spent beneath trees wherein the hairy man roosted, holding on tightly as he slept.

And closely akin to the visions of the hairy man was the call still sounding in the depths of the forest. It filled him with a great unrest and strange desires. It caused him to feel a vague, sweet gladness, and he was aware of wild yearnings and stirrings for he knew not what. Sometimes he pursued the call into the forest, looking for it as though it were a tangible thing, barking softly or defiantly, as the mood might dictate. He would thrust his nose into the cool wood moss, or into the black soil where long grasses grew, and snort joy at the fat earth smells; or he would crouch for hours, as if in concealment, behind fungus-covered trunks of fallen trees, wide-eyed and wide-eared to all that moved and sounded about him. It might be, lying thus, that he hoped to surprise this call he could not understand. But he did not know why he did these various things. He was impelled to do them, and did not reason about them at all.

Irresistible impulses seized him. He would be lying in camp, dozing lazily in the heat of the day, when suddenly his head would lift and his ears cock up, intent and listening, and he would spring to his feet and dash away, and on and on, for hours, through the forest aisles and across the open spaces where the niggerheads bunched. He loved to run down dry water-courses, and to creep and spy upon the bird life in the woods. For a day at a time he would lie in the underbrush where he could watch the partridges drumming and strutting up and down. But especially he loved to run in the dim twilight of the summer midnights, listening to the subdued and sleepy murmurs of the forest, reading signs and sounds as man may read a book, and seeking for the mysterious something that called—called, waking or sleeping, at all times, for him to come.

One night he sprang from sleep with a start, eager-eyed, nostrils quivering and scenting, his mane bristling in recurrent waves. From the forest came the call (or one note of it, for the call was many noted), distinct and definite as never before,—a long-drawn howl, like, yet unlike, any noise made by husky dog. And he knew it, in the old familiar way, as a sound heard before. He sprang through the sleeping camp and in swift silence dashed through the woods. As he drew closer to the cry he went more slowly, with caution in every movement, till he came to an open place among the trees, and looking out saw, erect on haunches, with nose pointed to the sky, a long, lean, timber wolf.

He had made no noise, yet it ceased from its howling and tried to sense his presence. Buck stalked into the open, half crouching, body gathered compactly together, tail straight and stiff, feet falling with unwonted care. Every movement advertised commingled threatening and overture of friendliness. It was the menacing truce that marks the meeting of wild beasts that prey. But the wolf fled at sight of him. He followed, with wild leapings, in a frenzy to overtake. He ran him into a blind channel, in the bed of the creek, where a timber jam barred the way. The wolf whirled about, pivoting on his hind legs after the fashion of Joe and of all cornered husky dogs, snarling and bristling, clipping his teeth together in a continuous and rapid succession of snaps.

Buck did not attack, but circled him about and hedged him in with friendly advances. The wolf was suspicious and afraid; for Buck made three of him in weight, while his head barely reached Buck's shoulder. Watching his chance, he darted away, and the chase resumed. Time and again he was cornered, and the thing repeated, though he was in poor condition, or Buck could not so easily have overtaken him. He would run till Buck's head was even with his flank, when he would whirl around at bay, only to dash away again at the first opportunity.

But in the end Buck's pertinacity was rewarded; for the wolf, finding that no harm was intended, finally sniffed noses with him. Then they became friendly, and played about in the nervous, half-coy way with which fierce beasts belie their fierceness. After some time of this the wolf started off at an easy lope in a manner that plainly showed he was going somewhere. He made it clear to Buck that he was to come, and they ran side by side through the sombre twilight, straight up the creek bed, into the gorge from which it issued, and across the bleak divide where it took its rise.

On the opposite slope of the watershed they came down into a level country where were great stretches of forest and many streams, and through these great stretches they ran steadily, hour after hour, the sun rising higher and the day growing warmer. Buck was wildly glad. He knew he was at last answering the call, running by the side of his wood brother toward the place from where the call surely came. Old memories were coming upon him fast, and he was stirring to them as of old he stirred to the realities of which they were the shadows. He had done this thing before, somewhere in that other and dimly remembered world, and he was doing it again, now, running free in the open, the unpacked earth underfoot, the wide sky overhead.

They stopped by a running stream to drink, and, stopping, Buck remembered John Thornton. He sat down. The wolf started on toward the place from where the call surely came, then returned to him, sniffing noses and making actions as though to encourage him. But Buck turned about and started slowly on the back track. For the better part of an hour the wild brother ran by his side, whining softly. Then he sat down, pointed his nose upward, and howled. It was a mournful howl, and as Buck held steadily on his way he heard it grow faint and fainter until it was lost in the distance.

John Thornton was eating dinner when Buck dashed into camp and sprang upon him in a frenzy of affection, overturning him, scrambling upon him, licking his face, biting his hand—"playing the general tom-fool," as John Thornton characterized it, the while he shook Buck back and forth and cursed him lovingly.

For two days and nights Buck never left camp, never let Thornton out of his sight. He followed him about at his work, watched him while he ate, saw him into his blankets at night and out of them in the morning. But after two days the call in the forest began to sound more imperiously than ever. Buck's restlessness came back on him, and he was haunted by recollections of the wild brother, and of the smiling land beyond the divide and the run side by side through the wide forest stretches. Once again he took to wandering in the woods, but the wild brother came no more; and though he listened through long vigils, the mournful howl was never raised.

He began to sleep out at night, staying away from camp for days at a time; and once he crossed the divide at the head of the creek and went down into the land of timber and streams. There he wandered for a week, seeking vainly for fresh sign of the wild brother, killing his meat as he travelled and travelling with the long, easy lope that seems never to tire. He fished for salmon in a broad stream that emptied somewhere into the sea, and by this stream he killed a large black bear, blinded by the mosquitoes while likewise fishing, and raging through the forest helpless and terrible. Even so, it was a hard fight, and it aroused the last latent remnants of Buck's ferocity. And two days later, when he returned to his kill and found a dozen wolverines quarrelling over the spoil, he scattered them like chaff; and those that fled left two behind who would quarrel no more.

The blood-longing became stronger than ever before. He was a killer, a thing that preyed, living on things that lived, unaided, alone, by virtue of his own strength and prowess, surviving triumphantly in a hostile environment where only the strong survived. Because of all this he became possessed of a great pride in himself, which communicated itself like a contagion to his physical being. It advertised itself in all his movements, was apparent in the play of every muscle, spoke plainly as speech in the way he carried himself, and made his glorious furry coat if anything more glorious. But for the stray brown on his muzzle and above his eyes, and for the splash of white hair that ran mid-most down his chest, he might well have been mistaken for a gigantic wolf, larger than the largest of the breed. From his St. Bernard father he had inherited size and weight, but it was his shepherd mother who had given shape to that size and weight. His muzzle was the long wolf muzzle, save that it was larger than the muzzle of any wolf; and his head, somewhat broader, was the wolf head on a massive scale.

His cunning was wolf cunning, and wild cunning; his intelligence, shepherd intelligence and St. Bernard intelligence; and all this, plus an experience gained in the fiercest of schools, made him as formidable a creature as any that roamed the wild. A carnivorous animal, living on a straight meat diet, he was in full flower, at the high tide of his life, overspilling with vigor and virility. When Thornton passed a caressing hand along his back, a snapping and cracking followed the hand, each hair discharging its pent magnetism at the contact. Every part, brain and body, nerve tissue and fibre, was keyed to the most exquisite pitch; and between all the parts there was a perfect equilibrium or adjustment. To sights and sounds and events which required action, he responded with lightning-like rapidity. Quickly as a husky dog could leap to defend from attack or to attack, he could leap twice as quickly. He saw the movement, or heard sound, and responded in less time than another dog required to compass the mere seeing or hearing. He perceived and determined and responded in the same instant. In point of fact the three actions of perceiving, determining, and responding were sequential; but so infinitesimal were the intervals of time between them that they appeared simultaneous. His muscles were surcharged with vitality, and snapped into play sharply, like steel springs. Life streamed through him in splendid flood, glad and rampant, until it seemed that it would burst him asunder in sheer ecstasy and pour forth generously over the world.

"Never was there such a dog," said John Thornton one day, as the partners watched Buck marching out of camp.

"When he was made, the mould was broke," said Pete.

"Py jingo! I t'ink so mineself," Hans affirmed.

They saw him marching out of camp, but they did not see the instant and terrible transformation which took place as soon as he was within the secrecy of the forest. He no longer marched. At once he became a thing of the wild, stealing along softly, cat-footed, a passing shadow that appeared and disappeared among the shadows. He knew how to take advantage of every cover, to crawl on his belly like a snake, and like a snake to leap and strike. He could take a ptarmigan from its nest, kill a rabbit as it slept, and snap in mid air the little chipmunks fleeing a second too late for the trees. Fish, in open pools, were not too quick for him; nor were beaver, mending their dams, too wary. He killed to eat, not from wantonness; but he preferred to eat what he killed himself. So a lurking humor ran through his deeds, and it was his delight to steal upon the squirrels, and, when he all but had them, to let them go, chattering in mortal fear to the treetops.

As the fall of the year came on, the moose appeared in greater abundance, moving slowly down to meet the winter in the lower and less rigorous valleys. Buck had already dragged down a stray part-grown calf; but he wished strongly for larger and more formidable quarry, and he came upon it one day on the divide at the head of the creek. A band of twenty moose had crossed over from the land of streams and timber, and chief among them was a great bull. He was in a savage temper, and, standing over six feet from the ground, was as formidable an antagonist as even Buck could desire. Back and forth the bull tossed his great palmated antlers, branching to fourteen points and embracing seven feet within the tips. His small eyes burned with a vicious and bitter light, while he roared with fury at sight of Buck.

From the bull's side, just forward of the flank, protruded a feathered arrow-end, which accounted for his savageness. Guided by that instinct which came from the old hunting days of the primordial world, Buck proceeded to cut the bull out from the herd. It was no slight task. He would bark and dance about in front of the bull, just out of reach of the great antlers and of the terrible splay hoofs which could have stamped his life out with a single blow. Unable to turn his back on the fanged danger and go on, the bull would be driven into paroxysms of rage. At such moments he charged Buck, who retreated craftily, luring him on by a simulated inability to escape. But when he was thus separated from his fellows, two or three of the younger bulls would charge back upon Buck and enable the wounded bull to rejoin the herd.

There is a patience of the wild—dogged, tireless, persistent as life itself—that holds motionless for endless hours the spider in its web, the snake in its coils, the panther in its ambuscade; this patience belongs peculiarly to life when it hunts its living food; and it belonged to Buck as he clung to the flank of the herd, retarding its march, irritating the young bulls, worrying the cows with their half-grown calves, and driving the wounded bull mad with rage. For half a day this continued. Buck multiplied himself, attacking from all sides, enveloping the herd in a whirlwind of menace, cutting out his victim as fast as it could rejoin its mates, wearing out the patience of creatures preyed upon, which is a lesser patience than that of creatures preying.

As the day wore along and the sun dropped to its bed in the northwest (the darkness had come back and the fall nights were six hours long), the young bulls retraced their steps more and more reluctantly to the aid of their beset leader. The down-coming winter was harrying them on to the lower levels, and it seemed they could never shake off this tireless creature that held them back. Besides, it was not the life of the herd, or of the young bulls, that was threatened. The life of only one member was demanded, which was a remoter interest than their lives, and in the end they were content to pay the toll.

As twilight fell the old bull stood with lowered head, watching his mates—the cows he had known, the calves he had fathered, the bulls he had mastered—as they shambled on at a rapid pace through the fading light. He could not follow, for before his nose leaped the merciless fanged terror that would not let him go. Three hundredweight more than half a ton he weighed; he had lived a long, strong life, full of fight and struggle, and at the end he faced death at the teeth of a creature whose head did not reach beyond his great knuckled knees.

From then on, night and day, Buck never left his prey, never gave it a moment's rest, never permitted it to browse the leaves of trees or the shoots of young birch and willow. Nor did he give the wounded bull opportunity to slake his burning thirst in the slender trickling streams they crossed. Often, in desperation, he burst into long stretches of flight. At such times Buck did not attempt to stay him, but loped easily at his heels, satisfied with the way the game was played, lying down when the moose stood still, attacking him fiercely when he strove to eat or drink.

The great head drooped more and more under its tree of horns, and the shambling trot grew weak and weaker. He took to standing for long periods, with nose to the ground and dejected ears dropped limply; and Buck found more time in which to get water for himself and in which to rest. At such moments, panting with red lolling tongue and with eyes fixed upon the big bull, it appeared to Buck that a change was coming over the face of things. He could feel a new stir in the land. As the moose were coming into the land, other kinds of life were coming in. Forest and stream and air seemed palpitant with their presence. The news of it was borne in upon him, not by sight, or sound, or smell, but by some other and subtler sense. He heard nothing, saw nothing, yet knew that the land was somehow different; that through it strange things were afoot and ranging; and he resolved to investigate after he had finished the business in hand.

At last, at the end of the fourth day, he pulled the great moose down. For a day and a night he remained by the kill, eating and sleeping, turn and turn about. Then, rested, refreshed and strong, he turned his face toward camp and John Thornton. He broke into the long easy lope, and went on, hour after hour, never at loss for the tangled way, heading straight home through strange country with a certitude of direction that put man and his magnetic needle to shame.

As he held on he became more and more conscious of the new stir in the land. There was life abroad in it different from the life which had been there throughout the summer. No longer was this fact borne in upon him in some subtle, mysterious way. The birds talked of it, the squirrels chattered about it, the very breeze whispered of it. Several times he stopped and drew in the fresh morning air in great sniffs, reading a message which made him leap on with greater speed. He was oppressed with a sense of calamity happening, if it were not calamity already happened; and as he crossed the last watershed and dropped down into the valley toward camp, he proceeded with greater caution.

Three miles away he came upon a fresh trail that sent his neck hair rippling and bristling. It led straight toward camp and John Thornton. Buck hurried on, swiftly and stealthily, every nerve straining and tense, alert to the multitudinous details which told a story—all but the end. His nose gave him a varying description of the passage of the life on the heels of which he was travelling. He remarked the pregnant silence of the forest. The bird life had flitted. The squirrels were in hiding. One only he saw,—a sleek gray fellow, flattened against a gray dead limb so that he seemed a part of it, a woody excrescence upon the wood itself.

As Buck slid along with the obscureness of a gliding shadow, his nose was jerked suddenly to the side as though a positive force had gripped and pulled it. He followed the new scent into a thicket and found Nig. He was lying on his side, dead where he had dragged himself, an arrow protruding, head and feathers, from either side of his body.

A hundred yards farther on, Buck came upon one of the sled-dogs Thornton had bought in Dawson. This dog was thrashing about in a death-struggle, directly on the trail, and Buck passed around him without stopping. From the camp came the faint sound of many voices, rising and falling in a sing-song chant. Bellying forward to the edge of the clearing, he found Hans, lying on his face, feathered with arrows like a porcupine. At the same instant Buck peered out where the spruce-bough lodge had been and saw what made his hair leap straight up on his neck and shoulders. A gust of overpowering rage swept over him. He did not know that he growled, but he growled aloud with a terrible ferocity. For the last time in his life he allowed passion to usurp cunning and reason, and it was because of his great love for John Thornton that he lost his head.

The Yeehats were dancing about the wreckage of the spruce-bough lodge when they heard a fearful roaring and saw rushing upon them an animal the like of which they had never seen before. It was Buck, a live hurricane of fury, hurling himself upon them in a frenzy to destroy. He sprang at the foremost man (it was the chief of the Yeehats), ripping the throat wide open till the rent jugular spouted a fountain of blood. He did not pause to worry the victim, but ripped in passing, with the next bound tearing wide the throat of a second man. There was no withstanding him. He plunged about in their very midst, tearing, rending, destroying, in constant and terrific motion which defied the arrows they discharged at him. In fact, so inconceivably rapid were his movements, and so closely were the Indians tangled together, that they shot one another with the arrows; and one young hunter, hurling a spear at Buck in mid air, drove it through the chest of another hunter with such force that the point broke through the skin of the back and stood out beyond. Then a panic seized the Yeehats, and they fled in terror to the woods, proclaiming as they fled the advent of the Evil Spirit.

And truly Buck was the Fiend incarnate, raging at their heels and dragging them down like deer as they raced through the trees. It was a fateful day for the Yeehats. They scattered far and wide over the country, and it was not till a week later that the last of the survivors gathered together in a lower valley and counted their losses. As for Buck, wearying of the pursuit, he returned to the desolated camp. He found Pete where he had been killed in his blankets in the first moment of surprise. Thornton's desperate struggle was fresh-written on the earth, and Buck scented every detail of it down to the edge of a deep pool. By the edge, head and fore feet in the water, lay Skeet, faithful to the last. The pool itself, muddy and discolored from the sluice boxes, effectually hid what it contained, and it contained John Thornton; for Buck followed his trace into the water, from which no trace led away.

All day Buck brooded by the pool or roamed restlessly about the camp. Death, as a cessation of movement, as a passing out and away from the lives of the living, he knew, and he knew John Thornton was dead. It left a great void in him, somewhat akin to hunger, but a void which ached and ached, and which food could not fill. At times, when he paused to contemplate the carcasses of the Yeehats, he forgot the pain of it; and at such times he was aware of a great pride in himself,—a pride greater than any he had yet experienced. He had killed man, the noblest game of all, and he had killed in the face of the law of club and fang. He sniffed the bodies curiously. They had died so easily. It was harder to kill a husky dog than them. They were no match at all, were it not for their arrows and spears and clubs. Thence-forward he would be unafraid of them except when they bore in their hands their arrows, spears, and clubs.

Night came on, and a full moon rose high over the trees into the sky, lighting the land till it lay bathed in ghostly day. And with the coming of the night, brooding and mourning by the pool, Buck became alive to a stirring of the new life in the forest other than that which the Yeehats had made. He stood up, listening and scenting. From far away drifted a faint, sharp yelp, followed by a chorus of similar sharp yelps. As the moments passed the yelps grew closer and louder. Again Buck knew them as things heard in that other world which persisted in his memory. He walked to the centre of the open space and listened. It was the call, the many-noted call, sounding more luringly and compellingly than ever before. And as never before, he was ready to obey. John Thornton was dead. The last tie was broken. Man and the claims of man no longer bound him.

Hunting their living meat, as the Yeehats were hunting it, on the flanks of the migrating moose, the wolf pack had at last crossed over from the land of streams and timber and invaded Buck's valley. Into the clearing where the moonlight streamed, they poured in a silvery flood; and in the centre of the clearing stood Buck, motionless as a statue, waiting their coming. They were awed, so still and large he stood, and a moment's pause fell, till the boldest one leaped straight for him. Like a flash Buck struck, breaking the neck. Then he stood, without movement, as before, the stricken wolf rolling in agony behind him. Three others tried it in sharp succession; and one after the other they drew back, streaming blood from slashed throats or shoulders.

This was sufficient to fling the whole pack forward, pell-mell, crowded together, blocked and confused by its eagerness to pull down the prey. Buck's marvellous quickness and agility stood him in good stead. Pivoting on his hind legs, and snapping and gashing, he was everywhere at once, presenting a front which was apparently unbroken so swiftly did he whirl and guard from side to side. But to prevent them from getting behind him, he was forced back, down past the pool and into the creek bed, till he brought up against a high gravel bank. He worked along to a right angle in the bank which the men had made in the course of mining, and in this angle he came to bay, protected on three sides and with nothing to do but face the front.

And so well did he face it, that at the end of half an hour the wolves drew back discomfited. The tongues of all were out and lolling, the white fangs showing cruelly white in the moonlight. Some were lying down with heads raised and ears pricked forward; others stood on their feet, watching him; and still others were lapping water from the pool. One wolf, long and lean and gray, advanced cautiously, in a friendly manner, and Buck recognized the wild brother with whom he had run for a night and a day. He was whining softly, and, as Buck whined, they touched noses.

Then an old wolf, gaunt and battle-scarred, came forward. Buck writhed his lips into the preliminary of a snarl, but sniffed noses with him. Whereupon the old wolf sat down, pointed nose at the moon, and broke out the long wolf howl. The others sat down and howled. And now the call came to Buck in unmistakable accents. He, too, sat down and howled. This over, he came out of his angle and the pack crowded around him, sniffing in half-friendly, half-savage manner. The leaders lifted the yelp of the pack and sprang away into the woods. The wolves swung in behind, yelping in chorus. And Buck ran with them, side by side with the wild brother, yelping as he ran.

And here may well end the story of Buck. The years were not many when the Yeehats noted a change in the breed of timber wolves; for some were seen with splashes of brown on head and muzzle, with a rift of white centring down the chest. But more remarkable than this, the Yeehats tell of a Ghost Dog that runs at the head of the pack. They are afraid of this Ghost Dog, for it has cunning greater than they, stealing from their camps in fierce winters, robbing their traps, slaying their dogs, and defying the bravest hunters.

Nay, the tale grows worse. Hunters there are who fail to return to the camp, and hunters there have been whom their tribesmen found with throats slashed cruelly open and with wolf prints about them in the snow greater than the prints of any wolf. Each fall, when the Yeehats follow the movement of the moose, there is a certain valley which they never enter. And women there are who become sad when the word goes over the fire of how the Evil Spirit came to select that valley for an abiding-place.

In the summers there is one visitor, however, to that valley, of which the Yeehats do not know. It is a great, gloriously coated wolf, like, and yet unlike, all other wolves. He crosses alone from the smiling timber land and comes down into an open space among the trees. Here a yellow stream flows from rotted moose-hide sacks and sinks into the ground, with long grasses growing though it and vegetable mould overrunning it and hiding its yellow from the sun; and here he muses for a time, howling once, long and mournfully, ere he departs.

But he is not always alone. When the long winter nights come on and the wolves follow their meat into the lower valleys, he may be seen running at the head of the pack through the pale moonlight or glimmering borealis, leaping gigantic above his fellows, his great throat a-bellow as he sings a song of the younger world, which is the song of the pack.

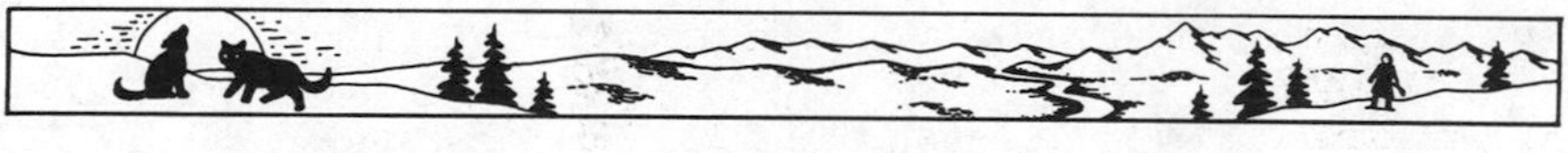

[illegible]

[illegible]

[illegible]

[illegible]

[illegible]

WHITE FANG

Part One—The Wild

I

The Trail of the Meat

Dark spruce forest frowned on either side the frozen waterway. The trees had been stripped by a recent wind of their white covering of frost, and they seemed to lean toward each other, black and ominous, in the fading light. A vast silence reigned over the land. The land itself was a desolation, lifeless, without movement, so lone and cold that the spirit of it was not even that of sadness. There was a hint in it of laughter, but of a laughter more terrible than any sadness—a laughter that was mirthless as the smile of the Sphinx, a laughter cold as the frost and partaking of the grimness of infallibility. It was the masterful and incommunicable wisdom of eternity laughing at the futility of life and the effort of life. It was the Wild, the savage, frozen-hearted Northland Wild.

But there *was* life, abroad in the land and defiant. Down the frozen waterway toiled a string of wolfish dogs. Their bristly fur was rimed with frost. Their breath froze in the air as it left their mouths, spouting forth in spumes of vapor that settled upon the hair of their bodies and formed into crystals of frost. Leather harness was on the dogs, and leather traces attached them to a sled which dragged along behind. The sled was without runners. It was made of stout birch-bark, and its full surface rested on the snow. The front end of the sled was turned up, like a scroll, in order to force down and under the bore of soft snow that surged like a wave before it. On the sled, securely lashed, was a long and narrow oblong box. There were other things on the sled—blankets, an axe, and a coffee-pot and frying-pan; but prominent, occupying most of the space, was the long and narrow oblong box.

In advance of the dogs, on wide snowshoes, toiled a man. At the rear of the sled toiled a second man. On the sled, in the box, lay a third man whose toil was over,—a man whom the Wild had conquered and beaten down until he would never move nor struggle again. It is not the way of the Wild to like movement. Life is an offence to it, for life is movement; and the Wild aims always to destroy movement. It freezes the water to prevent it running to the sea; it drives the sap out of the trees till they are frozen to their mighty hearts; and most ferociously and terribly of all does the Wild harry and crush into submission man—man, who is the most restless of life, ever in revolt against the dictum that all movement must in the end come to the cessation of movement.

But at front and rear, unawed and indomitable, toiled the two men who were not yet dead. Their bodies were covered with fur and soft-tanned leather. Eyelashes and cheeks and lips were so coated with the crystals from their frozen breath that their faces were not discernible. This gave them the seeming of ghostly masques, undertakers in a spectral world at the funeral of some ghost. But under it all they were men, penetrating the land of desolation and mockery and silence, puny adventurers bent on colossal adventure, pitting themselves against the might of a world as remote and alien and pulseless as the abysses of space.

They travelled on without speech, saving their breath for the work of their bodies. On every side was the silence, pressing upon them with a tangible presence. It affected their minds as the many atmospheres of deep water affect the body of the diver. It crushed them with the weight of unending vastness and unalterable decree. It crushed them into the remotest recesses of their own minds, pressing out of them, like juices from the grape, all the false ardors and exaltations and undue self-values of the human soul, until they perceived themselves finite and small, specks and motes, moving with weak cunning and little wisdom amidst the play and interplay of the great blind elements and forces.

An hour went by, and a second hour. The pale light of the short sunless day was beginning to fade, when a faint far cry arose on the still air. It soared upward with a swift rush, till it reached its topmost note, where it persisted, palpitant and tense, and then slowly died away. It might have been a lost soul wailing, had it not been invested with a certain sad fierceness and hungry eagerness. The front man turned his head until his eyes met the eyes of the man behind. And then, across the narrow oblong box, each nodded to the other.

A second cry arose, piercing the silence with needlelike shrillness. Both men located the sound. It was to the rear, somewhere in the snow expanse they had just traversed. A third and answering cry arose, also to the rear and to the left of the second cry.

"They're after us, Bill," said the man at the front.

His voice sounded hoarse and unreal, and he had spoken with apparent effort.

"Meat is scarce," answered his comrade. "I ain't seen a rabbit sign for days."

Thereafter they spoke no more, though their ears were keen for the hunting-cries that continued to rise behind them.

At the fall of darkness they swung the dogs into a cluster of spruce trees on the edge of the waterway and made a camp. The coffin, at the side of the fire, served for seat and table. The wolf-dogs, clustered on the far side of the fire, snarled and bickered among themselves, but evinced no inclination to stray off into the darkness.

"Seems to me, Henry, they're stayin' remarkable close to camp," Bill commented.

Henry, squatting over the fire and settling the pot of coffee with a piece of ice, nodded. Nor did he speak till he had taken his seat on the coffin and begun to eat.

"They know where their hides is safe," he said. "They'd sooner eat grub than be grub. They're pretty wise, them dogs."

Bill shook his head. "Oh, I don't know."

His comrade looked at him curiously. "First time I ever heard you say anythin' about their not bein' wise."

"Henry," said the other, munching with deliberation the beans he was eating, "did you happen to notice the way them dogs kicked up when I was a-feedin' 'em?"

"They did cut up more'n usual," Henry acknowledged.

"How many dogs've we got, Henry?"

"Six."

"Well, Henry . . ." Bill stopped for a moment, in order that his words might gain greater significance. "As I was sayin', Henry, we've got six dogs. I took six fish out of the bag. I gave one fish to each dog, an', Henry, I was one fish short."

"You counted wrong."

"We've got six dogs," the other reiterated dispassionately. "I took out six fish. One Ear didn't get no fish. I come back to the bag afterward an' got 'm his fish."

"We've only got six dogs," Henry said.

"Henry," Bill went on, "I won't say they was all dogs, but there was seven of 'm that got fish."

Henry stopped eating to glance across the fire and count the dogs.

"There's only six now," he said.

"I saw the other one run off across the snow," Bill announced with cool positiveness. "I saw seven."

His comrade looked at him commiseratingly, and said, "I'll be almighty glad when this trip's over."

"What d'ye mean by that?" Bill demanded.

"I mean that this load of ourn is gettin' on your nerves, an' that you're beginnin' to see things."

"I thought of that," Bill answered gravely. "An' so, when I saw it run off across the snow, I looked in the snow an' saw its tracks. Then I counted the dogs an' there was still six of 'em. The tracks is there in the snow now. D'ye want to look at 'em? I'll show 'm to you."

Henry did not reply, but munched on in silence, until, the meal finished, he topped it with a final cup of coffee. He wiped his mouth with the back of his hand and said:

"Then you're thinkin' as it was—"

A long wailing cry, fiercely sad, from somewhere in the darkness, had interrupted him. He stopped to listen to it, then he finished his sentence with a wave of his hand toward the sound of the cry, "—one of them?"

Bill nodded. "I'd a blame sight sooner think that than anything else. You noticed yourself the row the dogs made."

Cry after cry, and answering cries, were turning the silence into a bedlam. From every side the cries arose, and the dogs betrayed their fear by huddling together and so close to the fire that their hair was scorched by the heat. Bill threw on more wood, before lighting his pipe.

"I'm thinkin' you're down in the mouth some," Henry said.

"Henry . . ." He sucked meditatively at his pipe for some time before he went on. "Henry, I was a-thinkin' what a blame sight luckier he is than you an' me'll ever be."

He indicated the third person by a downward thrust of the thumb to the box on which they sat.

"You an' me, Henry, when we die, we'll be lucky if we get enough stones over our carcases to keep the dogs off of us."

"But we ain't got people an' money an' all the rest, like him," Henry rejoined. "Long-distance funerals is somethin' you an' me can't exactly afford."

"What gets me, Henry, is what a chap like this, that's a lord or something in his own country, and that's never had to bother about grub nor blankets, why he comes a-buttin' round the God-forsaken ends of the earth—that's what I can't exactly see."

"He might have lived to a ripe old age if he'd stayed to home," Henry agreed.

Bill opened his mouth to speak, but changed his mind. Instead, he pointed toward the wall of darkness that pressed about them from every side. There was no suggestion of form in the utter blackness; only could be seen a pair of eyes gleaming like live coals. Henry indicated with his head a second pair, and a third. A circle of the gleaming eyes had drawn about their camp. Now and again a pair of eyes moved, or disappeared to appear again a moment later.

The unrest of the dogs had been increasing, and they stampeded, in a surge of sudden fear, to the near side of the fire, cringing and crawling about the legs of the men. In the scramble one of the dogs had been overturned on the edge of the fire, and it had yelped with pain and fright as the smell of its singed coat possessed the air. The commotion caused the circle of eyes to shift restlessly for a moment and even to withdraw a bit, but it settled down again as the dogs became quiet.

"Henry, it's a blame misfortune to be out of ammunition."

Bill had finished his pipe and was helping his companion spread the bed of fur and blanket upon the spruce boughs which he had laid over the snow before supper. Henry grunted, and began unlacing his moccasins.

"How many cartridges did you say you had left?" he asked.

"Three," came the answer. "An' I wisht 'twas three hundred. Then I'd show 'em what for, damn 'em!"

He shook his fist angrily at the gleaming eyes, and began securely to prop his moccasins before the fire.

"An' I wisht this cold snap'd break," he went on. "It's ben fifty below for two weeks now. An' I wisht I'd never started on this trip, Henry. I don't like the looks of it. It don't feel right, somehow. An' while I'm wishin', I wisht the trip was over an' done with, an' you an' me a-sittin' by the fire in Fort McGurry just about now an' playin' cribbage—that's what I wisht."

Henry grunted and crawled into bed. As he dozed off he was aroused by his comrade's voice.

"Say, Henry, that other one that come in an' got a fish—why didn't the dogs pitch into it? That's what's botherin' me."

"You're botherin' too much, Bill," came the sleepy response. "You was never like this before. You jes' shut up now, an' go to sleep, an' you'll be all hunkydory in the mornin'. Your stomach's sour, that's what's botherin' you."

The men slept, breathing heavily, side by side, under the one covering. The fire died down, and the gleaming eyes drew closer the circle they had flung about the camp. The dogs clustered together in fear, now and again snarling menacingly as a pair of eyes drew close. Once their uproar became so loud that Bill woke up. He got out of bed carefully, so as not to disturb the sleep of his comrade, and threw more wood on the fire. As it began to flame up, the circle of eyes drew farther back. He glanced casually at the huddling dogs. He rubbed his eyes and looked at them more sharply. Then he crawled back into the blankets.

"Henry," he said. "Oh, Henry."

Henry groaned as he passed from sleep to waking, and demanded, "What's wrong now?"

"Nothin'," came the answer; "only there's seven of 'em again. I just counted."

Henry acknowledged receipt of the information with a grunt that slid into a snore as he drifted back into sleep.

In the morning it was Henry who awoke first and routed his companion out of bed. Daylight was yet three hours away, though it was already six o'clock; and in the darkness Henry went about preparing breakfast, while Bill rolled the blankets and made the sled ready for lashing.

"Say, Henry," he asked suddenly, "how many dogs did you say we had?"

"Six."

"Wrong," Bill proclaimed triumphantly.

"Seven again?" Henry queried.

"No, five; one's gone."

"The hell!" Henry cried in wrath, leaving the cooking to come and count the dogs.

"You're right, Bill," he concluded. "Fatty's gone."

"An' he went like greased lightnin' once he got started. Couldn't've seen 'm for smoke."

"No chance at all," Henry concluded. "They jes' swallowed 'm alive. I bet he was yelpin' as he went down their throats, damn 'em!"

"He always was a fool dog," said Bill.

"But no fool dog ought to be fool enough to go off an' commit suicide that way." He looked over the remainder of the team with a speculative eye that summed up instantly the salient traits of each animal. "I bet none of the others would do it."

"Couldn't drive 'em away from the fire with a club," Bill agreed. "I always did think there was somethin' wrong with Fatty, anyway."

And this was the epitaph of a dead dog on the Northland trail—less scant than the epitaph of many another dog, of many a man.

II

The She-Wolf

Breakfast eaten and the slim camp-outfit lashed to the sled, the men turned their backs on the cheery fire and launched out into the darkness. At once began to rise the cries that were fiercely sad—cries that called through the darkness and cold to one another and answered back. Conversation ceased. Daylight came at nine o'clock. At midday the sky to the south warmed to rose-color, and marked where the bulge of the earth intervened between the meridian sun and the northern world. But the rose-color swiftly faded. The gray light of day that remained lasted until three o'clock, when it, too, faded, and the pall of the Arctic night descended upon the lone and silent land.

As darkness came on, the hunting-cries to right and left and rear drew closer—so close that more than once they sent surges of fear through the toiling dogs, throwing them into short-lived panics.

At the conclusion of one such panic, when he and Henry had got the dogs back in the traces, Bill said:

"I wisht they'd strike game somewheres, an' go away an' leave us alone."

"They do get on the nerves horrible," Henry sympathized.

They spoke no more until camp was made.

Henry was bending over and adding ice to the bubbling pot of beans when he was startled by the sound of a blow, an exclamation from Bill, and a sharp snarling cry of pain from among the dogs. He straightened up in time to see a dim form disappearing across the snow into the shelter of the dark. Then he saw Bill, standing amid the dogs, half triumphant, half crest-fallen, in one hand a stout club, in the other the tail and part of the body of a sun-cured salmon.

"It got half of it," he announced; "but I got a whack at it jes' the same. D'ye hear it squeal?"

"What'd it look like?" Henry asked.

"Couldn't see. But it had four legs an' a mouth an' hair an' looked like any dog."

"Must be a tame wolf, I reckon."

"It's damned tame, whatever it is, comin' in here at feedin' time an' gettin' its whack of fish."

That night, when supper was finished and they sat on the oblong box and pulled at their pipes, the circle of gleaming eyes drew in even closer than before.

"I wisht they'd spring up a bunch of moose or somethin', an' go away an' leave us alone," Bill said.

Henry grunted with an intonation that was not all sympathy, and for a quarter of an hour they sat on in silence, Henry staring at the fire, and Bill at the circle of eyes that burned in the darkness just beyond the firelight.

"I wisht we was pullin' into McGurry right now," he began again.

"Shut up your wishin' an' your croakin'," Henry burst out angrily. "Your stomach's sour. That's what's ailin' you. Swallow a spoonful of sody, an' you'll sweeten up wonderful an' be more pleasant company."

In the morning, Henry was aroused by fervid blasphemy that proceeded from the mouth of Bill. Henry propped himself up on an elbow and looked to see his comrade standing among the dogs beside the replenished fire, his arms raised in objurgation, his face distorted with passion.

"Hello!" Henry called. "What's up now?"

"Frog's gone," came the answer.

"No."

"I tell you yes."

Henry leaped out of the blankets and to the dogs. He counted them with care, and then joined his partner in cursing the powers of the Wild that had robbed them of another dog.

"Frog was the strongest dog of the bunch," Bill pronounced finally.

"An' he was no fool dog neither," Henry added.

And so was recorded the second epitaph in two days.

A gloomy breakfast was eaten, and the four remaining dogs were harnessed to the sled. The day was a repetition of the days that had gone before. The men toiled without speech across the face of the frozen world. The silence was unbroken save by the cries of their pursuers, that, unseen, hung upon their rear. With the coming of night in the mid-afternoon, the cries sounded closer as the pursuers drew in according to their custom; and the dogs grew excited and frightened, and were guilty of panics that tangled the traces and further depressed the two men.

"There, that'll fix you fool critters," Bill said with satisfaction that night, standing erect at completion of his task.

Henry left his cooking to come and see. Not only had his partner tied the dogs up, but he had tied them, after the Indian fashion, with sticks. About the neck of each dog he had fastened a leather thong. To this, and so close to the neck that the dog could not get his teeth to it, he had tied a stout stick four or five feet in length. The other end of the stick, in turn, was made fast to a stake in the ground by means of a leather thong. The dog was unable to gnaw through the leather at his own end of the stick. The stick prevented him from getting at the leather that fastened the other end.

Henry nodded his head approvingly.

"It's the only contraption that'll ever hold One Ear," he said. "He can gnaw through leather as clean as a knife an' jes' about half as quick. They all 'll be here in the mornin' hunkydory."

"You jes' bet they will," Bill affirmed. "If one of 'em turns up missin', I'll go without my coffee."

"They jes' know we ain't loaded to kill," Henry remarked at bed-time, indicating the gleaming circle that hemmed them in. "If we could put a couple of shots into 'em, they'd be more respectful. They come closer every night. Get the firelight out of your eyes an' look hard—there! Did you see that one?"

For some time the two men amused themselves with watching the movement of vague forms on the edge of the firelight. By looking closely and steadily at where a pair of eyes burned in the darkness, the form of the animal would slowly take shape. They could even see these forms move at times.

A sound among the dogs attracted the men's attention. One Ear was uttering quick, eager whines, lunging at the length of his stick toward the darkness, and desisting now and again in order to make frantic attacks on the stick with his teeth.

"Look at that, Bill," Henry whispered.

Full into the firelight, with a stealthy, sidelong movement, glided a doglike animal. It moved with commingled mistrust and daring, cautiously observing the men, its attention fixed on the dogs. One Ear strained the full length of the stick toward the intruder and whined with eagerness.

"That fool One Ear don't seem scairt much," Bill said in a low tone.

"It's a she-wolf," Henry whispered back, "an' that accounts for Fatty an' Frog. She's the decoy for the pack. She draws out the dog an' then all the rest pitches in an' eats 'm up."

The fire crackled. A log fell apart with a loud spluttering noise. At the sound of it the strange animal leaped back into the darkness.

"Henry, I'm a-thinkin'," Bill announced.

"Thinkin' what?"

"I'm a-thinkin' that was the one I lambasted with the club."

"Ain't the slightest doubt in the world," was Henry's response.

"An' right here I want to remark," Bill went on, "that that animal's familyarity with campfires is suspicious an' immoral."

"It knows for certain more'n a self-respectin' wolf ought to know," Henry agreed. "A wolf that knows enough to come in with the dogs at feedin' time has had experiences."

"Ol' Villan had a dog once that run away with the wolves," Bill cogitated aloud. "I ought to know. I shot it out of the pack in a moose pasture over on Little Stick. An' Ol' Villan cried like a baby. Hadn't seen it for three years, he said. Ben with the wolves all that time."

"I reckon you've called the turn, Bill. That wolf's a dog, an' it's eaten fish many's the time from the hand of man."

"An' if I get a chance at it, that wolf that's a dog'll be jes' meat," Bill declared. "We can't afford to lose no more animals."

"But you've only got three cartridges," Henry objected.

"I'll wait for a dead sure shot," was the reply.

In the morning Henry renewed the fire and cooked breakfast to the accompaniment of his partner's snoring.

"You was sleepin' jes' too comfortable for anythin'," Henry told him, as he routed him out for breakfast. "I hadn't the heart to rouse you."

Bill began to eat sleepily. He noticed that his cup was empty and started to reach for the pot. But the pot was beyond arm's length and beside Henry.

"Say, Henry," he chided gently, "ain't you forgot somethin'?"

Henry looked about with great carefulness and shook his head. Bill held up the empty cup.

"You don't get no coffee," Henry announced.

"Ain't run out?" Bill asked anxiously.

"Nope."

"Ain't thinkin' it'll hurt my digestion?"

"Nope."

A flush of angry blood pervaded Bill's face.

"Then it's jes' warm an' anxious I am to be hearin' you explain yourself," he said.

"Spanker's gone," Henry answered.

Without haste, with the air of one resigned to misfortune, Bill turned his head, and from where he sat counted the dogs.

"How'd it happen?" he asked apathetically.

Henry shrugged his shoulders. "Don't know. Unless One Ear gnawed 'm loose. He couldn't a-done it himself, that's sure."

"The darned cuss." Bill spoke gravely and slowly, with no hint of the anger that was raging within. "Jes' because he couldn't chew himself loose, he chews Spanker loose."

"Well, Spanker's troubles is over, anyway; I guess he's digested by this time an' cavortin' over the landscape in the bellies of twenty different wolves," was Henry's epitaph on this, the latest lost dog. "Have some coffee, Bill."

But Bill shook his head.

"Go on," Henry pleaded, elevating the pot.

Bill shoved his cup aside. "I'll be ding-dong-danged if I do. I said I wouldn't if ary dog turned up missin', an' I won't."

"It's darn good coffee," Henry said enticingly.

But Bill was stubborn, and he ate a dry breakfast, washed down with mumbled curses at One Ear for the trick he had played.

"I'll tie 'em up out of reach of each other tonight," Bill said, as they took the trail.

They had travelled little more than a hundred yards, when Henry, who was in front, bent down and picked up something with which his snowshoe had collided. It was dark, and he could not see it, but he recognized it by the touch. He flung it back, so that it struck the sled and bounced along until it fetched up on Bill's snowshoes.

"Mebbe you'll need that in your business," Henry said.

Bill uttered an exclamation. It was all that was left of Spanker—the stick with which he had been tied.

"They ate 'm hide an' all," Bill announced. "The stick's as clean as a whistle. They've ate the leather offen both ends. They're damn hungry, Henry, an' they'll have you an' me guessin' before this trip's over."

Henry laughed defiantly. "I ain't been trailed this way by wolves before, but I've gone through a whole lot worse an' kept my health. Takes more'n a handful of them pesky critters to do for yours truly, Bill, my son."

"I don't know, I don't know," Bill muttered ominously.

"Well, you'll know all right when we pull into McGurry."

"I ain't feelin' special enthusiastic," Bill persisted.

"You're off color, that's what's the matter with you," Henry dogmatized. "What you need is quinine, an' I'm goin' to dose you up stiff as soon as we make McGurry."

Bill grunted his disagreement with the diagnosis, and lapsed into silence. The day was like all the days. Light came at nine o'clock. At twelve o'clock the southern horizon was warmed by the unseen sun; and then began the cold gray of afternoon that would merge, three hours later, into night.

It was just after the sun's futile effort to appear, that Bill slipped the rifle from under the sled-lashings and said:

"You keep right on, Henry, I'm goin' to see what I can see."

"You'd better stick by the sled," his partner protested. "You've only got three cartridges, an' there's no tellin' what might happen."

"Who's croakin' now?" Bill demanded triumphantly.

Henry made no reply, and plodded on alone, though often he cast anxious glances back into the gray solitude where his partner had disappeared. An hour later, taking advantage of the cut-offs around which the sled had to go, Bill arrived.

"They're scattered an' rangin' along wide," he said; "keepin' up with us an' lookin' for game at the same time. You see, they're sure of us, only they know they've got to wait to get us. In the meantime they're willin' to pick up anythin' eatable that comes handy."

"You mean they *think* they're sure of us," Henry objected pointedly.

But Bill ignored him. "I seen some of them. They're pretty thin. They ain't had a bite in weeks, I reckon, outside of Fatty an' Frog an' Spanker; an' there's so many of 'em that that didn't go far. They're remarkable thin. Their ribs is like washboards, an' their stomachs is right up against their backbones. They're pretty desperate, I can tell you. They'll be goin' mad, yet, an' then watch out."

A few minutes later, Henry, who was now travelling behind the sled, emitted a low, warning whistle. Bill turned and looked, then quietly stopped the dogs. To the rear, from around the last bend and plainly into view, on the very trail they had just covered, trotted a furry, slinking form. Its nose was to the trail, and it trotted with a peculiar, sliding, effortless gait. When they halted, it halted, throwing up its head and regarding them steadily with nostrils that twitched as it caught and studied the scent of them.

"It's the she-wolf," Bill whispered.

The dogs had lain down in the snow, and he walked past them to join his partner at the sled. Together they watched the strange animal that had pursued them for days and that had already accomplished the destruction of half their dog-team.

After a searching scrutiny, the animal trotted forward a few steps. This is repeated several times, till it was a short hundred yards away. It paused, head up, close by a clump of spruce trees, and with sight and scent studied the outfit of the watching men. It looked at them in a strangely wistful way, after the manner of a dog; but in its wistfulness there was none of the dog affection. It was a wistfulness bred of hunger, as cruel as its own fangs, as merciless as the frost itself.

It was large for a wolf, its gaunt frame advertising the lines of an animal that was among the largest of its kind.

"Stands pretty close to two feet an' a half at the shoulders," Henry commented. "An' I'll bet it ain't far from five feet long."

"Kind of strange color for a wolf," was Bill's criticism. "I never seen a red wolf before. Looks almost cinnamon to me."

The animal was certainly not cinnamon-colored. Its coat was the true wolf-coat. The dominant color was gray, and yet there was to it a faint reddish hue—a hue that was baffling, that appeared and disappeared, that was more like an illusion of the vision, now gray, distinctly gray, and again giving hints and glints of a vague redness of color not classifiable in terms of ordinary experience.

"Looks for all the world like a big husky sled-dog," Bill said. "I wouldn't be s'prised to see it wag its tail.

"Hello, you husky!" he called. "Come here, you, whatever-your-name-is."

"Ain't a bit scairt of you," Henry laughed.

Bill waved his hand at it threateningly and shouted loudly; but the animal betrayed no fear. The only change in it that they could notice was an accession of alertness. It still regarded them with the merciless wistfulness of hunger. They were meat, and it was hungry; and it would like to go in and eat them if it dared.

"Look here, Henry," Bill said, unconsciously lowering his voice to a whisper because of what he meditated. "We've got three cartridges. But it's a dead shot. Couldn't miss it. It's got away with three of our dogs, an' we oughter put a stop to it. What d'ye say?"

Henry nodded his consent. Bill cautiously slipped the gun from under the sled-lashing. The gun was on the way to his shoulder, but it never got there. For in that instant the she-wolf leaped sidewise from the trail into the clump of spruce trees and disappeared.

The two men looked at each other. Henry whistled long and comprehendingly.

"I might have knowed it," Bill chided himself aloud, as he replaced the gun. "Of course a wolf that knows enough to come in with the dogs at feedin' time, 'd know all about shooting-irons. I tell you right now, Henry, that critter's the cause of all our trouble. We'd have six dogs at the present time, 'stead of three, if it wasn't for her. An' I tell you right now, Henry, I'm goin' to get her. She's too smart to be shot in the open. But I'm goin' to lay for her. I'll bushwhack her as sure as my name is Bill."

"You needn't stray off too far in doin' it," his partner admonished. "If that pack ever starts to jump you, them three cartridges 'd be wuth no more'n three whoops in hell. Them animals is damn hungry, an' once they start in, they'll sure get you, Bill."

They camped early that night. Three dogs could not drag the sled so fast nor for so long hours as could six, and they were showing unmistakable signs of playing out. And the men went early to bed, Bill first seeing to it that the dogs were tied out of gnawing-reach of one another.

But the wolves were growing bolder, and the men were aroused more than once from their sleep. So near did the wolves approach, that the dogs became frantic with terror, and it was necessary to replenish the fire from time to time in order to keep the adventurous marauders at safer distance.

"I've hearn sailors talk of sharks followin' a ship," Bill remarked, as he crawled back into the blankets after one such replenishing of the fire. "Well, them wolves is land sharks. They know their business better'n we do, an' they ain't a-holdin' our trail this way for their health. They're goin' to get us. They're sure goin' to get us, Henry."

"They've half got you a'ready, a-talkin' like that," Henry retorted sharply. "A man's half licked when he says he is. An' you're half eaten from the way you're goin' on about it."

"They've got away with better men than you an' me," Bill answered.

"Oh, shet up your croakin'. You make me all-fired tired."

Henry rolled over angrily on his side, but was surprised that Bill made no similar display of temper. This was not Bill's way, for he was easily angered by sharp words. Henry thought long over it before he went to sleep, and as his eyelids fluttered down and he dozed off, the thought in his mind was: "There's no mistakin' it, Bill's almighty blue. I'll have to cheer him up tomorrow."

III

The Hunger Cry

THE day began auspiciously. They had lost no dogs during the night, and they swung out upon the trail and into the silence, the darkness, and the cold with spirits that were fairly light. Bill seemed to have forgotten his forebodings of the previous night, and even waxed facetious with the dogs when, at midday, they overturned the sled on a bad piece of trail.

It was an awkward mix-up. The sled was upside down and jammed between a tree-trunk and a huge rock, and they were forced to unharness the dogs in order to straighten out the tangle. The two men were bent over the sled and trying to right it, when Henry observed One Ear sidling away.

"Here, you, One Ear!" he cried, straightening up and turning around on the dog.

But One Ear broke into a run across the snow, his traces trailing behind him. And there, out in the snow of their back-track, was the she-wolf waiting for him. As he neared her, he became suddenly cautious. He slowed down to an alert and mincing walk and then stopped. He regarded her carefully and dubiously, yet desirefully. She seemed to smile at him, showing her teeth in an ingratiating rather than a menacing way. She moved toward him a few steps, playfully, and then halted. One Ear drew near to her, still alert and cautious, his tail and ears in the air, his head held high.

He tried to sniff noses with her, but she retreated playfully and coyly. Every advance on his part was accompanied by a corresponding retreat on her part. Step by step she was luring him away from the security of his human companionship. Once, as though a warning had in vague ways flitted through his intelligence, he turned his head and looked back at the overturned sled, at his team-mates, and at the two men who were calling to him.

But whatever idea was forming in his mind, was dissipated by the she-wolf, who advanced upon him, sniffed noses with him for a fleeting instant, and then resumed her coy retreat before his renewed advances.

In the meantime, Bill had bethought himself of the rifle. But it was jammed beneath the overturned sled, and by the time Henry had helped him to right the load, One Ear and the she-wolf were too close together and the distance too great to risk a shot.

Too late, One Ear learned his mistake. Before they saw the cause, the two men saw him turn and start to run back toward them. Then, approaching at right angles to the trail and cutting off his retreat, they saw a dozen wolves, lean and gray, bounding across the snow. On the instant, the she-wolf's coyness and playfulness disappeared. With a snarl she sprang upon One Ear. He thrust her off with his shoulder, and, his retreat cut off and still intent on regaining the sled, he altered his course in an attempt to circle around to it. More wolves were appearing every moment and joining in the chase. The she-wolf was one leap behind One Ear and holding her own.

"Where are you goin'?" Henry suddenly demanded, laying his hand on his partner's arm.

Bill shook it off. "I won't stand it," he said. "They ain't a-goin' to get any more of our dogs if I can help it."

Gun in hand, he plunged into the underbrush that lined the side of the trail. His intention was apparent enough. Taking the sled as the centre of the circle that One Ear was making, Bill planned to tap that circle at a point in advance of the pursuit. With his rifle, in the broad daylight, it might be possible for him to awe the wolves and save the dog.

"Say, Bill!" Henry called after him. "Be careful! Don't take no chances!"

Henry sat down on the sled and watched. There was nothing else for him to do. Bill had already gone from sight; but now and again, appearing and disappearing amongst the underbrush and the scattered clumps of spruce, could be seen One Ear. Henry judged his case to be hopeless. The dog was thoroughly alive to its danger, but it was running on the outer circle while the wolf-pack was running on the inner and shorter circle. It was vain to think of One Ear so outdistancing his pursuers as to be able to cut across their circle in advance of them and to regain the sled.

The different lines were rapidly approaching a point. Somewhere out there in the snow, screened from his sight by trees and thickets, Henry knew that the wolf-pack, One Ear, and Bill were coming together. All too quickly, far more quickly than he had expected, it happened. He heard a shot, then two shots in rapid succession, and he knew that Bill's ammunition was gone. Then he heard a great out-cry of snarls and yelps. He recognized One Ear's yell of pain and terror, and he heard a wolf-cry that bespoke a stricken animal. And that was all. The snarls ceased. The yelping died away. Silence settled down again over the lonely land.

He sat for a long while upon the sled. There was no need for him to go and see what had happened. He knew it as though it had taken place before his eyes. Once, he roused with a start and hastily got the axe out from underneath the lashings. But for some time longer he sat and brooded, the two remaining dogs crouching and trembling at his feet.

At last he arose in a weary manner, as though all the resilience had gone out of his body, and proceeded to fasten the dogs to the sled. He passed a rope over his shoulder, a man-trace, and pulled with the dogs. He did not go far. At the first hint of darkness he hastened to make a camp, and he saw to it that he had a generous supply of firewood. He fed the dogs, cooked and ate his supper, and made his bed close to the fire.

But he was not destined to enjoy that bed. Before his eyes closed the wolves had drawn too near for safety. It no longer required an effort of the vision to see them. They were all about him and the fire, in a narrow circle, and he could see them plainly in the firelight, lying down, sitting up, crawling forward on their bellies, or slinking back and forth. They even slept. Here and there he could see one curled up in the snow like a dog, taking the sleep that was now denied himself.

He kept the fire brightly blazing, for he knew that it alone intervened between the flesh of his body and their hungry fangs. His two dogs stayed close by him, one on either side, leaning against him for protection, crying and whimpering, and at times snarling desperately when a wolf approached a little closer than usual. At such moments, when his dogs snarled, the whole circle would be agitated, the wolves coming to their feet and pressing tentatively forward, a chorus of snarls and eager yelps rising about him. Then the circle would lie down again, and here and there a wolf would resume its broken nap.

But this circle had a continuous tendency to draw in upon him. Bit by bit, an inch at a time, with here a wolf bellying forward, and there a wolf bellying forward, the circle would narrow until the brutes were almost within springing distance. Then he would seize brands from the fire and hurl them into the pack. A hasty drawing back always resulted, accompanied by angry yelps and frightened snarls when a well-aimed brand struck and scorched a too daring animal.

Morning found the man haggard and worn, wide-eyed from want of sleep. He cooked breakfast in the darkness, and at nine o'clock, when, with the coming of daylight, the wolf-pack drew back, he set about the task he had planned through the long hours of the night. Chopping down young saplings, he made them cross-bars of a scaffold by lashing them high up to the trunks of standing trees. Using the sled-lashing for a heaving rope, and with the aid of the dogs, he hoisted the coffin to the top of the scaffold.

"They got Bill, an' they may get me, but they'll sure never get you, young man," he said, addressing the dead body in its tree-sepulchre.

Then he took the trail, the lightened sled bounding along behind the willing dogs; for they, too, knew that safety lay only in the gaining of Fort McGurry. The wolves were now more open in their pursuit, trotting sedately behind and ranging along on either side, their red tongues lolling out, their lean sides showing the undulating ribs with every movement. They were very lean, mere skin-bags stretched over bony frames, with strings for muscles—so lean that Henry found it in his mind to marvel that they still kept their feet and did not collapse forthright in the snow.

He did not dare travel until dark. At midday, not only did the sun warm the southern horizon, but it even thrust its upper rim, pale and golden, above the sky-line. He received it as a sign. The days were growing longer. The sun was returning. But scarcely had the cheer of its light departed, than he went into camp. There were still several hours of gray daylight and sombre twilight, and he utilized them in chopping an enormous supply of firewood.

With night came horror. Not only were the starving wolves growing bolder, but lack of sleep was telling upon Henry. He dozed despite himself, crouching by the fire, the blankets about his shoulders, the axe between his knees, and on either side a dog pressing close against him. He awoke once and saw in front of him, not a dozen feet away, a big gray wolf, one of the largest of the pack. And even as he looked, the brute deliberately stretched himself after the manner of a lazy dog, yawning full in his face and looking upon him with a possessive eye, as if, in truth, he were merely a delayed meal that was soon to be eaten.

This certitude was shown by the whole pack. Fully a score he could count, staring hungrily at him or calmly sleeping in the snow. They reminded him of children gathered about a spread table and awaiting permission to begin to eat. And he was the food they were to eat! He wondered how and when the meal would begin.

As he piled wood on the fire he discovered an appreciation of his own body which he had never felt before. He watched his moving muscles and was interested in the cunning mechanism of his fingers. By the light of the fire he crooked his fingers slowly and repeatedly, now one at a time, now all together, spreading them wide or making quick gripping movements. He studied the nail-formation, and prodded the finger-tips, now sharply, and again softly, gauging the while the nerve-sensations produced. It fascinated him, and he grew suddenly fond of this subtle flesh of his that worked so beautifully and smoothly and delicately. Then he would cast a glance of fear at the wolf-circle drawn expectantly about him, and like a blow the realization would strike him that this wonderful body of his, this living flesh, was no more than so much meat, a quest of ravenous animals, to be torn and slashed by their hungry fangs, to be sustenance to them as the moose and the rabbit had often been sustenance to him.

He came out of a doze that was half nightmare, to see the red-hued she-wolf before him. She was not more than half a dozen feet away, sitting in the snow and wistfully regarding him. The two dogs were whimpering and snarling at his feet, but she took no notice of them. She was looking at the man, and for some time he returned her look. There was nothing threatening about her. She looked at him merely with a great wistfulness, but he knew it to be the wistfulness of an equally great hunger. He was the food, and the sight of him excited in her the gustatory sensations. Her mouth opened, the saliva drooled forth, and she licked her chops with the pleasure of anticipation.

A spasm of fear went through him. He reached hastily for a brand to throw at her. But even as he reached, and before his fingers had closed on the missile, she sprang back into safety; and he knew that she was used to having things thrown at her. She had snarled as she sprang away, baring her white fangs to their roots, all her wistfulness vanishing, being replaced by a carnivorous malignity that made him shudder. He glanced at the hand that held the brand, noticing the cunning delicacy of the fingers that gripped it, how they adjusted themselves to all the inequalities of the surface, curling over and under and about the rough wood, and one little finger, too close to the burning portion of the brand, sensitively and automatically writhing back from the hurtful heat to a cooler gripping-place; and in the same instant he seemed to see a vision of those same sensitive and delicate fingers being crushed and torn by the white teeth of the she-wolf. Never had he been so fond of this body of his as now when his tenure of it was so precarious.

All night, with burning brands, he fought off the hungry pack. When he dozed despite himself, the whimpering and snarling of the dogs aroused him. Morning came, but for the first time the light of day failed to scatter the wolves. The man waited in vain for them to go. They remained in a circle about him and his fire, displaying an arrogance of possession that shook his courage born of the morning light.

He made one desperate attempt to pull out on the trail. But the moment he left the protection of the fire, the boldest wolf leaped for him, but leaped short. He saved himself by springing back, the jaws snapping together a scant six inches from his thigh. The rest of the pack was now up and surging upon him, and a throwing of firebrands right and left was necessary to drive them back to a respectful distance.

Even in the daylight he did not dare leave the fire to chop fresh wood. Twenty feet away towered a huge dead spruce. He spent half the day extending his campfire to the tree, at any moment a half dozen burning fagots ready at hand to fling at his enemies. Once at the tree, he studied the surrounding forest in order to fell the tree in the direction of the most firewood.

The night was a repetition of the night before, save that the need for sleep was becoming overpowering. The snarling of his dogs was losing its efficacy. Besides, they were snarling all the time, and his benumbed and drowsy senses no longer took note of changing pitch and intensity. He awoke with a start. The she-wolf was less than a yard from him. Mechanically, at short range, without letting go of it, he thrust a brand full into her open and snarling mouth. She sprang away, yelling with pain, and while he took delight in the smell of burning flesh and hair, he watched her shaking her head and growling wrathfully a score of feet away.

But this time, before he dozed again, he tied a burning pine-knot to his right hand. His eyes were closed but a few minutes when the burn of the flame on his flesh awakened him. For several hours he adhered to this programme. Every time he was thus awakened he drove back the wolves with flying brands, replenished the fire, and rearranged the pine-knot on his hand. All worked well, but there came a time when he fastened the pine-knot insecurely. As his eyes closed it fell away from his hand.

He dreamed. It seemed to him that he was in Fort McGurry. It was warm and comfortable, and he was playing cribbage with the Factor. Also, it seemed to him that the fort was besieged by wolves. They were howling at the very gates, and sometimes he and the Factor paused from the game to listen and laugh at the futile efforts of the wolves to get in. And then, so strange was the dream, there was a crash. The door was burst open. He could see the wolves flooding into the big living-room of the fort. They were leaping straight for him and the Factor. With the bursting open of the door, the noise of their howling had increased tremendously. This howling now bothered him. His dream was merging into something else—he knew not what; but through it all, following him, persisted the howling.

And then he awoke to find the howling real. There was a great snarling and yelping. The wolves were rushing him. They were all about him and upon him. The teeth of one had closed upon his arm. Instinctively he leaped into the fire, and as he leaped, he felt the sharp slash of teeth that tore through the flesh of his leg. Then began a fire fight. His stout mittens temporarily protected his hands, and he scooped live coals into the air in all directions, until the camp-fire took on the semblance of a volcano.

But it could not last long. His face was blistering in the heat, his eyebrows and lashes were singed off, and the heat was becoming unbearable to his feet. With a flaming brand in each hand, he sprang to the edge of the fire. The wolves had been driven back. On every side, wherever the live coals had fallen, the snow was sizzling, and every little while a retiring wolf, with wild leap and snort and snarl, announced that one such live coal had been stepped upon.

Flinging his brands at the nearest of his enemies, the man thrust his smouldering mittens into the snow and stamped about to cool his feet. His two dogs were missing, and he well knew that they had served as a course in the protracted meal which had begun days before with Fatty, the last course of which would likely be himself in the days to follow.

"You ain't got me yet!" he cried, savagely shaking his fist at the hungry beasts; and at the sound of his voice the whole circle was agitated, there was a general snarl, and the she-wolf slid up close to him across the snow and watched him with hungry wistfulness.

He set to work to carry out a new idea that had come to him. He extended the fire into a large circle. Inside this circle he crouched, his sleeping outfit under him as a protection against the melting snow. When he had thus disappeared within his shelter of flame, the whole pack came curiously to the rim of the fire to see what had become of him. Hitherto they had been denied access to the fire, and they now settled down in a close-drawn circle, like so many dogs, blinking and yawning and stretching their lean bodies in the unaccustomed warmth. Then the she-wolf sat down, pointed her nose at a star, and began to howl. One by one the wolves joined her, till the whole pack, on haunches, with noses pointed skyward, was howling its hunger cry.

Dawn came, and daylight. The fire was burning low. The fuel had run out, and there was need to get more. The man attempted to step out of his circle of flame, but the wolves surged to meet him. Burning brands made them spring aside, but they no longer sprang back. In vain he strove to drive them back. As he gave up and stumbled inside his circle, a wolf leaped for him, missed, and landed with all four feet in the coals. It cried out with terror, at the same time snarling, and scrambled back to cool its paws in the snow.

The man sat down on his blankets in a crouching position. His body leaned forward from the hips. His shoulders, relaxed and drooping, and his head on his knees advertised that he had given up the struggle. Now and again he raised his head to note the dying down of the fire. The circle of flame and coals was breaking into segments with openings in between. These openings grew in size, the segments diminished.

"I guess you can come an' get me any time," he mumbled. "Anyway, I'm goin' to sleep."

Once he wakened, and in an opening in the circle, directly in front of him, he saw the she-wolf gazing at him.

Again he awakened, a little later, though it seemed hours to him. A mysterious change had taken place—so mysterious a change that he was shocked wider awake. Something had happened. He could not understand at first. Then he discovered it. The wolves were gone. Remained only the trampled snow to show how closely they had pressed him. Sleep was welling up and gripping him again, his head was sinking down upon his knees, when he roused with a sudden start.

There were cries of men, the churn of sleds, the creaking of harnesses, and the eager whimpering of straining dogs. Four sleds pulled in from the river bed to the camp among the trees. Half a dozen men were about the man who crouched in the centre of the dying fire. They were shaking and prodding him into consciousness. He looked at them like a drunken man and maundered in strange, sleepy speech:

"Red she-wolf. . . . Come in with the dogs at feedin' time. . . . First she ate the dog-food. . . . Then she ate the dogs. . . . An' after that she ate Bill. . . ."

"Where's Lord Alfred?" one of the men bellowed in his ear, shaking him roughly.

He shook his head slowly. "No, she didn't eat him. . . . He's roostin' in a tree at the last camp."

"Dead?" the man shouted.

"An' in a box," Henry answered. He jerked his shoulder petulantly away from the grip of his questioner. "Say, you lemme alone. . . . I'm jes' plumb tuckered out. . . . Goo' night, everybody."

His eyes fluttered and went shut. His chin fell forward on his chest. And even as they eased him down upon the blankets his snores were rising on the frosty air.

But there was another sound. Far and faint it was, in the remote distance, the cry of the hungry wolf-pack as it took the trail of other meat than the man it had just missed.

Part Two—Born of the Wild

I

The Battle of the Fangs

It was the she-wolf who had first caught the sound of men's voices and the whining of the sled-dogs; and it was the she-wolf who was first to spring away from the cornered man in his circle of dying flame. The pack had been loath to forego the kill it had hunted down, and it lingered for several minutes, making sure of the sounds; and then it, too, sprang away on the trail made by the she-wolf.

Running at the forefront of the pack was a large gray wolf—one of its several leaders. It was he who directed the pack's course on the heels of the she-wolf. It was he who snarled warningly at the younger members of the pack or slashed at them with his fangs when they ambitiously tried to pass him. And it was he who increased the pace when he sighted the she-wolf, now trotting slowly across the snow.

She dropped in alongside by him, as though it were her appointed position, and took the pace of the pack. He did not snarl at her, nor show his teeth, when any leap of hers chanced to put her in advance of him. On the contrary, he seemed kindly disposed toward her—too kindly to suit her, for he was prone to run near to her, and when he ran too near it was she who snarled and showed her teeth. Nor was she above slashing his shoulder sharply on occasion. At such times he betrayed no anger. He merely sprang to the side and ran stiffly ahead for several awkward leaps, in carriage and conduct resembling an abashed country swain.

This was his one trouble in the running of the pack; but she had other troubles. On her other side ran a gaunt old wolf, grizzled and marked with the scars of many battles. He ran always on her right side. The fact that he had but one eye, and that the left eye, might account for this. He, also, was addicted to crowding her, to veering toward her till his scarred muzzle touched her body, or shoulder, or neck. As with the running mate on the left, she repelled these attentions with her teeth; but when both bestowed their attentions at the same time she was roughly jostled, being compelled, with quick snaps to either side, to drive both lovers away and at the same time to maintain her forward leap with the pack and see the way of her feet before her. At such times her running mates flashed their teeth and growled threateningly across at each other. They might have fought, but even wooing and its rivalry waited upon the more pressing hunger-need of the pack.

After each repulse, when the old wolf sheered abruptly away from the sharp-toothed object of his desire, he shouldered against a young three-year-old that ran on his blind right side. This young wolf had attained his full size; and, considering the weak and famished condition of the pack, he possessed more than the average vigor and spirit. Nevertheless, he ran with his head even with the shoulder of his one-eyed elder. When he ventured to run abreast of the older wolf, (which was seldom), a snarl and a snap sent him back even with the shoulder again. Sometimes, however, he dropped cautiously and slowly behind and edged in between the old leader and the she-wolf. This was doubly resented, even triply resented. When she snarled her displeasure, the old leader would whirl on the three-year-old. Sometimes she whirled with him. And sometimes the young leader on the left whirled, too.

At such times, confronted by three sets of savage teeth, the young wolf stopped precipitately, throwing himself back on his haunches, with fore-legs stiff, mouth menacing, and mane bristling. This confusion in the front of the moving pack always caused confusion in the rear. The wolves behind collided with the young wolf and expressed their displeasure by administering sharp nips on his hind-legs and flanks. He was laying up trouble for himself, for lack of food and short tempers went together; but with the boundless faith of youth he persisted in repeating the manoeuvreevery little while, though it never succeeded in gaining anything for him but discomfiture.

Had there been food, love-making and fighting would have gone on apace, and the pack-formation would have been broken up. But the situation of the pack was desperate. It was lean with long-standing hunger. It ran below its ordinary speed. At the rear limped the weak members, the very young and the very old. At the front were the strongest. Yet all were more like skeletons than full-bodied wolves. Nevertheless, with the exception of the ones that limped, the movements of the animals were effortless and tireless. Their stringy muscles seemed founts of inexhaustible energy. Behind every steel-like contraction of a muscle, lay another steel-like contraction, and another, and another, apparently without end.

They ran many miles that day. They ran through the night. And the next day found them still running. They were running over the surface of a world frozen and dead. No life stirred. They alone moved through the vast inertness. They alone were alive, and they sought for other things that were alive in order that they might devour them and continue to live.

They crossed low divides and ranged a dozen small streams in a lower-lying country before their quest was rewarded. Then they came upon moose. It was a big bull they first found. Here was meat and life, and it was guarded by no mysterious fires nor flying missiles of flame. Splay hoofs and palmated antlers they knew, and they flung their customary patience and caution to the wind. It was a brief fight and fierce. The big bull was beset on every side. He ripped them open or split their skulls with shrewdly driven blows of his great hoofs. He crushed them and broke them on his large horns. He stamped them into the snow under him in the wallowing struggle. But he was foredoomed, and he went down with the she-wolf tearing savagely at his throat, and with other teeth fixed everywhere upon him, devouring him alive, before ever his last struggles ceased or his last damage had been wrought.

There was food in plenty. The bull weighed over eight hundred pounds—fully twenty pounds of meat per mouth for the forty-odd wolves of the pack. But if they could fast prodigiously, they could feed prodigiously, and soon a few scattered bones were all that remained of the splendid live brute that had faced the pack a few hours before.

There was now much resting and sleeping. With full stomachs, bickering and quarrelling began among the younger males, and this continued through the few days that followed before the breaking-up of the pack. The famine was over. The wolves were now in the country of game, and though they still hunted in pack, they hunted more cautiously, cutting out heavy cows or crippled old bulls from the small moose-herds they ran across.

There came a day, in this land of plenty, when the wolf-pack split in half and went in different directions. The she-wolf, the young leader on her left, and the one-eyed elder on her right, led their half of the pack down to the Mackenzie River and across into the lake country to the east. Each day this remnant of the pack dwindled. Two by two, male and female, the wolves were deserting. Occasionally a solitary male was driven out by the sharp teeth of his rivals. In the end there remained only four: the she-wolf, the young leader, the one-eyed one, and the ambitious three-year-old.

The she-wolf had by now developed a ferocious temper. Her three suitors all bore the marks of her teeth. Yet they never replied in kind, never defended themselves against her. They turned their shoulders to her most savage slashes, and with wagging tails and mincing steps strove to placate her wrath. But if they were all mildness toward her, they were all fierceness toward one another. The three-year-old grew too ambitious in his fierceness. He caught the one-eyed elder on his blind side and ripped his ear into ribbons. Though the grizzled old fellow could see only on one side, against the youth and vigor of the other he brought into play the wisdom of long years of experience. His lost eye and his scarred muzzle bore evidence to the nature of his experience. He had survived too many battles to be in doubt for a moment about what to do.

The battle began fairly, but it did not end fairly. There was no telling what the outcome would have been, for the third wolf joined the elder, and together, old leader and young leader, they attacked the ambitious three-year-old and proceeded to destroy him. He was beset on either side by the merciless fangs of his erstwhile comrades. Forgotten were the days they had hunted together, the game they had pulled down, the famine they had suffered. That business was a thing of the past. The business of love was at hand—ever a sterner and crueler business than that of food-getting.

And in the meanwhile, the she-wolf, the cause of it all, sat down contentedly on her haunches and watched. She was even pleased. This was her day,—and it came not often,—when manes bristled, and fang smote fang or ripped and tore the yielding flesh, all for the possession of her.

And in the business of love the three-year-old, who had made this his first adventure upon it, yielded up his life. On either side of his body stood his two rivals. They were gazing at the she-wolf, who sat smiling in the snow. But the elder leader was wise, very wise, in love even as in battle. The younger leader turned his head to lick a wound on his shoulder. The curve of his neck was turned toward his rival. With his one eye the elder saw the opportunity. He darted in low and closed with his fangs. It was a long, ripping slash, and deep as well. His teeth, in passing, burst the wall of the great vein of the throat. Then he leaped clear.

The young leader snarled terribly, but his snarl broke mid-most into a tickling cough. Bleeding and coughing, already stricken, he sprang at the elder and fought while life faded from him, his legs going weak beneath him, the light of day dulling on his eyes, his blows and springs falling shorter and shorter.

And all the while the she-wolf sat on her haunches and smiled. She was made glad in vague ways by the battle, for this was the love-making of the Wild, the sex-tragedy of the natural world that was tragedy only to those that died. To those that survived it was not tragedy, but realization and achievement.

When the young leader lay in the snow and moved no more, One Eye stalked over to the she-wolf. His carriage was one of mingled triumph and caution. He was plainly expectant of a rebuff, and he was just as plainly surprised when her teeth did not flash out at him in anger. For the first time she met him with a kindly manner. She sniffed noses with him, and even condescended to leap about and frisk and play with him in quite puppyish fashion. And he, for all his gray years and sage experience, behaved quite as puppyishly and even a little more foolishly.

Forgotten already were the vanquished rivals and the love-tale red-written on the snow. Forgotten, save once, when old One Eye stopped for a moment to lick his stiffening wounds. Then it was that his lips half writhed into a snarl, and the hair of his neck and shoulders involuntarily bristled, while he half crouched for a spring, his claws spasmodically clutching into the snow-surface for firmer footing. But it was all forgotten the next moment, as he sprang after the she-wolf, who was coyly leading him a chase through the woods.

After that they ran side by side, like good friends who have come to an understanding. The days passed by, and they kept together, hunting their meat and killing and eating it in common. After a time the she-wolf began to grow restless. She seemed to be searching for something that she could not find. The hollows under fallen trees seemed to attract her, and she spent much time nosing about among the larger snow-piled crevices in the rocks and in the caves of overhanging banks. Old One Eye was not interested at all, but he followed her good-naturedly in her quest, and when her investigations in particular places were unusually protracted, he would lie down and wait until she was ready to go on.

They did not remain in one place, but travelled across country until they regained the Mackenzie River, down which they slowly went, leaving it often to hunt game along the small streams that entered it, but always returning to it again. Sometimes they chanced upon other wolves, usually in pairs; but there was no friendliness of intercourse displayed on either side, no gladness at meeting, no desire to return to the pack-formation. Several times they encountered solitary wolves. These were always males, and they were pressingly insistent on joining with One Eye and his mate. This he resented, and when she stood shoulder to shoulder with him, bristling and showing her teeth, the aspiring solitary ones would back off, turn tail, and continue on their lonely way.

One moonlight night, running through the quiet forest, One Eye suddenly halted. His muzzle went up, his tail stiffened, and his nostrils dilated as he scented the air. One foot also he held up, after the manner of a dog. He was not satisfied, and he continued to smell the air, striving to understand the message borne upon it to him. One careless sniff had satisfied his mate, and she trotted on to reassure him. Though he followed her, he was still dubious, and he could not forbear an occasional halt in order more carefully to study the warning.

She crept out cautiously on the edge of a large open space in the midst of the trees. For some time she stood alone. Then One Eye, creeping and crawling, every sense on the alert, every hair radiating infinite suspicion, joined her. They stood side by side, watching and listening and smelling.

To their ears came the sounds of dogs wrangling and scuffling, the guttural cries of men, the sharper voices of scolding women, and once the shrill and plaintive cry of a child. With the exception of the huge bulks of the skin lodges, little could be seen save the flames of the fire, broken by the movements of intervening bodies, and the smoke rising slowly on the quiet air. But to their nostrils came the myriad smells of an Indian camp, carrying a story that was largely incomprehensible to One Eye, but every detail of which the she-wolf knew.

She was strangely stirred, and sniffed and sniffed with an increasing delight. But old One Eye was doubtful. He betrayed his apprehension, and started tentatively to go. She turned and touched his neck with her muzzle in a reassuring way, then regarded the camp again. A new wistfulness was in her face, but it was not the wistfulness of hunger. She was thrilling to a desire that urged her to go forward, to be in closer to that fire, to be squabbling with the dogs, and to be avoiding and dodging the stumbling feet of men.

One Eye moved impatiently beside her; her unrest came back upon her, and she knew again her pressing need to find the thing for which she searched. She turned and trotted back into the forest, to the great relief of One Eye, who trotted a little to the fore until they were well within the shelter of the trees.

As they slid along, noiseless as shadows, in the moonlight, they came upon a runway. Both noses went down to the footprints in the snow. These footprints were very fresh. One Eye ran ahead cautiously, his mate at his heels. The broad pads of their feet were spread wide and in contact with the snow were like velvet. One Eye caught sight of a dim movement of white in the midst of the white. His sliding gait had been deceptively swift, but it was as nothing to the speed at which he now ran. Before him was bounding the faint patch of white he had discovered.

They were running along a narrow alley flanked on either side by a growth of young spruce. Through the trees the mouth of the alley could be seen, opening out on a moonlit glade. Old One Eye was rapidly overhauling the fleeing shape of white. Bound by bound he gained. Now he was upon it. One leap more and his teeth would be sinking into it. But that leap was never made. High in the air, and straight up, soared the shape of the white, now a struggling snowshoe rabbit that leaped and bounded, executing a fantastic dance there above him in the air and never once returning to earth.

One Eye sprang back with a snort of sudden fright, then shrank down to the snow and crouched, snarling threats at this thing of fear he did not understand. But the she-wolf coolly thrust past him. She poised for a moment, then sprang for the dancing rabbit. She, too, soared high, but not so high as the quarry, and her teeth clipped emptily together with a metallic snap. She made another leap, and another.

Her mate had slowly relaxed from his crouch and was watching her. He now evinced displeasure at her repeated failures, and himself made a mighty spring upward. His teeth closed upon the rabbit, and he bore it back to earth with him. But at the same time there was a suspicious crackling movement beside him, and his astonished eye saw a young spruce sapling bending down above him to strike him. His jaws let go their grip, and he leaped backward to escape this strange danger, his lips drawn back from his fangs, his throat snarling, every hair bristling with rage and fright. And in that moment the sapling reared its slender length upright and the rabbit soared dancing in the air again.

The she-wolf was angry. She sank her fangs into her mate's shoulder in reproof; and he, frightened, unaware of what constituted this new onslaught, struck back ferociously and in still greater fright, ripping down the side of the she-wolf's muzzle. For him to resent such reproof was equally unexpected to her, and she sprang upon him in snarling indignation. Then he discovered his mistake and tried to placate her. But she proceeded to punish him roundly, until he gave over all attempts at placation, and whirled in a circle, his head away from her, his shoulders receiving the punishment of her teeth.

In the meantime the rabbit danced above them in the air. The she-wolf sat down in the snow, and old One Eye, now more in fear of his mate than of the mysterious sapling, again sprang for the rabbit. As he sank back with it between his teeth, he kept his eye on the sapling. As before, it followed him back to earth. He crouched down under the impeding blow, his hair bristling, but his teeth still keeping tight hold of the rabbit. But the blow did not fall. The sapling remained bent above him. When he moved it moved, and he growled at it through his clenched jaws; when he remained still, it remained still, and he concluded it was safer to continue remaining still. Yet the warm blood of the rabbit tasted good in his mouth.

It was his mate who relieved him from the quandary in which he found himself. She took the rabbit from him, and while the sapling swayed and teetered threateningly above her she calmly gnawed off the rabbit's head. At once the sapling shot up, and after that gave no more trouble, remaining in the decorous and perpendicular position in which nature had intended it to grow. Then, between them, the she-wolf and One Eye devoured the game which the mysterious sapling had caught for them.

There were other run-ways and alleys where rabbits were hanging in the air, and the wolf-pair prospected them all, the she-wolf leading the way, old One Eye following and observant, learning the method of robbing snares—a knowledge destined to stand him in good stead in the days to come.

II

The Lair

FOR two days the she-wolf and One Eye hung about the Indian camp. He was worried and apprehensive, yet the camp lured his mate and she was loath to depart. But when, one morning, the air was rent with the report of a rifle close at hand, and a bullet smashed against a tree trunk several inches from One Eye's head, they hesitated no more, but went off on a long, swinging lope that put quick miles between them and the danger.

They did not go far—a couple of days' journey. The she-wolf's need to find the thing for which she searched had now become imperative. She was getting very heavy, and could run but slowly. Once, in the pursuit of a rabbit, which she ordinarily would have caught with ease, she gave over and lay down and rested. One Eye came to her; but when he touched her neck gently with his muzzle she snapped at him with such quick fierceness that he tumbled over backward and cut a ridiculous figure in his effort to escape her teeth. Her temper was now shorter than ever; but he had become more patient than ever and more solicitous.

And then she found the thing for which she sought. It was a few miles up a small stream that in the summer time flowed into the Mackenzie, but that then was frozen over and frozen down to its rocky bottom—a dead stream of solid white from source to mouth. The she-wolf was trotting wearily along, her mate well in advance, when she came upon the overhanging, high clay-bank. She turned aside and trotted over to it. The wear and tear of spring storms and melting snows had underwashed the bank and in one place had made a small cave out of a narrow fissure.

She paused at the mouth of the cave and looked the wall over carefully. Then, on one side and the other, she ran along the base of the wall to where its abrupt bulk merged from the softer-lined landscape. Returning to the cave, she entered its narrow mouth. For a short three feet she was compelled to crouch, then the walls widened and rose higher in a little round chamber nearly six feet in diameter. The roof barely cleared her head. It was dry and cosey. She inspected it with painstaking care, while One Eye, who had returned, stood in the entrance and patiently watched her. She dropped her head, with her nose to the ground and directed toward a point near to her closely bunched feet, and around this point she circled several times; then, with a tired sigh that was almost a grunt, she curled her body in, relaxed her legs, and dropped down, her head toward the entrance. One Eye, with pointed, interested ears, laughed at her, and beyond, outlined against the white light, she could see the brush of his tail waving good-naturedly. Her own ears, with a snuggling movement, laid their sharp points backward and down against the head for a moment, while her mouth opened and her tongue lolled peaceably out, and in this way she expressed that she was pleased and satisfied.

One Eye was hungry. Though he lay down in the entrance and slept, his sleep was fitful. He kept awaking and cocking his ears at the bright world without, where the April sun was blazing across the snow. When he dozed, upon his ears would steal the faint whispers of hidden trickles of running water, and he would rouse and listen intently. The sun had come back, and all the awakening Northland world was calling to him. Life was stirring. The feel of spring was in the air, the feel of growing life under the snow, of sap ascending in the trees, of buds bursting the shackles of the frost.

He cast anxious glances at his mate, but she showed no desire to get up. He looked outside, and half a dozen snow-birds fluttered across his field of vision. He started to get up, then looked back to his mate again, and settled down and dozed. A shrill and minute singing stole upon his hearing. Once, and twice, he sleepily brushed his nose with his paw. Then he woke up. There, buzzing in the air at the tip of his nose, was a lone mosquito. It was a full-grown mosquito, one that had lain frozen in a dry log all winter and that had now been thawed out by the sun. He could resist the call of the world no longer. Besides, he was hungry.

He crawled over to his mate and tried to persuade her to get up. But she only snarled at him, and he walked out alone into the bright sunshine to find the snow-surface soft underfoot and the travelling difficult. He went up the frozen bed of the stream, where the snow, shaded by the trees, was yet hard and crystalline. He was gone eight hours, and he came back through the darkness hungrier than when he had started. He had found game, but he had not caught it. He had broken through the melting snow-crust, and wallowed, while the snowshoe rabbits had skimmed along on top lightly as ever.

He paused at the mouth of the cave with a sudden shock of suspicion. Faint, strange sounds came from within. They were sounds not made by his mate, and yet they were remotely familiar. He bellied cautiously inside and was met by a warning snarl from the she-wolf. This he received without perturbation, though he obeyed it by keeping his distance; but he remained interested in the other sounds—faint, muffled sobbings and slubberings.

His mate warned him irritably away, and he curled up and slept in the entrance. When morning came and a dim light pervaded the lair, he again sought after the source of the remotely familiar sounds. There was a new note in his mate's warning snarl. It was a jealous note, and he was very careful in keeping a respectful distance. Nevertheless, he made out, sheltering between her legs against the length of her body, five strange little bundles of life, very feeble, very helpless, making tiny whimpering noises, with eyes that did not open to the light. He was surprised. It was not the first time in his long and successful life that this thing had happened. It had happened many times, yet each time it was as fresh a surprise as ever to him.

His mate looked at him anxiously. Every little while she emitted a low growl, and at times, when it seemed to her he approached too near, the growl shot up in her throat to a sharp snarl. Of her own experience she had no memory of the thing happening; but in her instinct, which was the experience of all the mothers of wolves, there lurked a memory of fathers that had eaten their new-born and helpless progeny. It manifested itself as a fear strong within her, that made her prevent One Eye from more closely inspecting the cubs he had fathered.

But there was no danger. Old One Eye was feeling the urge of an impulse, that was, in turn, an instinct that had come down to him from all the fathers of wolves. He did not question it, nor puzzle over it. It was there, in the fibre of his being; and it was the most natural thing in the world that he should obey it by turning his back on his new-born family and by trotting out and away on the meat-trail whereby he lived.

Five or six miles from the lair, the stream divided, its forks going off among the mountains at a right angle. Here, leading up the left fork, he came upon a fresh track. He smelled it and found it so recent that he crouched swiftly, and looked in the direction in which it disappeared. Then he turned deliberately and took the right fork. The footprint was much larger than the one his own feet made, and he knew that in the wake of such a trail there was little meat for him.

Half a mile up the right fork, his quick ears caught the sound of gnawing teeth. He stalked the quarry and found it to be a porcupine, standing upright against a tree and trying his teeth on the bark. One Eye approached carefully but hopelessly. He knew the breed, though he had never met it so far north before; and never in his long life had porcupine served him for a meal. But he had long since learned that there was such a thing as Chance, or Opportunity, and he continued to draw near. There was never any telling what might happen, for with live things events were somehow always happening differently.

The porcupine rolled itself into a ball, radiating long, sharp needles in all directions that defied attack. In his youth One Eye had once sniffed too near a similar, apparently inert ball of quills, and had the tail flick out suddenly in his face. One quill he had carried away in his muzzle, where it had remained for weeks, a rankling flame, until it finally worked out. So he lay down, in a comfortable crouching position, his nose fully a foot away, and out of the line of the tail. Thus he waited, keeping perfectly quiet. There was no telling. Something might happen. The porcupine might unroll. There might be opportunity for a deft and ripping thrust of paw into the tender, unguarded belly.

But at the end of half an hour he arose, growled wrathfully at the motionless ball, and trotted on. He had waited too often and futilely in the past for porcupines to unroll, to waste any more time. He continued up the right fork. The day wore along, and nothing rewarded his hunt.

The urge of his awakened instinct of fatherhood was strong upon him. He must find meat. In the afternoon he blundered upon a ptarmigan. He came out of a thicket and found himself face to face with the slow-witted bird. It was sitting on a log, not a foot beyond the end of his nose. Each saw the other. The bird made a startled rise, but he struck it with his paw, and smashed it down to earth, then pounced upon it, and caught it in his teeth as it scuttled across the snow trying to rise in the air again. As his teeth crunched through the tender flesh and fragile bones, he began naturally to eat. Then he remembered, and, turning on the back-track, started for home, carrying the ptarmigan in his mouth.

A mile above the forks, running velvet-footed as was his custom, a gliding shadow that cautiously prospected each new vista of the trail, he came upon later imprints of the large tracks he had discovered in the early morning. As the track led his way, he followed, prepared to meet the maker of it at every turn of the stream.

He slid his head around a corner of rock, where began an unusually large bend in the stream, and his quick eyes made out something that sent him crouching swiftly down. It was the maker of the track, a large female lynx. She was crouching as he had crouched once that day, in front of her the tight-rolled ball of quills. If he had been a gliding shadow before, he now became the ghost of such a shadow, as he crept and circled around, and came up well to leeward of the silent, motionless pair.

He lay down in the snow, depositing the ptarmigan beside him, and with eyes peering through the needles of a low-growing spruce he watched the play of life before him—the waiting lynx and the waiting porcupine, each intent on life; and, such was the curiousness of the game, the way of life for one lay in the eating of the other, and the way of life for the other lay in being not eaten. While old One Eye, the wolf, crouching in the covert, played his part, too, in the game, waiting for some strange freak of Chance, that might help him on the meat-trail which was his way of life.

Half an hour passed, an hour; and nothing happened. The ball of quills might have been a stone for all it moved; the lynx might have been frozen to marble; and old One Eye might have been dead. Yet all three animals were keyed to a tenseness of living that was almost painful, and scarcely ever would it come to them to be more alive than they were then in their seeming petrifaction.

One Eye moved slightly and peered forth with increased eagerness. Something was happening. The porcupine had at last decided that its enemy had gone away. Slowly, cautiously, it was unrolling its ball of impregnable armor. It was agitated by no tremor of anticipation. Slowly, slowly, the bristling ball straightened out and lengthened. One Eye, watching, felt a sudden moistness in his mouth and a drooling of saliva, involuntary, excited by the living meat that was spreading itself like a repast before him.

Not quite entirely had the porcupine unrolled when it discovered its enemy. In that instant the lynx struck. The blow was like a flash of light. The paw, with rigid claws curving like talons, shot under the tender belly and came back with a swift ripping movement. Had the porcupine been entirely unrolled, or had it not discovered its enemy a fraction of a second before the blow was struck, the paw would have escaped unscathed; but a side-flick of the tail sank sharp quills into it as it was withdrawn.

Everything had happened at once,—the blow, the counter-blow, the squeal of agony from the porcupine, the big cat's squall of sudden hurt and astonishment. One Eye half arose in his excitement, his ears up, his tail straight out and quivering behind him. The lynx's bad temper got the best of her. She sprang savagely at the thing that had hurt her. But the porcupine, squealing and grunting, with disrupted anatomy trying feebly to roll up into its ball-protection, flicked out its tail again, and again the big cat squalled with hurt and astonishment. Then she fell to backing away and sneezing, her nose bristling with quills like a monstrous pin-cushion. She brushed her nose with her paws, trying to dislodge the fiery darts, thrust it into the snow, and rubbed it against twigs and branches, all the time leaping about, ahead, sidewise, up and down, in a frenzy of pain and fright.

She sneezed continually, and her stub of a tail was doing its best toward lashing about by giving quick, violent jerks. She quit her antics, and quieted down for a long minute. One Eye watched. And even he could not repress a start and an involuntary bristling of hair along his back when she suddenly leaped, without warning, straight up in the air, at the same time emitting a long and most terrible squall. Then she sprang away, up the trail, squalling with every leap she made.

It was not until her racket had faded away in the distance and died out that One Eye ventured forth. He walked as delicately as though all the snow were carpeted with porcupine quills, erect and ready to pierce the soft pads of his feet. The porcupine met his approach with a furious squealing and a clashing of its long teeth. It had managed to roll up in a ball again, but it was not quite the old compact ball; its muscles were too much torn for that. It had been ripped almost in half, and was still bleeding profusely.

One Eye scooped out mouthfuls of the blood-soaked snow, and chewed and tasted and swallowed. This served as a relish, and his hunger increased mightily; but he was too old in the world to forget his caution. He waited. He lay down and waited, while the porcupine grated its teeth and uttered grunts and sobs and occasional sharp little squeals. In a little while, One Eye noticed that the quills were drooping and that a great quivering had set up. The quivering came to an end suddenly. There was a final defiant clash of the long teeth. Then all the quills drooped quite down, and the body relaxed and moved no more.

With a nervous, shrinking paw, One Eye stretched out the porcupine to its full length and turned it over on its back. Nothing had happened. It was surely dead. He studied it intently for a moment, then took a careful grip with his teeth and started off down the stream, partly carrying, partly dragging the porcupine, with head turned to the side so as to avoid stepping on the prickly mass. He recollected something, dropped the burden, and trotted back to where he had left the ptarmigan. He did not hesitate a moment. He knew clearly what was to be done, and this he did by promptly eating the ptarmigan. Then he returned and took up his burden.

When he dragged the result of his day's hunt into the cave, the she-wolf inspected it, turned her muzzle to him, and lightly licked him on the neck. But the next instant she was warning him away from the cubs with a snarl that was less harsh than usual and that was more apologetic than menacing. Her instinctive fear of the father of her progeny was toning down. He was behaving as a wolf father should, and manifesting no unholy desire to devour the young lives she had brought into the world.

III

The Gray Cub

HE was different from his brothers and sisters. Their hair already betrayed the reddish hue inherited from their mother, the she-wolf; while he alone, in this particular, took after his father. He was the one little gray cub of the litter. He had bred true to the straight wolf-stock—in fact, he had bred true, physically, to old One Eye himself, with but a single exception, and that was that he had two eyes to his father's one.

The gray cub's eyes had not been open long, yet already he could see with steady clearness. And while his eyes were still closed, he had felt, tasted, and smelled. He knew his two brothers and his two sisters very well. He had begun to romp with them in a feeble, awkward way, and even to squabble, his little throat vibrating with a queer rasping noise, (the forerunner of the growl), as he worked himself into a passion. And long before his eyes had opened, he had learned by touch, taste, and smell to know his mother—a fount of warmth and liquid food and tenderness. She possessed a gentle, caressing tongue that soothed him when it passed over his soft little body, and that impelled him to snuggle close against her and to doze off to sleep.

Most of the first month of his life had been passed thus in sleeping; but now he could see quite well, and he stayed awake for longer periods of time, and he was coming to learn his world quite well. His world was gloomy; but he did not know that, for he knew no other world. It was dim-lighted; but his eyes had never had to adjust themselves to any other light. His world was very small. Its limits were the walls of the lair;

but as he had no knowledge of the wide world outside, he was never oppressed by the narrow confines of his existence.

But he had early discovered that one wall of his world was different from the rest. This was the mouth of the cave and the source of light. He had discovered that it was different from the other walls long before he had any thoughts of his own, any conscious volitions. It had been an irresistible attraction before ever his eyes opened and looked upon it. The light from it had beat upon his sealed lids, and the eyes and the optic nerves had pulsated to little, sparklike flashes, warm-colored and strangely pleasing. The life of his body, and of every fibre of his body, the life that was the very substance of his body and that was apart from his own personal life, had yearned toward this light and urged his body toward it in the same way that the cunning chemistry of a plant urges it toward the sun.

Always, in the beginning, before his conscious life dawned, he had crawled toward the mouth of the cave. And in this his brothers and sisters were one with him. Never, in that period, did any of them crawl toward the dark corners of the back-wall. The light drew them as if they were plants; the chemistry of the life that composed them demanded the light as a necessity of being; and their little puppet-bodies crawled blindly and chemically, like the tendrils of a vine. Later on, when each developed individuality and became personally conscious of impulsions and desires, the attraction of the light increased. They were always crawling and sprawling toward it, and being driven back from it by their mother.

It was in this way that the gray cub learned other attributes of his mother than the soft, soothing tongue. In his insistent crawling toward the light, he discovered in her a nose that with a sharp nudge administered rebuke, and later, a paw, that crushed him down or rolled him over and over with swift, calculating stroke. Thus he learned hurt; and on top of it he learned to avoid hurt, first, by not incurring the risk of it; and second, when he had incurred the risk, by dodging and by retreating. These were conscious actions, and were the results of his first generalizations upon the world. Before that he had recoiled automatically from hurt, as he had crawled automatically toward the light. After that he recoiled from hurt because he *knew* that it was hurt.

He was a fierce little cub. So were his brothers and sisters. It was to be expected. He was a carnivorous animal. He came of a breed of meat-killers and meat-eaters. His father and mother lived wholly upon meat. The milk he had sucked with his first flickering life was milk transformed directly from meat, and now, at a month old, when his eyes had been open for but a week, he was beginning himself to eat meat—meat half-digested by the she-wolf and disgorged for the five growing cubs that already made too great demand upon her breast.

But he was, further, the fiercest of the litter. He could make a louder rasping growl than any of them. His tiny rages were much more terrible than theirs. It was he that first learned the trick of rolling a fellow-cub over with a cunning paw-stroke. And it was he that first gripped another cub by the ear and pulled and tugged and growled through jaws tight-clenched. And certainly it was he that caused the mother the most trouble in keeping her litter from the mouth of the cave.

The fascination of the light for the gray cub increased from day to day. He was perpetually departing on yard-long adventures toward the cave's entrance, and as perpetually being driven back. Only he did not know it for an entrance. He did not know anything about entrances—passages whereby one goes from one place to another place. He did not know any other place, much less of a way to get there. So to him the entrance of the cave was a wall—a wall of light. As the sun was to the outside dweller, this wall was to him the sun of his world. It attracted him as a candle attracts a moth. He was always striving to attain it. The life that was so swiftly expanding within him, urged him continually toward the wall of light. The life that was within him knew that it was the one way out, the way he was predestined to tread. But he himself did not know anything about it. He did not know there was any outside at all.

There was one strange thing about this wall of light. His father (he had already come to recognize his father as the one other dweller in the world, a creature like his mother, who slept near the light and was a bringer of meat)—his father had a way of walking right into the white far wall and disappearing. The gray cub could not understand this. Though never permitted by his mother to approach that wall, he had approached the other walls, and encountered hard obstruction on the end of his tender nose. This hurt. And after several such adventures, he left the walls alone. Without thinking about it, he accepted this disappearing into the wall as a peculiarity of his father, as milk and half-digested meat were peculiarities of his mother.

In fact, the gray cub was not given to thinking—at least, to the kind of thinking customary of men. His brain worked in dim ways. Yet his conclusions were as sharp and distinct as those achieved by men. He had a method of accepting things, without questioning the why and wherefore. In reality, this was the act of classification. He was never disturbed over *why* a thing happened. *How* it happened was sufficient for him. Thus, when he had bumped his nose on the back-wall a few times, he accepted that he would not disappear into walls. In the same way he accepted that his father could disappear into walls. But he was not in the least disturbed by desire to find out the reason for the difference between his father and himself. Logic and physics were no part of his mental make-up.

Like most creatures of the Wild, he early experienced famine. There came a time when not only did the meat-supply cease, but the milk no longer came from his mother's breast. At first, the cubs whimpered and cried, but for the most part they slept. It was not long before they were reduced to a coma of hunger. There were no more spats and squabbles, no more tiny rages nor attempts at growling; while the adventures toward the far white wall ceased altogether. The cubs slept, while the life that was in them flickered and died down.

One Eye was desperate. He ranged far and wide, and slept but little in the lair that had now become cheerless and miserable. The she-wolf, too, left her litter and went out in search of meat. In the first days after the birth of the cubs, One Eye had journeyed several times back to the Indian camp and robbed the rabbit snares; but, with the melting of the snow and the opening of the streams, the Indian camp had moved away, and that source of supply was closed to him.

When the gray cub came back to life and again took interest in the far white wall, he found that the population of his world had been reduced. Only one sister remained to him. The rest were gone. As he grew stronger, he found himself compelled to play alone, for the sister no longer lifted her head nor moved about. His little body rounded out with the meat he now ate; but the food had come too late for her. She slept continuously, a tiny skeleton flung round with skin in which the flame flickered lower and lower and at last went out.

Then there came a time when the gray cub no longer saw his father appearing and disappearing in the wall nor lying down asleep in the entrance. This had happened at the end of a second and less severe famine. The she-wolf knew why One Eye never came back, but there was no way by which she could tell what she had seen to the gray cub. Hunting herself for meat, up the left fork of the stream where lived the lynx, she had followed a day-old trail of One Eye. And she had found him, or what remained of him, at the end of the trail. There were many signs of the battle that had been fought, and of the lynx's withdrawal to her lair after having won the victory. Before she went away, the she-wolf had found this lair, but the signs told her that the lynx was inside, and she had not dared to venture in.

After that, the she-wolf in her hunting avoided the left fork. For she knew that in the lynx's lair was a litter of kittens, and she knew the lynx for a fierce, bad-tempered creature and a terrible fighter. It was all very well for half a dozen wolves to drive a lynx, spitting and bristling, up a tree; but it was quite a different matter for a lone wolf to encounter a lynx—especially when the lynx was known to have a litter of hungry kittens at her back.

But the Wild is the Wild, and motherhood is motherhood, at all times fiercely protective whether in the Wild or out of it; and the time was to come when the she-wolf, for her gray cub's sake, would venture the left fork, and the lair in the rocks, and the lynx's wrath.

IV

The Wall of the World

By the time his mother began leaving the cave on hunting expeditions, the cub had learned well the law that forbade his approaching the entrance. Not only had this law been forcibly and many times impressed on him by his mother's nose and paw, but in him the instinct of fear was developing. Never, in his brief cave-life, had he encountered anything of which to be afraid. Yet fear was in him. It had come down to him from a remote ancestry through a thousand thousand lives. It was a heritage he had received directly from One Eye and the she-wolf; but to them, in turn, it had been passed down through all the generations of wolves that had gone before. Fear!—that legacy of the Wild which no animal may escape nor exchange for pottage.

So the gray cub knew fear, though he knew not the stuff of which fear was made. Possibly he accepted it as one of the restrictions of life. For he had already learned that there were such restrictions. Hunger he had known; and when he could not appease his hunger he had felt restriction. The hard obstruction of the cave-wall, the sharp nudge of his mother's nose, the smashing stroke of her paw, the hunger unappeased of several famines, had borne in upon him that all was not freedom in the world, that to life there were limitations and restraints. These limitations and restraints were laws. To be obedient to them was to escape hurt and make for happiness.

He did not reason the question out in this man-fashion. He merely classified the things that hurt and the things that did not hurt. And after such classification he avoided the things that hurt, the restrictions and restraints, in order to enjoy the satisfactions and the remunerations of life.

Thus it was that in obedience to the law laid down by his mother, and in obedience to the law of that unknown and nameless thing, fear, he kept away from the mouth of the cave. It remained to him a white wall of light. When his mother was absent, he slept most of the time, while during the intervals that he was awake he kept very quiet, suppressing the whimpering cries that tickled in his throat and strove for noise.

Once, lying awake, he heard a strange sound in the white wall. He did not know that it was a wolverine, standing outside, all a-tremble with its own daring, and cautiously scenting out the contents of the cave. The cub knew only that the sniff was strange, a something unclassified, therefore unknown and terrible—for the unknown was one of the chief elements that went into the making of fear.

The hair bristled up on the gray cub's back, but it bristled silently. How was he to know that this thing that sniffed was a thing at which to bristle? It was not born of any knowledge of his, yet it was the visible expression of the fear that was in him, and for which, in his own life, there was no accounting. But fear was accompanied by another instinct—that of concealment. The cub was in a frenzy of terror, yet he lay without movement or sound, frozen, petrified into immobility, to all appearances dead. His mother, coming home, growled as she smelt the wolverine's track, and bounded into the cave and licked and nozzled him with undue vehemence of affection. And the cub felt that somehow he had escaped a great hurt.

But there were other forces at work in the cub, the greatest of which was growth. Instinct and law demanded of him obedience. But growth demanded disobedience. His mother and fear impelled him to keep away from the white wall. Growth is life, and life is forever destined to make for light. So there was no damming up the tide of life that was rising within him—rising with every mouthful of meat he swallowed, with every breath he drew. In the end, one day, fear and obedience were swept away by the rush of life, and the cub straddled and sprawled toward the entrance.

Unlike any other wall with which he had had experience, this wall seemed to recede from him as he approached. No hard surface collided with the tender little nose he thrust out tentatively before him. The substance of the wall seemed as permeable and yielding as light. And as condition, in his eyes, had the seeming of form, so he entered into what had been wall to him and bathed in the substance that composed it.

It was bewildering. He was sprawling through solidity. And ever the light grew brighter. Fear urged him to go back, but growth drove him on. Suddenly he found himself at the mouth of the cave. The wall, inside which he had thought himself, as suddenly leaped back before him to an immeasurable distance. The light had become painfully bright. He was dazzled by it. Likewise he was made dizzy by this abrupt and tremendous extension of space. Automatically, his eyes were adjusting themselves to the brightness, focussing themselves to meet the increased distance of objects. At first, the wall had leaped beyond his vision. He now saw it again; but it had taken upon itself a remarkable remoteness. Also, its appearance had changed. It was now a variegated wall, composed of the trees that fringed the stream, the opposing mountain that towered above the trees, and the sky that out-towered the mountain.

A great fear came upon him. This was more of the terrible unknown. He crouched down on the lip of the cave and gazed out on the world. He was very much afraid. Because it was unknown, it was hostile to him. Therefore the hair stood up on end along his back and his lips wrinkled weakly in an attempt at a ferocious and intimidating snarl. Out of his puniness and fright he challenged and menaced the whole wide world.

Nothing happened. He continued to gaze, and in his interest he forgot to snarl. Also, he forgot to be afraid. For the time, fear had been routed by growth, while growth had assumed the guise of curiosity. He began to notice near objects—an open portion of the stream that flashed in the sun, the blasted pine tree that stood at the base of the slope, and the slope itself, that ran right up to him and ceased two feet beneath the lip of the cave on which he crouched.

Now the gray cub had lived all his days on a level floor. He had never experienced the hurt of a fall. He did not know what a fall was. So he stepped boldly out upon the air. His hind-legs still rested on the cave-lip, so he fell forward head downward. The earth struck him a harsh blow on the nose that made him yelp. Then he began rolling down the slope, over and over. He was in a panic of terror. The unknown had caught him at last. It had gripped savagely hold of him and was about to wreak upon him some terrific hurt. Growth was now routed by fear, and he ki-yi'd like any frightened puppy.

The unknown bore him on he knew not to what frightful hurt, and he yelped and ki-yi'd unceasingly. This was a different proposition from crouching in frozen fear while the unknown lurked just alongside. Now the unknown had caught tight hold of him. Silence would do no good. Besides, it was not fear, but terror, that convulsed him.

But the slope grew more gradual, and its base was grass-covered. Here the cub lost momentum. When at last he came to a stop, he gave one last agonized yelp and then a long, whimpering wail. Also, and quite as a matter of course, as though in his life he had already made a thousand toilets, he proceeded to lick away the dry clay that soiled him.

After that he sat up and gazed about him, as might the first man of the earth who landed upon Mars. The cub had broken through the wall of the world, the unknown had let go its hold of him, and here he was without hurt. But the first man on Mars would have experienced less unfamiliarity than did he. Without any antecedent knowledge, without any warning whatever that such existed, he found himself an explorer in a totally new world.

Now that the terrible unknown had let go of him, he forgot that the unknown had any terrors. He was aware only of curiosity in all the things about him. He inspected the grass beneath him, the mossberry plant just beyond, and the dead trunk of the blasted pine that stood on the edge of an open space among the trees. A squirrel, running around the base of the trunk, came full upon him, and gave him a great fright. He cowered down and snarled. But the squirrel was as badly scared. It ran up the tree, and from a point of safety chattered back savagely.

This helped the cub's courage, and though the woodpecker he next encountered gave him a start, he proceeded confidently on his way. Such was his confidence, that when a moose-bird impudently hopped up to him, he reached out at it with a playful paw. The result was a sharp peck on the end of his nose that made him cower down and ki-yi. The noise he made was too much for the moose-bird, who sought safety in flight.

But the cub was learning. His misty little mind had already made an unconscious classification. There were live things and things not alive. Also, he must watch out for the live things. The things not alive remained always in one place; but the live things moved about, and there was no telling what they might do. The thing to expect of them was the unexpected, and for this he must be prepared.

He travelled very clumsily. He ran into sticks and things. A twig that he thought a long way off, would the next instant hit him on the nose or rake along his ribs. There were inequalities of surface. Sometimes he overstepped and stubbed his nose. Quite as often he understepped and stubbed his feet. Then there were the pebbles and stones that turned under him when he trod upon them; and from them he came to know that the things not alive were not all in the same state of stable equilibrium as was his cave; also, that small things not alive were more liable than large things to fall down or turn over. But with every mishap he was learning. The longer he walked, the better he walked. He was adjusting himself. He was learning to calculate his own muscular movements, to know his physical limitations, to measure distances between objects, and between objects and himself.

His was the luck of the beginner. Born to be a hunter of meat, (though he did not know it), he blundered upon meat just outside his own cave-door on his first foray into the world. It was by sheer blundering that he chanced upon the shrewdly hidden ptarmigan nest. He fell into it. He had essayed to walk along the trunk of a fallen pine. The rotten bark gave way under his feet, and with a despairing yelp he pitched down the rounded descent, smashed through the leafage and stalks of a small bush, and in the heart of the bush, on the ground, fetched up amongst seven ptarmigan chicks.

They made noises, and at first he was frightened at them. Then he perceived that they were very little, and he became bolder. They moved. He placed his paw on one, and its movements were accelerated. This was a source of enjoyment to him. He smelled it. He picked it up in his mouth. It struggled and tickled his tongue. At the same time he was made aware of a sensation of hunger. His jaws closed together. There was a crunching of fragile bones, and warm blood ran in his mouth. The taste of it was good. This was meat, the same as his mother gave him, only it was alive between his teeth and therefore better. So he ate the ptarmigan. Nor did he stop till he had devoured the whole brood. Then he licked his chops in quite the same way his mother did, and began to crawl out of the bush.

He encountered a feathered whirlwind. He was confused and blinded by the rush of it and the beat of angry wings. He hid his head between his paws and yelped. The blows increased. The mother-ptarmigan was in a fury. Then he became angry. He rose up, snarling, striking out with his paws. He sank his tiny teeth into one of the wings and pulled and tugged sturdily. The ptarmigan struggled against him, showering blows upon him with her free wing. It was his first battle. He was elated. He forgot all about the unknown. He no longer was afraid of anything. He was fighting, tearing at a live thing that was striking at him. Also, this live thing was meat. The lust to kill was on him. He had just destroyed little live things. He would now destroy a big live thing. He was too busy and happy to know that he was happy. He was thrilling and exulting in ways new to him and greater to him than any he had known before.

He held on to the wing and growled between his tight-clenched teeth. The ptarmigan dragged him out of the bush. When she turned and tried to drag him back into the bush's shelter, he pulled her away from it and on into the open. And all the time she was making outcry and striking with her wing, while feathers were flying like a snow-fall. The pitch to which he was aroused was tremendous. All the fighting blood of his breed was up in him and surging through him. This was living, though he did not know it. He was realizing his own meaning in the world; he was doing that for which he was made—killing meat and battling to kill it. He was justifying his existence, than which life can do no greater; for life achieves its summit when it does to the uttermost that which it was equipped to do.

After a time, the ptarmigan ceased her struggling. He still held her by the wing, and they lay on the ground and looked at each other. He tried to growl threateningly, ferociously. She pecked on his nose, which by now, what of previous adventures, was sore. He winced but held on. She pecked him again and again. From wincing he went to whimpering. He tried to back away from her, oblivious of the fact that by his hold on her he dragged her after him. A rain of pecks fell on his ill-used nose. The flood of fight ebbed down in him, and, releasing his prey, he turned tail and scampered off across the open in inglorious retreat.

He lay down to rest on the other side of the open, near the edge of the bushes, his tongue lolling out, his chest heaving and panting, his nose still hurting him and causing him to continue his whimper. But as he lay there, suddenly there came to him a feeling as of something terrible impending. The unknown with all its terrors rushed upon him, and he shrank back instinctively into the shelter of the bush. As he did so, a draught of air fanned him, and a large, winged body swept ominously and silently past. A hawk, driving down out of the blue, had barely missed him.

While he lay in the bush, recovering from this fright and peering fearfully out, the mother-ptarmigan on the other side of the open space fluttered out of the ravaged nest. It was because of her loss that she paid no attention to the winged bolt of the sky. But the cub saw, and it was a warning and a lesson to him—the swift downward swoop of the hawk, the short skim of its body just above the ground, the strike of its talons in the body of the ptarmigan, the ptarmigan's squawk of agony and fright, and the hawk's rush upward into the blue, carrying the ptarmigan away with it.

It was a long time before the cub left his shelter. He had learned much. Live things were meat. They were good to eat. Also, live things when they were large enough, could give hurt. It was better to eat small live things like ptarmigan chicks, and to let alone large live things like ptarmigan hens. Nevertheless he felt a little prick of ambition, a sneaking desire to have another battle with that ptarmigan hen—only the hawk had carried her away. Maybe there were other ptarmigan hens. He would go and see.

He came down a shelving bank to the stream. He had never seen water before. The footing looked good. There were no inequalities of surface. He stepped boldly out on it; and went down, crying with fear, into the embrace of the unknown. It was cold, and he gasped, breathing quickly. The water rushed into his lungs instead of the air that had always accompanied his act of breathing. The suffocation he experienced was like the pang of death. To him it signified death. He had no conscious knowledge of death, but like every animal of the Wild, he possessed the instinct of death. To him it stood as the greatest of hurts. It was the very essence of the unknown; it was the sum of the terrors of the unknown, the one culminating and unthinkable catastrophe that could happen to him, about which he knew nothing and about which he feared everything.

He came to the surface, and the sweet air rushed into his open mouth. He did not go down again. Quite as though it had been a long-established custom of his, he struck out with all his legs and began to swim. The near bank was a yard away; but he had come up with his back to it, and the first thing his eyes rested upon was the opposite bank, toward which he immediately began to swim. The stream was a small one, but in the pool it widened out to a score of feet.

Midway in the passage, the current picked up the cub and swept him down-stream. He was caught in the miniature rapid at the bottom of the pool. Here was little chance for swimming. The quiet water had become suddenly angry. Sometimes he was under, sometimes on top. At all times he was in violent motion, now being turned over or around, and again, being smashed against a rock. And with every rock he struck, he yelped. His progress was a series of yelps, from which might have been adduced the number of rocks he encountered.

Below the rapid was a second pool, and here, captured by the eddy, he was gently borne to the bank and as gently deposited on a bed of gravel. He crawled frantically clear of the water and lay down. He had learned some more about the world. Water was not alive. Yet it moved. Also, it looked as solid as the earth, but was without any solidity at all. His conclusion was that things were not always what they appeared to be. The cub's fear of the unknown was an inherited distrust, and it had now been strengthened by experience. Thenceforth, in the nature of things, he would possess an abiding distrust of appearances. He would have to learn the reality of a thing before he could put his faith into it.

One other adventure was destined for him that day. He had recollected that there was such a thing in the world as his mother. And then there came to him a feeling that he wanted her more than all the rest of the things in the world. Not only was his body tired with the adventures it had undergone, but his little brain was equally tired. In all the days he had lived it had not worked so hard as on this one day. Furthermore, he was sleepy. So he started out to look for the cave and his mother, feeling at the same time an overwhelming rush of loneliness and helplessness.

He was sprawling along between some bushes, when he heard a sharp, intimidating cry. There was a flash of yellow before his eyes. He saw a weasel leaping swiftly away from him. It was a small live thing, and he had no fear. Then, before him, at his feet, he saw an extremely small live thing, only several inches long—a young weasel, that, like himself, had disobediently gone out adventuring. It tried to retreat before him. He turned it over with his paw. It made a queer, grating noise. The next moment the flash of yellow reappeared before his eyes. He heard again the intimidating cry, and at the same instant received a severe blow on the side of the neck and felt the sharp teeth of the mother-weasel cut into his flesh.

While he yelped and ki-yi'd and scrambled backward, he saw the mother-weasel leap upon her young one and disappear with it into the neighboring thicket. The cut of her teeth in his neck still hurt, but his feelings were hurt more grievously, and he sat down and weakly whimpered. This mother-weasel was so small and so savage! He was yet to learn that for size and weight the weasel was the most ferocious, vindictive, and terrible of all the killers of the Wild. But a portion of this knowledge was quickly to be his.

He was still whimpering when the mother-weasel reappeared. She did not rush him, now that her young one was safe. She approached more cautiously, and the cub had full opportunity to observe her lean, snakelike body, and her head, erect, eager, and snakelike itself. Her sharp, menacing cry sent the hair bristling along his back, and he snarled warningly at her. She came closer and closer. There was a leap, swifter than his unpractised sight, and the lean, yellow body disappeared for a moment out of the field of his vision. The next moment she was at his throat, her teeth buried in his hair and flesh.

At first he snarled and tried to fight; but he was very young, and this was only his first day in the world, and his snarl became a whimper, his fight a struggle to escape. The weasel never relaxed her hold. She hung on striving to press down with her teeth to the great vein where his life-blood bubbled. The weasel was a drinker of blood, and it was ever her preference to drink from the throat of life itself.

The gray cub would have died, and there would have been no story to write about him, had not the she-wolf come bounding through the bushes. The weasel let go the cub and flashed at the she-wolf's throat, missing, but getting a hold on the jaw instead. The she-wolf flirted her head like the snap of a whip, breaking the weasel's hold and flinging it high in the air. And, still in the air, the she-wolf's jaws closed on the lean, yellow body, and the weasel knew death between the crunching teeth.

The cub experienced another access of affection on the part of his mother. Her joy at finding him seemed greater even than his joy at being found. She nozzled him and caressed him and licked the cuts made in him by the weasel's teeth. Then, between them, mother and cub, they ate the blood-drinker, and after that went back to the cave and slept.

V

The Law of Meat

THE cub's development was rapid. He rested for two days, and then ventured forth from the cave again. It was on this adventure that he found the young weasel whose mother he had helped eat, and he saw to it that the young weasel went the way of its mother. But on this trip he did not get lost. When he grew tired, he found his way back to the cave and slept. And every day thereafter found him out and ranging a wider area.

He began to get an accurate measurement of his strength and his weakness, and to know when to be bold and when to be cautious. He found it expedient to be cautious all the time, except for the rare moments, when, assured of his own intrepidity, he abandoned himself to petty rages and lusts.

He was always a little demon of fury when he chanced upon a stray ptarmigan. Never did he fail to respond savagely to the chatter of the squirrel he had first met on the blasted pine. While the sight of a moose-bird almost invariably put him into the wildest of rages; for he never forgot the peck on the nose he had received from the first of that ilk he encountered.

But there were times when even a moose-bird failed to affect him, and those were times when he felt himself to be in danger from some other prowling meat-hunter. He never forgot the hawk, and its moving shadow always sent him crouching into the nearest thicket. He no longer sprawled and straddled, and already he was developing the gait of his mother, slinking and furtive, apparently without exertion, yet sliding along with a swiftness that was as deceptive as it was imperceptible.

In the matter of meat, his luck had been all in the beginning. The seven ptarmigan chicks and the baby weasel represented the sum of his killings. His desire to kill strengthened with the days, and he cherished hungry ambitions for the squirrel that chattered so volubly and always informed all wild creatures that the wolf-cub was approaching. But as birds flew in the air, squirrels could climb trees, and the cub could only try to crawl unobserved upon the squirrel when it was on the ground.

The cub entertained a great respect for his mother. She could get meat, and she never failed to bring him his share. Further, she was unafraid of things. It did not occur to him that this fearlessness was founded upon experience and knowledge. Its effect on him was that of an impression of power. His mother represented power; and as he grew older he felt this power in the sharper admonition of her paw; while the reproving nudge of her nose gave place to the slash of her fangs. For this, likewise, he respected his mother. She compelled obedience from him, and the older he grew the shorter grew her temper.

Famine came again, and the cub with clearer consciousness knew once more the bite of hunger. The she-wolf ran herself thin in the quest for meat. She rarely slept any more in the cave, spending most of her time on the meat-trail and spending it vainly. This famine was not a long one, but it was severe while it lasted. The cub found no more milk in his mother's breast, nor did he get one mouthful of meat for himself.

Before, he had hunted in play, for the sheer joyousness of it; now he hunted in deadly earnestness, and found nothing. Yet the failure of it accelerated his development. He studied the habits of the squirrel with greater carefulness, and strove with greater craft to steal upon it and surprise it. He studied the wood-mice and tried to dig them out of their burrows; and he learned much about the ways of moose-birds and woodpeckers. And there came a day when the hawk's shadow did not drive him crouching into the bushes. He had grown stronger, and wiser, and more confident. Also, he was desperate. So he sat on his haunches, conspicuously, in an open space, and challenged the hawk down out of the sky. For he knew that there, floating in the blue above him, was meat, the meat his stomach yearned after so insistently. But the hawk refused to come down and give battle, and the cub crawled away into a thicket and whimpered his disappointment and hunger.

The famine broke. The she-wolf brought home meat. It was strange meat, different from any she had ever brought before. It was a lynx kitten, partly grown, like the cub, but not so large. And it was all for him. His mother had satisfied her hunger elsewhere; though he did not know that it was the rest of the lynx litter that had gone to satisfy her. Nor did he know the desperateness of her deed. He knew only that the velvet-furred kitten was meat, and he ate and waxed happier with every mouthful.

A full stomach conduces to inaction, and the cub lay in the cave, sleeping against his mother's side. He was aroused by her snarling. Never had he heard her snarl so terribly. Possibly in her whole life it was the most terrible snarl she ever gave. There was reason for it, and none knew it better than she. A lynx's lair is not despoiled with impunity. In the full glare of the afternoon light, crouching in the entrance of the cave, the cub saw the lynx-mother. The hair rippled up all along his back at the sight. Here was fear, and it did not require his instinct to tell him of it. And if sight alone were not sufficient, the cry of rage the intruder gave, beginning with a snarl and rushing abruptly upward into a hoarse screech, was convincing enough in itself.

The cub felt the prod of the life that was in him, and stood up and snarled valiantly by his mother's side. But she thrust him ignominiously away and behind her. Because of the low-roofed entrance the lynx could not leap in, and when she made a crawling rush of it the she-wolf sprang upon her and pinned her down. The cub saw little of the battle. There was a tremendous snarling and spitting and screeching. The two animals threshed about, the lynx ripping and tearing with her claws and using her teeth as well, while the she-wolf used her teeth alone.

Once, the cub sprang in and sank his teeth into the hind leg of the lynx. He clung on, growling savagely. Though he did not know it, by the weight of his body he clogged the action of the leg and thereby saved his mother much damage. A change in the battle crushed him under both their bodies and wrenched loose his hold. The next moment the two mothers separated, and, before they rushed together again, the lynx lashed out at the cub with a huge fore-paw that ripped his shoulder open to the bone and sent him hurtling sidewise against the wall. Then was added to the uproar the cub's shrill yelp of pain and fright. But the fight lasted so long that he had time to cry himself out and to experience a second burst of courage; and the end of the battle found him again clinging to a hind-leg and furiously growling between his teeth.

The lynx was dead. But the she-wolf was very weak and sick. At first she caressed the cub and licked his wounded shoulder; but the blood she had lost had taken with it her strength, and for all of a day and a night she lay by her dead foe's side, without movement, scarcely breathing. For a week she never left the cave, except for water, and then her movements were slow and painful. At the end of that time, the lynx was devoured, while the she-wolf's wounds had healed sufficiently to permit her to take the meat-trail again.

The cub's shoulder was stiff and sore, and for some time he limped from the terrible slash he had received. But the world now seemed changed. He went about in it with greater confidence, with a feeling of prowess that had not been his in the days before the battle with the lynx. He had looked upon life in a more ferocious aspect; he had fought; he had buried his teeth in the flesh of a foe; and he had survived. And because of all this, he carried himself more boldly, with a touch of defiance that was new in him. He was no longer afraid of minor things, and much of his timidity had vanished, though the unknown never ceased to press upon him with its mysteries and terrors, intangible and ever-menacing.

He began to accompany his mother on the meat-trail, and he saw much of the killing of meat and began to play his part in it. And in his own dim way he learned the law of meat. There were two kinds of life,—his own kind and the other kind. His own kind included his mother and himself. The other kind included all live things that moved. But the other kind was divided. One portion was what his own kind killed and ate. This portion was composed of the non-killers and the small killers. The other portion killed and ate his own kind, or was killed and eaten by his own kind. And out of this classification arose the law. The aim of life was meat. Life itself was meat. Life lived on life. There were the eaters and the eaten. The law was: EAT OR BE EATEN. He did not formulate the law in clear, set terms and moralize about it. He did not even think the law; he merely lived the law without thinking about it at all.

He saw the law operating around him on every side. He had eaten the ptarmigan chicks. The hawk had eaten the ptarmigan-mother. The hawk would also have eaten him. Later, when he had grown more formidable, he wanted to eat the hawk. He had eaten the lynx kitten. The lynx-mother would have eaten him had she not herself been killed and eaten. And so it went. The law was being lived about him by all live things, and he himself was part and parcel of the law. He was a killer. His only food was meat, live meat, that ran away swiftly before him, or flew into the air, or climbed trees, or hid in the ground, or faced him and fought with him, or turned the tables and ran after him.

Had the cub thought in man-fashion, he might have epitomized life as a voracious appetite, and the world as a place wherein ranged a multitude of appetites, pursuing and being pursued, hunting and being hunted, eating and being eaten, all in blindness and confusion, with violence and disorder, a chaos of gluttony and slaughter, ruled over by chance, merciless, planless, endless.

But the cub did not think in man-fashion. He did not look at things with wide vision. He was single-purposed, and entertained but one thought or desire at a time. Besides the law of meat, there was a myriad other and lesser laws for him to learn and obey. The world was filled with surprise. The stir of the life that was in him, the play of his muscles, was an unending happiness. To run down meat was to experience thrills and elations. His rages and battles were pleasures. Terror itself, and the mystery of the unknown, lent to his living.

And there were easements and satisfactions. To have a full stomach, to doze lazily in the sunshine—such things were remuneration in full for his ardors and toils, while his ardors and toils were in themselves self-remunerative. They were expressions of life, and life is always happy when it is expressing itself. So the cub had no quarrel with his hostile environment. He was very much alive, very happy, and very proud of himself.

PART THREE—THE GODS OF THE WILD

I

The Makers of Fire

THE cub came upon it suddenly. It was his own fault. He had been careless. He had left the cave and run down to the stream to drink. It might have been that he took no notice because he was heavy with sleep. (He had been out all night on the meat-trail, and had but just then awakened). And his carelessness might have been due to the familiarity of the trail to the pool. He had travelled it often, and nothing had ever happened on it.

He went down past the blasted pine, crossed the open space, and trotted in amongst the trees. Then, at the same instant, he saw and smelt. Before him, sitting silently on their haunches, were five live things, the like of which he had never seen before. It was his first glimpse of mankind. But at the sight of him the five men did not spring to their feet, nor show their teeth, nor snarl. They did not move, but sat there, silent and ominous.

Nor did the cub move. Every instinct of his nature would have impelled him to dash wildly away, had there not suddenly and for the first time arisen in him another and counter instinct. A great awe descended upon him. He was beaten down to movelessness by an overwhelming sense of his own weakness and littleness. Here was mastery and power, something far and away beyond him.

The cub had never seen man, yet the instinct concerning man was his. In dim ways he recognized in man the animal that had fought itself to primacy over the other animals of the Wild. Not alone out of his own eyes, but out of the eyes of all his ancestors was the cub now looking upon man—out of eyes that had circled in the darkness around countless winter campfires, that had peered from safe distances and from the hearts of thickets at the strange, two-legged animal that was lord over living things. The spell of the cub's heritage was upon him, the fear and the respect born of the centuries of struggle and the accumulated experience of the generations. The heritage was too compelling for a wolf that was only a cub. Had he been full-grown, he would have run away. As it was, he cowered down in a paralysis of fear, already half proffering the submission that his kind had proffered from the first time a wolf came in to sit by man's fire and be made warm.

One of the Indians arose and walked over to him and stooped above him. The cub cowered closer to the ground. It was the unknown, objectified at last, in concrete flesh and blood, bending over him and reaching down to seize hold of him. His hair bristled involuntarily; his lips writhed back and his little fangs were bared. The hand, poised like doom above him, hesitated, and the man spoke, laughing, "*Wabam wabisca ip pit tah.*" ("Look! The white fangs!")

The other Indians laughed loudly, and urged the man on to pick up the cub. As the hand descended closer and closer, there raged within the cub a battle of the instincts. He experienced two great impulsions,—to yield and to fight. The resulting action was a compromise. He did both. He yielded till the hand almost touched him. Then he fought, his teeth flashing in a snap that sank them into the hand. The next moment he received a clout alongside the head that knocked him over on his side. Then all fight fled out of him. His puppyhood and the instinct of submission took charge of him. He sat up on his haunches and ki-yi'd. But the man whose hand he had bitten was angry. The cub received a clout on the other side of his head. Whereupon he sat up and ki-yi'd louder than ever.

The four Indians laughed more loudly, while even the man who had been bitten began to laugh. They surrounded the cub and laughed at him, while he wailed out his terror and his hurt. In the midst of it, he heard something. The Indians heard it, too. But the cub knew what it was, and with a last, long wail that had in it more of triumph than grief, he ceased his noise and waited for the coming of his mother, of his ferocious and indomitable mother who fought and killed all things and was never afraid. She was snarling as she ran. She had heard the cry of her cub and was dashing to save him.

She bounded in amongst them, her anxious and militant motherhood making her anything but a pretty sight. But to the cub the spectacle of her protective rage was pleasing. He uttered a glad little cry and bounded to meet her, while the man-animals went back hastily several steps. The she-wolf stood over against her cub, facing the men, with bristling hair, a snarl rumbling deep in her throat. Her face was distorted and malignant with menace, even the bridge of the nose wrinkling from tip to eyes so prodigious was her snarl.

Then it was that a cry went up from one of the men. "Kiche!" was what he uttered. It was an exclamation of surprise. The cub felt his mother wilting at the sound.

"Kiche!" the man cried again, this time with sharpness and authority.

And then the cub saw his mother, the she-wolf, the fearless one, crouching down till her belly touched the ground, whimpering, wagging her tail, making peace signs. The cub could not understand. He was appalled. The awe of man rushed over him again. His instinct had been true. His mother verified it. She, too, rendered submission to the man-animals.

The man who had spoken came over to her. He put his hand upon her head, and she only crouched closer. She did not snap, nor threaten to snap. The other men came up, and surrounded her, and felt her, and pawed her, which actions she made no attempt to resent. They were greatly excited, and made many noises with their mouths. These noises were not indications of danger, the cub decided, as he crouched near his mother, still bristling from time to time but doing his best to submit.

"It is not strange," an Indian was saying. "Her father was a wolf. It is true, her mother was a dog; but did not my brother tie her out in the woods all of three nights in the mating season? Therefore was the father of Kiche a wolf."

"It is a year, Gray Beaver, since she ran away," spoke a second Indian.

"It is not strange, Salmon Tongue," Gray Beaver answered. "It was the time of the famine, and there was no meat for the dogs."

"She has lived with the wolves," said a third Indian.

"So it would seem, Three Eagles," Gray Beaver answered, laying his hand on the cub; "and this be the sign of it."

The cub snarled a little at the touch of the hand, and the hand flew back to administer a clout. Whereupon the cub covered its fangs and sank down submissively, while the hand, returning, rubbed behind his ears, and up and down his back.

"This be the sign of it," Gray Beaver went on. "It is plain that his mother is Kiche. But his father was a wolf. Wherefore is there in him little dog and much wolf. His fangs be white, and White Fang shall be his name. I have spoken. He is my dog. For was not Kiche my brother's dog? And is not my brother dead?"

The cub, who had thus received a name in the world, lay and watched. For a time the man-animals continued to make their mouth-noises. Then Gray Beaver took a knife from a sheath that hung around his neck, and went into the thicket and cut a stick. White Fang watched him. He notched the stick at each end and in the notches fastened strings of rawhide. One string he tied around the throat of Kiche. Then he led her to a small pine, around which he tied the other string.

White Fang followed and lay down beside her. Salmon Tongue's hand reached out to him and rolled him over on his back. Kiche looked on anxiously. White Fang felt fear mounting in him again. He could not quite suppress a snarl, but he made no offer to snap. The hand, with fingers crooked and spread apart, rubbed his stomach in a playful way and rolled him from side to side. It was ridiculous and ungainly, lying there on his back with legs sprawling in the air. Besides, it was a position of such utter helplessness that White Fang's whole nature revolted against it. He could do nothing to defend himself. If this man-animal intended harm, White Fang knew that he could not escape it. How could he spring away with his four legs in the air above him? Yet submission made him master his fear, and he only growled softly. This growl he could not suppress; nor did the man-animal resent it by giving him a blow on the head. And furthermore, such was the strangeness of it, White Fang experienced an unaccountable sensation of pleasure as the hand rubbed back and forth. When he was rolled on his side he ceased the growl; when the fingers pressed and prodded at the base of his ears the pleasurable sensation increased; and when, with a final rub and scratch, the man left him alone and went away, all fear had died out of White Fang. He was to know fear many times in his dealings with man; yet it was a token of the fearless companionship with man that was ultimately to be his.

After a time, White Fang heard strange noises approaching. He was quick in his classification, for he knew them at once for man-animal noises. A few minutes later the remainder of the tribe, strung out as it was on the march, trailed in. There were more men and many women and children, forty souls of them, and all heavily burdened with camp equipage and outfit. Also there were many dogs; and these, with the exception of the part-grown puppies, were likewise burdened with camp outfit. On their backs, in bags that fastened tightly around underneath, the dogs carried from twenty to thirty pounds of weight.

White Fang had never seen dogs before, but at sight of them he felt that they were his own kind, only somehow different. But they displayed little difference from the wolf when they discovered the cub and his mother. There was a rush. White Fang bristled and snarled and snapped in the face of the open-mouthed oncoming wave of dogs, and went down and under them, feeling the sharp slash of teeth in his body, himself biting and tearing at the legs and bellies above him. There was a great uproar. He could hear the snarl of Kiche as she fought for him; and he could hear the cries of the man-animals, the sound of clubs striking upon bodies, and the yelps of pain from the dogs so struck.

Only a few seconds elapsed before he was on his feet again. He could now see the man-animals driving back the dogs with clubs and stones, defending him, saving him from the savage teeth of his kind that somehow was not his kind. And though there was no reason in his brain for a clear conception of so abstract a thing as justice, nevertheless, in his own way, he felt the justice of the man-animals, and he knew them for what they were—makers of law and executors of law. Also, he appreciated the power with which they administered the law. Unlike any animals he had ever encountered, they did not bite nor claw. They enforced their live strength with the power of dead things. Dead things did their bidding. Thus, sticks and stones, directed by these strange creatures, leaped through the air like living things, inflicting grievous hurts upon the dogs.

To his mind this was power unusual, power inconceivable and beyond the natural, power that was godlike. White Fang, in the very nature of him, could never know anything about gods; at the best he could know only things that were beyond knowing; but the wonder and awe that he had of these man-animals in ways resembled what would be the wonder and awe of man at sight of some celestial creature, on a mountain top, hurling thunderbolts from either hand at an astonished world.

The last dog had been driven back. The hubbub died down. And White Fang licked his hurts and meditated upon this, his first taste of pack-cruelty and his introduction to the pack. He had never dreamed that his own kind consisted of more than One Eye, his mother, and himself. They had constituted a kind apart, and here, abruptly, he had discovered many more creatures apparently of his own kind. And there was a subconscious resentment that these, his kind, at first sight had pitched upon him and tried to destroy him. In the same way he resented his mother being tied with a stick, even though it was done by the superior man-animals. It savored of the trap, of bondage. Yet of the trap and of bondage he knew nothing. Freedom to roam and run and lie down at will, had been his heritage; and here it was being infringed upon. His mother's movements were restricted to the length of a stick, and by the length of that same stick was he restricted, for he had not yet got beyond the need of his mother's side.

He did not like it. Nor did he like it when the man-animals arose and went on with their march; for a tiny man-animal took the other end of the stick and led Kiche captive behind him, and behind Kiche followed White Fang, greatly perturbed and worried by this new adventure he had entered upon.

They went down the valley of the stream, far beyond White Fang's widest ranging, until they came to the end of the valley, where the stream ran into the Mackenzie River. Here, where canoes were cached on poles high in the air and where stood fish-racks for the drying of fish, camp was made; and White Fang looked on with wondering eyes. The superiority of these man-animals increased with every moment. There was their mastery over all these sharp-fanged dogs. It breathed of power. But greater than that, to the wolf-cub, was their mastery over things not alive; their capacity to communicate motion to unmoving things; their capacity to change the very face of the world.

It was this last that especially affected him. The elevation of frames of poles caught his eye; yet this in itself was not so remarkable, being done by the same creatures that flung sticks and stones to great distances. But when the frames of poles were made into tepees by being covered with cloth and skins, White Fang was astounded. It was the colossal bulk of them that impressed him. They arose around him, on every side, like some monstrous quick-growing form of life. They occupied nearly the whole circumference of his field of vision. He was afraid of them. They loomed ominously above him; and when the breeze stirred them into huge movements, he cowered down in fear, keeping his eyes warily upon them, and prepared to spring away if they attempted to precipitate themselves upon him.

But in a short while his fear of the tepees passed away. He saw the women and children passing in and out of them without harm, and he saw the dogs trying often to get into them, and being driven away with sharp words and flying stones. After a time, he left Kiche's side and crawled cautiously toward the wall of the nearest tepee. It was the curiosity of growth that urged him on—the necessity of learning and living and doing that brings experience. The last few inches to the wall of the tepee were crawled with painful slowness and precaution. The day's events had prepared him for the unknown to manifest itself in most stupendous and unthinkable ways. At last his nose touched the canvas. He waited. Nothing happened. Then he smelled the strange fabric, saturated with the man-smell. He closed on the canvas with his teeth and gave a gentle tug. Nothing happened, though the adjacent portions of the tepee moved. He tugged harder. There was a greater movement. It was delightful. He tugged still harder, and repeatedly, until the whole tepee was in motion. Then the sharp cry of a squaw inside sent him scampering back to Kiche. But after that he was afraid no more of the looming bulks of the tepees.

A moment later he was straying away again from his mother. Her stick was tied to a peg in the ground and she could not follow him. A part-grown puppy, somewhat larger and older than he, came toward him slowly, with ostentatious and belligerent importance. The puppy's name, as White Fang was afterward to hear him called, was Lip-lip. He had had experience in puppy fights and was already something of a bully.

Lip-lip was White Fang's own kind, and, being only a puppy, did not seem dangerous; so White Fang prepared to meet him in friendly spirit. But when the stranger's walk became stiff-legged and his lips lifted clear of his teeth, White Fang stiffened, too, and answered with lifted lips. They half circled about each other, tentatively, snarling and bristling. This lasted several minutes, and White Fang was beginning to enjoy it, as a sort of game. But suddenly, with remarkable swiftness, Lip-lip leaped in, delivered a slashing snap, and leaped away again. The snap had taken effect on the shoulder that had been hurt by the lynx and that was still sore deep down near the bone. The surprise and hurt of it brought a yelp out of White Fang; but the next moment, in a rush of anger, he was upon Lip-lip and snapping viciously.

But Lip-lip had lived his life in camp and had fought many puppy fights. Three times, four times, and half a dozen times, his sharp little teeth scored on the newcomer, until White Fang, yelping shamelessly, fled to the protection of his mother. It was the first of the many fights he was to have with Lip-lip, for they were enemies from the start, born so, with natures destined perpetually to clash.

Kiche licked White Fang soothingly with her tongue, and tried to prevail upon him to remain with her. But his curiosity was rampant, and several minutes later he was venturing forth on a new quest. He came upon one of the man-animals, Gray Beaver, who was squatting on his hams and doing something with sticks and dry moss spread before him on the ground. White Fang came near to him and watched. Gray Beaver made mouth-noises which White Fang interpreted as not hostile, so he came still nearer.

Women and children were carrying more sticks and branches to Gray Beaver. It was evidently an affair of moment. White Fang came in until he touched Gray Beaver's knee, so curious was he, and already forgetful that this was a terrible man-animal. Suddenly he saw a strange thing like mist beginning to arise from the sticks and moss beneath Gray Beaver's hands. Then, amongst the sticks themselves, appeared a live thing, twisting and turning, of a color like the color of the sun in the sky. White Fang knew nothing about fire. It drew him as the light in the mouth of the cave had drawn him in his early puppyhood. He crawled the several steps toward the flame. He heard Gray Beaver chuckle above him, and he knew the sound was not hostile. Then his nose touched the flame, and at the same instant his little tongue went out to it.

For a moment he was paralyzed. The unknown, lurking in the midst of the sticks and moss, was savagely clutching him by the nose. He scrambled backward, bursting out in an astonished explosion of ki-yi's. At the sound, Kiche leaped snarling to the end of her stick, and there raged terribly because she could not come to his aid. But Gray

Beaver laughed loudly, and slapped his thighs, and told the happening to all the rest of the camp, till everybody was laughing uproariously. But White Fang sat on his haunches and ki-yi'd and ki-yi'd, a forlorn and pitiable little figure in the midst of the man-animals.

It was the worst hurt he had ever known. Both nose and tongue had been scorched by the live thing, sun-colored, that had grown up under Gray Beaver's hands. He cried and cried interminably, and every fresh wail was greeted by bursts of laughter on the part of the man-animals. He tried to soothe his nose with his tongue, but the tongue was burnt too, and the two hurts coming together produced greater hurt; whereupon he cried more hopelessly and helplessly than ever.

And then shame came to him. He knew laughter and the meaning of it. It is not given us to know how some animals know laughter, and know when they are being laughed at; but it was this same way that White Fang knew it. And he felt shame that the man-animals should be laughing at him. He turned and fled away, not from the hurt of the fire, but from the laughter that sank even deeper, and hurt in the spirit of him. And he fled to Kiche, raging at the end of her stick like an animal gone mad—to Kiche, the one creature in the world who was not laughing at him.

Twilight drew down and night came on, and White Fang lay by his mother's side. His nose and tongue still hurt, but he was perplexed by a greater trouble. He was homesick. He felt a vacancy in him, a need for the hush and quietude of the stream and the cave in the cliff. Life had become too populous. There were so many of the man-animals, men, women, and children, all making noises and irritations. And there were the dogs, ever squabbling and bickering, bursting into uproars and creating confusions. The restful loneliness of the only life he had known was gone. Here the very air was palpitant with life. It hummed and buzzed unceasingly. Continually changing its intensity and abruptly variant in pitch, it impinged on his nerves and senses, made him nervous and restless and worried him with a perpetual imminence of happening.

He watched the man-animals coming and going and moving about the camp. In fashion distantly resembling the way men look upon the gods they create, so looked White Fang upon the man-animals before him. They were superior creatures, of a verity, gods. To his dim comprehension they were as much wonder-workers as gods are to men. They were creatures of mastery, possessing all manner of unknown and impossible potencies, overlords of the alive and the not alive,—making obey that which moved, imparting movement to that which did not move, and making life, sun-colored and biting life, to grow out of dead moss and wood. They were fire-makers! They were gods!

II

The Bondage

The days were thronged with experience for White Fang. During the time that Kiche was tied by the stick, he ran about over all the camp, inquiring, investigating, learning. He quickly came to know much of the ways of the man-animals, but familiarity did not breed contempt. The more he came to know them, the more they vindicated their superiority, the more they displayed their mysterious powers, the greater loomed their god-likeness.

To man has been given the grief, often, of seeing his gods overthrown and his altars crumbling; but to the wolf and the wild dog that have come in to crouch at man's feet, this grief has never come. Unlike man, whose gods are of the unseen and the overguessed, vapors and mists of fancy eluding the garmenture of reality, wandering wraiths of desired goodness and power, intangible outcroppings of self into the realm of spirit—unlike man, the wolf and the wild dog that have come in to the fire find their gods in the living flesh, solid to the touch, occupying earth-space and requiring time for the accomplishment of their ends and their existence. No effort of faith is necessary to believe in such a god; no effort of will can possibly induce disbelief in such a god. There is no getting away from it. There it stands, on its two hind-legs, club in hand, immensely potential, passionate and wrathful and loving, god and mystery and power all wrapped up and around by flesh that bleeds when it is torn and that is good to eat like any flesh.

And so it was with White Fang. The man-animals were gods unmistakable and unescapable. As his mother, Kiche, had rendered her allegiance to them at the first cry of her name, so he was beginning to render his allegiance. He gave them the trail as a privilege indubitably theirs. When they walked, he got out of their way. When they called, he came. When they threatened, he cowered down. When they commanded him to go, he went away hurriedly. For behind any wish of theirs was power to enforce that wish, power that hurt, power that expressed itself in clouts and clubs, in flying stones and stinging lashes of whips.

He belonged to them as all dogs belonged to them. His actions were theirs to command. His body was theirs to maul, to stamp upon, to tolerate. Such was the lesson that was quickly borne in upon him. It came hard, going as it did, counter to much that was strong and dominant in his own nature; and, while he disliked it in the learning of it, unknown to himself he was learning to like it. It was a placing of his destiny in another's hands, a shifting of the responsibilities of existence. This in itself was compensation, for it is always easier to lean upon another than to stand alone.

But it did not all happen in a day, this giving over of himself, body and soul, to the man-animals. He could not immediately forego his wild heritage and his memories of the Wild. There were days when he crept to the edge of the forest and stood and listened to something calling him far and away. And always he returned, restless and uncomfortable, to whimper softly and wistfully at Kiche's side and to lick her face with eager, questioning tongue.

White Fang learned rapidly the ways of the camp. He knew the injustice and greediness of the older dogs when meat or fish was thrown out to be eaten. He came to know that men were more just, children more cruel, and women more kindly and more likely to toss him a bit of meat or bone. And after two or three painful adventures with the mothers of part-grown puppies, he came into the knowledge that it was always good policy to let such mothers alone, to keep away from them as far as possible, and to avoid them when he saw them coming.

But the bane of his life was Lip-lip. Larger, older, and stronger, Lip-lip had selected White Fang for his special object of persecution. White Fang fought willingly enough, but he was outclassed. His enemy was too big. Lip-lip became a nightmare to him. Whenever he ventured away from his mother, the bully was sure to appear, trailing at his heels, snarling at him, picking upon him, and watchful of an opportunity, when no man-animal was near, to spring upon him and force a fight. As Lip-lip invariably won, he enjoyed it hugely. It became his chief delight in life, as it became White Fang's chief torment.

But the effect upon White Fang was not to cow him. Though he suffered most of the damage and was always defeated, his spirit remained unsubdued. Yet a bad effect was produced. He became malignant and morose. His temper had been savage by birth, but it became more savage under this unending persecution. The genial, playful, puppyish side of him found little expression. He never played and gambolled about with the other puppies of the camp. Lip-lip would not permit it. The moment White Fang appeared near them, Lip-lip was upon him, bullying and hectoring him, or fighting with him until he had driven him away.

The effect of all this was to rob White Fang of much of his puppyhood and to make him in his comportment older than his age. Denied the outlet, through play, of his energies, he recoiled upon himself and developed his mental processes. He became cunning; he had idle time in which to devote himself to thoughts of trickery. Prevented from obtaining his share of meat and fish when a general feed was given to the camp-dogs, he became a clever thief. He had to forage for himself, and he foraged well, though he was ofttimes a plague to the squaws in consequence. He learned to sneak about camp, to be crafty, to know what was going on everywhere, to see and to hear everything and to reason accordingly, and successfully to devise ways and means of avoiding his implacable persecutor.

It was early in the days of his persecution that he played his first really big crafty game and got therefrom his first taste of revenge. As Kiche, when with the wolves, had lured out to destruction dogs from the camps of men, so White Fang, in manner somewhat similar, lured Lip-lip into Kiche's avenging jaws. Retreating before Lip-lip, White Fang made an indirect flight that led in and out and around the various tepees of the camp. He was a good runner, swifter than any other puppy of his size, and swifter than Lip-lip. But he did not run his best in this chase. He barely held his own, one leap ahead of his pursuer.

Lip-lip, excited by the chase and by the persistent nearness of his victim, forgot caution and locality. When he remembered locality, it was too late. Dashing at top speed around a tepee, he ran full tilt into Kiche lying at the end of her stick. He gave one yelp of consternation, and then her punishing jaws closed upon him. She was tied, but he could not get away from her easily. She rolled him off his legs so that he could not run, while she repeatedly ripped and slashed him with her fangs.

When at last he succeeded in rolling clear of her, he crawled to his feet, badly dishevelled, hurt both in body and in spirit. His hair was standing out all over him in tufts where her teeth had mauled. He stood where he had arisen, opened his mouth, and broke out the long, heart-broken puppy wail. But even this he was not allowed to complete. In the middle of it, White Fang, rushing in, sank his teeth into Lip-lip's hind leg. There was no fight left in Lip-lip, and he ran away shamelessly, his victim hot on his heels and worrying him all the way back to his own tepee. Here the squaws came to his aid, and White Fang, transformed into a raging demon, was finally driven off only by a fusillade of stones.

Came the day when Gray Beaver, deciding that the liability of her running away was past, released Kiche. White Fang was delighted with his mother's freedom. He accompanied her joyfully about the camp; and, so long as he remained close by her side, Lip-lip kept a respectful distance. White Fang even bristled up to him and walked stiff-legged, but Lip-lip ignored the challenge. He was no fool himself, and whatever vengeance he desired to wreak, he could wait until he caught White Fang alone.

Later on that day, Kiche and White Fang strayed into the edge of the woods next to the camp. He had led his mother there, step by step, and now, when she stopped, he tried to inveigle her farther. The stream, the lair, and the quiet woods were calling to him, and he wanted her to come. He ran on a few steps, stopped, and looked back. She had not moved. He whined pleadingly, and scurried playfully in and out of the underbrush. He ran back to her, licked her face, and ran on again. And still she did not move. He stopped and regarded her, all of an intentness and eagerness, physically expressed, that slowly faded out of him as she turned her head and gazed back at the camp.

There was something calling to him out there in the open. His mother heard it, too. But she heard also that other and louder call, the call of the fire and of man—the call which it has been given alone of all animals to the wolf to answer, to the wolf and the wild-dog, who are brothers.

Kiche turned and slowly trotted back toward camp. Stronger than the physical restraint of the stick was the clutch of the camp upon her. Unseen and occultly, the gods still gripped with their power and would not let her go. White Fang sat down in the shadow of a birch and whimpered softly. There was a strong smell of pine, and subtle woods fragrances filled the air, reminding him of his old life of freedom before the days of his bondage. But he was still only a part-grown puppy, and stronger than the call either of man or of the Wild was the call of his mother. All the hours of his short life he had depended upon her. The time was yet to come for independence. So he arose and trotted forlornly back to camp, pausing once, and twice, to sit down and whimper and to listen to the call that still sounded in the depths of the forest.

In the Wild the time of a mother with her young is short; but under the dominion of man it is sometimes even shorter. Thus it was with White Fang. Gray Beaver was in the debt of Three Eagles. Three Eagles was going away on a trip up the Mackenzie to the Great Slave Lake. A strip of scarlet cloth, a bearskin, twenty cartridges, and Kiche, went to pay the debt. White Fang saw his mother taken aboard Three Eagles' canoe, and tried to follow her. A blow from Three Eagles knocked him backward to the land. The canoe shoved off. He sprang into the water and swam after it, deaf to the sharp cries of Gray Beaver to return. Even a man-animal, a god, White Fang ignored, such was the terror he was in of losing his mother.

But gods are accustomed to being obeyed, and Gray Beaver wrathfully launched a canoe in pursuit. When he overtook White Fang, he reached down and by the nape of the neck lifted him clear of the water. He did not deposit him at once in the bottom of the canoe. Holding him suspended with one hand, with the other hand he proceeded to give him a beating. And it *was* a beating. His hand was heavy. Every blow was shrewd to hurt; and he delivered a multitude of blows.

Impelled by the blows that rained upon him, now from this side, now from that, White Fang swung back and forth like an erratic and jerky pendulum. Varying were the emotions that surged through him. At first, he had known surprise. Then came a momentary fear, when he yelped several times to the impact of the hand. But this was quickly followed by anger. His free nature asserted itself, and he showed his teeth and snarled fearlessly in the face of the wrathful god. This but served to make the god more wrathful. The blows came faster, heavier, more shrewd to hurt.

Gray Beaver continued to beat, White Fang continued to snarl. But this could not last forever. One or the other must give over, and that one was White Fang. Fear surged through him again. For the first time he was being really man-handled. The occasional blows of sticks and stones he had previously experienced were as caresses compared with this. He broke down and began to cry and yelp. For a time each blow brought a yelp from him; but fear passed into terror, until finally his yelps were voiced in unbroken succession, unconnected with the rhythm of the punishment.

At last Gray Beaver withheld his hand. White Fang, hanging limply, continued to cry. This seemed to satisfy his master, who flung him down roughly in the bottom of the canoe. In the meantime the canoe had drifted down the stream. Gray Beaver picked up the paddle. White Fang was in his way. He spurned him savagely with his foot. In that moment White Fang's free nature flashed forth again, and he sank his teeth into the moccasined foot.

The beating that had gone before was as nothing compared with the beating he now received. Gray Beaver's wrath was terrible; likewise was White Fang's fright. Not only the hand, but the hard wooden paddle was used upon him; and he was bruised and sore in all his small body when he was again flung down in the canoe. Again, and this time with purpose, did Gray Beaver kick him. White Fang did not repeat his attack on the foot. He had learned another lesson of his bondage. Never, no matter what the circumstance, must he dare to bite the god who was lord and master over him; the body of the lord and master was sacred, not to be defiled by the teeth of such as he. That was evidently the crime of crimes, the one offence there was no condoning nor overlooking.

When the canoe touched the shore, White Fang lay whimpering and motionless, waiting the will of Gray Beaver. It was Gray Beaver's will that he should go ashore, for ashore he was flung, striking heavily on his side and hurting his bruises afresh. He crawled tremblingly to his feet and stood whimpering. Lip-lip, who had watched the whole proceeding from the bank, now rushed upon him, knocking him over and sinking his teeth into him. White Fang was too helpless to defend himself, and it would have gone hard with him had not Gray Beaver's foot shot out, lifting Lip-lip into the air with its violence so that he smashed down to earth a dozen feet away. This was the man-animal's justice; and even then, in his own pitiable plight, White Fang experienced a little grateful thrill. At Gray Beaver's heels he limped obediently through the village to the tepee. And so it came that White Fang learned that the right to punish was something the gods reserved for themselves and denied to the lesser creatures under them.

That night, when all was still, White Fang remembered his mother and sorrowed for her. He sorrowed too loudly and woke up Gray Beaver, who beat him. After that he mourned gently when the gods were around. But sometimes, straying off to the edge of the woods by himself, he gave vent to his grief, and cried it out with loud whimperings and wailings.

It was during this period that he might have hearkened to the memories of the lair and the stream and run back to the Wild. But the memory of his mother held him. As the hunting man-animals went out and came back, so she would come back to the village sometime. So he remained in his bondage waiting for her.

But it was not altogether an unhappy bondage. There was much to interest him. Something was always happening. There was no end to the strange things these gods did, and he was always curious to see. Besides, he was learning how to get along with Gray Beaver. Obedience, rigid, undeviating obedience, was what was exacted of him; and in return he escaped beatings and his existence was tolerated.

Nay, Gray Beaver himself sometimes tossed him a piece of meat, and defended him against the other dogs in the eating of it. And such a piece of meat was of value. It was worth more, in some strange way, than a dozen pieces of meat from the hand of a squaw. Gray Beaver never petted nor caressed. Perhaps it was the weight of his hand, perhaps his justice, perhaps the sheer power of him, and perhaps it was all these things that influenced White Fang; for a certain tie of attachment was forming between him and his surly lord.

Insidiously, and by remote ways, as well as by the power of stick and stone and clout of hand, were the shackles of White Fang's bondage being riveted upon him. The qualities in his kind that in the beginning made it possible for them to come in to the fires of men, were qualities capable of development. They were developing in him, and the camp-life, replete with misery as it was, was secretly endearing itself to him all the time. But White Fang was unaware of it. He knew only grief for the loss of Kiche, hope for her return, and a hungry yearning for the free life that had been his.

III

The Outcast

Lip-lip continued so to darken his days that White Fang became wickeder and more ferocious than it was his natural right to be. Savageness was a part of his make-up, but the savageness thus developed exceeded his make-up. He acquired a reputation for wickedness amongst the man-animals themselves. Wherever there was trouble and uproar in camp, fighting and squabbling or the outcry of a squaw over a bit of stolen meat, they were sure to find White Fang mixed up in it and usually at the bottom of it. They did not bother to look after the causes of his conduct. They saw only the effects, and the effects were bad. He was a sneak and a thief, a mischief-maker, a fomenter of trouble; and irate squaws told him to his face, the while he eyed them alert and ready to dodge any quick-flung missile, that he was a wolf and worthless and bound to come to an evil end.

He found himself an outcast in the midst of the populous camp. All the young dogs followed Lip-lip's lead. There was a difference between White Fang and them. Perhaps they sensed his wild-wood breed, and instinctively felt for him the enmity that the domestic dog feels for the wolf. But be that as it may, they joined with Lip-lip in the persecution. And, once declared against him, they found good reason to continue declared against him. One and all, from time to time, they felt his teeth; and to his credit, he gave more than he received. Many of them he could whip in single fight; but single fight was denied him. The beginning of such a fight was a signal for all the young dogs in camp to come running and pitch upon him.

Out of this pack-persecution he learned two important things: how to take care of himself in a mass-fight against him; and how, on a single dog, to inflict the greatest amount of damage in the briefest space of time. To keep one's feet in the midst of the hostile mass meant life, and this he learned well. He became cat-like in his ability to stay on his feet. Even grown dogs might hurtle him backward or sideways with the impact of their heavy bodies; and backward or sideways he would go, in the air or sliding on the ground, but always with his legs under him and his feet downward to the mother earth.

When dogs fight, there are usually preliminaries to the actual combat—snarlings and bristlings and stiff-legged struttings. But White Fang learned to omit these preliminaries. Delay meant the coming against him of all the young dogs. He must do his work quickly and get away. So he learned to give no warning of his intention. He rushed in and snapped and slashed on the instant, without notice, before his foe could prepare to meet him. Thus he learned how to inflict quick and severe damage. Also he learned the value of surprise. A dog, taken off its guard, its shoulder slashed open or its ear ripped in ribbons before it knew what was happening, was a dog half whipped.

Furthermore, it was remarkably easy to overthrow a dog taken by surprise; while a dog, thus overthrown, invariably exposed for a moment the soft underside of its neck —the vulnerable point at which to strike for its life. White Fang knew this point. It was a knowledge bequeathed to him directly from the hunting generations of wolves. So it was that White Fang's method, when he took the offensive, was: first, to find a young dog alone; second, to surprise it and knock it off its feet; and third, to drive in with his teeth at the soft throat.

Being but partly grown, his jaws had not yet become large enough nor strong enough to make his throat-attack deadly; but many a young dog went around camp with a lacerated throat in token of White Fang's intention. And one day, catching one of his enemies alone on the edge of the woods, he managed, by repeatedly overthrowing him and attacking the throat, to cut the great vein and let out the life. There was a great row that night. He had been observed, the news had been carried to the dead dog's master, the squaws remembered all the instances of stolen meat, and Gray Beaver was beset by many angry voices. But he resolutely held the door of his tepee, inside which he had placed the culprit, and refused to permit the vengeance for which his tribespeople clamored.

White Fang became hated by man and dog. During this period of his development he never knew a moment's security. The tooth of every dog was against him, the hand of every man. He was greeted with snarls by his kind, with curses and stones by his gods. He lived tensely. He was always keyed up, alert for attack, wary of being attacked, with an eye for sudden and unexpected missiles, prepared to act precipitately and coolly, to leap in with a flash of teeth, or to leap away with a menacing snarl.

As for snarling, he could snarl more terribly than any dog, young or old, in camp. The intent of the snarl is to warn or frighten, and judgment is required to know when it should be used. White Fang knew how to make it and when to make it. Into his snarl he incorporated all that was vicious, malignant, and horrible. With nose serrulated by continuous spasms, hair bristling in recurrent waves, tongue whipping out like a red snake and whipping back again, ears flattened down, eyes gleaming hatred, lips wrinkled back, and fangs exposed and dripping, he could compel a pause on the part of almost any assailant. A temporary pause, when taken off his guard, gave him the vital moment in which to think and determine his action. But often a pause so gained lengthened out until it evolved into a complete cessation from the attack. And before more than one of the grown dogs White Fang's snarl enabled him to beat an honorable retreat.

An outcast himself from the pack of the part-grown dogs, his sanguinary methods and remarkable efficiency made the pack pay for its persecution of him. Not permitted himself to run with the pack, the curious state of affairs obtained that no member of the pack could run outside the pack. White Fang would not permit it. What of his bushwhacking and waylaying tactics, the young dogs were afraid to run by themselves. With the exception of Lip-lip, they were compelled to bunch together for mutual protection against the terrible enemy they had made. A puppy alone by the river bank meant a puppy dead or a puppy that aroused the camp with its shrill pain and terror as it fled back from the wolf-cub that had waylaid it.

But White Fang's reprisals did not cease, even when the young dogs had learned thoroughly that they must stay together. He attacked them when he caught them alone, and they attacked him when they were bunched. The sight of him was sufficient to start them rushing after him, at which times his swiftness usually carried him into safety. But woe to the dog that outran his fellows in such pursuit! White Fang had learned to turn suddenly upon the pursuer that was ahead of the pack and thoroughly to rip him up before the pack could arrive. This occurred with great frequency, for, once in full cry, the dogs were prone to forget themselves in the excitement of the chase, while White Fang never forgot himself. Stealing backward glances as he ran, he was always ready to whirl around and down the overzealous pursuer that outran his fellows.

Young dogs are bound to play, and out of the exigencies of the situation they realized their play in this mimic warfare. Thus it was that the hunt of White Fang became their chief game—a deadly game, withal, and at all times a serious game. He, on the other hand, being the fastest-footed, was unafraid to venture anywhere. During the period that he waited vainly for his mother to come back, he led the pack many a wild chase through the adjacent woods. But the pack invariably lost him. Its noise and outcry warned him of its presence, while he ran alone, velvet-footed, silently, a moving shadow among the trees after the manner of his father and mother before him. Further, he was more directly connected with the Wild than they; and he knew more of its secrets and stratagems. A favorite trick of his was to lose his trail in running water and then lie quietly in a near-by thicket while their baffled cries arose around him.

Hated by his kind and by mankind, indomitable, perpetually warred upon and himself waging perpetual war, his development was rapid and one-sided. This was no soil for kindliness and affection to blossom in. Of such things he had not the faintest glimmering. The code he learned was to obey the strong and to oppress the weak. Gray Beaver was a god, and strong. Therefore White Fang obeyed him. But the dog younger or smaller than himself was weak, a thing to be destroyed. His development was in the direction of power. In order to face the constant danger of hurt and even of destruction, his predatory and protective faculties were unduly developed. He became quicker of movement than the other dogs, swifter of foot, craftier, deadlier, more lithe, more lean with ironlike muscle and sinew, more enduring, more cruel, more ferocious, and more intelligent. He had to become all these things, else he would not have held his own nor survived the hostile environment in which he found himself.

IV

The Trail of the Gods

In the fall of the year, when the days were shortening and the bite of the frost was coming into the air, White Fang got his chance for liberty. For several days there had been a great hubbub in the village. The summer camp was being dismantled, and the tribe, bag and baggage, was preparing to go off to the fall hunting. White Fang watched it all with eager eyes, and when the tepees began to come down and the canoes were loading at the bank, he understood. Already the canoes were departing, and some had disappeared down the river.

Quite deliberately he determined to stay behind. He waited his opportunity to slink out of camp to the woods. Here, in the running stream where ice was beginning to form, he hid his trail. Then he crawled into the heart of a dense thicket and waited. The time passed by, and he slept intermittently for hours. Then he was aroused by Gray Beaver's voice calling him by name. There were other voices. White Fang could hear Gray Beaver's squaw taking part in the search, and Mit-sah, who was Gray Beaver's son.

White Fang trembled with fear, and though the impulse came to crawl out of his hiding-place, he resisted it. After a time the voices died away, and some time after that he crept out to enjoy the success of his undertaking. Darkness was coming on, and for a while he played about among the trees, pleasuring in his freedom. Then, and quite suddenly, he became aware of loneliness. He sat down to consider, listening to the silence of the forest and perturbed by it. That nothing moved nor sounded, seemed ominous. He felt the lurking of danger, unseen and unguessed. He was suspicious of the looming bulks of the trees and of the dark shadows that might conceal all manner of perilous things.

Then it was cold. Here was no warm side of a tepee against which to snuggle. The frost was in his feet, and he kept lifting first one fore-foot and then the other. He curved his bushy tail around to cover them, and at the same time he saw a vision. There was nothing strange about it. Upon his inward sight was impressed a succession of memory-pictures. He saw the camp again, the tepees, and the blaze of the fire. He heard the shrill voices of the women, the gruff basses of the men, and the snarling of the dogs. He was hungry, and he remembered pieces of meat and fish that had been thrown him. Here was no meat, nothing but a threatening and inedible silence.

His bondage had softened him. Irresponsibility had weakened him. He had forgotten how to shift for himself. The night yawned about him. His senses, accustomed to the hum and bustle of the camp, used to the continuous impact of sights and sounds, were now left idle. There was nothing to do, nothing to see nor hear. They strained to catch some interruption of the silence and immobility of nature. They were appalled by inaction and by the feel of something terrible impending.

He gave a great start of fright. A colossal and formless something was rushing across the field of his vision. It was a tree-shadow flung by the moon, from whose face the clouds had been brushed away. Reassured, he whimpered softly; then he suppressed the whimper for fear that it might attract the attention of the lurking dangers.

A tree, contracting in the cool of the night, made a loud noise. It was directly above him. He yelped in his fright. A panic seized him, and he ran madly toward the village. He knew an overpowering desire for the protection and companionship of man. In his nostrils was the smell of the camp-smoke. In his ears the camp sounds and cries were ringing loud. He passed out of the forest and into the moonlit open where were no shadows nor darknesses. But no village greeted his eyes. He had forgotten. The village had gone away.

His wild flight ceased abruptly. There was no place to which to flee. He slunk forlornly through the deserted camp, smelling the rubbish-heaps and the discarded rags and tags of the gods. He would have been glad for the rattle of stones about him, flung by an angry squaw, glad for the hand of Gray Beaver descending upon him in wrath; while he would have welcomed with delight Lip-lip and the whole snarling, cowardly pack.

He came to where Gray Beaver's tepee had stood. In the centre of the space it had occupied, he sat down. He pointed his nose at the moon. His throat was afflicted by rigid spasms, his mouth opened, and in a heart-broken cry bubbled up his loneliness and fear, his grief for Kiche, all his past sorrows and miseries as well as his apprehension of sufferings and dangers to come. It was the long wolf-howl, full-throated and mournful, the first howl he had ever uttered.

The coming of daylight dispelled his fears, but increased his loneliness. The naked earth, which so shortly before had been so populous, thrust his loneliness more forcibly upon him. It did not take him long to make up his mind. He plunged into the forest and followed the river bank down the stream. All day he ran. He did not rest. He seemed made to run on forever. His iron-like body ignored fatigue. And even after fatigue came, his heritage of endurance braced him to endless endeavor and enabled him to drive his complaining body onward.

Where the river swung in against precipitous bluffs, he climbed the high mountains behind. Rivers and streams that entered the main river he forded or swam. Often he took to the rim-ice that was beginning to form, and more than once he crashed through and struggled for life in the icy current. Always he was on the lookout for the trail of the gods where it might leave the river and proceed inland.

White Fang was intelligent beyond the average of his kind; yet his mental vision was not wide enough to embrace the other bank of the Mackenzie. What if the trail of the gods led out on that side? It never entered his head. Later on, when he had travelled more and grown older and wiser and come to know more of trails and rivers, it might be that he could grasp and apprehend such a possibility. But that mental power was yet in the future. Just now he ran blindly, his own bank of the Mackenzie alone entering into his calculations.

All night he ran, blundering in the darkness into mishaps and obstacles that delayed but did not daunt. By the middle of the second day he had been running continuously for thirty hours, and the iron of his flesh was giving out. It was the endurance of his mind that kept him going. He had not eaten in forty hours, and he was weak with hunger. The repeated drenchings in the icy water had likewise had their effect on him. His handsome coat was draggled. The broad pads of his feet were bruised and bleeding. He had begun to limp, and this limp increased with the hours. To make it worse, the light of the sky was obscured and snow began to fall—a raw, moist, melting, clinging snow, slippery under foot, that hid from him the landscape he traversed, and that covered over the inequalities of the ground so that the way of his feet was more difficult and painful.

Gray Beaver had intended camping that night on the far bank of the Mackenzie, for it was in that direction that the hunting lay. But on the near bank, shortly before dark, a moose, coming down to drink, had been espied by Kloo-kooch, who was Gray Beaver's squaw. Now, had not the moose come down to drink, had not Mit-sah been steering out of the course because of the snow, had not Kloo-kooch sighted the moose, and had not Gray Beaver killed it with a lucky shot from his rifle, all subsequent things would have happened differently. Gray Beaver would not have camped on the near side of the Mackenzie, and White Fang would have passed by and gone on, either to die or to find his way to his wild brothers and become one of them,—a wolf to the end of his days.

Night had fallen. The snow was flying more thickly, and White Fang, whimpering softly to himself as he stumbled and limped along, came upon a fresh trail in the snow. So fresh was it that he knew it immediately for what it was. Whining with eagerness, he followed back from the river bank and in among the trees. The camp-sounds came to his ears. He saw the blaze of the fire, Kloo-kooch cooking, and Gray Beaver squatting on his hams and mumbling a chunk of raw tallow. There was fresh meat in camp!

White Fang expected a beating. He crouched and bristled a little at the thought of it.

Then he went forward again. He feared and disliked the beating he knew to be waiting for him. But he knew, further, that the comfort of the fire would be his, the protection of the gods, the companionship of the dogs—the last, a companionship of enmity, but none the less a companionship and satisfying to his gregarious needs.

He came cringing and crawling into the firelight. Gray Beaver saw him, and stopped munching the tallow. White Fang crawled slowly, cringing and grovelling in the abjectness of his abasement and submission. He crawled straight toward Gray Beaver, every inch of his progress becoming slower and more painful. At last he lay at the master's feet, into whose possession he now surrendered himself, voluntarily, body and soul. Of his own choice, he came in to sit by man's fire and to be ruled by him. White Fang trembled, waiting for the punishment to fall upon him. There was a movement of the hand above him. He cringed involuntarily under the expected blow. It did not fall. He stole a glance upward. Gray Beaver was breaking the lump of tallow in half! Gray Beaver was offering him one piece of the tallow! Very gently and somewhat suspiciously, he first smelled the tallow and then proceeded to eat it. Gray Beaver ordered meat to be brought to him, and guarded him from the other dogs while he ate. After that, grateful and content, White Fang lay at Gray Beaver's feet, gazing at the fire that warmed him, blinking and dozing, secure in the knowledge that the morrow would find him, not wandering forlorn through bleak forest-stretches, but in the camp of the man-animals, with the gods to whom he had given himself and upon whom he was now dependent.

V

The Covenant

When December was well along, Gray Beaver went on a journey up the Mackenzie, Mit-sah and Kloo-kooch went with him. One sled he drove himself, drawn by dogs he had traded for or borrowed. A second and smaller sled was driven by Mit-sah, and to this was harnessed a team of puppies. It was more of a toy affair than anything else, yet it was the delight of Mit-sah, who felt that he was beginning to do a man's work in the world. Also, he was learning to drive dogs and to train dogs; while the puppies themselves were being broken in to the harness. Furthermore, the sled was of some service, for it carried nearly two hundred pounds of outfit and food.

White Fang had seen the camp-dogs toiling in the harness, so that he did not resent overmuch the first placing of the harness upon himself. About his neck was put a moss-stuffed collar, which was connected by two pulling-traces to a strap that passed around his chest and over his back. It was to this that was fastened the long rope by which he pulled at the sled.

There were seven puppies in the team. The others had been born earlier in the year and were nine and ten months old, while White Fang was only eight months old. Each dog was fastened to the sled by a single rope. No two ropes were of the same length, while the difference in length between any two ropes was at least that of a dog's body. Every rope was brought to a ring at the front end of the sled. The sled itself was without runners, being a birchbark toboggan, with upturned forward end to keep it from ploughing under the snow. This construction enabled the weight of the sled and load to be distributed over the largest snow-surface; for the snow was crystal-powder and very soft. Observing the same principle of widest distribution of weight, the dogs at the ends of their ropes radiated fan-fashion from the nose of the sled, so that no dog trod in another's footsteps.

There was, furthermore, another virtue in the fan-formation. The ropes of varying length prevented the dogs' attacking from the rear those that ran in front of them. For a dog to attack another, it would have to turn upon one at a shorter rope. In which case it would find itself face to face with the dog attacked, and also it would find itself facing the whip of the driver. But the most peculiar virtue of all lay in the fact that the dog that strove to attack one in front of him must pull the sled faster, and that the faster the sled travelled, the faster could the dog attacked run away. Thus, the dog behind could never catch up with the one in front. The faster he ran, the faster ran the one he was after, and the faster ran all the dogs. Incidentally, the sled went faster, and thus, by cunning indirection, did man increase his mastery over the beasts.

Mit-sah resembled his father, much of whose gray wisdom he possessed. In the past he had observed Lip-lip's persecution of White Fang; but at that time Lip-lip was another man's dog, and Mit-sah had never dared more than to shy an occasional stone at him. But now Lip-lip was his dog, and he proceeded to wreak his vengeance on him by putting him at the end of the longest rope. This made Lip-lip the leader, and was apparently an honor; but in reality it took away from him all honor, and instead of being bully and master of the pack, he now found himself hated and persecuted by the pack.

Because he ran at the end of the longest rope, the dogs had always the view of him running away before them. All that they saw of him was his bushy tail and fleeing hind legs—a view far less ferocious and intimidating than his bristling mane and gleaming fangs. Also, dogs being so constituted in their mental ways, the sight of him running away gave desire to run after him and a feeling that he ran away from them.

The moment the sled started, the team took after Lip-lip in a chase that extended throughout the day. At first he had been prone to turn upon his pursuers, jealous of his dignity and wrathful; but at such times Mit-sah would throw the stinging lash of the thirty-foot cariboo-gut whip into his face and compel him to turn tail and run on. Lip-lip might face the pack, but he could not face that whip, and all that was left him to do was to keep his long rope taut and his flanks ahead of the teeth of his mates.

But a still greater cunning lurked in the recesses of the Indian mind. To give point to unending pursuit of the leader, Mit-sah favored him over the other dogs. These favors aroused in them jealousy and hatred. In their presence Mit-sah would give him meat and would give it to him only. This was maddening to them. They would rage around just outside the throwing-distance of the whip, while Lip-lip devoured the meat and Mit-sah protected him. And when there was no meat to give, Mit-sah would keep the team at a distance and make believe to give meat to Lip-lip.

White Fang took kindly to the work. He had travelled a greater distance than the other dogs in the yielding of himself to the rule of the gods, and he had learned more thoroughly the futility of opposing their will. In addition, the persecution he had suffered from the pack had made the pack less to him in the scheme of things, and man more. He had not learned to be dependent on his kind for companionship. Besides, Kiche was well-nigh forgotten; and the chief outlet of expression that remained to him was in the allegiance he tendered the gods he had accepted as masters. So he worked hard, learned discipline, and was obedient. Faithfulness and willingness characterized his toil. These are essential traits of the wolf and the wild-dog when they have become domesticated, and these traits White Fang possessed in unusual measure.

A companionship did exist between White Fang and the other dogs, but it was one of warfare and enmity. He had never learned to play with them. He knew only how to fight, and fight with them he did, returning to them a hundred-fold the snaps and slashes they had given him in the days when Lip-lip was leader of the pack. But Lip-lip was no longer leader—except when he fled away before his mates at the end of his rope, the sled bounding along behind. In camp he kept close to Mit-sah or Gray Beaver or Kloo-kooch. He did not dare venture away from the gods, for now the fangs of all dogs were against him, and he tasted to the dregs the persecution that had been White Fang's.

With the overthrow of Lip-lip, White Fang could have become leader of the pack. But he was too morose and solitary for that. He merely thrashed his team-mates. Otherwise he ignored them. They got out of his way when he came along; nor did the boldest of them ever dare to rob him of his meat. On the contrary, they devoured their own meat hurriedly, for fear that he would take it away from them. White Fang knew the law well: *to oppress the weak and obey the strong.* He ate his share of meat as rapidly as he could. And then woe the dog that had not yet finished! A snarl and a flash of fangs, and that dog would wail his indignation to the uncomforting stars while White Fang finished his portion for him.

Every little while, however, one dog or another would flame up in revolt and be promptly subdued. Thus White Fang was kept in training. He was jealous of the isolation in which he kept himself in the midst of the pack, and he fought often to maintain it. But such fights were of brief duration. He was too quick for the others. They were slashed open and bleeding before they knew what had happened, were whipped almost before they had begun to fight.

As rigid as the sled-discipline of the gods, was the discipline maintained by White Fang amongst his fellows. He never allowed them any latitude. He compelled them to an unremitting respect for him. They might do as they pleased amongst themselves. That was no concern of his. But it *was* his concern that they leave him alone in his isolation, get out of his way when he elected to walk among them, and at all times acknowledge his mastery over them. A hint of stiff-leggedness on their part, a lifted lip or a bristle of hair, and he would be upon them, merciless and cruel, swiftly convincing them of the error of their way.

He was a monstrous tyrant. His mastery was rigid as steel. He oppressed the weak with a vengeance. Not for nothing had he been exposed to the pitiless struggle for life in the days of his cubhood, when his mother and he, alone and unaided, held their own and survived in the ferocious environment of the Wild. And not for nothing had he learned to walk softly when superior strength went by. He oppressed the weak, but he respected the strong. And in the course of the long journey with Gray Beaver he walked softly indeed amongst the full-grown dogs in the camps of the strange man-animals they encountered.

The months passed by. Still continued the journey of Gray Beaver. White Fang's strength was developed by the long hours on trail and the steady toil at the sled; and it would have seemed that his mental development was well-nigh complete. He had come to know quite thoroughly the world in which he lived. His outlook was bleak and materialistic. The world as he saw it was a fierce and brutal world, a world without warmth, a world in which caresses and affection and the bright sweetnesses of the spirit did not exist.

He had no affection for Gray Beaver. True, he was a god, but a most savage god. White Fang was glad to acknowledge his lordship, but it was a lordship based upon superior intelligence and brute strength. There was something in the fibre of White Fang's being that made this lordship a thing to be desired, else he would not have come back from the Wild when he did to tender his allegiance. There were deeps in his nature which had never been sounded. A kind word, a caressing touch of the hand, on the part of Gray Beaver, might have sounded these deeps; but Gray Beaver did not caress nor speak kind words. It was not his way. His primacy was savage, and savagely he ruled, administering justice with a club, punishing transgression with the pain of a blow, and rewarding merit, not by kindness, but by withholding a blow.

So White Fang knew nothing of the heaven a man's hand might contain for him. Besides, he did not like the hands of the man-animals. He was suspicious of them. It was true that they sometimes gave meat, but more often they gave hurt. Hands were things to keep away from. They hurled stones, wielded sticks and clubs and whips, administered slaps and clouts, and, when they touched him, were cunning to hurt with pinch and twist and wrench. In strange villages he had encountered the hands of the children and learned that they were cruel to hurt. Also, he had once nearly had an eye poked out by a toddling papoose. From these experiences he became suspicious of all children. He could not tolerate them. When they came near with their ominous hands, he got up.

It was in a village at the Great Slave Lake, that, in the course of resenting the evil of the hands of the man-animals, he came to modify the law that he had learned from Gray Beaver; namely, that the unpardonable crime was to bite one of the gods. In this village, after the custom of all dogs in all villages, White Fang went foraging for food. A boy was chopping frozen moose-meat with an axe, and the chips were flying in the snow. White Fang, sliding by in quest of meat, stopped and began to eat the chips. He observed the boy lay down the axe and take up a stout club. White Fang sprang clear, just in time to escape the descending blow. The boy pursued him, and he, a stranger in the village, fled between two tepees, to find himself cornered against a high earth bank.

There was no escape for White Fang. The only way out was between the two tepees, and this the boy guarded. Holding his club prepared to strike, he drew in on his cornered quarry. White Fang was furious. He faced the boy, bristling and snarling, his sense of justice outraged. He knew the law of forage. All the wastage of meat, such as the frozen chips, belonged to the dog that found it. He had done no wrong, broken no law, yet here was this boy preparing to give him a beating. White Fang scarcely knew what happened. He did it in a surge of rage. And he did it so quickly that the boy did not know, either. All the boy knew was that he had in some unaccountable way been overturned into the snow, and that his club-hand had been ripped wide open by White Fang's teeth.

But White Fang knew that he had broken the law of the gods. He had driven his teeth into the sacred flesh of one of them, and could expect nothing but a most terrible punishment. He fled away to Gray Beaver, behind whose protecting legs he crouched when the bitten boy and the boy's family came, demanding vengeance. But they went away with vengeance unsatisfied. Gray Beaver defended White Fang. So did Mit-sah and Kloo-kooch. White Fang, listening to the wordy war and watching the angry gestures, knew that his act was justified. And so it came that he learned there were gods and gods. There were his gods, and there were other gods, and between them there was a difference. Justice or injustice, it was all the same, he must take all things from the hands of his own gods. But he was not compelled to take injustice from the other gods. It was his privilege to resent it with his teeth. And this also was a law of the gods.

Before the day was out, White Fang was to learn more about this law. Mit-sah, alone, gathering firewood in the forest, encountered the boy that had been bitten. With him were other boys. Hot words passed. Then all the boys attacked Mit-sah. It was going hard with him. Blows were raining upon him from all sides. White Fang looked on at first. This was an affair of the gods, and no concern of his. Then he realized that this was Mit-sah, one of his own particular gods, who was being maltreated. It was no reasoned impulse that made White Fang do what he then did. A mad rush of anger sent him leaping in amongst the combatants. Five minutes later the landscape was covered with fleeing boys, many of whom dripped blood upon the snow in token that White Fang's teeth had not been idle. When Mit-sah told his story in camp, Gray Beaver ordered meat to be given to White Fang. He ordered much meat to be given, and White Fang, gorged and sleepy by the fire, knew that the law had received its verification.

It was in line with these experiences that White Fang came to learn the law of property and the duty of the defence of property. From the protection of his god's body to the protection of his god's possessions was a step, and this step he made. What was his god's was to be defended against all the world—even to the extent of biting other gods. Not only was such an act sacrilegious in its nature, but it was fraught with peril. The gods were all-powerful, and a dog was no match against them; yet White Fang learned to face them, fiercely belligerent and unafraid. Duty rose above fear, and thieving gods learned to leave Gray Beaver's property alone.

One thing, in this connection, White Fang quickly learned, and that was that a thieving god was usually a cowardly god and prone to run away at the sounding of the alarm. Also, he learned that but brief time elapsed between his sounding of the alarm and Gray Beaver's coming to his aid. He came to know that it was not fear of him that drove the thief away, but fear of Gray Beaver. White Fang did not give the alarm by barking. He never barked. His method was to drive straight at the intruder, and to sink his teeth in if he could. Because he was morose and solitary, having nothing to do with the other dogs, he was unusually fitted to guard his master's property; and in this he was encouraged and trained by Gray Beaver. One result of this was to make White Fang more ferocious and indomitable, and more solitary.

The months went by, binding stronger and stronger the covenant between dog and man. This was the ancient covenant that the first wolf that came in from the Wild entered into with man. And, like all succeeding wolves and wild dogs that had done likewise, White Fang worked the covenant out for himself. The terms were simple. For the possession of a flesh-and-blood god, he exchanged his own liberty. Food and fire, protection and companionship, were some of the things he received from the god. In return, he guarded the god's property, defended his body, worked for him, and obeyed him.

The possession of a god implies service. White Fang's was a service of duty and awe, but not of love. He did not know what love was. He had no experience of love. Kiche was a remote memory. Besides, not only had he abandoned the Wild and his kind when he gave himself up to man, but the terms of the covenant were such that if he ever met Kiche again he would not desert his god to go with her. His allegiance to man seemed somehow a law of his being greater than the love of liberty, of kind and kin.

VI
The Famine

THE spring of the year was at hand when Gray Beaver finished his long journey. It was April, and White Fang was a year old when he pulled into the home village and was loosed from the harness by Mit-sah. Though a long way from his full growth, White Fang, next to Lip-lip, was the largest yearling in the village. Both from his father, the wolf, and from Kiche, he had inherited stature and strength, and already he was measuring up alongside the full-grown dogs. But he had not yet grown compact. His body was slender and rangy, and his strength more stringy than massive. His coat was the true wolf-gray, and to all appearances he was true wolf himself. The quarter-strain of dog he had inherited from Kiche had left no mark on him physically, though it played its part in his mental make-up.

He wandered through the village, recognizing with staid satisfaction the various gods he had known before the long journey. Then there were the dogs, puppies growing up like himself, and grown dogs that did not look so large and formidable as the memory-pictures he retained of them. Also, he stood less in fear of them than formerly, stalking among them with a certain careless ease that was as new to him as it was enjoyable.

There was Baseek, a grizzled old fellow that in his younger days had but to uncover his fangs to send White Fang cringing and crouching to the right-about. From him White Fang had learned much of his own insignificance; and from him he was now to learn much of the change and development that had taken place in himself. While Baseek had been growing weaker with age, White Fang had been growing stronger with youth.

It was at the cutting-up of a moose, fresh-killed, that White Fang learned of the changed relations in which he stood to the dog-world. He had got for himself a hoof and part of the shin-bone, to which quite a bit of meat was attached. Withdrawn from the immediate scramble of the other dogs,—in fact, out of sight behind a thicket,—he was devouring his prize, when Baseek rushed in upon him. Before he knew what he was doing, he had slashed the intruder twice and sprung clear. Baseek was surprised by the other's temerity and swiftness of attack. He stood, gazing stupidly across at White Fang, the raw, red shin-bone between them.

Baseek was old, and already he had come to know the increasing valor of the dogs it had been his wont to bully. Bitter experiences these, which, perforce, he swallowed, calling upon all his wisdom to cope with them. In the old days, he would have sprung upon White Fang in a fury of righteous wrath. But now his waning powers would not permit such a course. He bristled fiercely and looked ominously across the shin-bone at White Fang. And White Fang, resurrecting quite a deal of the old awe, seemed to wilt and to shrink in upon himself and grow small, as he cast about in his mind for a way to beat a retreat not too inglorious.

And right here Baseek erred. Had he contented himself with looking fierce and ominous, all would have been well. White Fang, on the verge of retreat, would have retreated, leaving the meat to him. But Baseek did not wait. He considered the victory already his and stepped forward to the meat. As he bent his head carelessly to smell it, White Fang bristled slightly. Even then it was not too late for Baseek to retrieve the situation. Had he merely stood over the meat, head up and glowering, White Fang would ultimately have slunk away. But the fresh meat was strong in Baseek's nostrils, and greed urged him to take a bite of it.

This was too much for White Fang. Fresh upon his months of mastery over his own team-mates, it was beyond his self-control to stand idly by while another devoured the meat that belonged to him. He struck, after his custom, without warning. With the first slash, Baseek's right ear was ripped into ribbons. He was astounded at the suddenness of it. But more things, and most grievous ones, were happening with equal suddenness. He was knocked off his feet. His throat was bitten. While he was struggling to his feet the young dog sank teeth twice into his shoulder. The swiftness of it was bewildering. He made a futile rush at White Fang, clipping the empty air with an outraged snap. The next moment his nose was laid open and he was staggering backward away from the meat.

The situtation was now reversed. White Fang stood over the shin-bone, bristling and menacing, while Baseek stood a little way off, preparing to retreat. He dared not risk a fight with this young lightning-flash, and again he knew, and more bitterly, the enfeeblement of oncoming age. His attempt to maintain his dignity was heroic. Calmly turning his back upon young dog and shin-bone, as though both were beneath his notice and unworthy of consideration, he stalked grandly away. Nor, until well out of sight, did he stop to lick his bleeding wounds.

The effect on White Fang was to give him a greater faith in himself, and a greater pride. He walked less softly among the grown dogs; his attitude toward them was less compromising. Not that he went out of his way looking for trouble. Far from it. But upon his way he demanded consideration. He stood upon his right to go his way unmolested and to give trail to no dog. He had to be taken into account, that was all. He was no longer to be disregarded and ignored, as was the lot of puppies and as continued to be the lot of the puppies that were his team-mates. They got out of the way, gave trail to the grown dogs, and gave up meat to them under compulsion. But White Fang, uncompanionable, solitary, morose, scarcely looking to right or left, redoubtable, forbidding of aspect, remote and alien, was accepted as an equal by his puzzled elders. They quickly learned to leave him alone, neither venturing hostile acts nor making overtures of friendliness. If they left him alone, he left them alone—a state of affairs that they found, after a few encounters, to be preeminently desirable.

In midsummer White Fang had an experience. Trotting along in his silent way to investigate a new tepee which had been erected on the edge of the village while he was away with the hunters after moose, he came full upon Kiche. He paused and looked at her. He remembered her vaguely, but he *remembered* her, and that was more than could be said for her. She lifted her lip at him in the old snarl of menace, and his memory became clear. His forgotten cubhood, all that was associated with that familiar snarl, rushed back to him. Before he had known the gods, she had been to him the centre-pin of the universe. The old familiar feelings of that time came back upon him, surged up within him. He bounded toward her joyously, and she met him with shrewd fangs that laid his cheek open to the bone. He did not understand. He backed way, bewildered and puzzled.

But it was not Kiche's fault. A wolf-mother was not made to remember her cubs of a year or so before. So she did not remember White Fang. He was a strange animal, an intruder; and her present litter of puppies gave her the right to resent such intrusion.

One of the puppies sprawled up to White Fang. They were half-brothers, only they did not know it. White Fang sniffed the puppy curiously, whereupon Kiche rushed upon him, gashing his face a second time. He backed farther away. All the old memories and associations died down again and passed into the grave from which they had been resurrected. He looked at Kiche licking her puppy and stopping now and then to snarl at him. She was without value to him. He had learned to get along without her. Her meaning was forgotten. There was no place for her in his scheme of things, as there was no place for him in hers.

He was still standing, stupid and bewildered, the memories forgotten, wondering what it was all about, when Kiche attacked him a third time, intent on driving him away altogether from the vicinity. And White Fang allowed himself to be driven away. This was a female of his kind, and it was a law of his kind that the males must not fight the females. He did not know anything about this law, for it was no generalization of the mind, not a something acquired by experience in the world. He knew it as a secret prompting, as an urge of instinct—of the same instinct that made him howl at the moon and stars of nights and that made him fear death and the unknown.

The months went by. White Fang grew stronger, heavier, and more compact, while his character was developing along the lines laid down by his heredity and his environment. His heredity was a life-stuff that may be likened to clay. It possessed many possibilities, was capable of being moulded into many different forms. Environment served to model the clay, to give it a particular form. Thus, had White Fang never come in to the fires of man, the Wild would have moulded him into a true wolf. But the gods had given him a different environment, and he was moulded into a dog that was rather wolfish, but that was a dog and not a wolf.

And so, according to the clay of his nature and the pressure of his surroundings, his character was being moulded into a certain particular shape. There was no escaping it. He was becoming more morose, more uncompanionable, more solitary, more ferocious; while the dogs were learning more and more that it was better to be at peace with him than at war, and Gray Beaver was coming to prize him more greatly with the passage of each day.

White Fang, seeming to sum up strength in all his qualities, nevertheless suffered from one besetting weakness. He could not stand being laughed at. The laughter of men was a hateful thing. They might laugh among themselves about anything they pleased except himself, and he did not mind. But the moment laughter was turned upon him he would fly into a most terrible rage. Grave, dignified, sombre, a laugh made him frantic to ridiculousness. It so outraged him and upset him that for hours he would behave like a demon. And woe to the dog that at such times ran foul of him. He knew the law too well to take it out on Gray Beaver; behind Gray Beaver were a club and god-head. But behind the dogs there was nothing but space, and into this space they fled when White Fang came on the scene, made mad by laughter.

In the third year of his life there came a great famine to the Mackenzie Indians. In the summer the fish failed. In the winter the cariboo forsook their accustomed track. Moose were scarce, the rabbits almost disappeared, hunting and preying animals perished. Denied their usual food-supply, weakened by hunger, they fell upon and devoured one another. Only the strong survived. White Fang's gods were also hunting animals. The old and the weak of them died of hunger. There was wailing in the village, where the women and children went without in order that what little they had might go into the bellies of the lean and hollow-eyed hunters who trod the forest in the vain pursuit of meat.

To such extremity were the gods driven that they ate the soft-tanned leather of their moccasins and mittens, while the dogs ate the harnesses off their backs and the very whip-lashes. Also, the dogs ate one another, and also the gods ate the dogs. The weakest and the more worthless were eaten first. The dogs that still lived, looked on and understood. A few of the boldest and wisest forsook the fires of the gods, which had now become a shambles, and fled into the forest, where, in the end, they starved to death or were eaten by wolves.

In this time of misery, White Fang, too, stole away into the woods. He was better fitted for the life than the other dogs, for he had the training of his cubhood to guide him. Especially adept did he become in stalking small living things. He would lie concealed for hours, following every movement of a cautious tree-squirrel, waiting, with a patience as huge as the hunger he suffered from, until the squirrel ventured out upon the ground. Even then, White Fang was not premature. He waited until he was sure of striking before the squirrel could gain a tree-refuge. Then, and not until then, would he flash from his hiding-place, a gray projectile, incredibly swift, never failing its mark—the fleeing squirrel that fled not fast enough.

Successful as he was with squirrels, there was one difficulty that prevented him from living and growing fat on them. There were not enough squirrels. So he was driven to hunt still smaller things. So acute did his hunger become at times that he was not above rooting out wood-mice from their burrows in the ground. Nor did he scorn to do battle with a weasel as hungry as himself and many times more ferocious.

In the worst pinches of the famine he stole back to the fires of the gods. But he did not go in to the fires. He lurked in the forest, avoiding discovery and robbing the snares at the rare intervals when game was caught. He even robbed Gray Beaver's snare of a rabbit at a time when Gray Beaver staggered and tottered through the forest, sitting down often to rest, what of weakness and of shortness of breath.

One day White Fang encountered a young wolf, gaunt and scrawny, loose-jointed with famine. Had he not been hungry himself, White Fang might have gone with him and eventually found his way into the pack amongst his wild brethren. As it was, he ran the young wolf down and killed and ate him.

Fortune seemed to favor him. Always, when hardest pressed for food, he found something to kill. Again, when he was weak, it was his luck that none of the larger preying animals chanced upon him. Thus, he was strong from the two days' eating a lynx had afforded him, when the hungry wolf-pack ran full tilt upon him. It was a long, cruel chase, but he was better nourished than they, and in the end outran them. And not only did he outrun them, but, circling widely back on his track, he gathered in one of his exhausted pursuers.

After that he left that part of the country and journeyed over to the valley wherein he had been born. Here, in the old lair, he encountered Kiche. Up to her old tricks, she, too, had fled the inhospitable fires of the gods and gone back to her old refuge to give birth to her young. Of this litter but one remained alive when White Fang came upon the scene, and this one was not destined to live long. Young life had little chance in such a famine.

Kiche's greeting of her grown son was anything but affectionate. But White Fang did not mind. He had outgrown his mother. So he turned tail philosophically and trotted on up the stream. At the forks he took the turning to the left, where he found the lair of the lynx with whom his mother and he had fought long before. Here, in the abandoned lair, he settled down and rested for a day.

During the early summer, in the last days of the famine, he met Lip-lip, who had likewise taken to the woods, where he had eked out a miserable existence. White Fang came upon him unexpectedly. Trotting in opposite directions along the base of a high bluff, they rounded a corner of rock and found themselves face to face. They paused with instant alarm, and looked at each other suspiciously.

White Fang was in splendid condition. His hunting had been good, and for a week he had eaten his fill. He was even gorged from his latest kill. But in the moment he looked at Lip-lip his hair rose on end all along his back. It was an involuntary bristling on his part, the physical state that in the past had always accompanied the mental state produced in him by Lip-lip's bullying and persecution. As in the past he had bristled and snarled at sight of Lip-lip, so now, and automatically, he bristled and snarled. He did not waste any time. The thing was done thoroughly and with despatch. Lip-lip essayed to back away, but White Fang struck him hard, shoulder to shoulder. Lip-lip was overthrown and rolled upon his back. White Fang's teeth drove into the scrawny throat. There was a death-struggle, during which White Fang walked around, stiff-legged and observant. Then he resumed his course and trotted on along the base of the bluff.

One day, not long after, he came to the edge of the forest, where a narrow stretch of open land sloped down to the Mackenzie. He had been over this ground before, when it was bare, but now a village occupied it. Still hidden amongst the trees, he paused to study the situation. Sights and sounds and scents were familiar to him. It was the old village changed to a new place. But sights and sounds and smells were different from those he had last had when he fled away from it. There was no whimpering nor wailing. Contented sounds saluted his ear, and when he heard the angry voice of a woman he knew it to be the anger that proceeds from a full stomach. And there was a smell in the air of fish. There was food. The famine was gone. He came out boldly from the forest and trotted into camp straight to Gray Beaver's tepee. Gray Beaver was not there; but Kloo-kooch welcomed him with glad cries and the whole of a fresh-caught fish, and he lay down to wait Gray Beaver's coming.

Part Four—The Superior Gods

I

The Enemy of his Kind

Had there been in White Fang's nature any possibility, no matter how remote, of his ever coming to fraternize with his kind, such possibility was irretrievably destroyed when he was made leader of the sled-team. For now the dogs hated him—hated him for the extra meat bestowed upon him by Mit-sah; hated him for all the real and fancied favors he received; hated him for that he fled always at the head of the team, his waving brush of a tail and his perpetually retreating hind-quarters forever maddening their eyes.

And White Fang just as bitterly hated them back. Being sled-leader was anything but gratifying to him. To be compelled to run away before the yelling pack, every dog of which, for three years, he had trashed and mastered, was almost more than he could endure. But endure it he must, or perish, and the life that was in him had no desire to perish. The moment Mit-sah gave his order for the start, that moment the whole team, with eager, savage cries, sprang forward at White Fang.

There was no defence for him. If he turned upon them, Mit-sah would throw the stinging lash of the whip into his face. Only remained to him to run away. He could not encounter that howling horde with his tail and hind-quarters. These were scarcely fit weapons with which to meet the many merciless fangs. So run away he did, violating his own nature and pride with every leap he made, and leaping all day long.

One cannot violate the promptings of one's nature without having that nature recoil upon itself. Such a recoil is like that of a hair, made to grow out from the body, turning unnaturally upon the direction of its growth and growing into the body—a rankling, festering thing of hurt. And so with White Fang. Every urge of his being impelled him to spring upon the pack that cried at his heels, but it was the will of the gods that this should not be; and behind the will, to enforce it, was the whip of cariboo-gut with its biting thirty-foot lash. So White Fang could only eat his heart in bitterness and develop a hatred and malice commensurate with the ferocity and indomitability of his nature.

If ever a creature was the enemy of its kind, White Fang was that creature. He asked no quarter, gave none. He was continually marred and scarred by the teeth of the pack, and as continually he left his own marks upon the pack. Unlike most leaders, who, when camp was made and the dogs were unhitched, huddled near to the gods for protection, White Fang disdained such protection. He walked boldly about the camp, inflicting punishment in the night for what he had suffered in the day. In the time before he was made leader of the team, the pack had learned to get out of his way. But now it was different. Excited by the day-long pursuit of him, swayed subconsciously by the insistent iteration on their brains of the sight of him fleeing away, mastered by the feeling of mastery enjoyed all day, the dogs could not bring themselves to give way to him. When he appeared amongst them, there was always a squabble. His progress was marked by snarl and snap and growl. The very atmosphere he breathed was surcharged with hatred and malice, and this but served to increase the hatred and malice within him.

When Mit-sah cried out his command for the team to stop, White Fang obeyed. At first this caused trouble for the other dogs. All of them would spring upon the hated leader, only to find the tables turned. Behind him would be Mit-sah, the great whip singing in his hand. So the dogs came to understand that when the team stopped by order, White Fang was to be let alone. But when White Fang stopped without orders, then it was allowed them to spring upon him and destroy him if they could. After several experiences, White Fang never stopped without orders. He learned quickly. It was in the nature of things that he must learn quickly, if he were to survive the unusually severe conditions under which life was vouchsafed him.

But the dogs could never learn the lesson to leave him alone in camp. Each day, pursuing him and crying defiance at him, the lesson of the previous night was erased, and that night would have to be learned over again, to be as immediately forgotten. Besides, there was a greater consistence in their dislike of him. They sensed between themselves and him a difference of kind—cause sufficient in itself for hostility. Like him, they were domesticated wolves. But they had been domesticated for generations. Much of the Wild had been lost, so that to them the Wild was the unknown, the terrible, the ever menacing and ever warring. But to him, in appearance and action and impulse, still clung the Wild. He symbolized it, was it personification; so that when they showed their teeth to him they were defending themselves against the powers of destruction that lurked in the shadows of the forest and in the dark beyond the camp-fire.

But there was one lesson the dogs did learn, and that was to keep together. White Fang was too terrible for any of them to face single-handed. They met him with the mass-formation, otherwise he would have killed them, one by one, in a night. As it was, he never had a chance to kill them. He might roll a dog off its feet, but the pack would be upon him before he could follow up and deliver the deadly throat-stroke. At the first hint of conflict, the whole team drew together and faced him. The dogs had quarrels among themselves, but these were forgotten when trouble was brewing with White Fang.

On the other hand, try as they would, they could not kill White Fang. He was too quick for them, too formidable, too wise. He avoided tight places and always backed out of it when they bade fair to surround him. While, as for getting him off his feet, there was no dog among them capable of doing the trick. His feet clung to the earth with the same tenacity that he clung to life. For that matter, life and footing were synonymous in this unending warfare with the pack, and none knew it better than White Fang.

So he became the enemy of his kind, domesticated wolves that they were, softened by the fires of man, weakened in the sheltering shadow of man's strength. White Fang was bitter and implacable. The clay of him was so moulded. He declared a vendetta against all dogs. And so terribly did he live this vendetta that Gray Beaver, fierce savage himself, could not but marvel at White Fang's ferocity. Never, he swore, had there been the like of this animal; and the Indians in strange villages swore likewise when they considered the tale of his killings amongst their dogs.

When White Fang was nearly five years old, Gray Beaver took him on another great journey, and long remembered was the havoc he worked amongst the dogs of the many villages along the Mackenzie, across the Rockies, and down the Porcupine to the Yukon. He revelled in the vengeance he wreaked upon his kind. They were ordinary, unsuspecting dogs. They were not prepared for his swiftness and directness, for his attack without warning. They did not know him for what he was, a lightning-flash of slaughter. They bristled up to him, stiff-legged and challenging, while he, wasting no time on elaborate preliminaries, snapping into action like a steel spring, was at their throats and destroying them before they knew what was happening and while they were yet in the throes of surprise.

He became an adept at fighting. He economized. He never wasted his strength, never tussled. He was in too quickly for that, and, if he missed, was out again too quickly. The dislike of the wolf for close quarters was his to an unusual degree. He could not endure a prolonged contact with another body. It smacked of danger. It made him frantic. He must be away, free, on his own legs, touching no living thing. It was the Wild still clinging to him, asserting itself through him. This feeling had been accentuated by the Ishmaelite life he had led from his puppyhood. Danger lurked in contacts. It was the trap, ever the trap, the fear of it lurking deep in the life of him, woven into the fibre of him.

In consequence, the strange dogs he encountered had no chance against him. He eluded their fangs. He got them, or got away, himself untouched in either event. In the natural course of things there were exceptions to this. There were times when several dogs, pitching on to him, punished him before he could get away; and there were times when a single dog scored deeply on him. But these were accidents. In the main, so efficient a fighter had he become, he went his way unscathed.

Another advantage he possessed was that of correctly judging time and distance. Not that he did this consciously, however. He did not calculate such things. It was all automatic. His eyes saw correctly, and the nerves carried the vision correctly to his brain. The parts of him were better adjusted than those of the average dog. They worked together more smoothly and steadily. His was a better, far better, nervous, mental, and muscular coördination. When his eyes conveyed to his brain the moving image of an action, his brain, without conscious effort, knew the space that limited that action and the time required for its completion. Thus, he could avoid the leap of another dog, or the drive of its fangs, and at the same moment could seize the infinitesimal fraction of time in which to deliver his own attack. Body and brain, his was a more perfected mechanism. Not that he was to be praised for it. Nature had been more generous to him than to the average animal, that was all.

It was in the summer that White Fang arrived at Fort Yukon. Gray Beaver had crossed the great water-shed between the Mackenzie and the Yukon in the late winter, and spent the spring in hunting among the western outlying spurs of the Rockies. Then, after the break-up of the ice on the Porcupine, he had built a canoe and paddled down that stream to where it effected its junction with the Yukon just under the Arctic Circle. Here stood the old Hudson's Bay Company fort; and here were many Indians, much food, and unprecedented excitement. It was the summer of 1898, and thousands of gold-hunters were going up the Yukon to Dawson and the Klondike. Still hundreds of miles from their goal, nevertheless many of them had been on the way for a year, and the least any of them had travelled to get that far was five thousand miles, while some had come from the other side of the world.

Here Gray Beaver stopped. A whisper of the gold-rush had reached his ears, and he had come with several bales of furs, and another of gut-sewn mittens and moccasins. He would not have ventured so long a trip had he not expected generous profits. But what he had expected was nothing to what he realized. His wildest dream had not exceeded a hundred per cent profit; he made a thousand per cent. And like a true Indian, he settled down to trade carefully and slowly, even if it took all summer and the rest of the winter to dispose of his goods.

It was at Fort Yukon that White Fang saw his first white men. As compared with the Indians he had known, they were to him another race of beings, a race of superior gods. They impressed him as possessing superior power, and it is on power that godhead rests. White Fang did not reason it out, did not in his mind make the sharp generalization that the white gods were more powerful. It was a feeling, nothing more, and yet none the less potent. As, in his puppyhood, the looming bulks of the tepees, man-reared, had affected him as manifestations of power, so was he affected now by the houses and the huge fort all of massive logs. Here was power. Those white gods were strong. They possessed greater mastery over matter than the gods he had known, most powerful among which was Gray Beaver. And yet Gray Beaver was as a child-god among these white-skinned ones.

To be sure, White Fang only felt these things. He was not conscious of them. Yet it is upon feeling, more often than thinking, that animals act; and every act White Fang now performed was based upon the feeling that the white men were the superior gods. In the first place he was very suspicious of them. There was no telling what unknown terrors were theirs, what unknown hurts they could administer. He was curious to observe them, fearful of being noticed by them. For the first few hours he was content with slinking around and watching them from a safe distance. Then he saw that no harm befell the dogs that were near to them, and he came in closer.

In turn, he was an object of great curiosity to them. His wolfish appearance caught their eyes at once, and they pointed him out to one another. This act of pointing put White Fang on his guard, and when they tried to approach him he showed his teeth and backed away. Not one succeeded in laying a hand on him, and it was well that they did not.

White Fang soon learned that very few of these gods—not more than a dozen—lived at this place. Every two or three days a steamer (another and colossal manifestation of power) came in to the bank and stopped for several hours. The white men came from off these steamers and went away on them again. There seemed untold numbers of these white men. In the first day or so, he saw more of them than he had seen Indians in all his life; and as the days went by they continued to come up the river, stop, and then go on up the river and out of sight.

But if the white gods were all-powerful, their dogs did not amount to much. This White Fang quickly discovered by mixing with those that came ashore with their masters. They were of irregular shapes and sizes. Some were short-legged—too short; others were long-legged—too long. They had hair instead of fur, and a few had very little hair at that. And none of them knew how to fight.

As an enemy of his kind, it was in White Fang's province to fight with them. This he did, and he quickly achieved for them a mighty contempt. They were soft and helpless, made much noise, and floundered around clumsily, trying to accomplish by main strength what he accomplished by dexterity and cunning. They rushed bellowing at him. He sprang to the side. They did not know what had become of him; and in that moment he struck them on the shoulder, rolling them off their feet and delivering his stroke at the throat.

Sometimes this stroke was successful, and a stricken dog rolled in the dirt, to be pounced upon and torn to pieces by the pack of Indian dogs that waited. White Fang was wise. He had long since learned that the gods were made angry when their dogs were killed. The white men were no exception to this. So he was content, when he had overthrown and slashed wide the throat of one of their dogs, to drop back and let the pack go in and do the cruel finishing work. It was then that the white men rushed in, visiting their wrath heavily on the pack, while White Fang went free. He would stand off at a little distance and look on, while stones, clubs, axes, and all sorts of weapons fell upon his fellows. White Fang was very wise.

But his fellows grew wise, in their own way; and in this White Fang grew wise with them. They learned that it was when a steamer first tied to the bank that they had their fun. After the first two or three strange dogs had been downed and destroyed, the white men hustled their own animals back on board and wreaked savage vengeance on the offenders. One white man, having seen his dog, a setter, torn to pieces before his eyes, drew a revolver. He fired rapidly, six times, and six of the pack lay dead or dying —another manifestation of power that sank deep into White Fang's consciousness.

White Fang enjoyed it all. He did not love his kind, and he was shrewd enough to escape hurt himself. At first, the killing of the white men's dogs had been a diversion. After a time it became his occupation. There was no work for him to do. Gray Beaver was busy trading and getting wealthy. So White Fang hung around the landing with the disreputable gang of Indian dogs, waiting for steamers. With the arrival of a steamer the fun began. After a few minutes, by the time the white men had got over their surprise, the gang scattered. The fun was over until the next steamer should arrive.

But it can scarcely be said that White Fang was a member of the gang. He did not mingle with it, but remained aloof, always himself, and was even feared by it. It is true, he worked with it. He picked the quarrel with the strange dog while the gang waited. And when he had overthrown the strange dog the gang went in to finish it. But it is equally true that he then withdrew, leaving the gang to receive the punishment of the outraged gods.

It did not require much exertion to pick these quarrels. All he had to do, when the strange dogs came ashore, was to show himself. When they saw him they rushed for him. It was their instinct. He was the Wild—the unknown, the terrible, the ever menacing, the thing that prowled in the darkness around the fires of the primeval world when they, cowering close to the fires, were reshaping their instincts, learning to fear the Wild out of which they had come, and which they had deserted and betrayed. Generation by generation, down all the generations, had this fear of the Wild been stamped into their natures. For centuries the Wild had stood for terror and destruction. And during all this time free license had been theirs, from their masters, to kill the things of the Wild. In doing this they had protected both themselves and the gods whose companionship they shared.

And so, fresh from the soft southern world, these dogs, trotting down the gangplank and out upon the Yukon shore, had but to see White Fang to experience the irresistible impulse to rush upon him and destroy him. They might be town-reared dogs, but the instinctive fear of the Wild was theirs just the same. Not alone with their own eyes did they see the wolfish creature in the clear light of day, standing before them. They saw him with the eyes of their ancestors, and by their inherited memory they knew White Fang for the wolf, and they remembered the ancient feud.

All of which served to make White Fang's days enjoyable. If the sight of him drove these strange dogs upon him, so much the better for him, so much the worse for them. They looked upon him as legitimate prey, and as legitimate prey he looked upon them.

Not for nothing had he first seen the light of day in a lonely lair and fought his first fights with the ptarmigan, the weasel, and the lynx. And not for nothing had his puppyhood been made bitter by the persecution of Lip-lip and the whole puppy-pack. It might have been otherwise, and he would then have been otherwise. Had Lip-lip not existed, he would have passed his puppyhood with the other puppies and grown up more doglike and with more liking for dogs. Had Gray Beaver possessed the plummet of affection and love, he might have sounded the deeps of White Fang's nature and brought up to the surface all manner of kindly qualities. But these things had not been so. The clay of White Fang had been moulded until he became what he was, morose and lonely, unloving and ferocious, the enemy of all his kind.

II

The Mad God

A small number of white men lived in Fort Yukon. These men had been long in the country. They called themselves Sour-doughs, and took great pride in so classifying themselves. For other men, new in the land, they felt nothing but disdain. The men who came ashore from the steamers were newcomers. They were known as *chechaquos,* and they always wilted at the application of the name. They made their bread with baking-powder. This was the invidious distinction between them and the Sour-doughs, who, forsooth, made their bread from sour-dough because they had no baking-powder.

All of which is neither here nor there. The men in the fort disdained the newcomers and enjoyed seeing them come to grief. Especially did they enjoy the havoc worked amongst the newcomers' dogs by White Fang and his direputable gang. When a steamer arrived, the men of the fort made it a point always to come down to the bank and see the fun. They looked forward to it with as much anticipation as did the Indian dogs, while they were not slow to appreciate the savage and crafty part played by White Fang.

But there was one man amongst them who particularly enjoyed the sport. He would come running at the first sound of a steamboat's whistle; and when the last fight was over and White Fang and the pack had scattered, he would return slowly to the fort, his face heavy with regret. Sometimes, when a soft Southland dog went down, shrieking its death-cry under the fangs of the pack, this man would be unable to contain himself, and would leap into the air and cry out with delight. And always he had a sharp and covetous eye for White Fang.

This man was called "Beauty" by the other men of the fort. No one knew his first name, and in general he was known in the country as Beauty Smith. But he was anything save a beauty. To antithesis was due his naming. He was preeminently unbeautiful. Nature had been niggardly with him. He was a small man to begin with; and upon his meagre frame was deposited an even more strikingly meagre head. Its apex might be likened to a point. In fact, in his boyhood, before he had been named Beauty by his fellows, he had been called "Pinhead."

Backward, from the apex, his head slanted down to his neck; and forward, it slanted uncompromisingly to meet a low and remarkably wide forehead. Beginning here, as though regretting her parsimony, Nature had spread his features with a lavish hand. His eyes were large, and between them was the distance of two eyes. His face, in relation to the rest of him, was prodigious. In order to discover the necessary area, Nature had given him an enormous prognathous jaw. It was wide and heavy, and protruded outward and down until it seemed to rest on his chest. Possibly this appearance was due to the weariness of the slender neck, unable properly to support so great a burden.

This jaw gave the impression of ferocious determination. But something lacked.

Perhaps it was from excess. Perhaps the jaw was too large. At any rate, it was a lie. Beauty Smith was known far and wide as the weakest of weak-kneed and snivelling cowards. To complete his description, his teeth were large and yellow, while the two eye-teeth, larger than their fellows, showed under his lean lips like fangs. His eyes were yellow and muddy, as though Nature had run short on pigments and squeezed together the dregs of all her tubes. It was the same with his hair, sparse and irregular of growth, muddy-yellow and dirty-yellow, rising on his head and sprouting out of his face in unexpected tufts and bunches, in appearance like clumped and wind-blown grain.

In short, Beauty Smith was a monstrosity, and the blame of it lay elsewhere. He was not responsible. The clay of him had been so moulded in the making. He did the cooking for the other men in the fort, the dish-washing and the drudgery. They did not despise him. Rather did they tolerate him in a broad human way, as one tolerates any creature evilly treated in the making. Also, they feared him. His cowardly rages made them dread a shot in the back or poison in their coffee. But somebody had to do the cooking, and whatever else his shortcomings, Beauty Smith could cook.

This was the man that looked at White Fang, delighted in his ferocious prowess, and desired to possess him. He made overtures to White Fang from the first. White Fang began by ignoring him. Later on, when the overtures became more insistent, White Fang bristled and bared his teeth and backed away. He did not like the man. The feel of him was bad. He sensed the evil in him, and feared the extended hand and the attempts at soft-spoken speech. Because of all this, he hated the man.

With the simpler creatures, good and bad are things simply understood. The good stands for all things that bring easement and satisfaction and surcease from pain. Therefore, the good is liked. The bad stands for all things that are fraught with discomfort, menace, and hurt, and is hated accordingly. White Fang's feel of Beauty Smith was bad. From the man's distorted body and twisted mind, in occult ways, like mists rising from malarial marshes, came emanations of the unhealth within. Not by reasoning, not by the five senses alone, but by other and remoter and uncharted senses, came the feeling to White Fang that the man was ominous with evil, pregnant with hurtfulness, and therefore a thing bad, and wisely to be hated.

White Fang was in Gray Beaver's camp when Beauty Smith first visited it. At the faint sound of his distant feet, before he came in sight, White Fang knew who was coming and began to bristle. He had been lying down in an abandon of comfort, but he arose quickly, and, as the man arrived, slid away in true wolf-fashion to the edge of the camp. He did not know what they said, but he could see the man and Gray Beaver talking together. Once, the man pointed at him, and White Fang snarled back as though the hand were just descending upon him instead of being, as it was, fifty feet away. The man laughed at this; and White Fang slunk away to the sheltering woods, his head turned to observe as he glided softly over the ground.

Gray Beaver refused to sell the dog. He had grown rich with his trading and stood in need of nothing. Besides, White Fang was a valuable animal, the strongest sled-dog he had ever owned, and the best leader. Furthermore, there was no dog like him on the Mackenzie nor the Yukon. He could fight. He killed other dogs as easily as men killed mosquitoes. (Beauty Smith's eyes lighted up at this, and he licked his thin lips with an eager tongue.) No, White Fang was not for sale at any price.

But Beauty Smith knew the ways of Indians. He visited Gray Beaver's camp often, and hidden under his coat was always a black bottle or so. One of the potencies of whiskey is the breeding of thirst. Gray Beaver got the thirst. His fevered membranes and burnt stomach began to clamor for more and more of the scorching fluid; while his brain, thrust all awry by the unwonted stimulant, permitted him to go any length to obtain it. The money he had received for his furs and mittens and moccasins began to go. It went faster and faster, and the shorter his money-sack grew, the shorter grew his temper.

In the end his money and goods and temper were all gone. Nothing remained to him but his thirst, a prodigious possession in itself that grew more prodigious with every sober breath he drew. Then it was that Beauty Smith had talk with him again about the sale of White Fang; but this time the price offered was in bottles, not dollars, and Gray Beaver's ears were more eager to hear.

"You ketch um dog you take um all right," was his last word.

The bottles were delivered, but after two days, "You ketch um dog," were Beauty Smith's words to Gray Beaver.

White Fang slunk into camp one evening and dropped down with a sigh of content. The dreaded white god was not there. For days his manifestations of desire to lay hands on him had been growing more insistent, and during that time White Fang had been compelled to avoid the camp. He did not know what evil was threatened by those insistent hands. He knew only that they did threaten evil of some sort, and that it was best for him to keep out of their reach.

But scarcely had he lain down when Gray Beaver staggered over to him and tied a leather thong around his neck. He sat down beside White Fang, holding the end of the thong in his hand. In the other hand he held a bottle, which, from time to time, was inverted above his head to the accompaniment of gurgling noises.

An hour of this passed, when the vibrations of feet in contact with the ground foreran the one who approached. White Fang heard it first, and he was bristling with recognition while Gray Beaver still nodded stupidly. White Fang tried to draw the thong softly out of his master's hand; but the relaxed fingers closed tightly and Gray Beaver roused himself.

Beauty Smith strode into camp and stood over White Fang. He snarled softly up at the thing of fear, watching keenly the deportment of the hands. One hand extended outward and began to descend upon his head. His soft snarl grew tense and harsh. The hand continued slowly to descend, while he crouched beneath it, eying it malignantly, his snarl growing shorter and shorter as, with quickening breath, it approached its culmination. Suddenly he snapped, striking with his fangs like a snake. The hand was jerked back, and the teeth came together emptily with a sharp click. Beauty Smith was frightened and angry. Gray Beaver clouted White Fang alongside the head, so that he cowered down close to the earth in respectful obedience.

White Fang's suspicious eyes followed every movement. He saw Beauty Smith go away and return with a stout club. Then the end of the thong was given over to him by Gray Beaver. Beauty Smith started to walk away. The thong grew taut. White Fang resisted it. Gray Beaver clouted him right and left to make him get up and follow. He obeyed, but with a rush, hurling himself upon the stranger who was dragging him away. Beauty Smith did not jump away. He had been waiting for this. He swung the club smartly, stopping the rush midway and smashing White Fang down upon the ground. Gray Beaver laughed and nodded approval. Beauty Smith tightened the thong again, and White Fang crawled limply and dizzily to his feet.

He did not rush a second time. One smash from the club was sufficient to convince him that the white god knew how to handle it, and he was too wise to fight the inevitable. So he followed morosely at Beauty Smith's heels, his tail between his legs, yet snarling softly under his breath. But Beauty Smith kept a wary eye on him, and the club was held always ready to strike.

At the fort Beauty Smith left him securely tied and went into bed. White Fang waited an hour. Then he applied his teeth to the thong, and in the space of ten seconds was free. He had wasted no time with his teeth. There had been no useless gnawing. The thong was cut across, diagonally, almost as clean as though done by a knife. White Fang looked up at the fort, at the same time bristling and growling. Then he turned and trotted back to Gray Beaver's camp. He owed no allegiance to this strange and terrible god. He had given himself to Gray Beaver, and to Gray Beaver he considered he still belonged.

But what had occurred before was repeated—with a difference. Gray Beaver again made him fast with a thong, and in the morning turned him over to Beauty Smith. And here was where the difference came in. Beauty Smith gave him a beating. Tied securely, White Fang could only rage futilely and endure the punishment. Club and whip were both used upon him, and he experienced the worst beating he had ever received in his life. Even the big beating given him in his puppyhood by Gray Beaver was mild compared with this.

Beauty Smith enjoyed the task. He delighted in it. He gloated over his victim, and his eyes flamed dully, as he swung the whip or club and listened to White Fang's cries of pain and to his helpless bellows and snarls. For Beauty Smith was cruel in the way that cowards are cruel. Cringing and snivelling himself before the blows or angry speech of a man, he revenged himself, in turn, upon creatures weaker than he. All life likes power, and Beauty Smith was no exception. Denied the expression of power amongst his own kind, he fell back upon the lesser creatures and there vindicated the life that was in him. But Beauty Smith had not created himself, and no blame was to be attached to him. He had come into the world with a twisted body and a brute intelligence. This had constituted the clay of him, and it had not been kindly moulded by the world.

White Fang knew why he was being beaten. When Gray Beaver tied the thong around his neck, and passed the end of the thong into Beauty Smith's keeping, White Fang knew that it was his god's will for him to go with Beauty Smith. And when Beauty Smith left him tied outside the fort, he knew that it was Beauty Smith's will that he should remain there. Therefore, he had disobeyed the will of both the gods, and earned the consequent punishment. He had seen dogs change owners in the past, and he had seen the runaways beaten as he was being beaten. He was wise, and yet in the nature of him there were forces greater than wisdom. One of these was fidelity. He did not love Gray Beaver; yet, even in the face of his will and his anger, he was faithful to him. He could not help it. This faithfulness was a quality of the clay that composed him. It was the quality that was peculiarly the possession of his kind; the quality that set apart his species from all other species; the quality that had enabled the wolf and the wild dog to come in from the open and be the companions of man.

After the beating, White Fang was dragged back to the fort. But this time Beauty Smith left him tied with a stick. One does not give up a god easily, and so with White Fang. Gray Beaver was his own particular god, and, in spite of Gray Beaver's will, White Fang still clung to him and would not give him up. Gray Beaver had betrayed and forsaken him, but that had no effect upon him. Not for nothing had he surrendered himself body and soul to Gray Beaver. There had been no reservation on White Fang's part, and the bond was not to be broken easily.

So, in the night, when the men in the fort were asleep, White Fang applied his teeth to the stick that held him. The wood was seasoned and dry, and it was tied so closely to his neck that he could scarcely get his teeth to it. It was only by the severest muscular exertion and neck-arching that he succeeded in getting the wood between his teeth, and barely between his teeth at that; and it was only by the exercise of an immense patience, extending through many hours, that he succeeded in gnawing through the stick. This was something that dogs were not supposed to do. It was unprecedented. But White Fang did it, trotting away from the fort in the early morning, with the end of the stick hanging to his neck.

He was wise. But had he been merely wise he would not have gone back to Gray Beaver, who had already twice betrayed him. But there was his faithfulness, and he went back to be betrayed yet a third time. Again he yielded to the tying of a thong around his neck by Gray Beaver, and again Beauty Smith came to claim him. And this time he was beaten even more severely than before.

Gray Beaver looked on stolidly while the white man wielded the whip. He gave no protection. It was no longer his dog. When the beating was over White Fang was sick. A soft Southland dog would have died under it, but not he. His school of life had been sterner, and he was himself of sterner stuff. He had too great vitality. His clutch on life was too strong. But he was very sick. At first he was unable to drag himself along, and Beauty Smith had to wait half an hour on him. And then, blind and reeling, he followed at Beauty Smith's heels back to the fort.

But now he was tied with a chain that defied his teeth, and he strove in vain, by lunging, to draw the staple from the timber into which it was driven. After a few days, sober and bankrupt, Gray Beaver departed up the Porcupine on his long journey to the Mackenzie. White Fang remained on the Yukon, the property of a man more than half mad and all brute. But what is a dog to know in its consciousness of madness? To White Fang, Beauty Smith was a veritable, if terrible, god. He was a mad god at best, but White Fang knew nothing of madness; he knew only that he must submit to the will of this new master, obey his every whim and fancy.

III

The Reign of Hate

UNDER the tutelage of the mad god, White Fang became a fiend. He was kept chained in a pen at the rear of the fort, and here Beauty Smith teased and irritated and drove him wild with petty torments. The man early discovered White Fang's susceptibility to laughter, and made it a point, after painfully tricking him, to laugh at him. This laughter was uproarious and scornful, and at the same time the god pointed his finger derisively at White Fang. At such times reason fled from White Fang, and in his transports of rage he was even more mad than Beauty Smith.

Formerly, White Fang had been merely the enemy of his kind, withal a ferocious enemy. He now became the enemy of all things, and more ferocious than ever. To such an extent was he tormented, that he hated blindly and without the faintest spark of reason. He hated the chain that bound him, the men who peered in at him through the slats of the pen, the dogs that accompanied the men and that snarled malignantly at him in his helplessness. He hated the very wood of the pen that confined him. And first, last, and most of all, he hated Beauty Smith.

But Beauty Smith had a purpose in all that he did to White Fang. One day a number of men gathered about the pen. Beauty Smith entered, club in hand, and took the chain from off White Fang's neck. When his master had gone out, White Fang turned loose and tore around the pen, trying to get at the men outside. He was magnificently terrible. Fully five feet in length, and standing two and one-half feet at the shoulder, he far outweighed a wolf of corresponding size. From his mother he had inherited the heavier proportions of the dog, so that he weighed, without any fat and without an ounce of superfluous flesh, over ninety pounds. It was all muscle, bone, and sinew—fighting flesh in the finest condition.

The door of the pen was being opened again. White Fang paused. Something unusual was happening. He waited. The door was opened wider. Then a huge dog was thrust inside, and the door was slammed shut behind him. White Fang had never seen such a dog (it was a mastiff); but the size and fierce aspect of the intruder did not deter him. Here was something, not wood nor iron, upon which to wreak his hate. He leaped in with a flash of fangs that ripped down the side of the mastiff's neck. The mastiff shook his head, growled hoarsely, and plunged at White Fang. But White Fang was here, there, and everywhere, always evading and eluding, and always leaping in and slashing with his fangs and leaping out again in time to escape punishment.

The men outside shouted and applauded, while Beauty Smith, in an ecstasy of delight, gloated over the ripping and mangling performed by White Fang. There was no hope for the mastiff from the first. He was too ponderous and slow. In the end, while Beauty Smith beat White Fang back with a club, the mastiff was dragged out by its owner. Then there was a payment of bets, and money clinked in Beauty Smith's hand.

White Fang came to look forward eagerly to the gathering of the men around his pen. It meant a fight; and this was the only way that was now vouchsafed him of expressing the life that was in him. Tormented, incited to hate, he was kept a prisoner so that there was no way of satisfying that hate except at the times his master saw fit to put another dog against him. Beauty Smith had estimated his powers well, for he was invariably the victor. One day, three dogs were turned in upon him in succession. Another day, a full-grown wolf, fresh-caught from the Wild, was shoved in through the door of the pen. And on still another day two dogs were set against him at the same time. This was his severest fight, and although in the end he killed them both he was himself half killed in doing it.

In the fall of the year, when the first snows were falling and mush-ice was running in the river, Beauty Smith took passage for himself and White Fang on a steamboat bound up the Yukon to Dawson. White Fang had now achieved a reputation in the land. As "The Fighting Wolf" he was known far and wide, and the cage in which he was kept on the steamboat's deck was usually surrounded by curious men. He raged and snarled at them, or lay quietly and studied them with cold hatred. Why should he not hate them? He never asked himself the question. He knew only hate and lost himself in the passion of it. Life had become a hell to him. He had not been made for the close confinement wild beasts endure at the hands of men. And yet it was in precisely this way that he was treated. Men stared at him, poked sticks between the bars to make him snarl, and then laughed at him.

They were his environment, these men, and they were moulding the clay of him into a more ferocious thing than had been intended by Nature. Nevertheless, Nature had given him plasticity. Where many another animal would have died or had its spirit broken, he adjusted himself and lived, and at no expense of the spirit. Possibly Beauty

Smith, archfiend and tormentor, was capable of breaking White Fang's spirit, but as yet there were no signs of his succeeding.

If Beauty Smith had in him a devil, White Fang had another; and the two of them raged against each other unceasingly. In the days before, White Fang had had the wisdom to cower down and submit to a man with a club in his hand; but this wisdom now left him. The mere sight of Beauty Smith was sufficient to send him into transports of fury. And when they came to close quarters, and he had been beaten back by the club, he went on growling and snarling and showing his fangs. The last growl could never be extracted from him. No matter how terribly he was beaten, he had always another growl; and when Beauty Smith gave up and withdrew, the defiant growl followed after him, or White Fang sprang at the bars of the cage bellowing his hatred.

When the steamboat arrived at Dawson, White Fang went ashore. But he still lived a public life, in a cage, surrounded by curious men. He was exhibited as "The Fighting Wolf," and men paid fifty cents in gold dust to see him. He was given no rest. Did he lie down to sleep, he was stirred up by a sharp stick—so that the audience might get its money's worth. In order to make the exhibition interesting, he was kept in a rage most of the time. But worse than all this, was the atmosphere in which he lived. He was regarded as the most fearful of wild beasts, and this was borne in to him through the bars of the cage. Every word, every cautious action, on the part of the men, impressed upon him his own terrible ferocity. It was so much added fuel to the flame of his fierceness. There could be but one result, and that was that his ferocity fed upon itself and increased. It was another instance of the plasticity of his clay, of his capacity for being moulded by the pressure of environment.

In addition to being exhibited, he was a professional fighting animal. At irregular intervals, whenever a fight could be arranged, he was taken out of his cage and led off into the woods a few miles from town. Usually this occured at night, so as to avoid interference from the mounted police of the Territory. After a few hours of waiting, when daylight had come, the audience and the dog with which he was to fight arrived. In this manner it came about that he fought all sizes and breeds of dogs. It was a savage land, the men were savage, and the fights were usually to the death.

Since White Fang continued to fight, it is obvious that it was the other dogs that died. He never knew defeat. His early training, when he fought with Lip-lip and the whole puppy-pack, stood him in good stead. There was the tenacity with which he clung to the earth. No dog could make him lose his footing. This was the favorite trick of the wolf breeds—to rush in upon him, either directly or with an unexpected swerve, in the hope of striking his shoulder and overthrowing him. Mackenzie hounds, Eskimo and Labrador dogs, huskies and Malemutes—all tried it on him, and all failed. He was never known to lose his footing. Men told this to one another, and looked each time to see it happen; but White Fang always disappointed them.

Then there was his lightning quickness. It gave him a tremendous advantage over his antagonists. No matter what their fighting experience, they had never encountered a dog that moved so swiftly as he. Also to be reckoned with, was the immediateness of his attack. The average dog was accustomed to the preliminaries of snarling and bristling and growling, and the average dog was knocked off his feet and finished before he had begun to fight or recovered from his surprise. So often did this happen, that it became the custom to hold White Fang until the other dog went through the preliminaries, was good and ready, and even made the first attack.

But greatest of all the advantages in White Fang's favor, was his experience. He knew more about fighting than did any of the dogs that faced him. He had fought more fights, knew how to meet more tricks and methods, and had more tricks himself, while his own method was scarcely to be improved upon.

As the time went by, he had fewer and fewer fights. Men despaired of matching him with an equal, and Beauty Smith was compelled to pit wolves against him. These were trapped by the Indians for the purpose, and a fight between White Fang and a wolf was always sure to draw a crowd. Once, a full-grown female lynx was secured, and this time White Fang fought for his life. Her quickness matched his; her ferocity equalled his; while he fought with his fangs alone, and she fought with her sharp-clawed feet as well.

But after the lynx, all fighting ceased for White Fang. There were no more animals with which to fight—at least, there was none considered worthy of fighting with him. So he remained on exhibition until spring, when one Tim Keenan, a faro-dealer, arrived in the land. With him came the first bulldog that had ever entered the Klondike. That this dog and White Fang should come together was inevitable, and for a week the anticipated fight was the mainspring of conversation in certain quarters of the town.

IV

The Clinging Death

BEAUTY Smith slipped the chain from his neck and stepped back.

For once White Fang did not make an immediate attack. He stood still, ears pricked forward, alert and curious, surveying the strange animal that faced him. He had never seen such a dog before. Tim Keenan shoved the bulldog forward with a muttered "Go to it." The animal waddled toward the centre of the circle, short and squat and ungainly. He came to a stop and blinked across at White Fang.

There were cries from the crowd of "Go to him, Cherokee!" "Sick 'm, Cherokee!" "Eat 'm up!"

But Cherokee did not seem anxious to fight. He turned his head and blinked at the men who shouted, at the same time wagging his stump of a tail good-naturedly. He was not afraid, but merely lazy. Besides, it did not seem to him that it was intended he should fight with the dog he saw before him. He was not used to fighting with that kind of dog, and he was waiting for them to bring on the real dog.

Tim Keenan stepped in and bent over Cherokee, fondling him on both sides of the shoulders with hands that rubbed against the grain of the hair and that made slight, pushing-forward movements. These were so many suggestions. Also, their effect was irritating, for Cherokee began to growl, very softly, deep down in his throat. There was a correspondence in rhythm between the growls and the movements of the man's hands. The growl rose in the throat with the culmination of each forward-pushing movement, and ebbed down to start up afresh with the beginning of the next movement. The end of each movement was the accent of the rhythm, the movement ending abruptly and the growling rising with a jerk.

This was not without its effect on White Fang. The hair began to rise on his neck and across the shoulders. Tim Keenan gave a final shove forward and stepped back again. As the impetus that carried Cherokee forward died down, he continued to go forward of his own volition, in a swift, bow-legged run. Then White Fang struck. A cry of startled admiration went up. He had covered the distance and gone in more like a cat than a dog; and with the same cat-like swiftness he had slashed with his fangs and leaped clear.

The bulldog was bleeding back of one ear from a rip in his thick neck. He gave no sign, did not even snarl, but turned and followed after White Fang. The display on both sides, the quickness of the one and the steadiness of the other, had excited the partisan spirit of the crowd, and the men were making new bets and increasing original bets. Again, and yet again, White Fang sprang in, slashed, and got away untouched; and still his strange foe followed after him, without too great haste, not slowly, but deliberately and determinedly, in a businesslike sort of way. There was purpose in his method—something for him to do that he was intent upon doing and from which nothing could distract him.

His whole demeanor, every action, was stamped with this purpose. It puzzled White Fang. Never had he seen such a dog. It had no hair protection. It was soft, and bled easily. There was no thick mat of fur to baffle White Fang's teeth, as they were often baffled by dogs of his own breed. Each time that his teeth struck they sank easily into the yielding flesh, while the animal did not seem able to defend itself. Another disconcerting thing was that it made no outcry, such as he had been accustomed to with the other dogs he had fought. Beyond a growl or a grunt, the dog took its punishment silently. And never did it flag in its pursuit of him.

Not that Cherokee was slow. He could turn and whirl swiftly enough, but White Fang was never there. Cherokee was puzzled, too. He had never fought before with a dog with which he could not close. The desire to close had always been mutual. But here was a dog that kept at a distance, dancing and dodging here and there and all about. And when it did get its teeth into him, it did not hold on but let go instantly and darted away again.

But White Fang could not get at the soft underside of the throat. The bulldog stood too short, while its massive jaws were an added protection. White Fang darted in and out unscathed, while Cherokee's wounds increased. Both sides of his neck and head were ripped and slashed. He bled freely, but showed no signs of being disconcerted. He continued his plodding pursuit, though once, for the moment baffled, he came to a full stop and blinked at the men who looked on, at the same time wagging his stump of a tail as an expression of his willingness to fight.

In that moment White Fang was in upon him and out, in passing ripping his trimmed remnant of an ear. With a slight manifestation of anger, Cherokee took up the pursuit again, running on the inside of the circle White Fang was making, and striving to fasten his deadly grip on White Fang's throat. The bulldog missed by a hair's-breadth, and cries of praise went up as White Fang doubled suddenly out of danger in the opposite direction.

The time went by. White Fang still danced on, dodging and doubling, leaping in and out, and ever inflicting damage. And still the bulldog, with grim certitude, toiled after him. Sooner or later he would accomplish his purpose, get the grip that would win the battle. In the meantime he accepted all the punishment the other could deal him. His tufts of ears had become tassels, his neck and shoulders were slashed in a score of places, and his very lips were cut and bleeding—all from those lightning snaps that were beyond his foreseeing and guarding.

Time and again White Fang had attempted to knock Cherokee off his feet; but the difference in their height was too great. Cherokee was too squat, too close to the ground. White Fang tried the trick once too often. The chance came in one of his quick doublings and counter-circlings. He caught Cherokee with head turned away as he whirled more slowly. His shoulder was exposed. White Fang drove in upon it; but his own shoulder was high above, while he struck with such force that his momentum carried him on across over the other's body. For the first time in his fighting history, men saw White Fang lose his footing. His body turned a half-somersault in the air, and he would have landed on his back had he not twisted, catlike, still in the air, in the effort to bring his feet to the earth. As it was, he struck heavily on his side. The next instant he was on his feet, but in that instant Cherokee's teeth closed on his throat.

It was not a good grip, being too low down toward the chest; but Cherokee held on. White Fang sprang to his feet and tore wildly around, trying to shake off the bulldog's body. It made him frantic, this clinging, dragging weight. It bound his movements, restricted his freedom. It was like the trap, and all his instinct resented it and revolted against it. It was a mad revolt. For several minutes he was to all intents insane. The basic life that was in him took charge of him. The will to exist of his body surged over him. He was dominated by this mere flesh-love of life. All intelligence was gone. It was as though he had no brain. His reason was unseated by the blind yearning of the flesh to exist and move, at all hazards to move, to continue to move, for movement was the expression of its existence.

Round and round he went, whirling and turning and reversing, trying to shake off the fifty-pound weight that dragged at his throat. The bulldog did little but keep his grip. Sometimes, and rarely, he managed to get his feet to the earth and for a moment to brace himself against White Fang. But the next moment his footing would be lost and he would be dragging around in the whirl of one of White Fang's mad gyrations. Cherokee identified himself with his instinct. He knew that he was doing the right thing by holding on, and there came to him certain blissful thrills of satisfaction. At such moments he even closed his eyes and allowed his body to be hurled hither and thither, willy-nilly, careless of any hurt that might thereby come to it. That did not count. The grip was the thing, and the grip he kept.

White Fang ceased only when he had tired himself out. He could do nothing, and he could not understand. Never, in all his fighting, had this thing happened. The dogs he had fought with did not fight that way. With them it was snap and slash and get away, snap and slash and get away. He lay partly on his side, panting for breath. Cherokee, still holding his grip, urged against him, trying to get him over entirely on his side. White Fang resisted, and he could feel the jaws shifting their grip, slightly relaxing and coming together again in a chewing movement. Each shift brought the grip closer in to his throat. The bulldog's method was to hold what he had, and when opportunity favored to work in for more. Opportunity favored when White Fang remained quiet. When White Fang struggled, Cherokee was content merely to hold on.

The bulging back of Cherokee's neck was the only portion of his body that White Fang's teeth could reach. He got hold toward the base where the neck comes out from the shoulders; but he did not know the chewing method of fighting, nor were his jaws adapted to it. He spasmodically ripped and tore with his fangs for a space. Then a change in their position diverted him. The bulldog had managed to roll him over on his back, and still hanging on to his throat, was on top of him. Like a cat, White Fang bowed his hind-quarters in, and, with the feet digging into his enemy's abdomen above him, he began to claw with long, tearing strokes. Cherokee might well have been disembowelled had he not quickly pivoted on his grip and got his body off of White Fang's and at right angles to it.

There was no escaping that grip. It was like Fate itself, and as inexorable. Slowly it shifted up along the jugular. All that saved White Fang from death was the loose skin of his neck and the thick fur that covered it. This served to form a large roll in Cherokee's mouth, the fur of which well-nigh defied his teeth. But bit by bit, whenever the chance offered, he was getting more of the loose skin and fur in his mouth. The result was that he was slowly throttling White Fang. The latter's breath was drawn with greater and greater difficulty as the moments went by.

It began to look as though the battle were over. The backers of Cherokee waxed jubilant and offered ridiculous odds. White Fang's backers were correspondingly depressed, and refused bets of ten to one and twenty to one, though one man was rash enough to close a wager of fifty to one. This man was Beauty Smith. He took a step into the ring and pointed his finger at White Fang. Then he began to laugh derisively and scornfully. This produced the desired effect. White Fang went wild with rage. He called up his reserves of strength and gained his feet. As he struggled around the ring, the fifty pounds of his foe ever dragging on his throat, his anger passed on into panic. The basic life of him dominated him again, and his intelligence fled before the will of his flesh to live. Round and round and back again, stumbling and falling and rising, even uprearing at times on his hind-legs and lifting his foe clear of the earth, he struggled vainly to shake off the clinging death.

At last he fell, toppling backward, exhausted; and the bulldog promptly shifted his grip, getting in closer, mangling more and more of the fur-folded flesh, throttling White Fang more severely than ever. Shouts of applause went up for the victor, and there were many cries of "Cherokee!" "Cherokee!" To this Cherokee responded by vigorous wagging of the stump of his tail. But the clamor of approval did not distract him. There was no sympathetic relation between his tail and his massive jaws. The one might wag, but the others held their terrible grip on White Fang's throat.

It was at this time that a diversion came to the spectators. There was a jingle of bells. Dog-musher's cries were heard. Everybody, save Beauty Smith, looked apprehensively, the fear of the police strong upon them. But they saw, up the trail, and not down, two men running with sled and dogs. They were evidently coming down the creek from some prospecting trip. At sight of the crowd they stopped their dogs and came over and joined it, curious to see the cause of the excitement. The dog-musher wore a mustache, but the other, a taller and younger man, was smooth-shaven, his skin rosy from the pounding of his blood and the running in the frosty air.

White Fang had practically ceased struggling. Now and again he resisted spasmodically and to no purpose. He could get little air, and that little grew less and less under the merciless grip that ever tightened. In spite of his armor of fur, the great vein of his throat would have long since been torn open, had not the first grip of the bulldog been so low down as to be practically on the chest. It had taken Cherokee a long time to shift that grip upward, and this had also tended further to clog his jaws with fur and skin-fold.

In the meantime, the abysmal brute in Beauty Smith had been rising up into his brain and mastering the small bit of sanity that he possessed at best. When he saw White Fang's eyes beginning to glaze, he knew beyond doubt that the fight was lost. Then he broke loose. He sprang upon White Fang and began savagely to kick him. There were hisses from the crowd and cries of protest, but that was all. While this went on, and Beauty Smith continued to kick White Fang, there was a commotion in the crowd. The tall young newcomer was forcing his way through, shouldering men right and left without ceremony or gentleness. When he broke through into the ring, Beauty Smith was just in the act of delivering another kick. All his weight was on one foot, and he was in a state of unstable equilibrium. At that moment the newcomer's fist landed a smashing blow full in his face. Beauty Smith's remaining leg left the ground, and his whole body seemed to lift into the air as he turned over backward and struck the snow. The newcomer turned upon the crowd.

"You cowards!" he cried. "You beasts!"

He was in a rage himself—a sane rage. His gray eyes seemed metallic and steel-like as they flashed upon the crowd. Beauty Smith regained his feet and came toward him, sniffling and cowardly. The newcomer did not understand. He did not know how abject a coward the other was, and thought he was coming back intent on fighting. So, with a "You beast!" he smashed Beauty Smith over backward with a second blow in the face. Beauty Smith decided that the snow was the safest place for him, and lay where he had fallen, making no effort to get up.

"Come on, Matt, lend a hand," the newcomer called to the dog-musher, who had followed him into the ring.

Both men bent over the dogs. Matt took hold of White Fang, ready to pull when Cherokee's jaws should be loosened. This the younger man endeavored to accomplish by clutching the bulldog's jaws in his hands and trying to spread them. It was a vain undertaking. As he pulled and tugged and wrenched, he kept exclaiming with every expulsion of breath, "Beasts!"

The crowd began to grow unruly, and some of the men were protesting against the spoiling of the sport; but they were silenced when the newcomer lifted his head from his work for a moment and glared at them.

"You damn beasts!" he finally exploded, and went back to his task.

"It's no use, Mr. Scott, you can't break 'm apart that way," Matt said at last.

The pair paused and surveyed the locked dogs.

"Ain't bleedin' much," Matt announced. "Ain't got all the way in yet."

"But he's liable to any moment," Scott answered. "There, did you see that! He shifted his grip in a bit."

The younger man's excitement and apprehension for White Fang was growing. He struck Cherokee about the head savagely again and again. But that did not loosen the jaws. Cherokee wagged the stump of his tail in advertisement that he understood the meaning of the blows, but that he knew he was himself in the right and only doing his duty by keeping his grip.

"Won't some of you help?" Scott cried desperately at the crowd.

But no help was offered. Instead, the crowd began sarcastically to cheer him on and showered him with facetious advice.

"You'll have to get a pry," Matt counselled.

The other reached into the holster at his hip, drew his revolver, and tried to thrust its muzzle between the bulldog's jaws. He shoved, and shoved hard, till the grating of the steel against the locked teeth could be distinctly heard. Both men were on their knees, bending over the dogs. Tim Keenan strode into the ring. He paused beside Scott and touched him on the shoulder, saying ominously:

"Don't break them teeth, stranger."

"Then I'll break his neck," Scott retorted, continuing his shoving and wedging with the revolver muzzle.

"I said don't break them teeth," the faro-dealer repeated more ominously than before.

But if it was a bluff he intended, it did not work. Scott never desisted from his efforts, though he looked up coolly and asked:

"Your dog?"

The faro-dealer grunted.

"Then get in here and break this grip."

"Well, stranger," the other drawled irritatingly, "I don't mind telling you that's something I ain't worked out for myself. I don't know how to turn the trick."

"Then get out of the way," was the reply, "and don't bother me. I'm busy."

Tim Keenan continued standing over him, but Scott took no further notice of his presence. He had managed to get the muzzle in between the jaws on one side, and was trying to get it out between the jaws on the other side. This accomplished, he pried gently and carefully, loosening the jaws a bit at a time, while Matt, a bit at a time, extricated White Fang's mangled neck.

"Stand by to receive your dog," was Scott's peremptory order to Cherokee's owner.

The faro-dealer stooped down obediently and got a firm hold on Cherokee.

"Now!" Scott warned, giving the final pry.

The dogs were drawn apart, the bulldog struggling vigorously.

"Take him away," Scott commanded, and Tim Keenan dragged Cherokee back into the crowd.

White Fang made several ineffectual efforts to get up. Once he gained his feet, but his legs were too weak to sustain him, and he slowly wilted and sank back into the snow. His eyes were half closed, and the surface of them was glassy. His jaws were apart, and through them the tongue protruded, draggled and limp. To all appearances he looked like a dog that had been strangled to death. Matt examined him.

"Just about all in," he announced; "but he's breathin' all right."

Beauty Smith had regained his feet and come over to look at White Fang.

"Matt, how much is a good sled-dog worth?" Scott asked.

The dog-musher, still on his knees and stooped over White Fang, calculated for a moment.

"Three hundred dollars," he answered.

"And how much for one that's all chewed up like this one?" Scott asked, nudging White Fang with his foot.

"Half of that," was the dog-musher's judgment.

Scott turned upon Beauty Smith.

"Did you hear, Mr. Beast? I'm going to take your dog from you, and I'm going to give you a hundred and fifty for him."

He opened his pocket-book and counted out the bills.

Beauty Smith put his hands behind his back, refusing to touch the proffered money.

"I ain't a-sellin'," he said.

"Oh, yes you are," the other assured him. "Because I'm buying. Here's your money. The dog's mine."

Beauty Smith, his hands still behind him, began to back away.

Scott sprang toward him, drawing his fist back to strike. Beauty Smith cowered down in anticipation of the blow.

"I've got my rights," he whimpered.

"You've forfeited your rights to own that dog," was the rejoinder. "Are you going to take the money? or do I have to hit you again?"

"All right," Beauty Smith spoke up with the alacrity of fear. "But I take the money under protest," he added. "The dog's a mint. I ain't a-goin' to be robbed. A man's got his rights."

"Correct," Scott answered, passing the money over to him. "A man's got his rights. But you're not a man. You're a beast."

"Wait till I get back to Dawson," Beauty Smith threatened. "I'll have the law on you."

"If you open your mouth when you get back to Dawson, I'll have you run out of town. Understand?"

Beauty Smith replied with a grunt.

"Understand?" the other thundered with abrupt fierceness.

"Yes," Beauty Smith grunted, shrinking away.

"Yes what?"

"Yes, sir," Beauty Smith snarled.

"Look out! He'll bite!" someone shouted, and a guffaw of laughter went up.

Scott turned his back on him, and returned to help the dog-musher, who was working over White Fang.

Some of the men were already departing; others stood in groups, looking on and talking. Tim Keenan joined one of the groups.

"Who's that mug?" he asked.

"Weedon Scott," someone answered.

"And who in hell is Weedon Scott?" the faro-dealer demanded.

"Oh, one of them crack-a-jack minin' cxperts. He's in with all the big bugs. If you want to keep out of trouble, you'll steer clear of him, that's my talk. He's all hunky with the officials. The Gold Commissioner's a special pal of his."

"I thought he must be somebody," was the faro-dealer's comment. "That's why I kept my hands offen him at the start."

V

The Indomitable

"It's hopeless," Weedon Scott confessed.

He sat on the step of his cabin and stared at the dog-musher, who responded with a shrug that was equally hopeless.

Together they looked at White Fang at the end of his stretched chain, bristling, snarling, ferocious, straining to get at the sled-dogs. Having received sundry lessons from Matt, said lessons being imparted by means of a club, the sled-dogs had learned to leave White Fang alone; and even then they were lying down at a distance, apparently oblivious of his existence.

"It's a wolf and there's no taming it," Weedon Scott announced.

"Oh, I don't know about that," Matt objected. "Might be a lot of dog in 'm, for all you can tell. But there's one thing I know sure, an' that there's no gettin' away from."

The dog-musher paused and nodded his head confidentially at Moosehide Mountain.

"Well, don't be a miser with what you know," Scott said sharply, after waiting a suitable length of time. "Spit it out. What is it?"

The dog-musher indicated White Fang with a backward thrust of his thumb.

"Wolf or dog, it's all the same—he's ben tamed a'ready."

"No!"

"I tell you yes, an' broke to harness. Look close there. D'ye see them marks across the chest?"

"You're right, Matt. He was a sled-dog before Beauty Smith got hold of him."

"An' there's not much reason against his bein' a sled-dog again."

"What d'ye think?" Scott queried eagerly. Then the hope died down as he added, shaking his head, "We've had him two weeks now, and if anything, he's wilder than ever at the present moment."

"Give 'm a chance," Matt counselled. "Turn 'm loose for a spell."

The other looked at him incredulously.

"Yes," Matt went on, "I know you've tried to, but you didn't take a club."

"You try it then."

The dog-musher secured a club and went over to the chained animal. White Fang watched the club after the manner of a caged lion watching the whip of its trainer.

"See 'm keep his eye on that club," Matt said. "That's a good sign. He's no fool. Don't dast tackle me so long as I got that club handy. He's not clean crazy, sure."

As the man's hand approached his neck, White Fang bristled and snarled and crouched down. But while he eyed the approaching hand, he at the same time contrived to keep track of the club in the other hand, suspended threateningly above him. Matt unsnapped the chain from the collar and stepped back.

White Fang could scarcely realize that he was free. Many months had gone by since he passed into the possession of Beauty Smith, and in all that period he had never known a moment of freedom except at the times he had been loosed to fight with other dogs. Immediately after such fights he had always been imprisoned again.

He did not know what to make of it. Perhaps some new deviltry of the gods was about to be perpetrated on him. He walked slowly and cautiously, prepared to be assailed at any moment. He did not know what to do, it was all so unprecedented. He took the precaution to sheer off from the two watching gods, and walked carefully to the corner of the cabin. Nothing happened. He was plainly perplexed, and he came back again, pausing a dozen feet away and regarding the two men intently.

"Won't he run away?" his new owner asked.

Matt shrugged his shoulders. "Got to take a gamble. Only way to find out is to find out."

"Poor devil," Scott murmured pityingly. "What he needs is some show of human kindness," he added, turning and going into the cabin.

He came out with a piece of meat, which he tossed to White Fang. He sprang away from it, and from a distance studied it suspiciously.

"Hi-yu, Major!" Matt shouted warningly, but too late.

Major had made a spring for the meat. At the instant his jaws closed on it, White Fang struck him. He was overthrown. Matt rushed in, but quicker than he was White Fang. Major staggered to his feet, but the blood spouting from his throat reddened the snow in a widening path.

"It's too bad, but it served him right," Scott said hastily.

But Matt's foot had already started on its way to kick White Fang. There was a leap, a flash of teeth, a sharp exclamation. White Fang, snarling fiercely, scrambled backward for several yards, while Matt stooped and investigated his leg.

"He got me all right," he announced, pointing to the torn trousers and undercloths, and the growing stain of red.

"I told you it was hopeless, Matt," Scott said in a discouraged voice. "I've thought about it off and on, while not wanting to think of it. But we've come to it now. It's the only thing to do."

As he talked, with reluctant movements he drew his revolver, threw open the cylinder, and assured himself of its contents.

"Look here, Mr. Scott," Matt objected; "that dog's ben through hell. You can't expect 'm to come out a white an' shinin' angel. Give 'm time."

"Look at Major," the other rejoined.

The dog-musher surveyed the stricken dog. He had sunk down on the snow in the circle of his blood, and was plainly in the last gasp.

"Served 'm right. You said so yourself, Mr. Scott. He tried to take White Fang's meat, an' he's dead-O. That was to be expected. I wouldn't give two whoops in hell for a dog that wouldn't fight for his own meat."

"But look at yourself, Matt. It's all right about the dogs, but we must draw the line somewhere."

"Served me right," Matt argued stubbornly. "What'd I want to kick 'm for? You said yourself he'd done right. Then I had no right to kick 'm."

"It would be a mercy to kill him," Scott insisted. "He's untamable."

"Now look here, Mr. Scott, give the poor devil a fightin' chance. He ain't had no chance yet. He's just come through hell, an' this is the first time he's ben loose. Give 'm a fair chance, an' if he don't deliver the goods, I'll kill 'm myself. There!"

"God knows I don't want to kill him or have him killed," Scott answered, putting away the revolver. "We'll let him run loose and see what kindness can do for him. And here's a try at it."

He walked over to White Fang and began talking to him gently and soothingly.

"Better have a club handy," Matt warned.

Scott shook his head and went on trying to win White Fang's confidence.

White Fang was suspicious. Something was impending. He had killed this god's dog, bitten his companion god, and what else was to be expected than some terrible punishment? But in the face of it he was indomitable. He bristled and showed his teeth, his eyes vigilant, his whole body wary and prepared for anything. The god had no club, so he suffered him to approach quite near. The god's hand had come out and was descending upon his head. White Fang shrank together and grew tense as he crouched under it. Here was danger, some treachery or something. He knew the hands of the gods, their proved mastery, their cunning to hurt. Besides, there was his old antipathy to being touched. He snarled more menacingly, crouched still lower, and still the hand descended. He did not want to bite the hand, and he endured the peril of it until his instinct surged up in him, mastering him with its insatiable yearning for life.

Weedon Scott had believed that he was quick enough to avoid any snap or slash. But he had yet to learn the remarkable quickness of White Fang, who struck with the certainty and swiftness of a coiled snake.

Scott cried out sharply with surprise, catching his torn hand and holding it tightly in his other hand. Matt uttered a great oath and sprang to his side. White Fang crouched down and backed away, bristling, showing his fangs, his eyes malignant with menace. Now he could expect a beating as fearful as any he had received from Beauty Smith.

"Here! What are you doing?" Scott cried suddenly.

Matt had dashed into the cabin and come out with a rifle.

"Nothin'," he said slowly, with a careless calmness that was assumed; "only goin' to keep that promise I made. I reckon it's up to me to kill 'm as I said I'd do."

"No you don't!"

"Yes, I do. Watch me."

As Matt had pleaded for White Fang when he had been bitten, it was now Weedon Scott's turn to plead.

"You said to give him a chance. Well, give it to him. We've only just started, and we can't quit at the beginning. It served me right, this time. And—look at him!"

White Fang, near the corner of the cabin and forty feet away, was snarling with blood-curdling viciousness, not at Scott, but at the dog-musher.

"Well, I'll be everlastin'ly gosh-swoggled!" was the dog-musher's expression of astonishment.

"Look at the intelligence of him," Scott went on hastily. "He knows the meaning of firearms as well as you do. He's got intelligence, and we've got to give that intelligence a chance. Put up the gun."

"All right, I'm willin'," Matt agreed, leaning the rifle against the woodpile.

"But will you look at that!" he exclaimed the next moment.

White Fang had quieted down and ceased snarling.

"This is worth investigatin'. Watch."

Matt reached for the rifle, and at the same moment White Fang snarled. He stepped away from the rifle, and White Fang's lifted lips descended, covering his teeth.

"Now, just for fun."

Matt took the rifle and began slowly to raise it to his shoulder. White Fang's snarling began with the movement, and increased as the movement approached its culmination. But the moment before the rifle came to a level on him, he leaped sidewise behind the corner of the cabin. Matt stood staring along the sights at the empty space of snow which had been occupied by White Fang.

The dog-musher put the rifle down solemnly, then turned and looked at his employer.

"I agree with you, Mr. Scott. That dog's too intelligent to kill."

VI

The Love-Master

As White Fang watched Weedon Scott approach, he bristled and snarled to advertise that he would not submit to punishment. Twenty-four hours had passed since he had slashed open the hand that was now bandaged and held up by a sling to keep the blood out of it. In the past White Fang had experienced delayed punishments, and he apprehended that such a one was about to befall him. How could it be otherwise? He had committed what was to him sacrilege, sunk his fangs into the holy flesh of a god, and of a white-skinned superior god at that. In the nature of things, and of intercourse with gods, something terrible awaited him.

The god sat down several feet away. White Fang could see nothing dangerous in that. When the gods administered punishment they stood on their legs. Besides, this god had no club, no whip, no firearm. And furthermore, he himself was free. No chain nor stick bound him. He could escape into safety while the god was scrambling to his feet. In the meantime he would wait and see.

The god remained quiet, made no movement; and White Fang's snarl slowly dwindled to a growl that ebbed down in his throat and ceased. Then the god spoke, and at the first sound of his voice, the hair rose on White Fang's neck and the growl rushed up in his throat. But the god made no hostile movement, and went on calmly talking. For a time White Fang growled in unison with him, a correspondence of rhythm being established between growl and voice. But the god talked on interminably. He talked to White Fang as White Fang had never been talked to before. He talked softly and soothingly, with a gentleness that somehow, somewhere, touched White Fang. In spite of himself and all the pricking warnings of his instinct, White Fang began to have confidence in this god. He had a feeling of security that was belied by all his experience with men.

After a long time, the god got up and went into the cabin. White Fang scanned him apprehensively when he came out. He had neither whip nor club nor weapon. Nor was his uninjured hand behind his back hiding something. He sat down as before, in the same spot, several feet away. He held out a small piece of meat. White Fang pricked his ears and investigated it suspiciously, managing to look at the same time both at the meat and the god, alert for any overt act, his body tense and ready to spring away at the first sign of hostility.

Still the punishment delayed. The god merely held near to his nose a piece of meat. And about the meat there seemed nothing wrong. Still White Fang suspected; and though the meat was proffered to him with short inviting thrusts of the hand, he refused to touch it. The gods were all-wise, and there was no telling what masterful treachery lurked behind that apparently harmless piece of meat. In past experience, especially in dealing with squaws, meat and punishment had often been disastrously related.

In the end, the god tossed the meat on the snow at White Fang's feet. He smelled the meat carefully; but he did not look at it. While he smelled it he kept his eyes on the god. Nothing happened. He took the meat into his mouth and swallowed it. Still nothing happened. The god was actually offering him another piece of meat. Again he refused to take it from the hand, and again it was tossed to him. This was repeated a number of times. But there came a time when the god refused to toss it. He kept it in his hand and steadfastly proffered it.

The meat was good meat, and White Fang was hungry. Bit by bit, infinitely cautious, he approached the hand. At last the time came that he decided to eat the meat from the hand. He never took his eyes from the god, thrusting his head forward with ears flattened back and hair involuntarily rising and cresting on his neck. Also a low growl rumbled in his throat as warning that he was not to be trifled with. He ate the meat, and nothing happened. Piece by piece, he ate all the meat, and nothing happened. Still the punishment delayed.

He licked his chops and waited. The god went on talking. In his voice was kindness —something of which White Fang had no experience whatever. And within him it aroused feelings which he had likewise never experienced before. He was aware of a certain strange satisfaction, as though some need were being gratified, as though some void in his being were being filled. Then again came the prod of his instinct and the warning of past experience. The gods were ever crafty, and they had unguessed ways of attaining their ends.

Ah, he had thought so! There it came now, the god's hand, cunning to hurt, thrusting out at him, descending upon his head. But the god went on talking. His voice was soft and soothing. In spite of the menacing hand, the voice inspired confidence. And in spite of the assuring voice, the hand inspired distrust. White Fang was torn by conflicting feelings, impulses. It seemed he would fly to pieces, so terrible was the control he was exerting, holding together by an unwonted indecision the counter-forces that struggled within him for mastery.

He compromised. He snarled and bristled and flattened his ears. But he neither snapped nor sprang away. The hand descended. Nearer and nearer it came. It touched the ends of his upstanding hair. He shrank down under it. It followed down after him, pressing more closely against him. Shrinking, almost shivering, he still managed to hold himself together. It was a torment, this hand that touched him and violated his instinct. He could not forget in a day all the evil that had been wrought him at the hands of men. But it was the will of the god, and he strove to submit.

The hand lifted and descended again in a patting, caressing movement. This continued, but every time the hand lifted, the hair lifted under it. And every time the hand descended, the ears flattened down and a cavernous growl surged in his throat. White Fang growled and growled with insistent warning. By this means he announced that he was prepared to retaliate for any hurt he might receive. There was no telling when the god's ulterior motive might be disclosed. At any moment that soft, confidence-inspiring voice might break forth in a roar of wrath, that gentle and caressing hand transform itself into a viselike grip to hold him helpless and administer punishment.

But the god talked on softly, and ever the hand rose and fell with non-hostile pats. White Fang experienced dual feelings. It was distasteful to his instinct. It restrained him, opposed the will of him toward personal liberty. And yet it was not physically painful. On the contrary, it was even pleasant, in a physical way. The patting movement slowly and carefully changed to a rubbing of the ears about their bases, and the physical pleasure even increased a little. Yet he continued to fear, and he stood on guard, expectant of unguessed evil, alternately suffering and enjoying as one feeling or the other came uppermost and swayed him.

"Well, I'll be gosh-swoggled!"

So spoke Matt, coming out of the cabin, his sleeves rolled up, a pan of dirty dishwater in his hands, arrested in the act of emptying the pan by the sight of Weedon Scott patting White Fang.

At the instant his voice broke the silence, White Fang leaped back, snarling savagely at him.

Matt regarded his employer with grieved disapproval.

"If you don't mind my expressin' my feelin's, Mr. Scott, I'll make free to say you're seventeen kinds of a damn fool an' all of 'em different, and then some."

Weedon Scott smiled with a superior air, gained his feet, and walked over to White Fang. He talked soothingly to him, but not for long, then slowly put out his hand, rested it on White Fang's head, and resumed the interrupted patting. White Fang endured it, keeping his eyes fixed suspiciously, not upon the man that petted him, but upon the man that stood in the doorway.

"You may be a number one, tip-top minin' expert, all right all right," the dog-musher delivered himself oracularly, "but you missed the chance of your life when you was a boy an' didn't join a circus."

White Fang snarled at the sound of his voice, but this time did not leap away from under the hand that was caressing his head and the back of his neck with long, soothing strokes.

It was the beginning of the end for White Fang—the ending of the old life and the reign of hate. A new and incomprehensibly fairer life was dawning. It required much thinking and endless patience on the part of Weedon Scott to accomplish this. And on the part of White Fang it required nothing less than a revolution. He had to ignore the urges and promptings of instinct and reason, defy experience, give the lie to life itself.

Life, as he had known it, not only had had no place in it for much that he now did; but all the currents had gone counter to those to which he now abandoned himself. In short, when all things were considered, he had to achieve an orientation far vaster than the one he had achieved at the time he came voluntarily in from the Wild and accepted Gray Beaver as his lord. At that time he was a mere puppy, soft from the making, without form, ready for the thumb of circumstance to begin its work upon him. But now it was different. The thumb of circumstance had done its work only too well. By it he had been formed and hardened into the Fighting Wolf, fierce and implacable, unloving and unlovable. To accomplish the change was like a reflux of being, and this when the plasticity of youth was no longer his; when the fibre of him had become tough and knotty; when the warp and the woof of him had made of him an adamantine texture, harsh and unyielding; when the face of his spirit had become iron and all his instincts and axioms had crystallized into set rules, cautions, dislikes, and desires.

Yet again, in his new orientation, it was the thumb of circumstance that pressed and prodded him, softening that which had become hard and remoulding it into fairer form. Weedon Scott was in truth this thumb. He had gone to the roots of White Fang's nature, and with kindness touched to life potencies that had languished and well-nigh perished. One such potency was *love.* It took the place of *like,* which latter had been the highest feeling that thrilled him in his intercourse with the gods.

But this love did not come in a day. It began with *like* and out of it slowly developed. White Fang did not run away, though he was allowed to remain loose, because he liked this new god. This was certainly better than the life he had lived in the cage of Beauty Smith, and it was necessary that he should have some god. The lordship of man was a need of his nature. The seal of his dependence on man had been set upon him in that early day when he turned his back on the Wild and crawled to Gray Beaver's feet to receive the expected beating. This seal had been stamped upon him again, and ineradicably, on his second return from the Wild, when the long famine was over and there was fish once more in the village of Gray Beaver.

And so, because he needed a god and because he preferred Weedon Scott to Beauty Smith, White Fang remained. In acknowledgment of fealty, he proceeded to take upon himself the guardianship of his master's property. He prowled about the cabin while the sled-dogs slept, and the first night-visitor to the cabin fought him off with a club until Weedon Scott came to the rescue. But White Fang soon learned to differentiate between thieves and honest men, to appraise the true value of step and carriage. The man who travelled, loud-stepping, the direct line to the cabin door, he let alone—though he watched him vigilantly until the door opened and he received the indorsement of the master. But the man who went softly, by circuitous ways, peering with caution, seeking after secrecy—that was the man who received no suspension of judgment from White Fang, and who went away abruptly, hurriedly, and without dignity.

Weedon Scott had set himself the task of redeeming White Fang—or rather, of redeeming mankind from the wrong it had done White Fang. It was a matter of principle and conscience. He felt that the ill done White Fang was a debt incurred by man and that it must be paid. So he went out of his way to be especially kind to the Fighting Wolf. Each day he made it a point to caress and pet White Fang, and to do it at length.

At first suspicious and hostile, White Fang grew to like this petting. But there was one thing that he never outgrew—his growling. Growl he would, from the moment the petting began until it ended. But it was a growl with a new note in it. A stranger could not hear this note, and to such a stranger the growling of White Fang was an exhibition of primordial savagery, nerve-racking and blood-curdling. But White Fang's throat had become harsh-fibred from the making of ferocious sounds through the many years since his first little rasp of anger in the lair of his cubhood, and he could not soften the sounds of that throat now to express the gentleness he felt. Nevertheless, Weedon Scott's ear and sympathy were fine enough to catch the new note all but drowned in the fierceness—the note that was the faintest hint of a croon of content and that none but he could hear.

As the days went by, the evolution of *like* into *love* was accelerated. White Fang himself began to grow aware of it, though in his consciousness he knew not what love was. It manifested itself to him as a void in his being—a hungry, aching, yearning void that clamored to be filled. It was a pain and an unrest; and it received easement only by the touch of the new god's presence. At such times love was a joy to him, a wild, keen-thrilling satisfaction. But when away from his god, the pain and the unrest returned; the void in him sprang up and pressed against him with its emptiness, and the hunger gnawed and gnawed unceasingly.

White Fang was in the process of finding himself. In spite of the maturity of his years and of the savage rigidity of the mould that had formed him, his nature was undergoing an expansion. There was a burgeoning within him of strange feelings and unwonted impulses. His old code of conduct was changing. In the past he had liked comfort and surcease from pain, disliked discomfort and pain, and he had adjusted his actions accordingly. But now it was different. Because of this new feeling within him, he ofttimes elected discomfort and pain for the sake of his god. Thus, in the early morning, instead of roaming and foraging, or lying in a sheltered nook, he would wait for hours on the cheerless cabin-stoop for a sight of the god's face. At night, when the god returned home, White Fang would leave the warm sleeping-place he had burrowed in the snow in order to receive the friendly snap of fingers and the word of greeting. Meat, even meat itself, he would forego to be with his god, to receive a caress from him or to accompany him down into the town.

Like had been replaced by *love.* And love was the plummet dropped down into the deeps of him where like had never gone. And responsive, out of his deeps had come the new thing—love. That which was given unto him did he return. This was a god indeed, a love-god, a warm and radiant god, in whose light White Fang's nature expanded as a flower expands under the sun.

But White Fang was not demonstrative. He was too old, too firmly moulded, to become adept at expressing himself in new ways. He was too self-possessed, too strongly poised in his own isolation. Too long had he cultivated reticence, aloofness, and moroseness. He had never barked in his life, and he could not now learn to bark a welcome when his god approached. He was never in the way, never extravagant nor foolish in the expression of his love. He never ran to meet his god. He waited at a distance; but he always waited, was always there. His love partook of the nature of worship, dumb, inarticulate, a silent adoration. Only by the steady regard of his eyes did he express his love, and by the unceasing following with his eyes of his god's every movement. Also, at times, when his god looked at him and spoke to him, he betrayed an awkward self-consciousness, caused by the struggle of his love to express itself and his physical inability to express it.

He learned to adjust himself in many ways to his new mode of life. It was borne in upon him that he must let his master's dogs alone. Yet his dominant nature asserted itself, and he had first to thrash them into an acknowledgment of his superiority and leadership. This accomplished, he had little trouble with them. They gave trail to him when he came and went or walked among them, and when he asserted his will they obeyed.

In the same way, he came to tolerate Matt—as a possession of his master. His master rarely fed him. Matt did that, it was his business; yet White Fang divined that it was his master's food he ate and that it was his master who thus fed him vicariously. Matt it was who tried to put him into the harness and make him haul sled with the other dogs. But Matt failed. It was not until Weedon Scott put the harness on White Fang and worked him, that he understood. He took it as his master's will that Matt should drive him and work him just as he drove and worked his master's other dogs.

Different from the Mackenzie toboggans were the Klondike sleds with runners under them. And different was the method of driving the dogs. There was no fan-formation of the team. The dogs worked in single file, one behind another, hauling on double traces. And here, in the Klondike, the leader was indeed the leader. The wisest as well as strongest dog was the leader, and the team obeyed him and feared him. That White Fang should quickly gain this post was inevitable. He could not be satisfied with less, as Matt learned after much inconvenience and trouble. White Fang picked out the post for himself, and Matt backed his judgment with strong language after the experiment had been tried. But, though he worked in the sled in the day, White Fang did not forego the guarding of his master's property in the night. Thus he was on duty all the time, ever vigilant and faithful, the most valuable of all the dogs.

"Makin' free to spit out what's in me," Matt said, one day, "I beg to state that you was a wise guy all right when you paid the price you did for that dog. You clean swindled Beauty Smith on top of pushin' his face in with your fist."

A recrudescence of anger glinted in Weedon Scott's gray eyes, and he muttered savagely, "The beast!"

In the late spring a great trouble came to White Fang. Without warning, the love-master disappeared. There had been warning, but White Fang was unversed in such things and did not understand the packing of a grip. He remembered afterward that this packing had preceeded the master's disappearance; but at the time he suspected nothing. That night he waited for the master to return. At midnight the chill wind that blew drove him to shelter at the rear of the cabin. There he drowsed, only half asleep, his ears keyed for the first sound of the familiar step. But, at two in the morning, his anxiety drove him out to the cold front stoop, where he crouched and waited.

But no master came. In the morning the door opened and Matt stepped outside. White Fang gazed at him wistfully. There was no common speech by which he might learn what he wanted to know. The days came and went, but never the master. White Fang, who had never known sickness in his life, became sick. He became very sick, so sick that Matt was finally compelled to bring him inside the cabin. Also, in writing to his employer, Matt devoted a postscript to White Fang.

Weedon Scott reading the letter down in Circle City, came upon the following:

"That damn wolf wont work. Wont eat. Aint got no spunk left. All the dogs is licking him. Wants to know what has become of you, and I dont know how to tell him. Mebbe he is going to die."

It was as Matt had said. White Fang had ceased eating, lost heart, and allowed every dog of the team to thrash him. In the cabin he lay on the floor near the stove, without interest in food, in Matt, nor in life. Matt might talk gently to him or swear at him, it was all the same; he never did more than turn his dull eyes upon the man, then drop his head back to its customary position on his fore-paws.

And then, one night, Matt, reading to himself with moving lips and mumbled sounds, was startled by a low whine from White Fang. He had got upon his feet, his ears cocked toward the door, and he was listening intently. A moment later, Matt heard a footstep. The door opened, and Weedon Scott stepped in. The two men shook hands. Then Scott looked around the room.

"Where's the wolf?" he asked.

Then he discovered him, standing where he had been lying, near to the stove. He had not rushed forward after the manner of other dogs. He stood, watching and waiting.

"Holy smoke!" Matt exclaimed. "Look at 'm wag his tail!"

Weedon Scott strode half across the room toward him, at the same time calling him. White Fang came to him, not with a great bound, yet quickly. He was awkward from self-consciousness, but as he drew near, his eyes took on a strange expression. Something, an incommunicable vastness of feeling, rose up into his eyes as a light and shone forth.

"He never looked at me that way all the time you was gone," Matt commented.

Weedon Scott did not hear. He was squatting down on his heels, face to face with White Fang and petting him—rubbing at the roots of the ears, making long, caressing strokes down the neck to the shoulders, tapping the spine gently with the balls of his fingers. And White Fang was growling responsively, the crooning note of the growl more pronounced than ever.

But that was not all. What of his joy, the great love in him, ever surging and struggling to express itself, succeeded in finding a new mode of expression. He suddenly thrust his head forward and nudged his way in between the master's arm and body. And here, confined, hidden from view all except his ears, no longer growling, he continued to nudge and snuggle.

The two men looked at each other. Scott's eyes were shining.

"Gosh!" said Matt in an awe-stricken voice.

A moment later, when he had recovered himself, he said, "I always insisted that wolf was a dog. Look at 'm!"

With the return of the love-master, White Fang's recovery was rapid. Two nights and a day he spent in the cabin. Then he sallied forth. The sled-dogs had forgotten his prowess. They remembered only the latest, which was his weakness and sickness. At the sight of him as he came out of the cabin, they sprang upon him.

"Talk about your rough-houses," Matt murmured gleefully, standing in the doorway and looking on. "Give 'm hell, you wolf! Give 'm hell!—and then some!"

White Fang did not need the encouragement. The return of the love-master was enough. Life was flowing through him again, splendid and indomitable. He fought from sheer joy, finding in it an expression of much that he felt and that otherwise was without speech. There could be but one ending. The team dispersed in ignominious defeat, and it was not until after dark that the dogs came sneaking back, one by one, by meekness and humility signifying their fealty to White Fang.

Having learned to snuggle, White Fang was guilty of it often. It was the final word. He could not go beyond it. The one thing of which he had always been particularly jealous, was his head. He had always disliked to have it touched. It was the Wild in him, the fear of hurt and of the trap, that had given rise to the panicky impulses to avoid contacts. It was the mandate of his instinct that that head must be free. And now, with the love-master, his snuggling was the deliberate act of putting himself into a position of hopeless helplessness. It was an expression of perfect confidence, of absolute self-surrender, as though he said: "I will put myself into thy hands. Work thou thy will with me."

One night, not long after the return, Scott and Matt sat at a game of cribbage preliminary to going to bed. "Fifteen-two, fifteen-four an' a pair makes six," Matt was pegging up, when there was an outcry and sound of snarling without. They looked at each other as they started to rise to their feet.

"The wolf's nailed somebody," Matt said.

A wild scream of fear and anguish hastened them.

"Bring a light!" Scott shouted, as he sprang outside.

Matt followed with the lamp, and by its light they saw a man lying on his back in the snow. His arms were folded, one above the other, across his face and throat. Thus he was trying to shield himself from White Fang's teeth. And there was need for it. White Fang was in a rage, wickedly making his attack on the most vulnerable spot. From shoulder to wrist of the crossed arms, the coat-sleeve, blue flannel shirt and undershirt were ripped in rags, while the arms themselves were terribly slashed and streaming blood.

All this the two men saw in the first instant. The next instant Weedon Scott had White Fang by the throat and was dragging him clear. White Fang struggled and snarled, but made no attempt to bite, while he quickly quieted down at a sharp word from the master.

Matt helped the man to his feet. As he arose he lowered his crossed arms, exposing the bestial face of Beauty Smith. The dog-musher let go of him precipitately, with action similar to that of a man who has picked up live fire. Beauty Smith blinked in the lamplight and looked about him. He caught sight of White Fang and terror rushed into his face.

At the same moment Matt noticed two objects lying in the snow. He held the lamp close to them, indicating them with his toe for his employer's benefit—a steel dog-chain and a stout club.

Weedon Scott saw and nodded. Not a word was spoken. The dog-musher laid his hand on Beauty Smith's shoulder and faced him to the right-about. No word needed to be spoken. Beauty Smith started.

In the meantime the love-master was patting White Fang and talking to him.

"Tried to steal you, eh? And you wouldn't have it! Well, well, he made a mistake, didn't he?"

"Must 'a' thought he had hold of seventeen devils," the dog-musher sniggered.

White Fang, still wrought up and bristling, growled and growled, the hair slowly lying down, the crooning note remote and dim, but growing in his throat.

PART FIVE—THE TAME

I

The Long Trail

IT was in the air. White Fang sensed the coming calamity, even before there was tangible evidence of it. In vague ways it was borne in upon him that a change was impending. He knew not how nor why, yet he got his feel of the oncoming event from the gods themselves. In ways subtler than they knew, they betrayed their intentions to the wolf-dog that haunted the cabin-stoop, and that, though he never came inside the cabin, knew what went on inside their brains.

"Listen to that, will you!" the dog-musher exclaimed at supper one night.

Weedon Scott listened. Through the door came a low, anxious whine, like a sobbing under the breath that has just grown audible. Then came the long sniff, as White Fang reassured himself that his god was still inside and had not yet taken himself off in mysterious and solitary flight.

"I do believe that wolf's on to you," the dog-musher said.

Weedon Scott looked across at his companion with eyes that almost pleaded, though this was given the lie by his words.

"What the devil can I do with a wolf in California?" he demanded.

"That's what I say," Matt answered. "What the devil can you do with a wolf in California?"

But this did not satisfy Weedon Scott. The other seemed to be judging him in a non-committal sort of way.

"White-man's dogs would have no show against him," Scott went on. "He'd kill them on sight. If he didn't bankrupt me with damage suits, the authorities would take him away from me and electrocute him."

"He's a downright murderer, I know," was the dog-musher's comment.

Weedon Scott looked at him suspiciously.

"It would never do," he said decisively.

"It would never do," Matt concurred. "Why, you'd have to hire a man 'specially to take care of 'm."

The other's suspicion was allayed. He nodded cheerfully. In the silence that followed, the low, half-sobbing whine was heard at the door and then the long, questing sniff.

"There's no denyin' he thinks a hell of a lot of you," Matt said.

The other glared at him in sudden wrath. "Damn it all, man! I know my own mind and what's best!"

"I'm agreein' with you, only . . ."

"Only what?" Scott snapped out.

"Only . . ." the dog-musher began softly, then changed his mind and betrayed a rising anger of his own. "Well, you needn't get so all-fired het up about it. Judgin' by your actions one'd think you didn't know your own mind."

Weedon Scott debated with himself for a while, and then said more gently: "You are right, Matt. I don't know my own mind, and that's what's the trouble."

"Why, it would be rank ridiculousness for me to take that dog along," he broke out after another pause.

"I'm agreein' with you," was Matt's answer, and again his employer was not quite satisfied with him.

"But how in the name of the great Sardanapalus he knows you're goin' is what gets me," the dog-musher continued innocently.

"It's beyond me, Matt," Scott answered, with a mournful shake of the head.

Then came the day when, through the open cabin door, White Fang saw the fatal grip on the floor and the love-master packing things into it. Also, there were comings and goings, and the erst-while placid atmosphere of the cabin was vexed with strange perturbations and unrest. Here was indubitable evidence. White Fang had already sensed it. He now reasoned it. His god was preparing for another flight. And since he had not taken him with him before, so, now, he could look to be left behind.

That night he lifted the long wolf-howl. As he had howled, in his puppy days, when he fled back from the Wild to the village to find it vanished and naught but a rubbish-heap to mark the site of Gray Beaver's tepee, so now he pointed his muzzle to the cold stars and told to them his woe.

Inside the cabin the two men had just gone to bed.

"He's gone off his food again," Matt remarked from his bunk.

There was a grunt from Weedon Scott's bunk, and a stir of blankets.

"From the way he cut up the other time you went away, I wouldn't wonder this time but what he died."

The blankets in the other bunk stirred irritably.

"Oh, shut up!" Scott cried out through the darkness. "You nag worse than a woman."

"I'm agreein' with you," the dog-musher answered, and Weedon Scott was not quite sure whether or not the other had snickered.

The next day White Fang's anxiety and restlessness were even more pronounced. He dogged his master's heels whenever he left the cabin, and haunted the front stoop when he remained inside. Through the open door he could catch glimpses of the luggage on the floor. The grip had been joined by two large canvas bags and a box. Matt was rolling the master's blankets and fur robe inside a small tarpaulin. White Fang whined as he watched the operation.

Later on, two Indians arrived. He watched them closely as they shouldered the luggage and were led off down the hill by Matt, who carried the bedding and the grip. But White Fang did not follow them. The master was still in the cabin. After a time, Matt returned. The master came to the door and called White Fang inside.

"You poor devil," he said gently, rubbing White Fang's ears and tapping his spine. "I'm hitting the long trail, old man, where you cannot follow. Now give me a growl—the last, good, good-by growl."

But White Fang refused to growl. Instead, and after a wistful, searching look, he snuggled in, burrowing his head out of sight between the master's arm and body.

"There she blows!" Matt cried. From the Yukon arose the hoarse bellowing of a river steamboat. "You've got to cut it short. Be sure and lock the front door. I'll go out the back. Get a move on!"

The two doors slammed at the same moment, and Weedon Scott waited for Matt to come around to the front. From inside the door came a low whining and sobbing. Then there were long, deep-drawn sniffs.

"You must take good care of him, Matt," Scott said, as they started down the hill. "Write and let me know how he gets along."

"Sure," the dog-musher answered. "But listen to that, will you!"

Both men stopped. White Fang was howling as dogs howl when their masters lie dead. He was voicing an utter woe, his cry bursting upward in great, heart-breaking rushes, dying down into quavering misery, and bursting upward again with rush upon rush of grief.

The *Aurora* was the first steamboat of the year for the Outside, and her decks were jammed with prosperous adventurers and broken gold seekers, all equally as mad to get to the Outside as they had been originally to get to the Inside. Near the gang-plank, Scott was shaking hands with Matt, who was preparing to go ashore. But Matt's hand went limp in the other's grasp as his gaze shot past and remained fixed on something behind him. Scott turned to see. Sitting on the deck several feet away and watching wistfully was White Fang.

The dog-musher swore softly, in awe-stricken accents. Scott could only look in wonder.

"Did you lock the front door?" Matt demanded.

The other nodded, and asked, "How about the back?"

"You just bet I did," was the fervent reply.

White Fang flattened his ears ingratiatingly, but remained where he was, making no attempt to approach.

"I'll have to take 'm ashore with me."

Matt made a couple of steps toward White Fang, but the latter slid away from him. The dog-musher made a rush of it, and White Fang dodged between the legs of a group of men. Ducking, turning, doubling, he slid about the deck, eluding the other's efforts to capture him.

But when the love-master spoke, White Fang came to him with prompt obedience.

"Won't come to the hand that's fed 'm all these months," the dog-musher muttered resentfully. "And you—you ain't never fed 'm after them first days of gettin' acquainted. I'm blamed if I can see how he works it out that you're the boss."

Scott, who had been patting White Fang, suddenly bent closer and pointed out fresh-made cuts on his muzzle, and a gash between the eyes.

Matt bent over and passed his hand along White Fang's belly.

"We plumb forgot the window. He's all cut an' gouged underneath. Must 'a' butted clean through it, b'gosh!"

But Weedon Scott was not listening. He was thinking rapidly. The *Aurora's* whistle hooted a final announcement of departure. Men were scurrying down the gang-plank to the shore. Matt loosened the bandana from his own neck and started to put it around White Fang's. Scott grasped the dog-musher's hand.

"Good-by, Matt, old man. About the wolf—you needn't write. You see, I've . . . !"

"What!" the dog-musher exploded. "You don't mean to say . . . ?"

"The very thing I mean. Here's your bandana. *I'll* write to *you* about him."

Matt paused halfway down the gang-plank.

"He'll never stand the climate!" he shouted back. "Unless you clip 'm in warm weather!"

The gang-plank was hauled in, and the *Aurora* swung out from the bank. Weedon Scott waved a last good-by. Then he turned and bent over White Fang, standing by his side.

"Now growl, damn you, growl," he said, as he patted the responsive head and rubbed the flattening ears.

II
The Southland

WHITE Fang landed from the steamer in San Francisco. He was appalled. Deep in him, below any reasoning process or act of consciousness, he had associated power with godhead. And never had the white men seemed such marvellous gods as now, when he trod the slimy pavement of San Francisco. The log cabins he had known were replaced by towering buildings. The streets were crowded with perils—wagons, carts, automobiles; great, straining horses pulling huge trucks; and monstrous cable and electric cars hooting and clanging through the midst, screeching their insistent menace after the manner of the lynxes he had known in the northern woods.

All this was the manifestation of power. Through it all, behind it all, was man, governing and controlling, expressing himself, as of old, by his mastery over matter. It was colossal, stunning. White Fang was awed. Fear sat upon him. As in his cubhood he had been made to feel his smallness and puniness on the day he first came in from the Wild to the village of Gray Beaver, so now, in his full-grown stature and pride of strength, he was made to feel small and puny. And there were so many gods! He was made dizzy by the swarming of them. The thunder of the streets smote upon his ears. He was bewildered by the tremendous and endless rush and movement of things. As never before, he felt his dependence on the love-master, close at whose heels he followed, no matter what happened never losing sight of him.

But White Fang was to have no more than a nightmare vision of the city—an experience that was like a bad dream, unreal and terrible, that haunted him for long after in his dreams. He was put into a baggage-car by the master, chained in a corner in the midst of heaped trunks and valises. Here a squat and brawny god held sway, with much noise, hurling trunks and boxes about, dragging them in through the door and tossing them into the piles, or flinging them out of the door, smashing and crashing, to other gods who awaited them.

And here, in this inferno of luggage, was White Fang deserted by the master. Or at least White Fang thought he was deserted, until he smelled out the master's canvas clothes-bags alongside of him and proceeded to mount guard over them.

" 'Bout time you come," growled the god of the car, an hour later, when Weedon Scott appeared at the door. "That dog of yourn won't let me lay a finger on your stuff."

White Fang emerged from the car. He was astonished. The nightmare city was gone. The car had been to him no more than a room in a house, and when he had entered it the city had been all around him. In the interval the city had disappeared. The roar of it no longer dinned upon his ears. Before him was smiling country, streaming with sunshine, lazy with quietude. But he had little time to marvel at the transformation. He accepted it as he accepted all the unaccountable doings and manifestations of the gods. It was their way.

There was a carriage waiting. A man and a woman approached the master. The woman's arms went out and clutched the master around the neck—a hostile act! The next moment Weedon Scott had torn loose from the embrace and closed with White Fang, who had become a snarling, raging demon.

"It's all right, mother," Scott was saying as he kept tight hold of White Fang and placated him. "He thought you were going to injure me, and he wouldn't stand for it. It's all right. It's all right. He'll learn soon enough."

"And in the meantime I may be permitted to love my son when his dog is not around," she laughed, though she was pale and weak from the fright.

She looked at White Fang, who snarled and bristled and glared malevolently.

"He'll have to learn, and he shall, without postponement," Scott said.

He spoke softly to White Fang until he had quieted him, then his voice became firm. "Down, sir! Down with you!"

This had been one of the things taught him by the master, and White Fang obeyed, though he lay down reluctantly and sullenly.

"Now, mother."

Scott opened his arms to her, but kept his eyes on White Fang.

"Down!" he warned. "Down!"

White Fang, bristling silently, half-crouching as he rose, sank back and watched the hostile act repeated. But no harm came of it, nor of the embrace from the strange man-god that followed. Then the clothes-bags were taken into the carriage, the strange gods and the love-master followed, and White Fang pursued, now running vigilantly behind, now bristling up to the running horses and warning them that he was there to see that no harm befell the god they dragged so swiftly across the earth.

At the end of fifteen minutes, the carriage swung in through a stone gateway and on between a double row of arched and interlacing walnut trees. On either side stretched lawns, their broad sweep broken, here and there, by great, sturdy-limbed oaks. In the near distance, in contrast with the young green of the tended grass, sunburnt hay-fields showed tan and gold; while beyond were the tawny hills and upland pastures. From the head of the lawn, on the first soft swell from the valley-level, looked down the deep-porched, many-windowed house.

Little opportunity was given White Fang to see all this. Hardly had the carriage entered the grounds, when he was set upon by a sheep-dog, bright-eyed, sharp-muzzled, righteously indignant and angry. It was between him and the master, cutting him off. White Fang snarled no warning, but his hair bristled as he made his silent and deadly rush. This rush was never completed. He halted with awkward abruptness, with stiff fore-legs bracing himself against his momentum, almost sitting down on his haunches, so desirous was he of avoiding contact with the dog he was in the act of attacking. It was a female, and the law of his kind thrust a barrier between. For him to attack her would require nothing less than a violation of his instinct.

But with the sheep-dog it was otherwise. Being a female, she possessed no such instinct. On the other hand, being a sheep-dog, her instinctive fear of the Wild, and especially of the wolf, was unusually keen. White Fang was to her a wolf, the hereditary marauder who had preyed upon her flocks from the time sheep were first herded and guarded by some dim ancestor of hers. And so, as he abandoned his rush at her and braced himself to avoid the contact, she sprang upon him. He snarled involuntarily as he felt her teeth in his shoulder, but beyond this made no offer to hurt her. He backed away, stiff-legged with self-consciousness, and tried to go around her. He dodged this way and that, and curved and turned, but to no purpose. She remained always between him and the way he wanted to go.

"Here, Collie!" called the strange man in the carriage.

Weedon Scott laughed.

"Never mind, father. It is good discipline. White Fang will have to learn many things, and it's just as well that he begins now. He'll adjust himself all right."

The carriage drove on, and still Collie blocked White Fang's way. He tried to outrun her by leaving the drive and circling across the lawn; but she ran on the inner and smaller circle, and was always there, facing him with her two rows of gleaming teeth. Back he circled, across the drive to the other lawn, and again she headed him off.

The carriage was bearing the master away. White Fang caught glimpses of it disappearing amongst the trees. The situation was desperate. He essayed another circle. She followed, running swiftly. And then, suddenly, he turned upon her. It was his old fighting trick. Shoulder to shoulder, he struck her squarely. Not only was she overthrown. So fast had she been running that she rolled along, now on her back, now on her side, as she struggled to stop, clawing gravel with her feet and crying shrilly her hurt pride and indignation.

White Fang did not wait. The way was clear, and that was all he had wanted. She took after him, never ceasing her outcry. It was the straight away now, and when it came to real running, White Fang could teach her things. She ran frantically, hysterically, straining to the utmost, advertising the effort she was making with every leap; and all the time White Fang slid smoothly away from her, silently, without effort, gliding like a ghost over the ground.

As he rounded the house to the *porte-cochŕe*, he came upon the carriage. It had stopped, and the master was alighting. At this moment, still running at top speed, White Fang became suddenly aware of an attack from the side. It was a deer-hound rushing upon him. White Fang tried to face it. But he was going too fast, and the hound was too close. It struck him on the side; and such was his forward momentum and the unexpectedness of it, White Fang was hurled to the ground and rolled clear over. He came out of the tangle a spectacle of malignancy, ears flattened back, lips writhing, nose wrinkling, his teeth clipping together as the fangs barely missed the hound's soft throat.

The master was running up, but was too far away; and it was Collie that saved the hound's life. Before White Fang could spring in and deliver the fatal stroke, and just as he was in the act of springing in, Collie arrived. She had been out-manoeuvred and out-run, to say nothing of her having been unceremoniously tumbled in the gravel, and her arrival was like that of a tornado—made up of offended dignity, justifiable wrath, and instinctive hatred for this marauder from the Wild. She struck White Fang at right angles in the midst of his spring, and again he was knocked off his feet and rolled over.

The next moment the master arrived, and with one hand held White Fang, while the father called off the dogs.

"I say, this is a pretty warm reception for a poor lone wolf from the Arctic," the master said, while White Fang calmed down under his caressing hand. "In all his life he's only been known once to go off his feet, and here he's been rolled twice in thirty seconds."

The carriage had driven away, and other strange gods had appeared from out the house. Some of these stood respectfully at a distance; but two of them, women, perpetrated the hostile act of clutching the master around the neck. White Fang, however, was beginning to tolerate this act. No harm seemed to come of it, while the noises the gods made were certainly not threatening. These gods also made overtures to White Fang, but he warned them off with a snarl, and the master did likewise with word of mouth. At such times White Fang leaned in close against the master's legs and received reassuring pats on the head.

The hound, under the command, "Dick! Lie down, sir!" had gone up the steps and lain down to one side on the porch, still growling and keeping a sullen watch on the intruder. Collie had been taken in charge by one of the woman-gods, who held arms around her neck and petted and caressed her; but Collie was very much perplexed and worried, whining and restless, outraged by the permitted presence of this wolf and confident that the gods were making a mistake.

All the gods started up the steps to enter the house. White Fang followed closely at the master's heels. Dick, on the porch, growled, and White Fang, on the steps, bristled and growled back.

"Take Collie inside and leave the two of them to fight it out," suggested Scott's father. "After that they'll be friends."

"Then White Fang, to show his friendship, will have to be chief mourner at the funeral," laughed the master.

The elder Scott looked incredulously, first at White Fang, then at Dick, and finally at his son.

"You mean that . . . ?"

Weedon nodded his head. "I mean just that. You'd have a dead Dick inside one minute—two minutes at the farthest."

He turned to White Fang. "Come on, you wolf. It's you that'll have to come inside."

White Fang walked stiff-legged up the steps and across the porch, with tail rigidly erect, keeping his eyes on Dick to guard against a flank attack, and at the same time prepared for whatever fierce manifestation of the unknown that might pounce out upon him from the interior of the house. But no thing of fear pounced out, and when he had gained the inside he scouted carefully around, looking for it and finding it not. Then he lay down with a contented grunt at the master's feet, observing all that went on, ever ready to spring to his feet and fight for life with the terrors he felt must lurk under the trap-roof of the dwelling.

III

The God's Domain

NOT only was White Fang adaptable by nature, but he had travelled much, and knew the meaning and necessity of adjustment. Here, in Sierra Vista, which was the name of Judge Scott's place, White Fang quickly began to make himself at home. He had no further serious trouble with the dogs. They knew more about the ways of the South-land gods than did he, and in their eyes he had qualified when he accompanied the gods inside the house. Wolf that he was, and unprecedented as it was, the gods had sanctioned his presence, and they, the dogs of the gods, could only recognize this sanction.

Dick, perforce, had to go through a few stiff formalities at first, after which he calmly accepted White Fang as an addition to the premises. Had Dick had his way, they would have been good friends; but White Fang was averse to friendship. All he asked of other dogs was to be let alone. His whole life he had kept aloof from his kind, and he still desired to keep aloof. Dick's overtures bothered him, so he snarled Dick away. In the north he had learned the lesson that he must let the master's dogs alone, and he did not forget that lesson now. But he insisted on his own privacy and self-seclusion, and so thoroughly ignored Dick that that good-natured creature finally gave him up and scarcely took as much interest in him as in the hitching-post near the stable.

Not so with Collie. While she accepted him because it was the mandate of the gods, that was no reason that she should leave him in peace. Woven into her being was the memory of countless crimes he and his had perpetrated against her ancestry. Not in a day nor a generation were the ravaged sheep-folds to be forgotten. All this was a spur to her, pricking her to retaliation. She could not fly in the face of the gods who permitted him, but that did not prevent her from making life miserable for him in petty ways. A feud, ages old, was between them, and she, for one, would see to it that he was reminded.

So Collie took advantage of her sex to pick upon White Fang and maltreat him. His instinct would not permit him to attack her, while her persistence would not permit him to ignore her. When she rushed at him he turned his fur-protected shoulder to her sharp teeth and walked away stiff-legged and stately. When she forced him too hard, he was compelled to go about in a circle, his shoulder presented to her, his head turned from her, and on his face and in his eyes a patient and bored expression. Sometimes, however, a nip on his hind-quarters hastened his retreat and made it anything but stately. But as a rule he managed to maintain a dignity that was almost solemnity. He ignored her existence whenever it was possible, and made it a point to keep out of her way. When he saw or heard her coming, he got up and walked off.

There was much in other matters for White Fang to learn. Life in the Northland was simplicity itself when compared with the complicated affairs of Sierra Vista. First of all, he had to learn the family of the master. In a way he was prepared to do this. As Mit-sah and Kloo-kooch had belonged to Gray Beaver, sharing his food, his fire, and his blankets, so now, at Sierra Vista, belonged to the love-master all the denizens of the house.

But in this matter there was a difference, and many differences. Sierra Vista was a far vaster affair than the tepee of Gray Beaver. There were many persons to be considered. There was Judge Scott, and there was his wife. There were the master's two sisters, Beth and Mary. There was his wife, Alice, and then there were his children, Weedon and Maud, toddlers of four and six. There was no way for anybody to tell him about all these people, and of blood-ties and relationship he knew nothing whatever and never would be capable of knowing. Yet he quickly worked it out that all of them belonged to the master. Then, by observation, whenever opportunity offered, by study of action, speech, and the very intonations of the voice, he slowly learned the intimacy and the degree of favor they enjoyed with the master. And by this ascertained standard, White Fang treated them accordingly. What was of value to the master he valued; what was dear to the master was to be cherished by White Fang and guarded carefully.

Thus it was with the two children. All his life he had disliked children. He hated and feared their hands. The lessons were not tender that he had learned of their tyranny and cruelty in the days of the Indian villages. When Weedon and Maud had first approached him, he growled warningly and looked malignant. A cuff from the master and a sharp word had then compelled him to permit their caresses, though he growled and growled under their tiny hands, and in the growl there was no crooning note. Later, he observed that the boy and girl were of great value in the master's eyes. Then it was that no cuff nor sharp word was necessary before they could pat him.

Yet White Fang was never effusively affectionate. He yielded to the master's children with an ill but honest grace, and endured their fooling as one would endure a painful operation. When he could no longer endure, he would get up and stalk determinedly away from them. But after a time, he grew even to like the children. Still he was not demonstrative. He would not go up to them. On the other hand, instead of walking away at sight of them, he waited for them to come to him. And still later, it was noticed that a pleased light came into his eyes when he saw them approaching, and that he looked after them with an appearance of curious regret when they left him for other amusements.

All this was a matter of development, and took time. Next in his regard, after the children, was Judge Scott. There were two reasons, possibly, for this. First, he was evidently a valuable possession of the master's, and next, he was undemonstrative. White Fang liked to lie at his feet on the wide porch when he read the newspaper, from time to time favoring White Fang with a look or a word—untroublesome tokens that he recognized White Fang's presence and existence. But this was only when the master was not around. When the master appeared, all other beings ceased to exist so far as White Fang was concerned.

White Fang allowed all the members of the family to pet him and make much of him; but he never gave to them what he gave to the master. No caress of theirs could put the love-croon into his throat, and, try as they would, they could never persuade him into snuggling against them. This expression of abandon and surrender, of absolute trust, he reserved for the master alone. In fact, he never regarded the members of the family in any other light than possessions of the love-master.

Also White Fang had early come to differentiate between the family and the servants of the household. The latter were afraid of him, while he merely refrained from attacking them. This because he considered that they were likewise possessions of the master. Between White Fang and them existed a neutrality and no more. They cooked for the master and washed the dishes and did other things, just as Matt had done up in the Klondike. They were, in short, appurtenances of the household.

Outside the household there was even more for White Fang to learn. The master's domain was wide and complex, yet it had its metes and bounds. The land itself ceased at the county road. Outside was the common domain of all gods—the roads and streets. Then inside other fences were the particular domains of other gods. A myriad laws governed all these things and determined conduct; yet he did not know the speech of the gods, nor was there any way for him to learn save by experience. He obeyed his natural impulses until they ran him counter to some law. When this had been done a few times, he learned the law and after that observed it.

But most potent in his education were the cuff of the master's hand, the censure of the master's voice. Because of White Fang's very great love, a cuff from the master hurt him far more than any beating Gray Beaver or Beauty Smith had ever given him. They had hurt only the flesh of him; beneath the flesh the spirit had still raged, splendid and invincible. But with the master the cuff was always too light to hurt the flesh. Yet it went deeper. It was an expression of the master's disapproval, and White Fang's spirit wilted under it.

In point of fact, the cuff was rarely administered. The master's voice was sufficient. By it White Fang knew whether he did right or not. By it he trimmed his conduct and adjusted his actions. It was the compass by which he steered and learned to chart the manners of a new land and life.

In the Northland, the only domesticated animal was the dog. All other animals lived in the Wild, and were, when not too formidable, lawful spoil for any dog. All his days White Fang had foraged among the live things for food. It did not enter his head that in the Southland it was otherwise. But this he was to learn early in his residence in Santa Clara Valley. Sauntering around the corner of the house in the early morning, he came upon a chicken that had escaped from the chicken-yard. White Fang's natural impulse was to eat it. A couple of bounds, a flash of teeth and a frightened squawk, and he had scooped in the adventurous fowl. It was farm-bred and fat and tender; and White Fang licked his chops and decided that such fare was good.

Later in the day, he chanced upon another stray chicken near the stables. One of the grooms ran to the rescue. He did not know White Fang's breed, so for weapon he took a light buggy-whip. At the first cut of the whip, White Fang left the chicken for the man. A club might have stopped White Fang, but not a whip. Silently, without flinching, he took a second cut in his forward rush, and as he leaped for the throat the groom cried out, "My God!" and staggered backward. He dropped the whip and shielded his throat with his arms. In consequence, his forearm was ripped open to the bone.

The man was badly frightened. It was not so much White Fang's ferocity as it was his silence that unnerved the groom. Still protecting his throat and face with his torn and bleeding arm, he tried to retreat to the barn. And it would have gone hard with him had not Collie appeared on the scene. As she had saved Dick's life, she now saved the groom's. She rushed upon White Fang in frenzied wrath. She had been right. She had known better than the blundering gods. All her suspicions were justified. Here was the ancient marauder up to his old tricks again.

The groom escaped into the stables, and White Fang backed away before Collie's wicked teeth, or presented his shoulder to them and circled round and round. But Collie did not give over, as was her wont, after a decent interval of chastisement. On the contrary, she grew more excited and angry every moment, until, in the end, White Fang flung dignity to the winds and frankly fled away from her across the fields.

"He'll learn to leave chickens alone," the master said. "But I can't give him the lesson until I catch him in the act."

Two nights later came the act, but on a more generous scale than the master had anticipated. White Fang had observed closely the chicken-yards and the habits of the chickens. In the nighttime, after they had gone to roost, he climbed to the top of a pile of newly hauled lumber. From there he gained the roof of a chicken-house, passed over the ridgepole and dropped to the ground inside. A moment later he was inside the house, and the slaughter began.

In the morning, when the master came out on to the porch, fifty white Leghorn hens, laid out in a row by the groom, greeted his eyes. He whistled to himself, softly, first with surprise, and then, at the end, with admiration. His eyes were likewise greeted by White Fang, but about the latter there were no signs of shame nor guilt. He carried himself with pride, as though, forsooth, he had achieved a deed praiseworthy and meritorious. There was about him no consciousness of sin. The master's lips tightened as he faced the disagreeable task. Then he talked harshly to the unwitting culprit, and in his voice there was nothing but godlike wrath. Also, he held White Fang's nose down to the slain hens, and at the same time cuffed him soundly.

White Fang never raided a chicken-roost again. It was against the law, and he had learned it. Then the master took him into the chicken-yards. White Fang's natural impulse, when he saw the live food fluttering about him and under his very nose, was to spring upon it. He obeyed the impulse, but was checked by the master's voice. They continued in the yards for half an hour. Time and again the impulse surged over White Fang, and each time, as he yielded to it, he was checked by the master's voice. Thus it was he learned the law, and ere he left the domain of the chickens, he had learned to ignore their existence.

"You can never cure a chicken-killer." Judge Scott shook his head sadly at the luncheon table, when his son narrated the lesson he had given White Fang. "Once they've got the habit and the taste of blood . . ." Again he shook his head sadly.

But Weedon Scott did not agree with his father.

"I'll tell you what I'll do," he challenged finally. "I'll lock White Fang in with the chickens all afternoon."

"But think of the chickens," objected the Judge.

"And furthermore," the son went on, "for every chicken he kills, I'll pay you one dollar gold coin of the realm."

"But you should penalize father, too," interposed Beth.

Her sister seconded her, and a chorus of approval arose from around the table. Judge Scott nodded his head in agreement.

"All right." Weedon Scott pondered for a moment. "And if, at the end of the afternoon, White Fang hasn't harmed a chicken, for every ten minutes of the time he has spent in the yard, you will have to say to him, gravely and with deliberation, just as if you were sitting on the bench and solemnly passing judgment, 'White Fang, you are smarter than I thought.' "

From hidden points of vantage the family watched the performance. But it was a fizzle. Locked in the yard and there deserted by the master, White Fang lay down and went to sleep. Once he got up and walked over to the trough for a drink of water. The chickens he calmly ignored. So far as he was concerned they did not exist. At four o'clock he executed a running jump, gained the roof of the chicken house and leaped to the ground outside, whence he sauntered gravely to the house. He had learned the law. And on the porch, before the delighted family, Judge Scott, face to face with White Fang said slowly and solemnly, sixteen times, "White Fang, you are smarter than I thought."

But it was the multiplicity of laws that befuddled White Fang and often brought him into disgrace. He had to learn that he must not touch the chickens that belonged to other gods. Then there were cats, and rabbits, and turkeys; all these he must let alone. In fact, when he had but partly learned the law, his impression was that he must leave all live things alone. Out in the back-pasture, a quail could flutter up under his nose unharmed. All tense and trembling with eagerness and desire, he mastered his instinct and stood still. He was obeying the will of the gods.

And then, one day, again out in the back-pasture, he saw Dick start a jackrabbit and run it. The master himself was looking on and did not interfere. Nay, he encouraged White Fang to join in the chase. And thus he learned that there was no taboo on jackrabbits. In the end he worked out the complete law. Between him and all domestic animals there must be no hostilities. If not amity, at least neutrality must obtain. But the other animals—the squirrels, and quail, and cottontails, were creatures of the Wild who had never yielded allegiance to man. They were the lawful prey of any dog. It was only the tame that the gods protected, and between the tame deadly strife was not permitted. The gods held the power of life and death over their subjects, and the gods were jealous of their power.

Life was complex in the Santa Clara Valley after the simplicities of the Northland. And the chief thing demanded by these intricacies of civilization was control, restraint—a poise of self that was as delicate as the fluttering of gossamer wings and at the same time as rigid as steel. Life had a thousand faces, and White Fang found he must meet them all—thus, when he went to town, in to San Jose, running behind the carriage or loafing about the streets when the carriage stopped. Life flowed past him, deep and wide and varied, continually impinging upon his senses, demanding of him instant and endless adjustments and correspondences, and compelling him, almost always to suppress his natural impulses.

There were butcher-shops where meat hung within reach. This meat he must not touch. There were cats at the houses the master visited that must be let alone. And there were dogs everywhere that snarled at him and that he must not attack. And then, on the crowded sidewalks, there were persons innumerable whose attention he attracted. They would stop and look at him, point him out to one another, examine him, talk to him, and, worst of all, pat him. And these perilous contacts from all these strange hands he must endure. Yet this endurance he achieved. Furthermore he got over being awkward and self-conscious. In a lofty way he received the attentions of the multitudes of strange gods. With condescension he accepted their condescension. On the other hand, there was something about him that prevented great familiarity. They patted him on the head and passed on, contented and pleased with their own daring.

But it was not all easy for White Fang. Running behind the carriage in the outskirts of San Jose, he encountered certain small boys who made a practice of flinging stones at him. Yet he knew that it was not permitted him to pursue and drag them down. Here he was compelled to violate his instinct of self-preservation, and violate it he did, for he was becoming tame and qualifying himself for civilization.

Nevertheless, White Fang was not quite satisfied with the arrangement. He had no abstract ideas about justice and fair play. But there is a certain sense of equity that resides in life, and it was this sense in him that resented the unfairness of his being permitted no defence against the stone-throwers. He forgot that in the covenant entered into between him and the gods they were pledged to care for him and defend him. But one day the master sprang from the carriage, whip in hand, and gave the stone-throwers a thrashing. After that they threw stones no more, and White Fang understood and was satisfied.

One other experience of similar nature was his. On the way to town, hanging around the saloon at the cross-roads, were three dogs that made a practice of rushing out upon him when he went by. Knowing his deadly method of fighting, the master had never ceased impressing upon White Fang the law that he must not fight. As a result, having learned the lesson well, White Fang was hard put whenever he passed the cross-roads saloon. After the first rush, each time, his snarl kept the three dogs at a distance, but they trailed along behind, yelping and bickering and insulting him. This endured for some time. The men at the saloon even urged the dogs on to attack White Fang. One day they openly sicked the dogs on him. The master stopped the carriage.

"Go to it," he said to White Fang.

But White Fang could not believe. He looked at the master, and he looked at the dogs. Then he looked back eagerly and questioningly at the master.

The master nodded his head. "Go to them, old fellow. Eat them up."

White Fang no longer hesitated. He turned and leaped silently among his enemies. All three faced him. There was a great snarling and growling, a clashing of teeth and a flurry of bodies. The dust of the road arose in a cloud and screened the battle. But at the end of several minutes two dogs were struggling in the dirt and the third was in full flight. He leaped a ditch, went through a rail fence, and fled across a field. White Fang followed, sliding over the ground in wolf fashion and with wolf speed, swiftly and without noise, and in the centre of the field he dragged down and slew the dog.

With this triple killing his main troubles with dogs ceased. The word went up and down the valley, and men saw to it that their dogs did not molest the Fighting Wolf.

IV

The Call of Kind

THE months came and went. There was plenty of food and no work in the Southland, and White Fang lived fat and prosperous and happy. Not alone was he in the geographical Southland, for he was in the Southland of life. Human kindness was like a sun shining upon him, and he flourished like a flower planted in good soil.

And yet he remained somehow different from other dogs. He knew the law even better than did the dogs that had known no other life, and he observed the law more punctiliously; but still there was about him a suggestion of lurking ferocity, as though the Wild still lingered in him and the wolf in him merely slept.

He never chummed with other dogs. Lonely he had lived, so far as his kind was concerned, and lonely he would continue to live. In his puppyhood, under the persecution of Lip-lip and the puppy-pack, and in his fighting days with Beauty Smith, he had acquired a fixed aversion for dogs. The natural course of his life had been diverted, and, recoiling from his kind, he had clung to the human.

Besides, all Southland dogs looked upon him with suspicion. He aroused in them their instinctive fear of the Wild, and they greeted him always with snarl and growl and belligerent hatred. He, on the other hand, learned that it was not necessary to use his teeth upon them. His naked fangs and writhing lips were uniformly efficacious, rarely failing to send a bellowing on-rushing dog back on its haunches.

But there was one trial in White Fang's life—Collie. She never gave him a moment's peace. She was not so amenable to the law as he. She defied all efforts of the master to make her become friends with White Fang. Ever in his ears was sounding her sharp and nervous snarl. She had never forgiven him the chicken-killing episode, and persistently held to the belief that his intentions were bad. She found him guilty before the act, and treated him accordingly. She became a pest to him, like a policeman following him around the stable and the grounds, and, if he even so much as glanced curiously at a pigeon or chicken, bursting into an outcry of indignation and wrath. His favorite way of ignoring her was to lie down, with his head on his fore-paws, and pretend sleep. This always dumfounded and silenced her.

With the exception of Collie, all things went well with White Fang. He had learned control and poise, and he knew the law. He achieved a staidness, and calmness, and philosophic tolerance. He no longer lived in a hostile environment. Danger and hurt and death did not lurk everywhere about him. In time, the unknown, as a thing of terror and menace ever impending, faded away. Life was soft and easy. It flowed along smoothly, and neither fear nor foe lurked by the way.

He missed the snow without being aware of it. "An unduly long summer" would have been his thought had he thought about it; as it was, he merely missed the snow in a vague, subconscious way. In the same fashion, especially in the heat of summer when he suffered from the sun, he experienced faint longings for the Northland. Their only effect upon him, however, was to make him uneasy and restless without his knowing what was the matter.

White Fang had never been very demonstrative. Beyond his snuggling and the throwing of a crooning note into his love-growl, he had no way of expressing his love. Yet it was given him to discover a third way. He had always been susceptible to the laughter of the gods. Laughter had affected him with madness, made him frantic with rage. But he did not have it in him to be angry with the love-master, and when that god elected to laugh at him in a good-natured, bantering way, he was nonplussed. He could feel the pricking and stinging of the old anger as it strove to rise up in him, but it strove against love. He could not be angry; yet he had to do something. At first he was dignified, and the master laughed the harder. Then he tried to be more dignified, and the master laughed harder than before. In the end, the master laughed him out of his dignity. His jaws slightly parted, his lips lifted a little, and a quizzical expression that was more love than humor came into his eyes. He had learned to laugh.

Likewise he learned to romp with the master, to be tumbled down and rolled over, and be the victim of innumerable rough tricks. In return he feigned anger, bristling and growling ferociously, and clipping his teeth together in snaps that had all the seeming of deadly intention. But he never forgot himself. Those snaps were always delivered on the empty air. At the end of such a romp, when blow and cuff and snap and snarl were fast and furious, they would break off suddenly and stand several feet apart, glaring at each other. And then, just as suddenly, like the sun rising on a stormy sea, they would begin to laugh. This would always culminate with the master's arms going around White Fang's neck and shoulders while the latter crooned and growled his love-song.

But nobody else ever romped with White Fang. He did not permit it. He stood on his dignity, and when they attempted it, his warning snarl and bristling mane were anything but playful. That he allowed the master these liberties was no reason that he should be a common dog, loving here and loving there, everybody's property for a romp and good time. He loved with single heart and refused to cheapen himself or his love.

The master went out on horseback a great deal, and to accompany him was one of White Fang's chief duties in life. In the Northland he had evidenced his fealty by toiling in the harness; but there were no sleds in the Southland, nor did dogs pack burdens on their backs. So he rendered fealty in the new way, by running with the master's horse. The longest day never played White Fang out. His was the gait of the wolf, smooth, tireless, and effortless, and at the end of fifty miles he would come in jauntily ahead of the horse.

It was in connection with the riding, that White Fang achieved one other mode of expression—remarkable in that he did it but twice in all his life. The first time occurred when the master was trying to teach a spirited thoroughbred the method of opening and closing gates without the rider's dismounting. Time and again and many times he ranged the horse up to the gate in the effort to close it, and each time the horse became frightened and backed and plunged away. It grew more nervous and excited every moment. When it reared, the master put the spurs to it and made it drop its fore-legs back to earth, whereupon it would begin kicking with its hind-legs. White Fang watched the performance with increasing anxiety until he could contain himself no longer, when he sprang in front of the horse and barked savagely and warningly.

Though he often tried to bark thereafter, and the master encouraged him, he succeeded only once, and then it was not in the master's presence. A scamper across the pasture, a jackrabbit rising suddenly under the horse's feet, a violent sheer, a stumble, a fall to earth, and a broken leg for the master were the cause of it. White Fang sprang in a rage at the throat of the offending horse, but was checked by the master's voice.

"Home! Go home!" the master commanded, when he had ascertained his injury.

White Fang was disinclined to desert him. The master thought of writing a note, but searched his pockets vainly for pencil and paper. Again he commanded White Fang to go home.

The latter regarded him wistfully, started away, then returned and whined softly. The master talked to him gently but seriously, and he cocked his ears and listened with painful intentness.

"That's all right, old fellow, you just run along home," ran the talk. "Go on home and tell them what's happened to me. Home with you, you wolf. Get along home!"

White Fang knew the meaning of "home," and though he did not understand the remainder of the master's language, he knew it was his will that he should go home. He turned and trotted reluctantly away. Then he stopped, undecided, and looked back over his shoulder.

"Go home!" came the sharp command, and this time he obeyed.

The family was on the porch, taking the cool of the afternoon, when White Fang arrived. He came in among them, panting, covered with dust.

"Weedon's back," Weedon's mother announced.

The children welcomed White Fang with glad cries and ran to meet him. He avoided them and passed down the porch, but they cornered him against a rocking-chair and the railing. He growled and tried to push by them. Their mother looked apprehensively in their direction.

"I confess, he makes me nervous around the children," she said. "I have a dread that he will turn upon them unexpectedly some day."

Growling savagly, White Fang sprang out of the corner, overturning the boy and the girl. The mother called them to her and comforted them, telling them not to bother White Fang.

"A wolf is a wolf," commented Judge Scott. "There is no trusting one."

"But he is not all wolf," interposed Beth, standing for her brother in his absence.

"You have only Weedon's opinion for that," rejoined the Judge. "He merely surmises that there is some strain of dog in White Fang; but as he will tell you himself, he knows nothing about it. As for his appearance—"

He did not finish the sentence. White Fang stood before him, growling fiercely.

"Go away! Lie down, sir!" Judge Scott commanded.

White Fang turned to the love-master's wife. She screamed with fright as he seized her dress in his teeth and dragged on it till the frail fabric tore away. By this time he had become the centre of interest. He had ceased from his growling and stood, head up, looking into their faces. His throat worked spasmodically, but made no sound, while he struggled with all his body, convulsed with the effort to rid himself of the incommunicable something that strained for utterance.

"I hope he is not going mad," said Weedon's mother. "I told Weedon that I was afraid the warm climate would not agree with an Arctic animal."

"He's trying to speak, I do believe," Beth announced.

At this moment speech came to White Fang, rushing up in a great burst of barking.

"Something has happened to Weedon," his wife said decisively.

They were all on their feet, now, and White Fang ran down the steps, looking back for them to follow. For the second and last time in his life he had barked and made himself understood.

After this event he found a warmer place in the hearts of the Sierra Vista people, and even the groom whose arm he had slashed admitted that he was a wise dog even if he was a wolf. Judge Scott still held to the same opinion, and proved it to everybody's dissatisfaction by measurements and descriptions taken from the encyclopaedia and various works on natural history.

The days came and went, streaming their unbroken sunshine over the Santa Clara

Valley. But as they grew shorter and White Fang's second winter in the Southland came on, he made a strange discovery. Collie's teeth were no longer sharp. There was a playfulness about her nips and a gentleness that prevented them from really hurting him. He forgot that she had made life a burden to him, and when she disported herself around him he responded solemnly, striving to be playful and becoming no more than ridiculous.

One day she led him off on a long chase through the back-pasture and into the woods. It was the afternoon that the master was to ride, and White Fang knew it. The horse stood saddled and waiting at the door. White Fang hesitated. But there was that in him deeper than all the law he had learned, than the customs that had moulded him, than his love for the master, than the very will to live of himself; and when, in the moment of his indecision, Collie nipped him and scampered off, he turned and followed after. The master rode alone that day; and in the woods, side by side, White Fang ran with Collie, as his mother, Kiche, and old One Eye had run long years before in the silent Northland forest.

V

The Sleeping Wolf

It was about this time that the newspapers were full of the daring escape of a convict from San Quentin prison. He was a ferocious man. He had been ill-made in the making. He had not been born right, and he had not been helped any by the moulding he had received at the hands of society. The hands of society are harsh, and this man was a striking sample of its handiwork. He was a beast—a human beast, it is true, but nevertheless so terrible a beast that he can best be characterized as carnivorous.

In San Quentin prison he had proved incorrigible. Punishment failed to break his spirit. He could die dumb-mad and fighting to the last, but he could not live and be beaten. The more fiercely he fought, the more harshly society handled him, and the only effect of harshness was to make him fiercer. Straightjackets, starvation, and beatings and clubbings were the wrong treatment for Jim Hall; but it was the treatment he received. It was the treatment he had received from the time he was a little pulpy boy in a San Francisco slum—soft clay in the hands of society and ready to be formed into something.

It was during Jim Hall's third term in prison that he encountered a guard that was almost as great a beast as he. The guard treated him unfairly, lied about him to the warden, lost him his credits, persecuted him. The difference between them was that the guard carried a bunch of keys and a revolver. Jim Hall had only his naked hands and his teeth. But he sprang upon the guard one day and used his teeth on the other's throat just like any jungle animal.

After this, Jim Hall went to live in the incorrigible cell. He lived there three years. The cell was of iron, the floor, the walls, the roof. He never left this cell. He never saw the sky nor the sunshine. Day was a twilight and night was a black silence. He was in an iron tomb, buried alive. He saw no human face, spoke to no human thing. When his food was shoved in to him, he growled like a wild animal. He hated all things. For days and nights he bellowed his rage at the universe. For weeks and months he never made a sound, in the black silence eating his very soul. He was a man and a monstrosity, as fearful a thing of fear as ever gibbered in the visions of a maddened brain.

And then, one night, he escaped. The warden said it was impossible, but nevertheless the cell was empty, and half in half out of it lay the body of a dead guard. Two other dead guards marked his trail through the prison to the outer walls, and he had killed with his hands to avoid noise.

He was armed with the weapons of the slain guards—a live arsenal that fled through the hills pursued by the organized might of society. A heavy price of gold was upon his head. Avaricious farmers hunted him with shot-guns. His blood might pay off a mortgage or send a son to college. Public-spirited citizens took down their rifles and went out after him. A pack of bloodhounds followed the way of his bleeding feet. And the sleuth-hounds of the law, the paid fighting animals of society, with telephone, and telegraph, and special train, clung to his trail night and day.

Sometimes they came upon him, and men faced him like heroes, or stampeded through barb-wire fences to the delight of the commonwealth reading the account at the breakfast table. It was after such encounters that the dead and wounded were carted back to the towns, and their places filled by men eager for the man-hunt.

And then Jim Hall disappeared. The bloodhounds vainly quested on the lost trail. Inoffensive ranchers in remote valleys were held up by armed men and compelled to identify themselves; while the remains of Jim Hall were discovered on a dozen mountainsides by greedy claimants for blood-money.

In the meantime the newspapers were read at Sierra Vista, not so much with interest as with anxiety. The women were afraid. Judge Scott pooh-poohed and laughed, but not with reason, for it was in his last days on the bench that Jim Hall had stood before him and received sentence. And in open courtroom, before all men, Jim Hall had proclaimed that the day would come when he would wreak vengeance on the judge that sentenced him.

For once, Jim Hall was right. He was innocent of the crime for which he was sentenced. It was a case, in the parlance of thieves and police, of "railroading." Jim Hall was being "railroaded" to prison for a crime he had not committed. Because of the two prior convictions against him, Judge Scott imposed upon him a sentence of fifty years.

Judge Scott did not know all things, and he did not know that he was party to a police conspiracy, that the evidence was hatched and perjured, that Jim Hall was guiltless of the crime charged. And Jim Hall, on the other hand, did not know that Judge Scott was merely ignorant. Jim Hall believed that the judge knew all about it and was hand in glove with the police in the perpetration of the monstrous injustice. So it was, when the doom of fifty years of living death was uttered by Judge Scott, that Jim Hall, hating all things in the society that misused him, rose up and raged in the courtroom until dragged down by half a dozen of his blue-coated enemies. To him, Judge Scott was the keystone in the arch of injustice, and upon Judge Scott he emptied the vials of his wrath and hurled the threats of his revenge yet to come. Then Jim Hall went to his living death . . . and escaped.

Of all this White Fang knew nothing. But between him and Alice, the master's wife, there existed a secret. Each night, after Sierra Vista had gone to bed, she arose and let in White Fang to sleep in the big hall. Now White Fang was not a house-dog, nor was he permitted to sleep in the house; so each morning, early, she slipped down and let him out before the family was awake.

On one such night, while all the house slept, White Fang awoke and lay very quietly. And very quietly he smelled the air and read the message it bore of a strange god's presence. And to his ears came sounds of the strange god's movements. White Fang burst into no furious outcry. It was not his way. The strange god walked softly, but more softly walked White Fang, for he had no clothes to rub against the flesh of his body. He followed silently. In the Wild he had hunted live meat that was infinitely timid, and he knew the advantage of surprise.

The strange god paused at the foot of the great staircase and listened, and White Fang was as dead, so without movement was he as he watched and waited. Up that staircase the way led to the love-master and to the love-master's dearest possessions. White Fang bristled, but waited. The strange god's foot lifted. He was beginning the ascent.

Then it was that White Fang struck. He gave no warning, with no snarl anticipated his own action. Into the air he lifted his body in the spring that landed him on the strange god's back. White Fang clung with his fore-paws to the man's shoulders, at the same time burying his fangs into the back of the man's neck. He clung on for a moment, long enough to drag the god over backward. Together they crashed to the floor. White Fang leaped clear, and, as the man struggled to rise, was in again with the slashing fangs.

Sierra Vista awoke in alarm. The noise from downstairs was as that of a score of battling fiends. There were revolver shots. A man's voice screamed once in horror and anguish. There was a great snarling and growling, and over all arose a smashing and crashing of furniture and glass.

But almost as quickly as it had arisen, the commotion died away. The struggle had not lasted more than three minutes. The frightened household clustered at the top of the stairway. From below, as from out an abyss of blackness, came up a gurgling sound, as of air bubbling through water. Sometimes this gurgle became sibilant, almost a whistle. But this, too, quickly died down and ceased. Then naught came up out of the blackness save a heavy panting of some creature struggling sorely for air.

Weedon Scott pressed a button, and the staircase and downstairs hall were flooded with light. Then he and Judge Scott, revolvers in hand, cautiously descended. There was no need for this caution. White Fang had done his work. In the midst of the wreckage of overthrown and smashed furniture, partly on his side, his face hidden by an arm, lay a man. Weedon Scott bent over, removed the arm, and turned the man's face upward. A gaping throat explained the manner of his death.

"Jim Hall," said Judge Scott, and father and son looked significantly at each other.

Then they turned to White Fang. He, too, was lying on his side. His eyes were closed, but the lids slightly lifted in an effort to look at them as they bent over him, and the tail was perceptibly agitated in a vain effort to wag. Weedon Scott patted him, and his throat rumbled an acknowledging growl. But it was a weak growl at best, and it quickly ceased. His eyelids drooped and went shut, and his whole body seemed to relax and flatten out upon the floor.

"He's all in, poor devil," muttered the master.

"We'll see about that," asserted the Judge, as he started for the telephone.

"Frankly, he has one chance in a thousand," announced the surgeon, after he had worked an hour and a half on White Fang.

Dawn was breaking through the windows and dimming the electric lights. With the exception of the children, the whole family was gathered about the surgeon to hear his verdict.

"One broken hind-leg," he went on. "Three broken ribs, one at least of which has pierced the lungs. He has lost nearly all the blood in his body. There is a large likelihood of internal injuries. He must have been jumped upon. To say nothing of three bullet holes clear through him. One chance in a thousand is really optimistic. He hasn't a chance in ten thousand."

"But he musn't lose any chance that might be of help to him," Judge Scott exclaimed. "Never mind expense. Put him under the X-ray—anything. Weedon, telegraph at once to San Francisco for Doctor Nichols. No reflection on you, doctor, you understand; but he must have the advantage of every chance."

The surgeon smiled indulgently. "Of course I understand. He deserves all that can be done for him. He must be nursed as you would nurse a human being, a sick child. And don't forget what I told you about temperature. I'll be back at ten o'clock again."

White Fang received the nursing. Judge Scott's suggestion of a trained nurse was indignantly clamored down by the girls, who themselves undertook the task. And White Fang won out on the one chance in ten thousand denied him by the surgeon.

The latter was not to be censured for his misjudgment. All his life he had tended and operated on the soft humans of civilization, who lived sheltered lives and had descended out of many sheltered generations. Compared with White Fang, they were frail and flabby, and clutched life without any strength in their grip. White Fang had come straight from the Wild, where the weak perish early and shelter is vouchsafed to none. In neither his father nor his mother was there any weakness, nor in the generations before them. A constitution of iron and the vitality of the Wild were White Fang's inheritance, and he clung to life, the whole of him and every part of him, in spirit and in flesh, with the tenacity that of old belonged to all creatures.

Bound down a prisoner, denied even movement by the plaster casts and bandages, White Fang lingered out the weeks. He slept long hours and dreamed much, and through his mind passed an unending pageant of Northland visions. All the ghosts of the past arose and were with him. Once again he lived in the lair with Kiche, crept trembling to the knees of Gray Beaver to tender his allegiance, ran for his life before Lip-lip and all the howling bedlam of the puppy-pack.

He ran again through the silence, hunting his living food through the months of famine; and again he ran at the head of the team, the gut-whips of Mit-sah and Gray Beaver snapping behind, their voices crying "Raa! Raa!" when they came to a narrow passage and the team closed together like a fan to go through. He lived again all his days with Beauty Smith and the fights he had fought. At such times he whimpered and snarled in his sleep, and they that looked on said that his dreams were bad.

But there was one particular nightmare from which he suffered—the clanking, clanging monsters of electric cars that were to him colossal screaming lynxes. He would lie in a screen of bushes, watching for a squirrel to venture far enough out on the ground from its tree-refuge. Then, when he sprang out upon it, it would transform itself into an electric car, menacing and terrible, towering over him like a mountain, screaming and clanging and spitting fire at him. It was the same when he challenged the hawk down out of the sky. Down out of the blue it would rush, as it dropped upon him changing itself into the ubiquitous electric car. Or again, he would be in the pen of Beauty Smith. Outside the pen, men would be gathering, and he knew that a fight was on. He watched the door for his antagonist to enter. The door would open, and thrust in upon him would come the awful electric car. A thousand times this occurred, and each time the terror it inspired was as vivid and great as ever.

Then came the day when the last bandage and the last plaster cast were taken off. It was a gala day. All Sierra Vista was gathered around. The master rubbed his ears, and he crooned his love-growl. The master's wife called him the "Blessed Wolf," which name was taken up with acclaim and all the women called him the Blessed Wolf.

He tried to rise to his feet, and after several attempts fell down from weakness. He had lain so long that his muscles had lost their cunning, and all the strength had gone out of them. He felt a little shame because of his weakness, as though, forsooth, he were failing the gods in the service he owed them. Because of this he made heroic efforts to arise, and at last he stood on his four legs, tottering and swaying back and forth.

"The Blessed Wolf!" chorused the women.

Judge Scott surveyed them triumphantly.

"Out of your own mouths be it," he said. "Just as I contended right along. No mere dog could have done what he did. He's a wolf."

"A Blessed Wolf," amended the Judge's wife.

"Yes, Blessed Wolf," agreed the Judge. "And henceforth that shall be my name for him."

"He'll have to learn to walk again," said the surgeon; "so he might as well start in right now. It won't hurt him. Take him outside."

And outside he went, like a king, with all Sierra Vista about him and tending on him. He was very weak, and when he reached the lawn he lay down and rested for a while.

Then the procession started on, little spurts of strength coming into White Fang's muscles as he used them and the blood began to surge through them. The stables were reached, and there in the doorway lay Collie, a half-dozen pudgy puppies playing about her in the sun.

White Fang looked on with a wondering eye. Collie snarled warningly at him, and he was careful to keep his distance. The master with his toe helped one sprawling puppy toward him. He bristled suspiciously, but the master warned him that all was well. Collie, clasped in the arms of one of the women, watched him jealously and with a snarl warned him that all was not well.

The puppy sprawled in front of him. He cocked his ears and watched it curiously. Then their noses touched, and he felt the warm little tongue of the puppy on his jowl. White Fang's tongue went out, he knew not why, and he licked the puppy's face.

Hand-clapping and pleased cries from the gods greeted the performance. He was surprised, and looked at them in a puzzled way. Then his weakness asserted itself, and he lay down, his ears cocked, his head on one side, as he watched the puppy. The other puppies came sprawling toward him, to Collie's great disgust; and he gravely permitted them to clamber and tumble over him. At first, amid the applause of the gods, he betrayed a trifle of his old self-consciousness and awkwardness. This passed away as the puppies' antics and mauling continued, and he lay with half-shut, patient eyes, drowsing in the sun.

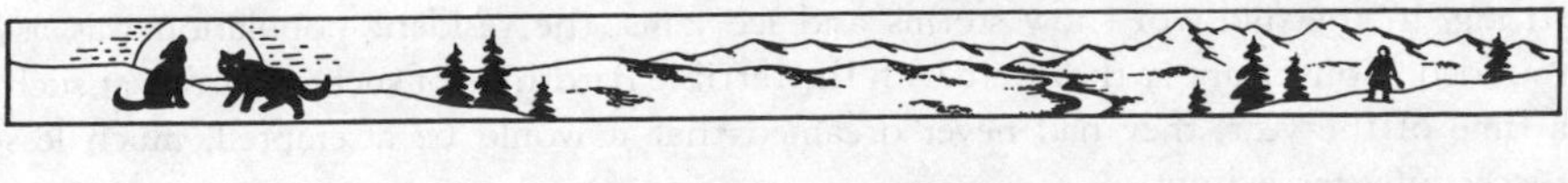

LONDON ON LONDON

This true description of London's journey downriver through the Klondike—and his attempts to sell an article about this adventure—was written well after gaining literary fame. It has the feeling of a successful man looking back on a folly of his youth with a self deprecating humor, but it also shows us the energy and intensity so inherent in his personality, as well as his writing. Once again, we see London's unique use of the landscape as character, so dominant in the stories that follow.

THE PROSPECTOR

AFTER the laundry, my sister and her husband grubstaked me into the Klondike. It was the first gold rush into that region, the early fall rush of 1897. I was twenty-one years old, and in spledid physical condition. I remember, at the end of the twenty-eight-mile portage across Chilkoot from Dyea Beach to Lake Linderman, I was packing up with the Indians and outpacking many an Indian. The last pack into Linderman was three miles. I back-tripped it four times a day, and on each forward trip carried one hundred and fifty pounds. This means that over the worst trails I daily traveled twenty-four miles, twelve of which were under a burden of one hundred and fifty pounds.

Yes, I had let career go hang, and was on the adventure-path again in quest of fortune . . .

THROUGH THE RAPIDS ON THE WAY TO KLONDIKE

WE were in a hurry. Every one was in a hurry. This hurry is characteristic of a gold rush, and especially so of the Klondike rush of '97. October was at hand, the land covered with snow, the river threatening to freeze up at any moment, and Dawson still hundreds of miles to the north.

Never in the history of all the Northland had such wild risks been taken, and never had it been penetrated by a more reckless company of men. The Klondike veterans who had come out with glowing accounts and heavy bags of Arctic gold, and who were responsible for the wave of adventure that swept over the land, laughed at us when we said we would pack our outfits over the passes and boat them down to Dawson in the fall of the year. But we did do it, and when we arrived at Dawson, several thousand strong, in the midst of snow storms and ice jams, the resident population was astounded. Conversant as they were with the terrible hardships of such a journey at such a time of the year, they had never dreamed that it would be attempted, much less successfully carried out.

Naturally, some fell by the way, others were frozen in from one end of the river to the other, thousands, worn out and disheartened, turned back from the passes; but our party was numbered among the lucky. And this, by showing how great was the understanding and how pressing the necessity, having once started, of going through, brings me to the narrative proper—the running of the Box Canyon and the White Horse Rapids.

To show the deep respect felt for these places by the Old Timers, I quote from Miner W. Bruce, an Alaskan pioneer, whose book we consulted throughout the trip.

"If a man is a skilful navigator he can run his boat through the canyon and land on the right hand side. If not, he had better make a portage. From this point he should follow the left hand side two miles to the head of White Horse Rapids. Great precaution should be exercised in reaching the point where the landing is made above the White Horse. Through the White Horse, in a low stage of water, the boat can be dropped with a line; but if the water is high, a portage must be made."

The Sixty Mile River, really a head reach of the Yukon, flows out of Marsh Lake with a varying width of from an eighth to a quarter of a mile. As it is deep and swift, an idea may be gained of the quantity of water in transit. Suddenly, it narrows to one hundred yards, rounds a bend where a landing may be made in an eddy, and dashes between towering rock walls, about eighty feet apart. This enormous volume of water, thus contracted to so small a passageway, attains a terrific speed, marked by great boilings and upheavals, and waves which stiffly stand up like walls. By some peculiar action or pressure against the rocky sides, the center of the rapids rises up in the form of a backbone, varying from six to eight feet in height. This is called the "Ridge."

Midway in this mile of canyon, the walls open out on either hand, like an immense circular court. The water dashes into this, forming a mighty maelstrom. It is said that in former years two Swedes were caught in this whirlpool. Their boat was most seaworthy, and at first they tried to get out; but failing in this, they took turns in bailing and praying, and waiting for something to turn up. Round and round they dashed for some four hours, and then, by a peculiar freak of the waters, were whirled on down the canyon, finally escaping with no damage done save to their nerves.

Tying our boat, the *Yukon Belle,* in the eddy above the Box, my three comrades and myself walked ahead to investigate. Hundreds were portaging their outfits on their backs. For us this would mean two days of severest toil, while if we cared to take the chances and run through, it would mean only two minutes. According to our custom, we put it to the vote, and the latter method was unanimously carried.

Lashing the steering oar so that it could not possibly escape, I allotted my comrades their places; for I was captain. Merritt Sloper, direct from adventures in South America and who knew a little of boating, took his position in the bow with a paddle. Thompson and Goodman, landlubbers who had never rowed before this trip, were stationed side by side at the oars. That the run may better be appreciated, it is well to explain that our twenty-seven-foot boat was carrying over five thousand pounds in addition to human freight, and hence did not possess the buoyancy so requisite for such an undertaking.

"Be sure to keep on the Ridge," cried the men on the bank as we cast off.

The water, though swift, had a slick, oily appearance until we dashed into the very jaws of the Box, where it instantly took on the aspect of chaos broken loose. Afraid that the rowers might catch a crab or make some other disastrous fumble, I called the oars in.

Then we met it on the fly. I caught a glimpse of the spectators fringing the brink of the cliffs above, and another glimpse of the rock walls dashing by like twin lightning express trains; then my whole energy was concentrated in keeping to the Ridge. This was serrated with stiff waves, which the boat, dead with weight, could not mount, being forced to jab her nose through at every lunge. For all the peril, I caught myself smiling at the ridiculous capers cut by Sloper, perched in the very bow and working his paddle like mad. Just as he would let drive for a tremendous stroke, the stern would fall in a trough, jerking the bow clear up, and he would miss the water utterly. And at the next stroke, perhaps, the nose would dive clean under, almost sweeping him away—and he only weighed one hundred pounds. But never did he lose his presence of mind or grit. Once, he turned and cried some warning at the top of his lungs, but it was drowned in the pandemonium of sound. The next instant we fell off the ridge. The water came inboard in all directions, and the boat, caught in a transverse current, threatened to twist broadside. This would mean destruction. I threw myself against the sweep till I could hear it cracking, while Sloper snapped his paddle short off.

And all this time we were flying down the gutter, less than two yards from the wall. Several times it seemed all up with us; but finally, mounting the Ridge almost sidewise, we took a header through a tremendous comber and shot into the whirlpool of the great circular court.

Ordering out the oars for steerage-way, and keeping a close eye on the split currents, I caught one free breath before we flew into the second half of the canyon. Though we crossed the Ridge from left to right and back again, it was merely a repetition of the first half. A moment later the *Yukon Belle* rubbed softly against the bank. We had run the mile of canyon in two minutes by the watch.

Sloper and I walked back by way of the portage and ran a friend's boat through. This was quite ticklish, for the little craft was but twenty-two feet over all, and proportionately heavier loaded than ours. Then we bailed out and ran two miles of ordinary rapids to the head of the White Horse, passing several wrecks in which a number of lives had been lost.

Of the two the White Horse was more dangerous than the Box. Save for a few who had been drowned, it had never been run in previous years. It had been the custom to portage everything around, even to the boats, which were skidding along on spruce tree trunks. But we were in a hurry and rather enthusiastic over our previous good luck; so not a pound was taken from the boats.

The dangerous point in these rapids is at the tail end, called the "Mane of the Horse," from a succession of foamy, mountainous waves. Extending three-quarters of the way across, a rocky reef throws the whole river against the right bank; then comes the jump, and it is thrown back to the left, forming another whirlpool, more risky by far than that of the Box.

When we struck the "Mane," the *Yukon Belle* forgot her heavy load, taking a series of leaps almost clear of the water, alternating with as many burials in the troughs. To this day I cannot see how it happened, but I lost control. A cross current caught our stern and we began to swing broadside. Then we jumped into the whirlpool, though I did not guess it at the time. Sloper snapped a second paddle and received another ducking.

It must be remembered that we were traveling at racehorse speed, and that things happened in a tithe of the time taken to tell them. From every quarter the water came aboard, threatening to swamp us. The *Yukon Belle* headed directly for the jagged left bank, and though I was up against the steering sweep till it cracked, I could not turn her nose downstream. Onlookers from the shore tried to snapshot us, but failed to gauge our speed or get more than a wild view of angry waters and flying foam.

The bank was alarmingly close, but the boat still had the bit in her teeth. It was all happening so quickly, that I for the first time realized I was trying to buck the whirlpool. Like a flash I was bearing against the opposite side of the sweep. The boat answered, at the same time following the bent of the whirlpool, and headed upstream. But the shave was so close that Sloper leaped to the top of a rock. Then, on seeing we had missed by a couple of inches, he pluckily tumbled aboard, all in a heap, like a man boarding a comet.

Though tearing like mad through a whirlpool, we breathed freer. Completing the circle, we were thrown into the "Mane," which we shot a second time and safely landed in a friendly eddy below.

It was late fall when Jack London reached the gold fields and he had time to stake out only a few claims when the northern winter closed in. With his friends he moved into an old deserted cabin and settled down to await the coming of spring. Situated as it was on the banks of the Stewart River where a number of trails crossed, this cabin became a meeting place for all those in the vicinity and for all those travelling through. Jack spent his winter reading, talking to the seasoned prospectors, and listening to their stories. When spring came Jack fell ill and was forced to leave for home—without a penny to show for his efforts. A number of years had yet to pass before he would realize just how valuable this Alaskan adventure would be to his literary career.

. . . At the end of the year, owing to an outbreak of scurvy, I was compelled to come out, and on a homeward journey of 1,900 miles in an open boat, made the only notes of the trip. It was in the Klondike that I found myself. There nobody talks. Everybody thinks. You get your true perspective. I got mine.

FROM DAWSON TO THE SEA

It was well into June when we cast off the boat's painter, and, with the last goodbyes ringing in our ears, began the 2,000-mile journey down the Yukon to St. Michael. As the six-mile current took us briskly in tow, we turned about for a final glimpse of Dawson-dreary, desolate Dawson, built in a swamp, flooded to the second story, populated by dogs, mosquitoes and gold-seekers. Our friends attempted a half-hearted cheer, and filled the air with messages for those at home.

Our boat was home-made, weak-kneed and leaky, but in thorough harmony with the wilderness we were traversing. A smooth and polished creation of the boat-builder's art might have been more beautiful, but we were quite agreed that it would have been less comfortable and a positive discord to our rough-hewn environment. In the bow was the woodshed, while amidships, built of pine boughs and blankets, was the bed chamber. Then came the rower's bench, and, jammed between this and the steersman, was our snug little kitchen. It was a veritable home, and we had little need of going ashore, save out of curiosity or to lay in a fresh supply of firewood.

The three of us had sworn to make of this a pleasure trip, in which all labor was to be performed by gravitation, and all profit reaped by ourselves. And what a profit it was to us who had been accustomed to pack great loads on our backs or drag all day at the sleds for a paltry 25 or 30 miles. We now hunted, played cards, smoked, ate and slept, sure of our six miles an hour, of our 144 a day.

Scarcely pausing at the deserted mining camp of Forty-Mile or at Fort Cudahy, we arrived at Eagle City, the first town on the American side of the boundary. What with the strange actions and heavy exactions of the Northwest Territory officials, we gave vent to a most excessive enthusiasm on once more treading the soil of Uncle Sam. The 50 inhabitants, while waiting for some steamer to bring them food, were engaged in bucking a faro layout. But they were boomers, halting the game in a vain attempt to sell us corner lots.

Three hundred miles below Dawson we encountered Circle City, the largest camp on the Yukon previous to the Klondike discoveries, and so named because of its proximity to the Arctic Circle. It lay on the edge of the great Yukon Flats, a dismal domain, about which little is known. The "Flats" are a vast area of low country, extending for hundreds of miles in every direction, into which the Yukon plunges and is practically lost. The river, hitherto flowing between mountains, rugged and sternly outlined, with few islands on its breast, now begins its heart-breaking dividing and subdividing. One finds himself in a gigantic puzzle, consisting of thousands of miles of territory, and cut up into countless myriads of islands and channels. Men have been known to lose their way and wander for weeks in this perplexing maze. Great "blind" sloughs, on every hand, lie in wait for the unwary. And most exasperating it is to labor several score of miles into one of these, to find that it is "blind" (has no outlet) and that you must retrace your steps. The islands are well wooded, but, having also been well flooded, are miserable to land upon. The region is one of the greatest nesting grounds in the world, abounding with all kinds of ducks, brant, geese and swans. The adventurer who faces this soggy wilderness of water, mud, dank vegetation and mosquitoes, does not care to linger by the way, but, with an intense longing and exceeding haste, keeps to the largest channels and swiftest currents.

Eighty-five miles within the Flats, where the Yukon crosses the Arctic Circle and makes it magnificent bend to the west and south, and the Porcupine threads the lacustrine wilderness and enters from the east, we landed at the old Hudson Bay Company post of Fort Yukon. The North American Trading and Transportation and the Alaska Commercial companies' caches are located here, also an Indian village. During the winter, while Dawson was on the ragged edge of famine, these caches were stocked to overflowing; yet it was impossible to sled the provisions such a distance up the river, while the steamers had found it equally impossible to get up before navigation closed.

The steamer Bella, a year late, was industriously loading up. It was a peculiar scene of animation and excitement. Four o'clock in the morning, under the Arctic circle, yet the sun was high in the heavens and it was already uncomfortably warm. It seemed more like some festival day at 3 o'clock in the afternoon. All was gaiety, noise and laughter. The bucks were skylarking or flirting with the maidens; the older squaws were gossiping in bunches, while the younger ones shrank and giggled in the corners. The children played or squabbled, and the babies rolled in the muck with the tawny wolf-dogs. Fantastic forms, dimly outlined, flitted to and fro, surged together, eddied, parted, in the smoke-laden atmosphere. Only by nosing and poking about could one see anything; for the reeking smoke rose from untold smudges, bringing grief to the mosquito, tears to the soft eyes of the white men and giving to the whole affair a mysterious air of unreality.

Through all this portion of the trip it was hard to realize our far-northerly latitude. It was more like an enchanted land, teeming with paradoxes. For instance, gasping for breath in the noonday heat and sweltering in a tropic temperature under Arctic skies or panting on top of the blankets at midnight, the red-disked sun poised like a ball of blood above the northern horizon. And the strange beauty and charm of the noonday nights—drifting, always drifting with the stream. Now slipping down a narrow channel where the wooded shores seem to meet overhead; now flashing into the open, where a thousand streams converge and form a mighty river; and again the diverging courses, the tiny channel, the overhanging forest, the smell of the land and the damp warmth of the vegetation. And above all, the hum of life, bursting into sudden gushes of song, slowly swelling to a great, dull roar of satisfaction or dying away into sweetly cadenced silence. Not a sound as we round the tail of a bar, disturbing a solitary crane from his ghostly reveries. A partridge drums in the forest, a moose lunges noisily as it takes to the water, and again silence. Then an owl hoots from some gloomy recess or a raven croaks gutturally overhead. Suddenly, the wild cry of a loon sweeps across a grassy stretch of river, awakening myriad answers. The robins open their full, rich throats, and the woods burst into music. The tree squirrels play half a dozen instruments at once, while the blackbirds sing shrill choruses to the sharp-marked time of the woodpecker. The pure treble of the songbirds is accompanied by the steady boom boom of the partridge, till all is lost in the general pandemonium. Then the wild fowl of the swamp join the quick crescendo, and the finale, swelled to bursting, slowly dies away. A kildee calls timidly to its mate, and silence falls.

After 300 miles of the Flats, we made Minook, the principal mining camp on the Lower River. It has since received the less euphemistic name of Rampart City. While the news of Dawson was by no means fresh, the men of the Lower River had had none all winter; so we landed amid a bombardment of queries. They were mostly perturbed over the war, the Thanksgiving football game and the execution of Durant. True to Northland tradition, we expanded items into chapters, yet failed utterly in satisfying their unholy lust for news.

Running the rapids below Minook, where the Yukon at some period cut its way through the Rampart Mountains, we made Tanana station. Here also was the Indian town of Nuklukyeto, while several miles below stood the old mission of St. James. Great was the merrymaking as we arrived in the wee, sma' hours. The spring run of salmon was expected at any moment, and the mission, Tanana and Tozikakats were all assembled, to say nothing of the general sprinkling contributed by the several hundred miles of Yukon on either side of the station. We landed our heavy craft amid the litter of flimsy bark canoes which lined the bank, and found ourselves in the great fishing camp. Picking our steps among the tents and wading through the sprawling babies and fighting dogs, we made our way to a large log structure where a dance was in progress. After much pushing and shoving, we forced an entrance through the swarming children. The long, low room was literally packed with dancers. There was no light, no ventilation, save through the crowded doorway, and, in the semi-darkness, strapping bucks and wild-eyed squaws sweated, howled and reveled in a dance which defies description. With the peculiar elation of the travelers who scales the virgin peak, we prepared to enjoy the novelty of the situation; but, imagine our disappointment on discovering that even here, 1,000 miles beyond the uttermost bounds of civilization, the adventurous white man already had penetrated. In the crowded room, dizzy with heat and the smell of bodies, we at last discerned the fair bronzed skin, the blue eyes, the blond mustache of the ubiquitous Anglo-Saxon. A glance demonstrated how thoroughly at home he was.

One hundred miles below Nuklukyeto, our midnight watch was beguiled by a wild chant, which rose and fell uncannily as it floated across the water. An hour later we rounded a bend and landed at a fishing village, so engrossed in its religious rites that our arrival was unnoted. Climbing the bank, we came full upon the weird scene. It brought us back to the orgies of the cavemen and more closely in touch with our common ancestor, probably arboreal, which Mr. Darwin has so fittingly described. Several score of bucks were giving tongue to unwritten music, evidently born when the world was very young, and still apulse with the spirit of primeval man. Urged on by the chief medicine man, the women had abandoned themselves to the religious ecstacy, their raven hair unbound and falling to their hips, while their bodies were swaying and undulating to the swing of the song.

Nor was the ubiquitous Anglo-Saxon absent; for there, between the flaps of a tent, with a nursing child at the breast, we found him staring at us through the eyes of a half-caste woman. Slender-formed, with her Caucasian features and delicate oval face, she seemed as a pearl cast among swine. Lafcadio Hearn had dwelt with great pathos upon the Japanese half-caste; but how much harder the lot of the Yukon Indian half-breed. It is a life of severest toil, coupled with extreme privation and misery. What white woman would care or dare to strap her suckling babe to her back, and, with the temperature ranging from 50 to 70 degrees below zero, travel 40 miles a day with the dogs? Such is but an instance of their continual life, whether at the hunting or the fishing, or when famine pinches or sickness is in the camps. Yet their lot is a common one, from the Coast Indians of the Panhandle to the Esquimaux of the Arctic Ocean, from the Rocky Mountains to the most westerly Aleutian isle.

In the course of trading with the natives, one soon learns much of the sickness and misery with which their lives are girt. From one end of the land to the other, the piteous cry for medicine goes up. In the most cursory intercourse, one stumbles upon pathetic little keynotes that serve as inklings to the solemn chords of heartache with which their lives vibrate. At the mouth of the Koyokuk, I wandered into a summer camp in the hope of picking up some specimens of beadwork. At one of the neatest tents of the encampment, I opened negotiations with a young half-breed woman for some exceptionally fine work, and, when I went away, I was filled with wonder at the bargain she had got. Nor was I at loss, for, before me, on a bearskin mat, had played a most beautiful child—flaxen-haired, blue-eyed and rosy-complexioned, a typical Saxon lass. As often as I stiffened the lines of the barter in accordance with Indian trading, I softened as I rescued my sheathknife or tobacco pouch from the baby fingers, or gazed into the blue eyes of the white father. And, when I hardened my heart for the articles of the final agreement, the mother said, "O you big white man, why so hard? I do much work, Oh, so much work. I get fish and moose and flour for two, and no man to help me."

I pointed to the child with a glance of interrogation, and she answered, "He go way —one—two—three years now."

And the bargain she made caused great envy among her dark sisters huddled in the doorway.

All through the interior, save in the sheltered nooks and on the northern slopes of the loftier peaks, the snow had quite disappeared by the middle of June. But from Tozikakat it began to grow more plentiful, till at Koyokuk, even the southern exposure was no longer bare—a sign that we were approaching the coast, or rather, the coast climate, for we were still 700 miles above the mouth of the river. It is naturally thus with a marine climate, where, because of the great body of water, the heat is neither absorbed nor radiated as rapidly as in the interior. Hence, the winters are much colder and the summers equally warmer at Dawson than at St. Michael. Along the shores of Bering Sea, even a month after the sun has passd its northern solstice, great bodies of snow are to be found lying at the water's edge.

At Nulato, 650 miles above the mouth, we found two small steamers fitting out and extensive preparations being made for the exploration of the Koyokuk, which is looked upon as the coming Alaskan Klondike. We were just in time for service at the Roman Catholic mission, and, strange it was, gazing upon the finely chiseled features of the be-moccasined, black-stoled priest, and listening to the strange unison of the shrill voices of the Indian women and the deep basses of the fathers. Father Monroe, a cultured, and as rumor puts it, a very wealthy Frenchman, has devoted his life to the cause of the missions, and for five long years has labored zealously at Nulato. The Indians are always more energetic, thrifty, and of better appearance at the missions than elsewhere, though Christianity seems never to get a really deep hold on them. Several of my souvenirs will testify to the readiness with which they will trade a crucifix for an old pack of cards.

It has been a very early spring, and the breaking of the Yukon was accompanied by the greatest high-water known for years. From Dawson to Kutlik, every station and long-established village had been severely flooded, many being washed away. If signs are to be trusted, the ice-run for the last 500 miles of river must have been terrific. Many portions of the mainland and whole islands had been swept clear of the timber which always clusters thickly in the bottoms. The large trees are uprooted or literally gnawed in two by the grinding ice, while the smaller ones bend before it and are rubbed clean of bark, reminding one of well-picked bones on some endless battlefield.

Game and fish were quite abundant the whole length of river, and every camp had a fresh bearskin or so stretched on the drying frames. While we did much of our own hunting, we did not waste time in gathering eggs or fishing, preferring to trade for such staples. However, we were usually disappointed in the eggs, not relishing the embryonic diet of ducks and geese which the natives so delight in. But the fish were excellent, especially the salmon. Oh, you, who pay big for the silver salmon of the fish market and then say it is good, come north and buy a great king salmon, weighing from 40 to 50 pounds of clean meat, for a tin cup or so of flour. They are to be found in the pink of condition in the icy waters of the Yukon, cold, firm-fleshed and, above all, delicious. But it takes one quite a time to learn to trade with the Indians. He must have the foresight of Joseph and the patience of Job, else will he be mulcted as the Gentile should be. The practiced hand endeavors to exhibit a well-disguised desire for the article he does not wish, and but ordinary interest in that which he is after. The native will then elevate the price of the former and correspondingly depress that of the latter. When he has thus brought the thing you wish absurdly low, snap it quick and pay on the spot. He will be chagrined, but a bargain's a bargain.

The hunting we could not forego, though the shotgun was old and decrepit, and one trigger persisted in discharging both barrels. Very pleasant it was during midnight lookouts, listening to the comrades snoring beneath the mosquito tent, drifting along the low-flooded banks, watching the sun above the northern horizon and dropping the startled wild fowl as they rose from the river.

By the time we arrived at Anvik, 600 miles from the mouth, we began to realize the mighty river we were voyaging on. At Fort Yukon, 1,300 miles from the mouth, it is 8 miles wide; at the Koyokuk it narrows to 2 or 3 miles; and from Koserefski it maintains a width of from 8 to 10 miles, till it is lost in the Great Delta, where its southern and northern mouths are over 80 miles apart. But at Anvik it is 40 miles wide, with a spring rise of from 30 to 40 feet. This great width is due to a division which makes possible one of the largest inland islands of the world—an island that is not even named.

A totally different native population is encountered from Anvik to the sea. The clean-limbed stalwart Indians disappear, being replaced by the Malemutes, who are a sort of mongrel cross of Thlinket and Esquimau. Poverty-stricken, with little energy and no ambition, they have not furnished much inducement to the white traders; hence, they continue to exist on a straight fish and meat diet, washed down with incalculable quantities of vile-smelling seal oil. Their houses are merely holes in the ground, shored with driftwood timbers. In the center of this they build an open fire, the smoke of which escapes through a venthole in the roof. In the winter time, the men, women and children crowd into these burrows like sardines. The sanitary, social and moral conditions may be conjectured.

They have quite a reverence for their dead, however; their burial places being neat, clean and pleasing to the eye. Rough palings surround the graves, which are usually covered with a rain shed. Fantastic designs are often painted upon them by the means of soot and seal oil. Occasionally, a curiously carved totem pole is raised; but, by the crosses the great majority rest in the consecrated ground of the Catholic Church. It is hard to say what becomes of the Protestant converts, but the more impressive ritual of the Catholic service, opposed to the bare, Puritanical mode of Protestant worship, and so pregnant with mysticism to the barbaric mind, may perhaps explain it.

From the Mission of the Holy Cross to the Russian Mission of Icogmute, we found the mountains dwindling sadly, and at Andrefsky we bade farewell to the last barren hills and plunged into the dismal solitude of the Great Delta of the Yukon. It was a repetition of the Flats, but fraught with more serious consequences. A mistake in this uncharted wilderness and one would blunder into the Southern Channel, wandering no man knows whither, till he emerged, without guide or landmark, on the bleak coast of Bering Sea. Disdaining Malemute guides, we were two days in traveling these 120 miles. We gave vent to much foolish enthusiasm when we felt the first pulse of the tide; and when in Kutlik we slept in sight of open sea, deemed ourselves to be nearly home.

The 80-mile run up the coast was full of excitement. As we skirted dangerous Point Romanoff, we picked up a Jesuit priest who was having a hard time in the surf. And for all the cloth he was a jolly fellow, pulling an oar, smoking a pipe or telling a tale with the next one. He was an illustration of the many strange types to be found in the Northland. An Italian by blood, a Frenchman by birth, a Spaniard by education and an American by residence, he was a marvelous scholar and his whole life was one continuous romance; but sworn to the oaths of his order, he had sacrificed twelve prime years of his life in bleak Alaska, and in all things, even to reducing the Innuit language to a grammar, was happy.

Our last taste of Bering Sea was a fitting close to the trip. Midnight found us wallowing in the sea, a rocky coast to leeward and a dirty sky to windward, with splutters of rain and wind squalls which soon developed into a gale. Removing the sprit and bagging the after-leech, we shortened to storm canvas and ran before it, reaching the harbor of St. Michael just 21 days from the time we cast off the lines at Dawson.

Back in California . . . recovering from scurvy, I found that my father was dead and that I was the head and the sole bread-winner of a household. When I state that I had passed coal on a steamship from Bering Sea to British Columbia, and traveled in the steerage from there to San Francisco, it will be understood that I brought nothing back from the Klondike but my scurvy.

Times were hard. Work of any sort was difficult to get. And work of any sort was what I had to take, for I was still an unskilled laborer. I had no thought of career. That was over and done with. I had to find food for two mouths besides my own and keep a roof over our heads—yes, and buy a winter suit, my one suit being decidedly summery. I had to get some sort of work immediately. After that, when I had caught my breath, I might think about my future.

Unskilled labor is the first to feel the slackness of hard times, and I had no trades save those of sailor and laundryman. With my new responsibilities I didn't dare go to sea, and I failed to find a job at laundrying. I failed to find a job at anything. I had my name down in five employment bureaus. I advertised in three newspapers. I sought out the few friends I knew who might be able to get me work; but they were either uninterested or unable to find anything for me.

The situation was desperate. I pawned my watch, my bicycle, and a mackintosh of which my father had been very proud and which he had left to me. It was and is my sole legacy in this world. It had cost fifteen dollars, and the pawnbroker let me have two dollars on it. And—oh, yes—a water-front comrade of earlier years drifted along one day with a dress suit wrapped in newspapers. He could give no adequate explanation of how he had come to possess it, nor did I press for an explanation. I wanted the suit myself. No; not to wear. I traded him a lot of rubbish which, being unpawnable, was useless to me. He peddled the rubbish for several dollars, while I pledged the dress suit with my pawnbroker for five dollars. And for all I know, the pawnbroker still has the suit. I had never intended to redeem it.

But I couldn't get any work. Yet I was a bargain in the labor market. I was twenty-two years old, weighed one hundred and sixty-five pounds stripped, every pound of which was excellent for toil; and the last traces of my scurvy were vanishing before a treatment of potatoes chewed raw. I tackled every opening for employment. I tried to become a studio model, but there were too many fine-bodied young fellows out of jobs. I answered advertisements of elderly invalids in need of companions. And I almost became a sewing machine agent, on commission, without salary. But poor people don't buy sewing machines in hard times, so I was forced to forego that employment.

Of course, it must be remembered that along with such frivolous occupations, I was trying to get work as wop, lumper, and roustabout. But winter was coming on, and the surplus labor army was pouring into the cities. Also, I, who had romped along carelessly through the countries of the world and the kingdom of the mind, was not a member of any union.

I sought odd jobs. I worked days, and half-days, at anything I could get. I mowed lawns, trimmed hedges, took up carpets, beat them, and laid them again. Further, I took the civil service examinations for mail carrier and passed first. But alas, there was no vacancy, and I must wait. And while I waited, and in between the odd jobs I managed to procure, I started to earn ten dollars by writing a newspaper account of the voyage I had made, in an open boat down the Yukon . . . I didn't know the first thing about the newspaper game, but I was confident I'd get ten dollars for my article.

But I didn't . . .

Sept. 17, 1898
962 E. 16th St.
Oakland, Calif.

Editor of the "Bulletin"

Dear Sir:

I have just returned from a year's residence in the Klondike entering the country by the way of Dyea and Chilcoot Pass. I left by the way of St. Michael, thus making altogether a journey of 2,500 miles on the Yukon in a small boat. I have sailed and traveled quite extensively in other parts of the world and have learned to size upon that which is interesting, to grasp the true romance of things, and to understand the people I may be thrown amongst.

I have just completed an article of 4,000 words, describing the trip from Dawson to St. Michael in a row boat. Kindly let me know if there would be any demand in your columns for it—of course thoroughly understanding that the acceptance of the manuscript is to depend upon its literary and intrinsic value.

Yours very respectfully,
Jack London

[In pencil]
Interest in Alaska has subsided in an amazing degree. Then again so much has been written that I do not think it would pay us to buy your story.

Editor

And here is the funny thing. Some are born to fortune, and some have fortune thrust upon them. But in my case I was clubbed into fortune, and bitter necessity wielded the club. I had long since abandoned all thought of writing as a career. My honest intention in writing that article was to earn ten dollars. And that was the limit of my intention. It would help to tide me along until I got steady employment. Had a vacancy occurred in the post office at that time, I should have jumped at it.

But the vacancy did not occur, nor did a steady job; and I employed the time between odd jobs with writing a twenty-one-thousand-word serial for the "Youth's Companion." I turned it out and typed it in seven days. I fancy that was what was the matter with it, for it came back.

It took some time for it to go and come, and in the meantime I tried my hand at short stories . . . .

And just then came the call from the post office to go to work. It placed me in a most trying predicament. The sixty-five dollars I could earn regularly every month was a terrible temptation. I couldn't decide what to do. And I'll never be able to forgive the postmaster of Oakland. I answered the call, and I talked to him like a man. I frankly told him the situation. It looked as if I might win out at writing. The chance was good, but not certain. Now, if he would pass me by and select the next man on the eligible list, and give me a call at the next vacancy—

But he shut me off with: "Then you don't want the position?"

"But I do," I protested. "Don't you see, if you will pass me over this time—"

"If you want it you will take it," he said coldly.

Happily for me, the cursed brutality of the man made me angry.

"Very well," I said. "I won't take it."

My difficulty was that I had no one to advise me. I didn't know a soul who had written or who had ever tried to write. I didn't even know one reporter. Also, to succeed at the writing game, I found I had to unlearn about everything the teachers and professors of literature of the high school and university had taught me. I was very indignant about this at the time; though now I can understand it. They did not know the trick of successful writing in the years of 1895 and 1896. They knew all about "Snow Bound" and "Sartor Resartus"; but the American editors of 1899 did not want such truck. They wanted the 1899 truck, and offered to pay so well for it that the teachers and professors of literature would have quit their jobs could they have supplied it.

I struggled along, stood off the butcher and the grocer, pawned my watch and bicycle and my father's mackintosh, and I worked. I really did work, and went on short commons of sleep.

Having burned my one ship, I plunged into writing. I am afraid I always was an extremist. Early and late I was at it—writing, typing, studying grammar, studying writing and all the forms of writing, and studying the writers who succeeded in order to find out how they succeeded. I managed on five hours' sleep in the twenty-four, and came pretty close to working the nineteen waking hours left to me. My light burned till two and three in the morning . . .

The trouble with the beginner at the writing game is the long, dry spells, when there is never an editor's check and everything pawnable is pawned. I wore my summer suit pretty well through that winter, and the following summer experienced the longest, dryest spell of all, in the period when salaried men are gone on vacation and manuscripts lie in editorial offices until vacation is over.

I had no one to give me tips, no one's experience to profit by. So I sat down and wrote in order to get an experience of my own. I wrote everything—short stories, articles, anecdotes, jokes, essays, sonnets, ballads, vilanelles, triolets, songs, light plays in iambic tetrameter, and heavy tragedies in blank verse. These various creations I stuck into envelopes, enclosed return postage, and dropped into the mail. Oh, I was prolific. Day by day my manuscripts mounted up, till the problem of finding stamps for them became as great as that of making life livable for my widow landlady.

All my manuscripts came back. They continued to come back. The process seemed like the working of a soulless machine. I dropped the manuscript into the mail box. After the lapse of a certain approximate length of time, the manuscript was brought back to me by the postman. Accompanying it was a stereotyped rejection slip. A part of the machine, some cunning arrangement of cogs and cranks at the other end, (it could not have been a living, breathing man with blood in his veins), had transferred the manuscript to another envelope, taken the stamps from the inside and pasted them outside, and added the rejection slip.

This went on for some months. I was still in the dark, I had not yet gained the smallest particle of experience. Concerning which was the more marketable, poetry or prose, jokes or sonnets, short stories or essays, I knew no more than when I began. I had vague ideas, however, dim and hazy ideas to the effect that a minimum rate of ten dollars a thousand words was paid; that if I only published two or three things the editors would clamor for my wares; that a manuscript held in some editor's hands for the small matter of four or five months did not necessarily mean a manuscript that was sold.

Concerning this minimum rate of ten dollars a thousand words, a thing in which I fondly believed, I must confess that I had gleaned it from some Sunday supplement.

Likewise I must confess the beautiful and touching modesty with which I aspired. Let other men, thought I, receive the maximum rate, whatever marvelous sum it may be. As for myself, I shall always be content to receive the minimum rate. And, once I get started, I shall do no more than three thousand words a day, five days only in the week. This will give me plenty of recreation, while I shall be earning six hundred dollars a month without overstocking the market.

As I say, the machine worked on for several months, and then, one morning, the postman brought me a letter, mark you, a letter, not a long thick one but a short thin one, and from a magazine. My stamp problem and my landlady problem were pressing me cruelly, and this short, thin letter from a magazine would of a certainty solve both problems in short order.

I could not open the letter right away. It seemed a sacred thing. It contained the written words of an editor. The magazine he represented I imagined ranked in the first class. I knew it held a four-thousand-word story of mine. What will it be? I asked. The minimum rate, I answered, modest as ever; forty dollars of course. Having thus guarded myself against an possible kind of disappointment, I opened the letter and read what I thought would be blazed in letters of fire on my memory for all time. Alas! the years are few, yet I have forgotten. But the gist of the letter was coldly to the effect that my story was available, that they would print it in the next number, and that they would pay me for it the sum of five dollars.

Five dollars! A dollar and a quarter a thousand! That I did not die right there and then convinces me that I am possessed of a singular ruggedness of soul which will permit me to survive and ultimately qualify for the oldest inhabitant.

Five dollars! When? The editor did not state. I didn't have even a stamp with which to convey my acceptation or rejection of his offer. Just then the landlady's little girl knocked at the back door. Both problems were clamoring more compellingly than ever for solution. It was plain there was no such thing as a minimum rate. Nothing remained but to get out and shovel coal. I had done it before and earned more money at it. I resolved to do it again; and I certainly should have, had it not been for the "Black Cat."

Yes, the "Black Cat." The postman brought me an offer from it of forty dollars for a four-thousand-word story, which same was more lengthy than strengthy, if I would grant permission to cut it down half. This was equivalent to a twenty-dollar rate. Grant permission? I told them they could cut it down two-halves if they'd only send the money along, which they did, by return mail. . . . I forgot my coal-shoveling resolution and continued to whang away at the typewriter . . .

. . . Critics have complained about the swift education one of my characters, Martin Eden, achieved. In three years, from a sailor with a common school education, I made a successful writer of him. The critics say this is impossible. Yet I was Martin Eden. At the end of three working years, two of which were spent in high school and the university and one spent at writing, and all three in studying immensely and intensely, I was publishing stories in magazines such as the *Atlantic Monthly,* was correcting proofs of my first book (issued by Houghton, Mifflin Co.), was selling sociological articles to *Cosmopolitan* and *McClure's,* had declined an associate editorship proffered me by telegraph from New York City, and was getting ready to marry.

This, then, was the childhood and youth of an extraordinary man—a childhood of poverty and struggle, yet one brimming with adventure and achievement. The time was 1899, he was twenty-five years old, and because of his tremendous intellectual accomplishment life held great promise. From this vantage point Jack London leaped up the stairway to success. His stories were sought by all the leading magazines. His novels were serialized before publication and sold hundreds of thousands of copies after publication. His name became a household word. Among other things he became a war correspondent, a world traveller, and a rabid socialist. His restless, turbulent spirit kept driving him forward, never giving his fertile, creative mind rest. Sixteen short years later his tiring body broke down, unable to stand the furious, strenuous pace. Jack London was buried on his famous ranch in the Valley of the Moon. He had left to posterity a rich literary heritage.

THE MAN

The Man

Though he never wrote an "official" autobiography, the two books included here present as complete a picture as London was to give of himself. Both contain the uncompromising honesty and exuberant energy so characteristic of his best writing; both were written during difficult periods in his life; both show an artist unafraid to confront his personal demons.

But there the similarity ends. London's views of the world and his own place in it were often contradictory, sometimes diametrically opposed. Socialist and capitalist, egalitarian and superman, artist and adventurer, it should be no surprise that London needed two ways of telling his own story, one through fiction, and one through a memoir.

Martin Eden may be the best novel London produced. The story of a man who begins as a sailor, educates himself, and becomes a famous but disillusioned writer is of course London's own story, told with a sensitivity only hinted at in his writing up to that time. It is, too, a very romantic work for him, not only in the growth of the title character, but in its evocations of the society he inhabits. Turn-of-the-century San Francisco Bay, with its waterfront saloons, bohemian wine parties, and Knob Hill socialite gatherings becomes a character itself, realistic yet lovingly rendered.

There is nothing romantic about *John Barleycorn.* Subtitled "Alcoholic Memoirs," it details London's lifelong battle with the bottle. Starting with his first taste of liquor—as well as his first hangover—at the age of five, London details the use of alcohol as an initiation into manhood. An alcoholic most of his adult life, he never actually quit drinking, only moderated it as his health demanded. Yet *John Barleycorn* goes beyond the "alcoholic memoir" to portray a man in perpetual struggle with his own impulses.

MARTIN EDEN

I

The one opened the door with a latch-key and went in, followed by a young fellow who awkwardly removed his cap. He wore rough clothes that smacked of the sea, and he was manifestly out of place in the spacious hall in which he found himself. He did not know what to do with his cap, and was stuffing it into his coat pocket when the other took it from him. The act was done quietly and naturally, and the awkward young fellow appreciated it. "He understands," was his thought. "He'll see me through all right."

He walked at the other's heels with a swing to his shoulders, and his legs spread unwittingly, as if the level floors were tilting up and sinking down to the heave and lunge of the sea. The wide rooms seemed too narrow for his rolling gait, and to himself he was in terror lest his broad shoulders should collide with the doorways or sweep the bric-a-brac from the low mantel. He recoiled from side to side between the various objects and multiplied the hazards that in reality lodged only in his mind. Between a grand piano and a centre-table piled high with books was space for a half a dozen to walk abreast, yet he essayed it with trepidation. His heavy arms hung loosely at his sides. He did not know what to do with those arms and hands, and when, to his excited vision, one arm seemed liable to brush against the books on the table, he lurched away like a frightened horse, barely missing the piano stool. He watched the easy walk of the other in front of him, and for the first time realized that his walk was different from that of other men. He experienced a momentary pang of shame that he should walk so uncouthly. The sweat burst through the skin of his forehead in tiny beads, and he paused and mopped his bronzed face with his handkerchief.

"Hold on, Arthur, my boy," he said, attempting to mask his anxiety with facetious utterance. "This is too much all at once for yours truly. Give me a chance to get my nerve. You know I didn't want to come, an' I guess your fam'ly ain't hankerin' to see me neither."

"That's all right," was the reassuring answer. "You mustn't be frightened at us. We're just homely people—Hello, there's a letter for me."

He stepped back to the table, tore open the envelope, and began to read, giving the stranger an opportunity to recover himself. And the stranger understood and appreciated. His was the gift of sympathy, understanding; and beneath his alarmed exterior that sympathetic process went on. He mopped his forehead dry and glanced about him with a controlled face, though in the eyes there was an expression such as wild animals betray when they fear the trap. He was surrounded by the unknown, apprehensive of what might happen, ignorant of what he should do, aware that he walked and bore himself awkwardly, fearful that every attribute and power of him was similarly afflicted. He was keenly sensitive, hopelessly self-conscious, and the amused glance that the other stole privily at him over the top of the letter burned into him like a dagger-thrust. He saw the glance, but he gave no sign, for among the things he had learned was discipline. Also, that dagger-thrust went to his pride. He cursed himself for having come, and at the same time resolved that, happen what would, having come, he would carry it through. The lines of his face hardened, and into his eyes came a fighting light. He looked about more unconcernedly, sharply observant, every detail of the pretty interior registering itself on his brain. His eyes were wide apart; nothing in their field of vision escaped; and as they drank in the beauty before them the fighting light died out and a warm glow took its place. He was responsive to beauty, and here was cause to respond.

An oil painting caught and held him. A heavy surf thundered and burst over an outjutting rock; lowering storm-clouds covered the sky; and, outside the line of surf, a pilot-schooner, close-hauled, heeled over till every detail of her deck was visible, was surging along against a stormy sunset sky. There was beauty, and it drew him irresistibly. He forgot his awkward walk and came closer to the painting, very close. The beauty faded out of the canvas. His face expressed his bepuzzlement. He stared at what seemed a careless daub of paint, then stepped away. Immediately all the beauty flashed back into the canvas. "A trick picture," was his thought, as he dismissed it, though in the midst of the multitudinous impressions he was receiving he found time to feel a prod of indignation that so much beauty should be sacrificed to make a trick. He did not know painting. He had been brought up on chromos and lithographs that were always definite and sharp, near or far. He had seen oil paintings, it was true, in the show windows of shops, but the glass of the windows had prevented his eager eyes from approaching too near.

He glanced around at his friend reading the letter and saw the books on the table. Into his eyes leaped a wistfulness and a yearning as promptly as the yearning leaps into the eyes of a starving man at sight of food. An impulsive stride, with one lurch to right and left of the shoulders, brought him to the table, where he began affectionately handling the books. He glanced at the titles and the authors' names, read fragments of text, caressing the volumes with his eyes and hands, and, once, recognized a book he had read. For the rest, they were strange books and strange authors. He chanced upon a volume of Swinburne and began reading steadily, forgetful of where he was, his face glowing. Twice he closed the book on his forefinger to look at the name of the author. Swinburne! he would remember that name. That fellow had eyes, and he had certainly seen color and flashing light. But who was Swinburne? Was he dead a hundred years or so, like most of the poets? Or was he alive still, and writing? He turned to the title-page . . . yes, he had written other books; well, he would go to the free library the first thing in the morning and try to get hold of some of Swinburne's stuff. He went back to the text and lost himself. He did not notice that a young woman had entered the room. The first he knew was when he heard Arthur's voice saying:—

"Ruth, this is Mr. Eden."

The book was closed on his forefinger, and before he turned he was thrilling to the first new impression, which was not of the girl, but of her brother's words. Under that muscled body of his he was a mass of quivering sensibilities. At the slightest impact of the outside world upon his consciousness, his thoughts, sympathies, and emotions leapt and played like lambent flame. He was extraordinarily receptive and responsive, while his imagination, pitched high, was ever at work establishing relations of likeness and difference. "Mr. Eden," was what he had thrilled to—he who had been called "Eden," or "Martin Eden," or just "Martin," all his life. And "*Mister!*" It was certainly going some, was his internal comment. His mind seemed to turn, on the instant, into a vast camera obscura, and he saw arrayed around his consciousness endless pictures from his life, of stoke-holes and forecastles, camps and beaches, jails and boozing-kens, fever-hospitals and slum streets, wherein the thread of association was the fashion in which he had been addressed in those various situations.

And then he turned and saw the girl. The phantasmagoria of his brain vanished at sight of her. She was a pale, ethereal creature, with wide, spiritual blue eyes and a wealth of golden hair. He did not know how she was dressed, except that the dress was as wonderful as she. He likened her to a pale gold flower upon a slender stem. No, she was a spirit, a divinity, a goddess; such sublimated beauty was not of the earth. Or perhaps the books were right, and there were many such as she in the upper walks of life. She might well be sung by that chap Swinburne. Perhaps he had had somebody like her in mind when he painted that girl, Iseult, in the book there on the table. All this plethora of sight, and feeling, and thought occurred on the instant. There was no pause of the realities wherein he moved. He saw her hand coming out to his, and she looked him straight in the eyes as she shook hands, frankly, like a man. The women he had known did not shake hands that way. For that matter, most of them did not shake hands at all. A flood of associations, visions of various ways he had made the acquaintance of women, rushed into his mind and threatened to swamp it. But he shook them aside and looked at her. Never had he seen such a woman. The women he had known! Immediately, beside her, on either hand, ranged the women he had known. For an eternal second he stood in the midst of a portrait gallery, wherein she occupied the central place, while about her were limned many women, all to be weighed and measured by a fleeting glance, herself the unit of weight and measure. He saw the weak and sickly faces of the girls of the factories, and the simpering, boisterous girls from the south of Market. There were women of the cattle camps, and swarthy cigarette-smoking women of Old Mexico. These, in turn, were crowded out by Japanese women, doll-like, stepping mincingly on wooden clogs; by Eurasians, delicate featured, stamped with degeneracy; by full-bodied South-Sea-Island women, flower-crowned and brown-skinned. All these were blotted out by a grotesque and terrible nightmare brood—frowsy, shuffling creatures from the pavements of Whitechapel, gin-bloated hags of the stews, and all the vast hell's following of harpies, vile-mouthed and filthy, that under the guise of monstrous female form prey upon sailors, the scrapings of the ports, the scum and slime of the human pit.

"Won't you sit down, Mr. Eden?" the girl was saying. "I have been looking forward to meeting you ever since Arthur told us. It was brave of you—"

He waved his hand deprecatingly and muttered that it was nothing at all, what he had done, and that any fellow would have done it. She noticed that the hand he waved was covered with fresh abrasions, in the process of healing, and a glance at the other loose-hanging hand showed it to be in the same condition. Also, with quick, critical eye, she noted a scar on his cheek, another that peeped out from under the hair of the forehead, and a third that ran down and disappeared under the starched collar. She repressed a smile at sight of the red line that marked the chafe of the collar against the bronzed neck. He was evidently unused to stiff collars. Likewise her feminine eye took in the clothes he wore, the cheap and unaesthetic cut, the wrinkling of the coat across the shoulders, and the series of wrinkles in the sleeves that advertised bulging biceps muscles.

While he waved his hand and muttered that he had done nothing at all, he was obeying her behest by trying to get into a chair. He found time to admire the ease with which she sat down, then lurched toward a chair facing her, overwhelmed with consciousness of the awkward figure he was cutting. This was a new experience for him. All his life, up to then, he had been unaware of being either graceful or awkward. Such thoughts of self had never entered his mind. He sat down gingerly on the edge of the chair, greatly worried by his hands. They were in the way wherever he put them. Arthur was leaving the room, and Martin Eden followed his exit with longing eyes. He felt lost, alone there in the room with that pale spirit of a woman. There was no barkeeper upon whom to call for drinks, no small boy to send around the corner for a can of beer and by means of that social fluid start the amenities of friendship flowing.

"You have such a scar on your neck, Mr. Eden," the girl was saying. "How did it happen? I am sure it must have been some adventure."

"A Mexican with a knife, miss," he answered, moistening his parched lips and clearing his throat. "It was just a fight. After I got the knife away, he tried to bite off my nose."

Baldly as he had stated it, in his eyes was a rich vision of that hot, starry night at Salina Cruz, the white strip of beach, the lights of the sugar steamers in the harbor, the voices of the drunken sailors in the distance, the jostling stevedores, the flaming passion in the Mexican's face, the glint of the beast-eyes in the starlight, the sting of the steel in his neck, and the rush of blood, the crowd and the cries, the two bodies, his and the Mexican's, locked together, rolling over and over and tearing up the sand, and from away off somewhere the mellow tinkling of a guitar. Such was the picture, and he thrilled to the memory of it, wondering if the man could paint it who had painted the pilot-schooner on the wall. The white beach, the stars, and the lights of the sugar steamers would look great, he thought, and midway on the sand the dark group of figures that surrounded the fighters. The knife occupied a place in the picture, he decided, and would show well, with a sort of gleam, in the light of the stars. But of all this no hint had crept into his speech. "He tried to bite off my nose," he concluded.

"Oh," the girl said, in a faint, far voice, and he noticed the shock in her sensitive face.

He felt a shock himself, and a blush of embarrassment shone faintly on his sunburned cheeks, though to him it burned as hotly as when his cheeks had been exposed to the open furnace-door in the fire-room. Such sordid things as stabbing affrays were evidently not fit subjects for conversation with a lady. People in the books, in her walk of life, did not talk about such things—perhaps they did not know about them, either.

There was a brief pause in the conversation they were trying to get started. Then she asked tentatively about the scar on his cheek. Even as she asked, he realized that she was making an effort to talk his talk, and he resolved to get away from it and talk hers.

"It was just an accident," he said, putting his hand to his cheek. "One night, in a calm, with a heavy sea running, the main-boom-lift carried away, an' next the tackle. The lift was wire, an' it was threshin' around like a snake. The whole watch was tryin' to grab it, an' I rushed in an' got swatted."

"Oh," she said, this time with an accent of comprehension, though secretly his speech had been so much Greek to her and she was wondering what a *lift* was and what *swatted* meant.

"This man Swineburne," he began, attempting to put his plan into execution and pronouncing the *i* long.

"Who?"

"Swineburne," he repeated, with the same mispronunciation. "The poet."

"Swinburne," she corrected.

"Yes, that's the chap," he stammered, his cheeks hot again. "How long since he died?"

"Why, I haven't heard that he was dead." She looked at him curiously. "Where did you make his acquaintance?"

"I never clapped eyes on him," was the reply. "But I read some of his poetry out of that book there on the table just before you come in. How do you like his poetry?"

And thereat she began to talk quickly and easily upon the subject he had suggested. He felt better, and settled back slightly from the edge of the chair, holding tightly to its arms with his hands, as if it might get away from him and buck him to the floor. He had succeeded in making her talk her talk, and while she rattled on, he strove to follow her, marvelling at all the knowledge that was stowed away in that pretty head of hers, and drinking in the pale beauty of her face. Follow her he did, though bothered by unfamiliar words that fell glibly from her lips and by critical phrases and thought-processes that were foreign to his mind, but that nevertheless stimulated his mind and set it tingling. Here was intellectual life, he thought, and here was beauty, warm and wonderful as he had never dreamed it could be. He forgot himself and stared at her with hungry eyes. Here was something to live for, to win to, to fight for—ay, and die for. The books were true. There were such women in the world. She was one of them. She lent wings to his imagination, and great, luminous canvases spread themselves before him, whereon loomed vague, gigantic figures of love and romance, and of heroic deeds for woman's sake—for a pale woman, a flower of gold. And through the swaying, palpitant vision, as through a fairy mirage, he stared at the real woman, sitting there and talking of literature and art. He listened as well, but he stared, unconscious of the fixity of his gaze or of the fact that all that was essentially masculine in his nature was shining in his eyes. But she, who knew little of the world of men, being a woman, was keenly aware of his burning eyes. She had never had men look at her in such fashion, and it embarrassed her. She stumbled and halted in her utterance. The thread of argument slipped from her. He frightened her, and at the same time it was strangely pleasant to be so looked upon. Her training warned her of peril and of wrong, subtle, mysterious, luring; while her instincts rang clarion-voiced through her being, impelling her to hurdle caste and place and gain to this traveller from another world, to this uncouth young fellow with lacerated hands and a line of raw red caused by the unaccustomed linen at his throat, who, all too evidently, was soiled and tainted by ungracious existence. She was clean, and her cleanness revolted; but she was a woman, and she was just beginning to learn the paradox of woman.

"As I was saying—what was I saying?" She broke off abruptly and laughed merrily at her predicament.

"You was saying that this man Swinburne failed bein' a great poet because—an' that was as far as you got, miss," he prompted, while to himself he seemed suddenly hungry, and delicious little thrills crawled up and down his spine at the sound of her laughter. Like silver, he thought to himself, like tinkling silver bells; and on the instant, and for an instant, he was transported to a far land, where under pink cherry blossoms, he smoked a cigarette and listened to the bells of the peaked pagoda calling straw-sandalled devotees to worship.

"Yes, thank you," she said. "Swinburne fails, when all is said, because he is, well, indelicate. There are many of his poems that should never be read. Every line of the really great poets is filled with beautiful truth, and calls to all that is high and noble in the human. Not a line of the great poets can be spared without impoverishing the world by that much."

"I thought it was great," he said hesitatingly, "the little I read. I had no idea he was such a—a scoundrel. I guess that crops out in his other books."

"There are many lines that could be spared from the book you were reading," she said, her voice primly firm and dogmatic.

"I must 'a' missed 'em," he announced. "What I read was the real goods. It was all lighted up an' shining, an' it shun right into me an' lighted me up inside, like the sun or a searchlight. That's the way it landed on me, but I guess I ain't up much on poetry, miss."

He broke off lamely. He was confused, painfully conscious of his inarticulateness. He had felt the bigness and glow of life in what he had read, but his speech was inadequate. He could not express what he felt, and to himself he likened himself to a sailor, in a strange ship, on a dark night, groping about in the unfamiliar running rigging. Well, he decided, it was up to him to get acquainted in this new world. He had never seen anything that he couldn't get the hang of when he wanted to and it was about time for him to want to learn to talk the things that were inside of him so that she could understand. *She* was bulking large on his horizon.

"Now Longfellow—" she was saying.

"Yes, I've read 'm," he broke in impulsively, spurred on to exhibit and make the most of his little store of book knowledge, desirous of showing her that he was not wholly a stupid clod. " 'The Psalm of Life,' 'Excelsior,' an'. . . . I guess that's all."

She nodded her head and smiled, and he felt, somehow, that her smile was tolerant, pitifully tolerant. He was a fool to attempt to make a pretence that way. That Longfellow chap most likely had written countless books of poetry.

"Excuse me, miss, for buttin' in that way. I guess the real facts is that I don't know nothin' much about such things. It ain't in my class. But I'm goin' to make it in my class."

It sounded like a threat. His voice was determined, his eyes were flashing, the lines of his face had grown harsh. And to her it seemed that the angle of his jaw had changed; its pitch had become unpleasantly aggressive. At the same time a wave of intense virility seemed to surge out from him and impinge upon her.

"I think you could make it in—in your class," she finished with a laugh. "You are very strong."

Her gaze rested for a moment on the muscular neck, heavy corded, almost bull-like, bronzed by the sun, spilling over with rugged health and strength. And though he sat there, blushing and humble, again she felt drawn to him. She was surprised by a wanton thought that rushed into her mind. It seemed to her that if she could lay her two hands upon that neck that all its strength and vigor would flow out to her. She was shocked by this thought. It seemed to reveal to her an undreamed depravity in her nature. Besides, strength to her was a gross and brutish thing. Her ideal of masculine beauty had always been slender gracefulness. Yet the thought still persisted. It bewildered her that she should desire to place her hands on that sunburned neck. In truth, she was far from robust, and the need of her body and mind was for strength. But she did not know it. She knew only that no man had ever affected her before as this one had, who shocked her from moment to moment with his awful grammar.

"Yes, I ain't no invalid," he said. "When it comes down to hard-pan, I can digest scrap-iron. But just now I've got dyspepsia. Most of what you was sayin' I can't digest. Never trained that way, you see. I like books and poetry, and what time I've had I've read 'em, but I've never thought about 'em the way you have. That's why I can't talk about 'em. I'm like a navigator adrift on a strange sea without chart or compass. Now I want to get my bearin's. Mebbe you can put me right. How did you learn all this you've ben talkin'?"

"By going to school, I fancy, and by studying," she answered.

"I went to school when I was a kid," he began to object.

"Yes; but I mean high school, and lectures, and the university."

"You've gone to the university?" he demanded in frank amazement. He felt that she had become remoter from him by at least a million miles.

"I'm going there now. I'm taking special courses in English."

He did not know what "English" meant, but he made a mental note of that item of ignorance and passed on.

"How long would I have to study before I could go to the university?" he asked.

She beamed encouragement upon his desire for knowledge, and said: "That depends upon how much studying you have already done. You have never attended high school? Of course not. But did you finish grammar school?"

"I had two years to run, when I left," he answered. "But I was always honorably promoted at school."

The next moment, angry with himself for the boast, he had gripped the arms of the chair so savagely that every finger-end was stinging. At the same moment he became aware that a woman was entering the room. He saw the girl leave her chair and trip swiftly across the floor to the newcomer. They kissed each other, and, with arms around each other's waists, they advanced toward him. That must be her mother, he thought. She was a tall, blond woman, slender, and stately, and beautiful. Her gown was what he might expect in such a house. His eyes delighted in the graceful lines of it. She and her dress together reminded him of women on the stage. Then he remembered seeing similar grand ladies and gowns entering the London theatres while he stood and watched and the policemen shoved him back into the drizzle beyond the awning. Next his mind leaped to the Grand Hotel at Yokohama, where, too, from the sidewalk, he had seen grand ladies. Then the city and the harbor of Yokohama, in a thousand pictures, began flashing before his eyes. But he swiftly dismissed the kaleidoscope of memory, oppressed by the urgent need of the present. He knew that he must stand up to be introduced, and he struggled painfully to his feet, where he stood with trousers bagging at the knees, his arms loose-hanging and ludicrous, his face set hard for the impending ordeal.

II

THE process of getting into the dining room was a nightmare to him. Between halts and stumbles, jerks and lurches, locomotion had at times seemed impossible. But at last he had made it, and was seated alongside of Her. The array of knives and forks frightened him. They bristled with unknown perils, and he gazed at them, fascinated, till their dazzle became a background across which moved a succession of forecastle pictures, wherein he and his mates sat eating salt beef with sheath-knives and fingers, or scooping thick peasoup out of pannikins by means of battered iron spoons. The stench of bad beef was in his nostrils, while in his ears, to the accompaniment of creaking timbers and groaning bulkheads, echoed the loud mouth-noises of the eaters. He watched them eating, and decided that they ate like pigs. Well, he would be careful here. He would make no noise. He would keep his mind upon it all the time.

He glanced around the table. Opposite him was Arthur, and Arthur's brother,

Norman. They were her brothers, he reminded himself, and his heart warmed toward them. How they loved each other, the members of this family! There flashed into his mind the picture of her mother, of the kiss of greeting, and of the pair of them walking toward him with arms entwined. Not in his world were such displays of affection between parents and children made. It was a revelation of the heights of existence that were attained in the world above. It was the finest thing yet that he had seen in this small glimpse of that world. He was moved deeply by appreciation of it, and his heart was melting with sympathetic tenderness. He had starved for love all his life. His nature craved love. It was an organic demand of his being. Yet he had gone without, and hardened himself in the process. He had not known that he needed love. Nor did he know it now. He merely saw it in operation, and thrilled to it, and thought it fine, and high, and splendid.

He was glad that Mr. Morse was not there. It was difficult enough getting acquainted with her, and her mother, and her brother, Norman. Arthur he already knew somewhat. The father would have been too much for him, he felt sure. It seemed to him that he had never worked so hard in his life. The severest toil was child's play compared with this. Tiny nodules of moisture stood out on his forehead, and his shirt was wet with sweat from the exertion of doing so many unaccustomed things at once. He had to eat as he had never eaten before, to handle strange tools, to glance surreptitiously about and learn how to accomplish each new thing, to receive the flood of impressions that was pouring in upon him and being mentally annotated and classified; to be conscious of a yearning for her that perturbed him in the form of a dull, aching restlessness; to feel the prod of desire to win to the walk in life whereon she trod, and to have his mind ever and again straying off in speculation and vague plans of how to reach to her. Also, when his secret glance went across to Norman opposite him, or to any one else, to ascertain just what knife or fork was to be used in any particular occasion, that person's features were seized upon by his mind, which automatically strove to appraise them and to divine what they were—all in relation to her. Then he had to talk, to hear what was said to him and what was said back and forth, and to answer, when it was necessary, with a tongue prone to looseness of speech that required a constant curb. And to add confusion to confusion, there was the servant, an unceasing menace, that appeared noiselessly at his shoulder, a dire Sphinx that propounded puzzles and conundrums demanding instantaneous solution. He was oppressed throughout the meal by the thought of finger-bowls. Irrelevantly, insistently, scores of times, he wondered when they would come on and what they looked like. He had heard of such things, and now, sooner or later, somewhere in the next few minutes, he would see them, sit at table with exalted beings who used them—ay, and he would use them himself. And most important of all, far down and yet always at the surface of his thought, was the problem of how he should comport himself toward these persons. What should his attitude be? He wrestled continually and anxiously with the problem. There were cowardly suggestions that he should make believe, assume a part; and there were still more cowardly suggestions that warned him he would fail in such course, that his nature was not fitted to live up to it, and that he would make a fool of himself.

It was during the first part of the dinner, struggling to decide upon his attitude, that he was very quiet. He did not know that his quietness was giving the lie to Arthur's words of the day before, when that brother of hers had announced that he was going to bring a wild man home to dinner and for them not to be alarmed, because they would find him an interesting wild man. Martin Eden could not have found it in him, just then, to believe that her brother could be guilty of such treachery—especially when he had been the means of getting this particular brother out of an unpleasant row. So he sat at table, perturbed by his own unfitness and at the same time charmed by all that went on about him. For the first time he realized that eating was something more than a utilitarian function. He was unaware of what he ate. It was merely food. He was feasting his love of beauty at this table where eating was an aesthetic function. It was an intellectual function, too. His mind was stirred. He heard words spoken that were meaningless to him, and other words that he had seen only in books and that no man or woman he had known was of large enough mental caliber to pronounce. When he heard such words dropping carelessly from the lips of the members of this marvellous family, her family, he thrilled with delight. The romance, and beauty, and high vigor of the books were coming true. He was in that rare and blissful state wherein a man sees his dreams stalk out from the crannies of fantasy and become fact.

Never had he been at such an altitude of living, and he kept himself in the background, listening, observing, and pleasuring, replying in reticent monosyllables, saying "Yes, miss," and "No, miss," to her, and "Yes, ma'am," and "No, ma'am," to her mother. He curbed the impulse, arising out of his sea-training, to say "Yes, sir," and "No, sir," to her brothers. He felt that it would be inappropriate and a confession of inferiority on his part—which would never do if he was to win to her. Also, it was a dictate of his pride. "By God!" he cried to himself, once; "I'm just as good as them, and if they do know lots that I don't, I could learn 'm a few myself, all the same!" And the next moment, when she or her mother addressed him as "Mr. Eden," his aggressive pride was forgotten, and he was glowing and warm with delight. He was a civilized man, that was what he was, shoulder to shoulder, at dinner, with people he had read about in books. He was in the books himself, adventuring through the printed pages of bound volumes.

But while he belied Arthur's description, and appeared a gentle lamb rather than a wild man, he was racking his brains for a course of action. He was no gentle lamb, and the part of second fiddle would never do for the high-pitched dominance of his nature. He talked only when he had to, and then his speech was like his walk to the table, filled with jerks and halts as he groped in his polyglot vocabulary for words, debating over words he knew were fit but which he feared he could not pronounce, rejecting other words he knew would not be understood or would be raw and harsh. But all the time he was oppressed by the consciousness that this carefulness of diction was making a booby of him, preventing him from expressing what he had in him. Also, his love of freedom chafed against the restriction in much the same way his neck chafed against the starched fetter of a collar. Besides, he was confident that he could not keep it up. He was by nature powerful of thought and sensibility, and the creative spirit was restive and urgent. He was swiftly mastered by the concept or sensation in him that struggled in birth-throes to receive expression and form, and then he forgot himself and where he was, and the old words—the tools of speech he knew—slipped out.

Once, he declined something from the servant who interrupted and pestered at his shoulder, and he said, shortly and emphatically, "Pow!"

On the instant those at the table were keyed up and expectant, the servant was smugly pleased, and he was wallowing in mortification. But he recovered himself quickly.

"It's the Kanaka for 'finish,' " he explained, "and it just come out naturally. It's spelt p-a-u."

He caught her curious and speculative eyes fixed on his hands, and, being in explanatory mood, he said:—

"I just come down the Coast on one of the Pacific mail steamers. She was behind time, an' around the Puget Sound ports we worked like niggers, storing cargo—mixed freight, if you know what that means. That's how the skin got knocked off."

"Oh, it wasn't that," she hastened to explain, in turn. "Your hands seemed too small for your body."

His cheeks were hot. He took it as an exposure of another of his deficiencies.

"Yes," he said depreciatingly. "They ain't big enough to stand the strain. I can hit like a mule with my arms and shoulders. They are too strong, an' when I smash a man on the jaw the hands get smashed, too."

He was not happy at what he had said. He was filled with disgust at himself. He had loosed the guard upon his tongue and talked about things that were not nice.

"It was brave of you to help Arthur the way you did—and you a stranger," she said tactfully, aware of his discomfiture though not of the reason for it.

He, in turn, realized what she had done, and in the consequent warm surge of gratefulness that overwhelmed him forgot his loose-worded tongue.

"It wasn't nothin' at all," he said. "Any guy 'ud do it for another. That bunch of hoodlums was lookin' for trouble, an' Arthur wasn't botherin' 'em none. They butted in on 'm, an' then I butted in on them an' poked a few. That's where some of the skin off my hands went, along with some of the teeth of the gang. I wouldn't 'a' missed it for anything. When I seen—"

He paused, open-mouthed, on the verge of the pit of his own depravity and utter worthlessness to breathe the same air she did. And while Arthur took up the tale, for the twentieth time, of his adventure with the drunken hoodlums on the ferry-boat and of how Martin Eden had rushed in and rescued him, that individual, with frowning brows, meditated upon the fool he had made of himself, and wrestled more determinedly with the problem of how he should conduct himself toward these people. He certainly had not succeeded so far. He wasn't of their tribe, and he couldn't talk their lingo, was the way he put it to himself. He couldn't fake being their kind. The masquerade would fail, and besides, masquerade was foreign to his nature. There was no room in him for sham or artifice. Whatever happened, he must be real. He couldn't talk their talk just yet, though in time he would. Upon that he was resolved. But in the meantime, talk he must, and it must be his own talk, toned down, of course, so as to be comprehensible to them and so as not to shock them too much. And furthermore, he wouldn't claim, not even by tacit acceptance, to be familiar with anything that was unfamiliar. In pursuance of this decision, when the two brothers, talking university shop, had used "trig" several times, Martin Eden demanded:—

"What is *trig?*"

"Trigonometry," Norman said; "a higher form of math."

"And what is *math?*" was the next question, which, somehow, brought the laugh on Norman.

"Mathematics, arithmetic," was the answer.

Martin Eden nodded. He had caught a glimpse of the apparently illimitable vistas of knowledge. What he saw took on tangibility. His abnormal power of vision made abstractions take on concrete form. In the alchemy of his brain, trigonometry and mathematics and the whole field of knowledge which they betokened were transmuted into so much landscape. The vistas he saw were vistas of green foliage and forest glades, all softly luminous or shot through with flashing lights. In the distance, detail was veiled and blurred by a purple haze, but behind this purple haze, he knew, was the glamour of the unknown, the lure of romance. It was like wine to him. Here was adventure, something to do with head and hand, a world to conquer—and straightway from the back of his consciousness rushed the thought, *conquering, to win to her, that lily-pale spirit sitting beside him.*

The glimmering vision was rent asunder and dissipated by Arthur, who, all evening, had been trying to draw his wild man out. Martin Eden remembered his decision. For the first time he became himself, consciously and deliberately at first, but soon lost in the joy of creating, in making life as he knew it appear before his listeners' eyes. He had been a member of the crew of the smuggling schooner *Halcyon* when she was captured by a revenue cutter. He saw with wide eyes, and he could tell what he saw. He brought the pulsing sea before them, and the men and the ships upon the sea. He communicated his power of vision, till they saw with his eyes what he had seen. He selected from the vast mass of detail with an artist's touch, drawing pictures of life that glowed and burned with light and color, injecting movement so that his listeners surged along with him on the flood of rough eloquence, enthusiasm, and power. At times he shocked them with the vividness of the narrative and his terms of speech, but beauty always followed fast upon the heels of violence, and tragedy was relieved by humor, by interpretations of the strange twists and quirks of sailors' minds.

And while he talked, the girl looked at him with startled eyes. His fire warmed her. She wondered if she had been cold all her days. She wanted to lean toward this burning, blazing man that was like a volcano spouting forth strength, robustness, and health. She felt that she must lean toward him, and resisted by an effort. Then, too, there was the counter impulse to shrink away from him. She was repelled by those lacerated hands, grimed by toil so that the very dirt of life was ingrained in the flesh itself, by that red chafe of the collar and those bulging muscles. His roughness frightened her; each roughness of speech was an insult to her ear, each rough phase of his life an insult to her soul. And ever and again would come the draw of him, till she thought he must be evil to have such power over her. All that was most firmly established in her mind was rocking. His romance and adventure were battering at the conventions. Before his facile perils and ready laugh, life was no longer an affair of serious effort and restraint, but a toy, to be played with and turned topsy-turvy, carelessly to be lived and pleasured in, and carelessly to be flung aside. "Therefore, play!" was the cry that rang through her. "Lean toward him, if so you will, and place your two hands upon his neck!" She wanted to cry out at the recklessness of the thought, and in vain she appraised her own cleanness and culture and balanced all that she was against what he was not. She glanced about her and saw the others gazing at him with rapt attention; and she would have despaired had not she seen horror in her mother's eyes—fascinated horror, it was true, but none the less horror. This man from outer darkness was evil. Her mother saw it, and her mother was right. She would trust her mother's judgment in this as she had always trusted it in all things. The fire of him was no longer warm, and the fear of him was no longer poignant.

Later, at the piano, she played for him, and at him, aggressively, with the vague intent of emphasizing the impassableness of the gulf that separated them. Her music was a club that she swung brutally upon his head; and though it stunned him and crushed him down, it incited him. He gazed upon her in awe. In his mind, as in her own, the gulf widened; but faster than it widened, towered his ambition to win across it. But he was too complicated a plexus of sensibilities to sit staring at a gulf a whole evening, especially when there was music. He was remarkably susceptible to music. It was like strong drink, firing him to audacities of feeling,—a drug that laid hold of his imagination and went cloud-soaring through the sky. It banished sordid fact, flooded his mind with beauty, loosed romance and to its heels added wings. He did not understand the music she played. It was different from the dance-hall piano-banging and blatant brass bands he had heard. But he had caught hints of such music from the books, and he accepted her playing largely on faith, patiently waiting, at first, for the lilting measures of pronounced and simple rhythm, puzzled because those measures were not long continued. Just as he caught the swing of them and started, his imagination attuned in flight, always they vanished away in a chaotic scramble of sounds that was meaningless to him, and that dropped his imagination, an inert weight, back to earth.

Once, it entered his mind that there was a deliberate rebuff in all this. He caught her spirit of antagonism and strove to divine the message that her hands pronounced upon the keys. Then he dismissed the thought as unworthy and impossible, and yielded himself more freely to the music. The old delightful condition began to be induced. His feet were no longer clay, and his flesh became spirit; before his eyes and behind his eyes shone a great glory; and then the scene before him vanished and he was away, rocking over the world that was to him a very dear world. The known and the unknown were commingled in the dream-pageant that thronged his vision. He entered strange ports of sun-washed lands, and trod market-places among barbaric peoples that no man had ever seen. The scent of the spice islands was in his nostrils as he had known it on warm, breathless nights at sea, or he beat up against the southeast trades through long tropic days, sinking palm-tufted coral islets in the turquoise sea behind and lifting palm-tufted coral islets in the turquoise sea ahead. Swift as thought the pictures came and went. One instant he was astride a broncho and flying through the fairy-colored Painted Desert country; the next instant he was gazing down through shimmering heat into the whited sepulchre of Death Valley, or pulling an oar on a freezing ocean where great ice islands towered and glistened in the sun. He lay on a coral beach where the cocoanuts grew down to the mellow-sounding surf. The hulk of an ancient wreck burned with blue fires, in the light of which danced the *hula* dancers to the barbaric love-calls of the singers, who chanted to tinkling *ukuleles* and rumbling tom-toms. It was a sensuous, tropic night. In the background a volcano crater was silhouetted against the stars. Overhead drifted a pale crescent moon, and the Southern Cross burned low in the sky.

He was a harp; all life that he had known and that was his consciousness was the strings; and the flood of music was a wind that poured against those strings and set them vibrating with memories and dreams. He did not merely feel. Sensation invested itself in form and color and radiance, and what his imagination dared, it objectified in some sublimated and magic way. Past, present, and future mingled; and he went on oscillating across the broad, warm world, through high adventure and noble deeds to Her—ay, and with her, winning her, his arms about her, and carrying her on in flight through the empery of his mind.

And she, glancing at him across her shoulder, saw something of all this in his face. It was a transfigured face, with great shining eyes that gazed beyond the veil of sound and saw behind it the leap and pulse of life and the gigantic phantoms of the spirit. She was startled. The raw, stumbling lout was gone. The ill-fitting clothes, battered hands, and sunburned face remained; but these seemed the prison-bars through which she saw a great soul looking forth, inarticulate and dumb because of those feeble lips that would not give it speech. Only for a flashing moment did she see this, then she saw the lout returned, and she laughed at the whim of her fancy. But the impression of that fleeting glimpse lingered, and when the time came for him to beat a stumbling retreat and go, she lent him the volume of Swinburne, and another of Browning—she was studying Browning in one of her English courses. He seemed such a boy, as he stood blushing and stammering his thanks, that a wave of pity, maternal in its prompting, welled up in her. She did not remember the lout, nor the imprisoned soul, nor the man who had stared at her in all masculineness and delighted and frightened her. She saw before her only a boy, who was shaking her hand with a hand so calloused that it felt like a nutmeg-grater and rasped her skin, and who was saying jerkily:—

"The greatest time of my life. You see, I ain't used to things. . . ." He looked about him helplessly. "To people and houses like this. It's all new to me, and I like it."

"I hope you'll call again," she said, as he was saying good night to her brothers.

He pulled on his cap, lurched desperately through the doorway, and was gone.

"Well, what do you think of him?" Arthur demanded.

"He is most interesting, a whiff of ozone," she answered. "How old is he?"

"Twenty—almost twenty-one. I asked him this afternoon. I didn't think he was that young."

And I am three years older, was the thought in her mind as she kissed her brothers good night.

III

As Martin Eden went down the steps, his hand dropped into his coat pocket. It came out with a brown rice paper and a pinch of Mexican tobacco, which were deftly rolled together into a cigarette. He drew the first whiff of smoke deep into his lungs and expelled it in a long and lingering exhalation. "By God!" he said aloud, in a voice of awe and wonder. "By God!" he repeated. And yet again he murmured, "By God!" Then his hand went to his collar, which he ripped out of the shirt and stuffed into his pocket. A cold drizzle was falling, but he bared his head to it and unbuttoned his vest, swinging along in splendid unconcern. He was only dimly aware that it was raining. He was in an ecstasy, dreaming dreams and reconstructing the scenes just past.

He had met the woman at last—the woman that he had thought little about, not being given to thinking about women, but whom he had expected, in a remote way, he would sometime meet. He had sat next to her at table. He had felt her hand in his, he had looked into her eyes and caught a vision of a beautiful spirit;—but no more beautiful than the eyes through which it shone, nor than the flesh that gave it expression and form. He did not think of her flesh as flesh,—which was new to him; for of the women he had known that was the only way he thought. Her flesh was somehow different. He did not conceive of her body as a body, subject to the ills and frailties of bodies. Her body was more than the garb of her spirit. It was an emanation of her spirit, a pure and gracious crystallization of her divine essence. This feeling of the divine startled him. It shocked him from his dreams to sober thought. No word, no clew, no hint, of the divine had ever reached him before. He had never believed in the divine. He had always been irreligious, scoffing good-naturedly at the sky-pilots and their immortality of the soul. There was no life beyond, he had contended; it was here and now, then darkness everlasting. But what he had seen in her eyes was soul—

immortal soul that could never die. No man he had known, nor any woman, had given him the message of immortality. But she had. She had whispered it to him the first moment she looked at him. Her face shimmered before his eyes as he walked along,—pale and serious, sweet and sensitive, smiling with pity and tenderness as only a spirit could smile, and pure as he had never dreamed purity could be. Her purity smote him like a blow. It startled him. He had known good and bad; but purity, as an attribute of existence, had never entered his mind. And now, in her, he conceived purity to be the superlative of goodness and of cleanness, the sum of which constituted eternal life.

And promptly urged his ambition to grasp at eternal life. He was not fit to carry water for her—he knew that; it was a miracle of luck and a fantastic stroke that had enabled him to see her and be with her and talk with her that night. It was accidental. There was no merit in it. He did not deserve such fortune. His mood was essentially religious. He was humble and meek, filled with self-disparagement and abasement. In such frame of mind sinners come to the penitent form. He was convicted of sin. But as the meek and lowly at the penitent form catch splendid glimpses of their future lordly existence, so did he catch similar glimpses of the state he would gain to by possessing her. But this possession of her was dim and nebulous and totally different from possession as he had known it. Ambition soared on mad wings, and he saw himself climbing the heights with her, sharing thoughts with her, pleasuring in beautiful and noble things with her. It was a soul-possession he dreamed, refined beyond any grossness, a free comradeship of spirit that he could not put into definite thought. He did not think it. For that matter, he did not think at all. Sensation usurped reason, and he was quivering and palpitant with emotions he had never known, drifting deliciously on a sea of sensibility where feeling itself was exalted and spiritualized and carried beyond the summits of life.

He staggered along like a drunken man, murmuring fervently aloud: "By God! By God!"

A policeman on a street corner eyed him suspiciously, then noted his sailor roll.

"Where did you get it?" the policeman demanded.

Martin Eden came back to earth. His was a fluid organism, swiftly adjustable, capable of flowing into and filling all sorts of nooks and crannies. With the policeman's hail he was immediately his ordinary self, grasping the situation clearly.

"It's a beaut, ain't it?" he laughed back. "I didn't know I was talkin' out loud."

"You'll be singing next," was the policeman's diagnosis.

"No, I won't. Gimme a match an' I'll catch the next car home."

He lighted his cigarette, said good night, and went on. "Now wouldn't that rattle you?" he ejaculated under his breath. "That copper thought I was drunk." He smiled to himself and meditated. "I guess I was," he added; "but I didn't think a woman's face'd do it."

He caught a Telegraph Avenue car that was going to Berkeley. It was crowded with youths and young men who were singing songs and ever and again barking out college yells. He studied them curiously. They were university boys. They went to the same university that she did, were in her class socially, could know her, could see her every day if they wanted to. He wondered that they did not want to, that they had been out having a good time instead of being with her that evening, talking with her, sitting around her in a worshipful and adoring circle. His thoughts wandered on. He noticed one with narrow-slitted eyes and a loose-lipped mouth. That fellow was vicious, he decided. On shipboard he would be a sneak, a whiner, a tattler. He, Martin Eden, was a better man than that fellow. The thought cheered him. It seemed to draw him nearer to Her. He began comparing himself with the students. He grew conscious of the muscled mechanism of his body and felt confident that he was physically their master. But their heads were filled with knowledge that enabled them to talk her talk,—the thought depressed him. But what was a brain for? he demanded passionately. What they had done, he could do. They had been studying about life from the books while he had been busy living life. His brain was just as full of knowledge as theirs, though it was a different kind of knowledge. How many of them could tie a lanyard knot, or take a wheel or a lookout? His life spread out before him in a series of pictures of danger and daring, hardship and toil. He remembered his failures and scrapes in the process of learning. He was that much to the good, anyway. Later on they would have to begin living life and going through the mill as he had gone. Very well. While they were busy with that, he could be learning the other side of life from the books.

As the car crossed the zone of scattered dwellings that separated Oakland from Berkeley, he kept a lookout for a familiar, two-story building along the front of which ran the proud sign, HIGGINBOTHAM'S CASH STORE. Martin Eden got off at this corner. He stared up for a moment at the sign. It carried a message to him beyond its mere wording. A personality of smallness and egotism and petty underhandedness seemed to emanate from the letters themselves. Bernard Higginbotham had married his sister, and he knew him well. He let himself in with a latch-key and climbed the stairs to the second floor. Here lived his brother-in-law. The grocery was below. There was a smell of stale vegetables in the air. As he groped his way across the hall he stumbled over a toy-cart, left there by one of his numerous nephews and nieces, and brought up against a door with a resounding bang. "The pincher," was his thought; "too miserly to burn two cents' worth of gas and save his boarders' necks."

He fumbled for the knob and entered a lighted room, where sat his sister and Bernard Higginbotham. She was patching a pair of his trousers, while his lean body was distributed over two chairs, his feet dangling in dilapidated carpet-slippers over the edge of the second chair. He glanced across the top of the paper he was reading, showing a pair of dark, insincere, sharp-staring eyes. Martin Eden never looked at him without experiencing a sense of repulsion. What his sister had seen in the man was beyond him. The other affected him as so much vermin, and always aroused in him an impulse to crush him under his foot. "Some day I'll beat the face off of him," was the way he often consoled himself for enduring the man's existence. The eyes, weasel-like and cruel, were looking at him complainingly.

"Well," Martin demanded. "Out with it."

"I had that door painted only last week," Mr. Higginbotham half whined, half bullied; "and you know what union wages are. You should be more careful."

Martin had intended to reply, but he was struck by the hopelessness of it. He gazed across the monstrous sordidness of soul to a chromo on the wall. It surprised him. He had always liked it, but it seemed that now he was seeing it for the first time. It was cheap, that was what it was, like everything else in this house. His mind went back to the house he had just left, and he saw, first, the paintings, and next, Her, looking at him with melting sweetness as she shook his hand at leaving. He forgot where he was and Bernard Higginbotham's existence, till that gentleman demanded:—

"Seen a ghost?"

Martin came back and looked at the beady eyes, sneering, truculent, cowardly, and there leaped into his vision, as on a screen, the same eyes when their owner was making a sale in the store below—subservient eyes, smug, and oily, and flattering.

"Yes," Martin answered. "I seen a ghost. Good night. Good night, Gertrude."

He started to leave the room, tripping over a loose seam in the slatternly carpet.

"Don't bang the door," Mr. Higginbotham cautioned him.

He felt the blood crawl in his veins, but controlled himself and closed the door softly behind him.

Mr. Higginbotham looked at his wife exultantly.

"He's ben drinkin'," he proclaimed in a hoarse whisper. "I told you he would."

She nodded her head resignedly.

"His eyes was pretty shiny," she confessed; "and he didn't have no collar, though he went away with one. But mebbe he didn't have more'n a couple of glasses."

"He couldn't stand up straight," asserted her husband. "I watched him. He couldn't walk across the floor without stumblin'. You heard 'm yourself almost fall down in the hall."

"I think it was over Alice's cart," she said. "He couldn't see it in the dark."

Mr. Higginbotham's voice and wrath began to rise. All day he effaced himself in the store, reserving for the evening, with his family, the privilege of being himself.

"I tell you that precious brother of yours was drunk."

His voice was cold, sharp, and final, his lips stamping the enunciation of each word like the die of a machine. His wife sighed and remained silent. She was a large, stout woman, always dressed slatternly and always tired from the burdens of her flesh, her work, and her husband.

"He's got it in him, I tell you, from his father," Mr. Higginbotham went on accusingly. "An' he'll croak in the gutter the same way. You know that."

She nodded, sighed, and went on stitching. They were agreed that Martin had come home drunk. They did not have it in their souls to know beauty or they would have known that those shining eyes and that glowing face betokened youth's first vision of love.

"Settin' a fine example to the children," Mr. Higginbotham snorted, suddenly, in the silence for which his wife was responsible and which he resented. Sometimes he almost wished she would oppose him more. "If he does it again, he's got to get out. Understand! I won't put up with his shinanigan—debotchin' innocent children with his boozing." Mr. Higginbotham liked the word, which was a new one in his vocabulary, recently gleaned from a newspaper column. "That's what it is, debotchin'—there ain't no other name for it."

Still his wife sighed, shook her head sorrowfully, and stitched on. Mr. Higginbotham resumed the newspaper.

"Has he paid last week's board?" he shot across the top of the newspaper.

She nodded, then added, "He still has some money."

"When is he goin' to sea again?"

"When his pay-day's spent, I guess," she answered. "He was over to San Francisco yesterday looking for a ship. But he's got money, yet, an' he's particular about the kind of ship he signs for."

"It's not for a deck-swab like him to put on airs," Mr. Higginbotham snorted. "Particular! Him!"

"He said something about a schooner that's gettin' ready to go off to some outlandish place to look for buried treasure, that he'd sail on her if his money held out."

"If he only wanted to steady down, I'd give him a job drivin' the wagon," her husband said, but with no trace of benevolence in his voice. "Tom's quit."

His wife looked alarm and interrogation.

"Quit to-night. Is goin' to work for Carruthers. They paid 'm more'n I could afford."

"I told you you'd lose 'm," she cried out. "He was worth more'n you was giving him."

"Now look here, old woman," Higginbotham bullied, "for the thousandth time I've told you to keep your nose out of the business. I won't tell you again."

"I don't care," she sniffled. "Tom was a good boy."

Her husband glared at her. This was unqualified defiance.

"If that brother of yours was worth his salt, he could take the wagon," he snorted.

"He pays his board, just the same," was the retort. "An' he's my brother, an' so long as he don't owe you money you've got no right to be jumping on him all the time. I've got some feelings, if I have been married to you for seven years."

"Did you tell 'm you'd charge him for gas if he goes on readin' in bed?" he demanded.

Mrs. Higginbotham made no reply. Her revolt faded away, her spirit wilting down into her tired flesh. Her husband was triumphant. He had her. His eyes snapped vindictively, while his ears joyed in the sniffles she emitted. He extracted great happiness from squelching her, and she squelched easily these days, though it had been different in the first years of their married life, before the brood of children and his incessant nagging had sapped her energy.

"Well, you tell 'm to-morrow, that's all," he said. "An' I just want to tell you, before I forget it, that you'd better send for Marian to-morrow to take care of the children. With Tom quit, I'll have to be out on the wagon, an' you can make up your mind to it to be down below waitin' on the counter."

"But to-morrow's wash day," she objected weakly.

"Get up early, then, an' do it first. I won't start out till ten o'clock."

He crinkled the paper viciously and resumed his reading.

IV

Martin Eden, with blood still crawling from contact with his brother-in-law, felt his way along the unlighted back hall and entered his room, a tiny cubbyhole with space for a bed, a wash-stand, and one chair. Mr. Higginbotham was too thrifty to keep a servant when his wife could do the work. Besides, the servant's room enabled them to take in two boarders instead of one. Martin placed the Swinburne and Browning on the chair, took off his coat, and sat down on the bed. A screeching of asthmatic springs greeted the weight of his body, but he did not notice them. He started to take off his shoes, but fell to staring at the white plaster wall opposite him, broken by long streaks of dirty brown where rain had leaked through the roof. On this befouled background visions began to flow and burn. He forgot his shoes and stared long, till his lips began to move and he murmured, "Ruth."

"Ruth." He had not thought a simple sound could be so beautiful. It delighted his ear, and he grew intoxicated with the repetition of it. "Ruth." It was a talisman, a magic word to conjure with. Each time he murmured it, her face shimmered before him, suffusing the foul wall with a golden radiance. This radiance did not stop at the wall. It extended on into infinity, and through its golden depths his soul went questing after hers. The best that was in him was pouring out in splendid flood. The very thought of her ennobled and purified him, made him better, and made him want to be better. This was new to him. He had never known women who had made him better. They had always had the counter effect of making him beastly. He did not know that many of them had done their best, bad as it was. Never having been conscious of himself, he did not know that he had that in his being that drew love from women and which had been the cause of their reaching out for his youth. Though they had often bothered him, he had never bothered about them; and he would never have dreamed that there were women who had been better because of him. Always in sublime carelessness had he lived, till now, and now it seemed to him that they had always reached out and dragged at him with vile hands. This was not just to them, nor to himself. But he, who for the first time was becoming conscious of himself, was in no condition to judge, and he burned with shame as he stared at the vision of his infamy.

He got up abruptly and tried to see himself in the dirty looking-glass over the washstand. He passed a towel over it and looked again, long and carefully. It was the first time he had ever really seen himself. His eyes were made for seeing, but up to that moment they had been filled with the ever changing panorama of the world, at which he had been too busy gazing, ever to gaze at himself. He saw the head and face of a young fellow of twenty, but, being unused to such appraisement, he did not know how to value it. Above a square-domed forehead he saw a mop of brown hair, nut-brown, with a wave to it and hints of curls that were a delight to any woman, making hands tingle to stroke it and fingers tingle to pass caresses through it. But he passed it by as without merit, in Her eyes, and dwelt long and thoughtfully on the high, square forehead,—striving to penetrate it and learn the quality of its content. What kind of a brain lay behind there? was his insistent interrogation. What was it capable of? How far would it take him? Would it take him to her?

He wondered if there was soul in those steel-gray eyes that were often quite blue of color and that were strong with the briny airs of the sun-washed deep. He wondered, also, how his eyes looked to her. He tried to imagine himself she, gazing into those eyes of his, but failed in the jugglery. He could successfully put himself inside other men's minds, but they had to be men whose ways of life he knew. He did not know her way of life. She was wonder and mystery, and how could he guess one thought of hers? Well, they were honest eyes, he concluded, and in them was neither smallness nor meanness. The brown sunburn of his face surprised him. He had not dreamed he was so black. He rolled up his shirt-sleeve and compared the white underside of the arm with his face. Yes, he was a white man, after all. But the arms were sunburned, too. He twisted his arm, rolled the biceps over with his other hand, and gazed underneath where he was least touched by the sun. It was very white. He laughed at his bronzed face in the glass at the thought that it was once as white as the underside of his arm; nor did he dream that in the world there were few pale spirits of women who could boast fairer or smoother skins than he—fairer than where he had escaped the ravages of the sun.

His might have been a cherub's mouth, had not the full, sensuous lips a trick, under stress, of drawing firmly across the teeth. At times, so tightly did they draw, the mouth became stern and harsh, even ascetic. They were the lips of a fighter and of a lover. They could taste the sweetness of life with relish, and they could put the sweetness aside and command life. The chin and jaw, strong and just hinting of square aggressiveness, helped the lips to command life. Strength balanced sensuousness and had upon it a tonic effect, compelling him to love beauty that was healthy and making him vibrate to sensations that were wholesome. And between the lips were teeth that had never known nor needed the dentist's care. They were white and strong and regular, he decided, as he looked at them. But as he looked, he began to be troubled. Somewhere, stored away in the recesses of his mind and vaguely remembered, was the impression that there were people who washed their teeth every day. They were the people from up above—people in her class. She must wash her teeth every day, too. What would she think if she learned that he had never washed his teeth in all the days of his life? He resolved to get a tooth-brush and form the habit. He would begin at once, to-morrow. It was not by mere achievement that he could hope to win to her. He must make a personal reform in all things, even to tooth-washing and neck-gear, though a starched collar affected him as a renunciation of freedom.

He held up his hand, rubbing the ball of the thumb over the calloused palm and gazing at the dirt that was ingrained in the flesh itself and which no brush could scrub away. How different was her palm! He thrilled deliciously at the remembrance. Like a rose-petal, he thought; cool and soft as a snowflake. He had never thought that a mere woman's hand could be so sweetly soft. He caught himself imagining the wonder of a caress from such a hand, and flushed guiltily. It was too gross a thought for her. In ways it seemed to impugn her high spirituality. She was a pale, slender spirit, exalted far beyond the flesh; but nevertheless the softness of her palm persisted in his thoughts. He was used to the harsh callousness of factory girls and working women. Well he knew why their hands were rough; but this hand of hers . . . It was soft because she had never used it to work with. The gulf yawned between her and him at the awesome thought of a person who did not have to work for a living. He suddenly saw the aristocracy of the people who did not labor. It towered before him on the wall, a figure in brass, arrogant and powerful. He had worked himself; his first memories seemed connected with work, and all his family had worked. There was Gertrude. When her hands were not hard from the endless housework, they were swollen and red like boiled beef, what of the washing. And there was his sister Marian. She had worked in the cannery the preceding summer, and her slim, pretty hands were all scarred with the tomato-knives. Besides, the tips of two of her fingers had been left in the cutting machine at the paper-box factory the preceding winter. He remembered the hard palms of his mother as she lay in her coffin. And his father had worked to the last fading gasp; the horned growth on his hands must have been half an inch thick when he died. But Her hands were soft, and her mother's hands, and her brothers'. This last came to him as a surprise; it was tremendously indicative of the highness of their caste, of the enormous distance that stretched between her and him.

He sat back on the bed with a bitter laugh, and finished taking off his shoes. He was a fool; he had been made drunken by a woman's face and by a woman's soft, white hands. And then, suddenly, before his eyes, on the foul plaster-wall appeared a vision. He stood in front of a gloomy tenement house. It was night-time, in the East End of London, and before him stood Margey, a little factory girl of fifteen. He had seen her home after the bean-feast. She lived in that gloomy tenement, a place not fit for swine. His hand was going out to hers as he said good night. She had put her lips up to be kissed, but he wasn't going to kiss her. Somehow he was afraid of her. And then her hand closed on his and pressed feverishly. He felt her callouses grind and grate on his, and a great wave of pity welled over him. He saw her yearning, hungry eyes, and her ill-fed female form which had been rushed from childhood into a frightened and ferocious maturity; then he put his arms about her in large tolerance and stooped and kissed her on the lips. Her glad little cry rang in his ears, and he felt her clinging to him like a cat. Poor little starveling! He continued to stare at the vision of what had happened in the long ago. His flesh was crawling as it had crawled that night when she clung to him, and his heart was warm with pity. It was a gray scene, greasy gray, and the rain drizzled greasily on the pavement stones. And then a radiant glory shone on the wall, and up through the other vision, displacing it, glimmered Her pale face under its crown of golden hair, remote and inaccessible as a star.

He took the Browning and the Swinburne from the chair and kissed them. Just the same, she told me to call again, he thought. He took another look at himself in the glass, and said aloud, with great solemnity:—

"Martin Eden, the first thing to-morrow you go to the free library an' read up on etiquette. Understand!"

He turned off the gas, and the springs shrieked under his body.

"But you've got to quit cussin', Martin, old boy; you've got to quit cussin'," he said aloud.

Then he dozed off to sleep and to dream dreams that for madness and audacity rivalled those of poppy-eaters.

V

HE awoke next morning from rosy scenes of dream to a steamy atmosphere that smelled of soapsuds and dirty clothes, and that was vibrant with the jar and jangle of tormented life. As he came out of his room he heard the slosh of water, a sharp exclamation, and a resounding smack as his sister visited her irritation upon one of her numerous progeny. The squall of the child went through him like a knife. He was aware that the whole thing, the very air he breathed, was repulsive and mean. How different, he thought, from the atmosphere of beauty and repose of the house wherein Ruth dwelt. There it was all spiritual. Here it was all material, and meanly material.

"Come here, Alfred," he called to the crying child, at the same time thrusting his hand into his trousers pocket, where he carried his money loose in the same large way that he lived life in general. He put a quarter in the youngster's hand and held him in his arms a moment, soothing his sobs. "Now run along and get some candy, and don't forget to give some to your brothers and sisters. Be sure and get the kind that lasts longest."

His sister lifted a flushed face from the wash-tub and looked at him.

"A nickel'd ha' ben enough," she said. "It's just like you, no idea of the value of money. The child'll eat himself sick."

"That's all right, sis," he answered jovially. "My money'll take care of itself. If you weren't so busy, I'd kiss you good morning."

He wanted to be affectionate to this sister, who was good, and who, in her way, he knew, loved him. But, somehow, she grew less herself as the years went by, and more and more baffling. It was the hard work, the many children, and the nagging of her husband, he decided, that had changed her. It came to him, in a flash of fancy, that her nature seemed taking on the attributes of stale vegetables, smelly soapsuds, and of the greasy dimes, nickels, and quarters she took in over the counter of the store.

"Go along an' get your breakfast," she said roughly, though secretly pleased. Of all her wandering brood of brothers he had always been her favorite. "I declare I *will* kiss you," she said, with a sudden stir at her heart.

With thumb and forefinger she swept the dripping suds first from one arm and then from the other. He put his arms round her massive waist and kissed her wet, steamy lips. The tears welled into her eyes—not so much from strength of feeling as from the weakness of chronic overwork. She shoved him away from her, but not before he caught a glimpse of her moist eyes.

"You'll find breakfast in the oven," she said hurriedly. "Jim ought to be up now. I had to get up early for the washing. Now get along with you and get out of the house early. It won't be nice to-day, what of Tom quittin' an' nobody but Bernard to drive the wagon."

Martin went into the kitchen with a sinking heart, the image of her red face and slatternly form eating its way like acid into his brain. She might love him if she only had some time, he concluded. But she was worked to death. Bernard Higginbotham was a brute to work her so hard. But he could not help but feel, on the other hand, that there had not been anything beautiful in that kiss. It was true, it was an unusual kiss. For years she had kissed him only when he returned from voyages or departed on voyages. But this kiss had tasted of soapsuds, and the lips, he had noticed, were flabby. There had been no quick, vigorous lip-pressure such as should accompany any kiss. Hers was the kiss of a tired woman who had been tired so long that she had forgotten how to kiss. He remembered her as a girl, before her marriage, when she would dance with the best, all night, after a hard day's work at the laundry, and think nothing of leaving the dance to go to another day's hard work. And then he thought of Ruth and the cool sweetness that must reside in her lips as it resided in all about her. Her kiss would be like her hand-shake or the way she looked at one, firm and frank. In imagination he dared to think of her lips on his, and so vividly did he imagine that he went dizzy at the thought and seemed to rift through clouds of rose-petals, filling his brain with their perfume.

In the kitchen he found Jim, the other boarder, eating mush very languidly, with a sick, far-away look in his eyes. Jim was a plumber's apprentice whose weak chin and hedonistic temperament, coupled with a certain nervous stupidity, promised to take him nowhere in the race for bread and butter.

"Why don't you eat?" he demanded, as Martin dipped dolefully into the cold, half-cooked oatmeal mush. "Was you drunk again last night?"

Martin shook his head. He was oppressed by the utter squalidness of it all. Ruth Morse seemed farther removed than ever.

"I was," Jim went on with a boastful, nervous giggle. "I was loaded right to the neck. Oh, she was a daisy. Billy brought me home."

Martin nodded that he heard,—it was a habit of nature with him to pay heed to whoever talked to him,—and poured a cup of lukewarm coffee.

"Goin' to the Lotus Club dance to-night?" Jim demanded. "They're goin' to have beer, an' if that Temescal bunch comes, there'll be a rough-house. I don't care, though. I'm takin' my lady friend just the same. Cripes, but I've got a taste in my mouth!"

He made a wry face and attempted to wash the taste away with coffee.

"D'ye know Julia?"

Martin shook his head.

"She's my lady friend," Jim explained, "and she's a peach. I'd introduce you to her, only you'd win her. I don't see what the girls see in you, honest I don't; but the way you win them away from the fellers is sickenin'."

"I never got any away from you," Martin answered uninterestedly. The breakfast had to be got through somehow.

"Yes, you did, too," the other asserted warmly. "There was Maggie."

"Never had anything to do with her. Never danced with her except that one night."

"Yes, an' that's just what did it," Jim cried out. "You just danced with her an' looked at her, an' it was all off. Of course you didn't mean nothin' by it, but it settled me for keeps. Wouldn't look at me again. Always askin' about you. She'd have made fast dates enough with you if you'd wanted to."

"But I didn't want to."

"Wasn't necessary. I was left at the pole." Jim looked at him admiringly. "How d'ye do it, anyway, Mart?"

"By not carin' about 'em," was the answer.

"You mean makin' b'lieve you don't care about them?" Jim queried eagerly.

Martin considered for a moment, then answered, "Perhaps that will do, but with me I guess it's different. I never have cared—much. If you can put it on, it's all right, most likely."

"You should 'a' ben up at Riley's barn last night," Jim announced inconsequently. "A lot of the fellers put on the gloves. There was a peach from West Oakland. They called 'm 'The Rat.' Slick as silk. No one could touch 'm. We was all wishin' you was there. Where was you anyway?"

"Down in Oakland," Martin replied.

"To the show?"

Martin shoved his plate away and got up.

"Comin' to the dance to-night?" the other called after him.

"No, I think not," he answered.

He went downstairs and out into the street, breathing great breaths of air. He had been suffocating in that atmosphere, while the apprentice's chatter had driven him frantic. There had been times when it was all he could do to refrain from reaching over and mopping Jim's face in the mush-plate. The more he had chattered, the more remote had Ruth seemed to him. How could he, herding with such cattle, ever become worthy of her? He was appalled at the problem confronting him, weighted down by the incubus of his working-class station. Everything reached out to hold him down—his sister, his sister's house and family, Jim the apprentice, everybody he knew, every tie of life. Existence did not taste good in his mouth. Up to then he had accepted existence, as he had lived it with all about him, as a good thing. He had never questioned it, except when he read books; but then, they were only books, fairy stories of a fairer and impossible world. But now he had seen that world, possible and real, with a flower of a woman called Ruth in the midmost centre of it; and thenceforth he must know bitter tastes, and longings sharp as pain, and hopelessness that tantalized because it fed on hope.

He had debated between the Berkeley Free Library and the Oakland Free Library, and decided upon the latter because Ruth lived in Oakland. Who could tell?—a library was a most likely place for her, and he might see her there. He did not know the way of libraries, and he wandered through endless rows of fiction, till the delicate-featured French-looking girl who seemed in charge, told him that the reference department was upstairs. He did not know enough to ask the man at the desk, and began his adventures in the philosophy alcove. He had heard of book philosophy, but had not imagined there had been so much written about it. The high, bulging shelves of heavy tomes humbled him and at the same time stimulated him. Here was work for the vigor of his brain. He found books on trigonometry in the mathematics section, and ran the pages, and stared at the meaningless formulas and figures. He could read English, but he saw there an alien speech. Norman and Arthur knew that speech. He had heard them talking it. And they were her brothers. He left the alcove in despair. From every side the books seemed to press upon him and crush him. He had never dreamed that the fund of human knowledge bulked so big. He was frightened. How could his brain ever master it all? Later, he remembered that there were other men, many men, who had mastered it; and he breathed a great oath, passionately, under his breath, swearing that his brain could do what theirs had done.

And so he wandered on, alternating between depression and elation as he stared at the shelves packed with wisdom. In one miscellaneous section he came upon a "Norrie's Epitome." He turned the pages reverently. In a way, it spoke a kindred speech. Both he and it were of the sea. Then he found a "Bowditch" and books by Lecky and Marshall. There it was; he would teach himself navigation. He would quit drinking, work up, and become a captain. Ruth seemed very near to him in that moment. As a captain, he could marry her (if she would have him). And if she wouldn't, well—he would live a good life among men, because of Her, and he would quit drinking anyway. Then he remembered the underwriters and the owners, the two masters a captain must serve, either of which could and would break him and whose interests were diametrically opposed. He cast his eyes about the room and closed the lids down on a vision of ten thousand books. No; no more of the sea for him. There was power in all that wealth of books, and if he would do great things, he must do them on the land. Besides, captains were not allowed to take their wives to sea with them.

Noon came, and afternoon. He forgot to eat, and sought on for the books on etiquette; for, in addition to career, his mind was vexed by a simple and very concrete problem: *When you meet a young lady and she asks you to call, how soon can you call?* was the way he worded it to himself. But when he found the right shelf, he sought vainly for the answer. He was appalled at the vast edifice of etiquette, and lost himself in the mazes of visiting-card conduct between persons in polite society. He abandoned his search. He had not found what he wanted, though he had found that it would take all of a man's time to be polite, and that he would have to live a preliminary life in which to learn how to be polite.

"Did you find what you wanted?" the man at the desk asked him as he was leaving.

"Yes, sir," he answered. "You have a fine library here."

The man nodded. "We should be glad to see you here often. Are you a sailor?"

"Yes, sir," he answered. "And I'll come again."

Now, how did he know that? he asked himself as he went down the stairs.

And for the first block along the street he walked very stiff and straight and awkwardly, until he forgot himself in his thoughts, whereupon his rolling gait gracefully returned to him.

VI

A TERRIBLE restlessness that was akin to hunger afflicted Martin Eden. He was famished for a sight of the girl whose slender hands had gripped his life with a giant's grasp. He could not steel himself to call upon her. He was afraid that he might call too soon, and so be guilty of an awful breach of that awful thing called etiquette. He spent long hours in the Oakland and Berkeley libraries, and made out application blanks for membership for himself, his sisters Gertrude and Marian, and Jim, the latter's consent being obtained at the expense of several glasses of beer. With four cards permitting him to draw books, he burned the gas late in the servant's room, and was charged fifty cents a week for it by Mr. Higginbotham.

The many books he read but served to whet his unrest. Every page of every book was a peep-hole into the realm of knowledge. His hunger fed upon what he read, and increased. Also, he did not know where to begin, and continually suffered from lack of preparation. The commonest references, that he could see plainly every reader was expected to know, he did not know. And the same was true of the poetry he read which maddened him with delight. He read more of Swinburne than was contained in the volume Ruth had lent him; and "Dolores" he understood thoroughly. But surely Ruth did not understand it, he concluded. How could she, living the refined life she did? Then he chanced upon Kipling's poems, and was swept away by the lilt and swing and glamour with which familiar things had been invested. He was amazed at the man's sympathy with life and at his incisive psychology. *Psychology* was a new word in Martin's vocabulary. He had bought a dictionary, which deed had decreased his supply of money and brought nearer the day on which he must sail in search of more. Also, it incensed Mr. Higginbotham, who would have preferred the money taking the form of board.

He dared not go near Ruth's neighborhood in the daytime, but night found him lurking like a thief around the Morse home, stealing glimpses at the windows and loving the very walls that sheltered her. Several times he barely escaped being caught by her brothers, and once he trailed Mr. Morse down town and studied his face in the lighted streets, longing all the while for some quick danger of death to threaten so that he might spring in and save her father. On another night, his vigil was rewarded by a glimpse of Ruth through a second-story window. He saw only her head and shoulders, and her arms raised as she fixed her hair before a mirror. It was only for a moment, but it was a long moment to him, during which his blood turned to wine and sang through his veins. Then she pulled down the shade. But it was her room—he had learned that; and thereafter he strayed there often, hiding under a dark tree on the opposite side of the street and smoking countless cigarettes. One afternoon he saw her mother coming out of a bank, and received another proof of the enormous distance that separated Ruth from him. She was of the class that dealt with banks. He had never been inside a bank in his life, and he had an idea that such institutions were frequented only by the very rich and the very powerful.

In one way, he had undergone a moral revolution. Her cleanness and purity had reacted upon him, and he felt in his being a crying need to be clean. He must be that if he were ever to be worthy of breathing the same air with her. He washed his teeth, and scrubbed his hands with a kitchen scrub-brush till he saw a nail-brush in a drug-store window and divined its use. While purchasing it, the clerk glanced at his nails, suggested a nail-file, and so he became possessed of an additional toilet-tool. He ran across a book in the library on the care of the body, and promptly developed a penchant for a cold-water bath every morning, much to the amazement of Jim, and to the bewilderment of Mr. Higginbotham, who was not in sympathy with such high-fangled notions and who seriously debated whether or not he should charge Martin extra for the water. Another stride was in the direction of creased trousers. Now that Martin was aroused in such matters, he swiftly noted the difference between the baggy knees of the trousers worn by the working class and the straight line from knee to foot of those worn by the men above the working class. Also, he learned the reason why, and invaded his sister's kitchen in search of irons and ironing-board. He had misadventures at first, hopelessly burning one pair and buying another, which expenditure again brought nearer the day on which he must put to sea.

But the reform went deeper than mere outward appearance. He still smoked, but he drank no more. Up to that time, drinking had seemed to him the proper thing for men to do, and he had prided himself on his strong head which enabled him to drink most men under the table. Whenever he encountered a chance shipmate, and there were many in San Francisco, he treated them and was treated in turn, as of old, but he ordered for himself root beer or ginger ale and good-naturedly endured their chaffing. And as they waxed maudlin he studied them, watching the beast rise and master them and thanking God that he was no longer as they. They had their limitations to forget, and when they were drunk, their dim, stupid spirits were even as gods, and each ruled in his heaven of intoxicated desire. With Martin the need for strong drink had vanished. He was drunken in new and more profound ways—with Ruth, who had fired him with love and with a glimpse of higher and eternal life; with books, that had set a myriad maggots of desire gnawing in his brain; and with the sense of personal cleanliness he was achieving, that gave him even more superb health than what he had enjoyed and that made his whole body sing with physical well-being.

One night he went to the theatre, on the blind chance that he might see her there, and from the second balcony he did see her. He saw her come down the aisle, with Arthur and a strange young man with a football mop of hair and eyeglasses, the sight of whom spurred him to instant apprehension and jealousy. He saw her take her seat in the orchestra circle, and little else than her did he see that night—a pair of slender white shoulders and a mass of pale gold hair, dim with distance. But there were others who saw, and now and again, glancing at those about him, he noted two young girls who looked back from the row in front, a dozen seats along, and who smiled at him with bold eyes. He had always been easy-going. It was not in his nature to give rebuff. In the old days he would have smiled back, and gone further and encouraged smiling. But now it was different. He did smile back, then looked away, and looked no more deliberately. But several times, forgetting the existence of the two girls, his eyes caught their smiles. He could not re-thumb himself in a day, nor could he violate the intrinsic kindliness of his nature; so, at such moments, he smiled at the girls in warm human friendliness. It was nothing new to him. He knew they were reaching out their woman's hands to him. But it was different now. Far down there in the orchestra circle was the one woman in all the world, so different, so terrifically different, from these two girls of his class, that he could feel for them only pity and sorrow. He had it in his heart to wish that they could possess, in some small measure, her goodness and glory. And not for the world could he hurt them because of their outreaching. He was not flattered by it; he even felt a slight shame at his lowliness that permitted it. He knew, did he belong in Ruth's class, that there would be no overtures from these girls; and with each glance of theirs he felt the fingers of his own class clutching at him to hold him down.

He left his seat before the curtain went down on the last act, intent on seeing Her as she passed out. There were always numbers of men who stood on the sidewalk outside, and he could pull his cap down over his eyes and screen himself behind some one's shoulder so that she should not see him. He emerged from the theatre with the first of the crowd; but scarcely had he taken his position on the edge of the sidewalk when the two girls appeared. They were looking for him, he knew; and for the moment he could have cursed that in him which drew women. Their casual edging across the sidewalk to the curb, as they drew near, apprised him of discovery. They slowed down, and were in the thick of the crowd as they came up with him. One of them brushed against him and apparently for the first time noticed him. She was a slender, dark girl, with black, defiant eyes. But they smiled at him, and he smiled back.

"Hello," he said.

It was automatic; he had said it so often before under similar circumstances of first meetings. Besides, he could do no less. There was that large tolerance and sympathy in his nature that would permit him to do no less. The black-eyed girl smiled gratification and greeting, and showed signs of stopping, while her companion, arm linked in arm, giggled and likewise showed signs of halting. He thought quickly. It would never do for Her to come out and see him talking there with them. Quite naturally, as a matter of course, he swung in alongside the dark-eyed one and walked with her. There was no awkwardness on his part, no numb tongue. He was at home here, and he held his own royally in the badinage, bristling with slang and sharpness, that was always the preliminary to getting acquainted in these swift-moving affairs. At the corner where the main stream of people flowed onward, he started to edge out into the cross street. But the girl with the black eyes caught his arm, following him and dragging her companion after her, as she cried:—

"Hold on, Bill! What's yer rush? You're not goin' to shake us so sudden as all that?"

He halted with a laugh, and turned, facing them. Across their shoulders he could see the moving throng passing under the street lamps. Where he stood it was not so light, and, unseen, he would be able to see Her as she passed by. She would certainly pass by, for that way led home.

"What's her name?" he asked of the giggling girl, nodding at the dark-eyed one.

"You ask her," was the convulsed response.

"Well, what is it?" he demanded, turning squarely on the girl in question.

"You ain't told me yours, yet," she retorted.

"You never asked it," he smiled. "Besides, you guessed the first rattle. It's Bill, all right, all right."

"Aw, go 'long with you." She looked him in the eyes, her own sharply passionate and inviting. "What is it, honest?"

Again she looked. All the centuries of woman since sex began were eloquent in her eyes. And he measured her in a careless way, and knew, bold now, that she would begin to retreat, coyly and delicately, as he pursued, ever ready to reverse the game should he turn faint-hearted. And, too, he was human, and could feel the draw of her, while his ego could not but appreciate the flattery of her kindness. Oh, he knew it all, and knew them well, from A to Z. Good, as goodness might be measured in their particular class, hard-working for meagre wages and scorning the sale of self for easier ways, nervously desirous for some small pinch of happiness in the desert of existence, and facing a future that was a gamble between the ugliness of unending toil and the black pit of more terrible wretchedness, the way whereto being briefer though better paid.

"Bill," he answered, nodding his head. "Sure, Pete, Bill an' no other."

"No joshin'?" she queried.

"It ain't Bill at all," the other broke in.

"How do you know?" he demanded. "You never laid eyes on me before."

"No need to, to know you're lyin'," was the retort.

"Straight, Bill, what is it?" the first girl asked.

"Bill'll do," he confessed.

She reached out to his arm and shook him playfully. "I knew you was lyin', but you look good to me just the same."

He captured the hand that invited, and felt on the palm familiar markings and distortions.

"When'd you chuck the cannery?" he asked.

"How'd yeh know?" and "My, ain't cheh a mind-reader!" the girls chorussed.

And while he exchanged the stupidities of stupid minds with them, before his inner sight towered the book-shelves of the library, filled with the wisdom of the ages. He smiled bitterly at the incongruity of it, and was assailed by doubts. But between inner vision and outward pleasantry he found time to watch the theatre crowd streaming by. And then he saw Her, under the lights, between her brother and the strange young man with glasses, and his heart seemed to stand still. He had waited long for this moment. He had time to note the light, fluffy something that hid her queenly head, the tasteful lines of her wrapped figure, the gracefulness of her carriage and of the hand that caught up her skirts; and then she was gone and he was left staring at the two girls of the cannery, at their tawdry attempts at prettiness of dress, their tragic efforts to be clean and trim, the cheap cloth, the cheap ribbons, and the cheap rings on the fingers. He felt a tug at his arm, and heard a voice saying:—

"Wake up, Bill! What's the matter with you?"

"What was you sayin'?" he asked.

"Oh, nothin'," the dark girl answered, with a toss of her head. "I was only remarkin'—"

"What?"

"Well, I was whisperin' it'd be a good idea if you could dig up a gentleman friend—for her" (indicating her companion), "and then, we could go off an' have ice-cream soda somewhere, or coffee, or anything."

He was afflicted by a sudden spiritual nausea. The transition from Ruth to this had been too abrupt. Ranged side by side with the bold, defiant eyes of the girl before him, he saw Ruth's clear, luminous eyes, like a saint's, gazing at him out of unplumbed depths of purity. And, somehow, he felt within him a stir of power. He was better than this. Life meant more to him than it meant to these two girls whose thoughts did not go beyond ice-cream and a gentleman friend. He remembered that he had led always a secret life in his thoughts. These thoughts he had tried to share, but never had he found a woman capable of understanding—nor a man. He had tried, at times, but had only puzzled his listeners. And as his thoughts had been beyond them, so, he argued now, he must be beyond them. He felt power move in him, and clenched his fists. If life meant more to him, then it was for him to demand more from life, but he could not demand it from such companionship as this. Those bold black eyes had nothing to offer. He knew the thoughts behind them—of ice-cream and of something else. But those saint's eyes alongside—they offered all he knew and more than he could guess. They offered books and painting, beauty and repose, and all the fine elegance of higher existence. Behind those black eyes he knew every thought process. It was like clock-work. He could watch every wheel go around. Their bid was low pleasure, narrow as the grave, that palled, and the grave was at the end of it. But the bid of the saint's eyes was mystery, and wonder unthinkable, and eternal life. He had caught glimpses of the soul in them, and glimpses of his own soul, too.

"There's only one thing wrong with the programme," he said aloud. "I've got a date already."

The girl's eyes blazed her disappointment.

"To sit up with a sick friend, I suppose?" she sneered.

"No, a real, honest date with—" he faltered, "with a girl."

"You're not stringin' me?" she asked earnestly.

He looked her in the eyes and answered: "It's straight, all right. But why can't we meet some other time? You ain't told me your name yet. An' where d'ye live?"

"Lizzie," she replied, softening toward him, her hand pressing his arm, while her body leaned against his. "Lizzie Connolly. And I live at Fifth an' Market."

He talked on a few minutes before saying good night. He did not go home immediately; and under the tree where he kept his vigils he looked up at a window and murmured: "That date was with you, Ruth. I kept it for you."

VII

A WEEK of heavy reading had passed since the evening he first met Ruth Morse, and still he dared not call. Time and again he nerved himself up to call, but under the doubts that assailed him his determination died away. He did not know the proper time to call, nor was there any one to tell him, and he was afraid of committing himself to an irretrievable blunder. Having shaken himself free from his old companions and old ways of life, and having no new companions, nothing remained for him but to read, and the long hours he devoted to it would have ruined a dozen pairs of ordinary eyes. But his eyes were strong, and they were backed by a body superbly strong. Furthermore, his mind was fallow. It had lain fallow all his life so far as the abstract thought of the books was concerned, and it was ripe for the sowing. It had never been jaded by study, and it bit hold of the knowledge in the books with sharp teeth that would not let go.

It seemed to him, by the end of the week, that he had lived centuries, so far behind were the old life and outlook. But he was baffled by lack of preparation. He attempted to read books that required years of preliminary specialization. One day he would read a book of antiquated philosophy, and the next day one that was ultra-modern, so that his head would be whirling with the conflict and contradiction of ideas. It was the same with the economists. On the one shelf at the library he found Karl Marx, Ricardo, Adam Smith, and Mill, and the abstruse formulas of the one gave no clew that the ideas of another were obsolete. He was bewildered, and yet he wanted to know. He had become interested, in a day, in economics, industry, and politics. Passing through the City Hall Park, he had noticed a group of men, in the centre of which were half a dozen, with flushed faces and raised voices, earnestly carrying on a discussion. He joined the listeners, and heard a new, alien tongue in the mouths of the philosophers of the people. One was a tramp, another was a labor agitator, a third was a law-school student, and the remainder was composed of wordy workingmen. For the first time he heard of socialism, anarchism, and single tax, and learned that there were warring social philosophies. He heard hundreds of technical words that were new to him, belonging to fields of thought that his meagre reading had never touched upon. Because of this he could not follow the arguments closely, and he could only guess at and surmise the ideas wrapped up in such strange expressions. Then there was a black-eyed restaurant waiter who was a theosophist, a union baker who was an agnostic, an old man who baffled all of them with the strange philosophy that *what is is right,* and another old man who discoursed interminably about the cosmos and the father-atom and the mother-atom.

Martin Eden's head was in a state of addlement when he went away after several hours, and he hurried to the library to look up the definitions of a dozen unusual words. And when he left the library, he carried under his arm four volumes: Madam Blavatsky's "Secret Doctrine," "Progress and Poverty," "The Quintessence of Socialism," and "Warfare of Religion and Science." Unfortunately, he began on the "Secret Doctrine." Every line bristled with many-syllabled words he did not understand. He sat up in bed, and the dictionary was in front of him more often than the book. He looked up so many new words that when they recurred, he had forgotten their meaning and had to look them up again. He devised the plan of writing the definitions in a notebook, and filled page after page with them. And still he could not understand. He read until three in the morning, and his brain was in a turmoil, but not one essential thought in the text had he grasped. He looked up, and it seemed that the room was lifting, heeling, and plunging like a ship upon the sea. Then he hurled the "Secret Doctrine" and many curses across the room, turned off the gas, and composed himself to sleep. Nor did he have much better luck with the other three books. It was not that his brain was weak or incapable; it could think these thoughts were it not for lack of training in thinking and lack of the thought-tools with which to think. He guessed this, and for a while entertained the idea of reading nothing but the dictionary until he had mastered every word in it.

Poetry, however, was his solace, and he read much of it, finding his greatest joy in the simpler poets, who were more understandable. He loved beauty, and there he found beauty. Poetry, like music, stirred him profoundly, and, though he did not know it, he was preparing his mind for the heavier work that was to come. The pages of his mind were blank, and, without effort, much he read and liked, stanza by stanza, was impressed upon those pages, so that he was soon able to extract great joy from chanting aloud or under his breath the music and the beauty of the printed words he had read. Then he stumbled upon Gayley's "Classic Myths" and Bulfinch's "Age of Fable," side by side on a library shelf. It was illumination, a great light in the darkness of his ignorance, and he read poetry more avidly than ever.

The man at the desk in the library had seen Martin there so often that he had become quite cordial, always greeting him with a smile and a nod when he entered. It was because of this that Martin did a daring thing. Drawing out some books at the desk, and while the man was stamping the cards, Martin blurted out:—

"Say, there's something I'd like to ask you."

The man smiled and paid attention.

"When you meet a young lady an' she asks you to call, how soon can you call?"

Martin felt his shirt press and cling to his shoulders, what of the sweat of the effort.

"Why I'd say any time," the man answered.

"Yes, but this is different," Martin objected. "She—I—well, you see, it's this way: maybe she won't be there. She goes to the university."

"Then call again."

"What I said ain't what I meant," Martin confessed falteringly, while he made up his mind to throw himself wholly upon the other's mercy. "I'm just a rough sort of a fellow, an' I ain't never seen anything of society. This girl is all that I ain't, an' I ain't anything that she is. You don't think I'm playin' the fool, do you?" he demanded abruptly.

"No, no; not at all, I assure you," the other protested. "Your request is not exactly in the scope of the reference department, but I shall be only too pleased to assist you."

Martin looked at him admiringly.

"If I could tear it off that way, I'd be all right," he said.

"I beg pardon?"

"I mean if I could talk easy that way, an' polite, an' all the rest."

"Oh," said the other, with comprehension.

"What is the best time to call? The afternoon?—not too close to meal-time? Or the evening? Or Sunday?"

"I'll tell you," the librarian said with a brightening face. "You call her up on the telephone and find out."

"I'll do it," he said, picking up his books and starting away.

He turned back and asked:—

"When you're speakin' to a young lady—say, for instance, Miss Lizzie Smith—do you say 'Miss Lizzie'? or 'Miss Smith'?"

"Say 'Miss Smith,' " the librarian stated authoritatively. "Say 'Miss Smith' always—until you come to know her better."

So it was that Martin Eden solved the problem.

"Come down any time; I'll be at home all afternoon," was Ruth's reply over the telephone to his stammered request as to when he could return the borrowed books.

She meet him at the door herself, and her woman's eyes took in immediately the creased trousers and the certain slight but indefinable change in him for the better. Also, she was struck by his face. It was almost violent, this health of his, and it seemed to rush out of him and at her in waves of force. She felt the urge again of the desire to lean toward him for warmth, and marvelled again at the effect his presence produced upon her. And he, in turn, knew again the swimming sensation of bliss when he felt the contact of her hand in greeting. The difference between them lay in that she was cool and self-possessed while his face flushed to the roots of the hair. He stumbled with his old awkwardness after her, and his shoulders swung and lurched perilously.

Once they were seated in the living-room, he began to get on easily—more easily by far than he had expected. She made it easy for him; and the gracious spirit with which she did it made him love her more madly than ever. They talked first of the borrowed books, of the Swinburne he was devoted to, and of the Browning he did not understand; and she led the conversation on from subject to subject, while she pondered the problem of how she could be of help to him. She had thought of this often since their first meeting. She wanted to help him. He made a call upon her pity and tenderness that no one had ever made before, and the pity was not so much derogatory of him as maternal in her. Her pity could not be of the common sort, when the man who drew it was so much man as to shock her with maidenly fears and set her mind and pulse thrilling with strange thoughts and feelings. The old fascination of his neck was there, and there was sweetness in the thought of laying her hands upon it. It seemed still a wanton impulse, but she had grown more used to it. She did not dream that in such guise new-born love would epitomize itself. Nor did she dream that the feeling he excited in her was love. She thought she was merely interested in him as an unusual type possessing various potential excellencies, and she even felt philanthropic about it.

She did not know she desired him; but with him it was different. He knew that he loved her, and he desired her as he had never before desired anything in his life. He had loved poetry for beauty's sake; but since he met her the gates to the vast field of love-poetry had been opened wide. She had given him understanding even more than Bulfinch and Gayley. There was a line that a week before he would not have favored with a second thought—"God's own mad lover dying on a kiss"; but now it was ever insistent in his mind. He marvelled at the wonder of it and the truth; and as he gazed upon her he knew that he could die gladly upon a kiss. He felt himself God's own mad lover, and no accolade of knighthood could have given him greater pride. And at last he knew the meaning of life and why he had been born.

As he gazed at her and listened, his thoughts grew daring. He reviewed all the wild delight of the pressure of her hand in his at the door, and longed for it again. His gaze wandered often toward her lips, and he yearned for them hungrily. But there was nothing gross or earthly about this yearning. It gave him exquisite delight to watch every movement and play of those lips as they enunciated the words she spoke; yet they were not ordinary lips such as all men and women had. Their substance was not mere human clay. They were lips of pure spirit, and his desire for them seemed absolutely different from the desire that had led him to other women's lips. He could kiss her lips, rest his own physical lips upon them, but it would be with the lofty and awful fervor with which one would kiss the robe of God. He was not conscious of this transvaluation of values that had taken place in him, and was unaware that the light that shone in his eyes when he looked at her was quite the same light that shines in all men's eyes when the desire of love is upon them. He did not dream how ardent and masculine his gaze was, nor that the warm flame of it was affecting the alchemy of her spirit. Her penetrative virginity exalted and disguised his own emotions, elevating his thoughts to a star-cool chastity, and he would have been startled to learn that there was that shining out of his eyes, like warm waves, that flowed through her and kindled a kindred warmth. She was subtly perturbed by it, and more than once, though she knew not why, it disrupted her train of thought with its delicious intrusion and compelled her to grope for the remainder of ideas partly uttered. Speech was always easy with her, and these interruptions would have puzzled her had she not decided that it was because he was a remarkable type. She was very sensitive to impressions, and it was not strange, after all, that this aura of a traveller from another world should so affect her.

The problem in the background of her consciousness was how to help him, and she turned the conversation in that direction; but it was Martin who came to the point first.

"I wonder if I can get some advice from you," he began, and received an acquiescence of willingness that made his heart bound. "You remember the other time I was here I said I couldn't talk about books an' things because I didn't know how? Well, I've ben doin' a lot of thinkin' ever since. I've ben to the library a whole lot, but most of the books I've tackled have ben over my head. Mebbe I'd better begin at the beginnin'. I ain't never had no advantages. I've worked pretty hard ever since I was a kid, an' since I've ben to the library, lookin' with new eyes at books—an' lookin' at new books, too—I've just about concluded that I ain't ben reading the right kind. You know the books you find in cattle-camps an' fo'c's'ls ain't the same you've got in this house, for instance. Well, that's the sort of readin' matter I've ben accustomed to. And yet—an' I ain't just makin' a brag of it—I've ben different from the people I've herded with. Not that I'm any better than the sailors an' cow-punchers I travelled with,—I was cow-punchin' for a short time, you know,—but I always liked books, read everything I could lay hands on, an'—well, I guess I think differently from most of 'em.

"Now, to come to what I'm drivin' at. I was never inside a house like this. When I come a week ago, an' saw all this, an' you, an' your mother, an' brothers, an' everything—well, I liked it. I'd heard about such things an' read about such things in some of the books, an' when I looked around at your house, why, the books come true. But the thing I'm after is I liked it. I wanted it. I want it now. I want to breathe air like you get in this house—air that is filled with books, and pictures, and beautiful things, where people talk in low voices an' are clean, an' their thoughts are clean. The air I always breathed was mixed up with grub an' house-rent an' scrappin' an' booze an' that's all they talked about, too. Why, when you was crossin' the room to kiss your mother, I thought it was the most beautiful thing I ever seen. I've seen a whole lot of life, an' somehow I've seen a whole lot more of it than most of them that was with me. I like to see, an' I want to see more, an' I want to see it different.

"But I ain't got to the point yet. Here it is. I want to make my way to the kind of life you have in this house. There's more in life than booze, an' hard work, an' knockin' about. Now, how am I goin' to get it? Where do I take hold an' begin? I'm willin' to work my passage, you know, an' I can make most men sick when it comes to hard work. Once I get started, I'll work night an' day. Mebbe you think it's funny, me askin' you about all this. I know you're the last person in the world I ought to ask, but I don't know anybody else I could ask—unless it's Arthur. Mebbe I ought to ask him. If I was—"

His voice died away. His firmly planned intention had come to a halt on the verge of the horrible probability that he should have asked Arthur and that he had made a fool of himself. Ruth did not speak immediately. She was too absorbed in striving to reconcile the stumbling, uncouth speech and its simplicity of thought with what she saw in his face. She had never looked in eyes that expressed greater power. Here was a man who could do anything, was the message she read there, and it accorded ill with the weakness of his spoken thought. And for that matter so complex and quick was her own mind that she did not have a just appreciation of simplicity. And yet she had caught an impression of power in the very groping of this mind. It had seemed to her like a giant writhing and straining at the bonds that held him down. Her face was all sympathy when she did speak.

"What you need, you realize yourself, and it is education. You should go back and finish grammar school, and then go through the high school and university."

"But that takes money," he interrupted.

"Oh!" she cried. "I had not thought of that. But then you have relatives, somebody who could assist you?"

He shook his head.

"My father and mother are dead. I've two sisters, one married, an' the other'll get married soon, I suppose. Then I've a string of brothers,—I'm the youngest,—but they never helped nobody. They've just knocked around over the world, lookin' out for number one. The oldest died in India. Two are in South Africa now, an' another's on a whaling voyage, an' one's travellin' with a circus—he does trapeze work. An' I guess I'm just like them. I've taken care of myself since I was eleven—that's when my mother died. I've got to study by myself, I guess, an' what I want to know is where to begin."

"I should say the first thing of all would be to get a grammar. Your grammar is—" She had intended saying "awful," but she amended it to "is not particularly good."

He flushed and sweated.

"I know I must talk a lot of slang an' words you don't understand. But then they're the only words I know—how to speak. I've got other words in my mind, picked 'em up from books, but I can't pronounce 'em, so I don't use 'em."

"It isn't what you say, so much as how you say it. You don't mind my being frank, do you? I don't want to hurt you."

"No, no," he cried, while he secretly blessed her for her kindness. "Fire away. I've got to know, an' I'd sooner know from you than anybody else."

"Well, then, you say, 'You was'; it should be, 'You were.' You say 'I seen' for 'I saw.' You use the double negative—"

"What's the double negative?" he demanded; then added humbly, "You see, I don't even understand your explanations."

"I'm afraid I didn't explain that," she smiled. "A double negative is—let me see—well, you say, 'never helped nobody.' 'Never' is a negative. 'Nobody' is another negative. It is a rule that two negatives make a positive. 'Never helped nobody' means that, not helping nobody, they must have helped somebody."

"That's pretty clear," he said. "I never thought of it before. But it don't mean they *must* have helped somebody, does it? Seems to me that 'never helped nobody' just naturally fails to say whether or not they helped somebody. I never thought of it before, and I'll never say it again."

She was pleased and surprised with the quickness and surety of his mind. As soon as he had got the clew he not only understood but corrected her error.

"You'll find it all in the grammar," she went on. "There's something else I noticed in your speech. You say 'don't' when you shouldn't. 'Don't' is a contraction and stands for two words. Do you know them?"

He thought a moment, then answered, " 'Do not.' "

She nodded her head, and said, "And you use 'don't' when you mean 'does not.' "

He was puzzled over this, and did not get it so quickly.

"Give me an illustration," he asked.

"Well—" She puckered her brows and pursed up her mouth as she thought, while he looked on and decided that her expression was most adorable. " 'It don't do to be hasty.' Change 'don't' to 'do not,' and it reads, 'It do not do to be hasty,' which is perfectly absurd."

He turned it over in his mind and considered.

"Doesn't it jar on your ear?" she suggested.

"Can't say that it does," he replied judicially.

"Why didn't you say, 'Can't say that it do'?" she queried.

"That sounds wrong," he said slowly. "As for the other I can't make up my mind. I guess my ear ain't had the trainin' yours has."

"There is no such word as 'ain't,' " she said, prettily emphatic.

Martin flushed again.

"And you say 'ben' for 'been,' " she continued; " 'I come' for 'I came'; and the way you chop your endings is something dreadful."

"How do you mean?" He leaned forward, feeling that he ought to get down on his knees before so marvellous a mind. "How do I chop?"

"You don't complete the endings. 'A-n-d' spells 'and.' You pronounce it 'an'.' 'I-n-g' spells 'ing.' Sometimes you pronounce it 'ing' and sometimes you leave off the 'g.' And then you slur by dropping initial letters and diphthongs. 'T-h-e-m' spells 'them.' You pronounce it—oh, well, it is not necessary to go over all of them. What you need is the grammar. I'll get one and show you how to begin."

As she arose, there shot through his mind something that he had read in the etiquette books, and he stood up awkwardly, worrying as to whether he was doing the right thing, and fearing that she might take it as a sign that he was about to go.

"By the way, Mr. Eden," she called back, as she was leaving the room. "What is *booze?* You used it several times, you know."

"Oh, booze," he laughed. "It's slang. It means whiskey an' beer—anything that will make you drunk."

"And another thing," she laughed back. "Don't use 'you' when you are impersonal. 'You' is very personal, and your use of it just now was not precisely what you meant."

"I don't just see that."

"Why, you said just now, to me, 'whiskey and beer—anything that will make you drunk'—make *me* drunk, don't you see?"

"Well, it would, wouldn't it?"

"Yes, of course," she smiled. "But it would be nicer not to bring me into it. Substitute 'one' for 'you' and see how much better it sounds."

When she returned with the grammar, she drew a chair near his—he wondered if he should have helped her with the chair—and sat down beside him. She turned the pages of the grammar, and their heads were inclined toward each other. He could hardly follow her outlining of the work he must do, so amazed was he by her delightful propinquity. But when she began to lay down the importance of conjugation, he forgot all about her. He had never heard of conjugation, and was fascinated by the glimpse he was catching into the tie-ribs of language. He leaned closer to the page, and her hair touched his cheek. He had fainted but once in his life, and he thought he was going to faint again. He could scarcely breathe, and his heart was pounding the blood up into his throat and suffocating him. Never had she seemed so accessible as now. For the moment the great gulf that separated them was bridged. But there was no diminution in the loftiness of his feeling for her. She had not descended to him. It was he who had been caught up into the clouds and carried to her. His reverence for her, in that moment, was of the same order as religious awe and fervor. It seemed to him that he had intruded upon the holy of holies, and slowly and carefully he moved his head aside from the contact which thrilled him like an electric shock and of which she had not been aware.

VIII

SEVERAL weeks went by, during which Martin Eden studied his grammar, reviewed the books on etiquette, and read voraciously the books that caught his fancy. Of his own class he saw nothing. The girls of the Lotus Club wondered what had become of him and worried Jim with questions, and some of the fellows who put on the glove at Riley's were glad that Martin came no more. He made another discovery of treasure-trove in the library. As the grammar had shown him the tie-ribs of language, so that book showed him the tie-ribs of poetry, and he began to learn metre and construction and form, beneath the beauty he loved finding the why and wherefore of that beauty. Another modern book he found treated poetry as a representative art, treated it exhaustively, with copious illustrations from the best in literature. Never had he read fiction with so keen zest as he studied these books. And his fresh mind, untaxed for twenty years and impelled by maturity of desire, gripped hold of what he read with a virility unusual to the student mind.

When he looked back now from his vantage-ground, the old world he had known, the world of land and sea and ships, of sailor-men and harpy-women, seemed a very small world; and yet it blended in with this new world and expanded. His mind made for unity, and he was surprised when at first he began to see points of contact between the two worlds. And he was ennobled, as well, by the loftiness of thought and beauty he found in the books. This led him to believe more firmly than ever that up above him, in society like Ruth and her family, all men and women thought these thoughts and lived them. Down below where he lived was the ignoble, and he wanted to purge himself of the ignoble that had soiled all his days, and to rise to that sublimated realm where dwelt the upper classes. All his childhood and youth had been troubled by a vague unrest; he had never known what he wanted, but he had wanted something that he had hunted vainly for until he met Ruth. And now his unrest had become sharp and painful, and he knew at last, clearly and definitely, that it was beauty, and intellect, and love that he must have.

During those several weeks he saw Ruth half a dozen times, and each time was an added inspiration. She helped him with his English, corrected his pronunciation, and started him on arithmetic. But their intercourse was not all devoted to elementary study. He had seen too much of life, and his mind was too matured, to be wholly content with fractions, cube root, parsing, and analysis; and there were times when their conversation turned on other themes—the last poetry he had read, the latest poet she had studied. And when she read aloud to him her favorite passages, he ascended to the topmost heaven of delight. Never, in all the women he had heard speak, had he heard a voice like hers. The least sound of it was a stimulus to his love, and he thrilled and throbbed with every word she uttered. It was the quality of it, the repose, and the musical modulation—the soft, rich, indefinable product of culture and a gentle soul. As he listened to her, there rang in the ears of his memory the harsh cries of barbarian women and of hags, and, in lesser degrees of harshness, the strident voices of working women and of the girls of his own class. Then the chemistry of vision would begin to work, and they would troop in review across his mind, each, by contrast, multiplying Ruth's glories. Then, too, his bliss was heightened by the knowledge that her mind was comprehending what she read and was quivering with appreciation of the beauty of the written thought. She read to him much from "The Princess," and often he saw her eyes swimming with tears, so finely was her aesthetic nature strung. At such moments her own emotions elevated him till he was as a god, and, as he gazed at her and listened, he seemed gazing on the face of life and reading its deepest secrets. And then, becoming aware of the heights of exquisite sensibility he attained, he decided that this was love and that love was the greatest thing in the world. And in review would pass along the corridors of memory all previous thrills and burnings he had known,—the drunkenness of wine, the caresses of women, the rough play and give and take of physical contests,—and they seemed trivial and mean compared with this sublime ardor he now enjoyed.

The situation was obscured to Ruth. She had never had any experiences of the heart. Her only experiences in such matters were of the books, where the facts of ordinary day were translated by fancy into a fairy realm of unreality; and she little knew that this rough sailor was creeping into her heart and storing there pent forces that would some day burst forth and surge through her in waves of fire. She did not know the actual fire of love. Her knowledge of love was purely theoretical, and she conceived of it as lambent flame, gentle as the fall of dew or the ripple of quiet water, and cool as the velvet-dark of summer nights. Her idea of love was more that of placid affection, serving the loved one softly in an atmosphere, flower-scented and dim-lighted, of ethereal calm. She did not dream of the volcanic convulsions of love, its scorching heat and sterile wastes of parched ashes. She knew neither her own potencies, nor the potencies of the world; and the deeps of life were to her seas of illusion. The conjugal affection of her father and mother constituted her ideal of love-affinity, and she looked forward some day to emerging, without shock or friction, into that same quiet sweetness of existence with a loved one.

So it was that she looked upon Martin Eden as a novelty, a strange individual, and she identified with novelty and strangeness the effects he produced upon her. It was only natural. In similar ways she had experienced unusual feelings when she looked at wild animals in the menagerie, or when she witnessed a storm of wind, or shuddered at the bright-ribbed lightning. There was something cosmic in such things, and there was something cosmic in him. He came to her breathing of large airs and great spaces. The blaze of tropic suns was in his face, and in his swelling, resilient muscles was the primordial vigor of life. He was marred and scarred by that mysterious world of rough men and rougher deeds, the outposts of which began beyond her horizon. He was untamed, wild, and in secret ways her vanity was touched by the fact that he came so mildly to her hand. Likewise she was stirred by the common impulse to tame the wild thing. It was an unconscious impulse, and farthest from her thoughts that her desire was to re-thumb the clay of him into a likeness of her father's image, which image she believed to be the finest in the world. Nor was there any way, out of her inexperience, for her to know that the cosmic feel she caught of him was that most cosmic of things, love, which with equal power drew men and women together across the world, compelled stags to kill each other in the rutting season, and drove even the elements irresistibly to unite.

His swift development was a source of surprise and interest. She detected unguessed finenesses in him that seemed to bud, day by day, like flowers in congenial soil. She read Browning aloud to him, and was often puzzled by the strange interpretations he gave to mooted passages. It was beyond her to realize that, out of his experience of men and women and life, his interpretations were far more frequently correct than hers. His conceptions seemed naïve to her, though she was often fired by his daring flights of comprehension, whose orbit-path was so wide among the stars that she could not follow and could only sit and thrill to the impact of unguessed power. Then she played to him—no longer at him—and probed him with music that sank to depths beyond her plumb-line. His nature opened to music as a flower to the sun, and the transition was quick from his working-class ragtime and jingles to her classical display pieces that she knew nearly by heart. Yet he betrayed a democratic fondness for Wagner, and the "Tannhäuser" overture, when she had given him the clew to it, claimed him as nothing else she played. In an immediate way it personified his life. All his past was the *Venusburg* motif, while her he identified somehow with the *Pilgrim's Chorus* motif; and from the exalted state this elevated him to, he swept onward and upward into that vast shadow-realm of spirit-groping, where good and evil war eternally.

Sometimes he questioned, and induced in her mind temporary doubts as to the correctness of her own definitions and conceptions of music. But her singing he did not question. It was too wholly her, and he sat always amazed at the divine melody of her pure soprano voice. And he could not help but contrast it with the weak pipings and shrill quaverings of factory girls, ill-nourished and untrained, and with the raucous shriekings from gin-cracked throats of the women of the seaport towns. She enjoyed singing and playing to him. In truth, it was the first time she had ever had a human soul to play with, and the plastic clay of him was a delight to mould; for she thought she was moulding it, and her intentions were good. Besides, it was pleasant to be with him. He did not repel her. That first repulsion had been really a fear of her undiscovered self, and the fear had gone to sleep. Though she did not know it, she had a feeling in him of proprietary right. Also, he had a tonic effect upon her. She was studying hard at the university, and it seemed to strengthen her to emerge from the dusty books and have the fresh sea-breeze of his personality blow upon her. Strength! Strength was what she needed, and he gave it to her in generous measure. To come into the same room with him, or to meet him at the door, was to take heart of life. And when he had gone, she would return to her books with a keener zest and fresh store of energy.

She knew her Browning, but it had never sunk into her that it was an awkward thing to play with souls. As her interest in Martin increased, the remodelling of his life became a passion with her.

"There is Mr. Butler," she said one afternoon, when grammar and arithmetic and poetry had been put aside. "He had comparatively no advantages at first. His father had been a bank cashier, but he lingered for years, dying of consumption in Arizona, so that when he was dead, Mr. Butler, Charles Butler he was called, found himself alone in the world. His father had come from Australia, you know, and so he had no relatives in California. He went to work in a printing-office,—I have heard him tell of it many times,—and he got three dollars a week, at first. His income to-day is at least thirty thousand a year. How did he do it? He was honest, and faithful, and industrious, and economical. He denied himself the enjoyments that most boys indulge in. He made it a point to save so much every week, no matter what he had to do without in order to save it. Of course, he was soon earning more than three dollars a week, and as his wages increased he saved more and more.

"He worked in the daytime, and at night he went to night school. He had his eyes fixed always on the future. Later on he went to night high school. When he was only seventeen, he was earning excellent wages at setting type, but he was ambitious. He wanted a career, not a livelihood, and he was content to make immediate sacrifices for his ultimate gain. He decided upon the law, and he entered father's office as an office boy—think of that!—and got only four dollars a week. But he had learned how to be economical, and out of that four dollars he went on saving money."

She paused for breath, and to note how Martin was receiving it. His face was lighted up with interest in the youthful struggles of Mr. Butler; but there was a frown upon his face as well.

"I'd say they was pretty hard lines for a young fellow," he remarked. "Four dollars a week! How could he live on it? You can bet he didn't have any frills. Why, I pay five dollars a week for board now, an' there's nothin' excitin' about it, you can lay to that. He must have lived like a dog. The food he ate—"

"He cooked for himself," she interrupted, "on a little kerosene stove."

"The food he ate must have been worse than what a sailor gets on the worst-feedin' deep-water ships, than which there ain't much that can be possibly worse."

"But think of him now!" she cried enthusiastically. "Think of what his income affords him. His early denials are paid for a thousand-fold."

Martin looked at her sharply.

"There's one thing I'll bet you," he said, "and it is that Mr. Butler is nothin' gay-hearted now in his fat days. He fed himself like that for years an' years, on a boy's stomach, an' I bet his stomach's none too good now for it."

Her eyes dropped before his searching gaze.

"I'll bet he's got dyspepsia right now!" Martin challenged.

"Yes, he has," she confessed; "but—"

"An' I bet," Martin dashed on, "that he's solemn an' serious as an old owl, an' doesn't care a rap for a good time, for all his thirty thousand a year. An' I'll bet he's not particularly joyful at seein' others have a good time. Ain't I right?"

She nodded her head in agreement, and hastened to explain:—

"But he is not that type of man. By nature he is sober and serious. He always was that."

"You can bet he was," Martin proclaimed. "Three dollars a week, an' four dollars a week, an' a young boy cookin' for himself on an oil-burner an' layin' up money, workin' all day an' studyin' all night, just workin' an' never playin', never havin' a good time, an' never learnin' how to have a good time—of course his thirty thousand came along too late."

His sympathetic imagination was flashing upon his inner sight all the thousands of details of the boy's existence and of his narrow spiritual development into a thirty-thousand-dollar-a-year man. With the swiftness and wide-reaching of multitudinous thought Charles Butler's whole life was telescoped upon his vision.

"Do you know," he added, "I feel sorry for Mr. Butler. He was too young to know better, but he robbed himself of life for the sake of thirty thousand a year that's clean wasted upon him. Why, thirty thousand, lump sum, wouldn't buy for him right now what ten cents he was layin' up would have bought him, when he was a kid, in the way of candy an' peanuts or a seat in nigger heaven."

It was just such uniqueness of points of view that startled Ruth. Not only were they new to her, and contrary to her own beliefs, but she always felt in them germs of truth that threatened to unseat or modify her own convictions. Had she been fourteen instead of twenty-four, she might have been changed by them; but she was twenty-four, conservative by nature and upbringing, and already crystallized into the cranny of life where she had been born and formed. It was true, his bizarre judgments troubled her in the moments they were uttered, but she ascribed them to his novelty of type and strangeness of living, and they were soon forgotten. Nevertheless, while she disapproved of them, the strength of their utterance, and the flashing of eyes and earnestness of face that accompanied them, always thrilled her and drew her toward him. She would never have guessed that this man who had come from beyond her horizon, was, in such moments, flashing on beyond her horizon with wider and deeper concepts. Her own limits were the limits of her horizon; but limited minds can recognize limitations only in others. And so she felt that her outlook was very wide indeed, and that where his conflicted with hers marked his limitations; and she dreamed of helping him to see as she saw, of widening his horizon until it was identified with hers.

"But I have not finished my story," she said. "He worked, so father says, as no other office boy he ever had. Mr. Butler was always eager to work. He never was late, and he was usually at the office a few minutes before his regular time. And yet he saved his time. Every spare moment was devoted to study. He studied book-keeping and type-writing, and he paid for lessons in shorthand by dictating at night to a court reporter who needed practice. He quickly became a clerk, and he made himself invaluable. Father appreciated him and saw that he was bound to rise. It was on father's suggestion that he went to law college. He became a lawyer, and hardly was he back in the office when father took him in as junior partner. He is a great man. He refused the United States Senate several times, and father says he could become a justice of the Supreme Court any time a vacancy occurs, if he wants to. Such a life is an inspiration to all of us. It shows us that a man with will may rise superior to his environment."

"He is a great man," Martin said sincerely.

But it seemed to him there was something in the recital that jarred upon his sense of beauty and life. He could not find an adequate motive in Mr. Butler's life of pinching and privation. Had he done it for love of a woman, or for attainment of beauty, Martin would have understood. God's own mad lover should do anything for the kiss, but not for thirty thousand dollars a year. He was dissatisfied with Mr. Butler's career. There was something paltry about it, after all. Thirty thousand a year was all right, but dyspepsia and inability to be humanly happy robbed such princely income of all its value.

Much of this he strove to express to Ruth, and shocked her and made it clear that more remodelling was necessary. Hers was that common insularity of mind that makes human creatures believe that their color, creed, and politics are best and right and that other human creatures scattered over the world are less fortunately placed than they. It was the same insularity of mind that made the ancient Jew thank God he was not born a woman, and sent the modern missionary god-substituting to the ends of the earth; and it made Ruth desire to shape this man from other crannies of life into the likeness of the men who lived in her particular cranny of life.

IX

BACK from sea Martin Eden came, homing for California with a lover's desire. His store of money exhausted, he had shipped before the mast on the treasure-hunting schooner; and the Solomon Islands, after eight months of failure to find treasure, had witnessed the breaking up of the expedition. The men had been paid off in Australia, and Martin had immediately shipped on a deep-water vessel for San Francisco. Not alone had those eight months earned him enough money to stay on land for many weeks, but they had enabled him to do a great deal of studying and reading.

His was the student's mind, and behind his ability to learn was the indomitability of his nature and his love for Ruth. The grammar he had taken along he went through again and again until his unjaded brain had mastered it. He noticed the bad grammar used by his shipmates, and made a point of mentally correcting and reconstructing their crudities of speech. To his great joy he discovered that his ear was becoming sensitive and that he was developing grammatical nerves. A double negative jarred him like a discord, and often, from lack of practice, it was from his own lips that the jar came. His tongue refused to learn new tricks in a day.

After he had been through the grammar repeatedly, he took up the dictionary and added twenty words a day to his vocabulary. He found that this was no light task, and at wheel or lookout he steadily went over and over his lengthening list of pronunciations and definitions, while he invariably memorized himself to sleep. "Never did anything," "if I were," and "those things," were phrases, with many variations, that he repeated under his breath in order to accustom his tongue to the language spoken by Ruth. "And" and "ing," with the "d" and "g" pronounced emphatically, he went over thousands of times; and to his surprise he noticed that he was beginning to speak cleaner and more correct English than the officers themselves and the gentleman-adventurers in the cabin who had financed the expedition.

The captain was a fishy-eyed Norwegian who somehow had fallen into possession of a complete Shakespeare, which he never read, and Martin had washed his clothes for him and in return been permitted access to the precious volumes. For a time, so steeped was he in the plays and in the many favorite passages that impressed themselves almost without effort on his brain, that all the world seemed to shape itself into forms of Elizabethan tragedy or comedy and his very thoughts were in blank verse. It trained his ear and gave him a fine appreciation for noble English; withal it introduced into his mind much that was archaic and obsolete.

The eight months had been well spent, and, in addition to what he had learned of right speaking and high thinking, he had learned much of himself. Along with his humbleness because he knew so little, there arose a conviction of power. He felt a sharp gradation between himself and his shipmates, and was wise enough to realize that the difference lay in potentiality rather than achievement. What he could do, they could do; but within him he felt a confused ferment working that told him there was more in him than he had done. He was tortured by the exquisite beauty of the world, and wished that Ruth were there to share it with him. He decided that he would describe to her many of the bits of South Sea beauty. The creative spirit in him flamed up at the thought and urged that he recreate this beauty for a wider audience than Ruth. And then, in splendor and glory, came the great idea. He would write. He would be one of the eyes through which the world saw, one of the ears through which it heard, one of the hearts through which it felt. He would write—everything—poetry and prose, fiction and description, and plays like Shakespeare. There was career and the way to win to Ruth. The men of literature were the world's giants, and he conceived them to be far finer than the Mr. Butlers who earned thirty thousand a year and could be Supreme Court justices if they wanted to.

Once the idea had germinated, it mastered him, and the return voyage to San Francisco was like a dream. He was drunken with unguessed power and felt that he could do anything. In the midst of the great and lonely sea he gained perspective. Clearly, and for the first time, he saw Ruth and her world. It was all visualized in his mind as a concrete thing which he could take up in his two hands and turn around and about and examine. There was much that was dim and nebulous in that world, but he saw it as a whole and not in detail, and he saw, also, the way to master it. To write! The thought was fire in him. He would begin as soon as he got back. The first thing he would do would be to describe the voyage of the treasure-hunters. He would sell it to some San Francisco newspaper. He would not tell Ruth anything about it, and she would be surprised and pleased when she saw his name in print. While he wrote, he could go on studying. There were twenty-four hours in each day. He was invincible. He knew how to work, and the citadels would go down before him. He would not have to go to sea again—as a sailor; and for the instant he caught a vision of a steam yacht. There were other writers who possessed steam yachts. Of course, he cautioned himself, it would be slow succeeding at first, and for a time he would be content to earn enough money by his writing to enable him to go on studying. And then, after some time,—a very indeterminate time,—when he had learned and prepared himself, he would write the great things and his name would be on all men's lips. But greater than that, infinitely greater and greatest of all, he would have proved himself worthy of Ruth. Fame was all very well, but it was for Ruth that his splendid dream arose. He was not a fame-monger, but merely one of God's mad lovers.

Arrived in Oakland, with his snug pay-day in his pocket, he took up his old room at Bernard Higginbotham's and set to work. He did not even let Ruth know he was back. He would go and see her when he finished the article on the treasure-hunters. It was not so difficult to abstain from seeing her, because of the violent heat of creative fever that burned in him. Besides, the very article he was writing would bring her nearer to him. He did not know how long an article he should write, but he counted the words in a double-page article in the Sunday supplement of the *San Francisco Examiner*, and guided himself by that. Three days, at white heat, completed his narrative; but when he had copied it carefully, in a large scrawl that was easy to read, he learned from a rhetoric he picked up in the library that there were such things as paragraphs and quotation marks. He had never thought of such things before; and he promptly set to work writing the article over, referring continually to the pages of the rhetoric and learning more in a day about composition than the average schoolboy in a year. When he had copied the article a second time and rolled it up carefully, he read in a newspaper an item on hints to beginners, and discovered the iron law that manuscripts should never be rolled and that they should be written on one side of the paper. He had violated the law on both counts. Also, he learned from the item that first-class papers paid a minimum of ten dollars a column. So, while he copied the manuscript a third time, he consoled himself by multiplying ten columns by ten dollars. The product was always the same, one hundred dollars, and he decided that that was better than seafaring. If it hadn't been for his blunders, he would have finished the article in three days. One hundred dollars in three days! It would have taken him three months and longer on the sea to earn a similar amount. A man was a fool to go to sea when he could write, he concluded, though the money in itself meant nothing to him. Its value was in the liberty it would get him, the presentable garments it would buy him, all of which would bring him nearer, swiftly nearer, to the slender, pale girl who had turned his life back upon itself and given him inspiration.

He mailed the manuscript in a flat envelope, and addressed it to the editor of the *San Francisco Examiner.* He had an idea that anything accepted by a paper was published immediately, and as he had sent the manuscript in on Friday he expected it to come out on the following Sunday. He conceived that it would be fine to let that event apprise Ruth of his return. Then, Sunday afternoon, he would call and see her. In the meantime he was occupied by another idea, which he prided himself upon as being a particularly sane, careful, and modest idea. He would write an adventure story for boys and sell it to *The Youth's Companion.* He went to the free reading-room and looked through the files of *The Youth's Companion.* Serial stories, he found, were usually published in that weekly in five instalments of about three thousand words each. He discovered several serials that ran to seven instalments, and decided to write one of that length.

He had been on a whaling voyage in the Arctic, once—a voyage that was to have been for three years and which had terminated in shipwreck at the end of six months. While his imagination was fanciful, even fantastic at times, he had a basic love of reality that compelled him to write about the things he knew. He knew whaling, and out of the real materials of his knowledge he proceeded to manufacture the fictitious adventures of the two boys he intended to use as joint heroes. It was easy work, he decided on Saturday evening. He had completed on that day the first instalment of three thousand words—much to the amusement of Jim, and to the open derision of Mr. Higginbotham, who sneered throughout meal-time at the "litery" person they had discovered in the family.

Martin contented himself by picturing his brother-in-law's surprise on Sunday morning when he opened his *Examiner* and saw the article on the treasure-hunters. Early that morning he was out himself to the front door, nervously racing through the many-sheeted newspaper. He went through it a second time, very carefully, then folded it up and left it where he had found it. He was glad he had not told any one about his article. On second thought he concluded that he had been wrong about the speed with which things found their way into newspaper columns. Besides, there had not been any news value in his article, and most likely the editor would write to him about it first.

After breakfast he went on with his serial. The words flowed from his pen, though he broke off from the writing frequently to look up definitions in the dictionary or to refer to the rhetoric. He often read or re-read a chapter at a time, during such pauses; and he consoled himself that while he was not writing the great things he felt to be in him, he was learning composition, at any rate, and training himself to shape up and express his thoughts. He toiled on till dark, when he went out to the reading-room and explored magazines and weeklies until the place closed at ten o'clock. This was his programme for a week. Each day he did three thousand words, and each evening he puzzled his way through the magazines, taking note of the stories, articles, and poems that editors saw fit to publish. One thing was certain: What these multitudinous writers did he could do, and only give him time and he would do what they could not do. He was cheered to read in *Book News*, in a paragraph on the payment of magazine writers, not that Rudyard Kipling received a dollar per word, but that the minimum rate paid by first-class magazines was two cents a word. *The Youth's Companion* was certainly first class, and at that rate the three thousand words he had written that day would bring him sixty dollars—two months' wages on the sea!

On Friday night he finished the serial, twenty-one thousand words long. At two cents a word, he calculated, that would bring him four hundred and twenty dollars. Not a bad week's work. It was more money than he had ever possessed at one time. He did not know how he could spend it all. He had tapped a gold mine. Where this came from he could always get more. He planned to buy some more clothes, to subscribe to many magazines, and to buy dozens of reference books that at present he was compelled to go to the library to consult. And still there was a large portion of the four hundred and twenty dollars unspent. This worried him until the thought came to him of hiring a servant for Gertrude and of buying a bicycle for Marian.

He mailed the bulky manuscript to *The Youth's Companion*, and on Saturday afternoon, after having planned an article on pearl-diving, he went to see Ruth. He had telephoned, and she went herself to greet him at the door. The old familiar blaze of health rushed out from him and struck her like a blow. It seemed to enter into her body and course through her veins in a liquid glow, and to set her quivering with its imparted strength. He flushed warmly as he took her hand and looked into her blue eyes, but the fresh bronze of eight months of sun hid the flush, though it did not protect the neck from the gnawing chafe of the stiff collar. She noted the red line of it with amusement which quickly vanished as she glanced at his clothes. They really fitted him,—it was his first made-to-order suit,—and he seemed slimmer and better modelled. In addition, his cloth cap had been replaced by a soft hat, which she commanded him to put on and then complimented him on his appearance. She did not remember when she had felt so happy. This change in him was her handiwork, and she was proud of it and fired with ambition further to help him.

But the most radical change of all, and the one that pleased her most, was the change in his speech. Not only did he speak more correctly, but he spoke more easily, and there were many new words in his vocabulary. When he grew excited or enthusiastic, however, he dropped back into the old slurring and the dropping of final consonants. Also, there was an awkward hesitancy, at times, as he essayed the new words he had learned. On the other hand, along with his ease of expression, he displayed a lightness and facetiousness of thought that delighted her. It was his old spirit of humor and badinage that had made him a favorite in his own class, but which he had hitherto been unable to use in her presence through lack of words and training. He was just beginning to orientate himself and to feel that he was not wholly an intruder. But he was very tentative, fastidiously so, letting Ruth set the pace of sprightliness and fancy, keeping up with her but never daring to go beyond her.

He told her of what he had been doing, and of his plan to write for a livelihood and of going on with his studies. But he was disappointed at her lack of approval. She did not think much of his plan.

"You see," she said frankly, "writing must be a trade, like anything else. Not that I know anything about it, of course. I only bring common judgment to bear. You couldn't hope to be a blacksmith without spending three years at learning the trade—or is it five years! Now writers are so much better paid than blacksmiths that there must be ever so many more men who would like to write, who—try to write."

"But then, may not I be peculiarly constituted to write?" he queried, secretly exulting at the language he had used, his swift imagination throwing the whole scene and atmosphere upon a vast screen along with a thousand other scenes from his life—scenes that were rough and raw, gross and bestial.

The whole composite vision was achieved with the speed of light, producing no pause in the conversation, nor interrupting his calm train of thought. On the screen of his imagination he saw himself and this sweet and beautiful girl, facing each other and conversing in good English, in a room of books and paintings and tone and culture, and all illuminated by a bright light of steadfast brilliance; while ranged about and fading away to the remote edges of the screen were antithetical scenes, each scene a picture, and he the onlooker, free to look at will upon what he wished. He saw these other scenes through drifting vapors and swirls of sullen fog dissolving before shafts of red and garish light. He saw cowboys at the bar, drinking fierce whiskey, the air filled with obscenity and ribald language, and he saw himself with them, drinking and cursing with the wildest, or sitting at table with them, under smoking kerosene lamps, while the chips clicked and clattered and the cards were dealt around. He saw himself, stripped to the waist, with naked fists, fighting his great fight with Liverpool Red in the forecastle of the *Susquehanna*; and he saw the bloody deck of the *John Rogers*, that gray morning of attempted mutiny, the mate kicking in death-throes on the main-hatch, the revolver in the old man's hand spitting fire and smoke, the men with passion-wrenched faces, of brutes screaming vile blasphemies and falling about him—and then he returned to the central scene, calm and clean in the steadfast light, where Ruth sat and talked with him amid books and paintings; and he saw the grand piano upon which she would later play to him; and he heard the echoes of his own selected and correct words, "But then, may I not be peculiarly constituted to write?"

"But no matter how peculiarly constituted a man may be for blacksmithing," she was laughing, "I never heard of one becoming a blacksmith without first serving his apprenticeship."

"What would you advise?" he asked. "And don't forget that I feel in me this capacity to write—I can't explain it; I just know that it is in me."

"You must get a thorough education," was the answer, "whether or not you ultimately become a writer. This education is indispensable for whatever career you select, and it must not be slipshod or sketchy. You should go to high school."

"Yes—" he began; but she interrupted with an afterthought:—

"Of course, you could go on with your writing, too."

"I would have to," he said grimly.

"Why?" She looked at him, prettily puzzled, for she did not quite like the persistence with which he clung to his notion.

"Because, without writing there wouldn't be any high school. I must live and buy books and clothes, you know."

"I'd forgotten that," she laughed. "Why weren't you born with an income?"

"I'd rather have good health and imagination," he answered. "I can make good on the income, but the other things have to be made good for—" He almost said "you," then amended his sentence to, "have to be made good for one."

"Don't say 'make good,' " she cried, sweetly petulant. "It's slang, and it's horrid."

He flushed, and stammered, "That's right, and I only wish you'd correct me every time."

"I—I'd like to," she said haltingly. "You have so much in you that is good that I want to see you perfect."

He was clay in her hands immediately, as passionately desirous of being moulded by her as she was desirous of shaping him into the image of her ideal of man. And when she pointed out the opportuneness of the time, that the entrance examinations to high school began on the following Monday, he promptly volunteered that he would take them.

Then she played and sang to him, while he gazed with hungry yearning at her, drinking in her loveliness and marvelling that there should not be a hundred suitors listening there and longing for her as he listened and longed.

X

HE stopped to dinner that evening, and, much to Ruth's satisfaction, made a favorable impression on her father. They talked about the sea as a career, a subject which Martin had at his finger-ends, and Mr. Morse remarked afterward that he seemed a very clear-headed young man. In his avoidance of slang and his search after right words, Martin was compelled to talk slowly, which enabled him to find the best thoughts that were in him. He was more at ease than that first night at dinner, nearly a year before, and his shyness and modesty even commended him to Mrs. Morse, who was pleased at his manifest improvement.

"He is the first man that ever drew passing notice from Ruth," she told her husband. "She has been so singularly backward where men are concerned that I have been worried greatly."

Mr. Morse looked at his wife curiously.

"You mean to use this young sailor to wake her up?" he questioned.

"I mean that she is not to die an old maid if I can help it," was the answer. "If this young Eden can arouse her interest in mankind in general, it will be good thing."

"A very good thing," he commented. "But suppose,—and we must suppose, sometimes, my dear,—suppose he arouses her interest too particularly in him?"

"Impossible," Mrs. Morse laughed. "She is three years older than he, and, besides, it is impossible. Nothing will ever come of it. Trust that to me."

And so Martin's rôle was arranged for him, while he, led on by Arthur and Norman, was meditating an extravagance. They were going out for a ride into the hills Sunday morning on their wheels, which did not interest Martin until he learned that Ruth, too, rode a wheel and was going along. He did not ride, nor own a wheel, but if Ruth rode, it was up to him to begin, was his decision; and when he said good night, he stopped in at a cyclery on his way home and spent forty dollars for a wheel. It was more than a month's hard-earned wages, and it reduced his stock of money amazingly; but when he added the hundred dollars he was to receive from the *Examiner* to the four hundred and twenty dollars that was the least *The Youth's Companion* could pay him, he felt that he had reduced the perplexity the unwonted amount of money had caused him. Nor did he mind, in the course of learning to ride the wheel home, the fact that he ruined his suit of clothes. He caught the tailor by telephone that night from Mr. Higginbotham's store and ordered another suit. Then he carried the wheel up the narrow stairway that clung like a fire-escape to the rear wall of the building, and when he had moved his bed out from the wall, found there was just space enough in the small room for himself and the wheel.

Sunday he had intended to devote to studying for the high school examination, but the pearl-diving article lured him away, and he spent the day in the white-hot fever of re-creating the beauty and romance that burned in him. The fact that the *Examiner* of that morning had failed to publish his treasure-hunting article did not dash his spirits. He was at too great a height for that, and having been deaf to a twice-repeated summons, he went without the heavy Sunday dinner with which Mr. Higginbotham invariably graced his table. To Mr. Higginbotham such a dinner was advertisement of his worldly achievement and prosperity, and he honored it by delivering platitudinous sermonettes upon American institutions and the opportunity said institutions gave to any hard-working man to rise—the rise, in his case, which he pointed out unfailingly, being from a grocer's clerk to the ownership of Higginbotham's Cash Store.

Martin Eden looked with a sigh at his unfinished "Pearl-diving" on Monday morning, and took the car down to Oakland to the high school. And when, days later, he applied for the results of his examinations, he learned that he had failed in everything save grammar.

"Your grammar is excellent," Professor Hilton informed him, staring at him through heavy spectacles; "but you know nothing, positively nothing, in the other branches, and your United States history is abominable—there is no other word for it, abominable. I should advise you—"

Professor Hilton paused and glared at him, unsympathetic and unimaginative as one of his own test-tubes. He was professor of physics in the high school, possessor of a large family, a meagre salary, and a select fund of parrot-learned knowledge.

"Yes, sir," Martin said humbly, wishing somehow that the man at the desk in the library was in Professor Hilton's place just then.

"And I should advise you to go back to the grammar school for at least two years. Good day."

Martin was not deeply affected by his failure, though he was surprised at Ruth's shocked expression when he told her Professor Hilton's advice. Her disappointment was so evident that he was sorry he had failed, but chiefly so for her sake.

"You see I was right," she said. "You know far more than any of the students entering high school, and yet you can't pass the examinations. It is because what education you have is fragmentary, sketchy. You need the discipline of study, such as only skilled teachers can give you. You must be thoroughly grounded. Professor Hilton is right, and if I were you, I'd go to night school. A year and a half of it might enable you to catch up that additional six months. Besides, that would leave you your days in which to write, or, if you could not make your living by your pen, you would have your days in which to work in some position."

But if my days are taken up with work and my nights with school, when am I going to see you?—was Martin's first thought, though he refrained from uttering it. Instead, he said:—

"It seems so babyish for me to be going to night school. But I wouldn't mind that if I thought it would pay. But I don't think it will pay. I can do the work quicker than they can teach me. It would be a loss of time—" he thought of her and his desire to have her—"and I can't afford the time. I haven't the time to spare, in fact."

"There is so much that is necessary." She looked at him gently, and he felt that he was a brute to oppose her. "Physics and chemistry—you can't do them without laboratory study; and you'll find algebra and geometry almost hopeless without instruction. You need the skilled teachers, the specialists in the art of imparting knowledge."

He was silent for a minute, casting about for the least vainglorious way in which to express himself.

"Please don't think I'm bragging," he began. "I don't intend it that way at all. But I have a feeling that I am what I may call a natural student. I can study by myself. I take to it kindly, like a duck to water. You see yourself what I did with grammar. And I've learned much of other things—you would never dream how much. And I'm only getting started. Wait till I get—" He hesitated and assured himself of the pronunciation before he said "momentum. I'm getting my first real feel of things now. I'm beginning to size up the situation—"

"Please don't say 'size up,' " she interrupted.

"To get a line on things," he hastily amended.

"That doesn't mean anything in correct English," she objected.

He floundered for a fresh start.

"What I'm driving at is that I'm beginning to get the lay of the land."

Out of pity she forebore, and he went on.

"Knowledge seems to me like a chart-room. Whenever I go into the library, I am impressed that way. The part played by teachers is to teach the student the contents of the chart-room in a systematic way. The teachers are guides to the chart-room, that's all. It's not something that they have in their own heads. They don't make it up, don't create it. It's all in the chart-room and they know their way about in it, and it's their business to show the place to strangers who might else get lost. Now I don't get lost easily. I have the bump of location. I usually know where I'm at—What's wrong now?"

"Don't say 'where I'm at.' "

"That's right," he said gratefully, "where I am. But where am I at—I mean, where am I? Oh, yes, in the chart-room. Well, some people—"

"Persons," she corrected.

"Some persons need guides, most persons do; but I think I can get along without them. I've spent a lot of time in the chart-room now, and I'm on the edge of knowing my way about, what charts I want to refer to, what coasts I want to explore. And from the way I line it up, I'll explore a whole lot more quickly by myself. The speed of a fleet, you know, is the speed of the slowest ship, and the speed of the teachers is affected the same way. They can't go any faster than the ruck of their scholars, and I can set a faster pace for myself than they set for a whole schoolroom."

" 'He travels the fastest who travels alone,' " she quoted at him.

But I'd travel faster with you just the same, was what he wanted to blurt out, as he caught a vision of a world without end of sunlit spaces and starry voids through which he drifted with her, his arm around her, her pale gold hair blowing about his face. In the same instant he was aware of the pitiful inadequacy of speech. God! If he could so frame words that she could see what he then saw! And he felt the stir in him, like a throe of yearning pain, of the desire to paint these visions that flashed unsummoned on the mirror of his mind. Ah, that was it! He caught at the hem of the secret. It was the very thing that the great writers and master-poets did. That was why they were giants. They knew how to express what they thought, and felt, and saw. Dogs asleep in the sun often whined and barked, but they were unable to tell what they saw that made them whine and bark. He had often wondered what it was. And that was all he was, a dog asleep in the sun. He saw noble and beautiful visions, but he could only whine and bark at Ruth. But he would cease sleeping in the sun. He would stand up, with open eyes, and he would struggle and toil and learn until, with eyes unblinded and tongue untied, he could share with her his visioned wealth. Other men had discovered the trick of expression, of making words obedient servitors, and of making combinations of words mean more than the sum of their separate meanings. He was stirred profoundly by the passing glimpse at the secret, and he was again caught up in the vision of sunlit spaces and starry voids—until it came to him that it was very quiet, and he saw Ruth regarding him with an amused expression and a smile in her eyes.

"I have had a great visioning," he said, and at the sound of his words in his own ears his heart gave a leap. Where had those words come from? They had adequately expressed the pause his vision had put in the conversation. It was a miracle. Never had he so loftily framed a lofty thought. But never had he attempted to frame lofty thoughts in words. That was it. That explained it. He had never tried. But Swinburne had, and Tennyson, and Kipling, and all the other poets. His mind flashed on to his "Pearl-diving." He had never dared the big things, the spirit of the beauty that was a fire in him. That article would be a different thing when he was done with it. He was appalled by the vastness of the beauty that rightfully belonged in it, and again his mind flashed and dared, and he demanded of himself why he could not chant that beauty in noble verse as the great poets did. And there was all the mysterious delight and spiritual wonder of his love for Ruth. Why could he not chant that, too, as the poets did? They had sung of love. So would he. By God!—

And in his frightened ears he heard his exclamation echoing. Carried away, he had breathed it aloud. The blood surged into his face, wave upon wave, mastering the bronze of it till the blush of shame flaunted itself from collar-rim to the roots of his hair.

"I—I—beg your pardon," he stammered. "I was thinking."

"It sounded as if you were praying," she said bravely, but she felt herself inside to be withering and shrinking. It was the first time she had heard an oath from the lips of a man she knew, and she was shocked, not merely as a matter of principle and training, but shocked in spirit by this rough blast of life in the garden of her sheltered maidenhood.

But she forgave, and with surprise at the ease of her forgiveness. Somehow it was not so difficult to forgive him anything. He had not had a chance to be as other men, and he was trying so hard, and succeeding, too. It never entered her head that there could be any other reason for her being kindly disposed toward him. She was tenderly disposed toward him, but she did not know it. She had no way of knowing it. The placid poise of twenty-four years without a single love affair did not fit her with a keen perception of her own feelings, and she who had never warmed to actual love was unaware that she was warming now.

XI

Martin went back to his pearl-diving article, which would have been finished sooner if it had not been broken in upon so frequently by his attempts to write poetry. His poems were love poems, inspired by Ruth, but they were never completed. Not in a day could he learn to chant in noble verse. Rhyme and metre and structure were serious enough in themselves, but there was, over and beyond them, an intangible and evasive something that he caught in all great poetry, but which he could not catch and imprison in his own. It was the elusive spirit of poetry itself that he sensed and sought after but could not capture. It seemed a glow to him, a warm and trailing vapor, ever beyond his reaching, though sometimes he was rewarded by catching at shreds of it and weaving them into phrases that echoed in his brain with haunting notes or drifted across his vision in misty wafture of unseen beauty. It was baffling. He ached with desire to express and could but gibber prosaically as everybody gibbered. He read his fragments aloud. The metre marched along on perfect feet, and the rhyme pounded a longer and equally faultless rhythm, but the glow and high exaltation that he felt within were lacking. He could not understand, and time and again, in despair, defeated and depressed, he returned to his article. Prose was certainly an easier medium.

Following the "Pearl-diving," he wrote an article on the sea as a career, another on turtle-catching, and a third on the northeast trades. Then he tried, as an experiment, a short story, and before he broke his stride he had finished six short stories and despatched them to various magazines. He wrote prolifically, intensely, from morning till night, and late at night, except when he broke off to go to the reading-room, draw books from the library, or to call on Ruth. He was profoundly happy. Life was pitched high. He was in a fever that never broke. The joy of creation that is supposed to belong to the gods was his. All the life about him—the odors of stale vegetables and soapsuds, the slatternly form of his sister, and the jeering face of Mr. Higginbotham—was a dream. The real world was in his mind, and the stories he wrote were so many pieces of reality out of his mind.

The days were too short. There was so much he wanted to study. He cut his sleep down to five hours and found that he could get along upon it. He tried four hours and a half, and regretfully came back to five. He could joyfully have spent all his waking hours upon any one of his pursuits. It was with regret that he ceased from writing to study, that he ceased from study to go to the library, that he tore himself away from that chart-room of knowledge or from the magazines in the reading-room that were filled with the secrets of writers who succeeded in selling their wares. It was like severing heart-strings, when he was with Ruth, to stand up and go; and he scorched through the dark streets so as to get home to his books at the least possible expense of time. And hardest of all was it to shut up the algebra or physics, put note-book and pencil aside, and close his tired eyes in sleep. He hated the thought of ceasing to live, even for so short a time, and his sole consolation was that the alarm clock was set five hours ahead. He would lose only five hours anyway, and then the jangling bell would jerk him out of unconsciousness and he would have before him another glorious day of nineteen hours.

In the meantime the weeks were passing, his money was ebbing low, and there was no money coming in. A month after he had mailed it, the adventure serial for boys was returned to him by *The Youth's Companion.* The rejection slip was so tactfully worded that he felt kindly toward the editor. But he did not feel so kindly toward the editor of the *San Francisco Examiner.* After waiting two whole weeks, Martin had written to him. A week later he wrote again. At the end of the month, he went over to San Francisco and personally called upon the editor. But he did not meet that exalted personage, thanks to a Cerberus of an office boy, of tender years and red hair, who guarded the portals. At the end of the fifth week the manuscript came back to him, by mail, without comment. There was no rejection slip, no explanation, nothing. In the same way his other articles were tied up with the other leading San Francisco papers. When he recovered them, he sent them to the magazines in the East, from which they were returned more promptly, accompanied always by the printed rejection slips.

The short stories were returned in similar fashion. He read them over and over, and liked them so much that he could not puzzle out the cause of their rejection, until, one day, he read in a newspaper that manuscripts should always be typewritten. That explained it. Of course editors were so busy that they could not afford the time and strain of reading handwriting. Martin rented a typewriter and spent a day mastering the machine. Each day he typed what he composed, and he typed his earlier manuscripts as fast as they were returned him. He was surprised when the typed ones began to come back. His jaw seemed to become squarer, his chin more aggressive, and he bundled the manuscripts off to new editors.

The thought came to him that he was not a good judge of his own work. He tried it out on Gertrude. He read his stories aloud to her. Her eyes glistened, and she looked at him proudly as she said:—

"Ain't it grand, you writin' those sort of things."

"Yes, yes," he demanded impatiently. "But the story—how did you like it?"

"Just grand," was the reply. "Just grand, an' thrilling, too. I was all worked up."

He could see that her mind was not clear. The perplexity was strong in her good-natured face. So he waited.

"But, say, Mart," after a long pause, "how did it end? Did that young man who spoke so highfalutin' get her?"

And, after he had explained the end, which he thought he had made artistically obvious, she would say:—

"That's what I wanted to know. Why didn't you write that way in the story?"

One thing he learned, after he had read her a number of stories, namely, that she liked happy endings.

"That story was perfectly grand," she announced, straightening up from the wash-tub with a tired sigh and wiping the sweat from her forehead with a red, steamy hand; "but it makes me sad. I want to cry. There is too many sad things in the world anyway. It makes me happy to think about happy things. Now if he'd married her, and—You don't mind, Mart?" she queried apprehensively. "I just happen to feel that way, because I'm tired, I guess. But the story was grand just the same, perfectly grand. Where are you goin' to sell it?"

"That's a horse of another color," he laughed.

"But if you *did* sell it, what do you think you'd get for it?"

"Oh, a hundred dollars. That would be the least, the way prices go."

"My! I do hope you'll sell it!"

"Easy money, eh?" Then he added proudly: "I wrote it in two days. That's fifty dollars a day."

He longed to read his stories to Ruth, but did not dare. He would wait till some were published, he decided, then she would understand what he had been working for. In the meantime he toiled on. Never had the spirit of adventure lured him more strongly than on this amazing exploration of the realm of mind. He bought the text-books on physics and chemistry, and, along with his algebra, worked out problems and demonstrations. He took the laboratory proofs on faith, and his intense power of vision enabled him to see the reactions of chemicals more understandingly than the average student saw them in the laboratory. Martin wandered on through the heavy pages, overwhelmed by the clews he was getting to the nature of things. He had accepted the world as the world, but now he was comprehending the organization of it, the play and interplay of force and matter. Spontaneous explanations of old matters were continually arising in his mind. Levers and purchases fascinated him, and his mind roved backward to hand-spikes and blocks and tackles at sea. The theory of navigation, which enabled the ships to travel unerringly their courses over the pathless ocean, was made clear to him. The mysteries of storm, and rain, and tide were revealed, and the reason for the existence of trade-winds made him wonder whether he had written his article on the northeast trade too soon. At any rate he knew he could write it better now. One afternoon he went out with Arthur to the University of California, and, with bated breath and a feeling of religious awe, went through the laboratories, saw demonstrations, and listened to a physics professor lecturing to his classes.

But he did not neglect his writing. A stream of short stories flowed from his pen, and he branched out into the easier forms of verse—the kind he saw printed in the magazines—though he lost his head and wasted two weeks on a tragedy in blank verse, the swift rejection of which, by half a dozen magazines, dumfounded him. Then he discovered Henley and wrote a series of sea-poems on the model of "Hospital Sketches." They were simple poems, of light and color, and romance and adventure. "Sea Lyrics," he called them, and he judged them to be the best work he had yet done. There were thirty, and he completed them in a month, doing one a day after having done his regular day's work on fiction, which day's work was the equivalent to a week's work of the average successful writer. The toil meant nothing to him. It was not toil. He was finding speech, and all the beauty and wonder that had been pent for years behind his inarticulate lips was now pouring forth in a wild and virile flood.

He showed the "Sea Lyrics" to no one, not even to the editors. He had become distrustful of editors. But it was not distrust that prevented him from submitting the "Lyrics." They were so beautiful to him that he was impelled to save them to share with Ruth in some glorious, far-off time when he would dare to read to her what he had written. Against that time he kept them with him, reading them aloud, going over them until he knew them by heart.

He lived every moment of his waking hours, and he lived in his sleep, his subjective mind rioting through his five hours of surcease and combining the thoughts and events of the day into grotesque and impossible marvels. In reality, he never rested, and a weaker body or a less firmly poised brain would have been prostrated in a general break-down. His late afternoon calls on Ruth were rarer now, for June was approaching, when she would take her degree and finish with the university. Bachelor of Arts!—when he thought of her degree, it seemed she fled beyond him faster than he could pursue.

One afternoon a week she gave to him, and arriving late, he usually stayed for dinner and for music afterward. Those were his red-letter days. The atmosphere of the house, in such contrast with that in which he lived, and the mere nearness to her, sent him forth each time with a firmer grip on his resolve to climb the heights. In spite of the beauty in him, and the aching desire to create, it was for her that he struggled. He was a lover first and always. All other things he subordinated to love. Greater than his adventure in the world of thought was his love-adventure. The world itself was not so amazing because of the atoms and molecules that composed it according to the propulsions of irresistible force; what made it amazing was the fact that Ruth lived in it. She was the most amazing thing he had ever known, or dreamed, or guessed.

But he was oppressed always by her remoteness. She was so far from him, and he did not know how to approach her. He had been a success with girls and women in his own class; but he had never loved any of them, while he did love her, and besides, she was not merely of another class. His very love elevated her above all classes. She was a being apart, so far apart that he did not know how to draw near to her as a lover should draw near. It was true, as he acquired knowledge and language, that he was drawing nearer, talking her speech, discovering ideas and delights in common; but this did not satisfy his lover's yearning. His lover's imagination had made her holy, too holy, too spiritualized, to have any kinship with him in the flesh. It was his own love that thrust her from him and made her seem impossible for him. Love itself denied him the one thing that it desired.

And then, one day, without warning, the gulf between them was bridged for a moment, and thereafter, though the gulf remained, it was ever narrower. They had been eating cherries—great, luscious, black cherries with a juice of the color of dark wine. And later, as she read aloud to him from "The Princess," he chanced to notice the stain of the cherries on her lips. For the moment her divinity was shattered. She was clay, after all, mere clay, subject to the common law of clay as his clay was subject, or anybody's clay. Her lips were flesh like his, and cherries dyed them as cherries dyed his. And if so with her lips, then was it so with all of her. She was woman, all woman, just like any woman. It came upon him abruptly. It was a revelation that stunned him. It was as if he had seen the sun fall out of the sky, or had seen worshipped purity polluted.

Then he realized the significance of it, and his heart began pounding and challenging him to play the lover with this woman who was not a spirit from other worlds but a mere woman with lips a cherry could stain. He trembled at the audacity of his thought; but all his soul was singing, and reason, in a triumphant paean, assured him he was right. Something of this change in him must have reached her, for she paused from her reading, looked up at him, and smiled. His eyes dropped from her blue eyes to her lips, and the sight of the stain maddened him. His arms all but flashed out to her and around her, in the way of his old careless life. She seemed to lean toward him, to wait, and all his will fought to hold him back.

"You were not following a word," she pouted.

Then she laughed at him, delighting in his confusion, and as he looked into her frank eyes and knew that she had divined nothing of what he felt, he became abashed. He had indeed in thought dared too far. Of all the women he had known there was no woman who would not have guessed—save her. And she had not guessed. There was the difference. She *was* different. He was appalled by his own grossness, awed by her clear innocence, and he gazed again at her across the gulf. The bridge had broken down.

But still the incident had brought him nearer. The memory of it persisted, and in the moments when he was most cast down, he dwelt upon it eagerly. The gulf was never again so wide. He had accomplished a distance vastly greater than a bachelorship of arts, or a dozen bachelorships. She was pure, it was true, as he had never dreamed of purity; but cherries stained her lips. She was subject to the laws of the universe just as inexorably as he was. She had to eat to live, and when she got her feet wet, she caught cold. But that was not the point. If she could feel hunger and thirst, and heat and cold, then could she feel love—and love for a man. Well, he was a man. And why could he not be *the* man? "It's up to me to make good," he would murmur fervently. "I will be *the* man. I will make myself *the* man. I will make good."

XII

EARLY one evening, struggling with a sonnet that twisted all awry the beauty and thought that trailed in glow and vapor through his brain, Martin was called to the telephone.

"It's a lady's voice, a fine lady's," Mr. Higginbotham, who had called him, jeered.

Martin went to the telephone in the corner of the room, and felt a wave of warmth rush through him as he heard Ruth's voice. In his battle with the sonnet he had forgotten her existence, and at the sound of her voice his love for her smote him like a sudden blow. And such a voice!—delicate and sweet, like a strain of music heard far off and faint, or, better, like a bell of silver, a perfect tone, crystal-pure. No mere woman had a voice like that. There was something celestial about it, and it came from other worlds. He could scarcely hear what it said, so ravished was he, though he controlled his face, for he knew that Mr. Higginbotham's ferret eyes were fixed upon him.

It was not much that Ruth wanted to say—merely that Norman had been going to take her to a lecture that night, but that he had a headache, and she was so disappointed, and she had the tickets, and that if he had no other engagement, would he be good enough to take her?

Would he! He fought to suppress the eagerness in his voice. It was amazing. He had always seen her in her own house. And he had never dared to ask her to go anywhere with him. Quite irrelevantly, still at the telephone and talking with her, he felt an overpowering desire to die for her, and visions of heroic sacrifice shaped and dissolved in his whirling brain. He loved her so much, so terribly, so hopelessly. In that moment of mad happiness that she should go out with him, go to a lecture with him—with him, Martin Eden—she soared so far above him that there seemed nothing else for him to do than die for her. It was the only fit way in which he could express the tremendous and lofty emotion he felt for her. It was the sublime abnegation of true love that comes to all lovers, and it came to him there, at the telephone, in a whirlwind of fire and glory; and to die for her, he felt, was to have lived and loved well. And he was only twenty-one, and he had never been in love before.

His hand trembled as he hung up the receiver, and he was weak from the organ which had stirred him. His eyes were shining like an angel's, and his face was transfigured, purged of all earthly dross, and pure and holy.

"Makin' dates outside, eh?" his brother-in-law sneered. "You know what that means. You'll be in the police court yet."

But Martin could not come down from the height. Not even the bestiality of the allusion could bring him back to earth. Anger and hurt were beneath him. He had seen a great vision and was as a god, and he could feel only profound and awful pity for this maggot of a man. He did not look at him, and though his eyes passed over him, he did not see him; and as in a dream he passed out of the room to dress. It was not until he had reached his own room and was tying his necktie that he became aware of a sound that lingered unpleasantly in his ears. On investigating this sound he identified it as the final snort of Bernard Higginbotham, which somehow had not penetrated to his brain before.

As Ruth's front door closed behind them and he came down the steps with her, he found himself greatly perturbed. It was not unalloyed bliss, taking her to the lecture. He did not know what he ought to do. He had seen, on the streets, with persons of her class, that the women took the men's arms. But then, again, he had seen them when they didn't; and he wondered if it was only in the evening that arms were taken, or only between husbands and wives and relatives.

Just before he reached the sidewalk, he remembered Minnie. Minnie had always been a stickler. She had called him down the second time she walked out with him, because he had gone along on the inside, and she had laid the law down to him that a gentleman always walked on the outside—when he was with a lady. And Minnie had made a practice of kicking his heels, whenever they crossed from one side of the street to the other, to remind him to get over on the outside. He wondered where she had got that item of etiquette, and whether it had filtered down from above and was all right.

It wouldn't do any harm to try it, he decided, by the time they had reached the sidewalk; and he swung behind Ruth and took up his station on the outside. Then the other problem presented itself. Should he offer her his arm? He had never offered anybody his arm in his life. The girls he had known never took the fellows' arms. For the first several times they walked freely, side by side, and after that it was arms around the waists, and heads against the fellows' shoulders where the streets were unlighted. But this was different. She wasn't that kind of a girl. He must do something.

He crooked the arm next to her—crooked it very slightly and with secret tentativeness, not invitingly, but just casually, as though he was accustomed to walk that way. And then the wonderful thing happened. He felt her hand upon his arm. Delicious thrills ran through him at the contact, and for a few sweet moments it seemed that he had left the solid earth and was flying with her through the air. But he was soon back again, perturbed by a new complication. They were crossing the street. This would put him on the inside. He should be on the outside. Should he therefore drop her arm and change over? And if he did so, would he have to repeat the manoeuvre the next time? And the next? There was something wrong about it, and he resolved not to caper about and play the fool. Yet he was not satisfied with his conclusion, and when he found himself on the inside, he talked quickly and earnestly, making a show of being carried away by what he was saying, so that, in case he was wrong in not changing sides, his enthusiasm would seem the cause for his carelessness.

As they crossed Broadway, he came face to face with a new problem. In the blaze of the electric lights, he saw Lizzie Connolly and her giggly friend. Only for an instant he hesitated, then his hand went up and his hat came off. He could not be disloyal to his kind, and it was to more than Lizzie Connolly that his hat was lifted. She nodded and looked at him boldly, not with soft and gentle eyes like Ruth's, but with eyes that were handsome and hard, and that swept on past him to Ruth and itemized her face and dress and station. And he was aware that Ruth looked, too, with quick eyes that were timid and mild as a dove's, but which saw, in a look that was a flutter on and past, the working-class girl in her cheap finery and under the strange hat that all working-class girls were wearing just then.

"What a pretty girl!" Ruth said a moment later.

Martin could have blessed her, though he said:—

"I don't know. I guess it's all a matter of personal taste, but she doesn't strike me as being particularly pretty."

"Why, there isn't one woman in ten thousand with features as regular as hers. They are splendid. Her face is as clear-cut as a cameo. And her eyes are beautiful."

"Do you think so?" Martin queried absently, for to him there was only one beautiful woman in the world, and she was beside him, her hand upon his arm.

"Do I think so? If that girl had proper opportunity to dress, Mr. Eden, and if she were taught how to carry herself, you would be fairly dazzled by her, and so would all men."

"She would have to be taught how to speak," he commented, "or else most of the men wouldn't understand her. I'm sure you couldn't understand a quarter of what she said if she just spoke naturally."

"Nonsense! You are as bad as Arthur when you try to make your point."

"You forget how I talked when you first met me. I have learned a new language since then. Before that time I talked as that girl talks. Now I can manage to make myself understood sufficiently in your language to explain that you do not know that other girl's language. And do you know why she carries herself the way she does? I think about such things now, though I never used to think about them, and I am beginning to understand—much."

"But why does she?"

"She has worked long hours for years at machines. When one's body is young, it is very pliable, and hard work will mould it like putty according to the nature of the work. I can tell at a glance the trades of many workingmen I meet on the street. Look at me. Why am I rolling all about the shop? Because of the years I put in on the sea. If I'd put in the same years cow-punching, with my body young and pliable, I wouldn't be rolling now, but I'd be bow-legged. And so with that girl. You noticed that her eyes were what I might call hard. She has never been sheltered. She has had to take care of herself, and a young girl can't take care of herself and keep her eyes soft and gentle like—like yours, for example."

"I think you are right," Ruth said in a low voice. "And it is too bad. She is such a pretty girl."

He looked at her and saw her eyes luminous with pity. And then he remembered that he loved her and was lost in amazement at his fortune that permitted him to love her and to take her on his arm to a lecture.

Who are you, Martin Eden? he demanded of himself in the looking-glass, that night when he got back to his room. He gazed at himself long and curiously. Who are you? What are you? Where do you belong? You belong by rights to girls like Lizzie Connolly. You belong with the legions of toil, with all that is low, and vulgar, and unbeautiful. You belong with the oxen and the drudges, in dirty surroundings among smells and stenches. There are the stale vegetables now. Those potatoes are rotting. Smell them, damn you, smell them. And yet you dare to open the books, to listen to beautiful music, to learn to love beautiful paintings, to speak good English, to think thoughts that none of your own kind thinks, to tear yourself away from the oxen and the Lizzie Connollys and to love a pale spirit of a woman who is a million miles beyond you and who lives in the stars! Who are you? and what are you? damn you! And are you going to make good?

He shook his fist at himself in the glass, and sat down on the edge of the bed to dream for a space with wide eyes. Then he got out note-book and algebra and lost himself in quadratic equations, while the hours slipped by, and the stars dimmed, and the gray of dawn flooded against his window.

XIII

It was the knot of wordy socialists and working-class philosophers that held forth in the City Hall Park on warm afternoons that was responsible for the great discovery. Once or twice in the month, while riding through the park on his way to the library, Martin dismounted from his wheel and listened to the arguments, and each time he tore himself away reluctantly. The tone of discussion was much lower than at Mr. Morse's table. The men were not grave and dignified. They lost their tempers easily and called one another names, while oaths and obscene allusions were frequent on their lips. Once or twice he had seen them come to blows. And yet, he knew not why, there seemed something vital about the stuff of these men's thoughts. Their logomachy was far more stimulating to his intellect than the reserved and quiet dogmatism of Mr. Morse. These men, who slaughtered English, gesticulated like lunatics, and fought one another's ideas with primitive anger, seemed somehow to be more alive than Mr. Morse and his crony, Mr. Butler.

Martin had heard Herbert Spencer quoted several times in the park, but one afternoon a disciple of Spencer's appeared, a seedy tramp with a dirty coat buttoned tightly at the throat to conceal the absence of a shirt. Battle royal was waged, amid the smoking of many cigarettes and the expectoration of much tobacco-juice, wherein the tramp successfully held his own, even when a socialist workman sneered, "There is no god but the Unknowable, and Herbert Spencer is his prophet." Martin was puzzled as to what the discussion was about, but when he rode on to the library he carried with him a new-born interest in Herbert Spencer, and because of the frequency with which the tramp had mentioned "First Principles," Martin drew out that volume.

So the great discovery began. Once before he had tried Spencer, and choosing the "Principles of Psychology" to begin with, he had failed as abjectly as he had failed with Madam Blavatsky. There had been no understanding the book, and he had returned it unread. But this night, after algebra and physics, and an attempt at a sonnet, he got into bed and opened "First Principles." Morning found him still reading. It was impossible for him to sleep. Nor did he write that day. He lay on the bed till his body grew tired, when he tried the hard floor, reading on his back, the book held in the air above him, or changing from side to side. He slept that night, and did his writing next morning, and then the book tempted him and he fell, reading all afternoon, oblivious to everything and oblivious to the fact that that was the afternoon Ruth gave to him. His first consciousness of the immediate world about him was when Bernard Higginbotham jerked open the door and demanded to know if he thought they were running a restaurant.

Martin Eden had been mastered by curiosity all his days. He wanted to know, and it was this desire that had sent him adventuring over the world. But he was now learning from Spencer that he never had known, and that he never could have known had he continued his sailing and wandering forever. He had merely skimmed over the surface of things, observing detached phenomena, accumulating fragments of facts, making superficial little generalizations—and all and everything quite unrelated in a capricious and disorderly world of whim and chance. The mechanism of the flight of birds he had watched and reasoned about with understanding; but it had never entered his head to try to explain the process whereby birds, as organic flying mechanisms, had been developed. He had never dreamed there was such a process. That birds should have come to be, was unguessed. They always had been. They just happened.

And as it was with birds, so had it been with everything. His ignorant and unprepared attempts at philosophy had been fruitless. The mediaeval metaphysics of Kant had given him the key to nothing, and had served the sole purpose of making him doubt his own intellectual powers. In similar manner his attempt to study evolution had been confined to a hopelessly technical volume by Romanes. He had understood nothing, and the only idea he had gathered was that evolution was a dry-as-dust theory, of a lot of little men possessed of huge and unintelligible vocabularies. And now he learned that evolution was no mere theory but an accepted process of development; that scientists no longer disagreed about it, their only differences being over the method of evolution.

And here was the man Spencer, organizing all knowledge for him, reducing everything to unity, elaborating ultimate realities, and presenting to his startled gaze a universe so concrete of realization that it was like the model of a ship such as sailors make and put into glass bottles. There was no caprice, no chance. All was law. It was in obedience to law that the bird flew, and it was in obedience to the same law that fermenting slime had writhed and squirmed and put out legs and wings and become a bird.

Martin had ascended from pitch to pitch of intellectual living, and here he was at a higher pitch than ever. All the hidden things were laying their secrets bare. He was drunken with comprehension. At night, asleep, he lived with the gods in colossal nightmare; and awake, in the day, he went around like a somnambulist, with absent stare, gazing upon the world he had just discovered. At table he failed to hear the conversation about petty and ignoble things, his eager mind seeking out and following cause and effect in everything before him. In the meat on the platter he saw the shining sun and traced its energy back through all its transformations to its source a hundred million miles away, or traced its energy ahead to the moving muscles in his arms that enabled him to cut the meat, and to the brain wherewith he willed the muscles to move to cut the meat, until, with inward gaze, he saw the same sun shining in his brain. He was entranced by illumination, and did not hear the "Bughouse," whispered by Jim, nor see the anxiety on his sister's face, nor notice the rotary motion of Bernard Higginbotham's finger, whereby he imparted the suggestion of wheels revolving in his brother-in-law's head.

What, in a way, most profoundly impressed Martin, was the correlation of knowledge—of all knowledge. He had been curious to know things, and whatever he acquired he had filed away in separate memory compartments in his brain. Thus, on the subject of sailing he had an immense store. On the subject of woman he had a fairly large store. But these two subjects had been unrelated. Between the two memory compartments there had been no connection. That, in the fabric of knowledge, there should be any connection whatever between a woman with hysterics and a schooner carrying a weather-helm or heaving to in a gale, would have struck him as ridiculous and impossible. But Herbert Spencer had shown him not only that it was not ridiculous, but that it was impossible for there to be no connection. All things were related to all other things from the farthermost star in the wastes of space to the myriads of atoms in the grain of sand under one's foot. This new concept was a perpetual amazement to Martin, and he found himself engaged continually in tracing the relationship between all things under the sun and on the other side of the sun. He drew up lists of the most incongruous things and was unhappy until he succeeded in establishing kinship between them all—kinship between love, poetry, earthquake, fire, rattlesnakes, rainbows, precious gems, monstrosities, sunsets, the roaring of lions, illuminating gas, cannibalism, beauty, murder, lovers, fulcrums, and tobacco. Thus, he unified the universe and held it up and looked at it, or wandered through its byways and alleys and jungles, not as a terrified traveller in the thick of mysteries seeking an unknown goal, but observing and charting and becoming familiar with all there was to know. And the more he knew, the more passionately he admired the universe, and life, and his own life in the midst of it all.

"You fool!" he cried at his image in the looking-glass. "You wanted to write, and you tried to write, and you had nothing in you to write about. What did you have in you?—some childish notions, a few half-baked sentiments, a lot of undigested beauty, a great black mass of ignorance, a heart filled to bursting with love, and an ambition as big as your love and as futile as your ignorance. And you wanted to write! Why, you're just on the edge of beginning to get something in you to write about. You wanted to create beauty, but how could you when you knew nothing about the nature of beauty? You wanted to write about life when you knew nothing of the essential characteristics of life. You wanted to write about the world and the scheme of existence when the world was a Chinese puzzle to you and all that you could have written would have been about what you did not know of the scheme of existence. But cheer up, Martin, my boy. You'll write yet. You know a little, a very little, and you're on the right road now to know more. Some day, if you're lucky, you may come pretty close to knowing all that may be known. Then you will write."

He brought his great discovery to Ruth, sharing with her all his joy and wonder in it. But she did not seem to be so enthusiastic over it. She tacitly accepted it and, in a way, seemed aware of it from her own studies. It did not stir her deeply, as it did him, and he would have been surprised had he not reasoned it out that it was not new and fresh to her as it was to him. Arthur and Norman, he found, believed in evolution and had read Spencer, though it did not seem to have made any vital impression upon them, while the young fellow with the glasses and the mop of hair, Will Olney, sneered disagreeably at Spencer and repeated the epigram, "There is no god but the Unknowable, and Herbert Spencer is his prophet."

But Martin forgave him the sneer, for he had begun to discover that Olney was not in love with Ruth. Later, he was dumfounded to learn from various little happenings not only that Olney did not care for Ruth, but that he had a positive dislike for her. Martin could not understand this. It was a bit of phenomena that he could not correlate with all the rest of the phenomena in the universe. But nevertheless he felt sorry for the young fellow because of the great lack in his nature that prevented him from a proper appreciation of Ruth's fineness and beauty. They rode out into the hills several Sundays on their wheels, and Martin had ample opportunity to observe the armed truce that existed between Ruth and Olney. The latter chummed with Norman, throwing Arthur and Martin into company with Ruth, for which Martin was duly grateful.

Those Sundays were great days for Martin, greatest because he was with Ruth, and great, also, because they were putting him more on a par with the young men of her class. In spite of their long years of disciplined education, he was finding himself their intellectual equal, and the hours spent with them in conversation was so much practice for him in the use of the grammar he had studied so hard. He had abandoned the etiquette books, falling back upon observation to show him the right things to do. Except when carried away by his enthusiasm, he was always on guard, keenly watchful of their actions and learning their little courtesies and refinements of conduct.

The fact that Spencer was very little read was for some time a source of surprise to Martin. "Herbert Spencer," said the man at the desk in the library, "oh, yes, a great mind." But the man did not seem to know anything of the content of that great mind. One evening, at dinner, when Mr. Butler was there, Martin turned the conversation upon Spencer. Mr. Morse bitterly arraigned the English philosopher's agnosticism, but confessed that he had not read "First Principles"; while Mr. Butler stated that he had no patience with Spencer, had never read a line of him, and had managed to get along quite well without him. Doubts arose in Martin's mind, and had he been less strongly individual he would have accepted the general opinion and given Herbert Spencer up. As it was, he found Spencer's explanation of things convincing; and, as he phrased it to himself, to give up Spencer would be equivalent to a navigator throwing the compass and chronometer overboard. So Martin went on into a thorough study of evolution, mastering more and more the subject himself, and being convinced by the corroborative testimony of a thousand independent writers. The more he studied, the more vistas he caught of fields of knowledge yet unexplored, and the regret that days were only twenty-four hours long became a chronic complaint with him.

One day, because the days were so short, he decided to give up algebra and geometry. Trigonometry he had not even attempted. Then he cut chemistry from his study-list, retaining only physics.

"I am not a specialist," he said, in defence, to Ruth. "Nor am I going to try to be a specialist. There are too many special fields for any one man, in a whole lifetime, to master a tithe of them. I must pursue general knowledge. When I need the work of specialists, I shall refer to their books."

"But that is not like having the knowledge yourself," she protested.

"But it is unnecessary to have it. We profit from the work of the specialists. That's what they are for. When I came in, I noticed the chimney-sweeps at work. They're specialists, and when they get done, you will enjoy clean chimneys without knowing anything about the construction of chimneys."

"That's far-fetched, I am afraid."

She looked at him curiously, and he felt a reproach in her gaze and manner. But he was convinced of the rightness of his position.

"All thinkers on general subjects, the greatest minds in the world, in fact, rely on the specialists. Herbert Spencer did that. He generalized upon the findings of thousands of investigators. He would have had to live a thousand lives in order to do it all himself. And so with Darwin. He took advantage of all that had been learned by the florists and cattle-breeders."

"You're right, Martin," Olney said. "You know what you're after, and Ruth doesn't. She doesn't know what she is after for herself even.

"—Oh, yes," Olney rushed on, heading off her objection, "I know you call it general culture. But it doesn't matter what you study if you want general culture. You can study French, or you can study German, or cut them both out and study Esperanto, you'll get the culture tone just the same. You can study Greek or Latin, too, for the same purpose, though it will never be any use to you. It will be culture, though. Why, Ruth studied Saxon, became clever in it,—that was two years ago,—and all that she remembers of it now is 'Whan that sweet Aprile with his schowers soote'—isn't that the way it goes?

"But it's given you the culture tone just the same," he laughed, again heading her off. "I know. We were in the same classes."

"But you speak of culture as if it should be a means to something," Ruth cried out. Her eyes were flashing, and in her cheeks were two spots of color. "Culture is the end in itself."

"But that is not what Martin wants."

"How do you know?"

"What do you want, Martin?" Olney demanded, turning squarely upon him.

Martin felt very uncomfortable, and looked entreaty at Ruth.

"Yes, what do you want?" Ruth asked. "That will settle it."

"Yes, of course, I want culture," Martin faltered. "I love beauty, and culture will give me a finer and keener appreciation of beauty."

She nodded her head and looked triumph.

"Rot, and you know it," was Olney's comment. "Martin's after career, not culture. It just happens that culture, in his case, is incidental to career. If he wanted to be a chemist, culture would be unnecessary. Martin wants to write, but he's afraid to say so because it will put you in the wrong.

"And why does Martin want to write?" he went on. "Because he isn't rolling in wealth. Why do you fill your head with Saxon and general culture? Because you don't have to make your way in the world. Your father sees to that. He buys your clothes for you, and all the rest. What rotten good is our education, yours and mine and Arthur's and Norman's? We're soaked in general culture, and if our daddies went broke to-day, we'd be falling down to-morrow on teachers' examinations. The best job you could get, Ruth, would be a country school or music teacher in a girls' boarding-school."

"And pray what would you do?" she asked.

"Not a blessed thing. I could earn a dollar and a half a day, common labor, and I might get in as instructor in Hanley's cramming joint—I say might, mind you, and I might be chucked out at the end of the week for sheer inability."

Martin followed the discussion closely, and while he was convinced that Olney was right, he resented the rather cavalier treatment he accorded Ruth. A new conception of love formed in his mind as he listened. Reason had nothing to do with love. It mattered not whether the woman he loved reasoned correctly or incorrectly. Love was above reason. If it just happened that she did not fully appreciate his necessity for a career, that did not make her a bit less lovable. She was all lovable, and what she thought had nothing to do with her lovableness.

"What's that?" he replied to a question from Olney that broke in upon his train of thought.

"I was saying that I hoped you wouldn't be fool enough to tackle Latin."

"But Latin is more than culture," Ruth broke in. "It is equipment."

"Well, are you going to tackle it?" Olney persisted.

Martin was sore beset. He could see that Ruth was hanging eagerly upon his answer.

"I am afraid I won't have time," he said finally. "I'd like to, but I won't have time."

"You see Martin's not seeking culture," Olney exulted. "He's trying to get somewhere, to do something."

"Oh, but it's mental training. It's mind discipline. It's what makes disciplined minds." Ruth looked expectantly at Martin, as if waiting for him to change his judgment. "You know, the foot-ball players have to train before the big game. And that is what Latin does for the thinker. It trains."

"Rot and bosh! That's what they told us when we were kids. But there is one thing they didn't tell us then. They let us find it out for ourselves afterwards." Olney paused for effect, then added, "And what they didn't tell us was that every gentleman should have studied Latin, but that no gentleman should know Latin."

"Now that's unfair," Ruth cried. "I knew you were turning the conversation just in order to get off something."

"It's clever all right," was the retort, "but it's fair, too. The only men who know their Latin are the apothecaries, the lawyers, and the Latin professors. And if Martin wants to be one of them, I miss my guess. But what's all that got to do with Herbert Spencer anyway? Martin's just discovered Spencer, and he's wild over him. Why? Because Spencer is taking him somewhere. Spencer couldn't take me anywhere, nor you. We haven't got anywhere to go. You'll get married some day, and I'll have nothing to do but keep track of the lawyers and business agents who will take care of the money my father's going to leave me."

Olney got up to go, but turned at the door and delivered a parting shot.

"You leave Martin alone, Ruth. He knows what's best for himself. Look at what he's done already. He makes me sick sometimes, sick and ashamed of myself. He knows more now about the world, and life, and man's place, and all the rest, than Arthur, or Norman, or I, or you, too, for that matter, and in spite of all our Latin, and French, and Saxon, and culture."

"But Ruth is my teacher," Martin answered chivalrously. "She is responsible for what little I have learned."

"Rats!" Olney looked at Ruth, and his expression was malicious. "I suppose you'll be telling me next that you read Spencer on her recommendation—only you didn't. And she doesn't know anything more about Darwin and evolution than I do about King Solomon's mines. What's that jawbreaker definition about something or other, of Spencer's, that you sprang on us the other day—that indefinite, incoherent homogeneity thing? Spring it on her, and see if she understands a word of it. That isn't culture, you see. Well, tra la, and if you tackle Latin, Martin, I won't have any respect for you."

And all the while, interested in the discussion, Martin had been aware of an irk in it as well. It was about studies and lessons, dealing with the rudiments of knowledge, and the schoolboyish tone of it conflicted with the big things that were stirring in him—with the grip upon life that was even then crooking his fingers like eagle's talons, with the cosmic thrills that made him ache, and with the inchoate consciousness of mastery of it all. He likened himself to a poet, wrecked on the shores of a strange land, filled with power of beauty, stumbling and stammering and vainly trying to sing in the rough, barbaric tongue of his brethren in the new land. And so with him. He was alive, painfully alive, to the great universal things, and yet he was compelled to potter and grope among schoolboy topics and debate whether or not he should study Latin.

"What in hell has Latin to do with it?" he demanded before his mirror that night. "I wish dead people would stay dead. Why should I and the beauty in me be ruled by the dead? Beauty is alive and everlasting. Languages come and go. They are the dust of the dead."

And his next thought was that he had been phrasing his ideas very well, and he went to bed wondering why he could not talk in similar fashion when he was with Ruth. He was only a schoolboy, with a schoolboy's tongue, when he was in her presence.

"Give me time," he said aloud. "Only give me time."

Time! Time! Time! was his unending plaint.

XIV

It was not because of Olney, but in spite of Ruth, and his love for Ruth, that he finally decided not to take up Latin. His money meant time. There was so much that was more important than Latin, so many studies that clamored with imperious voices. And he must write. He must earn money. He had had no acceptances. Twoscore of manuscripts were travelling the endless round of the magazines. How did the others do it? He spent long hours in the free reading-room, going over what others had written, studying their work eagerly and critically, comparing it with his own, and wondering, wondering, about the secret trick they had discovered which enabled them to sell their work.

He was amazed at the immense amount of printed stuff that was dead. No light, no life, no color, was shot through it. There was no breath of life in it, and yet it sold, at two cents a word, twenty dollars a thousand—the newspaper clipping had said so. He was puzzled by countless short stories, written lightly and cleverly he confessed, but without vitality or reality. Life was so strange and wonderful, filled with an immensity of problems, of dreams, and of heroic toils, and yet these stories dealt only with the commonplaces of life. He felt the stress and strain of life, its fevers and sweats and wild insurgences—surely this was the stuff to write about! He wanted to glorify the leaders of forlorn hopes, the mad lovers, the giants that fought under stress and strain, amid terror and tragedy, making life crackle with the strength of their endeavor. And yet the magazine short stories seemed intent on glorifying the Mr. Butlers, the sordid dollar-chasers, and the commonplace little love affairs of commonplace little men and women. Was it because the editors of the magazines were commonplace? he demanded. Or were they afraid of life, these writers and editors and readers?

But his chief trouble was that he did not know any editors or writers. And not merely did he not know any writers, but he did not know anybody who had ever attempted to write. There was nobody to tell him, to hint to him, to give him the least word of advice. He began to doubt that editors were real men. They seemed cogs in a machine. That was what it was, a machine. He poured his soul into stories, articles, and poems, and intrusted them to the machine. He folded them just so, put the proper stamps inside the long envelope along with the manuscript, sealed the envelope, put more stamps outside, and dropped it into the mail-box. It travelled across the continent, and after a certain lapse of time the postman returned him the manuscript in another long envelope, on the outside of which were the stamps he had enclosed. There was no human editor at the other end, but a mere cunning arrangement of cogs that changed the manuscript from one envelope to another and stuck on the stamps. It was like the slot machines wherein one dropped pennies, and, with a metallic whirl of machinery had delivered to him a stick of chewing-gum or a tablet of chocolate. It depended upon which slot one dropped the penny in, whether he got chocolate or gum. And so with the editorial machine. One slot brought checks and the other brought rejection slips. So far he had found only the latter slot.

It was the rejection slips that completed the horrible machinelikeness of the process. These slips were printed in stereotyped forms and he had received hundreds of them—as many as a dozen or more on each of his earlier manuscripts. If he had received one line, one personal line, along with one rejection of all his rejections, he would have been cheered. But not one editor had given that proof of existence. And he could conclude only that there were no warm human men at the other end, only mere cogs, well oiled and running beautifully in the machine.

He was a good fighter, whole-souled and stubborn, and he would have been content to continue feeding the machine for years; but he was bleeding to death, and not years but weeks would determine the fight. Each week his board bill brought him nearer destruction, while the postage on forty manuscripts bled him almost as severely. He no longer bought books, and he economized in petty ways and sought to delay the inevitable end; though he did not know how to economize, and brought the end nearer by a week when he gave his sister Marian five dollars for a dress.

He struggled in the dark, without advice, without encouragement, and in the teeth of discouragement. Even Gertrude was beginning to look askance. At first she had tolerated with sisterly fondness what she conceived to be his foolishness; but now, out of sisterly solicitude, she grew anxious. To her it seemed that his foolishness was becoming a madness. Martin knew this and suffered more keenly from it than from the open and nagging contempt of Bernard Higginbotham. Martin had faith in himself, but he was alone in this faith. Not even Ruth had faith. She had wanted him to devote himself to study, and, though she had not openly disapproved of his writing, she had never approved.

He had never offered to show her his work. A fastidious delicacy had prevented him. Besides, she had been studying heavily at the university, and he felt averse to robbing her of her time. But when she had taken her degree, she asked him herself to let her see something of what he had been doing. Martin was elated and diffident. Here was a judge. She was a bachelor of arts. She had studied literature under skilled instructors. Perhaps the editors were capable judges, too. But she would be different from them. She would not hand him a stereotyped rejection slip, nor would she inform him that lack of preference for his work did not necessarily imply lack of merit in his work. She would talk, a warm human being, in her quick, bright way, and, most important of all, she would catch glimpses of the real Martin Eden. In his work she would discern what his heart and soul were like, and she would come to understand something, a little something, of the stuff of his dreams and the strength of his power.

Martin gathered together a number of carbon copies of his short stories, hesitated a moment, then added his "Sea Lyrics." They mounted their wheels on a late June afternoon and rode for the hills. It was the second time he had been out with her alone, and as they rode along through the balmy warmth, just chilled by the sea-breeze to refreshing coolness, he was profoundly impressed by the fact that it was a very beautiful and well-ordered world and that it was good to be alive and to love. They left their wheels by the roadside and climbed to the brown top of an open knoll where the sunburnt grass breathed a harvest breath of dry sweetness and content.

"Its work is done," Martin said, as they seated themselves, she upon his coat, and he sprawling close to the warm earth. He sniffed the sweetness of the tawny grass, which entered his brain and set his thoughts whirling on from the particular to the universal. "It has achieved its reason for existence," he went on, patting the dry grass affectionately. "It quickened with ambition under the dreary downpour of last winter, fought the violent early spring, flowered, and lured the insects and the bees, scattered its seeds, squared itself with its duty and the world, and—"

"Why do you always look at things with such dreadfully practical eyes?" she interrupted.

"Because I've been studying evolution, I guess. It's only recently that I got my eyesight, if the truth were told."

"But it seems to me you lose sight of beauty by being so practical, that you destroy beauty like the boys who catch butterflies and rub the down off their beautiful wings."

He shook his head.

"Beauty has significance, but I never knew its significance before. I just accepted beauty as something meaningless, as something that was just beautiful without rhyme or reason. I did not know anything about beauty. But now I know, or, rather, am just beginning to know. This grass is more beautiful to me now that I know why it is grass, and all the hidden chemistry of sun and rain and earth that makes it become grass. Why, there is romance in the life-history of any grass, yes, and adventure, too. The very thought of it stirs me. When I think of the play of force and matter, and all the tremendous struggle of it, I feel as if I could write an epic on the grass."

"How well you talk," she said absently, and he noted that she was looking at him in a searching way.

He was all confusion and embarrassment on the instant, the blood flushing red on his neck and brow.

"I hope I am learning to talk," he stammered. "There seems to be so much in me I want to say. But it is all so big. I can't find ways to say what is really in me. Sometimes it seems to me that all the world, all life, everything, had taken up residence inside of me and was clamoring for me to be the spokesman. I feel—oh, I can't describe it. I feel the bigness of it, but when I speak, I babble like a little child. It is a great task to transmute feeling and sensation into speech, written or spoken, that will, in turn, in him who reads or listens, transmute itself back into the selfsame feeling and sensation. It is a lordly task. See, I bury my face in the grass, and the breath I draw in through my nostrils sets me quivering with a thousand thoughts and fancies. It is a breath of the universe I have breathed. I know song and laughter, and success and pain, and struggle and death; and I see visions that arise in my brain somehow out of the scent of the grass, and I would like to tell them to you, to the world. But how can I? My tongue is tied. I have tried, by the spoken word, just now, to describe to you the effect on me of the scent of the grass. But I have not succeeded. I have no more than hinted in awkward speech. My words seem gibberish to me. And yet I am stifled with desire to tell. Oh!—" he threw up his hands with a despairing gesture—"it is impossible! It is not understandable! It is incommunicable!"

"But you do talk well," she insisted. "Just think how you have improved in the short time I have known you. Mr. Butler is a noted public speaker. He is always asked by the State Committee to go out on stump during campaign. Yet you talked just as well as he the other night at dinner. Only he was more controlled. You get too excited; but you will get over that with practice. Why, you would make a good public speaker. You can go far—if you want to. You are masterly. You can lead men, I am sure, and there is no reason why you should not succeed at anything you set your hand to, just as you have succeeded with grammar. You would make a good lawyer. You should shine in politics. There is nothing to prevent you from making as great a success as Mr. Butler has made. And minus the dyspepsia," she added with a smile.

They talked on; she, in her gently persistent way, returning always to the need of thorough grounding in education and to the advantages of Latin as part of the foundation for any career. She drew her ideal of the successful man, and it was largely in her father's image, with a few unmistakable lines and touches of color from the image of Mr. Butler. He listened eagerly, with receptive ears, lying on his back and looking up and joying in each movement of her lips as she talked. But his brain was not receptive. There was nothing alluring in the pictures she drew, and he was aware of a dull pain of disappointment and of a sharper ache of love for her. In all she said there was no mention of his writing, and the manuscripts he had brought to read lay neglected on the ground.

At last, in a pause, he glanced at the sun, measured its height above the horizon, and suggested his manuscripts by picking them up.

"I had forgotten," she said quickly. "And I am so anxious to hear."

He read to her a story, one that he flattered himself was among his very best. He called it "The Wine of Life," and the wine of it, that had stolen into his brain when he wrote it, stole into his brain now as he read it. There was a certain magic in the original conception, and he had adorned it with more magic of phrase and touch. All the old fire and passion with which he had written it were reborn in him, and he was swayed and swept away so that he was blind and deaf to the faults of it. But it was not so with Ruth. Her trained ear detected the weaknesses and exaggerations, the overemphasis of the tyro, and she was instantly aware each time the sentence-rhythm tripped and faltered. She scarcely noted the rhythm otherwise, except when it became too pompous, at which moments she was disagreeably impressed with its amateurishness. That was her final judgment on the story as a whole—amateurish, though she did not tell him so. Instead, when he had done, she pointed out the minor flaws and said that she liked the story.

But he was disappointed. Her criticism was just. He acknowledged that, but he had a feeling that he was not sharing his work with her for the purpose of schoolroom correction. The details did not matter. They could take care of themselves. He could mend them, he could learn to mend them. Out of life he had captured something big and attempted to imprison it in the story. It was the big thing out of life he had read to her, not sentence-structure and semicolons. He wanted her to feel with him this big thing that was his, that he had seen with his own eyes, grappled with his own brain, and placed there on the page with his own hands in printed words. Well, he had failed, was his secret decision. Perhaps the editors were right. He had felt the big thing, but he had failed to transmute it. He concealed his disappointment, and joined so easily with her in her criticism that she did not realize that deep down in him was running a strong undercurrent of disagreement.

"This next thing I've called 'The Pot'," he said, unfolding the manuscript. "It has been refused by four or five magazines now, but still I think it is good. In fact, I don't know what to think of it, except that I've caught something there. Maybe it won't affect you as it does me. It's a short thing—only two thousand words."

"How dreadful!" she cried, when he had finished. "It is horrible, unutterably horrible!"

He noted her pale face, her eyes wide and tense, and her clenched hands, with secret satisfaction. He had succeeded. He had communicated the stuff of fancy and feeling from out of his brain. It had struck home. No matter whether she liked it or not, it had gripped her and mastered her, made her sit there and listen and forget details.

"It is life," he said, "and life is not always beautiful. And yet, perhaps because I am strangely made, I find something beautiful there. It seems to me that the beauty is tenfold enhanced because it is there—"

"But why couldn't the poor woman—" she broke in disconnectedly. Then she left the revolt of her thought unexpressed to cry out: "Oh! It is degrading! It is not nice! It is nasty!"

For the moment it seemed to him that his heart stood still. *Nasty!* He had never dreamed it. He had not meant it. The whole sketch stood before him in letters of fire, and in such blaze of illumination he sought vainly for nastiness. Then his heart began to beat again. He was not guilty.

"Why didn't you select a nice subject?" she was saying. "We know there are nasty things in the world, but that is no reason—"

She talked on in her indignant strain, but he was not following her. He was smiling to himself as he looked up into her virginal face, so innocent, so penetratingly innocent, that its purity seemed always to enter into him, driving out of him all dross and bathing him in some ethereal effulgence that was as cool and soft and velvety as starshine. *We know there are nasty things in the world!* He cuddled to him the notion of her knowing, and chuckled over it as a love joke. The next moment, in a flashing vision of multitudinous detail, he sighted the whole sea of life's nastiness that he had known and voyaged over and through, and he forgave her for not understanding the story. It was through no fault of hers that she could not understand. He thanked God that she had been born and sheltered to such innocence. But he knew life, its foulness as well as its fairness, its greatness in spite of the slime that infested it, and by God he was going to have his say on it to the world. Saints in heaven—how could they be anything but fair and pure? No praise to them. But saints in slime—ah, that was the everlasting wonder! That was what made life worth while. To see moral grandeur rising out of cesspools of iniquity; to rise himself and first glimpse beauty, faint and far, through mud-dripping eyes; to see out of weakness, and frailty, and viciousness, and all abysmal brutishness, arising strength, and truth, and high spiritual endowment—

He caught a stray sequence of sentences she was uttering.

"The tone of it all is low. And there is so much that is high. Take 'In Memoriam.' "

He was impelled to suggest "Locksley Hall," and would have done so, had not his vision gripped him again and left him staring at her, the female of his kind, who, out of the primordial ferment, creeping and crawling up the vast ladder of life for a thousand thousand centuries, had emerged on the topmost rung, having become one Ruth, pure, and fair, and divine, and with power to make him know love, and to aspire toward purity, and to desire to taste divinity—him, Martin Eden, who, too, had come up in some amazing fashion from out of the ruck and the mire and the countless mistakes and abortions of unending creation. There was the romance, and the wonder, and the glory. There was the stuff to write, if he could only find speech. Saints in heaven!—They were only saints and could not help themselves. But he was a man.

"You have strength," he could hear her saying, "but it is untutored strength."

"Like a bull in a china shop," he suggested, and won a smile.

"And you must develop discrimination. You must consult taste, and fineness, and tone."

"I dare too much," he muttered.

She smiled approbation, and settled herself to listen to another story.

"I don't know what you'll make of this," he said apologetically. "It's a funny thing. I'm afraid I got beyond my depth in it, but my intentions were good. Don't bother about the little features of it. Just see if you catch the feel of the big thing in it. It is big, and it is true, though the chance is large that I have failed to make it intelligible."

He read, and as he read he watched her. At last he had reached her, he thought. She sat without movement, her eyes steadfast upon him, scarcely breathing, caught up and out of herself, he thought, by the witchery of the thing he had created. He had entitled the story "Adventure," and it was the apotheosis of adventure—not of the adventure of the storybooks, but of real adventure, the savage taskmaster, awful of punishment and awful of reward, faithless and whimsical, demanding terrible patience and heart-breaking days and nights of toil, offering the blazing sunlight glory or dark death at the end of thirst and famine or of the long drag and monstrous delirium of rotting fever, through blood and sweat and stinging insects leading up by long chains of petty and ignoble contacts to royal culminations and lordly achievements.

It was this, all of it, and more, that he had put into his story, and it was this, he believed, that warmed her as she sat and listened. Her eyes were wide, color was in her pale cheeks, and before he finished it seemed to him that she was almost panting. Truly, she was warmed; but she was warmed, not by the story, but by him. She did not think much of the story; it was Martin's intensity of power, the old excess of strength that seemed to pour from his body and on and over her. The paradox of it was that it was the story itself that was freighted with his power, that was the channel, for the time being, through which his strength poured out to her. She was aware only of the strength, and not of the medium, and when she seemed most carried away by what he had written, in reality she had been carried away by something quite foreign to it—by a thought, terrible and perilous, that had formed itself unsummoned in her brain. She had caught herself wondering what marriage was like, and the becoming conscious of the waywardness and ardor of the thought had terrified her. It was unmaidenly. It was not like her. She had never been tormented by womanhood, and she had lived in a dreamland of Tennysonian poesy, dense even to the full significance of that delicate master's delicate allusions to the grossnesses that intrude upon the relations of queens and knights. She had been asleep, always, and now life was thundering imperatively at all her doors. Mentally she was in a panic to shoot the bolts and drop the bars into place, while wanton instincts urged her to throw wide her portals and bid the deliciously strange visitor to enter in.

Martin waited with satisfaction for her verdict. He had no doubt of what it would be, and he was astounded when he heard her say:—

"It is beautiful."

"It *is* beautiful," she repeated, with emphasis, after a pause.

Of course it was beautiful; but there was something more than mere beauty in it, something more stingingly splendid which had made beauty its handmaiden. He sprawled silently on the ground, watching the grisly form of a great doubt rising before him. He had failed. He was inarticulate. He had seen one of the greatest things in the world, and he had not expressed it.

"What did you think of the—" He hesitated, abashed at his first attempt to use a strange word. "Of the *motif?*" he asked.

"It was confused," she answered. "That is my only criticism in the large way. I followed the story, but there seemed so much else. It is too wordy. You clog the action by introducing so much extraneous material."

"That was the major *motif,*" he hurriedly explained, "the big underrunning *motif,* the cosmic and universal thing. I tried to make it keep time with the story itself, which was only superficial after all. I was on the right scent, but I guess I did it badly. I did not succeed in suggesting what I was driving at. But I'll learn in time."

She did not follow him. She was a bachelor of arts, but he had gone beyond her limitations. This she did not comprehend, attributing her incomprehension to his incoherence.

"You were too voluble," she said. "But it was beautiful, in places."

He heard her voice as from far off, for he was debating whether he would read her the "Sea Lyrics." He lay in dull despair, while she watched him searchingly, pondering again upon unsummoned and wayward thoughts of marriage.

"You want to be famous?" she asked abruptly.

"Yes, a little bit," he confessed. "That is part of the adventure. It is not the being famous, but the process of becoming so, that counts. And after all, to be famous would be, for me, only a means to something else. I want to be famous very much, for that matter, and for that reason."

"For your sake," he wanted to add, and might have added had she proved enthusiastic over what he had read to her.

But she was too busy in her mind, carving out a career for him that would at least be possible, to ask what the ultimate something was which he had hinted at. There was no career for him in literature. Of that she was convinced. He had proved it to-day, with his amateurish and sophomoric productions. He could talk well, but he was incapable of expressing himself in a literary way. She compared Tennyson, and Browning, and her favorite prose masters with him, and to his hopeless discredit. Yet she did not tell him her whole mind. Her strange interest in him led her to temporize. His desire to write was, after all, a little weakness which he would grow out of in time. Then he would devote himself to the more serious affairs of life. And he would succeed, too. She knew that. He was so strong that he could not fail—if only he would drop writing.

"I wish you would show me all you write, Mr. Eden," she said.

He flushed with pleasure. She was interested, that much was sure. And at least she had not given him a rejection slip. She had called certain portions of his work beautiful, and that was the first encouragement he had ever received from any one.

"I will," he said passionately. "And I promise you, Miss Morse, that I will make good. I have come far, I know that; and I have far to go, and I will cover it if I have to do it on my hands and knees." He held up a bunch of manuscript. "Here are the 'Sea Lyrics.' When you get home, I'll turn them over to you to read at your leisure. And you must be sure to tell me just what you think of them. What I need, you know, above all things, is criticism. And do, please, be frank with me."

"I will be perfectly frank," she promised, with an uneasy conviction that she had not been frank with him and with a doubt if she could be quite frank with him the next time.

XV

THE first battle, fought and finished," Martin said to the looking-glass ten days later. "But there will be a second battle, and a third battle, and battles to the end of time, unless—"

He had not finished the sentence, but looked about the mean little room and let his eyes dwell sadly upon a heap of returned manuscripts, still in their long envelopes, which lay in a corner on the floor. He had no stamps with which to continue them on their travels, and for a week they had been piling up. More of them would come in on the morrow, and on the next day, and the next, till they were all in. And he would be unable to start them out again. He was a month's rent behind on the type-writer, which he could not pay, having barely enough for the week's board which was due and for the employment office fees.

He sat down and regarded the table thoughtfully. There were ink stains upon it, and he suddenly discovered that he was fond of it.

"Dear old table," he said, "I've spent some happy hours with you, and you've been a pretty good friend when all is said and done. You never turned me down, never passed me out a reward-of-unmerit rejection slip, never complained about working overtime."

He dropped his arms upon the table and buried his face in them. His throat was aching, and he wanted to cry. It reminded him of his first fight, when he was six years old, when he punched away with the tears running down his cheeks while the other boy, two years his elder, had beaten and pounded him into exhaustion. He saw the ring of boys, howling like barbarians as he went down at last, writhing in the throes of nausea, the blood streaming from his nose and the tears from his bruised eyes.

"Poor little shaver," he murmured. "And you're just as badly licked now. You're beaten to a pulp. You're down and out."

But the vision of that first fight still lingered under his eyelids, and as he watched he saw it dissolve and reshape into the series of fights which had followed. Six months later Cheese-Face (that was the boy) had whipped him again. But he had blacked Cheese-Face's eye that time. That was going some. He saw them all, fight after fight, himself always whipped and Cheese-Face exulting over him. But he had never run away. He felt strengthened by the memory of that. He had always stayed and taken his medicine. Cheese-Face had been a little fiend at fighting, and had never once shown mercy to him. But he had stayed! He had stayed with it!

Next, he saw a narrow alley, between ramshackle frame buildings. The end of the alley was blocked by a one-story brick building, out of which issued the rhythmic thunder of the presses, running off the first edition of the *Enquirer.* He was eleven, and Cheese-Face was thirteen, and they both carried the *Enquirer.* That was why they were there, waiting for their papers. And, of course, Cheese-Face had picked on him again, and there was another fight that was indeterminate, because at quarter to four the door of the press-room was thrown open and the gang of boys crowded in to fold their papers.

"I'll lick you to-morrow," he heard Cheese-Face promise; and he heard his own voice, piping and trembling with unshed tears, agreeing to be there on the morrow.

And he had come there the next day, hurrying from school to be there first, and beating Cheese-Face by two minutes. The other boys said he was all right, and gave him advice, pointing out his faults as a scrapper and promising him victory if he carried out their instructions. The same boys gave Cheese-Face advice, too. How they had enjoyed the fight! He paused in his recollections long enough to envy them the spectacle he and Cheese-Face had put up. Then the fight was on, and it went on, without rounds, for thirty minutes, until the press-room door was opened.

He watched the youthful apparition of himself, day after day, hurrying from school to the *Enquirer* alley. He could not walk very fast. He was stiff and lame from the incessant fighting. His forearms were black and blue from wrist to elbow, what of the countless blows he had warded off, and here and there the tortured flesh was beginning to fester. His head and arms and shoulders ached, the small of his back ached,—he ached all over, and his brain was heavy and dazed. He did not play at school. Nor did he study. Even to sit still all day at his desk, as he did, was a torment. It seemed centuries since he had begun the round of daily fights, and time stretched away into a nightmare and infinite future of daily fights. Why couldn't Cheese-Face be licked? he often thought; that would put him, Martin, out of his misery. It never entered his head to cease fighting, to allow Cheese-Face to whip him.

And so he dragged himself to the *Enquirer* alley, sick in body and soul, but learning the long patience, to confront his eternal enemy, Cheese-Face, who was just as sick as he, and just a bit willing to quit if it were not for the gang of newsboys that looked on and made pride painful and necessary. One afternoon, after twenty minutes of desperate efforts to annihilate each other according to set rules that did not permit kicking, striking below the belt, nor hitting when one was down, Cheese-Face, panting for breath and reeling, offered to call it quits. And Martin, head on arms, thrilled at the picture he caught of himself, at that moment in the afternoon of long ago, when he reeled and panted and choked with the blood that ran into his mouth and down his throat from his cut lips; when he tottered toward Cheese-Face, spitting out a mouthful of blood so that he could speak, crying out that he would never quit, though Cheese-Face could give in if he wanted to. And Cheese-Face did not give in, and the fight went on.

The next day and the next, days without end, witnessed the afternoon fight. When he put up his arms, each day, to begin, they pained exquisitely, and the first few blows, struck and received, racked his soul; after that things grew numb, and he fought on blindly, seeing as in a dream, dancing and wavering, the large features and burning, animal-like eyes of Cheese-Face. He concentrated upon that face; all else about him was a whirling void. There was nothing else in the world but that face, and he would never know rest, blessed rest, until he had beaten that face into a pulp with his bleeding knuckles, or until the bleeding knuckles that somehow belonged to that face had beaten him into a pulp. And then, one way or the other, he would have rest. But to quit,—for him, Martin, to quit,—that was impossible!

Came the day when he dragged himself into the *Enquirer* alley, and there was no Cheese-Face. Nor did Cheese-Face come. The boys congratulated him, and told him that he had licked Cheese-Face. But Martin was not satisfied. He had not licked Cheese-Face, nor had Cheese-Face licked him. The problem had not been solved. It was not until afterward that they learned that Cheese-Face's father had died suddenly that very day.

Martin skipped on through the years to the night in the nigger heaven at the Auditorium. He was seventeen and just back from sea. A row started. Somebody was bullying somebody, and Martin interfered, to be confronted by Cheese-Face's blazing eyes.

"I'll fix you after de show," his ancient enemy hissed.

Martin nodded. The nigger-heaven bouncer was making his way toward the disturbance.

"I'll meet you outside, after the last act," Martin whispered, the while his face showed undivided interest in the buck-and-wing dancing on the stage.

The bouncer glared and went away.

"Got a gang?" he asked Cheese-Face, at the end of the act.

"Sure."

"Then I got to get one," Martin announced.

Between the acts he mustered his following—three fellows he knew from the nail works, a railroad fireman, and half a dozen of the Boo Gang, along with as many more from the dread Eighteen-and-Market Gang.

When the theatre let out, the two gangs strung along inconspicuously on opposite sides of the street. When they came to a quiet corner, they united and held a council of war.

"Eighth Street Bridge is the place," said a red-headed fellow belonging to Cheese-Face's gang. "You kin fight in the middle, under the electric light, an' whichever way the bulls come in we kin sneak the other way."

"That's agreeable to me," Martin said, after consulting with the leaders of his own gang.

The Eighth Street Bridge, crossing an arm of San Antonio Estuary, was the length of three city blocks. In the middle of the bridge, and at each end, were electric lights. No policeman could pass those end-lights unseen. It was the safe place for the battle that revived itself under Martin's eyelids. He saw the two gangs, aggressive and sullen, rigidly keeping apart from each other and backing their respective champions; and he saw himself and Cheese-Face stripping. A short distance away lookouts were set, their task being to watch the lighted ends of the bridge. A member of the Boo Gang held Martin's coat, and shirt, and cap, ready to race with them into safety in case the police interfered. Martin watched himself go into the centre, facing Cheese-Face, and he heard himself say, as he held up his hand warningly:—

"They ain't no hand-shakin' in this. Understand? They ain't nothin' but scrap. No throwin' up the sponge. This is a grudge-fight an' it's to a finish. Understand? Somebody's goin' to get licked."

Cheese-Face wanted to demur,—Martin could see that,—but Cheese-Face's old perilous pride was touched before the two gangs.

"Aw, come on," he replied. "Wot's the good of chewin' de rag about it? I'm wit' cheh to de finish."

Then they fell upon each other, like young bulls, in all the glory of youth, with naked fists, with hatred, with desire to hurt, to maim, to destroy. All the painful, thousand years' gains of man in his upward climb through creation were lost. Only the electric light remained, a milestone on the path of the great human adventure. Martin and Cheese-Face were two savages, of the stone age, of the squatting place and the tree refuge. They sank lower and lower into the muddy abyss, back into the dregs of the raw beginnings of life, striving blindly and chemically, as atoms strive, as the star-dust of the heavens strives, colliding, recoiling, and colliding again and eternally again.

"God! We are animals! Brute-beasts!" Martin muttered aloud, as he watched the progress of the fight. It was to him, with his splendid power of vision, like gazing into a kinetoscope. He was both onlooker and participant. His long months of culture and refinement shuddered at the sight; then the present was blotted out of his consciousness and the ghosts of the past possessed him, and he was Martin Eden, just returned from sea and fighting Cheese-Face on the Eighth Street Bridge. He suffered and toiled and sweated and bled, and exulted when his naked knuckles smashed home.

They were twin whirlwinds of hatred, revolving about each other monstrously. The time passed, and the two hostile gangs became very quiet. They had never witnessed such intensity of ferocity, and they were awed by it. The two fighters were greater brutes than they. The first splendid velvet edge of youth and condition wore off, and they fought more cautiously and deliberately. There had been no advantage gained either way. "It's anybody's fight," Martin heard some one saying. Then he followed up a feint, right and left, was fiercely countered, and felt his cheek laid open to the bone. No bare knuckle had done that. He heard mutters of amazement at the ghastly damage wrought, and was drenched with his own blood. But he gave no sign. He became immensely wary, for he was wise with knowledge of the low cunning and foul vileness of his kind. He watched and waited, until he feigned a wild rush, which he stopped midway, for he had seen the glint of metal.

"Hold up yer hand!" he screamed. "Them's brass knuckles, an' you hit me with 'em!"

Both gangs surged forward, growling and snarling. In a second there would be a free-for-all fight, and he would be robbed of his vengeance. He was beside himself.

"You guys keep out!" he screamed hoarsely. "Understand? Say, d'ye understand?"

They shrank away from him. They were brutes, but he was the arch-brute, a thing of terror that towered over them and dominated them.

"This is my scrap, an' they ain't goin' to be no buttin' in. Gimme them knuckles."

Cheese-Face, sobered and a bit frightened, surrendered the foul weapon.

"You passed 'em to him, you red-head sneakin' in behind the push there," Martin went on, as he tossed the knuckles into the water. "I seen you, an' I was wonderin' what you was up to. If you try anything like that again, I'll beat cheh to death. Understand?"

They fought on, through exhaustion and beyond, to exhaustion immeasurable and inconceivable, until the crowd of brutes, its blood-lust sated, terrified by what it saw, begged them impartially to cease. And Cheese-Face, ready to drop and die, or to stay on his legs and die, a grisly monster out of whose features all likeness to Cheese-Face had been beaten, wavered and hesitated; but Martin sprang in and smashed him again and again.

Next, after a seeming century or so, with Cheese-Face weakening fast, in a mix-up of blows there was a loud snap, and Martin's right arm dropped to his side. It was a broken bone. Everybody heard it and knew; and Cheese-Face knew, rushing like a tiger in the other's extremity and raining blow on blow. Martin's gang surged forward to interfere. Dazed by the rapid succession of blows, Martin warned them back with vile and earnest curses sobbed out and groaned in ultimate desolation and despair.

He punched on, with his left hand only, and as he punched, doggedly, only half-conscious, as from a remote distance he heard murmurs of fear in the gangs, and one who said with shaking voice: "This ain't a scrap, fellows. It's murder, an' we ought to stop it."

But no one stopped it, and he was glad, punching on wearily and endlessly with his one arm, battering away at a bloody something before him that was not a face but a horror, an oscillating, hideous, gibbering, nameless thing that persisted before his wavering vision and would not go away. And he punched on and on, slower and slower, as the last shreds of vitality oozed from him, through centuries and aeons and enormous lapses of time, until, in a dim way, he became aware that the nameless thing was sinking, slowly sinking down to the rough board-planking of the bridge. And the next moment he was standing over it, staggering and swaying on shaky legs, clutching at the air for support, and saying in a voice he did not recognize:—

"D'ye want any more? Say, d'ye want any more?"

He was still saying it, over and over,—demanding, entreating, threatening, to know if it wanted any more,—when he felt the fellows of his gang laying hands on him, patting him on the back and trying to put his coat on him. And then came a sudden rush of blackness and oblivion.

The tin alarm-clock on the table ticked on, but Martin Eden, his face buried on his arms, did not hear it. He heard nothing. He did not think. So absolutely had he relived life that he had fainted just as he fainted years before on the Eighth Street Bridge. For a full minute the blackness and the blankness endured. Then, like one from the dead, he sprang upright, eyes flaming, sweat pouring down his face, shouting:—

"I licked you, Cheese-Face! It took me eleven years, but I licked you!"

His knees were trembling under him, he felt faint, and he staggered back to the bed, sinking down and sitting on the edge of it. He was still in the clutch of the past. He looked about the room, perplexed, alarmed, wondering where he was, until he caught sight of the pile of manuscripts in the corner. Then the wheels of memory slipped ahead through four years of time, and he was aware of the present, of the books he had opened and the universe he had won from their pages, of his dreams and ambitions, and of his love for a pale wraith of a girl, sensitive and sheltered and ethereal, who would die of horror did she witness but one moment of what he had just lived through —one moment of all the muck of life through which he had waded.

He arose to his feet and confronted himself in the looking-glass.

"And so you arise from the mud, Martin Eden," he said solemnly. "And you cleanse your eyes in a great brightness, and thrust your shoulders among the stars, doing what all life has done, letting the 'ape and tiger die' and wresting highest heritage from all powers that be."

He looked more closely at himself and laughed.

"A bit of hysteria and melodrama, eh?" he queried. "Well, never mind. You licked Cheese-Face, and you'll lick the editors if it takes twice eleven years to do it in. You can't stop here. You've got to go on. It's to a finish, you know."

XVI

THE alarm-clock went off, jerking Martin out of sleep with a suddenness that would have given headache to one with less splendid constitution. Though he slept soundly, he awoke instantly, like a cat, and he awoke eagerly, glad that the five hours of unconsciousness were gone. He hated the oblivion of sleep. There was too much to do, too much of life to live. He grudged every moment of life sleep robbed him of, and before the clock had ceased its clattering he was head and ears in the wash-basin and thrilling to the cold bite of the water.

But he did not follow his regular programme. There was no unfinished story waiting his hand, no new story demanding articulation. He had studied late, and it was nearly time for breakfast. He tried to read a chapter in Fiske, but his brain was restless and he closed the book. To-day witnessed the beginning of the new battle, wherein for some time there would be no writing. He was aware of a sadness akin to that with which one leaves home and family. He looked at the manuscripts in the corner. That was it. He was going away from them, his pitiful, dishonored children that were welcome nowhere. He went over and began to rummage among them, reading snatches here and there, his favorite portions. "The Pot" he honored with reading aloud, as he did "Adventure." "Joy," his latest-born, completed the day before and tossed into the corner for lack of stamps, won his keenest approbation.

"I can't understand," he murmured. "Or maybe it's the editors who can't understand. There's nothing wrong with that. They publish worse every month. Everything they publish is worse—nearly everything, anyway."

After breakfast he put the type-writer in its case and carried it down into Oakland.

"I owe a month on it," he told the clerk in the store. "But you tell the manager I'm going to work and that I'll be in in a month or so and straighten up."

He crossed on the ferry to San Francisco and made his way to an employment office. "Any kind of work, no trade," he told the agent; and was interrupted by a newcomer, dressed rather foppishly, as some workingmen dress who have instincts for finer things. The agent shook his head despondently.

"Nothin' doin', eh?" said the other. "Well, I got to get somebody to-day."

He turned and stared at Martin, and Martin, staring back, noted the puffed and discolored face, handsome and weak, and knew that he had been making a night of it.

"Lookin' for a job?" the other queried. "What can you do?"

"Hard labor, sailorizing, run a type-writer, no shorthand, can sit on a horse, willing to do anything and tackle anything," was the answer.

The other nodded.

"Sounds good to me. My name's Dawson, Joe Dawson, an' I'm tryin' to scare up a laundryman."

"Too much for me." Martin caught an amusing glimpse of himself ironing fluffy white things that women wear. But he had taken a liking to the other, and he added: "I might do the plain washing. I learned that much at sea."

Joe Dawson thought visibly for a moment.

"Look here, let's get together an' frame it up. Willin' to listen?"

Martin nodded.

"This is a small laundry, up country, belongs to Shelly Hot Springs,—hotel, you know. Two men do the work, boss and assistant. I'm the boss. You don't work for me, but you work under me. Think you'd be willin' to learn?"

Martin paused to think. The prospect was alluring. A few months of it, and he would have time to himself for study. He could work hard and study hard.

"Good grub an' a room to yourself," Joe said.

That settled it. A room to himself where he could burn the midnight oil unmolested.

"But work like hell," the other added.

Martin caressed his swelling shoulder-muscles significantly. "That came from hard work."

"Then let's get to it." Joe held his hand to his head for a moment. "Gee, but it's a stem-winder. Can hardly see. I went down the line last night—everything—everything. Here's the frame-up. The wages for two is a hundred and board. I've ben drawin' down sixty, the second man forty. But he knew the biz. You're green. If I break you in, I'll be doing plenty of your work at first. Suppose you begin at thirty, an' work up to the forty. I'll play fair. Just as soon as you can do your share you get the forty."

"I'll go you," Martin announced, stretching out his hand, which the other shook. "Any advance?—for railroad ticket and extras?"

"I blew it in," was Joe's sad answer, with another reach at his aching head. "All I got is a return ticket."

"And I'm broke—when I pay my board."

"Jump it," Joe advised.

"Can't. Owe it to my sister."

Joe whistled a long, perplexed whistle, and racked his brains to little purpose.

"I've got the price of the drinks," he said desperately. "Come on, an' mebbe we'll cook up something."

Martin declined.

"Water-wagon?"

This time Martin nodded, and Joe lamented, "Wish I was.

"But I somehow just can't," he said in extenuation. "After I've ben workin' like hell all week I just got to booze up. If I didn't, I'd cut my throat or burn up the premises. But I'm glad you're on the wagon. Stay with it."

Martin knew of the enormous gulf between him and this man—the gulf the books had made; but he found no difficulty in crossing back over that gulf. He had lived all his life in the working-class world, and the *camaraderie* of labor was second nature with him. He solved the difficulty of transportation that was too much for the other's aching head. He would send his trunk up to Shelly Hot Springs on Joe's ticket. As for himself, there was his wheel. It was seventy miles, and he could ride it on Sunday and be ready for work Monday morning. In the meantime he would go home and pack up. There was no one to say good-by to. Ruth and her whole family were spending the long summer in the Sierras, at Lake Tahoe.

He arrived at Shelly Hot Springs, tired and dusty, on Sunday night. Joe greeted him exuberantly. With a wet towel bound about his aching brow, he had been at work all day.

"Part of last week's washin' mounted up, me bein' away to get you," he explained. "Your box arrived all right. It's in your room. But it's a hell of a thing to call a trunk. An' what's in it? Gold bricks?"

Joe sat on the bed while Martin unpacked. The box was a packing-case for breakfast food, and Mr. Higginbotham had charged him half a dollar for it. Two rope handles, nailed on by Martin, had technically transformed it into a trunk eligible for the baggage-car. Joe watched, with bulging eyes, a few shirts and several changes of underclothes come out of the box, followed by books, and more books.

"Books clean to the bottom?" he asked.

Martin nodded, and went on arranging the books on a kitchen table which served in the room in place of a washstand.

"Gee!" Joe exploded, then waited in silence for the deduction to arise in his brain. At last it came.

"Say, you don't care for the girls—much?" he queried.

"No," was the answer. "I used to chase a lot before I tackled the books. But since then there's no time."

"And there won't be any time here. All you can do is work an' sleep."

Martin thought of his five hours' sleep a night, and smiled. The room was situated over the laundry and was in the same building with the engine that pumped water, made electricity, and ran the laundry machinery. The engineer, who occupied the adjoining room, dropped in to meet the new hand and helped Martin rig up an electric bulb, on an extension wire, so that it travelled along a stretched cord from over the table to the bed.

The next morning, at quarter-past six, Martin was routed out for a quarter-to-seven breakfast. There happened to be a bath-tub for the servants in the laundry building, and he electrified Joe by taking a cold bath.

"Gee, but you're a hummer!" Joe announced, as they sat down to breakfast in a corner of the hotel kitchen.

With them was the engineer, the gardener, and the assistant gardener, and two or three men from the stable. They ate hurriedly and gloomily, with but little conversation, and as Martin ate and listened he realized how far he had travelled from their status. Their small mental caliber was depressing to him, and he was anxious to get away from them. So he bolted his breakfast, a sickly, sloppy affair, as rapidly as they, and heaved a sigh of relief when he passed out through the kitchen door.

It was a perfectly appointed, small steam laundry, wherein the most modern machinery did everything that was possible for machinery to do. Martin, after a few instructions, sorted the great heaps of soiled clothes, while Joe started the masher and made up fresh supplies of soft-soap, compounded of biting chemicals that compelled him to swathe his mouth and nostrils and eyes in bath-towels till he resembled a mummy. Finished the sorting, Martin lent a hand in wringing the clothes. This was done by dumping them into a spinning receptacle that went at a rate of a few thousand revolutions a minute, tearing the water from the clothes by centrifugal force. Then Martin began to alternate between the dryer and the wringer, between times "shaking out" socks and stockings. By the afternoon, one feeding and one stacking up, they were running socks and stockings through the mangle while the irons were heating. Then it was hot irons and underclothes till six o'clock, at which time Joe shook his head dubiously.

"Way behind," he said. "Got to work after supper."

And after supper they worked until ten o'clock, under the blazing electric lights, until the last piece of underclothing was ironed and folded away in the distributing room. It was a hot California night, and though the windows were thrown wide, the room, with its red-hot ironing-stove, was a furnace. Martin and Joe, down to undershirts, bare armed, sweated and panted for air.

"Like trimming cargo in the tropics," Martin said, when they went upstairs.

"You'll do," Joe answered. "You take hold like a good fellow. If you keep up the pace, you'll be on thirty dollars only one month. The second month you'll be gettin' your forty. But don't tell me you never ironed before. I know better."

"Never ironed a rag in my life, honestly, until to-day," Martin protested.

He was surprised at his weariness when he got into his room, forgetful of the fact that he had been on his feet and working without let up for fourteen hours. He set the alarm at six, and measured back five hours to one o'clock. He could read until then. Slipping off his shoes, to ease his swollen feet, he sat down at the table with his books. He opened Fiske, where he had left off two days before, and began to read. But he found trouble with the first paragraph and began to read it through a second time. Then he awoke, in pain from his stiffened muscles and chilled by the mountain wind that had begun to blow in through the window. He looked at the clock. It marked two. He had been asleep four hours. He pulled off his clothes and crawled into bed, where he was asleep the moment after his head touched the pillow.

Tuesday was a day of similar unremitting toil. The speed with which Joe worked won Martin's admiration. Joe was a dozen of demons for work. He was keyed up to concert pitch, and there was never a moment in the long day when he was not fighting for moments. He concentrated himself upon his work and upon how to save time, pointing out to Martin where he did in five motions what could be done in three, or in three motions what could be done in two. "Elimination of waste motion," Martin phrased it as he watched and patterned after. He was a good workman himself, quick and deft, and it had always been a point of pride with him that no man should do any of his work for him or outwork him. As a result, he concentrated with a similar singleness of purpose, greedily snapping up the hints and suggestions thrown out by his working mate. He "rubbed out" collars and cuffs, rubbing the starch out from between the double thicknesses of linen so that there would be no blisters when it came to the ironing, and doing it at a pace that elicited Joe's praise.

There was never an interval when something was not at hand to be done. Joe waited for nothing, waited on nothing, and went on the jump from task to task. They starched two hundred white shirts, with a single gathering movement seizing a shirt so that the wristbands, neckband, yoke, and bosom protruded beyond the circling right hand. At the same moment the left hand held up the body of the shirt so that it would not enter the starch, and at the same moment the right hand dipped into the starch—starch so hot that, in order to wring it out, their hands had to be thrust, and thrust continually, into a bucket of cold water. And that night they worked till half-past ten, dipping "fancy starch"—all the frilled and airy, delicate wear of ladies.

"Me for the tropics and no clothes," Martin laughed.

"And me out of a job," Joe answered seriously. "I don't know nothin' but laundrying."

"And you know it well."

"I ought to. Began in the Contra Costa in Oakland when I was eleven, shakin' out for the mangle. That was eighteen years ago, an' I've never done a tap of anything else. But this job is the fiercest I ever had. Ought to be one more man on it at least. We work to-morrow night. Always run the mangle Wednesday nights—collars an' cuffs."

Martin set his alarm, drew up to the table, and opened Fiske. He did not finish the first paragraph. The lines blurred and ran together and his head nodded. He walked up and down, batting his head savagely with his fists, but he could not conquer the numbness of sleep. He propped the book before him, and propped his eyelids with his fingers, and fell asleep with his eyes wide open. Then he surrendered, and, scarcely conscious of what he did, got off his clothes and into bed. He slept seven hours of heavy, animal-like sleep, and awoke by the alarm, feeling that he had not had enough.

"Doin' much readin'?" Joe asked.

Martin shook his head.

"Never mind. We got to run the mangle to-night, but Thursday we'll knock off at six. That'll give you a chance."

Martin washed woollens that day, by hand, in a large barrel, with strong soft-soap, by means of a hub from a wagon wheel, mounted on a plunger-pole that was attached to a spring-pole overhead.

"My invention," Joe said proudly. "Beats a wash-board an' your knuckles, and, besides, it saves at least fifteen minutes in the week, an' fifteen minutes ain't to be sneezed at in this shebang."

Running the collars and cuffs through the mangle was also Joe's idea. That night, while they toiled on under the electric lights, he explained it.

"Something no laundry ever does, except this one. An' I got to do it if I'm goin' to get done Saturday afternoon at three o'clock. But I know how, an' that's the difference. Got to have right heat, right pressure, and run 'em through three times. Look at that!" He held a cuff aloft. "Couldn't do it better by hand or on a tiler."

Thursday, Joe was in a rage. A bundle of extra "fancy starch" had come in.

"I'm goin' to quit," he announced. "I won't stand for it. I'm goin' to quit it cold. What's the good of me workin' like a slave all week, a-savin' minutes, an' them a-comin' an' ringin' in fancy-starch extras on me? This is a free country, an' I'm goin' to tell that fat Dutchman what I think of him. An' I won't tell 'm in French. Plain United States is good enough for me. Him a-ringin' in fancy starch extras!

"We got to work to-night," he said the next moment, reversing his judgment and surrendering to fate.

And Martin did no reading that night. He had seen no daily paper all week, and, strangely to him, felt no desire to see one. He was not interested in the news. He was too tired and jaded to be interested in anything, though he planned to leave Saturday afternoon, if they finished at three, and ride on his wheel to Oakland. It was seventy miles, and the same distance back on Sunday afternoon would leave him anything but rested for the second week's work. It would have been easier to go on the train, but the round trip was two dollars and a half, and he was intent on saving money.

XVII

MARTIN learned to do many things. In the course of the first week, in one afternoon, he and Joe accounted for the two hundred white shirts. Joe ran the tiler, a machine wherein a hot iron was hooked on a steel string which furnished the pressure. By this means he ironed the yoke, wristbands, and neckband, setting the latter at right angles to the shirt, and put the glossy finish on the bosom. As fast as he finished them, he flung the shirts on a rack between him and Martin, who caught them up and "backed" them. This task consisted of ironing all the unstarched portions of the shirts.

It was exhausting work, carried on, hour after hour, at top speed. Out on the broad verandas of the hotel, men and women, in cool white, sipped iced drinks and kept their circulation down. But in the laundry the air was sizzling. The huge stove roared red hot and white hot, while the irons, moving over the damp cloth, sent up clouds of steam. The heat of these irons was different from that used by housewives. An iron that stood the ordinary test of a wet finger was too cold for Joe and Martin, and such test was useless. They went wholly by holding the irons close to their cheeks, gauging the heat by some secret mental process that Martin admired but could not understand. When the fresh irons proved too hot, they hooked them on iron rods and dipped them into cold water. This again required a precise and subtle judgment. A fraction of a second too long in the water and the fine and silken edge of the proper heat was lost, and Martin found time to marvel at the accuracy he developed—an automatic accuracy, founded upon criteria that were machine-like and unerring.

But there was little time in which to marvel. All Martin's consciousness was concentrated in the work. Ceaselessly active, head and hand, an intelligent machine, all that constituted him a man was devoted to furnishing that intelligence. There was no room in his brain for the universe and its mighty problems. All the broad and spacious corridors of his mind were closed and hermetically sealed. The echoing chamber of his soul was a narrow room, a conning tower, whence were directed his arm and shoulder muscles, his ten nimble fingers, and the swift-moving iron along its steaming path in broad, sweeping strokes, just so many strokes and no more, just so far with each stroke and not a fraction of an inch farther, rushing along interminable sleeves, sides, backs, and tails, and tossing the finished shirts, without rumpling, upon the receiving frame. And even as his hurrying soul tossed, it was reaching for another shirt. This went on, hour after hour, while outside all the world swooned under the overhead California sun. But there was no swooning in that superheated room. The cool guests on the verandas needed clean linen.

The sweat poured from Martin. He drank enormous quantities of water, but so great was the heat of the day and of his exertions, that the water sluiced through the interstices of his flesh and out at all his pores. Always, at sea, except at rare intervals, the work he performed had given him ample opportunity to commune with himself. The master of the ship had been lord of Martin's time; but here the manager of the hotel was lord of Martin's thoughts as well. He had no thoughts save for the nerve-racking, body-destroying toil. Outside of that it was impossible to think. He did not know that he loved Ruth. She did not even exist, for his driven soul had no time to remember her. It was only when he crawled to bed at night, or to breakfast in the morning, that she asserted herself to him in fleeting memories.

"This is hell, ain't it?" Joe remarked once.

Martin nodded, but felt a rasp of irritation. The statement had been obvious and unnecessary. They did not talk while they worked. Conversation threw them out of their stride, as it did this time, compelling Martin to miss a stroke of his iron and to make two extra motions before he caught his stride again.

On Friday morning the washer ran. Twice a week they had to put through hotel linen,—the sheets, pillow-slips, spreads, table-cloths, and napkins. This finished, they buckled down to "fancy starch." It was slow work, fastidious and delicate, and Martin did not learn it so readily. Besides, he could not take chances. Mistakes were disastrous.

"See that," Joe said, holding up a filmy corset-cover that he could have crumpled from view in one hand. "Scorch that an' it's twenty dollars out of your wages."

So Martin did not scorch that, and eased down on his muscular tension, though nervous tension rose higher than ever, and he listened sympathetically to the other's blasphemies as he toiled and suffered over the beautiful things that women wear when they do not have to do their own laundrying. "Fancy starch" was Martin's nightmare, and it was Joe's, too. It was "fancy starch" that robbed them of their hard-won minutes. They toiled at it all day. At seven in the evening they broke off to run the hotel linen through the mangle. At ten o'clock, while the hotel guests slept, the two laundrymen sweated on at "fancy starch" till midnight, till one, till two. At half-past two they knocked off.

Saturday morning it was "fancy starch," and odds and ends, and at three in the afternoon the week's work was done.

"You ain't a-goin' to ride them seventy miles into Oakland on top of this?" Joe demanded, as they sat on the stairs and took a triumphant smoke.

"Got to," was the answer.

"What are you goin' for?—a girl?"

"No; to save two and a half on the railroad ticket. I want to renew some books at the library."

"Why don't you send 'em down an' up by express? That'll cost only a quarter each way."

Martin considered it.

"An' take a rest to-morrow," the other urged. "You need it. I know I do. I'm plumb tuckered out."

He looked it. Indomitable, never resting, fighting for seconds and minutes all week, circumventing delays and crushing down obstacles, a fount of resistless energy, a high-driven human motor, a demon for work, now that he had accomplished the week's task he was in a state of collapse. He was worn and haggard, and his handsome face drooped in lean exhaustion. He puffed his cigarette spiritlessly, and his voice was peculiarly dead and monotonous. All the snap and fire had gone out of him. His triumph seemed a sorry one.

"An' next week we got to do it all over again," he said sadly. "An' what's the good of it all, hey? Sometimes I wish I was a hobo. They don't work, an' they get their livin'. Gee! I wish I had a glass of beer; but I can't get up the gumption to go down to the village an' get it. You'll stay over, an' send your books down by express, or else you're a damn fool."

"But what can I do here all day Sunday?" Martin asked.

"Rest. You don't know how tired you are. Why, I'm that tired Sunday I can't even read the papers. I was sick once—typhoid. In the hospital two months an' a half. Didn't do a tap of work all that time. It was beautiful.

"It was beautiful," he repeated dreamily, a minute later.

Martin took a bath, after which he found that the head laundryman had disappeared. Most likely he had gone for the glass of beer, Martin decided, but the half-mile walk down to the village to find out seemed a long journey to him. He lay on his bed with his shoes off, trying to make up his mind. He did not reach out for a book. He was too tired to feel sleepy, and he lay, scarcely thinking, in a semi-stupor of weariness, until it was time for supper. Joe did not appear for that function, and when Martin heard the gardener remark that most likely he was ripping the slats off the bar, Martin understood. He went to bed immediately afterward, and in the morning decided that he was greatly rested. Joe being still absent, Martin procured a Sunday paper and lay down in a shady nook under the trees. The morning passed, he knew not how. He did not sleep, nobody disturbed him, and he did not finish the paper. He came back to it in the afternoon, after dinner, and fell asleep over it.

So passed Sunday, and Monday morning he was hard at work, sorting clothes, while Joe, a towel bound tightly around his head, with groans and blasphemies, was running the washer and mixing soft-soap.

"I simply can't help it," he explained. "I got to drink when Saturday night comes around."

Another week passed, a great battle that continued under the electric lights each night and that culminated on Saturday afternoon at three o'clock, when Joe tasted his moment of wilted triumph and then drifted down to the village to forget. Martin's Sunday was the same as before. He slept in the shade of the trees, toiled aimlessly through the newspaper, and spent long hours lying on his back, doing nothing, thinking nothing. He was too dazed to think, though he was aware that he did not like himself. He was self-repelled, as though he had undergone some degradation or was intrinsically foul. All that was god-like in him was blotted out. The spur of ambition was blunted; he had no vitality with which to feel the prod of it. He was dead. His soul seemed dead. He was a beast, a work-beast. He saw no beauty in the sunshine sifting down through the green leaves, nor did the azure vault of the sky whisper as of old and hint of cosmic vastness and secrets trembling to disclosure. Life was intolerably dull and stupid, and its taste was bad in his mouth. A black screen was drawn across his mirror of inner vision, and fancy lay in a darkened sick-room where entered no ray of light. He envied Joe, down in the village, rampant, tearing the slats off the bar, his brain gnawing with maggots, exulting in maudlin ways over maudlin things, fantastically and gloriously drunk and forgetful of Monday morning and the week of deadening toil to come.

A third week went by, and Martin loathed himself, and loathed life. He was oppressed by a sense of failure. There was reason for the editors refusing his stuff. He could see that clearly now, and laugh at himself and the dreams he had dreamed. Ruth returned his "Sea Lyrics" by mail. He read her letter apathetically. She did her best to say how much she liked them and that they were beautiful. But she could not lie, and she could not disguise the truth from herself. She knew they were failures, and he read her disapproval in every perfunctory and unenthusiastic line of her letter. And she was right. He was firmly convinced of it as he read the poems over. Beauty and wonder had departed from him, and as he read the poems he caught himself puzzling as to what he had had in mind when he wrote them. His audacities of phrase struck him as grotesque, his felicities of expression were monstrosities, and everything was absurd, unreal, and impossible. He would have burned the "Sea Lyrics" on the spot, had his will been strong enough to set them aflame. There was the engine-room, but the exertion of carrying them to the furnace was not worth while. All his exertion was used in washing other persons' clothes. He did not have any left for private affairs.

He resolved that when Sunday came he would pull himself together and answer Ruth's letter. But Saturday afternoon, after work was finished and he had taken a bath, the desire to forget overpowered him. "I guess I'll go down and see how Joe's getting on," was the way he put it to himself; and in the same moment he knew that he lied. But he did not have the energy to consider the lie. If he had had the energy, he would have refused to consider the lie, because he wanted to forget. He started for the village slowly and casually, increasing his pace in spite of himself as he neared the saloon.

"I thought you was on the water-wagon," was Joe's greeting.

Martin did not deign to offer excuses, but called for whiskey, filling his own glass brimming before he passed the bottle.

"Don't take all night about it," he said roughly.

The other was dawdling with the bottle, and Martin refused to wait for him, tossing the glass off in a gulp and refilling it.

"Now, I can wait for you," he said grimly; "but hurry up."

Joe hurried, and they drank together.

"The work did it, eh?" Joe queried.

Martin refused to discuss the matter.

"It's fair hell, I know," the other went on, "but I kind of hate to see you come off the wagon, Mart. Well, here's how!"

Martin drank on silently, biting out his orders and invitations and awing the barkeeper, an effeminate country youngster with watery blue eyes and hair parted in the middle.

"It's something scandalous the way they work us poor devils," Joe was remarking. "If I didn't bowl up, I'd break loose an' burn down the shebang. My bowlin' up is all that saves 'em, I can tell you that."

But Martin made no answer. A few more drinks, and in his brain he felt the maggots of intoxication beginning to crawl. Ah, it was living, the first breath of life he had breathed in three weeks. His dreams came back to him. Fancy came out of the darkened room and lured him on, a thing of flaming brightness. His mirror of vision was silver-clear, a flashing, dazzling palimpsest of imagery. Wonder and beauty walked with him, hand in hand, and all power was his. He tried to tell it to Joe, but Joe had visions of his own, infallible schemes whereby he would escape the slavery of laundry-work and become himself the owner of a great steam laundry.

"I tell yeh, Mart, they won't be no kids workin' in my laundry—not on yer life. An' they won't be no workin' a livin' soul after six P.M. You hear me talk! They'll be machinery enough an' hands enough to do it all in decent workin' hours, an' Mart, s'help me, I'll make yeh superintendent of the shebang—the whole of it, all of it. Now here's the scheme. I get on the water-wagon an' save my money for two years—save an' then—"

But Martin turned away, leaving him to tell it to the barkeeper, until that worthy was called away to furnish drinks to two farmers who, coming in, accepted Martin's invitation. Martin dispensed royal largess, inviting everybody up, farmhands, a stableman, and the gardener's assistant from the hotel, the barkeeper, and the furtive hobo who slid in like a shadow and like a shadow hovered at the end of the bar.

XVIII

MONDAY morning, Joe groaned over the first truck load of clothes to the washer.

"I say," he began.

"Don't talk to me," Martin snarled.

"I'm sorry, Joe," he said at noon, when they knocked off for dinner.

Tears came into the other's eyes.

"That's all right, old man," he said. "We're in hell, an' we can't help ourselves. An', you know, I kind of like you a whole lot. That's what made it hurt. I cottoned to you from the first."

Martin shook his hand.

"Let's quit," Joe suggested. "Let's chuck it, an' go hoboin'. I ain't never tried it, but it must be dead easy. An' nothin' to do. Just think of it, nothin' to do. I was sick once, typhoid, in the hospital, an' it was beautiful. I wish I'd get sick again."

The week dragged on. The hotel was full, and extra "fancy starch" poured in upon them. They performed prodigies of valor. They fought late each night under the electric lights, bolted their meals, and even got in a half hour's work before breakfast. Martin no longer took his cold baths. Every moment was drive, drive, drive, and Joe was the masterful shepherd of moments, herding them carefully, never losing one, counting them over like a miser counting gold, working on in a frenzy, toil-mad, a feverish machine, aided ably by that other machine that thought of itself as once having been one Martin Eden, a man.

But it was only at rare moments that Martin was able to think. The house of thought was closed, its windows boarded up, and he was its shadowy caretaker. He was a shadow. Joe was right. They were both shadows, and this was the unending limbo of toil. Or was it a dream? Sometimes, in the steaming, sizzling heat, as he swung the heavy irons back and forth over the white garments, it came to him that it was a dream. In a short while, or maybe after a thousand years or so, he would awake, in his little room with the ink-stained table, and take up his writing where he had left off the day before. Or maybe that was a dream, too, and the awakening would be the changing of the watches, when he would drop down out of his bunk in the lurching forecastle and go up on deck, under the tropic stars, and take the wheel and feel the cool tradewind blowing through his flesh.

Came Saturday and its hollow victory at three o'clock.

"Guess I'll go down an' get a glass of beer," Joe said, in the queer, monotonous tones that marked his week-end collapse.

Martin seemed suddenly to wake up. He opened the kit bag and oiled his wheel, putting graphite on the chain and adjusting the bearings. Joe was halfway down to the saloon when Martin passed by, bending low over the handle-bars, his legs driving the ninety-six gear with rhythmic strength, his face set for seventy miles of road and grade and dust. He slept in Oakland that night, and on Sunday covered the seventy miles back. And on Monday morning, weary, he began the new week's work, but he had kept sober.

A fifth week passed, and a sixth, during which he lived and toiled as a machine, with just a spark of something more in him, just a glimmering bit of soul, that compelled him, at each week-end, to scorch off the hundred and forty miles. But this was not rest. It was super-machinelike, and it helped to crush out the glimmering bit of soul that was all that was left him from former life. At the end of the seventh week, without intending it, too weak to resist, he drifted down to the village with Joe and drowned life and found life until Monday morning.

Again, at the week-ends, he ground out the one hundred and forty miles, obliterating the numbness of too great exertion by the numbness of still greater exertion. At the end of three months he went down a third time to the village with Joe. He forgot, and lived again, and, living, he saw, in clear illumination, the beast he was making of himself—not by the drink, but by the work. The drink was an effect, not a cause. It followed inevitably upon the work, as the night follows upon the day. Not by becoming a toil-beast could he win to the heights, was the message the whiskey whispered to him, and he nodded approbation. The whiskey was wise. It told secrets on itself.

He called for paper and pencil, and for drinks all around, and while they drank his very good health, he clung to the bar and scribbled.

"A telegram, Joe," he said. "Read it."

Joe read it with a drunken, quizzical leer. But what he read seemed to sober him. He looked at the other reproachfully, tears oozing into his eyes and down his cheeks.

"You ain't goin' back on me, Mart?" he queried hopelessly.

Martin nodded, and called one of the loungers to him to take the message to the telegraph office.

"Hold on," Joe muttered thickly. "Lemme think."

He held on to the bar, his legs wobbling under him, Martin's arm around him and supporting him, while he thought.

"Make that two laundrymen," he said abruptly. "Here, lemme fix it."

"What are you quitting for?" Martin demanded.

"Same reason as you."

"But I'm going to sea. You can't do that."

"Nope," was the answer, "but I can hobo all right, all right."

Martin looked at him searchingly for a moment, then cried:—

"By God, I think you're right! Better a hobo than a beast of toil. Why, man, you'll live. And that's more than you ever did before."

"I was in hospital, once," Joe corrected. "It was beautiful. Typhoid—did I tell you?"

While Martin changed the telegram to "two laundrymen," Joe went on:—

"I never wanted to drink when I was in hospital. Funny, ain't it? But when I've ben workin' like a slave all week, I just got to bowl up. Ever noticed that cooks drink like hell?—an' bakers, too? It's the work. They've sure got to. Here, lemme pay half of that telegram."

"I'll shake you for it," Martin offered.

"Come on, everybody drink," Joe called, as they rattled the dice and rolled them out on the damp bar.

Monday morning Joe was wild with anticipation. He did not mind his aching head, nor did he take interest in his work. Whole herds of moments stole away and were lost while their careless shepherd gazed out of the window at the sunshine and the trees.

"Just look at it!" he cried. "An' it's all mine! It's free. I can lie down under them trees an' sleep for a thousan' years if I want to. Aw, come on, Mart, let's chuck it. What's the good of waitin' another moment. That's the land of nothin' to do out there, an' I got a ticket for it—an' it ain't no return ticket, b'gosh!"

A few minutes later, filling the truck with soiled clothes for the washer, Joe spied the hotel manager's shirt. He knew its mark, and with a sudden glorious consciousness of freedom he threw it on the floor and stamped on it.

"I wish you was in it, you pig-headed Dutchman!" he shouted. "In it, an' right there where I've got you! Take that! an' that! an' that! damn you! Hold me back, somebody! Hold me back!"

Martin laughed and held him to his work. On Tuesday night the new laundrymen arrived, and the rest of the week was spent breaking them into the routine. Joe sat around and explained his system, but he did no more work.

"Not a tap," he announced. "Not a tap. They can fire me if they want to, but if they do, I'll quit. No more work in mine, thank you kindly. Me for the freight cars an' the shade under the trees. Go to it, you slaves! That's right. Slave an' sweat! Slave an' sweat! An' when you're dead, you'll rot the same as me, an' what's it matter how you live?—eh? Tell me that—what's it matter in the long run?"

On Saturday they drew their pay and came to the parting of the ways.

"They ain't no use in me askin' you to change your mind an' hit the road with me?" Joe asked hopelessly.

Martin shook his head. He was standing by his wheel, ready to start. They shook hands, and Joe held on to his for a moment, as he said:—

"I'm goin' to see you again, Mart, before you an' me die. That's straight dope. I feel it in my bones. Good-by, Mart, an' be good. I like you like hell, you know."

He stood, a forlorn figure, in the middle of the road, watching until Martin turned a bend and was gone from sight.

"He's a good Indian, that boy," he muttered. "A good Indian."

Then he plodded down the road himself, to the water-tank, where half a dozen empties lay on a side-track waiting for the up freight.

XIX

RUTH and her family were home again, and Martin, returned to Oakland, saw much of her. Having gained her degree, she was doing no more studying; and he, having worked all vitality out of his mind and body, was doing no writing. This gave them time for each other that they had never had before, and their intimacy ripened fast.

At first, Martin had done nothing but rest. He had slept a great deal, and spent long hours musing and thinking and doing nothing. He was like one recovering from some terrible bout of hardship. The first signs of reawakening came when he discovered more than languid interest in the daily paper. Then he began to read again—light novels, and poetry; and after several days more he was head over heels in his long-neglected Fiske. His splendid body and health made new vitality, and he possessed all the resiliency and rebound of youth.

Ruth showed her disappointment plainly when he announced that he was going to sea for another voyage as soon as he was well rested.

"Why do you want to do that?" she asked.

"Money," was the answer. "I'll have to lay in a supply for my next attack on the editors. Money is the sinews of war, in my case—money and patience."

"But if all you wanted was money, why didn't you stay in the laundry?"

"Because the laundry was making a beast of me. Too much work of that sort drives to drink."

She stared at him with horror in her eyes.

"Do you mean—?" she quavered.

It would have been easy for him to get out of it; but his natural impulse was for frankness, and he remembered his old resolve to be frank, no matter what happened.

"Yes," he answered. "Just that. Several times."

She shivered and drew away from him.

"No man that I have ever known did that—ever did that."

"Then they never worked in the laundry at Shelly Hot Springs," he laughed bitterly. "Toil is a good thing. It is necessary for human health, so all the preachers say, and Heaven knows I've never been afraid of it. But there is such a thing as too much of a good thing, and the laundry up there is one of them. And that's why I'm going to sea one more voyage. It will be my last, I think, for when I come back, I shall break into the magazines. I am certain of it."

She was silent, unsympathetic, and he watched her moodily, realizing how impossible it was for her to understand what he had been through.

"Some day I shall write it up—'The Degradation of Toil' or the 'Psychology of Drink in the Working-class,' or something like that for a title."

Never, since the first meeting, had they seemed so far apart as that day. His confession, told in frankness, with the spirit of revolt behind, had repelled her. But she was more shocked by the repulsion itself than by the cause of it. It pointed out to her how near she had drawn to him, and once accepted, it paved the way for greater intimacy. Pity, too, was aroused, and innocent, idealistic thoughts of reform. She would save this raw young man who had come so far. She would save him from the curse of his early environment, and she would save him from himself in spite of himself. And all this affected her as a very noble state of consciousness; nor did she dream that behind it and underlying it were the jealousy and desire of love.

They rode on their wheels much in the delightful fall weather, and out in the hills they read poetry aloud, now one and now the other, noble, uplifting poetry that turned one's thoughts to higher things. Renunciation, sacrifice, patience, industry, and high endeavor were the principles she thus indirectly preached—such abstractions being objectified in her mind by her father, and Mr. Butler, and by Andrew Carnegie, who, from a poor immigrant boy had arisen to be the bookgiver of the world.

All of which was appreciated and enjoyed by Martin. He followed her mental processes more clearly now, and her soul was no longer the sealed wonder it had been. He was on terms of intellectual equality with her. But the points of disagreement did not affect his love. His love was more ardent than ever, for he loved her for what she was, and even her physical frailty was an added charm in his eyes. He read of sickly Elizabeth Barrett, who for years had not placed her feet upon the ground, until that day of flame when she eloped with Browning and stood upright, upon the earth, under the open sky; and what Browning had done for her, Martin decided he could do for Ruth. But first, she must love him. The rest would be easy. He would give her strength and health. And he caught glimpses of their life, in the years to come, wherein, against a background of work and comfort and general well-being, he saw himself and Ruth reading and discussing poetry, she propped amid a multitude of cushions on the ground while she read aloud to him. This was the key to the life they would live. And always he saw that particular picture. Sometimes it was she who leaned against him while he read, one arm about her, her head upon his shoulder. Sometimes they pored together over the printed pages of beauty. Then, too, she loved nature, and with generous imagination he changed the scene of their reading—sometimes they read in closed-in valleys with precipitous walls, or in high mountain meadows, and, again, down by the gray sand-dunes with a wreath of billows at their feet, or afar on some volcanic tropic isle where waterfalls descended and became mist, reaching the sea in vapor veils that swayed and shivered to every vagrant wisp of wind. But always, in the foreground, lords of beauty and eternally reading and sharing, lay he and Ruth, and always in the background that was beyond the background of nature, dim and hazy, were work and success and money earned that made them free of the world and all its treasures.

"I should recommend my little girl to be careful," her mother warned her one day.

"I know what you mean. But it is impossible. He is not—"

Ruth was blushing, but it was the blush of maidenhood called upon for the first time to discuss the sacred things of life with a mother held equally sacred.

"Your kind." Her mother finished the sentence for her.

Ruth nodded.

"I did not want to say it, but he is not. He is rough, brutal, strong—too strong. He has not—"

She hesitated and could not go on. It was a new experience, talking over such matters with her mother. And again her mother completed her thought for her.

"He has not lived a clean life, is what you wanted to say."

Again Ruth nodded, and again a blush mantled her face.

"It is just that," she said. "It has not been his fault, but he has played much with—"

"With pitch?"

"Yes, with pitch. And he frightens me. Sometimes I am positively in terror of him, when he talks in that free and easy way of the things he has done—as if they did not matter. They do matter, don't they?"

They sat with their arms twined around each other, and in the pause her mother patted her hand and waited for her to go on.

"But I am interested in him dreadfully," she continued. "In a way he is my protégé. Then, too, he is my first boy friend—but not exactly friend; rather protégé and friend combined. Sometimes, too, when he frightens me, it seems that he is a bulldog I have taken for a plaything, like some of the 'frat' girls, and he is tugging hard, and showing his teeth, and threatening to break loose."

Again her mother waited.

"He interests me, I suppose, like the bulldog. And there is much good in him, too; but there is much in him that I would not like in—in the other way. You see, I have been thinking. He swears, he smokes, he drinks, he has fought with his fists (he has told me so, and he likes it; he says so). He is all that a man should not be—a man I would want for my—" her voice sank very low—"husband. Then he is too strong. My prince must be tall, and slender, and dark—a graceful, bewitching prince. No, there is no danger of my falling in love with Martin Eden. It would be the worst fate that could befall me."

"But it is not that that I spoke about," her mother equivocated. "Have you thought about him? He is so ineligible in every way, you know, and suppose he should come to love you?"

"But he does—already," she cried.

"It was to be expected," Mrs. Morse said gently. "How could it be otherwise with any one who knew you?"

"Olney hates me!" she exclaimed passionately. "And I hate Olney. I feel always like a cat when he is around. I feel that I must be nasty to him, and even when I don't happen to feel that way, why, he's nasty to me, anyway. But I am happy with Martin Eden. No one ever loved me before—no man, I mean, in that way. And it is sweet to be loved—that way. You know what I mean, mother dear. It is sweet to feel that you are really and truly a woman." She buried her face in her mother's lap, sobbing. "You think I am dreadful, I know, but I am honest, and I tell you just how I feel."

Mrs. Morse was strangely sad and happy. Her child-daughter, who was a bachelor of arts, was gone; but in her place was a woman-daughter. The experiment had succeeded. The strange void in Ruth's nature had been filled, and filled without danger or penalty. This rough sailor-fellow had been the instrument, and, though Ruth did not love him, he had made her conscious of her womanhood.

"His hand trembles," Ruth was confessing, her face, for shame's sake, still buried. "It is most amusing and ridiculous, but I feel sorry for him, too. And when his hands are too trembly, and his eyes too shiny, why, I lecture him about his life and the wrong way he is going about it to mend it. But he worships me, I know. His eyes and his hands do not lie. And it makes me feel grown-up, the thought of it, the very thought of it; and I feel that I am possessed of something that is by rights my own—that makes me like the other girls—and—and young women. And, then, too, I knew that I was not like them before, and I knew that it worried you. You thought you did not let me know that dear worry of yours, but I did, and I wanted to—'to make good,' as Martin Eden says."

It was a holy hour for mother and daughter, and their eyes were wet as they talked on in the twilight, Ruth all white innocence and frankness, her mother sympathetic, receptive, yet calmly explaining and guiding.

"He is four years younger than you," she said. "He has no place in the world. He has neither position nor salary. He is impractical. Loving you, he should, in the name of common sense, be doing something that would give him the right to marry, instead of paltering around with those stories of his and with childish dreams. Martin Eden, I am afraid, will never grow up. He does not take to responsibility and a man's work in the world like your father did, or like all our friends, Mr. Butler for one. Martin Eden, I am afraid, will never be a money-earner. And this world is so ordered that money is necessary to happiness—oh, no, not these swollen fortunes, but enough of money to permit of common comfort and decency. He—he has never spoken?"

"He has not breathed a word. He has not attempted to; but if he did, I would not let him, because, you see, I do not love him."

"I am glad of that. I should not care to see my daughter, my one daughter, who is so clean and pure, love a man like him. There are noble men in the world who are clean and true and manly. Wait for them. You will find one some day, and you will love him and be loved by him, and you will be happy with him as your father and I have been happy with each other. And there is one thing you must always carry in mind—"

"Yes, mother."

Mrs. Morse's voice was low and sweet as she said, "And that is the children."

"I—have thought about them," Ruth confessed, remembering the wanton thoughts that had vexed her in the past, her face again red with maiden shame that she should be telling such things.

"And it is that, the children, that makes Mr. Eden impossible," Mrs. Morse went on incisively. "Their heritage must be clean, and he is, I am afraid, not clean. Your father has told me of sailors' lives, and—and you understand."

Ruth pressed her mother's hand in assent, feeling that she really did understand, though her conception was of something vague, remote, and terrible that was beyond the scope of imagination.

"You know I do nothing without telling you," she began. "—Only, sometimes you must ask me, like this time. I wanted to tell you, but I did not know how. It is false modesty, I know it is that, but you can make it easy for me. Sometimes, like this time, you must ask me, you must give me a chance.

"Why, mother, you are a woman, too!" she cried exultantly, as they stood up, catching her mother's hands and standing erect, facing her in the twilight, conscious of a strangely sweet equality between them. "I should never have thought of you in that way if we had not had this talk. I had to learn that I was a woman to know that you were one, too."

"We are women together," her mother said, drawing her to her and kissing her. "We are women together," she repeated, as they went out of the room, their arms around each other's waists, their hearts swelling with a new sense of companionship.

"Our little girl has become a woman," Mrs. Morse said proudly to her husband an hour later.

"That means," he said, after a long look at his wife, "that means she is in love."

"No, but that she is loved," was the smiling rejoinder. "The experiment has succeeded. She is awakened at last."

"Then we'll have to get rid of him." Mr. Morse spoke briskly, in matter-of-fact, businesslike tones.

But his wife shook her head. "It will not be necessary. Ruth says he is going to sea in a few days. When he comes back, she will not be here. We will send her to Aunt Clara's. And, besides, a year in the East, with the change in climate, people, ideas, and everything, is just the thing she needs."

XX

THE desire to write was stirring in Martin once more. Stories and poems were springing into spontaneous creation in his brain, and he made notes of them against the future time when he would give them expression. But he did not write. This was his little vacation; he had resolved to devote it to rest and love, and in both matters he prospered. He was soon spilling over with vitality, and each day he saw Ruth, at the moment of meeting, she experienced the old shock of his strength and health.

"Be careful," her mother warned her once again. "I am afraid you are seeing too much of Martin Eden."

But Ruth laughed from security. She was sure of herself, and in a few days he would be off to sea. Then, by the time he returned, she would be away on her visit East. There was a magic, however, in the strength and health of Martin. He, too, had been told of her contemplated Eastern trip, and he felt the need for haste. Yet he did not know how to make love to a girl like Ruth. Then, too, he was handicapped by the possession of a great fund of experience with girls and women who had been absolutely different from her. They had known about love and life and flirtation, while she knew nothing about such things. Her prodigious innocence appalled him, freezing on his lips all ardors of speech, and convincing him, in spite of himself, of his own unworthiness. Also he was handicapped in another way. He had himself never been in love before. He had liked women in that turgid past of his, and been fascinated by some of them, but he had not known what it was to love them. He had whistled in a masterful, careless way, and they had come to him. They had been diversions, incidents, part of the game men play, but a small part at most. And now, and for the first time, he was a suppliant, tender and timid and doubting. He did not know the way of love, nor its speech, while he was frightened at his loved one's clear innocence.

In the course of getting acquainted with a varied world, whirling on through the ever changing phases of it, he had learned a rule of conduct which was to the effect that when one played a strange game, he should let the other fellow play first. This had stood him in good stead a thousand times and trained him as an observer as well. He knew how to watch the thing that was strange, and to wait for a weakness, for a place of entrance, to divulge itself. It was like sparring for an opening in fist-fighting. And when such an opening came, he knew by long experience to play for it and to play hard.

So he waited with Ruth and watched, desiring to speak his love but not daring. He was afraid of shocking her, and he was not sure of himself. Had he but known it, he was following the right course with her. Love came into the world before articulate speech, and in its own early youth it had learned ways and means that it had never forgotten. It was in this old, primitive way that Martin wooed Ruth. He did not know he was doing it at first, though later he divined it. The touch of his hand on hers was vastly more potent than any word he could utter, the impact of his strength on her imagination was more alluring than the printed poems and spoken passions of a thousand generations of lovers. Whatever his tongue could express would have appealed, in part, to her judgment; but the touch of hand, the fleeting contact, made its way directly to her instinct. Her judgment was as young as she, but her instincts were as old as the race and older. They had been young when love was young, and they were wiser than convention and opinion and all the new-born things. So her judgment did not act. There was no call upon it, and she did not realize the strength of the appeal Martin made from moment to moment to her love-nature. That he loved her, on the other hand, was as clear as day, and she consciously delighted in beholding his love-manifestations—the glowing eyes with their tender lights, the trembling hands, and the never failing swarthy flush that flooded darkly under his sunburn. She even went farther, in a timid way inciting him, but doing it so delicately that he never suspected, and doing it half-consciously, so that she scarcely suspected herself. She thrilled with these proofs of her power that proclaimed her a woman, and she took an Eve-like delight in tormenting him and playing upon him.

Tongue-tied by inexperience and by excess of ardor, wooing unwittingly and awkwardly, Martin continued his approach by contact. The touch of his hand was pleasant to her, and something deliciously more than pleasant. Martin did not know it, but he did know that it was not distasteful to her. Not that they touched hands often, save at meeting and parting; but that in handling the bicycles, in strapping on the books of verse they carried into the hills, and in conning the pages of books side by side, there were opportunities for hand to stray against hand. And there were opportunities, too, for her hair to brush his cheek, and for shoulder to touch shoulder, as they leaned together over the beauty of the books. She smiled to herself at vagrant impulses which arose from nowhere and suggested that she rumple his hair; while he desired greatly, when they tired of reading, to rest his head in her lap and dream with closed eyes about the future that was to be theirs. On Sunday picnics at Shellmound Park and Schuetzen Park, in the past, he had rested his head on many laps, and, usually, he had slept soundly and selfishly while the girls shaded his face from the sun and looked down and loved him and wondered at his lordly carelessness of their love. To rest his head in a girl's lap had been the easiest thing in the world until now, and now he found Ruth's lap inaccessible and impossible. Yet it was right here, in his reticence, that the strength of his wooing lay. It was because of this reticence that he never alarmed her. Herself fastidious and timid, she never awakened to the perilous trend of their intercourse. Subtly and unaware she grew toward him and closer to him, while he, sensing the growing closeness, longed to dare but was afraid.

Once he dared, one afternoon, when he found her in the darkened living room with a blinding headache.

"Nothing can do it any good," she had answered his inquiries. "And besides, I don't take headache powders. Doctor Hall won't permit me."

"I can cure it, I think, and without drugs," was Martin's answer. "I am not sure, of course, but I'd like to try. It's simply massage. I learned the trick first from the Japanese. They are a race of masseurs, you know. Then I learned it all over again with variations from the Hawaiians. They call it *lomi-lomi.* It can accomplish most of the things drugs accomplish and a few things that drugs can't."

Scarcely had his hands touched her head when she sighed deeply.

"That is so good," she said.

She spoke once again, half an hour later, when she asked, "Aren't you tired?"

The question was perfunctory, and she knew what the answer would be. Then she lost herself in drowsy contemplation of the soothing balm of his strength. Life poured from the ends of his fingers, driving the pain before it, or so it seemed to her, until with the easement of pain, she fell asleep and he stole away.

She called him up by telephone that evening to thank him.

"I slept until dinner," she said. "You cured me completely, Mr. Eden, and I don't know how to thank you."

He was warm, and bungling of speech, and very happy, as he replied to her, and there was dancing in his mind, throughout the telephone conversation, the memory of Browning and of sickly Elizabeth Barrett. What had been done could be done again, and he, Martin Eden, could do it and would do it for Ruth Morse. He went back to his room and to the volume of Spencer's "Sociology" lying open on the bed. But he could not read. Love tormented him and overrode his will, so that, despite all determination, he found himself at the little ink-stained table. The sonnet he composed that night was the first of a love-cycle of fifty sonnets which was completed within two months. He had the "Love-sonnets from the Portuguese" in mind as he wrote, and he wrote under the best conditions for great work, at a climacteric of living, in the throes of his own sweet love-madness.

The many hours he was not with Ruth he devoted to the "Love-cycle," to reading at home, or to the public reading-rooms, where he got more closely in touch with the magazines of the day and the nature of their policy and content. The hours he spent with Ruth were maddening alike in promise and in inconclusiveness. It was a week after he cured her headache that a moonlight sail on Lake Merritt was proposed by Norman and seconded by Arthur and Olney. Martin was the only one capable of handling a boat, and he was pressed into service. Ruth sat near him in the stern, while the three young fellows lounged amidships, deep in a wordy wrangle over "frat" affairs.

The moon had not yet risen, and Ruth, gazing into the starry vault of the sky and exchanging no speech with Martin, experienced a sudden feeling of loneliness. She glanced at him. A puff of wind was heeling the boat over till the deck was awash, and he, one hand on tiller and the other on mainsheet, was luffing slightly, at the same time peering ahead to make out the near-lying north shore. He was unaware of her gaze, and she watched him intently, speculating fancifully about the strange warp of soul that led him, a young man with signal powers, to fritter away his time on the writing of stories and poems foredoomed to mediocrity and failure.

Her eyes wandered along the strong throat, dimly seen in the starlight, and over the firm-poised head, and the old desire to lay her hands upon his neck came back to her. The strength she abhorred attracted her. Her feeling of loneliness became more pronounced, and she felt tired. Her position on the heeling boat irked her, and she remembered the headache he had cured and the soothing rest that resided in him. He was sitting beside her, quite beside her, and the boat seemed to tilt her toward him. Then arose in her the impulse to lean against him, to rest herself against his strength—a vague, half-formed impulse, which, even as she considered it, mastered her and made her lean toward him. Or was it the heeling of the boat? She did not know. She never knew. She knew only that she was leaning against him and that the easement and soothing rest were very good. Perhaps it had been the boat's fault, but she made no effort to retrieve it. She leaned lightly against his shoulder, but she leaned, and she continued to lean when he shifted his position to make it more comfortable for her.

It was a madness, but she refused to consider the madness. She was no longer herself but a woman, with a woman's clinging need; and though she leaned ever so lightly, the need seemed satisfied. She was no longer tired. Martin did not speak. Had he, the spell would have been broken. But his reticence of love prolonged it. He was dazed and dizzy. He could not understand what was happening. It was too wonderful to be anything but a delirium. He conquered a mad desire to let go sheet and tiller and to clasp her in his arms. His intuition told him it was the wrong thing to do, and he was glad that sheet and tiller kept his hands occupied and fended off temptation. But he luffed the boat less delicately, spilling the wind shamelessly from the sail so as to prolong the tack to the north shore. The shore would compel him to go about, and the contact would be broken. He sailed with skill, stopping way on the boat without exciting the notice of the wranglers, and mentally forgiving his hardest voyages in that they had made this marvellous night possible, giving him mastery over sea and boat and wind so that he could sail with her beside him, her dear weight against him on his shoulder.

When the first light of the rising moon touched the sail, illuminating the boat with pearly radiance, Ruth moved away from him. And, even as she moved, she felt him move away. The impulse to avoid detection was mutual. The episode was tacitly and secretly intimate. She sat apart from him with burning cheeks, while the full force of it came home to her. She had been guilty of something she would not have her brothers see, nor Olney see. Why had she done it? She had never done anything like it in her life, and yet she had been moonlight-sailing with young men before. She had never desired to do anything like it. She was overcome with shame and with the mystery of her own burgeoning womanhood. She stole a glance at Martin, who was busy putting the boat about on the other tack, and she could have hated him for having made her do an immodest and shameful thing. And he, of all men! Perhaps her mother was right, and she was seeing too much of him. It would never happen again, she resolved, and she would see less of him in the future. She entertained a wild idea of explaining to him the first time they were alone together, of lying to him, of mentioning casually the attack of faintness that had overpowered her just before the moon came up. Then she remembered how they had drawn mutually away before the revealing moon, and she knew he would know it for a lie.

In the days that swiftly followed she was no longer herself but a strange, puzzling creature, wilful over judgment and scornful of self-analysis, refusing to peer into the future or to think about herself and whither she was drifting. She was in a fever of tingling mystery, alternately frightened and charmed, and in constant bewilderment. She had one idea firmly fixed, however, which insured her security. She would not let Martin speak his love. As long as she did this, all would be well. In a few days he would be off to sea. And even if he did speak, all would be well. It could not be otherwise, for she did not love him. Of course, it would be a painful half hour for him, and an embarrassing half hour for her, because it would be her first proposal. She thrilled deliciously at the thought. She was really a woman, with a man ripe to ask for her in marriage. It was a lure to all that was fundamental in her sex. The fabric of her life, of all that constituted her, quivered and grew tremulous. The thought fluttered in her mind like a flame-attracted moth. She went so far as to imagine Martin proposing, herself putting the words into his mouth; and she rehearsed her refusal, tempering it with kindness and exhorting him to true and noble manhood. And especially he must stop smoking cigarettes. She would make a point of that. But no, she must not let him speak at all. She could stop him, and she had told her mother that she would. All flushed and burning, she regretfully dismissed the conjured situation. Her first proposal would have to be deferred to a more propitious time and a more eligible suitor.

XXI

CAME a beautiful fall day, warm and languid, palpitant with the hush of the changing season, a California Indian summer day, with hazy sun and wandering wisps of breeze that did not stir the slumber of the air. Filmy purple mists, that were not vapors but fabrics woven of color, hid in the recesses of the hills. San Francisco lay like a blur of smoke upon her heights. The intervening bay was a dull sheen of molten metal, whereon sailing craft lay motionless or drifted with the lazy tide. Far Tamalpais, barely seen in the silver haze, bulked hugely by the Golden Gate, the latter a pale gold pathway under the westering sun. Beyond, the Pacific, dim and vast, was raising on its sky-line tumbled cloud-masses that swept landward, giving warning of the first blustering breath of winter.

The erasure of summer was at hand. Yet summer lingered, fading and fainting among her hills, deepening the purple of her valleys, spinning a shroud of haze from waning powers and sated raptures, dying with the calm content of having lived and lived well. And among the hills, on their favorite knoll, Martin and Ruth sat side by side, their heads bent over the same pages, he reading aloud from the love-sonnets of the woman who had loved Browning as it is given to few men to be loved.

But the reading languished. The spell of passing beauty all about them was too strong. The golden year was dying as it had lived, a beautiful and unrepentant voluptuary, and reminiscent rapture and content freighted heavily the air. It entered into them, dreamy and languorous, weakening the fibres of resolution, suffusing the face of morality, or of judgment, with haze and purple mist. Martin felt tender and melting, and from time to time warm glows passed over him. His head was very near to hers, and when wandering phantoms of breeze stirred her hair so that it touched his face, the printed pages swam before his eyes.

"I don't believe you know a word of what you are reading," she said once when he had lost his place.

He looked at her with burning eyes, and was on the verge of becoming awkward, when a retort came to his lips.

"I don't believe you know either. What was the last sonnet about?"

"I don't know," she laughed frankly. "I've already forgotten. Don't let us read any more. The day is too beautiful."

"It will be our last in the hills for some time," he announced gravely. "There's a storm gathering out there on the sea-rim."

The book slipped from his hands to the ground, and they sat idly and silently, gazing out over the dreamy bay with eyes that dreamed and did not see. Ruth glanced sidewise at his neck. She did not lean toward him. She was drawn by some force outside of herself and stronger than gravitation, strong as destiny. It was only an inch to lean, and it was accomplished without volition on her part. Her shoulder touched his as lightly as a butterfly touches a flower, and just as lightly was the counter-pressure. She felt his shoulder press hers, and a tremor run through him. Then was the time for her to draw back. But she had become an automaton. Her actions had passed beyond the control of her will—she never thought of control or will in the delicious madness that was upon her. His arm began to steal behind her and around her. She waited its slow progress in a torment of delight. She waited, she knew not for what, panting, with dry, burning lips, a leaping pulse, and a fever of expectancy in all her blood. The girdling arm lifted higher and drew her toward him, drew her slowly and caressingly. She could wait no longer. With a tired sigh, and with an impulsive movement all her own, unpremeditated, spasmodic, she rested her head upon his breast. His head bent over swiftly, and, as his lips approached, hers flew to meet them.

This must be love, she thought, in the one rational moment that was vouchsafed her. If it was not love, it was too shameful. It could be nothing else than love. She loved the man whose arms were around her and whose lips were pressed to hers. She pressed more tightly to him, with a snuggling movement of her body. And a moment later, tearing herself half out of his embrace, suddenly and exultantly she reached up and placed both hands upon Martin Eden's sunburnt neck. So exquisite was the pang of love and desire fulfilled that she uttered a low moan, relaxed her hands, and lay half-swooning in his arms.

Not a word had been spoken, and not a word was spoken for a long time. Twice he bent and kissed her, and each time her lips met his shyly and her body made its happy, nestling movement. She clung to him, unable to release herself, and he sat, half supporting her in his arms, as he gazed with unseeing eyes at the blur of the great city across the bay. For once there were no visions in his brain. Only colors and lights and glows pulsed there, warm as the day and warm as his love. He bent over her. She was speaking.

"When did you love me?" she whispered.

"From the first, the very first, the first moment I laid eyes on you. I was mad for love of you then, and in all the time that has passed since then I have only grown the madder. I am maddest, now, dear. I am almost a lunatic, my head is so turned with joy."

"I am glad I am a woman, Martin—dear," she said, after a long sigh.

He crushed her in his arms again and again, and then asked:—

"And you? When did you first know?"

"Oh, I knew it all the time, almost from the first."

"And I have been as blind as a bat!" he cried, a ring of vexation in his voice. "I never dreamed it until just now, when I—when I kissed you."

"I didn't mean that." She drew herself partly away and looked at him. "I meant I knew you loved me almost from the first."

"And you?" he demanded.

"It came to me suddenly." She was speaking very slowly, her eyes warm and fluttery and melting, a soft flush on her cheeks that did not go away. "I never knew until just now when—you put your arms around me. And I never expected to marry you, Martin, not until just now. How did you make me love you?"

"I don't know," he laughed, "unless just by loving you, for I loved you hard enough to melt the heart of a stone, much less the heart of the living, breathing woman you are."

"This is so different from what I thought love would be," she announced irrelevantly.

"What did you think it would be like?"

"I didn't think it would be like this." She was looking into his eyes at the moment, but her own dropped as she continued, "You see, I didn't know what this was like."

He offered to draw her toward him again, but it was no more than a tentative muscular movement of the girdling arm, for he feared that he might be greedy. Then he felt her body yielding, and once again she was close in his arms and lips were pressed on lips.

"What will my people say?" she queried, with sudden apprehension, in one of the pauses.

"I don't know. We can find out very easily any time we are so minded."

"But if mamma objects? I am sure I am afraid to tell her."

"Let me tell her," he volunteered valiantly. "I think your mother does not like me, but I can win her around. A fellow who can win you can win anything. And if we don't—"

"Yes?"

"Why, we'll have each other. But there's no danger of not winning your mother to our marriage. She loves you too well."

"I should not like to break her heart," Ruth said pensively.

He felt like assuring her that mothers' hearts were not so easily broken, but instead he said, "And love is the greatest thing in the world."

"Do you know, Martin, you sometimes frighten me. I am frightened now, when I think of you and of what you have been. You must be very, very good to me. Remember, after all, that I am only a child. I never loved before."

"Nor I. We are both children together. And we are fortunate above most, for we have found our first love in each other."

"But that is impossible!" she cried, withdrawing herself from his arms with a swift, passionate movement. "Impossible for you. You have been a sailor, and sailors, I have heard, are—are—"

Her voice faltered and died away.

"Are addicted to having a wife in every port?" he suggested. "Is that what you mean?"

"Yes," she answered in a low voice.

"But that is not love." He spoke authoritatively. "I have been in many ports, but I never knew a passing touch of love until I saw you that first night. Do you know, when I said good night and went away, I was almost arrested."

"Arrested?"

"Yes. The policeman thought I was drunk; and I was, too—with love for you."

"But you said we were children, and I said it was impossible, for you, and we have strayed away from the point."

"I said that I never loved anybody but you," he replied. "You are my first, my very first."

"And yet you have been a sailor," she objected.

"But that doesn't prevent me from loving you the first."

"And there have been women—other women—oh!"

And to Martin Eden's supreme surprise, she burst into a storm of tears that took more kisses than one and many caresses to drive away. And all the while there was running through his head Kipling's line: *"And the Colonel's lady and Judy O'Grady are sisters under their skins."* It was true, he decided; though the novels he had read had led him to believe otherwise. His idea, for which the novels were responsible, had been that only formal proposals obtained in the upper classes. It was all right enough, down whence he had come, for youths and maidens to win each other by contact; but for the exalted personages up above on the heights to make love in similar fashion had seemed unthinkable. Yet the novels were wrong. Here was a proof of it. The same pressures and caresses, unaccompanied by speech, that were efficacious with the girls of the working-class, were equally efficacious with the girls above the working-class. They were all of the same flesh, after all, sisters under their skins; and he might have known as much himself had he remembered his Spencer. As he held Ruth in his arms and soothed her, he took great consolation in the thought that the Colonel's lady and Judy O'Grady were pretty much alike under their skins. It brought Ruth closer to him, made her possible. Her dear flesh was as anybody's flesh, as his flesh. There was no bar to their marriage. Class difference was the only difference, and class was extrinsic. It could be shaken off. A slave, he had read, had risen to the Roman purple. That being so, then he could rise to Ruth. Under her purity, and saintliness, and culture, and ethereal beauty of soul, she was, in things fundamentally human, just like Lizzie Connolly and all Lizzie Connollys. All that was possible of them was possible of her. She could love, and hate, maybe have hysterics; and she could certainly be jealous, as she was jealous now, uttering her last sobs in his arms.

"Besides, I am older than you," she remarked suddenly, opening her eyes and looking up at him, "three years older."

"Hush, you are only a child, and I am forty years older than you, in experience," was his answer.

In truth, they were children together, so far as love was concerned, and they were as naïve and immature in the expression of their love as a pair of children, and this despite the fact that she was crammed with a university education and that his head was full of scientific philosophy and the hard facts of life.

They sat on through the passing glory of the day, talking as lovers are prone to talk, marvelling at the wonder of love and at destiny that had flung them so strangely together, and dogmatically believing that they loved to a degree never attained by lovers before. And they returned insistently, again and again, to a rehearsal of their first impressions of each other and to hopeless attempts to analyze just precisely what they felt for each other and how much there was of it.

The cloud-masses on the western horizon received the descending sun, and the circle of the sky turned to rose, while the zenith glowed with the same warm color. The rosy light was all about them, flooding over them, as she sang, "Goodby, Sweet Day." She sang softly, leaning in the cradle of his arm, her hands in his, their hearts in each other's hands.

XXII

Mrs. Morse did not require a mother's intuition to read the advertisement in Ruth's face when she returned home. The flush that would not leave the cheeks told the simple story, and more eloquently did the eyes, large and bright, reflecting an unmistakable inward glory.

"What has happened?" Mrs. Morse asked, having bided her time till Ruth had gone to bed.

"You know?" Ruth queried, with trembling lips.

For reply, her mother's arm went around her, and a hand was softly caressing her hair.

"He did not speak," she blurted out. "I did not intend that it should happen, and I would never have let him speak—only he didn't speak."

"But if he did not speak, then nothing could have happened, could it?"

"But it did, just the same."

"In the name of goodness, child, what are you babbling about?" Mrs. Morse was bewildered. "I don't think I know what happened, after all. What did happen?"

Ruth looked at her mother in surprise.

"I thought you knew. Why, we're engaged, Martin and I."

Mrs. Morse laughed with incredulous vexation.

"No, he didn't speak," Ruth explained. "He just loved me, that was all. I was as surprised as you are. He didn't say a word. He just put his arm around me. And—and I was not myself. And he kissed me, and I kissed him. I couldn't help it. I just had to. And then I knew I loved him."

She paused, waiting with expectancy the benediction of her mother's kiss, but Mrs. Morse was coldly silent.

"It is a dreadful accident, I know," Ruth recommenced with a sinking voice. "And I don't know how you will ever forgive me. But I couldn't help it. I did not dream that I loved him until that moment. And you must tell father for me."

"Would it not be better not to tell your father? Let me see Martin Eden, and talk with him, and explain. He will understand and release you."

"No! no!" Ruth cried, starting up. "I do not want to be released. I love him, and love is very sweet. I am going to marry him—of course, if you will let me."

"We have other plans for you, Ruth, dear, your father and I—oh, no, no; no man picked out for you, or anything like that. Our plans go no farther than your marrying some man in your own station in life, a good and honorable gentleman, whom you will select yourself, when you love him."

"But I love Martin already," was the plaintive protest.

"We would not influence your choice in any way; but you are our daughter, and we could not bear to see you make a marriage such as this. He has nothing but roughness and coarseness to offer you in exchange for all that is refined and delicate in you. He is no match for you in any way. He could not support you. We have no foolish ideas about wealth, but comfort is another matter, and our daughter should at least marry a man who can give her that—and not a penniless adventurer, a sailor, a cowboy, a smuggler, and Heaven knows what else, who, in addition to everything, is hare-brained and irresponsible."

Ruth was silent. Every word she recognized as true.

"He wastes his time over his writing, trying to accomplish what geniuses and rare men with college educations sometimes accomplish. A man thinking of marriage should be preparing for marriage. But not he. As I have said, and I know you agree with me, he is irresponsible. And why should he not be? It is the way of sailors. He has never learned to be economical or temperate. The spendthrift years have marked him. It is not his fault, of course, but that does not alter his nature. And have you thought of the years of licentiousness he inevitably has lived? Have you thought of that, daughter? You know what marriage means."

Ruth shuddered and clung close to her mother.

"I have thought." Ruth waited a long time for the thought to frame itself. "And it is terrible. It sickens me to think of it. I told you it was a dreadful accident, my loving him; but I can't help myself. Could you help loving father? Then it is the same with me. There is something in me, in him—I never knew it was there until to-day—but it is there, and it makes me love him. I never thought to love him, but, you see, I do," she concluded, a certain faint triumph in her voice.

They talked long, and to little purpose, in conclusion agreeing to wait an indeterminate time without doing anything.

The same conclusion was reached, a little later that night, between Mrs. Morse and her husband, after she had made due confession of the miscarriage of her plans.

"It could hardly have come otherwise," was Mr. Morse's judgment. "This sailor-fellow has been the only man she was in touch with. Sooner or later she was going to awaken anyway; and she did awaken, and lo! here was this sailor-fellow, the only accessible man at the moment, and of course she promptly loved him, or thought she did, which amounts to the same thing."

Mrs. Morse took it upon herself to work slowly and indirectly upon Ruth, rather than to combat her. There would be plenty of time for this, for Martin was not in position to marry.

"Let her see all she wants of him," was Mr. Morse's advice. "The more she knows him, the less she'll love him, I wager. And give her plenty of contrast. Make a point of having young people at the house. Young women and young men, all sorts of young men, clever men, men who have done something or who are doing things, men of her own class, gentlemen. She can gauge him by them. They will show him up for what he is. And after all, he is a mere boy of twenty-one. Ruth is no more than a child. It is calf love with the pair of them, and they will grow out of it."

So the matter rested. Within the family it was accepted that Ruth and Martin were engaged, but no announcement was made. The family did not think it would ever be necessary. Also, it was tacitly understood that it was to be a long engagement. They did not ask Martin to go to work, nor to cease writing. They did not intend to encourage him to mend himself. And he aided and abetted them in their unfriendly designs, for going to work was farthest from his thoughts.

"I wonder if you'll like what I have done!" he said to Ruth several days later. "I've decided that boarding with my sister is too expensive, and I am going to board myself. I've rented a little room out in North Oakland, retired neighborhood and all the rest, you know, and I've bought an oil-burner on which to cook."

Ruth was overjoyed. The oil-burner especially pleased her.

"That was the way Mr. Butler began his start," she said.

Martin frowned inwardly at the citation of that worthy gentleman, and went on: "I put stamps on all my manuscripts and started them off to the editors again. Then to-day I moved in, and to-morrow I start to work."

"A position!" she cried, betraying the gladness of her surprise in all her body, nestling closer to him, pressing his hand, smiling. "And you never told me! What is it?"

He shook his head.

"I meant that I was going to work at my writing." Her face fell, and he went on hastily. "Don't misjudge me. I am not going in this time with any iridescent ideas. It is to be a cold, prosaic, matter-of-fact business proposition. It is better than going to sea again, and I shall earn more money than any position in Oakland can bring an unskilled man.

"You see, this vacation I have taken has given me perspective. I haven't been working the life out of my body, and I haven't been writing, at least not for publication. All I've done has been to love you and to think. I've read some, too, but it has been part of my thinking, and I have read principally magazines. I have generalized about myself, and the world, my place in it, and my chance to win to a place that will be fit for you. Also, I've been reading Spencer's 'Philosophy of Style,' and found out a lot of what was the matter with me—or my writing, rather; and for that matter with most of the writing that is published every month in the magazines.

"But the upshot of it all—of my thinking and reading and loving—is that I am going to move to Grub Street. I shall leave masterpieces alone and do hack-work—jokes, paragraphs, feature articles, humorous verse, and society verse—all the rot for which there seems so much demand. Then there are the newspaper syndicates, and the newspaper short-story syndicates, and the syndicates for the Sunday supplements. I can go ahead and hammer out the stuff they want, and earn the equivalent of a good salary by it. There are free-lances, you know, who earn as much as four or five hundred a month. I don't care to become as they; but I'll earn a good living, and have plenty of time to myself, which I wouldn't have in any position.

"Then, I'll have my spare time for study and for real work. In between the grind I'll try my hand at masterpieces, and I'll study and prepare myself for the writing of masterpieces. Why, I am amazed at the distance I have come already. When I first tried to write, I had nothing to write about except a few paltry experiences which I neither understood nor appreciated. But I had no thoughts. I really didn't. I didn't even have the words with which to think. My experiences were so many meaningless pictures. But as I began to add to my knowledge, and to my vocabulary, I saw something more in my experiences than mere pictures. I retained the pictures and I found their interpretation. That was when I began to do good work, when I wrote 'Adventure,' 'Joy,' 'The Pot,' 'The Wine of Life,' 'The Jostling Street,' the 'Love-cycle,' and the 'Sea Lyrics.' I shall write more like them, and better; but I shall do it in my spare time. My feet are on the solid earth, now. Hack-work and income first, masterpieces afterward. Just to show you, I wrote half a dozen jokes last night for the comic weeklies; and just as I was going to bed, the thought struck me to try my hand at a triolet—a humorous one; and inside an hour I had written four. They ought to be worth a dollar apiece. Four dollars right there for a few afterthoughts on the way to bed.

"Of course it's all valueless, just so much dull and sordid plodding; but it is no more dull and sordid than keeping books at sixty dollars a month, adding up endless columns of meaningless figures until one dies. And furthermore, the hack-work keeps me in touch with things literary and gives me time to try bigger things."

"But what good are these bigger things, these masterpieces?" Ruth demanded. "You can't sell them."

"Oh, yes, I can," he began; but she interrupted.

"All those you named, and which you say yourself are good—you have not sold any of them. We can't get married on masterpieces that won't sell."

"Then we'll get married on triolets that will sell," he asserted stoutly, putting his arm around her and drawing a very unresponsive sweetheart toward him.

"Listen to this," he went on in attempted gayety. "It's not art, but it's a dollar.

"He came in
When I was out,
To borrow some tin
Was why he came in,
And he went without;
So I was in
And he was out."

The merry lilt with which he had invested the jingle was at variance with the dejection that came into his face as he finished. He had drawn no smile from Ruth. She was looking at him in an earnest and troubled way.

"It may be a dollar," she said, "but it is a jester's dollar, the fee of a clown. Don't you see, Martin, the whole thing is lowering. I want the man I love and honor to be something finer and higher than a perpetrator of jokes and doggerel."

"You want him to be like—say Mr. Butler?" he suggested.

"I know you don't like Mr. Butler," she began.

"Mr. Butler's all right," he interrupted. "It's only his indigestion I find fault with. But to save me I can't see any difference between writing jokes or comic verse and running a type-writer, taking dictation, or keeping sets of books. It is all a means to an end. Your theory is for me to begin with keeping books in order to become a successful lawyer or man of business. Mine is to begin with hack-work and develop into an able author."

"There is a difference," she insisted.

"What is it?"

"Why, your good work, what you yourself call good, you can't sell. You have tried,—you know that,—but the editors won't buy it."

"Give me time, dear," he pleaded. "The hack-work is only makeshift, and I don't take it seriously. Give me two years. I shall succeed in that time, and the editors will be glad to buy my good work. I know what I am saying; I have faith in myself. I know what I have in me; I know what literature is, now; I know the average rot that is poured out by a lot of little men; and I know that at the end of two years I shall be on the highroad to success. As for business, I shall never succeed at it. I am not in sympathy with it. It strikes me as dull, and stupid, and mercenary, and tricky. Anyway I am not adapted for it. I'd never get beyond a clerkship, and how could you and I be happy on the paltry earnings of a clerk? I want the best of everything in the world for you, and the only time when I won't want it will be when there is something better. And I'm going to get it, going to get all of it. The income of a successful author makes Mr. Butler look cheap. A 'best-seller' will earn anywhere between fifty and a hundred thousand dollars—sometimes more and sometimes less; but, as a rule, pretty close to those figures."

She remained silent; her disappointment was apparent.

"Well?" he asked.

"I had hoped and planned otherwise. I had thought, and I still think, that the best thing for you would be to study shorthand—you already know type-writing—and go into father's office. You have a good mind, and I am confident you would succeed as a lawyer."

XXIII

THAT Ruth had little faith in his power as a writer, did not alter her nor diminish her in Martin's eyes. In the breathing spell of the vacation he had taken, he had spent many hours in self-analysis, and thereby learned much of himself. He had discovered that he loved beauty more than fame, and that what desire he had for fame was largely for Ruth's sake. It was for this reason that his desire for fame was strong. He wanted to be great in the world's eyes: "to make good," as he expressed it, in order that the woman he loved should be proud of him and deem him worthy.

As for himself, he loved beauty passionately, and the joy of serving her was to him sufficient wage. And more than beauty he loved Ruth. He considered love the finest thing in the world. It was love that had worked the revolution in him, changing him from an uncouth sailor to a student and an artist; therefore, to him, the finest and greatest of the three, greater than learning and artistry, was love. Already he had discovered that his brain went beyond Ruth's, just as it went beyond the brains of her brothers, or the brain of her father. In spite of every advantage of university training, and in the face of her bachelorship of arts, his power of intellect overshadowed hers, and his year or so of self-study and equipment gave him a mastery of the affairs of the world and art and life that she could never hope to possess.

All this he realized, but it did not affect his love for her, nor her love for him. Love was too fine and noble, and he was too loyal a lover for him to besmirch love with criticism. What did love have to do with Ruth's divergent views on art, right conduct, the French Revolution, or equal suffrage? They were mental processes, but love was beyond reason; it was superrational. He could not belittle love. He worshipped it. Love lay on the mountain-tops beyond the valley-land of reason. It was a sublimated condition of existence, the topmost peak of living, and it came rarely. Thanks to the school of scientific philosophers he favored, he knew the biological significance of love; but by a refined process of the same scientific reasoning he reached the conclusion that the human organism achieved its highest purpose in love, that love must not be questioned, but must be accepted as the highest guerdon of life. Thus, he considered the lover blessed over all creatures, and it was a delight to him to think of "God's own mad lover," rising above the things of earth, above wealth and judgment, public opinion and applause, rising above life itself and "dying on a kiss."

Much of this Martin had already reasoned out, and some of it he reasoned out later. In the meantime he worked, taking no recreation except when he went to see Ruth, and living like a Spartan. He paid two dollars and a half a month rent for the small room he got from his Portuguese landlady, Maria Silva, a virago and a widow, hard working and harsher tempered, rearing her large brood of children somehow, and drowning her sorrow and fatigue at irregular intervals in a gallon of the thin, sour wine that she bought from the corner grocery and saloon for fifteen cents. From detesting her and her foul tongue at first, Martin grew to admire her as he observed the brave fight she made. There were but four rooms in the little house—three, when Martin's was subtracted. One of these, the parlor, gay with an ingrain carpet and dolorous with a funeral card and a death-picture of one of her numerous departed babes, was kept strictly for company. The blinds were always down, and her barefooted tribe was never permitted to enter the sacred precinct save on state occasions. She cooked, and all ate, in the kitchen, where she likewise washed, starched, and ironed clothes on all days of the week except Sunday; for her income came largely from taking in washing from her more prosperous neighbors. Remained the bedroom, small as the one occupied by Martin, into which she and her seven little ones crowded and slept. It was an everlasting miracle to Martin how it was accomplished, and from her side of the thin partition he heard nightly every detail of the going to bed, the squalls and squabbles, the soft chattering, and the sleepy, twittering noises as of birds. Another source of income to Maria were her cows, two of them, which she milked night and morning and which gained a surreptitious livelihood from vacant lots and the grass that grew on either side the public sidewalks, attended always by one or more of her ragged boys, whose watchful guardianship consisted chiefly in keeping their eyes out for the poundmen.

In his own small room Martin lived, slept, studied, wrote, and kept house. Before the one window, looking out on the tiny front porch, was the kitchen table that served as desk, library, and type-writing stand. The bed, against the rear wall, occupied two-thirds of the total space of the room. The table was flanked on one side by a gaudy bureau, manufactured for profit and not for service, the thin veneer of which was shed day by day. This bureau stood in the corner, and in the opposite corner, on the table's other flank, was the kitchen—the oil-stove on a dry-goods box, inside of which were dishes and cooking utensils, a shelf on the wall for provisions, and a bucket of water on the floor. Martin had to carry his water from the kitchen sink, there being no tap in his room. On days when there was much steam to his cooking, the harvest of veneer from the bureau was unusually generous. Over the bed, hoisted by a tackle to the ceiling, was his bicycle. At first he had tried to keep it in the basement; but the tribe of Silva, loosening the bearings and puncturing the tires, had driven him out. Next he attempted the tiny front porch, until a howling southeaster drenched the wheel a night-long. Then he had retreated with it to his room and slung it aloft.

A small closet contained his clothes and the books he had accumulated and for which there was no room on the table or under the table. Hand in hand with reading, he had developed the habit of making notes, and so copiously did he make them that there would have been no existence for him in the confined quarters had he not rigged several clothes-lines across the room on which the notes were hung. Even so, he was crowded until navigating the room was a difficult task. He could not open the door without first closing the closet door, and *vice versa.* It was impossible for him anywhere to traverse the room in a straight line. To go from the door to the head of the bed was a zigzag course that he was never quite able to accomplish in the dark without collisions. Having settled the difficulty of the conflicting doors, he had to steer sharply to the right to avoid the kitchen. Next, he sheered to the left, to escape the foot of the bed; but this sheer, if too generous, brought him against the corner of the table. With a sudden twitch and lurch, he terminated the sheer and bore off to the right along a sort of canal, one bank of which was the bed, the other the table. When the one chair in the room was at its usual place before the table, the canal was unnavigable. When the chair was not in use, it reposed on top of the bed, though sometimes he sat on the chair when cooking, reading a book while the water boiled, and even becoming skilful enough to manage a paragraph or two while steak was frying. Also, so small was the little corner that constituted the kitchen, he was able, sitting down, to reach anything he needed. In fact, it was expedient to cook sitting down; standing up, he was too often in his own way.

In conjunction with a perfect stomach that could digest anything, he possessed knowledge of the various foods that were at the same time nutritious and cheap. Pea-soup was a common article in his diet, as well as potatoes and beans, the latter large and brown and cooked in Mexican style. Rice, cooked as American housewives never cook it and can never learn to cook it, appeared on Martin's table at least once a day. Dried fruits were less expensive than fresh, and he had usually a pot of them, cooked and ready at hand, for they took the place of butter on his bread. Occasionally he graced his table with a piece of round-steak, or with a soup-bone. Coffee, without cream or milk, he had twice a day, in the evening substituting tea; but both coffee and tea were excellently cooked.

There was need for him to be economical. His vacation had consumed nearly all he had earned in the laundry, and he was so far from his market that weeks must elapse before he could hope for the first returns from his hack-work. Except at such times as he saw Ruth, or dropped in to see his sister Gertrude, he lived a recluse, in each day accomplishing at least three days' labor of ordinary men. He slept a scant five hours, and only one with a constitution of iron could have held himself down, as Martin did, day after day, to nineteen consecutive hours of toil. He never lost a moment. On the looking-glass were lists of definitions and pronunciations; when shaving, or dressing, or combing his hair, he conned these lists over. Similar lists were on the wall over the oil-stove, and they were similarly conned while he was engaged in cooking or in washing the dishes. New lists continually displaced the old ones. Every strange or partly familiar word encountered in his reading was immediately jotted down, and later, when a sufficient number had been accumulated, were typed and pinned to the wall or looking-glass. He even carried them in his pockets, and reviewed them at odd moments on the street, or while waiting in butcher shop or grocery to be served.

He went farther in the matter. Reading the works of men who had arrived, he noted every result achieved by them, and worked out the tricks by which they had been achieved—the tricks of narrative, of exposition, of style, the points of view, the contrasts, the epigrams; and of all these he made lists for study. He did not ape. He sought principles. He drew up lists of effective and fetching mannerisms, till out of many such, culled from many writers, he was able to induce the general principle of mannerism, and, thus equipped, to cast about for new and original ones of his own, and to weigh and measure and appraise them properly. In similar manner he collected lists of strong phrases, the phrases of living language, phrases that bit like acid and scorched like flame, or that glowed and were mellow and luscious in the midst of the arid desert of common speech. He sought always for the principle that lay behind and beneath. He wanted to know how the thing was done; after that he could do it for himself. He was not content with the fair face of beauty. He dissected beauty in his crowded little bedroom laboratory, where cooking smells alternated with the outer bedlam of the Silva tribe; and, having dissected and learned the anatomy of beauty, he was nearer being able to create beauty itself.

He was so made that he could work only with understanding. He could not work blindly, in the dark, ignorant of what he was producing and trusting to chance and the star of his genius that the effect produced should be right and fine. He had no patience with chance effects. He wanted to know why and how. His was deliberate creative genius, and, before he began a story or poem, the thing itself was already alive in his brain, with the end in sight and the means of realizing that end in his conscious possession. Otherwise the effort was doomed to failure. On the other hand, he appreciated the chance effects in words and phrases that came lightly and easily into his brain, and that later stood all tests of beauty and power and developed tremendous and incommunicable connotations. Before such he bowed down and marvelled, knowing that they were beyond the deliberate creation of any man. And no matter how much he dissected beauty in search of the principles that underlie beauty and make beauty possible, he was aware, always, of the innermost mystery of beauty to which he did not penetrate and to which no man had ever penetrated. He knew full well, from his Spencer, that man can never attain ultimate knowledge of anything, and that the mystery of beauty was no less than that of life—nay, more—that the fibres of beauty and life were intertwisted, and that he himself was but a bit of the same nonunderstandable fabric, twisted of sunshine and star-dust and wonder.

In fact, it was when filled with these thoughts that he wrote his essay entitled "Star-dust," in which he had his fling, not at the principles of criticism, but at the principal critics. It was brilliant, deep, philosophical, and deliciously touched with laughter. Also it was promptly rejected by the magazines as often as it was submitted. But having cleared his mind of it, he went serenely on his way. It was a habit he developed, of incubating and maturing his thought upon a subject, and of then rushing into the typewriter with it. That it did not see print was a matter of small moment with him. The writing of it was the culminating act of a long mental process, the drawing together of scattered threads of thought and the final generalizing upon all the data with which his mind was burdened. To write such an article was the conscious effort by which he freed his mind and made it ready for fresh material and problems. It was in a way akin to that common habit of men and women troubled by real or fancied grievances, who periodically and volubly break their long-suffering silence and "have their say" till the last word is said.

XXIV

THE weeks passed. Martin ran out of money, and publishers' checks were far away as ever. All his important manuscripts had come back and been started out again, and his hack-work fared no better. His little kitchen was no longer graced with a variety of foods. Caught in the pinch with a part sack of rice and a few pounds of dried apricots, rice and apricots was his menu three times a day for five days handrunning. Then he started to realize on his credit. The Portuguese grocer, to whom he had hitherto paid cash, called a halt when Martin's bill reached the magnificent total of three dollars and eighty-five cents.

"For you see," said the grocer, "you no catcha da work, I losa da mon'."

And Martin could reply nothing. There was no way of explaining. It was not true business principle to allow credit to a strong-bodied young fellow of the working-class who was too lazy to work.

"You catcha da job, I let you have mora da grub," the grocer assured Martin. "No job, no grub. Thata da business." And then, to show that it was purely business foresight and not prejudice, "Hava da drink on da house—good friends justa da same."

So Martin drank, in his easy way, to show that he was good friends with the house, and then went supperless to bed.

The fruit store, where Martin had bought his vegetables, was run by an American whose business principles were so weak that he let Martin run a bill of five dollars before stopping his credit. The baker stopped at two dollars, and the butcher at four dollars. Martin added his debts and found that he was possessed of a total credit in all the world of fourteen dollars and eighty-five cents. He was up with his type-writer rent, but he estimated that he could get two months' credit on that, which would be eight dollars. When that occurred, he would have exhausted all possible credit.

The last purchase from the fruit store had been a sack of potatoes, and for a week he had potatoes, and nothing but potatoes, three times a day. An occasional dinner at Ruth's helped to keep strength in his body, though he found it tantalizing enough to refuse further helping when his appetite was raging at sight of so much food spread before it. Now and again, though afflicted with secret shame, he dropped in at his sister's at meal-time and ate as much as he dared—more than he dared at the Morse table.

Day by day he worked on, and day by day the postman delivered to him rejected manuscripts. He had no money for stamps, so the manuscripts accumulated in a heap under the table. Came a day when for forty hours he had not tasted food. He could not hope for a meal at Ruth's, for she was away to San Rafael on a two weeks' visit; and for very shame's sake he could not go to his sister's. To cap misfortune, the postman, in his afternoon round, brought him five returned manuscripts. Then it was that Martin wore his overcoat down into Oakland, and came back without it, but with five dollars tinkling in his pocket. He paid a dollar each on account to the four tradesmen, and in his kitchen fried steak and onions, made coffee, and stewed a large pot of prunes. And having dined, he sat down at his table-desk and completed before midnight an essay which he entitled "The Dignity of Usury." Having typed it out, he flung it under the table, for there had been nothing left from the five dollars with which to buy stamps.

Later on he pawned his watch, and still later his wheel, reducing the amount available for food by putting stamps on all his manuscripts and sending them out. He was disappointed with his hack-work. Nobody cared to buy. He compared it with what he found in the newspapers, weeklies, and cheap magazines, and decided that his was better, far better, than the average; yet it would not sell. Then he discovered that most of the newspapers printed a great deal of what was called "plate" stuff, and he got the address of the association that furnished it. His own work that he sent in was returned, along with a stereotyped slip informing him that the staff supplied all the copy that was needed.

In one of the great juvenile periodicals he noted whole columns of incident and anecdote. Here was a chance. His paragraphs were returned, and though he tried repeatedly he never succeeded in placing one. Later on, when it no longer mattered, he learned that the associate editors and sub-editors augmented their salaries by supplying those paragraphs themselves. The comic weeklies returned his jokes and humorous verse, and the light society verse he wrote for the large magazines found no abiding-place. Then there was the newspaper storiette. He knew that he could write better ones than were published. Managing to obtain the addresses of two newspaper syndicates, he deluged them with storiettes. When he had written twenty and failed to place one of them, he ceased. And yet, from day to day, he read storiettes in the dailies and weeklies, scores and scores of storiettes, not one of which would compare with his. In his despondency, he concluded that he had no judgment whatever, that he was hypnotized by what he wrote, and that he was a self-deluded pretender.

The inhuman editorial machine ran smoothly as ever. He folded the stamps in with his manuscript, dropped it into the letter-box, and from three weeks to a month afterward the postman came up the steps and handed him the manuscript. Surely there were no live, warm editors at the other end. It was all wheels and cogs and oil-cups—a clever mechanism operated by automatons. He reached stages of despair wherein he doubted if editors existed at all. He had never received a sign of the existence of one, and from absence of judgment in rejecting all he wrote it seemed plausible that editors were myths, manufactured and maintained by office boys, typesetters, and pressmen.

The hours he spent with Ruth were the only happy ones he had, and they were not all happy. He was afflicted always with a gnawing restlessness, more tantalizing than in the old days before he possessed her love; for now that he did possess her love, the possession of her was far away as ever. He had asked for two years; time was flying, and he was achieving nothing. Again, he was always conscious of the fact that she did not approve what he was doing. She did not say so directly. Yet indirectly she let him understand it as clearly and definitely as she could have spoken it. It was not resentment with her, but disapproval; though less sweet-natured women might have resented where she was no more than disappointed. Her disappointment lay in that this man she had taken to mould, refused to be moulded. To a certain extent she had found his clay plastic, then it had developed stubbornness, declining to be shaped in the image of her father or of Mr. Butler.

What was great and strong in him, she missed, or, worse yet, misunderstood. This man, whose clay was so plastic that he could live in any number of pigeonholes of human existence, she thought wilful and most obstinate because she could not shape him to live in her pigeonhole, which was the only one she knew. She could not follow the flights of his mind, and when his brain got beyond her, she deemed him erratic. Nobody else's brain ever got beyond her. She could always follow her father and mother, her brothers and Olney; wherefore, when she could not follow Martin, she believed the fault lay with him. It was the old tragedy of insularity trying to serve as mentor to the universal.

"You worship at the shrine of the established," he told her once, in a discussion they had over Praps and Vanderwater. "I grant that as authorities to quote they are most excellent—the two foremost literary critics in the United States. Every school teacher in the land looks up to Vanderwater as the Dean of American criticism. Yet I read his stuff, and it seems to me the perfection of the felicitous expression of the inane. Why, he is no more than a ponderous bromide, thanks to Gelett Burgess. And Praps is no better. His 'Hemlock Mosses,' for instance, is beautifully written. Not a comma is out of place; and the tone—ah!—is lofty, so lofty. He is the best-paid critic in the United States. Though, Heaven forbid! he's not a critic at all. They do criticism better in England.

"But the point is, they sound the popular note, and they sound it so beautifully and morally and contentedly. Their reviews remind me of a British Sunday. They are the popular mouthpieces. They back up your professors of English, and your professors of English back them up. And there isn't an original idea in any of their skulls. They know only the established,—in fact, they are the established. They are weak minded, and the established impresses itself upon them as easily as the name of the brewery is impressed on a beer bottle. And their function is to catch all the young fellows attending the university, to drive out of their minds any glimmering originality that may chance to be there, and to put upon them the stamp of the established."

"I think I am nearer the truth," she replied, "when I stand by the established, than you are, raging around like an iconoclastic South Sea Islander."

"It was the missionary who did the image breaking," he laughed. "And unfortunately, all the missionaries are off among the heathen, so there are none left at home to break those old images, Mr. Vanderwater and Mr. Praps."

"And the college professors, as well," she added.

He shook his head emphatically. "No; the science professors should live. They're really great. But it would be a good deed to break the heads of nine-tenths of the English professors—little, microscopic-minded parrots!"

Which was rather severe on the professors, but which to Ruth was blasphemy. She could not help but measure the professors, neat, scholarly, in fitting clothes, speaking in well-modulated voices, breathing of culture and refinement, with this almost indescribable young fellow whom somehow she loved, whose clothes never would fit him, whose heavy muscles told of damning toil, who grew excited when he talked, substituting abuse for calm statement and passionate utterance for cool self-possession. They at least earned good salaries and were—yes, she compelled herself to face it—were gentlemen; while he could not earn a penny, and he was not as they.

She did not weigh Martin's words nor judge his argument by them. Her conclusion that his argument was wrong was reached—unconsciously, it is true—by a comparison of externals. They, the professors, were right in their literary judgments because they were successes. Martin's literary judgments were wrong because he could not sell his wares. To use his own phrase, they made good, and he did not make good. And besides, it did not seem reasonable that he should be right—he who had stood, so short a time before, in that same living room, blushing and awkward, acknowledging his introduction, looking fearfully about him at the bric-a-brac his swinging shoulders threatened to break, asking how long since Swinburne died, and boastfully announcing that he had read "Excelsior" and the "Psalm of Life."

Unwittingly, Ruth herself proved his point that she worshipped the established. Martin followed the processes of her thoughts, but forbore to go farther. He did not love her for what she thought of Praps and Vanderwater and English professors, and he was coming to realize, with increasing conviction, that he possessed brain-areas and stretches of knowledge which she could never comprehend nor know existed.

In music she thought him unreasonable, and in the matter of opera not only unreasonable but wilfully perverse.

"How did you like it?" she asked him one night, on the way home from the opera.

It was a night when he had taken her at the expense of a month's rigid economizing on food. After vainly waiting for him to speak about it, herself still tremulous and stirred by what she had just seen and heard, she had asked the question.

"I liked the overture," was his answer. "It was splendid."

"Yes, but the opera itself?"

"That was splendid too; that is, the orchestra was, though I'd have enjoyed it more if those jumping-jacks had kept quiet or gone off the stage."

Ruth was aghast.

"You don't mean Tetralani or Barillo?" she queried.

"All of them—the whole kit and crew."

"But they are great artists," she protested.

"They spoiled the music just the same, with their antics and unrealities."

"But don't you like Barillo's voice?" Ruth asked. "He is next to Caruso, they say."

"Of course I liked him, and I liked Tetralani even better. Her voice is exquisite—or at least I think so."

"But, but—" Ruth stammered. "I don't know what you mean, then. You admire their voices, yet say they spoiled the music."

"Precisely that. I'd give anything to hear them in concert, and I'd give even a bit more not to hear them when the orchestra is playing. I'm afraid I am a hopeless realist. Great singers are not great actors. To hear Barillo sing a love passage with the voice of an angel, and to hear Tetralani reply like another angel, and to hear it all accompanied by a perfect orgy of glowing and colorful music—is ravishing, most ravishing. I do not admit it. I assert it. But the whole effect is spoiled when I look at them—at Tetralani, five feet ten in her stocking feet and weighing a hundred and ninety pounds, and at Barillo, a scant five feet four, greasy-featured, with the chest of a squat, undersized blacksmith, and at the pair of them, attitudinizing, clasping their breasts, flinging their arms in the air like demented creatures in an asylum; and when I am expected to accept all this as the faithful illusion of a love-scene between a slender and beautiful princess and a handsome, romantic, young prince—why, I can't accept it, that's all. It's rot; it's absurd; it's unreal. That's what's the matter with it. It's not real. Don't tell me that anybody in this world ever made love that way. Why, if I'd made love to you in such fashion, you'd have boxed my ears."

"But you misunderstand," Ruth protested. "Every form of art has its limitations." (She was busy recalling a lecture she had heard at the university on the conventions of the arts.) "In painting there are only two dimensions to the canvas, yet you accept the illusion of three dimensions which the art of a painter enables him to throw into the canvas. In writing, again, the author must be omnipotent. You accept as perfectly legitimate the author's account of the secret thoughts of the heroine, and yet all the time you know that the heroine was alone when thinking these thoughts, and that neither the author nor any one else was capable of hearing them. And so with the stage, with sculpture, with opera, with every art form. Certain irreconcilable things must be accepted."

"Yes, I understood that," Martin answered. "All the arts have their conventions." (Ruth was surprised at his use of the word. It was as if he had studied at the university himself, instead of being ill-equipped from browsing at haphazard through the books in the library.) "But even the conventions must be real. Trees, painted on flat cardboard and stuck up on each side of the stage, we accept as a forest. It is a real enough convention. But, on the other hand, we would not accept a sea scene as a forest. We can't do it. It violates our senses. Nor would you, or, rather, should you, accept the ravings and writhings and agonized contortions of those two lunatics to-night as a convincing portrayal of love."

"But you don't hold yourself superior to all the judges of music?" she protested.

"No, no, not for a moment. I merely maintain my right as an individual. I have just been telling you what I think, in order to explain why the elephantine gambols of Madame Tetralani spoil the orchestra for me. The world's judges of music may all be right. But I am I, and I won't subordinate my taste to the unanimous judgment of mankind. If I don't like a thing, I don't like it, that's all; and there is no reason under the sun why I should ape a liking for it just because the majority of my fellow-creatures like it, or make believe they like it. I can't follow the fashions in the things I like or dislike."

"But music, you know, is a matter of training," Ruth argued; "and opera is even more a matter of training. May it not be—"

"That I am not trained in opera?" he dashed in.

She nodded.

"The very thing," he agreed. "And I consider I am fortunate in not having been caught when I was young. If I had, I could have wept sentimental tears to-night, and the clownish antics of that precious pair would have but enhanced the beauty of their voices and the beauty of the accompanying orchestra. You are right. It's mostly a matter of training. And I am too old, now. I must have the real or nothing. An illusion that won't convince is a palpable lie, and that's what grand opera is to me when little Barillo throws a fit, clutches mighty Tetralani in his arms (also in a fit), and tells her how passionately he adores her."

Again Ruth measured his thoughts by comparison of externals and in accordance with her belief in the established. Who was he that he should be right and all the cultured world wrong? His words and thoughts made no impression upon her. She was too firmly entrenched in the established to have any sympathy with revolutionary ideas. She had always been used to music, and she had enjoyed opera ever since she was a child, and all her world had enjoyed it, too. Then by what right did Martin Eden emerge, as he had so recently emerged, from his rag-time and working-class songs, and pass judgment on the world's music? She was vexed with him, and as she walked beside him she had a vague feeling of outrage. At the best, in her most charitable frame of mind, she considered the statement of his views to be a caprice, an erratic and uncalled-for prank. But when he took her in his arms at the door and kissed her good night in tender lover-fashion, she forgot everything in the outrush of her own love to him. And later, on a sleepless pillow, she puzzled, as she had often puzzled of late, as to how it was that she loved so strange a man, and loved him despite the disapproval of her people.

And next day Martin Eden cast hack-work aside, and at white heat hammered out an essay to which he gave the title, "The Philosophy of Illusion." A stamp started it on its travels, but it was destined to receive many stamps and to be started on many travels in the months that followed.

XXV

Maria Silva was poor, and all the ways of poverty were clear to her. Poverty, to Ruth, was a word signifying a not-nice condition of existence. That was her total knowledge on the subject. She knew Martin was poor, and his condition she associated in her mind with the boyhood of Abraham Lincoln, of Mr. Butler, and of other men who had become successes. Also, while aware that poverty was anything but delectable, she had a comfortable middle-class feeling that poverty was salutary, that it was a sharp spur that urged on to success all men who were not degraded and hopeless drudges. So that her knowledge that Martin was so poor that he had pawned his watch and overcoat did not disturb her. She even considered it the hopeful side of the situation, believing that sooner or later it would arouse him and compel him to abandon his writing.

Ruth never read hunger in Martin's face, which had grown lean and had enlarged the slight hollows in the cheeks. In fact, she marked the change in his face with satisfaction. It seemed to refine him, to remove from him much of the dross of flesh and the too animal-like vigor that lured her while she detested it. Sometimes, when with her, she noted an unusual brightness in his eyes, and she admired it, for it made him appear more the poet and the scholar—the things he would have liked to be and which she would have liked him to be. But Maria Silva read a different tale in the hollow cheeks and the burning eyes, and she noted the changes in them from day to day, by them following the ebb and flow of his fortunes. She saw him leave the house with his overcoat and return without it, though the day was chill and raw, and promptly she saw his cheeks fill out slightly and the fire of hunger leave his eyes. In the same way she had seen his wheel and watch go, and after each event she had seen his vigor bloom again.

Likewise she watched his toils, and knew the measure of the midnight oil he burned. Work! She knew that he outdid her, though his work was of a different order. And she was surprised to behold that the less food he had, the harder he worked. On occasion, in a casual sort of way, when she thought hunger pinched hardest, she would send him in a loaf of new baking, awkwardly covering the act with banter to the effect that it was better than he could bake. And again, she would send one of her toddlers in to him with a great pitcher of hot soup, debating inwardly the while whether she was justified in taking it from the mouths of her own flesh and blood. Nor was Martin ungrateful, knowing as he did the lives of the poor, and that if ever in the world there was charity, this was it.

On a day when she had filled her brood with what was left in the house, Maria invested her last fifteen cents in a gallon of cheap wine. Martin, coming into her kitchen to fetch water, was invited to sit down and drink. He drank her very good health, and in return she drank his. Then she drank to prosperity in his undertakings, and he drank to the hope that James Grant would show up and pay her for his washing. James Grant was a journeyman carpenter who did not always pay his bills and who owed Maria three dollars.

Both Maria and Martin drank the sour new wine on empty stomachs, and it went swiftly to their heads. Utterly differentiated creatures that they were, they were lonely in their misery, and though the misery was tacitly ignored, it was the bond that drew them together. Maria was amazed to learn that he had been in the Azores, where she had lived until she was eleven. She was doubly amazed that he had been in the Hawaiian Islands, whither she had migrated from the Azores with her people. But her amazement passed all bounds when he told her he had been on Maui, the particular island whereon she had attained womanhood and married. Kahului, where she had first met her husband,—he, Martin, had been there twice! Yes, she remembered the sugar steamers, and he had been on them—well, well, it was a small world. And Wailuku! That place, too! Did he know the head-luna of the plantation? Yes, and had had a couple of drinks with him.

And so they reminiscenced and drowned their hunger in the raw, sour wine. To Martin the future did not seem so dim. Success trembled just before him. He was on the verge of clasping it. Then he studied the deep-lined face of the toilworn woman before him, remembered her soups and loaves of new baking, and felt spring up in him the warmest gratitude and philanthropy.

"Maria," he exclaimed suddenly. "What would you like to have?"

She looked at him, bepuzzled.

"What would you like to have now, right now, if you could get it?"

"Shoe alla da roun' for da childs—seven pairs da shoe."

"You shall have them," he announced, while she nodded her head gravely. "But I mean a big wish, something big that you want."

Her eyes sparkled good-naturedly. He was choosing to make fun with her, Maria, with whom few made fun these days.

"Think hard," he cautioned, just as she was opening her mouth to speak.

"Alla right," she answered. "I thinka da hard. I lika da house, dis house—all mine, no paya da rent, seven dollar da month."

"You shall have it," he granted, "and in a short time. Now wish the great wish. Make believe I am God, and I say to you anything you want you can have. Then you wish that thing, and I listen."

Maria considered solemnly for a space.

"You no 'fraid?" she asked warningly.

"No, no," he laughed, "I'm not afraid. Go ahead."

"Most verra big," she warned again.

"All right. Fire away."

"Well, den—" She drew a big breath like a child, as she voiced to the uttermost all she cared to demand of life. "I lika da have one milka ranch—good milka ranch. Plenty cow, plenty land, plenty grass. I lika da have near San Le-an; my sister liva dere. I sella da milk in Oakland. I maka da plentee mon. Joe an' Nick no runna da cow. Dey go-a to school. Bimeby maka da good engineer, worka da railroad. Yes, I lika da milka ranch."

She paused and regarded Martin with twinkling eyes.

"You shall have it," he answered promptly.

She nodded her head and touched her lips courteously to the wine-glass and to the giver of the gift she knew would never be given. His heart was right, and in her own heart she appreciated his intention as much as if the gift had gone with it.

"No, Maria," he went on; "Nick and Joe won't have to peddle milk, and all the kids can go to school and wear shoes the whole year round. It will be a first-class milk ranch —everything complete. There will be a house to live in and a stable for the horses, and cow-barns, of course. There will be chickens, pigs, vegetables, fruit trees, and everything like that; and there will be enough cows to pay for a hired man or two. Then you won't have anything to do but take care of the children. For that matter, if you find a good man, you can marry and take it easy while he runs the ranch."

And from such largess, dispensed from his future, Martin turned and took his one good suit of clothes to the pawnshop. His plight was desperate for him to do this, for it cut him off from Ruth. He had no second-best suit that was presentable, and though he could go to the butcher and the baker, and even on occasion to his sister's, it was beyond all daring to dream of entering the Morse home so disreputably apparelled.

He toiled on, miserable and well-nigh hopeless. It began to appear to him that the second battle was lost and that he would have to go to work. In doing this he would satisfy everybody—the grocer, his sister, Ruth, and even Maria, to whom he owed a month's room rent. He was two months behind with his type-writer, and the agency was clamoring for payment or for the return of the machine. In desperation, all but ready to surrender, to make a truce with fate until he could get a fresh start, he took the civil service examinations for the Railway Mail. To his surprise, he passed first. The job was assured, though when the call would come to enter upon his duties nobody knew.

It was at this time, at the lowest ebb, that the smoothrunning editorial machine broke down. A cog must have slipped or an oil-cup run dry, for the postman brought him one morning a short, thin envelope. Martin glanced at the upper left-hand corner and read the name and address of the *Transcontinental Monthly.* His heart gave a great leap, and he suddenly felt faint, the sinking feeling accompanied by a strange trembling of the knees. He staggered into his room and sat down on the bed, the envelope still unopened, and in that moment came understanding to him how people suddenly fall dead upon receipt of extraordinarily good news.

Of course this was good news. There was no manuscript in that thin envelope, therefore it was an acceptance. He knew the story in the hands of the *Transcontinental.* It was "The Ring of Bells," one of his horror stories, and it was an even five thousand words. And, since first-class magazines always paid on acceptance, there was a check inside. Two cents a word—twenty dollars a thousand; the check must be a hundred dollars. One hundred dollars! As he tore the envelope open, every item of all his debts surged in his brain—$3.85 to the grocer; butcher, $4.00 flat; baker, $2.00; fruit store, $5.00; total, $14.85. Then there was room rent, $2.50; another month in advance, $2.50; two months' type-writer, $8.00; a month in advance, $4.00; total, $31.85. And finally to be added, his pledges, plus interest, with the pawnbroker—watch, $5.50; overcoat, $5.50; wheel, $7.75; suit of clothes, $5.50 (60% interest, but what did it matter?)—grand total, $56.10. He saw, as if visible in the air before him, in illuminated figures, the whole sum, and the subtraction that followed and that gave a remainder of $43.90. When he had squared every debt, redeemed every pledge, he would still have jingling in his pockets a princely $43.90. And on top of that he would have a month's rent paid in advance on the type-writer and on the room.

By this time he had drawn the single sheet of type-written letter out and spread it open. There was no check. He peered into the envelope, held it to the light, but could not trust his eyes, and in trembling haste tore the envelope apart. There was no check. He read the letter, skimming it line by line, dashing through the editor's praise of his story to the meat of the letter, the statement why the check had not been sent. He found no such statement, but he did find that which made him suddenly wilt. The letter slid from his hand. His eyes went lack-lustre, and he lay back on the pillow, pulling the blanket about him and up to his chin.

Five dollars for "The Ring of Bells"—five dollars for five thousand words! Instead of two cents a word, ten words for a cent! And the editor had praised it, too. And he would receive the check when the story was published. Then it was all poppycock, two cents a word for minimum rate and payment upon acceptance. It was a lie, and it had led him astray. He would never have attempted to write had he known that. He would have gone to work—to work for Ruth. He went back to the day he first attempted to write, and was appalled at the enormous waste of time—and all for ten words for a cent. And the other high rewards of writers, that he had read about, must be lies, too. His second-hand ideas of authorship were wrong, for here was the proof of it.

The *Transcontinental* sold for twenty-five cents, and its dignified and artistic cover proclaimed it as among the first-class magazines. It was a staid, respectable magazine, and it had been published continuously since long before he was born. Why, on the outside cover were printed every month the words of one of the world's great writers, words proclaiming the inspired mission of the *Transcontinental* by a star of literature whose first coruscations had appeared inside those self-same covers. And the high and lofty, heaven-inspired *Transcontinental* paid five dollars for five thousand words! The great writer had recently died in a foreign land—in dire poverty, Martin remembered, which was not to be wondered at, considering the magnificent pay authors receive.

Well, he had taken the bait, the newspaper lies about writers and their pay, and he had wasted two years over it. But he would disgorge the bait now. Not another line would he ever write. He would do what Ruth wanted him to do, what everybody wanted him to do—get a job. The thought of going to work reminded him of Joe—Joe, tramping through the land of nothing-to-do. Martin heaved a great sigh of envy. The reaction of nineteen hours a day for many days was strong upon him. But then, Joe was not in love, had none of the responsibilities of love, and he could afford to loaf through the land of nothing-to-do. He, Martin, had something to work for, and go to work he would. He would start out early next morning to hunt a job. And he would let Ruth know, too, that he had mended his ways and was willing to go into her father's office.

Five dollars for five thousand words, ten words for a cent, the market price for art. The disappointment of it, the lie of it, the infamy of it, were uppermost in his thoughts; and under his closed eyelids, in fiery figures, burned the "$3.85" he owed the grocer. He shivered, and was aware of an aching in his bones. The small of his back ached especially. His head ached, the top of it ached, the back of it ached, the brains inside of it ached and seemed to be swelling, while the ache over his brows was intolerable. And beneath the brows, planted under his lids, was the merciless "$3.85." He opened his eyes to escape it, but the white light of the room seemed to sear the balls and forced him to close his eyes, when the "$3.85" confronted him again.

Five dollars for five thousand words, ten words for a cent—that particular thought took up its residence in his brain, and he could no more escape it than he could the "$3.85" under his eyelids. A change seemed to come over the latter, and he watched curiously, till "$2.00" burned in its stead. Ah, he thought, that was the baker. The next sum that appeared was "$2.50." It puzzled him, and he pondered it as if life and death hung on the solution. He owed somebody two dollars and a half, that was certain, but who was it? To find it was the task set him by an imperious and malignant universe, and he wandered through the endless corridors of his mind, opening all manner of lumber rooms and chambers stored with odds and ends of memories and knowledge as he vainly sought the answer. After several centuries it came to him, easily, without effort, that it was Maria. With a great relief he turned his soul to the screen of torment under his lids. He had solved the problem; now he could rest. But no, the "$2.50" faded away, and in its place burned "$8.00." Who was that? He must go the dreary round of his mind again and find out.

How long he was gone on this quest he did not know, but after what seemed an enormous lapse of time, he was called back to himself by a knock at the door, and by Maria's asking if he was sick. He replied in a muffled voice he did not recognize, saying that he was merely taking a nap. He was surprised when he noted the darkness of night in the room. He had received the letter at two in the afternoon, and he realized that he was sick.

Then the "$8.00" began to smoulder under his lids again, and he returned himself to servitude. But he grew cunning. There was no need for him to wander through his mind. He had been a fool. He pulled a lever and made his mind revolve about him, a monstrous wheel of fortune, a merry-go-round of memory, a revolving sphere of wisdom. Faster and faster it revolved, until its vortex sucked him in and he was flung whirling through black chaos.

Quite naturally he found himself at a mangle, feeding starched cuffs. But as he fed he noticed figures printed on the cuffs. It was a new way of marking linen, he thought, until, looking closer, he saw "$3.85" on one of the cuffs. Then it came to him that it was the grocer's bill, and that these were his bills flying around on the drum of the mangle. A crafty idea came to him. He would throw the bills on the floor and so escape paying them. No sooner thought than done, and he crumpled the cuffs spitefully as he flung them upon an unusually dirty floor. Ever the heap grew, and though each bill was duplicated a thousand times, he found only one for two dollars and a half, which was what he owed Maria. That meant that Maria would not press for payment, and he resolved generously that it would be the only one he would pay; so he began searching through the cast-out heap for hers. He sought it desperately, for ages, and was still searching when the manager of the hotel entered, the fat Dutchman. His face blazed with wrath, and he shouted in stentorian tones that echoed down the universe, "I shall deduct the cost of those cuffs from your wages!" The pile of cuffs grew into a mountain, and Martin knew that he was doomed to toil for a thousand years to pay for them. Well, there was nothing left to do but kill the manager and burn down the laundry. But the big Dutchman frustrated him, seizing him by the nape of the neck and dancing him up and down. He danced him over the ironing tables, the stove, and the mangles, and out into the wash-room and over the wringer and washer. Martin was danced until his teeth rattled and his head ached, and he marvelled that the Dutchman was so strong.

And then he found himself before the mangle, this time receiving the cuffs an editor of a magazine was feeding from the other side. Each cuff was a check, and Martin went over them anxiously, in a fever of expectation, but they were all blanks. He stood there and received the blanks for a million years or so, never letting one go by for fear it might be filled out. At last he found it. With trembling fingers he held it to the light. It was for five dollars. "Ha! Ha!" laughed the editor across the mangle. "Well, then, I shall kill you," Martin said. He went out into the wash-room to get the axe, and found Joe starching manuscripts. He tried to make him desist, then swung the axe for him. But the weapon remained poised in mid-air, for Martin found himself back in the ironing room in the midst of a snow-storm. No, it was not snow that was falling, but checks of large denomination, the smallest not less than a thousand dollars. He began to collect them and sort them out, in packages of a hundred, tying each package securely with twine.

He looked up from his task and saw Joe standing before him juggling flat-irons, starched shirts, and manuscripts. Now and again he reached out and added a bundle of checks to the flying miscellany that soared through the roof and out of sight in a tremendous circle. Martin struck at him, but he seized the axe and added it to the flying circle. Then he plucked Martin and added him. Martin went up through the roof, clutching at manuscripts, so that by the time he came down he had a large armful. But no sooner down than up again, and a second and a third time and countless times he flew around the circle. From far off he could hear a childish treble singing: "Waltz me around again, Willie, around, around, around."

He recovered the axe in the midst of the Milky Way of checks, starched shirts, and manuscripts, and prepared, when he came down, to kill Joe. But he did not come down. Instead, at two in the morning, Maria, having heard his groans through the thin partition, came into his room, to put hot flat-irons against his body and damp cloths upon his aching eyes.

XXVI

Martin Eden did not go out to hunt for a job in the morning. It was late afternoon before he came out of his delirium and gazed with aching eyes about the room. Mary, one of the tribe of Silva, eight years old, keeping watch, raised a screech at sight of his returning consciousness. Maria hurried into the room from the kitchen. She put her work-calloused hand upon his hot forehead and felt his pulse.

"You lika da eat?" she asked.

He shook his head. Eating was farthest from his desire, and he wondered that he should ever have been hungry in his life.

"I'm sick, Maria," he said weakly. "What is it? Do you know?"

"Grip," she answered. "Two or three days you alla da right. Better you no eat now. Bimeby plenty can eat, to-morrow can eat maybe."

Martin was not used to sickness, and when Maria and her little girl left him, he essayed to get up and dress. By a supreme exertion of will, with reeling brain and eyes that ached so that he could not keep them open, he managed to get out of bed, only to be left stranded by his senses upon the table. Half an hour later he managed to regain the bed, where he was content to lie with closed eyes and analyze his various pains and weaknesses. Maria came in several times to change the cold cloths on his forehead. Otherwise she left him in peace, too wise to vex him with chatter. This moved him to gratitude, and he murmured to himself, "Maria, you getta da milka ranch, all righta, all right."

Then he remembered his long-buried past of yesterday. It seemed a life-time since he had received that letter from the *Transcontinental*, a life-time since it was all over and done with and a new page turned. He had shot his bolt, and shot it hard, and now he was down on his back. If he hadn't starved himself, he wouldn't have been caught by La Grippe. He had been run down, and he had not had the strength to throw off the germ of disease which had invaded his system. This was what resulted.

"What does it profit a man to write a whole library and lose his own life?" he demanded aloud. "This is no place for me. No more literature in mine. Me for the counting-house and ledger, the monthly salary, and the little home with Ruth."

Two days later, having eaten an egg and two slices of toast and drunk a cup of tea, he asked for his mail, but found his eyes still hurt too much to permit him to read.

"You read for me, Maria," he said. "Never mind the big, long letters. Throw them under the table. Read me the small letters."

"No can," was the answer. "Teresa, she go to school, she can."

So Teresa Silva, aged nine, opened his letters and read them to him. He listened absently to a long dun from the type-writer people, his mind busy with ways and means of finding a job. Suddenly he was shocked back to himself.

" 'We offer you forty dollars for all serial rights in your story,' " Teresa slowly spelled out, " 'provided you allow us to make the alterations suggested.' "

"What magazine is that?" Martin shouted. "Here, give it to me!"

He could see to read, now, and he was unaware of the pain of the action. It was the *White Mouse* that was offering him forty dollars, and the story was "The Whirlpool," another of his early horror stories. He read the letter through again and again. The editor told him plainly that he had not handled the idea properly, but that it was the idea they were buying because it was original. If they could cut the story down one-third, they would take it and send him forty dollars on receipt of his answer.

He called for pen and ink, and told the editor he could cut the story down three-thirds if he wanted to, and to send the forty dollars right along.

The letter despatched to the letter-box by Teresa, Martin lay back and thought. It wasn't a lie, after all. The *White Mouse* paid on acceptance. There were three thousand words in "The Whirlpool." Cut down a third, there would be two thousand. At forty dollars that would be two cents a word. Pay on acceptance and two cents a word—the newspapers had told the truth. And he had thought the *White Mouse* a third-rater! It was evident that he did not know the magazines. He had deemed the *Transcontinental* a first-rater, and it paid a cent for ten words. He had classed the *White Mouse* as of no account, and it paid twenty times as much as the *Transcontinental* and also had paid on acceptance.

Well, there was one thing certain: when he got well, he would not go out looking for a job. There were more stories in his head as good as "The Whirlpool," and at forty dollars apiece he could earn far more than in any job or position. Just when he thought the battle lost, it was won. He had proved for his career. The way was clear. Beginning with the *White Mouse* he would add magazine after magazine to his growing list of patrons. Hack-work could be put aside. For that matter, it had been wasted time, for it had not brought him a dollar. He would devote himself to work, good work, and he would pour out the best that was in him. He wished Ruth was there to share in his joy, and when he went over the letters left lying on his bed, he found one from her. It was sweetly reproachful, wondering what had kept him away for so dreadful a length of time. He reread the letter adoringly, dwelling over her handwriting, loving each stroke of her pen, and in the end kissing her signature.

And when he answered, he told her recklessly that he had not been to see her because his best clothes were in pawn. He told her that he had been sick, but was once more nearly well, and that inside ten days or two weeks (as soon as a letter could travel to New York City and return) he would redeem his clothes and be with her.

But Ruth did not care to wait ten days or two weeks. Besides, her lover was sick. The next afternoon, accompanied by Arthur, she arrived in the Morse carriage, to the unqualified delight of the Silva tribe and of all the urchins on the street, and to the consternation of Maria. She boxed the ears of the Silvas who crowded about the visitors on the tiny front porch, and in more than usual atrocious English tried to apologize for her appearance. Sleeves rolled up from soap-flecked arms and a wet gunny-sack around her waist told of the task at which she had been caught. So flustered was she by two such grand young people asking for her lodger, that she forgot to invite them to sit down in the little parlor. To enter Martin's room, they passed through the kitchen, warm and moist and steamy from the big washing in progress. Maria, in her excitement, jammed the bedroom and bedroom-closet doors together, and for five minutes, through the partly open door, clouds of steam, smelling of soap-suds and dirt, poured into the sick chamber.

Ruth succeeded in veering right and left and right again, and in running the narrow passage between table and bed to Martin's side; but Arthur veered too wide and fetched up with clatter and bang of pots and pans in the corner where Martin did his cooking. Arthur did not linger long. Ruth occupied the only chair, and having done his duty, he went outside and stood by the gate, the centre of seven marvelling Silvas, who watched him as they would have watched a curiosity in a side-show. All about the carriage were gathered the children from a dozen blocks, waiting and eager for some tragic and terrible dénouement. Carriages were seen on their street only for weddings and funerals. Here was neither marriage nor death; therefore, it was something transcending experience and well worth waiting for.

Martin had been wild to see Ruth. His was essentially a love-nature, and he possessed more than the average man's need for sympathy. He was starving for sympathy, which, with him, meant intelligent understanding; and he had yet to learn that Ruth's sympathy was largely sentimental and tactful, and that it proceeded from gentleness of nature rather than from understanding of the objects of her sympathy. So it was while Martin held her hand and gladly talked, that her love for him prompted her to press his hand in return, and that her eyes were moist and luminous at sight of his helplessness and of the marks suffering had stamped upon his face.

But while he told her of his two acceptances, of his despair when he received the one from the *Transcontinental,* and of the corresponding delight with which he received the one from the *White Mouse,* she did not follow him. She heard the words he uttered and understood their literal import, but she was not with him in his despair and his delight. She could not get out of herself. She was not interested in selling stories to magazines. What was important to her was matrimony. She was not aware of it, however, any more than she was aware that her desire that Martin take a position was the instinctive and preparative impulse of motherhood. She would have blushed had she been told as much in plain, set terms, and next, she might have grown indignant and asserted that her sole interest lay in the man she loved and her desire for him to make the best of himself. So, while Martin poured out his heart to her, elated with the first success his chosen work in the world had received, she paid heed to his bare words only, gazing now and again about the room, shocked by what she saw.

For the first time Ruth gazed upon the sordid face of poverty. Starving lovers had always seemed romantic to her, but she had had no idea how starving lovers lived. She had never dreamed it could be like this. Ever her gaze shifted from the room to him and back again. The steamy smell of dirty clothes, which had entered with her from the kitchen, was sickening. Martin must be soaked with it, Ruth concluded, if that awful woman washed frequently. Such was the contagiousness of degradation. When she looked at Martin, she seemed to see the smirch left upon him by his surroundings. She had never seen him unshaven, and the three days' growth of beard on his face was repulsive to her. Not alone did it give him the same dark and murky aspect of the Silva house, inside and out, but it seemed to emphasize that animal-like strength of his which she detested. And here he was, being confirmed in his madness by the two acceptances he took such pride in telling her about. A little longer and he would have surrendered and gone to work. Now he would continue on in this horrible house, writing and starving for a few more months.

"What is that smell?" she asked suddenly.

"Some of Maria's washing smells, I imagine," was the answer. "I am growing quite accustomed to them."

"No, no; not that. It is something else. A stale, sickish smell."

Martin sampled the air before replying.

"I can't smell anything else, except stale tobacco smoke," he announced.

"That's it. It is terrible. Why do you smoke so much, Martin?"

"I don't know, except that I smoke more than usual when I am lonely. And then, too, it's such a long-standing habit. I learned when I was only a youngster."

"It is not a nice habit, you know," she reproved. "It smells to heaven."

"That's the fault of the tobacco. I can afford only the cheapest. But wait until I get that forty-dollar check. I'll use a brand that is not offensive even to the angels. But that wasn't so bad, was it, two acceptances in three days? That forty-five dollars will pay about all my debts."

"For two years' work?" she queried.

"No, for less than a week's work. Please pass me that book over on the far corner of the table, the account book with the gray cover." He opened it and began turning over the pages rapidly. "Yes, I was right. Four days for 'The Ring of Bells,' two days for 'The Whirlpool.' That's forty-five dollars for a week's work, one hundred and eighty dollars a month. That beats any salary I can command. And, besides, I'm just beginning. A thousand dollars a month is not too much to buy for you all I want you to have. A salary of five hundred a month would be too small. That forty-five dollars is just a starter. Wait till I get my stride. Then watch my smoke."

Ruth misunderstood his slang, and reverted to cigarettes.

"You smoke more than enough as it is, and the brand of tobacco will make no difference. It is the smoking itself that is not nice, no matter what the brand may be. You are a chimney, a living volcano, a perambulating smoke-stack, and you are a perfect disgrace, Martin dear, you know you are."

She leaned toward him, entreaty in her eyes, and as he looked at her delicate face and into her pure, limpid eyes, as of old he was struck with his own unworthiness.

"I wish you wouldn't smoke any more," she whispered. "Please, for—my sake."

"All right, I won't," he cried. "I'll do anything you ask, dear love, anything; you know that."

A great temptation assailed her. In an insistent way she had caught glimpses of the large, easy-going side of his nature, and she felt sure, if she asked him to cease attempting to write, that he would grant her wish. In the swift instant that elapsed, the words trembled on her lips. But she did not utter them. She was not quite brave enough; she did not quite dare. Instead, she leaned toward him to meet him, and in his arms murmured:—

"You know, it is really not for my sake, Martin, but for your own. I am sure smoking hurts you; and besides, it is not good to be a slave to anything, to a drug least of all."

"I shall always be your slave," he smiled.

"In which case, I shall begin issuing my commands."

She looked at him mischievously, though deep down she was already regretting that she had not preferred her largest request.

"I live but to obey, your majesty."

"Well, then, my first commandment is, Thou shalt not omit to shave every day. Look how you have scratched my cheek."

And so it ended in caresses and love-laughter. But she had made one point, and she could not expect to make more than one at a time. She felt a woman's pride in that she had made him stop smoking. Another time she would persuade him to take a position, for had he not said he would do anything she asked?

She left his side to explore the room, examining the clothes-lines of notes overhead, learning the mystery of the tackle used for suspending his wheel under the ceiling, and being saddened by the heap of manuscripts under the table which represented to her just so much wasted time. The oilstove won her admiration, but on investigating the food shelves she found them empty.

"Why, you haven't anything to eat, you poor dear," she said with tender compassion. "You must be starving."

"I store my food in Maria's safe and in her pantry," he lied. "It keeps better there. No danger of my starving. Look at that."

She had come back to his side, and she saw him double his arm at the elbow, the biceps crawling under his shirt-sleeve and swelling into a knot of muscle, heavy and hard. The sight repelled her. Sentimentally, she disliked it. But her pulse, her blood, every fibre of her, loved it and yearned for it, and, in the old, inexplicable way, she leaned toward him, not away from him. And in the moment that followed, when he crushed her in his arms, the brain of her, concerned with the superficial aspects of life, was in revolt; while the heart of her, the woman of her, concerned with life itself, exulted triumphantly. It was in moments like this that she felt to the uttermost the greatness of her love for Martin, for it was almost a swoon of delight to her to feel his strong arms about her, holding her tightly, hurting her with the grip of their fervor. At such moments she found justification for her treason to her standards, for her violation of her own high ideals, and, most of all, for her tacit disobedience to her mother and father. They did not want her to marry this man. It shocked them that she should love him. It shocked her, too, sometimes, when she was apart from him, a cool and reasoning creature. With him, she loved him—in truth, at times a vexed and worried love; but love it was, a love that was stronger than she.

"This La Grippe is nothing," he was saying. "It hurts a bit, and gives one a nasty headache, but it doesn't compare with break-bone fever."

"Have you had that, too?" she queried absently, intent on the heaven-sent justification she was finding in his arms.

And so, with absent queries, she led him on, till suddenly his words startled her.

He had had the fever in a secret colony of thirty lepers on one of the Hawaiian Islands.

"But why did you go there?" she demanded.

Such royal carelessness of body seemed criminal.

"Because I didn't know," he answered. "I never dreamed of lepers. When I deserted the schooner and landed on the beach, I headed inland for some place of hiding. For three days I lived off guavas, *ohia-* apples, and bananas, all of which grew wild in the jungle. On the fourth day I found the trail—a mere foot-trail. It led inland, and it led up. It was the way I wanted to go, and it showed signs of recent travel. At one place it ran along the crest of a ridge that was no more than a knife-edge. The trail wasn't three feet wide on the crest, and on either side the ridge fell away in precipices hundreds of feet deep. One man, with plenty of ammunition, could have held it against a hundred thousand.

"It was the only way in to the hiding-place. Three hours after I found the trail I was there, in a little mountain valley, a pocket in the midst of lava peaks. The whole place was terraced for taro-patches, fruit trees grew there, and there were eight or ten grass huts. But as soon as I saw the inhabitants I knew what I'd struck. One sight of them was enough."

"What did you do?" Ruth demanded breathlessly, listening, like any Desdemona, appalled and fascinated.

"Nothing for me to do. Their leader was a kind old fellow, pretty far gone, but he ruled like a king. He had discovered the little valley and founded the settlement—all of which was against the law. But he had guns, plenty of ammunition, and those Kanakas, trained to the shooting of wild cattle and wild pig, were dead shots. No, there wasn't any running away for Martin Eden. He stayed—for three months."

"But how did you escape?"

"I'd have been there yet, if it hadn't been for a girl there, a half-Chinese, quarter-white, and quarter-Hawaiian. She was a beauty, poor thing, and well educated. Her mother, in Honolulu, was worth a million or so. Well, this girl got me away at last. Her mother financed the settlement, you see, so the girl wasn't afraid of being punished for letting me go. But she made me swear, first, never to reveal the hiding-place; and I never have. This is the first time I have even mentioned it. The girl had just the first signs of leprosy. The fingers of her right hand were slightly twisted, and there was a small spot on her arm. That was all. I guess she is dead, now."

"But weren't you frightened? And weren't you glad to get away without catching that dreadful disease?"

"Well," he confessed, "I was a bit shivery at first; but I got used to it. I used to feel sorry for that poor girl, though. That made me forget to be afraid. She was such a beauty, in spirit as well as in appearance, and she was only slightly touched; yet she was doomed to lie there, living the life of a primitive savage and rotting slowly away. Leprosy is far more terrible than you can imagine it."

"Poor thing," Ruth murmured softly. "It's a wonder she let you get away."

"How do you mean?" Martin asked unwittingly.

"Because she must have loved you," Ruth said, still softly. "Candidly, now, didn't she?"

Martin's sunburn had been bleached by his work in the laundry and by the indoor life he was living, while the hunger and the sickness had made his face even pale; and across this pallor flowed the slow wave of a blush. He was opening his mouth to speak, but Ruth shut him off.

"Never mind, don't answer; it's not necessary," she laughed.

But it seemed to him there was something metallic in her laughter, and that the light in her eyes was cold. On the spur of the moment it reminded him of a gale he had once experienced in the North Pacific. And for the moment the apparition of the gale rose before his eyes—a gale at night, with a clear sky and under a full moon, the huge seas glinting coldly in the moonlight. Next, he saw the girl in the leper refuge and remembered it was for love of him that she had let him go.

"She was noble," he said simply. "She gave me life."

That was all of the incident, but he heard Ruth muffle a dry sob in her throat, and noticed that she turned her face away to gaze out of the window. When she turned it back to him, it was composed, and there was no hint of the gale in her eyes.

"I'm such a silly," she said plaintively. "But I can't help it. I do so love you, Martin, I do, I do. I shall grow more catholic in time, but at present I can't help being jealous of those ghosts of the past, and you know your past is full of ghosts.

"It must be," she silenced his protest. "It could not be otherwise. And there's poor Arthur motioning me to come. He's tired waiting. And now good-by, dear.

"There's some kind of a mixture, put up by the druggists, that helps men to stop the use of tobacco," she called back from the door, "and I am going to send you some."

The door closed, but opened again.

"I do, I do," she whispered to him; and this time she was really gone.

Maria, with worshipful eyes that none the less were keen to note the texture of Ruth's garments and the cut of them (a cut unknown that produced an effect mysteriously beautiful), saw her to the carriage. The crowd of disappointed urchins stared till the carriage disappeared from view, then transferred their stare to Maria, who had abruptly become the most important person on the street. But it was one of her progeny who blasted Maria's reputation by announcing that the grand visitors had been for her lodger. After that Maria dropped back into her old obscurity and Martin began to notice the respectful manner in which he was regarded by the small fry of the neighborhood. As for Maria, Martin rose in her estimation a full hundred per cent, and had the Portuguese grocer witnessed that afternoon carriage-call he would have allowed Martin an additional three-dollars-and-eighty-five-cents' worth of credit.

XXVII

The sun of Martin's good fortune rose. The day after Ruth's visit, he received a check for three dollars from a New York scandal weekly in payment for three of his triolets. Two days later a newspaper published in Chicago accepted his "Treasure Hunters," promising to pay ten dollars for it on publication. The price was small, but it was the first article he had written, his very first attempt to express his thought on the printed page. To cap everything, the adventure serial for boys, his second attempt, was accepted before the end of the week by a juvenile monthly calling itself *Youth and Age.* It was true the serial was twenty-one thousand words, and they offered to pay him sixteen dollars on publication, which was something like seventy-five cents a thousand words; but it was equally true that it was the second thing he had attempted to write and that he was himself thoroughly aware of its clumsy worthlessness.

But even his earliest efforts were not marked with the clumsiness of mediocrity. What characterized them was the clumsiness of too great strength—the clumsiness which the tyro betrays when he crushes butterflies with battering rams and hammers out vignettes with a war-club. So it was that Martin was glad to sell his early efforts for songs. He knew them for what they were, and it had not taken him long to acquire this knowledge. What he pinned his faith to was his later work. He had striven to be something more than a mere writer of magazine fiction. He had sought to equip himself with the tools of artistry. On the other hand, he had not sacrificed strength. His conscious aim had been to increase his strength by avoiding excess of strength. Nor had he departed from his love of reality. His work was realism, though he had endeavored to fuse with it the fancies and beauties of imagination. What he sought was an impassioned realism, shot through with human aspiration and faith. What he wanted was life as it was, with all its spirit-groping and soul-reaching left in.

He had discovered, in the course of his reading, two schools of fiction. One treated of man as a god, ignoring his earthly origin; the other treated of man as a clod, ignoring his heaven-sent dreams and divine possibilities. Both the god and the clod schools erred, in Martin's estimation, and erred through too great singleness of sight and purpose. There was a compromise that approximated the truth, though it flattered not the school of god, while it challenged the brute-savageness of the school of clod. It was his story, "Adventure," which had dragged with Ruth, that Martin believed had achieved his ideal of the true in fiction; and it was in an essay, "God and Clod," that he had expressed his views on the whole general subject.

But "Adventure," and all that he deemed his best work, still went begging among the editors. His early work counted for nothing in his eyes except for the money it brought, and his horror stories, two of which he had sold, he did not consider high work nor his best work. To him they were frankly imaginative and fantastic, though invested with all the glamour of the real, wherein lay their power. This investiture of the grotesque and impossible with reality, he looked upon as a trick—a skilful trick at best. Great literature could not reside in such a field. Their artistry was high, but he denied the worthwhileness of artistry when divorced from humanness. The trick had been to fling over the face of his artistry a mask of humanness, and this he had done in the half-dozen or so stories of the horror brand he had written before he emerged upon the high peaks of "Adventure," "Joy," "The Pot," and "The Wine of Life."

The three dollars he received for the triolets he used to eke out a precarious existence against the arrival of the *White Mouse* check. He cashed the first check with the suspicious Portuguese grocer, paying a dollar on account and dividing the remaining two dollars between the baker and the fruit store. Martin was not yet rich enough to afford meat, and he was on slim allowance when the *White Mouse* check arrived. He was divided on the cashing of it. He had never been in a bank in his life, much less been in one on business, and he had a naïve and childlike desire to walk into one of the big banks down in Oakland and fling down his indorsed check for forty dollars. On the other hand, practical common sense ruled that he should cash it with his grocer and thereby make an impression that would later result in an increase of credit. Reluctantly Martin yielded to the claims of the grocer, paying his bill with him in full, and receiving in change a pocketful of jingling coin. Also, he paid the other tradesmen in full, redeemed his suit and his bicycle, paid one month's rent on the type-writer, and paid Maria the overdue month for his room and a month in advance. This left him in his pocket, for emergencies, a balance of nearly three dollars.

In itself, this small sum seemed a fortune. Immediately on recovering his clothes he had gone to see Ruth, and on the way he could not refrain from jingling the little handful of silver in his pocket. He had been so long without money that, like a rescued starving man who cannot let the unconsumed food out of his sight, Martin could not keep his hand off the silver. He was not mean, nor avaricious, but the money meant more than so many dollars and cents. It stood for success, and the eagles stamped upon the coins were to him so many winged victories.

It came to him insensibly that it was a very good world. It certainly appeared more beautiful to him. For weeks it had been a very dull and sombre world; but now, with nearly all debts paid, three dollars jingling in his pocket, and in his mind the consciousness of success, the sun shone bright and warm, and even a rain-squall that soaked unprepared pedestrians seemed a merry happening to him. When he starved, his thoughts had dwelt often upon the thousands he knew were starving the world over; but now that he was feasted full, the fact of the thousands starving was no longer pregnant in his brain. He forgot about them, and, being in love, remembered the countless lovers in the world. Without deliberately thinking about it, *motifs* for love-lyrics began to agitate his brain. Swept away by the creative impulse, he got off the electric car, without vexation, two blocks beyond his crossing.

He found a number of persons in the Morse home. Ruth's two girl-cousins were visiting her from San Rafael, and Mrs. Morse, under pretext of entertaining them, was pursuing her plan of surrounding Ruth with young people. The campaign had begun during Martin's enforced absence, and was already in full swing. She was making a point of having at the house men who were doing things. Thus, in addition to the cousins Dorothy and Florence, Martin encountered two university professors, one of Latin, the other of English; a young army officer just back from the Philippines, one-time schoolmate of Ruth's; a young fellow named Melville, private secretary to Joseph Perkins, head of the San Francisco Trust Company; and finally of the men, a live bank cashier, Charles Hapgood, a youngish man of thirty-five, graduate of Stanford University, member of the Nile Club and the Unity Club, and a conservative speaker for the Republican Party during campaigns—in short, a rising young man in every way. Among the women was one who painted portraits, another who was a professional musician, and still another who possessed the degree of Doctor of Sociology and who was locally famous for her social settlement work in the slums of San Francisco. But the women did not count for much in Mrs. Morse's plan. At the best, they were necessary accessories. The men who did things must be drawn to the house somehow.

"Don't get excited when you talk," Ruth admonished Martin, before the ordeal of introduction began.

He bore himself a bit stiffly at first, oppressed by a sense of his own awkwardness, especially of his shoulders, which were up to their old trick of threatening destruction to furniture and ornaments. Also, he was rendered self-conscious by the company. He had never before been in contact with such exalted beings nor with so many of them. Hapgood, the bank cashier, fascinated him, and he resolved to investigate him at the first opportunity. For underneath Martin's awe lurked his assertive ego, and he felt the urge to measure himself with these men and women and to find out what they had learned from the books and life which he had not learned.

Ruth's eyes roved to him frequently to see how he was getting on, and she was surprised and gladdened by the ease with which he got acquainted with her cousins. He certainly did not grow excited, while being seated removed from him the worry of his shoulders. Ruth knew them for clever girls, superficially brilliant, and she could scarcely understand their praise of Martin later that night at going to bed. But he, on the other hand, a wit in his own class, a gay quizzer and laughter-maker at dances and Sunday picnics, had found the making of fun and the breaking of good-natured lances simple enough in this environment. And on this evening success stood at his back, patting him on the shoulder and telling him that he was making good, so that he could afford to laugh and make laughter and remain unabashed.

Later, Ruth's anxiety found justification. Martin and Professor Caldwell had got together in a conspicuous corner, and though Martin no longer wove the air with his hands, to Ruth's critical eye he permitted his own eyes to flash and glitter too frequently, talked too rapidly and warmly, grew too intense, and allowed his aroused blood to redden his cheeks too much. He lacked decorum and control, and was in decided contrast to the young professor of English with whom he talked.

But Martin was not concerned with appearances! He had been swift to note the other's trained mind and to appreciate his command of knowledge. Furthermore, Professor Caldwell did not realize Martin's concept of the average English professor. Martin wanted him to talk shop, and, though he seemed averse at first, succeeded in making him do it. For Martin did not see why a man should not talk shop.

"It's absurd and unfair," he had told Ruth weeks before, "this objection to talking shop. For what reason under the sun do men and women come together if not for the exchange of the best that is in them? And the best that is in them is what they are interested in, the thing by which they make their living, the thing they've specialized on and sat up days and nights over, and even dreamed about. Imagine Mr. Butler living up to social etiquette and enunciating his views on Paul Verlaine or the German drama or the novels of D'Annunzio. We'd be bored to death. I, for one, if I must listen to Mr. Butler, prefer to hear him talk about his law. It's the best that is in him, and life is so short that I want the best of every man and woman I meet."

"But," Ruth had objected, "there are the topics of general interest to all."

"There, you mistake," he had rushed on. "All persons in society, all cliques in society—or, rather, nearly all persons and cliques—ape their betters. Now, who are the best betters? The idlers, the wealthy idlers. They do not know, as a rule, the things known by the persons who are doing something in the world. To listen to conversation about such things would mean to be bored, wherefore the idlers decree that such things are shop and must not be talked about. Likewise they decree the things that are not shop and which may be talked about, and those things are the latest operas, latest novels, cards, billiards, cocktails, automobiles, horse shows, trout fishing, tuna-fishing, big-game shooting, yacht sailing, and so forth—and mark you, these are the things the idlers know. In all truth, they constitute the shop-talk of the idlers. And the funniest part of it is that many of the clever people, and all the would-be clever people, allow the idlers so to impose upon them. As for me, I want the best a man's got in him, call it shop vulgarity or anything you please."

And Ruth had not understood. This attack of his on the established had seemed to her just so much wilfulness of opinion.

So Martin contaminated Professor Caldwell with his own earnestness, challenging him to speak his mind. As Ruth paused beside them she heard Martin saying:—

"You surely don't pronounce such heresies in the University of California?"

Professor Caldwell shrugged his shoulders. "The honest taxpayer and the politician, you know. Sacramento gives us our appropriations and therefore we kowtow to Sacramento, and to the Board of Regents, and to the party press, or to the press of both parties."

"Yes, that's clear; but how about you?" Martin urged. "You must be a fish out of the water."

"Few like me, I imagine, in the university pond. Sometimes I am fairly sure I am out of water, and that I should belong in Paris, in Grub Street, in a hermit's cave, or in some sadly wild Bohemian crowd, drinking claret,—dago-red they call it in San Francisco,—dining in cheap restaurants in the Latin Quarter, and expressing vociferously radical views upon all creation. Really, I am frequently almost sure that I was cut out to be a radical. But then, there are so many questions on which I am not sure. I grow timid when I am face to face with my human frailty, which ever prevents me from grasping all the factors in any problem—human, vital problems, you know."

And as he talked on, Martin became aware that to his own lips had come the "Song of the Trade Wind":—

"I am strongest at noon,
But under the moon
I stiffen the bunt of the sail."

He was almost humming the words, and it dawned upon him that the other reminded him of the trade wind, of the Northeast Trade, steady, and cool, and strong. He was equable, he was to be relied upon, and withal there was a certain bafflement about him. Martin had the feeling that he never spoke his full mind, just as he had often had the feeling that the trades never blew their strongest but always held reserves of strength that were never used. Martin's trick of visioning was active as ever. His brain was a most accessible storehouse of remembered fact and fancy, and its contents seemed ever ordered and spread for his inspection. Whatever occurred in the instant present, Martin's mind immediately presented associated antithesis or similitude which ordinarily expressed themselves to him in vision. It was sheerly automatic, and his visioning was an unfailing accompaniment to the living present. Just as Ruth's face, in a momentary jealousy, had called before his eyes a forgotten moonlight gale, and as Professor Caldwell made him see again the Northeast Trade herding the white billows across the purple sea, so, from moment to moment, not disconcerting but rather identifying and classifying, new memory-visions rose before him, or spread under his eyelids, or were thrown upon the screen of his consciousness. These visions came out of the actions and sensations of the past, out of things and events and books of yesterday and last week—a countless host of apparitions that, waking or sleeping, forever thronged his mind.

So it was, as he listened to Professor Caldwell's easy flow of speech—the conversation of a clever, cultured man—that Martin kept seeing himself down all his past. He saw himself when he had been quite the hoodlum, wearing a "stiff-rim" Stetson hat and a square-cut, double-breasted coat, with a certain swagger to the shoulders and possessing the ideal of being as tough as the police permitted. He did not disguise it to himself, nor attempt to palliate it. At one time in his life he had been just a common hoodlum, the leader of a gang that worried the police and terrorized honest, working-class householders. But his ideals had changed. He glanced about him at the well-bred, well-dressed men and women, and breathed into his lungs the atmosphere of culture and refinement, and at the same moment the ghost of his early youth, in stiff-rim and square-cut, with swagger and toughness, stalked across the room. This figure, of the corner hoodlum, he saw merge into himself, sitting and talking with an actual university professor.

For, after all, he had never found his permanent abiding place. He had fitted in wherever he found himself, been a favorite always and everywhere by virtue of holding his own at work and at play and by his willingness and ability to fight for his rights and command respect. But he had never taken root. He had fitted in sufficiently to satisfy his fellows but not to satisfy himself. He had been perturbed always by a feeling of unrest, had heard always the call of something from beyond, and had wandered on through life seeking it until he found books and art and love. And here he was, in the midst of all this, the only one of all the comrades he had adventured with who could have made themselves eligible for the inside of the Morse home.

But such thoughts and visions did not prevent him from following Professor Caldwell closely. And as he followed, comprehendingly and critically, he noted the unbroken field of the other's knowledge. As for himself, from moment to moment the conversation showed him gaps and open stretches, whole subjects with which he was unfamiliar. Nevertheless, thanks to his Spencer, he saw that he possessed the outlines of the field of knowledge. It was a matter only of time, when he would fill in the outline. Then watch out, he thought—ware shoal, everybody! He felt like sitting at the feet of the professor, worshipful and absorbent; but, as he listened, he began to discern a weakness in the other's judgments—a weakness so stray and elusive that he might not have caught it had it not been ever present. And when he did catch it, he leapt to equality at once.

Ruth came up to them a second time, just as Martin began to speak.

"I'll tell you where you are wrong, or, rather, what weakens your judgments," he said. "You lack biology. It has no place in your scheme of things. —Oh, I mean the real interpretative biology, from the ground up, from the laboratory and the test-tube and the vitalized inorganic right on up to the widest aesthetic and sociological generalizations."

Ruth was appalled. She had sat two lecture courses under Professor Caldwell and looked up to him as the living repository of all knowledge.

"I scarcely follow you," he said dubiously.

Martin was not so sure but what he had followed him.

"Then I'll try to explain," he said. "I remember reading in Egyptian history something to the effect that understanding could not be had of Egyptian art without first studying the land question."

"Quite right," the professor nodded.

"And it seems to me," Martin continued, "that knowledge of the land question, in turn, of all questions, for that matter, cannot be had without previous knowledge of the stuff and the constitution of life. How can we understand laws and institutions, religions and customs, without understanding, not merely the nature of the creatures that made them, but the nature of the stuff out of which the creatures are made? Is literature less human than the architecture and sculpture of Egypt? Is there one thing in the known universe that is not subject to the law of evolution?—Oh, I know there is an elaborate evolution of the various arts laid down, but it seems to me to be too mechanical. The human himself is left out. The evolution of the tool, of the harp, of music and song and dance, are all beautifully elaborated; but how about the evolution of the human himself, the development of the basic and intrinsic parts that were in him before he made his first tool or gibbered his first chant? It is that which you do not consider, and which I call biology. It is biology in its largest aspects.

"I know I express myself incoherently, but I've tried to hammer out the idea. It came to me as you were talking, so I was not primed and ready to deliver it. You spoke yourself of the human frailty that prevented one from taking all the factors into consideration. And you, in turn,—or so it seems to me,—leave out the biological factor, the very stuff out of which has been spun the fabric of all the arts, the warp and the woof of all human actions and achievements."

To Ruth's amazement, Martin was not immediately crushed, and that the professor replied in the way he did struck her as forbearance for Martin's youth. Professor Caldwell sat for a full minute, silent and fingering his watch chain.

"Do you know," he said at last, "I've had that same criticism passed on me once before—by a very great man, a scientist and evolutionist, Joseph Le Conte. But he is dead, and I thought to remain undetected; and now you come along and expose me. Seriously, though—and this is confession—I think there is something in your contention—a great deal, in fact. I am too classical, not enough up-to-date in the interpretative branches of science, and I can only plead the disadvantages of my education and a temperamental slothfulness that prevents me from doing the work. I wonder if you'll believe that I've never been inside a physics or chemistry laboratory? It is true, nevertheless. Le Conte was right, and so are you, Mr. Eden, at least to an extent—how much I do not know."

Ruth drew Martin away with her on a pretext; when she had got him aside, whispering:—

"You shouldn't have monopolized Professor Caldwell that way. There may be others who want to talk with him."

"My mistake," Martin admitted contritely. "But I'd got him stirred up, and he was so interesting that I did not think. Do you know, he is the brightest, the most intellectual, man I have ever talked with. And I'll tell you something else. I once thought that everybody who went to universities, or who sat in the high places in society, was just as brilliant and intelligent as he."

"He's an exception," she answered.

"I should say so. Whom do you want me to talk to now?—Oh, say, bring me up against that cashier-fellow."

Martin talked for fifteen minutes with him, nor could Ruth have wished better behavior on her lover's part. Not once did his eyes flash nor his cheeks flush, while the calmness and poise with which he talked surprised her. But in Martin's estimation the whole tribe of bank cashiers fell a few hundred per cent, and for the rest of the evening he labored under the impression that bank cashiers and talkers of platitudes were synonymous phrases. The army officer he found good-natured and simple, a healthy, wholesome young fellow, content to occupy the place in life into which birth and luck had flung him. On learning that he had completed two years in the university, Martin was puzzled to know where he had stored it away. Nevertheless Martin liked him better than the platitudinous bank cashier.

"I really don't object to platitudes," he told Ruth later; "but what worries me into nervousness is the pompous, smugly complacent, superior certitude with which they are uttered and the time taken to do it. Why, I could give that man the whole history of the Reformation in the time he took to tell me that the Union-Labor Party had fused with the Democrats. Do you know, he skins his words as a professional poker-player skins the cards that are dealt out to him. Some day I'll show you what I mean."

"I'm sorry you don't like him," was her reply. "He's a favorite of Mr. Butler's. Mr. Butler says he is safe and honest—calls him the Rock, Peter, and says that upon him any banking institution can well be built."

"I don't doubt it—from the little I saw of him and the less I heard from him; but I don't think so much of banks as I did. You don't mind my speaking my mind this way, dear?"

"No, no; it is most interesting."

"Yes," Martin went on heartily, "I'm no more than a barbarian getting my first impressions of civilization. Such impressions must be entertainingly novel to the civilized person."

"What did you think of my cousins?" Ruth queried.

"I liked them better than the other women. There's plenty of fun in them along with paucity of pretence."

"Then you did like the other women?"

He shook his head.

"That social-settlement woman is no more than a sociological poll-parrot. I swear, if you winnowed her out between the stars, like Tomlinson, there would be found in her not one original thought. As for the portrait-painter, she was a positive bore. She'd make a good wife for the cashier. And the musician woman! I don't care how nimble her fingers are, how perfect her technique, how wonderful her expression—the fact is, she knows nothing about music."

"She plays beautifully," Ruth protested.

"Yes, she's undoubtedly gymnastic in the externals of music, but the intrinsic spirit of music is unguessed by her. I asked her what music meant to her—you know I'm always curious to know that particular thing; and she did not know what it meant to her, except that she adored it, that it was the greatest of the arts, and that it meant more than life to her."

"You were making them talk shop," Ruth charged him.

"I confess it. And if they were failures on shop, imagine my sufferings if they had discoursed on other subjects. Why, I used to think that up here, where all the advantages of culture were enjoyed—" He paused for a moment, and watched the youthful shade of himself, in stiff-rim and square-cut, enter the door and swagger across the room. "As I was saying, up here I thought all men and women were brilliant and radiant. But now, from what little I've seen of them, they strike me as a pack of ninnies, most of them, and ninety per cent of the remainder as bores. Now there's Professor Caldwell—he's different. He's a man, every inch of him and every atom of his gray matter."

Ruth's face brightened.

"Tell me about him," she urged. "Not what is large and brilliant—I know those qualities; but whatever you feel is adverse. I am most curious to know."

"Perhaps I'll get myself in a pickle." Martin debated humorously for a moment. "Suppose you tell me first. Or maybe you find in him nothing less than the best."

"I attended two lecture courses under him, and I have known him for two years; that is why I am anxious for your first impression."

"Bad impression, you mean? Well, here goes. He is all the fine things you think about him, I guess. At least, he is the finest specimen of intellectual man I have met; but he is a man with a secret shame.

"Oh, no, no!" he hastened to cry. "Nothing paltry nor vulgar. What I mean is that he strikes me as a man who has gone to the bottom of things, and is so afraid of what he saw that he makes believe to himself that he never saw it. Perhaps that's not the clearest way to express it. Here's another way. A man who has found the path to the hidden temple but has not followed it; who has, perhaps, caught glimpses of the temple and striven afterward to convince himself that it was only a mirage of foliage. Yet another way. A man who could have done things but who placed no value on the doing, and who, all the time, in his innermost heart, is regretting that he has not done them; who has secretly laughed at the rewards for doing, and yet, still more secretly, has yearned for the rewards and for the joy of doing."

"I don't read him that way," she said. "And for that matter, I don't see just what you mean."

"It is only a vague feeling on my part," Martin temporized. "I have no reason for it. It is only a feeling, and most likely it is wrong. You certainly should know him better than I."

From the evening at Ruth's Martin brought away with him strange confusions and conflicting feelings. He was disappointed in his goal, in the persons he had climbed to be with. On the other hand, he was encouraged with his success. The climb had been easier than he expected. He was superior to the climb, and (he did not, with false modesty, hide it from himself) he was superior to the beings among whom he had climbed—with the exception, of course, of Professor Caldwell. About life and the books he knew more than they, and he wondered into what nooks and crannies they had cast aside their educations. He did not know that he was himself possessed of unusual brain vigor; nor did he know that the persons who were given to probing the depths and to thinking ultimate thoughts were not to be found in the drawing rooms of the world's Morses; nor did he dream that such persons were as lonely eagles sailing solitary in the azure sky far above the earth and its swarming freight of gregarious life.

XXVIII

BUT success had lost Martin's address, and her messengers no longer came to his door. For twenty-five days, working Sundays and holidays, he toiled on "The Shame of the Sun," a long essay of some thirty thousand words. It was a deliberate attack on the mysticism of the Maeterlinck school—an attack from the citadel of positive science upon the wonder-dreamers, but an attack nevertheless that retained much of beauty and wonder of the sort compatible with ascertained fact. It was a little later that he followed up the attack with two short essays, "The Wonder-Dreamers" and "The Yardstick of the Ego." And on essays, long and short, he began to pay the travelling expenses from magazine to magazine.

During the twenty-five days spent on "The Shame of the Sun," he sold hack-work to the extent of six dollars and fifty cents. A joke had brought in fifty cents, and a second one, sold to a high-grade comic weekly, had fetched a dollar. Then two humorous poems had earned two dollars and three dollars respectively. As a result, having exhausted his credit with the tradesmen (though he had increased his credit with the grocer to five dollars), his wheel and suit of clothes went back to the pawnbroker. The type-writer people were again clamoring for money, insistently pointing out that according to the agreement rent was to be paid strictly in advance.

Encouraged by his several small sales, Martin went back to hack-work. Perhaps there was a living in it, after all. Stored away under his table were the twenty storiettes which had been rejected by the newspaper short-story syndicate. He read them over in order to find out how not to write newspaper storiettes, and so doing, reasoned out the perfect formula. He found that the newspaper storiette should never be tragic, should never end unhappily, and should never contain beauty of language, subtlety of thought, nor real delicacy of sentiment. Sentiment it must contain, plenty of it, pure and noble, of the sort that in his own early youth had brought his applause from "nigger heaven"—the "For-God-my-country-and-the-Czar" and "I-may-be-poor-but-I-am-honest" brand of sentiment.

Having learned such precautions, Martin consulted "The Duchess" for tone, and proceeded to mix according to formula. The formula consists of three parts: (1) a pair of lovers are jarred apart; (2) by some deed or event they are reunited; (3) marriage bells. The third part was an unvarying quantity, but the first and second parts could be varied an infinite number of times. Thus, the pair of lovers could be jarred apart by misunderstood motives, by accident of fate, by jealous rivals, by irate parents, by crafty guardians, by scheming relatives, and so forth and so forth; they could be reunited by a brave deed of the man lover, by a similar deed of the woman lover, by change of heart in one lover or the other, by forced confession of crafty guardian, scheming relative, or jealous rival, by voluntary confession of same, by discovery of some unguessed secret, by lover storming girl's heart, by lover making long and noble self-sacrifice, and so on, endlessly. It was very fetching to make the girl propose in the course of being reunited, and Martin discovered, bit by bit, other decidedly piquant and fetching ruses. But marriage bells at the end was the one thing he could take no liberties with; though the heavens rolled up as a scroll and the stars fell, the wedding bells must go on ringing just the same. In quantity, the formula prescribed twelve hundred words minimum dose, fifteen hundred words maximum dose.

Before he got very far along in the art of the storiette, Martin worked out half a dozen stock forms, which he always consulted when constructing storiettes. These forms were like the cunning tables used by mathematicians, which may be entered from top, bottom, right, and left, which entrances consist of scores of lines and dozens of columns, and from which may be drawn, without reasoning or thinking, thousands of different conclusions, all unchallengably precise and true. Thus, in the course of half an hour with his forms, Martin could frame up a dozen or so storiettes, which he put aside and filled in at his convenience. He found that he could fill one in, after a day of serious work, in the hour before going to bed. As he later confessed to Ruth, he could almost do it in his sleep. The real work was in constructing the frames, and that was merely mechanical.

He had no doubt whatever of the efficacy of his formula, and for once he knew the editorial mind when he said positively to himself that the first two he sent off would bring checks. And checks they brought, for four dollars each, at the end of twelve days.

In the meantime he was making fresh and alarming discoveries concerning the magazines. Though the *Transcontinental* had published "The Ring of Bells," no check was forthcoming. Martin needed it, and he wrote for it. An evasive answer and a request for more of his work was all he received. He had gone hungry two days waiting for the reply, and it was then that he put his wheel back in pawn. He wrote regularly, twice a week, to the *Transcontinental* for his five dollars, though it was only semi-occasionally that he elicited a reply. He did not know that the *Transcontinental* had been staggering along precariously for years, that it was a fourth-rater, or a tenth-rater, without standing, with a crazy circulation that partly rested on petty bullying and partly on patriotic appealing, and with advertisements that were scarcely more than charitable donations. Nor did he know that the *Transcontinental* was the sole livelihood of the editor and the business manager, and that they could wring their livelihood out of it only by moving to escape paying rent and by never paying any bill they could evade. Nor could he have guessed that the particular five dollars that belonged to him had been appropriated by the business manager for the painting of his house in Alameda, which painting he performed himself, on weekday afternoons, because he could not afford to pay union wages and because the first scab he had employed had had a ladder jerked out from under him and been sent to the hospital with a broken collar-bone.

The ten dollars for which Martin had sold "Treasure Hunters" to the Chicago newspaper did not come to hand. The article had been published, as he had ascertained at the file in the Central Reading-room, but no word could he get from the editor. His letters were ignored. To satisfy himself that they had been received, he registered several of them. It was nothing less than robbery, he concluded—a cold-blooded steal; while he starved, he was pilfered of his merchandise, of his goods, the sale of which was the sole way of getting bread to eat.

Youth and Age was a weekly, and it had published two-thirds of his twenty-one-thousand-word serial when it went out of business. With it went all hopes of getting his sixteen dollars.

To cap the situation, "The Pot," which he looked upon as one of the best things he had written, was lost to him. In despair, casting about frantically among the magazines, he had sent it to *The Billow*, a society weekly in San Francisco. His chief reason for submitting it to that publication was that, having only to travel across the bay from Oakland, a quick decision could be reached. Two weeks later he was overjoyed to see, in the latest number on the news-stand, his story printed in full, illustrated, and in the place of honor. He went home with leaping pulse, wondering how much they would pay him for one of the best things he had done. Also, the celerity with which it had been accepted and published was a pleasant thought to him. That the editor had not informed him of the acceptance made the surprise more complete. After waiting a week, two weeks, and half a week longer, desperation conquered diffidence, and he wrote to the editor of *The Billow*, suggesting that possibly through some negligence of the business manager his little account had been overlooked.

Even if it isn't more than five dollars, Martin thought to himself, it will buy enough beans and pea-soup to enable me to write half a dozen like it, and possibly as good.

Back came a cool letter from the editor that at least elicited Martin's admiration.

"We thank you," it ran, "for your excellent contribution. All of us in the office enjoyed it immensely, and, as you see, it was given the place of honor and immediate publication. We earnestly hope that you liked the illustrations.

"On rereading your letter it seems to us that you are laboring under the misapprehension that we pay for unsolicited manuscripts. This is not our custom, and of course yours was unsolicited. We assumed, naturally, when we received your story, that you understood the situation. We can only deeply regret this unfortunate misunderstanding, and assure you of our unfailing regard. Again, thanking you for your kind contribution, and hoping to receive more from you in the near future, we remain, etc."

There was also a postscript to the effect that though *The Billow* carried no free list, it took great pleasure in sending him a complimentary subscription for the ensuing year.

After that experience, Martin typed at the top of the first sheet of all his manuscripts: "Submitted at your usual rate."

Some day, he consoled himself, they will be submitted at *my* usual rate.

He discovered in himself, at this period, a passion for perfection, under the sway of which he rewrote and polished "The Jostling Street," "The Wine of Life," "Joy," the "Sea Lyrics," and others of his earlier work. As of old, nineteen hours of labor a day was all too little to suit him. He wrote prodigiously, and he read prodigiously, forgetting in his toil the pangs caused by giving up his tobacco. Ruth's promised cure for the habit, flamboyantly labelled, he stowed away in the most inaccessible corner of his bureau. Especially during his stretches of famine he suffered from lack of the weed; but no matter how often he mastered the craving, it remained with him as strong as ever. He regarded it as the biggest thing he had ever achieved. Ruth's point of view was that he was doing no more than was right. She brought him the antitobacco remedy, purchased out of her glove money, and in a few days forgot all about it.

His machine-made storiettes, though he hated them and derided them, were successful. By means of them he redeemed all his pledges, paid most of his bills, and bought a new set of tires for his wheel. The storiettes at least kept the pot a-boiling and gave him time for ambitious work; while the one thing that upheld him was the forty dollars he had received from *The White Mouse.* He anchored his faith to that, and was confident that the really first-class magazines would pay an unknown writer at least an equal rate, if not a better one. But the thing was, how to get into the first-class magazines. His best stories, essays, and poems went begging among them, and yet, each month, he read reams of dull, prosy, inartistic stuff between all their various covers. If only one editor, he sometimes thought, would descend from his high seat of pride to write me one cheering line! No matter if my work is unusual, no matter if it is unfit, for prudential reasons, for their pages, surely there must be some sparks in it, somewhere, a few, to warm them to some sort of appreciation. And thereupon he would get out one or another of his manuscripts, such as "Adventure," and read it over and over in a vain attempt to vindicate the editorial silence.

As the sweet California spring came on, his period of plenty came to an end. For several weeks he had been worried by a strange silence on the part of the newspaper storiette syndicate. Then, one day, came back to him through the mail ten of his immaculate machine-made storiettes. They were accompanied by a brief letter to the effect that the syndicate was overstocked, and that some months would elapse before it would be in the market again for manuscripts. Martin had even been extravagant on the strength of those ten storiettes. Toward the last the syndicate had been paying him five dollars each for them and accepting every one he sent. So he had looked upon the ten as good as sold, and he had lived accordingly, on a basis of fifty dollars in the bank. So it was that he entered abruptly upon a lean period, wherein he continued selling his earlier efforts to publications that would not pay and submitting his later work to magazines that would not buy. Also, he resumed his trips to the pawnbroker down in Oakland. A few jokes and snatches of humorous verse, sold to the New York weeklies, made existence barely possible for him. It was at this time that he wrote letters of inquiry to the several great monthly and quarterly reviews, and learned in reply that they rarely considered unsolicited articles, and that most of their contents were written upon order by well-known specialists who were authorities in their various fields.

XXIX

It was a hard summer for Martin. Manuscript readers and editors were away on vacation, and publications that ordinarily returned a decision in three weeks now retained his manuscript for three months or more. The consolation he drew from it was that a saving in postage was effected by the deadlock. Only the robber-publications seemed to remain actively in business, and to them Martin disposed of all his early efforts, such as "Pearl-diving," "The Sea as a Career," "Turtle-catching," and "The Northeast Trades." For these manuscripts he never received a penny. It is true, after six months' correspondence, he effected a compromise, whereby he received a safety razor for "Turtle-catching," and that *The Acropolis,* having agreed to give him five dollars cash and five yearly subscriptions for "The Northeast Trades," fulfilled the second part of the agreement.

For a sonnet on Stevenson he managed to wring two dollars out of a Boston editor who was running a magazine with a Matthew Arnold taste and a penny-dreadful purse. "The Peri and the Pearl," a clever skit of a poem of two hundred lines, just finished, white hot from his brain, won the heart of the editor of a San Francisco magazine published in the interest of a great railroad. When the editor wrote, offering him payment in transportation, Martin wrote back to inquire if the transportation was transferable. It was not, and so, being prevented from peddling it, he asked for the return of the poem. Back it came, with the editor's regrets, and Martin sent it to San Francisco again, this time to *The Hornet,* a pretentious monthly that had been fanned into a constellation of the first magnitude by the brilliant journalist who founded it. But *The Hornet's* light had begun to dim long before Martin was born. The editor promised Martin fifteen dollars for the poem, but, when it was published, seemed to forget about it. Several of his letters being ignored, Martin indicted an angry one which drew a reply. It was written by a new editor, who coolly informed Martin that he declined to be held responsible for the old editor's mistakes, and that he did not think much of "The Peri and the Pearl" anyway.

But *The Globe,* a Chicago magazine, gave Martin the most cruel treatment of all. He had refrained from offering his "Sea Lyrics" for publication, until driven to it by starvation. After having been rejected by a dozen magazines, they had come to rest in *The Globe* office. There were thirty poems in the collection, and he was to receive a dollar apiece for them. The first month four were published, and he promptly received a check for four dollars; but when he looked over the magazine, he was appalled at the slaughter. In some cases the titles had been altered: "Finis," for instance, being changed to "The Finish," and "The Song of the Outer Reef" to "The Song of the Coral Reef." In one case, an absolutely different title, a misappropriate title, was substituted. In place of his own, "Medusa Lights," the editor had printed, "The Backward Track." But the slaughter in the body of the poems was terrifying. Martin groaned and sweated and thrust his hands through his hair. Phrases, lines, and stanzas were cut out, interchanged, or juggled about in the most incomprehensible manner. Sometimes lines and stanzas not his own were substituted for his. He could not believe that a sane editor could be guilty of such maltreatment, and his favorite hypothesis was that his poems must have been doctored by the office boy or the stenographer. Martin wrote immediately, begging the editor to cease publishing the lyrics and to return them to him. He wrote again and again, begging, entreating, threatening, but his letters were ignored. Month by month the slaughter went on till the thirty poems were published, and month by month he received a check for those which had appeared in the current number.

Despite these various misadventures, the memory of the *White Mouse* forty-dollar check sustained him, though he was driven more and more to hack-work. He discovered a bread-and-butter field in the agricultural weeklies and trade journals, though among the religious weeklies he found he could easily starve. At his lowest ebb, when his black suit was in pawn, he made a ten-strike—or so it seemed to him—in a prize contest arranged by the County Committee of the Republican Party. There were three branches of the contest, and he entered them all, laughing at himself bitterly the while in that he was driven to such straits to live. His poem won the first prize of ten dollars, his campaign song the second prize of five dollars, his essay on the principles of the Republican Party the first prize of twenty-five dollars. Which was very gratifying to him until he tried to collect. Something had gone wrong in the County Committee, and, though a rich banker and a state senator were members of it, the money was not forthcoming. While this affair was hanging fire, he proved that he understood the principles of the Democratic Party by winning the first prize for his essay in a similar contest. And, moreover, he received the money, twenty-five dollars. But the forty dollars won in the first contest he never received.

Driven to shifts in order to see Ruth, and deciding that the long walk from north Oakland to her house and back again consumed too much time, he kept his black suit in pawn in place of his bicycle. The latter gave him exercise, saved him hours of time for work, and enabled him to see Ruth just the same. A pair of knee duck trousers and an old sweater made him a presentable wheel costume, so that he could go with Ruth on afternoon rides. Besides, he no longer had opportunity to see much of her in her own home, where Mrs. Morse was thoroughly prosecuting her campaign of entertainment. The exalted beings he met there, and to whom he had looked up but a short time before, now bored him. They were no longer exalted. He was nervous and irritable, what of his hard times, disappointments, and close application to work, and the conversation of such people was maddening. He was not unduly egotistic. He measured the narrowness of their minds by the minds of the thinkers in the books he read. At Ruth's home he never met a large mind, with the exception of Professor Caldwell, and Caldwell he had met there only once. As for the rest, they were numskulls, ninnies, superficial, dogmatic, and ignorant. It was their ignorance that astounded him. What was the matter with them? What had they done with their educations? They had had access to the same books he had. How did it happen that they had drawn nothing from them?

He knew that the great minds, the deep and rational thinkers, existed. He had his proofs from the books, the books that had educated him beyond the Morse standard. And he knew that higher intellects than those of the Morse circle were to be found in the world. He read English society novels, wherein he caught glimpses of men and women talking politics and philosophy. And he read of salons in great cities, even in the United States, where art and intellect congregated. Foolishly, in the past, he had conceived that all well-groomed persons above the working class were persons with power of intellect and vigor of beauty. Culture and collars had gone together, to him, and he had been deceived into believing that college educations and mastery were the same things.

Well, he would fight his way on and up higher. And he would take Ruth with him. Her he dearly loved, and he was confident that she would shine anywhere. As it was clear to him that he had been handicapped by his early environment, so now he perceived that she was similarly handicapped. She had not had a chance to expand. The books on her father's shelves, the paintings on the walls, the music on the piano—all was just so much meretricious display. To real literature, real painting, real music, the Morses and their kind, were dead. And bigger than such things was life, of which they were densely, hopelessly ignorant. In spite of their Unitarian proclivities and their masks of conservative broadmindedness, they were two generations behind interpretative science: their mental processes were mediaeval, while their thinking on the ultimate data of existence and of the universe struck him as the same metaphysical method that was as young as the youngest race, as old as the cave-man, and older—the same that moved the first Pleistocene ape-man to fear the dark; that moved the first hasty Hebrew savage to incarnate Eve from Adam's rib; that moved Descartes to build an idealistic system of the universe out of the projections of his own puny ego; and that moved the famous British ecclesiastic to denounce evolution in satire so scathing as to win immediate applause and leave his name a notorious scrawl on the page of history.

So Martin thought, and he thought further, till it dawned upon him that the difference between these lawyers, officers, business men, and bank cashiers he had met and the members of the working class he had known was on a par with the difference in the food they ate, clothes they wore, neighborhoods in which they lived. Certainly, in all of them was lacking the something more which he found in himself and in the books. The Morses had shown him the best their social position could produce, and he was not impressed by it. A pauper himself, a slave to the money-lender, he knew himself the superior of those he met at the Morses'; and, when his one decent suit of clothes was out of pawn, he moved among them a lord of life, quivering with a sense of outrage akin to what a prince would suffer if condemned to live with goatherds.

"You hate and fear the socialists," he remarked to Mr. Morse, one evening at dinner; "but why? You know neither them nor their doctrines."

The conversation had been swung in that direction by Mrs. Morse, who had been invidiously singing the praises of Mr. Hapgood. The cashier was Martin's black beast, and his temper was a trifle short where the talker of platitudes was concerned.

"Yes," he had said, "Charley Hapgood is what they call a rising young man—somebody told me as much. And it is true. He'll make the Governor's Chair before he dies, and, who knows? maybe the United States Senate."

"What makes you think so?" Mrs. Morse had inquired.

"I've heard him make a campaign speech. It was so cleverly stupid and unoriginal, and also so convincing, that the leaders cannot help but regard him as safe and sure, while his platitudes are so much like the platitudes of the average voter that—oh, well, you know you flatter any man by dressing up his own thoughts for him and presenting them to him."

"I actually think you are jealous of Mr. Hapgood," Ruth had chimed in.

"Heaven forbid!"

The look of horror on Martin's face stirred Mrs. Morse to belligerence.

"You surely don't mean to say that Mr. Hapgood is stupid?" she demanded icily.

"No more than the average Republican," was the retort, "or average Democrat, either. They are all stupid when they are not crafty, and very few of them are crafty. The only wise Republicans are the millionaires and their conscious henchmen. They know which side their bread is buttered on, and they know why."

"I am a Republican," Mr. Morse put in lightly. "Pray, how do you classify me?"

"Oh, you are an unconscious henchman."

"Henchman?"

"Why, yes. You do corporation work. You have no working-class nor criminal practice. You don't depend upon wife-beaters and pickpockets for your income. You get your livelihood from the masters of society, and whoever feeds a man is that man's master. Yes, you are a henchman. You are interested in advancing the interests of the aggregations of capital you serve."

Mr. Morse's face was a trifle red.

"I confess, sir," he said, "that you talk like a scoundrelly socialist."

Then it was that Martin made his remark:—

"You hate and fear the socialists; but why? You know neither them nor their doctrines."

"Your doctrine certainly sounds like socialism," Mr. Morse replied, while Ruth gazed anxiously from one to the other, and Mrs. Morse beamed happily at the opportunity afforded of rousing her liege lord's antagonism.

"Because I say Republicans are stupid, and hold that liberty, equality, and fraternity are exploded bubbles, does not make me a socialist," Martin said with a smile. "Because I question Jefferson and the unscientific Frenchmen who informed his mind, does not make me a socialist. Believe me, Mr. Morse, you are far nearer socialism than I who am its avowed enemy."

"Now you please to be facetious," was all the other could say.

"Not at all. I speak in all seriousness. You still believe in equality, and yet you do the work of the corporations, and the corporations, from day to day, are busily engaged in burying equality. And you call me a socialist because I deny equality, because I affirm just what you live up to. The Republicans are foes to equality, though most of them fight the battle against equality with the very word itself the slogan on their lips. In the name of equality they destroy equality. That was why I called them stupid. As for myself, I am an individualist. I believe the race is to the swift, the battle to the strong. Such is the lesson I have learned from biology, or at least think I have learned. As I said, I am an individualist, and individualism is the hereditary and eternal foe of socialism."

"But you frequent socialist meetings," Mr. Morse challenged.

"Certainly, just as spies frequent hostile camps. How else are you to learn about the enemy? Besides, I enjoy myself at their meetings. They are good fighters, and, right or wrong, they have read the books. Any one of them knows far more about sociology and all the other ologies than the average captain of industry. Yes, I have been to half a dozen of their meetings, but that doesn't make me a socialist any more than hearing Charley Hapgood orate made me a Republican."

"I can't help it," Mr. Morse said feebly, "but I still believe you incline that way."

Bless me, Martin thought to himself, he doesn't know what I was talking about. He hasn't understood a word of it. What did he do with his education, anyway?

Thus, in his development, Martin found himself face to face with economic morality, or the morality of class; and soon it became to him a grisly monster. Personally, he was an intellectual moralist, and more offending to him than platitudinous pomposity was the morality of those about him, which was a curious hotchpotch of the economic, the metaphysical, the sentimental, and the imitative.

A sample of this curious messy mixture he encountered nearer home. His sister Marian had been keeping company with an industrious young mechanic, of German extraction, who, after thoroughly learning the trade, had set up for himself in a bicycle-repair shop. Also, having got the agency for a low-grade make of wheel, he was prosperous. Marian had called on Martin in his room a short time before to announce her engagement, during which visit she had playfully inspected Martin's palm and told his fortune. On her next visit she brought Hermann von Schmidt along with her. Martin did the honors and congratulated both of them in language so easy and graceful as to affect disagreeably the peasant-mind of his sister's lover. This bad impression was further heightened by Martin's reading aloud the half-dozen stanzas of verse with which he had commemorated Marian's previous visit. It was a bit of society verse, airy and delicate, which he had named "The Palmist." He was surprised, when he finished reading it, to note no enjoyment in his sister's face. Instead, her eyes were fixed anxiously upon her betrothed, and Martin, following her gaze, saw spread on that worthy's asymmetrical features nothing but black and sullen disapproval. The incident passed over, they made an early departure, and Martin forgot all about it, though for the moment he had been puzzled that any woman, even of the working class, should not have been flattered and delighted by having poetry written about her.

Several evenings later Marian again visited him, this time alone. Nor did she waste time in coming to the point, upbraiding him sorrowfully for what he had done.

"Why, Marian," he chided, "you talk as though you were ashamed of your relatives, or of your brother at any rate."

"And I am, too," she blurted out.

Martin was bewildered by the tears of mortification he saw in her eyes. The mood, whatever it was, was genuine.

"But, Marian, why should your Hermann be jealous of my writing poetry about my own sister?"

"He ain't jealous," she sobbed. "He says it was indecent, ob—obscene."

Martin emitted a long, low whistle of incredulity, then proceeded to resurrect and read a carbon copy of "The Palmist."

"I can't see it," he said finally, proffering the manuscript to her. "Read it yourself and show me whatever strikes you as obscene—that was the word, wasn't it?"

"He says so, and he ought to know," was the answer, with a wave aside of the manuscript, accompanied by a look of loathing. "And he says you've got to tear it up. He says he won't have no wife of his with such things written about her which anybody can read. He says it's a disgrace, an' he won't stand for it."

"Now, look here, Marian, this is nothing but nonsense," Martin began; then abruptly changed his mind.

He saw before him an unhappy girl, knew the futility of attempting to convince her husband or her, and, though the whole situation was absurd and preposterous, he resolved to surrender.

"All right," he announced, tearing the manuscript into half a dozen pieces and throwing it into the waste-basket.

He contented himself with the knowledge that even then the original typewritten manuscript was reposing in the office of a New York magazine. Marian and her husband would never know, and neither himself nor they nor the world would lose if the pretty, harmless poem ever were published.

Marian, starting to reach into the waste-basket, refrained.

"Can I?" she pleaded.

He nodded his head, regarding her thoughtfully as she gathered the torn pieces of manuscript and tucked them into the pocket of her jacket—ocular evidence of the success of her mission. She reminded him of Lizzie Connolly, though there was less of fire and gorgeous flaunting life in her than in that other girl of the working class whom he had seen twice. But they were on a par, the pair of them, in dress and carriage, and he smiled with inward amusement at the caprice of his fancy which suggested the appearance of either of them in Mrs. Morse's drawing-room. The amusement faded, and he was aware of a great loneliness. This sister of his and the Morse drawing-room were milestones of the road he had travelled. And he had left them behind. He glanced affectionately about him at his few books. They were all the comrades left to him.

"Hello, what's that?" he demanded in startled surprise.

Marian repeated her question.

"Why don't I go to work?" He broke into a laugh that was only half-hearted. "That Hermann of yours has been talking to you."

She shook her head.

"Don't lie," he commanded, and the nod of her head affirmed his charge.

"Well, you tell that Hermann of yours to mind his own business; that when I write poetry about the girl he's keeping company with it's his business, but that outside of that he's got no say so. Understand?

"So you don't think I'll succeed as a writer, eh?" he went on. "You think I'm no good?—that I've fallen down and am a disgrace to the family?"

"I think it would be much better if you got a job," she said firmly, and he saw she was sincere. "Hermann says—"

"Damn Hermann!" he broke out good-naturedly. "What I want to know is when you're going to get married. Also, you find out from your Hermann if he will deign to permit you to accept a wedding present from me."

He mused over the incident after she had gone, and once or twice broke out into laughter that was bitter as he saw his sister and her betrothed, all the members of his own class and the members of Ruth's class, directing their narrow little lives by narrow little formulas—herd-creatures, flocking together and patterning their lives by one another's opinions, failing of being individuals and of really living life because of the childlike formulas by which they were enslaved. He summoned them before him in apparitional procession: Bernard Higginbotham arm in arm with Mr. Butler, Hermann von Schmidt cheek by jowl with Charley Hapgood, and one by one and in pairs he judged them and dismissed them—judged them by the standards of intellect and morality he had learned from the books. Vainly he asked: Where are the great souls, the great men and women? He found them not among the careless, gross, and stupid intelligences that answered the call of vision to his narrow room. He felt a loathing for them such as Circe must have felt for her swine. When he had dismissed the last one and thought himself alone, a late-comer entered, unexpected and unsummoned. Martin watched him and saw the stiff-rim, the square-cut, double-breasted coat and the swaggering shoulders, of the youthful hoodlum who had once been he.

"You were like all the rest, young fellow," Martin sneered. "Your morality and your knowledge were just the same as theirs. You did not think and act for yourself. Your opinions, like your clothes, were ready made; your acts were shaped by popular approval. You were cock of your gang because others acclaimed you the real thing. You fought and ruled the gang, not because you liked to—you know you really despised it,

—but because the other fellows patted you on the shoulder. You licked Cheese-Face because you wouldn't give in, and you wouldn't give in partly because you were abysmal brute and for the rest because you believed what every one about you believed, that the measure of manhood was the carnivorous ferocity displayed in injuring and marring fellow-creatures' anatomies. Why, you whelp, you even won other fellows' girls away from them, not because you wanted the girls, but because in the marrow of those about you, those who set your moral pace, was the instinct of the wild stallion and the bull-seal. Well, the years have passed, and what do you think about it now?"

As if in reply, the vision underwent a swift metamorphosis. The stiff-rim and the square-cut vanished, being replaced by milder garments; the toughness went out of the face, the hardness out of the eyes; and the face, chastened and refined, was irradiated from an inner life of communion with beauty and knowledge. The apparition was very like his present self, and, as he regarded it, he noted the student-lamp by which it was illuminated, and the book over which it pored. He glanced at the title and read, "The Science of AEsthetics." Next, he entered into the apparition, trimmed the student-lamp, and himself went on reading "The Science of AEsthetics."

XXX

ON a beautiful fall day, a day of similar Indian summer to that which had seen their love declared the year before, Martin read his "Love-cycle" to Ruth. It was in the afternoon, and, as before, they had ridden out to their favorite knoll in the hills. Now and again she had interrupted his reading with exclamations of pleasure, and now, as he laid the last sheet of manuscript with its fellows, he waited her judgment.

She delayed to speak, and at last she spoke haltingly, hesitating to frame in words the harshness of her thought.

"I think they are beautiful, very beautiful," she said; "but you can't sell them, can you? You see what I mean," she said, almost pleaded. "This writing of yours is not practical. Something is the matter—maybe it is with the market—that prevents you from earning a living by it. And please, dear, don't misunderstand me. I am flattered, and made proud, and all that—I could not be a true woman were it otherwise—that you should write these poems to me. But they do not make our marriage possible. Don't you see, Martin? Don't think me mercenary. It is love, the thought of our future, with which I am burdened. A whole year has gone by since we learned we loved each other, and our wedding day is no nearer. Don't think me immodest in thus talking about our wedding, for really I have my heart, all that I am, at stake. Why don't you try to get work on a newspaper, if you are so bound up in your writing? Why not become a reporter?—for a while, at least?"

"It would spoil my style," was his answer, in a low, monotonous voice. "You have no idea how I've worked for style."

"But those storiettes," she argued. "You called them hack-work. You wrote many of them. Didn't they spoil your style?"

"No, the cases are different. The storiettes were ground out, jaded, at the end of a long day of application to style. But a reporter's work is all hack from morning till night, is the one paramount thing of life. And it is a whirlwind life, the life of the moment, with neither past nor future, and certainly without thought of any style but reportorial style, and that certainly is not literature. To become a reporter now, just as my style is taking form, crystallizing, would be to commit literary suicide. As it is, every storiette, every word of every storiette, was a violation of myself, of my self-respect, of my respect for beauty. I tell you it was sickening. I was guilty of sin. And I was secretly glad when the markets failed, even if my clothes did go into pawn. But the joy of writing the 'Love-cycle'! The creative joy in its noblest form! That was compensation for everything."

Martin did not know that Ruth was unsympathetic concerning the creative joy. She used the phrase—it was on her lips he had first heard it. She had read about it, studied about it, in the university in the course of earning her Bachelorship of Arts; but she was not original, not creative, and all manifestations of culture on her part were but harpings of the harpings of others.

"May not the editor have been right in his revision of your 'Sea Lyrics'?" she questioned. "Remember, an editor must have proved qualifications or else he would not be an editor."

"That's in line with the persistence of the established," he rejoined, his heat against the editor-folk getting the better of him. "What is, is not only right, but is the best possible. The existence of anything is sufficient vindication of its fitness to exist—to exist, mark you, as the average person unconsciously believes, not merely in present conditions, but in all conditions. It is their ignorance, of course, that makes them believe such rot—their ignorance, which is nothing more nor less than the henidical mental process described by Weininger. They think they think, and such thinkless creatures are the arbiters of the lives of the few who really think."

He paused, overcome by the consciousness that he had been talking over Ruth's head.

"I'm sure I don't know who this Weininger is," she retorted. "And you are so dreadfully general that I fail to follow you. What I was speaking of was the qualification of editors—"

"And I'll tell you," he interrupted. "The chief qualification of ninety-nine per cent of all editors is failure. They have failed as writers. Don't think they prefer the drudgery of the desk and the slavery to their circulation and to the business manager to the joy of writing. They have tried to write, and they have failed. And right there is the cursed paradox of it. Every portal to success in literature is guarded by those watch-dogs, the failures in literature. The editors, sub-editors, associate editors, most of them, and the manuscript-readers for the magazines and book-publishers, most of them, nearly all of them, are men who wanted to write and who have failed. And yet they, of all creatures under the sun the most unfit, are the very creatures who decide what shall and what shall not find its way into print—they, who have proved themselves not original, who have demonstrated that they lack the divine fire, sit in judgment upon originality and genius. And after them come the reviewers, just so many more failures. Don't tell me that they have not dreamed the dream and attempted to write poetry or fiction; for they have, and they have failed. Why, the average review is more nauseating than cod-liver oil. But you know my opinion on the reviewers and the alleged critics. There are great critics, but they are as rare as comets. If I fail as a writer, I shall have proved for the career of editorship. There's bread and butter and jam, at any rate."

Ruth's mind was quick, and her disapproval of her lover's views was buttressed by the contradiction she found in his contention.

"But, Martin, if that be so, if all the doors are closed as you have shown so conclusively, how is it possible that any of the great writers ever arrived?"

"They arrived by achieving the impossible," he answered. "They did such blazing, glorious work as to burn to ashes those that opposed them. They arrived by course of miracle, by winning a thousand-to-one wager against them. They arrived because they were Carlyle's battle-scarred giants who will not be kept down. And that is what I must do; I must achieve the impossible."

"But if you fail? You must consider me as well, Martin."

"If I fail?" He regarded her for a moment as though the thought she had uttered was unthinkable. Then intelligence illumined his eyes. "If I fail, I shall become an editor, and you will be an editor's wife."

She frowned at his facetiousness—a pretty, adorable frown that made him put his arm around her and kiss it away.

"There, that's enough," she urged, by an effort of will withdrawing herself from the fascination of his strength. "I have talked with father and mother. I never before asserted myself so against them. I demanded to be heard. I was very undutiful. They are against you, you know; but I assured them over and over of my abiding love for you, and at last father agreed that if you wanted to, you could begin right away in his office. And then, of his own accord, he said he would pay you enough at the start so that we could get married and have a little cottage somewhere. Which I think was very fine of him—don't you?"

Martin, with the dull pain of despair at his heart, mechanically reaching for the tobacco and paper (which he no longer carried) to roll a cigarette, muttered something inarticulate, and Ruth went on.

"Frankly, though, and don't let it hurt you—I tell you, to show you precisely how you stand with him—he doesn't like your radical views, and he thinks you are lazy. Of course I know you are not. I know you work hard."

How hard, even she did not know, was the thought in Martin's mind.

"Well, then," he said, "how about my views? Do you think they are so radical?"

He held her eyes and waited the answer.

"I think them, well, very disconcerting," she replied.

The question was answered for him, and so oppressed was he by the grayness of life that he forgot the tentative proposition she had made for him to go to work. And she, having gone as far as she dared, was willing to wait the answer till she should bring the question up again.

She had not long to wait. Martin had a question of his own to propound to her. He wanted to ascertain the measure of her faith in him, and within the week each was answered. Martin precipitated it by reading to her his "The Shame of the Sun."

"Why don't you become a reporter?" she asked when he had finished. "You love writing so, and I am sure you would succeed. You could rise in journalism and make a name for yourself. There are a number of great special correspondents. Their salaries are large, and their field is the world. They are sent everywhere, to the heart of Africa, like Stanley, or to interview the Pope, or to explore unknown Thibet."

"Then you don't like my essay?" he rejoined. "You believe that I have some show in journalism but none in literature?"

"No, no; I do like it. It reads well. But I am afraid it's over the heads of your readers. At least it is over mine. It sounds beautiful, but I don't understand it. Your scientific slang is beyond me. You are an extremist, you know, dear, and what may be intelligible to you may not be intelligible to the rest of us."

"I imagine it's the philosophic slang that bothers you," was all he could say.

He was flaming from the fresh reading of the ripest thought he had expressed, and her verdict stunned him.

"No matter how poorly it is done," he persisted, "don't you see anything in it?—in the thought of it, I mean?"

She shook her head.

"No, it is so different from anything I have read. I read Maeterlinck and understand him—"

"His mysticism, you understand that?" Martin flashed out.

"Yes, but this of yours, which is supposed to be an attack upon him, I don't understand. Of course, if originality counts—"

He stopped her with an impatient gesture that was not followed by speech. He became suddenly aware that she was speaking and that she had been speaking for some time.

"After all, your writing has been a toy to you," she was saying. "Surely you have played with it long enough. It is time to take up life seriously—*our* life, Martin. Hitherto you have lived solely your own."

"You want me to go to work?" he asked.

"Yes. Father has offered—"

"I understand all that," he broke in; "but what I want to know is whether or not you have lost faith in me?"

She pressed his hand mutely, her eyes dim.

"In your writing, dear," she admitted in a half-whisper.

"You've read lots of my stuff," he went on brutally. "What do you think of it? Is it utterly hopeless? How does it compare with other men's work?"

"But they sell theirs, and you—don't."

"That doesn't answer my question. Do you think that literature is not at all my vocation?"

"Then I will answer." She steeled herself to do it. "I don't think you were made to write. Forgive me, dear. You compel me to say it; and you know I know more about literature than you do."

"Yes, you are a Bachelor of Arts," he said meditatively; "and you ought to know."

"But there is more to be said," he continued, after a pause painful to both. "I know what I have in me. No one knows that so well as I. I know I shall succeed. I will not be kept down. I am afire with what I have to say in verse, and fiction, and essay. I do not ask you to have faith in that, though. I do not ask you to have faith in me, nor in my writing. What I do ask of you is to love me and have faith in love.

"A year ago I begged for two years. One of those years is yet to run. And I do believe, upon my honor and my soul, that before that year is run I shall have succeeded. You remember what you told me long ago, that I must serve my apprenticeship to writing. Well, I have served it. I have crammed it and telescoped it. With you at the end awaiting me, I have never shirked. Do you know, I have forgotten what it is to fall peacefully asleep. A few million years ago I knew what it was to sleep my fill and to awake naturally from very glut of sleep. I am awakened always now by an alarm clock. If I fall asleep early or late, I set the alarm accordingly; and this, and the putting out of the lamp, are my last conscious actions.

"When I begin to feel drowsy, I change the heavy book I am reading for a lighter one. And when I doze over that, I beat my head with my knuckles in order to drive sleep away. Somewhere I read of a man who was afraid to sleep. Kipling wrote the story. This man arranged a spur so that when unconsciousness came, his naked body pressed against the iron teeth. Well, I've done the same. I look at the time, and I resolve that not until midnight, or not until one o'clock, or two o'clock, or three o'clock, shall the spur be removed. And so it rowels me awake until the appointed time. That spur has been my bed-mate for months. I have grown so desperate that five and a half hours of sleep is an extravagance. I sleep four hours now. I am starved for sleep. There are times when I am light-headed from want of sleep, times when death, with its rest and sleep, is a positive lure to me, times when I am haunted by Longfellow's lines:—

" 'The sea is still and deep;
All things within its bosom sleep;
A single step and all is o'er,
A plunge, a bubble, and no more.'

"Of course, this is sheer nonsense. It comes from nervousness, from an overwrought mind. But the point is: Why have I done this? For you. To shorten my apprenticeship. To compel Success to hasten. And my apprenticeship is now served. I know my equipment. I swear that I learn more each month than the average college man learns in a year. I know it, I tell you. But were my need for you to understand not so desperate I should not tell you. It is not boasting. I measure the results by the books. Your brothers, to-day, are ignorant barbarians compared with me and the knowledge I have wrung from the books in the hours they were sleeping. Long ago I wanted to be famous. I care very little for fame now. What I want is you; I am more hungry for you than for food, or clothing, or recognition. I have a dream of laying my head on your breast and sleeping an aeon or so, and the dream will come true ere another year is gone."

His power beat against her, wave upon wave; and in the moment his will opposed hers most she felt herself most strongly drawn toward him. The strength that had always poured out from him to her was now flowering in his impassioned voice, his flashing eyes, and the vigor of life and intellect surging in him. And in that moment, and for the moment, she was aware of a rift that showed in her certitude—a rift through which she caught sight of the real Martin Eden, splendid and invincible; and as animal-trainers have their moments of doubt, so she, for the instant, seemed to doubt her power to tame this wild spirit of a man.

"And another thing," he swept on. "You love me. But why do you love me? The thing in me that compels me to write is the very thing that draws your love. You love me because I am somehow different from the men you have known and might have loved. I was not made for the desk and counting-house, for petty business squabbling and legal jangling. Make me do such things, make me like those other men, doing the work they do, breathing the air they breathe, developing the point of view they have developed, and you have destroyed the difference, destroyed me, destroyed the thing you love. My desire to write is the most vital thing in me. Had I been a mere clod, neither would I have desired to write, nor would you have desired me for a husband."

"But you forget," she interrupted, the quick surface of her mind glimpsing a parallel. "There have been eccentric inventors, starving their families while they sought such chimeras as perpetual motion. Doubtless their wives loved them, and suffered with them and for them, not because of but in spite of their infatuation for perpetual motion."

"True," was the reply. "But there have been inventors who were not eccentric and who starved while they sought to invent practical things; and sometimes, it is recorded, they succeeded. Certainly I do not seek any impossibilities—"

"You have called it 'achieving the impossible,' " she interpolated.

"I spoke figuratively. I seek to do what men have done before me—to write and to live by my writing."

Her silence spurred him on.

"To you, then, my goal is as much a chimera as perpetual motion?" he demanded.

He read her answer in the pressure of her hand on his—the pitying mother-hand for the hurt child. And to her, just then, he was the hurt child, the infatuated man striving to achieve the impossible.

Toward the close of their talk she warned him again of the antagonism of her father and mother.

"But you love me?" he asked.

"I do! I do!" she cried.

"And I love you, not them, and nothing they do can hurt me." Triumph sounded in his voice. "For I have faith in your love, not fear of their enmity. All things may go astray in this world, but not love. Love cannot go wrong unless it be a weakling that faints and stumbles by the way."

XXXI

MARTIN had encountered his sister Gertrude by chance on Broadway—as it proved, a most propitious yet disconcerting chance. Waiting on the corner for a car, she had seen him first, and noted the eager, hungry lines of his face and the desperate, worried look of his eyes. In truth, he was desperate and worried. He had just come from a fruitless interview with the pawnbroker, from whom he had tried to wring an additional loan on his wheel. The muddy fall weather having come on, Martin had pledged his wheel some time since and retained his black suit.

"There's the black suit," the pawnbroker, who knew his every asset, had answered. "You needn't tell me you've gone and pledged it with that Jew, Lipka. Because if you have—"

The man had looked the threat, and Martin hastened to cry:—

"No, no; I've got it. But I want to wear it on a matter of business."

"All right," the mollified usurer had replied. "And I want it on a matter of business before I can let you have any more money. You don't think I'm in it for my health?"

"But it's a forty-dollar wheel, in good condition," Martin had argued. "And you've only let me have seven dollars on it. No, not even seven. Six and a quarter; you took the interest in advance."

"If you want some more, bring the suit," had been the reply that sent Martin out of the stuffy little den, so desperate at heart as to reflect it in his face and touch his sister to pity.

Scarcely had they met when the Telegraph Avenue car came along and stopped to take on a crowd of afternoon shoppers. Mrs. Higginbotham divined from the grip on her arm as he helped her on, that he was not going to follow her. She turned on the step and looked down upon him. His haggard face smote her to the heart again.

"Ain't you comin'?" she asked.

The next moment she had descended to his side.

"I'm walking—exercise, you know," he explained.

"Then I'll go along for a few blocks," she announced. "Mebbe it'll do me good. I ain't ben feelin' any too spry these last few days."

Martin glanced at her and verified her statement in her general slovenly appearance, in the unhealthy fat, in the drooping shoulders, the tired face with the sagging lines, and in the heavy fall of her feet, without elasticity—a very caricature of the walk that belongs to a free and happy body.

"You'd better stop here," he said, though she had already come to a halt at the first corner, "and take the next car."

"My goodness!—if I ain't all tired a'ready!" she panted. "But I'm just as able to walk as you in them soles. They're that thin they'll bu'st long before you git out to North Oakland."

"I've a better pair at home," was the answer.

"Come out to dinner to-morrow," she invited irrelevantly. "Mr. Higginbotham won't be there. He's goin' to San Leandro on business."

Martin shook his head, but he had failed to keep back the wolfish, hungry look that leapt into his eyes at the suggestion of dinner.

"You haven't a penny, Mart, and that's why you're walkin'. Exercise!" She tried to sniff contemptuously, but succeeded in producing only a sniffle. "Here, lemme see."

And, fumbling in her satchel, she pressed a five-dollar piece into his hand. "I guess I forgot your last birthday, Mart," she mumbled lamely.

Martin's hand instinctively closed on the piece of gold. In the same instant he knew he ought not to accept, and found himself struggling in the throes of indecision. That bit of gold meant food, life, and light in his body and brain, power to go on writing, and—who was to say?—maybe to write something that would bring in many pieces of gold. Clear on his vision burned the manuscripts of two essays he had just completed. He saw them under the table on top of the heap of returned manuscripts for which he had no stamps, and he saw their titles, just as he had typed them—"The High Priests of Mystery," and "The Cradle of Beauty." He had never submitted them anywhere. They were as good as anything he had done in that line. If only he had stamps for them! Then the certitude of his ultimate success rose up in him, an able ally of hunger, and with a quick movement he slipped the coin into his pocket.

"I'll pay you back, Gertrude, a hundred times over," he gulped out, his throat painfully contracted and in his eyes a swift hint of moisture.

"Mark my words!" he cried with abrupt positiveness. "Before the year is out I'll put an even hundred of those little yellow-boys into your hand. I don't ask you to believe me. All you have to do is wait and see."

Nor did she believe. Her incredulity made her uncomfortable, and failing of other expedient, she said:—

"I know you're hungry, Mart. It's sticking out all over you. Come in to meals any time. I'll send one of the children to tell you when Mr. Higginbotham ain't to be there. An' Mart—"

He waited, though he knew in his secret heart what she was about to say, so visible was her thought process to him.

"Don't you think it's about time you got a job?"

"You don't think I'll win out?" he asked.

She shook her head.

"Nobody has faith in me, Gertrude, except myself." His voice was passionately rebellious. "I've done good work already, plenty of it, and sooner or later it will sell."

"How do you know it is good?"

"Because—" He faltered as the whole vast field of literature and the history of literature stirred in his brain and pointed the futility of his attempting to convey to her the reasons for his faith. "Well, because it's better than ninety-nine per cent of what is published in the magazines."

"I wish't you'd listen to reason," she answered feebly, but with unwavering belief in the correctness of her diagnosis of what was ailing him. "I wish't you'd listen to reason," she repeated, "an' come to dinner to-morrow."

After Martin had helped her on the car, he hurried to the post-office and invested three of the five dollars in stamps; and when, later in the day, on the way to the Morse home, he stopped in at the post-office to weigh a large number of long, bulky envelopes, he affixed to them all the stamps save three of the two-cent denomination.

It proved a momentous night for Martin, for after dinner he met Russ Brissenden. How he chanced to come there, whose friend he was or what acquaintance brought him, Martin did not know. Nor had he the curiosity to inquire about him of Ruth. In short, Brissenden struck Martin as anaemic and feather-brained, and was promptly dismissed from his mind. An hour later he decided that Brissenden was a boor as well, what of the way he prowled about from one room to another, staring at the pictures or poking his nose into books and magazines he picked up from the table or drew from the shelves. Though a stranger in the house he finally isolated himself in the midst of the company, huddling into a capacious Morris chair and reading steadily from a thin volume he had drawn from his pocket. As he read, he abstractedly ran his fingers, with a caressing movement, through his hair. Martin noticed him no more that evening, except once when he observed him chaffing with great apparent success with several of the young women.

It chanced that when Martin was leaving, he overtook Brissenden already half down the walk to the street.

"Hello, is that you?" Martin said.

The other replied with an ungracious grunt, but swung alongside. Martin made no further attempt at conversation, and for several blocks unbroken silence lay upon them.

"Pompous old ass!"

The suddenness and the virulence of the exclamation startled Martin. He felt amused, and at the same time was aware of a growing dislike for the other.

"What do you go to such a place for?" was abruptly flung at him after another block of silence.

"Why do you?" Martin countered.

"Bless me, I don't know," came back. "At least this is my first indiscretion. There are twenty-four hours in each day, and I must spend them somehow. Come and have a drink."

"All right," Martin answered.

The next moment he was nonplussed by the readiness of his acceptance. At home was several hours' hack-work waiting for him before he went to bed, and after he went to bed there was a volume of Weismann waiting for him, to say nothing of Herbert Spencer's Autobiography, which was as replete for him with romance as any thrilling novel. Why should he waste any time with this man he did not like? was his thought. And yet, it was not so much the man nor the drink as was it what was associated with the drink—the bright lights, the mirrors and dazzling array of glasses, the warm and glowing faces and the resonant hum of the voices of men. That was it, it was the voices of men, optimistic men, men who breathed success and spent their money for drinks like men. He was lonely, that was what was the matter with him; that was why he had snapped at the invitation as a bonita strikes at a white rag on a hook. Not since with Joe, at Shelly Hot Springs, with the one exception of the wine he took with the Portuguese grocer, had Martin had a drink at a public bar. Mental exhaustion did not produce a craving for liquor such as physical exhaustion did, and he had felt no need for it. But just now he felt desire for the drink, or, rather, for the atmosphere wherein drinks were dispensed and disposed of. Such a place was the Grotto, where Brissenden and he lounged in capacious leather chairs and drank Scotch and soda.

They talked. They talked about many things, and now Brissenden and now Martin took turn in ordering Scotch and soda. Martin, who was extremely strong-headed, marvelled at the other's capacity for liquor, and ever and anon broke off to marvel at the other's conversation. He was not long in assuming that Brissenden knew everything, and in deciding that here was the second intellectual man he had met. But he noted that Brissenden had what Professor Caldwell lacked—namely, fire, the flashing insight and perception, the flaming uncontrol of genius. Living language flowed from him. His thin lips, like the dies of a machine, stamped out phrases that cut and stung; or again, pursing caressingly about the inchoate sound they articulated, the thin lips shaped soft and velvety things, mellow phrases of glow and glory, of haunting beauty, reverberant of the mystery and inscrutableness of life; and yet again the thin lips were like a bugle, from which rang the crash and tumult of cosmic strife, phrases that sounded clear as silver, that were luminous as starry spaces, that epitomized the final word of science and yet said something more—the poet's word, the transcendental truth, elusive and without words which could express, and which none the less found expression in the subtle and all but ungraspable connotations of common words. He, by some wonder of vision, saw beyond the farthest outpost of empiricism, where was no language for narration, and yet, by some golden miracle of speech, investing known words with unknown significances, he conveyed to Martin's consciousness messages that were incommunicable to ordinary souls.

Martin forgot his first impression of dislike. Here was the best the books had to offer coming true. Here was an intelligence, a living man for him to look up to. "I am down in the dirt at your feet," Martin repeated to himself again and again.

"You've studied biology," he said aloud, in significant allusion.

To his surprise Brissenden shook his head.

"But you are stating truths that are substantiated only by biology," Martin insisted, and was rewarded by a blank stare. "Your conclusions are in line with the books which you must have read."

"I am glad to hear it," was the answer. "That my smattering of knowledge should enable me to short-cut my way to truth is most reassuring. As for myself, I never bother to find out if I am right or not. It is all valueless anyway. Man can never know the ultimate verities."

"You are a disciple of Spencer!" Martin cried triumphantly.

"I haven't read him since adolescence, and all I read then was his 'Education.' "

"I wish I could gather knowledge as carelessly," Martin broke out half an hour later. He had been closely analyzing Brissenden's mental equipment. "You are a sheer dogmatist, and that's what makes it so marvellous. You state dogmatically the latest facts which science has been able to establish only by *à posteriori* reasoning. You jump at correct conclusions. You certainly short-cut with a vengeance. You feel your way with the speed of light, by some hyperrational process, to truth."

"Yes, that was what used to bother Father Joseph, and Brother Dutton," Brissenden replied. "Oh, no," he added; "I am not anything. It was a lucky trick of fate that sent me to a Catholic college for my education. Where did you pick up what you know?"

And while Martin told him, he was busy studying Brissenden, ranging from his long, lean, aristocratic face and drooping shoulders to the overcoat on a neighboring chair, its pockets sagged and bulged by the freightage of many books. Brissenden's face and long, slender hands were browned by the sun—excessively browned, Martin thought. This sunburn bothered Martin. It was patent that Brissenden was no outdoor man. Then how had he been ravaged by the sun? Something morbid and significant attached to that sunburn, was Martin's thought as he returned to a study of the face, narrow, with high cheek-bones and cavernous hollows, and graced with as delicate and fine an aquiline nose as Martin had ever seen. There was nothing remarkable about the size of the eyes. They were neither large nor small, while their color was a nondescript brown; but in them smouldered a fire, or, rather, lurked an expression dual and strangely contradictory. Defiant, indomitable, even harsh to excess, they at the same time aroused pity. Martin found himself pitying him he knew not why, though he was soon to learn.

"Oh, I'm a lunger," Brissenden announced, offhand, a little later, having already stated that he came from Arizona. "I've been down there a couple of years living on the climate."

"Aren't you afraid to venture it up in this climate?"

"Afraid?"

There was no special emphasis of his repetition of Martin's word. But Martin saw in that ascetic face the advertisement that there was nothing of which it was afraid. The eyes had narrowed till they were eagle-like, and Martin almost caught his breath as he noted the eagle beak with its dilated nostrils, defiant, assertive, aggressive. Magnificent, was what he commented to himself, his blood thrilling at the sight. Aloud, he quoted:—

" 'Under the bludgeoning of Chance
My head is bloody but unbowed.' "

"You like Henley," Brissenden said, his expression changing swiftly to large graciousness and tenderness. "Of course, I couldn't have expected anything else of you. Ah, Henley! A brave soul. He stands out among contemporary rhymesters—magazine rhymesters—as a gladiator stands out in the midst of a band of eunuchs."

"You don't like the magazines," Martin softly impeached.

"Do you?" was snarled back at him so savagely as to startle him.

"I—I write, or, rather, try to write, for the magazines," Martin faltered.

"That's better," was the mollified rejoinder. "You try to write, but you don't succeed. I respect and admire your failure. I know what you write. I can see it with half an eye, and there's one ingredient in it that shuts it out of the magazines. It's guts, and magazines have no use for that particular commodity. What they want is wish-wash and slush, and God knows they get it, but not from you."

"I'm not above hack-work," Martin contended.

"On the contrary—" Brissenden paused and ran an insolent eye over Martin's objective poverty, passing from the well-worn tie and the saw-edged collar to the shiny sleeves of the coat and on to the slight fray of one cuff, winding up and dwelling upon Martin's sunken cheeks. "On the contrary, hack-work is above you, so far above you that you can never hope to rise to it. Why, man, I could insult you by asking you to have something to eat."

Martin felt the heat in his face of the involuntary blood, and Brissenden laughed triumphantly.

"A full man is not insulted by such an invitation," he concluded.

"You are a devil," Martin cried irritably.

"Anyway, I didn't ask you."

"You didn't dare."

"Oh, I don't know about that. I invite you now."

Brissenden half rose from his chair as he spoke, as if with the intention of departing to the restaurant forthwith.

Martin's fists were tight-clenched, and his blood was drumming in his temples.

"Bosco! He eats 'em alive! Eats 'em alive!" Brissenden exclaimed, imitating the *spieler* of a locally famous snake-eater.

"I could certainly eat you alive," Martin said, in turn running insolent eyes over the other's disease-ravaged frame.

"Only I'm not worthy of it?"

"On the contrary," Martin considered, "because the incident is not worthy." He broke into a laugh, hearty and wholesome. "I confess you made a fool of me, Brissenden. That I am hungry and you are aware of it are only ordinary phenomena, and there's no disgrace. You see, I laugh at the conventional little moralities of the herd; then you drift by, say a sharp, true word, and immediately I am the slave of the same little moralities."

"You were insulted," Brissenden affirmed.

"I certainly was, a moment ago. The prejudice of early youth, you know. I learned such things then, and they cheapen what I have since learned. They are the skeletons in my particular closet."

"But you've got the door shut on them now?"

"I certainly have."

"Sure?"

"Sure."

"Then let's go and get something to eat."

"I'll go you," Martin answered, attempting to pay for the current Scotch and soda with the last change from his two dollars and seeing the waiter bullied by Brissenden into putting that change back on the table.

Martin pocketed it with a grimace, and felt for a moment the kindly weight of Brissenden's hand upon his shoulder.

XXXII

Promptly, the next afternoon, Maria was excited by Martin's second visitor. But she did not lose her head this time, for she seated Brissenden in her parlor's grandeur of respectability.

"Hope you don't mind my coming?" Brissenden began.

"No, no, not at all," Martin answered, shaking hands and waving him to the solitary chair, himself taking to the bed. "But how did you know where I lived?"

"Called up the Morses. Miss Morse answered the 'phone. And here I am." He tugged at his coat pocket and flung a thin volume on the table. "There's a book, by a poet. Read it and keep it." And then, in reply to Martin's protest: "What have I to do with books? I had another hemorrhage this morning. Got any whiskey? No, of course not. Wait a minute."

He was off and away. Martin watched his long figure go down the outside steps, and, on turning to close the gate, noted with a pang the shoulders, which had once been broad, drawn in now over the collapsed ruin of the chest. Martin got two tumblers, and fell to reading the book of verse, Henry Vaughn Marlow's latest collection.

"No Scotch," Brissenden announced on his return. "The beggar sells nothing but American whiskey. But here's a quart of it."

"I'll send one of the youngsters for lemons, and we'll make a toddy," Martin offered.

"I wonder what a book like that will earn Marlow?" he went on, holding up the volume in question.

"Possibly fifty dollars," came the answer. "Though he's lucky if he pulls even on it, or if he can inveigle a publisher to risk bringing it out."

"Then one can't make a living out of poetry?"

Martin's tone and face alike showed his dejection.

"Certainly not. What fool expects to? Out of rhyming, yes. There's Bruce, and Virginia Spring, and Sedgwick. They do very nicely. But poetry—do you know how Vaughn Marlow makes his living?—teaching in a boys' cramming-joint down in Pennsylvania, and of all private little hells such a billet is the limit. I wouldn't trade places with him if he had fifty years of life before him. And yet his work stands out from the ruck of the contemporary versifiers as a balas ruby among carrots. And the reviews he gets! Damn them, all of them, the crass manikins!"

"Too much is written by the men who can't write about the men who do write," Martin concurred. "Why, I was appalled at the quantities of rubbish written about Stevenson and his work."

"Ghouls and harpies!" Brissenden snapped out with clicking teeth. "Yes, I know the spawn—complacently pecking at him for his Father Damien letter, analyzing him, weighing him—"

"Measuring him by the yardstick of their own miserable egos," Martin broke in.

"Yes, that's it, a good phrase,—mouthing and besliming the True, and Beautiful, and Good, and finally patting him on the back and saying, 'Good dog, Fido.' Faugh! 'The little chattering daws of men,' Richard Realf called them the night he died."

"Pecking at star-dust," Martin took up the strain warmly; "at the meteoric flight of the master-men. I once wrote a squib on them—the critics, or the reviewers, rather."

"Let's see it," Brissenden begged eagerly.

So Martin unearthed a carbon copy of "Star-dust," and during the reading of it Brissenden chuckled, rubbed his hands, and forgot to sip his toddy.

"Strikes me you're a bit of star-dust yourself, flung into a world of cowled gnomes who cannot see," was his comment at the end of it. "Of course it was snapped up by the first magazine?"

Martin ran over the pages of his manuscript book.

"It has been refused by twenty-seven of them."

Brissenden essayed a long and hearty laugh, but broke down in a fit of coughing.

"Say, you needn't tell me you haven't tackled poetry," he gasped. "Let me see some of it."

"Don't read it now," Martin pleaded. "I want to talk with you. I'll make up a bundle and you can take it home."

Brissenden departed with the "Love-cycle," and "The Peri and the Pearl," returning next day to greet Martin with:—

"I want more."

Not only did he assure Martin that he was a poet, but Martin learned that Brissenden also was one. He was swept off his feet by the other's work, and astounded that no attempt had been made to publish it.

"A plague on all their houses!" was Brissenden's answer to Martin's volunteering to market his work for him. "Love Beauty for its own sake," was his counsel, "and leave the magazines alone. Back to your ships and your sea—that's my advice to you, Martin Eden. What do you want in these sick and rotten cities of men? You are cutting your throat every day you waste in them trying to prostitute beauty to the needs of magazinedom. What was it you quoted me the other day?—Oh, yes, 'Man, the latest of the ephemera.' Well, what do you, the latest of the ephemera, want with fame? If you got it, it would be poison to you. You are too simple, too elemental, and too rational, by my faith, to prosper on such pap. I hope you never do sell a line to the magazines. Beauty is the only master to serve. Serve her and damn the multitude! Success! What in hell's success if it isn't right there in your Stevenson sonnet, which outranks Henley's 'Apparition,' in that 'Love-cycle,' in those sea-poems?

"It is not in what you succeed in doing that you get your joy, but in the doing of it. You can't tell me. I know it. You know it. Beauty hurts you. It is an everlasting pain in you, a wound that does not heal, a knife of flame. Why should you palter with magazines? Let beauty be your end. Why should you mint beauty into gold? Anyway, you can't; so there's no use in my getting excited over it. You can read the magazines for a thousand years and you won't find the value of one line of Keats. Leave fame and coin alone, sign away on a ship tomorrow, and go back to your sea."

"Not for fame, but for love," Martin laughed. "Love seems to have no place in your Cosmos; in mine, Beauty is the handmaiden of Love."

Brissenden looked at him pityingly and admiringly. "You are so young, Martin boy, so young. You will flutter high, but your wings are of the finest gauze, dusted with the fairest pigments. Do not scorch them. But of course you have scorched them already. It required some glorified petticoat to account for that 'Love-cycle,' and that's the shame of it."

"It glorifies love as well as the petticoat," Martin laughed.

"The philosophy of madness," was the retort. "So have I assured myself when wandering in hasheesh dreams. But beware. These bourgeois cities will kill you. Look at that den of traitors where I met you. Dry rot is no name for it. One can't keep his sanity in such an atmosphere. It's degrading. There's not one of them who is not degrading, man and woman, all of them animated stomachs guided by the high intellectual and artistic impulses of clams—"

He broke off suddenly and regarded Martin. Then, with a flash of divination, he saw the situation. The expression on his face turned to wondering horror.

"And you wrote that tremendous 'Love-cycle' to her—that pale, shrivelled, female thing!"

The next instant Martin's right hand had shot to a throttling clutch on his throat, and he was being shaken till his teeth rattled. But Martin, looking into his eyes, saw no fear there,—naught but a curious and mocking devil. Martin remembered himself, and flung Brissenden, by the neck, sidelong upon the bed, at the same moment releasing his hold.

Brissenden panted and gasped painfully for a moment, then began to chuckle.

"You had made me eternally your debtor had you shaken out the flame," he said.

"My nerves are on a hair-trigger these days," Martin apologized. "Hope I didn't hurt you. Here, let me mix a fresh toddy."

"Ah, you young Greek!" Brissenden went on. "I wonder if you take just pride in that body of yours. You are devilish strong. You are a young panther, a lion cub. Well, well, it is you who must pay for that strength."

"What do you mean?" Martin asked curiously, passing him a glass. "Here, down this and be good."

"Because—" Brissenden sipped his toddy and smiled appreciation of it. "Because of the women. They will worry you until you die, as they have already worried you, or else I was born yesterday. Now there's no use in your choking me; I'm going to have my say. This is undoubtedly your calf love; but for Beauty's sake show better taste next time. What under heaven do you want with a daughter of the bourgeoisie? Leave them alone. Pick out some great, wanton flame of a woman, who laughs at life and jeers at death and loves one while she may. There are such women, and they will love you just as readily as any pusillanimous product of bourgeois-sheltered life."

"Pusillanimous?" Martin protested.

"Just so, pusillanimous; prattling out little moralities that have been prattled into them, and afraid to live life. They will love you, Martin, but they will love their little moralities more. What you want is the magnificent abandon of life, the great free souls, the blazing butterflies and not the little gray moths. Oh, you will grow tired of them, too, of all the female things, if you are unlucky enough to live. But you won't live. You won't go back to your ships and sea; therefore, you'll hang around these pest-holes of cities until your bones are rotten, and then you'll die."

"You can lecture me, but you can't make me talk back," Martin said. "After all, you have but the wisdom of your temperament, and the wisdom of my temperament is just as unimpeachable as yours."

They disagreed about love, and the magazines, and many things, but they liked each other, and on Martin's part it was no less than a profound liking. Day after day they were together, if for no more than the hour Brissenden spent in Martin's stuffy room. Brissenden never arrived without his quart of whiskey, and when they dined together down-town, he drank Scotch and soda throughout the meal. He invariably paid the way for both, and it was through him that Martin learned the refinements of food, drank his first champagne, and made acquaintance with Rhenish wines.

But Brissenden was always an enigma. With the face of an ascetic, he was, in all the failing blood of him, a frank voluptuary. He was unafraid to die, bitter and cynical of all the ways of living; and yet, dying, he loved life, to the last atom of it. He was possessed by a madness to live, to thrill, "to squirm my little space in the cosmic dust whence I came," as he phrased it once himself. He had tampered with drugs and done many strange things in quest of new thrills, new sensations. As he told Martin, he had once gone three days without water, had done so voluntarily, in order to experience the exquisite delight of such a thirst assuaged. Who or what he was, Martin never learned. He was a man without a past, whose future was the imminent grave and whose present was a bitter fever of living.

XXXIII

MARTIN was steadily losing his battle. Economize as he would, the earnings from hack-work did not balance expenses. Thanksgiving found him with his black suit in pawn and unable to accept the Morses' invitation to dinner. Ruth was not made happy by his reason for not coming, and the corresponding effect on him was one of desperation. He told her that he would come, after all; that he would go over to San Francisco, to the *Transcontinental* office, collect the five dollars due him, and with it redeem his suit of clothes.

In the morning he borrowed ten cents from Maria. He would have borrowed it, by preference, from Brissenden, but that erratic individual had disappeared. Two weeks had passed since Martin had seen him, and he vainly cudgelled his brains for some cause of offence. The ten cents carried Martin across the ferry to San Francisco, and as he walked up Market Street he speculated upon his predicament in case he failed to collect the money. There would then be no way for him to return to Oakland, and he knew no one in San Francisco from whom to borrow another ten cents.

The door to the *Transcontinental* office was ajar, and Martin, in the act of opening it, was brought to a sudden pause by a loud voice from within, which exclaimed:—

"But that is not the question, Mr. Ford." (Ford, Martin knew, from his correspondence, to be the editor's name.) "The question is, are you prepared to pay?—cash, and cash down, I mean? I am not interested in the prospects of the *Transcontinental* and what you expect to make it next year. What I want is to be paid for what I do. And I tell you, right now, the Christmas *Transcontinental* don't go to press till I have the money in my hand. Good day. When you get the money, come and see me."

The door jerked open, and the man flung past Martin with an angry countenance and went down the corridor, muttering curses and clenching his fists. Martin decided not to enter immediately, and lingered in the hallways for a quarter of an hour. Then he shoved the door open and walked in. It was a new experience, the first time he had been inside an editorial office. Cards evidently were not necessary in that office, for the boy carried word to an inner room that there was a man who wanted to see Mr. Ford. Returning, the boy beckoned him from halfway across the room and led him to the private office, the editorial sanctum. Martin's first impression was of the disorder and cluttered confusion of the room. Next he noticed a bewhiskered, youthful-looking man, sitting at a roll-top desk, who regarded him curiously. Martin marvelled at the calm repose of his face. It was evident that the squabble with the printer had not affected his equanimity.

"I—I am Martin Eden," Martin began the conversation. ("And I want my five dollars," was what he would have liked to say.)

But this was his first editor, and under the circumstances he did not desire to scare him too abruptly. To his surprise, Mr. Ford leaped into the air with a "You don't say so!" and the next moment, with both hands, was shaking Martin's hand effusively.

"Can't say how glad I am to see you, Mr. Eden. Often wondered what you were like."

Here he held Martin off at arm's length and ran his beaming eyes over Martin's second-best suit, which was also his worst suit, and which was ragged and past repair, though the trousers showed the careful crease he had put in with Maria's flat-irons.

"I confess, though, I conceived you to be a much older man than you are. Your story, you know, showed such breadth, and vigor, such maturity and depth of thought. A masterpiece, that story—I knew it when I had read the first half-dozen lines. Let me tell you how I first read it. But no; first let me introduce you to the staff."

Still talking, Mr. Ford led him into the general office, where he introduced him to the associate editor, Mr. White, a slender, frail little man whose hand seemed strangely cold, as if he were suffering from a chill, and whose whiskers were sparse and silky.

"And Mr. Ends, Mr. Eden. Mr. Ends is our business manager, you know."

Martin found himself shaking hands with a cranky-eyed, bald-headed man, whose face looked youthful enough from what little could be seen of it, for most of it was covered by a snow-white beard, carefully trimmed—by his wife, who did it on Sundays, at which times she also shaved the back of his neck.

The three men surrounded Martin, all talking admiringly and at once, until it seemed to him that they were talking against time for a wager.

"We often wondered why you didn't call," Mr. White was saying.

"I didn't have the carfare, and I live across the Bay," Martin answered bluntly, with the idea of showing them his imperative need for the money.

Surely, he thought to himself, my glad rags in themselves are eloquent advertisement of my need. Time and again, whenever opportunity offered, he hinted about the purpose of his business. But his admirers' ears were deaf. They sang his praises, told him what they had thought of his story at first sight, what they subsequently thought, what their wives and families thought; but not one hint did they breathe of intention to pay him for it.

"Did I tell you how I first read your story?" Mr. Ford said. "Of course I didn't. I was coming west from New York, and when the train stopped at Ogden, the train-boy on the new run brought aboard the current number of the *Transcontinental.*"

My God! Martin thought; you can travel in a Pullman while I starve for the paltry five dollars you owe me. A wave of anger rushed over him. The wrong done him by the *Transcontinental* loomed colossal, for strong upon him were all the dreary months of vain yearning, of hunger and privation, and his present hunger awoke and gnawed at him, reminding him that he had eaten nothing since the day before, and little enough then. For the moment he saw red. These creatures were not even robbers. They were sneak-thieves. By lies and broken promises they had tricked him out of his story. Well, he would show them. And a great resolve surged into his will to the effect that he would not leave the office until he got his money. He remembered, if he did not get it, that there was no way for him to go back to Oakland. He controlled himself with an effort, but not before the wolfish expression of his face had awed and perturbed them.

They became more voluble than ever. Mr. Ford started anew to tell how he had first read "The Ring of Bells," and Mr. Ends at the same time was striving to repeat his niece's appreciation of "The Ring of Bells," said niece being a school-teacher in Alameda.

"I'll tell you what I came for," Martin said finally. "To be paid for that story all of you like so well. Five dollars, I believe, is what you promised me would be paid on publication."

Mr. Ford, with an expression on his mobile features of immediate and happy acquiescence, started to reach for his pocket, then turned suddenly to Mr. Ends, and said that he had left his money home. That Mr. Ends resented this, was patent; and Martin saw the twitch of his arm as if to protect his trousers pocket. Martin knew that the money was there.

"I am sorry," said Mr. Ends, "but I paid the printer not an hour ago, and he took my ready change. It was careless of me to be so short; but the bill was not yet due, and the printer's request, as a favor, to make an immediate advance, was quite unexpected."

Both men looked expectantly at Mr. White, but that gentleman laughed and shrugged his shoulders. His conscience was clean at any rate. He had come into the *Transcontinental* to learn magazine-literature, instead of which he had principally learned finance. The *Transcontinental* owed him four months' salary, and he knew that the printer must be appeased before the associate editor.

"It's rather absurd, Mr. Eden, to have caught us in this shape," Mr. Ford preambled airily. "All carelessness, I assure you. But I'll tell you what we'll do. We'll mail you a check the first thing in the morning. You have Mr. Eden's address, haven't you, Mr. Ends?"

Yes, Mr. Ends had the address, and the check would be mailed the first thing in the morning. Martin's knowledge of banks and checks was hazy, but he could see no reason why they should not give him the check on this day just as well as on the next.

"Then it is understood, Mr. Eden, that we'll mail you the check to-morrow?" Mr. Ford said.

"I need the money to-day," Martin answered stolidly.

"The unfortunate circumstances—if you had chanced here any other day," Mr. Ford began suavely, only to be interrupted by Mr. Ends, whose cranky eyes justified themselves in his shortness of temper.

"Mr. Ford has already explained the situation," he said with asperity. "And so have I. The check will be mailed—"

"I also have explained," Martin broke in, "and I have explained that I want the money to-day."

He had felt his pulse quicken a trifle at the business manager's brusqueness, and upon him he kept an alert eye, for it was in that gentleman's trousers pocket that he divined the *Transcontinental*' s ready cash was reposing.

"It is too bad—" Mr. Ford began.

But at that moment, with an impatient movement, Mr. Ends turned as if about to leave the room. At the same instant Martin sprang for him, clutching him by the throat with one hand in such fashion that Mr. Ends' snow-white beard, still maintaining its immaculate trimness, pointed ceilingward at an angle of forty-five degrees. To the horror of Mr. White and Mr. Ford, they saw their business manager shaken like an Astrakhan rug.

"Dig up, you venerable discourager of rising young talent!" Martin exhorted. "Dig up, or I'll shake it out of you, even if it's all in nickels." Then, to the two affrighted onlookers: "Keep away! If you interfere, somebody's liable to get hurt."

Mr. Ends was choking, and it was not until the grip on his throat was eased that he was able to signify his acquiescence in the digging-up programme. All together, after repeated digs, his trousers pocket yielded four dollars and fifteen cents.

"Inside out with it," Martin commanded.

An additional ten cents fell out. Martin counted the result of his raid a second time to make sure.

"You next!" he shouted at Mr. Ford. "I want seventy-five cents more."

Mr. Ford did not wait, but ransacked his pockets, with the result of sixty cents.

"Sure that is all?" Martin demanded menacingly, possessing himself of it. "What have you got in your vest pockets?"

In token of his good faith, Mr. Ford turned two of his pockets inside out. A strip of cardboard fell to the floor from one of them. He recovered it and was in the act of returning it, when Martin cried:—

"What's that?—A ferry ticket? Here, give it to me. It's worth ten cents. I'll credit you with it. I've now got four dollars and ninety-five cents, including the ticket. Five cents is still due me."

He looked fiercely at Mr. White, and found that fragile creature in the act of handing him a nickel.

"Thank you," Martin said, addressing them collectively. "I wish you a good day."

"Robber!" Mr. Ends snarled after him.

"Sneak-thief!" Martin retorted, slamming the door as he passed out.

Martin was elated—so elated that when he recollected that *The Hornet* owed him fifteen dollars for "The Peri and the Pearl," he decided forthwith to go and collect it. But *The Hornet* was run by a set of clean-shaven, strapping young men, frank buccaneers who robbed everything and everybody, not excepting one another. After some breakage of the office furniture, the editor (an ex-college athlete), ably assisted by the business manager, an advertising agent, and the porter, succeeded in removing Martin from the office and in accelerating, by initial impulse, his descent of the first flight of stairs.

"Come again, Mr. Eden; glad to see you any time," they laughed down at him from the landing above.

Martin grinned as he picked himself up.

"Phew!" he murmured back. "The *Transcontinental* crowd were nanny-goats, but you fellows are a lot of prize-fighters."

More laughter greeted this.

"I must say, Mr. Eden," the editor of *The Hornet* called down, "that for a poet you can go some yourself. Where did you learn that right cross—if I may ask?"

"Where you learned that half-Nelson," Martin answered. "Anyway, you're going to have a black eye."

"I hope your neck doesn't stiffen up," the editor wished solicitously. "What do you say we all go out and have a drink on it—not the neck, of course, but the little rough-house?"

"I'll go you if I lose," Martin accepted.

And robbers and robbed drank together, amicably agreeing that the battle was to the strong, and that the fifteen dollars for "The Peri and the Pearl" belonged by right to *The Hornet*' s editorial staff.

XXXIV

ARTHUR remained at the gate while Ruth climbed Maria's front steps. She heard the rapid click of the type-writer, and when Martin let her in, found him on the last page of a manuscript. She had come to make certain whether or not he would be at their table for Thanksgiving dinner; but before she could broach the subject Martin plunged into the one with which he was full.

"Here, let me read you this," he cried, separating the carbon copies and running the pages of manuscript into shape. "It's my latest, and different from anything I've done.

It is so altogether different that I am almost afraid of it, and yet I've a sneaking idea it is good. You be judge. It's an Hawaiian story. I've called it 'Wiki-Wiki.' "

His face was bright with the creative glow, though she shivered in the cold room and had been struck by the coldness of his hands at greeting. She listened closely while he read, and though he from time to time had seen only disapprobation in her face, at the close he asked:—

"Frankly, what do you think of it?"

"I—I don't know," she answered. "Will it—do you think it will sell?"

"I'm afraid not," was the confession. "It's too strong for the magazines. But it's true, on my word it's true."

"But why do you persist in writing such things when you know they won't sell?" she went on inexorably. "The reason for your writing is to make a living, isn't it?"

"Yes, that's right; but the miserable story got away with me. I couldn't help writing it. It demanded to be written."

"But that character, that Wiki-Wiki, why do you make him talk so roughly? Surely it will offend your readers, and surely that is why the editors are justified in refusing your work."

"Because the real Wiki-Wiki would have talked that way."

"But it is not good taste."

"It is life," he replied bluntly. "It is real. It is true. And I must write life as I see it."

She made no answer, and for an awkward moment they sat silent. It was because he loved her that he did not quite understand her, and she could not understand him because he was so large that he bulked beyond her horizon.

"Well, I've collected from the *Transcontinental*," he said in an effort to shift the conversation to a more comfortable subject. The picture of the bewhiskered trio, as he had last seen them, mulcted of four dollars and ninety cents and a ferry ticket, made him chuckle.

"Then you'll come!" she cried joyously. "That was what I came to find out."

"Come?" he muttered absently. "Where?"

"Why, to dinner to-morrow. You know you said you'd recover your suit if you got that money."

"I forgot all about it," he said humbly. "You see, this morning the poundman got Maria's two cows and the baby calf, and—well, it happened that Maria didn't have any money, and so I had to recover her cows for her. That's where the *Transcontinental* fiver went—'The Ring of Bells' went into the poundman's pocket."

"Then you won't come?"

He looked down at his clothing.

"I can't."

Tears of disappointment and reproach glistened in her blue eyes, but she said nothing.

"Next Thanksgiving you'll have dinner with me in Delmonico's," he said cheerily; "or in London, or Paris, or anywhere you wish. I know it."

"I saw in the paper a few days ago," she announced abruptly, "that there had been several local appointments to the Railway Mail. You passed first, didn't you?"

He was compelled to admit that the call had come for him, but that he had declined it. "I was so sure—I am so sure—of myself," he concluded. "A year from now I'll be earning more than a dozen men in the Railway Mail. You wait and see."

"Oh," was all she said, when he finished. She stood up, pulling at her gloves. "I must go, Martin. Arthur is waiting for me."

He took her in his arms and kissed her, but she proved a passive sweetheart. There was no tenseness in her body, her arms did not go around him, and her lips met his without their wonted pressure.

She was angry with him, he concluded, as he returned from the gate. But why? It was unfortunate that the poundman had gobbled Maria's cows. But it was only a stroke of fate. Nobody could be blamed for it. Nor did it enter his head that he could have done aught otherwise than what he had done. Well, yes, he was to blame a little, was his next thought, for having refused the call to the Railway Mail. And she had not liked "Wiki-Wiki."

He turned at the head of the steps to meet the letter-carrier on his afternoon round. The ever recurrent fever of expectancy assailed Martin as he took the bundle of long envelopes. One was not long. It was short and thin, and outside was printed the address of *The New York Outview.* He paused in the act of tearing the envelope open. It could not be an acceptance. He had no manuscripts with that publication. Perhaps—his heart almost stood still at the wild thought—perhaps they were ordering an article from him; but the next instant he dismissed the surmise as hopelessly impossible.

It was a short, formal letter, signed by the office editor, merely informing him that an anonymous letter which they had received was enclosed, and that he could rest assured the *Outview*' s staff never under any circumstances gave consideration to anonymous correspondence.

The enclosed letter Martin found to be crudely printed by hand. It was a hotchpotch of illiterate abuse of Martin, and of assertion that the "so-called Martin Eden" who was selling stories to magazines was no writer at all, and that in reality he was stealing stories from old magazines, typing them, and sending them out as his own. The envelope was postmarked "San Leandro." Martin did not require a second thought to discover the author. Higginbotham's grammar, Higginbotham's colloquialisms, Higginbotham's mental quirks and processes, were apparent throughout. Martin saw in every line, not the fine Italian hand, but the coarse grocer's fist, of his brother-in-law.

But why? he vainly questioned. What injury had he done Bernard Higginbotham? The thing was so unreasonable, so wanton. There was no explaining it. In the course of the week a dozen similar letters were forwarded to Martin by the editors of various Eastern magazines. The editors were behaving handsomely, Martin concluded. He was wholly unknown to them, yet some of them had even been sympathetic. It was evident that they detested anonymity. He saw that the malicious attempt to hurt him had failed. In fact, if anything came of it, it was bound to be good, for at least his name had been called to the attention of a number of editors. Sometime, perhaps, reading a submitted manuscript of his, they might remember him as the fellow about whom they had received an anonymous letter. And who was to say that such a remembrance might not sway the balance of their judgment just a trifle in his favor?

It was about this time that Martin took a great slump in Maria's estimation. He found her in the kitchen one morning, groaning with pain, tears of weakness running down her cheeks, vainly endeavoring to put through a large ironing. He promptly diagnosed her affliction as La Grippe, dosed her with hot whiskey (the remnants in the bottles for which Brissenden was responsible), and ordered her to bed. But Maria was refractory. The ironing had to be done, she protested, and delivered that night, or else there would be no food on the morrow for the seven small and hungry Silvas.

To her astonishment (and it was something that she never ceased from relating to her dying day), she saw Martin Eden seize an iron from the stove and throw a fancy shirt-waist on the ironing-board. It was Kate Flanagan's best Sunday waist, than whom there was no more exacting and fastidiously dressed woman in Maria's world. Also, Miss Flanagan had sent special instruction that said waist must be delivered by that night. As every one knew, she was keeping company with John Collins, the blacksmith, and, as Maria knew privily, Miss Flanagan and Mr. Collins were going next day to Golden Gate Park. Vain was Maria's attempt to rescue the garment. Martin guided her tottering footsteps to a chair, from where she watched him with bulging eyes. In a quarter of the time it would have taken her she saw the shirt-waist safely ironed, and ironed as well as she could have done it, as Martin made her grant.

"I could work faster," he explained, "if your irons were only hotter."

To her, the irons he swung were much hotter than she ever dared to use.

"Your sprinkling is all wrong," he complained next. "Here, let me teach you how to sprinkle. Pressure is what's wanted. Sprinkle under pressure if you want to iron fast."

He procured a packing-case from the woodpile in the cellar, fitted a cover to it, and raided the scrap-iron the Silva tribe was collecting for the junkman. With fresh-sprinkled garments in the box, covered with the board and pressed by the iron, the device was complete and in operation.

"Now you watch me, Maria," he said, stripping off to his undershirt and gripping an iron that was what he called "really hot."

"An' when he feenish da iron' he washa da wools," as she described it afterward. "He say, 'Maria, you are da greata fool. I showa you how to washa da wools,' an' he showa me, too. Ten minutes he maka da machine—one barrel, one wheel-hub, two poles, justa like dat."

Martin had learned the contrivance from Joe at the Shelly Hot Springs. The old wheel-hub, fixed on the end of the upright pole, constituted the plunger. Making this, in turn, fast to the spring-pole attached to the kitchen rafters, so that the hub played upon the woollens in the barrel, he was able, with one hand, thoroughly to pound them.

"No more Maria washa da wools," her story always ended. "I maka da kids worka da pole an' da hub an' da barrel. Him da smarta man, Mister Eden."

Nevertheless, by his masterly operation and improvement of her kitchen-laundry, he fell an immense distance in her regard. The glamour of romance with which her imagination had invested him faded away in the cold light of fact that he was an ex-laundryman. All his books, and his grand friends who visited him in carriages or with countless bottles of whiskey, went for naught. He was, after all, a mere workingman, a member of her own class and caste. He was more human and approachable, but he was no longer mystery.

Martin's alienation from his family continued. Following upon Mr. Higginbotham's unprovoked attack, Mr. Hermann von Schmidt showed his hand. The fortunate sale of several storiettes, some humorous verse, and a few jokes gave Martin a temporary splurge of prosperity. Not only did he partially pay up his bills, but he had sufficient balance left to redeem his black suit and wheel. The latter, by virtue of a twisted crank-hanger, required repairing, and, as a matter of friendliness with his future brother-in-law, he sent it to Von Schmidt's shop.

The afternoon of the same day Martin was pleased by the wheel being delivered by a small boy. Von Schmidt was also inclined to be friendly, was Martin's conclusion from this unusual favor. Repaired wheels usually had to be called for. But when he examined the wheel, he discovered no repairs had been made. A little later in the day he telephoned his sister's betrothed, and learned that that person didn't want anything to do with him in "any shape, manner, or form."

"Hermann von Schmidt," Martin answered cheerfully, "I've a good mind to come over and punch that Dutch nose of yours."

"You come to my shop," came the reply, "an' I'll send for the police. An' I'll put you through, too. Oh, I know you, but you can't make no rough-house with me. I don't want nothin' to do with the likes of you. You're a loafer, that's what, an' I ain't asleep. You ain't goin' to do no spongin' off me just because I'm marryin' your sister. Why don't you go to work an' earn an honest livin', eh? Answer me that."

Martin's philosophy asserted itself, dissipating his anger, and he hung up the receiver with a long whistle of incredulous amusement. But after the amusement came the reaction, and he was oppressed by his loneliness. Nobody understood him, nobody seemed to have any use for him, except Brissenden, and Brissenden had disappeared, God alone knew where.

Twilight was falling as Martin left the fruit store and turned homeward, his marketing on his arm. At the corner an electric car had stopped, and at sight of a lean, familiar figure alighting, his heart leapt with joy. It was Brissenden, and in the fleeting glimpse, ere the car started up, Martin noted the overcoat pockets, one bulging with books, the other bulging with a quart bottle of whiskey.

XXXV

Brissenden gave no explanation of his long absence, nor did Martin pry into it. He was content to see his friend's cadaverous face opposite him through the steam rising from a tumbler of toddy.

"I, too, have not been idle," Brissenden proclaimed, after hearing Martin's account of the work he had accomplished.

He pulled a manuscript from his inside coat pocket and passed it to Martin, who looked at the title and glanced up curiously.

"Yes, that's it," Brissenden laughed. "Pretty good title, eh? 'Ephemera'—it is the one word. And you're responsible for it, what of your *man*, who is always the erected, the vitalized inorganic, the latest of the ephemera, the creature of temperature strutting his little space on the thermometer. It got into my head and I had to write it to get rid of it. Tell me what you think of it."

Martin's face, flushed at first, paled as he read on. It was perfect art. Form triumphed over substance, if triumph it could be called where the last conceivable atom of substance had found expression in so perfect construction as to make Martin's head swim with delight, to put passionate tears into his eyes, and to send chills creeping up and down his back. It was a long poem of six or seven hundred lines, and it was a fantastic, amazing, unearthly thing. It was terrific, impossible; and yet there it was, scrawled in black ink across the sheets of paper. It dealt with man and his soul-gropings in their ultimate terms, plumbing the abysses of space for the testimony of remotest suns and rainbow spectrums. It was a mad orgy of imagination, wassailing in the skull of a dying man who half sobbed under his breath and was quick with the wild flutter of fading heart-beats. The poem swung in majestic rhythm to the cool tumult of interstellar conflict, to the onset of starry hosts, to the impact of cold suns and the flaming up of nebulae in the darkened void; and through it all, unceasing and faint, like a silver shuttle, ran the frail, piping voice of man, a querulous chirp amid the screaming of planets and the crash of systems.

"There is nothing like it in literature," Martin said, when at last he was able to speak. "It's wonderful!—wonderful! It has gone to my head. I am drunken with it. That great, infinitesimal question—I can't shake it out of my thoughts. That questing, eternal, ever recurring, thin little wailing voice of man is still ringing in my ears. It is like the dead-march of a gnat amid the trumpeting of elephants and the roaring of lions. It is insatiable with microscopic desire. I know I'm making a fool of myself, but the thing has obsessed me. You are—I don't know what you are—you are wonderful, that's all. But how do you do it? How do you do it?"

Martin paused from his rhapsody, only to break out afresh.

"I shall never write again. I am a dauber in clay. You have shown me the work of the real artificer-artisan. Genius! This is something more than genius. It transcends genius. It is truth gone mad. It is true, man, every line of it. I wonder if you realize that, you dogmatist. Science cannot give you the lie. It is the truth of the sneer, stamped out from the black iron of the Cosmos and interwoven with mighty rhythms of sound into a fabric of splendor and beauty. And now I won't say another word. I am overwhelmed, crushed. Yes, I will, too. Let me market it for you."

Brissenden grinned. "There's not a magazine in Christendom that would dare to publish it—you know that."

"I know nothing of the sort. I know there's not a magazine in Christendom that wouldn't jump at it. They don't get things like that every day. That's no mere poem of the year. It's the poem of the century."

"I'd like to take you up on the proposition."

"Now don't get cynical," Martin exhorted. "The magazine editors are not wholly fatuous. I know that. And I'll close with you on the bet. I'll wager anything you want that 'Ephemera' is accepted either on the first or second offering."

"There's just one thing that prevents me from taking you." Brissenden waited a moment. "The thing is big—the biggest I've ever done. I know that. It's my swan song. I am almighty proud of it. I worship it. It's better than whiskey. It is what I dreamed of—the great and perfect thing—when I was a simple young man, with sweet illusions and clean ideals. And I've got it, now, in my last grasp, and I'll not have it pawed over and soiled by a lot of swine. No, I won't take the bet. It's mine. I made it, and I've shared it with you."

"But think of the rest of the world," Martin protested. "The function of beauty is joy-making."

"It's my beauty."

"Don't be selfish."

"I'm not selfish." Brissenden grinned soberly in the way he had when pleased by the thing his thin lips were about to shape. "I'm as unselfish as a famished hog."

In vain Martin strove to shake him from his decision. Martin told him that his hatred of the magazines was rabid, fanatical, and that his conduct was a thousand times more despicable than that of the youth who burned the temple of Diana at Ephesus. Under the storm of denunciation Brissenden complacently sipped his toddy and affirmed that everything the other said was quite true, with the exception of the magazine editors. His hatred of them knew no bounds, and he excelled Martin in denunciation when he turned upon them.

"I wish you'd type it for me," he said. "You know how a thousand times better than any stenographer. And now I want to give you some advice." He drew a bulky manuscript from his outside coat pocket. "Here's your 'Shame of the Sun.' I've read it not once, but twice and three times—the highest compliment I can pay you. After what you've said about 'Ephemera' I must be silent. But this I will say: when 'The Shame of the Sun' is published, it will make a hit. It will start a controversy that will be worth thousands to you just in advertising."

Martin laughed. "I suppose your next advice will be to submit it to the magazines."

"By all means no—that is, if you want to see it in print. Offer it to the first-class houses. Some publisher's reader may be mad enough or drunk enough to report favorably on it. You've read the books. The meat of them has been transmuted in the alembic of Martin Eden's mind and poured into 'The Shame of the Sun,' and one day Martin Eden will be famous, and not the least of his fame will rest upon that work. So you must get a publisher for it—the sooner the better."

Brissenden went home late that night; and just as he mounted the first step of the car, he swung suddenly back on Martin and thrust into his hand a small, tightly crumpled wad of paper.

"Here, take this," he said. "I was out to the races to-day, and I had the right dope."

The bell clanged and the car pulled out, leaving Martin wondering as to the nature of the crinkly, greasy wad he clutched in his hand. Back in his room he unrolled it and found a hundred-dollar bill.

He did not scruple to use it. He knew his friend had always plenty of money, and he knew also, with profound certitude, that his success would enable him to repay it. In the morning he paid every bill, gave Maria three months' advance on the room, and redeemed every pledge at the pawnshop. Next he bought Marian's wedding present, and simpler presents, suitable to Christmas, for Ruth and Gertrude. And finally, on the balance remaining to him, he herded the whole Silva tribe down into Oakland. He was a winter late in redeeming his promise, but redeemed it was, for the last, least Silva got a pair of shoes, as well as Maria herself. Also, there were horns, and dolls, and toys of various sorts, and parcels and bundles of candies and nuts that filled the arms of all the Silvas to overflowing.

It was with this extraordinary procession trooping at his and Maria's heels into a confectioner's in quest of the biggest candy-cane ever made, that he encountered Ruth and her mother. Mrs. Morse was shocked. Even Ruth was hurt, for she had some regard for appearances, and her lover, cheek by jowl with Maria, at the head of that army of Portuguese ragamuffins, was not a pretty sight. But it was not that which hurt so much as what she took to be his lack of pride and self-respect. Further, and keenest of all, she read into the incident the impossibility of his living down his working-class origin. There was stigma enough in the fact of it, but shamelessly to flaunt it in the face of the world—her world—was going too far. Though her engagement to Martin had been kept secret, their long intimacy had not been unproductive of gossip; and in the shop, glancing covertly at her lover and his following, had been several of her acquaintances. She lacked the easy largeness of Martin and could not rise superior to her environment. She had been hurt to the quick, and her sensitive nature was quivering with the shame of it. So it was, when Martin arrived later in the day, that he kept her present in his breast-pocket, deferring the giving of it to a more propitious occasion. Ruth in tears—passionate, angry tears—was a revelation to him. The spectacle of her suffering convinced him that he had been a brute, yet in the soul of him he could not see how nor why. It never entered his head to be ashamed of those he knew, and to take the Silvas out to a Christmas treat could in no way, so it seemed to him, show lack of consideration for Ruth. On the other hand, he did see Ruth's point of view, after she had explained it; and he looked upon it as a feminine weakness, such as afflicted all women and the best of women.

XXXVI

COME on,—I'll show you the real dirt," Brissenden said to him, one evening in January.

They had dined together in San Francisco, and were at the Ferry Building, returning to Oakland, when the whim came to him to show Martin the "real dirt." He turned and fled across the water-front, a meagre shadow in a flapping overcoat, with Martin straining to keep up with him. At a wholesale liquor store he bought two gallon-demijohns of old port, and with one in each hand boarded a Mission Street car, Martin at his heels burdened with several quart-bottles of whiskey.

If Ruth could see me now, was his thought, while he wondered as to what constituted the real dirt.

"Maybe nobody will be there," Brissenden said, when they dismounted and plunged off to the right into the heart of the working-class ghetto, south of Market Street. "In which case you'll miss what you've been looking for so long."

"And what the deuce is that?" Martin asked.

"Men, intelligent men, and not the gibbering nonentities I found you consorting with in that trader's den. You read the books and you found yourself all alone. Well, I'm going to show you to-night some other men who've read the books, so that you won't be lonely any more.

"Not that I bother my head about their everlasting discussions," he said at the end of a block. "I'm not interested in book philosophy. But you'll find these fellows intelligences and not bourgeois swine. But watch out, they'll talk an arm off of you on any subject under the sun.

"Hope Norton's there," he panted a little later, resisting Martin's effort to relieve him of the two demijohns. "Norton's an idealist—a Harvard man. Prodigious memory. Idealism led him to philosophic anarchy, and his family threw him off. Father's a railroad president and many times millionnaire, but the son's starving in 'Frisco, editing an anarchist sheet for twenty-five a month."

Martin was little acquainted in San Francisco, and not at all south of Market; so he had no idea of where he was being led.

"Go ahead," he said; "tell me about them beforehand. What do they do for a living? How do they happen to be here?"

"Hope Hamilton's there." Brissenden paused and rested his hands. "Strawn-Hamilton's his name—hyphenated, you know—comes of old Southern stock. He's a tramp—laziest man I ever knew, though he's clerking, or trying to, in a socialist coöperative store for six dollars a week. But he's a confirmed hobo. Tramped into town. I've seen him sit all day on a bench and never a bite pass his lips, and in the evening, when I invited him to dinner—restaurant two blocks away—have him say, 'Too much trouble, old man. Buy me a package of cigarettes instead.' He was a Spencerian like you till Kreis turned him to materialistic monism. I'll start him on monism if I can. Norton's another monist—only he affirms naught but spirit. He can give Kreis and Hamilton all they want, too."

"Who is Kreis?" Martin asked.

"His rooms we're going to. One time professor—fired from university—usual story. A mind like a steel trap. Makes his living any old way. I know he's been a street fakir when he was down. Unscrupulous. Rob a corpse of a shroud—anything. Difference between him and the bourgeoisie is that he robs without illusion. He'll talk Nietzsche, or Schopenhauer, or Kant, or anything, but the only thing in this world, not excepting Mary, that he really cares for, is his monism. Haeckel is his little tin god. The only way to insult him is to take a slap at Haeckel.

"Here's the hang-out." Brissenden rested his demijohn at the upstairs entrance, preliminary to the climb. It was the usual two-story corner building, with a saloon and grocery underneath. "The gang lives here—got the whole upstairs to themselves. But Kreis is the only one who has two rooms. Come on."

No lights burned in the upper hall, but Brissenden threaded the utter blackness like a familiar ghost. He stopped to speak to Martin.

"There's one fellow—Stevens—a theosophist. Makes a pretty tangle when he gets going. Just now he's dish-washer in a restaurant. Likes a good cigar. I've seen him eat in a ten-cent hash-house and pay fifty cents for the cigar he smoked afterward. I've got a couple in my pocket for him, if he shows up.

"And there's another fellow—Parry—an Australian, a statistician and a sporting encyclopaedia. Ask him the grain output of Paraguay for 1903, or the English importation of sheetings into China for 1890, or at what weight Jimmy Britt fought Battling Nelson, or who was welter-weight champion of the United States in '68, and you'll get the correct answer with the automatic celerity of a slot-machine. And there's Andy, a stone-mason, has ideas on everything, a good chess-player; and another fellow, Harry, a baker, red hot socialist and strong union man. By the way, you remember the Cooks' and Waiters' strike—Hamilton was the chap who organized that union and precipitated the strike—planned it all out in advance, right here in Kreis's rooms. Did it just for the fun of it, but was too lazy to stay by the union. Yet he could have risen high if he wanted to. There's no end to the possibilities in that man—if he weren't so insuperably lazy."

Brissenden advanced through the darkness till a thread of light marked the threshold of a door. A knock and an answer opened it, and Martin found himself shaking hands with Kreis, a handsome brunette man, with dazzling white teeth, a drooping black mustache, and large, flashing black eyes. Mary, a matronly young blonde, was washing dishes in the little back room that served for kitchen and dining room. The front room served as bedchamber and living room. Overhead was the week's washing, hanging in festoons so low that Martin did not see at first the two men talking in a corner. They hailed Brissenden and his demijohns with acclamation, and, on being introduced, Martin learned they were Andy and Parry. He joined them and listened attentively to the description of a prize-fight Parry had seen the night before; while Brissenden, in his glory, plunged into the manufacture of a toddy and the serving of wine and whiskey-and-sodas. At his command, "Bring in the clan," Andy departed to go the round of the rooms for the lodgers.

"We're lucky that most of them are here," Brissenden whispered to Martin. "There's Norton and Hamilton; come on and meet them. Stevens isn't around, I hear. I'm going to get them started on monism if I can. Wait till they get a few jolts in them and they'll warm up."

At first the conversation was desultory. Nevertheless Martin could not fail to appreciate the keen play of their minds. They were men with opinions, though the opinions often clashed, and, though they were witty and clever, they were not superficial. He swiftly saw, no matter upon what they talked, that each man applied the correlation of knowledge and had also a deep-seated and unified conception of society and the Cosmos. Nobody manufactured their opinions for them; they were all rebels of one variety or another, and their lips were strangers to platitudes. Never had Martin, at the Morses', heard so amazing a range of topics discussed. There seemed no limit save time to the things they were alive to. The talk wandered from Mrs. Humphry Ward's new book to Shaw's latest play, through the future of the drama to reminiscences of Mansfield. They appreciated or sneered at the morning editorials, jumped from labor conditions in New Zealand to Henry James and Brander Matthews, passed on to the German designs in the Far East and the economic aspect of the Yellow Peril, wrangled over the German elections and Bebel's last speech, and settled down to local politics, the latest plans and scandals in the union labor party administration, and the wires that were pulled to bring about the Coast Seamen's strike. Martin was struck by the inside knowledge they possessed. They knew what was never printed in the newspapers—the wires and strings and the hidden hands that made the puppets dance. To Martin's surprise, the girl, Mary, joined in the conversation, displaying an intelligence he had never encountered in the few women he had met. They talked together on Swinburne and Rossetti, after which she led him beyond his depth into the by-paths of French literature. His revenge came when she defended Maeterlinck and he brought into action the carefully-thought-out thesis of "The Shame of the Sun."

Several other men had dropped in, and the air was thick with tobacco smoke, when Brissenden waved the red flag.

"Here's fresh meat for your axe, Kreis," he said; "a rose-white youth with the ardor of a lover for Herbert Spencer. Make a Haeckelite of him—if you can."

Kreis seemed to wake up and flash like some metallic, magnetic thing, while Norton looked at Martin sympathetically, with a sweet, girlish smile, as much as to say that he would be amply protected.

Kreis began directly on Martin, but step by step Norton interfered, until he and Kreis were off and away in a personal battle. Martin listened and fain would have rubbed his eyes. It was impossible that this should be, much less in the labor ghetto south of Market. The books were alive in these men. They talked with fire and enthusiasm, the intellectual stimulant stirring them as he had seen drink and anger stir other men. What he heard was no longer the philosophy of the dry, printed word, written by half-mythical demigods like Kant and Spencer. It was living philosophy, with warm, red blood, incarnated in these two men till its very features worked with excitement. Now and again other men joined in, and all followed the discussion with cigarettes going out in their hands and with alert, intent faces.

Idealism had never attracted Martin, but the exposition it now received at the hands of Norton was a revelation. The logical plausibility of it, that made an appeal to his intellect, seemed missed by Kreis and Hamilton, who sneered at Norton as a metaphysician, and who, in turn, sneered back at them as metaphysicians. *Phenomenon* and *noumenon* were bandied back and forth. They charged him with attempting to explain consciousness by itself. He charged them with word-jugglery, with reasoning from words to theory instead of from facts to theory. At this they were aghast. It was the cardinal tenet of their mode of reasoning to start with facts and to give names to the facts.

When Norton wandered into the intricacies of Kant, Kreis reminded him that all good little German philosophies when they died went to Oxford. A little later Norton reminded them of Hamilton's Law of Parsimony, the application of which they immediately claimed for every reasoning process of theirs. And Martin hugged his knees and exulted in it all. But Norton was no Spencerian, and he, too, strove for Martin's philosophic soul, talking as much at him as to his two opponents.

"You know Berkeley has never been answered," he said, looking directly at Martin. "Herbert Spencer came the nearest, which was not very near. Even the stanchest of Spencer's followers will not go farther. I was reading an essay of Saleeby's the other day, and the best Saleeby could say was that Herbert Spencer *nearly* succeeded in answering Berkeley."

"You know what Hume said?" Hamilton asked. Norton nodded, but Hamilton gave it for the benefit of the rest. "He said that Berkeley's arguments admit of no answer and produce no conviction."

"In his, Hume's, mind," was the reply. "And Hume's mind was the same as yours, with this difference: he was wise enough to admit there was no answering Berkeley."

Norton was sensitive and excitable, though he never lost his head, while Kreis and Hamilton were like a pair of cold-blooded savages, seeking out tender places to prod and poke. As the evening grew late, Norton, smarting under the repeated charges of being a metaphysician, clutching his chair to keep from jumping to his feet, his gray eyes snapping and his girlish face grown harsh and sure, made a grand attack upon their position.

"All right, you Haeckelites, I may reason like a medicine man, but, pray, how do you reason? You have nothing to stand on, you unscientific dogmatists with your positive science which you are always lugging about into places it has no right to be. Long before the school of materialistic monism arose, the ground was removed so that there could be no foundation. Locke was the man, John Locke. Two hundred years ago—more than that, even—in his 'Essay concerning the Human Understanding,' he proved the non-existence of innate ideas. The best of it is that that is precisely what you claim. To-night, again and again, you have asserted the non-existence of innate ideas.

"And what does that mean? It means that you can never know ultimate reality. Your brains are empty when you are born. Appearances, or phenomena, are all the content your minds can receive from your five senses. Then noumena, which are not in your minds when you are born, have no way of getting in—"

"I deny—" Kreis started to interrupt.

"You wait till I'm done," Norton shouted. "You can know only that much of the play and interplay of force and matter as impinges in one way or another on your senses. You see, I am willing to admit, for the sake of the argument, that matter exists; and what I am about to do is to efface you by your own argument. I can't do it any other way, for you are both congenitally unable to understand a philosophic abstraction.

"And now, what do you know of matter, according to your own positive science? You know it only by its phenomena, its appearances. You are aware only of its changes, or of such changes in it as cause changes in your consciousness. Positive science deals only with phenomena, yet you are foolish enough to strive to be ontologists and to deal with noumena. Yet, by the very definition of positive science, science is concerned only with appearances. As somebody has said, phenomenal knowledge cannot transcend phenomena.

"You cannot answer Berkeley, even if you have annihilated Kant, and yet, perforce, you assume that Berkeley is wrong when you affirm that science proves the non-existence of God, or, as much to the point, the existence of matter. —You know I granted the reality of matter only in order to make myself intelligible to your understanding. Be positive scientists, if you please; but ontology has no place in positive science, so leave it alone. Spencer is right in his agnosticism, but if Spencer—"

But it was time to catch the last ferry-boat for Oakland, and Brissenden and Martin slipped out, leaving Norton still talking and Kreis and Hamilton waiting to pounce on him like a pair of hounds as soon as he finished.

"You have given me a glimpse of fairyland," Martin said on the ferry-boat. "It makes life worth while to meet people like that. My mind is all worked up. I never appreciated idealism before. Yet I can't accept it. I know that I shall always be a realist. I am so made, I guess. But I'd like to have made a reply to Kreis and Hamilton, and I think I'd have had a word or two for Norton. I didn't see that Spencer was damaged any. I'm as excited as a child on its first visit to the circus. I see I must read up some more. I'm going to get hold of Saleeby. I still think Spencer is unassailable, and next time I'm going to take a hand myself."

But Brissenden, breathing painfully, had dropped off to sleep, his chin buried in a scarf and resting on his sunken chest, his body wrapped in the long overcoat and shaking to the vibration of the propellers.

XXXVII

THE first thing Martin did next morning was to go counter both to Brissenden's advice and command. "The Shame of the Sun" he wrapped and mailed to *The Acropolis.* He believed he could find magazine publication for it, and he felt that recognition by the magazines would commend him to the book-publishing houses. "Ephemera" he likewise wrapped and mailed to a magazine. Despite Brissenden's prejudice against the magazines, which was a pronounced mania with him, Martin decided that the great poem should see print. He did not intend, however, to publish it without the other's permission. His plan was to get it accepted by one of the high magazines, and, thus armed, again to wrestle with Brissenden for consent.

Martin began, that morning, a story which he had sketched out a number of weeks before and which ever since had been worrying him with its insistent clamor to be created. Apparently it was to be a rattling sea story, a tale of twentieth-century adventure and romance, handling real characters, in a real world, under real conditions. But beneath the swing and go of the story was to be something else—something that the superficial reader would never discern and which, on the other hand, would not diminish in any way the interest and enjoyment for such a reader. It was this, and not the mere story, that impelled Martin to write it. For that matter, it was always the great, universal motif that suggested plots to him. After having found such a motif, he cast about for the particular persons and particular location in time and space wherewith and wherein to utter the universal thing. "Overdue" was the title he had decided for it, and its length he believed would not be more than sixty thousand words—a bagatelle for him with his splendid vigor of production. On this first day he took hold of it with conscious delight in the mastery of his tools. He no longer worried for fear that the sharp, cutting edges should slip and mar his work. The long months of intense application and study had brought their reward. He could now devote himself with sure hand to the larger phases of the thing he shaped; and as he worked, hour after hour, he felt, as never before, the sure and cosmic grasp with which he held life and the affairs of life.

"Overdue" would tell a story that would be true of its particular characters and its particular events; but it would tell, too, he was confident, great vital things that would be true of all time, and all sea, and all life—thanks to Herbert Spencer, he thought, leaning back for a moment from the table. Ay, thanks to Herbert Spencer and to the master-key of life, evolution, which Spencer had placed in his hands.

He was conscious that it was great stuff he was writing. "It will go! It will go!" was the refrain that kept sounding in his ears. Of course it would go. At last he was turning out the thing at which the magazines would jump. The whole story worked out before him in lightning flashes. He broke off from it long enough to write a paragraph in his note-book. This would be the last paragraph in "Overdue"; but so thoroughly was the whole book already composed in his brain that he could write, weeks before he had arrived at the end, the end itself. He compared the tale, as yet unwritten, with the tales of the sea-writers, and he felt it to be immeasurably superior. "There's only one man who could touch it," he murmured aloud, "and that's Conrad. And it ought to make even him sit up and shake hands with me, and say, 'Well done, Martin, my boy.' "

He toiled on all day, recollecting, at the last moment, that he was to have dinner at the Morses'. Thanks to Brissenden, his black suit was out of pawn and he was again eligible for dinner parties. Down town he stopped off long enough to run into the library and search for Saleeby's books. He drew out "The Cycle of Life," and on the car turned to the essay Norton had mentioned on Spencer. As Martin read, he grew angry. His face flushed, his jaw set, and unconsciously his hand clenched, unclenched, and clenched again as if he were taking fresh grips upon some hateful thing out of which he was squeezing the life. When he left the car, he strode along the sidewalk as a wrathful man will stride, and he rang the Morse bell with such viciousness that it roused him to consciousness of his condition, so that he entered in good nature, smiling with amusement at himself. No sooner, however, was he inside than a great depression descended upon him. He fell from the height where he had been up-borne all day on the wings of inspiration. "Bourgeois," "trader's den"—Brissenden's epithets repeated themselves in his mind. But what of that? he demanded angrily. He was marrying Ruth, not her family.

It seemed to him that he had never seen Ruth more beautiful, more spiritual and ethereal and at the same time more healthy. There was color in her cheeks, and her eyes drew him again and again—the eyes in which he had first read immortality. He had forgotten immortality of late, and the trend of his scientific reading had been away from it; but here, in Ruth's eyes, he read an argument without words that transcended all worded arguments. He saw that in her eyes before which all discussion fled away, for he saw love there. And in his own eyes was love; and love was unanswerable. Such was his passionate doctrine.

The half hour he had with her, before they went in to dinner, left him supremely happy and supremely satisfied with life. Nevertheless, at table, the inevitable reaction and exhaustion consequent upon the hard day seized hold of him. He was aware that his eyes were tired and that he was irritable. He remembered it was at this table, at which he now sneered and was so often bored, that he had first eaten with civilized beings in what he had imagined was an atmosphere of high culture and refinement. He caught a glimpse of that pathetic figure of him, so long ago, a self-conscious savage, sprouting sweat at every pore in an agony of apprehension, puzzled by the bewildering minutiae of eating-implements, tortured by the ogre of a servant, striving at a leap to live at such dizzy social altitude, and deciding in the end to be frankly himself, pretending no knowledge and no polish he did not possess.

He glanced at Ruth for reassurance, much in the same manner that a passenger, with sudden panic thought of possible shipwreck, will strive to locate the life-preservers. Well, that much had come out of it—love and Ruth. All the rest had failed to stand the test of the books. But Ruth and love had stood the test; for them he found a biological sanction. Love was the most exalted expression of life. Nature had been busy designing him, as she had been busy with all normal men, for the purpose of loving. She had spent ten thousand centuries—ay, a hundred thousand and a million centuries—upon the task, and he was the best she could do. She had made love the strongest thing in him, increased its power a myriad per cent with her gift of imagination, and sent him forth into the ephemera to thrill and melt and mate. His hand sought Ruth's hand beside him hidden by the table, and a warm pressure was given and received. She looked at him a swift instant, and her eyes were radiant and melting. So were his in the thrill that pervaded him; nor did he realize how much that was radiant and melting in her eyes had been aroused by what she had seen in his.

Across the table from him, cater-cornered, at Mr. Morse's right, sat Judge Blount, a local superior court judge. Martin had met him a number of times and had failed to like him. He and Ruth's father were discussing labor union politics, the local situation, and socialism, and Mr. Morse was endeavoring to twit Martin on the latter topic. At last Judge Blount looked across the table with benignant and fatherly pity. Martin smiled to himself.

"You'll grow out of it, young man," he said soothingly. "Time is the best cure for such youthful distempers." He turned to Mr. Morse. "I do not believe discussion is good in such cases. It makes the patient obstinate."

"That is true," the other assented gravely. "But it is well to warn the patient occasionally of his condition."

Martin laughed merrily, but it was with an effort. The day had been too long, the day's effort too intense, and he was deep in the throes of the reaction.

"Undoubtedly you are both excellent doctors," he said; "but if you care a whit for the opinion of the patient, let him tell you that you are poor diagnosticians. In fact, you are both suffering from the disease you think you find in me. As for me, I am immune. The socialist philosophy that riots half-baked in your veins has passed me by."

"Clever, clever," murmured the judge. "An excellent ruse in controversy, to reverse positions."

"Out of your mouth." Martin's eyes were sparkling, but he kept control of himself. "You see, Judge, I've heard your campaign speeches. By some henidical process—henidical, by the way, is a favorite word of mine which nobody understands—by some henidical process you persuade yourself that you believe in the competitive system and the survival of the strong, and at the same time you indorse with might and main all sorts of measures to shear the strength from the strong."

"My young man—"

"Remember, I've heard your campaign speeches," Martin warned. "It's on record, your position on interstate commerce regulation, on regulation of the railway trust and Standard Oil, on the conservation of the forests, on a thousand and one restrictive measures that are nothing else than socialistic."

"Do you mean to tell me that you do not believe in regulating these various outrageous exercises of power?"

"That's not the point. I mean to tell you that you are a poor diagnostician. I mean to tell you that I am not suffering from the microbe of socialism. I mean to tell you that it is you who are suffering from the emasculating ravages of that same microbe. As for me, I am an inveterate opponent of socialism just as I am an inveterate opponent of your own mongrel democracy that is nothing else than pseudo-socialism masquerading under a garb of words that will not stand the test of the dictionary.

"I am a reactionary—so complete a reactionary that my position is incomprehensible to you who live in a veiled lie of social organization and whose sight is not keen enough to pierce the veil. You make believe that you believe in the survival of the strong and the rule of the strong. I believe. That is the difference. When I was a trifle younger,—a few months younger,—I believed the same thing. You see, the ideas of you and yours had impressed me. But merchants and traders are cowardly rulers at best; they grunt and grub all their days in the trough of money-getting, and I have swung back to aristocracy, if you please. I am the only individualist in this room. I look to the state for nothing. I look only to the strong man, the man on horseback, to save the state from its own rotten futility.

"Nietzsche was right. I won't take the time to tell you who Nietzsche was, but he was right. The world belongs to the strong—to the strong who are noble as well and who do not wallow in the swine-trough of trade and exchange. The world belongs to the true noblemen, to the great blond beasts, to the noncompromisers, to the 'yes-sayers.' And they will eat you up, you socialists who are afraid of socialism and who think yourselves individualists. Your slave-morality of the meek and lowly will never save you. —Oh, it's all Greek, I know, and I won't bother you any more with it. But remember one thing. There aren't half a dozen individualists in Oakland, but Martin Eden is one of them."

He signified that he was done with the discussion, and turned to Ruth.

"I'm wrought up to-day," he said in an undertone. "All I want to do is to love, not talk."

He ignored Mr. Morse, who said:—

"I am unconvinced. All socialists are Jesuits. That is the way to tell them."

"We'll make a good Republican out of you yet," said Judge Blount.

"The man on horseback will arrive before that time," Martin retorted with good humor, and returned to Ruth.

But Mr. Morse was not content. He did not like the laziness and the disinclination for sober, legitimate work of this prospective son-in-law of his, for whose ideas he had no respect and of whose nature he had no understanding. So he turned the conversation to Herbert Spencer. Judge Blount ably seconded him, and Martin, whose ears had pricked at the first mention of the philosopher's name, listened to the judge enunciate a grave and complacent diatribe against Spencer. From time to time Mr. Morse glanced at Martin, as much as to say, "There, my boy, you see."

"Chattering daws," Martin muttered under his breath and went on talking with Ruth and Arthur.

But the long day and the "real dirt" of the night before were telling upon him; and, besides, still burning in his mind was what had made him angry when he read it on the car.

"What is the matter?" Ruth asked suddenly, alarmed by the effort he was making to contain himself.

"There is no god but the Unknowable, and Herbert Spencer is its prophet," Judge Blount was saying at that moment.

Martin turned upon him.

"A cheap judgment," he remarked quietly. "I heard it first in the City Hall Park, on the lips of a workingman who ought to have known better. I have heard it often since, and each time the clap-trap of it nauseates me. You ought to be ashamed of yourself. To hear that great and noble man's name upon your lips is like finding a dew-drop in a cesspool. You are disgusting."

It was like a thunderbolt. Judge Blount glared at him with apoplectic countenance, and silence reigned. Mr. Morse was secretly pleased. He could see that his daughter was shocked. It was what he wanted to do—to bring out the innate ruffianism of this man he did not like.

Ruth's hand sought Martin's beseechingly under the table, but his blood was up. He was inflamed by the intellectual pretence and fraud of those who sat in the high places. A Superior Court Judge! It was only several years before that he had looked up from the mire at such glorious entities and deemed them gods.

Judge Blount recovered himself and attempted to go on, addressing himself to Martin with an assumption of politeness that the latter understood was for the benefit of the ladies. Even this added to his anger. Was there no honesty in the world?

"You can't discuss Spencer with me," he cried. "You do not know any more about Spencer than do his own countrymen. But it is no fault of yours, I grant. It is just a phase of the contemptible ignorance of the times. I ran across a sample of it on my way here this evening. I was reading an essay by Saleeby on Spencer. You should read it. It is accessible to all men. You can buy it in any book-store or draw it from the public library. You would feel ashamed of your paucity of abuse and ignorance of that noble man compared with what Saleeby has collected on the subject. It is a record of shame that would shame your shame.

" 'The philosopher of the half-educated,' he was called by an academic philosopher who was not worthy to pollute the atmosphere he breathed. I don't think you have read ten pages of Spencer, but there have been critics, assumably more intelligent than you, who have read no more than you of Spencer, who publicly challenged his followers to adduce one single idea from all his writings—from Herbert Spencer's writings, the man who has impressed the stamp of his genius over the whole field of scientific research and modern thought; the father of psychology; the man who revolutionized pedagogy, so that to-day the child of the French peasant is taught the three R's according to principles laid down by him. And the little gnats of men sting his memory when they get their very bread and butter from the technical application of his ideas. What little of worth resides in their brains is largely due to him. It is certain that had he never lived, most of what is correct in their parrot-learned knowledge would be absent.

"And yet a man like Principal Fairbanks of Oxford—a man who sits in an even higher place than you, Judge Blount—has said that Spencer will be dismissed by posterity as a poet and dreamer rather than a thinker. Yappers and blatherskites, the whole brood of them! ' "First Principles" is not wholly destitute of a certain literary power,' said one of them. And others of them have said that he was an industrious plodder rather than an original thinker. Yappers and blatherskites! Yappers and blatherskites!"

Martin ceased abruptly, in a dead silence. Everybody in Ruth's family looked up to Judge Blount as a man of power and achievement, and they were horrified at Martin's outbreak. The remainder of the dinner passed like a funeral, the judge and Mr. Morse confining their talk to each other, and the rest of the conversation being extremely desultory. Then afterward, when Ruth and Martin were alone, there was a scene.

"You are unbearable," she wept.

But his anger still smouldered, and he kept muttering, "The beasts! The beasts!"

When she averred he had insulted the judge, he retorted:—

"By telling the truth about him?"

"I don't care whether it was true or not," she insisted. "There are certain bounds of decency, and you had no license to insult anybody."

"Then where did Judge Blount get the license to assault truth?" Martin demanded. "Surely to assault truth is a more serious misdemeanor than to insult a pygmy personality such as the judge's. He did worse than that. He blackened the name of a great, noble man who is dead. Oh, the beasts! The beasts!"

His complex anger flamed afresh, and Ruth was in terror of him. Never had she seen him so angry, and it was all mystified and unreasonable to her comprehension. And yet, through her very terror ran the fibres of fascination that had drawn and that still drew her to him—that had compelled her to lean towards him, and, in that mad culminating moment, lay her hands upon his neck. She was hurt and outraged by what had taken place, and yet she lay in his arms and quivered while he went on muttering, "The beasts! The beasts!" And she still lay there when he said: "I'll not bother your table again, dear. They do not like me, and it is wrong of me to thrust my objectionable presence upon them. Besides, they are just as objectionable to me. Faugh! They are sickening. And to think of it, I dreamed in my innocence that the persons who sat in the high places, who lived in fine houses and had educations and bank accounts, were worth while!"

XXXVIII

"Come on, let's go down to the local."

So spoke Brissenden, faint from a hemorrhage of half an hour before—the second hemorrhage in three days. The perennial whiskey glass was in his hands, and he drained it with shaking fingers.

"What do I want with socialism?" Martin demanded.

"Outsiders are allowed five-minute speeches," the sick man urged. "Get up and spout. Tell them why you don't want socialism. Tell them what you think about them and their ghetto ethics. Slam Nietzsche into them and get walloped for your pains. Make a scrap of it. It will do them good. Discussion is what they want, and what you want, too. You see, I'd like to see you a socialist before I'm gone. It will give you a sanction for your existence. It is the one thing that will save you in the time of disappointment that is coming to you."

"I never can puzzle out why you, of all men, are a socialist," Martin pondered. "You detest the crowd so. Surely there is nothing in the canaille to recommend it to your aesthetic soul." He pointed an accusing finger at the whiskey glass which the other was refilling. "Socialism doesn't seem to save you."

"I'm very sick," was the answer. "With you it is different. You have health and much to live for, and you must be handcuffed to life somehow. As for me, you wonder why I am a socialist. I'll tell you. It is because socialism is inevitable; because the present rotten and irrational system cannot endure; because the day is past for your man on horseback. The slaves won't stand for it. They are too many, and willy-nilly they'll drag down the would-be equestrian before ever he gets astride. You can't get away from them, and you'll have to swallow the whole slave-morality. It's not a nice mess, I'll allow. But it's been a-brewing and swallow it you must. You are antediluvian anyway, with your Nietzsche ideas. The past is past, and the man who says history repeats itself is a liar. Of course I don't like the crowd, but what's a poor chap to do? We can't have the man on horseback, and anything is preferable to the timid swine that now rule. But come on, anyway. I'm loaded to the guards now, and if I sit here any longer, I'll get drunk. And you know the doctor says—damn the doctor! I'll fool him yet."

It was Sunday night, and they found the small hall packed by the Oakland socialists, chiefly members of the working class. The speaker, a clever Jew, won Martin's admiration at the same time that he aroused his antagonism. The man's stooped and narrow shoulders and weazened chest proclaimed him the true child of the crowded ghetto, and strong on Martin was the age-long struggle of the feeble, wretched slaves against the lordly handful of men who had ruled over them and would rule over them to the end of time. To Martin this withered wisp of a creature was a symbol. He was the figure that stood forth representative of the whole miserable mass of weaklings and inefficients who perished according to biological law on the ragged confines of life. They were the unfit. In spite of their cunning philosophy and of their antlike proclivities for coöperation, Nature rejected them for the exceptional man. Out of the plentiful spawn of life she flung from her prolific hand she selected only the best. It was by the same method that men, aping her, bred race-horses and cucumbers. Doubtless, a creator of a Cosmos could have devised a better method; but creatures of this particular Cosmos must put up with this particular method. Of course, they could squirm as they perished, as the socialists squirmed, as the speaker on the platform and the perspiring crowd were squirming even now as they counselled together for some new device with which to minimize the penalties of living and outwit the Cosmos.

So Martin thought, and so he spoke when Brissenden urged him to give them hell. He obeyed the mandate, walking up to the platform, as was the custom, and addressing the chairman. He began in a low voice, haltingly, forming into order the ideas which had surged in his brain while the Jew was speaking. In such meetings five minutes was the time allotted to each speaker; but when Martin's five minutes were up, he was in full stride, his attack upon their doctrines but half completed. He had caught their interest, and the audience urged the chairman by acclamation to extend Martin's time. They appreciated him as a foeman worthy of their intellect, and they listened intently, following every word. He spoke with fire and conviction, mincing no words in his attack upon the slaves and their morality and tactics and frankly alluding to his hearers as the slaves in question. He quoted Spencer and Malthus, and enunciated the biological law of development.

"And so," he concluded, in a swift résumé, "no state composed of the slave-types can endure. The old law of development still holds. In the struggle for existence, as I have shown, the strong and the progeny of the strong tend to survive, while the weak and the progeny of the weak are crushed and tend to perish. The result is that the strong and the progeny of the strong survive, and, so long as the struggle obtains, the strength of each generation increases. That is development. But you slaves—it is too bad to be slaves, I grant—but you slaves dream of a society where the law of development will be annulled, where no weaklings and inefficients will perish, where every inefficient will have as much as he wants to eat as many times a day as he desires, and where all will marry and have progeny—the weak as well as the strong. What will be the result? No longer will the strength and life-value of each generation increase. On the contrary, it will diminish. There is the Nemesis of your slave philosophy. Your society of slaves—of, by, and for, slaves—must inevitably weaken and go to pieces as the life which composes it weakens and goes to pieces.

"Remember, I am enunciating biology and not sentimental ethics. No state of slaves can stand—"

"How about the United States?" a man yelled from the audience.

"And how about it?" Martin retorted. "The thirteen colonies threw off their rulers and formed the Republic so-called. The slaves were their own masters. There were no more masters of the sword. But you couldn't get along without masters of some sort, and there arose a new set of masters—not the great, virile, noble men, but the shrewd and spidery traders and money-lenders. And they enslaved you over again—but not frankly, as the true, noble men would do with weight of their own right arms, but secretly, by spidery machinations and by wheedling and cajolery and lies. They have purchased your slave judges, they have debauched your slave legislatures, and they have forced to worse horrors than chattel slavery your slave boys and girls. Two million of your children are toiling to-day in this trader-oligarchy of the United States. Ten millions of you slaves are not properly sheltered nor properly fed.

"But to return. I have shown that no society of slaves can endure, because, in its very nature, such society must annul the law of development. No sooner can a slave society be organized than deterioration sets in. It is easy for you to talk of annulling the law of development, but where is the new law of development that will maintain your strength? Formulate it. Is it already formulated? Then state it."

Martin took his seat amidst an uproar of voices. A score of men were on their feet clamoring for recognition from the chair. And one by one, encouraged by vociferous applause, speaking with fire and enthusiasm and excited gestures, they replied to the attack. It was a wild night—but it was wild intellectually, a battle of ideas. Some strayed from the point, but most of the speakers replied directly to Martin. They shook him with lines of thought that were new to him; and gave him insights, not into new biological laws, but into new applications of the old laws. They were too earnest to be always polite, and more than once the chairman rapped and pounded for order.

It chanced that a cub reporter sat in the audience, detailed there on a day dull of news and impressed by the urgent need of journalism for sensation. He was not a bright cub reporter. He was merely facile and glib. He was too dense to follow the discussion. In fact, he had a comfortable feeling that he was vastly superior to these wordy maniacs of the working class. Also, he had a great respect for those who sat in the high places and dictated the policies of nations and newspapers. Further, he had an ideal, namely, of achieving that excellence of the perfect reporter who is able to make something—even a great deal—out of nothing.

He did not know what all the talk was about. It was not necessary. Words like *revolution* gave him his cue. Like a paleontologist, able to reconstruct an entire skeleton from one fossil bone, he was able to reconstruct a whole speech from the one word *revolution.* He did it that night, and he did it well; and since Martin had made the biggest stir, he put it all into his mouth and made him the arch-anarch of the show, transforming his reactionary individualism into the most lurid, red-shirt socialist utterance. The cub reporter was an artist, and it was a large brush with which he laid on the local color—wild-eyed long-haired men, neurasthenic and degenerate types of men, voices shaken with passion, clenched fists raised on high, and all projected against a background of oaths, yells, and the throaty rumbling of angry men.

XXXIX

OVER the coffee, in his little room, Martin read next morning's paper. It was a novel experience to find himself head-lined, on the first page at that; and he was surprised to learn that he was the most notorious leader of the Oakland socialists. He ran over the violent speech the cub reporter had constructed for him, and, though at first he was angered by the fabrication, in the end he tossed the paper aside with a laugh.

"Either the man was drunk or criminally malicious," he said that afternoon, from his perch on the bed, when Brissenden had arrived and dropped limply into the one chair.

"But what do you care?" Brissenden asked. "Surely you don't desire the approval of the bourgeois swine that read the newspapers?"

Martin thought for a while, then said:—

"No, I really don't care for their approval, not a whit. On the other hand, it's very likely to make my relations with Ruth's family a trifle awkward. Her father always contended I was a socialist, and this miserable stuff will clinch his belief. Not that I care for his opinion—but what's the odds? I want to read you what I've been doing to-day. It's 'Overdue,' of course, and I'm just about halfway through."

He was reading aloud when Maria thrust open the door and ushered in a young man in a natty suit who glanced briskly about him, noting the oil-burner and the kitchen in the corner before his gaze wandered on to Martin.

"Sit down," Brissenden said.

Martin made room for the young man on the bed and waited for him to broach his business.

"I heard you speak last night, Mr. Eden, and I've come to interview you," he began.

Brissenden burst out in a hearty laugh.

"A brother socialist?" the reporter asked, with a quick glance at Brissenden that appraised the color-value of that cadaverous and dying man.

"And he wrote that report," Martin said softly. "Why, he is only a boy!"

"Why don't you poke him?" Brissenden asked. "I'd give a thousand dollars to have my lungs back for five minutes."

The cub reporter was a trifle perplexed by this talking over him and around him and at him. But he had been commended for his brilliant description of the socialist meeting and had further been detailed to get a personal interview with Martin Eden, the leader of the organized menace to society.

"You do not object to having your picture taken, Mr. Eden?" he said. "I've a staff photographer outside, you see, and he says it will be better to take you right away before the sun gets lower. Then we can have the interview afterward."

"A photographer," Brissenden said meditatively. "Poke him, Martin! Poke him!"

"I guess I'm getting old," was the answer. "I know I ought, but I really haven't the heart. It doesn't seem to matter."

"For his mother's sake," Brissenden urged.

"It's worth considering," Martin replied; "but it doesn't seem worth while enough to rouse sufficient energy in me. You see, it does take energy to give a fellow a poking. Besides, what does it matter?"

"That's right—that's the way to take it," the cub announced airily, though he had already begun to glance anxiously at the door.

"But it wasn't true, not a word of what he wrote," Martin went on, confining his attention to Brissenden.

"It was just in a general way a description, you understand," the cub ventured, "and besides, it's good advertising. That's what counts. It was a favor to you."

"It's good advertising, Martin, old boy," Brissenden repeated solemnly.

"And it was a favor to me—think of that!" was Martin's contribution.

"Let me see—where were you born, Mr. Eden?" the cub asked, assuming an air of expectant attention.

"He doesn't take notes," said Brissenden. "He remembers it all."

"That is sufficient for me." The cub was trying not to look worried. "No decent reporter needs to bother with notes."

"That was sufficient—for last night." But Brissenden was not a disciple of quietism, and he changed his attitude abruptly. "Martin, if you don't poke him, I'll do it myself, if I fall dead on the floor the next moment."

"How will a spanking do?" Martin asked.

Brissenden considered judicially, and nodded his head.

The next instant Martin was seated on the edge of the bed with the cub face downward across his knees.

"Now don't bite," Martin warned, "or else I'll have to punch your face. It would be a pity, for it is such a pretty face."

His uplifted hand descended, and thereafter rose and fell in a swift and steady rhythm. The cub struggled and cursed and squirmed, but did not offer to bite. Brissenden looked on gravely, though once he grew excited and gripped the whiskey bottle, pleading, "Here, just let me swat him once."

"Sorry my hand played out," Martin said, when at last he desisted. "It is quite numb."

He uprighted the cub and perched him on the bed.

"I'll have you arrested for this," he snarled, tears of boyish indignation running down his flushed cheeks. "I'll make you sweat for this. You'll see."

"The pretty thing," Martin remarked. "He doesn't realize that he has entered upon the downward path. It is not honest, it is not square, it is not manly, to tell lies about one's fellow-creatures the way he has done, and he doesn't know it."

"He has to come to us to be told," Brissenden filled in a pause.

"Yes, to me whom he has maligned and injured. My grocery will undoubtedly refuse me credit now. The worst of it is that the poor boy will keep on this way until he deteriorates into a first-class newspaper man and also a first-class scoundrel."

"But there is yet time," quoth Brissenden. "Who knows but what you may prove the humble instrument to save him. Why didn't you let me swat him just once? I'd like to have had a hand in it."

"I'll have you arrested, the pair of you, you b-b-big brutes," sobbed the erring soul.

"No, his mouth is too pretty and too weak." Martin shook his head lugubriously. "I'm afraid I've numbed my hand in vain. The young man cannot reform. He will become eventually a very great and successful newspaper man. He has no conscience. That alone will make him great."

With that the cub passed out the door, in trepidation to the last for fear that Brissenden would hit him in the back with the bottle he still clutched.

In the next morning's paper Martin learned a great deal more about himself that was new to him. "We are the sworn enemies of society," he found himself quoted as saying in a column interview. "No, we are not anarchists but socialists." When the reporter pointed out to him that there seemed little difference between the two schools, Martin had shrugged his shoulders in silent affirmation. His face was described as bilaterally asymmetrical, and various other signs of degeneration were described. Especially notable were his thuglike hands and the fiery gleams in his blood-shot eyes.

He learned, also, that he spoke nightly to the workmen in the City Hall Park, and that among the anarchists and agitators that there inflamed the minds of the people he drew the largest audiences and made the most revolutionary speeches. The cub painted a high-light picture of his poor little room, its oil-stove and the one chair, and of the death's-head tramp who kept him company and who looked as if he had just emerged from twenty years of solitary confinement in some fortress dungeon.

The cub had been industrious. He had scurried around and nosed out Martin's family history, and procured a photograph of Higginbotham's Cash Store with Bernard Higginbotham himself standing out in front. That gentleman was depicted as an intelligent, dignified business man who had no patience with his brother-in-law's socialistic views, and no patience with the brother-in-law, either, whom he was quoted as characterizing as a lazy good-for-nothing who wouldn't take a job when it was offered to him and who would go to jail yet. Hermann von Schmidt, Marian's husband, had likewise been interviewed. He had called Martin the black sheep of the family and repudiated him. "He tried to sponge off of me, but I put a stop to that good and quick," Von Schmidt had said to the reporter. "He knows better than to come bumming around here. A man who won't work is no good, take that from me."

This time Martin was genuinely angry. Brissenden looked upon the affair as a good joke, but he could not console Martin, who knew that it would be no easy task to explain to Ruth. As for her father, he knew that he must be overjoyed with what had happened and that he would make the most of it to break off the engagement. How much he would make of it he was soon to realize. The afternoon mail brought a letter from Ruth. Martin opened it with a premonition of disaster, and read it standing at the open door when he had received it from the postman. As he read, mechanically his hand sought his pocket for the tobacco and brown paper of his old cigarette days. He was not aware that the pocket was empty or that he had even reached for the materials with which to roll a cigarette.

It was not a passionate letter. There were no touches of anger in it. But all the way through, from the first sentence to the last, was sounded the note of hurt and disappointment. She had expected better of him. She had thought he had got over his youthful wildness, that her love for him had been sufficiently worth while to enable him to live seriously and decently. And now her father and mother had taken a firm stand and commanded that the engagement be broken. That they were justified in this she could not but admit. Their relation could never be a happy one. It had been unfortunate from the first. But one regret she voiced in the whole letter, and it was a bitter one to Martin. "If only you had settled down to some position and attempted to make something of yourself," she wrote. "But it was not to be. Your past life had been too wild and irregular. I can understand that you are not to be blamed. You could act only according to your nature and your early training. So I do not blame you, Martin. Please remember that. It was simply a mistake. As father and mother have contended, we were not made for each other, and we should both be happy because it was discovered not too late." . . . "There is no use trying to see me," she said toward the last. "It would be an unhappy meeting for both of us, as well as for my mother. I feel, as it is, that I have caused her great pain and worry. I shall have to do much living to atone for it."

He read it through to the end, carefully, a second time, then sat down and replied. He outlined the remarks he had uttered at the socialist meeting, pointing out that they were in all ways the converse of what the newspaper had put in his mouth. Toward the end of the letter he was God's own lover pleading passionately for love. "Please answer," he said, "and in your answer you have to tell me but one thing. Do you love me? That is all—the answer to that one question."

But no answer came the next day, nor the next. "Overdue" lay untouched upon the table, and each day the heap of returned manuscripts under the table grew larger. For the first time Martin's glorious sleep was interrupted by insomnia, and he tossed through long, restless nights. Three times he called at the Morse home, but was turned away by the servant who answered the bell. Brissenden lay sick in his hotel, too feeble to stir out, and, though Martin was with him often, he did not worry him with his troubles.

For Martin's troubles were many. The aftermath of the cub reporter's deed was even wider than Martin had anticipated. The Portuguese grocer refused him further credit, while the greengrocer, who was an American and proud of it, had called him a traitor to his country and refused further dealings with him—carrying his patriotism to such a degree that he cancelled Martin's account and forbade him ever to attempt to pay it. The talk in the neighborhood reflected the same feeling, and indignation against Martin ran high. No one would have anything to do with a socialist traitor. Poor Maria was dubious and frightened, but she remained loyal. The children of the neighborhood recovered from the awe of the grand carriage which once had visited Martin, and from safe distances they called him "hobo" and "bum." The Silva tribe, however, stanchly defended him, fighting more than one pitched battle for his honor, and black eyes and bloody noses became quite the order of the day and added to Maria's perplexities and troubles.

Once, Martin met Gertrude on the street, down in Oakland, and learned what he knew could not be otherwise—that Bernard Higginbotham was furious with him for having dragged the family into public disgrace, and that he had forbidden him the house.

"Why don't you go away, Martin?" Gertrude had begged. "Go away and get a job somewhere and steady down. Afterwards, when this all blows over, you can come back."

Martin shook his head, but gave no explanations. How could he explain? He was appalled at the awful intellectual chasm that yawned between him and his people. He could never cross it and explain to them his position,—the Nietzschean position, in regard to socialism. There were not words enough in the English language, nor in any language, to make his attitude and conduct intelligible to them. Their highest concept of right conduct, in his case, was to get a job. That was their first word and their last. It constituted their whole lexicon of ideas. Get a job! Go to work! Poor, stupid slaves, he thought, while his sister talked. Small wonder the world belonged to the strong. The slaves were obsessed by their own slavery. A job was to them a golden fetich before which they fell down and worshipped.

He shook his head again, when Gertrude offered him money, though he knew that within the day he would have to make a trip to the pawnbroker.

"Don't come near Bernard now," she admonished him. "After a few months, when he is cooled down, if you want to, you can get the job of drivin' delivery-wagon for him. Any time you want me, just send for me an' I'll come. Don't forget."

She went away weeping audibly, and he felt a pang of sorrow shoot through him at sight of her heavy body and uncouth gait. As he watched her go, the Nietzschean edifice seemed to shake and totter. The slave-class in the abstract was all very well, but it was not wholly satisfactory when it was brought home to his own family. And yet, if there was ever a slave trampled by the strong, that slave was his sister Gertrude. He grinned savagely at the paradox. A fine Nietzscheman he was, to allow his intellectual concepts to be shaken by the first sentiment or emotion that strayed along—ay, to be shaken by the slave-morality itself, for that was what his pity for his sister really was. The true noble men were above pity and compassion. Pity and compassion had been generated in the subterranean barracoons of the slaves and were no more than the agony and sweat of the crowded miserables and weaklings.

XL

"OVERDUE" still continued to lie forgotten on the table. Every manuscript that he had had out now lay under the table. Only one manuscript he kept going, and that was Brissenden's "Ephemera." His bicycle and black suit were again in pawn, and the type-writer people were once more worrying about the rent. But such things no longer bothered him. He was seeking a new orientation, and until that was found his life must stand still.

After several weeks, what he had been waiting for happened. He met Ruth on the street. It was true, she was accompanied by her brother, Norman, and it was true that they tried to ignore him and that Norman attempted to wave him aside.

"If you interfere with my sister, I'll call an officer," Norman threatened. "She does not wish to speak with you, and your insistence is insult."

"If you persist, you'll have to call that officer, and then you'll get your name in the papers," Martin answered grimly. "And now, get out of my way and get the officer if you want to. I'm going to talk with Ruth.

"I want to have it from your own lips," he said to her.

She was pale and trembling, but she held up and looked inquiringly.

"The question I asked in my letter," he prompted.

Norman made an impatient movement, but Martin checked him with a swift look. She shook her head.

"Is all this of your own free will?" he demanded.

"It is." She spoke in a low, firm voice and with deliberation. "It is of my own free will. You have disgraced me so that I am ashamed to meet my friends. They are all talking about me, I know. That is all I can tell you. You have made me very unhappy, and I never wish to see you again."

"Friends! Gossip! Newspaper misreports! Surely such things are not stronger than love! I can only believe that you never loved me."

A blush drove the pallor from her face.

"After what has passed?" she said faintly. "Martin, you do not know what you are saying. I am not common."

"You see, she doesn't want to have anything to do with you," Norman blurted out, starting on with her.

Martin stood aside and let them pass, fumbling unconsciously in his coat pocket for the tobacco and brown papers that were not there.

It was a long walk to North Oakland, but it was not until he went up the steps and entered his room that he knew he had walked it. He found himself sitting on the edge of the bed and staring about him like an awakened somnambulist. He noticed "Overdue" lying on the table and drew up his chair and reached for his pen. There was in his nature a logical compulsion toward completeness. Here was something undone. It had been deferred against the completion of something else. Now that something else had been finished, and he would apply himself to this task until it was finished. What he would do next he did not know. All that he did know was that a climacteric in his life had been attained. A period had been reached, and he was rounding it off in workmanlike fashion. He was not curious about the future. He would soon enough find out what it held in store for him. Whatever it was, it did not matter. Nothing seemed to matter.

For five days he toiled on at "Overdue," going nowhere, seeing nobody, and eating meagrely. On the morning of the sixth day the postman brought him a thin letter from the editor of *The Parthenon.* A glance told him that "Ephemera" was accepted. "We have submitted the poem to Mr. Cartwright Bruce," the editor went on to say, "and he has reported so favorably upon it that we cannot let it go. As an earnest of our pleasure in publishing the poem, let me tell you that we have set it for the August number, our July number being already made up. Kindly extend our pleasure and our thanks to Mr. Brissenden. Please send by return mail his photograph and biographical data. If our honorarium is unsatisfactory, kindly telegraph us at once and state what you consider a fair price."

Since the honorarium they had offered was three hundred and fifty dollars, Martin thought it not worth while to telegraph. Then, too, there was Brissenden's consent to be gained. Well, he had been right, after all. Here was one magazine editor who knew real poetry when he saw it. And the price was splendid, even though it was for the poem of a century. As for Cartwright Bruce, Martin knew that he was the one critic for whose opinions Brissenden had any respect.

Martin rode down town on an electric car, and as he watched the houses and cross-streets slipping by he was aware of a regret that he was not more elated over his friend's success and over his own signal victory. The one critic in the United States had pronounced favorably on the poem, while his own contention that good stuff could find its way into the magazines had proved correct. But enthusiasm had lost its spring in him, and he found that he was more anxious to see Brissenden than he was to carry the good news. The acceptance of *The Parthenon* had recalled to him that during his five days' devotion to "Overdue" he had not heard from Brissenden nor even thought about him. For the first time Martin realized the daze he had been in, and he felt shame for having forgotten his friend. But even the shame did not burn very sharply. He was numb to emotions of any sort save the artistic ones concerned in the writing of "Overdue." So far as other affairs were concerned, he had been in a trance. For that matter, he was still in a trance. All this life through which the electric car whirred seemed remote and unreal, and he would have experienced little interest and less shock if the great stone steeple of the church he passed had suddenly crumbled to mortar-dust upon his head.

At the hotel he hurried up to Brissenden's room, and hurried down again. The room was empty. All luggage was gone.

"Did Mr. Brissenden leave any address?" he asked the clerk, who looked at him curiously for a moment.

"Haven't you heard?" he asked.

Martin shook his head.

"Why, the papers were full of it. He was found dead in bed. Suicide. Shot himself through the head."

"Is he buried yet?" Martin seemed to hear his voice, like some one else's voice, from a long way off, asking the question.

"No. The body was shipped East after the inquest. Lawyers engaged by his people saw to the arrangements."

"They were quick about it, I must say," Martin commented.

"Oh, I don't know. It happened five days ago."

"Five days ago?"

"Yes, five days ago."

"Oh," Martin said as he turned and went out.

At the corner he stepped into the Western Union and sent a telegram to *The Parthenon*, advising them to proceed with the publication of the poem. He had in his pocket but five cents with which to pay his carfare home, so he sent the message collect.

Once in his room, he resumed his writing. The days and nights came and went, and he sat at his table and wrote on. He went nowhere, save to the pawnbroker, took no exercise, and ate methodically when he was hungry and had something to cook, and just as methodically went without when he had nothing to cook. Composed as the story was, in advance, chapter by chapter, he nevertheless saw and developed an opening that increased the power of it, though it necessitated twenty thousand additional words. It was not that there was any vital need that the thing should be well done, but that his artistic canons compelled him to do it well. He worked on in the daze, strangely detached from the world around him, feeling like a familiar ghost among these literary trappings of his former life. He remembered that some one had said that a ghost was the spirit of a man who was dead and who did not have sense enough to know it; and he paused for the moment to wonder if he were really dead and unaware of it.

Came the day when "Overdue" was finished. The agent of the type-writer firm had come for the machine, and he sat on the bed while Martin, on the one chair, typed the last pages of the final chapter. "Finis," he wrote, in capitals, at the end, and to him it was indeed finis. He watched the type-writer carried out the door with a feeling of relief, then went over and lay down on the bed. He was faint from hunger. Food had not passed his lips in thirty-six hours, but he did not think about it. He lay on his back, with closed eyes, and did not think at all, while the daze or stupor slowly welled up, saturating his consciousness. Half in delirium, he began muttering aloud the lines of an anonymous poem Brissenden had been fond of quoting to him. Maria, listening anxiously outside his door, was perturbed by his monotonous utterance. The words in themselves were not significant to her, but the fact that he was saying them was. "I have done," was the burden of the poem.

> " 'I have done—
> Put by the lute.
> Song and singing soon are over
> As the airy shades that hover
> In among the purple clover.
> I have done—
> Put by the lute.
> Once I sang as early thrushes
> Sing among the dewy bushes;
> Now I'm mute.

I am like a weary linnet,
For my throat has no song in it;
I have had my singing minute.
I have done.
Put by the lute.' "

Maria could stand it no longer, and hurried away to the stove, where she filled a quart-bowl with soup, putting into it the lion's share of chopped meat and vegetables which her ladle scraped from the bottom of the pot. Martin roused himself and sat up and began to eat, between spoonfuls reassuring Maria that he had not been talking in his sleep and that he did not have any fever.

After she left him he sat drearily, with drooping shoulders, on the edge of the bed, gazing about him with lack-lustre eyes that saw nothing until the torn wrapper of a magazine, which had come in the morning's mail and which lay unopened, shot a gleam of light into his darkened brain. It is *The Parthenon*, he thought, the August *Parthenon*, and it must contain "Ephemera." If only Brissenden were here to see!

He was turning the pages of the magazine, when suddenly he stopped. "Ephemera" had been featured, with gorgeous head-piece and Beardsley-like margin decorations. On one side of the head-piece was Brissenden's photograph, on the other side was the photograph of Sir John Value, the British Ambassador. A preliminary editorial note quoted Sir John Value as saying that there were no poets in America, and the publication of "Ephemera" was *The Parthenon's* "There, take that, Sir John Value!" Cartwright Bruce was described as the greatest critic in America, and he was quoted as saying that "Ephemera" was the greatest poem ever written in America. And finally, the editor's foreword ended with: "We have not yet made up our minds entirely as to the merits of "Ephemera"; perhaps we shall never be able to do so. But we have read it often, wondering at the words and their arrangement, wondering where Mr. Brissenden got them, and how he could fasten them together." Then followed the poem.

"Pretty good thing you died, Briss, old man," Martin murmured, letting the magazine slip between his knees to the floor.

The cheapness and vulgarity of it was nauseating, and Martin noted apathetically that he was not nauseated very much. He wished he could get angry, but did not have energy enough to try. He was too numb. His blood was too congealed to accelerate to the swift tidal flow of indignation. After all, what did it matter? It was on a par with all the rest that Brissenden had condemned in bourgeois society.

"Poor Briss," Martin communed; "he would never have forgiven me."

Rousing himself with an effort, he possessed himself of a box which had once contained type-writer paper. Going through its contents, he drew forth eleven poems which his friend had written. These he tore lengthwise and crosswise and dropped into the waste basket. He did it languidly, and, when he had finished, sat on the edge of the bed staring blankly before him.

How long he sat there he did not know, until, suddenly, across his sightless vision he saw form a long horizontal line of white. It was curious. But as he watched it grow in definiteness he saw that it was a coral reef smoking in the white Pacific surges. Next, in the line of breakers, he made out a small canoe, an outrigger canoe. In the stern he saw a young bronzed god in scarlet hip-cloth, dipping a flashing paddle. He recognized him. He was Moti, the youngest son of Tati, the chief, and this was Tahiti, and beyond that smoking reef lay the sweet land of Papara and the chief's grass house by the river's mouth. It was the end of the day, and Moti was coming home from the fishing. He was waiting for the rush of a big breaker whereon to jump the reef. Then he saw himself, sitting forward in the canoe as he had often sat in the past, dipping a paddle that waited Moti's word to dig in like mad when the turquoise wall of the great breaker rose behind them. Next, he was no longer an onlooker but was himself in the canoe, Moti was crying out, they were both thrusting hard with their paddles, racing on the steep face of the flying turquoise. Under the bow the water was hissing as from a steam jet, the air was filled with driven spray, there was a rush and rumble and long-echoing roar, and the canoe floated on the placid water of the lagoon. Moti laughed and shook the salt water from his eyes, and together they paddled in to the pounded-coral beach where Tati's grass walls through the cocoanut-palms showed golden in the setting sun.

The picture faded, and before his eyes stretched the disorder of his squalid room. He strove in vain to see Tahiti again. He knew there was singing among the trees and that the maidens were dancing in the moonlight, but he could not see them. He could see only the littered writing-table, the empty space where the type-writer had stood, and the unwashed window-pane. He closed his eyes with a groan, and slept.

XLI

HE slept heavily all night, and did not stir until aroused by the postman on his morning round. Martin felt tired and passive, and went through his letters aimlessly. One thin envelope, from a robber magazine, contained a check for twenty-two dollars. He had been dunning for it for a year and a half. He noted its amount apathetically. The old-time thrill at receiving a publisher's check was gone. Unlike his earlier checks, this one was not pregnant with promise of great things to come. To him it was a check for twenty-two dollars, that was all, and it would buy him something to eat.

Another check was in the same mail, sent from a New York weekly in payment for some humorous verse which had been accepted months before. It was for ten dollars. An idea came to him, which he calmly considered. He did not know what he was going to do, and he felt in no hurry to do anything. In the meantime he must live. Also he owed numerous debts. Would it not be a paying investment to put stamps on the huge pile of manuscripts under the table and start them on their travels again? One or two of them might be accepted. That would help him to live. He decided on the investment, and, after he had cashed the checks at the bank down in Oakland, he bought ten dollars' worth of postage stamps. The thought of going home to cook breakfast in his stuffy little room was repulsive to him. For the first time he refused to consider his debts. He knew that in his room he could manufacture a substantial breakfast at a cost of from fifteen to twenty cents. But, instead, he went into the Forum Café and ordered a breakfast that cost two dollars. He tipped the waiter a quarter, and spent fifty cents for a package of Egyptian cigarettes. It was the first time he had smoked since Ruth had asked him to stop. But he could see now no reason why he should not, and besides, he wanted to smoke. And what did the money matter? For five cents he could have bought a package of Durham and brown papers and rolled forty cigarettes—but what of it? Money had no meaning to him now except what it would immediately buy. He was chartless and rudderless, and he had no port to make, while drifting involved the least living, and it was living that hurt.

The days slipped along, and he slept eight hours regularly every night. Though now, while waiting for more checks, he ate in the Japanese restaurants where meals were served for ten cents, his wasted body filled out, as did the hollows in his cheeks. He no longer abused himself with short sleep, overwork, and overstudy. He wrote nothing, and the books were closed. He walked much, out in the hills, and loafed long hours in the quiet parks. He had no friends nor acquaintances, nor did he make any. He had no inclination. He was waiting for some impulse, from he knew not where, to put his stopped life into motion again. In the meantime his life remained run down, planless, and empty and idle.

Once he made a trip to San Francisco to look up the "real dirt." But at the last moment, as he stepped into the upstairs entrance, he recoiled and turned and fled through the swarming ghetto. He was frightened at the thought of hearing philosophy discussed, and he fled furtively, for fear that some one of the "real dirt" might chance along and recognize him.

Sometimes he glanced over the magazines and newspapers to see how "Ephemera" was being maltreated. It had made a hit. But what a hit! Everybody had read it, and everybody was discussing whether or not it was really poetry. The local papers had taken it up, and daily there appeared columns of learned criticisms, facetious editorials, and serious letters from subscribers. Helen Della Delmar (proclaimed with a flourish of trumpets and rolling of tomtoms to be the greatest woman poet in the United States) denied Brissenden a seat beside her on Pegasus and wrote voluminous letters to the public, proving that he was no poet.

The Parthenon came out in its next number patting itself on the back for the stir it had made, sneering at Sir John Value, and exploiting Brissenden's death with ruthless commercialism. A newspaper with a sworn circulation of half a million published an original and spontaneous poem by Helen Della Delmar, in which she gibed and sneered at Brissenden. Also, she was guilty of a second poem, in which she parodied him.

Martin had many times to be glad that Brissenden was dead. He had hated the crowd so, and here all that was finest and most sacred of him had been thrown to the crowd. Daily the vivisection of Beauty went on. Every nincompoop in the land rushed into free print, floating their wizened little egos into the public eye on the surge of Brissenden's greatness. Quoth one paper: "We have received a letter from a gentleman who wrote a poem just like it, only better, some time ago." Another paper, in deadly seriousness, reproving Helen Della Delmar for her parody, said: "But unquestionably Miss Delmar wrote it in a moment of badinage and not quite with the respect that one great poet should show to another and perhaps to the greatest. However, whether Miss Delmar be jealous or not of the man who invented 'Ephemera,' it is certain that she, like thousands of others, is fascinated by his work, and that the day may come when she will try to write lines like his."

Ministers began to preach sermons against "Ephemera," and one, who too stoutly stood for much of its content, was expelled for heresy. The great poem contributed to the gayety of the world. The comic verse-writers and the cartoonists took hold of it with screaming laughter, and in the personal columns of society weeklies jokes were perpetrated on it to the effect that Charley Frensham told Archie Jennings, in confidence, that five lines of "Ephemera" would drive a man to beat a cripple, and that ten lines would send him to the bottom of the river.

Martin did not laugh; nor did he grit his teeth in anger. The effect produced upon him was one of great sadness. In the crash of his whole world, with love on the pinnacle, the crash of magazinedom and the dear public was a small crash indeed.

Brissenden had been wholly right in his judgment of the magazines, and he, Martin, had spent arduous and futile years in order to find it out for himself. The magazines were all Brissenden had said they were and more. Well, he was done, he solaced himself. He had hitched his wagon to a star and been landed in a pestiferous marsh. The visions of Tahiti—clean, sweet Tahiti—were coming to him more frequently. And there were the low Paumotus, and the high Marquesas; he saw himself often, now, on board trading schooners or frail little cutters, slipping out at dawn through the reef at Papeete and beginning the long beat through the pearl-atolls to Nukahiva and the Bay of Taiohae, where Tamari, he knew, would kill a pig in honor of his coming, and where Tamari's flower-garlanded daughters would seize his hands and with song and laughter garland him with flowers. The South Seas were calling, and he knew that sooner or later he would answer the call.

In the meantime he drifted, resting and recuperating after the long traverse he had made through the realm of knowledge. When *The Parthenon* check of three hundred and fifty dollars was forwarded to him, he turned it over to the local lawyer who had attended to Brissenden's affairs for his family. Martin took a receipt for the check, and at the same time gave a note for the hundred dollars Brissenden had let him have.

The time was not long when Martin ceased patronizing the Japanese restaurants. At the very moment when he had abandoned the fight, the tide turned. But it had turned too late. Without a thrill he opened a thin envelope from *The Millennium*, scanned the face of a check that represented three hundred dollars, and noted that it was the payment on acceptance for "Adventure." Every debt he owed in the world, including the pawnshop with its usurious interest, amounted to less than a hundred dollars. And when he had paid everything, and lifted the hundred-dollar note with Brissenden's lawyer, he still had over a hundred dollars in pocket. He ordered a suit of clothes from the tailor and ate his meals in the best cafés in town. He still slept in his little room at Maria's, but the sight of his new clothes caused the neighborhood children to cease from calling him "hobo" and "tramp" from the roofs of woodsheds and over back fences.

"Wiki-Wiki," his Hawaiian short story, was bought by *Warren's Monthly* for two hundred and fifty dollars. *The Northern Review* took his essay, "The Cradle of Beauty," and *Mackintosh's Magazine* took "The Palmist"—the poem he had written to Marian. The editors and readers were back from their summer vacations, and manuscripts were being handled quickly. But Martin could not puzzle out what strange whim animated them to this general acceptance of the things they had persistently rejected for two years. Nothing of his had been published. He was not known anywhere outside of Oakland, and in Oakland, with the few who thought they knew him, he was notorious as a red-shirt and a socialist. So there was no explaining this sudden acceptability of his wares. It was sheer jugglery of fate.

After it had been refused by a number of magazines, he had taken Brissenden's rejected advice and started "The Shame of the Sun" on the round of publishers. After several refusals, Singletree, Darnley & Co. accepted it, promising fall publication. When Martin asked for an advance on royalties, they wrote that such was not their custom, that books of that nature rarely paid for themselves, and that they doubted if his book would sell a thousand copies. Martin figured what the book would earn him on such a sale. Retailed at a dollar, on a royalty of fifteen per cent, it would bring him one hundred and fifty dollars. He decided that if he had it to do over again he would confine himself to fiction. "Adventure," one-fourth as long, had brought him twice as much from *The Millennium*. That newspaper paragraph he had read so long ago had been true, after all. The first-class magazines did pay on acceptance, and they paid well. Not two cents a word, but four cents a word, had *The Millennium* paid him. And, furthermore, they bought good stuff, too, for were they not buying his? This last thought he accompanied with a grin.

He wrote to Singletree, Darnley & Co., offering to sell out his rights in "The Shame of the Sun" for a hundred dollars, but they did not care to take the risk. In the meantime he was not in need of money, for several of his later stories had been accepted and paid for. He actually opened a bank account, where, without a debt in the world, he had several hundred dollars to his credit. "Overdue," after having been declined by a number of magazines, came to rest at the Meredith-Lowell Company. Martin remembered the five dollars Gertrude had given him, and his resolve to return it to her a hundred times over; so he wrote for an advance on royalties of five hundred dollars. To his surprise a check for that amount, accompanied by a contract, came by return mail. He cashed the check into five-dollar gold pieces and telephoned Gertrude that he wanted to see her.

She arrived at the house panting and short of breath from the haste she had made. Apprehensive of trouble, she had stuffed the few dollars she possessed into her hand-satchel; and so sure was she that disaster had overtaken her brother, that she stumbled forward, sobbing, into his arms, at the same time thrusting the satchel mutely at him.

"I'd have come myself," he said. "But I didn't want a row with Mr. Higginbotham, and that is what would have surely happened."

"He'll be all right after a time," she assured him, while she wondered what the trouble was that Martin was in. "But you'd best get a job first an' steady down. Bernard does like to see a man at honest work. That stuff in the newspapers broke 'm all up. I never saw 'm so mad before."

"I'm not going to get a job," Martin said with a smile. "And you can tell him so from me. I don't need a job, and there's the proof of it."

He emptied the hundred gold pieces into her lap in a glinting, tinkling stream.

"You remember that fiver you gave me the time I didn't have carfare? Well, there it is, with ninety-nine brothers of different ages but all of the same size."

If Gertrude had been frightened when she arrived, she was now in a panic of fear. Her fear was such that it was certitude. She was not suspicious. She was convinced. She looked at Martin in horror, and her heavy limbs shrank under the golden stream as though it were burning her.

"It's yours," he laughed.

She burst into tears, and began to moan, "My poor boy, my poor boy!"

He was puzzled for a moment. Then he divined the cause of her agitation and handed her the Meredith-Lowell letter which had accompanied the check. She stumbled through it, pausing now and again to wipe her eyes, and when she had finished, said:—

"An' does it mean that you come by the money honestly?"

"More honestly than if I'd won it in a lottery. I earned it."

Slowly faith came back to her, and she reread the letter carefully. It took him long to explain to her the nature of the transaction which had put the money into his possession, and longer still to get her to understand that the money was really hers and that he did not need it.

"I'll put it in the bank for you," she said finally.

"You'll do nothing of the sort. It's yours, to do with as you please, and if you won't take it, I'll give it to Maria. She'll know what to do with it. I'd suggest, though, that you hire a servant and take a good long rest."

"I'm goin' to tell Bernard all about it," she announced, when she was leaving.

Martin winced, then grinned.

"Yes, do," he said. "And then, maybe, he'll invite me to dinner again."

"Yes, he will—I'm sure he will!" she exclaimed fervently, as she drew him to her and kissed and hugged him.

XLII

One day Martin became aware that he was lonely. He was healthy and strong, and had nothing to do. The cessation from writing and studying, the death of Brissenden, and the estrangement from Ruth had made a big hole in his life; and his life refused to be pinned down to good living in cafés and the smoking of Egyptian cigarettes. It was true the South Seas were calling to him, but he had a feeling that the game was not yet played out in the United States. Two books were soon to be published, and he had more books that might find publication. Money could be made out of them, and he would wait and take a sackful of it into the South Seas. He knew a valley and a bay in the Marquesas that he could buy for a thousand Chili dollars. The valley ran from the horseshoe, land-locked bay to the tops of the dizzy, cloud-capped peaks and contained perhaps ten thousand acres. It was filled with tropical fruits, wild chickens, and wild pigs, with an occasional herd of wild cattle, while high up among the peaks were herds of wild goats harried by packs of wild dogs. The whole place was wild. Not a human lived in it. And he could buy it and the bay for a thousand Chili dollars.

The bay, as he remembered it, was magnificent, with water deep enough to accommodate the largest vessel afloat, and so safe that the South Pacific Directory recommended it as the best careening place for ships for hundreds of miles around. He would buy a schooner—one of those yacht-like, coppered crafts that sailed like witches—and go trading copra and pearling among the islands. He would make the valley and the bay his headquarters. He would build a patriarchal grass house like Tati's, and have it and the valley and the schooner filled with dark-skinned servitors. He would entertain there the factor of Taiohae, captains of wandering traders, and all the best of the South Pacific riffraff. He would keep open house and entertain like a prince. And he would forget the books he had opened and the world that had proved an illusion.

To do all this he must wait in California to fill the sack with money. Already it was beginning to flow in. If one of the books made a strike, it might enable him to sell the whole heap of manuscripts. Also he could collect the stories and the poems into books, and make sure of the valley and the bay and the schooner. He would never write again. Upon that he was resolved. But in the meantime, awaiting the publication of the books, he must do something more than live dazed and stupid in the sort of uncaring trance into which he had fallen.

He noted, one Sunday morning, that the Bricklayers' Picnic took place that day at Shell Mound Park, and to Shell Mound Park he went. He had been to the working-class picnics too often in his earlier life not to know what they were like, and as he entered the park he experienced a recrudescence of all the old sensations. After all, they were his kind, these working people. He had been born among them, he had lived among them, and though he had strayed for a time, it was well to come back among them.

"If it ain't Mart!" he heard some one say, and the next moment a hearty hand was on his shoulder. "Where you ben all the time? Off to sea? Come on an' have a drink."

It was the old crowd in which he found himself—the old crowd, with here and there a gap, and here and there a new face. The fellows were not bricklayers, but, as in the old days, they attended all Sunday picnics for the dancing, and the fighting, and the fun. Martin drank with them, and began to feel really human once more. He was a fool to have ever left them, he thought; and he was very certain that his sum of happiness would have been greater had he remained with them and let alone the books and the people who sat in the high places. Yet the beer seemed not so good as of yore. It didn't taste as it used to taste. Brissenden had spoiled him for steam beer, he concluded, and wondered if, after all, the books had spoiled him for companionship with these friends of his youth. He resolved that he would not be so spoiled, and he went on to the dancing pavilion. Jimmy, the plumber, he met there, in the company of a tall, blond girl who promptly forsook him for Martin.

"Gee, it's like old times," Jimmy explained to the gang that gave him the laugh as Martin and the blonde whirled away in a waltz. "An' I don't give a rap. I'm too damned glad to see 'm back. Watch 'm waltz, eh? It's like silk. Who'd blame any girl?"

But Martin restored the blonde to Jimmy, and the three of them, with half a dozen friends, watched the revolving couples and laughed and joked with one another. Everybody was glad to see Martin back. No book of his had been published; he carried no fictitious value in their eyes. They liked him for himself. He felt like a prince returned from exile, and his lonely heart burgeoned in the geniality in which it bathed. He made a mad day of it, and was at his best. Also, he had money in his pockets, and, as in the old days when he returned from sea with a pay-day, he made the money fly.

Once, on the dancing-floor, he saw Lizzie Connolly go by in the arms of a young workingman; and, later, when he made the round of the pavilion, he came upon her sitting by a refreshment table. Surprise and greetings over, he led her away into the grounds, where they could talk without shouting down the music. From the instant he spoke to her, she was his. He knew it. She showed it in the proud humility of her eyes, in every caressing movement of her proudly carried body, and in the way she hung upon his speech. She was not the young girl as he had known her. She was a woman, now, and Martin noted that her wild, defiant beauty had improved, losing none of its wildness, while the defiance and the fire seemed more in control. "A beauty, a perfect beauty," he murmured admiringly under his breath. And he knew she was his, that all he had to do was to say "Come," and she would go with him over the world wherever he led.

Even as the thought flashed through his brain he received a heavy blow on the side of his head that nearly knocked him down. It was a man's fist, directed by a man so angry and in such haste that the fist had missed the jaw for which it was aimed. Martin turned as he staggered, and saw the fist coming at him in a wild swing. Quite as a matter of course he ducked, and the fist flew harmlessly past, pivoting the man who had driven it. Martin hooked with his left, landing on the pivoting man with the weight of his body behind the blow. The man went to the ground sidewise, leaped to his feet, and made a mad rush. Martin saw his passion-distorted face and wondered what could be the cause of the fellow's anger. But while he wondered, he shot in a straight left, the weight of his body behind the blow. The man went over backward and fell in a crumpled heap. Jimmy and others of the gang were running toward them.

Martin was thrilling all over. This was the old days with a vengeance, with their dancing, and their fighting, and their fun. While he kept a wary eye on his antagonist, he glanced at Lizzie. Usually the girls screamed when the fellows got to scrapping, but she had not screamed. She was looking on with bated breath, leaning slightly forward, so keen was her interest, one hand pressed to her breast, her cheek flushed, and in her eyes a great and amazed admiration.

The man had gained his feet and was struggling to escape the restraining arms that were laid on him.

"She was waitin' for me to come back!" he was proclaiming to all and sundry. "She was waitin' for me to come back, an' then that fresh guy comes buttin' in. Let go o' me, I tell yeh. I'm goin' to fix 'm."

"What's eatin' yer?" Jimmy was demanding, as he helped hold the young fellow back. "That guy's Mart Eden. He's nifty with his mitts, lemme tell you that, an' he'll eat you alive if you monkey with 'm."

"He can't steal her on me that way," the other interjected.

"He licked the Flyin' Dutchman, an' you know *him,*" Jimmy went on expostulating. "An' he did it in five rounds. You couldn't last a minute against him. See?"

This information seemed to have a mollifying effect, and the irate young man favored Martin with a measuring stare.

"He don't look it," he sneered; but the sneer was without passion.

"That's what the Flyin' Dutchman thought," Jimmy assured him. "Come on, now, let's get outa this. There's lots of other girls. Come on."

The young fellow allowed himself to be led away toward the pavilion, and the gang followed after him.

"Who is he?" Martin asked Lizzie. "And what's it all about, anyway?"

Already the zest of combat, which of old had been so keen and lasting, had died down, and he discovered that he was self-analytical, too much so to live, single heart and single hand, so primitive an existence.

Lizzie tossed her head.

"Oh, he's nobody," she said. "He's just ben keepin' company with me.

"I had to, you see," she explained after a pause. "I was gettin' pretty lonesome. But I never forgot." Her voice sank lower, and she looked straight before her. "I'd throw 'm down for you any time."

Martin, looking at her averted face, knowing that all he had to do was to reach out his hand and pluck her, fell to pondering whether, after all, there was any real worth in refined, grammatical English, and, so, forgot to reply to her.

"You put it all over him," she said tentatively, with a laugh.

"He's a husky young fellow, though," he admitted generously. "If they hadn't taken him away, he might have given me my hands full."

"Who was that lady friend I seen you with that night?" she asked abruptly.

"Oh, just a lady friend," was his answer.

"It was a long time ago," she murmured contemplatively. "It seems like a thousand years."

But Martin went no further into the matter. He led the conversation off into other channels. They had lunch in the restaurant, where he ordered wine and expensive delicacies and afterward he danced with her and with no one but her, till she was tired. He was a good dancer, and she whirled around and around with him in a heaven of delight, her head against his shoulder, wishing that it could last forever. Later in the afternoon they strayed off among the trees, where, in the good old fashion, she sat down while he sprawled on his back, his head in her lap. He lay and dozed, while she fondled his hair, looked down on his closed eyes, and loved him without reserve. Looking up suddenly, he read the tender advertisement in her face. Her eyes fluttered down, then they opened and looked into his with soft defiance.

"I've kept straight all these years," she said, her voice so low that it was almost a whisper.

In his heart Martin knew that it was the miraculous truth. And at his heart pleaded a great temptation. It was in his power to make her happy. Denied happiness himself, why should he deny happiness to her? He could marry her and take her down with him to dwell in the grass-walled castle in the Marquesas. The desire to do it was strong, but stronger still was the imperative command of his nature not to do it. In spite of himself he was still faithful to Love. The old days of license and easy living were gone. He could not bring them back, nor could he go back to them. He was changed—how changed he had not realized until now.

"I am not a marrying man, Lizzie," he said lightly.

The hand caressing his hair paused perceptibly, then went on with the same gentle stroke. He noticed her face harden, but it was with the hardness of resolution, for still the soft color was in her cheeks and she was all glowing and melting.

"I did not mean that—" she began, then faltered. "Or anyway I don't care.

"I don't care," she repeated. "I'm proud to be your friend. I'd do anything for you. I'm made that way, I guess."

Martin sat up. He took her hand in his. He did it deliberately, with warmth but without passion; and such warmth chilled her.

"Don't let's talk about it," she said.

"You are a great and noble woman," he said. "And it is I who should be proud to know you. And I am, I am. You are a ray of light to me in a very dark world, and I've got to be straight with you, just as straight as you have been."

"I don't care whether you're straight with me or not. You could do anything with me. You could throw me in the dirt an' walk on me. An' you're the only man in the world that can," she added with a defiant flash. "I ain't taken care of myself ever since I was a kid for nothin'."

"And it's just because of that that I'm not going to," he said gently. "You are so big and generous that you challenge me to equal generousness. I'm not marrying, and I'm not—well, loving without marrying, though I've done my share of that in the past. I'm sorry I came here to-day and met you. But it can't be helped now, and I never expected it would turn out this way.

"But look here, Lizzie. I can't begin to tell you how much I like you. I do more than like you. I admire and respect you. You are magnificent, and you are magnificently good. But what's the use of words? Yet there's something I'd like to do. You've had a hard life; let me make it easy for you." (A joyous light welled into her eyes, then faded out again.) "I'm pretty sure of getting hold of some money soon—lots of it."

In that moment he abandoned the idea of the valley and the bay, the grass-walled castle and the trim, white schooner. After all, what did it matter? He could go away, as he had done so often, before the mast, on any ship bound anywhere.

"I'd like to turn it over to you. There must be something you want—to go to school or business college. You might like to study and be a stenographer. I could fix it for you. Or maybe your father and mother are living—I could set them up in a grocery store or something. Anything you want, just name it, and I can fix it for you."

She made no reply, but sat, gazing straight before her, dry-eyed and motionless, but with an ache in the throat which Martin divined so strongly that it made his own throat ache. He regretted that he had spoken. It seemed so tawdry what he had offered her—mere money—compared with what she offered him. He offered her an extraneous thing with which he could part without a pang, while she offered him herself, along with disgrace and shame, and sin, and all her hopes of heaven.

"Don't let's talk about it," she said with a catch in her voice that she changed to a cough. She stood up. "Come on, let's go home. I'm all tired out."

The day was done, and the merrymakers had nearly all departed. But as Martin and Lizzie emerged from the trees they found the gang waiting for them. Martin knew immediately the meaning of it. Trouble was brewing. The gang was his body-guard. They passed out through the gates of the park with, straggling in the rear, a second gang, the friends that Lizzie's young man had collected to avenge the loss of his lady. Several constables and special police officers, anticipating trouble, trailed along to prevent it, and herded the two gangs separately aboard the train for San Francisco. Martin told Jimmy that he would get off at Sixteenth Street Station and catch the electric car into Oakland. Lizzie was very quiet and without interest in what was impending. The train pulled in to Sixteenth Street Station, and the waiting electric car could be seen, the conductor of which was impatiently clanging the gong.

"There she is," Jimmy counselled. "Make a run for it, an' we'll hold 'em back. Now you go! Hit her up!"

The hostile gang was temporarily disconcerted by the manoeuvre, then it dashed from the train in pursuit. The staid and sober Oakland folk who sat upon the car scarcely noted the young fellow and the girl who ran for it and found a seat in front on the outside. They did not connect the couple with Jimmy, who sprang on the steps, crying to the motorman:—

"Slam on the juice, old man, and beat it outa here!"

The next moment Jimmy whirled about, and the passengers saw him land his fist on the face of a running man who was trying to board the car. But fists were landing on faces the whole length of the car. Thus, Jimmy and his gang, strung out on the long, lower steps, met the attacking gang. The car started with a great clanging of its gong, and, as Jimmy's gang drove off the last assailants, they, too, jumped off to finish the job. The car dashed on, leaving the flurry of combat far behind, and its dumfounded passengers never dreamed that the quiet young man and the pretty working-girl sitting in the corner on the outside seat had been the cause of the row.

Martin had enjoyed the fight, with a recrudescence of the old fighting thrills. But they quickly died away, and he was oppressed by a great sadness. He felt very old—centuries older than those careless, care-free young companions of his other days. He had travelled far, too far to go back. Their mode of life, which had once been his, was now distasteful to him. He was disappointed in it all. He had developed into an alien. As the steam beer had tasted raw, so their companionship seemed raw to him. He was too far removed. Too many thousands of opened books yawned between them and him. He had exiled himself. He had travelled in the vast realm of intellect until he could no longer return home. On the other hand, he was human, and his gregarious need for companionship remained unsatisfied. He had found no new home. As the gang could not understand him, as his own family could not understand him, as the bourgeoisie could not understand him, so this girl beside him, whom he honored high, could not understand him nor the honor he paid her. His sadness was not untouched with bitterness as he thought it over.

"Make it up with him," he advised Lizzie, at parting, as they stood in front of the workingman's shack in which she lived, near Sixth and Market. He referred to the young fellow whose place he had usurped that day.

"I can't—now," she said.

"Oh, go on," he said jovially. "All you have to do is whistle and he'll come running."

"I didn't mean that," she said simply.

And he knew what she had meant.

She leaned toward him as he was about to say good night. But she leaned not imperatively, not seductively, but wistfully and humbly. He was touched to the heart. His large tolerance rose up in him. He put his arms around her, and kissed her, and knew that upon his own lips rested as true a kiss as man ever received.

"My God!" she sobbed. "I could die for you. I could die for you."

She tore herself from him suddenly and ran up the steps. He felt a quick moisture in his eyes.

"Martin Eden," he communed. "You're not a brute, and you're a damn poor Nietzscheman. You'd marry her if you could and fill her quivering heart full with happiness. But you can't, you can't. And it's a damn shame."

" 'A poor old tramp explains his poor old ulcers,' " he muttered, remembering his Henley. " 'Life is, I think, a blunder and a shame.' It is—a blunder and a shame."

XLIII

"The Shame of the Sun" was published in October. As Martin cut the cords of the express package and the half-dozen complimentary copies from the publishers spilled out on the table, a heavy sadness fell upon him. He thought of the wild delight that would have been his had this happened a few short months before, and he contrasted that delight that should have been with his present uncaring coldness. His book, his first book, and his pulse had not gone up a fraction of a beat, and he was only sad. It meant little to him now. The most it meant was that it might bring some money, and little enough did he care for money.

He carried a copy out into the kitchen and presented it to Maria.

"I did it," he explained, in order to clear up her bewilderment. "I wrote it in the room there, and I guess some few quarts of your vegetable soup went into the making of it. Keep it. It's yours. Just to remember me by, you know."

He was not bragging, not showing off. His sole motive was to make her happy, to make her proud of him, to justify her long faith in him. She put the book in the front room on top of the family Bible. A sacred thing was this book her lodger had made, a fetich of friendship. It softened the blow of his having been a laundryman, and though she could not understand a line of it, she knew that every line of it was great. She was a simple, practical, hard-working woman, but she possessed faith in large endowment.

Just as emotionlessly as he had received "The Shame of the Sun" did he read the reviews of it that came in weekly from the clipping bureau. The book was making a hit, that was evident. It meant more gold in the money sack. He could fix up Lizzie, redeem all his promises, and still have enough left to build his grass-walled castle.

Singletree, Darnley & Co. had cautiously brought out an edition of fifteen hundred copies, but the first reviews had started a second edition of twice the size through the presses; and ere this was delivered a third edition of five thousand had been ordered. A London firm made arrangements by cable for an English edition, and hot-footed upon this came the news of French, German, and Scandinavian translations in progress. The attack upon the Maeterlinck school could not have been made at a more opportune moment. A fierce controversy was precipitated. Saleeby and Haeckel indorsed and defended "The Shame of the Sun," for once finding themselves on the same side of a question. Crookes and Wallace ranged up on the opposing side, while Sir Oliver Lodge attempted to formulate a compromise that would jibe with his particular cosmic theories. Maeterlinck's followers rallied around the standard of mysticism. Chesterton set the whole world laughing with a series of alleged non-partisan essays on the subject, and the whole affair, controversy and controversialists, was well-nigh swept into the pit by a thundering broadside from George Bernard Shaw. Needless to say the arena was crowded with hosts of lesser lights, and the dust and sweat and din became terrific.

"It is a most marvellous happening," Singletree, Darnley & Co. wrote Martin, "a critical philosophic essay selling like a novel. You could not have chosen your subject better, and all contributory factors have been unwarrantedly propitious. We need scarcely to assure you that we are making hay while the sun shines. Over forty thousand copies have already been sold in the United States and Canada, and a new edition of twenty thousand is on the presses. We are overworked, trying to supply the demand. Nevertheless we have helped to create that demand. We have already spent five thousand dollars in advertising. The book is bound to be a record-breaker.

"Please find herewith a contract in duplicate for your next book which we have taken the liberty of forwarding to you. You will please note that we have increased your royalties to twenty per cent, which is about as high as a conservative publishing house dares go. If our offer is agreeable to you, please fill in the proper blank space with the title of your book. We make no stipulations concerning its nature. Any book on any subject. If you have one already written, so much the better. Now is the time to strike. The iron could not be hotter.

"On receipt of signed contract we shall be pleased to make you an advance on royalties of five thousand dollars. You see, we have faith in you, and we are going in on this thing big. We should like, also, to discuss with you the drawing up of a contract for a term of years, say ten, during which we shall have the exclusive right of publishing in book-form all that you produce. But more of this anon."

Martin laid down the letter and worked a problem in mental arithmetic, finding the product of fifteen cents times sixty thousand to be nine thousand dollars. He signed the new contract, inserting "The Smoke of Joy" in the blank space, and mailed it back to the publishers along with the twenty storiettes he had written in the days before he discovered the formula for the newspaper storiette. And promptly as the United States mail could deliver and return, came Singletree, Darnley & Co.'s check for five thousand dollars.

"I want you to come down town with me, Maria, this afternoon about two o'clock," Martin said, the morning the check arrived. "Or, better, meet me at Fourteenth and Broadway at two o'clock. I'll be looking out for you."

At the appointed time she was there; but *shoes* was the only clew to the mystery her mind had been capable of evolving, and she suffered a distinct shock of disappointment when Martin walked her right by a shoe-store and dived into a real estate office. What happened thereupon resided forever after in her memory as a dream. Fine gentlemen smiled at her benevolently as they talked with Martin and one another; a typewriter clicked; signatures were affixed to an imposing document; her own landlord was there, too, and affixed his signature; and when all was over and she was outside on the sidewalk, her landlord spoke to her, saying, "Well, Maria, you won't have to pay me no seven dollars and a half this month."

Maria was too stunned for speech.

"Or next month, or the next, or the next," her landlord said.

She thanked him incoherently, as if for a favor. And it was not until she had returned home to North Oakland and conferred with her own kind, and had the Portuguese grocer investigate, that she really knew that she was the owner of the little house in which she had lived and for which she had paid rent so long.

"Why don't you trade with me no more?" the Portuguese grocer asked Martin that evening, stepping out to hail him when he got off the car; and Martin explained that he wasn't doing his own cooking any more, and then went in and had a drink of wine on the house. He noted it was the best wine the grocer had in stock.

"Maria," Martin announced that night, "I'm going to leave you. And you're going to leave here yourself soon. Then you can rent the house and be a landlord yourself. You've a brother in San Leandro or Haywards, and he's in the milk business. I want you to send all your washing back unwashed—understand?—unwashed, and to go out to San Leandro to-morrow, or Haywards, or wherever it is, and see that brother of yours. Tell him to come to see me. I'll be stopping at the Metropole down in Oakland. He'll know a good milk-ranch when he sees one."

And so it was that Maria became a landlord and the sole owner of a dairy, with two hired men to do the work for her and a bank account that steadily increased despite the fact that her whole brood wore shoes and went to school. Few persons ever meet the fairy princes they dream about; but Maria, who worked hard and whose head was hard, never dreaming about fairy princes, entertained hers in the guise of an ex-laundryman.

In the meantime the world had begun to ask: "Who is this Martin Eden?" He had declined to give any biographical data to his publishers, but the newspapers were not to be denied. Oakland was his own town, and the reporters nosed out scores of individuals who could supply information. All that he was and was not, all that he had done and most of what he had not done, was spread out for the delectation of the public, accompanied by snapshots and photographs—the latter procured from the local photographer who had once taken Martin's picture and who promptly copyrighted it and put it on the market. At first, so great was his disgust with the magazines and all bourgeois society, Martin fought against publicity; but in the end, because it was easier than not to, he surrendered. He found that he could not refuse himself to the special writers who travelled long distances to see him. Then again, each day was so many hours long, and, since he no longer was occupied with writing and studying, those hours had to be occupied somehow; so he yielded to what was to him a whim, permitted interviews, gave his opinions on literature and philosophy, and even accepted invitations of the bourgeoisie. He had settled down into a strange and comfortable state of mind. He no longer cared. He forgave everybody, even the cub reporter who had painted him red and to whom he now granted a full page with specially posed photographs.

He saw Lizzie occasionally, and it was patent that she regretted the greatness that had come to him. It widened the space between them. Perhaps it was with the hope of narrowing it that she yielded to his persuasions to go to night school and business college and to have herself gowned by a wonderful dressmaker who charged outrageous prices. She improved visibly from day to day, until Martin wondered if he was doing right, for he knew that all her compliance and endeavor was for his sake. She was trying to make herself of worth in his eyes—of the sort of worth he seemed to value. Yet he gave her no hope, treating her in brotherly fashion and rarely seeing her.

"Overdue" was rushed upon the market by the Meredith-Lowell Company in the height of his popularity, and being fiction, in point of sales it made even a bigger strike than "The Shame of the Sun." Week after week his was the credit of the unprecedented performance of having two books at the head of the list of best-sellers. Not only did the story take with the fiction-readers, but those who read "The Shame of the Sun" with avidity were likewise attracted to the sea-story by the cosmic grasp of mastery with which he had handled it. First, he had attacked the literature of mysticism, and had done it exceeding well; and, next, he had successfully supplied the very literature he had exposited, thus proving himself to be that rare genius, a critic and a creator in one.

Money poured in on him, fame poured in on him; he flashed, comet-like, through the world of literature, and he was more amused than interested by the stir he was making. One thing was puzzling him, a little thing that would have puzzled the world had it known. But the world would have puzzled over his bepuzzlement rather than over the little thing that to him loomed gigantic. Judge Blount invited him to dinner. That was the little thing, or the beginning of the little thing, that was soon to become the big thing. He had insulted Judge Blount, treated him abominably, and Judge Blount, meeting him on the street, invited him to dinner. Martin bethought himself of the numerous occasions on which he had met Judge Blount at the Morses' and when Judge Blount had not invited him to dinner. Why had he not invited him to dinner then? he asked himself. He had not changed. He was the same Martin Eden. What made the difference? The fact that the stuff he had written had appeared inside the covers of books? But it was work performed. It was not something he had done since. It was achievement accomplished at the very time Judge Blount was sharing this general view and sneering at his Spencer and his intellect. Therefore it was not for any real value, but for a purely fictitious value that Judge Blount invited him to dinner.

Martin grinned and accepted the invitation, marvelling the while at his complacence. And at the dinner, where, with their womenkind, were half a dozen of those that sat in high places, and where Martin found himself quite the lion, Judge Blount, warmly seconded by Judge Hanwell, urged privately that Martin should permit his name to be put up for the Styx—the ultra-select club to which belonged, not the mere men of wealth, but the men of attainment. And Martin declined, and was more puzzled than ever.

He was kept busy disposing of his heap of manuscripts. He was overwhelmed by requests from editors. It had been discovered that he was a stylist, with meat under his style. *The Northern Review,* after publishing "The Cradle of Beauty," had written him for half a dozen similar essays, which would have been supplied out of the heap, had not *Burton's Magazine,* in a speculative mood, offered him five hundred dollars each for five essays. He wrote back that he would supply the demand, but at a thousand dollars an essay. He remembered that all these manuscripts had been refused by the very magazines that were now clamoring for them. And their refusals had been cold-blooded, automatic, stereotyped. They had made him sweat, and now he intended to make them sweat. *Burton's Magazine* paid his price for five essays, and the remaining four, at the same rate, were snapped up by *Mackintosh's Monthly, The Northern Review* being too poor to stand the pace. Thus went out to the world "The High Priests of Mystery," "The Wonder-Dreamers," "The Yardstick of the Ego," "Philosophy of Illusion," "God and Clod," "Art and Biology," "Critics and Test-tubes," "Star-dust," and "The Dignity of Usury,"—to raise storms and rumblings and mutterings that were many a day in dying down.

Editors wrote to him telling him to name his own terms, which he did, but it was always for work performed. He refused resolutely to pledge himself to any new thing. The thought of again setting pen to paper maddened him. He had seen Brissenden torn to pieces by the crowd, and despite the fact that him the crowd acclaimed, he could not get over the shock nor gather any respect for the crowd. His very popularity seemed a disgrace and a treason to Brissenden. It made him wince, but he made up his mind to go on and fill the money-bag.

He received letters from editors like the following: "About a year ago we were unfortunate enough to refuse your collection of love-poems. We were greatly impressed by them at the time, but certain arrangements already entered into prevented our taking them. If you still have them, and if you will be kind enough to forward them, we shall be glad to publish the entire collection on your own terms. We are also prepared to make a most advantageous offer for bringing them out in book-form."

Martin recollected his blank-verse tragedy, and sent it instead. He read it over before mailing, and was particularly impressed by its sophomoric amateurishness and general worthlessness. But he sent it; and it was published, to the everlasting regret of the editor. The public was indignant and incredulous. It was too far a cry from Martin Eden's high standard to that serious bosh. It was asserted that he had never written it, that the magazine had faked it very clumsily, or that Martin Eden was emulating the elder Dumas and at the height of success was hiring his writing done for him. But when he explained that the tragedy was an early effort of his literary childhood, and that the magazine had refused to be happy unless it got it, a great laugh went up at the magazine's expense and a change in the editorship followed. The tragedy was never brought out in book-form, though Martin pocketed the advance royalties that had been paid.

Coleman's Weekly sent Martin a lengthy telegram, costing nearly three hundred dollars, offering him a thousand dollars an article for twenty articles. He was to travel over the United States, with all expenses paid, and select whatever topics interested him. The body of the telegram was devoted to hypothetical topics in order to show him the freedom of range that was to be his. The only restriction placed upon him was that he must confine himself to the United States. Martin sent his inability to accept and his regrets by wire "collect."

"Wiki-Wiki," published in *Warren's Monthly*, was an instantaneous success. It was brought out forward in a wide-margined, beautifully decorated volume that struck the holiday trade and sold like wildfire. The critics were unanimous in the belief that it would take its place with those two classics by two great writers, "The Bottle Imp" and "The Magic Skin."

The public, however, received the "Smoke of Joy" collection rather dubiously and coldly. The audacity and unconventionality of the storiettes was a shock to bourgeois morality and prejudice; but when Paris went mad over the immediate translation that was made, the American and English reading public followed suit and bought so many copies that Martin compelled the conservative house of Singletree, Darnley & Co. to pay a flat royalty of twenty-five per cent for a third book, and thirty per cent flat for a fourth. These two volumes comprised all the short stories he had written and which had received, or were receiving, serial publication. "The Ring of Bells" and his horror stories constituted one collection; the other collection was composed of "Adventure," "The Pot," "The Wine of Life," "The Whirlpool," "The Jostling Street," and four other stories. The Lowell-Meredith Company captured the collection of all his essays, and the Maxmillian Company got his "Sea Lyrics" and the "Love-cycle," the latter receiving serial publication in the *Ladies' Home Companion* after the payment of an extortionate price.

Martin heaved a sigh of relief when he had disposed of the last manuscript. The grass-walled castle and the white, coppered schooner were very near to him. Well, at any rate he had discovered Brissenden's contention that nothing of merit found its way into the magazines. His own success demonstrated that Brissenden had been wrong. And yet, somehow, he had a feeling that Brissenden had been right, after all. "The Shame of the Sun" had been the cause of his success more than the stuff he had written. That stuff had been merely incidental. It had been rejected right and left by the magazines. The publication of "The Shame of the Sun" had started a controversy and precipitated the landslide in his favor. Had there been no "Shame of the Sun" there would have been no landslide, and had there been no miracle in the go of "The Shame of the Sun" there would have been no landslide. Singletree, Darnley & Co. attested that miracle. They had brought out a first edition of fifteen hundred copies and been dubious of selling it. They were experienced publishers and no one had been more astounded than they at the success which had followed. To them it had been in truth a miracle. They never got over it, and every letter they wrote him reflected their reverent awe of that first mysterious happening. They did not attempt to explain it. There was no explaining it. It had happened. In the face of all experience to the contrary, it had happened.

So it was, reasoning thus, that Martin questioned the validity of his popularity. It was the bourgeoisie that bought his books and poured its gold into his money-sack, and from what little he knew of the bourgeoisie it was not clear to him how it could possibly appreciate or comprehend what he had written. His intrinsic beauty and power meant nothing to the hundreds of thousands who were acclaiming him and buying his books. He was the fad of the hour, the adventurer who had stormed Parnassus while the gods nodded. The hundreds of thousands read him and acclaimed him with the same brute non-understanding with which they had flung themselves on Brissenden's "Ephemera" and torn it to pieces—a wolf-rabble that fawned on him instead of fanging him. Fawn or fang, it was all a matter of chance. One thing he knew with absolute certitude: "Ephemera" was infinitely greater than anything he had done. It was infinitely greater than anything he had in him. It was a poem of centuries. Then the tribute the mob paid him was a sorry tribute indeed, for that same mob had wallowed "Ephemera" into the mire. He sighed heavily and with satisfaction. He was glad the last manuscript was sold and that he would soon be done with it all.

XLIV

MR. Morse met Martin in the office of the Hotel Metropole. Whether he had happened there just casually, intent on other affairs, or whether he had come there for the direct purpose of inviting him to dinner, Martin never could quite make up his mind, though he inclined toward the second hypothesis. At any rate, invited to dinner he was by Mr. Morse—Ruth's father, who had forbidden him the house and broken off the engagement.

Martin was not angry. He was not even on his dignity. He tolerated Mr. Morse, wondering the while how it felt to eat such humble pie. He did not decline the invitation. Instead, he put it off with vagueness and indefiniteness and inquired after the family, particularly after Mrs. Morse and Ruth. He spoke her name without hesitancy, naturally, though secretly surprised that he had had no inward quiver, no old, familiar increase of pulse and warm surge of blood.

He had many invitations to dinner, some of which he accepted. Persons got themselves introduced to him in order to invite him to dinner. And he went on puzzling over the little thing that was becoming a great thing. Bernard Higginbotham invited him to dinner. He puzzled the harder. He remembered the days of his desperate starvation when no one invited him to dinner. That was the time he needed dinners, and went weak and faint for lack of them and lost weight from sheer famine. That was the paradox of it. When he wanted dinners, no one gave them to him, and now that he could buy a hundred thousand dinners and was losing his appetite, dinners were thrust upon him right and left. But why? There was no justice in it, no merit on his part. He was no different. All the work he had done was even at that time work performed. Mr. and Mrs. Morse had condemned him for an idler and a shirk and through Ruth had urged that he take a clerk's position in an office. Furthermore, they had been aware of his work performed. Manuscript after manuscript of his had been turned over to them by Ruth. They had read them. It was the very same work that had put his name in all the papers, and it was his name being in all the papers that led them to invite him.

One thing was certain: the Morses had not cared to have him for himself or for his work. Therefore they could not want him now for himself or for his work, but for the fame that was his, because he was somebody amongst men, and—why not?—because he had a hundred thousand dollars or so. That was the way bourgeois society valued a man, and who was he to expect it otherwise? But he was proud. He disdained such valuation. He desired to be valued for himself, or for his work, which, after all, was an expression of himself. That was the way Lizzie valued him. The work, with her, did not even count. She valued him, himself. That was the way Jimmy, the plumber, and all the old gang valued him. That had been proved often enough in the days when he ran with them; it had been proved that Sunday at Shell Mound Park. His work could go hang. What they liked, and were willing to scrap for, was just Mart Eden, one of the bunch and a pretty good guy.

Then there was Ruth. She had liked him for himself, that was indisputable. And yet, much as she had liked him she had liked the bourgeois standard of valuation more. She had opposed his writing, and principally, it seemed to him, because it did not earn money. That had been her criticism of his "Love-cycle." She, too, had urged him to get a job. It was true, she refined it to "position," but it meant the same thing, and in his own mind the old nomenclature stuck. He had read her all that he wrote—poems, stories, essays—"Wiki-Wiki," "The Shame of the Sun," everything. And she had always and consistently urged him to get a job, to go to work—good God! as if he hadn't been working, robbing sleep, exhausting life, in order to be worthy of her.

So the little thing grew bigger. He was healthy and normal, ate regularly, slept long hours, and yet the growing little thing was becoming an obsession. *Work performed.* The phrase haunted his brain. He sat opposite Bernard Higginbotham at a heavy Sunday dinner over Higginbotham's Cash Store, and it was all he could do to restrain himself from shouting out:—

"It was work performed! And now you feed me, when then you let me starve, forbade me your house, and damned me because I wouldn't get a job. And the work was already done, all done. And now, when I speak, you check the thought unuttered on your lips and hang on my lips and pay respectful attention to whatever I choose to say. I tell you your party is rotten and filled with grafters, and instead of flying into a rage you hum and haw and admit there is a great deal in what I say. And why? Because I'm famous; because I've a lot of money. Not because I'm Martin Eden, a pretty good fellow and not particularly a fool. I could tell you the moon is made of green cheese and you would subscribe to the notion, at least you would not repudiate it, because I've got dollars, mountains of them. And it was all done long ago; it was work performed, I tell you, when you spat upon me as the dirt under your feet."

But Martin did not shout out. The thought gnawed in his brain, an unceasing torment, while he smiled and succeeded in being tolerant. As he grew silent, Bernard Higginbotham got the reins and did the talking. He was a success himself, and proud of it. He was self-made. No one had helped him. He owed no man. He was fulfilling his duty as a citizen and bringing up a large family. And there was Higginbotham's Cash Store, that monument of his own industry and ability. He loved Higginbotham's Cash Store as some men loved their wives. He opened up his heart to Martin, showed with what keenness and with what enormous planning he had made the store. And he had plans for it, ambitious plans. The neighborhood was growing up fast. The store was really too small. If he had more room, he would be able to put in a score of labor-saving and money-saving improvements. And he would do it yet. He was straining every effort for the day when he could buy the adjoining lot and put up another two-story frame building. The upstairs he could rent, and the whole ground-floor of both buildings would be Higginbotham's Cash Store. His eyes glistened when he spoke of the new sign that would stretch clear across both buildings.

Martin forgot to listen. The refrain of "Work performed," in his own brain, was drowning the other's clatter. The refrain maddened him, and he tried to escape from it.

"How much did you say it would cost?" he asked suddenly.

His brother-in-law paused in the middle of an expatiation on the business opportunities of the neighborhood. He hadn't said how much it would cost. But he knew. He had figured it out a score of times.

"At the way lumber is now," he said, "four thousand could do it."

"Including the sign?"

"I didn't count on that. It'd just have to come, onc't the buildin' was there."

"And the ground?"

"Three thousand more."

He leaned forward, licking his lips, nervously spreading and closing his fingers, while he watched Martin write a check. When it was passed over to him, he glanced at the amount—seven thousand dollars.

"I—I can't afford to pay more than six per cent," he said huskily.

Martin wanted to laugh, but, instead, demanded:—

"How much would that be?"

"Lemme see. Six per cent—six times seven—four hundred an' twenty."

"That would be thirty-five dollars a month, wouldn't it?"

Higginbotham nodded.

"Then, if you've no objection, we'll arrange it this way." Martin glanced at Gertrude. "You can have the principal to keep for yourself, if you'll use the thirty-five dollars a month for cooking and washing and scrubbing. The seven thousand is yours if you'll guarantee that Gertrude does no more drudgery. Is it a go?"

Mr. Higginbotham swallowed hard. That his wife should do no more housework was an affront to his thrifty soul. The magnificent present was the coating of a pill, a bitter pill. That his wife should not work! It gagged him.

"All right, then," Martin said. "I'll pay the thirty-five a month, and—"

He reached across the table for the check. But Bernard Higginbotham got his hand on it first, crying:—

"I accept! I accept!"

When Martin got on the electric car, he was very sick and tired. He looked up at the assertive sign.

"The swine," he groaned. "The swine, the swine."

When *Mackintosh's Magazine* published "The Palmist," featuring it with decorations by Berthier and with two pictures by Wenn, Hermann von Schmidt forgot that he had called the verses obscene. He announced that his wife had inspired the poem, saw to it that the news reached the ears of a reporter, and submitted to an interview by a staff writer who was accompanied by a staff photographer and a staff artist. The result was a full page in a Sunday supplement, filled with photographs and idealized drawings of Marian, with many intimate details of Martin Eden and his family, and with the full text of "The Palmist" in large type, and republished by special permission of *Mackintosh's Magazine.* It caused quite a stir in the neighborhood, and good housewives were proud to have the acquaintance of the great writer's sister, while those who had not made haste to cultivate it. Hermann von Schmidt chuckled in his little repair shop and decided to order a new lathe. "Better than advertising," he told Marian, "and it costs nothing."

"We'd better have him to dinner," she suggested.

And to dinner Martin came, making himself agreeable with the fat wholesale butcher and his fatter wife—important folk, they, likely to be of use to a rising young man like Hermann von Schmidt. No less a bait, however, had been required to draw them to his house than his great brother-in-law. Another man at table who had swallowed the same bait was the superintendent of the Pacific Coast agencies for the Asa Bicycle Company. Him Von Schmidt desired to please and propitiate because from him could be obtained the Oakland agency for the bicycle. So Hermann von Schmidt found it a goodly asset to have Martin for a brother-in-law, but in his heart of hearts he couldn't understand where it all came in. In the silent watches of the night, while his wife slept, he had floundered through Martin's books and poems, and decided that the world was a fool to buy them.

And in his heart of hearts Martin understood the situation only too well, as he leaned back and gloated at Von Schmidt's head, in fancy punching it well-nigh off of him, sending blow after blow home just right—the chuckle-headed Dutchman! One thing he did like about him, however. Poor as he was, and determined to rise as he was, he nevertheless hired one servant to take the heavy work off of Marian's hands. Martin talked with the superintendent of the Asa agencies, and after dinner he drew him aside with Hermann, whom he backed financially for the best bicycle store with fittings in Oakland. He went further, and in a private talk with Hermann told him to keep his eyes open for an automobile agency and garage, for there was no reason that he should not be able to run both establishments successfully.

With tears in her eyes and her arms around his neck, Marian, at parting, told Martin how much she loved him and always had loved him. It was true, there was a perceptible halt midway in her assertion, which she glossed over with more tears and kisses and incoherent stammerings, and which Martin inferred to be her appeal for forgiveness for the time she had lacked faith in him and insisted on his getting a job.

"He can't never keep his money, that's sure," Hermann von Schmidt confided to his wife. "He got mad when I spoke of interest, an' he said damn the principal and if I mentioned it again, he'd punch my Dutch head off. That's what he said—my Dutch head. But he's all right, even if he ain't no business man. He's given me my chance, an' he's all right."

Invitations to dinner poured in on Martin; and the more they poured, the more he puzzled. He sat, the guest of honor, at an Arden Club banquet, with men of note whom he had heard about and read about all his life; and they told him how, when they had read "The Ring of Bells" in the *Transcontinental*, and "The Peri and the Pearl" in *The Hornet*, they had immediately picked him for a winner. My God! and I was hungry and in rags, he thought to himself. Why didn't you give me a dinner then? Then was the time. It was work performed. If you are feeding me now for work performed, why did you not feed me then when I needed it? Not one word in "The Ring of Bells," nor in "The Peri and the Pearl" has been changed. No; you're not feeding me now for work performed. You are feeding me because everybody else is feeding me and because it is an honor to feed me. You are feeding me now because you are herd animals; because you are part of the mob; because the one blind, automatic thought in the mob-mind just now is to feed me. And where does Martin Eden and the work Martin Eden performed come in in all this? he asked himself plaintively, then arose to respond cleverly and wittily to a clever and witty toast.

So it went. Wherever he happened to be—at the Press Club, at the Redwood Club, at pink teas and literary gatherings—always were remembered "The Ring of Bells" and "The Peri and the Pearl" when they were first published. And always was Martin's maddening and unuttered demand: Why didn't you feed me then? It was work performed. "The Ring of Bells" and "The Peri and the Pearl" are not changed one iota. They were just as artistic, just as worth while, then as now. But you are not feeding me for their sake, nor for the sake of anything else I have written. You're feeding me because it is the style of feeding just now, because the whole mob is crazy with the idea of feeding Martin Eden.

And often, at such times, he would abruptly see slouch in among the company a young hoodlum in square-cut coat and under a stiff-rim Stetson hat. It happened to him at the Gallina Society in Oakland one afternoon. As he rose from his chair and stepped forward across the platform, he saw stalk through the wide door at the rear of the great room the young hoodlum with the square-cut coat and stiff-rim hat. Five hundred fashionably gowned women turned their heads, so intent and steadfast was Martin's gaze, to see what he was seeing. But they saw only the empty centre aisle. He saw the young tough lurching down that aisle and wondered if he would remove the stiff-rim which never yet had he seen him without. Straight down the aisle he came, and up the platform. Martin could have wept over that youthful shade of himself, when he thought of all that lay before him. Across the platform he swaggered, right up to Martin, and into the foreground of Martin's consciousness disappeared. The five hundred women applauded softly with gloved hands, seeking to encourage the bashful great man who was their guest. And Martin shook the vision from his brain, smiled, and began to speak.

The Superintendent of Schools, good old man, stopped Martin on the street and remembered him, recalling seances in his office when Martin was expelled from school for fighting.

"I read your 'Ring of Bells' in one of the magazines quite a time ago," he said. "It was as good as Poe. Splendid, I said at the time, splendid!"

Yes, and twice in the months that followed you passed me on the street and did not know me, Martin almost said aloud. Each time I was hungry and heading for the pawnbroker. Yet it was work performed. You did not know me then. Why do you know me now?

"I was remarking to my wife only the other day," the other was saying, "wouldn't it be a good idea to have you out to dinner some time? And she quite agreed with me. Yes, she quite agreed with me."

"Dinner?" Martin said so sharply that it was almost a snarl.

"Why, yes, yes, dinner, you know—just pot luck with us, with your old superintendent, you rascal," he uttered nervously, poking Martin in an attempt at jocular fellowship.

Martin went down the street in a daze. He stopped at the corner and looked about him vacantly.

"Well, I'll be damned!" he murmured at last. "The old fellow was afraid of me."

XLV

Kreis came to Martin one day—Kreis, of the "real dirt"; and Martin turned to him with relief, to receive the glowing details of a scheme sufficiently wild-catty to interest him as a fictionist rather than an investor. Kreis paused long enough in the midst of his exposition to tell him that in most of his "Shame of the Sun" he had been a chump.

"But I didn't come here to spout philosophy," Kreis went on. "What I want to know is whether or not you will put a thousand dollars in on this deal?"

"No, I'm not chump enough for that, at any rate," Martin answered. "But I'll tell you what I will do. You gave me the greatest night of my life. You gave me what money cannot buy. Now I've got money, and it means nothing to me. I'd like to turn over to you a thousand dollars of what I don't value for what you gave me that night and which was beyond price. You need the money. I've got more than I need. You want it. You came for it. There's no use scheming it out of me. Take it."

Kreis betrayed no surprise. He folded the check away in his pocket.

"At that rate I'd like the contract of providing you with many such nights," he said.

"Too late." Martin shook his head. "That night was the one night for me. I was in paradise. It's commonplace with you, I know. But it wasn't to me. I shall never live at such a pitch again. I'm done with philosophy. I want never to hear another word of it."

"The first dollar I ever made in my life out of my philosophy," Kreis remarked, as he paused in the doorway. "And then the market broke."

Mrs. Morse drove by Martin on the street one day, and smiled and nodded. He smiled back and lifted his hat. The episode did not affect him. A month before it might have disgusted him, or made him curious and set him to speculating about her state of consciousness at that moment. But now it was not provocative of a second thought. He forgot about it the next moment. He forgot about it as he would have forgotten the Central Bank Building or the City Hall after having walked past them. Yet his mind was preternaturally active. His thoughts went ever around and around in a circle. The centre of that circle was "work performed"; it ate at his brain like a deathless maggot. He awoke to it in the morning. It tormented his dreams at night. Every affair of life around him that penetrated through his senses immediately related itself to "work performed." He drove along the path of relentless logic to the conclusion that he was nobody, nothing. Mart Eden, the hoodlum, and Mart Eden, the sailor, had been real, had been he; but Martin Eden! the famous writer, did not exist. Martin Eden, the famous writer, was a vapor that had arisen in the mob-mind and by the mob-mind had been thrust into the corporeal being of Mart Eden, the hoodlum and sailor. But it couldn't fool him. He was not that sun-myth that the mob was worshipping and sacrificing dinners to. He knew better.

He read the magazines about himself, and pored over portraits of himself published therein until he was unable to associate his identity with those portraits. He was the fellow who had lived and thrilled and loved; who had been easy-going and tolerant of the frailties of life; who had served in the forecastle, wandered in strange lands, and led his gang in the old fighting days. He was the fellow who had been stunned at first by the thousands of books in the free library, and who had afterward learned his way among them and mastered them; he was the fellow who had burned the midnight oil and bedded with a spur and written books himself. But the one thing he was not was that colossal appetite that all the mob was bent upon feeding.

There were things, however, in the magazines that amused him. All the magazines were claiming him. *Warren's Monthly* advertised to its subscribers that it was always on the quest after new writers, and that, among others, it had introduced Martin Eden to the reading public. *The White Mouse* claimed him; so did *The Northern Review* and *Mackintosh's Magazine,* until silenced by *The Globe,* which pointed triumphantly to its files where the mangled "Sea Lyrics" lay buried. *Youth and Age,* which had come to life again after having escaped paying its bills, put in a prior claim, which nobody but farmers' children ever read. The *Transcontinental* made a dignified and convincing statement of how it first discovered Martin Eden, which was warmly disputed by *The Hornet,* with the exhibit of "The Peri and the Pearl." The modest claim of Singletree, Darnley & Co. was lost in the din. Besides, that publishing firm did not own a magazine wherewith to make its claim less modest.

The newspapers calculated Martin's royalties. In some way the magnificent offers certain magazines had made him leaked out, and Oakland ministers called upon him in a friendly way, while professional begging letters began to clutter his mail. But worse than all this were the women. His photographs were published broadcast, and special writers exploited his strong, bronzed face, his scars, his heavy shoulders, his clear, quiet eyes, and the slight hollows in his cheeks like an ascetic's. At this last he remembered his wild youth and smiled. Often, among the women he met, he would see now one, now another, looking at him, appraising him, selecting him. He laughed to himself. He remembered Brissenden's warning and laughed again. The women would never destroy him, that much was certain. He had gone past that stage.

Once, walking with Lizzie toward night school, she caught a glance directed toward him by a well-gowned, handsome woman of the bourgeoisie. The glance was a trifle too long, a shade too considerative. Lizzie knew it for what it was, and her body tensed angrily. Martin noticed, noticed the cause of it, told her how used he was becoming to it and that he did not care anyway.

"You ought to care," she answered with blazing eyes. "You're sick. That's what's the matter."

"Never healthier in my life. I weigh five pounds more than I ever did."

"It ain't your body. It's your head. Something's wrong with your think-machine. Even I can see that, an' I ain't nobody."

He walked on beside her, reflecting.

"I'd give anything to see you get over it," she broke out impulsively. "You ought to care when women look at you that way, a man like you. It's not natural. It's all right enough for sissy-boys. But you ain't made that way. So help me, I'd be willing an' glad if the right woman came along an' made you care."

When he left Lizzie at night school, he returned to the Metropole.

Once in his rooms, he dropped into a Morris chair and sat staring straight before him. He did not doze. Nor did he think. His mind was a blank, save for the intervals when unsummoned memory pictures took form and color and radiance just under his eyelids. He saw these pictures, but he was scarcely conscious of them—no more so than if they had been dreams. Yet he was not asleep. Once, he roused himself and glanced at his watch. It was just eight o'clock. He had nothing to do, and it was too early for bed. Then his mind went blank again, and the pictures began to form and vanish under his eyelids. There was nothing distinctive about the pictures. They were always masses of leaves and shrub-like branches shot through with hot sunshine.

A knock at the door aroused him. He was not asleep, and his mind immediately connected the knock with a telegram, or letter, or perhaps one of the servants bringing back clean clothes from the laundry. He was thinking about Joe and wondering where he was, as he said, "Come in."

He was still thinking about Joe, and did not turn toward the door. He heard it close softly. There was a long silence. He forgot that there had been a knock at the door, and was still staring blankly before him when he heard a woman's sob. It was involuntary, spasmodic, checked, and stifled—he noted that as he turned about. The next instant he was on his feet.

"Ruth!" he said, amazed and bewildered.

Her face was white and strained. She stood just inside the door, one hand against it for support, the other pressed to her side. She extended both hands toward him piteously, and started forward to meet him. As he caught her hands and led her to the Morris chair he noticed how cold they were. He drew up another chair and sat down on the broad arm of it. He was too confused to speak. In his own mind his affair with Ruth was closed and sealed. He felt much in the same way that he would have felt had the Shelly Hot Springs Laundry suddenly invaded the Hotel Metropole with a whole week's washing ready for him to pitch into. Several times he was about to speak, and each time he hesitated.

"No one knows I am here," Ruth said in a faint voice, with an appealing smile.

"What did you say?" he asked.

He was surprised at the sound of his own voice.

She repeated her words.

"Oh," he said, then wondered what more he could possibly say.

"I saw you come in, and I waited a few minutes."

"Oh," he said again.

He had never been so tongue-tied in his life. Positively he did not have an idea in his head. He felt stupid and awkward, but for the life of him he could think of nothing to say. It would have been easier had the intrusion been the Shelly Hot Springs laundry. He could have rolled up his sleeves and gone to work.

"And then you came in," he said finally.

She nodded, with a slightly arch expression, and loosened the scarf at her throat.

"I saw you first from across the street when you were with that girl."

"Oh, yes," he said simply. "I took her down to night school."

"Well, aren't you glad to see me?" she said at the end of another silence.

"Yes, yes." He spoke hastily. "But wasn't it rash of you to come here?"

"I slipped in. Nobody knows I am here. I wanted to see you. I came to tell you I have been very foolish. I came because I could no longer stay away, because my heart compelled me to come, because—because I wanted to come."

She came forward, out of her chair and over to him. She rested her hand on his shoulder a moment, breathing quickly, and then slipped into his arms. And in his large, easy way, desirous of not inflicting hurt, knowing that to repulse this proffer of herself was to inflict the most grievous hurt a woman could receive, he folded his arms around her and held her close. But there was no warmth in the embrace, no caress in the contact. She had come into his arms, and he held her, that was all. She nestled against him, and then, with a change of position, her hands crept up and rested upon his neck. But his flesh was not fire beneath those hands, and he felt awkward and uncomfortable.

"What makes you tremble so?" he asked. "Is it a chill? Shall I light the grate?"

He made a movement to disengage himself, but she clung more closely to him, shivering violently.

"It is merely nervousness," she said with chattering teeth. "I'll control myself in a minute. There, I am better already."

Slowly her shivering died away. He continued to hold her, but he was no longer puzzled. He knew now for what she had come.

"My mother wanted me to marry Charley Hapgood," she announced.

"Charley Hapgood, that fellow who speaks always in platitudes?" Martin groaned. Then he added, "And now, I suppose, your mother wants you to marry me."

He did not put it in the form of a question. He stated it as a certitude, and before his eyes began to dance the rows of figures of his royalties.

"She will not object, I know that much," Ruth said.

"She considers me quite eligible?"

Ruth nodded.

"And yet I am not a bit more eligible now than I was when she broke our engagement," he meditated. "I haven't changed any. I'm the same Martin Eden, though for that matter I'm a bit worse—I smoke now. Don't you smell my breath?"

In reply she pressed her open fingers against his lips, placed them graciously and playfully, and in expectancy of the kiss that of old had always been a consequence. But there was no caressing answer of Martin's lips. He waited until the fingers were removed and then went on.

"I am not changed. I haven't got a job. I'm not looking for a job. Furthermore, I am not going to look for a job. And I still believe that Herbert Spencer is a great and noble man and that Judge Blount is an unmitigated ass. I had dinner with him the other night, so I ought to know."

"But you didn't accept father's invitation," she chided.

"So you know about that? Who sent him? Your mother?"

She remained silent.

"Then she did send him. I thought so. And now I suppose she has sent you."

"No one knows that I am here," she protested. "Do you think my mother would permit this?"

"She'd permit you to marry me, that's certain."

She gave a sharp cry. "Oh, Martin, don't be cruel. You have not kissed me once. You are as unresponsive as a stone. And think what I have dared to do." She looked about her with a shiver, though half the look was curiosity. "Just think of where I am."

"I could die for you! I could die for you!"— Lizzie's words were ringing in his ears.

"Why didn't you dare it before?" he asked harshly. "When I hadn't a job? When I was starving? When I was just as I am now, as a man, as an artist, the same Martin Eden? That's the question I've been propounding to myself for many a day—not concerning you merely, but concerning everybody. You see I have not changed, though my sudden apparent appreciation in value compels me constantly to reassure myself on that point. I've got the same flesh on my bones, the same ten fingers and toes. I am the same. I have not developed any new strength nor virtue. My brain is the same old brain. I haven't made even one new generalization on literature or philosophy. I am personally of the same value that I was when nobody wanted me. And what is puzzling me is why they want me now. Surely they don't want me for myself, for myself is the same old self they did not want. Then they must want me for something else, for something that is outside of me, for something that is not I! Shall I tell you what that something is? It is for the recognition I have received. That recognition is not I. It resides in the minds of others. Then again for the money I have earned and am earning. But that money is not I. It resides in banks and in the pockets of Tom, Dick, and Harry. And is it for that, for the recognition and the money, that you now want me?"

"You are breaking my heart," she sobbed. "You know I love you, that I am here because I love you."

"I am afraid you don't see my point," he said gently. "What I mean is: if you love me, how does it happen that you love me now so much more than you did when your love was weak enough to deny me?"

"Forget and forgive," she cried passionately. "I loved you all the time, remember that, and I am here, now, in your arms."

"I'm afraid I am a shrewd merchant, peering into the scales, trying to weigh your love and find out what manner of thing it is."

She withdrew herself from his arms, sat upright, and looked at him long and searchingly. She was about to speak, then faltered and changed her mind.

"You see, it appears this way to me," he went on. "When I was all that I am now, nobody out of my own class seemed to care for me. When my books were all written, no one who had read the manuscripts seemed to care for them. In point of fact, because of the stuff I had written they seemed to care even less for me. In writing the stuff it seemed that I had committed acts that were, to say the least, derogatory. 'Get a job,' everybody said."

She made a movement of dissent.

"Yes, yes," he said; "except in your case you told me to get a position. The homely word *job,* like much that I have written, offends you. It is brutal. But I assure you it was no less brutal to me when everybody I knew recommended it to me as they would recommend right conduct to an immoral creature. But to return. The publication of what I had written, and the public notice I received, wrought a change in the fibre of your love. Martin Eden, with his work all performed, you would not marry. Your love for him was not strong enough to enable you to marry him. But your love is now strong enough, and I cannot avoid the conclusion that its strength arises from the publication and the public notice. In your case I do not mention royalties, though I am certain that they apply to the change wrought in your mother and father. Of course, all this is not flattering to me. But worst of all, it makes me question love, sacred love. Is love so gross a thing that it must feed upon publication and public notice? It would seem so. I have sat and thought upon it till my head went around."

"Poor, dear head." She reached up a hand and passed the fingers soothingly through his hair. "Let it go around no more. Let us begin anew, now. I loved you all the time. I know that I was weak in yielding to my mother's will. I should not have done so. Yet I have heard you speak so often with broad charity of the fallibility and frailty of humankind. Extend that charity to me. I acted mistakenly. Forgive me."

"Oh, I do forgive," he said impatiently. "It is easy to forgive where there is really nothing to forgive. Nothing that you have done requires forgiveness. One acts according to one's lights, and more than that one cannot do. As well might I ask you to forgive me for my not getting a job."

"I meant well," she protested. "You know that. I could not have loved you and not meant well."

"True; but you would have destroyed me out of your well-meaning.

"Yes, yes," he shut off her attempted objection. "You would have destroyed my writing and my career. Realism is imperative to my nature, and the bourgeois spirit hates realism. The bourgeoisie is cowardly. It is afraid of life. And all your effort was to make me afraid of life. You would have formalized me. You would have compressed me into a two-by-four pigeonhole of life, where all life's values are unreal, and false, and vulgar." He felt her stir protestingly. "Vulgarity—a hearty vulgarity, I'll admit—is the basis of bourgeois refinement and culture. As I say, you wanted to formalize me, to make me over into one of your own class, with your class-ideals, class-values, and class-prejudices." He shook his head sadly. "And you do not understand, even now, what I am saying. My words do not mean to you what I endeavor to make them mean. What I say is so much fantasy to you. Yet to me it is vital reality. At the best you are a trifle puzzled and amused that this raw boy, crawling up out of the mire of the abyss, should pass judgment upon your class and call it vulgar."

She leaned her head wearily against his shoulder, and her body shivered with recurrent nervousness. He waited for a time for her to speak, and then went on.

"And now you want to renew our love. You want us to be married. You want me. And yet, listen—if my books had not been noticed, I'd nevertheless have been just what I am now. And you would have stayed away. It is all those damned books—"

"Don't swear," she interrupted.

Her reproof startled him. He broke into a harsh laugh.

"That's it," he said, "at a high moment, when what seems your life's happiness is at stake, you are afraid of life in the same old way—afraid of life and a healthy oath."

She was stung by his words into realization of the puerility of her act, and yet she felt that he had magnified it unduly and was consequently resentful. They sat in silence for a long time, she thinking desperately and he pondering upon his love which had departed. He knew, now, that he had not really loved her. It was an idealized Ruth he had loved, an ethereal creature of his own creating, the bright and luminous spirit of his love-poems. The real bourgeois Ruth, with all the bourgeois failings and with the hopeless cramp of the bourgeois psychology in her mind, he had never loved.

She suddenly began to speak.

"I know that much you have said is so. I have been afraid of life. I did not love you well enough. I have learned to love better. I love you for what you are, for what you were, for the ways even by which you have become. I love you for the ways wherein you differ from what you call my class, for your beliefs which I do not understand but which I know I can come to understand. I shall devote myself to understanding them. And even your smoking and your swearing—they are part of you and I will love you for them, too. I can still learn. In the last ten minutes I have learned much. That I have dared to come here is a token of what I have already learned. Oh, Martin!—"

She was sobbing and nestling close against him.

For the first time his arms folded her gently and with sympathy, and she acknowledged it with a happy movement and a brightening face.

"It is too late," he said. He remembered Lizzie's words. "I am a sick man—oh, not my body. It is my soul, my brain. I seem to have lost all values. I care for nothing. If you had been this way a few months ago, it would have been different. It is too late, now."

"It is not too late," she cried. "I will show you. I will prove to you that my love has grown, that it is greater to me than my class and all that is dearest to me. All that is dearest to the bourgeoisie I will flout. I am no longer afraid of life. I will leave my father and mother, and let my name become a by-word with my friends. I will come to you here and now, in free love if you will, and I will be proud and glad to be with you. If I have been a traitor to love, I will now, for love's sake, be a traitor to all that made that earlier treason."

She stood before him, with shining eyes.

"I am waiting, Martin," she whispered, "waiting for you to accept me. Look at me."

It was splendid, he thought, looking at her. She had redeemed herself for all that she had lacked, rising up at last, true woman, superior to the iron rule of bourgeois convention. It was splendid, magnificent, desperate. And yet, what was the matter with him? He was not thrilled nor stirred by what she had done. It was splendid and magnificent only intellectually. In what should have been a moment of fire, he coldly appraised her. His heart was untouched. He was unaware of any desire for her. Again he remembered Lizzie's words.

"I am sick, very sick," he said with a despairing gesture. "How sick I did not know till now. Something has gone out of me. I have always been unafraid of life, but I never dreamed of being sated with life. Life has so filled me that I am empty of any desire for anything. If there were room, I should want you, now. You see how sick I am."

He leaned his head back and closed his eyes; and like a child, crying, that forgets its grief in watching the sunlight percolate through the tear-dimmed films over the pupils, so Martin forgot his sickness, the presence of Ruth, everything, in watching the masses of vegetation, shot through hotly with sunshine that took form and blazed against the background of his eyelids. It was not restful, that green foliage. The sunlight was too raw and glaring. It hurt him to look at it, and yet he looked, he knew not why.

He was brought back to himself by the rattle of the door-knob. Ruth was at the door.

"How shall I get out?" she questioned tearfully. "I am afraid."

"Oh, forgive me," he cried, springing to his feet. "I'm not myself, you know. I forgot you were here." He put his hand to his head. "You see, I'm not just right. I'll take you home. We can go out by the servants' entrance. No one will see us. Pull down that veil and everything will be all right."

She clung to his arm through the dim-lighted passages and down the narrow stairs.

"I am safe now," she said, when they emerged on the sidewalk, at the same time starting to take her hand from his arm.

"No, no, I'll see you home," he answered.

"No, please don't," she objected. "It is unnecessary."

Again she started to remove her hand. He felt a momentary curiosity. Now that she was out of danger she was afraid. She was in almost a panic to be quit of him. He could see no reason for it and attributed it to her nervousness. So he restrained her withdrawing hand and started to walk on with her. Halfway down the block, he saw a man in a long overcoat shrink back into a doorway. He shot a glance in as he passed by, and, despite the high turned-up collar, he was certain that he recognized Ruth's brother, Norman.

During the walk Ruth and Martin held little conversation. She was stunned. He was apathetic. Once, he mentioned that he was going away, back to the South Seas, and, once, she asked him to forgive her having come to him. And that was all. The parting at her door was conventional. They shook hands, said good night, and he lifted his hat. The door swung shut, and he lighted a cigarette and turned back for his hotel. When he came to the doorway into which he had seen Norman shrink, he stopped and looked in in a speculative humor.

"She lied," he said aloud. "She made believe to me that she had dared greatly, and all the while she knew the brother that brought her was waiting to take her back." He burst into laughter. "Oh, these bourgeois! When I was broke, I was not fit to be seen with his sister. When I have a bank account, he brings her to me."

As he swung on his heel to go on, a tramp, going in the same direction, begged him over his shoulder.

"Say, mister, can you give me a quarter to get a bed?" were the words.

But it was the voice that made Martin turn around. The next instant he had Joe by the hand.

"D'ye remember that time we parted at the Hot Springs?" the other was saying. "I said then we'd meet again. I felt it in my bones. An' here we are."

"You're looking good," Martin said admiringly, "and you've put on weight."

"I sure have." Joe's face was beaming. "I never knew what it was to live till I hit hoboin'. I'm thirty pounds heavier an' feel tiptop all the time. Why, I was worked to skin an' bone in them old days. Hoboin' sure agrees with me."

"But you're looking for a bed just the same," Martin chided, "and it's a cold night."

"Huh? Lookin' for a bed?" Joe shot a hand into his hip pocket and brought it out filled with small change. "That beats hard graft," he exulted. "You just looked good; that's why I battered you."

Martin laughed and gave in.

"You've several full-sized drunks right there," he insinuated.

Joe slid the money back into his pocket.

"Not in mine," he announced. "No gettin' oryide for me, though there ain't nothin' to stop me except I don't want to. I've ben drunk once since I seen you last, an' then it was unexpected, bein' on an empty stomach. When I work like a beast, I drink like a beast. When I live like a man, I drink like a man—a jolt now an' again when I feel like it, an' that's all."

Martin arranged to meet him next day, and went on to the hotel. He paused in the office to look up steamer sailings. The *Mariposa* sailed for Tahiti in five days.

"Telephone over to-morrow and reserve a stateroom for me," he told the clerk. "No deck-stateroom, but down below, on the weather-side,—the port-side, remember that, the port-side. You'd better write it down."

Once in his room he got into bed and slipped off to sleep as gently as a child. The occurrences of the evening had made no impression on him. His mind was dead to impressions. The glow of warmth with which he met Joe had been most fleeting. The succeeding minute he had been bothered by the ex-laundryman's presence and by the compulsion of conversation. That in five more days he sailed for his loved South Seas meant nothing to him. So he closed his eyes and slept normally and comfortably for eight uninterrupted hours. He was not restless. He did not change his position, nor did he dream. Sleep had become to him oblivion, and each day that he awoke, he awoke with regret. Life worried and bored him, and time was a vexation.

XLVI

"Say, Joe," was his greeting to his old-time working-mate next morning, "there's a Frenchman out on Twenty-eighth Street. He's made a pot of money, and he's going back to France. It's a dandy, well-appointed, small steam laundry. There's a start for you if you want to settle down. Here, take this; buy some clothes with it and be at this man's office by ten o'clock. He looked up the laundry for me, and he'll take you out and show you around. If you like it, and think it is worth the price—twelve thousand—let me know and it is yours. Now run along. I'm busy. I'll see you later."

"Now look here, Mart," the other said slowly, with kindling anger, "I come here this mornin' to see you. Savve? I didn't come here to get no laundry. I come here for a talk for old friends' sake, and you shove a laundry at me. I tell you what you can do. You can take that laundry an' go to hell."

He was starting to fling out of the room when Martin caught him by the shoulder and whirled him around.

"Now look here, Joe," he said; "if you act that way, I'll punch your head. And for old friends' sake I'll punch it hard. Savve?—you will, will you?"

Joe had clinched and attempted to throw him, and he was twisting and writhing out of the advantage of the other's hold. They reeled about the room, locked in each other's arms, and came down with a crash across the splintered wreckage of a wicker chair. Joe was underneath, with arms spread out and held and with Martin's knee on his chest. He was panting and gasping for breath when Martin released him.

"Now we'll talk a moment," Martin said. "You can't get fresh with me. I want that laundry business finished first of all. Then you can come back and we'll talk for old sake's sake. I told you I was busy. Look at that."

A servant had just come in with the morning mail, a great mass of letters and magazines.

"How can I wade through that and talk with you? You go and fix up that laundry, and then we'll get together."

"All right," Joe admitted reluctantly. "I thought you was turnin' me down, but I guess I was mistaken. But you can't lick me, Mart, in a stand-up fight. I've got the reach on you."

"We'll put on the gloves sometime and see," Martin said with a smile.

"Sure; as soon as I get that laundry going." Joe extended his arm. "You see that reach? It'll make you go a few."

Martin heaved a sigh of relief when the door closed behind the laundryman. He was becoming anti-social. Daily he found it a severer strain to be decent with people. Their presence perturbed him, and the effort of conversation irritated him. They made him restless, and no sooner was he in contact with them than he was casting about for excuses to get rid of them.

He did not proceed to attack his mail, and for a half hour he lolled in his chair, doing nothing, while no more than vague, half-formed thoughts occasionally filtered through his intelligence, or rather, at wide intervals, themselves constituted the flickering of his intelligence.

He roused himself and began glancing through his mail. There were a dozen requests for autographs—he knew them at sight; there were professional begging letters; and there were letters from cranks, ranging from the man with a working model of perpetual motion, and the man who demonstrated that the surface of the earth was the inside of a hollow sphere, to the man seeking financial aid to purchase the Peninsula of Lower California for the purpose of communist colonization. There were letters from women seeking to know him, and over one such he smiled, for enclosed was her receipt for pew-rent, sent as evidence of her good faith and as proof of her respectability.

Editors and publishers contributed to the daily heap of letters, the former on their knees for his manuscripts, the latter on their knees for his books—his poor disdained manuscripts that had kept all he possessed in pawn for so many dreary months in order to find them in postage. There were unexpected checks for English serial rights and for advance payments on foreign translations. His English agent announced the sale of German translation rights in three of his books, and informed him that Swedish editions, from which he could expect nothing because Sweden was not a party to the Berne Convention, were already on the market. Then there was a nominal request for his permission for a Russian translation, that country being likewise outside the Berne Convention.

He turned to the huge bundle of clippings which had come in from his press bureau, and read about himself and his vogue, which had become a furore. All his creative output had been flung to the public in one magnificent sweep. That seemed to account for it. He had taken the public off its feet, the way Kipling had, that time when he lay near to death and all the mob, animated by a mob-mind thought, began suddenly to read him. Martin remembered how that same world-mob, having read him and acclaimed him and not understood him in the least, had, abruptly, a few months later, flung itself upon him and torn him to pieces. Martin grinned at the thought. Who was he that he should not be similarly treated in a few more months? Well, he would fool the mob. He would be away, in the South Seas, building his grass house, trading for pearls and copra, jumping reefs in frail outriggers, catching sharks and bonitas, hunting wild goats among the cliffs of the valley that lay next to the valley of Taiohae.

In the moment of that thought the desperateness of his situation dawned upon him. He saw, cleared eyed, that he was in the Valley of the Shadow. All the life that was in him was fading, fainting, making toward death. He realized how much he slept, and how much he desired to sleep. Of old, he had hated sleep. It had robbed him of precious moments of living. Four hours of sleep in the twenty-four had meant being robbed of four hours of life. How he had grudged sleep! Now it was life he grudged. Life was not good; its taste in his mouth was without tang, and bitter. This was his peril. Life that did not yearn toward life was in fair way toward ceasing. Some remote instinct for preservation stirred in him, and he knew he must get away. He glanced about the room, and the thought of packing was burdensome. Perhaps it would be better to leave that to the last. In the meantime he might be getting an outfit.

He put on his hat and went out, stopping in at a gun-store, where he spent the remainder of the morning buying automatic rifles, ammunition, and fishing tackle. Fashions changed in trading, and he knew he would have to wait till he reached Tahiti before ordering his trade-goods. They could come up from Australia, anyway. This solution was a source of pleasure. He had avoided doing something, and the doing of anything just now was unpleasant. He went back to the hotel gladly, with a feeling of satisfaction in that the comfortable Morris chair was waiting for him; and he groaned inwardly, on entering his room, at sight of Joe in the Morris chair.

Joe was delighted with the laundry. Everything was settled, and he would enter into possession next day. Martin lay on the bed, with closed eyes, while the other talked on. Martin's thoughts were far away—so far away that he was rarely aware that he was thinking. It was only by an effort that he occasionally responded. And yet this was Joe, whom he had always liked. But Joe was too keen with life. The boisterous impact of it on Martin's jaded mind was a hurt. It was an aching probe to his tired sensitiveness. When Joe reminded him that sometime in the future they were going to put on the gloves together, he could almost have screamed.

"Remember, Joe, you're to run the laundry according to those old rules you used to lay down at Shelly Hot Springs," he said. "No overworking. No working at night. And no children at the mangles. No children anywhere. And a fair wage."

Joe nodded and pulled out a note-book.

"Look at here. I was workin' out them rules before breakfast this A.M. What d'ye think of them?"

He read them aloud, and Martin approved, worrying at the same time as to when Joe would take himself off.

It was late afternoon when he awoke. Slowly the fact of life came back to him. He glanced about the room. Joe had evidently stolen away after he had dozed off. That was considerate of Joe, he thought. Then he closed his eyes and slept again.

In the days that followed Joe was too busy organizing and taking hold of the laundry to bother him much; and it was not until the day before sailing that the newspapers made the announcement that he had taken passage on the *Mariposa.* Once, when the instinct of preservation fluttered, he went to a doctor and underwent a searching physical examination. Nothing could be found the matter with him. His heart and lungs were pronounced magnificent. Every organ, so far as the doctor could know, was normal and was working normally.

"There is nothing the matter with you, Mr. Eden," he said, "positively nothing the matter with you. You are in the pink of condition. Candidly, I envy you your health. It is superb. Look at that chest. There, and in your stomach, lies the secret of your remarkable constitution. Physically, you are a man in a thousand—in ten thousand. Barring accidents, you should live to be a hundred."

And Martin knew that Lizzie's diagnosis had been correct. Physically he was all right. It was his "think-machine" that had gone wrong, and there was no cure for that except to get away to the South Seas. The trouble was that now, on the verge of departure, he had no desire to go. The South Seas charmed him no more than did bourgeois civilization. There was no zest in the thought of departure, while the act of departure appalled him as a weariness of the flesh. He would have felt better if he were already on board and gone.

The last day was a sore trial. Having read of his sailing in the morning papers, Bernard Higginbotham, Gertrude, and all the family came to say good-by, as did Hermann von Schmidt and Marian. Then there was business to be transacted, bills to be paid, and everlasting reporters to be endured. He said good-by to Lizzie Connolly, abruptly, at the entrance to night school, and hurried away. At the hotel he found Joe, too busy all day with the laundry to have come to him earlier. It was the last straw, but Martin gripped the arms of his chair and talked and listened for half an hour.

"You know, Joe," he said, "that you are not tied down to that laundry. There are no strings on it. You can sell it any time and blow the money. Any time you get sick of it and want to hit the road, just pull out. Do what will make you the happiest."

Joe shook his head.

"No more road in mine, thank you kindly. Hoboin's all right, exceptin' for one thing —the girls. I can't help it, but I'm a ladies' man. I can't get along without 'em, and you've got to get along without 'em when you're hoboin'. The times I've passed by houses where dances an' parties was goin' on, an' heard the women laugh, an' saw their white dresses and smiling faces through the windows—Gee! I tell you them moments was plain hell. I like dancin' an' picnics, an' walking in the moonlight, an' all the rest too well. Me for the laundry, and a good front, with big iron dollars clinkin' in my jeans. I seen a girl already, just yesterday, and, d'ye know, I'm feelin' already I'd just as soon marry her as not. I've ben whistlin' all day at the thought of it. She's a beaut, with the kindest eyes and softest voice you ever heard. Me for her, you can stack on that. Say, why don't you get married with all this money to burn? You could get the finest girl in the land."

Martin shook his head with a smile, but in his secret heart he was wondering why any man wanted to marry. It seemed an amazing and incomprehensible thing.

From the deck of the *Mariposa,* at the sailing hour, he saw Lizzie Connolly hiding on the skirts of the crowd on the wharf. Take her with you, came the thought. It is easy to be kind. She will be supremely happy. It was almost a temptation one moment, and the succeeding moment it became a terror. He was in a panic at the thought of it. His tired soul cried out in protest. He turned away from the rail with a groan, muttering, "Man, you are too sick, you are too sick."

He fled to his stateroom, where he lurked until the steamer was clear of the dock. In the dining saloon, at luncheon, he found himself in the place of honor, at the captain's right; and he was not long in discovering that he was the great man on board. But no more unsatisfactory great man ever sailed on a ship. He spent the afternoon in a deck-chair, with closed eyes, dozing brokenly most of the time, and in the evening went early to bed.

After the second day, recovered from seasickness, the full passenger list was in evidence, and the more he saw of the passengers the more he disliked them. Yet he knew that he did them injustice. They were good and kindly people, he forced himself to acknowledge, and in the moment of acknowledgment he qualified—good and kindly like all the bourgeoisie, with all the psychological cramp and intellectual futility of their kind. They bored him when they talked with him, their little superficial minds were so filled with emptiness; while the boisterous high spirits and the excessive energy of the younger people shocked him. They were never quiet, ceaselessly playing deck-quoits, tossing rings, promenading, or rushing to the rail with loud cries to watch the leaping porpoises and the first schools of flying fish.

He slept much. After breakfast he sought his deck-chair with a magazine he never finished. The printed pages tired him. He puzzled that men found so much to write about, and, puzzling, dozed in his chair. When the gong awoke him for luncheon, he was irritated that he must awaken. There was no satisfaction in being awake.

Once, he tried to arouse himself from his lethargy, and went forward into the forecastle with the sailors. But the breed of sailors seemed to have changed since the days he had lived in the forecastle. He could find no kinship with these stolid-faced, ox-minded bestial creatures. He was in despair. Up above nobody had wanted Martin Eden for his own sake, and he could not go back to those of his own class who had wanted him in the past. He did not want them. He could not stand them any more than he could stand the stupid first-cabin passengers and the riotous young people.

Life was to him like strong, white light that hurts the tired eyes of a sick person. During every conscious moment life blazed in a raw glare around him and upon him. It hurt. It hurt intolerably. It was the first time in his life that Martin had travelled first class. On ships at sea he had always been in the forecastle, the steerage, or in the black depths of the coal-hold, passing coal. In those days, climbing up the iron ladders from out the pit of stifling heat, he had often caught glimpses of the passengers, in cool white, doing nothing but enjoy themselves, under awnings spread to keep the sun and wind away from them, with subservient stewards taking care of their every want and whim, and it had seemed to him that the realm in which they moved and had their being was nothing else than paradise. Well, here he was, the great man on board, in the midmost centre of it, sitting at the captain's right hand, and yet vainly harking back to forecastle and stoke-hole in quest of the Paradise he had lost. He had found no new one, and now he could not find the old one.

He strove to stir himself and find something to interest him. He ventured the petty officers' mess, and was glad to get away. He talked with a quartermaster off duty, an intelligent man who promptly prodded him with the socialist propaganda and forced into his hands a bunch of leaflets and pamphlets. He listened to the man expounding the slave-morality, and as he listened, he thought languidly of his own Nietzsche philosophy. But what was it worth, after all? He remembered one of Nietzsche's mad utterances wherein that madman had doubted truth. And who was to say? Perhaps Nietzsche had been right. Perhaps there was no truth in anything, no truth in truth—no such thing as truth. But his mind wearied quickly, and he was content to go back to his chair and doze.

Miserable as he was on the steamer, a new misery came upon him. What when the steamer reached Tahiti? He would have to go ashore. He would have to order his trade-goods, to find a passage on a schooner to the Marquesas, to do a thousand and one things that were awful to contemplate. Whenever he steeled himself deliberately to think, he could see the desperate peril in which he stood. In all truth, he was in the Valley of the Shadow, and his danger lay in that he was not afraid. If he were only afraid, he would make toward life. Being unafraid, he was drifting deeper into the shadow. He found no delight in the old familiar things of life. The *Mariposa* was now in the northeast trades, and this wine of wind, surging against him, irritated him. He had his chair moved to escape the embrace of this lusty comrade of old days and nights.

The day the *Mariposa* entered the doldrums, Martin was more miserable than ever. He could no longer sleep. He was soaked with sleep, and perforce he must now stay awake and endure the white glare of life. He moved about restlessly. The air was sticky and humid, and the rain-squalls were unrefreshing. He ached with life. He walked around the deck until that hurt too much, then sat in his chair until he was compelled to walk again. He forced himself at last to finish the magazine, and from the steamer library he culled several volumes of poetry. But they could not hold him, and once more he took to walking.

He stayed late on deck, after dinner, but that did not help him, for when he went below, he could not sleep. This surcease from life had failed him. It was too much. He turned on the electric light and tried to read. One of the volumes was a Swinburne. He lay in bed, glancing through its pages, until suddenly he became aware that he was reading with interest. He finished the stanza, attempted to read on, then came back to it. He rested the book face downward on his breast and fell to thinking. That was it.

The very thing. Strange that it had never come to him before. That was the meaning of it all; he had been drifting that way all the time, and now Swinburne showed him that it was the happy way out. He wanted rest, and here was rest awaiting him. He glanced at the open port-hole. Yes, it was large enough. For the first time in weeks he felt happy. At last he had discovered the cure of his ill. He picked up the book and read the stanza slowly aloud:—

" 'From too much love of living,
From hope and fear set free,
We thank with brief thanksgiving
Whatever gods may be
That no life lives forever;
That dead men rise up never;
That even the weariest river
Winds somewhere safe to sea.' "

He looked again at the open port. Swinburne had furnished the key. Life was ill, or, rather, it had become ill—an unbearable thing. "That dead men rise up never!" That line stirred him with a profound feeling of gratitude. It was the one beneficent thing in the universe. When life became an aching weariness, death was ready to soothe away to everlasting sleep. But what was he waiting for? It was time to go.

He arose and thrust his head out the port-hole, looking down into the milky wash. The *Mariposa* was deeply loaded, and, hanging by his hands, his feet would be in the water. He could slip in noiselessly. No one would hear. A smother of spray dashed up, wetting his face. It tasted salt on his lips, and the taste was good. He wondered if he ought to write a swan-song, but laughed the thought away. There was no time. He was too impatient to be gone.

Turning off the light in his room so that it might not betray him, he went out the port-hole feet first. His shoulders stuck, and he forced himself back so as to try it with one arm down by his side. A roll of the steamer aided him, and he was through, hanging by his hands. When his feet touched the sea, he let go. He was in a milky froth of water. The side of the *Mariposa* rushed past him like a dark wall, broken here and there by lighted ports. She was certainly making time. Almost before he knew it, he was astern, swimming gently on the foam-crackling surface.

A bonita struck at his white body, and he laughed aloud. It had taken a piece out, and the sting of it reminded him of why he was there. In the work to do he had forgotten the purpose of it. The lights of the *Mariposa* were growing dim in the distance, and there he was, swimming confidently, as though it were his intention to make for the nearest land a thousand miles or so away.

It was the automatic instinct to live. He ceased swimming, but the moment he felt the water rising above his mouth the hands struck out sharply with a lifting movement. The will to live, was his thought, and the thought was accompanied by a sneer. Well, he had will,—ay, will strong enough that with one last exertion it could destroy itself and cease to be.

He changed his position to a vertical one. He glanced up at the quiet stars, at the same time emptying his lungs of air. With swift, vigorous propulsion of hands and feet, he lifted his shoulders and half his chest out of water. This was to gain impetus for the descent. Then he let himself go and sank without movement, a white statue, into the sea. He breathed in the water deeply, deliberately, after the manner of a man taking an anaesthetic. When he strangled, quite involuntarily his arms and legs clawed the water and drove him up to the surface and into the clear sight of the stars.

The will to live, he thought disdainfully, vainly endeavoring not to breathe the air into his bursting lungs. Well, he would have to try a new way. He filled his lungs with air, filled them full. This supply would take him far down. He turned over and went down head first, swimming with all his strength and all his will. Deeper and deeper he went. His eyes were open, and he watched the ghostly, phosphorescent trails of the darting bonita. As he swam, he hoped that they would not strike at him, for it might snap the tension of his will. But they did not strike, and he found time to be grateful for this last kindness of life.

Down, down, he swam till his arms and legs grew tired and hardly moved. He knew that he was deep. The pressure on his ear-drums was a pain, and there was a buzzing in his head. His endurance was faltering, but he compelled his arms and legs to drive him deeper until his will snapped and the air drove from his lungs in a great explosive rush. The bubbles rubbed and bounded like tiny balloons against his cheeks and eyes as they took their upward flight. Then came pain and strangulation. This hurt was not death, was the thought that oscillated through his reeling consciousness. Death did not hurt. It was life, the pangs of life, this awful, suffocating feeling; it was the last blow life could deal him.

His wilful hands and feet began to beat and churn about, spasmodically and feebly. But he had fooled them and the will to live that made them beat and churn. He was too deep down. They could never bring him to the surface. He seemed floating languidly in a sea of dreamy vision. Colors and radiances surrounded him and bathed him and pervaded him. What was that? It seemed a lighthouse; but it was inside his brain—a flashing, bright white light. It flashed swifter and swifter. There was a long rumble of sound, and it seemed to him that he was falling down a vast and interminable stairway. And somewhere at the bottom he fell into darkness. That much he knew. He had fallen into darkness. And at the instant he knew, he ceased to know.

JOHN BARLEYCORN

I

IT ALL came to me one election day. It was on a warm California afternoon, and I had ridden down into the Valley of the Moon from the ranch to the little village to vote yes and no to a host of proposed amendments to the Constitution of the State of California. Because of the warmth of the day I had had several drinks before casting my ballot, and divers drinks after casting it. Then I had ridden up through the vine-clad hills and rolling pastures of the ranch and arrived at the farmhouse in time for another drink and supper.

"How did you vote on the suffrage amendment?" Charmian asked.

"I voted for it."

She uttered an exclamation of surprise. For be it known, in my younger days, despite my ardent democracy, I had been opposed to woman suffrage. In my later and more tolerant years I had been unenthusiastic in my acceptance of it as an inevitable social phenomenon.

"Now just why did you vote for it?" Charmian asked.

I answered. I answered at length. I answered indignantly. The more I answered, the more indignant I became. (No; I was not drunk. The horse I had ridden was well-named "The Outlaw." I'd like to see any drunken man ride her.)

And yet—how shall I say?—I was lighted up, I was feeling "good," I was pleasantly jingled.

"When the women get the ballot, they will vote for prohibition," I said. "It is the wives, and sisters, and mothers, and they only, who will drive the nails into the coffin of John Barleycorn—"

"But I thought you were a friend to John Barleycorn," Charmian interpolated.

"I am. I was. I am not. I never am. I am never less his friend than when he is with me and when I seem most his friend. He is the king of liars. He is the frankest truth-sayer. He is the august companion with whom one walks with the gods. He is also in league with the Noseless One. His way leads to truth naked, and to death. He gives clear vision, and muddy dreams. He is the enemy of life, and the teacher of wisdom beyond life's vision. He is a red-handed killer, and he slays youth."

And Charmian looked at me, and I knew she wondered where I had got it.

I continued to talk. As I say, I was lighted up. In my brain every thought was at home. Every thought, in its little cell, crouched ready-dressed at the door, like prisoners at midnight waiting a jail-break. And every thought was a vision, bright-imaged, sharp-cut, unmistakable. My brain was illuminated by the clear, white light of alcohol. John Barleycorn was on a truth-telling rampage, giving away the choicest secrets on himself. And I was his spokesman. There moved the multitudes of memories of my past life, all orderly arranged like soldiers in some vast review. It was mine to pick and choose. I was a lord of thought, the master of my vocabulary and of the totality of my experience, unerringly capable of selecting my data and building my exposition. For so John Barleycorn tricks and lures, setting the maggots of intelligence gnawing, whispering his fatal intuitions of truth, flinging purple passages into the monotony of one's days.

I outlined my life to Charmian, and expounded the makeup of my constitution. I was no hereditary alcoholic. I had been born with no organic, chemical predisposition toward alcohol. In this matter I was normal in my generation. Alcohol was an acquired taste. It had been painfully acquired. Alcohol had been a dreadfully repugnant thing—more nauseous than any physic. Even now I did not like the taste of it. I drank it only for its "kick." And from the age of five to that of twenty-five, I had not learned to care for its kick. Twenty years of unwilling apprenticeship had been required to make my system rebelliously tolerant of alcohol, to make me, in the heart and the deeps of me, desirous of alcohol.

I sketched my first contacts with alcohol, told of my first intoxications and revulsions, and pointed out always the one thing that in the end had won me over—namely, the accessibility of alcohol. Not only had it always been accessible, but every interest of my developing life had drawn me to it. A newsboy on the streets, a sailor, a miner, a wanderer in far lands, always where men came together to exchange ideas, to laugh and boast and dare, to relax, to forget the dull toil of tiresome nights and days, always they came together over alcohol. The saloon was the place of congregation. Men gathered to it as primitive men gathered about the fire of the squatting-place or the fire at the mouth of the cave.

I reminded Charmian of the canoe-houses from which she had been barred in the South Pacific, where the kinky-haired cannibals escaped from their womenkind and feasted and drank by themselves, the sacred precincts taboo to women under pain of death. As a youth, by way of the saloon I had escaped from the narrowness of women's influence into the wide free world of men. All ways led to the saloon. The thousand roads of romance and adventure drew together in the saloon, and thence led out and on over the world.

"The point is," I concluded my sermon, "that it is the accessibility of alcohol that has given me my taste for alcohol. I did not care for it. I used to laugh at it. Yet here I am, at the last, possessed with the drinker's desire. It took twenty years to implant that desire; and for ten years more that desire has grown. And the effect of satisfying that desire is anything but good. Temperamentally I am wholesome-hearted and merry. Yet when I walk with John Barleycorn I suffer all the damnation of intellectual pessimism.

"—But," I hastened to add (I always hasten to add), "—John Barleycorn must have his due. He does tell the truth. That is the curse of it. The so-called truths of life are not true. They are the vital lies by which life lives, and John Barleycorn gives them the lie."

"Which does not make toward life," Charmian said.

"Very true," I answered. "And that is the perfectest hell of it. John Barleycorn makes toward death. That is why I voted for the amendment to-day. I read back in my life and saw how the accessibility of alcohol had given me the taste for it. You see, comparatively few alcoholics are born in a generation. And by alcoholic I mean a man whose chemistry craves alcohol and drives him resistlessly to it. The great majority of habitual drinkers are born not only without desire for alcohol but with actual repugnance toward it. Not the first, nor the twentieth, nor the hundredth drink, succeeded in giving them the liking. But they learned, just as men learn to smoke; though it is far easier to learn to smoke than to learn to drink. They learned because alcohol was so accessible. The women know the game. They pay for it—the wives and sisters and mothers. And when they come to vote they will vote for prohibition. And the best of it is that there will be no hardship worked on the coming generation. Not having access to alcohol, not being predisposed toward alcohol, it will never miss alcohol. It will mean life more abundant for the manhood of the young boys born and growing up—ay, and life more abundant for the young girls born and growing up to share the lives of the young men."

"Why not write all this up for the sake of the young men and women coming?" Charmian asked. "Why not write it so as to help the wives and sisters and mothers to the way they should vote?"

"The 'Memoirs of an Alcoholic.' " I sneered—or, rather, John Barleycorn sneered; for he sat with me there at table in my pleasant, philanthropic jingle, and it is a trick of John Barleycorn to turn the smile to a sneer without an instant's warning.

"No," said Charmian, ignoring John Barleycorn's roughness as so many women have learned to do. "You have shown yourself no alcoholic, no dipsomaniac, but merely an habitual drinker, one who has made John Barleycorn's acquaintance through long years of rubbing shoulders with him. Write it up and call it 'Alcoholic Memoirs.' "

II

AND, ere I begin, I must ask the reader to walk with me in all sympathy; and, since sympathy is merely understanding, begin by understanding me and whom and what I write about. In the first place, I am a seasoned drinker. I have no constitutional predisposition for alcohol. I am not stupid. I am not a swine. I know the drinking game from A to Zed, and I have used my judgment in drinking. I never have to be put to bed. Nor do I stagger. In short, I am a normal, average man; and I drink in the normal, average way, as drinking goes. And this is the very point: I am writing of the effects of alcohol on the normal, average man. I have no word to say for or about the microscopically unimportant excessivist, the dipsomaniac.

There are, broadly speaking, two types of drinkers. There is the man whom we all know, stupid, unimaginative, whose brain is bitten numbly by numb maggots; who walks generously with wide-spread, tentative legs, falls frequently in the gutter, and who sees, in the extremity of his ecstasy, blue mice and pink elephants. He is the type that gives rise to the jokes in the funny papers.

The other type of drinker has imagination, vision. Even when most pleasantly jingled he walks straight and naturally, never staggers nor falls, and knows just where he is and what he is doing. It is not his body but his brain that is drunken. He may bubble with wit, or expand with good fellowship. Or he may see intellectual specters and phantoms that are cosmic and logical and that take the forms of syllogisms. It is when in this condition that he strips away the husks of life's healthiest illusions and gravely considers the iron collar of necessity welded about the neck of his soul. This is the hour of John Barleycorn's subtlest power. It is easy for any man to roll in the gutter. But it is a terrible ordeal for a man to stand upright on his two legs unswaying, and decide that in all the universe he finds for himself but one freedom, namely, the anticipating of the day of his death. With this man this is the hour of the white logic (of which more anon), when he knows that he may know only the laws of things—the meaning of things never. This is his danger hour. His feet are taking hold of the path that leads down into the grave.

All is clear to him. All these baffling head-reaches after immortality are but the panics of souls frightened by the fear of death, and cursed with the thrice-cursed gift of imagination. They have not the instinct for death; they lack the will to die when the time to die is at hand. They trick themselves into believing they will outwit the game and win to a future, leaving the other animals to the darkness of the grave or the annihilating heats of the crematory. But he, this man in the hour of his white logic, knows that they trick and outwit themselves. The one event happeneth to all alike. There is no new thing under the sun, not even that yearned-for bauble of feeble souls —immortality. But he knows, *he* knows, standing upright on his two legs unswaying. He is compounded of meat and wine and sparkle, of sun-mote and world-dust, a frail mechanism made to run for a span, to be tinkered at by doctors of divinity and doctors of physic, and to be flung into the scrap-heap at the end.

Of course, all this is soul-sickness, life-sickness. It is the penalty the imaginative man must pay for his friendship with John Barleycorn. The penalty paid by the stupid man is simpler, easier. He drinks himself into sottish unconsciousness. He sleeps a drugged sleep, and, if he dream, his dreams are dim and inarticulate. But to the imaginative man, John Barleycorn sends the pitiless, spectral syllogisms of the white logic. He looks upon life and all its affairs with the jaundiced eye of a pessimistic German philosopher. He sees through all illusions. He trans-values all values. God is bad, truth is a cheat, and life is a joke. From his calm-mad heights, with the certitude of a god, he beholds all life as evil. Wife, children, friends—in the clear, white light of his logic they are exposed as frauds and shams. He sees through them, and all that he sees is their frailty, their meagerness, their sordidness, their pitifulness. No longer do they fool him. They are miserable little egotisms, like all the other little humans, fluttering their May-fly life-dance of an hour. They are without freedom. They are puppets of chance. So is he. He realizes that. But there is one difference. He sees; he knows. And he knows his one freedom: he may anticipate the day of his death. All of which is not good for a man who is made to live and love and be loved. Yet suicide, quick or slow, a sudden spill or a gradual oozing away through the years, is the price John Barleycorn exacts. No friend of his ever escapes making the just, due payment.

III

I WAS five years old the first time I got drunk. It was on a hot day, and my father was plowing in the field. I was sent from the house, half a mile away, to carry to him a pail of beer. "And be sure you don't spill it," was the parting injunction.

It was, as I remember it, a lard pail, very wide across the top, and without a cover. As I toddled along, the beer slopped over the rim upon my legs. And as I toddled, I pondered. Beer was a very precious thing. Come to think of it, it must be wonderfully good. Else why was I never permitted to drink of it in the house? Other things kept from me by the grown-ups I had found good. Then this, too, was good. Trust the grown-ups. They knew. And anyway, the pail was too full. I was slopping it against my legs and spilling it on the ground. Why waste it? And no one would know whether I had drunk or spilled it.

I was so small that in order to negotiate the pail, I sat down and gathered it into my lap. First I sipped the foam. I was disappointed. The preciousness evaded me. Evidently it did not reside in the foam. Besides, the taste was not good. Then I remembered seeing the grown-ups blow the foam away before they drank. I buried my face in the foam and lapped the solid liquid beneath. It wasn't good at all. But still I drank. The grown-ups knew what they were about. Considering my diminutiveness, the size of the pail in my lap, and my drinking out of it with my breath held and my face buried to the ears in foam, it was rather difficult to estimate how much I drank. Also, I was gulping it down like medicine, in nauseous haste to get the ordeal over.

I shuddered when I started on, and decided that the good taste would come afterward. I tried several times more in the course of that long half-mile. Then, astounded by the quantity of beer that was lacking, and remembering having seen stale beer made to foam afresh, I took a stick and stirred what was left till it foamed to the brim.

And my father never noticed. He emptied the pail with the wide thirst of the sweating plowman, returned it to me, and started up the plow. I endeavored to walk beside the horses. I remember tottering and falling against their heels in front of the shining share, and that my father hauled back on the lines so violently that the horses nearly sat down on me. He told me afterward that it was by only a matter of inches that I escaped disembowelling. Vaguely, too, I remember, my father carried me in his arms to the trees on the edge of the field, while all the world reeled and swung about me and I was aware of deadly nausea mingled with an appalling conviction of sin.

I slept the afternoon away under the trees, and when my father roused me at sundown it was a very sick little boy that got up and dragged wearily homeward. I was exhausted, oppressed by the weight of my limbs, and in my stomach was a harp-like vibration that extended to my throat and brain. My condition was like that of one who had gone through a battle with poison. In truth, I had been poisoned.

In the weeks and months that followed I had no more interest in beer than in the kitchen stove after it had burned me. The grown-ups were right. Beer was not for children. The grown-ups didn't mind it; but neither did they mind taking pills and castor oil. As for me, I could manage to get along quite well without beer. Yes, and to the day of my death I could have managed to get along quite well without it. But circumstance decreed otherwise. At every turn in the world in which I lived, John Barleycorn beckoned. There was no escaping him. All paths led to him. And it took twenty years of contact, of exchanging greetings and passing on with my tongue in my cheek, to develop in me a sneaking liking for the rascal.

IV

My next bout with John Barleycorn occurred when I was seven. This time my imagination was at fault, and I was frightened into the encounter. Still farming, my family had moved to a ranch on the bleak sad coast of San Mateo County south of San Francisco. It was a wild, primitive countryside in those days; and often I heard my mother pride herself that we were old American stock and not immigrant Irish and Italians like our neighbors. In all our section there was only one other old American family.

One Sunday morning found me, how or why I cannot now remember, at the Morrisey ranch. A number of young people had gathered there from the nearer ranches. Besides, the oldsters had been there, drinking since early dawn, and, some of them, since the night before. The Morriseys were a huge breed, and there were many strapping great sons and uncles, heavy-booted, big-fisted, rough-voiced.

Suddenly there were screams from the girls and cries of "Fight!" There was a rush. Men hurled themselves out of the kitchen. Two giants, flush-faced, with graying hair, were locked in each other's arms. One was Black Matt, who, everybody said, had killed two men in his time. The women screamed softly, crossed themselves, or prayed brokenly, hiding their eyes and peeping through their fingers. But not I. It is a fair presumption that I was the most interested spectator. Maybe I would see that wonderful thing, a man killed. Anyway, I would see a man-fight. Great was my disappointment. Black Matt and Tom Morrisey merely held on to each other and lifted their clumsy-booted feet in what seemed a grotesque, elephantine dance. They were too drunk to fight. Then the peacemakers got hold of them and led them back to cement the new friendship in the kitchen.

Soon they were all talking at once, rumbling and roaring as big-chested open-air men will when whisky has whipped their taciturnity. And I, a little shaver of seven, my heart in my mouth, my trembling body strung tense as a deer's on the verge of flight, peered wonderingly in at the open door and learned more of the strangeness of men. And I marveled at Black Matt and Tom Morrisey, sprawled over the table, arms about each other's necks, weeping lovingly.

The kitchen-drinking continued, and the girls outside grew timorous. They knew the drink game, and all were certain that something terrible was going to happen. They protested that they did not wish to be there when it happened, and some one suggested going to a big Italian rancho four miles away, where they could get up a dance. Immediately they paired off, lad and lassie, and started down the sandy road. And each lad walked with his sweetheart—trust a child of seven to listen and to know the love affairs of his countryside. And behold, I, too, was a lad with a lassie. A little Irish girl of my own age had been paired off with me. We were the only children in this spontaneous affair. Perhaps the oldest couple might have been twenty. There were chits of girls, quite grown up, of fourteen and sixteen, walking with their fellows. But we were uniquely young, this little Irish girl and I, and we walked hand in hand, and, sometimes, under the tutelage of our elders, with my arm around her waist. Only that wasn't comfortable. And I was very proud, on that bright Sunday morning, going down the long bleak road among the sandhills. I, too, had my girl, and was a little man.

The Italian rancho was a bachelor establishment. Our visit was hailed with delight. The red wine was poured in tumblers for all, and the long dining-room was partly cleared for dancing. And the young fellows drank and danced with the girls to the strains of an accordeon. To me that music was divine. I had never heard anything so glorious. The young Italian who furnished it would even get up and dance, his arms around his girl, playing the accordeon behind her back. All of which was very wonderful for me, who did not dance, but who sat at a table and gazed wide-eyed at the amazingness of life. I was only a little lad, and there was so much of life for me to learn. As the time passed, the Irish lads began helping themselves to the wine, and jollity and high spirits reigned. I noted that some of them staggered and fell down in the dances, and that one had gone to sleep in a corner. Also, some of the girls were complaining and wanting to leave, and others of the girls were titteringly complacent, willing for anything to happen.

When our Italian hosts had offered me wine in a general sort of way, I had declined. My beer experience had been enough for me, and I had no inclination to traffic further in the stuff nor in anything related to it. Unfortunately, one young Italian, Peter, an impish soul, seeing me sitting solitary, stirred by a whim of the moment, half-filled a tumbler with wine and passed it to me. He was sitting across the table from me. I declined. His face grew stern, and he insistently proffered the wine. And then terror descended upon me—a terror which I must explain.

My mother had theories. First, she steadfastly maintained that brunettes and all the tribe of dark-eyed humans were deceitful. Needless to say, my mother was a blond. Next, she was convinced that the dark-eyed Latin races were profoundly sensitive, profoundly treacherous, and profoundly murderous. Again and again, drinking in the strangeness and the fearsomeness of the world from her lips, I had heard her state that if one offended an Italian, no matter how slightly and unintentionally, he was certain to retaliate by stabbing one in the back. That was her particular phrase—"stab you in the back."

Now, although I had been eager to see Black Matt kill Tom Morrisey that morning, I did not care to furnish to the dancers the spectacle of a knife sticking in *my* back. I had not yet learned to distinguish between facts and theories. My faith was implicit in my mother's exposition of the Italian character. Besides, I had some glimmering inkling of the sacredness of hospitality. Here was a treacherous, sensitive, murderous Italian, offering me hospitality. I had been taught to believe that if I offended him he would strike at me with a knife precisely as a horse kicked out when one got too close to its heels and worried it. Then, too, this Italian, Peter, had those terrible black eyes I had heard my mother talk about. They were eyes different from the eyes I knew, from the blues and grays and hazels of my own family, from the pale and genial blues of the Irish. Perhaps Peter had had a few drinks. At any rate his eyes were brilliantly black and sparkling with deviltry. They were the mysterious, the unknown, and who was I, a seven-year-old, to analyze them and know their prankishness? In them I visioned sudden death, and I declined the wine half-heartedly. The expression in his eyes changed. They grew stern and imperious as he shoved the tumbler of wine closer.

What could I do? I have faced real death since in my life, but never have I known the fear of death as I knew it then. I put the glass to my lips, and Peter's eyes relented. I knew he would not kill me just then. That was a relief. But the wine was not. It was cheap, new wine, bitter and sour, made of the leavings and scrapings of the vineyards and the vats, and it tasted far worse than beer. There is only one way to take medicine, and that is to take it. And that is the way I took that wine. I threw my head back and gulped it down. I had to gulp again and hold the poison down, for poison it was to my child's tissues and membranes.

Looking back now, I can realize that Peter was astounded. He half-filled a second tumbler and shoved it across the table. Frozen with fear, in despair at the fate which had befallen me, I gulped the second glass down like the first. This was too much for Peter. He must share the infant prodigy he had discovered. He called Dominick, a young mustached Italian, to see the sight. This time it was a full tumbler that was given me. One will do anything to live. I gripped myself, mastered the qualms that rose in my throat, and downed the stuff.

Dominick had never seen an infant of such heroic caliber. Twice again he refilled the tumbler, each time to the brim, and watched it disappear down my throat. By this time my exploits were attracting attention. Middle-aged Italian laborers, old-country peasants who did not talk English and who could not dance with the Irish girls, surrounded me. They were swarthy and wild-looking; they wore belts and red shirts; and I knew they carried knives; and they ringed me around like a pirate chorus. And Peter and Dominick made me show off for them.

Had I lacked imagination, had I been stupid, had I been stubbornly mulish in having my own way, I should never have got in this pickle. And the lads and lassies were dancing, and there was no one to save me from my fate. How much I drank I do not know. My memory of it is of an age-long suffering of fear in the midst of a murderous crew, and of an infinite number of glasses of red wine passing across the bare boards of a wine-drenched table and going down my burning throat. Bad as the wine was, a knife in the back was worse, and I must survive at any cost.

Looking back with the drinker's knowledge, I know now why I did not collapse stupefied upon the table. As I have said, I was frozen, I was paralyzed, with fear. The only movement I made was to convey that never-ending procession of glasses to my lips. I was a poised and motionless receptacle for all that quantity of wine. It lay inert in my fear-inert stomach. I was too frightened, even, for my stomach to turn. So all that Italian crew looked on and marveled at the infant phenomenon that downed wine with the *sang-froid* of an automaton. It is not in the spirit of braggadocio that I dare to assert they had never seen anything like it.

The time came to go. The tipsy antics of the lads had led a majority of the soberer-minded lassies to compel a departure. I found myself at the door, beside my little maiden. She had not had my experience, so she was sober. She was fascinated by the titubations of the lads who strove to walk beside their girls, and began to mimic them. I thought this a great game, and I, too, began to stagger tipsily. But she had no wine to stir up, while my movements quickly set the fumes rising to my head. Even at the start, I was more realistic than she. In several minutes I was astonishing myself. I saw one lad, after reeling half a dozen steps, pause at the side of the road, gravely peer into the ditch, and gravely, and after apparent deep thought, fall into it. To me this was excruciatingly funny. I staggered to the edge of the ditch, fully intending to stop on the edge. I came to myself, in the ditch, in process of being hauled out by several anxious-faced girls.

I didn't care to play at being drunk any more. There was no more fun in me. My eyes were beginning to swim, and with wide-open mouth I panted for air. A girl led me by the hand on either side, but my legs were leaden. The alcohol I had drunk was striking my heart and brain like a club. Had I been a weakling of a child, I am confident that it would have killed me. As it was, I know I was nearer death than any of the scared girls dreamed. I could hear them bickering among themselves as to whose fault it was; some were weeping—for themselves, for me, and for the disgraceful way their lads had behaved. But I was not interested. I was suffocating, and I wanted air. To move was agony. It made me pant harder. Yet those girls persisted in making me walk, and it was four miles home. Four miles! I remember my swimming eyes saw a small bridge across the road an infinite distance away. In fact, it was not a hundred feet distant. When I reached it, I sank down and lay on my back panting. The girls tried to lift me, but I was helpless and suffocating. Their cries of alarm brought Larry, a drunken youth of seventeen, who proceeded to resuscitate me by jumping on my chest. Dimly I remember this, and the squalling of the girls as they struggled with him and dragged him away. And then I knew nothing, though I learned afterward that Larry wound up under the bridge and spent the night there.

When I came to, it was dark. I had been carried unconscious for four miles and been put to bed. I was a sick child, and, despite the terrible strain on my heart and tissues, I continually relapsed into the madness of delirium. All the content of the terrible and horrible in my child's mind spilled out. The most frightful visions were realities to me. I saw murders committed, and I was pursued by murderers. I screamed and raved and fought. My sufferings were prodigious. Emerging from such delirium, I would hear my mother's voice: "But the child's brain. He will lose his reason." And sinking back into delirium, I would take the idea with me and be immured in madhouses, and be beaten by keepers, and surrounded by screeching lunatics.

One thing that had strongly impressed my young mind was the talk of my elders about the dens of iniquity in San Francisco's Chinatown. In my delirium I wandered deep beneath the ground through a thousand of these dens, and behind locked doors of iron I suffered and died a thousand deaths. And when I would come upon my father, seated at table in these subterranean crypts, gambling with Chinese for great stakes of gold, all my outrage gave vent in the vilest cursing. I would rise in bed, struggling against the detaining hands, and curse my father till the rafters rang. All the inconceivable filth a child running at large in a primitive countryside may hear men utter, was mine; and though I had never dared utter such oaths, they now poured from me, at the top of my lungs, as I cursed my father sitting there underground and gambling with long-haired, long-nailed Chinamen.

It is a wonder that I did not burst my heart or brain that night. A seven-year-old child's arteries and nerve-centers are scarcely fitted to endure the terrific paroxysms that convulsed me. No one slept in the thin, frame farmhouse that night when John Barleycorn had his will of me. And Larry, under the bridge, had no delirium like mine. I am confident that his sleep was stupefied and dreamless, and that he awoke next day merely to heaviness and moroseness, and that if he lives to-day he does not remember that night, so passing was it as an incident. But my brain was seared forever by that experience. Writing now, thirty years afterward, every vision is as distinct, as sharp-cut, every pain as vital and terrible, as on that night.

I was sick for days afterward, and I needed none of my mother's injunctions to avoid John Barleycorn in the future. My mother had been dreadfully shocked. She held that I had done wrong, very wrong, and that I had gone contrary to all her teaching. And how was I, who was never allowed to talk back, who lacked the very words with which to express my psychology—how was I to tell my mother that it was her teaching that was directly responsible for my drunkenness? Had it not been for her theories about dark eyes and Italian character, I should never have wet my lips with the sour, bitter wine. And not until man-grown did I tell her the true inwardness of that disgraceful affair.

In those after-days of sickness, I was confused on some points, and very clear on others. I felt guilty of sin, yet smarted with a sense of injustice. It had not been my fault; yet I had done wrong. But very clear was my resolution never to touch liquor again. No mad dog was ever more afraid of water than was I of alcohol.

Yet the point I am making is that this experience, terrible as it was, could not in the end deter me from forming John Barleycorn's cheek-by-jowl acquaintance. All about me, even then, were the forces moving me toward him. In the first place, barring my mother, ever extreme in her views, it seemed to me all the grown-ups looked upon the affair with tolerant eyes. It was a joke, something funny that had happened. There was no shame attached. Even the lads and lassies giggled and snickered over their part in the affair, narrating with gusto how Larry had jumped on my chest and slept under the bridge, how So-and-So had slept out in the sandhills that night, and what had happened to the other lad who fell in the ditch. As I say, so far as I could see, there was no shame anywhere. It had been something ticklishly, devilishly fine—a bright and gorgeous episode in the monotony of life and labor on that bleak, fog-girt coast.

The Irish ranchers twitted me good-naturedly on my exploit, and patted me on the back until I felt that I had done something heroic. Peter and Dominick and the other Italians were proud of my drinking prowess. The face of morality was not set against drinking. Besides, everybody drank. There was not a teetotaler in the community. Even the teacher of our little country school, a graying man of fifty, gave us vacations on the occasions when he wrestled with John Barleycorn and was thrown. Thus there was no spiritual deterrence. My loathing for alcohol was purely physiological. I didn't like the damned stuff.

V

THIS physical loathing for alcohol I have never got over. But I have conquered it. To this day I re-conquer it every time I take a drink. The palate never ceases to rebel, and the palate can be trusted to know what is good for the body. But men do not knowingly drink for the effect alcohol produces on the body. What they drink for is the brain-effect; and if it must come through the body, so much the worse for the body.

And yes, despite my physical loathing for alcohol, the brightest spots in my child life were the saloons. Sitting on the heavy potato wagons, wrapped in fog, feet stinging from inactivity, the horses plodding slowly along the deep road through the sandhills, one bright vision made the way never too long. The bright vision was the saloon at Colma, where my father, or whoever drove, always got out to get a drink. And I got out to warm by the great stove and get a soda cracker. Just one soda cracker, but a fabulous luxury. Saloons were good for something. Back behind the plodding horses, I would take an hour in consuming that one cracker. I took the smallest of nibbles, never losing a crumb, and chewed the nibble till it became the thinnest and most delectable of pastes. I never voluntarily swallowed this paste. I just tasted it, and went on tasting it, turning it over with my tongue, spreading it on the inside of one cheek, then on the inside of the other cheek, until, at the end, it eluded me and in tiny drops and oozelets slipped and dribbled down my throat. Horace Fletcher had nothing on me when it came to soda crackers.

I liked saloons. Especially I liked the San Francisco saloons. They had the most delicious dainties for the taking—strange breads and crackers, cheeses, sausages, sardines—wonderful foods that I never saw on our meager home-table. And once, I remember, a barkeeper mixed me a sweet temperance drink of syrup and soda water. My father did not pay for it. It was the barkeeper's treat, and he became my ideal of a good, kind man. I dreamed day dreams of him for years. Although I was seven years old at the time, I can see him now with undiminished clearness, though I never laid eyes on him but that one time. The saloon was south of Market Street in San Francisco. It stood on the west side of the street. As you entered, the bar was on the left. On the right, against the wall, was the free-lunch counter. It was a long, narrow room, and at the rear, beyond the beer kegs on tap, were small round tables and chairs. The barkeeper was blue-eyed, and had fair, silky hair peeping out from under a black silk skullcap. I remember he wore a brown Cardigan jacket, and I know precisely the spot, in the midst of the array of bottles, from which he took the bottle of red-colored syrup. He and my father talked long, and I sipped my sweet drink and worshiped him. And for years afterward I worshiped the memory of him.

Despite my two disastrous experiences, here was John Barleycorn, prevalent and accessible everywhere in the community, luring and drawing me. Here were connotations of the saloon making deep indentations in a child's mind. Here was a child, forming its first judgments of the world, finding the saloon a delightful and desirable place. Stores, nor public buildings, nor all the dwellings of men ever opened their doors to me and let me warm by their fires or permitted me to eat the food of the gods from narrow shelves against the wall. Their doors were ever closed to me; the saloon's doors were ever open. And always and everywhere I found saloons, on highway and byway, up narrow alleys and on busy thoroughfares, bright-lighted and cheerful, warm in winter and in summer dark and cool. Yes, the saloon was a mighty fine place, and it was more than that.

By the time I was ten years old, my family had abandoned ranching and gone to live in the city. And here, at ten, I began on the streets as a newsboy. One of the reasons for this was that we needed the money. Another reason was that I needed the exercise. I had found my way to the free public library, and was reading myself into nervous prostration. On the poor-ranches on which I had lived there had been no books. In ways truly miraculous, I had been lent four books, marvelous books, and them I had devoured. One was the life of Garfield; the second, Paul du Chaillu's African travels; the third, a novel by Ouida with the last forty pages missing; and the fourth, Irving's "Alhambra." This last had been lent me by a school-teacher. I was not a forward child. Unlike Oliver Twist, I was incapable of asking for more. When I returned the "Alhambra" to the teacher I hoped she would lend me another book. And because she did not —most likely she deemed me unappreciative—I cried all the way home on the three-mile tramp from the school to the ranch. I waited and yearned for her to lend me another book. Scores of times I nerved myself almost to the point of asking her, but never quite reached the necessary pitch of effrontery.

And then came the city of Oakland, and on the shelves of that free-library I discovered all the great world beyond the skyline. Here were thousands of books as good as my four wonder-books, and some were even better. Libraries were not concerned with children in those days, and I had strange adventures. I remember, in the catalogue, being impressed by the title, "The Adventures of Peregrine Pickle." I filled an application blank and the librarian handed me the collected and entirely unexpurgated works of Smollett in one huge volume. I read everything, but principally history and adventure, and all the old travels and voyages. I read mornings, afternoons, and nights. I read in bed, I read at table, I read as I walked to and from school, and I read at recess while the other boys were playing. I began to get the "jerks." To everybody I replied: "Go away. You make me nervous."

And so, at ten, I was out on the streets, a newsboy. I had no time to read. I was busy getting exercise and learning how to fight, busy learning forwardness, and brass and bluff. I had an imagination and a curiosity about all things that made me plastic. Not least among the things I was curious about was the saloon. And I was in and out of many a one. I remember, in those days, on the east side of Broadway between Sixth and Seventh, from corner to corner, there was a solid block of saloons.

In the saloons life was different. Men talked with great voices, laughed great laughs, and there was an atmosphere of greatness. Here was something more than common every-day where nothing happened. Here life was always very live, and, sometimes, even lurid, when blows were struck, and blood was shed, and big policemen came shouldering in. Great moments, these, for me, my head filled with all the wild and valiant fighting of the gallant adventures on sea and land. There were no big moments when I trudged along the street throwing my papers in at doors. But in the saloons, even the sots, stupefied, sprawling across the tables or in the sawdust, were objects of mystery and wonder.

And more, the saloons were right. The city fathers sanctioned them and licensed them. They were not the terrible places I heard boys deem them who lacked my opportunities to know. Terrible they might be, but then that only meant they were terribly wonderful, and it is the terribly wonderful that a boy desires to know. In the same way pirates, and shipwrecks, and battles were terrible; and what healthy boy wouldn't give his immortal soul to participate in such affairs?

Besides, in saloons I saw reporters, editors, lawyers, judges, whose names and faces I knew. They put the seal of social approval on the saloon. They verified my own feeling of fascination in the saloon. They, too, must have found there that something different, that something beyond, which I sensed and groped after. What it was, I did not know; yet there it must be, for there men focused like buzzing flies about a honey pot. I had no sorrows, and the world was very bright, so I could not guess that what these men sought was forgetfulness of jaded toil and stale grief.

Not that I drank at that time. From ten to fifteen I rarely tasted liquor, but I was intimately in contact with drinkers and drinking places. The only reason I did not drink was because I didn't like the stuff. As the time passed, I worked as boy-helper on an ice-wagon, set up pins in a bowling-alley with a saloon attached, and swept out saloons at Sunday picnic grounds.

Big jovial Josie Harper ran a road-house at Telegraph Avenue and Thirty-ninth Street. Here for a year I delivered an evening paper, until my route was changed to the water-front and tenderloin of Oakland. The first month, when I collected Josie Harper's bill, she poured me a glass of wine. I was ashamed to refuse, so I drank it. But after that I watched the chance when she wasn't around so as to collect from her barkeeper.

The first day I worked in the bowling-alley, the barkeeper, according to custom, called us boys up to have a drink after we had been setting up pins for several hours. The others asked for beer. I said I'd take ginger ale. The boys snickered, and I noticed the barkeeper favored me with a strange, searching scrutiny. Nevertheless he opened a bottle of ginger ale. Afterward, back in the alleys, in the pauses between games, the boys enlightened me. I had offended the barkeeper. A bottle of ginger ale cost the saloon ever so much more than a glass of steam beer; and it was up to me, if I wanted to hold my job, to drink beer. Besides, beer was food. I could work better on it. There was no food in ginger ale. After that, when I couldn't sneak out of it, I drank beer and wondered what men found in it that was so good. I was always aware that I was missing something.

What I really liked in those days was candy. For five cents I could buy five "cannon-balls"—big lumps of the most delicious lastingness. I could chew and worry a single one for an hour. Then there was a Mexican who sold big slabs of brown chewing-taffy for five cents each. It required a quarter of a day properly to absorb one of them. And many a day I made my entire lunch off of one of those slabs. In truth, I found food there, but not in beer.

VI

But the time was rapidly drawing near when I was to begin my second series of bouts with John Barleycorn. When I was fourteen, my head filled with the tales of the old voyagers, my vision with tropic isles and far sea-rims, I was sailing a small centerboard skiff around San Francisco Bay and on the Oakland Estuary. I wanted to go to sea. I wanted to get away from monotony and the commonplace. I was in the flower of my adolescence, a-thrill with romance and adventure, dreaming of wild life in the wild man-world. Little I guessed how all the warp and woof of that man-world was entangled with alcohol.

So, one day, as I hoisted sail on my skiff, I met Scotty. He was a husky youngster of seventeen, a runaway apprentice, he told me, from an English ship in Australia. He had just worked his way on another ship to San Francisco; and now he wanted to see about getting a berth on a whaler. Across the estuary, near where the whalers lay, was lying the sloop-yacht *Idler.* The caretaker was a harpooner who intended sailing next voyage on the whale ship *Bonanza.* Would I take him, Scotty, over in my skiff to call upon the harpooner?

Would I? Hadn't I heard the stories and rumors about the *Idler?*— the big sloop that had come up from the Sandwich Islands where it had been engaged in smuggling opium. And the harpooner who was caretaker! How often had I seen him and envied him his freedom. He never had to leave the water. He slept aboard the *Idler* each night, while I had to go home upon the land to go to bed. The harpooner was only nineteen years old (and I have never had anything but his own word that he was a harpooner); but he had been too shining and glorious a personality for me ever to address as I paddled around the yacht at a wistful distance. Would I take Scotty, the runaway sailor, to visit the harpooner, on the opium-smuggler *Idler?* Would I!

The harpooner came on deck to answer our hail, and invited us aboard. I played the sailor and the man, fending off the skiff so that it would not mar the yacht's white paint, dropping the skiff astern on a long painter, and making the painter fast with two nonchalant half-hitches. We went below. It was the first sea-interior I had ever seen. The clothing on the wall smelled musty. But what of that? Was it not the sea-gear of men?—leather jackets lined with corduroy, blue coats of pilot cloth, sou'westers, sea-boots, oilskins. And everywhere was in evidence the economy of space—the narrow bunks, the swinging tables, the incredible lockers. There were the tell-tale compass, the sea-lamps in their gimbals, the blue-backed charts carelessly rolled and tucked away, the signal-flags in alphabetical order, and a mariner's dividers jammed into the woodwork to hold a calendar. At last I was living. Here I sat, inside my first ship, a smuggler, accepted as a comrade by a harpooner and a runaway English sailor who said his name was Scotty.

The first thing that the harpooner, aged nineteen, and the sailor, aged seventeen, did to show that they were men, was to behave like men. The harpooner suggested the eminent desirableness of a drink, and Scotty searched his pockets for dimes and nickels. Then the harpooner carried away a pink flask to be filled in some blind pig, for there were no licensed saloons in that locality. We drank the cheap rotgut out of tumblers. Was I any the less strong, any the less valiant, than the harpooner and the sailor? They were men. They proved it by the way they drank. Drink was the badge of manhood. So I drank with them, drink by drink, raw and straight, though the damned stuff couldn't compare with a stick of chewing taffy or a delectable "cannonball." I shuddered and swallowed my gorge with every drink, though I manfully hid all such symptoms.

Divers times we filled the flask that afternoon. All I had was twenty cents, but I put it up like a man, though with secret regret at the enormous store of candy it could have bought. The liquor mounted in the heads of all of us, and the talk of Scotty and the harpooner was upon running the Easting down, gales off the Horn and pamperos off the Plate, lower topsail breezes, southerly busters, North Pacific gales, and of smashed whaleboats in the Arctic ice.

"You can't swim in that ice water," said the harpooner confidentially to me. "You double up in a minute and go down. When a whale smashes your boat, the thing to do is to get your belly across an oar, so that when the cold doubles you you'll float."

"Sure," I said, with a grateful nod and an air of certitude that I, too, would hunt whales and be in smashed boats in the Arctic Ocean. And, truly, I registered his advice as singularly valuable information, and filed it away in my brain, where it persists to this day.

But I couldn't talk—at first. Heavens! I was only fourteen, and had never been on the ocean in my life. I could only listen to the two sea-dogs, and show my manhood by drinking with them, fairly and squarely, drink and drink.

The liquor worked its will with me; the talk of Scotty and the harpooner poured through the pent space of the *Idler's* cabin and through my brain like great gusts of wide, free wind; and in imagination I lived my years to come and rocked over the wild, mad, glorious world on multitudinous adventures.

We unbent. Our inhibitions and taciturnities vanished. We were as if we had known each other for years and years, and we pledged ourselves to years of future voyagings together. The harpooner told of misadventures and secret shames. Scotty wept over his poor old mother in Edinburg—a lady, he insisted, gently born—who was in reduced circumstances, who had pinched herself to pay the lump sum to the ship-owners for his apprenticeship, whose sacrificing dream had been to see him a merchantman officer and a gentleman, and who was heartbroken because he had deserted his ship in Australia and joined another as a common sailor before the mast. And Scotty proved it. He drew her last sad letter from his pocket and wept over it as he read it aloud. The harpooner and I wept with him, and swore that all three of us would ship on the whaleship *Bonanza,* win a big pay-day, and, still together, make a pilgrimage to Edinburg and lay our store of money in the dear lady's lap.

And, as John Barleycorn heated his way into my brain, thawing my reticence, melting my modesty, talking through me and with me and as me, my adopted twin brother and *alter ego,* I, too, raised my voice to show myself a man and an adventurer, and bragged in detail and at length of how I had crossed San Francisco Bay in my open skiff in a roaring southwester when even the schooner sailors doubted my exploit. Further, I —or John Barleycorn, for it was the same thing—told Scotty that he might be a deep sea sailor and know the last rope on the great deep sea ships, but that when it came to small-boat sailing I could beat him hands down and sail circles around him.

The best of it was that my assertion and brag were true. With reticence and modesty present, I could never have dared tell Scotty my small-boat estimate of him. But it is ever the way of John Barleycorn to loosen the tongue and babble the secret thought.

Scotty, or John Barleycorn, or the pair, was very naturally offended by my remarks. Nor was I loath. I could whip any runaway sailor seventeen years old. Scotty and I flared and raged like young cockerels, until the harpooner poured another round of drinks to enable us to forgive and make up. Which we did, arms around each other's necks, protesting vows of eternal friendship—just like Black Matt and Tom Morrisey, I remembered, in the ranch kitchen in San Mateo. And remembering, I knew that I was at last a man—despite my meager fourteen years—a man as big and manly as those two strapping giants who had quarreled and made up on that memorable Sunday morning of long ago.

By this time the singing stage was reached, and I joined Scotty and the harpooner in snatches of sea songs and chanties. It was here, in the cabin of the *Idler,* that I first heard "Blow the Man Down," "Flying Cloud," and "Whisky, Johnny, Whisky." Oh, it was brave. I was beginning to grasp the meaning of life. Here was no commonplace, no Oakland Estuary, no weary round of throwing newspapers at front doors, delivering ice, and setting up ninepins. All the world was mine, all its paths were under my feet, and John Barleycorn, tricking my fancy, enabled me to anticipate the life of adventure for which I yearned.

We were not ordinary. We were three tipsy young gods, incredibly wise, gloriously genial, and without limit to our powers. Ah!—and I say it now, after the years—could John Barleycorn keep one at such a height, I should never draw a sober breath again. But this is not a world of free freights. One pays according to an iron schedule—for every strength the balanced weakness; for every high a corresponding low; for every fictitious god-like moment an equivalent time in reptilian slime. For every feat of telescoping long days and weeks of life into mad, magnificent instants, one must pay with shortened life, and, oft-times, with savage usury added.

Intenseness and duration are as ancient enemies as fire and water. They are mutually destructive. They cannot co-exist. And John Barleycorn, mighty necromancer though he be, is as much a slave to organic chemistry as we mortals are. We pay for every nerve Marathon we run, nor can John Barleycorn intercede and fend off the just payment. He can lead us to the heights, but he cannot keep us there, else would we all be devotees. And there is no devotee but pays for the mad dances John Barleycorn pipes.

Yet the foregoing is all in after-wisdom spoken. It was no part of the knowledge of the lad, fourteen years old, who sat in the *Idler's* cabin between the harpooner and the sailor, the air rich in his nostrils with the musty smell of men's sea-gear, roaring in chorus: "Yankee ship come down de ribber—Pull, my bully boys, pull!"

We grew maudlin, and all talked and shouted at once. I had a splendid constitution, a stomach that would digest scrap-iron, and I was still running my Marathon in full vigor when Scotty began to fail and fade. His talk grew incoherent. He groped for words and could not find them, while the ones he found his lips were unable to form. His poisoned consciousness was leaving him. The brightness went out of his eyes, and he looked as stupid as were his efforts to talk. His face and body sagged as his consciousness sagged. (A man cannot sit upright save by an act of will). Scotty's reeling brain could not control his muscles. All his correlations were breaking down. He strove to take another drink, and feebly dropped the tumbler on the floor. Then, to my amazement, weeping bitterly, he rolled into a bunk on his back and immediately snored off to sleep.

The harpooner and I drank on, grinning in a superior way to each other over Scotty's plight. The last flask was opened, and we drank it between us, to the accompaniment of Scotty's stertorous breathing. Then the harpooner faded away into his bunk, and I was left alone, unthrown, on the field of battle.

I was very proud, and John Barleycorn was proud with me. I could carry my drink. I was a man. I had drunk two men, drink for drink, into unconsciousness. And I was still on my two feet, upright, making my way on deck to get air into my scorching lungs. It was in this bout on the *Idler* that I discovered what a good stomach and a strong head I had for drink—a bit of knowledge that was to be a source of pride in succeeding years, and that ultimately I was to come to consider a great affliction. The fortunate man is the one who cannot take more than a couple of drinks without becoming intoxicated. The unfortunate wight is the one who can take many glasses without betraying a sign; who *must* take numerous glasses in order to get the "kick."

The sun was setting when I came on the *Idler's* deck. There were plenty of bunks below. I did not need to go home. But I wanted to demonstrate to myself how much I was a man. There lay my skiff astern. The last of a strong ebb was running out in channel in the teeth of an ocean breeze of forty miles an hour. I could see the stiff whitecaps, and the suck and run of the current was plainly visible in the face and trough of each one.

I set sail, cast off, took my place at the tiller, the sheet in my hand, and headed across channel. The skiff heeled over and plunged into it madly. The spray began to fly. I was at the pinnacle of exaltation. I sang "Blow the Man Down" as I sailed. I was no boy of fourteen, living the mediocre ways of the sleepy town called Oakland. I was a man, a god, and the very elements rendered me allegiance as I bitted them to my will.

The tide was out. A full hundred yards of soft mud intervened between the boat wharf and the water. I pulled up my centerboard, ran full tilt into the mud, took in sail, and, standing in the stern as I had often done at low tide, I began to shove the skiff with an oar. It was then that my correlations began to break down. I lost my balance and pitched headforemost into the ooze. Then, and for the first time, as I floundered to my feet covered with slime, the blood running down my arms from a scrape against a barnacled stake, I knew that I was drunk. But what of it? Across the channel two strong sailormen lay unconscious in their bunks where I had drunk them. I *was* a man. I was still on my legs, if they *were* knee deep in mud. I disdained to get back into the skiff. I waded through the mud, shoving the skiff before me and yammering the chant of my manhood to the world.

I paid for it. I was sick for a couple of days, meanly sick, and my arms were painfully poisoned from the barnacle scratches. For a week I could not use them, and it was a torture to put on and take off my clothes.

I swore, "Never again!" The game wasn't worth it. The price was too stiff. I had no moral qualms. My revulsion was purely physical. No exalted moments were worth such hours of misery and wretchedness. When I got back to my skiff, I shunned the *Idler.* I would cross the opposite side of the channel to go around her. Scotty had disappeared. The harpooner was still about, but him I avoided. Once, when he landed on the boat-wharf, I hid in a shed so as to escape seeing him. I was afraid he would propose some more drinking, maybe have a flask full of whisky in his pocket.

And yet—and here enters the necromancy of John Barleycorn—that afternoon's drunk on the *Idler* had been a purple passage flung into the monotony of my days. It was memorable. My mind dwelt on it continually. I went over the details, over and over again. Among other things, I had got into the cogs and springs of men's actions. I had seen Scotty weep about his own worthlessness and the sad case of his Edinburg mother who was a lady. The harpooner had told me terribly wonderful things of himself. I had caught a myriad enticing and inflammatory hints of a world beyond my world, and for which I was certainly as fitted as the two lads who had drunk with me. I had got behind men's souls. I had got behind my own soul and found unguessed potencies and greatnesses.

Yes, that day stood out above all my other days. To this day it so stands out. The memory of it is branded in my brain. But the price exacted was too high. I refused to play and pay, and returned to my cannonballs and taffy-slabs. The point is that all the chemistry of my healthy, normal body drove me away from alcohol. The stuff didn't agree with me. It was abominable. But despite this, circumstance was to continue to drive me toward John Barleycorn, to drive me again and again, until, after long years, the time should come when I would look up John Barleycorn in every haunt of men—look him up and hail him gladly as benefactor and friend. And detest and hate him all the time. Yes, he is a strange friend, John Barleycorn.

VII

I WAS barely turned fifteen, and working long hours in a cannery. Month in and month out, the shortest day I ever worked was ten hours. When to ten hours of actual work at a machine is added the noon hour; the walking to work and walking home from work; the getting up in the morning, dressing, and eating; the eating at night, undressing, and going to bed, there remains no more than the nine hours out of the twenty-four required by a healthy youngster for sleep. Out of those nine hours, after I was in bed and ere my eyes drowsed shut, I managed to steal a little time for reading.

But many a night I did not knock off work until midnight. On occasion I worked eighteen and twenty hours on a stretch. Once I worked at my machine for thirty-six consecutive hours. And there were weeks on end when I never knocked off work earlier than eleven o'clock, got home and in bed at half after midnight, and was called at half-past five to dress, eat, walk to work, and be at my machine at seven o'clock whistle blow.

No moments here to be stolen for my beloved books. And what had John Barleycorn to do with so strenuous, Stoic toil of a lad just turned fifteen? He had everything to do with it. Let me show you. I asked myself if this were the meaning of life—to be a work-beast? I knew of no horse in the city of Oakland that worked the hours I worked. If this were living, I was entirely unenamored of it. I remembered my skiff, lying idle and accumulating barnacles at the boat-wharf; I remembered the wind that blew every day on the bay, the sunrises and sunsets I never saw; the bite of the salt air in my nostrils, the bite of the salt water on my flesh when I plunged overside; I remembered all the beauty and the wonder and the sense-delights of the world denied me. There was only one way to escape my deadening toil. I must get out and away on the water. I must earn my bread on the water. And the way of the water led inevitably to John Barleycorn. I did not know this. And when I did learn it, I was courageous enough not to retreat back to my bestial life at the machine.

I wanted to be where the winds of adventure blew. And the winds of adventure blew the oyster pirate sloops up and down San Francisco Bay, from raided oyster-beds and fights at night on shoal and flat, to markets in the morning against city wharves, where peddlers and saloon-keepers came down to buy. Every raid on an oyster-bed was a felony. The penalty was state imprisonment, the stripes and the lockstep. And what of that? The men in stripes worked a shorter day than I at my machine. And there was vastly more romance in being an oyster pirate or a convict than in being a machine slave. And behind it all, behind all of me with youth a-bubble, whispered Romance, Adventure.

So I interviewed my Mammy Jennie, my old nurse at whose black breast I had suckled. She was more prosperous than my folks. She was nursing sick people at a good weekly wage. Would she lend her "white child" the money? *Would she?* What she had was mine.

Then I sought out French Frank, the oyster pirate, who wanted to sell, I had heard, his sloop, the *Razzle Dazzle.* I found him lying at anchor on the Alameda side of the estuary, near the Webster Street bridge, with visitors aboard, whom he was entertaining with afternoon wine. He came on deck to talk business. He was willing to sell. But it was Sunday. Besides, he had guests. On the morrow he would make out the bill of sale and I could enter into possession. And in the meantime I must come below and meet his friends. They were two sisters, Mamie and Tess; a Mrs. Hadley, who chaperoned them; "Whisky" Bob, a youthful oyster pirate of sixteen; and "Spider" Healey, a black-whiskered wharf-rat of twenty. Mamie, who was Spider's niece, was called the Queen of the Oyster Pirates, and, on occasion, presided at their revels. French Frank was in love with her, though I did not know it at the time; and she steadfastly refused to marry him.

French Frank poured a tumbler of red wine from a big demijohn to drink to our transaction. I remembered the red wine of the Italian rancho, and shuddered inwardly. Whisky and beer were not quite so repulsive. But the Queen of the Oyster Pirates was looking at me, a part-emptied glass in her own hand. I had my pride. If I was only fifteen, at least I could not show myself any less a man than she. Besides, there were her sister, and Mrs. Hadley, and the young oyster pirate, and the whiskered wharf-rat, all with glasses in their hands. Was I a milk and water sop? No; a thousand times no, and a thousand glasses no. I downed the tumblerful like a man.

French Frank was elated by the sale, which I had bound with a twenty-dollar goldpiece. He poured more wine. I had learned my strong head and stomach, and I was certain I could drink with them in a temperate way and not poison myself for a week to come. I could stand as much as they; and besides, they had already been drinking for some time.

We got to singing. Spider sang "The Boston Burglar" and "Black Lulu." The Queen sang "Then I Wisht I were a Little Bird." And her sister Tess sang "Oh, Treat My Daughter Kind-i-ly." The fun grew fast and furious. I found myself able to miss drinks without being noticed or called to account. Also, standing in the companionway, head and shoulders out and glass in hand, I could fling the wine overboard.

I reasoned something like this: It is a queerness of these people that they like this vile-tasting wine. Well, let them. I cannot quarrel with their tastes. My manhood, according to their queer notions, must compel me to appear to like this wine. Very well. I shall so appear. But I shall drink no more than is unavoidable.

And the Queen began to make love to me, the latest recruit to the oyster pirate fleet, and no mere hand, but a master and owner. She went upon deck to take the air, and took me with her. She knew, of course, but I never dreamed, how French Frank was raging down below. Then Tess joined us, sitting on the cabin; and Spider, and Bob; and at the last, Mrs. Hadley and French Frank. And we sat there, glasses in hand, and sang, while the big demijohn went around; and I was the only strictly sober one.

And I enjoyed it as no one of them was able to enjoy it. Here, in this atmosphere of bohemianism, I could not but contrast the scene with my scene of the day before, sitting at my machine, in the stifling, shut-in air, repeating, endlessly repeating, at top speed, my series of mechanical motions. And here I sat now, glass in hand, in warm-glowing camaraderie, with the oyster pirates, adventurers who refused to be slaves to petty routine, who flouted restrictions and the law, who carried their lives and their liberty in their hands. And it was through John Barleycorn that I came to join this glorious company of free souls, unashamed and unafraid.

And the afternoon sea breeze blew its tang into my lungs, and curled the waves in mid-channel. Before it came the scow schooners, wing-and-wing, blowing their horns for the drawbridges to open. Red-stacked tugs tore by, rocking the *Razzle Dazzle* in the waves of their wake. A sugar bark towed from the "boneyard" to sea. The sun-wash was on the crisping water, and life was big. And Spider sang:

"Oh, it's Lulu, black Lulu, my darling,
Oh, it's where have you been so long?
Been layin' in jail,
A-waitin' for bail,
Till my bully comes rollin' along."

There it was, the smack and slap of the spirit of revolt, of adventure, of romance, of the things forbidden and done defiantly and grandly. And I knew that on the morrow I would not go back to my machine at the cannery. To-morrow I would be an oyster pirate, as free a freebooter as the century and the waters of San Francisco Bay would permit. Spider had already agreed to sail with me as my crew of one, and, also, as cook while I did the deck work. We would outfit our grub and water in the morning, hoist the big mainsail (which was a bigger piece of canvas than any I had ever sailed under), and beat our way out the estuary on the first of the sea breeze and the last of the ebb. Then we would slack sheets, and on the first of the flood run down the bay to the Asparagus Islands, where we would anchor miles off shore. And at last my dream would be realized: I would sleep upon the water. And next morning I would wake upon the water; and thereafter all my days and nights would be on the water.

And the Queen asked me to row her ashore in my skiff, when at sunset French Frank prepared to take his guests ashore. Nor did I catch the significance of his abrupt change of plan when he turned the task of rowing his skiff over to Whisky Bob, himself remaining on board the sloop. Nor did I understand Spider's grinning side-remark to me: "Gee! There's nothin' slow about *you.*" How could it possibly enter my boy's head that a grizzled man of fifty should be jealous of me?

VIII

We met by appointment, early Monday morning, to complete the deal, in Johnny Heinhold's "Last Chance"—a saloon, of course, for the transactions of men. I paid the money over, received the bill of sale, and French Frank treated. This struck me as an evident custom, and a logical one—the seller, who receives the money, to wet a piece of it in the establishment where the trade was consummated. But to my surprise, French Frank treated the house. He and I drank, which seemed just; but why should Johnny Heinhold, who owned the saloon and waited behind the bar, be invited to drink? I figured it immediately that he made a profit on the very drink he drank. I could, in a way, considering that they were friends and shipmates, understand Spider and Whisky Bob being asked to drink; but why should the longshoremen, Bill Kelly and Soup Kennedy, be asked?

Then there was Pat, the Queen's brother, making a total of eight of us. It was early morning and all ordered whisky. What could I do, here in this company of big men, all drinking whisky? "Whisky," I said, with the careless air of one who had said it a thousand times. And such whisky! I tossed it down. A-r-r-r-gh! I can taste it yet.

And I was appalled at the price French Frank had paid—eighty cents. *Eighty cents!* It was an outrage to my thrifty soul. Eighty cents—the equivalent of eight long hours of my toil at the machine, gone down our throats and gone like that, in a twinkling, leaving only a bad taste in my mouth. There was no discussion but that French Frank was a waster.

I was anxious to be gone, out into the sunshine, out over the water to my glorious boat. But all hands lingered. Even Spider, my crew, lingered. No hint broke through my obtuseness of why they lingered. I have often thought since of how they must have regarded me, the newcomer being welcomed into their company, standing at bar with them, and not standing for a single round of drinks.

French Frank, who, unknown to me, had swallowed his chagrin since the day before, now that the money for the *Razzle Dazzle* was in his pocket began to behave curiously toward me. I sensed the change in his attitude, saw the forbidding glitter in his eyes, and wondered. The more I saw of men, the queerer they became. Johnny Heinhold leaned across the bar and whispered in my ear: "He's got it in for you. Watch out."

I nodded comprehension of his statement, and acquiescence in it, as a man should nod who knows all about men. But secretly I was perplexed. Heavens! How was I, who had worked hard and read books of adventure, and who was only fifteen years old, who had not dreamed of giving the Queen of the Oyster Pirates a second thought, and who did not know that French Frank was madly and Latinly in love with her—how was I to guess that I had done him shame? And how was I to guess that the story of how the Queen had thrown him down on his own boat, the moment I hove in sight, was already the gleeful gossip of the waterfront? And by the same token, how was I to guess that her brother Pat's offishness with me was anything else than temperamental gloominess of spirit?

Whisky Bob got me aside a moment. "Keep your eyes open," he muttered. "Take my tip. French Frank's ugly. I'm going up river with him to get a schooner for oystering. When he gets down on the beds, watch out. He says he'll run you down. After dark, any time he's around, change your anchorage and douse your riding light. Savve?"

Oh, certainly, I savve'd. I nodded my head, and as one man to another thanked him for his tip; and drifted back to the group at the bar. No; I did not treat. I never dreamed that I was expected to treat. I left with Spider, and my ears burn now as I try to surmise the things they must have said about me.

I asked Spider, in an off-hand way, what was eating French Frank. "He's crazy jealous of you," was the answer. "Do you think so?" I stalled, and dismissed the matter as not worth thinking about.

But I leave it to any one—the swell of my fifteen-years-old manhood at learning that French Frank, the adventurer of fifty, the sailor of all the seas of all the world, was jealous of me—and jealous over a girl most romantically named the Queen of the Oyster Pirates. I had read of such things in books, and regarded them as personal probabilities of a distant maturity. Oh, I felt a rare young devil, as we hoisted the big mainsail that morning, broke out anchor, and filled away close-hauled on the three-mile beat to windward out into the bay.

Such was my escape from the killing machine-toil, and my introduction to the oyster pirates. True, the introduction had begun with drink, and the life promised to continue with drink. But was I to stay away from it for such reason? Wherever life ran free and great, there men drank. Romance and adventure seemed always to go down the street locked arm in arm with John Barleycorn. To know the two, I must know the third. Or else I must go back to my free-library books and read of the deeds of other men and do no deeds of my own save slave for ten cents an hour at a machine in a cannery.

No; I was not to be deterred from this brave life on the water by the fact that the water-dwellers had queer and expensive desires for beer and wine and whisky. What if their notions of happiness included the strange one of seeing me drink? When they persisted in buying the stuff and thrusting it upon me, why, I would drink it. It was the price I would pay for their comradeship. And I didn't have to get drunk. I had not got drunk the Sunday afternoon I arranged to buy the *Razzle Dazzle,* despite the fact that none of the rest was sober. Well, I could go on into the future that way, drinking the stuff when it gave them pleasure that I should drink it, but carefully avoiding over-drinking.

IX

GRADUAL as was my development as a heavy drinker among the oyster pirates, the real heavy drinking came suddenly and was the result, not of desire for alcohol, but of an intellectual conviction.

The more I saw of the life, the more I was enamored of it. I can never forget my thrills, the first night I took part in a concerted raid, when we assembled on board the *Annie*— rough men, big and unafraid, and weazened wharf rats, some of them ex-convicts, all of them enemies of the law and meriting jail, in sea-boots and sea-gear, talking in gruff, low voices, and "Big" George with revolvers strapped about his waist to show that he meant business.

Oh, I know, looking back, that the whole thing was sordid and silly. But I was not looking back in those days when I was rubbing shoulders with John Barleycorn and beginning to accept him. The life was brave and wild, and I was living the adventure I had read so much about.

Nelson, "Young Scratch" they called him to distinguish him from "Old Scratch," his father, sailed in the sloop *Reindeer,* partners with one "Clam." Clam was a dare-devil, but Nelson was a reckless maniac. He was twenty years old, with the body of a Hercules. When he was shot in Benicia, a couple of years later, the coroner said he was the greatest-shouldered man he had ever seen laid on a slab.

Nelson could not read nor write. He had been "dragged" up by his father on San Francisco Bay, and boats were second nature with him. His strength was prodigious, and his reputation along the waterfront for violence was anything but savory. He had Berserker rages and did mad, terrible things. I made his acquaintance the first cruise of the *Razzle Dazzle,* and saw him sail the *Reindeer* in a blow and dredge oysters all around the rest of us as we lay at two anchors, troubled with fear of going ashore.

He was some man, this Nelson; and when, passing by the Last Chance saloon, he spoke to me, I felt very proud. But try to imagine my pride when he promptly asked me in to have a drink. I stood at bar and drank a glass of beer with him, and talked manfully of oysters, and boats, and of the mystery of who had put the load of buckshot through the *Annie's* mainsail.

We talked and lingered at the bar. It seemed to me strange that we lingered. We had had our beer. But who was I to lead the way outside when great Nelson chose to lean against the bar? After a few minutes, to my surprise, he asked me to have another drink, which I did. And still we talked, and Nelson evinced no intention of leaving the bar.

Bear with me while I explain the way of my reasoning and of my innocence. First of all, I was very proud to be in the company of Nelson, who was the most heroic figure among the oyster pirates and bay adventurers. Unfortunately for my stomach and mucous membranes, Nelson had a strange quirk of nature that made him find happiness in treating me to beer. I had no moral disinclination for beer, and just because I didn't like the taste of it and the weight of it was no reason I should forego the honor of his company. It was his whim to drink beer, and to have me drink beer with him. Very well, I would put up with the passing discomfort.

So we continued to talk at bar, and to drink beer ordered and paid for by Nelson. I think, now, when I look back upon it, that Nelson was curious. He wanted to find out just what kind of a gink I was. He wanted to see how many times I'd let him treat without offering to treat in return.

After I had drunk half-a-dozen glasses, my policy of temperateness in mind, I decided that I had had enough for that time. So I mentioned that I was going aboard the *Razzle Dazzle*, then lying at the city wharf a hundred yards away.

I said good-by to Nelson, and went on down the wharf. But John Barleycorn, to the extent of six glasses, went with me. My brain tingled and was very much alive. I was uplifted by my sense of manhood. I, a truly-true oyster pirate, was going aboard my own boat after hobnobbing in the Last Chance with Nelson, the greatest oyster pirate of us all. Strong in my brain was the vision of us leaning against the bar and drinking beer. And curious it was, I decided, this whim of nature that made men happy in spending good money for beer for a fellow like me who didn't want it.

As I pondered this, I recollected that several times other men, in couples, had entered the Last Chance, and first one, then the other, had treated to drinks. I remembered, on the drunk on the *Idler*, how Scotty and the harpooner and myself had raked and scraped dimes and nickels with which to buy the whisky. Then came my boy code: when on a day a fellow gave another a "cannonball" or a chunk of taffy, on some other day he would expect to receive back a cannonball or a chunk of taffy.

That was why Nelson had lingered at the bar. Having bought a drink, he had waited for me to buy one. *I had let him buy six drinks and never once offered to treat.* And he was the great Nelson! I could feel myself blushing with shame. I sat down on the stringer-piece of the wharf and buried my face in my hands. And the heat of my shame burned up my neck and into my cheeks and forehead. I have blushed many times in my life, but never have I experienced so terrible a blush as that one.

And sitting there on the stringer-piece in my shame, I did a great deal of thinking and trans-valuing of values. I had been born poor. Poor I had lived. I had gone hungry on occasion. I had never had toys nor playthings like other children. My first memories of life were pinched by poverty. The pinch of poverty had been chronic. I was eight years old when I wore my first little undershirt actually sold in a store across the counter. And then it had been only one little undershirt. When it was soiled I had to return to the awful home-made things until it was washed. I had been so proud of it that I insisted on wearing it without any outer garment. For the first time I mutinied against my mother—mutinied myself into hysteria, until she let me wear the store undershirt so all the world could see.

Only a man who has undergone famine can properly value food; only sailors and desert-dwellers know the meaning of fresh water. And only a child, with a child's imagination, can come to know the meaning of things it has been long denied. I early discovered that the only things I could have were those I got for myself. My meager childhood developed meagerness. The first things I had been able to get for myself had been cigarette pictures, cigarette posters, and cigarette albums. I had not had the spending of the money I earned, so I traded "extra" newspapers for these treasures. I traded duplicates with the other boys, and circulating, as I did, all about town, I had greater opportunities for trading and acquiring.

It was not long before I had complete every series issued by every cigarette manufacturer—such as the Great Race Horses, Parisian Beauties, Women of All Nations, Flags of All Nations, Noted Actors, Champion Prize Fighters, etc. And each series I had three different ways: in the card from the cigarette package, in the poster, and in the album.

Then I began to accumulate duplicate sets, duplicate albums. I traded for other things that boys valued and which they usually bought with money given them by their parents. Naturally, they did not have the keen sense of values that I had, who was never given money to buy anything. I traded for postage stamps, for minerals, for curios, for birds' eggs, for marbles (I had a more magnificent collection of agates than I have ever seen any other boy possess—and the nucleus of the collection was a handful worth at least three dollars which I had kept as security for twenty cents I loaned to a messenger-boy who was sent to reform school before he could redeem them).

I'd trade anything and everything for anything else, and turn it over in a dozen more trades until it was transmuted into something that was worth something. I was famous as a trader. I was notorious as a miser. I could even make a junk man weep when I had dealings with him. Other boys called me in to sell for them their collections of bottles, rags, old iron, grain and gunny sacks, and five-gallon oil-cans—ay, and gave me a commission for doing it.

And this was the thrifty, close-fisted boy, accustomed to slave at a machine for ten cents an hour, who sat on the stringer-piece and considered the matter of beer at five cents a glass and gone in a moment with nothing to show for it. I was now with men I admired. I was proud to be with them. Had all my pinching and saving brought me the equivalent of one of the many thrills which had been mine since I came among the oyster pirates? Then what was worth while—money or thrills? These men had no horror of squandering a nickel, or many nickels. They were magnificently careless of money, calling up eight men to drink whisky at ten cents a glass, as French Frank had done. Why, Nelson had just spent sixty cents on beer for the two of us.

Which was it to be? I was aware that I was making a grave decision. I was deciding between money and men, between niggardliness and romance. Either I must throw overboard all my old values of money and look upon it as something to be flung about wastefully, or I must throw overboard my comradeship with those men whose peculiar quirks made them care for strong drink.

I retraced my steps up the wharf to the Last Chance where Nelson still stood outside. "Come on and have a beer," I invited. Again we stood at bar and drank and talked, but this time it was I who paid—ten cents! A whole hour of my labor at a machine for a drink of something I didn't want and which tasted rotten. But it wasn't difficult. I had achieved a concept. Money no longer counted. It was comradeship that counted.

"Have another," I said. And we had another, and I paid for it. Nelson, with the wisdom of the skilled drinker, said to the barkeeper, "Make mine a small one, Johnny." Johnny nodded and gave him a glass that contained only a third as much as the glasses we had been drinking. Yet the charge was the same—five cents.

By this time I was getting nicely jingled, so such extravagance didn't hurt me much. Besides, I was learning. There was more in this buying of drinks than mere quantity. I got my finger on it. There was a stage when the beer didn't count at all, but just the spirit of comradeship of drinking together. And, ha!—another thing! I, too, could call for small beers and minimize by two-thirds the detestable freightage with which comradeship burdened one.

"I had to go aboard to get some money," I remarked casually, as we drank, in the hope Nelson would take it as an explanation of why I had let him treat six consecutive times.

"Oh, well, you didn't have to do that," he answered. "Johnny'll trust a fellow like you—won't you, Johnny?"

"Sure," Johnny agreed, with a smile.

"How much you got down against me?" Nelson queried.

Johnny pulled out the book he kept behind the bar, found Nelson's page, and added up the account of several dollars. At once I became possessed with a desire to have a page in that book. Almost it seemed the final badge of manhood.

After a couple more drinks, for which I insisted on paying, Nelson decided to go. We parted true comradely, and I wandered down the wharf to the *Razzle Dazzle.* Spider was just building the fire for supper.

"Where'd you get it?" he grinned up at me through the open companion.

"Oh, I've been with Nelson," I said carelessly, trying to hide my pride.

Then an idea came to me. Here was another one of them. Now that I had achieved my concept, I might as well practice it thoroughly. "Come on," I said, "up to Johnny's and have a drink."

Going up the wharf, we met Clam coming down. Clam was Nelson's partner, and he was a fine, brave, handsome, mustached man of thirty—everything, in short, that his nickname did not connote. "Come on," I said, "and have a drink." He came. As we turned into the Last Chance, there was Pat, the Queen's brother, coming out.

"What's your hurry?" I greeted him. "We're having a drink. Come on along." "I've just had one," he demurred. "What of it?—we're having one now," I retorted. And Pat consented to join us, and I melted my way into his good graces with a couple of glasses of beer. Oh! I was learning things that afternoon about John Barleycorn. There was more in him than the bad taste when you swallowed him. Here, at the absurd cost of ten cents, a gloomy, grouchy individual, who threatened to become an enemy, was made into a good friend, even genial, his looks were kindly, and our voices mellowed together as we talked water-front and oyster-bed gossip.

"Small beer for me, Johnny," I said, when the others had ordered schooners. Yet I said it like the accustomed drinker, carelessly, casually, as a sort of spontaneous thought that had just occurred to me. Looking back, I am confident that the only one there who guessed I was a tyro at bar-drinking was Johnny Heinhold.

"Where'd he get it?" I overheard Spider confidentially ask Johnny.

"Oh, he's been sousin' here with Nelson all afternoon," was Johnny's answer.

I never let on that I'd heard, but *proud?* Ay, even the barkeeper was giving me commendation as a man. *"He's been sousin' here with Nelson all afternoon."* Magic words! The accolade delivered by a barkeeper with a beer glass!

I remembered that French Frank had treated Johnny the day I bought the *Razzle Dazzle.* The glasses were filled, and we were ready to drink. "Have something yourself, Johnny," I said, with an air of having intended to say it all the time but of having been a trifle remiss because of the interesting conversation I had been holding with Clam and Pat.

Johnny looked at me with quick sharpness, divining, I am positive, the strides I was making in my education, and poured himself whisky from his private bottle. This hit me for a moment on my thrifty side. He had taken a ten-cent drink when the rest of us were drinking five-cent drinks! But the hurt was only for a moment. I dismissed it as ignoble, remembered my concept, and did not give myself away.

"You'd better put me down in the book for this," I said, when we had finished the drink. And I had the satisfaction of seeing a fresh page devoted to my name and a charge penciled for a round of drinks amounting to thirty cents. And I glimpsed, as through a golden haze, a future wherein that page would be much-charged, and crossed off, and charged again.

I treated a second time around, and then, to my amazement, Johnny redeemed himself in that matter of the ten-cent drink. He treated us a round from behind the bar, and I decided that he had arithmetically evened things up handsomely.

"Let's go around to the St. Louis House," Spider suggested, when we got outside. Pat, who had been shoveling coal all day, had gone home, and Clam had gone upon the *Reindeer* to cook supper.

So around Spider and I went to the St. Louis House—my first visit—a huge bar-room, where perhaps fifty men, mostly longshoremen, were congregated. And there I met Stew Kennedy for the second time, and Bill Kelly. And Smith, of the *Annie,* drifted in—he of the belt-buckled revolvers. And Nelson showed up. And I met others, including the Vigy brothers, who ran the place, and, chiefest of all, Joe Goose, with the wicked eyes, the twisted nose, and the flowered vest, who played the harmonica like a roystering angel and went on the most atrocious tears that even the Oakland waterfront could conceive of and admire.

As I bought drinks—others treated as well—the thought flickered across my mind that Mammy Jennie wasn't going to be repaid much on her loan out of that week's earnings of the *Razzle Dazzle.* "But what of it?" I thought, or rather, John Barleycorn thought it for me. "You're a man and you're getting acquainted with men. Mammy Jennie doesn't need the money as promptly as all that. She isn't starving. You know that. She's got other money in bank. Let her wait, and pay her back gradually."

And thus it was I learned another trait of John Barleycorn. He inhibits morality. Wrong conduct that it is impossible for one to do sober, is done quite easily when one is not sober. In fact, it is the only thing one can do, for John Barleycorn's inhibition rises like a wall between one's immediate desires and long-learned morality.

I dismissed my thought of debt to Mammy Jennie and proceeded to get acquainted at the trifling expense of some trifling money and a jingle that was growing unpleasant. Who took me on board and put me to bed that night I do not know, but I imagine it must have been Spider.

X

AND so I won my manhood's spurs. My status on the water-front and with the oyster pirates became immediately excellent. I was looked upon as a good fellow, as well as no coward. And somehow, from the day I achieved that concept sitting on the stringer-piece of the Oakland City Wharf, I have never cared much for money. No one has ever considered me a miser since, while my carelessness of money is a source of anxiety and worry to some that know me.

So completely did I break with my parsimonious past that I sent word home to my mother to call in the boys of the neighborhood and give to them all my collections. I never even cared to learn what boys got what collections. I was a man, now, and I made a clean sweep of everything that bound me to my boyhood.

My reputation grew. When the story went around the water-front of how French Frank had tried to run me down with his schooner, and of how I had stood on the deck of the *Razzle Dazzle,* a cocked double-barreled shotgun in my hands, steering with my feet and holding her to her course, and compelled him to put up his wheel and keep away, the water-front decided that there was something to me despite my youth. And I continued to show what was in me. There were the times I brought the *Razzle Dazzle* in with a bigger load of oysters than any other two-man craft; there was the time when we raided far down in Lower Bay and mine was the only craft back at daylight to the anchorage off Asparagus Island; there was the Thursday night we raced for market and I brought the *Razzle Dazzle* in without a rudder, first of the fleet, and skimmed the cream of the Friday morning trade; and there was the time I brought her in from Upper Bay under a jib, when Scotty burned my mainsail. (Yes; it was Scotty of the *Idler* adventure. Irish had followed Spider on board the *Razzle Dazzle,* and Scotty, turning up, had taken Irish's place.)

But the things I did on the water only partly counted. What completed everything and won for me the title of "Prince of the Oyster Beds," was that I was a good fellow ashore with my money, buying drinks like a man. I little dreamed that the time would come when the Oakland waterfront, which had shocked me at first, would be shocked and annoyed by the deviltry of the things I did.

But always the life was tied up with drinking. The saloons are poor men's clubs. Saloons are congregating places. We engaged to meet one another in saloons. We celebrated our good fortune or wept our grief in saloons. We got acquainted in saloons.

Can I ever forget the afternoon I met "Old Scratch," Nelson's father? It was in the Last Chance. Johnny Heinhold introduced us. That Old Scratch was Nelson's father was noteworthy enough. But there was more to it than that. He was owner and master of the scow-schooner *Annie Mine,* and some day I might ship as a sailor with him. Still more, he was romance. He was a blue-eyed, yellow-haired, raw-boned Viking, big-bodied and strong-muscled despite his age. And he had sailed the seas in ships of all nations in the old savage sailing days.

I had heard many weird tales about him, and worshiped him from a distance. It took the saloon to bring us together. Even so, our acquaintance might have been no more than a handgrip and a word—he was a laconic old fellow—had it not been for the drinking.

"Have a drink," I said, with promptitude, after the pause which I had learned good form in drinking dictates. Of course, while we drank our beer, which I had paid for, it was incumbent on him to listen to me and to talk to me. And Johnny, like a true host, made the tactful remarks that enabled us to find mutual topics of conversation. And of course, having drunk my beer, Captain Nelson must now buy beer in turn. This led to more talking, and Johnny drifted out of the conversation to wait on other customers.

The more beer Captain Nelson and I drank the better we got acquainted. In me he found an appreciative listener, who, by virtue of book-reading, knew much about the sea-life he had lived. So he drifted back to his wild young days, and spun many a rare yarn for me, while we downed beer, treat by treat, all through a blessed summer afternoon. And it was only John Barleycorn that made possible that long afternoon with the old sea dog.

It was Johnny Heinhold who secretly warned me across the bar that I was getting pickled and advised me to take small beers. But as long as Captain Nelson drank large beers, my pride forbade anything else than large beers. And not until the skipper ordered his first small beer did I order one for myself. Oh, when we came to a lingering fond farewell, I was drunk. But I had the satisfaction of seeing Old Scratch as drunk as I. My youthful modesty scarcely let me dare believe that the hardened old bucaneer was even drunker.

And afterwards, from Spider, and Pat, and Clam, and Johnny Heinhold, and others, came the tips that Old Scratch liked me and had nothing but good words for the fine lad I was. Which was the more remarkable, because he was known as a savage, cantankerous old cuss who never liked anybody. (His very nickname, "Scratch," arose from a Berserker trick of his, in fighting, of tearing off his opponent's face). And that I had won to his friendship, all thanks were due to John Barleycorn. I have given the incident merely as an example of the multitudinous lures and draws and services by which John Barleycorn wins his followers.

XI

AND still there arose in me no desire for alcohol, no chemical demand. In years and years of heavy drinking, drinking did not beget the desire. Drinking was the way of the life I led, the way of the men with whom I lived. While away on my cruises on the bay, I took no drink along; and while out on the bay the thought of the desirableness of a drink never crossed my mind. It was not until I tied the *Razzle Dazzle* up to the wharf and got ashore in the congregating places of men, where drink flowed, that the buying of drinks for other men, and the accepting of drinks from other men, devolved upon me as a social duty and a manhood rite.

Then, too, there were the times, lying at the city wharf or across the estuary on the sandpit, when the Queen, and her sister, and her brother Pat, and Mrs. Hadley came aboard. It was my boat. I was host, and I could only dispense hospitality in the terms of their understanding of it. So I would rush Spider, or Irish, or Scotty, or whoever was my crew, with the can for beer and the demijohn for red wine. And again, lying at the wharf disposing of my oysters, there were dusky twilights when big policemen and plain clothes men stole on board. And because we lived in the shadow of the police, we opened oysters and fed them to them with squirts of pepper sauce, and rushed the growler or got stronger stuff in bottles.

Drink as I would, I couldn't come to like John Barleycorn. I valued him extremely well for his associations, but not for the taste of him. All the time I was striving to be a man amongst men, and all the time I nursed secret and shameful desires for candy. But I would have died before I'd let anybody guess it. I used to indulge in lonely debauches, on nights when I knew my crew was going to sleep ashore. I would go up to the Free Library, exchange my books, buy a quarter's worth of all sorts of candy that chewed and lasted, sneak aboard the *Razzle Dazzle*, lock myself in the cabin, go to bed, and lie there long hours of bliss, reading and chewing candy. And those were the only times I felt that I got my real money's worth. Dollars and dollars, across the bar, couldn't buy the satisfaction that twenty-five cents did in a candy store. As my drinking grew heavier, I began to note more and more that it was in the drinking bouts the purple passages occurred. Drunks were always memorable. At such times things happened. Men like Joe Goose dated existence from drunk to drunk. The longshoremen all looked forward to their Saturday night drunk. We of the oyster boats waited until we had disposed of our cargoes before we got really started, though a scattering of drinks and a meeting of a chance friend sometimes precipitated an accidental drunk.

In ways, the accidental drunks were the best. Stranger and more exciting things happened at such times. As, for instance, the Sunday when Nelson and French Frank and Captain Spink stole the stolen salmon boat from Whisky Bob and Nicky the Greek. Changes had taken place in the personnel of the oyster boats. Nelson had got into a fight with Bill Kelly on the *Annie* and was carrying a bullet-hole through his left hand. Also, having quarreled with Clam and broken partnership, Nelson had sailed the *Reindeer*, his arm in a sling, with a crew of two deep-water sailors, and he had sailed so madly as to frighten them ashore. Such was the tale of his recklessness they spread, that no one on the water-front would go out with Nelson. So the *Reindeer*, crewless, lay across the estuary at the sandpit. Beside her lay the *Razzle Dazzle* with a burned mainsail and with Scotty and me on board. Whisky Bob had fallen out with French Frank and gone on a raid "up river" with Nicky the Greek.

The result of this raid was a brand new Columbia River salmon boat, stolen from an Italian fisherman. We oyster pirates were all visited by the searching Italian, and we were convinced, from what we knew of their movements, that Whisky Bob and Nicky the Greek were the guilty parties. But where was the salmon boat? Hundreds of Greek and Italian fishermen, up river and down bay, had searched every slough and tule patch for it. When the owner despairingly offered a reward of fifty dollars, our interest increased and the mystery deepened.

One Sunday morning, old Captain Spink paid me a visit. The conversation was confidential. He had just been fishing in his skiff in the old Alameda ferry slip. As the tide went down, he had noticed a rope tied to a pile under water and leading downward. In vain he had tried to heave up what was fast on the other end. Farther along, to another pile, was a similar rope, leading downward and unheavable. Without doubt, it was the missing salmon boat. If we restored it to its rightful owner there was fifty dollars in it for us. But I had queer ethical notions about honor amongst thieves, and declined to have anything to do with the affair.

But French Frank had quarreled with Whisky Bob, and Nelson was also an enemy. (Poor Whisky Bob!—without viciousness, good-natured, generous, born weak, raised poorly, with an irresistible chemical demand for alcohol, still prosecuting his vocation of bay pirate, his body was picked up, not long afterward, beside a dock where it had sunk full of gunshot wounds.) Within an hour after I had rejected Captain Spink's proposal, I saw him sail down the estuary on board the *Reindeer* with Nelson. Also, French Frank went by on his schooner.

It was not long ere they sailed back up the estuary, curiously side by side. As they headed in for the sandpit, the submerged salmon boat could be seen, gunwales awash and held up from sinking by ropes fast to the schooner and the sloop. The tide was half out, and they sailed squarely in on the sand, grounding in a row with the salmon boat in the middle.

Immediately Hans, one of French Frank's sailors, was into a skiff and pulling rapidly for the north shore. The big demijohn in the stern-sheets told his errand. They couldn't wait a moment to celebrate the fifty dollars they had so easily earned. It is the way of the devotees of John Barleycorn. When good fortune comes, they drink. When they have no fortune they drink to the hope of good fortune. If fortune be ill, they drink to forget it. If they meet a friend, they drink. If they quarrel with a friend and lose him, they drink. If their love-making be crowned with success, they are so happy they needs must drink. If they be jilted, they drink for the contrary reason. And if they haven't anything to do at all, why they take a drink, secure in the knowledge that when they have taken a sufficient number of drinks the maggots will start crawling in their brains and they will have their hands full with things to do. When they are sober they want to drink; and when they have drunk they want to drink more.

Of course, as fellow comrades, Scotty and I were called in for the drinking. We helped to make a hole in that fifty dollars not yet received. The afternoon, from just an ordinary, common, summer, Sunday afternoon, became a gorgeous, purple afternoon. We all talked and sang and ranted and bragged, and ever French Frank and Nelson sent more drinks around. We lay in full sight of the Oakland water-front, and the noise of our revels attracted friends. Skiff after skiff crossed the estuary and hauled up on the sandpit, while Hans' work was cut out for him—ever to row back and forth for more supplies of booze.

Then Whisky Bob and Nicky the Greek arrived, sober, indignant, outraged in that their fellow pirates had raised their plant. French Frank, aided by John Barleycorn, orated hypocritically about virtue and honesty, and, despite his fifty years, got Whisky Bob out on the sand and proceeded to lick him. When Nicky the Greek jumped in with a short-handled shovel to Whisky Bob's assistance, short work was made of him by Hans. And of course, when the bleeding remnants of Bob and Nicky were sent packing in their skiff, the event must needs be celebrated in further carousal.

By this time, our visitors being numerous, we were a large crowd compounded of many nationalities and diverse temperaments, all aroused by John Barleycorn, all restraints cast off. Old quarrels revived, ancient hates flared up. Fight was in the air. And whenever a longshoreman remembered something against a scow-schooner sailor, or vice versa, or an oyster pirate remembered or was remembered, a fist shot out and another fight was on. And every fight was made up in more rounds of drinks, wherein the combatants, aided and abetted by the rest of us, embraced each other and pledged undying friendship.

And of all times, Soup Kennedy selected this time to come and retrieve an old shirt of his, left aboard the *Reindeer* from the trip he sailed with Clam. He had espoused Clam's side of the quarrel with Nelson. Also, he had been drinking in the St. Louis House, so that it was John Barleycorn who led him to the sandpit in quest of his old shirt. A few words started the fray. He locked with Nelson in the cockpit of the *Reindeer,* and in the mix-up barely escaped being brained by an iron bar wielded by irate French Frank—irate because a two-handed man had attacked a one-handed man. (If the *Reindeer* still floats, the dent of the iron bar remains in the hard-wood rail of her cockpit.)

But Nelson pulled his bandaged hand, bullet-perforated, out of its sling, and, held by us, wept and roared his Berserker belief that he could lick Soup Kennedy one-handed. And we let them loose on the sand. Once, when it looked as if Nelson were getting the worst of it, French Frank and John Barleycorn sprang unfairly into the fight. Scotty protested and reached for French Frank, who whirled upon him and fell on top of him in a pummeling clinch after a sprawl of twenty feet across the sand. In the course of separating these two, half-a-dozen fights started amongst the rest of us. These fights were finished, one way or the other, or we separated them with drinks, while all the time Nelson and Soup Kennedy fought on. Occasionally we returned to them and gave advice, such as, when they lay exhausted in the sand, unable to strike a blow, "Throw sand in his eyes." And they threw sand in each other's eyes, recuperated and fought on to successive exhaustions.

And now, of all this that is squalid, and ridiculous, and bestial, try to think what it meant to me, a youth not yet sixteen, burning with the spirit of adventure, fancy-filled with tales of bucaneers and sea-rovers, sacks of cities and conflicts of armed men, and imagination-maddened by the stuff I had drunk. It was life raw and naked, wild and free—the only life of that sort which my birth in time and space permitted me to attain. And more than that. It carried a promise. It was the beginning. From the sandpit the way led out through the Golden Gate to the vastness of adventure of all the world, where battles would be fought, not for old shirts and over stolen salmon boats, but for high purposes and romantic ends.

And because I told Scotty what I thought of his letting an old man like French Frank get away with him, we, too, brawled and added to the festivity of the sandpit. And Scotty threw up his job as crew, and departed in the night with a pair of blankets belonging to me. During the night, while the oyster pirates lay stupefied in their bunks, the schooner and the *Reindeer* floated on the high water and swung about to their anchors. The salmon boat, still filled with rocks and water, rested on the bottom.

In the morning, early, I heard wild cries from the *Reindeer*, and tumbled out in the chill gray to see a spectacle that made the water-front laugh for days. The beautiful salmon boat lay on the hard sand, squashed flat as a pancake, while on it were perched French Frank's schooner and the *Reindeer*. Unfortunately two of the *Reindeer's* planks had been crushed in by the stout oak stem of the salmon boat. The rising tide had flowed through the hole and just awakened Nelson by getting into his bunk with him. I lent a hand, and we pumped the *Reindeer* out and repaired the damage.

Then Nelson cooked breakfast, and while we ate we considered the situation. He was broke. So was I. The fifty dollars' reward would never be paid for that pitiful mess of splinters on the sand beneath us. He had a wounded hand and no crew. I had a burned mainsail and no crew. "What d 'ye say you and me?" Nelson queried. "I'll go you," was my answer. And thus I became partners with "Young Scratch" Nelson, the wildest, maddest of them all. We borrowed the money for an outfit of grub from Johnny Heinhold, filled our water-barrels, and sailed away that day for the oyster-beds.

XII

Nor have I ever regretted those months of mad deviltry I put in with Nelson. He *could* sail, even if he did frighten every man that sailed with him. To steer to miss destruction by an inch or an instant was his joy. To do what everybody else did not dare attempt to do was his pride. Never to reef down was his mania, and in all the time I spent with him, blow high or low, the *Reindeer* was never reefed. Nor was she ever dry. We strained her open and sailed her open and sailed her open continually. And we abandoned the Oakland water-front and went wider afield for our adventures.

And all this glorious passage in my life was made possible for me by John Barleycorn. And this is my complaint against John Barleycorn. Here I was, thirsting for the wild life of adventure, and the only way for me to win to it was through John Barleycorn's mediation. It was the way of the men who lived the life. Did I wish to live the life, I must live it the way they did. It was by virtue of drinking that I gained that partnership and comradeship with Nelson. Had I drunk only the beer he paid for, or had I declined to drink at all, I should never have been selected by him as a partner. He wanted a partner who would meet him on the social side, as well as the work side, of life.

I abandoned myself to the life, and developed the misconception that the secret of John Barleycorn lay in going on mad drunks, rising through the successive stages that only an iron constitution could endure to final stupefaction and swinish unconsciousness. I did not like the taste, so I drank for the sole purpose of getting drunk, of getting hopelessly, helplessly drunk. And I, who had saved and scraped, traded like a Shylock and made junkmen weep; I, who had stood aghast when French Frank, at a single stroke, spent eighty cents for whisky for eight men; I turned myself loose with a more lavish disregard for money than any of them.

I remember going ashore one night with Nelson. In my pocket was one hundred and eighty dollars. It was my intention, first, to buy me some clothes, after that some drinks. I needed the clothes. All I possessed were on me, and they were as follows: a pair of sea-boots that providentially leaked the water out as fast as it ran in, a pair of fifty-cent overalls, a forty-cent cotton shirt, and a sou'wester. I had no hat, so I had to wear the sou'wester, and it will be noted that I have listed neither underclothes nor socks. I didn't own any.

To reach the stores where clothes could be bought, we had to pass a dozen saloons. So I bought me the drinks first. I never got to the clothing stores. In the morning, broke, poisoned, but contented, I came back on board, and we set sail. I possessed only the clothes I had gone ashore in, and not a cent remained of the one hundred and eighty dollars. It might well be deemed impossible, by those who have never tried it, that in twelve hours a lad can spend all of one hundred and eighty dollars for drinks. I know otherwise.

And I had no regrets. I was proud. I had shown them I could spend with the rest of them. Amongst strong men I had proved myself strong. I had clinched again, as I had often clinched, my right to the title of "Prince." Also, my attitude may be considered, in part, as a reaction from my childhood's meagerness and my childhood's excessive toil.

Possibly my inchoate thought was: Better to reign among booze-fighters, a prince, than to toil twelve hours a day at a machine for ten cents an hour. There are no purple passages in machine toil. But if the spending of one hundred and eighty dollars in twelve hours isn't a purple passage, then I'd like to know what is.

Oh, I skip much of the details of my trafficking with John Barleycorn during this period, and shall only mention events that will throw light on John Barleycorn's ways. There were three things that enabled me to pursue this heavy drinking: first, a magnificent constitution far better than the average; second, the healthy, open-air life on the water; and third, the fact that I drank irregularly. While out on the water, we never carried any drink along.

The world was opening up to me. Already I knew several hundred miles of the waterways of it, and of the towns and cities and fishing hamlets on the shores. Came the whisper to range farther. I had not found it yet. There was more behind. But even this much of the world was too wide for Nelson. He wearied for his beloved Oakland water-front, and when he elected to return to it we separated in all friendliness.

I now made the old town of Benicia, on the Carquinez Straits, my headquarters. In a cluster of fishermen's arks, moored in the tules on the water-front, dwelt a congenial crowd of drinkers and vagabonds, and I joined them. I had longer spells ashore, between fooling with salmon fishing and making raids up and down bay and rivers as a deputy fish patrolman, and I drank more and learned more about drinking. I held my own with any one, drink for drink; and often drank more than my share to show the strength of my manhood. When, on a morning, my unconscious carcass was disentangled from the nets on the drying-frames, whither I had stupidly, blindly crawled the night before; and when the water-front talked it over with many a giggle and laugh and another drink, I was proud indeed. It was an exploit.

And when I never drew a sober breath, on one stretch, for three solid weeks, I was certain I had reached the top. Surely, in that direction, one could go no farther. It was time for me to move on. For always, drunk or sober, at the back of my consciousness something whispered that this carousing and bay-adventuring was not all of life. This whisper was my good fortune. I happened to be so made that I could hear it calling, always calling, out and away over the world. It was not canniness on my part. It was curiosity, desire to know, an unrest and a seeking for things wonderful that I seemed somehow to have glimpsed or guessed. What was this life for, I demanded, if this were all? No; there was something more, away and beyond. (And, in relation to my much later development as a drinker, this whisper, this promise of the things at the back of life, must be noted, for it was destined to play a dire part in my later wrestlings with John Barleycorn.)

But what gave immediacy to my decision to move on, was a trick John Barleycorn played me—a monstrous, incredible trick that showed abysses of intoxication hitherto undreamed. At one o'clock in the morning, after a prodigious drunk, I was tottering aboard a sloop at the end of the wharf, intending to go to sleep. The tides sweep through Carquinez Straits as in a mill-race, and the full ebb was on when I stumbled overboard. There was nobody on the wharf, nobody on the sloop. I was borne away by the current. I was not startled. I thought the misadventure delightful. I was a good swimmer, and in my inflamed condition the contact of the water with my skin soothed me like cool linen.

And then John Barleycorn played me his maniacal trick. Some maundering fancy of going out with the tide suddenly obsessed me. I had never been morbid. Thoughts of suicide had never entered my head. And now that they entered, I thought it fine, a splendid culmination, a perfect rounding off of my short but exciting career. I, who had never known girl's love, nor woman's love, nor the love of children; who had never played in the wide joy-fields of art, nor climbed the star-cool heights of philosophy, nor seen with my eyes more than a pin-point's surface of the gorgeous world; I decided that this was all, that I had seen all, lived all, been all, that was worth while, and that now was the time to cease. This was the trick of John Barleycorn, laying me by the heels of my imagination and in a drug-dream dragging me to death.

Oh, he was convincing. I had really experienced all of life, and it didn't amount to much. The swinish drunkenness in which I had lived for months (this was accompanied by the sense of degradation and the old feeling of conviction of sin) was the last and best, and I could see for myself what it was worth. There were all the broken-down old bums and loafers I had bought drinks for. That was what remained of life. Did I want to become like them? A thousand times no; and I wept tears of sweet sadness over my glorious youth going out with the tide. (And who has not seen the weeping-drunk, the melancholic drunk? They are to be found in all the barrooms, if they can find no other listener telling their sorrows to the barkeeper, who is paid to listen.)

The water was delicious. It was a man's way to die. John Barleycorn changed the tune he played in my drink-maddened brain. Away with tears and regret. It was a hero's death, and by the hero's own hand and will. So I struck up my death-chant and was singing it lustily, when the gurgle and splash of the current-riffles in my ears reminded me of my more immediate situation.

Below the town of Benicia, where the *Solano* wharf projects, the straits widen out into what bay-farers call the "Bight of Turner's Shipyard." I was in the shore-tide that swept under the *Solano* wharf and on into the bight. I knew of old the power of the suck which developed when the tide swung around the end of Dead Man's Island and drove straight for the wharf. I didn't want to go through those piles. It wouldn't be nice, and I might lose an hour in the bight on my way out with the tide.

I undressed in the water and struck out with a strong, single-overhand stroke, crossing the current at right angles. Nor did I cease until, by the wharf-lights, I knew I was safe to sweep by the end. Then I turned over and rested. The stroke had been a telling one, and I was a little time in recovering my breath.

I was elated, for I had succeeded in avoiding the suck. I started to raise my death-chant again—a purely extemporized farrago of a drug-crazed youth. "Don't sing . . . yet," whispered John Barleycorn. "The *Solano* runs all night. There are railroad men on the wharf. They will hear you, and come out in a boat and rescue you, and you don't want to be rescued." I certainly didn't. What? Be robbed of my hero's death? Never. And I lay on my back in the starlight, watching the familiar wharf-lights go by, red and green and white, and bidding sad, sentimental farewell to them, each and all.

When I was well clear, in mid-channel, I sang again. Sometimes I swam a few strokes, but in the main I contented myself with floating and dreaming long drunken dreams. Before daylight, the chill of the water and the passage of the hours had sobered me sufficiently to make me wonder what portion of the Straits I was in, and also to wonder if the turn of the tide wouldn't catch me and take me back ere I had drifted out into San Pablo Bay.

Next I discovered that I was very weary and very cold, and quite sober, and that I didn't in the least want to be drowned. I could make out the Selby Smelter on the Contra Costa shore and the Mare Island lighthouse. I started to swim for the Solano shore, but was too weak and chilled, and made so little headway, and at the cost of so painful effort that I gave it up and contented myself with floating, now and then giving a stroke to keep my balance in the tide-rips which were increasing their commotion on the surface of the water. And I knew fear. I was sober, now, and I didn't want to die. I discovered scores of reasons for living. And the more reasons I discovered, the more liable it seemed that I was going to drown anyway.

Daylight, after I had been four hours in the water, found me in a parlous condition in the tide-rips off Mare Island light, where the swift ebbs from Vallejo Straits and Carquinez Straits were fighting with each other, and where, at that particular moment, they were fighting the flood tide setting up against them from San Pablo Bay. A stiff breeze had sprung up, and the crisp little waves were persistently lapping into my mouth, and I was beginning to swallow salt water. With my swimmer's knowledge, I knew the end was near. And then the boat came—a Greek fisherman running in for Valejo; and again I had been saved from John Barleycorn by my constitution and physical vigor.

And in passing, let me note that this maniacal trick John Barleycorn played me is nothing uncommon. An absolute statistic of the percentage of suicides due to John Barleycorn would be appalling. In my case, healthy, normal, young, full of the joy of life, the suggestion to kill myself was unusual; but it must be taken into account that it came on the heels of a long carouse, when my nerves and brain were fearfully poisoned, and that the dramatic, romantic side of my imagination, drink-maddened to lunacy, was delighted with the suggestion. And yet, the older, more morbid drinkers, more jaded with life and more disillusioned, who kill themselves, do so usually after a long debauch, when their nerves and brains are thoroughly poison-soaked.

XIII

So I left Benicia, where John Barleycorn had nearly got me, and ranged wider afield in pursuit of the whisper from the back of life to come and find. And wherever I ranged, the way lay along alcohol-drenched roads. Men still congregated in saloons. They were the poorman's clubs, and they were the only clubs to which I had access. I could get acquainted in saloons. I could go into a saloon and talk with any man. In the strange towns and cities I wandered through, the only place for me to go was the saloon. I was no longer a stranger in any town the moment I had entered a saloon.

And right here let me break in with experiences no later than last year. I harnessed four horses to a light trap, took Charmian along, and drove for three months and a half over the wildest mountain parts of California and Oregon. Each morning I did my regular day's work of writing fiction. That completed, I drove on through the middle of the day and the afternoon to the next stop. But the irregularity of occurrence of stopping places, coupled with widely varying road conditions, made it necessary to plan, the day before, each day's drive and my work. I must know when I was to start driving in order to start writing in time to finish my day's output. Thus, on occasion, when the drive was to be long, I would be up and at my writing by five in the morning. On easier driving days I might not start writing till nine o'clock.

But how to plan? As soon as I arrived in a town, and put the horses up, on the way from the stable to the hotel I dropped into the saloons. First thing, a drink—oh, I wanted the drink, but also it must not be forgotten that, because of wanting to know things, it was in this very way I had learned to want a drink. Well, the first thing, a drink. "Have something yourself," to the barkeeper. And then, as we drink, my opening query about roads and stopping-places on ahead.

"Let me see," the barkeeper will say, "there's the road across Tarwater Divide. That used to be good. I was over it three years ago. But it was blocked this spring. . . . Say,

I'll tell you what. I'll ask Jerry—" And the barkeeper turns and addresses some men sitting at a table or leaning against the bar farther along, and who may be Jerry, or Tom, or Bill. "Say, Jerry, how about the Tarwater road? You was down to Wilkins last week."

And while Bill or Jerry or Tom is beginning to unlimber his thinking and speaking apparatus, I suggest that he join us in the drink. Then discussions arise about the advisability of this road or that, what the best stopping places may be, what running time I may expect to make, where the best trout streams are, and so forth, in which other men join, and which are punctuated with more drinks.

Two or three more saloons, and I accumulate a warm jingle and come pretty close to knowing everybody in town, all about the town, and a fair deal about the surrounding country. I know the lawyers, editors, business men, local politicians, and the visiting ranchers, hunters, and miners, so that by evening, when Charmian and I stroll down the main street and back, she is astounded by the number of my acquaintances in that totally strange town.

And thus is demonstrated a service John Barleycorn renders, a service by which he increases his power over men. And over the world, wherever I have gone, during all the years, it has been the same. It may be a cabaret in the Latin Quarter, a café in some obscure Italian village, a boozing-ken in sailortown, and it may be up at the club over Scotch and soda; but always it will be where John Barleycorn makes fellowship that I get immediately in touch, and meet, and know. And in the good days coming, when John Barleycorn will have been banished out of existence along with the other barbarians, some other institution than the saloon will have to obtain, some other congregating place of men where strange men and stranger men may get in touch, and meet, and know.

But to return to my narrative. When I turned my back on Benicia, my way led through saloons. I had developed no moral theories against drinking, and I disliked as much as ever the taste of the stuff. But I had grown respectfully suspicious of John Barleycorn. I could not forget that trick he had played on me—on *me*, who did not want to die. So I continued to drink, and to keep a sharp eye on John Barleycorn, resolved to resist all future suggestions of self-destruction.

In strange towns I made immediate acquaintances in the saloons. When I hoboed, and hadn't the price of a bed, a saloon was the only place that would receive me and give me a chair by the fire. I could go into a saloon and wash up, brush my clothes, and comb my hair. And saloons were always so damnably convenient. They were everywhere in my western country.

I couldn't go into the dwellings of strangers that way. Their doors were not open to me; no seats were there for me by their fires. Also, churches and preachers I had never known. And from what I didn't know I was not attracted toward them. Besides, there was no glamour about them, no haze of romance, no promise of adventure. They were the sort with whom things never happened. They lived and remained always in the one place, creatures of order and system, narrow, limited, restrained. They were without greatness, without imagination, without camaraderie. It was the good fellows, easy and genial, daring, and, on occasion, mad, that I wanted to know—the fellows, generous-hearted and handed, and not rabbit-hearted.

And here is another complaint I bring against John Barleycorn. It is these good fellows that he gets—the fellows with the fire and the go in them, who have bigness, and warmness, and the best of the human weaknesses. And John Barleycorn puts out the fire, and soddens the agility, and, when he does not more immediately kill them or make maniacs of them, he coarsens and grossens them, twists and malforms them out of the original goodness and fineness of their natures.

Oh!—and I speak out of later knowledge—heaven forefend me from the most of the average run of male humans who are not good fellows—the ones cold of heart and cold of head who don't smoke, drink, nor swear, nor do much of anything else that is brave, and resentful, and stinging, because in their feeble fibers there has never been the stir and prod of life to well over its boundaries and be devilish and daring. One doesn't meet these in saloons, nor rallying to lost causes, nor flaming on the adventure-paths, nor loving as God's own mad lovers. They are too busy keeping their feet dry, conserving their heart-beats, and making unlovely life-successes of their spirit-mediocrity.

And so I draw the indictment home to John Barleycorn. It is just these, the good fellows, the worth while, the fellows with the weakness of too much strength, too much spirit, too much fire and flame of fine devilishness, that he solicits and ruins. Of course, he ruins weaklings; but with them, the worst we breed, I am not here concerned. My concern is that it is so much of the best we breed whom John Barleycorn destroys. And the reason why these best are destroyed is because John Barleycorn stands on every highway and byway, accessible, law-protected, saluted by the policeman on the beat, speaking to them, leading them by the hand to the places where the good fellows and daring ones foregather and drink deep. With John Barleycorn out of the way, these daring ones would still be born, and they would do things instead of perishing.

Always I encountered the camaraderie of drink. I might be walking down the track to the water-tank to lie in wait for a passing freight-train, when I would chance upon a bunch of "alki-stiffs." An alki-stiff is a tramp who drinks druggist's alcohol. Immediately, with greeting and salutation, I am taken into the fellowship. The alcohol, shrewdly blended with water, is handed to me, and soon I am caught up in the revelry, with maggots crawling in my brain and John Barleycorn whispering to me that life is big, and that we are all brave and fine—free spirits sprawling like careless gods upon the turf and telling the two-by-four, cut-and-dried, conventional world to go hang.

XIV

BACK in Oakland from my wanderings, I returned to the water-front and renewed my comradeship with Nelson, who was now on shore all the time and living more madly than before. I, too, spent my time on shore with him, only occasionally going for cruises of several days on the bay to help out on short-handed scow-schooners.

The result was that I was no longer reinvigorated by periods of open-air abstinence and healthy toil. I drank every day, and whenever opportunity offered I drank to excess; for I still labored under the misconception that the secret of John Barleycorn lay in drinking to bestiality and unconsciousness. I became pretty thoroughly alcohol-soaked during this period. I practically lived in saloons; became a barroom loafer, and worse.

And right here was John Barleycorn getting me in a more insidious though no less deadly way than when he nearly sent me out with the tide. I had a few months still to run before I was seventeen; I scorned the thought of a steady job at anything; I felt myself a pretty tough individual in a group of pretty tough men; and I drank because these men drank and because I had to make good with them. I had never had a real boyhood, and in this, my precocious manhood, I was very hard and woefully wise. Though I had never known girl's love even, I had crawled through such depths that I was convinced absolutely that I knew the last word about love and life. And it wasn't a pretty knowledge. Without being pessimistic, I was quite satisfied that life was a rather cheap and ordinary affair.

You see, John Barleycorn was blunting me. The old stings and prods of the spirit were no longer sharp. Curiosity was leaving me. What did it matter what lay on the other side of the world? Men and women, without doubt, very much like the men and women I knew; marrying and giving in marriage and all the petty run of petty human concerns; and drinks, too. But the other side of the world was a long way to go for a drink. I had but to step to the corner and get all I wanted at Joe Vigy's. Johnny Heinhold still ran the Last Chance. And there were saloons on all the corners and between the corners.

The whispers from the back of life were growing dim as my mind and body soddened. The old unrest was drowsy. I might as well rot and die here in Oakland as anywhere else. And I should have so rotted and died and not in very long order either, at the pace John Barleycorn was leading me, had the matter depended wholly on him. I was learning what it was to have no appetite. I was learning what it was to get up shaky in the morning, with a stomach that quivered, with fingers touched with palsy, and to know the drinker's need for a stiff glass of whisky neat in order to brace up. (Oh! John Barleycorn is a wizard dopester. Brain and body, scorched and jangled and poisoned, return to be tuned up by the very poison that caused the damage.)

There is no end to John Barleycorn's tricks. He had tried to inveigle me into killing myself. At this period he was doing his best to kill me at a fairly rapid pace. But not satisfied with that, he tried another dodge. He very nearly got me, too, and right there I learned a lesson about him—became a wiser, a more skillful drinker. I learned there were limits to my gorgeous constitution, and that there were no limits to John Barleycorn. I learned that in a short hour or two he could master my strong head, my broad shoulders and deep chest, put me on my back, and with a devil's grip on my throat proceed to choke the life out of me.

Nelson and I were sitting in the Overland House. It was early in the evening, and the only reason we were there was because we were broke and it was election time. You see, in election time local politicians, aspirants for office, have a way of making the rounds of the saloons to get votes. One is sitting at a table, in a dry condition, wondering who is going to turn up and buy him a drink, or if his credit is good at some other saloon and if it's worth while to walk that far to find out, when suddenly the saloon doors swing wide and enters a bevy of well-dressed men, themselves usually wide and exhaling an atmosphere of prosperity and fellowship.

They have smiles and greetings for everybody—for you, without the price of a glass of beer in your pocket, for the timid hobo who lurks in the corner and who certainly hasn't a vote but who may establish a lodging-house registration. And do you know, when these politicians swing wide the doors and come in, with their broad shoulders, their deep chests, and their generous stomachs which cannot help making them optimists and masters of life, why, you perk right up. It's going to be a warm evening after all, and you know you'll get a souse started at the very least. And—who knows?—the gods may be kind, other drinks may come, and the night culminate in glorious greatness. And the next thing you know, you are lined up at the bar, pouring drinks down your throat and learning the gentlemen's names and the offices which they hope to fill.

It was during this period, when the politicians went their saloon rounds, that I was getting bitter bits of education and having illusions punctured—I, who had pored and thrilled over "The Rail-Splitter," and "From Canal Boy to President." Yes, I was learning how noble politics and politicians are.

Well, on this night, broke, thirsty, but with the drinker's faith in the unexpected drink, Nelson and I sat in the Overland House waiting for something to turn up, especially politicians. And there entered Joe Goose—he of the unquenchable thirst, the wicked eyes, the crooked nose, the flowered vest.

"Come on, fellows—free booze—all you want of it. I didn't want you to miss it."

"Where?" we wanted to know.

"Come on. I'll tell you as we go along. We haven't a minute to lose." And as we hurried up town, Joe Goose explained. "It's the Hancock Fire Brigade. All you have to do is wear a red shirt and a helmet, and carry a torch. They're going down on a special train to Haywards to parade."

(I think the place was Haywards. It may have been San Leandro or Niles. And, to save me, I can't remember whether the Hancock Fire Brigade was a Republican or a Democratic organization. But anyway, the politicians who ran it were short of torch-bearers, and anybody who would parade could get drunk if he wanted to.)

"The town'll be wide open," Joe Goose went on. "Booze? It'll run like water. The politicians have bought the stocks of the saloons. There'll be no charge. All you got to do is walk right up and call for it. We'll raise hell."

At the hall, on Eighth Street near Broadway, we got into the firemen's shirts and helmets, were equipped with torches, and, growling because we weren't given at least one drink before we started, were herded aboard the train. Oh, those politicians had handled our kind before. At Haywards there were no drinks either. Parade, first, and earn your booze, was the order of the night.

We paraded. Then the saloons were opened. Extra barkeepers had been engaged, and the drinkers jammed six deep before every drink-drenched and unwiped bar. There was no time to wipe the bar, nor wash glasses, nor do anything save fill glasses. The Oakland water-front can be real thirsty on occasion.

This method of jamming and struggling in front of the bar was too slow for us. The drink was ours. The politicians had bought it for us. We'd paraded and earned it, hadn't we? So we made a flank attack around the end of the bar, shoved the protesting barkeepers aside, and helped ourselves to bottles.

Outside, we knocked the necks of the bottles off against the concrete curbs, and drank. Now Joe Goose and Nelson had learned discretion with straight whisky, drunk in quantity. I hadn't: I still labored under the misconception that one was to drink all he could get—especially when it didn't cost anything. We shared our bottles with others, and drank a good portion ourselves, while I drank most of all. And I didn't like the stuff. I drank it as I had drunk beer at five, and wine at seven. I mastered my qualms and downed it like so much medicine. And when we wanted more bottles, we went into other saloons where the free drink was flowing, and helped ourselves.

I haven't the slightest idea of how much I drank—whether it was two quarts or five. I do know that I began the orgy with half-pint draughts and with no water afterward to wash the taste away and to dilute the whisky.

Now the politicians were too wise to leave the town filled with drunks from the water-front of Oakland. When train time came, there was a round-up of the saloons. Already I was feeling the impact of the whisky. Nelson and I were hustled out of a saloon, and found ourselves in the very last rank of a disorderly parade. I struggled along heroically, my correlations breaking down, my legs tottering under me, my head swimming, my heart pounding, my lungs panting for air.

My helplessness was coming on so rapidly that my reeling brain told me I would go down and out and never reach the train if I remained at the rear of the procession. I left the ranks and ran down a pathway beside the road under broad-spreading trees. Nelson pursued me, laughing. Certain things stand out, as in memories of nightmare. I remember those trees especially, and my desperate running along under them, and how, every time I fell, roars of laughter went up from the other drunks. They thought I was merely antic drunk. They did not dream that John Barleycorn had me by the throat in a death-clutch. But I knew it. And I remember the fleeting bitterness that was mine as I realized that I was in a struggle with death and that these others did not know. It was as if I were drowning before a crowd of spectators who thought I was cutting up tricks for their entertainment.

And running there under the trees, I fell and lost consciousness. What happened afterward, with one glimmering exception, I had to be told. Nelson, with his enormous strength, picked me up and dragged me on and aboard the train. When he had got me into a seat, I fought and panted so terribly for air that even with his obtuseness he knew I was in a bad way. And right there, at any moment, I know now, I might have died. I often think it is the nearest to death I have ever been. I have only Nelson's description of my behavior to go by.

I was scorching up, burning alive internally, in an agony of fire and suffocation, and I wanted air. I madly wanted air. My efforts to raise a window were vain, for all the windows in the car were screwed down. Nelson had seen drink-crazed men, and thought I wanted to throw myself out. He tried to restrain me, but I fought on. I seized some man's torch and smashed the glass.

Now there were pro-Nelson and anti-Nelson factions on the Oakland water-front, and men of both factions, with more drink in them than was good, filled the car. My smashing of the window was the signal for the anti's. One of them reached for me, and dropped me, and started the fight, of all of which I have no knowledge save what was told me afterward, and a sore jaw next day from the blow that put me out. The man who struck me went down across my body, Nelson followed him, and they say there were few unbroken windows in the wreckage of the car that followed as the free-for-all fight had its course.

This being knocked cold and motionless was perhaps the best thing that could have happened to me. My violent struggles had only accelerated my already dangerously accelerated heart, and increased the need for oxygen in my suffocating lungs.

After the fight was over and I came to, I did not come to myself. I was no more myself than a drowning man is who continues to struggle after he has lost consciousness. I have no memory of my actions, but I cried "Air! Air!" so insistently, that it dawned on Nelson that I did not contemplate self-destruction. So he cleared the jagged glass from the window ledge and let me stick my head and shoulders out. He realized, partially, the seriousness of my condition, and held me by the waist to prevent me from crawling farther out. And for the rest of the run in to Oakland I kept my head and shoulders out, fighting like a maniac whenever he tried to draw me inside.

And here my one glimmering streak of true consciousness came. My sole recollection, from the time I fell under the trees until I awoke the following evening, is of my head out the window, facing the wind caused by the train, cinders striking and burning and blinding me, while I breathed with will. All my will was concentrated on breathing —on breathing the air in the hugest lung-full gulps I could, pumping the greatest amount of air into my lungs in the shortest possible time. It was that or death, and I was a swimmer and diver and I knew it; and in the most intolerable agony of prolonged suffocation, during those moments I was conscious, I faced the wind and the cinders and breathed for life.

All the rest is a blank. I came to the following evening, in a water-front lodging-house. I was alone. No doctor had been called in. And I might well have died there, for Nelson and the others, deeming me merely "sleeping off my drunk," had let me lie there in a comatose condition for seventeen hours. Many a man, as every doctor knows, has died of the sudden impact of a quart or more of whisky. Usually one reads of them so dying, strong drinkers, on account of a wager. But I didn't know . . . then. And so I learned; and by no virtue nor prowess, but simply through good fortune and constitution. Again my constitution had triumphed over John Barleycorn. I had escaped from another death-pit, dragged myself through another morass, and perilously acquired the discretion that would enable me to drink wisely for many another year to come.

Heavens! That was twenty years ago, and I am still very much and wisely alive; and I have seen much, done much, lived much, in that intervening score of years; and I shudder when I think how close a shave I ran, how near I was to missing that splendid fifth of a century that has been mine. And, oh, it wasn't John Barleycorn's fault that he didn't get me that night of the Hancock Fire Brigade.

XV

It was during the early winter of 1892 that I resolved to go to sea. My Hancock Fire Brigade experience was very little responsible for this. I still drank and frequented saloons—practically lived in saloons. Whisky was dangerous, in my opinion, but not wrong. Whisky was dangerous, like other dangerous things in the natural world. Men died of whisky; but then, too, fishermen were capsized and drowned, hoboes fell under trains and were cut to pieces. To cope with winds and waves, railroad trains, and barrooms, one must use judgment. To get drunk after the manner of men was all right, but one must do it with discretion. No more quarts of whisky for me.

What really decided me to go to sea was that I had caught my first vision of the death-road which John Barleycorn maintains for his devotees. It was not a clear vision, however, and there were two phases of it, somewhat jumbled at the time. It struck me, from watching those with whom I associated, that the life we were living was more destructive than that lived by the average man.

John Barleycorn, by inhibiting morality, incited to crime. Everywhere I saw men doing, drunk, what they would never dream of doing sober. And this wasn't the worst of it. It was the penalty that must be paid. Crime was destructive. Saloon-mates I drank with, who were good fellows and harmless, sober, did most violent and lunatic things when they were drunk. And then the police gathered them in and they vanished from our ken. Sometimes I visited them behind the bars and said good-by ere they journeyed across the bay to put on the felon's stripes. And time and again I heard the one explanation: *If I hadn't been drunk I wouldn't a-done it.* And sometimes, under the spell of John Barleycorn, the most frightful things were done—things that shocked even my case-hardened soul.

The other phase of the death-road was that of the habitual drunkards, who had a way of turning up their toes without apparent provocation. When they took sick, even with trifling afflictions that any ordinary man could pull through, they just pegged out. Sometimes they were found unattended and dead in their beds; on occasion their bodies were dragged out of the water; and sometimes it was just plain accident, as when Bill Kelly, unloading cargo while drunk, had a finger jerked off, which, under the circumstances, might just as easily have been his head.

So I considered my situation and knew that I was getting into a bad way of living. It made toward death too quickly to suit my youth and vitality. And there was only one way out of this hazardous manner of living and that was to get out. The sealing-fleet was wintering in San Francisco Bay, and in the saloons I met skippers, mates, hunters, boat-steerers, and boat-pullers. I met the seal-hunter, Pete Holt, and agreed to be his boat-puller and to sign on any schooner he signed on. And I had to have half-a-dozen drinks with Pete Holt there and then to seal our agreement.

And at once awoke all my old unrest that John Barleycorn had put to sleep. I found myself actually bored with the saloon-life of the Oakland water-front, and wondered what I had ever found fascinating in it. Also, with this death-road concept in my brain, I began to grow afraid that something would happen to me before sailing day, which was set for some time in January. I lived more circumspectly, drank less deeply, and went home more frequently. When drinking grew too wild, I got out. When Nelson was in his maniacal cups, I managed to get separated from him.

On the twelfth of January, 1893, I was seventeen, and the twentieth of January I signed before the shipping commissioner the articles of the *Sophie Sutherland*, a three topmast sealing schooner bound on a voyage to the coast of Japan. And of course we had to drink on it. Joe Vigy cashed my advance note, and Pete Holt treated, and I treated, and Joe Vigy treated, and other hunters treated. Well, it was the way of men, and who was I, just turned seventeen, that I should decline the way of life of these fine, chesty, man-grown men?

XVI

THERE was nothing to drink on the *Sophie Sutherland*, and we had fifty-one days of glorious sailing, taking the southern passage in the northeast trades to Bonin Islands. This isolated group, belonging to Japan, had been selected as the rendezvous of the Canadian and American sealing-fleets. Here they filled their water-barrels and made repairs before starting on the hundred days' harrying of the seal-herd along the northern coasts of Japan to Behring Sea.

Those fifty-one days of fine sailing and intense sobriety had put me in splendid fettle. The alcohol had been worked out of my system, and from the moment the voyage began I had not known the desire for a drink. I doubt if I even thought once about a drink. Often, of course, the talk in the forecastle turned on drink, and the men told of their more exciting or humorous drunks, remembering such passages more keenly, with greater delight, than all the other passages of their adventurous lives.

In the forecastle, the oldest man, fat and fifty, was Louis. He was a broken skipper. John Barleycorn had thrown him, and he was winding up his career where he had begun it, in the forecastle. His case made quite an impression on me. John Barleycorn did other things beside kill a man. He hadn't killed Louis. He had done much worse. He had robbed him of power and place and comfort, crucified his pride, and condemned him to the hardship of the common sailor that would last as long as his healthy breath lasted, which promised to be for a long time.

We completed our run across the Pacific, lifted the volcanic peaks, jungle-clad, of the Bonin Islands, sailed in among the reefs to the land-locked harbor, and let our anchor rumble down where lay a score or more of sea-gipsies like ourself. The scents of strange vegetation blew off the tropic land. Aborigines, in queer outrigger canoes, and Japanese, in queerer sampans, paddled about the bay and came aboard. It was my first foreign land; I had won to the other side of the world, and I would see all I had read in the books come true. I was wild to get ashore.

Victor and Axel, a Swede and a Norwegian, and I planned to keep together. (And so well did we, that for the rest of the cruise we were known as the "Three Sports.") Victor pointed out a pathway that disappeared up a wild canyon, emerged on a steep, bare lava-slope, and thereafter appeared and disappeared, ever climbing, among the palms and flowers. We would go over that path, he said, and we agreed, and we would see beautiful scenery, and strange native villages, and find Heaven alone knew what adventure at the end. And Axel was keen to go fishing. The three of us agreed to that, too. We would get a sampan, and a couple of Japanese fishermen who knew the fishing grounds, and we would have great sport. As for me, I was keen for anything.

And then, our plans made, we rowed ashore over the banks of living coral and pulled our boat up the white beach of coral sand. We walked across the fringe of beach under the cocoanut palms and into the little town, and found several hundred riotous seamen from all the world, drinking prodigiously, singing prodigiously, dancing prodigiously—and all on the main street to the scandal of a helpless handful of Japanese police.

Victor and Axel said we'd have a drink before we started on our long walk. Could I decline to drink with these two chesty shipmates? Drinking together, glass in hand, put the seal on comradeship. It was the way of life. Our teetotaler owner-captain was laughed at, and sneered at, by all of us because of his teetotalism. I didn't in the least want a drink, but I did want to be a good fellow and a good comrade. Nor did Louis' case deter me, as I poured the biting, scorching stuff down my throat. John Barleycorn had thrown Louis to a nasty fall, but I was young. My blood ran full and red; I had a constitution of iron; and—well, youth ever grins scornfully at the wreckage of age.

Queer, fierce, alcoholic stuff it was that we drank. There was no telling where or how it had been manufactured—some native concoction, most likely. But it was hot as fire, pale as water, and quick as death with its kick. It had been filled into empty "square-face" bottles which had once contained Holland gin and which still bore the fitting legend: "Anchor Brand." It certainly anchored us. We never got out of the town. We never went fishing in the sampan. And though we were there ten days, we never trod that wild path along the lava-cliffs and among the flowers.

We met old acquaintances from other schooners, fellows we had met in the saloons of San Francisco before we sailed. And each meeting meant a drink; and there was much to talk about; and more drinks; and songs to be sung; and pranks and antics to be performed; until the maggots of imagination began to crawl, and it all seemed great and wonderful to me, these lusty, hard-bitten sea-rovers, of whom I made one, gathered in wassail on a coral strand. Old lines about knights at table in the great banquet-halls, and of those above the salt and below the salt, and of Vikings feasting fresh from sea and ripe for battle, came to me; and I knew that the old times were not dead and that we belonged to that self-same ancient breed.

By mid-afternoon Victor went mad with drink, and wanted to fight everybody and everything. I have since seen lunatics in the violent wards of asylums that seemed to behave in no wise different from Victor's way, save that perhaps he was more violent. Axel and I interfered as peace-makers, were roughed and jostled in the mix-ups, and finally, with infinite precaution and intoxicated cunning, succeeded in inveigling our chum down to the boat and in rowing him aboard our schooner.

But no sooner did Victor's feet touch the deck, than he began to clean up the ship. He had the strength of several men, and he ran amuck with it. I remember especially one man whom he got into the chain-boxes but failed to damage through inability to hit him. The man dodged and ducked, and Victor broke the knuckles of both his fists against the huge links of the anchor chain. By the time we dragged him out of that, his madness had shifted to the belief that he was a great swimmer, and the next moment he was overboard and demonstrating his ability by floundering like a sick porpoise and swallowing much salt water.

We rescued him, and by the time we got him below, undressed, and into his bunk, we were wrecks ourselves. But Axel and I wanted to see more of shore, and away we went, leaving Victor snoring. It was curious, the judgment passed on Victor by his shipmates, drinkers themselves. They shook their heads disapprovingly and muttered: "A man like that oughtn't to drink." Now Victor was the smartest sailor and best-tempered shipmate in the forecastle. He was an all-around splendid type of seaman; his mates recognized his worth, and respected him and liked him. Yet John Barleycorn metamorphosed him into a violent lunatic. And that was the very point these drinkers made. They knew that drink—and drink with a sailor is always excessive—made them mad, but only mildly mad. Violent madness was objectionable because it spoiled the fun of others and often culminated in tragedy. From their standpoint, mild madness was all right. But from the standpoint of the whole human race, is not all madness objectionable? And is there a greater maker of madness of all sorts than John Barleycorn?

But to return. Ashore, snugly ensconced in a Japanese house of entertainment, Axel and I compared bruises, and over a comfortable drink talked of the afternoon's happenings. We liked the quietness of that drink and took another. A shipmate dropped in, several shipmates dropped in, and we had more quiet drinks. Finally, just as we had engaged a Japanese orchestra, and as the first strains of the *samisens* and *taikos* were rising, through the paper-walls came a wild howl from the street. We recognized it. Still howling, disdaining doorways, with bloodshot eyes and wildly waving muscular arms, Victor burst upon us through the fragile walls. The old amuck rage was on him, and he wanted blood, anybody's blood. The orchestra fled; so did we. We went through doorways, and we went through paper-walls—anything to get away.

And after the place was half wrecked, and we had agreed to pay the damage, leaving Victor partly subdued and showing symptoms of lapsing into a comatose state, Axel and I wandered away in quest of a quieter drinking-place. The main street was a madness. Hundreds of sailors rollicked up and down. Because the chief of police with his small force was helpless, the Governor of the colony had issued orders to the captains to have all their men on board by sunset.

What! To be treated in such fashion! As the news spread among the schooners, they were emptied. Everybody came ashore. Men who had had no intention of coming ashore, climbed into the boats. The unfortunate governor's *ukase* had precipitated a general debauch for all hands. It was hours after sunset, and the men wanted to see anybody try to put them on board. They went around inviting the authorities to try to put them on board. In front of the governor's house they were gathered thickest, bawling sea-songs, circulating square-faces, and dancing uproarious Virginia reels and old-country dances. The police, including the reserves, stood in little forlorn groups, waiting for the command the governor was too wise to issue. And I thought this saturnalia was great. It was like the old days of the Spanish Main come back. It was license; it was adventure. And I was part of it, a chesty sea-rover along with all these other chesty sea-rovers among the paper houses of Japan.

The governor never issued the order to clear the streets, and Axel and I wandered on from drink to drink. After a time, in some of the antics, getting hazy myself, I lost him. I drifted along, making new acquaintances, downing more drinks, getting hazier and hazier. I remember, somewhere, sitting in a circle with Japanese fishermen, kanaka boat-steerers from our own vessels, and a young Danish sailor fresh from cowboying in the Argentine and with a penchant for native customs and ceremonials. And with due and proper and most intricate Japanese ceremonial, we of the circle drank *sake*, pale, mild, and lukewarm, from tiny porcelain bowls.

And, later, I remember the runaway apprentices—boys of eighteen and twenty, of middle class English families, who had jumped their ships and apprenticeships in various ports of the world and drifted into the forecastles of the sailing schooners. They were healthy, smooth-skinned, clear-eyed, and they were young—youths like me, learning the way of their feet in the world of men. And they *were* men. No mild *sake* for them, but square-faces illicitly refilled with corrosive fire that flamed through their veins and burst into conflagrations in their heads. I remember a melting song they sang, the refrain of which was:

I give it to thee with pride,
Wear it for your mother's sake
When you are on the tide.

They wept over it as they sang it, the graceless young scamps who had all broken their mothers' prides, and I sang with them, and wept with them, and luxuriated in the pathos and the tragedy of it, and struggled to make glimmering inebriated generalizations on life and romance. And one last picture I have, standing out very clear and bright in the midst of vagueness before and blackness afterward. We—the apprentices and I—are swaying and clinging to one another under the stars. We are singing a rollicking sea-song, all save one who sits on the ground and weeps; and we are marking the rhythm with waving square-faces. From up and down the street come far choruses of sea-voices similarly singing, and life is great, and beautiful, and romantic, and magnificently mad.

And next, after the blackness, I open my eyes in the early dawn to see a Japanese woman, solicitously anxious, bending over me. She is the port-pilot's wife, and I am lying in her doorway. I am chilled and shivering, sick with the after sickness of debauch. And I feel lightly clad. Those rascals of runaway apprentices! They have acquired the habit of running away. They have run away with my possessions. My watch is gone. My few dollars are gone. My coat is gone. So is my belt. And yes, my shoes.

And the foregoing is a sample of the ten days I spent in the Bonin Islands. Victor got over his lunacy, rejoined Axel and me, and after that we caroused somewhat more discreetly. And we never climbed that lava path among the flowers. The town and the square-faces were all we saw.

One who has been burned by fire must preach about the fire. I might have seen and healthily enjoyed a whole lot more of the Bonin Islands, if I had done what I ought to have done. But, as I see it, it is not a matter of what one ought to do, or ought not to do. It is what one *does* do. That is the everlasting, irrefragable fact. I did just what I did. I did what all those men did in the Bonin Islands. I did what millions of men over the world were doing at that particular point in time. I did it because the way led to it, because I was only a human boy, a creature of my environment, and neither an anemic nor a god. I was just human, and I was taking the path in the world that men took—men whom I admired, if you please; full-blooded men, lusty, breedy, chesty men, free spirits and anything but niggards in the way they foamed life away.

And the way was open. It was like an uncovered well in a yard where children play. It is small use to tell the brave little boys toddling their way along into knowledge of life that they mustn't play near the uncovered well. They *will* play near it. Any parent knows that. And we know that a certain percentage of them, the livest and most daring, will fall into the well. The thing to do—we all know it—is to cover up the well. The case is the same with John Barleycorn. All the no-saying and no-preaching in the world will fail to keep men, and youths growing into manhood, away from John Barleycorn when John Barleycorn is everywhere accessible, and where John Barleycorn is everywhere the connotation of manliness, and daring, and great-spiritedness.

The only rational thing for the twentieth century folk to do is to cover up the well; to make the twentieth century in truth the twentieth century, and to relegate to the nineteenth century and all the preceding centuries the things of those centuries, the witch-burnings, the intolerances, the fetiches, and, not least among such barbarisms, John Barleycorn.

XVII

NORTH we raced from the Bonin Islands to pick up the seal-herd, and north we hunted it for a hundred days into frosty, wintry weather and into and through vast fogs which hid the sun from us for a week at a time. It was wild and heavy work off the Siberian coast, without a drink or thought of drink. Then we sailed south to Yokohama, with a big catch of skins in our salt and a heavy pay-day coming.

I was eager to be ashore and see Japan, but the first day was devoted to ship's work, and not until evening did we sailors land. And here, by the very system of things, by the way life was organized and men transacted affairs, John Barleycorn reached out and tucked my arm in his. The captain had given money for us to the hunters, and the hunters were waiting in a certain Japanese public house for us to come and get it. We rode to the place in rickshaws. Our own crowd had taken possession of it. Drink was flowing. Everybody had money, and everybody was treating. After the hundred days of hard toil and absolute abstinence, in the pink of physical condition, bulging with health, overspilling with spirits that had been long pent by discipline and circumstance, of course we would have a drink or two. And after that we would see the town.

It was the old story. There were so many drinks to be drunk, and as the warm magic poured through our veins and mellowed our voices and affections we knew it was no time to make invidious distinctions—to drink with this shipmate and to decline to drink with that shipmate. We were all shipmates who had been through stress and storm together, who had pulled and hauled on the same sheets and tackles, relieved one another's wheels, lain out side by side on the same jib-boom when she was plunging into it and looked to see who was missing when she cleared and lifted. So we drank with all, and all treated, and our voices rose, and we remembered a myriad kindly acts of comradeship, and forgot our fights and wordy squabbles, and knew one another for the best fellows in the world.

Well, the night was young when we arrived in that public house, and for all of that first night that public house was what I saw of Japan—a drinking place which was very like a drinking place at home or anywhere else over the world.

We lay in Yokohama harbor for two weeks, and about all we saw of Japan was its drinking places where sailors congregated. Occasionally, some one of us varied the monotony with a more exciting drunk. In such fashion I managed a real exploit by swimming off to the schooner one dark midnight and going soundly to sleep while the water-police searched the harbor for my body and brought my clothes out for identification.

Perhaps it was for things like that, I imagined, that men got drunk. In our little round of living what I had done was a noteworthy event. All the harbor talked about it. I enjoyed several days of fame among the Japanese boatmen and ashore in the pubs. It was a red letter event. It was an event to be remembered and narrated with pride. I remember it to-day, twenty years afterward, with a secret glow of pride. It was a purple passage, just as Victor's wrecking of the tea house in the Bonin Islands and my being looted by the runaway apprentices were purple passages.

The point is that the charm of John Barleycorn was still a mystery to me. I was so organically a non-alcoholic that alcohol itself made no appeal; the chemical reactions it produced in me were not satisfying because I possessed no need for such chemical satisfaction. I drank because the men I was with drank, and because my nature was such that I could not permit myself to be less of a man than other men at their favorite pastime. And I still had a sweet tooth, and on privy occasions when there was no man to see, bought candy and blissfully devoured it.

We hove up anchor to a jolly chanty, and sailed out of Yokohama harbor for San Francisco. We took the northern passage, and with the stout west wind at our back made the run across the Pacific in thirty-seven days of brave sailing. We still had a big pay-day coming to us, and for thirty-seven days, without a drink to addle our mental processes, we incessantly planned the spending of our money.

The first statement of each man—ever an ancient one in homeward-bound forecastles—was: "No boarding-house sharks in mine." Next, in parentheses, was regret at having spent so much money in Yokohama. And after that, each man proceeded to paint his favorite phantom. Victor, for instance, said that immediately he landed in San Francisco he would pass right through the water-front and the Barbary Coast, and put an advertisement in the papers. His advertisement would be for board and room in some simple working-class family. "Then," said Victor, "I shall go to some dancing-school for a week or two, just to meet and get acquainted with the girls and fellows. Then I'll get the run of the different dancing-crowds, and be invited to their homes, and to parties, and all that, and with the money I've got I can last out till next January when I'll go sealing again."

No; he wasn't going to drink. He knew the way of it, particularly his way of it, wine in, wit out, and his money would be gone in no time. He had his choice, based on bitter experience, between three days' debauch among the sharks and harpies of the

Barbary Coast and a whole winter of wholesome enjoyment and sociability, and there wasn't any doubt of the way he was going to choose.

Said Axel Gunderson, who didn't care for dancing and social functions: "I've got a good pay-day. Now I can go home. It is fifteen years since I've seen my mother and all the family. When I pay off I shall send my money home to wait for me. Then I'll pick a good ship bound for Europe, and arrive there with another pay-day. Put them together, and I'll have more money than ever in my life before. I'll be a prince at home. You haven't any idea how cheap everything is in Norway. I can make presents to everybody, and spend my money like what would seem to them a millionaire, and live a whole year there before I'd have to go back to sea."

"The very thing I'm going to do," declared Red John. "It's three years since I've received a line from home and ten years since I was there. Things are just as cheap in Sweden, Axel, as in Norway, and my folks are real country folks and farmers. I'll send my pay-day home and ship on the same ship with you for around the Horn. We'll pick a good one."

And as Axel Gunderson and Red John painted the pastoral delights and festive customs of their respective countries, each fell in love with the other's home place, and they solemnly pledged to make the journey together, and to spend, together, six months in the one's Swedish home and six months in the other's Norwegian home. And for the rest of the voyage they could hardly be pried apart, so infatuated did they become with discussing their plans.

Long John was not a home-body. But he was tired of the forecastle. No boarding-house sharks in his. He, too, would get a room in a quiet family, and he would go to a navigation school and study to be a captain. And so it went. Each man swore that for once he would be sensible and not squander his money. No boarding-house sharks, no sailor-town, no drink, was the slogan of our forecastle.

The men became stingy. Never was there such economy. They refused to buy anything more from the slop-chest. Old rags had to last, and they sewed patch upon patch, turning out what are called "homeward-bound patches" of the most amazing dimensions. They saved on matches, even, waiting till two or three were ready to light their pipes from the same match.

As we sailed up the San Francisco water-front, the moment the port doctors passed us the boarding-house runners were alongside in whitehall boats. They swarmed on board, each drumming for his own boarding-house, and each with a bottle of free whisky inside his shirt. But we waved them grandly and blasphemously away. We wanted none of their boarding-houses and none of their whisky. We were sober, thrifty sailormen, with better use for our money.

Came the paying off before the Shipping Commissioner. We emerged upon the sidewalk, each with a pocketful of money. About us, like buzzards, clustered the sharks and harpies. And we looked at each other. We had been seven months together, and our paths were separating. One last farewell rite of comradeship remained. (Oh, it was the way, the custom). "Come on, boys," said our sailing-master. There stood the inevitable adjacent saloon. There were a dozen saloons all around. And when we had followed the sailing-master into the one of his choice, the sharks were thick on the sidewalk outside. Some of them even ventured inside, but we would have nothing to do with them.

There we stood at the long bar—the sailing-master, the mates, the six hunters, the six boat-steerers, and the five boat-pullers. There were only five of the last, for one of our number had been dropped overboard, with a sack of coal at his feet, between two snow squalls in a driving gale off Cape Jerimo. There were nineteen of us, and it was to be our last drink together. With seven months of men's work in the world, blow high, blow low, behind us, we were looking on each other for the last time. We knew it, for sailors' ways go wide. And the nineteen of us drank the sailing-master's treat. Then the mate looked at us with eloquent eyes and called for another round. We liked the mate just as well as the sailing-master, and we liked them both. Could we drink with one, and not the other?

And Pete Holt, my own hunter (lost next year in the *Mary Thomas* with all hands), called a round. The time passed, the drinks continued to come on the bar, our voices rose, and the maggots began to crawl. There were six hunters, and each insisted, in the sacred name of comradeship, that all hands drink with him just once. There were six boat-steerers and five boat-pullers and the same logic held with them. There was money in all our pockets, and our money was as good as any man's, and our hearts were as free and generous.

Nineteen rounds of drinks. What more would John Barleycorn ask in order to have his will with men? They were ripe to forget their dearly cherished plans. They rolled out of the saloon and into the arms of the sharks and harpies. They didn't last long. From two days to a week saw the end of their money and saw them being carted by the boarding-house master on board outward-bound ships. Victor was a fine body of a man, and through a lucky friendship managed to get into the life-saving service. He never saw the dancing-school nor placed his advertisement for a room in a working-class family. Nor did Long John win to navigation-school. By the end of the week he was a transient lumper on a river steamboat. Red John and Axel did not send their pay-days home to the old country. Instead, and along with the rest, they were scattered on board sailing ships bound for the four quarters of the globe, where they had been placed by the boarding-house masters and where they were working out advance money which they had neither seen nor spent.

What saved me was that I had a home and people to go to. I crossed the bay to Oakland, and, among other things, took a look at the death-road. Nelson was gone—shot to death while drunk and resisting the officers. His partner in that affair was lying in prison. Whisky Bob was gone. Old Cole, Old Smoudge and Bob Smith were gone. Another Smith, he of the belted guns and the *Annie,* was drowned. French Frank, they said, was lurking up river, afraid to come down because of something he had done. Others were wearing stripes in San Quentin or Folsom. Big Alec, the King of the Greeks, whom I had known well in the old Benicia days, and with whom I had drunk whole nights through, had killed two men and fled to foreign parts. Fitzsimmons, with whom I had sailed on the Fish Patrol, had been stabbed in the lung through the back and had died a lingering death from tuberculosis. And so it went, a very lively and well-patronized road, and, from what I knew of all of them, John Barleycorn was responsible, with the sole exception of Smith of the *Annie.*

XVIII

MY infatuation for the Oakland water-front was quite dead. I didn't like the looks of it nor the life. I didn't care for the drinking, nor the vagrancy of it, and I wandered back to the Oakland Free Library and read the books with greater understanding. Then, too, my mother said I had sown my wild oats and it was time I settled down to a regular job. Also, the family needed the money. So I got a job at the jute mills—a ten-hour day at ten cents an hour. Despite my increase in strength and general efficiency, I was receiving no more than when I worked in the cannery several years before. But, then, there was a promise of a raise to a dollar and a quarter a day after a few months.

And here, so far as John Barleycorn is concerned, began a period of innocence. I did not know what it was to take a drink from month end to month end. Not yet eighteen years old, healthy and with labor-hardened but unhurt muscles, like any young animal I needed diversion, excitement, something beyond the books and the mechanical toil.

I strayed into Young Men's Christian Associations. The life there was healthful and athletic, but too juvenile. For me it was too late. I was not boy, nor youth, despite my paucity of years. I had bucked big with men. I knew mysterious and violent things. I was from the other side of life so far as concerned the young men I encountered in the Y. M. C. A. I spoke another language, possessed a sadder and more terrible wisdom. (When I come to think it over, I realize, now, that I have never had a boyhood.) At any rate, the Y. M. C. A. young men were too juvenile for me, too unsophisticated. This I would not have minded, could they have met me and helped me mentally. But I had got more out of the books than they. Their meager physical experiences, plus their meager intellectual experiences, made a negative sum so vast that it overbalanced their wholesome morality and healthful sports.

In short, I couldn't play with the pupils of a lower grade. All the clean splendid young life that was theirs was denied me—thanks to my earlier tutelage under John Barleycorn. I knew too much too young. And yet, in the good time coming, when alcohol is eliminated from the needs and the institutions of men, it will be the Y.M. C.A., and similar unthinkably better and wiser and more virile congregating places, that will receive the men who now go to saloons to find themselves and one another. In the meantime, we live today, here and now, and we discuss to-day, here and now.

I was working ten hours a day in the jute mills. It was humdrum machine-toil. I wanted life. I wanted to realize myself in other ways than at a machine for ten cents an hour. And yet I had had my fill of saloons. I wanted something new. I was growing up. I was developing unguessed and troubling potencies and proclivities. And at this very stage, fortunately, I met Louis Shattuck and we became chums.

Louis Shattuck, without one vicious trait, was a real innocently devilish young fellow who was quite convinced that he was a sophisticated town-boy. And I wasn't a town-boy at all. Louis was handsome, and graceful, and filled with love for the girls. With him it was an exciting and all-absorbing pursuit. I didn't know anything about girls. I had been too busy being a man. This was an entirely new phase of existence which had escaped me. And when I saw Louis say good-by to me, raise his hat to a girl of his acquaintance, and walk on by her side down the sidewalk, I was made excited and envious. I, too, wanted to play this game.

"Well—there's only one thing to do," said Louis, "and that is, you must get a girl."

Which is more difficult than it sounds. Let me show you, at the expense of a slight going aside. Louis did not know girls in their home life. He had the entrée to no girl's home. And of course, I, a stranger in this new world, was similarly circumstanced. But further, Louis and I were unable to go to dancing-schools, or to public dances, which were very good places for getting acquainted. We didn't have the money. He was a blacksmith's apprentice, and was earning but slightly more than I. We both lived at home and paid our way. When we had done this, and bought our cigarettes, and the inevitable clothes and shoes, there remained to each of us, for personal spending, a sum that varied between seventy cents and a dollar for the week. We whacked this up, shared it, and sometimes loaned all of what was left of it when one of us needed it for some more gorgeous girl-adventure, such as carfare out to Blair's Park and back—twenty cents, bang, just like that; and ice-cream for two—thirty cents; or tamales, which came cheaper and which for two cost only twenty cents.

I did not mind this money meagerness. The disdain for money I had learned from the oyster pirates had never left me. I didn't care over-weeningly for it for personal gratification; and in my philosophy I completed the circle, finding myself as equable with the lack of a ten-cent piece as I was with the squandering of scores of dollars in calling all men and hangers-on up to the bar to drink with me.

But how to get a girl? There was no girl's home to which Louis could take me and where I might be introduced to girls. I knew none. And Louis' several girls he wanted for himself; and anyway, in the very human nature of boys' and girls' ways, he couldn't turn any of them over to me. He did persuade them to bring girlfriends for me; but I found them weak sisters, pale and ineffectual alongside the choice specimens he had.

"You'll have to do like I did," he said finally. "I got these by getting them. You'll have to get one the same way."

And he initiated me. It must be remembered that Louis and I were hard situated. We really had to struggle to pay our board and maintain a decent appearance. We met each other in the evening, after the day's work, on the street corner, or in a little candy store on a side street, our sole frequenting place. Here we bought our cigarettes, and, occasionally, a nickel's worth of "red-hots." (Oh, yes; Louis and I unblushingly ate candy—all we could get. Neither of us drank. Neither of us ever went into a saloon.)

But the girl. In quite primitive fashion, as Louis advised me, I was to select her and make myself acquainted with her. We strolled the streets in the early evenings. The girls, like us, strolled in pairs. And strolling girls *will* look at strolling boys who look. (And to this day, in any town, city, or village, in which I, in my middle age, find myself, I look on with the eye trained of old experience, and watch the sweet game played by the strolling boys and girls who just *must* stroll when the spring and summer evenings call.)

The trouble was that in this Arcadian phase of my history, I, who had come through, case-hardened, from the other side of life, was timid and bashful. Again and again Louis nerved me up. But I didn't know girls. They were strange and wonderful to me after my precocious man's life. I failed of the bold front and the necessary forwardness when the crucial moment came.

Then Louis would show me how—a certain, eloquent glance of eye, a smile, a daring, lifted hat, a spoken word, hesitancies, giggles, coy nervousness, and, behold, Louis acquainted and nodding me up to be introduced. But, when we paired off to stroll along boy and girl together, I noted that Louis had invariably picked the good-looker and left to me the little lame sister.

I improved, of course, after experiences too numerous to enter upon, so that there were divers girls to whom I could lift my hat and who would walk beside me in the early evenings. But girl's love did not immediately come to me. I was excited, interested, and I pursued the quest. And the thought of drink never entered my mind. Some of Louis' and my adventures have since given me serious pause when casting sociological generalizations. But it was all good and innocently youthful, and I learned one generalization, biological rather than sociological, namely, that the "Colonel's lady and Judy O'Grady are sisters under their skins."

And before long I learned girl's love, all the dear fond deliciousness of it, all the glory and the wonder. I shall call her Haydee. She was between fifteen and sixteen. Her little skirt reached her shoe-tops. We sat side by side in a Salvation Army meeting. She was not a convert, nor was her aunt, who sat on the other side of her and who, visiting from the country, where at that time the Salvation Army was not, had dropped in to the meeting for half an hour out of curiosity. And Louis sat beside me and observed—I do believe he did no more than observe, because Haydee was not his style of girl.

We did not speak, but in that great half-hour we glanced shyly at each other, and shyly avoided or as shyly returned and met each other's glances more than several times. She had a slender oval face. Her brown eyes were beautiful. Her nose was a dream, as was her sweet-lipped, petulant-hinting mouth. She wore a tam o'shanter, and I thought her brown hair the prettiest shade of brown I had ever seen. And from that single experience of half an hour I have ever since been convinced of the reality of love at first sight.

All too soon the aunt and Haydee departed. (This is permissible at any stage of a Salvation Army meeting.) I was no longer interested in the meeting, and after an appropriate interval of a couple of minutes or less, started to leave with Louis. As we passed out, at the back of the hall a woman recognized me with her eyes, arose, and followed me. I shall not describe her. She was of my own kind and friendship of the old time on the water-front. When Nelson was shot, he had died in her arms, and she knew me as his one comrade. And she must tell me how Nelson had died, and I did want to know; so I went with her across the width of life from dawning boy's love for a brown-haired girl in a tam o'shanter back to the old sad savagery I had known.

And when I had heard the tale, I hurried away to find Louis, fearing that I had lost my first love with the first glimpse of her. But Louis was dependable. Her name was—Haydee. He knew where she lived. Each day she passed the blacksmith-shop where he worked, going to or from the Lafayette school. Further, he had seen her on occasion with Ruth, another schoolgirl; and, still further, Nita, who sold us red-hots at the candy store, was a friend of Ruth. The thing to do was to go around to the candy store and see if we could get Nita to give a note to Ruth to give to Haydee. If that could be arranged, all I had to do was write the note.

And it so happened. And in stolen half-hours of meeting I came to know all the sweet madness of boy's love and girl's love. So far as it goes it is not the biggest love in the world, but I do dare to assert that it is the sweetest. Oh, as I look back on it! Never did girl have more innocent boy-lover than I who had been so wicked-wise and violent beyond my years. I didn't know the first thing about girls. I, who had been hailed Prince of the Oyster Pirates, who could go anywhere in the world as a man amongst men; who could sail boats, lay aloft in black and storm, or go into the toughest hangouts in sailor town and play my part in any rough-house that started or call all hands to the bar—I didn't know the first thing I might say or do with this slender little chit of a girl-woman whose scant skirt just reached her shoe-tops and who was as abysmally ignorant of life, as I was, or thought I was, profoundly wise.

I remember we sat on a bench in the starlight. There was fully a foot of space between us. We slightly faced each other, our near elbows on the back of the bench; and once or twice our elbows just touched. And all the time, deliriously happy, talking in the gentlest and most delicate terms that might not offend her sensitive ears, I was cudgeling my brains in an effort to divine what I was expected to do. What did girls expect of boys, sitting on a bench and tentatively striving to find out what love was? What did she expect me to do? Was I expected to kiss her? Did she expect me to try? And if she did expect me, and I didn't, what would she think of me?

Ah, she was wiser than I—I know it now—the little innocent girl-woman in her shoe-top skirt. She had known boys all her life. She encouraged me in the ways a girl may. Her gloves were off and in one hand, and I remember, lightly and daringly, in mock reproof for something I had said, how she tapped my lips with a tiny flirt of those gloves. I was like to swoon with delight. It was the most wonderful thing that had ever happened to me. And I remember yet the faint scent that clung to those gloves and that I breathed in the moment they touched my lips.

Then came the agony of apprehension and doubt. Should I imprison in my hand that little hand with the dangling, scented gloves which had just tapped my lips? Should I dare to kiss her there and then, or slip my arm around her waist? Or dared I even sit closer?

Well, I didn't dare. I did nothing. I merely continued to sit there and love with all my soul. And when we parted that evening I had not kissed her. I do remember the first time I kissed her, on another evening, at parting—a mighty moment, when I took all my heart of courage and dared. We never succeeded in managing more than a dozen stolen meetings, and we kissed perhaps a dozen times—as boys and girls kiss, briefly and innocently, and wonderingly. We never went anywhere—not even to a matinée. We once shared together five cents' worth of red-hots. But I have always fondly believed that she loved me. I know I loved her; and I dreamed day dreams of her for a year and more, and the memory of her is very dear.

XIX

WHEN I was with folk who did not drink, I never thought of drinking. Louis did not drink. Neither he nor I could afford it; but, more significant than that, we had no desire to drink. We were healthy, normal, non-alcoholic. Had we been alcoholic, we would have drunk whether or not we could have afforded it.

Each night, after the day's work, washed up, clothes changed and supper eaten, we met on the street corner or in the little candy store. But the warm, fall weather passed, and on bitter nights of frost or damp nights of drizzle the street corner was not a comfortable meeting place. And the candy store was unheated. Nita, or whoever waited on the counter, between waitings lurked in a back living-room that was heated. We were not admitted to this room, and in the store it was as cold as out-of-doors.

Louis and I debated the situation. There was only one solution: the saloon, the congregating place of men, the place where men hobnobbed with John Barleycorn. Well do I remember the damp and draughty evening, shivering without overcoats because we could not afford them, that Louis and I started out to select our saloon. Saloons are always warm and comfortable. Now Louis and I did not go into this saloon because we wanted a drink. Yet we knew that saloons were not charitable institutions. A man could not make a lounging place of a saloon without occasionally buying something over the bar.

Our dimes and nickels were few. We could ill spare any of them when they were so potent in buying carfare for oneself and a girl. (We never paid carfare when by ourselves, being content to walk.) So, in this saloon, we desired to make the most of our expenditure. We called for a deck of cards and sat down at a table and played euchre for an hour, in which time Louis treated once, and I treated once, to beer—the cheapest drink, ten cents for two. Prodigal! How we grudged it!

We studied the men who came into the place. They seemed all middle-aged and elderly workmen, most of them Germans, who flocked by themselves in old-acquaintance groups, and with whom we could have only the slightest contacts. We voted against that saloon, and went out cast-down with the knowledge that we had lost an evening and wasted twenty cents for beer that we didn't want.

We made several more tries on succeeding nights, and at last found our way into the National, a saloon on Tenth and Franklin. Here was a more congenial crowd. Here Louis met a fellow or two he knew, and here I met fellows I had gone to school with when a little lad in knee pants. We talked of old days, and of what had become of this fellow, and what that fellow was doing now, and of course we talked it over drinks. They treated, and we drank. Then, according to the code of drinking, we had to treat. It hurt, for it meant forty to fifty cents a clatter.

We felt quite enlivened when the short evening was over; but at the same time we were bankrupt. Our week's spending-money was gone. We decided that that was the saloon for us, and we agreed to be more circumspect thereafter in our drink-buying. Also, we had to economize for the rest of the week. We didn't even have carfare. We were compelled to break an engagement with two girls from West Oakland with whom we were attempting to be in love. They were to meet us up town the next evening, and we hadn't the carfare necessary to take them home. Like many others financially embarrassed, we had to disappear for a time from the gay whirl—at least until Saturday night pay-day. So Louis and I rendezvoused in a livery stable, and with coats buttoned and chattering teeth played euchre and casino until the time of our exile was over.

Then we returned to the National Saloon and spent no more than we could decently avoid spending for the comfort and warmth. Sometimes we had mishaps, as when one got stuck twice in succession in a five-handed game of Sancho Pedro for the drinks. Such a disaster meant anywhere between twenty-five to eighty cents, just according to how many of the players ordered ten-cent drinks. But we could temporarily escape the evil effects of such disaster by virtue of an account we ran behind the bar. Of course, this only set back the day of reckoning and seduced us into spending more than we would have spent on a cash basis. (When I left Oakland suddenly for the adventure-path the following spring, I well remember I owed that saloon keeper one dollar and seventy cents. Long after, when I returned, he was gone. I still owe him that dollar and seventy cents, and if he should chance to read these lines I want him to know that I'll pay on demand.)

The foregoing incident of the National Saloon I have given in order again to show the lure, or draw, or compulsion, toward John Barleycorn in society as at present organized with saloons on all the corners. Louis and I were two healthy youths. We didn't want to drink. We couldn't afford to drink. And yet we were driven by the circumstances of cold and rainy weather to seek refuge in a saloon, where we had to spend part of our pitiful dole for drink. It will be urged by some critics that we might have gone to the Y. M. C. A., to night school, and to the social circles and homes of young people. The only reply is that we didn't. That is the irrefragable fact. We didn't. And to-day, at this moment, there are hundreds of thousands of boys like Louis and me doing just what Louis and I did, with John Barleycorn, warm and comfortable, beckoning and welcoming, tucking their arms in his and beginning to teach them his mellow ways.

XX

THE jute mills failed of its agreement to increase my pay to a dollar and a quarter a day, and I, a free-born American boy whose direct ancestors had fought in all the wars from the old pre-Revolutionary Indian wars down, exercised my sovereign right of free contract by quitting the job.

I was still resolved to settle down, and I looked about me. One thing was clear. Unskilled labor didn't pay. I must learn a trade, and I decided on electricity. The need for electricians was constantly growing. But how to become an electrician? I hadn't the money to go to a technical school or university; besides, I didn't think much of schools. I was a practical man in a practical world. Also, I still believed in the old myths which were the heritage of the American boy when I was a boy.

A canal boy could become a president. Any boy, who took employment with any firm, could, by thrift, energy, and sobriety, learn the business and rise from position to position until he was taken in as a junior partner. After that the senior partnership was only a matter of time. Very often—so ran the myth—the boy, by reason of his steadiness and application, married his employer's daughter. By this time I had been encouraged to such faith in myself in the matter of girls that I was quite certain I would marry my employer's daughter. There wasn't a doubt of it. All the little boys in the myths did it as soon as they were old enough.

So I bade farewell forever to the adventure-path, and went out to the power-plant of one of our Oakland street-railways. I saw the superintendent himself, in a private office so fine that it almost stunned me. But I talked straight up. I told him I wanted to become a practical electrician, that I was unafraid of work, that I was used to hard work, and that all he had to do was look at me to see I was fit and strong. I told him that I wanted to begin right at the bottom and work up, that I wanted to devote my life to this one occupation and this one employment.

The superintendent beamed as he listened. He told me that I was the right stuff for success, and that he believed in encouraging American youth that wanted to rise. Why, employers were always on the lookout for young fellows like me, and alas, they found them all too rarely. My ambition was fine and worthy, and he would see to it that I got my chance. (And as I listened with swelling heart, I wondered if it was his daughter I was to marry.)

"Before you can go out on the road and learn the more complicated and higher details of the profession," he said, "you will, of course, have to work in the car house with the men who install and repair the motors. (By this time I was sure that it was his daughter, and I was wondering how much stock he might own in the company.)

"But," he said, "as you yourself so plainly see, you couldn't expect to begin as a helper to the car house electricians. That will come when you have worked up to it. You will really begin at the bottom. In the car house your first employment will be sweeping up, washing the windows, keeping things clean. And after you have shown yourself satisfactory at that, then you may become a helper to the car house electricians."

I didn't see how sweeping and scrubbing a building was any preparation for the trade of electrician; but I did know that in the books all the boys started with the most menial tasks and by making good ultimately won to the ownership of the whole concern.

"When shall I come to work?" I asked, eager to launch on this dazzling career.

"But," said the superintendent, "as you and I have already agreed, you must begin at the bottom. Not immediately can you in any capacity enter the car house. Before that you must pass through the engine room as an oiler."

My heart went down slightly and for the moment, as I saw the road lengthen between his daughter and me; then it rose again. I would be a better electrician with knowledge of steam engines. As an oiler in the great engine room I was confident that few things concerning steam would escape me. Heavens! My career shone more dazzling than ever.

"When shall I come to work?" I asked gratefully.

"But," said the superintendent, "you could not expect to enter immediately into the engine room. There must be preparation for that. And through the fire room, of course. Come, you see the matter clearly, I know. And you will see that even the mere handling of coal is a scientific matter and not to be sneezed at. Do you know that we weigh every pound of coal we burn? Thus, we learn the value of the coal we buy; we know to a tee the last penny of cost of every item of production, and we learn which firemen are the most wasteful, which firemen, out of stupidity or carelessness, get the least out of the coal they fire." The superintendent beamed again. "You see how very important the little matter of coal is, and by as much as you learn of this little matter you will become that much better a workman—more valuable to us, more valuable to yourself. Now, are you prepared to begin?"

"Any time," I said valiantly. "The sooner the better."

"Very well," he answered. "You will come to-morrow morning at seven o'clock."

I was taken out and shown my duties. Also, I was told the terms of my employment—a ten-hour day, every day in the month including Sundays and holidays, with one day off each month, with a salary of thirty dollars a month. It wasn't exciting. Years before, at the cannery, I had earned a dollar a day for a ten-hour day. I consoled myself with the thought that the reason my earning capacity had not increased with my years and strength was because I had remained an unskilled laborer. But it was different now. I was beginning to work for skill, for a trade, for career and fortune and the superintendent's daughter.

And I was beginning in the right way—right at the beginning. That was the thing. I was passing coal to the firemen, who shoveled it into the furnaces where its energy was transformed into steam, which, in the engine room, was transformed into the electricity with which the electricians worked. This passing of coal was surely the very beginning . . . unless the superintendent should take it into his head to send me to work in the mines from which the coal came in order to get a completer understanding of the genesis of electricity for street railways.

Work! I, who had worked with men, found that I didn't know the first thing about real work. A ten-hour day! I had to pass coal for the day and night shifts, and, despite working through the noon-hour, I never finished my task before eight at night. I was working a twelve- to thirteen-hour day, and I wasn't being paid overtime as in the cannery.

I might as well give the secret away right here. I was doing the work of two men. Before me, one mature able-bodied laborer had done the day shift and another equally mature able-bodied laborer had done the night shift. They had received forty dollars a month each. The superintendent, bent on an economical administration, had persuaded me to do the work of both men for thirty dollars a month. I thought he was making an electrician of me. In truth and fact, he was saving fifty dollars a month operating expenses to the company.

But I didn't know I was displacing two men. Nobody told me. On the contrary, the superintendent warned everybody not to tell me. How valiantly I went at it that first day. I worked at top speed, filling the iron wheelbarrow with coal, running it on the scales and weighing the load, then trundling it into the fire room and dumping it on the plates before the fires.

Work! I did more than the two men whom I had displaced. They had merely wheeled in the coal and dumped it on the plates. But while I did this for the day coal, the night coal I had to pile against the wall of the fire room. Now the fire room was small. It had been planned for a night coal-passer. So I had to pile the night coal higher and higher, buttressing up the heap with stout planks. Toward the top of the heap I had to handle the coal a second time, tossing it up with a shovel.

I dripped with sweat, but I never ceased from my stride, though I could feel exhaustion coming on. By ten o'clock in the morning, so much of my body's energy had I consumed, I felt hungry and snatched a thick double-slice of bread and butter from my dinner pail. This I devoured, standing, grimed with coal dust, my knees trembling under me. By eleven o'clock, in this fashion, I had consumed my whole lunch. But what of it? I realized that it would enable me to continue working through the noon hour. And I worked all afternoon. Darkness came on, and I worked under the electric lights. The day fireman went off and the night fireman came on. I plugged away.

At half-past eight, famished, tottering, I washed up, changed my clothes, and dragged my weary body to the car. It was three miles to where I lived, and I had received a pass with the stipulation that I could sit down as long as there were no paying passengers in need of a seat. As I sank into a corner outside seat I prayed that no passenger might require my seat. But the car filled up, and, half way in, a woman came on board, and there was no seat for her. I started to get up, and to my astonishment found that I could not. With the chill wind blowing on me, my spent body had stiffened into the seat. It took me the rest of the run in to unkink my complaining joints and muscles and get into a standing position on the lower step. And when the car stopped at my corner I nearly fell to the ground when I stepped off.

I hobbled two blocks to the house and limped into the kitchen. While my mother started to cook I plunged into bread and butter; but before my appetite was appeased, or the steak fried, I was sound asleep. In vain my mother strove to shake me awake enough to eat the meat. Failing in this, with the assistance of my father she managed to get me to my room, where I collapsed dead asleep on the bed. They undressed me and covered me up. In the morning came the agony of being awakened. I was terribly sore, and worst of all my wrists were swelling. But I made up for my lost supper, eating an enormous breakfast, and when I hobbled to catch my car I carried a lunch twice as big as the one the day before.

Work! Let any youth just turned eighteen try to out-shovel two man-grown coal-shovelers. Work! Long before midday I had eaten the last scrap of my huge lunch. But I was resolved to show them what a husky young fellow determined to rise could do. The worst of it was that my wrists were swelling and going back on me. There are few who do not know the pain of walking on a sprained ankle. Then imagine the pain of shoveling coal and trundling a loaded wheelbarrow with two sprained wrists.

Work! More than once I sank down on the coal where no one could see me, and cried with rage, and mortification, and exhaustion, and despair. That second day was my hardest, and all that enabled me to survive it and get in the last of the night coal at the end of thirteen hours was the day fireman, who bound both my wrists with broad leather straps. So tightly were they buckled that they were like slightly flexible plaster casts. They took the stresses and pressures which thitherto had been borne by my wrists, and they were so tight that there was no room for the inflammation to rise in the sprains.

And in this fashion I continued to learn to be an electrician. Night after night I limped home, fell asleep before I could eat my supper, and was helped into bed and undressed. Morning after morning, always with huger lunches in my dinner pail, I limped out of the house on my way to work.

I no longer read my library books. I made no dates with the girls. I was a proper work-beast. I worked, and ate, and slept, while my mind slept all the time. The whole thing was a nightmare. I worked every day, including Sunday, and I looked far ahead to my one day off at the end of a month, resolved to lie abed all that day and just sleep and rest up.

The strangest part of this experience was that I never took a drink nor thought of taking a drink. Yet I knew that men under hard pressure almost invariably drank. I had seen them do it, and in the past had often done it myself. But so sheerly non-alcoholic was I that it never entered my mind that a drink might be good for me. I instance this to show how entirely lacking from my make-up was any predisposition toward alcohol. And the point of this instance is that later on, after more years had passed, contact with John Barleycorn at last did induce in me the alcoholic desire.

I had often noticed the day fireman staring at me in a curious way. At last, one day, he spoke. He began by swearing me to secrecy. He had been warned by the superintendent not to tell me, and in telling me he was risking his job. He told me of the day coal-passer and the night coal-passer, and of the wages they had received. I was doing for thirty dollars a month what they had received eighty dollars for doing. He would have told me sooner, the fireman said, had he not been so certain that I would break down under the work and quit. As it was, I was killing myself, and all to no good purpose. I was merely cheapening the price of labor, he argued, and keeping two men out of a job.

Being an American boy, and a proud American boy, I did not immediately quit. This was foolish of me, I know; but I resolved to continue the work long enough to prove to the superintendent that I could do it without breaking down. Then I would quit, and he would realize what a fine young fellow he had lost.

All of which I faithfully and foolishly did. I worked on until the time came when I got in the last of the night coal by six o'clock. Then I quit the job of learning electricity by doing more than two men's work for a boy's wages, went home, and proceeded to sleep the clock around.

Fortunately, I had not stayed by the job long enough to injure myself—though I was compelled to wear straps on my wrists for a year afterward. But the effect of this work orgy in which I had indulged was to sicken me with work. I just wouldn't work. The thought of work was repulsive. I didn't care if I never settled down. Learning a trade could go hang. It was a whole lot better to royster and frolic over the world in the way I had previously done. So I headed out on the adventure-path again, starting to tramp East by beating my way on the railroads.

XXI

BUT behold! As soon as I went out on the adventure-path I met John Barleycorn again. I moved through a world of strangers, and the act of drinking together made one acquainted with men and opened the way to adventures. It might be in a saloon with jingled townsmen, or with a genial railroad man well lighted up and armed with pocket flasks, or with a bunch of alki-stiffs in a hang-out. Yes; and it might be in a prohibition state, such as Iowa was in 1894, when I wandered up the main street of Des Moines and was variously invited by strangers into various blind pigs—I remember drinking in barber-shops, plumbing establishments, and furniture stores.

Always it was John Barleycorn. Even a tramp, in those halcyon days, could get most frequently drunk. I remember, inside the prison at Buffalo, how some of us got magnificently jingled, and how, on the streets of Buffalo after our release, another jingle was financed with pennies begged on the maindrag.

I had no call for alcohol, but when I was with those who drank I drank with them. I insisted on traveling or loafing with the livest, keenest men, and it was just these live, keen ones that did most of the drinking. They were the more comradely men, the more venturous, the more individual. Perhaps it was too much temperament that made them turn from the commonplace and humdrum to find relief in the lying and fantastic sureties of John Barleycorn. Be that as it may, the men I liked best, desired most to be with, were invariably to be found in John Barleycorn's company.

In the course of my tramping over the United States I achieved a new concept. As a tramp, I was behind the scenes of society—ay, and down in the cellar. I could watch the machinery work. I saw the wheels of the social machine go around, and I learned that the dignity of manual labor wasn't what I had been told it was by the teachers, preachers, and politicians. The men without trades were helpless cattle. If one learned a trade, he was compelled to belong to a union in order to work at his trade. And his union was compelled to bully and slug the employers' unions in order to hold up wages or hold down hours. The employers' unions likewise bullied and slugged. I couldn't see any dignity at all. And when a workman got old, or had an accident, he was thrown into the scrap-heap like any worn-out machine. I saw too many of this sort who were making anything but dignified ends of life.

So my new concept was that manual labor was undignified, and that it didn't pay. No trade for me, was my decision, and no superintendent's daughter. And no criminality, I also decided. That would be almost as disastrous as to be a laborer. Brains paid, not brawn, and I resolved never again to offer my muscles for sale in the brawn market. Brain, and brain only, would I sell.

I returned to California with the firm intention of developing my brain. This meant school education. I had gone through the grammar school long ago, so I entered the Oakland High School. To pay my way, I worked as a janitor. My sister helped me, too; and I was not above mowing anybody's lawn or taking up and beating carpets when I had half a day to spare. I was working to get away from work, and I buckled down to it with a grim realization of the paradox.

Boy and girl love was left behind, and along with it, Haydee and Louis Shattuck, and the early evening strolls. I hadn't the time. I joined the Henry Clay Debating Society. I was received into the homes of some of the members, where I met nice girls whose skirts reached the ground. I dallied with little home clubs wherein we discussed poetry and art and the nuances of grammar. I joined the socialist local, where we studied and orated political economy, philosophy, and politics. I kept half-a-dozen membership cards working in the free library and did an immense amount of collateral reading.

And for a year and a half on end I never took a drink nor thought of taking a drink. I hadn't the time, and I certainly did not have the inclination. Between my janitor-work, my studies, and innocent amusements such as chess, I hadn't a moment to spare. I was discovering a new world, and such was the passion of my exploration that the old world of John Barleycorn held no inducements for me.

Come to think of it, I did enter a saloon. I went to see Johnny Heinhold in the Last Chance, and I went to borrow money. And right here is another phase of John Barleycorn. Saloon-keepers are notoriously good fellows. On an average they perform vastly greater generosities than do business men. When I simply had to have ten dollars, desperate, with no place to turn, I went to Johnny Heinhold. Several years had passed since I had been in his place or spent a cent across his bar. And when I went to borrow the ten dollars I didn't buy a drink, either. And Johnny Heinhold let me have the ten dollars, without security or interest.

More than once, in the brief days of my struggle for an education, I went to Johnny Heinhold to borrow money. When I entered the university, I borrowed forty dollars from him, without interest, without security, without buying a drink. And yet—and here is the point, the custom and the code—in the days of my prosperity, after the lapse of years, I have gone out of my way by many a long block to spend across Johnny Heinhold's bar deferred interest on the various loans. Not that Johnny Heinhold asked me to do it or expected me to do it. I did it, as I have said, in obedience to the code I had learned along with all the other things connected with John Barleycorn. In distress, when a man has no other place to turn, when he hasn't the slightest bit of security which a savage-hearted pawnbroker would consider, he can go to some saloon keeper he knows. Gratitude is inherently human. When the man so helped has money again, depend upon it that a portion will be spent across the bar of the saloon keeper who befriended him.

Why, I recollect the early days of my writing career, when the small sums of money I earned from the magazines came with tragic irregularity, while at the same time I was staggering along with a growing family—a wife, children, a mother, a nephew, and my Mammy Jennie and her old husband fallen on evil days. There were two places at which I could borrow money; a barber shop and a saloon. The barber charged me five per cent. per month in advance. That is to say, when I borrowed one hundred dollars, he handed me ninety-five. The other five dollars he retained as advance interest for the first month. And on the second month I paid him five dollars more, and continued so to do each month until I made a ten-strike with the editors and lifted the loan.

The other place to which I came in trouble was the saloon. This saloon keeper I had known by sight for a couple of years. I had never spent my money in his saloon, and even when I borrowed from him I didn't spend any money. Yet never did he refuse me any sum I asked of him. Unfortunately, before I became prosperous, he moved away to another city. And to this day I regret that he is gone. It is the code I have learned. The right thing to do, and the thing I'd do right now did I know where he is, would be to drop in on occasion and spend a few dollars across his bar for old sake's sake and gratitude.

This is not to exalt saloon keepers. I have written it to exalt the power of John Barleycorn, and to illustrate one more of the myriad ways by which a man is brought in contact with John Barleycorn, until in the end he finds he cannot get along without him.

But to return to the run of my narrative. Away from the adventure-path, up to my ears in study, every moment occupied, I lived oblivious to John Barleycorn's existence. Nobody about me drank. If any had drunk, and had they offered it to me, I surely would have drunk. As it was, when I had spare moments I spent them playing chess, or going with nice girls who were themselves students, or in riding a bicycle whenever I was fortunate enough to have it out of the pawnbroker's possession.

What I am insisting upon all the time is this: in me was not the slightest trace of alcoholic desire, and this despite the long and severe apprenticeship I had served under John Barleycorn. I had come back from the other side of life to be delighted with this Arcadian simplicity of student youths and student maidens. Also, I had found my way into the realm of the mind, and I was intellectually intoxicated. Alas! as I was to learn at a later period, intellectual intoxication, too, has its katzenjammer.

XXII

THREE years was the time required to go through high school. I grew impatient. Also, my schooling was becoming financially impossible. At such rate I could not last out, and I did greatly want to go to the state university. When I had done a year of high school, I decided to attempt a short cut. I borrowed the money and paid to enter the senior class of a "cramming joint" or academy. I was scheduled to graduate right into the university at the end of four months, thus saving two years.

And how I did cram! I had two years' new work to do in a third of a year. For five weeks I crammed, until simultaneous quadratic equations and chemical formulas fairly oozed from my ears. And then the master of the academy took me aside. He was very sorry, but he was compelled to give me back my tuition fee and to ask me to leave the school. It wasn't a matter of scholarship. I stood well in my classes, and did he graduate me into the university he was confident that in that institution I would continue to stand well. The trouble was that tongues were gossiping about my case. What! In four months accomplish two years' work! It would be a scandal, and the universities were becoming severer in their treatment of accredited prep schools. He couldn't afford such a scandal, therefore I must gracefully depart.

I did. And I paid back the borrowed money, and gritted my teeth, and started to cram by myself. There were three months yet before the university entrance-examinations. Without laboratories, without coaching, sitting in my bedroom, I proceeded to compress that two years' work into three months and to keep reviewed on the previous year's work.

Nineteen hours a day I studied. For three months I kept this pace, only breaking it on several occasions. My body grew weary, my mind grew weary, but I stayed with it. My eyes grew weary and began to twitch, but they did not break down. Perhaps, toward the last, I got a bit dotty. I know that at the time I was confident I had discovered the formula for squaring the circle; but I resolutely deferred the working of it out until after the examinations. Then I would show them.

Came the several days of the examinations, during which time I scarcely closed my eyes in sleep, devoting every moment to cramming and reviewing. And when I turned in my last examination paper I was in full possession of a splendid case of brain-fag. I didn't want to see a book. I didn't want to think nor to lay eyes on anybody who was liable to think.

There was but one prescription for such a condition, and I gave it to myself—the adventure-path. I didn't wait to learn the result of my examinations. I stowed a roll of blankets and some cold food into a borrowed whitehall boat and set sail. Out of the Oakland Estuary I drifted on the last of an early morning ebb, caught the first of the flood up bay, and raced along with a spanking breeze. San Pablo Bay was smoking, and the Carquinez Straits off the Selby Smelter were smoking, as I picked up ahead and left astern the old landmarks I had first learned with Nelson in the unreefed *Reindeer.*

Benicia showed before me. I opened the bight of Turner's Shipyard, rounded the *Solano* wharf, and surged along abreast of the patch of tules and the clustering fishermen's-arks where in the old days I had lived and drunk deep.

And right here something happened to me, the gravity of which I never dreamed for many a long year to come. I had no intention of stopping at Benicia. The tide favored, the wind was fair and howling—glorious sailing for a sailor. Bull Head and Army Points showed ahead, marking the entrance to Suisun Bay, which I know was smoking. And yet, when I laid eyes on those fishing-arks lying in the water-front tules, without debate, on the instant, I put down my tiller, came in on the sheet, and headed for the shore. On the instant, out of the profound of my brain-fag, I knew what I wanted. I wanted to drink. I wanted to get drunk.

The call was imperative. There was no uncertainty about it. More than anything else in the world, my frayed and frazzled mind wanted surcease from weariness in the way it knew surcease would come. And right here is the point. For the first time in my life I consciously, deliberately desired to get drunk. It was a new, a totally different manifestation of John Barleycorn's power. It was not a body need for alcohol. It was a mental desire. My overworked and jaded mind wanted to forget.

And here the point is drawn to its sharpest. Granted my prodigious brain-fag, nevertheless, had I never drunk in the past, the thought would never have entered my mind to get drunk now. Beginning with physical intolerance for alcohol, for years drinking only for the sake of comradeship and because alcohol was everywhere on the adventure-path, I had now reached the stage where my brain cried out, not merely for a drink, but for a drunk. And had I not been so long used to alcohol, my brain would not have so cried out. I should have sailed on past Bull Head, and in the smoking white of Suisun Bay, and in the wine of wind that filled my sail and poured through me, I should have forgotten my weary brain and rested and refreshed it.

So I sailed in to shore, made all fast, and hurried up among the arks. Charley Le Grant fell on my neck. His wife, Lizzie, folded me to her capacious breast. Billy Murphy, and Joe Lloyd, and all the survivors of the old guard, got around me and their arms around me. Charley seized the can and started for Jorgensen's saloon across the railroad tracks. That meant beer. I wanted whisky, so I called after him to bring a flask.

Many times that flask journeyed across the railroad tracks and back. More old friends of the old free and easy times dropped in, fishermen, Greeks, and Russians, and French. They took turns in treating, and treated all around in turn again. They came and went, but I stayed on and drank with all. I guzzled, I swilled. I ran the liquor down and joyed as the maggots mounted in my brain.

And Clam came in, Nelson's partner before me, handsome as ever, but more reckless, half insane, burning himself out with whisky. He had just had a quarrel with his partner on the sloop *Gazelle,* and knives had been drawn, and blows struck, and he was bent on maddening the fever of the memory with more whisky. And while we downed it, we remembered Nelson and that he had stretched out his great shoulders for the last long sleep in this very town of Benicia; and we wept over the memory of him, and remembered only the good things of him, and sent out the flask to be filled and drank again.

They wanted me to stay over, but through the open door I could see the brave wind on the water, and my ears were filled with the roar of it. And while I forgot that I had plunged into the books nineteen hours a day for three solid months, Charley Le Grant shifted my outfit into a big Columbia River salmon boat. He added charcoal and a fisherman's brazier, a coffee pot and frying-pan, and the coffee and the meat, and a black bass fresh from the water that day.

They had to help me down the rickety wharf and into the salmon boat. Likewise they stretched my boom and sprit until the sail set like a board. Some feared to set the sprit; but I insisted, and Charley had no doubts. He knew me of old, and knew that I could sail as long as I could see. They cast off my painter. I put the tiller up, filled away before it, and with dizzy eyes checked and steadied the boat on her course and waved farewell.

The tide had turned, and the fierce ebb, running in the teeth of a fiercer wind, kicked up a stiff, upstanding sea. Suisun Bay was white with wrath and sea-lump. But a salmon boat can sail, and I knew how to sail a salmon boat. So I drove her into it, and through it, and across, and maundered aloud and chanted my disdain for all the books and schools. Cresting seas filled me a foot or so with water, but I laughed at it sloshing about my feet, and chanted my disdain for the wind and the water. I hailed myself a master of life, riding on the back of the unleashed elements, and John Barleycorn rode with me. Amid dissertations on mathematics and philosophy and spoutings and quotations, I sang all the old songs learned in the days when I went from the cannery to the oyster boats to be a pirate—such songs as: "Black Lulu," "Flying Cloud," "Treat My Daughter Kind-i-ly," "The Boston Burglar," "Come All You Rambling Gambling Men," "I Wisht I Was a Little Bird," "Shenandoah," and "Ranzo, Boys, Ranzo."

Hours afterward, in the fires of sunset, where the Sacramento and the San Joaquin tumble their muddy floods together, I took the New York Cut-Off, skimmed across the smooth land-locked water past Black Diamond, on into the San Joaquin, and on to Antioch, where, somewhat sobered and magnificently hungry, I laid alongside a big potato sloop that had a familiar rig. Here were old friends aboard, who fried my black bass in olive oil. Then, too, there was a meaty fisherman's stew, delicious with garlic, and crusty Italian bread without butter, and all washed down with pint mugs of thick and heady claret.

My salmon boat was a-soak, but in the snug cabin of the sloop dry blankets and a dry bunk were mine; and we lay and smoked and yarned of old days, while overhead the wind screamed through the rigging and taut halyards drummed against the mast.

XXIII

My cruise in the salmon boat lasted a week, and I returned ready to enter the university. During the week's cruise I did not drink again. To accomplish this I was compelled to avoid looking up old friends, for as ever the adventure-path was beset with John Barleycorn. I had wanted the drink that first day, and in the days that followed I did not want it. My tired brain had recuperated. I had no moral scruples in the matter. I was not ashamed nor sorry because of that first day's orgy at Benicia, and I thought no more about it, returning gladly to my books and studies.

Long years were to pass ere I looked back upon that day and realized its significance. At the time, and for a long time afterward, I was to think of it only as a frolic. But still later, in the slough of brain-fag and intellectual weariness, I was to remember and know the craving for the anodyne that resides in alcohol.

In the meantime, after this one relapse at Benicia, I went on with my abstemiousness, primarily because I didn't want to drink. And next, I was abstemious because my way led among books and students, where no drinking was. Had I been out on the adventure-path, I should as a matter of course have been drinking. For that is the pity of the adventure-path, which is one of John Barleycorn's favorite stamping-grounds.

I completed the first half of my freshman year, and in January of 1897 took up my course for the second half. But the pressure from lack of money, plus a conviction that the university was not giving me all that I wanted in the time I could spare for it, forced me to leave. I was not very disappointed. For two years I had studied, and in those two years, what was far more valuable, I had done a prodigious amount of reading. Then, too, my grammar had improved. It is true, I had not yet learned that I must say "It is I"; but I no longer was guilty of the double negative in writing, though still prone to that error in excited speech.

I decided immediately to embark on my career. I had four preferences: first, music; second, poetry; third, the writing of philosophic, economic, and political essays; and, fourth, and last, and least, fiction writing. I resolutely cut out music as impossible, settled down in my bedroom, and tackled my second, third and fourth choices simultaneously. Heavens, how I wrote! Never was there a creative fever such as mine from which the patient escaped fatal results. The way I worked was enough to soften my brain and send me to a mad-house. I wrote, I wrote everything—ponderous essays, scientific and sociological, short stories, humorous verse, verse of all sorts from triolets and sonnets to blank verse tragedy and elephantine epics in Spenserian stanzas. On occasion I composed steadily, day after day, for fifteen hours a day. At times I forgot to eat, or refused to tear myself away from my passionate outpouring in order to eat.

And then there was the matter of typewriting. My brother-in-law owned a machine which he used in the daytime. In the night I was free to use it. That machine was a wonder. I could weep now as I recollect my wrestlings with it. It must have been a first model in the year one of the typewriter era. Its alphabet was all capitals. It was informed with an evil spirit. It obeyed no known laws of physics, and overthrew the hoary axiom that like things performed to like things produce like results. I'll swear that machine never did the same thing in the same way twice. Again and again it demonstrated that unlike actions produce like results.

How my back used to ache with it! Prior to that experience, my back had been good for every violent strain put upon it in a none too gentle career. But that typewriter proved to me that I had a pipe-stem for a back. Also, it made me doubt my shoulders. They ached as with rheumatism after every bout. The keys of that machine had to be hit so hard that to one outside the house it sounded like distant thunder or some one breaking up the furniture. I had to hit the keys so hard that I strained my first fingers to the elbows, while the ends of my fingers were blisters burst and blistered again. Had it been my machine I'd have operated it with a carpenter's hammer.

The worst of it was that I was actually typing my manuscripts at the same time I was trying to master that machine. It was a feat of physical endurance and a brain storm combined to type a thousand words, and I was composing thousands of words every day which just had to be typed for the waiting editors.

Oh, between the writing and the typewriting I was well aweary. I had brain-and nerve-fag, and body-fag as well, and yet the thought of drink never suggested itself. I was living too high to stand in need of an anodyne. All my waking hours, except those with that infernal typewriter, were spent in a creative heaven. And along with this I had no desire for drink, because I still believed in many things—in the love of all men and women in the matter of man and woman love; in fatherhood; in human justice; in art—in the whole host of fond illusions that keep the world turning around.

But the waiting editors elected to keep on waiting. My manuscripts made amazing round-trip records between the Pacific and the Atlantic. It might have been the weirdness of the typewriting that prevented the editors from accepting at least one little offering of mine. I don't know, and goodness knows the stuff I wrote was as weird as its typing. I sold my hard-bought school books for ridiculous sums to second-hand bookmen. I borrowed small sums of money wherever I could, and suffered my old father to feed me with the meager returns of his failing strength.

It didn't last long, only a few weeks, when I had to surrender and go to work. Yet I was unaware of any need for the drink-anodyne. I was not disappointed. My career was retarded, that was all. Perhaps I did need further preparation. I had learned enough from the books to realize that I had touched only the hem of knowledge's garment. I still lived on the heights. My waking hours, and most of the hours I should have used for sleep, were spent with the books.

XXIV

OUT in the country, at the Belmont Academy, I went to work in a small, perfectly appointed steam laundry. Another fellow and myself did all the work from sorting and washing to ironing the white shirts, collars and cuffs, and the "fancy starch" of the wives of the professors. We worked like tigers, especially as summer came on and the academy boys took to the wearing of duck trousers. It consumes a dreadful lot of time to iron one pair of duck trousers. And there were so many pairs of them. We sweated our way through long sizzling weeks at a task that was never done; and many a night, while the students snored in bed, my partner and I toiled on under the electric light at steam mangle or ironing board.

The hours were long, the work was arduous, despite the fact that we became past masters in the art of eliminating waste motion. And I was receiving thirty dollars a month and board—a slight increase over my coal-shoveling and cannery days, at least to the extent of board, which cost my employer little (we ate in the kitchen), but which was to me the equivalent of twenty dollars a month. My robuster strength of added years, my increased skill, and all I had learned from the books, were responsible for this increase of twenty dollars. Judging by my rate of development, I might hope before I died to be a night watchman for sixty dollars a month, or a policeman actually receiving a hundred dollars with pickings.

So relentlessly did my partner and I spring into our work throughout the week that by Saturday night we were frazzled wrecks. I found myself in the old familiar work-beast condition, toiling longer hours than the horses toiled, thinking scarcely more frequent thoughts than horses think. The books were closed to me. I had brought a trunkful to the laundry, but found myself unable to read them. I fell asleep the moment I tried to read; and if I did manage to keep my eyes open for several pages, I could not remember the contents of those pages. I gave over attempts on heavy study, such as jurisprudence, political economy, and biology, and tried lighter stuff, such as history. I fell asleep. I tried literature, and fell asleep. And finally, when I fell asleep over lively novels, I gave up. I never succeeded in reading one book in all the time I spent in the laundry.

And when Saturday night came, and the week's work was over until Monday morning, I knew only one desire besides the desire to sleep, and that was to get drunk. This was the second time in my life that I had heard the unmistakable call of John Barleycorn. The first time it had been because of brain-fag. But I had no overworked brain now. On the contrary, all I knew was the dull numbness of a brain that was not worked at all. That was the trouble. My brain had become so alert and eager, so quickened by the wonder of the new world the books had discovered to it, that it now suffered all the misery of stagnancy and inaction.

And I, the long-time intimate of John Barleycorn, knew just what he promised me—maggots of fancy, dreams of power, forgetfulness, anything and everything save whirling washers, revolving mangles, humming centrifugal wringers, and fancy starch and interminable processions of duck trousers moving in steam under my flying iron. And that's it. John Barleycorn makes his appeal to weakness and failure, to weariness and exhaustion. He is the easy way out. And he is lying all the time. He offers false strength to the body, false elevation to the spirit, making things seem what they are not and vastly fairer than what they are.

But it must not be forgotten that John Barleycorn is protean. As well as to weakness and exhaustion, does he appeal to too much strength, to superabundant vitality, to the ennui of idleness. He can tuck in his arm the arm of any man in any mood. He can throw the net of his lure over all men. He exchanges new lamps for old, the spangles of illusion for the drabs of reality, and in the end cheats all who traffic with him.

I didn't get drunk, however, for the simple reason that it was a mile and a half to the nearest saloon. And this, in turn, was because the call to get drunk was not very loud in my ears. Had it been loud, I would have traveled ten times the distance to win to the saloon. On the other hand, had the saloon been just around the corner, I should have got drunk. As it was, I would sprawl out in the shade on my one day of rest and dally with the Sunday papers. But I was too weary even for their froth. The comic supplement might bring a pallid smile to my face, and then I would fall asleep.

Although I did not yield to John Barleycorn while working in the laundry, a certain definite result was produced. I had heard the call, felt the gnaw of desire, yearned for the anodyne. I was being prepared for the stronger desire of later years.

And the point is that this development of desire was entirely in my brain. My body did not cry out for alcohol. As always, alcohol was repulsive to my body. When I was bodily weary from shoveling coal, the thought of taking a drink had never flickered into my consciousness. When I was brain-wearied after taking the entrance examinations to the university, I promptly got drunk. At the laundry, I was suffering physical exhaustion again, and physical exhaustion that was not nearly as profound as that of the coal-shoveling. But there was a difference. When I went coal-shoveling, my mind had not yet awakened. Between that time and the laundry my mind had found the kingdom of the mind. While shoveling coal, my mind was somnolent. While toiling in the laundry, my mind, informed and eager to do and be, was crucified.

And whether I yielded to drink, as at Benicia, or whether I refrained, as at the laundry, in my brain the seeds of desire for alcohol were germinating.

XXV

AFTER the laundry, my sister and her husband grubstaked me into the Klondike. It was the first gold rush into that region, the early fall rush of 1897. I was twenty-one years old, and in splendid physical condition. I remember, at the end of the twenty-eight-mile portage across Chilkoot from Dyea Beach to Lake Linderman, I was packing up with the Indians and outpacking many an Indian. The last pack into Linderman was three miles. I back-tripped it four times a day, and on each forward trip carried one hundred and fifty pounds. This means that over the worst trails I daily traveled twenty-four miles, twelve of which were under a burden of one hundred and fifty pounds.

Yes, I had let career go hang, and was on the adventure-path again in quest of fortune. And of course, on the adventure-path, I met John Barleycorn. Here were the chesty men again, rovers and adventurers, and while they didn't mind a grub famine, whisky they could not do without. Whisky went over the trail, while the flour lay cached and untouched by the trail-side.

As good fortune would have it, the three men in my party were not drinkers. Therefore I didn't drink save on rare occasions and disgracefully when with other men. In my personal medicine chest was a quart of whisky. I never drew the cork till six months afterward, in a lonely camp, where, without anesthetics, a doctor was compelled to operate on a man. The doctor and the patient emptied my bottle between them and then proceeded to the operation.

Back in California a year later, recovering from scurvy, I found that my father was dead and that I was the head and the sole bread-winner of a household. When I state that I had passed coal on a steamship from Behring Sea to British Columbia, and traveled in the steerage from there to San Francisco, it will be understood that I brought nothing back from the Klondike but my scurvy.

Times were hard. Work of any sort was difficult to get. And work of any sort was what I had to take, for I was still an unskilled laborer. I had no thought of career. That was over and done with. I had to find food for two mouths beside my own and keep a roof over our heads—yes, and buy a winter suit, my one suit being decidedly summery. I had to get some sort of work immediately. After that, when I had caught my breath, I might think about my future.

Unskilled labor is the first to feel the slackness of hard times, and I had no trades save those of sailor and laundryman. With my new responsibilities I didn't dare go to sea, and I failed to find a job at laundrying. I failed to find a job at anything. I had my name down in five employment bureaus. I advertised in three newspapers. I sought out the few friends I knew who might be able to get me work; but they were either uninterested or unable to find anything for me.

The situation was desperate. I pawned my watch, my bicycle, and a mackintosh of which my father had been very proud and which he had left to me. It was and is my sole legacy in this world. It had cost fifteen dollars, and the pawnbroker let me have two dollars on it. And—oh, yes—a waterfront comrade of earlier years drifted along one day with a dress suit wrapped in newspapers. He could give no adequate explanation of how he had come to possess it, nor did I press for an explanation. I wanted the suit myself. No; not to wear. I traded him a lot of rubbish which, being unpawnable, was useless to me. He peddled the rubbish for several dollars, while I pledged the dress suit with my pawnbroker for five dollars. And for all I know, the pawnbroker still has the suit. I had never intended to redeem it.

But I couldn't get any work. Yet I was a bargain in the labor market. I was twenty-two years old, weighed one hundred and sixty-five pounds stripped, every pound of which was excellent for toil; and the last traces of my scurvy were vanishing before a treatment of potatoes chewed raw. I tackled every opening for employment. I tried to become a studio model, but there were too many fine-bodied young fellows out of jobs. I answered advertisements of elderly invalids in need of companions. And I almost became a sewing machine agent, on commission, without salary. But poor people don't buy sewing machines in hard times, so I was forced to forego that employment.

Of course, it must be remembered that along with such frivolous occupations, I was trying to get work as wop, lumper, and roustabout. But winter was coming on, and the surplus labor army was pouring into the cities. Also, I, who had romped along carelessly through the countries of the world and the kingdom of the mind, was not a member of any union.

I sought odd jobs. I worked days, and half-days, at anything I could get. I mowed lawns, trimmed hedges, took up carpets, beat them, and laid them again. Further, I took the civil service examinations for mail carrier and passed first. But alas, there was no vacancy, and I must wait. And while I waited, and in between the odd jobs I managed to procure, I started to earn ten dollars by writing a newspaper account of a voyage I had made, in an open boat down the Yukon, of nineteen hundred miles in nineteen days. I didn't know the first thing about the newspaper game, but I was confident I'd get ten dollars for my article.

But I didn't. The first San Francisco newspaper to which I mailed it never acknowledged receipt of the manuscript, but held on to it. The longer it held on to it, the more certain I was that the thing was accepted.

And here is the funny thing. Some are born to fortune, and some have fortune thrust upon them. But in my case I was clubbed into fortune, and bitter necessity wielded the club. I had long since abandoned all thought of writing as a career. My honest intention in writing that article was to earn ten dollars. And that was the limit of my intention. It would help to tide me along until I got steady employment. Had a vacancy occurred in the post office at that time, I should have jumped at it.

But the vacancy did not occur, nor did a steady job; and I employed the time between odd jobs with writing a twenty-one-thousand-word serial for the "Youth's Companion." I turned it out and typed it in seven days. I fancy that was what was the matter with it, for it came back.

It took some time for it to go and come, and in the meantime I tried my hand at short stories. I sold one to the *Overland Monthly* for five dollars. The *Black Cat* gave me forty dollars for another. The *Overland Monthly* offered me seven dollars and a half, pay on publication, for all the stories I should deliver. I got my bicycle, my watch, and my father's mackintosh out of pawn and rented a typewriter. Also, I paid up the bills I owed to the several groceries that allowed me a small credit. I recall the Portuguese groceryman who never permitted my bill to go beyond four dollars. Hopkins, another grocer, could not be budged beyond five dollars.

And just then came the call from the post office to go to work. It placed me in a most trying predicament. The sixty-five dollars I could earn regularly every month was a terrible temptation. I couldn't decide what to do. And I'll never be able to forgive the postmaster of Oakland. I answered the call, and I talked to him like a man. I frankly told him the situation. It looked as if I might win out at writing. The chance was good, but not certain. Now, if he would pass me by and select the next man on the eligible list, and give me a call at the next vacancy—

But he shut me off with: "Then you don't want the position?"

"But I do," I protested. "Don't you see, if you will pass me over this time—"

"If you want it you will take it," he said coldly.

Happily for me, the cursed brutality of the man made me angry.

"Very well," I said. "I won't take it."

XXVI

Having burned my one ship, I plunged into writing. I am afraid I always was an extremist. Early and late I was at it—writing, typing, studying grammar, studying writing and all the forms of writing, and studying the writers who succeeded in order to find out how they succeeded. I managed on five hours' sleep in the twenty-four, and came pretty close to working the nineteen waking hours left to me. My light burned till two and three in the morning, which led a good neighbor woman into a bit of sentimental Sherlock Holmes deduction. Never seeing me in the daytime, she concluded that I was a gambler, and that the light in my window was placed there by my mother to guide her erring son home.

The trouble with the beginner at the writing game is the long, dry spells, when there is never an editor's check and everything pawnable is pawned. I wore my summer suit pretty well through that winter, and the following summer experienced the longest, dryest spell of all, in the period when salaried men are gone on vacation and manuscripts lie in editorial offices until vacation is over.

My difficulty was that I had no one to advise me. I didn't know a soul who had written or who had ever tried to write. I didn't even know one reporter. Also, to succeed at the writing game, I found I had to unlearn about everything the teachers and professors of literature of the high school and university had taught me. I was very indignant about this at the time; though now I can understand it. They did not know the trick of successful writing in the years of 1895 and 1896. They knew all about "Snow Bound" and "Sartor Resartus"; but the American editors of 1899 did not want such truck. They wanted the 1899 truck, and offered to pay so well for it that the teachers and professors of literature would have quit their jobs could they have supplied it.

I struggled along, stood off the butcher and the grocer, pawned my watch and bicycle and my father's mackintosh, and I worked. I really did work, and went on short commons of sleep. Critics have complained about the swift education one of my characters, Martin Eden, achieved. In three years, from a sailor with a common school education, I made a successful writer of him. The critics say this is impossible. Yet I was Martin Eden. At the end of three working years, two of which were spent in high school and the university and one spent at writing, and all three in studying immensely and intensely, I was publishing stories in magazines such as the *Atlantic Monthly,* was correcting proofs of my first book (issued by Houghton, Mifflin Co.), was selling sociological articles to *Cosmopolitan* and *McClure's*, had declined an associate editorship proffered me by telegraph from New York City, and was getting ready to marry.

Now the foregoing means work, especially the last year of it, when I was learning my trade as a writer. And in that year, running short on sleep and tasking my brain to its limit, I neither drank nor cared to drink. So far as I was concerned, alcohol did not exist. I did suffer from brain-fag on occasion, but alcohol never suggested itself as an ameliorative. Heavens! Editorial acceptances and checks were all the ameliorratives I needed. A thin envelope from an editor in the morning's mail was more stimulating than half-a-dozen cocktails. And if a check of decent amount came out of the envelope, such incident in itself was a whole drunk.

Furthermore, at that time in my life I did not know what a cocktail was. I remember, when my first book was published, several Alaskans who were members of the Bohemian Club entertained me one evening at the club in San Francisco. We sat in most wonderful leather chairs, and drinks were ordered. Never had I heard such an ordering of liqueurs and of highballs of particular brands of Scotch. I didn't know what a liqueur or a highball was, and I didn't know that "Scotch" meant whisky. I knew only poor men's drinks, the drinks of the frontier and of sailor-town—cheap beer and cheaper whisky that was just called whisky and nothing else. I was embarrassed to make a choice, and the waiter nearly collapsed when I ordered claret as an after-dinner drink.

XXVII

As I succeeded with my writing, my standard of living rose and my horizon broadened. I confined myself to writing and typing a thousand words a day, including Sundays and holidays; and I still studied hard, but not so hard as formerly. I allowed myself five and one-half hours of actual sleep. I added this half-hour because I was compelled. Financial success permitted me more time for exercise. I rode my wheel more, chiefly because it was permanently out of pawn; and I boxed and fenced, walked on my hands, jumped high and broad, put the shot and tossed the caber, and went swimming. And I learned that more sleep is required for physical exercise than for mental exercise. There were tired nights, bodily, when I slept six hours; and on occasion of very severe exercise I actually slept seven hours. But such sleep orgies were not frequent. There was so much to learn, so much to be done, that I felt wicked when I slept seven hours. And I blessed the man who invented alarm clocks.

And still no desire to drink. I possessed too many fine faiths, was living at too keen a pitch. I was a socialist, intent on saving the world, and alcohol could not give me the fervors that were mine from ideas and ideals. My voice, on account of my successful writing, had added weight, or so I thought. At any rate, my reputation as a writer drew me audiences that my reputation as a speaker never could have drawn. I was invited before clubs and organizations of all sorts to deliver my message. I fought the good fight, and went on studying and writing, and was very busy.

Up to this time I had had a very restricted circle of friends. But now I began to go about. I was invited out, especially to dinner; and I made many friends and acquaintances whose economic lives were easier than mine had been. And many of them drank. In their own houses they drank and offered me drink. They were not drunkards any of them. They just drank temperately, and I drank temperately with them as an act of comradeship and accepted hospitality. I did not care for it, neither wanted it nor did not want it, and so small was the impression made by it that I do not remember my first cocktail nor my first Scotch highball.

Well, I had a house. When one is asked into other houses, he naturally asks others into his house. Behold the rising standard of living. Having been given drink in other houses, I could expect nothing else of myself than to give drink in my own house. So I laid in a supply of beer and whisky and table claret. Never since that has my house not been well supplied.

And still, through all this period, I did not care in the slightest for John Barleycorn. I drank when others drank, and with them, as a social act. And I had so little choice in the matter that I drank whatever they drank. If they elected whisky, then whisky it was for me. If they drank root beer or sarsaparilla, I drank root beer or sarsaparilla with them. And when there were no friends in the house, why, I didn't drink anything. Whisky decanters were always in the room where I wrote, and for months and years I never knew what it was, when by myself, to take a drink.

When out at dinner, I noticed the kindly, genial glow of the preliminary cocktail. It seemed a very fitting and gracious thing. Yet so little did I stand in need of it, with my own high intensity and vitality, that I never thought it worth while to have a cocktail before my own meal when I ate alone.

On the other hand, I well remember a very brilliant man, somewhat older than I, who occasionally visited me. He liked whisky, and I recall sitting whole afternoons in my den, drinking steadily with him, drink for drink, until he was mildly lighted up and I was slightly aware that I had drunk some whisky. Now why did I do this? I don't know, save that the old schooling held, the training of the old days and nights, glass in hand, with men, the drinking ways of drink and drinkers.

Besides, I no longer feared John Barleycorn. Mine was that most dangerous stage when a man believes himself John Barleycorn's master. I had proved it to my satisfaction in the long years of work and study. I could drink when I wanted, refrain when I wanted, drink without getting drunk, and to cap everything I was thoroughly conscious that I had no liking for the stuff. During this period I drank precisely for the same reason I had drunk with Scotty and the harpooner and with the oyster pirates—because it was an act performed by men with whom I wanted to behave as a man. These brilliant ones, these adventurers of the mind, drank. Very well. There was no reason I should not drink with them,—I who knew so confidently that I had nothing to fear from John Barleycorn.

And the foregoing was my attitude of mind for years. Occasionally I got well jingled, but such occasions were rare. It interfered with my work, and I permitted nothing to interfere with my work. I remember, when spending several months in the East End of London, during which time I wrote a book and adventured much amongst the worst of the slum classes, that I got drunk several times and was mightily wroth with myself because it interfered with my writing. Yet these very times were because I was out on the adventure-path, where John Barleycorn is always to be found.

Then, too, with the certitude of long training and unholy intimacy, there were occasions when I engaged in drinking-bouts with men. Of course, this was on the adventure-path in various parts of the world, and it was a matter of pride. It is a queer man-pride that leads one to drink with men in order to show as strong a head as they. But this queer man-pride is no theory. It is a fact.

For instance, a wild band of young revolutionists invited me as the guest of honor to a beer bust. It is the only technical beer bust I ever attended. I did not know the true inwardness of the affair when I accepted. I imagined that the talk would be wild and high, that some of them might drink more than they ought, and that I would drink discreetly. But it seemed these beer busts were a diversion of these high-spirited young fellows whereby they whiled away the tedium of existence by making fools of their betters. As I learned afterward, they had got their previous guest of honor, a brilliant young radical, unskilled in drinking, quite pipped.

When I found myself with them, and the situation dawned on me, up rose my queer man-pride. I'd show them, the young rascals. I'd show them who was husky and chesty, who had the vitality and the constitution, the stomach and the head, who could make most of a swine of himself and show it least. These unlicked cubs who thought they could out-drink *me!*

You see, it was an endurance test, and no man likes to give another best. Faugh! It was steam beer. I had learned more expensive brews. Not for years had I drunk steam beer; but when I had, I had drunk with men, and I guessed I could show these youngsters some ability in beer-guzzling. And the drinking began, and I had to drink with the best of them. Some of them might lag, but the guest of honor was not permitted to lag.

And all my austere nights of midnight oil, all the books I had read, all the wisdom I had gathered, went glimmering before the ape and tiger in me that crawled up from the abysm of my heredity, atavistic, competitive and brutal, lustful with strength and desire to outswine the swine.

And when the session broke up I was still on my feet, and I walked erect, unswaying —which was more than can be said of some of my hosts. I recall one of them in indignant tears on the street corner, weeping as he pointed out my sober condition. Little he dreamed the iron clutch, born of old training, with which I held to my consciousness in my swimming brain, kept control of my muscles and my qualms, kept my voice unbroken and easy and my thoughts consecutive and logical. Yes, and mixed up with it all I was privily a-grin. They hadn't made a fool of me in that drinking bout. And I was proud of myself for the achievement. Darn it, I am still proud, so strangely is man compounded.

But I didn't write my thousand words next morning. I was sick, poisoned. It was a day of wretchedness. In the afternoon I had to give a public speech. I gave it, and I am confident it was as bad as I felt. Some of my hosts were there in the front rows to mark any signs on me of the night before. I don't known what signs they marked, but I marked signs on them and took consolation in the knowledge that they were just as sick as I.

Never again, I swore. And I have never been inveigled into another beer bust. For that matter, that was my last drinking bout of any sort. Oh, I have drunk ever since, but with more wisdom, more discretion, and never in a competitive spirit. It is thus the seasoned drinker grows seasoned.

To show that at this period in my life drinking was wholly a matter of companionship, I remember crossing the Atlantic in the old *Teutonic.* It chanced, at the start, that I chummed with an English cable operator and a younger member of a Spanish shipping firm. Now the only thing they drank was "horse's neck"—a long, soft, cool drink with an apple peel or an orange peel floating in it. And for that whole voyage I drank horse's necks with my two companions. On the other hand, had they drunk whisky, I should have drunk whisky with them. From this it must not be concluded that I was merely weak. I didn't care. I had no morality in the matter. I was strong with youth, and unafraid, and alcohol was an utterly negligible question so far as I was concerned.

XXVIII

Not yet was I ready to tuck my arm in John Barleycorn's. The older I got, the greater my success, the more money I earned, the wider was the command of the world that became mine and the more prominently did John Barleycorn bulk in my life. And still I maintained no more than a nodding acquaintance with him. I drank for the sake of sociability, and when alone I did not drink. Sometimes I got jingled, but I considered such jingles the mild price I paid for sociability.

To show how unripe I was for John Barleycorn, when, at this time, I descended into my slough of despond, I never dreamed of turning to John Barleycorn for a helping hand. I had life troubles and heart troubles which are neither here nor there in this narrative. But, combined with them, were intellectual troubles which are indeed germane.

Mine was no uncommon experience. I had read too much positive science and lived too much positive life. In the eagerness of youth I had made the ancient mistake of pursuing Truth too relentlessly. I had torn her veils from her, and the sight was too terrible for me to stand. In brief, I lost my fine faiths in pretty well everything except humanity, and the humanity I retained faith in was a very stark humanity indeed.

This long sickness of pessimism is too well known to most of us to be detailed here. Let it suffice to state that I had it very bad. I meditated suicide coolly, as a Greek philosopher might. My regret was that there were too many dependent directly upon me for food and shelter for me to quit living. But that was sheer morality. What really saved me was the one remaining illusion—the PEOPLE.

The things I had fought for and burned my midnight oil for, had failed me. Success—I despised it. Recognition—it was dead ashes. Society, men and women above the ruck and the muck of the water-front and the forecastle—I was appalled by their unlovely mental mediocrity. Love of woman—it was like all the rest. Money—I could sleep in only one bed at a time, and of what worth was an income of a hundred porterhouses a day when I could eat only one? Art, culture—in the face of the iron facts of biology such things were ridiculous, the exponents of such things only the more ridiculous.

From the foregoing it can be seen how very sick I was. I was born a fighter. The things I had fought for had proved not worth the fight. Remained the PEOPLE. My fight was finished, yet something was left still to fight for—the PEOPLE.

But while I was discovering this one last tie to bind me to life, in my extremity, in the depths of despond, walking in the valley of the shadow, my ears were deaf to John Barleycorn. Never the remotest whisper arose in my consciousness that John Barleycorn was the anodyne, that he could lie me along to live. One way only was uppermost in my thought—my revolver, the crashing eternal darkness of a bullet. There was plenty of whisky in the house—for my guests. I never touched it. I grew afraid of my revolver—afraid during the period in which the radiant, flashing vision of the PEOPLE was forming in my mind and will. So obsessed was I with the desire to die, that I feared I might commit the act in my sleep, and I was compelled to give my revolver away to others who were to lose it for me where my subconscious hand might not find it.

But the PEOPLE saved me. By the PEOPLE was I handcuffed to life. There was still one fight left in me, and here was the thing for which to fight. I threw all precaution to the winds, threw myself with fiercer zeal into the fight for socialism, laughed at the editors and publishers who warned me and who were the sources of my hundred porterhouses a day, and was brutally careless of whose feelings I hurt and of how savagely I hurt them. As the "well-balanced radicals" charged at the time, my efforts were so strenuous, so unsafe and unsane, so ultra-revolutionary, that I retarded the socialist development in the United States by five years. In passing, I wish to remark, at this late date, that it is my fond belief that I accelerated the socialist development in the United States by at least five minutes.

It was the PEOPLE, and no thanks to John Barleycorn, who pulled me through my long sickness. And when I was convalescent, came the love of woman to complete the cure and lull my pessimism asleep for many a long day, until John Barleycorn again awoke it. But, in the meantime, I pursued Truth less relentlessly, refraining from tearing her last veils aside even when I clutched them in my hand. I no longer cared to look upon Truth naked. I refused to permit myself to see a second time what I had once seen. And the memory of what I had that time seen I resolutely blotted from my mind.

And I was very happy. Life went well with me. I took delight in little things. The big things I declined to take too seriously. I still read the books, but not with the old eagerness. I still read the books to-day, but never again shall I read them with that old glory of youthful passion when I harked to the call from over and beyond that whispered me on to win to the mystery at the back of life and behind the stars.

The point of this chapter is that, in the long sickness that at some time comes to most of us, I came through without any appeal for aid to John Barleycorn. Love, socialism, the PEOPLE—healthful figments of man's mind—were the things that cured and saved me. If ever a man was not a born alcoholic, I believe that I am that man. And yet . . . well, let the succeeding chapters tell their tale, for in them will be shown how I paid for my previous quarter of a century of contact with ever-accessible John Barleycorn.

XXIX

After my long sickness my drinking continued to be convivial. I drank when others drank and I was with them. But, imperceptibly, my need for alcohol took form and began to grow. It was not a body need. I boxed, swam, sailed, rode horses, lived in the open an arrantly healthful life, and passed life insurance examinations with flying colors. In its inception, now that I look back upon it, this need for alcohol was a mental need, a nerve need, a good-spirits need. How can I explain?

It was something like this. Physiologically, from the standpoint of palate and stomach, alcohol was, as it had always been, repulsive. It tasted no better than beer did when I was five, than bitter claret did when I was seven. When I was alone, writing or studying, I had no need for it. But—I was growing old, or wise, or both, or senile as an alternative. When I was in company I was less pleased, less excited, with the things said and done. Erstwhile worth-while fun and stunts seemed no longer worth while; and it was a torment to listen to the insipidities and stupidities of women, to the pompous, arrogant sayings of the little half-baked men. It is the penalty one pays for reading the books too much, or for being oneself a fool. In my case it does not matter which was my trouble. The trouble itself was the fact. The condition of the fact was mine. For me the life, and light, and sparkle of human intercourse were dwindling.

I had climbed too high among the stars, or, maybe, I had slept too hard. Yet I was not hysterical nor in any way overwrought. My pulse was normal. My heart was an amazement of excellence to the insurance doctors. My lungs threw the said doctors into ecstasies. I wrote a thousand words every day. I was punctiliously exact in dealing with all the affairs of life that fell to my lot. I exercised in joy and gladness. I slept at night like a babe. But—

Well, as soon as I got out in the company of others I was driven to melancholy and spiritual tears. I could neither laugh with nor at the solemn utterances of men I esteemed ponderous asses; nor could I laugh with nor at, nor engage in my old-time lightsome persiflage, with the silly superficial chatterings of women, who, underneath all their silliness and softness, were as primitive, direct, and deadly in their pursuit of biological destiny as the monkey women were before they shed their furry coats and replaced them with the furs of other animals.

And I was not pessimistic. I swear I was not pessimistic. I was merely bored. I had seen the same show too often, listened too often to the same songs and the same jokes. I knew too much about the box-office receipts. I knew the cogs of the machinery behind the scenes so well, that the posing on the stage, and the laughter and the song, could not drown the creaking of the wheels behind.

It doesn't pay to go behind the scenes and see the angel-voiced tenor beat his wife. Well, I'd been behind, and I was paying for it. Or else I was a fool. It is immaterial which was my situation. The situation is what counts, and the situation was that social intercourse for me was getting painful and difficult. On the other hand, it must be stated that on rare occasions, on very rare occasions, I did meet rare souls, or fools like me, with whom I could spend magnificent hours among the stars, or in the paradise of fools. I was married to a rare soul, or a fool, who never bored me and who was always a source of new and unending surprise and delight. But I could not spend all my hours solely in her company. Nor would it have been fair, nor wise, to compel her to spend all her hours in my company. Besides, I had written a string of successful books, and society demands some portion of the recreative hours of a fellow that writes books. And any normal man, of himself and his needs, demands some hours of his fellow man.

And now we begin to come to it. How to face social intercourse with the glamour gone? John Barleycorn! The ever-patient one had waited a quarter of a century and more for me to reach my hand out in need of him. His thousand tricks had failed, thanks to my constitution and good luck, but he had more tricks in his bag. A cocktail or two, or several, I found, cheered me up for the foolishness of foolish people. A cocktail, or several, before dinner, enabled me to laugh whole-heartedly at things which had long since ceased being laughable. The cocktail was a prod, a spur, a kick, to my jaded mind and bored spirits. It recrudesced the laughter and the song, and put a lilt into my own imagination so that I could laugh and sing and say foolish things with the liveliest of them, or platitudes with verve and intensity to the satisfaction of the pompous mediocre ones who knew no other way to talk.

A poor companion without a cocktail, I became a very good companion with one. I achieved a false exhilaration, drugged myself to merriment. And the thing began so imperceptibly, that I, old intimate of John Barleycorn, never dreamed whither it was leading me. I was beginning to call for music and wine; soon I should be calling for madder music and more wine.

It was at this time I became aware of waiting with expectancy for the pre-dinner cocktail. I *wanted* it, and I was *conscious* that I wanted it. I remember, while war-corresponding in the Far East, of being irresistibly attracted to a certain home. Besides accepting all invitations to dinner, I made a point of dropping in almost every afternoon. Now, the hostess was a charming woman, but it was not for her sake that I was under her roof so frequently. It happened that she made by far the finest cocktail procurable in that large city where drink-mixing on the part of the foreign population was indeed an art. Up at the club, down at the hotels, and in other private houses, no such cocktails were created. Her cocktails were subtle. They were masterpieces. They were the least repulsive to the palate and carried the most "kick." And yet, I desired her cocktails only for sociability's sake, to key myself to sociable moods. When I rode away from that city, across hundreds of miles of rice-fields and mountains, and through months of campaigning, and on with the victorious Japanese into Manchuria, I did not drink. Several bottles of whisky were always to be found on the backs of my packhorses. Yet I never broached a bottle for myself, never took a drink by myself, and never knew a desire to take such a drink. Oh, if a white man came into my camp, I opened a bottle and we drank together according to the way of men, just as he would open a bottle and drink with me if I came into his camp. I carried that whisky for social purposes, and I so charged it up in my expense account to the newspaper for which I worked.

Only in retrospect can I mark the almost imperceptible growth of my desire. There were little hints then that I did not take, little straws in the wind that I did not see, little incidents the gravity of which I did not realize.

For instance, for some years it had been my practice each winter to cruise for six or eight weeks on San Francisco Bay. My stout sloop yacht, the *Spray*, had a comfortable cabin and a coal stove. A Korean boy did the cooking, and I usually took a friend or so along to share the joys of the cruise. Also, I took my machine along and did my thousand words a day. On the particular trip I have in mind, Cloudesley and Toddy came along. This was Toddy's first trip. On previous trips Cloudesley had elected to drink beer; so I had kept the yacht supplied with beer and had drunk beer with him.

But on this cruise the situation was different. Toddy was so nicknamed because of his diabolical cleverness in concocting toddies. So I brought whisky along—a couple of gallons. Alas! Many another gallon I bought, for Cloudesley and I got into the habit of drinking a certain hot toddy of huge dimensions that actually tasted delicious going down and that carried the most exhilarating kick imaginable.

I *liked* those toddies. I grew to look forward to the making of them. We drank them regularly, one before breakfast, one before dinner, one before supper, and a final one when we went to bed. We never got drunk. But I will say that four times a day we were very genial. And when, in the middle of the cruise, Toddy was called back to San Francisco on business, Cloudesley and I saw to it that the Korean boy mixed toddies regularly for us according to formula.

But that was only on the boat. Back on the land, in my house, I took no before-breakfast eye-opener, no bed-going nightcap. And I haven't drunk hot toddies since, and that was many a year ago. But the point is, I *liked* those toddies. The geniality of which they were provocative was marvelous. They were eloquent proselyters for John Barleycorn in their small insidious way. They were tickles of the something destined to grow into daily and deadly desire. And I didn't know, never dreamed—I, who had lived with John Barleycorn for so many years and laughed at all his unavailing attempts to win me.

XXX

PART of the process of recovering from my long sickness was to find delight in little things, in things unconnected with books and problems, in play, in games of tag in the swimming pool, in flying kites, in fooling with horses, in working out mechanical puzzles. As a result, I grew tired of the city. On the ranch, in the Valley of the Moon, I found my paradise. I gave up living in cities. All the cities held for me were music, the theater, and Turkish baths.

And all went well with me. I worked hard, played hard, and was very happy. I read more fiction and less fact. I did not study a tithe as much as I had studied in the past. I still took an interest in the fundamental problems of existence, but it was a very cautious interest; for I had burned my fingers that time I clutched at the veils of Truth and rent them from her. There was a bit of lie in this attitude of mine, a bit of hypocrisy; but the lie and the hypocrisy were those of a man desiring to live. I deliberately blinded myself to what I took to be the savage interpretation of biological fact. After all, I was merely forswearing a bad habit, foregoing a bad frame of mind. And I repeat, I was very happy. And I add, that in all my days, measuring them with cold, considerative judgment, this was, far and away beyond all other periods, the happiest period of my life.

But the time was at hand, rimeless and reasonless so far as I can see, when I was to begin to pay for my score of years of dallying with John Barleycorn. Occasionally guests journeyed to the ranch and remained a few days. Some did not drink. But to those who did drink, the absence of all alcohol on the ranch was a hardship. I could not violate my sense of hospitality by compelling them to endure this hardship. I ordered in a stock . . . for my guests.

I was never interested enough in cocktails to know how they were made. So I got a barkeeper in Oakland to make them in bulk and ship them to me. When I had no guests I didn't drink. But I began to notice, when I finished my morning's work, that I was glad if there were a guest, for then I could drink a cocktail with him.

Now I was so clean of alcohol that even a single cocktail was provocative of pitch. A single cocktail would glow the mind and tickle a laugh for the few minutes prior to sitting down to table and starting the delightful process of eating. On the other hand, such was the strength of my stomach, of my alcoholic resistance, that the single cocktail was only the glimmer of a glow, the faintest tickle of a laugh. One day a friend frankly and shamelessly suggested a second cocktail. I drank the second one with him. The glow was appreciably longer and warmer, the laughter deeper and more resonant. One does not forget such experiences. Sometimes I almost think that it was because I was so very happy that I started on my real drinking.

I remember one day Charmian and I took a long ride over the mountains on our horses. The servants had been dismissed for the day, and we returned late at night to a jolly chafing-dish supper. Oh, it was good to be alive that night while the supper was preparing, the two of us alone in the kitchen. I, personally, was at the top of life. Such things as the books and ultimate truth did not exist. My body was gloriously healthy, and healthily tired from the long ride. It had been a splendid day. The night was splendid. I was with the woman who was my mate, picnicking in gleeful abandon. I had no troubles. The bills were all paid, and a surplus of money was rolling in on me. The future ever widened before me. And right there, in the kitchen, delicious things bubbled in the chafing dish, our laughter bubbled, and my stomach was keen with a most delicious edge of appetite.

I felt so good, that somehow, somewhere, in me arose an insatiable greed to feel better. I was so happy that I wanted to pitch my happiness even higher. And I knew the way. Ten thousand contacts with John Barleycorn had taught me. Several times I wandered out of the kitchen to the cocktail bottle, and each time I left it diminished by one man's size cocktail. The result was splendid. I wasn't jingled, I wasn't lighted up; but I was warmed, I glowed, my happiness was pyramided. Munificent as life was to me, I added to that munificence. It was a great hour—one of my greatest. But I paid for it, long afterwards, as you shall see. One does not forget such experiences, and, in human stupidity, cannot be brought to realize that there is no immutable law which decrees that same things shall produce same results. For they don't, else would the thousandth pipe of opium be provocative of similar delights to the first, else would one cocktail, instead of several, produce an equivalent glow after a year of cocktails.

One day, just before I ate midday dinner, after my morning's writing was done, when I had no guest, I took a cocktail by myself. Thereafter, when there were no guests, I took this daily pre-dinner cocktail. And right there John Barleycorn had me. I was beginning to drink regularly. I was beginning to drink alone. And I was beginning to drink, not for hospitality's sake, not for the sake of the taste, but for the effect of the drink.

I *wanted* that daily pre-dinner cocktail. And it never crossed my mind that there was any reason I should not have it. I paid for it. I could pay for a thousand cocktails each day if I wanted. And what was a cocktail—one cocktail—to me who on so many occasions for so many years had drunk inordinate quantities of stiffer stuff and been unharmed?

The program of my ranch life was as follows: Each morning, at eight-thirty, having been reading or correcting proofs in bed since four or five, I went to my desk. Odds and ends of correspondence and notes occupied me till nine, and at nine sharp, invariably, I began my writing. By eleven, sometimes a few minutes earlier or later, my thousand words were finished. Another half hour at cleaning up my desk, and my day's work was done, so that at eleven-thirty I got into a hammock under the trees with my mail bag and the morning newspaper. At twelve-thirty I ate dinner and in the afternoon I swam and rode.

One morning, at eleven-thirty, before I got into the hammock, I took a cocktail. I repeated this on subsequent mornings, of course, taking another cocktail just before I ate at twelve-thirty. Soon I found myself, seated at my desk in the midst of my thousand words, looking forward to that eleven-thirty cocktail.

At last, now, I was thoroughly conscious that I desired alcohol. But what of it? I wasn't afraid of John Barleycorn. I had associated with him too long. I was wise in the matter of drink. I was discreet. Never again would I drink to excess. I knew the dangers and the pitfalls of John Barleycorn, the various ways by which he had tried to kill me in the past. But all that was past, long past. Never again would I drink myself to stupefaction. Never again would I get drunk. All I wanted, and all I would take, was just enough to glow and warm me, to kick geniality alive in me and put laughter in my throat and stir the maggots of imagination slightly in my brain. Oh, I was thoroughly master of myself, and of John Barleycorn.

XXXI

BUT the same stimulus to the human organism will not continue to produce the same response. By and by I discovered there was no kick at all in one cocktail. One cocktail left me dead. There was no glow, no laughter tickle. Two or three cocktails were required to produce the original effect of one. And I wanted that effect. I drank my first cocktail at eleven-thirty when I took the morning's mail into the hammock, and I drank my second cocktail an hour later just before I ate. I got into the habit of crawling out of the hammock ten minutes earlier so as to find time and decency for two more cocktails ere I ate. This became schedule—three cocktails in the hour that intervened between my desk and dinner. And these were two of the deadliest drinking habits: regular drinking and solitary drinking.

I was always willing to drink when any one was around. I drank by myself when no one was around. Then I made another step. When I had for guest a man of limited drinking caliber, I took two drinks to his one—one drink with him, the other drink without him and of which he did not know. I *stole* that other drink, and, worse than that, I began the habit of drinking alone when there was a guest, a man, a comrade, with whom I could have drunk. But John Barleycorn furnished the extenuation. It was a wrong thing to trip a guest up with excess of hospitality and get him drunk. If I persuaded him, with his limited caliber, into drinking up with me, I'd surely get him drunk. What could I do but steal that every second drink, or else deny myself the kick equivalent to what he had got out of half the number?

Please remember, as I recite this development of my drinking, that I am no fool, no weakling. As the world measures such things, I am a success—I dare say a success more conspicuous than the success of the average successful man, and a success that required a pretty fair amount of brains and will power. My body is a strong body. It has survived where weaklings died like flies. And yet these things which I am relating happened to my body and to me. I am a fact. My drinking is a fact. My drinking is a thing that has happened, and is no theory nor speculation; and, as I see it, it but lays the emphasis on the power of John Barleycorn—a savagery that we still permit to exist, a deadly institution that lingers from the mad old brutal days and that takes its heavy toll of youth and strength and high spirit, and of very much of all of the best we breed.

To return. After a boisterous afternoon in the swimming pool, followed by a glorious ride on horseback over the mountains or up or down the Valley of the Moon, I found myself so keyed and splendid that I desired to be more highly keyed, to feel more splendid. I knew the way. A cocktail before supper was not the way. Two or three, at the very least, was what was needed. I took them. Why not? It was living. I had always dearly loved to live. This also became part of the daily schedule.

Then, too, I was perpetually finding excuses for extra cocktails. It might be the assembling of a particularly jolly crowd; a touch of anger against my architect or against a thieving stone-mason working on my barn; the death of my favorite horse in a barbed wire fence; or news of good fortune in the morning mail from my dealings with editors and publishers. It was immaterial what the excuse might be, once the desire had germinated in me. The thing was: I *wanted* alcohol. At last, after a score and more of years of dallying and of not wanting, now I wanted it. And my strength was my weakness. I required two, three, or four drinks to get an effect commensurate with the effect the average man got out of one drink.

One rule I observed. I never took a drink until my day's work of writing a thousand words was done. And, when done, the cocktails reared a wall of inhibition in my brain between the day's work done and the rest of the day of fun to come. My work ceased from my consciousness. No thought of it flickered in my brain till next morning at nine o'clock when I sat at my desk and began my next thousand words. This was a desirable condition of mind to achieve. I conserved my energy by means of this alcoholic inhibition. John Barleycorn was not so black as he was painted. He did a fellow many a good turn, and this was one of them.

And I turned out work that was healthful, and wholesome, and sincere. It was never pessimistic. The way to life I had learned in my long sickness. I knew the illusions were right, and I exalted the illusions. Oh, I still turn out the same sort of work, stuff that is clean, alive, optimistic, and that makes toward life. And I am always assured by the critics of my superabundant and abounding vitality, and of how thoroughly I am deluded by these very illusions I exploit.

And while on this digression, let me repeat the question I have repeated to myself ten thousand times. *Why did I drink?* What need was there for it? I was happy. Was it because I was too happy? I was strong. Was it because I was too strong? Did I possess too much vitality? I don't know why I drank. I cannot answer, though I can voice the suspicion that ever grows in me. I had been in too familiar contact with John Barleycorn through too many years. A left-handed man, by long practice, can become a right-handed man. Had I, a non-alcoholic, by long practice, become an alcoholic?

I was so happy! I had won through my long sickness to the satisfying love of woman. I earned more money with less endeavor. I glowed with health. I slept like a babe. I continued to write successful books, and in sociological controversy I saw my opponents confuted with the facts of the times that daily reared new buttresses to my intellectual position. From day's end to day's end I never knew sorrow, disappointment, nor regret. I was happy all the time. Life was one unending song. I begrudged the very hours of blessed sleep because by that much was I robbed of the joy that would have been mine had I remained awake. And yet I drank. And John Barleycorn, all unguessed by me, was setting the stage for a sickness all his own.

The more I drank the more I was required to drink to get an equivalent effect. When I left the Valley of the Moon, and went to the city and dined out, a cocktail served at table was a wan and worthless thing. There was no pre-dinner kick in it. On my way to dinner I was compelled to accumulate the kick—two cocktails, three, and, if I met some fellows, four or five, or six, it didn't matter within several. Once, I was in a rush. I had no time decently to accumulate the several drinks. A brilliant idea came to me. I told the barkeeper to mix me a double cocktail. Thereafter, whenever I was in a hurry, I ordered double cocktails. It saved time.

One result of this regular heavy drinking was to jade me. My mind grew so accustomed to spring and liven by artificial means, that without artificial means it refused to spring and liven. Alcohol become more and more imperative in order to meet people, in order to become sociably fit. I had to get the kick and the hit of the stuff, the crawl of the maggots, the genial brain glow, the laughter tickle, the touch of devilishness and sting, the smile over the face of things, ere I could join my fellows and make one with them.

Another result was that John Barleycorn was beginning to trip me up. He was thrusting my long sickness back upon me, inveigling me into again pursuing Truth and snatching her veils away from her, tricking me into looking reality stark in the face. But this came on gradually. My thoughts were growing harsh again, though they grew harsh slowly.

Sometimes warnings crossed my mind. Where was this steady drinking leading? But trust John Barleycorn to silence such questions. "Come on and have a drink and I'll tell you all about it," is his way. And it works. For instance, the following is a case in point, and one which John Barleycorn never wearied of reminding me:

I had suffered an accident which required a ticklish operation. One morning, a week after I had come off the table, I lay on my hospital bed, weak and weary. The sunburn of my face, what little of it could be seen through a scraggly growth of beard, had faded to a sickly yellow. My doctor stood at my bedside on the verge of departure. He glared disapprovingly at the cigarette I was smoking.

"That's what you ought to quit," he lectured. "It will get you in the end. Look at me."

I looked. He was about my own age, broad-shouldered, deep-chested, eyes sparkling, and ruddy-cheeked with health. A finer specimen of manhood one would not ask.

"I used to smoke," he went on. "Cigars. But I gave even them up. And look at me."

The man was arrogant, and rightly arrogant, with conscious well-being. And within a month he was dead. It was no accident. Half-a-dozen different bugs of long scientific names had attacked and destroyed him. The complications were astonishing and painful, and for days before he died the screams of agony of that splendid manhood could be heard for a block around. He died screaming.

"You see," said John Barleycorn. "He took care of himself. He even stopped smoking cigars. And that's what he got for it. Pretty rotten, eh? But the bugs will jump. There's no forefending them. Your magnificent doctor took every precaution, yet they got him. When the bug jumps you can't tell where it will land. It may be you. Look what he missed. Will you miss all I can give you, only to have a bug jump on you and drag you down? There is no equity in life. It's all a lottery. But I put the lying smile on the face of life and laugh at the facts. Smile with me and laugh. You'll get yours in the end, but in the meantime laugh. It's a pretty dark world. I illuminate it for you. It's a rotten world, when things can happen such as happened to your doctor. There's only one thing to do; take another drink and forget it."

And of course I took another drink for the inhibition that accompanied it. I took another drink every time John Barleycorn reminded me of what had happened. Yet I drank rationally, intelligently. I saw to it that the quality of the stuff was of the best. I sought the kick and the inhibition, and avoided the penalties of poor quality and of drunkenness. It is to be remarked, in passing, that when a man begins to drink rationally and intelligently he betrays a grave symptom of how far along the road he has traveled.

But I continued to observe my rule of never taking my first drink of the day until the last word of my thousand words was written. On occasion, however, I took a day's vacation from my writing. At such times, since it was no violation of my rule, I didn't mind how early in the day I took that first drink. And persons who have never been through the drinking game wonder how the drinking habit grows!

XXXII

WHEN the *Snark* sailed on her long cruise from San Francisco there was nothing to drink on board. Or, rather, we were all of us unaware that there was anything to drink, nor did we discover it for many a month. This sailing with a "dry" boat was malice aforethought on my part. I had played John Barleycorn a trick. And it showed that I was listening ever so slightly to the faint warnings that were beginning to arise in my consciousness.

Of course, I veiled the situation to myself and excused myself to John Barleycorn. And I was very scientific about it. I said that I would drink only while in ports. During the dry sea-stretches my system would be cleansed of the alcohol that soaked it, so that when I reached a port I should be in shape to enjoy John Barleycorn more thoroughly. His bite would be sharper, his kick keener and more delicious.

We were twenty-seven days on the traverse between San Francisco and Honolulu. After the first day out, the thought of a drink never troubled me. This I take to show how intrinsically I am not an alcoholic. Sometimes, during the traverse, looking ahead and anticipating the delightful *lanai* luncheons and dinners of Hawaii (I had been there a couple of times before), I thought, naturally, of the drinks that would precede those meals. I did not think of those drinks with any yearning, with any irk at the length of the voyage. I merely thought they would be nice and jolly, part of the atmosphere of a proper meal.

Thus, once again I proved to my complete satisfaction that I was John Barleycorn's master. I could drink when I wanted, refrain when I wanted. Therefore I would continue to drink when I wanted.

Some five months were spent in the various islands of the Hawaiian group. Being ashore, I drank. I even drank a bit more than I had been accustomed to drink in California prior to the voyage. The people in Hawaii seemed to drink a bit more, on the average, than the people in more temperate latitudes. I do not intend the pun, and can awkwardly revise the statement to "latitudes more distant from the equator." Yet Hawaii is only sub-tropical. The deeper I got into the tropics the deeper I found men drank, the deeper I drank myself.

From Hawaii we sailed for the Marquesas. The traverse occupied sixty days. For sixty days we never raised land, a sail, nor a steamer smoke. But early in those sixty days, the cook, giving an overhauling to the galley, made a find. Down in the bottom of a deep locker he found a dozen bottles of angelica and muscatel. These had come down from the kitchen cellar of the ranch along with the home-preserved fruits and jellies. Six months in the galley-heat had effected some sort of a change in the thick sweet wine—brandied it, I imagine.

I took a taste. Delicious! And thereafter, once each day, at twelve o'clock, after our observations were worked up and the *Snark's* position charted, I drank half a tumbler of the stuff. It had a rare kick to it. It warmed the cockles of my geniality and put a fairer face on the truly fair face of the sea. Each morning, below, sweating out my thousand words, I found myself looking forward to that twelve o'clock event of the day.

The trouble was I had to share the stuff, and the length of the traverse was doubtful. I regretted that there were not more than a dozen bottles. And when they were gone I even regretted that I had shared any of it. I was thirsty for the alcohol, and eager to arrive in the Marquesas.

So it was that I reached the Marquesas the possessor of a real, man's size thirst. And in the Marquesas were several white men, a lot of sickly natives, much magnificent scenery, plenty of trade rum, an immense quantity of absinthe, but neither whisky nor gin. The trade rum scorched the skin of one's mouth. I know, because I tried it. But I had ever been plastic, and I accepted the absinthe. The trouble with the stuff was that I had to take such inordinate quantities in order to feel the slightest effect.

From the Marquesas I sailed with sufficient absinthe in ballast to last me to Tahiti, where I outfitted with Scotch and American whisky, and thereafter there were no dry stretches between ports. But please do not misunderstand. There was no drunkenness, as drunkenness is ordinarily understood—no staggering and rolling around, no befuddlement of the senses. The skilled and seasoned drinker, with a strong constitution, never descends to anything like that. He drinks to feel good, to get a pleasant jingle, and no more than that. The things he carefully avoids are the nausea of over-drinking, the after-effect of over-drinking, the helplessness and loss of pride of over-drinking.

What the skilled and seasoned drinker achieves is a discreet and canny semi-intoxication. And he does it by the twelve-month around without any apparent penalty. There are hundreds of thousands of men of this sort in the United States to-day, in clubs, hotels, and in their own homes—men who are never drunk, and who, though most of them will indignantly deny it, are rarely sober. And all of them fondly believe, as I fondly believed, that they are beating the game.

On the sea-stretches I was fairly abstemious; but ashore I drank more. I seemed to need more, anyway, in the tropics. This is a common experience, for the excessive consumption of alcohol in the tropics by white men is a notorious fact. The tropics is no place for white-skinned men. Their skin-pigment does not protect them against the excessive white light of the sun. The ultra-violet rays, and other high-velocity and invisible rays from the upper end of the spectrum, rip and tear through their tissues, just as the X-ray ripped and tore through the tissues of so many laboratory experimenters before they learned the danger.

White men in the tropics undergo radical changes of nature. They become savage, merciless. They commit monstrous acts of cruelty that they would never dream of committing in their original temperate climate. They become nervous, irritable, and less moral. And they drink as they never drank before. Drinking is one form of the many forms of degeneration that set in when white men are exposed too long to too much white light. The increase of alcoholic consumption is automatic. The tropics is no place for a long sojourn. They seem doomed to die anyway, and the heavy drinking expedites the process. They don't reason about it. They just do it.

The sun-sickness got me, despite the fact that I had been in the tropics only a couple of years. I drank heavily during this time, but right here I wish to forestall misunderstanding. The drinking was not the cause of the sickness, nor of the abandonment of the voyage. I was strong as a bull, and for many months I fought the sun-sickness that was ripping and tearing my surface and nervous tissues to pieces. All through the New Hebrides and the Solomons and up among the atolls on the Line, during this period, under a tropic sun, rotten with malaria, and suffering from a few minor afflictions such as Biblical leprosy with the silvery skin, I did the work of five men.

To navigate a vessel through the reefs and shoals and passages and unlighted coasts of the coral seas is a man's work in itself. I was the only navigator on board. There was no one to check me up on the working out of my observations, nor any one with whom I could advise in the ticklish darkness among uncharted reefs and shoals. And I stood all watches. There was no seaman on board whom I could trust to stand a mate's watch. I was mate as well as captain. Twenty-four hours a day were the watches I stood at sea, catching cat-naps when I might. Third, I was doctor. And let me say right here that the doctor's job on the *Snark* at that time was a man's job. All on board suffered from malaria—the real, tropical malaria that can kill in three months. All on board suffered from perforating ulcers and from the maddening itch of *ngari ngari.* A Japanese cook went insane from his too numerous afflictions. One of my Polynesian sailors lay at death's door with blackwater fever. Oh, yes, it was a full man's job, and I dosed and doctored, and pulled teeth, and dragged my patients through mild little things like ptomaine poisoning.

Fourth, I was a writer. I sweated out my thousand words a day, every day, except when the shock of fever smote me, or a couple of nasty squalls smote the *Snark*, in the morning. Fifth, I was a traveler and a writer, eager to see things and to gather material into my note books. And, sixth, I was master and owner of the craft that was visiting strange places where visitors are rare and where visitors are made much of. So here I had to hold up the social end, entertain on board, be entertained ashore by planters, traders, governors, captains of war vessels, kinky-headed cannibal kings, and prime ministers sometimes fortunate enough to be clad in cotton under shirts.

Of course I drank. I drank with my guests and hosts. Also, I drank by myself. Doing the work of five men, I thought, entitled me to drink. Alcohol was good for a man who overworked. I noted its effect on my small crew, when, breaking their backs and hearts at heaving up anchor in forty fathoms, they knocked off gasping and trembling at the end of half an hour and had new life put into them by stiff jolts of rum. They caught their breaths, wiped their mouths, and went to it again with a will. And when we careened the *Snark* and had to work in the water to our necks between shocks of fever, I noted how raw trade-rum helped the work along.

And here again we come to another side of many-sided John Barleycorn. On the face of it, he gives something for nothing. Where no strength remains he finds new strength. The wearied one rises to greater effort. For the time being there is an actual accession of strength. I remember passing coal on an ocean steamer through eight days of hell, during which time we coal-passers were kept to the job by being fed whisky. We toiled half drunk all the time. And without the whisky we could not have passed the coal.

This strength John Barleycorn gives is not fictitious strength. It is real strength. But it is manufactured out of the sources of strength, and it must ultimately be paid for, and with interest. But what weary human will look so far ahead? He takes this apparently miraculous accession of strength at its face value. And many an overworked business and professional man, as well as a harried common laborer, has traveled John Barleycorn's death-road because of this mistake.

XXXIII

I WENT to Australia to go into hospital and get tinkered up, after which I planned to go on with the voyage. And during the long weeks I lay in hospital, from the first day I never missed alcohol. I never thought about it. I knew I should have it again when I was on my feet. But when I regained my feet I was not cured of my major afflictions. Naaman's silvery skin was still mine. The mysterious sun-sickness, which the experts of Australia could not fathom, still ripped and tore my tissues. Malaria still festered in me and put me on my back in shivering delirium at the most unexpected moments, among other things compelling me to cancel a double lecture tour which had been arranged.

So I abandoned the *Snark* voyage and sought a cooler climate. The day I came out of hospital I took up drinking again as a matter of course. I drank wine at meals. I drank cocktails before meals. I drank Scotch highballs when anybody I chanced to be with was drinking them. I was so thoroughly the master of John Barleycorn, I could take up with him or let go of him whenever I pleased, just as I had done all my life.

After a time, for cooler climate, I went down to southernmost Tasmania in forty-three South. And I found myself in a place where there was nothing to drink. It didn't mean anything. I didn't drink. It was no hardship. I soaked in the cool air, rode horseback, and did my thousand words a day save when the fever shock came in the morning.

And for fear that the idea may still lurk in some minds that my preceding years of drinking were the cause of my disabilities, I here point out that my Japanese cabin-boy, Nakata, still with me, was rotten with fever, as was Charmian, who in addition was in the slough of a tropical neurasthenia that required several years of temperate climate to cure, and that neither she nor Nakata drank or ever had drunk.

When I returned to Hobart Town, where drink was obtainable, I drank as of old. The same when I arrived back in Australia. On the contrary, when I sailed from Australia on a tramp steamer commanded by an abstemious captain, I took no drink along, and had no drink for the forty-three days' passage. Arrived in Ecuador, squarely under the equatorial sun, where the humans were dying of yellow fever, smallpox, and the plague, I promptly drank again—every drink of every sort that had a kick in it. I caught none of these diseases. Neither did Charmian nor Nataka, who did not drink.

Enamored of the tropics, despite the damage done me, I stopped in various places, and was a long while getting back to the splendid, temperate climate of California. I did my thousand words a day, traveling or stopping over, suffered my last faint fever shock, saw my silvery skin vanish and my sun-torn tissues healthily knit again, and drank as a broad-shouldered, chesty man may drink.

XXXIV

BACK on the ranch, in the Valley of the Moon, I resumed my steady drinking. My program was no drink in the morning; first drink-time came with the completion of my thousand words. Then, between that and the midday meal, were drinks numerous enough to develop a pleasant jingle. Again, in the hour preceding the evening meal, I developed another pleasant jingle. Nobody ever saw me drunk, for the simple reason that I never was drunk. But I did get a jingle twice each day; and the amount of alcohol I consumed every day, if loosed in the system of one unaccustomed to drink, would have put such a one on his back and out.

It was the old proposition. The more I drank, the more I was compelled to drink in order to get an effect. The time came when cocktails were inadequate. I had neither the time in which to drink them nor the space to accommodate them. Whisky had a more powerful jolt. It gave quicker action with less quantity. Bourbon or rye, or cunningly aged blends, constituted the pre-midday drinking. In the late afternoon it was Scotch and soda.

My sleep, always excellent, now became not quite so excellent. I had been accustomed to read myself back to sleep when I chanced to awake. But now this began to fail me. When I had read two or three of the small hours away and was as wide awake as ever, I found that a drink furnished the soporific effect. Sometimes two or three drinks were required.

So short a period of sleep then intervened before early morning rising, that my system did not have time to work off the alcohol. As a result I awoke with mouth parched and dry, with a slight heaviness of head, and with a mild nervous palpitation in the stomach. In fact I did not feel good. I was suffering from the morning sickness of the steady, heavy drinker. What I needed was a pick-me-up, a bracer. Trust John Barleycorn, once he has broken down a man's defenses! So it was a drink before breakfast to put me right for breakfast—the old poison of the snake that has bitten one! Another custom, begun at this time, was that of the pitcher of water by the bed-side to furnish relief to my scorched and sizzling membranes.

I achieved a condition in which my body was never free from alcohol. Nor did I permit myself to be away from alcohol. If I traveled to out-of-the-way places, I declined to run the risk of finding them dry. I took a quart, or several quarts, along in my grip. In the past I had been amazed by other men guilty of this practice. Now I did it myself unblushingly. And when I got out with the fellows, I cast all rules by the board. I drank when they drank, what they drank, and in the same way they drank.

I was carrying a beautiful alcoholic conflagration around with me. The thing fed on its own heat and flamed the fiercer. There was no time, in all my waking time, that I didn't want a drink. I began to anticipate the completion of my daily thousand words by taking a drink when only five hundred words were written. It was not long until I prefaced the beginning of the thousand words with a drink.

The gravity of this I realized too well. I made new rules. Resolutely I would refrain from drinking until my work was done. But a new and most diabolical complication arose. The work refused to be done without drinking. It just couldn't be done. I had to drink in order to do it. I was beginning to fight now. I had the craving at last, and it was mastering me. I would sit at my desk and dally with pad and pen, but words refused to flow. My brain could not think the proper thoughts because continually it was obsessed with the one thought that across the room in the liquor cabinet stood John Barleycorn. When, in despair, I took my drink, at once my brain loosened up and began to roll off the thousand words.

In my town house, in Oakland, I finished the stock of liquor and wilfully refused to purchase more. It was no use, because, unfortunately, there remained in the bottom of the liquor cabinet a case of beer. In vain I tried to write. Now beer is a poor substitute for strong waters; besides, I didn't like beer; yet all I could think of was that beer so singularly accessible in the bottom of the cabinet. Not until I had drunk a pint of it did the words begin to reel off, and the thousand were reeled off to the tune of numerous pints. The worst of it was that the beer caused me severe heart-burn; but despite the discomfort I soon finished the case.

The liquor cabinet was now bare. I did not replenish it. By truly heroic perseverance, I finally forced myself to write the daily thousand words without the spur of John Barleycorn. But all the time I wrote I was keenly aware of the craving for a drink. And as soon as the morning's work was done, I was out of the house and away down-town to get my first drink. Merciful goodness!—if John Barleycorn could get such sway over me, a non-alcoholic, what must be the sufferings of the true alcoholic, battling against the organic demands of his chemistry while those closest to him sympathize little, understand less, and despise and deride him!

XXXV

BUT the freight has to be paid. John Barleycorn began to collect, and he collected not so much from the body as from the mind. The old long sickness, which had been purely an intellectual sickness, recrudesced. The old ghosts, long laid, lifted their heads again. But they were different and more deadly ghosts. The old ghosts, intellectual in their inception, had been laid by a sane and normal logic. But now they were raised by the White Logic of John Barleycorn, and John Barleycorn never lays the ghosts of his raising. For this sickness of pessimism, caused by drink, one must drink further in quest of the anodyne that John Barleycorn promises but never delivers.

How to describe this White Logic to those who have never experienced it? It is perhaps better first to state how impossible such a description is. Take Hasheesh Land, for instance, the land of enormous extensions of time and space. In past years I have made two memorable journeys into that far land. My adventures there are seared in sharpest detail on my brain. Yet I have tried vainly, with endless words, to describe any tiny particular phase to persons who have not traveled there.

I use all the hyperbole of metaphor, and tell what centuries of time and profounds of unthinkable agony and horror can obtain in each interval of all the intervals between the notes of a quick jig played quickly on the piano. I talk for an hour, elaborating that one phase of Hasheesh Land, and at the end I have told them nothing. And when I cannot tell them this one thing of all the vastness of terrible and wonderful things, I know I have failed to give them the slightest concept of Hasheesh Land.

But, let me talk with some other traveler in that weird region, and at once am I understood. A phrase, a word, conveys instantly to his mind what hours of words and phrases could not convey to the mind of the non-traveler. So it is with John Barleycorn's realm where the White Logic reigns. To those untraveled there, the traveler's account must always seem unintelligible and fantastic. At the best, I may only beg of the untraveled ones to strive to take on faith the narrative I shall relate.

For there are fatal intuitions of truth that reside in alcohol. Philip sober vouches for Philip drunk in this matter. There seem to be various orders of truth in this world. Some sorts of truth are truer than others. Some sorts of truth are lies, and these sorts are the very ones that have the greatest use-value to life that desires to realize and live. At once, O untraveled reader, you see how lunatic and blasphemous is the realm I am trying to describe to you in the language of John Barleycorn's tribe. It is not the language of your tribe, all of whose members resolutely shun the roads that lead to death and tread only the roads that lead to life. For there are roads and roads, and of truth there are orders and orders. But have patience. At least, through what seems no more than verbal yammerings, you may, perchance, glimpse faint far vistas of other lands and tribes.

Alcohol tells truth, but its truth is not normal. What is normal is healthful. What is healthful tends toward life. Normal truth is a different order, and a lesser order, of truth. Take a dray horse. Through all the vicissitudes of its life, from first to last, somehow, in unguessably dim ways, it must believe that life is good; that the drudgery in harness is good; that death, no matter how blind-instinctively apprehended, is a dread giant; that life is beneficent and worth-while; that, in the end, with fading life, it will not be knocked about and beaten and urged beyond its sprained and spavined best; that old age, even, is decent, dignified, and valuable, though old age means a ribby scarecrow in a hawker's cart, stumbling a step to every blow, stumbling dizzily on through merciless servitude and slow disintegration to the end—the end, the apportionment of its parts (of its subtle flesh, its pink and springy bone, its juices and ferments, and all the sensateness that informed it), to the chicken farm, the hide-house, the glue-rendering works, and the bone-meal fertilizer factory. To the last stumble of its stumbling end this dray horse must abide by the mandates of the lesser truth that is the truth of life and that makes life possible to persist.

This dray horse, like all other horses, like all other animals including man, is life-blinded and sense-struck. It will live, no matter what the price. The game of life is good, though all of life may be hurt, and though all lives lose the game in the end. This is the order of truth that obtains, not for the universe, but for the live things in it if they for a little space will endure ere they pass. This order of truth, no matter how erroneous it may be, is the sane and normal order of truth, the rational order of truth that life must believe in order to live.

To man, alone among the animals, has been given the awful privilege of reason. Man, with his brain, can penetrate the intoxicating show of things and look upon a universe brazen with indifference toward him and his dreams. He can do this, but it is not well for him to do it. To live, and live abundantly, to sting with life, to be alive (which is to be what he is), it is good that man be life-blinded and sense-struck. What is good is true. And this is the order of truth, lesser though it be, that man must know and guide his actions by, with unswerving certitude that it is absolute truth and that in the universe no other order of truth can obtain. It is good that man should accept at face value the cheats of sense and snares of flesh, and through the fogs of sentiency pursue the lures and lies of passion. It is good that he shall see neither shadows nor futilities, nor be appalled by his lusts and rapacities.

And man does this. Countless men have glimpsed that other and truer order of truth and recoiled from it. Countless men have passed through the long sickness and lived to tell of it and deliberately to forget it to the end of their days. They lived. They realized life, for life is what they were. They did right.

And now comes John Barleycorn with the curse he lays upon the imaginative man who is lusty with life and desire to live. John Barleycorn sends his White Logic, the argent messenger of truth beyond truth, the antithesis of life, cruel and bleak as interstellar space, pulseless and frozen as absolute zero, dazzling with the frost of irrefragable logic and unforgettable fact. John Barleycorn will not let the dreamer dream, the liver live. He destroys birth and death, and dissipates to mist the paradox of being, until his victim cries out, as in "The City of Dreadful Night" : "Our life's a cheat, our death a black abyss." And the feet of the victim of such dreadful intimacy take hold of the way of death.

XXXVI

Back to personal experiences and the effects in the past of John Barleycorn's White Logic on me. On my lovely ranch in the Valley of the Moon, brain-soaked with many months of alcohol, I am oppressed by the cosmic sadness that has always been the heritage of man. In vain do I ask myself why I should be sad. My nights are warm. My roof does not leak. I have food galore for all the caprices of appetite. Every creature-comfort is mine. In my body are no aches nor pains. The good old flesh-machine is running smoothly on. Neither brain nor muscle is overworked. I have land, money, power, recognition from the world, a consciousness that I do my meed of good in serving others, a mate whom I love, children that are of my own fond flesh. I have done, and am doing, what a good citizen of the world should do. I have built houses, many houses, and tilled many a hundred acres. And as for trees, have I not planted a hundred thousand? Everywhere, from any window of my house, I can gaze forth upon these trees of my planting, standing valiantly erect and aspiring toward the sun.

My life has indeed fallen in pleasant places. Not a hundred men in a million have been so lucky as I. Yet, with all this vast good fortune, am I sad. And I am sad because John Barleycorn is with me. And John Barleycorn is with me because I was born in what future ages will call the dark ages before the ages of rational civilization. John Barleycorn is with me because in all the unwitting days of my youth John Barleycorn was accessible, calling to me and inviting me on every corner and on every street between the corners. The pseudocivilization into which I was born permitted everywhere licensed shops for the sale of soul-poison. The system of life was so organized that I (and millions like me) was lured and drawn and driven to the poison shops.

Wander with me through one mood of the myriad of moods of sadness into which one is plunged by John Barleycorn. I ride out over my beautiful ranch. Between my legs is a beautiful horse. The air is wine. The grapes on a score of rolling hills are red with autumn flame. Across Sonoma Mountain wisps of sea fog are stealing. The afternoon sun smoulders in the drowsy sky. I have everything to make me glad I am alive. I am filled with dreams and mysteries. I am all sun and air and sparkle. I am vitalized, organic. I move, I have the power of movement, I command movement of the live thing I bestride. I am possessed with the pomps of being, and know proud passions and inspirations. I have ten thousand august connotations. I am a king in the kingdom of sense, and trample the face of the uncomplaining dust. . . .

And yet, with jaundiced eye I gaze upon all the beauty and wonder about me, and with jaundiced brain consider the pitiful figure I cut in this world that endured so long without me and that will again endure without me. I remember the men who broke their hearts and their backs over this stubborn soil that now belongs to me. As if anything imperishable could belong to the perishable! These men passed. I, too, shall pass. These men toiled, and cleared, and planted, gazed with aching eyes, while they rested their labor-stiffened bodies, on these same sunrises and sunsets, at the autumn glory of the grape, and at the fog-wisps stealing across the mountain. And they are gone. And I know that I, too, shall some day, and soon, be gone.

Gone? I am going now. In my jaw are cunning artifices of the dentists which replace the parts of me already gone. Never again will I have the thumbs of my youth. Old fights and wrestlings have injured them irreparably. That punch on the head of a man whose very name is forgotten, settled this thumb finally and forever. A slip-grip at catch-as-catch-can did for the other. My lean runner's stomach has passed into the limbo of memory. The joints of the legs that bear me up are not so adequate as they once were, when, in wild nights and days of toil and frolic, I strained and snapped and ruptured them. Never again can I swing dizzily aloft and trust all the proud quick that is I to a single rope-clutch in the driving blackness of storm. Never again can I run with the sled-dogs along the endless miles of Arctic trail.

I am aware that within this disintegrating body which has been dying since I was born I carry a skeleton; that under the rind of flesh which is called my face is a bony, noseless death's head. All of which does not shudder me. To be afraid is to be healthy. Fear of death makes for life. But the curse of the White Logic is that it does not make one afraid. The world-sickness of the White Logic makes one grin jocosely into the face of the Noseless One and to sneer at all the phantasmagoria of living.

I look about me as I ride, and on every hand I see the merciless and infinite waste of natural selection. The White Logic insists upon opening the long-closed books, and by paragraph and chapter states the beauty and wonder I behold in terms of futility and dust. About me is murmur and hum, and I know it for the gnat-swarm of the living, piping for a little space its thin plaint of troubled air.

I return across the ranch. Twilight is on, and the hunting-animals are out. I watch the piteous tragic play of life feeding on life. Here is no morality. Only in man is morality, and man created it—a code of action that makes toward living and that is of the lesser order of truth. Yet all this I knew before, in the weary days of my long sickness. These were the greater truths that I so successfully schooled myself to forget; the truths that were so serious that I refused to take them seriously, and played with gently, O so gently, as sleeping dogs at the back of consciousness which I did not care to waken. I did but stir them, and let them lie. I was too wise, too wicked wise, to wake them. But now White Logic willy nilly wakes them for me, for White Logic, most valiant, is unafraid of all the monsters of the earthly dream.

"Let the doctors of all the schools condemn me," White Logic whispers as I ride along. "What of it? I am truth. You know it. You cannot combat me. They say I make for death. What of it? It is truth. Life lies in order to live. Life is a perpetual lie-telling process. Life is a mad dance in the domain of flux, wherein appearances in mighty tides ebb and flow, chained to the wheels of moons beyond our ken. Appearances are ghosts. Life is ghost land, where appearances change, transfuse, permeate each the other and all the others, that are, that are not, that always flicker, fade, and pass, only to come again as new appearances, as other appearances. You are such an appearance, composed of countless appearances out of the past. All an appearance can know is mirage. You know mirages of desire. These very mirages are the unthinkable and incalculable congeries of appearances that crowd in upon you and form you out of the past, and that sweep you on to dissemination into other unthinkable and incalculable congeries of appearances to people the ghost land of the future. Life is apparitional, and passes. You are an apparition. Through all the apparitions that preceded you and that compose the parts of you, you rose gibbering from the evolutionary mire, and gibbering you will pass on, interfusing, permeating the procession of apparitions that will succeed you."

And of course it is all unanswerable, and as I ride along through the evening shadows I sneer at that Great Fetish which Comte called the world. And I remember what another pessimist of sentiency has uttered: "Transient are all. They, being born, must die; and, being dead, are glad to be at rest."

But here through the dusk comes one who is not glad to be at rest. He is a workman on the ranch, an old man, an immigrant Italian. He takes his hat off to me in all servility, because, forsooth, I am to him a lord of life. I am food to him, and shelter, and existence. He has toiled like a beast all his days, and lived less comfortably than my horses in their deep-strawed stalls. He is labor-crippled. He shambles as he walks. One shoulder is twisted higher than the other. His hands are gnarled claws, repulsive, horrible. As an apparition he is a pretty miserable specimen. His brain is as stupid as his body is ugly.

"His brain is so stupid that he does not know he is an apparition," the White Logic chuckles to me. "He is sense-drunk. He is the slave of the dream of life. His brain is filled with superrational sanctions and obsessions. He believes in a transcendent overworld. He has listened to the vagaries of the prophets, who have blown for him the sumptuous bubble of Paradise. He feels inarticulate affinities with self-conjured non-realities. He sees penumbral visions of himself titubating fantastically through days and nights of space and stars. Beyond the shadow of any doubt he is convinced that the universe was made for him, and that it is his destiny to live forever in the immaterial and supersensuous realms he and his kind have builded of the stuff of semblance and deception.

"But you, who have opened the books and who share my awful confidence—you know him for what he is, brother to you and the dust, a cosmic joke, a sport of chemistry, a garmented beast that arose out of the ruck of screaming beastliness by virtue and accident of two opposable great toes. He is brother as well to the gorilla and the chimpanzee. He thumps his chest in anger, and roars and quivers with cataleptic ferocity. He knows monstrous, atavistic promptings, and he is composed of all manner of shreds of abysmal and forgotten instincts."

"Yet he dreams he is immortal," I argue feebly. "It is vastly wonderful for so stupid a clod to bestride the shoulders of time and ride the eternities."

"Pah!" is the retort. "Would you then shut the books and exchange places with this thing that is only an appetite and a desire, a marionette of the belly and the loins?"

"To be stupid is to be happy," I contend.

"Then your ideal of happiness is a jelly-like organism floating in a tideless, tepid, twilight sea, eh?"

—Oh, the victim cannot combat John Barleycorn!

"One step removed from the annihilating bliss of Buddha's Nirvana," the White Logic adds. "Oh, well, here's the house. Cheer up and take a drink. We know, we illuminated, you and I, all the folly and the farce."

And in my book-walled den, the mausoleum of the thoughts of men, I take my drink, and other drinks, and roust out the sleeping dogs from the recesses of my brain and halloo them on over the walls of prejudice and law and through all the cunning labyrinths of superstition and belief.

"Drink," says the White Logic. "The Greeks believed that the gods gave them wine so that they might forget the miserableness of existence. And remember what Heine said."

Well do I remember that flaming Jew's "With the last breath all is done: joy, love, sorrow, macaroni, the theater, lime-trees, raspberry drops, the power of human relations, gossip, the barking of dogs, champagne."

"Your clear white light is sickness," I tell the White Logic. "You lie."

"By telling too strong a truth," he quips back.

"Alas, yes, so topsyturvy is existence," I acknowledge sadly.

"Ah, well, Liu Ling was wiser than you," the White Logic girds. "You remember him?"

I nod my head—Liu Ling, a hard drinker, one of the group of bibulous poets who called themselves the Seven Sages of the Bamboo Grove and who lived in China many an ancient century ago.

"It was Liu Ling," prompts the White Logic, "who declared that to a drunken man the affairs of this world appear but as so much duckweed on a river. Very well. Have another Scotch, and let semblance and deception become duckweed on a river."

And while I pour and sip my Scotch, I remember another Chinese philosopher, Chuang Tzu, who, four centuries before Christ, challenged this dreamland of the world, saying: "How then do I know but that the dead repent of having previously clung to life? Those who dream of the banquet, wake to lamentation and sorrow. Those who dream of lamentation and sorrow, wake to join the hunt. While they dream, they do not know that they dream. Some will even interpret the very dream they are dreaming; and only when they awake do they know it was a dream. . . . Fools think they are awake now, and flatter themselves they know if they are really princes or peasants. Confucius and you are both dreams; and I who say you are dreams—I am but a dream myself.

"Once upon a time, I, Chuang Tzu, dreamt I was a butterfly, fluttering hither and thither, to all intents and purposes a butterfly. I was conscious only of following my fancies as a butterfly, and was unconscious of my individuality as a man. Suddenly, I awaked, and there I lay, myself again. Now I do not know whether I was then a man dreaming I was a butterfly, or whether I am now a butterfly dreaming I am a man."

XXXVII

"Come," says the White Logic, "and forget these Asian dreamers of old time. Fill your glass and let us look at the parchments of the dreamers of yesterday who dreamed their dreams on your own warm hills."

I pore over the abstract of title of the vineyard called Tokay on the rancho called Petaluma. It is a sad long list of the names of men, beginning with Manuel Micheltoreno, one time Mexican "Governor, Commander-in-Chief, and Inspector of the Department of the Californias," who deeded ten square leagues of stolen Indian land to Colonel Don Mariano Guadalupe Vallejo for services rendered his country and for moneys paid by him for ten years to his soldiers.

Immediately this musty record of man's land-lust assumes the formidableness of a battle—the quick struggling with the dust. There are deeds of trust, mortgages, certificates of release, transfers, judgments, foreclosures, writs of attachment, orders of sale, tax liens, petitions for letters of administration, and decrees of distribution. It is like a monster ever unsubdued, this stubborn land that drowses in this Indian summer weather and that survives them all, the men who scratched its surface and passed.

Who was this James King of William, so curiously named? The oldest surviving settler in the Valley of the Moon knows him not. Yet only sixty years ago he loaned Mariano G. Vallejo eighteen thousand dollars on security of certain lands including the vineyard yet to be and to be called Tokay. Whence came Peter O'Connor, and whither vanished, after writing his little name of a day on the woodland that was to become a vineyard? Appears Louis Csomortanyi, a name to conjure with. He lasts through several pages of this record of the enduring soil.

Comes old American stock, thirsting across the Great American Desert, mule-backing across the Isthmus, windjamming around the Horn, to write brief and forgotten names where ten thousand generations of wild Indians are equally forgotten—names like Halleck, Hastings, Swett, Tait, Denman, Tracy, Grimwood, Carlton, Temple. There are no names like those to-day in the Valley of the Moon.

The names begin to appear fast and furiously, flashing from legal page to legal page and in a flash vanishing. But ever the persistent soil remains for others to scrawl themselves across. Come the names of men of whom I have vaguely heard but whom I have never known. Kohler and Frohling—who built the great stone winery on the vineyard called Tokay, but who built upon a hill up which other vinyardists refused to haul their grapes. So Kohler and Frohling lost the land; the earthquake of 1906 threw down the winery; and I now live in its ruins.

La Motte—he broke the soil, planted vines and orchards, instituted commercial fish-culture, built a mansion renowned in its day, was defeated by the soil, and passed. And my name of a day appears. On the site of his orchards and vineyards, of his proud mansion, of his very fish ponds, I have scrawled myself with a hundred thousand eucalyptus trees.

Cooper and Greenlaw—on what is called the Hill Ranch they left two of their dead, "Little Lillie" and "Little David," who rest to-day inside a tiny square of hand-hewn palings. Also, Cooper and Greenlaw in their time cleared the virgin forest from three fields of forty acres. To-day I have those three fields sown with Canada peas, and in the spring they shall be plowed under for green manure.

Haska—a dim legendary figure of a generation ago, who went back up the mountain and cleared six acres of brush in the tiny valley that took his name. He broke the soil, reared stone walls and a house, and planted apple trees. And already the site of the house is undiscoverable, the location of the stone walls may be deduced from the configuration of the landscape, and I am renewing the battle, putting in Angora goats to browse away the brush that has overrun Haska's clearing and choked Haska's apple trees to death. So I, too, scratch the land with my brief endeavor and flash my name across a page of legal script ere I pass and the page grows musty.

"Dreamers and ghosts," the White Logic chuckles.

"But surely the striving was not altogether vain," I contend.

"It was based on illusion and is a lie."

"A vital lie," I retort.

"And pray what is a vital lie but a lie?" the White Logic challenges. "Come. Fill your glass and let us examine these vital liars who crowd your bookshelves. Let us dabble in William James a bit."

"A man of health," I say. "From him we may expect no philosopher's stone, but at least we shall find a few robust tonic things to which to tie."

"Rationality gelded to sentiment," the White Logic grins. "At the end of all his thinking he still clung to the sentiment of immortality. Facts transmuted in the alembic of hope into terms of faith. The ripest fruit of reason the stultification of reason. From the topmost peak of reason James teaches to cease reasoning and to have faith that all is well and will be well—the old, oh, ancient old, acrobatic flip of the metaphysicians whereby they reasoned reason quite away in order to escape the pessimism consequent upon the grim and honest exercise of reason.

"Is this flesh of yours you? Or is it an extraneous something possessed by you? Your body—what is it? A machine for converting stimuli into reactions. Stimuli and reactions are remembered. They constitute experience. Then you are in your consciousness these experiences. You are at any moment what you are thinking at that moment. Your I is both subject and object; it predicates things of itself and is the things predicated. The thinker is the thought, the knower is what is known, the possessor is the things possessed.

"After all, as you know well, man is a flux of states of consciousness, a flow of passing thoughts, each thought of self another self, a myriad thoughts, a myriad selves, a continual becoming but never being, a will-of-the-wisp flitting of ghosts in ghostland. But this, man will not accept of himself. He refuses to accept his own passing. He will not pass. He will live again if he has to die to do it.

"He shuffles atoms and jets of light, remotest nebulae, drips of water, prick-points of sensation, slime-oozings and cosmic bulks, all mixed with pearls of faith, love of woman, imagined dignities, frightened surmises, and pompous arrogances, and of the stuff builds himself an immortality to startle the heavens and baffle the immensities. He squirms on his dunghill, and like a child lost in the dark among goblins, calls to the gods that he is their younger brother, a prisoner of the quick that is destined to be as free as they—monuments of egotism reared by the epiphenomena; dreams and the dust of dreams, that vanish when the dreamer vanishes and are no more when he is not.

"It is nothing new, these vital lies men tell themselves, muttering and mumbling them like charms and incantations against the powers of Night. The voodoos and medicine men and the devil-devil doctors were the fathers of metaphysics. Night and the Noseless One were ogres that beset the way of light and life. And the metaphysicians would win by if they had to tell lies to do it. They were vexed by the brazen law of the Ecclesiast that men die like the beasts of the field and their end is the same. Their creeds were their schemes, their religions their nostrums, their philosophies their devices, by which they half-believed they would outwit the Noseless One and the Night.

"Bog-lights, vapors of mysticism, psychic overtones, soul orgies, wailings among the shadows, weird gnosticisms, veils and tissues of words, gibbering subjectivisms, gropings and maunderings, ontological fantasies, pan-psychic hallucinations—this is the stuff, the phantasms of hope, that fills your book shelves. Look at them, all the sad wraiths of sad mad men and passionate rebels—your Schopenhauers, your Strindbergs, your Tolstois and Nietzsches.

"Come. Your glass is empty. Fill and forget."

I obey, for my brain is now well a-crawl with the maggots of alcohol, and as I drink to the sad thinkers on my shelves I quote Richard Hovey:

"Abstain not! Life and Love, like night and day,
Offer themselves to us on their own terms,
Not ours. Accept their bounty while ye may,
Before we be accepted by the worms."

"I will cap you," cries the White Logic.

"No," I answer, while the maggots madden me. "I know you for what you are, and I am unafraid. Under your mask of hedonism you are yourself the Noseless One and your way leads to the Night. Hedonism has no meaning. It, too, is a lie, at best the coward's smug compromise—"

"Now will I cap you!" the White Logic breaks in.

"But if you would not this poor life fulfil,
Lo, you are free to end it when you will,
Without the fear of waking after death."

And I laugh my defiance; for now, and for the moment, I know the White Logic to be the arch-impostor of them all, whispering his whispers of death. And he is guilty of his own unmasking, with his own genial chemistry turning the tables on himself, with his own maggots biting alive the old illusions, resurrecting and making to sound again the old voice from beyond of my youth, telling me again that still are mine the possibilities and powers which life and the books had taught me did not exist.

And the dinner-gong sounds to the reversed bottom of my glass. Jeering at the White Logic, I go out to join my guests at table, and with assumed seriousness to discuss the current magazines and the silly doings of the world's day, whipping every trick and ruse of controversy through all the paces of paradox and persiflage. And, when the whim changes, it is most easy and delightfully disconcerting to play with the respectable and cowardly bourgeois fetishes and to laugh and epigram at the flitting god-ghosts and the debaucheries and follies of wisdom.

The clown's the thing! The clown! If one must be a philosopher, let him be Aristophanes. And no one at the table thinks I am jingled. I am in fine fettle, that is all. I tire of the labor of thinking, and, when the table is finished, start practical jokes and set all playing at games, which we carry on with bucolic boisterousness.

And when the evening is over and good night said, I go back through my book-walled den to my sleeping porch and to myself and to the White Logic which, undefeated, has never left me. And as I fall to fuddled sleep I hear Youth crying, as Harry Kemp heard it:

"I heard Youth calling in the night:
'Gone is my former world-delight;
For there is naught my feet may stay;
The morn suffuses into day,
It dare not stand a moment still
But must the world with light fulfil.
More evanescent than the rose
My sudden rainbow comes and goes
Plunging bright ends across the sky—
Yea, I am Youth because I die!' "

XXXVIII

THE foregoing is a sample roaming with the White Logic through the dusk of my soul. To the best of my power I have striven to give the reader a glimpse of a man's secret dwelling when it is shared with John Barleycorn. And the reader must remember that this mood, which he has read in a quarter of an hour, is but one mood of the myriad moods of John Barleycorn, and that the procession of such moods may well last the clock around through many a day and week and month.

My alcoholic reminiscences draw to a close. I can say, as any strong, chesty drinker can say, that all that leaves me alive to-day on the planet is my unmerited luck—the luck of chest, and shoulders, and constitution. I dare to say that a not large percentage of youths, in the formative stage of fifteen to seventeen, could have survived the stress of heavy drinking that I survived between my fifteenth and seventeenth years; that a not large percentage of men could have punished the alcohol I have punished in my manhood years and lived to tell the tale. I survived, through no personal virtue, but because I did not have the chemistry of a dipsomaniac and because I possessed an organism unusually resistant to the ravages of John Barleycorn. And, surviving, I have watched the others die, not so lucky, down all the long sad road.

It was my unmitigated and absolute good fortune, good luck, chance, call it what you will, that brought me through the fires of John Barleycorn. My life, my career, my joy in living, have not been destroyed. They have been scorched, it is true; but, like the survivors of forlorn hopes, they have by unthinkably miraculous ways come through the fight to marvel at the tally of the slain.

And like such a survivor of old red War who cries out, "Let there be no more war!" so I cry out, "Let there be no more poison-fighting by our youths!" The way to stop war is to stop it. The way to stop drinking is to stop it. The way China stopped the general use of opium was by stopping the cultivation and importation of opium. The philosophers, priests, and doctors of China could have preached themselves breathless against opium for a thousand years, and the use of opium, so long as opium was ever-accessible and obtainable, would have continued unabated. We are so made, that is all. We have with great success made a practice of not leaving arsenic and strychnine, and typhoid and tuberculosis germs, lying around for our children to be destroyed by. Treat John Barleycorn the same way. Stop him. Don't let him lie around, licensed and legal, to pounce upon our youth. Not of alcoholics nor for alcoholics do I write, but for our youths, for those who possess no more than the adventure-stings and the genial predispositions, the social man-impulses, which are twisted all awry by our barbarian civilization which feeds them poison on all the corners. It is the healthy, normal boys, now born or being born, for whom I write.

It was for this reason, more than any other, and more ardently than any other, that I rode down into the Valley of the Moon, all a-jingle, and voted for equal suffrage. I voted that women might vote, because I knew that they, the wives and mothers of the race, would vote John Barleycorn out of existence and back into the historical limbo of our vanished customs of savagery. If I thus seem to cry out as one hurt, please remember that I have been sorely bruised and that I do dislike the thought that any son or daughter of mine or yours should be similarly bruised.

The women are the true conservators of the race. The men are the wastrels, the adventure-lovers and gamblers, and in the end it is by their women that they are saved. About man's first experiment in chemistry was the making of alcohol, and down all the generations to this day man has continued to manufacture and drink it. And there has never been a day when the women have not resented man's use of alcohol, though they have never had the power to give weight to their resentment. The moment women get the vote in any community, the first thing they proceed to do, or try to do, is to close the saloons. In a thousand generations to come men of themselves will not close the saloons. As well expect the morphine victims to legislate the sale of morphine out of existence.

The women know. They have paid an incalculable price of sweat and tears for man's use of alcohol. Ever jealous for the race, they will legislate for the babes of boys yet to be born; and for the babes of girls, too, for they must be the mothers, wives, and sisters of these boys.

And it will be easy. The only ones that will be hurt will be the topers and seasoned drinkers of a single generation. I am one of these, and I make solemn assurance, based upon long traffic with John Barleycorn, that it won't hurt me very much to stop drinking when no one else drinks and when no drink is obtainable. On the other hand, the overwhelming proportion of young men are so normally non-alcoholic, that, never having had access to alcohol, they will never miss it. They will know of the saloon only in the pages of history, and they will think of the saloon as a quaint old custom similar to bullbaiting and the burning of witches.

XXXIX

OF course, no personal tale is complete without bringing the narrative of the person down to the last moment. But mine is no tale of a reformed drunkard. I was never a drunkard, and I have not reformed.

It chanced, some time ago, that I made a voyage of one hundred and forty-eight days in a windjammer around the Horn. I took no private supply of alcohol along, and, though there was no day of those one hundred and forty-eight days that I could not have got a drink from the captain, I did not take a drink. I did not take a drink because I did not desire a drink. No one else drank on board. The atmosphere for drinking was not present, and in my system there was no organic need for alcohol. My chemistry did not demand alcohol.

So there arose before me a problem, a clear and simple problem: *This is so easy, why not keep it up when you get back on land?* I weighed this problem carefully. I weighed it for five months, in a state of absolute non-contact with alcohol. And out of the data of past experience, I reached certain conclusions.

In the first place, I am convinced that not one man in ten thousand, or in a hundred thousand, is a genuine, chemical dipsomaniac. Drinking, as I deem it, is practically entirely a habit of mind. It is unlike tobacco, or cocaine, or morphine, or all the rest of the long list of drugs. The desire for alcohol is quite peculiarly mental in its origin. It is a matter of mental training and growth, and it is cultivated in social soil. Not one drinker in a million began drinking alone. All drinkers begin socially, and this drinking is accompanied by a thousand social connotations such as I have described out of my own experience in the first part of this narrative. These social connotations are the stuff of which the drink habit is largely composed. The part that alcohol itself plays is inconsiderable, when compared with the part played by the social atmosphere in which it is drunk. The human is rarely born these days, who, without long training in the social relations of drinking, feels the irresistible chemical propulsion of his system toward alcohol. I do assume that such rare individuals are born, but I have never encountered one.

On this long, five-months' voyage, I found that among all my bodily needs not the slightest shred of a bodily need for alcohol existed. But this I did find: my need was mental and social. When I thought of alcohol, the connotation was fellowship. When I thought of fellowship, the connotation was alcohol. Fellowship and alcohol were Siamese twins. They always occurred linked together.

Thus, when reading in my deck-chair or when talking with others, practically any mention of any part of the world I knew instantly aroused the connotation of drinking and good fellows. Big nights and days and moments, all purple passages and freedoms, thronged my memory. "Venice" stares at me from the printed page, and I remember the café tables on the sidewalks. "The Battle of Santiago," some one says, and I answer, "Yes, I've been over the ground." But I do not see the ground, nor Kettle Hill, nor the Peace Tree. What I see is the Café Venus, on the plaza of Santiago, where one hot night I talked long and drank deep with a dying consumptive.

The East End of London, I read, or some one says; and first of all, under my eyelids, leap the visions of the shining pubs, and in my ears echo the calls for "two of bitter" and "three of Scotch." The Latin Quarter—at once I am in the student cabarets, bright faces and keen spirits around me, sipping cool, well-dripped absinthe while our voices mount and soar in Latin fashion as we settle God and art and democracy and the rest of the simple problems of existence.

In a pampero off the River Plate, we speculate, if we are disabled, of running in to Buenos Ayres, the "Paris of America," and I have visions of bright congregating-places of men, of the jollity of raised glasses, and of song and cheer and the hum of genial voices. When we have picked up the Northeast Trades in the Pacific, we try to persuade our dying captain to run for Honolulu, and while I persuade I see myself again drinking cocktails on the cool *lanais,* and fizzes out at Waikiki where the surf rolls in. Some one mentions the way wild ducks are cooked in the restaurants of San Francisco, and at once I am transported to the light and clatter of many tables, where I gaze at old friends across the golden brims of long-stemmed Rhine-wine glasses.

And so I pondered my problem. I should not care to revisit all these fair places of the world except in the fashion I visited them before. *Glass in hand!* There is a magic in the phrase. It means more than all the words in the dictionary can be made to mean. It is a habit of mind to which I have been trained all my life. It is now part of the stuff that composes me. I like the bubbling play of wit, the chesty laughs, the resonant voices of men, when, glass in hand, they shut the gray world outside and prod their brains with the fun and folly of an accelerated pulse.

No, I decided; I shall take my drink on occasion. With all the books on my shelves, with all the thoughts of the thinkers shaded by my particular temperament, I decided coolly and deliberately that I should continue to do what I had been trained to want to do. I would drink—but, oh, more skilfully, more discreetly, than ever before. Never again would I be a peripatetic conflagration. Never again would I invoke the White Logic. I had learned how not to invoke him.

The White Logic now lies decently buried alongside the Long Sickness. Neither will afflict me again. It is many a year since I laid the Long Sickness away; his sleep is sound. And just as sound is the sleep of the White Logic. And yet, in conclusion, I can well say that I wish my forefathers had banished John Barleycorn before my time. I regret that John Barleycorn flourished everywhere in the system of society in which I was born, else I should not have made his acquaintance, and I was long trained in his acquaintance.

London on London

Long before Jack Kerouac or Woody Guthrie, London went out on the road seeking new experiences, trying to find his place in the world. The following piece on "Kelly's Army," two thousand tramps marching across the country, is perhaps the first work in American literature dealing with the "hobo" and this lifestyle. It is also a devastating work of social criticism, heartfelt and biting, the result of London's newly found political and social awareness. The accompanying article, "Holding Her Down," is literally a how-to manual on train hopping.

The Tramp

Perhaps the greatest charm of tramp-life is the absence of monotony. In Hobo Land the face of life is protean—an ever changing phantasmagoria, where the impossible happens and the unexpected jumps out of the bushes at every turn of the road. The hobo never knows what is going to happen the next moment; hence, he lives only in the present moment. He has learned the futility of telic endeavor, and knows the delight of drifting along with the whimsicalities of Chance.

Often I think over my tramp days, and ever I marvel at the swift succession of pictures that flash up in my memory. It matters not where I begin to think; any day of all the days is a day apart, with a record of swift-moving pictures all its own . . .

TWO THOUSAND STIFFS

A "stiff" is a tramp. It was once my fortune to travel a few weeks with a "push" that numbered two thousand. This was known as "Kelly's Army." Across the wild and woolly West, clear from California, General Kelly and his heroes had captured trains; but they fell down when they crossed the Missouri and went up against the effete East. The East hadn't the slightest intention of giving free transportation to two thousand hoboes. Kelly's Army lay helplessly for some time at Council Bluffs. The day I joined it, made desperate by delay, it marched out to capture a train.

It was quite an imposing sight. General Kelly sat a magnificent black charger, and with waving banners, to the martial music of fife and drum corps, company by company, in two divisions, his two thousand stiffs countermarched before him and hit the wagon-road to the little burg of Weston, seven miles away. Being the latest recruit, I was in the last company, of the last regiment, of the Second Division, and, furthermore, in the last rank of the rear-guard. The army went into camp at Weston beside the railroad track—beside the tracks, rather, for two roads went through: the Chicago, Milwaukee, and St. Paul, and the Rock Island.

Our intention was to take the first train out, but the railroad officials "coppered" our play—and won. There was no first train. They tied up the two lines and stopped running trains. In the meantime, while we lay by the dead tracks, the good people of

Omaha and Council Bluffs were bestirring themselves. Preparations were making to form a mob, capture a train in Council Bluffs, run it down to us, and make us a present of it. The railroad officials coppered that play, too. They didn't wait for the mob. Early in the morning of the second day, an engine, with a single private car attached, arrived at the station and side-tracked. At this sign that life had renewed in the dead roads, the whole army lined up beside the track.

But never did life renew so monstrously on a dead railroad as it did on those two roads. From the west came the whistle of a locomotive. It was coming in our direction, bound east. We were bound east. A stir of preparation ran down our ranks. The whistle tooted fast and furiously, and the train thundered at top speed. The hobo didn't live that could have boarded it. Another locomotive whistled, and another train came through at top speed, and another, and another, train after train, train after train, till toward the last the trains were composed of passenger coaches, box-cars, flat-cars, dead engines, cabooses, mail-cars, wrecking appliances, and all the riff-raff of worn-out and abandoned rolling-stock that collects in the yards of great railways. When the yards at Council Bluffs had been completely cleaned, the private car and engine went east, and the tracks died for keeps.

That day went by, and the next, and nothing moved, and in the meantime, pelted by sleet, and rain, and hail, the two thousand hobos lay beside the track. But that night the good people of Council Bluffs went the railroad officials one better. A mob formed in Council Bluffs, crossed the river to Omaha, and there joined with another mob in a raid on the Union Pacific yards. First they captured an engine, next they knocked a train together, and then the united mobs piled aboard, crossed the Missouri, and ran down the Rock Island right of way to turn the train over to us. The railway officials tried to copper this play, but fell down, to the mortal terror of the section boss and one member of the section gang at Weston. This pair, under secret telegraphic orders, tried to wreck our train-load of sympathizers by tearing up the track. It happened that we were suspicious and had our patrols out. Caught red-handed at train-wrecking, and surrounded by twenty hundred infuriated hoboes, that section-gang boss and assistant prepared to meet death. I don't remember what saved them, unless it was the arrival of the train.

It was our turn to fall down, and we did, hard. In their haste, the two mobs had neglected to make up a sufficiently long train. There wasn't room for two thousand hoboes to ride. So the mobs and the hoboes had a talkfest, fraternized, sang songs, and parted, the mobs going back on their captured train to Omaha, the hoboes pulling out next morning on a hundred-and-forty-mile march to Des Moines. It was not until Kelly's Army crossed the Missouri that it began to walk, and after that it never rode again. It cost the railroads slathers of money, but they were acting on principle, and they won.

Underwood, Leola, Menden, Avoca, Walnut, Marno, Atlantic, Wyoto, Anita, Adair, Adam, Casey, Stuart, Dexter, Carlham, De Soto, Van Meter, Booneville, Commerce, Valley Junction—how the names of the towns come back to me as I con the map and trace our route through the fat Iowa country! And the hospitable Iowa farmer-folk! They turned out with their wagons and carried our baggage; gave us hot lunches at noon by the wayside; mayors of comfortable little towns made speeches of welcome and hastened us on our way; deputations of little girls and maidens came out to meet us, and the good citizens turned out by hundreds, locked arms, and marched with us down their main streets. It was circus day when we came to town, and every day was circus day, for there were many towns.

In the evenings our camps were invaded by whole populations. Every company had its campfire, and around each fire something was doing. The cooks in my company, Company L, were song-and-dance artists and contributed most of our entertainment. In another part of the encampment the glee club would be singing—one of its star voices was the "Dentist," drawn from Company L, and we were mighty proud of him. Also, he pulled teeth for the whole army, and, since the extractions usually occurred at meal-time, our digestions were stimulated by variety of incident. The Dentist had no anaesthetics, but two or three of us were always on tap to volunteer to hold down the patient. In addition to the stunts of the companies and the glee club, church services were usually held, local preachers officiating, and always there was a great making of political speeches. All these things ran neck and neck; it was a full-blown Midway. A lot of talent can be dug out of two thousand hoboes. I remember we had a picked baseball nine, and on Sundays we made a practice of putting it all over the local nines. Sometimes we did it twice on Sundays.

Last year, while on a lecturing trip, I rode into Des Moines in a Pullman—I don't mean a "side-door Pullman," but the real thing. On the outskirts of the city I saw the old stove-works, and my heart leaped. It was there, at the stove-works, a dozen years before, that the Army lay down and swore a mighty oath that its feet were sore and that it would walk no more. We took possession of the stove-works and told Des Moines that we had come to stay—that we'd walk in, but we'd be blessed if we'd walk out. Des Moines was hospitable, but this was too much of a good thing. Do a little mental arithmetic, gentle reader. Two thousand hoboes, eating three square meals, make six thousand meals per day, forty-two thousand meals per week, or one hundred and sixty-eight thousand meals per shortest month in the calendar. That's going some. We had no money. It was up to Des Moines.

Des Moines was desperate. We lay in camp, made political speeches, held sacred concerts, pulled teeth, played baseball and seven-up, and ate our six thousand meals per day, and Des Moines paid for it. Des Moines pleaded with the railroads, but they were obdurate; they had said we shouldn't ride, and that settled it. To permit us to ride would be to establish a precedent, and there weren't going to be any precedents. And still we went on eating. That was the terrifying factor in the situation. We were bound for Washington, and Des Moines would have had to float municipal bonds to pay all our railroad fares, even at special rates, and if we remained much longer, she'd have to float bonds anyway to feed us.

Then some local genius solved the problem. We wouldn't walk. Very good. We should ride. From Des Moines to Keokuk on the Mississippi flowed the Des Moines River. This particular stretch of river was three hundred miles long. We could ride on it, said the local genius; and, once equipped with floating stock, we could ride on down the Mississippi to the Ohio, and thence up the Ohio, winding up with a short portage over the mountains to Washington.

Des Moines took up a subscription. Public-spirited citizens contributed several thousand dollars. Lumber, rope, nails, and cotton for calking were bought in large quantities, and on the banks of the Des Moines was inaugurated a tremendous era of shipbuilding. Now the Des Moines is a picayune stream, unduly dignified by the appellation of "river." In our spacious western land it would be called a "creek." The oldest inhabitants shook their heads and said we couldn't make it, that there wasn't enough water to float us. Des Moines didn't care, so long as it got rid of us, and we were such well-fed optimists that we didn't care either.

On Wednesday, May 9, 1894, we got under way and started on our colossal picnic.

Des Moines had got off pretty easily, and she certainly owes a statue in bronze to the local genius who got her out of her difficulty. True, Des Moines had to pay for our boats; we had eaten sixty-six thousand meals at the stove-works; and we took twelve thousand additional meals along with us in our commissary—as a precaution against famine in the wilds; but then, think what it would have meant if we had remained at Des Moines eleven months instead of eleven days. Also, when we departed, we promised Des Moines we'd come back if the river failed to float us.

It was all very well having twelve thousand meals in the commissary, and no doubt the commissary "ducks" enjoyed them; for the commissary promptly got lost, and my boat, for one, never saw it again. The company formation was hopelessly broken up during the river-trip. In any camp of men there will alwyas be found a certain percentage of shirks, of helpless, of just ordinary, and of hustlers. There were ten men in my boat, and they were the cream of Company L. Every man was a hustler. For two reasons I was included in the ten. First, I was as good a hustler as ever "threw his feet," and next, I was "Sailor Jack." I understood boats and boating. The ten of us forgot the remaining forty men of Company L, and by the time we had missed one meal we promptly forgot the commissary. We were independent. We went down the river "on our own," hustling and "chewin's," beating every boat in the fleet, and, alas that I must say it, sometimes taking possession of the stores the farmer-folk had collected for the Army.

For a good part of the three hundred miles we were from half a day to a day or so in advance of the Army. We had managed to get hold of several American flags. When we approached a small town, or when we saw a group of farmers gathered on the bank, we ran up our flags, called ourselves the "advance boat," and demanded to know what provisions had been collected for the Army. We represented the Army, of course, and the provisions were turned over to us. But there wasn't anything small about us. We never took more than we could get away with. But we did take the cream of everything. For instance, if some philanthropic farmer had donated several dollars' worth of tobacco, we took it. So, also, we took butter and sugar, coffee and canned goods; but when the stores consisted of sacks of beans and flour, or two or three slaughtered steers, we resolutely refrained and went our way, leaving orders to turn such provisions over to the commissary boats whose business was to follow behind us.

My, but the ten of us did live on the fat of the land! For a long time General Kelly vainly tried to head us off. He sent two rowers, in a light, round-bottomed boat, to overtake us and put a stop to our piratical careers. They overtook us all right, but they were two and we were ten. They were empowered by General Kelly to make us prisoners, and they told us so. When we expressed disinclination to become prisoners, they hurried ahead to the next town to invoke the aid of the authorities. We went ashore immediately and cooked an early supper; and under the cloak of darkness we ran by the town and its authorities.

I kept a diary on part of the trip, and as I read it over now I note one persistently recurring phrase, namely, "Living fine." We did live fine. We even disdained to use coffee boiled in water. We made our coffee out of milk, calling the wonderful beverage, if I remember rightly, "pale Vienna."

While we were ahead, skimming the cream, and while the commissary was lost far behind, the main Army, coming along in the middle, starved. This was hard on the Army, I'll allow; but then, the ten of us were individualists. We had initiative and enterprise. We ardently believed that the grub was to the man who got there first, the pale Vienna to the strong. On one stretch the Army went forty-eight hours without grub; and then it arrived at a small village of some three hundred inhabitants, the name of which I do not remember, though I think it was Red Rock. This town, following the practice of all towns through which the Army passed, had appointed a committee of safety. Counting five to a family, Red Rock consisted of sixty households. Her committee of safety was scared stiff by the eruption of two thousand hungry hoboes who lined their boats two and three deep along the river bank. General Kelly was a fair man. He had no intention of working a hardship on the village. He did not expect sixty households to furnish two thousand meals. Besides, the Army had its treasure-chest.

But the committee of safety lost its head. "No encouragement to the invader" was its programme, and when General Kelly wanted to buy food, the committee turned him down. It had nothing to sell; General Kelly's money was "no good" in their burg. And then General kelly went into action. The bugles blew. The Army left the boats and on top of the bank formed in battle array. The committee was there to see. General Kelly's speech was brief.

"Boys," he said, "when did you eat last?"

"Day before yesterday," they shouted.

"Are you hungry?"

A mighty affirmation from two thousand throats shook the atmosphere. Then General Kelly turned to the committee of safety:—

"You see, gentlemen, the situation. My men have eaten nothing in forty-eight hours. If I turn them loose upon your town, I'll not be responsible for what happens. They are desperate. I offered to buy food for them, but you refused to sell. I now withdraw my offer. Instead, I shall demand. I give you five minutes to decide. Either kill me six steers and give me four thousand rations, or I turn the men loose. Five minutes, gentlemen."

The terrified committee of safety looked at the two thousand hungry hoboes and collapsed. It didn't wait the five minutes. It wasn't going to take any chances. The killing of the steers and the collecting of the requisition began forthwith, and the Army dined.

And still the ten graceless individualists soared along ahead and gathered in everything in sight. But General Kelly fixed us. He sent horsemen down each bank, warning farmers and townspeople against us. They did their work thoroughly, all right. The erstwhile hospitable farmers met us with the icy mit. Also, they summoned the constables when we tied up to the bank, and loosed the dogs. I know. Two of the latter caught me with a barbed-wire fence between me and the river. I was carrying two buckets of milk for the pale Vienna. I didn't damage the fence any; but we drank plebeian coffee boiled with vulgar water, and it was up to me to throw my feet for another pair of trousers. I wonder, gentle reader, if you ever essayed hastily to climb a barbed-wire fence with a bucket of milk in each hand. Ever since that day I have had a prejudice against barbed wire, and I have gathered statistics on the subject.

Unable to make an honest living so long as General Kelly kept his two horsemen ahead of us, we returned to the Army and raised a revolution. It was a small affair, but it devastated Company L of the Second Division. The captain of Company L refused to recognize us; said we were deserters, and traitors, and scalawags; and when he drew rations for Company L from the commissary, he wouldn't give us any. That captain didn't appreciate us, or he wouldn't have refused us grub. Promptly we intrigued with the first lieutenant. He joined us with the ten men in his boat, and in return we elected him captain of Company M. The Captain of Company L raised a roar. Down upon us came General Kelly, Colonel Speed, and Colonel Baker. The twenty of us stood firm, and our revolution was ratified.

But we never bothered with the commissary. Our hustlers drew better rations from the farmers. Our new captain, however, doubted us. He never knew when he'd see the ten of us again, once we got under way in the morning, so he called in a blacksmith to clinch his captaincy. In the stern of our boat, one on each side, were driven two heavy eye-bolts of iron. Correspondingly, on the bow of his boat, were fastened two huge iron hooks. The boats were brought together, end on, the hooks dropped into the eye-bolts, and there we were, hard and fast. We couldn't lose that captain. But we were irrepressible. Out of our very manacles we wrought an invincible device that enabled us to put it all over every other boat in the fleet.

Like all great inventions, this one of ours was accidental. We discovered it the first time we ran on a snag in a bit of a rapid. The head-boat hung up and anchored, and the tail-boat swung around in the current, pivoting the head-boat on the snag. I was at the stern of the tail-boat, steering. In vain we tried to shove off. Then I ordered the men from the head-boat into the tail-boat. Immediately the head-boat floated clear, and its men returned into it. After that, snags, reefs, shoals, and bars had no terrors for us. The instant the head-boat struck, the men in it leaped into the tail-boat. Of course, the head-boat floated over the obstruction and the tail-boat then struck. Like automatons, the twenty men now in the tail-boat leaped into the head-boat, and the tail-boat floated past.

The boats used by the Army were all alike, made by the mile and sawed off. They were flat-boats, and their lines were rectangles. Each boat was six feet wide, ten feet long, and a foot and a half deep. Thus, when our two boats were hooked together, I sat at the stern steering a craft twenty feet long, containing twenty husky hoboes who "spelled" each other at the oars and paddles, and loaded with blankets, cooking outfit, and our own private commissary.

Still we caused General Kelly trouble. He had called in his horsemen, and substituted three police-boats that travelled in the van and allowed no boats to pass them. The craft containing Company M crowded the police-boats hard. We could have passed them easily, but it was against the rules. So we kept a respectful distance astern and waited. Ahead we knew was virgin farming country, unbegged and generous; but we waited. White water was all we needed, and when we rounded a bend and a rapid showed up we knew what would happen. Smash! Police-boat number one goes on a boulder and hangs up. Bang! Police-boat number two follows suit. Whop! Police-boat number three encounters the common fate of all. Of course our boat does the same things; but one, two, the men are out of the head-boat and into the tail-boat; one, two, they are out of the tail-boat and into the head-boat; and one, two, the men who belong in the tail-boat are back in it and we are dashing on. "Stop! you blankety-blank-blanks!" shriek the police-boats. "How can we?—blank the blankety-blank river, anyway!" we wail plaintively as we surge past, caught in that remorseless current that sweeps us on out of sight and into the hospitable farmer-country that replenishes our private commissary with the cream of its contributions. Again we drink pale Vienna and realize that the grub is to the man who gets there.

Poor General Kelly! He devised another scheme. The whole fleet started ahead of us. Company M of the Second Division started in its proper place in the line, which was last. And it took us only one day to put the "kibosh" on that particular scheme. Twenty-five miles of bad water lay before us—all rapids, shoals, bars, and boulders. It was over that stretch of water that the oldest inhabitants of Des Moines had shaken their heads. Nearly two hundred boats entered the bad water ahead of us, and they piled up in the most astounding manner. We went through that stranded fleet like hemlock through the fire. There was no avoiding the boulders, bars, and snags except by getting out on the bank. We didn't avoid them. We went right over them, one, two, one, two, head-boat, tail-boat, head-boat, tail-boat, all hands back and forth and back again. We camped that night alone, and loafed in camp all of next day while the Army patched and repaired its wrecked boats and straggled up to us.

There was no stopping our cussedness. We rigged up a mast, piled on the canvas (blankets), and travelled short hours while the Army worked over-time to keep us in sight. Then General Kelly had recourse to diplomacy. No boat could touch us in the straight-away. Without discussion, we were the hottest bunch that ever came down the Des Moines. The ban of the police-boats was lifted. Colonel Speed was put aboard, and with this distinguished officer we had the honor of arriving first at Keokuk on the Mississippi. And right here I want to say to General Kelly and Colonel Speed that here's my hand. You were heroes, both of you, and you were men. And I'm sorry for at least ten per cent of the trouble that was given you by the head-boat of Company M.

At Keokuk the whole fleet was lashed together in a huge raft, and, after being wind-bound a day, a steamboat took us in tow down the Mississippi to Quincy, Illinois, where we camped across the river on Goose Island. Here the raft idea was abandoned, the boats being joined together in groups of four and decked over. Somebody told me that Quincy was the richest town of its size in the United States. When I heard this, I was immediately overcome by an irresistible impulse to throw my feet. No "blowed-in-the-grass profesh" could possibly pass up such a promising burg. I crossed the river to Quincy in a small dug-out; but I came back in a large river-boat, down to the gunwales with the results of my thrown feet. Of course I kept all the money I had collected, though I paid the boat-hire; also I took my pick of the underwear, socks, cast-off clothes, shirts, "kicks," and "sky-pieces"; and when Company M had taken all it wanted there was still a respectable heap that was turned over to Company L. Alas, I was young and prodigal in those days! I told a thousand "stories" to the good people of Quincy, and every story was "good"; but since I have come to write for the magazines I have often regretted the wealth of story, the fecundity of fiction, I lavished that day in Quincy, Illinois.

It was at Hannibal, Missouri, that the ten invincibles went to pieces. It was not planned. We just naturally flew apart. The Boiler-Maker and I deserted secretly. On the same day Scotty and Davy made a swift sneak for the Illinois shore; also McAvoy and Fish achieved their get-away. This accounts for six of the ten; what became of the remaining four I do not know. As a sample of life on The Road, I make the following quotation from my diary of the several days following my desertion.

"Friday, May 25th. Boiler-Maker and I left the camp on the island. We went ashore on the Illinois side in a skiff and walked six miles on the C.B. & Q. to Fell Creek. We had gone six miles out of our way, but we got on a hand-car and rode six miles to Hull's, on the Wabash. While there, we met McAvoy, Fish, Scotty, and Davy, who had also pulled out from the Army.

"Saturday, May 26th. At 2:11 A.M. we caught the Cannon-ball as she slowed up at the crossing. Scotty and Davy were ditched. The four of us were ditched at the Bluffs, forty miles farther on. In the afternoon Fish and McAvoy caught a freight while Boiler-Maker and I were away getting something to eat.

"Sunday, May 27th. At 3:21 A.M. we caught the Cannon-ball and found Scotty and Davy on the blind. We were all ditched at daylight at Jacksonville. The C. & A. runs through here, and we're going to take that. Boiler-Maker went off, but didn't return. Guess he caught a freight.

"Monday, May 28th. Boiler-Maker didn't show up. Scotty and Davy went off to sleep somewhere, and didn't get back in time to catch the K.C. passenger at 3:30 A.M. I caught her and rode her till after sunrise to Masson City, 25,000 inhabitants. Caught a cattle train and rode all night.

"Tuesday, May 29th. Arrived in Chicago at 7 A.M. . . ."

. . . On rods and blind baggages I fought my way from the open West, where men bucked big and the job hunted the man, to the congested labor centres of the East, where men were small potatoes and hunted the job for all they were worth. And on this new *blond-beast* adventure I found myself looking upon life from a new and totally different angle. I had dropped down from the proletariat into what sociologists love to call the "submerged tenth," and I was startled to discover the way in which that submerged tenth was recruited.

I found there all sorts of men, many of whom had once been as good as myself and just as *blond-beastly*; sailor-men, soldier-men, labor-men, all wrenched and distorted and twisted out of shape by toil and hardship and accident, and cast adrift by their masters like so many old horses. I battered on the drag and slammed back gates with them, or shivered with them in box cars and city parks, listening the while to life-histories which began under auspices as fair as mine, with digestions and bodies equal to and better than mine, and which ended there before my eyes in the shambles at the bottom of the Social Pit.

And as I listened my brain began to work. The woman of the streets and the man of the gutter drew very close to me. I saw the picture of the Social Pit as vividly as though it were a concrete thing, and at the bottom of the Pit I saw them, myself above them, not far, and hanging on to the slippery wall by main strength and sweat. And I confess a terror seized me. What when my strength failed? when I should be unable to work shoulder to shoulder with the strong men who were as yet babes unborn? And there and then I swore a great oath. It ran something like this: *All my days I have worked hard with my body, and according to the number of days I have worked, by just that much am I nearer the bottom of the Pit. I shall climb out of the Pit, but not by the muscles of my body shall I climb out. I shall do no more hard work, and may God strike me dead if I do another day's hard work with my body more than I absolutely have to do.* And I have been busy ever since running away from hard work.

Incidentally, while tramping some ten thousand miles through the United States and Canada, I strayed into Niagara Falls, was nabbed by a fee-hunting constable, denied the right to plead guilty or not guilty, sentenced out of hand to thirty days' imprisonment for having no fixed abode and no visible means of support, handcuffed and chained to a bunch of men similarly circumstanced, carted down country to Buffalo, registered at the Erie County Penitentiary, had my head clipped and my budding mustache shaved, was dressed in convict stripes, compulsorily vaccinated by a medical student who practised on such as we, made to march the lock-step, and put to work under the eyes of guards armed with Winchester rifles—all for adventuring in *blond-beastly* fashion. Concerning further details deponent sayeth not, though he may hint that some of his plethoric national patriotism simmered down and leaked out of the bottom of his soul somewhere—at least, since that experience he finds that he cares more for men and women and little children than for imaginary geographical lines.

* * *

To return to my conversion. I think it is apparent that my rampant individualism was pretty effectively hammered out of me, and something else as effectively hammered in. But, just as I had been an individualist without knowing it, I was now a Socialist without knowing it, withal, an unscientific one. I had been reborn, but not renamed, and I was running around to find out what manner of thing I was. I ran back to California and opened the books. I do not remember which ones I opened first. It is an unimportant detail anyway. I was already It, whatever It was, and by aid of the books I discovered that It was a Socialist. Since that day I have opened many books, but no economic argument, no lucid demonstration of the logic and inevitableness of Socialism affects me as profoundly and convincingly as I was affected on the day when I first saw the walls of the Social Pit rise around me and felt myself slipping down, down, into the shambles at the bottom.

THE BRAIN MERCHANT

So my new concept was that manual labor was undignified, and that it didn't pay. No trade for me, was my decision, and no superintendent's daughter. And no criminality, I also decided. That would be almost as disastrous as to be a laborer. Brains paid, not brawn, and I resolved never again to offer my muscles for sale in the brawn market. Brain, and brain only, would I sell.

In my nineteenth year I returned to Oakland and started at the High School, which ran the usual school magazine. This publication was a weekly—no, I guess a monthly—one, and I wrote stories for it; very little imaginary, just recitals of my sea and tramping experiences.

. . . To pay my way, I worked as a janitor. My sister helped me, too; and I was not above mowing anybody's lawn or taking up and beating carpets when I had half a day to spare . . . I joined the Henry Clay Debating Society. I was received into the homes of some of the members, where I met nice girls whose skirts reached the ground. I dallied with little home clubs wherein we discussed poetry and art and the nuances of grammar. I joined the socialist local, where we studied and orated political economy, philosophy, and politics. I kept half-a-dozen membership cards working in the Free Library and did an immense amount of collateral reading.

. . . At this time my socialistic utterances had attracted considerable attention, and I was known as the "Boy Socialist," a distinction that brought about my arrest for street-talking.

Three years was the time required to go through high school. I grew impatient. Also, my schooling was becoming financially impossible. At such rate I could not last out, and I did greatly want to go to the state university. When I had done a year of high school, I decided to attempt a short cut. I borrowed the money and paid to enter the senior class of a "cramming joint" or academy. I was scheduled to graduate right into the university at the end of four months, thus saving two years.

And how I did cram! I had two years' new work to do in a third of a year. For five weeks I crammed, until simultaneous quadratic equations and chemical formulas fairly oozed from my ears. And then the master of the academy took me aside. He was very sorry, but he was compelled to give me back my tuition fee and to ask me to leave the school. It wasn't a matter of scholarship. I stood well in my classes, and did he graduate me into the university he was confident that in that institution I would continue to stand well. The trouble was that tongues were gossiping about my case. What! In four months accomplish two years' work! It would be a scandal, and the universities were becoming severer in their treatment of accredited prep schools. He couldn't afford such a scandal, therefore I must gracefully depart.

I did. And I paid back the borrowed money, and gritted my teeth, and started to cram by myself. There were three months yet before the university entrance-examinations. Without laboratories, without coaching, sitting my bedroom, I proceeded to compress that two years' work into three months and to keep reviewed on the previous year's work.

Nineteen hours a day I studied. For three months I kept this pace, only breaking it on several occasions. My body grew weary, my mind grew weary, but I stayed with it. My eyes grew weary and began to twitch, but they did not break down. Perhaps, toward the last, I got a bit dotty. I know that at the time I was confident I had discovered the formula for squaring the circle; but I resolutely deferred the working of it out until after the examinations. Then I would show them.

Came the several days of the examinations, during which time I scarcely closed my eyes in sleep, devoting every moment to cramming and reviewing. And when I turned in my last examination paper I was in full possession of a splendid case of brain-fag. I didn't want to see a book. I didn't want to think nor to lay eyes on anybody who was liable to think.

There was but one prescription for such a condition, and I gave it to myself—the adventure-path. I didn't wait to learn the result of my examinations. I stowed a roll of blankets and some cold food into a borrowed whitehall boat and set sail. Out of the Oakland Estuary I drifted on the last of an early morning ebb, caught the first of the flood up bay, and raced along with a spanking breeze. San Pablo Bay was smoking, and the Carquinez Straits off the Selby Smelter were smoking, as I picked up ahead and left astern the old landmarks I had first learned with Nelson in the unreefed *Reindeer.*

My cruise in the salmon boat lasted a week and I returned ready to enter the university . . . My tried brain had recuperated . . . I thought no more about it, returning gladly to my books and studies.

I completed the first half of my freshman year, and in January of 1897 took up my course for the second half. But the pressure from lack of money, plus a conviction that the university was not giving me all that I wanted in the time I could spare for it, forced me to leave. I was not very disappointed. For two years I had studied, and in those two years, what was far more valuable, I had done a prodigious amount of reading. Then, too, my grammar had improved. It is true, I had not yet learned that I must say "It is I"; but I no longer was guilty of the double negative in writing, though still prone to that error in excited speech.

I decided immediately to embark on my career. I had four preferences: first, music; second, poetry; third, the writing of philosophic, economic, and political essays; and, fourth, and last, and least, fiction writing. I resolutely cut out music as impossible, settled down in my bedroom, and tackled my second, third and fourth choices simultaneously. Heavens, how I wrote! Never was there a creative fever such as mine from which the patient escaped fatal results. The way I worked was enough to soften my brain and send me to a mad-house. I wrote, I wrote everything . . . On occasion I composed steadily, day after day, for fifteen hours a day. At times I forgot to eat, or refused to tear myself away from my passionate outpouring in order to eat.

And then there was the matter of typewriting. My brother-in-law owned a machine which he used in the daytime. In the night I was free to use it. That machine was a wonder. I could weep now as I recollect my wrestlings with it. It must have been a first model in the year one of the typewriter era. Its alphabet was all capitals. It was informed with an evil spirit. It obeyed no known laws of physics, and overthrew the hoary axiom that like things performed to like things produce like results. I'll swear that machine never did the same thing in the same way twice. Again and again it demonstrated that unlike actions produce like results.

How my back used to ache with it! Prior to that experience, my back had been good for every violent strain put upon it in a none too gentle career. But that typewriter proved to me that I had a pipe-stem for a back. Also, it made me doubt my shoulders. They ached as with rheumatism after every bout. The keys of that machine had to be hit so hard that to one outside the house it sounded like distant thunder or some one breaking up the furniture. I had to hit the keys so hard that I strained my first fingers to the elbows, while the ends of my fingers were blisters burst and blistered again. Had it been my machine I'd have operated it with a carpenter's hammer.

The worst of it was that I was actually typing my manuscripts at the same time I was trying to master that machine. It was a feat of physical endurance and a brain storm combined to type a thousand words, and I was composing thousands of words every day which just had to be typed for the waiting editors.

But the waiting editors elected to keep on waiting. My manuscripts made amazing round-trip records between the Pacific and the Atlantic. It might have been the weirdness of the typewriting that prevented the editors from accepting at least one little offering of mine. I don't know, and goodness knows the stuff I wrote was as weird as its typing. I sold my heard-bought school books for ridiculous sums to second-hand bookmen. I borrowed small sums of money wherever I could, and suffered my old father to feed me with the meager returns of his failing strength.

It didn't last long, only a few weeks, when I had to surrender and go to work . . . I was not disappointed. My career was retarded, that was all. Perhaps I did need further preparation. I had learned enough from the books to realize that I had touched only the hem of knowledge's garment. I still lived on the heights. My waking hours, and most of the hours I should have used for sleep, were spent with the books.

Out in the country, at the Belmont Academy, I went to work in a small, perfectly appointed steam laundry. Another fellow and myself did all the work from sorting and washing to ironing the white shirts, collars and cuffs, and the "fancy starch" of the wives of the professors. We worked like tigers, especially as summer came on and the academy boys took to the wearing of duck trousers. It consumes a dreadful lot of time to iron one pair of duck trousers. And there were so many pairs of them. We sweated our way through long sizzling weeks at a task that was never done; and many a night, while the students snored in bed, my partner and I toiled on under the electric light at steam mangle or ironing board.

The hours were long, the work was arduous, despite the fact that we became past masters in the art of eliminating waste motion. And I was receiving thirty dollars a month and board—a slight increase over my coal-shoveling and cannery days, at least to the extent of board, which cost my employer little (we ate in the kitchen), but which was to me the equivalent of twenty dollars a month. My robuster strength of added years, my increased skill, and all I had learned from the books, were responsible for this increase of twenty dollars. Judging by my rate of development, I might hope before I died to be a night watchman for sixty dollars a month, or a policeman actually receiving a hundred dollars with pickings.

So relentlessly did my partner and I spring into our work throughout the week that by Saturday night we were frazzled wrecks. I found myself in the old familiar work-beast condition, toiling longer hours than the horses toiled, thinking scarcely more frequent thoughts than horses think. The books were closed to me. I had brought a trunkful to the laundry, but found myself unable to read them. I fell asleep the moment I tried to read; and if I did manage to keep my eyes open for several pages, I could not remember the contents of those pages. I gave over attempts on heavy study, such as jurisprudence, political economy, and biology, and tried lighter stuff, such as history. I fell asleep. I tried literature, and fell asleep. And finally, when I fell asleep over lively novels, I gave up. I never succeeded in reading one book in all the time I spent in the laundry.

And when Saturday night came, and the week's work was over until Monday morning, I knew only one desire besides the desire to sleep, and that was to get drunk. This was the second time in my life that I had heard the unmistakable call of John Barleycorn. The first time it had been because of brain-fag. But I had no overworked brain now. On the contrary, all I knew was the dull numbness of a brain that was not worked at all. That was the trouble. My brain had become so alert and eager, so quickened by the wonder of the new world the books had discovered to it, that it now suffered all the misery of stagnancy and inaction.

And I, the long-time intimate of John Barleycorn, knew just what he promised me—maggots of fancy, dreams of power, forgetfulness, anything and everything save whirling washers, revolving mangles, humming centrifugal wringers, and fancy starch and interminable processions of duck trousers moving in steam under my flying iron. And that's it. John Barleycorn makes his appeal to weakness and failure, to weariness and exhaustion. He is the easy way out. And he is lying all the time. He offers false strength to the body, false elevation to the spirit, making things seem what they are not and vastly fairer than what they are.

I didn't get drunk, however, for the simple reason that it was a mile and a half to the nearest saloon. And this, in turn, was because the call to get drunk was not very loud in my ears. Had it been loud, I would have traveled ten times the distance to win to the saloon. On the other hand, had the saloon been just around the corner, I should have got drunk. As it was, I would sprawl out in the shade on my one day of rest and dally with the Sunday papers. But I was too weary even for their froth. The comic supplement might bring a pallid smile to my face, and then I would fall asleep.

Then I left the laundry and wrote all the time, and lived and dreamed again. After three months' trial I gave up writing, having decided that I was a failure, and left for the Klondike to prospect for gold.

HOLDING HER DOWN

BARRING accidents, a good hobo, with youth and agility, can hold a train down despite all the efforts of the train-crew to "ditch" him—given, of course, night-time as an essential condition. When such a hobo, under such conditions, makes up his mind that he is going to hold her down, either he does hold her down, or chance trips him up. There is no legitimate way, short of murder, whereby the train-crew can ditch him. That train-crews have not stopped short of murder is a current belief in the tramp world. Not having had that particular experience in my tramp days I cannot vouch for it personally.

But this I have heard of the "bad" roads. When a tramp has "gone underneath," on the rods, and the train is in motion, there is apparently no way of dislodging him until the train stops. The tramp, snugly ensconced inside the truck, with the four wheels and all the framework around him, has the "cinch" on the crew—or so he thinks, until some day he rides the rods on a bad road. A bad road is usually one on which a short time previously one or several trainmen have been killed by tramps. Heaven pity the tramp who is caught "underneath" on such a road—for caught he is, though the train be going sixty miles an hour.

The "shack" (brakeman) takes a coupling-pin and a length of bell-cord to the platform in front of the truck in which the tramp is riding. The shack fastens the coupling-pin to the bell-cord, drops the former down between the platforms, and pays out the latter. The coupling-pin strikes the ties between the rails, rebounds against the bottom of the car, and again strikes the ties. The shack plays it back and forth, now to this side, now to the other, lets it out a bit and hauls it in a bit, giving his weapon opportunity for every variety of impact and rebound. Every blow of that flying coupling-pin is freighted with death, and at sixty miles an hour it beats a veritable tattoo of death. The next day the ramains of that tramp are gathered up along the right of way, and a line in the local paper mentions the unknown man, undoubtedly a tramp, assumably drunk, who had probably fallen asleep on the track.

As a characteristic illustration of how a capable hobo can hold her down, I am minded to give the following experience. I was in Ottawa, bound west over the Canadian Pacific. Three thousand miles of that road stretched before me; it was the fall of the year, and I had to cross Manitoba and the Rocky Mountains. I could expect "crimpy" weather, and every moment of delay increased the frigid hardships of the journey. Furthermore, I was disgusted. The distance between Montreal and Ottawa is one hundred and twenty miles. I ought to know, for I had just come over it and it had taken me six days. By mistake I had missed the main line and come over a small "jerk" with only two locals a day on it. And during these six days I had lived on dry crusts, and not enough of them, begged from the French peasants.

Furthermore, my disgust had been heightened by the one day I had spent in Ottawa trying to get an outfit of clothing for my long journey. Let me put it on record right here that Ottawa, with one exception, is the hardest town in the United States and Canada to beg clothes in; the one exception is Washington, D.C. The latter fair city is the limit. I spent two weeks there trying to beg a pair of shoes, and then had to go on to Jersey City before I got them.

But to return to Ottawa. At eight sharp in the morning I started out after clothes. I worked energetically all day. I swear I walked forty miles. I interviewed the housewives of a thousand homes. I did not even knock off work for dinner. And at six in the afternoon, after ten hours of unremitting and depressing toil, I was still shy one shirt, while the pair of trousers I had managed to acquire was tight and, moreover, was showing all the signs of an early disintegration.

At six I quit work and headed for the railroad yards . . .

When I arrived at the depot, I found, much to my disgust, a bunch of at least twenty tramps that were waiting to ride out the blind baggages of the overland. Now two or three tramps on the blind baggage are all right. They are inconspicuous. But a score! That meant trouble. No train-crew would ever let all of us ride.

I may as well explain here what a blind baggage is. Some mail-cars are built without doors in the ends; hence, such a car is "blind." The mail-cars that possess end doors, have those doors always locked. Suppose, after the train has started, that a tramp gets on to the platform of one of these blind cars. There is no door, or the door is locked. No conductor or brakeman can get to him to collect fare or throw him off. It is clear that the tramp is safe until the next time the train stops. Then he must get off, run ahead in the darkness, and when the train pulls by, jump on to the blind again. But there are ways and ways, as you shall see.

When the train pulled out, those twenty tramps swarmed upon the three blinds. Soem climbed on before the train had run a car-length. They were awkward dubs, and I saw their speedy finish. Of course, the train-crew was "on," and at the first stop the trouble began. I jumped off and ran forward along the track. I noticed that I was accompanied by a number of the tramps. They evidently knew their business. When one is beating an overland, he must always keep well ahead of the train at the stops. I ran ahead, and as I ran, one by one those that accompanied me dropped out. This dropping out was the measure of their skill and nerve in boarding a train.

For this is the way it works. When the train starts, the shack rides out the blind. There is no way for him to get back into the train proper except by jumping off the blind and catching a platform where the car-ends are not "blind." When the train is going as fast as the shack cares to risk, he therefore jumps off the blind, lets several cars go by, and gets on the train. So it is up to the tramp to run so far ahead that before the blind is opposite him the shack will have already vacated it.

I dropped the last tramp by about fifty feet, and waited. The train started. I saw the lantern of the shack on the first blind. He was riding her out. And I saw the dubs stand forlornly by the track as the blind went by. They made no attempt to get on. They were beaten by their own inefficiency at the very start. After them, in the line-up, came the tramps that knew a little something about the game. They let the first blind, occupied by the shack, go by, and jumped on the second and third blinds. Of course, the shack jumped off the first and on to the second as it went by, and scrambled around there, throwing off the men who had boarded it. But the point is that I was so far ahead that when the first blind came opposite me, the shack had already left it and was tangled up with the tramps on the second blind. A half dozen of the more skilful tramps, who had run far enough ahead, made the first blind, too.

At the next stop, as we ran forward along the track, I counted but fifteen of us. Five had been ditched. The weeding-out process had begun nobly, and it continued station by station. Now we were fourteen, now twelve, now eleven, now nine, now eight. It reminded me of the ten little niggers of the nursery rhyme. I was resolved that I should be the last little nigger of all. And why not? Was I not blessed with strength, agility, and youth? (I was eighteen, and in perfect condition.) And didn't I have my "nerve" with me? And furthermore, was I not a tramp-royal? Were not these other tramps mere dubs and "gay-cats" and amateurs alongside of me? If I weren't the last little nigger, I might as well quit the game and get a job on an alfalfa farm somewhere.

By the time our number had been reduced to four, the whole train-crew had become interested. From then on it was a contest of skill and wits, with the odds in favor of the crew. One by one the three other survivors turned up missing, until I alone remained. My, but I was proud of myself! No Croesus was ever prouder of his first million. I was holding her down in spite of two brakemen, a conductor, a fireman, and an engineer.

And here are a few samples of the way I held her down. Out ahead, in the darkness, —so far ahead that the shack riding out the blind must perforce get off before it reaches me,—I get on. Very well. I am good for another station. When that station is reached, I dart ahead again to repeat the manoeuvre. The train pulls out. I watch her coming. There is no light of a lantern on the blind. Has the crew abandoned the fight? I do not know. One never knows, and one must be prepared every moment for anything. As the first blind comes opposite me, and I run to leap aboard, I strain my eyes to see if the shack is on the platform. For all I know he may be there, with his lantern doused, and even as I spring upon the steps that lantern may smash down upon my head. I ought to know. I have been hit by lanterns two or three times.

But no, the first blind is empty. The train is gathering speed. I am safe for another station. But am I? I feel the train slacken speed. On the instant I am alert. A manoeuvre is being executed against me, and I do not know what it is. I try to watch on both sides at once, not forgetting to keep track of the tender in front of me. From any one, or all, of these three directions, I may be assailed.

Ah, there it comes. The shack has ridden out the engine. My first warning is when his feet strike the steps of the right-hand side of the blind. Like a flash I am off the blind to the left and running ahead past the engine. I lose myself in the darkness. The situation is where it has been ever since the train left Ottawa. I am ahead, and the train must come past me if it is to proceed on its journey. I have as good a chance as ever for boarding her.

I watch carefully. I see a lantern come forward to the engine, and I do not see it go back from the engine. It must therefore be still on the engine, and it is a fair assumption that attached to the handle of that lantern is a shack. That shack was lazy, or else he would have put out his lantern instead of trying to shield it as he came forward. The train pulls out. The first blind is empty, and I gain it. As before, the train slackens, the shack from the engine boards the blind from one side, and I go off the other side and run forward.

As I wait in the darkness I am conscious of a big thrill of pride. THe overland has stopped twice for me—for me, a poor hobo on the bum. I alone have twice stopped the overland with its many passengers and coaches, its government mail, and its two thousand steam horses straining in the engine. And I weigh only one hundred and sixty pounds, and I haven't a five-cent piece in my pocket!

Again I see the lantern come forward to the engine. But this time it comes conspicuously. A bit too conspicuously to suit me, and I wonder what is up. At any rate I have something else to be afraid of than the shack on the engine. The train pulls by. Just in time, before I make my spring, I see the dark form of a shack, without a lantern, on the first blind. I let it go by, and prepare to board the second blind. But the shack on the first blind has jumped off and is at my heels. Also, I have a fleeting glimpse of the lantern of the shack who rode out the engine. He has jumped off, and now both shacks are on the ground on the same side with me. The next moment the second blind comes by and I am aboard it. But I do not linger. I have figured out my countermove. As I dash across the platform I hear the impact of the shack's feet against the steps as he boards. I jump off the other side and run forward with the train. My plan is to run forward and get on the first blind. It is nip and tuck, for the train is gathering speed. Also, the shack is behind me and running after me. I guess I am the better sprinter, for I make the first blind. I stand on the steps and watch my pursuer. He is only about ten feet back and running hard; but now the train has approximated his own speed, and, relative to me, he is standing still. I encourage him, hold out my hand to him; but he explodes in a mighty oath, gives up and makes the train several cars back.

The train is speeding along, and I am still chuckling to myself, when, without warning, a spray of water strikes me. The fireman is playing the hose on me from the engine. I step forward from the car-platform to the rear of the tender, where I am sheltered under the overhang. The water flies harmlessly over my head. My fingers itch to climb up on the tender and lam that fireman with a chunk of coal; but I know if I do that, I'll be massacred by him and the engineer, and I refrain.

At the next stop I am off and ahead in the darkness. This time, when the train pulls out, both shacks are on the first blind. I divine their game. They have blocked the repetition of my previous play. I cannot again take the second blind, cross over, and run forward to the first. As soon as the first blind passes and I do not get on, they swing off, one on each side of the train. I board the second blind, and as I do so I know that a moment later, simultaneously, those two shacks will arrive on both sides of me. It is like a trap. Both ways are blocked. Yet there is another way out, and that way is up.

So I do not wait for my pursuers to arrive. I climb upon the upright ironwork of the platform and stand upon the wheel of the hand-brake. This has taken up the moment of grace and I hear the shacks strike the steps on either side. I don't stop to look. I raise my arms overhead until my hands rest against the down-curving ends of the roofs of the two cars. One hand, of course, is on the curved roof of one car, the other hand on the curved roof of the other car. By this time both shacks are coming up the steps. I know it, though I am too busy to see them. All this is happening in the space of only several seconds. I make a spring with my legs and "muscle" myself up with my arms. As I draw up my legs, both shacks reach for me and clutch empty air. I know this, for I look down and see them. Also I hear them swear.

I am now in a precarious position, riding the ends of the down-curving roofs of two cars at the same time. With a quick, tense movement, I transfer both legs to the curve of one roof and both hands to the curve of the other roof. Then, gripping the edge of that curving roof, I climb over the curve to the level roof above, where I sit down to catch my breath, holding on the while to a ventilator that projects above the surface. I am on top of the train—on the "decks," as the tramps call it, and this process I have described is by them called "decking her." And let me say right here that only a young and vigorous tramp is able to deck a passenger train, and also, that the young and vigorous tramp must have his nerve with him as well.

The train goes on gathering speed, and I know I am safe until the next stop—but only until the next stop. If I remain on the roof after the train stops, I know those shacks will fusillade me with rocks. A healthy shack can "dewdrop" a pretty heavy chunk of stone on top of a car—say anywhere from five to twenty pounds. On the other hand, the chances are large that at the next stop the shacks will be waiting for me to descend at the place I climbed up. It is up to me to climb down at some other platform.

Registering a fervent hope that there are no tunnels in the next half mile, I rise to my feet and walk down the train half a dozen cars. And let me say that one must leave timidity behind him on such a *passear*. The roofs of passenger coaches are not made for midnight promenades. And if any one thinks they are, let me advise him to try it. Just let him walk along the roof of a jolting, lurching car, with nothing to hold on to but the black and empty air, and when he comes to the down-curving end of the roof, all wet and slippery with dew, let him accelerate his speed so as to step across to the next roof, down-curving and wet and slippery. Believe me, he will learn whether his heart is weak or his head is giddy.

As the train slows down for a stop, half a dozen platforms from where I had decked her I come down. No one is on the platform. When the train comes to a standstill, I slip off to the ground. Ahead, and between me and the engine, are two moving lanterns. The shacks are looking for me on the roofs of the cars. I note that the car beside which I am standing is a "four-wheeler"—by which is meant that it has only four wheels to each truck. (When you go underneath on the rods, be sure to avoid the "six-wheelers,"—they lead to disasters.)

I duck under the train and make for the rods, and I can tell you I am mighty glad that the train is standing still. It is the first time I have ever gone underneath on the Canadian Pacific, and the internal arrangements are new to me. I try to crawl over the top of the truck, between the truck and the bottom of the car. But the space is not large enough for me to squeeze through. This is new to me. Down in the United States I am accustomed to going underneath on rapidly moving trains, seizing a gunnel and swinging my feet under to the brake-beam, and from there crawling over the top of the truck and down inside the truck to a seat on the cross-rod.

Feeling with my hands in the darkness, I learn that there is room between the brake-beam and the ground. It is a tight squeeze. I have to lie flat and worm my way through. Once inside the truck, I take my seat on the rod and wonder what the shacks are thinking has become of me. The train gets under way. They have given me up at last.

But have they? At the very next stop, I see a lantern thrust under the next truck to mine at the other end of the car. They are searching the rods for me. I must make my get-away pretty lively. I crawl on my stomach under the brake-beam. They see me and run for me, but I crawl on hands and knees across the rail on the opposite side and gain my feet. Then away I go for the head of the train. I run past the engine and hide in the sheltering darkness. It is the same old situation. I am ahead of the train, and the train must go past me.

The train pulls out. There is a lantern on the first blind. I lie low, and see the peering shack go by. But there is also a lantern on the second blind. That shack spots me and calls to the shack who has gone past on the first blind. Both jump off. Never mind, I'll take the third blind and deck her. But heavens, there is a lantern on the third blind, too. It is the conductor. I let it go by. At any rate I have now the full train-crew in front of me. I turn and run back in the opposite direction to what the train is going. I look over my shoulder. All three lanterns are on the ground and wobbling along in pursuit.

I sprint. Half the train has gone by, and it is going quite fast, when I spring aboard. I know that the two shacks and the conductor will arrive like ravening wolves in about two seconds. I spring upon the wheel of the hand-brake, get my hands on the curved ends of the roofs, and muscle myself up to the decks; while my disappointed pursuers, clustering on the platform beneath like dogs that have treed a cat, howl curses up at me and say unsocial things about my ancestors.

But what does that matter? It is five to one, including the engineer and fireman, and the majesty of the law and the might of a great corporation are behind them, and I am beating them out. I am too far down the train, and I run ahead over the roofs of the coaches until I am over the fifth or sixth platform from the engine. I peer down cautiously. A shack is on that platform. That he has caught sight of me, I know from the way he makes a swift sneak inside the car; and I know, also, that he is waiting inside the door, all ready to pounce out on me when I climb down. But I make believe that I don't know, and I remain there to encourage him in his error. I do not see him, yet I know that he opens the door once and peeps up to assure himself that I am still there.

The train slows down for a station. I dangle my legs down in a tentative way. The train stops. My legs are still dangling. I hear the door unlatch softly. He is all ready for me. Suddenly I spring up and run forward over the roof. This is right over his head, where he lurks inside the door. The train is standing still; the night is quiet, and I take care to make plenty of noise on the metal roof with my feet. I don't know, but my assumption is that he is now running forward to catch me as I descend at the next platform. But I don't descend there. Halfway along the roof of the coach, I turn, retrace my way softly, and quickly to the platform both the shack and I have just abandoned. The coast is clear. I descend to the ground on the off-side of the train and hide in the darkness. Not a soul has seen me.

I go over to the fence, at the edge of the right of way, and watch. Ah, ha! What's that? I see a lantern on top of the train, moving along from front to rear. They think I haven't come down, and they are searching the roofs for me. And better than that—on the ground on each side of the train, moving abreast with the lantern on top, are two other lanterns. It is a rabbit-drive, and I am the rabbit. When the shack on top flushes me, the ones on each side will nab me. I roll a cigarette and watch the procession go by. Once past me, I am safe to proceed to the front of the train. She pulls out, and I make the front blind without opposition. But before she is fully under way and just as I am lighting my cigarette, I am aware that the fireman has climbed over the coal to the back of the tender and is looking down at me. I am filled with apprehension. From his position he can mash me to a jelly with lumps of coal. Instead of which he addresses me, and I note with relief the admiration in his voice.

"You son-of-a-gun," is what he says.

It is a high compliment, and I thrill as a schoolboy thrills on receiving a reward of merit.

"Say," I call up to him, "don't you play the hose on me any more."

"All right," he answers, and goes back to his work.

I have made friends with the engineer, but the shacks are still looking for me. At the next stop, the shacks ride out all three blinds, and as before, I let them go by and deck in the middle of the train. The crew is on its mettle by now, and the train stops. The shacks are going to ditch me or know the reason why. Three times the mighty overland stops for me at that station, and each time I elude the shacks and make the decks. But it is hopeless, for they have finally come to an understanding of the situation. I have taught them that they cannot guard the train from me. They must do something else.

And they do it. When the train stops that last time, they take after me hot-footed. Ah, I see their game. They are trying to run me down. At first they herd me back toward the rear of the train. I know my peril. Once to the rear of the train, it will pull out with me left behind. I double, and twist, and turn, dodge through my pursuers, and gain the front of the train. One shack still hangs on after me. All right, I'll give him the run of his life, for my wind is good. I run straight ahead along the track. It doesn't matter. If he chases me ten miles, he'll nevertheless have to catch the train, and I can board her at any speed that he can.

So I run on, keeping just comfortably ahead of him and straining my eyes in the gloom for cattle-guards that may bring me to grief. Alas! I strain my eyes too far ahead, and trip over something just under my feet, I know not what, some little thing, and go down to earth in a long, stumbling fall. The next moment I am on my feet, but the shack has me by the collar. I do not struggle. I am busy with breathing deeply and with sizing him up. He is narrow-shouldered, and I have at least thirty pounds the better of him in weight. Besides, he is just as tired as I am, and if he tries to slug me, I'll teach him a few things.

But he doesn't try to slug me, and that problem is settled. Instead, he starts to lead me back toward the train, and another possible problem arises. I see the lanterns of the conductor and the other shack. We are approaching them. Not for nothing have I made the acquaintance of the New York police. Not for nothing, in box-cars, by water-tanks, and in prison-cells, have I listened to bloody tales of man-handling. What if these three men are about to man-handle me? Heaven knows I have given them provocation enough. I think quickly. We are drawing nearer and nearer to the other two trainmen. I line up the stomach and the jaw of my captor, and plan the right and left I'll give him at the first sign of trouble.

Pshaw! I know another trick I'd like to work on him, and I almost regret that I did not do it at the moment I was captured. I could make him sick, what of his clutch on my collar. His fingers, tight-gripping, are buried inside my collar. My coat is tightly buttoned. Did you ever see a tourniquet? Well, this is one. All I have to do is to duck my head under his arm and begin to twist. I must twist rapidly—very rapidly. I know how to do it; twisting in a violent, jerky way, ducking my head under his arm with each revolution. Before he knows it, those detaining fingers of his will be detained. He will be unable to withdraw them. It is a powerful leverage. Twenty seconds after I have started revolving, the blood will be bursting out of his finger-ends, the delicate tendons will be rupturing, and all the muscles and nerves will be mashing and crushing together in a shrieking mass. Try it sometime when somebody has you by the collar. But be quick—quick as lightning. Also, be sure to hug yourself while you are revolving—hug your face with your left arm and your abdomen with your right. You see, the other fellow might try to stop you with a punch from his free arm. It would be a good idea, too, to revolve away from that free arm rather than toward it. A punch going is never so bad as a punch coming.

That shack will never know how near he was to being made very, very sick. All that saves him is that it is not in their plan to man-handle me. When we draw near enough, he calls out that he has me, and they signal the train to come on. The engine passes us, and the three blinds. After that, the conductor and the other shack swing aboard. But still my captor holds on to me. I see the plan. He is going to hold me until the rear of the train goes by. Then he will hop on, and I shall be left behind—ditched.

But the train has pulled out fast, the engineer trying to make up for lost time. Also, it is a long train. It is going very lively, and I know the shack is measuring its speed with apprehension.

"Think you can make it?" I query innocently.

He releases my collar, makes a quick run, and swings aboard. A number of coaches are yet to pass by. He knows it, and remains on the steps, his head poked out and watching me. In that moment my next move comes to me. I'll make the last platform. I know she's going fast and faster, but I'll only get a roll in the dirt if I fail, and the optimism of youth is mine. I do not give myself away. I stand with a dejected droop of shoulder, advertising that I have abandoned hope. But at the same time I am feeling with my feet the good gravel. It is perfect footing. Also I am watching the poked-out head of the shack. I see it withdrawn. He is confident that the train is going too fast for me ever to make it.

And the train *is* going fast—faster than any train I have ever tackled. As the last coach comes by I sprint in the same direction with it. It is a swift, short sprint. I cannot hope to equal the speed of the train, but I can reduce the difference of our speed to the minimum, and, hence, reduce the shock of impact, when I leap on board. In the fleeting instant of darkness I do not see the iron hand-rail of the last platform; nor is there time for me to locate it. I reach for where I think it ought to be, and at the same instant my feet leave the ground. It is all in the toss. The next moment I may be rolling in the gravel with broken ribs, or arms, or head. But my fingers grip the hand-hold, there is a jerk on my arms that slightly pivots my body, and my feet land on the steps with sharp violence.

I sit down, feeling very proud of myself. In all my hoboing it is the best bit of train-jumping I have done. I know that late at night one is always good for several stations on the last platform, but I do not care to trust myself at the rear of the train. At the first stop I run forward on the off-side of the train, pass the Pullmans, and duck under and take a rod under a day-coach. At the next stop I run forward again and take another rod.

I am now comparatively safe. The shacks think I am ditched. But the long day and the strenuous night are beginning to tell on me. Also, it is not so windy nor cold underneath, and I begin to doze. This will never do. Sleep on the rods spells death, so I crawl out at a station and go forward to the second blind. Here I can lie down and sleep; and here I do sleep—how long I do not know—for I am awakened by a lantern thrust into my face. The two shacks are staring at me. I scramble up on the defensive, wondering as to which one is going to make the first "pass" at me. But slugging is far from their minds.

"I thought you was ditched," says the shack who had held me by the collar.

"If you hadn't let go of me when you did, you'd have been ditched along with me," I answer.

"How's that?" he asks.

"I'd have gone into a clinch with you, that's all," is my reply.

They hold a consultation, and their verdict is summed up in:—

"Well, I guess you can ride, Bo. There's no use trying to keep you off."

And they go away and leave me in peace to the end of their division.

I have given the foregoing as a sample of what "holding her down" means. Of course, I have selected a fortunate night out of my experiences, and said nothing of the nights—and many of them—when I was tripped up by accident and ditched.

In conclusion, I want to tell of what happened when I reached the end of the division. On single-track, transcontinental lines, the freight trains wait at the divisions and follow out after the passenger trains. When the division was reached, I left my train, and looked for the freight that would pull out behind it. I found the freight, made up on a side-track and waiting. I climbed into a box-car half full of coal and lay down. In no time I was asleep.

I was awakened by the sliding open of the door. Day was just dawning, cold and gray, and the freight had not yet started. A "con" (conductor) was poking his head inside the door.

"Get out of that, you blankety-blank-blank!" he roared at me.

I got, and outside I watched him go down the line inspecting every car in the train. When he got out of sight I thought to myself that he would never think I'd have the nerve to climb back into the very car out of which he had fired me. So back I climbed and lay down again.

Now that con's mental processes must have been paralleling mine, for he reasoned that it was the very thing I would do. For back he came and fired me out.

Now, surely, I reasoned, he will never dream that I'd do it a third time. Back I went, into the very same car. But I decided to make sure. Only one side-door could be opened. The other side-door was nailed up. Beginning at the top of the coal, I dug a hole alongside of that door and lay down in it. I heard the other door open. The con climbed up and looked in over the top of the coal. He couldn't see me. He called to me to get out. I tried to fool him by remaining quiet. But when he began tossing chunks of coal into the hole on top of me, I gave up and for the third time was fired out. Also, he informed me in warm terms of what would happen to me if he caught me in there again.

I changed my tactics. When a man is paralleling your mental processes, ditch him. Abruptly break off your line of reasoning, and go off on a new line. This I did. I hid between some cars on an adjacent side-track, and watched. Sure enough, that con came back again to the car. He opened the door, he climbed up, he called, he threw coal into the hole I had made. He even crawled over the coal and looked into the hole. That satisfied him. Five minutes later the freight was pulling out, and he was not in sight. I ran alongside the car, pulled the door open, and climbed in. He never looked for me again, and I rode that coal-car precisely one thousand and twenty-two miles, sleeping most of the time and getting out at divisions (where the freights always stop for an hour or so) to beg my food. And at the end of the thousand and twenty-two miles I lost that car through a happy incident. I got a "set-down," and the tramp doesn't live who won't miss a train for a set-down any time.

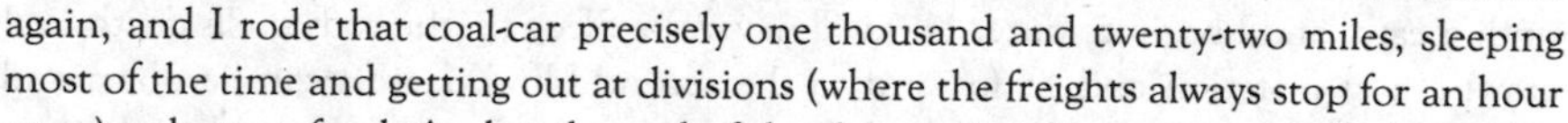

THE SEA

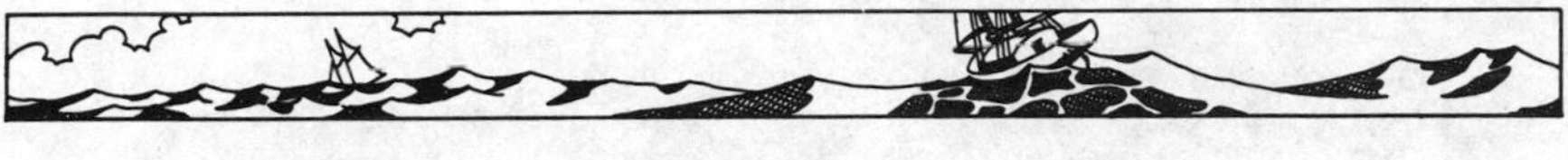

The Sea

As opposed to the limited time he spent in the Arctic snowfields, London was raised with an intimate knowledge and love of the sea. His own lifelong experiences ranged from negotiating the waterways and pirating the oyster beds of San Francisco Bay to hunting seals off the coast of Japan to sailing his own boat, the *Snark*, across the Pacific with his wife, Charmian.

In the process of educating himself, the young London immediately embraced the tradition of the sea as a setting for great literary adventure. Authors from Homer to Conrad used the sea as a symbol of the untamed, the absence of law and civilization, the primitive in all of us. Perhaps London's strongest influence was Melville, whose *Moby Dick* showed him that larger issues and ideas, struggles between good and evil, could be played out effectively against this primal backdrop.

The Sea Wolf is the culmination of all London knew and imagined about adventure on the oceans, and it is generally considered one of the great sea stories ever written. Not only are its epic proportions, realistic characterizations, and dangerous conflict truly captivating, but here we see London's writing at its best.

The two opposing characters seem to represent the contradictions London recognized in himself: elitist versus populist, civilized versus savage, cerebral versus visceral. Wolf Larsen, the ship's captain, is rough hewn, ruthless—the raw, natural, aggressive side of London that drove him toward adventure and success. Larsen's nemesis, Humphrey van Weyden, is the cultured, educated "gentleman" that London struggled successfully to become.

London recognized that at sea, away from order and authority, the rules of conduct changed. Survival depended not on laws, but on boldness and wits, on understanding adversary and environment, on finding the inner strength he believed is in us all.

THE CRUISE OF THE *Dazzler*

I

'Frisco Kid, and the New Boy

'FRISCO Kid was discontented—discontented and disgusted; though this would have seemed impossible to the boys who fished from the dock above and envied him mightily. He frowned, got up from where he had been sunning himself on top of the *Dazzler*'s cabin, and kicked off his heavy rubber boots. Then he stretched himself on the narrow side-deck and dangled his feet in the cool salt water.

"Now, that's freedom," thought the boys who watched him. Besides, those long seaboots, reaching the hips and buckled to the leather strap about the waist, held a strange and wonderful fascination for them. They did not know that 'Frisco Kid did not possess such things as shoes; that the boots were an old pair of Pete Le Maire's and were three sizes too large for him; nor could they guess how uncomfortable they were to wear on a hot summer day.

The cause of 'Frisco Kid's discontent was those very boys who sat on the string-piece and admired him; but his disgust was the result of quite another event. Further, the *Dazzler* was short one in its crew, and he had to do more work than was justly his share. He did not mind the cooking, nor the washing down of the decks and the pumping; but when it came to the paint-scrubbing and dish-washing, he rebelled. He felt that he had earned the right to be exempt from such scullion work. That was all the green boys were fit for; while he could make or take in sail, lift anchor, steer, and make landings.

"Stan' from un'er!" Pete Le Maire, captain of the *Dazzler* and lord and master of 'Frisco Kid, threw a bundle into the cockpit and came aboard by the starboard rigging.

"Come! Queeck!" he shouted to the boy who owned the bundle, and who now hesitated on the dock. It was a good fifteen feet to the deck of the sloop, and he could not reach the steel stay by which he must descend.

"Now! One, two, three!" the Frenchman counted good-naturedly, after the manner of all captains when their crews are short-handed.

The boy swung his body into space and gripped the rigging. A moment later he struck the deck, his hands tingling warmly from the friction.

"Kid, dis is ze new sailor. I make your acquaintance." Pete smirked and bowed, and stood aside. "Mistaire Sho Bronson," he added as an afterthought.

The two boys regarded each other silently for a moment. They were evidently about the same age, though the stranger looked the heartier and the stronger of the two. 'Frisco Kid put out his hand, and they shook.

"So you're thinking of tackling the water, eh?" he asked.

Joe Bronson nodded, and glanced curiously about him before answering. "Yes; I think the Bay life will suit me for a while, and then, when I've got used to it, I'm going to sea in the forecastle."

"In the what? In the *what,* did you say?"

"In the forecastle—the place where the sailors live," he explained, flushing and feeling doubtful of his pronunciation.

"Oh, the fo'c'sle. Know anything about going to sea?"

"Yes—no; that is, except what I've read."

'Frisco Kid whistled, turned on his heel in a lordly manner, and went into the cabin.

"Going to sea!" he remarked to himself as he built the fire and set about cooking supper; "in the 'forecastle,' too—and thinks he'll like it!"

In the meanwhile Pete Le Maire was showing the new-comer about the sloop as though he were a guest. Such affability and charm did he display that 'Frisco Kid, popping his head up through the scuttle to call them to supper, nearly choked in his effort to suppress a grin.

Joe Bronson enjoyed that supper. The food was rough but good, and the smack of the salt air and the sea-fittings around him gave zest to his appetite. The cabin was clean and snug, and, though not large, the accommodations surprised him. Every bit of space was utilized. The table swung to the centerboard-case on hinges, so that when not in use it actually occupied almost no room at all. On either side, and partly under the deck, were two bunks. The blankets were rolled back, and they sat on the well-scrubbed bunk boards while they ate. A swinging sea-lamp of brightly polished brass gave them light, which in the daytime could be obtained through the four deadeyes, or small round panes of heavy glass which were fitted into the walls of the cabin. On one side of the door were the stove and wood-box, on the other the cupboard. The front end of the cabin was ornamented with a couple of rifles and a shot-gun, while exposed by the rolled-back blankets of Pete's bunk was a cartridge-lined belt carrying a brace of revolvers.

It all seemed like a dream to Joe. Countless times he had imagined scenes somewhat similar to this; but here he was, right in the midst of it, and already it seemed as though he had known his two companions for years. Pete was smiling genially at him across the board. His was really a villainous countenance, but to Joe it seemed only "weather-beaten." 'Frisco Kid was describing to him, between mouthfuls, the last sou'easter the *Dazzler* had weathered, and Joe experienced an increasing awe for this boy who had lived so long upon the water and knew so much about it.

The captain, however, drank a glass of wine, and topped it off with a second and a third, and then, a vicious flush lighting his swarthy face, stretched out on top of his blankets, where he soon was snoring loudly.

"Better turn in and get a couple of hours' sleep," 'Frisco Kid said kindly, pointing Joe's bunk out to him. "We'll most likely be up the rest of the night."

Joe obeyed, but he could not fall asleep so readily as the others. He lay with his eyes wide open, watching the hands of the alarmclock that hung in the cabin, and thinking how quickly event had followed event in the last twelve hours. Only that very morning he had been a school-boy, and now he was a sailor, shipped on the *Dazzler*, and bound he knew not whither. His fifteen years increased to twenty at the thought of it, and he felt every inch a man—a sailor-man at that. He wished Charley and Fred could see him now. Well, they would hear of it quick enough. He could see them talking it over, and the other boys crowding around. "Who?" "What!—Joe Bronson?" "Yes, he's run away to sea. Used to chum with us, you know."

Joe pictured the scene proudly. Then he softened at the thought of his mother worrying, but hardened again at the recollection of his father. Not that his father was not good and kind; but he did not understand boys, Joe thought. That was where the trouble lay. Only that morning he had said that the world wasn't a play-ground, and that the boys who thought it was were liable to make sore mistakes and be glad to get home again. Well, *he* knew that there was plenty of hard work and rough experience in the world; but *he* also thought boys had some rights and should be allowed to do a lot of things without being questioned. He'd show him he could take care of himself; and, anyway, he could write home after he got settled down to his new life.

A skiff grazed the side of the *Dazzler* softly and interrupted his reveries. He wondered why he had not heard the sound of the rowlocks. Then two men jumped over the cock-pit-rail and came into the cabin.

"Bli' me, if 'ere they ain't snoozin'," said the first of the new-comers, deftly rolling 'Frisco Kid out of his blankets with one hand and reaching for the wine-bottle with the other.

Pete put his head up on the other side of the centerboard, his eyes heavy with sleep, and made them welcome.

" 'Oo 's this?" asked "the Cockney," as 'Frisco Kid called him, smacking his lips over the wine and rolling Joe out upon the floor. "Passenger?"

"No, no," Pete made haste to answer. "Ze new sailor-man. Vaire good boy."

"Good boy or not, he's got to keep his tongue a-tween his teeth," growled the second new-comer, who had not yet spoken, glaring fiercely at Joe.

"I say," queried the other man, " 'ow does 'e whack up on the loot? I 'ope as me an' Bill 'ave a square deal."

"Ze *Dazzler* she take one share—what you call—one third; den we split ze rest in five shares. Five men, five shares. Vaire good."

It was all Greek to Joe, except he knew that he was in some way the cause of the quarrel. In the end Pete had his way, and the newcomers gave in after much grumbling. After they had drunk their coffee all hands went on deck.

"Just stay in the cockpit an' keep out of their way," 'Frisco Kid whispered to Joe. "I'll teach you the ropes an' everything when we ain't in a hurry."

Joe's heart went out to him in sudden gratitude, for the strange feeling came to him that, of those on board, to 'Frisco Kid, and to 'Frisco Kid only, could he look for help in time of need. Already a dislike for Pete was growing up within him. Why, he could not say—he just simply felt it. A creaking of blocks for'ard, and the huge mainsail loomed above him in the night. Bill cast off the bow-line. The Cockney followed with the stern. 'Frisco Kid gave her the jib as Pete jammed up the tiller, and the *Dazzler* caught the breeze, heeling over for mid-channel. Joe heard some talking in low tones of not putting up the side-lights, and of keeping a sharp lookout, but all he could comprehend was that some law of navigation was being violated.

The water-front lights of Oakland began to slip past. Soon the stretches of docks and the shadowy ships began to be broken by dim sweeps of marsh-land, and Joe knew that they were heading out for San Francisco Bay. The wind was blowing from the north in mild squalls, and the *Dazzler* cut noiselessly through the landlocked water.

"Where are we going?" Joe asked the Cockney, in an endeavor to be friendly and at the same time satisfy his curiosity.

"Oh, my pardner 'ere, Bill—we're goin' to take a cargo from 'is factory," that worthy airily replied.

Joe thought he was rather a funny-looking individual to own a factory; but conscious that stranger things yet might be found in this new world he was entering, he said nothing. He had already exposed himself to 'Frisco Kid in the matter of his pronunciation of "fo'c'sle," and he had no desire further to show his ignorance.

A little after that he was sent in to blow out the cabin lamp. The *Dazzler* tacked about and began to work in toward the north shore. Everybody kept silent, save for occasional whispered questions and answers which passed between Bill and the captain. Finally the sloop was run into the wind and the jib and mainsail lowered cautiously.

"Short hawse, you know," Pete whispered to 'Frisco Kid, who went for'ard and dropped the anchor, paying out the slightest quantity of slack.

The *Dazzler*'s skiff was brought alongside, as was also the small boat the two strangers had come aboard in.

"See that that cub don't make a fuss," Bill commanded in an undertone, as he joined his partner in his own boat.

"Can you row?" 'Frisco Kid asked as they got into the other boat. Joe nodded his head. "Then take these oars, and don't make a racket."

'Frisco Kid took the second pair, while Pete steered. Joe noticed that the oars were muffled with sennit, and that even the rowlock sockets were protected by leather. It was impossible to make a noise except by a mis-stroke, and Joe had learned to row on Lake Merrit well enough to avoid that. They followed in the wake of the first boat, and glancing aside, he saw they were running along the length of a pier which jutted out from the land. A couple of ships, with riding-lanterns burning brightly, were moored to it, but they kept just beyond the edge of the light. He stopped rowing at the whispered command of 'Frisco Kid. Then the boats grounded like ghosts on a tiny beach, and they clambered out.

Joe followed the men, who picked their way carefully up a twenty-foot bank. At the top he found himself on a narrow railway track which ran between huge piles of rusty scrap-iron. These piles, separated by tracks, extended in every direction, he could not tell how far, though in the distance he could see the vague outlines of some great factory-like building. The men began to carry loads of the iron down to the beach, and Pete, gripping him by the arm and again warning him to not make any noise, told him to do likewise. At the beach they turned their loads over to 'Frisco Kid, who loaded them, first in one skiff and then in the other. As the boats settled under the weight, he kept pushing them farther and farther out, in order that they should keep clear of the bottom.

Joe worked away steadily, though he could not help marveling at the queerness of the whole business. Why should there be such a mystery about it, and why such care taken to maintain silence? He had just begun to ask himself these questions, and a horrible suspicion was forming itself in his mind, when he heard the hoot of an owl from the direction of the beach. Wondering at an owl being in so unlikely a place, he stooped to gather a fresh load of iron. But suddenly a man sprang out of the gloom, flashing a dark lantern full upon him. Blinded by the light, he staggered back. Then a revolver in the man's hand went off. All Joe realized was that he was being shot at, while his legs manifested an overwhelming desire to get away. Even if he had so wished, he could not very well have stayed to explain to the excited man with the smoking revolver. So he took to his heels for the beach, colliding with another man with a dark lantern who came running around the end of one of the piles of iron. This second man quickly regained his feet, and peppered away at Joe as he flew down the bank.

He dashed out into the water for the boat. Pete at the bow oars and 'Frisco Kid at the stroke had the skiff's nose pointed seaward and were calmly awaiting his arrival. They had their oars all ready for the start, but they held them quietly at rest, notwithstanding that both men on the bank had begun to fire at them. The other skiff lay closer inshore, partially aground. Bill was trying to shove it off, and was calling on the Cockney to lend a hand; but that gentleman had lost his head completely, and came floundering through the water hard after Joe. No sooner had Joe climbed in over the stern than he followed him. This extra weight on the stern of the heavily loaded craft nearly swamped them; as it was, a dangerous quantity of water was shipped. In the meantime the men on the bank had reloaded their pistols and opened fire again, this time with better aim. The alarm had spread. Voices and cries could be heard from the ships on the pier, along which men were running. In the distance a police whistle was being frantically blown.

"Get out!" 'Frisco Kid shouted. "You ain't a-going to sink us if I know it. Go and help your pardner!"

But the Cockney's teeth were chattering with fright, and he was too unnerved to move or speak.

"T'row ze crazy man out!" Pete ordered from the bow. At this moment a bullet shattered an oar in his hand, and he coolly proceeded to ship a spare one.

"Give us a hand, Joe," 'Frisco Kid commanded.

Joe understood, and together they seized the terror-stricken creature and flung him overboard. Two or three bullets splashed about him as he came to the surface just in time to be picked up by Bill, who had at last succeeded in getting clear.

"Now," Pete called, and a few strokes into the darkness quickly took them out of the zone of fire.

So much water had been shipped that the light skiff was in danger of sinking at any moment. While the other two rowed, and by the Frenchman's orders, Joe began to throw out the iron. This saved them for the time being; but just as they swept alongside the *Dazzler* the skiff lurched, shoved a side under, and turned turtle, sending the remainder of the iron to the bottom. Joe and 'Frisco Kid came up side by side, and together they clambered aboard with the skiff's painter in tow. Pete had already arrived, and now helped them out.

By the time they had canted the water out of the swamped boat, Bill and his partner appeared on the scene. All hands worked rapidly, and almost before Joe could realize, the mainsail and jib had been hoisted, the anchor broken out, and the *Dazzler* was leaping down the channel. Off a bleak piece of marshland, Bill and the Cockney said good-by and cast loose in their skiff. Pete, in the cabin, bewailed their bad luck in various languages, and sought consolation in the wine-bottle.

The wind freshened as they got clear of the land, and soon the *Dazzler* was heeling it with her lee deck buried and the water churning by half-way up the cockpit-rail. Side-lights had been hung out. 'Frisco Kid was steering, and by his side sat Joe, pondering over the events of the night.

He could no longer blind himself to the facts. His mind was in a whirl of apprehension. If he had done wrong, he reasoned, he had done it through ignorance; and he did not feel shame for the past so much as he did fear of the future. His companions were thieves and robbers—the Bay pirates, of whose unlawful deeds he had heard vague tales. And here he was, right in the midst of them, already possessing information which could send them to State's prison. This very fact, he knew, would force them to keep a sharp watch upon him and so lessen his chances of escape. But escape he would, at the very first opportunity.

At this point his thoughts were interrupted by a sharp squall, which hurled the *Dazzler* over till the sea rushed inboard. 'Frisco Kid luffed quickly, at the same time slacking off the mainsheet. Then, single-handed,—for Pete remained below, and Joe sat still looking idly on—he proceeded to reef down.

II

Joe Tries Taking French Leave

THE squall which had so nearly capsized the *Dazzler* was of short duration, but it marked the rising of the wind, and soon puff after puff was shrieking down upon them out of the north. The mainsail was spilling the wind, and slapping and thrashing about till it seemed it would tear itself to pieces. The sloop was rolling wildly in the quick sea which had come up. Everything was in confusion; but even Joe's untrained eye showed him that it was an orderly confusion. He could see that 'Frisco Kid knew just what to do, and just how to do it. As he watched him he learned a lesson, the lack of which has made failures of the lives of many men—*knowledge of one's own capacities.* 'Frisco Kid knew what he was able to do, and because of this he had confidence in himself. He was cool and self-possessed, working hurriedly but not carelessly. There was no bungling. Every reef-point was drawn down to stay. Other accidents might occur, but the next squall, or the next forty squalls, would not carry one of these reef-knots away.

He called Joe for'ard to help stretch the mainsail by means of swinging on the peak and throat halyards. To lay out on the long bow-sprit and put a single reef in the jib was a slight task compared with what had been already accomplished; so a few moments later they were again in the cockpit. Under the other lad's directions, Joe flattened down the jib-sheet, and, going into the cabin, let down a foot or so of center-board. The excitement of the struggle had chased all unpleasant thoughts from his mind. Patterning after the other boy, he had retained his coolness. He had executed his orders without fumbling, and at the same time without undue slowness. Together they had exerted their puny strength in the face of violent nature, and together they had outwitted her.

He came back to where his companion stood at the tiller steering, and he felt proud of him and of himself. And when he read the unspoken praise in 'Frisco Kid's eyes he blushed like a girl at her first compliment. But the next instant the thought flashed across him that this boy was a thief, a common thief, and he instinctively recoiled. His whole life had been sheltered from the harsher things of the world. His reading, which had been of the best, had laid a premium upon honesty and uprightness, and he had learned to look with abhorrence upon the criminal classes. So he drew a little away from 'Frisco Kid and remained silent. But 'Frisco Kid, devoting all his energies to the handling of the sloop, had no time in which to remark this sudden change of feeling on the part of his companion.

Yet there was one thing Joe found in himself that surprised him. While the thought of 'Frisco Kid being a thief was repulsive to him, 'Frisco Kid himself was not. Instead of feeling an honest desire to shun him, he felt drawn toward him. He could not help liking him, though he knew not why. Had he been a little older he would have understood that it was the lad's good qualities which appealed to him—his coolness and self-reliance, his manliness and bravery, and a certain kindliness and sympathy in his nature. As it was, he thought it his own natural badness which prevented him from disliking 'Frisco Kid, and while he felt shame at his own weakness, he could not smother the sort of regard which he felt growing up for this common thief, this Bay pirate.

"Take in two or three feet on the skiff's painter," commanded 'Frisco Kid, who had an eye for everything.

The skiff was towing with too long a painter, and was behaving very badly. Every once in a while it would hold back till the tow-rope tautened, then come leaping ahead and sheering and dropping slack till it threatened to shove its nose under the huge whitecaps which roared hungrily on every hand. Joe climbed over the cockpit-rail upon the slippery after-deck, and made his way to the bitt to which the skiff was fastened.

"Be careful," 'Frisco Kid warned, as a heavy puff struck the *Dazzler* and careened her dangerously over on her side. "Keep one turn round the bitt, and heave in on it when the painter slacks."

It was ticklish work for a greenhorn. Joe threw off all the turns save the last, which he held with one hand, while with the other he attempted to bring in on the painter. But at that instant it tightened with a tremendous jerk, the boat sheering sharply into the crest of a heavy sea. The rope slipped from his hands and began to fly out over the stern. He clutched it frantically, and was dragged after it over the sloping deck.

"Let her go! Let her go!" 'Frisco Kid roared.

Joe let go just as he was on the verge of going overboard, and the skiff dropped rapidly astern. He glanced in a shamefaced way at his companion, expecting to be sharply reprimanded for his awkwardness. But 'Frisco Kid smiled good-naturedly.

"That's all right," he said. "No bones broke, and nobody overboard. Better to lose a boat than a man any day. That's what I say. Besides, I shouldn't have sent you out there. And there's no harm done. We can pick it up all right. Go in and drop some more centerboard,—a couple of feet,—and then come out and do what I tell you. But don't be in a hurry. Take it easy and sure."

Joe dropped the centerboard, and returned, to be stationed at the jib-sheet.

"Hard a-lee!" 'Frisco Kid cried, throwing the tiller down and following it with his body. "Cast off! That's right! Now lend a hand on the main-sheet!"

Together, hand over hand, they came in on the reefed mainsail. Joe began to warm up with the work. The *Dazzler* turned on her heel like a race-horse and swept into the wind, her canvas snarling and her sheets slatting like hail.

"Draw down the jib-sheet!"

Joe obeyed, and the head-sail, filling, forced her off on the other tack. This manoeuver had turned Pete's bunk from the lee to the weather side, and rolled him out on the cabin floor, where he lay in a drunken stupor.

'Frisco Kid, with his back against the tiller, and holding the sloop off that it might cover their previous course, looked at him with an expression of disgust, and muttered: "The dog! We could well go to the bottom, for all he'd care or do!"

Twice they tacked, trying to go over the same ground, and then Joe discovered the skiff bobbing to windward in the starlit darkness.

"Plenty of time," 'Frisco Kid cautioned, shooting the *Dazzler* into the wind toward it and gradually losing headway.

"Now!"

Joe leaned over the side, grasped the trailing painter, and made it fast to the bitt. Then they tacked ship again and started on their way. Joe still felt sore over the trouble he had caused, but 'Frisco Kid quickly put him at ease.

"Oh, that's nothing," he said. "Everybody does that when they're beginning. Now, some men forget all about the trouble they had in learning, and get mad when a greeny makes a mistake. I never do. Why, I remember—"

And here he told Joe of many of the mishaps which fell to him when, as a little lad, he first went on the water, and of some of the severe punishments for the same which were measured out to him. He had passed the running end of a lanyard over the tiller-neck, and, as they talked, they sat side by side and close against each other, in the shelter of the cockpit.

"What place is that?" Joe asked as they flew by a lighthouse perched on a rocky headland.

"Goat Island. They've got a naval training-station for boys over on the other side, and a torpedo magazine. There's jolly good fishing, too—rock-cod. We'll pass to the lee of it and make across and anchor in the shelter of Angel Island. There's a quarantine station there. Then, when Pete gets sober, we'll know where he wants to go. You can turn in now and get some sleep. I can manage all right."

Joe shook his head. There had been too much excitement for him to feel in the least like sleeping. He could not bear to think of it, with the *Dazzler* leaping and surging along, and shattering the seas into clouds of spray on her weather bow. His clothes had half dried already, and he preferred to stay on deck and enjoy it. The lights of Oakland had dwindled till they made only a hazy flare against the sky; but to the south the San Francisco lights, topping hills and sinking into valleys, stretched miles upon miles. Starting from the great ferry building and passing on to Telegraph Hill, Joe was soon able to locate the principal places of the city. Somewhere over in that maze of light and shadow was the home of his father, and perhaps even now they were thinking and worrying about him; and over there his sister Bessie was sleeping cozily, to wake up in the morning and wonder why her brother Joe did not come down to breakfast. Joe shivered. It was almost morning. Then, slowly, his head drooped over on 'Frisco Kid's shoulder, and soon he was fast asleep.

"Come! Wake up! We're going into anchor."

Joe roused with a start, bewildered at the unusual scene; for sleep had banished his troubles for the time being, and he knew not where he was. Then he remembered. The wind had dropped with the night. Beyond, the heavy after-sea was still rolling, but the *Dazzler* was creeping up in the shelter of a rocky island. The sky was clear, and the air had the snap and vigor of early morning about it. The rippling water was laughing in the rays of the sun, just shouldering above the eastern sky-line. To the south lay Alcatraz Island, and from its gun-crowned heights a flourish of trumpets saluted the day. In the west the Golden Gate yawned between the Pacific Ocean and San Francisco Bay. A full-rigged ship, with her lightest canvas, even to the sky-sails, set, was coming slowly in on the flood-tide.

It was a pretty sight. Joe rubbed the sleep from his eyes and remained gazing till 'Frisco Kid told him to go for'ard and make ready for dropping the anchor.

"Overhaul about fifty fathoms of chain," he ordered, "and then stand by." He eased the sloop gently into the wind, at the same time casting off the jib-sheet. "Let go the jib-halyards and come in on the downhaul!"

Joe had seen the manoeuver performed the previous night, and so was able to carry it out with fair success.

"Now! Over with the mud-hook! Watch out for turns! Lively, now!"

The chain flew out with startling rapidity, and brought the *Dazzler* to rest. 'Frisco Kid went for'ard to help, and together they lowered the mainsail, furled it in shipshape manner, made all fast with the gaskets, and put the crutches under the main-boom.

"Here's a bucket." 'Frisco Kid passed him the article in question. "Wash down the decks, and don't be afraid of the water, nor of the dirt, neither. Here's a broom. Give it what for, and have everything shining. When you get that done, bail out the skiff; she opened her seams a little last night. I'm going below to cook breakfast."

The water was soon slushing merrily over the deck, while the smoke pouring from the cabin stove carried a promise of good things to come. Time and again Joe lifted his head from his task to take in the scene. It was one to appeal to any healthy boy, and he was no exception. The romance of it stirred him strangely, and his happiness would have been complete could he have escaped remembering who and what his companions were. But the thought of this, and of Pete in his bleary, drunken sleep below, marred the beauty of the day. He had been unused to such things, and was shocked at the harsh reality of life. But instead of hurting him, as it might a lad of weaker nature, it had the opposite effect. It strengthened his desire to be clean and strong, and to not be ashamed of himself in his own eyes. He glanced about him and sighed. Why could not men be honest and true? It seemed too bad that he must go away and leave all this; but the events of the night were strong upon him, and he knew that in order to be true to himself he must escape.

At this juncture he was called to breakfast. He discovered that 'Frisco Kid was as good a cook as he was sailor, and made haste to do justice to the fare. There were mush and condensed milk, beefsteak and fried potatoes, and all topped off with good French bread, butter, and coffee. Pete did not join them, though 'Frisco Kid attempted a couple of times to rouse him. He mumbled and grunted, half opened his bleared eyes, then went to snoring again.

"Can't tell when he's going to get those spells," 'Frisco Kid explained, when Joe, having finished washing the dishes, came on deck. "Sometimes he won't get that way for a month, and others he won't be decent for a week at a stretch. Sometimes he's good-natured, and sometimes he's dangerous. So the best thing to do is to let him alone and keep out of his way. And don't cross him, for if you do there's liable to be trouble."

"Come on; let's take a swim," he added, abruptly changing the subject to one more agreeable. "Can you swim?"

Joe nodded. "What's that place?" he asked as he poised before diving, pointing toward a sheltered beach on the island, where there were several buildings and a large number of tents.

"Quarantine station. Lots of smallpox coming in now on the China steamers, and they make them go there till the doctors say they're safe to land. I tell you, they're strict about it, too. Why—"

Splash! Had 'Frisco Kid finished his sentence just then, instead of diving overboard, much trouble might have been saved to Joe. But he did not finish it, and Joe dived after him.

"I'll tell you what," 'Frisco Kid suggested half an hour later, while they clung to the bob-stay preparatory to climbing out. "Let's catch a mess of fish for dinner, and then turn in and make up for the sleep we lost last night. What d'you say?"

They made a race to clamber aboard, but Joe was shoved over the side again. When he finally did arrive, the other lad had brought to light a pair of heavily leaded, large-hooked lines, and a mackerel-keg of salt sardines.

"Bait," he said. "Just shove a whole one on. They're not a bit partic'lar. Swallow the bait, hook and all, and go—that's their caper. The fellow that don't catch first fish has to clean 'em."

Both sinkers started on their long descent together, and seventy feet of line whizzed out before they came to rest. But at the instant his sinker touched the bottom Joe felt the struggling jerks of a hooked fish. As he began to haul in he glanced at 'Frisco Kid, and saw that he, too, had evidently captured a finny prize. The race between them was exciting. Hand over hand the wet lines flashed inboard; but 'Frisco Kid was more expert, and his fish tumbled into the cockpit first. Joe's followed an instant later—a three-pound rock-cod. He was wild with joy. It was magnificent, the largest fish he had ever landed or ever seen landed. Over went the lines again, and up they came with two mates of the ones already captured. It was sport royal. Joe would have certainly continued till he had fished the Bay empty had not 'Frisco Kid persuaded him to stop.

"We've got enough for three meals now," he said, "so there's no use in having them spoil. Besides, the more you catch, the more you clean, and you'd better start in right away. I'm going to bed."

Joe did not mind. In fact, he was glad he had not caught the first fish, for it helped out a little plan which had come to him while in swimming. He threw the last cleaned fish into a bucket of water, and glanced about him. The quarantine station was a bare half-mile away, and he could make out a soldier pacing up and down at sentry duty on the beach. Going into the cabin, he listened to the heavy breathing of the sleepers. He had to pass so close to 'Frisco Kid to get his bundle of clothes that he decided not to take them. Returning outside, he carefully pulled the skiff alongside, got aboard with a pair of oars, and cast off.

At first he rowed very gently in the direction of the station, fearing the chance of noise if he made undue haste. But gradually he increased the strength of his strokes till he had settled down to the regular stride. When he had covered half the distance he glanced about. Escape was sure now, for he knew, even if he were discovered, that it would be impossible for the *Dazzler* to get under way and head him off before he made the land and the protection of that man who wore the uniform of Uncle Sam.

The report of a gun came to him from the shore, but his back was in that direction and he did not bother to turn around. A second report followed, and a bullet cut the water within a couple of feet of his oar-blade. This time he did turn around. The soldier on the beach was leveling his rifle at him for a third shot.

III

Joe Loses Liberty, and Finds a Friend

Joe was in a predicament, and a very tantalizing one at that. A few minutes of hard rowing would bring him to the beach and to safety; but on that beach, for some unaccountable reason, stood a United States soldier who persisted in firing at him.

When Joe saw the gun aimed at him for the third time, he backed water hastily. As a result the skiff came to a standstill, and the soldier, lowering his rifle, regarded him intently.

"I want to come ashore! Important!" Joe shouted out to him.

The man in uniform shook his head.

"But it's important, I tell you! Won't you let me come ashore?"

He took a hurried look in the direction of the *Dazzler*. The shots had evidently awakened Pete; for the mainsail had been hoisted, and as he looked he saw the anchor broken out and the jib flung to the breeze.

"Can't land here!" the soldier shouted back. "Smallpox!"

"But I must!" he cried, choking down a half-sob and preparing to row.

"Then I'll shoot," was the cheering response, and the rifle came to shoulder again.

Joe thought rapidly. The island was large. Perhaps there were no soldiers farther on, and if he only once got ashore he did not care how quickly they captured him. He might catch the smallpox, but even that was better than going back to the Bay pirates. He whirled the skiff half about to the right, and threw all his strength against the oars. The cove was quite wide, and the nearest point which he must go around a good distance away. Had he been more of a sailor he would have gone in the other direction for the opposite point, and thus had the wind on his pursuers. As it was, the *Dazzler* had a beam wind in which to overtake him.

It was nip and tuck for a while. The breeze was light and not very steady, so sometimes he gained and sometimes they. Once it freshened till the sloop was within a hundred yards of him, and then it dropped suddenly flat, the *Dazzler*'s big mainsail flapping idly from side to side.

"Ah! you steal ze skiff, eh?" Pete howled at him, running into the cabin for his rifle. "I fix you! You come back queeck, or I kill you!" But he knew the soldier was watching them from the shore, and did not dare to fire, even over the lad's head.

Joe did not think of this, for he, who had never been shot at in all his previous life, had been under fire twice in the last twenty-four hours. Once more or less couldn't amount to much. So he pulled steadily away, while Pete raved like a wild man, threatening him with all manner of punishments once he laid hands upon him again. To complicate matters, 'Frisco Kid waxed mutinous.

"Just you shoot him and I'll see you hung for it, see if I don't," he threatened. "You'd better let him go. He's a good boy and all right, and not raised for the life you and I are leading."

"You too, eh!" the Frenchman shrieked, beside himself with rage. "Den I fix you, you rat!"

He made a rush for the boy, but 'Frisco Kid led him a lively chase from cockpit to bowsprit and back again. A sharp capful of wind arriving just then, Pete abandoned the one chase for the other. Springing to the tiller and slacking away on the main-sheet —for the wind favored—he headed the sloop down upon Joe. The latter made one tremendous spurt, then gave up in despair and hauled in his oars. Pete let go the main-sheet, lost steerage-way as he rounded up alongside the motionless skiff, and dragged Joe out.

"Keep mum," 'Frisco Kid whispered to him while the irate Frenchman was busy fastening the painter. "Don't talk back. Let him say all he wants to, and keep quiet. It'll be better for you."

But Joe's Anglo-Saxon blood was up and he did not heed.

"Look here, Mr. Pete, or whatever your name is," he commenced, "I give you to understand that I want to quit, and that I'm going to quit. So you'd better put me ashore at once. If you don't, I'll put you in prison, or my name's not Joe Bronson."

'Frisco Kid waited the outcome fearfully. Pete was aghast. He was being defied aboard his own vessel, and by a boy. Never had such a thing been heard of. He knew he was committing an unlawful act in detaining him, while at the same time he was afraid to let him go with the information he had gathered concerning the sloop and its occupation. The boy had spoken the unpleasant truth when he said he could send him to prison. The only thing for him to do was to bully him.

"You will, eh?" His shrill voice rose wrathfully. "Den you come too. You row ze boat last-a night—answer me dat! You steal ze iron—answer me dat! You run away—answer me dat! And den you say you put me in jail? Bah!"

"But I didn't know," Joe protested.

"Ha, ha! Dat is funny. You tell dat to ze judge; mebbe him laugh, eh?"

"I say I didn't," Joe reiterated manfully. "I didn't know I'd shipped along with a lot of pirates and thieves."

'Frisco Kid winced at this epithet, and had Joe been looking at him he would have seen the red flush of shame mount to his face.

"And now that I do know," he continued, "I wish to be put ashore. I don't know anything about the law, but I do know right and wrong, and I'm willing to take my chance with any judge for whatever wrong I have done—with all the judges in the United States, for that matter. And that's more than you can say, Mr. Pete."

"You say dat, eh? Vaire good. But you are one big t'ief—"

"I'm not! Don't you dare call me that again!" Joe's face was pale, and he was trembling—but not with fear.

"T'ief!" the Frenchman taunted back.

"You lie!"

Joe had not been a boy among boys for nothing. He knew the penalty which attached itself to the words he had just spoken, and he expected to receive it. So he was not overmuch surprised when he picked himself up from the floor of the cockpit an instant later, his head still ringing from a stiff blow between the eyes.

"Say dat one time more," Pete bullied, his fist raised and prepared to strike.

Tears of anger stood in Joe's eyes, but he was calm and in dead earnest. "When you say I am a thief, Pete, you lie. You can kill me, but still I will say you lie."

"No, you don't!" 'Frisco Kid had darted in like a wildcat, preventing a second blow and shoving the Frenchman back across the cockpit.

"You leave the boy alone," he continued, suddenly unshipping and arming himself with the heavy iron tiller, and standing between them. "This thing's gone just about as far as it's going to go. You big fool, can't you see the stuff the boy's made out of? He speaks true. He's right, and he knows it, and you could kill him and he wouldn't give in. There's my hand on it, Joe." He turned and extended his hand to Joe, who returned the grip. "You've got spunk, and you're not afraid to show it."

Pete's mouth twisted itself in a sickly smile, but the evil gleam in his eyes gave it the lie. He shrugged his shoulders and said: "Ah! So? He does not dee-sire dat I him call pet names. Ha, ha! It is only ze sailor-man play. Let us—what you call—forgive and forget, eh? Vaire good; forgive and forget."

He reached out his hand, but Joe refused to take it. 'Frisco Kid nodded approval, while Pete, still shrugging his shoulders and smiling, passed into the cabin.

"Slack off ze main-sheet," he called out, "and run down for Hunter's Point. For one time I will cook ze dinner, and den you will say dat it is ze vaire good dinner. Ah! Pete is ze great cook!"

"That's the way he always does—gets real good and cooks when he wants to make up," 'Frisco Kid hazarded, slipping the tiller into the rudder-head and obeying the order. "But even then you can't trust him."

Joe nodded his head, but did not speak. He was in no mood for conversation. He was still trembling from the excitement of the last few moments, while deep down he questioned himself on how he had behaved, and found naught to be ashamed of.

The afternoon sea-breeze had sprung up and was now rioting in from the Pacific. Angel Island was fast dropping astern, and the water-front of San Francisco showing up, as the *Dazzler* plowed along before it. Soon they were in the midst of the shipping, passing in and out among the vessels which had come from the uttermost ends of the earth. Later they crossed the fairway, where the ferry steamers, crowded with passengers, passed backward and forward between San Francisco and Oakland. One came so close that the passengers crowded to the side to see the gallant little sloop and the two boys in the cockpit. Joe gazed almost enviously at the row of down-turned faces. They all were going to their homes, while he—he was going he knew not whither, at the will of Pete Le Maire. He was half tempted to cry out for help; but the foolishness of such an act struck him, and he held his tongue. Turning his head, his eyes wandered along the smoky heights of the city, and he fell to musing on the strange ways of men and ships on the sea.

'Frisco Kid watched him from the corner of his eye, following his thoughts as accurately as though he spoke them aloud.

"Got a home over there somewhere?" he queried suddenly, waving his hand in the direction of the city.

Joe started, so correctly had his thought been anticipated. "Yes," he said simply.

"Tell us about it."

Joe rapidly described his home, though forced to go into greater detail because of the curious questions of his companion. 'Frisco Kid was interested in everything, especially in Mrs. Bronson and Bessie. Of the latter he could not seem to tire, and poured forth question after question concerning her. So peculiar and artless were some of them that Joe could hardly forbear to smile.

"Now tell me about your home," he said, when he at last had finished.

'Frisco Kid seemed suddenly to harden, and his face took on a stern look which the other had never seen there before. He swung his foot idly to and fro, and lifted a dull eye to the main-peak blocks, with which, by the way, there was nothing the matter.

"Go ahead," the other encouraged.

"I haven't no home."

The four words left his mouth as though they had been forcibly ejected, and his lips came together after them almost with a snap.

Joe saw he had touched a tender spot, and strove to ease the way out of it again. "Then the home you did have." He did not dream that there were lads in the world who never had known homes, or that he had only succeeded in probing deeper.

"Never had none."

"Oh!" His interest was aroused, and he now threw solicitude to the winds. "Any sisters?"

"Nope."

"Mother?"

"I was so young when she died that I don't remember her."

"Father?"

"I never saw much of him. He went to sea,—anyhow, he disappeared."

"Oh!" Joe did not know what to say, and an oppressive silence, broken only by the churn of the *Dazzler*'s forefoot, fell upon them.

Just then Pete came out to relieve at the tiller, while they went in to eat. Both lads hailed his advent with feelings of relief, and the awkwardness vanished over the dinner, which was all their skipper had claimed it to be. Afterward 'Frisco Kid relieved Pete, and while he was eating, Joe washed up the dishes and put the cabin shipshape. Then they all gathered in the stern, where the captain strove to increase the general cordiality by entertaining them with descriptions of life among the pearl-divers of the South Seas.

In this fashion the afternoon wore away. They had long since left San Francisco behind, rounded Hunter's Point, and were now skirting the San Mateo shore. Joe caught a glimpse, once, of a party of cyclists rounding a cliff on the San Bruno Road, and remembered the time when he had gone over the same ground on his own wheel. That was only a month or two before, but it seemed an age to him now, so much had there been to come between.

By the time supper had been eaten and the things cleared away, they were well down the Bay, off the marshes behind which Redwood City clustered. The wind had gone down with the sun, and the *Dazzler* was making but little headway, when they sighted a sloop bearing down upon them on the dying wind. 'Frisco Kid instantly named it as the *Reindeer*, to which Pete, after a deep scrutiny, agreed. He seemed greatly pleased at the meeting.

"Epont Nelson runs her," 'Frisco Kid informed Joe. "They've got something big down here, and they're always after Pete to tackle it with them. He knows more about it, whatever it is."

Joe nodded and looked at the approaching craft curiously. Though somewhat larger, it was built on about the same lines as the *Dazzler*—which meant, above everything else, that it was built for speed. The mainsail was so large that it was more like that of a racing-yacht, and it carried the points for no less than three reefs in case of rough weather. Aloft and on deck everything was in place; nothing was untidy or useless. From running-gear to standing-rigging, everything bore evidence of thorough order and smart seamanship.

The *Reindeer* came up slowly in the gathering twilight, and went to anchor not a biscuit-toss away. Pete followed suit with the *Dazzler*, and then went in the skiff to pay them a visit. The two lads stretched themselves out on top of the cabin and awaited his return.

"Do you like the life?" Joe broke silence.

The other turned on his elbow. "Well—I do, and then again I don't. The fresh air and the salt water, and all that, and the freedom—that's all right; but I don't like the—the—" He paused a moment, as though his tongue had failed in its duty, and then blurted out, "the stealing."

"Then why don't you quit it?" Joe liked the lad more than he dared confess, and he felt a sudden missionary zeal come upon him.

"I will, just as soon as I can turn my hand to something else."

"But why not now?"

Now is the accepted time, was ringing in Joe's ears, and if the other wished to leave, it seemed a pity that he did not, and at once.

"Where can I go? What can I do? There's nobody in all the world to lend me a hand, just as there never has been. I tried it once, and learned my lesson too well to do it again in a hurry."

"Well, when I get out of this I'm going home. Guess my father was right, after all. And I don't see—maybe—what's the matter with you going with me?" He said this last impulsively, without thinking, and 'Frisco Kid knew it.

"You don't know what you're talking about," he answered. "Fancy me going off with you! What'd your father say? And—and the rest? How would he think of me? And what'd he do?"

Joe felt sick at heart. He realized that in the spirit of the moment he had given an invitation which, on sober thought, he knew would be impossible to carry out. He tried to imagine his father receiving in his own house a stranger like 'Frisco Kid. No, that was not to be thought of. Then, forgetting his own plight, he fell to racking his brains for some other method by which 'Frisco Kid could get away from his present surroundings.

"He might turn me over to the police," the other went on, "and send me to a refuge. I'd die first, before I'd let that happen to me. And besides, Joe, I'm not of your kind, and you know it. Why, I'd be like a fish out of water, what with all the things I don't know. Nope; I guess I'll have to wait a little before I strike out. But there's only one thing for you to do, and that's to go straight home. First chance I get, I'll land you, and then deal with Pete—"

"No, you don't," Joe interrupted hotly. "When I leave I'm not going to leave you in trouble on my account. So don't you try anything like that. I'll get away, never fear; and if I can figure it out, I want you to come along too—come along, anyway, and figure it out afterwards. What d'you say?"

'Frisco Kid shook his head, and, gazing up at the starlit heavens, wandered off into day-dreams of the life he would like to lead, but from which he seemed inexorably shut out. The seriousness of life was striking deeper than ever into Joe's heart, and he lay silent, thinking hard. A mumble of heavy voices came to them from the *Reindeer*; from the land the solemn notes of a church bell floated across the water; while the summer night wrapped them slowly in its warm darkness.

IV

'Frisco Kid Tells His Story

AFTER the conversation died away, the two lads lay upon the cabin for perhaps an hour.

Then, without saying a word, 'Frisco Kid went below and struck a light. Joe could hear him fumbling about, and a little later heard his own name called softly. On going into the cabin, he saw 'Frisco Kid sitting on the edge of the bunk, a sailor's ditty-box on his knees, and in his hand a carefully folded page from a magazine.

"Does she look like this?" he asked, smoothing it out and turning it that the other might see.

It was a half-page illustration of two girls and a boy, grouped in an old-fashioned, roomy attic, and evidently holding a council of some sort. The girl who was talking faced the onlooker, while the backs of the two others were turned.

"Who?" Joe queried, glancing in perplexity from the picture to 'Frisco Kid's face.

"Like—like your sister—Bessie." The name seemed reluctant to come from his lips, and he expressed it with a certain shy reverence, as though it were something unspeakably sacred.

Joe was nonplussed for the moment. He could see no bearing between the two in point, and, anyway, girls were rather silly creatures to waste one's time over. "He's actually blushing," he thought, regarding the soft glow on the other's cheeks. He felt an irresistible desire to laugh, but tried to smother it down.

"No, no; don't!" 'Frisco Kid cried, snatching the paper away and putting it back in the ditty-box with shaking fingers. Then he added more slowly: "I thought I—I kind of thought you would understand, and—and—"

His lips trembled and his eyes glistened with unwonted moistness as he turned hastily away.

The next instant Joe was by his side on the bunk, his arm around him. Prompted by some instinctive monitor, he had done it before he thought. A week before he could not have imagined himself in such an absurd situation—his arm around a boy! but now it seemed the most natural thing in the world. He did not comprehend, but he knew that, whatever it was, it was something that seemed of deep importance to his companion.

"Go ahead and tell us," he urged. "I'll understand."

"No, you won't; you can't."

"Yes—sure. Go ahead."

'Frisco Kid choked and shook his head. "I don't think I could, anyway. It's more the things I feel, and I don't know how to put them in words." Joe's arm wrapped about him reassuringly, and he went on: "Well, it's this way. You see, I don't know much about the land, and people, and homes, and I never had no brothers, or sisters, or playmates. All the time I didn't know it, but I was lonely—sort of missed them down in here somewheres." He placed a hand over his breast to locate the seat of loss. "Did you ever feel downright hungry? Well, that's just the way I used to feel, only a different kind of hunger, and me not knowing what it was. But one day, oh, a long time back, I got a-hold of a magazine, and saw a picture—that picture, with the two girls and the boy talking together. I thought it must be fine to be like them, and I got to thinking about the things they said and did, till it came to me all of a sudden like, and I knew that it was just loneliness was the matter with me.

"But, more than anything else, I got to wondering about the girl who looks out of the picture right at you. I was thinking about her all the time, and by and by she became real to me. You see, it was making believe, and I knew it all the time; and then again I didn't. Whenever I'd think of the men, and the work, and the hard life, I'd know it was make-believe; but when I'd think of her, it wasn't. I don't know; I can't explain it."

Joe remembered all his own adventures which he had imagined on land and sea, and nodded. He at least understood that much.

"Of course it was all foolishness, but to have a girl like that for a friend seemed more like heaven to me than anything else I knew of. As I said, it was a long while back, and I was only a little kid. That's when Nelson gave me my name, and I've never been anything but 'Frisco Kid ever since. But the girl in the picture: I was always getting that picture out to look at her, and before long, if I wasn't square, why, I felt ashamed to look at her. Afterwards, when I was older, I came to look at it in another way. I thought, 'Suppose, Kid, some day you were to meet a girl like that, what would she think of you? Could she like you? Could she be even the least bit of a friend to you?' And then I'd make up my mind to be better, to try and do something with myself so that she or any of her kind of people would not be ashamed to know me.

"That's why I learned to read. That's why I ran away. Nicky Perrata, a Greek boy, taught me my letters, and it wasn't till after I learned to read that I found out there was anything really wrong in Bay-pirating. I'd been used to it ever since I could remember, and several people I knew made their living that way. But when I did find out, I ran away, thinking to quit it for good. I'll tell you about it sometime, and how I'm back at it again.

"Of course she seemed a real girl when I was a youngster, and even now she sometimes seems that way, I've thought so much about her. But while I'm talking to you it all clears up and she comes to me in this light: she stands just for—well, for a better, cleaner life than this, and one I'd like to live; and if I could live it, why, I'd come to know that kind of girls, and their kind of people—your kind, that's what I mean. So I was wondering about your sister and you, and that's why—I don't know; I guess I was just wondering. But I suppose you know lots of girls like that, don't you?"

Joe nodded his head in token that he did.

"Then tell me about them; something—anything," he added, as he noted the fleeting expression of doubt in the other's eyes.

"Oh, that's easy," Joe began valiantly. To a certain extent he did understand the lad's hunger, and it seemed a simple enough task to satisfy him. "To begin with, they're like—hem!—why, they're like—girls, just girls." He broke off with a miserable sense of failure.

'Frisco Kid waited patiently, his face a study in expectancy.

Joe struggled vainly to marshal his ideas. To his mind, in quick succession, came the girls with whom he had gone to school, the sisters of the boys he knew, and those who were his sister's friends—slim girls and plump girls, tall girls and short girls, blue-eyed and brown-eyed, curly-haired, black-haired, golden-haired; in short, a regular procession of girls of all sorts and descriptions. But, to save himself, he could say nothing about them. Anyway, he'd never been a "sissy," and why should he be expected to know anything about them? "All girls are alike," he concluded desperately. "They're just the same as the ones you know, Kid. Sure they are."

"But I don't know any."

Joe whistled. "And never did?"

"Yes, one—Carlotta Gispardi. But she couldn't speak English; and she died. I don't care; though I never knew any, I seem to know as much about them as you do."

"And I guess I know more about adventures all over the world than you do," Joe retorted.

Both boys laughed. But a moment later Joe fell into deep thought. It had come upon him quite swiftly that he had not been duly grateful for the good things of life he did possess. Already home, father, and mother had assumed a greater significance to him; but he now found himself placing a higher personal value upon his sister, his chums and friends. He never had appreciated them properly, he thought, but henceforth—well, there would be a different tale to tell.

The voice of Pete hailing them put a finish to the conversation, for they both ran on deck.

"Get up ze mainsail, and break out ze hook!" he shouted. "And den tail on to ze *Reindeer*! No side-lights!"

"Come! Cast off those gaskets! Lively!" 'Frisco Kid ordered. "Now lay onto the peak-halyards—there, that rope; cast it off the pin. And don't hoist ahead of me. There! Make fast! We'll stretch it afterwards. Run aft and come in on the main-sheet! Shove the helm up!"

Under the sudden driving power of the mainsail, the *Dazzler* strained and tugged at her anchor like an impatient horse, till the muddy iron left the bottom with a rush, and she was free.

"Let go the sheet! Come for'ard again, and lend a hand on the chain! Stand by to give her the jib!" 'Frisco Kid, the boy who mooned over a picture of a girl in a magazine, had vanished, and 'Frisco Kid the sailor, strong and dominant, was on deck. He ran aft and tacked about as the jib rattled aloft in the hands of Joe, who quickly joined him. Just then the *Reindeer*, like a monstrous bat, passed to leeward of them in the gloom.

"Ah! dose boys! Dey take all-a night!" they heard Pete exclaim; and then the gruff voice of Nelson, who said: "Never you mind, Frenchy. I learned the Kid his sailorizing, and I ain't never been ashamed of him yet."

The *Reindeer* was the faster boat, but by spilling the wind from her sails they managed so that the boys could keep them in sight. The breeze came steadily in from the west, with a promise of early increase. The stars were being blotted out by driving masses of clouds, which indicated a greater velocity in the upper strata. 'Frisco Kid surveyed the sky. "Going to have it good and stiff before morning," he prophesied, and Joe guessed so, too.

A couple of hours later both boats stood in for the land, and dropped anchor not more than a cable's-length from the shore. A little wharf ran out, the bare end of which was perceptible to them, though they could discern a small yacht lying to a buoy a short distance away.

As on the previous night, everything was in readiness for hasty departure. The anchors could be tripped and the sails flung out on a moment's notice. Both skiffs came over noiselessly from the *Reindeer*. Nelson had given one of his two men to Pete, so that each skiff was doubly manned. They were not a very prepossessing bunch of men—at least, Joe thought so, for their faces bore a savage seriousness which almost made him shiver. The captain of the *Dazzler* buckled on his pistol-belt and placed a rifle and a small double-block tackle in the boat. Nelson was also armed, while his men wore at their hips the customary sailor's sheath-knife. They were very slow and careful to avoid noise in getting into the boats, Pete pausing long enough to warn the boys to remain quietly aboard and not try any tricks.

"Now'd be your chance, Joe, if they hadn't taken the skiffs," 'Frisco Kid whispered, when the boats had vanished into the loom of the land.

"What's the matter with the *Dazzler*?" was the unexpected answer. "We could up sail and away before you could say Jack Robinson."

They crawled for'ard and began to hoist the mainsail. The anchor they could slip, if necessary, and save the time of pulling it up. But at the first rattle of the halyards on the sheaves a warning "Hist!" came to them through the darkness, followed by a loudly whispered "Drop that!"

Glancing in the direction from which these sounds proceeded, they made out a white face peering at them from over the rail of the other sloop.

"Aw, it's only the *Reindeer*'s boy," 'Frisco Kid said. "Come on."

Again they were interrupted at the first rattling of the blocks.

"I say, you fellers, you'd better let go them halyards pretty quick, I'm a-tellin' you, or I'll give you what for!"

This threat being dramatically capped by the click of a cocking pistol, 'Frisco Kid obeyed and went grumblingly back to the cockpit. "Oh, there's plenty more chances to come," he whispered consolingly to Joe. "Pete was cute, wasn't he? Kind of thought you'd be trying to make a break, and fixed it so you couldn't."

Nothing came from the shore to indicate how the pirates were faring. Not a dog barked, not a light flared; yet the air seemed quivering with an alarm about to burst forth. The night had taken on a strained feeling of intensity, as though it held in store all kinds of terrible things. The boys felt this keenly as they huddled against each other in the cockpit and waited.

"You were going to tell me about your running away," Joe ventured finally, "and why you came back again."

'Frisco Kid took up the tale at once, speaking in a muffled undertone close to the other's ear.

"You see, when I made up my mind to quit the life, there wasn't a soul to lend me a hand; but I knew that the only thing for me to do was to get ashore and find some kind of work, so I could study. Then I figured there'd be more chance in the country than in the city; so I gave Nelson the slip. I was on the *Reindeer* then—one night on the Alameda oyster-beds, and headed back from the Bay. But they were all Portuguese farmers thereabouts, and none of them had work for me. Besides, it was in the wrong time of the year—winter. That shows how much I knew about the land.

"I'd saved up a couple of dollars, and I kept traveling back, deeper and deeper into the country, looking for work and buying bread and cheese, and such things, from the store-keepers. I tell you it was cold, nights, sleeping out without blankets, and I was always glad when morning came. But worse than that was the way everybody looked on me. They were all suspicious, and not a bit afraid to show it, and sometimes they'd sick their dogs on me and tell me to get along. Seemed as though there wasn't no place for me on the land. Then my money gave out, and just about the time I was good and hungry I got captured."

"Captured! What for?"

"Nothing. Living, I suppose. I crawled into a haystack to sleep one night, because it was warmer, and along comes a village constable and arrests me for being a tramp. At first they thought I was a runaway, and telegraphed my description all over. I told them I didn't have no people, but they wouldn't believe me for a long while. And then, when nobody claimed me, the judge sent me to a boys' 'refuge' in San Francisco."

He stopped and peered intently in the direction of the shore. The darkness and the silence in which the men had been swallowed up were profound. Nothing was stirring save the rising wind.

"I thought I'd die in that 'refuge.' Just like being in jail. You were locked up and guarded like any prisoner. Even then, if I could have liked the other boys it wouldn't have been so bad. But they were mostly street-boys of the worst sort, without one spark of manhood or one idea of square dealing and fair play. There was only one thing I did like, and that was the books. Oh, I did lots of reading, I tell you. But that couldn't make up for the rest. I wanted the freedom, and the sunlight, and the salt water. And what had I done to be kept in prison and herded with such a gang? Instead of doing wrong, I had tried to do good, to make myself better, and that's what I got for it. I wasn't old enough, you see.

"Sometimes I'd see the sunshine dancing on the water and showing white on the sails, and the *Reindeer* cutting through it just as you please, and I'd get that sick I wouldn't know hardly what I did. And then the boys would come against me with some of their meannesses, and I'd start in to lick the whole kit of them. Then the men in charge'd lock me up and punish me. After I couldn't stand it no longer, I watched my chance, and cut and run for it. Seemed as though there wasn't no place on the land for me, so I picked up with Pete and went back on the Bay. That's about all there is to it, though I'm going to try it again when I get a little older—old enough to get a square deal for myself."

"You're going to go back on the land with me," Joe said authoritatively, laying a hand on his shoulder; "that's what you're going to do. As for—"

Bang! a revolver-shot rang out from the shore. Bang! bang! More guns were speaking sharply and hurriedly. A man's voice rose wildly on the air and died away. Somebody began to cry for help. Both boys were to their feet on the instant, hoisting the mainsail and getting everything ready to run. The *Reindeer* boy was doing likewise. A man, roused from his sleep on the yacht, thrust an excited head through the skylight, but withdrew it hastily at sight of the two stranger sloops. The intensity of waiting was broken, the time for action come.

V

Perilous Hours

HEAVING in on the anchor-chain till it was up and down, 'Frisco Kid and Joe ceased from their exertions. Everything was in readiness to give the *Dazzler* the jib and go. They strained their eyes in the direction of the shore. The clamor had died away, but here and there lights were beginning to flash. The creaking of a block and tackle came to their ears, and they heard Nelson's voice singing out "Lower away!" and "Cast off!"

"Pete forgot to oil it," 'Frisco Kid commented, referring to the tackle.

"Takin' their time about it, ain't they?" the boy on the *Reindeer* called over to them, sitting down on the cabin and mopping his face after the exertion of hoisting the mainsail single-handed.

"Guess they're all right," 'Frisco Kid rejoined.

"Say, you," the man on the yacht cried through the skylight, not venturing to show his head. "You'd better go away."

"And you'd better stay below and keep quiet," was the response.

"We'll take care of ourselves. See you do the same," replied the boy on the *Reindeer*.

"If I was only out of this, I'd show you," the man threatened.

"Lucky for you you're not," was the response.

"Here they come!"

The two skiffs shot out of the darkness and came alongside. Some kind of an altercation was going on, as Pete's shrill voice attested.

"No, no!" he cried. "Put it on ze *Dazzler*. Ze *Reindeer* she sail too fast-a, and run away, oh, so queeck, and never more I see it. Put it on ze *Dazzler*. Eh? W'at you say?"

"All right," Nelson agreed. "We'll whack up afterwards. But hurry up. Out with you, lads, and heave her up. My arm's broke."

The men tumbled out, ropes were cast inboard, and all hands, with the exception of Joe, tailed on. The shouting of men, the sound of oars, and the rattling and slapping of blocks and sails, told that the men on shore were getting under way for the pursuit.

"Now!" Nelson commanded. "All together! Don't let her come back or you'll smash the skiff. There she takes it! A long pull and a strong pull! Once again! And yet again! Get a turn there, somebody, and take a spell."

Though the task was but half accomplished, they were exhausted by the strenuous effort, and hailed the rest eagerly. Joe glanced over the side to discover what the heavy object might be, and saw the vague outlines of a very small office safe.

"Now, all together! Take her on the run, and don't let her stop! Yo, ho! heave, ho! Once again! And another! Over with her!"

Straining and gasping, with tense muscles and heaving chests, they brought the cumbersome weight over the side, rolled it on top of the rail, and lowered it into the cockpit on the run. The cabin doors were thrown apart, and it was moved along, end for end, till it lay on the cabin floor, snug against the end of the center-board-case. Nelson had followed it aboard to superintend. His left arm hung helpless at his side, and from the finger-tips blood dripped with monotonous regularity. He did not seem to mind it, however; nor even the mutterings of the human storm he had raised ashore, and which, to judge by the sounds, was even now threatening to break upon them.

"Lay your course for the Golden Gate," he said to Pete, as he turned to go. "I'll try to stand by you; but if you get lost in the dark, I'll meet you outside, off the Farralones, in the morning." He sprang into the skiff after the men, and, with a wave of his uninjured arm, cried heartily: "And then it's Mexico, my jolly rovers—Mexico and summer weather!"

Just as the *Dazzler*, freed from her anchor, paid off under the jib and filled away, a dark sail loomed under her stern, barely missing the skiff in tow. The cockpit of the stranger was crowded with men, who raised their voices angrily at sight of the pirates. Joe had half a mind to run for'ard and cut the halyards so that they might be captured. As he had told Pete the day before, he had done nothing to be ashamed of, and was not afraid to go before a court of justice. But the thought of 'Frisco Kid restrained him. He wished to take him ashore with him, but in so doing he did not wish to take him to jail. So he began to experience a keen interest in the escape of the *Dazzler*, after all.

The pursuing sloop rounded up hurriedly to come about after them, and in the darkness fouled the yacht which lay at anchor. The man aboard of her, thinking that at last his time had come, let out one wild yell, and ran on deck, screaming for help. In the confusion of the collision Pete and the boys slipped away into the night.

The *Reindeer* had already disappeared, and by the time Joe and 'Frisco Kid had the running-gear coiled down and everything in shape, they were standing out in open water. The wind was freshening constantly, and the *Dazzler* heeling a lively clip through the comparatively smooth water. Before an hour had passed, the lights of Hunter's Point were well on her starboard beam. 'Frisco Kid went below to make coffee, but Joe remained on deck, watching the lights of South San Francisco grow, and speculating on his destination. Mexico! They were going to sea in such a frail craft! Impossible! At least, it seemed so to him, for his conceptions of ocean travel were limited to steamers and full-rigged ships, and he did not know how the tiny fishing-boats ventured the open sea. He was beginning to feel half sorry that he had not cut the halyards, and longed to ask Pete a thousand questions; but just as the first was on his lips, that worthy ordered him to go below and get some coffee, and then to turn in. He was followed shortly afterward by 'Frisco Kid, Pete remaining at his lonely task of beating down the Bay and out to sea. Twice Pete heard the waves buffeted back from some flying forefoot, and once he saw a sail to leeward on the opposite tack, which luffed sharply and came about at sight of him. But the darkness favored, and he heard no more of it—perhaps because he worked into the wind closer by a point, and held on his way with a rebellious shaking after-leech.

Shortly after dawn the boys were called and came sleepily on deck. The day had broken cold and gray, while the wind had attained half a gale. Joe noted with astonishment the white tents of the quarantine station on Angel Island. San Francisco lay a smoky blur on the southern horizon, while the night, still lingering on the western edge of the world, slowly withdrew before their eyes. Pete was just finishing a long reach into the Raccoon Strait, and, at the same time, studiously regarding a plunging sloop-yacht half a mile astern.

"Dey t'ink to catch ze *Dazzler*, eh? Bah!" And he brought the craft in question about, laying a course straight for the Golden Gate.

The pursuing yacht followed suit. Joe watched her a few moments. She held an apparently parallel course to them, and forged ahead much faster.

"Why, at this rate they'll have us in no time!" he cried.

Pete laughed. "You t'ink so? Bah! Dey outfoot; we outpoint. Dey are scared of ze wind; we wipe ze eye of ze wind. Ah! you wait—you see."

"They're traveling ahead faster," 'Frisco Kid explained, "but we're sailing closer to the wind. In the end we'll beat them, even if they have the nerve to cross the bar, which I don't think they have. Look! See!"

Ahead could be seen the great ocean surges, flinging themselves skyward and bursting into roaring caps of smother. In the midst of it, now rolling her dripping bottom clear, now sousing her deck-load of lumber far above the guards, a coasting steam-schooner was lumbering heavily into port. It was magnificent, this battle between man and the elements. Whatever timidity he had entertained fled away, and Joe's nostrils began to dilate and his eyes to flash at the nearness of the impending struggle.

Pete called for his oilskins and sou'wester, and Joe also was equipped with a spare suit. Then he and 'Frisco Kid were sent below to lash and cleat the safe in place. In the midst of this task Joe glanced at the firm-name gilt-lettered on the face of it, and read, "Bronson & Tate." Why, that was his father and his father's partner. That was their safe! their money! 'Frisco Kid, nailing the last retaining-cleat on the floor of the cabin, looked up and followed his fascinated gaze.

"That's rough, isn't it?" he whispered. "Your father?"

Joe nodded. He could see it all now. They had run in to San Andreas, where his father worked the big quarries, and most probably the safe contained the wages of the thousand men or so whom his firm employed. "Don't say anything," he cautioned.

'Frisco Kid agreed knowingly. "Pete can't read, anyway," he added, "and the chances are that Nelson won't know what your name is. But, just the same, it's pretty rough. They'll break it open and divide up as soon as they can, so I don't see what you're going to do about it."

"Wait and see." Joe had made up his mind that he would do his best to stand by his father's property. At the worst, it could only be lost; and that would surely be the case were he not along; while, being along, he at least held a fighting chance to save or to be in position to recover it. Responsibilities were showering upon him thick and fast. Three days before he had had but himself to consider. Then, in some subtle way, he had felt a certain accountability for 'Frisco Kid's future welfare; and after that, and still more subtly, he had become aware of duties which he owed to his position, to his sister, to his chums, and to friends. And now, by a most unexpected chain of circumstances, came the pressing need of service for his father's sake. It was a call upon his deepest strength, and he responded bravely. While the future might be doubtful, he had no doubt of himself; and this very state of mind, this self-confidence, by a generous alchemy, gave him added strength. Nor did he fail to be vaguely aware of it, and to grasp dimly at the truth that confidence breeds confidence—strength, strength.

"Now she takes it!" Pete cried.

Both lads ran into the cockpit. They were on the edge of the breaking bar. A huge forty-footer reared a foam-crested head far above them, stealing their wind for the moment and threatening to crush the tiny craft like an egg-shell. Joe held his breath. It was the supreme moment. Pete luffed straight into it, and the *Dazzler* mounted the steep slope with a rush, poised a moment on the giddy summit, and fell into the yawning valley beyond. Keeping off in the intervals to fill the mainsail, and luffing into the combers, they worked their way across the dangerous stretch. Once they caught the tail-end of a whitecap and were well-nigh smothered in the froth; but otherwise the sloop bobbed and ducked with the happy facility of a cork.

To Joe it seemed as though he had been lifted out of himself, out of the world. Ah, this was life! This was action! Surely it could not be the old, commonplace world he had lived in so long! The sailors, grouped on the streaming deck-load of the steamer, waved their sou'westers, nor, on the bridge, was the captain above expressing his admiration for the plucky craft.

"Ah! You see! You see!" Pete pointed astern.

The sloop-yacht had been afraid to venture it, and was skirting back and forth on the inner edge of the bar. The chase was off. A pilot-boat, running for shelter from the coming storm, flew by them like a frightened bird, passing the steamer as though the latter were standing still.

Half an hour later the *Dazzler* passed beyond the last smoking sea and was sliding up and down on the long Pacific swell. The wind had increased its velocity and necessitated a reefing down of jib and mainsail. Then she laid off again, full and free on the starboard tack, for the Farralones, thirty miles away. By the time breakfast was cooked and eaten they picked up the *Reindeer*, hove to and working offshore to the south and west. The wheel was lashed down, and there was not a soul on deck.

Pete complained bitterly against such recklessness. "Dat is ze one fault of Nelson. He no care. He is afraid of not'ing. Some day he will die, oh, so vaire queeck! I know, I know."

Three times they circled about the *Reindeer*, running under her weather quarter and shouting in chorus, before they brought anybody on deck. Sail was then made at once, and together the two cockle-shells plunged away into the vastness of the Pacific. This was necessary, as 'Frisco Kid informed Joe, in order to have an offing before the whole fury of the storm broke upon them. Otherwise they would be driven on the lee shore of the California coast. "Grub and water," he said, could be obtained by running in to the land when fine weather came. He also congratulated Joe upon the fact that he was not sea-sick—which circumstance likewise brought praise from Pete, and put him in better humor with his mutinous sailor.

"I'll tell you what we'll do," 'Frisco Kid whispered, while cooking dinner. "To-night we'll drag Pete down—"

"Drag Pete down?"

"Yes, and tie him up good and snug—as soon as it gets dark. Then put out the lights and make a run for it. Get to port anyway, anywhere, just so long as we shake loose from Nelson. You'll save your father's money, and I'll go away somewhere, over on the other side of the world, and begin all over again."

"Then we'll have to call it off, that's all."

"Call what off?"

"Tying Pete up and running for it."

"No, sir; that's decided upon."

"Now, listen here: I'll not have a thing to do with it—I'll go on to Mexico first—if you don't make me one promise."

"And what's the promise?"

"Just this: you place yourself in my hands from the moment we get ashore, and trust to me. You don't know anything about the land, anyway—you said so. And I'll fix it with my father—I know I can—so that you can get to study, and get an education, and be something else than a Bay pirate or a sailor. That's what you'd like, isn't it?"

Though he said nothing, 'Frisco Kid showed how well he liked it by the expression of his face.

"And it'll be no more than your due, either," Joe continued. "You've stood by me, and you'll have recovered my father's money. He'll owe it to you."

"But I don't do things that way. Think I do a man a favor just to be paid for it?"

"Now you keep quiet. How much do you think it'd cost my father to recover that safe? Give me your promise, that's all, and when I've got things arranged, if you don't like them you can back out. Come on; that's fair."

They shook hands on the bargain, and proceeded to map out their line of action for the night.

But the storm yelling down out of the north-west had something entirely different in store for the *Dazzler* and her crew. By the time dinner was over they were forced to put double reefs in mainsail and jib, and still the gale had not reached its height. The sea, also, had been kicked up till it was a continuous succession of water mountains, frightful and withal grand to look upon from the low deck of the sloop. It was only when the sloops were tossed up on the crests of the waves at the same time that they caught sight of each other. Occasional fragments of seas swashed into the cockpit or dashed aft clear over the cabin, and before long Joe was stationed at the small pump to keep the well dry.

At three o'clock, watching his chance, Pete motioned to the *Reindeer* that he was going to heave to and get out a sea-anchor. This latter was of the nature of a large shallow canvas bag, with the mouth held open by triangularly lashed spars. To this the towing-ropes were attached, on the kite principle, so that the greatest resisting surface was presented to the water. The sloop, drifting so much faster, would thus be held bow on to both wind and sea—the safest possible position in a storm. Nelson waved his hand in response that he understood, and to go ahead.

Pete went for'ard to launch the sea-anchor himself, leaving it to 'Frisco Kid to put the helm down at the proper moment and run into the wind.

The Frenchman poised on the slippery fore-deck, waiting an opportunity. But at this moment the *Dazzler* lifted into an unusually large sea, and, as she cleared the summit, caught a heavy snort of the gale at the very instant she was righting herself to an even keel.

Thus there was not the slightest yield to this sudden pressure coming on her sails and mast-gear.

Snap! Crash! The steel weather-rigging was carried away at the lanyards, and mast, jib, mainsail, blocks, stays, sea-anchor, Pete—everything—went over the side. Almost by a miracle, the captain clutched at the bobstay and managed to get one hand up and over the bow-sprit. The boys ran for'ard to drag him into safety, and Nelson, observing the disaster, put up his helm and instantly ran the *Reindeer* down to the rescue of the imperiled crew.

VI

The End of the Cruise

PETE was uninjured from the fall overboard with the *Dazzler*'s mast, but the sea-anchor which had gone with him had not escaped so easily. The gaff of the mainsail had been driven through it, and it refused to work. The wreckage, thumping alongside, held the sloop in a quartering slant to the seas—not so dangerous a position as it might be, nor as safe, either.

"Good-by, old-a *Dazzler*. Never no more you wipe ze eye of ze wind. Never no more you kick your heels at ze crack gentleman-yachts."

So the captain lamented, standing in the cockpit and surveying the ruin with wet eyes. Even Joe, who bore him great dislike, felt sorry for him at this moment. As the horse is to the Arab, so the ship is to the sailor, and Pete suffered his loss keenly. A heavier blast of the wind caught the jagged crest of a wave and hurled it upon the helpless craft.

"Can't we save her?" Joe spluttered.

'Frisco Kid shook his head.

"Or the safe?"

"Impossible," he answered. "Couldn't lay another boat alongside for a United States mint. As it is, it'll keep us guessing to save ourselves."

Another sea swept over them, and the skiff, which had long since been swamped, dashed itself to pieces against the stern. Then the *Reindeer* towered above them on a mountain of water. Joe caught himself half shrinking back, for it seemed she would fall down squarely on top of them; but the next instant she dropped into the gaping trough, and they were looking down upon her far below. It was a striking picture—one Joe was destined never to forget. The *Reindeer* was wallowing in the snow-white smother, her rails flush with the sea, the water scudding across her deck in foaming cataracts. The air was filled with flying spray, which made the scene appear hazy and unreal. One of the men was clinging to the perilous after-deck and striving to cast off the water-logged skiff. The boy, leaning far over the cockpit-rail and holding on for dear life, was passing him a knife. The second man stood at the wheel, putting it up with flying hands, and forcing the sloop to pay off. By him, his injured arm in a sling, was Nelson, his sou'wester gone and his fair hair plastered in wet, wind-blown ringlets about his face. His whole attitude breathed indomitability, courage, strength. Joe looked upon him in sudden awe, and, realizing the enormous possibilities in the man, felt sorrow for the way in which they had been wasted. A pirate—a robber! In that flashing moment he caught a glimpse of truth, grasped at the mystery of success and failure. Of such stuff as Nelson were heroes made; but they possessed wherein he lacked —the power of choice, the careful poise of mind, the sober control of soul.

These were the thoughts which came to Joe in the flight of a second. Then the *Reindeer* swept skyward and hurtled across their bow to leeward on the breast of a mighty billow.

"Ze wild man! ze wild man!" Pete shrieked, watching her in amazement. "He t'inks he can jibe! He will die! We will all die! He must come about! Oh, ze fool! ze fool!"

But time was precious, and Nelson ventured the chance. At the right moment he jibed the mainsail over and hauled back on the wind.

"Here she comes! Make ready to jump for it!" 'Frisco Kid cried to Joe.

The *Reindeer* dashed by their stern, heeling over till the cabin windows were buried, and so close that it appeared she must run them down. But a freak of the waters lurched the two crafts apart. Nelson, seeing that the manoeuver had miscarried, instantly instituted another. Throwing the helm hard up, the *Reindeer* whirled on her heel, thus swinging her overhanging main-boom closer to the *Dazzler*. Pete was the nearest, and the opportunity could last no longer than a second. Like a cat he sprang, catching the foot-rope with both hands. Then the *Reindeer* forged ahead, dipping him into the sea at every plunge. But he clung on, working inboard every time he emerged, till he dropped into the cockpit, as Nelson squared off to run down to leeward and repeat the manoeuver.

"Your turn next," 'Frisco Kid said.

"No; yours," Joe replied.

"But I know more about the water," 'Frisco Kid insisted.

"I can swim as well as you," said the other.

It would have been hard to forecast the outcome of this dispute; but, as it was, the swift rush of events made any settlement useless. The *Reindeer* had jibed over and was plowing back at breakneck speed, careening at such an angle that it seemed she must surely capsize. It was a gallant sight.

The storm burst in fury, the shouting wind flattening the ragged crests till they boiled. The *Reindeer* dipped from view behind an immense wave. The wave rolled on, but where the sloop had been the boys noted with startled eyes only the angry waters. Doubting, they looked a second time. There was no *Reindeer*. They were alone on the ocean.

"God have mercy on their souls!"

Joe was too horrified at the suddenness of the catastrophe to utter a sound.

"Sailed her clean under, and, with the ballast she carried, went straight to bottom," 'Frisco Kid gasped when he could speak. "Pete always said Nelson would drown himself that way some day! And now they're all gone. It's dreadful—dreadful. But now we've got to look out for ourselves, I tell you! The back of the storm broke in that puff, but the sea'll kick up worse yet as the wind eases down. Lend a hand, and hang on with the other. We've got to get her head-on."

Together, knives in hand, they crawled for'ard, where the pounding wreckage hampered the boat sorely. 'Frisco Kid took the lead in the ticklish work, but Joe obeyed orders like a veteran. Every minute or so the bow was swept by the sea, and they were pounded and buffeted about like a pair of shuttlecocks. First the main portion of the wreckage was securely fastened to the for'ard bitts; then, breathless and gasping, more often under the water than out, it was cut and hack at the tangle of halyards, sheets, stays, and tackles. The cockpit was taking water rapidly, and it was a race between swamping and completing the task. At last, however, everything stood clear save the lee rigging. 'Frisco Kid slashed the lanyards. The storm did the rest. The *Dazzler* drifted swiftly to leeward of the wreckage, till the strain on the line fast to the for'ard bitts jerked her bow into place, and she ducked dead into the eye of the wind and sea.

Pausing but for a cheer at the success of their undertaking, the two lads raced aft, where the cockpit was half full and the dunnage of the cabin all afloat. With a couple of buckets procured from the stern lockers, they proceeded to fling the water overboard. It was heartbreaking work, for many a barrelful was flung back upon them again; but they persevered, and when night fell, the *Dazzler*, bobbing merrily at her sea-anchor, could boast that her pumps sucked once more. As 'Frisco Kid had said, the backbone of the storm was broken, though the wind had veered to the west, where it still blew stiffly.

"If she holds," 'Frisco Kid said, referring to the breeze, "we'll drift to the California coast, somewhere along in, to-morrow. There's nothing to do now but wait."

They said little, oppressed by the loss of their comrades and overcome with exhaustion, preferring to huddle against each other for the sake of warmth and companionship. It was a miserable night, and they shivered constantly from the cold. Nothing dry was to be obtained aboard, food, blankets, everything being soaked with the salt water. Sometimes they dozed; but these intervals were short and harassing, for it seemed as if each of the two boys took turns in waking with such a sudden start as to rouse the other.

At last day broke, and they looked about. Wind and sea had dropped considerably, and there was no question as to the safety of the *Dazzler*. The coast was nearer than they had expected, its cliffs showing dark and forbidding in the gray of dawn. But with the rising of the sun they could see the yellow beaches, flanked by the white surf, and, beyond—it seemed too good to be true—the clustering houses and smoking chimneys of a town.

"It's Santa Cruz!" 'Frisco Kid cried. "And we'll run no risk of being wrecked in the surf!"

"Then you think we'll save the safe?" Joe queried.

"Yes, indeed we will! There isn't much of a sheltered harbor for large vessels, but with this breeze we'll run right up the mouth of the San Lorenzo River. Then there's a little lake like, and boat-houses. Water smooth as glass. Come on. We'll be in in time for breakfast."

Bringing to light some spare coils of rope from the lockers, he put a clove-hitch on the standing part of the sea-anchor hawser, and carried the new running-line aft, making it fast to the stern bitts. Then he cast off from the for'ard bitts. Naturally the *Dazzler* swung off into the trough, completed the evolution, and pointed her nose toward shore. A couple of spare oars from below, and as many water-soaked blankets, sufficed to make a jury-mast and sail. When this was in place Joe cast loose from the wreckage, which was now towing astern, while 'Frisco Kid took the tiller.

"How's that?" said 'Frisco Kid, as he finished making the *Dazzler* fast fore and aft, and stepped upon the stringer-piece of the tiny wharf. "What 'll we do next, captain?"

Joe looked up in quick surprise. "Why—I—what's the matter?"

"Well, aren't you captain now? Haven't we reached land? I'm crew from now on, you know. What's your orders?"

Joe caught the spirit of it. "Pipe all hands for breakfast; that is—wait a minute."

Diving below, he possessed himself of the money he had stowed away in his bundle when he came aboard. Then he locked the cabin door, and they went uptown in search of restaurants. Over the breakfast Joe planned the next move, and, when they had done, communicated it to 'Frisco Kid.

In response to his inquiry the cashier told him when the morning train started for San Francisco. He glanced at the clock.

"I've just time to catch it," he said to 'Frisco Kid. "Here is the key to the cabin door. Keep it locked, and don't let anybody come aboard. Here's money. Eat at the restaurants. Dry your blankets and sleep in the cockpit. I'll be back to-morrow. And don't let anybody into that cabin. Good-by."

With a hasty hand-grip, he sped down the street to the depot. The conductor, when he punched his ticket, looked at him with surprise. And well he might, for it was not the custom of his passengers to travel in sea-boots and sou'westers. But Joe did not mind. He did not even notice. He had bought a paper and was absorbed in its contents. Before long his eyes caught an interesting paragraph:

SUPPOSED TO HAVE BEEN LOST

> The tug "Sea Queen," chartered by Bronson & Tate, has returned from a fruitless cruise outside the heads. No news of value could be obtained concerning the pirates who so daringly carried off their safe at San Andreas last Tuesday night. The lighthouse-keeper at the Farralones mentions having sighted the two sloops Wednesday morning, clawing offshore in the teeth of the gale. It is

> supposed by shipping men that they perished in the storm with their ill-gotten treasure. Rumor has it that, in addition to a large sum in gold, the safe contained papers of even greater importance.

When Joe had read this he felt a great relief. It was evident no one had been killed at San Andreas on the night of the robbery, else there would have been some comment on it in the paper. Nor, if they had had any clue to his own whereabouts, would they have omitted such a striking bit of information.

At the depot in San Francisco the curious onlookers were surprised to see a boy clad conspicuously in sea-boots and sou'wester hail a cab and dash away in it. But Joe was in a hurry. He knew his father's hours, and was fearful lest he should not catch him before he went to luncheon.

The office-boy scowled at him when he pushed open the door and asked to see Mr. Bronson; nor could the head clerk, when summoned by this strange-looking intruder, recognize him.

"Don't you know me, Mr. Willis?"

Mr. Willis looked a second time. "Why, it's Joe Bronson! Of all things under the sun, where did you drop from? Go right in. Your father's in there."

Mr. Bronson stopped dictating to his stenographer, looked up, and said: "Hello! where have you been?"

"To sea," Joe answered demurely enough, not sure of just what kind of a reception he was to get, and fingering his sou'wester nervously.

"Short trip, eh? How did you make out?"

"Oh, so-so." He had caught the twinkle in his father's eye, and knew that it was all clear sailing. "Not so bad—er—that is, considering."

"Considering?"

"Well, not exactly that; rather, it might have been worse, and, well—I don't know that it could have been better."

"You interest me; sit down." Then, turning to the stenographer, "You may go, Mr. Brown, and—hum—I sha'n't need you any more to-day."

It was all Joe could do to keep from crying, so kindly and naturally had his father received him—making him feel at once as if not the slightest thing uncommon had occurred. It was as if he had just returned from a vacation, or, man-grown, had come back from some business trip.

"Now go ahead, Joe. You were speaking to me a moment ago in conundrums, and have aroused my curiosity to a most uncomfortable degree."

Thereat Joe sat down and told what had happened, all that had happened, from the previous Monday night to that moment. Each little incident he related, every detail, not forgetting his conversations with 'Frisco Kid nor his plans concerning him. His face flushed and he was carried away with the excitement of the narrative, while Mr. Bronson was almost as interested, urging him on whenever he slackened his pace, but otherwise remaining silent.

"So you see," Joe said at last, "it couldn't possibly have turned out any better."

"Ah, well," Mr. Bronson deliberated judiciously, "it may be so, and then again it may not."

"I don't see it." Joe felt sharp disappointment at his father's qualified approval. It seemed to him that the return of the safe merited something stronger.

That Mr. Bronson fully comprehended the way Joe felt about it was clearly in evidence, for he went on: "As to the matter of the safe, all hail to you, Joe. Credit, and plenty of it, is your due. Mr. Tate and I have already spent five hundred dollars in attempting to recover it. So important was it that we have also offered five thousand dollars reward, and this morning were even considering the advisability of increasing the amount. But, my son,"—Mr. Bronson stood up, resting a hand affectionately on his boy's shoulder,—"there be certain things in this world which are of still greater importance than gold or papers which represent that which gold may buy. How about *yourself*? There's the point. Will you sell the best possibilities of your life right now for a million dollars?"

Joe shook his head.

"As I said, that's the point. A human life the treasure of the world cannot buy; nor can it redeem one which is misspent; nor can it make full and complete and beautiful a life which is dwarfed and warped and ugly. How about yourself? What is to be the effect of all these strange adventures on your life—*your* life, Joe? Are you going to pick yourself up to-morrow and try it over again? Or the next day, or the day after? Do you understand? Why, Joe, do you think for one moment that I could place against the best value of my son's life the paltry value of a safe? And *can* I say, until time has told me, whether this trip of yours could not possibly have been better? Such an experience is as potent for evil as for good. One dollar is exactly like another—there are many in the world; but no Joe is like my Joe, nor can there be any others in the world to take his place. Don't you see, Joe? Don't you understand?"

Mr. Bronson's voice broke slightly, and the next instant Joe was sobbing as though his heart would break. He had never understood this father of his before, and he knew now the pain he must have caused him, to say nothing of his mother and sister. But the four stirring days he had spent had given him a clearer view of the world and humanity, and he had always possessed the power of putting his thoughts into speech; so he spoke of these things and the lessons he had learned, the conclusions he had drawn from his conversations with 'Frisco Kid, from his intercourse with Pete, from the graphic picture he retained of the *Reindeer* and Nelson as they wallowed in the trough beneath him. And Mr. Bronson listened and, in turn, understood.

"But what of 'Frisco Kid, father?" Joe asked when he had finished.

"Hum! there's a great deal of promise in the boy, from what you say of him." Mr. Bronson hid the twinkle in his eye this time. "And, I must confess, he seems perfectly capable of shifting for himself."

"Sir?" Joe could not believe his ears.

"Let us see, then. He is at present entitled to the half of five thousand dollars, the other half of which belongs to you. It was you two who preserved the safe from the bottom of the Pacific, and if you only had waited a little longer, Mr. Tate and I might have increased the reward."

"Oh!" Joe caught a glimmering of the light. "Part of that is easily arranged, father. I simply refuse to take my half. As to the other—that isn't exactly what 'Frisco Kid desires. He wants friends—and—and—though you didn't say so, they are far higher than gold, nor can gold buy them. He wants friends and a chance for an education—not twenty-five hundred dollars."

"Don't you think it would be better that he choose for himself?"

"Ah, no. That's all arranged."

"Arranged?"

"Yes, sir. He's captain on sea, and I'm captain on land. So he's under my charge now."

"Then you have the power of attorney for him in the present negotiations? Good. I'll make a proposition. The twenty-five hundred dollars shall be held in trust by me, on his demand at any time. We'll settle about yours afterward. Then he shall be put on probation for, say, a year—as messenger first, and then in the office. You can either coach him in his studies, or he can attend night-school. And after that, if he comes through his period of probation with flying colors, I'll give him the same opportunities for an education that you possess. It all depends on himself. And now, Mr. Attorney, what have you to say to my offer in the interests of your client?"

"That I close with it at once—and thank you."

Father and son shook hands.

"And what are you going to do now, Joe?"

"I'm going to send a telegram to 'Frisco Kid first, and then hurry home."

"Then wait a minute till I call up San Andreas and tell Mr. Tate the good news, and I'll go with you."

"Mr. Willis," Mr. Bronson said as they left the outer office, "do you remain in charge, and kindly tell the clerks that they are free for the rest of the day.

"And I say," he called back as they entered the elevator, "don't forget the office-boy."

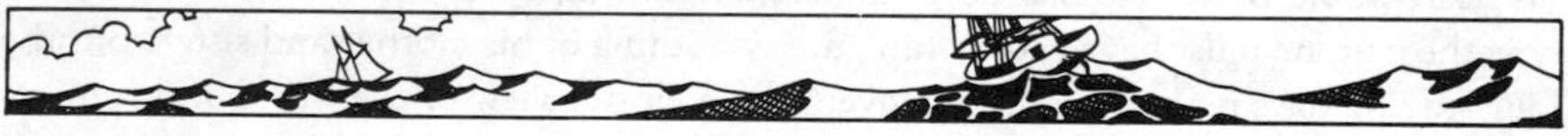

THE WHALE TOOTH

IT WAS in the early days in Fiji, when John Starhurst arose in the mission-house at Rewa Village and announced his intention of carrying the Gospel throughout all Viti Levu. Now Viti Levu means the "Great Land", it being the largest island in a group composed of many large islands, to say nothing of hundreds of small ones. Here and there on the coasts, living by most precarious tenure, was a sprinkling of missionaries, traders, bêche-de-mer fishers, and whaleship deserters. The smoke of the hot ovens arose under their windows, and the bodies of the slain were dragged by their doors on the way to the feasting.

The Lotu, or the Worship, was progressing slowly, and, often, in crablike fashion. Chiefs, who announced themselves Christians and were welcomed into the body of the chapel, had a distressing habit of backsliding in order to partake of the flesh of some favorite enemy. Eat or be eaten had been the law of the land; and eat or be eaten promised to remain the law of the land for a long time to come. There were chiefs, such as Tanoa, Tuiveikoso, and Tuikilakila, who had literally eaten hundreds of their fellow-men. But among these gluttons Ra Undreundre ranked highest. Ra Undreundre lived at Takiraki. He kept a register of his gustatory exploits. A row of stones outside his house marked the bodies he had eaten. This row was two hundred and thirty paces long, and the stones in it numbered eight hundred and seventy-two. Each stone represented a body. The row of stones might have been longer, had not Ra Undreundre unfortunately received a spear in the small of his back in a bush skirmish on Somo Somo and been served up on the table of Naungavuli, whose mediocre string of stones numbered only forty-eight.

The hard-worked, fever-stricken missionaries stuck doggedly to their task, at times despairing, and looking forward for some special manifestation, some outburst of Pentecostal fire that would bring a glorious harvest of souls. But cannibal Fiji had remained obdurate. The frizzle-headed man-eaters were loath to leave their fleshpots so long as the harvest of human carcasses was plentiful. Sometimes, when the harvest was too plentiful, they imposed on the missionaries by letting the word slip out that on such a day there would be a killing and a barbecue. Promptly the missionaries would buy the lives of the victims with stick tobacco, fathoms of calico and quarts of trade-beads. Natheless the chiefs drove a handsome trade in thus disposing of their surplus live meat. Also, they could always go out and catch more.

It was at this juncture the John Starhurst proclaimed that he would carry the Gospel from coast to coast of the Great Land, and that he would begin by penetrating the mountain fastnesses of the head-waters of the Rewa River. His words were received with consternation.

The native teachers wept softly. His two fellow-missionaries strove to dissuade him. The King of Rewa warned him that the mountain dwellers would surely kai-kai him—kai-kai meaning "to eat"—and that he, the King of Rewa, having become Lotu, would be put to the necessity of going to war with the mountain dwellers. That he could not conquer them he was perfectly aware. That they might come down the river and sack Rewa Village he was likewise perfectly aware. But what was he to do? If John Starhurst persisted in going out and being eaten, there would be a war that would cost hundreds of lives.

Later in the day a deputation of Rewa chiefs waited upon John Starhurst. He heard them patiently, and argued patiently with them, though he abated not a whit from his purpose. To his fellow-missionaries he explained that he was not bent upon martyrdom; that the call had come for him to carry the Gospel into Viti Levu, and that he was merely obeying the Lord's wish.

To the traders, who came and objected most strenuously of all, he said: "Your objections are valueless. They consist merely of the damage that may be done your businesses. You are interested in making money, but I am interested in saving souls. The heathen of this dark land must be saved."

John Starhurst was not a fanatic. He would have been the first man to deny the imputation. He was eminently sane and practical. He was sure that his mission would result in good, and he had private visions of igniting the Pentecostal spark in the souls of the mountaineers and of inaugurating a revival that would sweep down out of the mountains and across the length and breadth of the Great Land from sea to sea and to the isles in the midst of the sea. There were no wild lights in his mild gray eyes, but only calm resolution and an unfaltering trust in the Higher Power that was guiding him.

One man only he found who approved of his project, and that was Ra Vatu, who secretly encouraged him and offered to lend him guides to the first foothills. John Starhurst, in turn, was greatly pleased by Ra Vatu's conduct. From an incorrigible heathen, with a heart as black as his practices. Ra Vatu was beginning to emanate light. He even spoke of becoming Lotu. True, three years before he had expressed a similar intention, and would have entered the church had not John Starhurst entered objection to his bringing his four wives along with him. Ra Vatu had had economic and ethical objections to monogamy. Besides, the missionary's hair-splitting objection had offended him; and, to prove that he was a free agent and a man of honor, he had swung his huge war-club over Starhurst's head. Starhurst had escaped by rushing in under the club and holding on to him until help arrived. But all that was now forgiven and forgotten. Ra Vatu was coming into the church, not merely as a converted heathen, but as a converted polygamist as well. He was only waiting, he assured Starhurst, until his oldest wife, who was very sick, should die.

John Starhurst journeyed up the sluggish Rewa in one of Ra Vatu's canoes. This canoe was to carry him for two days, when, the head of navigation reached, it would return. Far in the distance, lifted into the sky, could be seen the great smoky mountains that marked the backbone of the Great Land. All day John Starhurst gazed at them with eager yearning.

Sometimes he prayed silently. At other times he was joined in prayer by Narau, a native teacher, who for seven years had been Lotu, ever since the day he had been saved from the hot oven by Dr James Ellery Brown at the trifling expense of one hundred sticks of tobacco, two cotton blankets and a large bottle of painkiller. At the last moment, after twenty hours of solitary supplication and prayer, Narau's ears had heard the call to go forth with John Starhurst on the mission to the mountains.

"Master, I will surely go with thee," he had announced.

John Starhurst had hailed him with sober delight. Truly, the Lord was with him thus to spur on so broken-spirited a creature as Narau.

"I am indeed without spirit, the weakest of the Lord's vessels," Narau explained, the first day in the canoe.

"You should have faith, stronger faith," the missionary chided him.

Another canoe journeyed up the Rewa that day. But it journeyed an hour astern, and it took care not to be seen. This canoe was also the property of Ra Vatu. In it was Erirola, Ra Vatu's first cousin and trusted henchman; and in the small basket that never left his hand was a whale tooth. It was a magnificent tooth, fully six inches long, beautifully proportioned, the ivory turned yellow and purple with age. This tooth was likewise the property of Ra Vatu; and in Fiji, when such a tooth goes forth, things usually happen. For this is the virtue of the whale tooth: Whoever accepts it cannot refuse the request that may accompany it or follow it. The request may be anything from a human life to a tribal alliance, and no Fijian is so dead to honor as to deny the request when once the tooth has been accepted. Sometimes the request hangs fire, or the fulfilment is delayed, with untoward consequences.

High up the Rewa, at the village of a chief, Mongondro by name, John Starhurst rested at the end of the second day of the journey. In the morning, attended by Narau, he expected to start on foot for the smoky mountains that were now green and velvety with nearness. Mongondro was a sweet-tempered, mild-mannered little old chief, short-sighted and afflicted with elephantiasis, and no longer inclined toward the turbulence of war. He received the missionary with warm hospitality, gave him food from his own table, and even discussed religious matters with him. Mongondro was of an inquiring bent of mind, and pleased John Starhurst greatly by asking him to account for the existence and beginning of things. When the missionary had finished his summary of the Creation according to Genesis, he saw that Mongondro was deeply affected. The little old chief smoked silently for some time. Then he took the pipe from his mouth and shook his head sadly.

"It cannot be," he said. "I, Mongondro, in my youth, was a good workman with the adze. Yet three months did it take me to make a canoe—a small canoe, a very small canoe. And you say that all this land and water was made by one man—"

"Nay, was made by one God, the only true God," the missionary interrupted.

"It is the same thing," Mongondro went on, "that all the land and all the water, the trees, the fish, and bush and mountains, the sun, the moon and the stars, were made in six days! No, no. I tell you that in my youth I was an able man, yet did it require me three months for one small canoe. It is a story to frighten children with; but no man can believe it."

"I am a man," the missionary said.

"True, you are a man. But it is not given to my dark understanding to know what you believe."

"I tell you, I do believe that everything was made in six days."

"So you say, so you say," the old cannibal murmured soothingly.

It was not until after John Starhurst and Narau had gone off to bed that Erirola crept into the chief's house, and, after diplomatic speech, handed the whale tooth to Mongondro.

The old chief held the tooth in his hands for a long time. It was a beautiful tooth, and he yearned for it. Also, he divined the request that must accompany it. "No, no; whale teeth were beautiful," and his mouth watered for it, but he passed it back to Erirola with many apologies.

In the early dawn John Starhurst was afoot, striding along the bush trail in his big leather boots, at his heels the faithful Narau, himself at the heels of a naked guide lent him by Mongondro to show the way to the next village, which was reached by midday. Here a new guide showed the way. A mile in the rear plodded Erirola, the whale tooth in the basket slung on his shoulder. For two days more he brought up the missionary's rear, offering the tooth to the village chiefs. But village after village refused the tooth. It followed so quickly the missionary's advent that they divined the request that would be made, and would have none of it.

They were getting deep into the mountains, and Erirola took a secret trail, cut in ahead of the missionary, and reached the stronghold of the Buli of Gatoka. Now the Buli was unaware of John Starhurst's imminent arrival. Also, the tooth was beautiful—an extraordinary specimen, while the coloring of it was of the rarest order. The tooth was presented publicly. The Buli of Gatoka, seated on his best mat, surrounded by his chief men, three busy fly-brushers at his back, deigned to receive from the hand of his herald the whale tooth presented by Ra Vatu and carried into the mountains by his cousin, Erirola. A clapping of hands went up at the acceptation of the present, the assembled headmen, heralds and fly-brushers crying aloud in chorus:

"A! woi! woi! woi! A! woi! woi! woi! A tabua levu! woi! woi! A mudua, mudua, mudua!"

"Soon will come a man, a white man," Erirola began, after the proper pause. "He is a missionary man, and he will come to-day. Ra Vatu is pleased to desire his boots. He wishes to present them to his good friend, Mongondro, and it is in his mind to send them with the feet along in them, for Mongondro is an old man and his teeth are not good. Be sure, O Buli, that the feet go along in the boots. As for the rest of him, it may stop here."

The delight in the whale tooth faded out of the Buli's eyes, and he glanced about him dubiously. Yet had he already accepted the tooth.

"A little thing like a missionary does not matter," Erirola prompted.

"No, a little thing like a missionary does not matter," the Buli answered, himself again. "Mongondro shall have the boots. Go, you young men, some three or four of you, and meet the missionary on the trail. Be sure you bring back the boots as well."

"It is too late," said Erirola. "Listen! He comes now."

Breaking through the thicket of brush, John Starhurst, with Narau close on his heels, strode upon the scene. The famous boots, having filled in wading the stream, squirted fine jets of water at every step. Starhurst looked about him with flashing eyes. Upborne by an unwavering trust, untouched by doubt or fear, he exulted in all he saw. He knew that since the beginning of time he was the first white man ever to tread the mountain stronghold of Gatoka.

The grass houses clung to the steep mountain side or overhung the rushing Rewa. On either side towered a mighty precipice. At the best, three hours of sunlight penetrated that narrow gorge. No coconuts nor bananas were to be seen, though dense, tropic vegetation overran everything, dripping in airy festoons from the sheer lips of the precipices and running riot in all the crannied ledges. At the far end of the gorge the Rewa leaped eight hundred feet in a single span, while the atmosphere of the rock fortress pulsed to the rhythmic thunder of the fall.

From the Buli's house John Starhurst saw emerging the Buli and his followers.

"I bring you good tidings," was the missionary's greeting.

"Who has sent you?" the Buli rejoined quietly.

"God."

"It is a new name in Viti Levu," the Buli grinned. "Of what islands, villages or passes may he be chief?"

"He is the chief over all islands, all villages, all passes," John Starhurst answered solemnly. "He is the Lord over heaven and earth, and I am come to bring His word to you."

"Has he sent whale teeth?" was the insolent query.

"No, but more precious than whale teeth is the—"

"It is the custom, between chiefs, to send whale teeth," the Buli interrupted. "Your chief is either a niggard, or you are a fool, to come empty-handed into the mountains. Behold, a more generous than you is before you."

So saying, he showed the whale tooth he had received from Erirola.

Narau groaned.

"It is the whale tooth of Ra Vatu," he whispered to Starhurst. "I know it well. Now are we undone."

"A gracious thing," the missionary answered, passing his hand through his long beard and adjusting his glasses. "Ra Vatu has arranged that we should be well received."

But Narau groaned again, and backed away from the heels he had dogged so faithfully.

"Ra Vatu is soon to become Lotu," Starhurst explained, "and I have come bringing the Lotu to you."

"I want none of your Lotu," said the Buli, proudly. "And it is in my mind that you will be clubbed this day."

The Buli nodded to one of his big mountaineers, who stepped forward, swinging a club. Narau bolted into the nearest house, seeking to hide among the women and mats;

but John Starhurst sprang in under the club and threw his arms around his executioner's neck. From this point of vantage he proceeded to argue. He was arguing for his life, and he knew it; but he was neither excited nor afraid.

"It would be an evil thing for you to kill me," he told the man. "I have done you no wrong, nor have I done the Buli wrong."

So well did he cling to the neck of the one man that they dared not strike with their clubs. And he continued to cling and to dispute for his life with those who clamored for his death.

"I am John Starhurst," he went on calmly. "I have labored in Fiji for three years, and I have done it for no profit. I am here among you for good. Why should any man kill me? To kill me will not profit any man."

The Buli stole a look at the whale tooth. He was well paid for the deed.

The missionary was surrounded by a mass of naked savages, all struggling to get at him. The death song, which is the song of the oven, was raised, and his expostulations could no longer be heard. But so cunningly did he twine and wreathe his body about his captor's that the death-blow could not be struck. Erirola smiled, and the Buli grew angry.

"Away with you!" he cried. "A nice story to go back to the coast—a dozen of you and one missionary, without weapons, weak as a woman, overcoming all of you."

"Wait, O Buli," John Starhurst called out from the thick of the scuffle, "and I will overcome even you. For my weapons are Truth and Right, and no man can withstand them."

"Come to me, then," the Buli answered, "for my weapon is only a poor miserable club, and, as you say, it cannot withstand you."

The group separated from him, and John Starhurst stood alone, facing the Buli, who was leaning on an enormous, knotted war-club.

"Come to me, missionary man, and overcome me," the Buli challenged.

"Even so will I come to you and overcome you," John Starhurst made answer, first wiping his spectacles and settling them properly, then beginning his advance.

The Buli raised the club and waited.

"In the first place, my death will profit you nothing," began the argument.

"I leave the answer to my club," was the Buli's reply.

And to every point he made the same reply, at the same time watching the missionary closely in order to forestall that cunning run-in under the lifted club. Then, and for the first time, John Starhurst knew that his death was at hand. He made no attempt to run in. Bareheaded, he stood in the sun and prayed aloud—the mysterious figure of the inevitable white man, who, with Bible, bullet or rum bottle, has confronted the amazed savage in his every stronghold. Even so stood John Starhurst in the rock fortress of the Buli of Gatoka.

"Forgive them, for they know not what they do," he prayed. "O Lord! have mercy upon Fiji. Have compassion for Fiji. O Jehovah, hear us for His sake, Thy Son, whom Thou didst give that through Him all men might also become Thy children. From Thee we came, and our mind is that to Thee we may return. The land is dark, O Lord, the land is dark. But Thou art mighty to save. Reach out Thy hand, O Lord, and save Fiji, poor cannibal Fiji."

The Buli grew impatient.

"Now will I answer thee," he muttered, at the same time swinging his club with both hands.

Narau, hiding among the women and the mats, heard the impact of the blow and shuddered. Then the death song arose, and he knew his beloved missionary's body was being dragged to the oven as he heard the words:

"Drag me gently. Drag me gently."

"For I am the champion of my land."

"Give thanks! Give thanks! Give thanks!"

Next, a single voice arose out of the din, asking:

"Where is the brave man?"

A hundred voices bellowed the answer:

"Gone to be dragged into the oven and cooked."

"Where is the coward?" the single voice demanded.

"Gone to report!" the hundred voices bellowed back. "Gone to report! Gone to report!"

Narau groaned in anguish of spirit. The words of the old song were true. He was the coward, and nothing remained to him but to go and report.

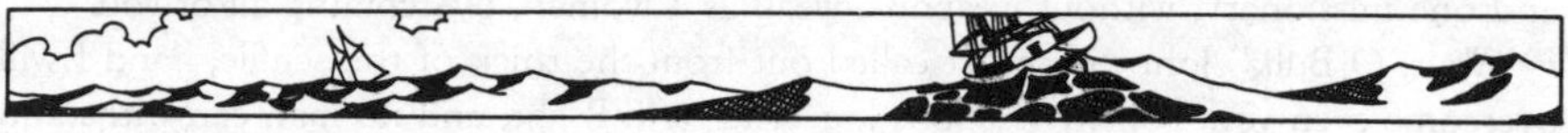

Mauki

He weighed one hundred and ten pounds. His hair was kinky and negroid, and he was black. He was peculiarly black. He was neither blue-black nor purple-black, but plum-black. His name was Mauki, and he was the son of a chief. He had three *tambos. Tambo* is Melanesian for *taboo,* and is first cousin to that Polynesian word. Mauki's three *tambos* were as follows: first, he must never shake hands with a woman, nor have a woman's hand touch him or any of his personal belongings; secondly, he must never eat clams nor any food from a fire in which clams had been cooked; thirdly, he must never touch a crocodile, nor travel in a canoe that carried any part of a crocodile even if as large as a tooth.

Of a different black were his teeth, which were deep black, or, perhaps better, *lamp-black.* They had been made so in a single night, by his mother, who had compressed about them a powdered mineral which was dug from the landslide back of Port Adams. Port Adams is a salt-water village on Malaita, and Malaita is the most savage island in the Solomons—so savage that no traders nor planters have yet gained a foothold on it; while, from the time of the earliest *bêche-de-mer* fishers and sandalwood traders down to the latest labor recruiters equipped with automatic rifles and gasolene engines, scores of white adventurers have been passed out by tomahawks and soft-nosed Snider bullets. So Malaita remains to-day, in the twentieth century, the stamping ground of the labor recruiters, who farm its coasts for laborers who engage and contract themselves to toil on the plantations of the neighboring and more civilized islands for a wage of thirty dollars a year. The natives of those neighboring and more civilized islands have themselves become too civilized to work on plantations.

Mauki's ears were pierced, not in one place, nor two places, but in a couple of dozen places. In one of the smaller holes he carried a clay pipe. The larger holes were too large for such use. The bowl of the pipe would have fallen through. In fact, in the largest hole in each ear he habitually wore round wooden plugs that were an even four inches in diameter. Roughly speaking, the circumference of said holes was twelve and one-half inches. Mauki was catholic in his tastes. In the various smaller holes he carried such things as empty rifle cartridges, horseshoe nails, copper screws, pieces of string, braids of sennit, strips of green leaf and, in the cool of the day, scarlet hibiscus flowers. From which it will be seen that pockets were not necessary to his well-being. Besides, pockets were impossible, for his only wearing apparel consisted of a piece of calico several inches wide. A pocket knife he wore in his hair, the blade snapped down on a kinky lock. His most prized possession was the handle of a china cup, which he suspended from a ring of turtle-shell, which, in turn, was passed through the partition-cartilage of his nose.

But in spite of embellishments, Mauki had a nice face. It was really a pretty face, viewed by any standard, and for a Melanesian it was a remarkably good-looking face. Its one fault was its lack of strength. It was softly effeminate, almost girlish. The features were small, regular and delicate. The chin was weak, and the mouth was weak. There was no strength nor character in the jaws, forehead and nose. In the eyes only could be caught any hint of the unknown quantities that were so large a part of his make-up and that other persons could not understand. These unknown quantities were pluck, pertinacity, fearlessness, imagination and cunning; and when they found expression in some consistent and striking action, those about him were astounded.

Mauki's father was chief over the village at Port Adams, and thus, by birth a salt-water man, Mauki was half amphibian. He knew the way of the fishes and oysters, and the reef was an open book to him. Canoes, also, he knew. He learned to swim when he was a year old. At seven years he could hold his breath a full minute and swim straight down to bottom through thirty feet of water. And at seven years he was stolen by the bushmen, who cannot even swim and who are afraid of salt water. Thereafter Mauki saw the sea only from a distance, through rifts in the jungle and from open spaces on the high mountain sides. He became the slave of old Fanfoa, head chief over a score of scattered bush-villages on the range-lips of Malaita, the smoke of which, on calm mornings, is about the only evidence the seafaring white men have of the teeming interior population. For the whites do not penetrate Malaita. They tried it once, in the days when the search was on for gold, but they always left their heads behind to grin from the smoky rafters of the bushmen's huts.

When Mauki was a young man of seventeen, Fanfoa got out of tobacco. He got dreadfully out of tobacco. It was hard times in all his villages. He had been guilty of a mistake. Suo was a harbor so small that a large schooner could not swing at anchor in it. It was surrounded by mangroves that overhung the deep water. It was a trap, and into the trap sailed two white men in a small ketch. They were after recruits, and they possessed much tobacco and trade-goods, to say nothing of three rifles and plenty of ammunition. Now there were no salt-water men living at Suo, and it was there that the bushmen could come down to the sea. The ketch did a splendid traffic. It signed on twenty recruits the first day. Even old Fanfoa signed on. And that same day the score of new recruits chopped off the two white men's heads, killed the boat's crew and burned the ketch. Thereafter, and for three months, there was tobacco and trade-goods in plenty and to spare in all the bush-villages. Then came the man-of-war that threw shells for miles into the hills, frightening the people out of their villages and into the deeper bush. Next the man-of-war sent landing parties ashore. The villages were all burned, along with the tobacco and trade-stuff. The coconuts and bananas were chopped down, the taro gardens uprooted, and the pigs and chickens killed.

It taught Fanfoa a lesson, but in the meantime he was out of tobacco. Also, his young men were too frightened to sign on with the recruiting vessels. That was why Fanfoa ordered his slave, Mauki, to be carried down and signed on for half a case of tobacco advance, along with knives, axes, calico and beads, which he would pay for with his toil on the plantations. Mauki was sorely frightened when they brought him on board the schooner. He was a lamb led to the slaughter. White men were ferocious creatures. They had to be, or else they would not make a practice of venturing along the Malaita coast and into all harbors, two on a schooner, when each schooner carried from fifteen to twenty blacks as boat's crew, and often as high as sixty or seventy black recruits. In addition to this, there was always the danger of the shore population, the sudden attack and the cutting off of the schooner and all hands. Truly, white men must be terrible. Besides, they were possessed of such devil-devils—rifles that shot very rapidly many times, things of iron and brass that made the schooners go when there was no wind, and boxes that talked and laughed just as men talked and laughed. Ay, and he had heard of one white man whose particular devil-devil was so powerful that he could take out all his teeth and put them back at will.

Down into the cabin they took Mauki. On deck, the one white man kept guard with two revolvers in his belt. In the cabin the other white man sat with a book before him, in which he inscribed strange marks and lines. He looked at Mauki as though he had been a pig or a fowl, glanced under the hollows of his arms, and wrote in the book. Then he held out the writing stick and Mauki just barely touched it with his hand, in so doing pledging himself to toil for three years on the plantations of the Moongleam Soap Company. It was not explained to him that the will of the ferocious white men would be used to enforce the pledge, and that, behind all, for the same use, was all the power and all the warships of Great Britain.

Other blacks there were on board, from unheard-of far places, and when the white man spoke to them, they tore the long feather from Mauki's hair, cut that same hair short, and wrapped about his waist a lava-lava of bright yellow calico.

After many days on the schooner, and after beholding more land and islands than he had ever dreamed of, he was landed on New Georgia, and put to work in the field clearing jungle and cutting cane grass. For the first time he knew what work was. Even as a slave to Fanfoa he had not worked like this. And he did not like work. It was up at dawn and in at dark, on two meals a day. And the food was tiresome. For weeks at a time they were given nothing but sweet potatoes to eat, and for weeks at a time it would be nothing but rice. He cut out the coconut from the shells day after day; and for long days and weeks he fed the fires that smoked the copra, till his eyes got sore and he was set to felling trees. He was a good axe-man, and later he was put in the bridge-building gang. Once, he was punished by being put in the road-building gang. At times he served as boat's crew in the whale-boats, when they brought in copra from distant beaches or when the white men went out to dynamite fish.

Among other things he learned *bêche-de-mer* English, with which he could talk with all white men, and with all recruits who otherwise would have talked in a thousand different dialects. Also, he learned certain things about the white men, principally that they kept their word. If they told a boy he was going to receive a stick of tobacco, he got it. If they told a boy they would knock seven bells out of him if he did a certain thing, when he did that thing seven bells invariably were knocked out of him. Mauki did not know what seven bells were, but they occurred in *bêche-de-mer,* and he imagined them to be the blood and teeth that sometimes accompanied the process of knocking out seven bells. One other thing he learned: no boy was struck or punished unless he did wrong. Even when the white men were drunk, as they were frequently, they never struck unless a rule had been broken.

Mauki did not like the plantation. He hated work, and he was the son of a chief. Furthermore, it was ten years since he had been stolen from Port Adams by Fanfoa, and he was homesick. He was even homesick for the slavery under Fanfoa. So he ran away. He struck back into the bush, with the idea of working southward to the beach and stealing a canoe in which to go home to Port Adams. But the fever got him, and he was captured and brought back more dead than alive.

A second time he ran away, in the company of two Malaita boys. They got down the coast twenty miles, and were hidden in the hut of a Malaita freeman, who dwelt in that village. But in the dead of night two white men came, who were not afraid of all the village people and who knocked seven bells out of the three runaways, tied them like pigs and tossed them into the whale-boat. But the man in whose house they had hidden—seven times seven bells must have been knocked out of him from the way the hair, skin and teeth flew, and he was discouraged for the rest of his natural life from harboring runaway laborers.

For a year Mauki toiled on. Then he was made a house-boy, and had good food and easy times, with light work in keeping the house clean and serving the white men with whiskey and beer at all hours of the day and most hours of the night. He liked it, but he liked Port Adams more. He had two years longer to serve, but two years were too long for him in the throes of homesickness. He had grown wiser with his year of service, and, being now a house-boy, he had opportunity. He had the cleaning of the rifles, and he knew where the key to the store-room was hung. He planned the escape, and one night ten Malaita boys and one boy from San Cristoval sneaked from the barracks and dragged one of the whale-boats down to the beach. It was Mauki who supplied the key that opened the padlock on the boat, and it was Mauki who equipped the boat with a dozen Winchesters, an immense amount of ammunition, a case of dynamite with detonators and fuse, and ten cases of tobacco.

The northwest monsoon was blowing, and they fled south in the night-time, hiding by day on detached and uninhabited islets, or dragging their whale-boat into the bush on the large islands. Thus they gained Guadalcanar, skirted halfway along it, and crossed the Indispensable Straits to Florida Island. It was here that they killed the San Cristoval boy, saving his head and cooking and eating the rest of him. The Malaita coast was only twenty miles away, but the last night a strong current and baffling winds prevented them from gaining across. Daylight found them still several miles from their goal. But daylight brought a cutter, in which were two white men, who were not afraid of eleven Malaita men armed with twelve rifles. Mauki and his companions were carried back to Tulagi, where lived the great white master of all the white men. And the great white master held a court, after which, one by one, the runaways were tied up and given twenty lashes each, and sentenced to a fine of fifteen dollars. Then they were sent back to New Georgia, where the white men knocked seven bells out of them all around and put them to work. But Mauki was no longer house-boy. He was put in the road-making gang. The fine of fifteen dollars had been paid by the men from whom he had run away, and he was told that he would have to work it out, which meant six months' additional toil. Further, his share of the stolen tobacco earned him another year of toil.

Port Adams was now three years and a half away, so he stole a canoe one night, hid on the islets in Manning Straits, passed through the Straits, and began working along the eastern coast of Ysabel, only to be captured, two-thirds of the way along, by the white men on Meringe Lagoon. After a week, he escaped from them and took to the bush. They were no bush natives on Ysabel, only salt-water men, who were all Christians. The white men put up a reward of five hundred sticks of tobacco, and every time Mauki ventured down to the sea to steal a canoe he was chased by the salt-water men. Four months of this passed when, the reward having been raised to a thousand sticks, he was caught and sent back to New Georgia and the road-building gang. Now a thousand sticks are worth fifty dollars, and Mauki had to pay the reward himself, which required a year and eight months' labor. So Port Adams was now five years away.

His homesickness was greater than ever, and it did not appeal to him to settle down and be good, work out his four years, and go home. The next time, he was caught in the very act of running away. His case was brought before Mr Haveby, the island manager of the Moongleam Soap Company, who adjudged him an incorrigible. The Company had plantations on the Santa Cruz Islands, hundreds of miles across the sea, and there it sent its Solomon Islands' incorrigibles. And there Mauki was sent, though he never arrived. The schooner stopped at Santa Anna, and in the night Mauki swam ashore, where he stole two rifles and a case of tobacco from the trader and got away in a canoe to Cristoval. Malaita was now to the north, fifty or sixty miles away. But when he attempted the passage, he was caught by a light gale and driven back to Santa Anna, where the trader clapped him in irons and held him against the return of the schooner from Santa Cruz. The two rifles the trader recovered, but the case of tobacco was charged up to Mauki at the rate of another year. The sum of years he now owed the Company was six.

On the way back to New Georgia, the schooner dropped anchor in Marau Sound, which lies at the southeastern extremity of Guadalcanar. Mauki swam ashore with handcuffs on his wrists and got away to the bush. The schooner went on, but the Moongleam trader ashore offered a thousand sticks, and to him Mauki was brought by the bushmen with a year and eight months tacked on to his account. Again, and before the schooner called in, he got away, this time in a whale-boat accompanied by a case of the trader's tobacco. But a northwest gale wrecked him upon Ugi, where the Christian natives stole his tobacco and turned him over to the Moongleam trader who resided there. The tobacco the natives stole meant another year for him, and the tale was now eight years and a half.

"We'll send him to Lord Howe," said Mr Haveby. "Bunster is there, and we'll let them settle it between them. It will be a case, I imagine, of Mauki getting Bunster, or Bunster getting Mauki, and good riddance in either event."

If one leaves Meringe Lagoon, on Ysabel, and steers a course due north, magnetic, at the end of one hundred and fifty miles he will lift the pounded coral beaches of Lord Howe above the sea. Lord Howe is a ring of land some one hundred and fifty miles in circumference, several hundred yards wide at its widest, and towering in places to a height of ten feet above sea-level. Inside this ring of sand is a mighty lagoon studded with coral patches. Lord Howe belongs to the Solomons neither geographically nor ethnologically. It is an atoll, while the Solomons are high islands; and its people and language are Polynesian, while the inhabitants of the Solomons are Melanesian. Lord

Howe has been populated by the westward Polynesian drift which continues to this day, big outrigger canoes being washed upon its beaches by the southeast trade. That there has been a slight Melanesian drift in the period of the northwest monsoon, is also evident.

Nobody ever comes to Lord Howe, or Ontong-Java as it is sometimes called. Thomas Cook & Son do not sell tickets to it, and tourists do not dream of its existence. Not even a white missionary has landed on its shore. Its five thousand natives are as peaceable as they are primitive. Yet they were not always peaceable. The *Sailing Directions* speak of them as hostile and treacherous. But the men who compile the *Sailing Directions* have never heard of the change that was worked in the hearts of the inhabitants, who, not many years ago, cut off a big bark and killed all hands with the exception of the second mate. This survivor carried the news to his brothers. The captains of three trading schooners returned with him to Lord Howe. They sailed their vessels right into the lagoon and proceeded to preach the white man's gospel that only white men shall kill white men and that the lesser breeds must keep hands off. The schooners sailed up and down the lagoon, harrying and destroying. There was no escape from the narrow sand-circle, no bush to which to flee. The men were shot down at sight, and there was no avoiding being sighted. The villages were burned, the canoes smashed, the chickens and pigs killed, and the precious coconut-trees chopped down. For a month this continued, when the schooners sailed away; but the fear of the white man had been seared into the souls of the islanders and never again were they rash enough to harm one.

Max Bunster was the one white man on Lord Howe, trading in the pay of the ubiquitous Moongleam Soap Company. And the Company billeted him on Lord Howe, because, next to getting rid of him, it was the most out-of-the-way place to be found. That the Company did not get rid of him was due to the difficulty of finding another man to take his place. He was a strapping big German, with something wrong in his brain. Semimadness would be a charitable statement of his condition. He was a bully and a coward, and a thrice-bigger savage than any savage on the island. Being a coward, his brutality was of the cowardly order. When he first went into the Company's employ, he was stationed on Savo. When a consumptive colonial was sent to take his place, he beat him up with his fists and sent him off a wreck in the schooner that brought him.

Mr Haveby next selected a young Yorkshire giant to relieve Bunster. The Yorkshire man had a reputation as a bruiser and preferred fighting to eating. But Bunster wouldn't fight. He was a regular little lamb—for ten days, at the end of which time the Yorkshire man was prostrated by a combined attack of dysentery and fever. Then Bunster went for him, among other things getting him down and jumping on him a score or so of times. Afraid of what would happen when his victim recovered, Bunster fled away in a cutter to Guvutu, where he signalized himself by beating up a young Englishman already crippled by a Boer bullet through both hips.

Then it was that Mr Haveby sent Bunster to Lord Howe, the falling-off place. He celebrated his landing by mopping up half a case of gin and by thrashing the elderly and wheezy mate of the schooner which had brought him. When the schooner departed, he called the kanakas down to the beach and challenged them to throw him in a wrestling bout, promising a case of tobacco to the one who succeeded. Three kanakas he threw, but was promptly thrown by a fourth, who, instead of receiving the tobacco, got a bullet through his lungs.

And so began Bunster's reign on Lord Howe. Three thousand people lived in the principal village; but it was deserted, even in broad day, when he passed through. Men, women and children fled before him. Even the dogs and pigs got out of the way, while the king was not above hiding under a mat. The two prime ministers lived in terror of Bunster, who never discussed any moot subject, but struck out with his fists instead.

And to Lord Howe came Mauki, to toil for Bunster for eight long years and a half. There was no escaping from Lord Howe. For better or worse, Bunster and he were tied together. Bunster weighed two hundred pounds. Mauki weighed one hundred and ten. Bunster was a degenerate brute. But Mauki was a primitive savage. While both had wills and ways of their own.

Mauki had no idea of the sort of master he was to work for. He had had no warnings, and he had concluded as a matter of course that Bunster would be like other white men, a drinker of much whiskey, a ruler and a lawgiver who always kept his word and who never struck a boy undeserved. Bunster had the advantage. He knew all about Mauki, and gloated over the coming into possession of him. The last cook was suffering from a broken arm and a dislocated shoulder, so Bunster made Mauki cook and general house-boy.

And Mauki soon learned that there were white men and white men. On the very day the schooner departed he was ordered to buy a chicken from Samisee, the native Tongan missionary. But Samisee had sailed across the lagoon and would not be back for three days. Mauki returned with the information. He climbed the steep stairway (the house stood on piles twelve feet above the sand), and entered the living-room to report. The trader demanded the chicken. Mauki opened his mouth to explain the missionary's absence. But Bunster did not care for explanations. He struck out with his fist. The blow caught Mauki on the mouth and lifted him into the air. Clear through the doorway he flew, across the narrow veranda, breaking the top railing, and down to the ground. His lips were a contused, shapeless mass, and his mouth was full of blood and broken teeth.

"That'll teach you that back talk don't go with me," the trader shouted, purple with rage, peering down at him over the broken railing.

Mauki had never met a white man like this, and he resolved to walk small and never offend. He saw the boat-boys knocked about, and one of them put in irons for three days with nothing to eat for the crime of breaking a rowlock while pulling. Then, too, he heard the gossip of the village and learned why Bunster had taken a third wife—by force, as was well known. The first and second wives lay in the graveyard, under the white coral sand, with slabs of coral rock at head and feet. They had died, it was said, from beatings he had given them. The third wife was certainly ill-used, as Mauki could see for himself.

But there was no way by which to avoid offending the white man, who seemed offended with life. When Mauki kept silent, he was struck and called a sullen brute. When he spoke, he was struck for giving back talk. When he was grave, Bunster accused him of plotting and gave him a thrashing in advance; and when he strove to be cheerful and to smile, he was charged with sneering at his lord and master and given a taste of stick. Bunster was a devil. The village would have done for him, had it not remembered the lesson of the three schooners. It might have done for him anyway, if there had been a bush to which to flee. As it was, the murder of the white man, of any white man, would bring a man-of-war that would kill the offenders and chop down the precious coconut-trees. Then there were the boat-boys, with minds fully made up to drown him by accident at the first opportunity to capsize the cutter. Only Bunster saw to it that the boat did not capsize.

Mauki was of a different breed, and, escape being impossible while Bunster lived, he was resolved to get the white man. The trouble was that he could never find a chance. Bunster was always on guard. Day and night his revolvers were ready to hand. He permitted nobody to pass behind his back, as Mauki learned after having been knocked down several times. Bunster knew that he had more to fear from the good-natured, even sweet-faced, Malaita boy than from the entire population of Lord Howe; and it gave added zest to the programme of torment he was carrying out. And Mauki walked small, accepted his punishments and waited.

All other white men had respected his *tambos,* but not so Bunster. Mauki's weekly allowance of tobacco was two sticks. Bunster passed them to his woman and ordered Mauki to receive them from her hand. But this could not be, and Mauki went without his tobacco. In the same way he was made to miss many a meal, and to go hungry many a day. He was ordered to make chowder out of the big clams that grew in the lagoon. This he could not do, for clams were *tambo.* Six times in succession he refused to touch the clams, and six times he was knocked senseless. Bunster knew that the boy would die first, but called his refusal mutiny, and would have killed him had there been another cook to take his place.

One of the trader's favorite tricks was to catch Mauki's kinky locks and bat his head against the wall. Another trick was to catch Mauki unawares and thrust the live end of a cigar against his flesh. This Bunster called vaccination, and Mauki was vaccinated a number of times a week. Once, in a rage, Bunster ripped the cup handle from Mauki's nose, tearing the hole clear out of the cartilage.

"Oh, what a mug!" was his comment, when he surveyed the damage he had wrought.

The skin of a shark is like sandpaper, but the skin of a ray fish is like a rasp. In the South Seas the natives use it as a wood file in smoothing down canoes and paddles. Bunster had a mitten made of ray fish skin. The first time he tried it on Mauki, with one sweep of the hand it fetched the skin off his back from neck to armpit. Bunster was delighted. He gave his wife a taste of the mitten, and tried it out thoroughly on the boat-boys. The prime ministers came in for a stroke each, and they had to grin and take it for a joke.

"Laugh, damn you, laugh!" was the cue he gave.

Mauki came in for the largest share of the mitten. Never a day passed without a caress from it. There were times when the loss of so much cuticle kept him awake at night, and often the half-healed surface was raked raw afresh by the facetious Mr Bunster. Mauki continued his patient wait, secure in the knowledge that sooner or later his time would come. And he knew just what he was going to do, down to the smallest detail, when the time did come.

One morning Bunster got up in a mood for knocking seven bells out of the universe. He began on Mauki, and wound up on Mauki, in the interval knocking down his wife and hammering all the boat-boys. At breakfast he called the coffee slops and threw the scalding contents of the cup into Mauki's face. By ten o'clock Bunster was shivering with ague, and half an hour later he was burning with fever. It was no ordinary attack. It quickly became pernicious, and developed into black-water fever. The days passed, and he grew weaker and weaker, never leaving his bed. Mauki waited and watched, the while his skin grew intact once more. He ordered the boys to beach the cutter, scrub her bottom, and give her a general overhauling. They thought the order emanated from Bunster, and they obeyed. But Bunster at the time was lying unconscious and giving no orders. This was Mauki's chance, but still he waited.

When the worst was past, and Bunster lay convalescent and conscious, but weak as a baby, Mauki packed his few trinkets, including the china cup handle, into his trade box. Then he went over to the village and interviewed the king and his two prime ministers.

"This fella Bunster, him good fella you like too much?" he asked.

They explained in one voice that they liked the trader not at all. The ministers poured forth a recital of all the indignities and wrongs that had been heaped upon them. The king broke down and wept. Mauki interrupted rudely.

"You savve me—me big fella marster my country. You no like 'm this fella white marster. Me no like 'm. Plenty good you put hundred coconut, two hundred coconut, three hundred coconut along cutter. Him finish, you go sleep 'm good fella. Altogether kanaka sleep 'm good fella. Bime by big fella noise along house, you no savve hear 'm that fella noise. You altogether sleep strong fella too much."

In like manner Mauki interviewed the boat-boys. Then he ordered Bunster's wife to return to her family house. Had she refused, he would have been in a quandary, for his *tambo* would not have permitted him to lay hands on her.

The house deserted, he entered the sleeping-room, where the trader lay in a doze. Mauki first removed the revolvers, then placed the ray fish mitten on his hand. Bunster's first warning was a stroke of the mitten that removed the skin the full length of his nose.

"Good fella, eh?" Mauki grinned, between two strokes, one of which swept the forehead bare and the other of which cleaned off one side of his face. "Laugh, damn you, laugh."

Mauki did his work thoroughly, and the kanakas, hiding in their houses, heard the "big fella noise" that Bunster made and continued to make for an hour or more.

When Mauki was done, he carried the boat compass and all the rifles and ammunition down to the cutter, which he proceeded to ballast with cases of tobacco. It was while engaged in this that a hideous, skinless thing came out of the house and ran screaming down the beach till it fell in the sand and mowed and gibbered under the scorching sun. Mauki looked toward it and hesitated. Then he went over and removed the head, which he wrapped in a mat and stowed in the stern-locker of the cutter.

So soundly did the kanakas sleep through that long hot day that they did not see the cutter run out through the passage and head south, close-hauled on the southeast trade. Nor was the cutter ever sighted on that long tack to the shores of Ysabel, and during the tedious head-beat from there to Malaita. He landed at Port Adams with a wealth of rifles and tobacco such as no one man had ever possessed before. But he did not stop there. He had taken a white man's head, and only the bush could shelter him. So back he went to the bush-villages, where he shot old Fanfoa and half a dozen of the chief men, and made himself the chief over all the villages. When his father died, Mauki's brother ruled in Port Adams, and, joined together, salt-water men and bushmen, the resulting combination was the strongest of the ten score fighting tribes in Malaita.

More than his fear of the British government was Mauki's fear of the all-powerful Moongleam Soap Company; and one day a message came up to him in the bush, reminding him that he owed the Company eight and one-half years of labor. He sent back a favorable answer, and then appeared the inevitable white man, the captain of the schooner, the only white man during Mauki's reign who ventured the bush and came out alive. This man not only came out, but he brought with him seven hundred and fifty dollars in gold sovereigns—the money price of eight years and a half of labor plus the cost price of certain rifles and cases of tobacco.

Mauki no longer weighs one hundred and ten pounds. His stomach is three times its former girth, and he has four wives. He has many other things—rifles and revolvers, the handle of a china cup, and an excellent collection of bushmen's heads. But more precious than the entire collection is another head, perfectly dried and cured, with sandy hair and a yellowish beard, which is kept wrapped in the finest of fibre lava-lavas. When Mauki goes to war with villages beyond his realm, he invariably gets out this head, and, alone in his grass palace, contemplates it long and solemnly. At such times the hush of death falls on the village, and not even a pickaninny dares make a noise. The head is esteemed the most powerful devil-devil on Malaita, and to the possession of it is ascribed all of Mauki's greatness.

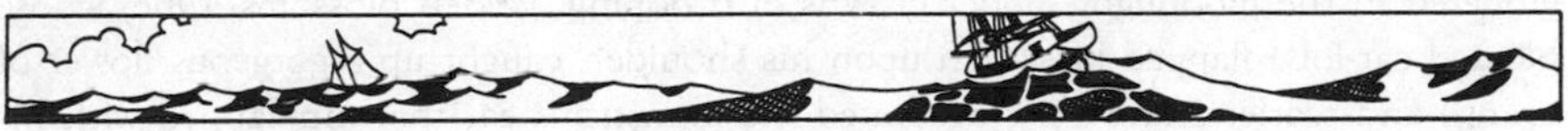

Koolau the Leper

"Because we are sick they take away our liberty. We have obeyed the law. We have done no wrong. And yet they would put us in prison. Molokai is a prison. That you know. Niuli, there, his sister was sent to Molokai seven years ago. He has not seen her since. Nor will he ever see her. She must stay there until she dies. This is not her will. It is not Niuli's will. It is the will of the white men who rule the land. And who are these white men?

"We know. We have it from our fathers and our fathers' fathers. They came like lambs, speaking softly. Well might they speak softly, for we were many and strong, and all the islands were ours. As I say, they spoke softly. They were of two kinds. The one kind asked our permission, our gracious permission, to preach to us the word of God. The other kind asked our permission, our gracious permission, to trade with us. That was the beginning. To-day all the islands are theirs, all the land, all the cattle—everything is theirs. They that preached the word of God and they that preached the word of Rum have foregathered and become great chiefs. They live like kings in houses of many rooms, with multitudes of servants to care for them. They who had nothing have everything, and if you, or I, or any Kanaka be hungry, they sneer and say, 'Well, why don't you work? There are the plantations.' "

Koolau paused. He raised one hand, and with gnarled and twisted fingers lifted up the blazing wreath of hibiscus that crowned his black hair. The moonlight bathed the scene in silver. It was a night of peace, though those who sat about him and listened had all the seeming of battle-wrecks. Their faces were leonine. Here a space yawned in a face where should have been a nose, and there an arm-stump showed where a hand had rotted off. They were men and women beyond the pale, the thirty of them, for upon them had been placed the mark of the beast.

They sat, flower-garlanded, in the perfumed, luminous night, and their lips made uncouth noises and their throats rasped approval of Koolau's speech. They were creatures who once had been men and women. But they were men and women no longer. They were monsters—in face and form grotesque caricatures of everything human. They were hideously maimed and distorted, and had the seeming of creatures that had been racked in millenniums of hell. Their hands, when they possessed them, were like harpy-claws. Their faces were the misfits and slips, crushed and bruised by some mad god at play in the machinery of life. Here and there were features which the mad god had smeared half away, and one woman wept scalding tears from twin pits of horror, where her eyes had once been. Some were in pain and groaned from their chests. Others coughed, making sounds like the tearing of tissue. Two were idiots, more like huge apes marred in the making, until even an ape were an angel. They mowed and gibbered in the moonlight, under crowns of drooping, golden blossoms. One, whose bloated ear-lobe flapped like a fan upon his shoulder, caught up a gorgeous flower of orange and scarlet and with it decorated the monstrous ear that flip-flapped with his every movement.

And over these things Koolau was king. And this was his kingdom—a flower-throttled gorge, with beetling cliffs and crags, from which floated the blattings of wild goats. On three sides the grim walls rose, festooned in fantastic draperies of tropic vegetation and pierced by cave-entrances—the rocky lairs of Koolau's subjects. On the fourth side the earth fell away into a tremendous abyss, and, far below, could be seen the summits of lesser peaks and crags, at whose bases foamed and rumbled the Pacific surge. In fine weather a boat could land on the rocky beach that marked the entrance of Kalalau Valley, but the weather must be very fine. And a cool-headed mountaineer might climb from the beach to the head of Kalalau Valley, to this pocket among the peaks where Koolau ruled; but such a mountaineer must be very cool of head, and he must know the wild-goat trails as well. The marvel was that the mass of human wreckage that constituted Koolau's people should have been able to drag its helpless misery over the giddy goat-trails to this inaccessible spot.

"Brothers," Koolau began.

But one of the mowing, apelike travesties emitted a wild shriek of madness, and Koolau waited while the shrill cachinnation was tossed back and forth among the rocky walls and echoed distantly through the pulseless night.

"Brothers, is it not strange? Ours was the land, and behold, the land is not ours. What did these preachers of the word of God and the word of Rum give us for the land? Have you received one dollar, as much as one dollar, any one of you, for the land? Yet it is theirs, and in return they tell us we can go to work on the land, their land, and that what we produce by our toil shall be theirs. Yet in the old days we did not have to work. Also, when we are sick, they take away our freedom."

"Who brought the sickness, Koolau?" demanded Kiloliana, a lean and wiry man with a face so like a laughing faun's that one might expect to see the cloven hoofs under him. They were cloven, it was true, but the cleavages were great ulcers and livid putrefactions. Yet this was Kiloliana, the most daring climber of them all, the man who knew every goat-trail and who had led Koolau and his wretched followers into the recesses of Kalalau.

"Ay, well questioned," Koolau answered. "Because we would not work the miles of sugar-cane where once our horses pastured, they brought the Chinese slaves from over seas. And with them came the Chinese sickness—that which we suffer from and because of which they would imprison us on Molokai. We were born on Kauai. We have been to the other islands, some here and some there, to Oahu, to Maui, to Hawaii, to Honolulu. Yet always did we come back to Kauai. Why did we come back? There must be a reason. Because we love Kauai. We were born here. Here we have lived. And here shall we die—unless—unless—there be weak hearts amongst us. Such we do not want. They are fit for Molokai. And if there be such, let them not remain. To-morrow the soldiers land on the shore. Let the weak hearts go down to them. They will be sent swiftly to Molokai. As for us, we shall stay and fight. But know that we will not die. We have rifles. You know the narrow trails where men must creep, one by one. I, alone, Koolau, who was once a cowboy on Niihau, can hold the trail against a thousand men. Here is Kapahei, who was once a judge over men and a man with honor, but who is now a hunted rat, like you and me. Hear him. He is wise."

Kapahei arose. Once he had been a judge. He had gone to college at Punahou. He had sat at meat with lords and chiefs and the high representatives of alien powers who protected the interests of traders and missionaries. Such had been Kapahei. But now, as Koolau had said, he was a hunted rat, a creature outside the law, sunk so deep in the mire of human horror that he was above the law as well as beneath it. His face was featureless, save for gaping orifices and for the lidless eyes that burned under hairless brows.

"Let us not make trouble," he began. "We ask to be left alone. But if they do not leave us alone, then is the trouble theirs, and the penalty. My fingers are gone, as you see." He held up his stumps of hands that all might see. "Yet have I the joint of one thumb left, and it can pull a trigger as firmly as did its lost neighbor in the old days. We love Kauai. Let us live here, or die here, but do not let us go to the prison of Molokai. The sickness is not ours. We have not sinned. The men who preached the word of God and the word of Rum brought the sickness with the coolie slaves who work the stolen land. I have been a judge. I know the law and the justice, and I say to you it is unjust to steal a man's land, to make that man sick with the Chinese sickness, and then to put that man in prison for life."

"Life is short, and the days are filled with pain," said Koolau. "Let us drink and dance and be happy as we can."

From one of the rocky lairs calabashes were produced and passed around. The calabashes were filled with the fierce distillation of the root of the *ti*- plant; and as the liquid fire coursed through them and mounted to their brains, they forgot that they had once been men and women, for they were men and women once more. The woman who wept scalding tears from open eyepits was indeed a woman apulse with life as she plucked the strings of an *ukulele* and lifted her voice in a barbaric love-call such as might have come from the dark forest-depths of the primeval world. The air tingled with her cry, softly imperious and seductive. Upon a mat, timing his rhythm to the woman's song, Kiloliana danced. It was unmistakable. Love danced in all his movements, and, next, dancing with him on the mat, was a woman whose heavy hips and generous breast gave the lie to her disease-corroded face. It was a dance of the living dead, for in their disintegrating bodies life still loved and longed. Ever the woman whose sightless eyes ran scalding tears chanted her love-cry, ever the dancers danced of love in the warm night, and ever the calabashes went around till in all their brains were maggots crawling of memory and desire. And with the woman on the mat danced a slender maid whose face was beautiful and unmarred, but whose twisted arms that rose and fell marked the disease's ravage. And the two idiots, gibbering and mouthing strange noises, danced apart, grotesque, fantastic, travestying love as they themselves had been travestied by life.

But the woman's love-cry broke midway, the calabashes were lowered, and the dancers ceased, as all gazed into the abyss above the sea, where a rocket flared like a wan phantom through the moonlit air.

"It is the soldiers," said Koolau. "To-morrow there will be fighting. It is well to sleep and be prepared."

The lepers obeyed, crawling away to their lairs in the cliff, until only Koolau remained, sitting motionless in the moonlight, his rifle across his knees, as he gazed far down to the boats landing on the beach.

The far head of Kalalau Valley had been well chosen as a refuge. Except Kiloliana, who knew back-trails up the precipitous walls, no man could win to the gorge save by advancing across a knife-edged ridge. This passage was a hundred yards in length. At best, it was a scant twelve inches wide. On either side yawned the abyss. A slip, and to right or left the man would fall to his death. But once across he would find himself in an earthly paradise. A sea of vegetation laved the landscape, pouring its green billows from wall to wall, dripping from the cliff-lips in great vine-masses, and flinging a spray of ferns and air-plants into the multitudinous crevices. During the many months of Koolau's rule, he and his followers had fought with this vegetable sea. The choking jungle, with its riot of blossoms, had been driven back from the bananas, oranges and mangoes that grew wild. In little clearings grew the wild arrowroot; on stone terraces, filled with soil scrapings, were the *taro* patches and the melons; and in every open space where the sunshine penetrated, were *papaia* trees burdened with their golden fruit.

Koolau had been driven to this refuge from the lower valley by the beach. And if he were driven from it in turn, he knew of gorges among the jumbled peaks of the inner fastnesses where he could lead his subjects and live. And now he lay with his rifle beside him, peering down through a tangled screen of foliage at the soldiers on the beach. He noted that they had large guns with them, from which the sunshine flashed as from mirrors. The knife-edged passage lay directly before him. Crawling upward along the trail that led to it he could see tiny specks of men. He knew they were not the soldiers, but the police. When they failed, then the soldiers would enter the game.

He affectionately rubbed a twisted hand along his rifle barrel and made sure that the sights were clean. He had learned to shoot as a wild-cattle hunter on Niihau, and on that island his skill as a marksman was unforgotten. As the toiling specks of men grew nearer and larger, he estimated the range, judged the deflection of the wind that swept at right angles across the line of fire, and calculated the chances of overshooting marks that were so far below his level. But he did not shoot. Not until they reached the beginning of the passage did he make his presence known. He did not disclose himself, but spoke from the thicket.

"What do you want?" he demanded.

"We want Koolau, the leper," answered the man who led the native police, himself a blue-eyed American.

"You must go back," Koolau said.

He knew the man, a deputy sheriff, for it was by him that he had been harried out of Niihau, across Kauai, to Kalalau Valley and out of the valley to the gorge.

"Who are you?" the sheriff asked.

"I am Koolau, the leper," was the reply.

"Then come out. We want you. Dead or alive, there is a thousand dollars on your head. You cannot escape."

Koolau laughed aloud in the thicket.

"Come out!" the sheriff commanded, and was answered by silence.

He conferred with the police, and Koolau saw that they were preparing to rush him.

"Koolau," the sheriff called. "Koolau, I am coming across to get you."

"Then look first and well about you at the sun and sea and sky, for it will be the last time you behold them."

"That's all right, Koolau," the sheriff said soothingly. "I know you're a dead shot. But you won't shoot me. I have never done you any wrong."

Koolau grunted in the thicket.

"I say, you know, I've never done you any wrong, have I?" the sheriff persisted.

"You do me wrong when you try to put me in prison," was the reply. "And you do me wrong when you try for the thousand dollars on my head. If you will live, stay where you are."

"I've got to come across and get you. I'm sorry. But it is my duty."

"You will die before you get across."

The sheriff was no coward. Yet was he undecided. He gazed into the gulf on either side, and ran his eyes along the knife-edge he must travel. Then he made up his mind.

"Koolau," he called.

But the thicket remained silent.

"Koolau, don't shoot. I am coming."

The sheriff turned, gave some orders to the police, then started on his perilous way. He advanced slowly. It was like walking a tight rope. He had nothing to lean upon but the air. The lava rock crumbled under his feet, and on either side the dislodged fragments pitched downward through the depths. The sun blazed upon him, and his face was wet with sweat. Still he advanced, until the halfway point was reached.

"Stop!" Koolau commanded from the thicket. "One more step and I shoot."

The sheriff halted, swaying for balance as he stood poised above the void. His face was pale, but his eyes were determined. He licked his dry lips before he spoke.

"Koolau, you won't shoot me. I know you won't."

He started once more. The bullet whirled him half about. On his face was an expression of querulous surprise as he reeled to the fall. He tried to save himself by throwing his body across the knife-edge; but at that moment he knew death. The next moment the knife-edge was vacant. Then came the rush, five policemen, in single file, with superb steadiness, running along the knife-edge. At the same instant the rest of the posse opened fire on the thicket. It was madness. Five times Koolau pulled the trigger, so rapidly that his shots constituted a rattle. Changing his position and crouching low under the bullets that were biting and singing through the bushes, he peered out. Four of the police had followed the sheriff. The fifth lay across the knife-edge, still alive. On the farther side, no longer firing, were the surviving police. On the naked rock there was no hope for them. Before they could clamber down Koolau could have picked off the last man. But he did not fire, and, after a conference, one of them took off a white undershirt and waved it as a flag. Followed by another, he advanced along the knife-edge to their wounded comrade. Koolau gave no sign, but watched them slowly withdraw and become specks as they descended into the lower valley.

Two hours later, from another thicket, Koolau watched a body of police trying to make the ascent from the opposite side of the valley. He saw the wild goats flee before them as they climbed higher and higher, until he doubted his judgment and sent for Kiloliana who crawled in beside him.

"No, there is no way," said Kiloliana.

"The goats?" Koolau questioned.

"They come over from the next valley, but they cannot pass to this. There is no way. Those men are not wiser than goats. They may fall to their deaths. Let us watch."

"They are brave men," said Koolau. "Let us watch."

Side by side they lay among the morning-glories, with the yellow blossoms of the *hau* dropping upon them from overhead, watching the motes of men toil upward, till the thing happened, and three of them, slipping, rolling, sliding, dashed over a clifflip and fell sheer half a thousand feet.

Kiloliana chuckled.

"We will be bothered no more," he said.

"They have war guns," Koolau made answer. "The soldiers have not yet spoken."

In the drowsy afternoon, most of the lepers lay in their rock dens asleep. Koolau, his rifle on his knees, fresh-cleaned and ready, dozed in the entrance to his own den. The maid with the twisted arm lay below in the thicket and kept watch on the knife-edge passage. Suddenly Koolau was startled wide awake by the sound of an explosion on the beach. The next instant the atmosphere was incredibly rent asunder. The terrible sound frightened him. It was as if all the gods had caught the envelope of the sky in their hands and were ripping it apart as a woman rips apart a sheet of cotton cloth. But it was such an immense ripping, growing swiftly nearer. Koolau glanced up apprehensively, as if expecting to see the thing. Then high up on the cliff overhead the shell burst in a fountain of black smoke. The rock was shattered, the fragments falling to the foot of the cliff.

Koolau passed his hand across his sweaty brow. He was terribly shaken. He had had no experience with shell-fire, and this was more dreadful than anything he had imagined.

"One," said Kapahei, suddenly bethinking himself to keep count.

A second and a third shell flew screaming over the top of the wall, bursting beyond view. Kapahei methodically kept the count. The lepers crowded into the open space before the caves. At first they were frightened, but as the shells continued their flight overhead the leper folk became reassured and began to admire the spectacle. The two idiots shrieked with delight, prancing wild antics as each air-tormenting shell went by. Koolau began to recover his confidence. No damage was being done. Evidently they could not aim such large missiles at such long range with the precision of a rifle.

But a change came over the situation. The shells began to fall short. One burst below in the thicket by the knife-edge. Koolau remembered the maid who lay there on watch, and ran down to see. The smoke was still rising from the bushes when he crawled in. He was astounded. The branches were splintered and broken. Where the girl had lain was a hole in the ground. The girl herself was in shattered fragments. The shell had burst right on her.

First peering out to make sure no soldiers were attempting the passage, Koolau started back on the run for the caves. All the time the shells were moaning, whining, screaming by, and the valley was rumbling and reverberating with the explosions. As he came in sight of the caves, he saw the two idiots cavorting about, clutching each other's hands with their stumps of fingers. Even as he ran, Koolau saw a spout of black smoke rise from the ground, near to the idiots. They were flung apart bodily by the explosion. One lay motionless, but the other was dragging himself by his hands toward the cave. His legs trailed out helplessly behind him, while the blood was pouring from his body. He seemed bathed in blood, and as he crawled he cried like a little dog. The rest of the lepers, with the exception of Kapahei, had fled into the caves.

"Seventeen," said Kapahei. "Eighteen," he added.

This last shell had fairly entered into one of the caves. The explosion caused all the caves to empty. But from the particular cave no one emerged. Koolau crept in through the pungent, acrid smoke. Four bodies, frightfully mangled, lay about. One of them was the sightless woman whose tears till now had never ceased.

Outside, Koolau found his people in a panic and already beginning to climb the goat trail that led out of the gorge and on among the jumbled heights and chasms. The wounded idiot, whining feebly and dragging himself along on the ground by his hands, was trying to follow. But at the first pitch of the wall his helplessness overcame him and he fell back.

"It would be better to kill him," said Koolau to Kapahei, who still sat in the same place.

"Twenty-two," Kapahei answered. "Yes, it would be a wise thing to kill him. Twenty-three—twenty-four."

The idiot whined sharply when he saw the rifle leveled at him. Koolau hesitated, then lowered the gun.

"It is a hard thing to do," he said.

"You are a fool, twenty-six, twenty-seven," said Kapahei. "Let me show you."

He arose and, with a heavy fragment of rock in his hand, approached the wounded thing. As he lifted his arm to strike, a shell burst full upon him, relieving him of the necessity of the act and at the same time putting an end to his count.

Koolau was alone in the gorge. He watched the last of his people drag their crippled bodies over the brow of the height and disappear. Then he turned and went down to the thicket where the maid had been killed. The shell-fire still continued, but he remained; for far below he could see the soldiers climbing up. A shell burst twenty feet away. Flattening himself into the earth, he heard the rush of the fragments above his body. A shower of *hau* blossoms rained upon him. He lifted his head to peer down the trail, and sighed. He was very much afraid. Bullets from rifles would not have worried him, but this shell-fire was abominable. Each time a shell shrieked by he shivered and crouched; but each time he lifted his head again to watch the trail.

At last the shells ceased. This, he reasoned, was because the soldiers were drawing near. They crept along the trail in single file, and he tried to count them until he lost track. At any rate, there were a hundred or so of them—all come after Koolau the leper. He felt a fleeting prod of pride. With war guns and rifles, police and soldiers, they came for him, and he was only one man, a crippled wreck of a man at that. They offered a thousand dollars for him, dead or alive. In all his life he had never possessed that much money. The thought was a bitter one. Kapahei had been right. He, Koolau, had done no wrong. Because the *haoles* wanted labor with which to work the stolen land, they had brought in the Chinese coolies, and with them had come the sickness. And now, because he had caught the sickness, he was worth a thousand dollars—but not to himself. It was his worthless carcass, rotten with disease or dead from a bursting shell, that was worth all that money.

When the soldiers reached the knife-edged passage, he was prompted to warn them. But his gaze fell upon the body of the murdered maid, and he kept silent. When six had ventured on the knife-edge, he opened fire. Nor did he cease when the knife-edge was bare. He emptied his magazine, reloaded, and emptied it again. He kept on shooting.

All his wrongs were blazing in his brain, and he was in a fury of vengeance. All down the goat trail the soldiers were firing, and though they lay flat and sought to shelter themselves in the shallow inequalities of the surface, they were exposed marks to him. Bullets whistled and thudded about him, and an occasional ricochet sang sharply through the air. One bullet ploughed a crease through his scalp, and a second burned across his shoulder-blade without breaking the skin.

It was a massacre, in which one man did the killing. The soldiers began to retreat, helping along their wounded. As Koolau picked them off he became aware of the smell of burnt meat. He glanced about him at first, and then discovered that it was his own hands. The heat of the rifle was doing it. The leprosy had destroyed most of the nerves in his hands. Though his flesh burned and he smelled it, there was no sensation.

He lay in the thicket, smiling, until he remembered the war guns. Without doubt they would open up on him again, and this time upon the very thicket from which he had inflicted the damage. Scarcely had he changed his position to a nook behind a small shoulder of the wall where he had noted that no shells fell, than the bombardment recommenced. He counted the shells. Sixty more were thrown into the gorge before the war-guns ceased. The tiny area was pitted with their explosions, until it seemed impossible that any creature could have survived. So the soldiers thought, for, under the burning afternoon sun, they climbed the goat trail again. And again the knife-edged passage was disputed, and again they fell back to the beach.

For two days longer Koolau held the passage, though the soldiers contented themselves with flinging shells into his retreat. Then Pahau, a leper boy, came to the top of the wall at the back of the gorge and shouted down to him that Kiloliana, hunting goats that they might eat, had been killed by a fall, and that the women were frightened and knew not what to do. Koolau called the boy down and left him with a spare gun with which to guard the passage. Koolau found his people disheartened. The majority of them were too helpless to forage food for themselves under such forbidding circumstances, and all were starving. He selected two women and a man who were not too far gone with the disease, and sent them back to the gorge to bring up food and mats. The rest he cheered and consoled until even the weakest took a hand in building rough shelters for themselves.

But those he had dispatched for food did not return, and he started back for the gorge. As he came out on the brow of the wall, half a dozen rifles cracked. A bullet tore through the fleshy part of his shoulder, and his cheek was cut by a sliver of rock where a second bullet smashed against the cliff. In the moment that this happened, and he leaped back, he saw that the gorge was alive with soldiers. His own people had betrayed him. The shell-fire had been too terrible, and they had preferred the prison of Molokai.

Koolau dropped back and unslung one of his heavy cartridge-belts. Lying among the rocks, he allowed the head and shoulders of the first soldier to rise clearly into view before pulling trigger. Twice this happened, and then, after some delay, in place of a head and shoulders a white flag was thrust above the edge of the wall.

"What do you want?" he demanded.

"I want you, if you are Koolau the leper," came the answer.

Koolau forgot where he was, forgot everything, as he lay and marvelled at the strange persistence of these *haoles* who would have their will though the sky fell in. Ay, they would have their will over all men and all things, even though they died in getting it. He could not but admire them, too, what of that will in them that was stronger than life and that bent all things to their bidding. He was convinced of the hopelessness of his struggle. There was no gainsaying that terrible will of the *haoles.* Though he killed a thousand, yet would they rise like the sands of the sea and come upon him, ever more and more. They never knew when they were beaten. That was their fault and their virtue. It was where his own kind lacked. He could see, now, how the handful of the preachers of God and the preachers of Rum had conquered the land. It was because—

"Well, what have you got to say? Will you come with me?"

It was the voice of the invisible man under the white flag. There he was, like any *haole*, driving straight toward the end determined.

"Let us talk," said Koolau.

The man's head and shoulders arose, then his whole body. He was a smooth-faced, blue-eyed youngster of twenty-five, slender and natty in his captain's uniform. He advanced until halted, then seated himself a dozen feet away:

"You are a brave man," said Koolau wonderingly. "I could kill you like a fly."

"No, you couldn't," was the answer.

"Why not?"

"Because you are a man, Koolau, though a bad one. I know your story. You kill fairly."

Koolau grunted, but was secretly pleased.

"What have you done with my people?" he demanded. "The boy, the two women and the man?"

"They gave themselves up, as I have now come for you to do."

Koolau laughed incredulously.

"I am a free man," he announced. "I have done no wrong. All I ask is to be left alone. I have lived free, and I shall die free. I will never give myself up."

"Then your people are wiser than you," answered the young captain. "Look—they are coming now."

Koolau turned and watched the remnant of his band approach. Groaning and sighing, a ghastly procession, it dragged its wretchedness past. It was given to Koolau to taste a deeper bitterness, for they hurled imprecations and insults at him as they went by; and the panting hag who brought up the rear halted, and with skinny, harpy-claws extended, shaking her snarling death's head from side to side, she laid a curse upon him. One by one they dropped over the lip-edge and surrendered to the hiding soldiers.

"You can go now," said Koolau to the captain. "I will never give myself up. That is my last word. Good-by."

The captain slipped over the cliff to his soldiers. The next moment, and without a flag of truce, he hoisted his hat on his scabbard, and Koolau's bullet tore through it. That afternoon they shelled him out from the beach, and as he retreated into the inaccessible pockets beyond, the soldiers followed him.

For six weeks they hunted him from pocket to pocket, over the volcanic peaks and along the goat trails. When he hid in the lantana jungle, they formed lines of beaters, and through lantana jungle and guava scrub they drove him like a rabbit. But ever he turned and doubled and eluded. There was no cornering him. When pressed too closely, his sure rifle held them back and they carried their wounded down the goat trails to the beach. There were times when they did the shooting as his brown body showed for a moment through the underbrush. Once, five of them caught him on an exposed goat trail between pockets. They emptied their rifles at him as he limped and climbed along his dizzy way. Afterward they found blood-stains and knew that he was wounded. At the end of six weeks they gave up. The soldiers and police returned to

Honolulu, and Kalalau Valley was left to him for his own, though head-hunters ventured after him from time to time and to their own undoing.

Two years later, and for the last time, Koolau crawled into a thicket and lay down among the *ti-* leaves and wild ginger blossoms. Free he had lived, and free he was dying. A slight drizzle of rain began to fall, and he drew a ragged blanket about the distorted wreck of his limbs. His body was covered with an oilskin coat. Across his chest he laid his Mauser rifle, lingering affectionately for a moment to wipe the dampness from the barrel. The hand with which he wiped had no fingers left upon it with which to pull the trigger.

He closed his eyes, for, from the weakness in his body and the fuzzy turmoil in his brain, he knew that his end was near. Like a wild animal he had crept into hiding to die. Half-conscious, aimless and wandering, he lived back in his life to his early manhood on Niihau. As life faded and the drip of the rain grew dim in his ears, it seemed to him that he was once more in the thick of the horse-breaking, with raw colts rearing and bucking under him, his stirrups tied together beneath, or charging madly about the breaking corral and driving the helping cowboys over the rails. The next instant, and with seeming naturalness, he found himself pursuing the wild bulls of the upland pastures, roping them and leading them down to the valleys. Again the sweat and dust of the branding pen stung his eyes and bit his nostrils.

All his lusty, whole-bodied youth was his, until the sharp pangs of impending dissolution brought him back. He lifted his monstrous hands and gazed at them in wonder. But how? Why? Why should the wholeness of that wild youth of his change to this? Then he remembered, and once again, and for a moment, he was Koolau, the leper. His eyelids fluttered wearily down and the drip of the rain ceased in his ears. A prolonged trembling set up in his body. This, too, ceased. He half-lifted his head, but it fell back. Then his eyes opened, and did not close. His last thought was of his Mauser, and he pressed it against his chest with his folded, fingerless hands.

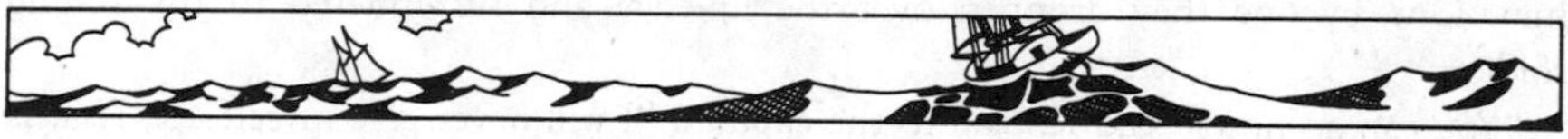

THE SHERIFF OF KONA

"You cannot escape liking the climate," Cudworth said, in reply to my panegyric on the Kona coast. "I was a young fellow, just out of college, when I came here eighteen years ago. I never went back, except, of course, to visit. And I warn you, if you have some spot dear to you on earth, not to linger here too long, else you will find this dearer."

We had finished dinner, which had been served on the big *lanai,* the one with a northerly exposure, though *exposure* is indeed a misnomer in so delectable a climate.

The candles had been put out, and a slim, white-clad Japanese slipped like a ghost through the silvery moonlight, presented us with cigars, and faded away into the darkness of the bungalow. I looked through a screen of banana and lehua trees, and down across the guava scrub to the quiet sea a thousand feet beneath. For a week, ever since I had landed from the tiny coasting-steamer, I had been stopping with Cudworth, and during that time no wind had ruffled that unvexed sea. True, there had been breezes, but they were the gentlest zephyrs that ever blew through summer isles. They were not winds; they were sighs—long, balmy sighs of a world at rest.

"A lotus land," I said.

"Where each day is like every day, and every day is a paradise of days," he answered. "Nothing ever happens. It is not too hot. It is not too cold. It is always just right. Have you noticed how the land and the sea breathe turn and turn about?"

Indeed I had noticed that delicious, rhythmic, breathing. Each morning I had watched the sea-breeze begin at the shore and slowly extend seaward as it blew the mildest, softest whiff of ozone to the land. It played over the sea, just faintly darkening its surface, with here and there and everywhere long lanes of calm, shifting, changing, drifting, according to the capricious kisses of the breeze. And each evening I had watched the sea breath die away to heavenly calm, and heard the land breath softly make its way through the coffee trees and monkey-pods.

"It is a land of perpetual calm," I said. "Does it ever blow here?—ever really blow? You know what I mean."

Cudworth shook his head and pointed eastward.

"How can it blow, with a barrier like that to stop it?"

Far above towered the huge bulks of Mauna Kea and Mauna Loa, seeming to blot out half the starry sky. Two miles and a half above our heads they reared their own heads, white with snow that the tropic sun had failed to melt.

"Thirty miles away, right now, I'll wager, it is blowing forty miles an hour."

I smiled incredulously.

Cudworth stepped to the *lanai* telephone. He called up, in succession, Waimea, Kohala and Hamakua. Snatches of his conversation told me that the wind was blowing: "Rip-snorting and back-jumping, eh? . . . How long? . . . Only a week? . . . Hello, Abe, is that you? . . . Yes, yes . . . You *will* plant coffee on the Hamakua coast . . . Hang your wind-breaks! You should see *my* trees."

"Blowing a gale," he said to me, turning from hanging up the receiver. "I always have to joke Abe on his coffee. He has five hundred acres, and he's done marvels in wind-breaking, but how he keeps the roots in the ground is beyond me. Blow? It always blows on the Hamakua side. Kohala reports a schooner under double reefs beating up the channel between Hawaii and Maui, and making heavy weather of it."

"It is hard to realize," I said lamely. "Doesn't a little whiff of it ever eddy around somehow, and get down here?"

"Not a whiff. Our land-breeze is absolutely of no kin, for it begins this side of Mauna Kea and Mauna Loa. You see, the land radiates its heat quicker than the sea, and so, at night, the land breathes over the sea. In the day the land becomes warmer than the sea, and the sea breathes over the land . . . Listen! Here comes the land-breath now, the mountain wind."

I could hear it coming, rustling softly through the coffee trees, stirring the monkey-pods, and sighing through the sugar-cane. On the *lanai* the hush still reigned. Then it came, the first feel of the mountain wind, faintly balmy, fragrant and spicy, and cool, deliciously cool, a silken coolness, a wine-like coolness—cool as only the mountain wind of Kona can be cool.

"Do you wonder that I lost my heart to Kona eighteen years ago?" he demanded. "I could never leave it now. I think I should die. It would be terrible. There was another man who loved it, even as I. I think he loved it more, for he was born here on the Kona coast. He was a great man, my best friend, my more than brother. But he left it, and he did not die."

"Love?" I queried. "A woman?"

Cudworth shook his head.

"Nor will he ever come back, though his heart will be here until he dies."

He paused and gazed down upon the beachlights of Kailua. I smoked silently and waited.

"He was already in love . . . with his wife. Also, he had three children, and he loved them. They are in Honolulu now. The boy is going to college."

"Some rash act?" I questioned, after a time, impatiently.

He shook his head. "Neither guilty of anything criminal, nor charged with anything criminal. He was the Sheriff of Kona."

"You choose to be paradoxical," I said.

"I suppose it does sound that way," he admitted, "and that is the perfect hell of it."

He looked at me searchingly for a moment, and then abruptly took up the tale.

"He was a leper. No, he was not born with it—no one is born with it; it came upon him. This man—what does it matter? Lyte Gregory was his name. Every *kamaina* knows the story. He was straight American stock, but he was built like the chieftains of old Hawaii. He stood six feet three. His stripped weight was two hundred and twenty pounds, not an ounce of which was not clean muscle or bone. He was the strongest man I have ever seen. He was an athlete and a giant. He was a god. He was my friend. And his heart and his soul were as big and as fine as his body.

"I wonder what you would do if you saw your friend, your brother, on the slippery lip of a precipice, slipping, slipping, and you were able to do nothing. That was just it. I could do nothing. I saw it coming, and I could do nothing. My God, man! what could I do? There it was, malignant and incontestable, the mark of the thing on his brow. No one else saw it. It was because I loved him so, I do believe, that I alone saw it. I could not credit the testimony of my senses. It was too incredibly horrible. Yet there it was, on his brow, on his ears. I had seen it, the slight puff of the earlobes—oh, so impercep-tibly slight. I watched it for months. Then, next, hoping against hope, the darkening of the skin above both eyebrows—oh, so faint, just like the dimmest touch of sunburn. I should have thought it sunburn but that there was a shine to it, such an invisible shine, like a little highlight seen for a moment and gone the next. I tried to believe it was sunburn, only I could not. I knew better. No one noticed it but me. No one ever noticed it except Stephen Kaluna, and I did not know that till afterward. But I saw it coming, the whole damnable, unnamable awfulness of it; but I refused to think about the future. I was afraid. I could not. And of nights I cried over it.

"He was my friend. We fished sharks on Niihau together. We hunted wild cattle on Mauna Kea and Mauna Loa. We broke horses and branded steers on the Carter Ranch. We hunted goats through Haleakala. He taught me diving and surfing until I was nearly as clever as he, and he was cleverer than the average Kanaka. I have seen him dive in fifteen fathoms, and he could stay down two minutes. He was an amphibian and a mountaineer. He could climb wherever a goat dared climb. He was afraid of nothing. He was on the wrecked *Luga*, and he swam thirty miles in thirty-six hours in a heavy sea. He could fight his way out through breaking combers that would batter you and me to a jelly. He was a great, glorious man-god. We went through the Revolution together. We were both romantic loyalists. He was shot twice and sentenced to death. But he was too great a man for the republicans to kill. He laughed at them. Later, they gave him honor and made him Sheriff of Kona. He was a simple man, a boy that never grew up. His was no intricate brain pattern. He had no twists nor quirks in his mental processes. He went straight to the point, and his points were always simple.

"And he was sanguine. Never have I known so confident a man, nor a man so satisfied and happy. He did not ask anything from life. There was nothing left to be desired. For him life had no arrears. He had been paid in full, cash down, and in advance. What more could he possibly desire than that magnificent body, that iron constitution, that immunity from all ordinary ills, and that lowly wholesomeness of soul? Physically he was perfect. He had never been sick in his life. He did not know what a headache was. When I was so afflicted he used to look at me in wonder, and make me laugh with his clumsy attempts at sympathy. He did not understand such a thing as a headache. He could not understand. Sanguine? No wonder. How could he be otherwise with that tremendous vitality and incredible health?

"Just to show you what faith he had in his glorious star, and, also, what sanction he had for that faith. He was a youngster at the time—I had just met him—when he went into a poker game at Wailuku. There was a big German in it, Schultz his name was, and he played a brutal, domineering game. He had had a run of luck as well, and he was quite insufferable, when Lyte Gregory dropped in and took a hand. The very first hand it was Schultz's blind. Lyte came in, as well as the others, and Schultz raised them out —all except Lyte. He did not like the German's tone, and he raised him back. Schultz raised in turn, and in turn Lyte raised Schultz. So they went, back and forth. The stakes were big. And do you know what Lyte held? A pair of kings and three little clubs. It wasn't poker. Lyte wasn't playing poker. He was playing his optimism. He didn't know what Schultz held, but he raised and raised until he made Schultz squeal, and Schultz held three aces all the time. Think of it! A man with a pair of kings compelling three aces to see before the draw!

"Well, Schultz called for two cards. Another German was dealing, Schultz's friend at that. Lyte knew then that he was up against three of a kind. Now what did he do? What would you have done? Drawn three cards and held up the kings, of course. Not Lyte, he was playing optimism. He threw the kings away, held up the three little clubs and drew two cards. He never looked at them. He looked across at Schultz to bet, and Schultz did bet, big. Since he himself held three aces, he knew he had Lyte, because he played Lyte for threes, and, necessarily, they would have to be smaller threes. Poor Schultz! He was perfectly correct under the premises. His mistake was that he thought Lyte was playing poker. They bet back and forth for five minutes, until Schultz's certainty began to ooze out. And all the time Lyte had never looked at his two cards, and Schultz knew it. I could see Schultz think, and revive, and splurge with his bets again. But the strain was too much for him.

" 'Hold on, Gregory,' he said at last. 'I've got you beaten from the start. I don't want any of your money. I've got—'

" 'Never mind what you've got,' Lyte interrupted. 'You don't know what I've got. I guess I'll take a look.'

"He looked, and raised the German a hundred dollars. Then they went at it again, back and forth and back and forth, until Schultz weakened and called, and laid down his three aces. Lyte faced his five cards. They were all black. He had drawn two more clubs. Do you know, he just about broke Schultz's nerve as a poker player. He never played in the same form again. He lacked confidence after that, and was a bit wobbly.

" 'But how could you do it?" I asked Lyte afterward. 'You knew he had you beaten when he drew two cards. Besides, you never looked at your own draw.'

" 'I didn't have to look,' was Lyte's answer. 'I knew they were two clubs all the time. They just had to be two clubs. Do you think I was going to let that big Dutchman beat me? It was impossible that he should beat me. It is not my way to be beaten. I just have to win. Why, I'd have been the most surprised man in this world if they hadn't been all clubs.'

"That was Lyte's way, and maybe it will help you to appreciate his colossal optimism. As he put it, he just had to succeed, to fare well, to prosper. And in that same incident, as in ten thousand others, he found his sanction. The thing was that he did succeed, did prosper. That was why he was afraid of nothing. Nothing could ever happen to him. He knew it, because nothing had ever happened to him. That time the *Luga* was lost and he swam thirty miles, he was in the water two whole nights and a day. And during all that terrible stretch of time he never lost hope once, never once doubted the outcome. He just knew he was going to make the land. He told me so himself, and I know it was the truth.

"Well, that is the kind of a man Lyte Gregory was. He was of a different race from ordinary, ailing mortals. He was a lordly being, untouched by common ills and misfortunes. Whatever he wanted he got. He won his wife—one of the Caruthers, a little beauty—from a dozen rivals. And she settled down and made him the finest wife in the world. He wanted a boy. He got it. He wanted a girl and another boy. He got them. And they were just right, without spot or blemish, with chests like little barrels, and with all the inheritance of his own health and strength.

"And then it happened. The mark of the beast was laid upon him. I watched it for a year. It broke my heart. But he did not know it, nor did anybody else guess it except that cursed *hapa-haole*, Stephen Kaluna. He knew it, but I did not know that he did. And—yes—Doc Strowbridge knew it. He was the federal physician, and he had developed the leper eye. You see, part of his business was to examine suspects and order them to the receiving station at Honolulu. And Stephen Kaluna had developed the leper eye. The disease ran strong in his family, and four or five of his relatives were already on Molokai.

"The trouble arose over Stephen Kaluna's sister. When she became suspect, and before Doc Strowbridge could get hold of her, her brother spirited her away to some hiding place. Lyte was Sheriff of Kona, and it was his business to find her.

"We were all over at Hilo that night, in Ned Austin's. Stephen Kaluna was there when we came in, by himself, in his cups, and quarrelsome. Lyte was laughing over some joke—that huge, happy laugh of a giant boy. Kaluna spat contemptuously on the floor. Lyte noticed, so did everybody; but he ignored the fellow. Kaluna was looking for trouble. He took it as a personal grudge that Lyte was trying to apprehend his sister. In half a dozen ways he advertised his displeasure at Lyte's presence, but Lyte ignored him. I imagined Lyte was a bit sorry for him, for the hardest duty of his office was the apprehension of lepers. It is not a nice thing to go into a man's house and tear away a father, mother or child, who has done no wrong, and to send such a one to perpetual banishment on Molokai. Of course, it is necessary as a protection to society, and Lyte, I do believe, would have been the first to apprehend his own father did he become suspect.

"Finally, Kaluna blurted out: 'Look here, Gregory, you think you're going to find Kalaniweo, but you're not.'

"Kalaniweo was his sister. Lyte glanced at him when his name was called, but he made no answer. Kaluna was furious. He was working himself up all the time.

" 'I'll tell you one thing,' he shouted. 'You'll be on Molokai yourself before ever you get Kalaniweo there. I'll tell you what you are. You've no right to be in the company of honest men. You've made a terrible fuss talking about your duty, haven't you? You've sent many lepers to Molokai, and knowing all the time you belonged there yourself.'

"I'd seen Lyte angry more than once, but never quite so angry as at that moment. Leprosy with us, you know, is not a thing to jest about. He made one leap across the floor, dragging Kaluna out of his chair with a clutch on his neck. He shook him back and forth savagely, till you could hear the half-caste's teeth rattling.

" 'What do you mean?' Lyte was demanding. 'Spit it out, man, or I'll choke it out of you!'

"You know, in the West there is a certain phrase that a man must smile while uttering. So with us of the islands, only our phrase is related to leprosy. No matter what Kaluna was, he was no coward. As soon as Lyte eased the grip on his throat he answered:

" 'I'll tell you what I mean. You are a leper yourself.'

"Lyte suddenly flung the half-caste sidewise into a chair, letting him down easily enough. Then Lyte broke out into honest, hearty laughter. But he laughed alone, and when he discovered it he looked around at our faces. I had reached his side and was trying to get him to come away, but he took no notice of me. He was gazing, fascinated, at Kaluna, who was brushing at his own throat in a flurried, nervous way, as if to brush off the contamination of the fingers that had clutched him. The action was unreasoned, genuine.

"Lyte looked around at us, slowly passing from face to face.

" 'My God, fellows! My God!' he said.

"He did not speak it. It was more a hoarse whisper of fright and horror. It was fear that fluttered in his throat, and I don't think that ever in his life before he had known fear.

"Then his colossal optimism asserted itself, and he laughed again.

" 'A good joke—whoever put it up,' he said. 'The drinks are on me. I had a scare for a moment. But, fellows, don't do it again, to anybody. It's too serious. I tell you I died a thousand deaths in that moment. I thought of my wife and the kids, and . . ."

"His voice broke, and the half-caste, still throat-brushing, drew his eyes. He was puzzled and worried.

" 'John,' he said, turning toward me.

"His jovial, rotund voice rang in my ears. But I could not answer. I was swallowing hard at that moment, and besides, I knew my face didn't look just right.

" 'John,' he called again, taking a step nearer.

"He called timidly, and of all nightmares of horrors the most frightful was to hear timidity in Lyte Gregory's voice.

" 'John, John, what does it mean?' he went on, still more timidly. 'It's a joke, isn't it? John, here's my hand. If I were a leper would I offer you my hand? Am I a leper, John?'

"He held out his hand, and what in high heaven or hell did I care? He was my friend. I took his hand, though it cut me to the heart to see the way his face brightened.

" 'It was only a joke, Lyte," I said. 'We fixed it up on you. But you're right. It's too serious. We won't do it again.'

"He did not laugh this time. He smiled, as a man awakened from a bad dream and still oppressed by the substance of the dream.

" 'All right, then,' he said. 'Don't do it again, and I'll stand for the drinks. But I may as well confess that you fellows had me going south for a moment. Look at the way I've been sweating.'

"He sighed and wiped the sweat from his forehead as he started to step toward the bar.

" 'It is no joke,' Kaluna said abruptly.

"I looked murder at him, and I felt murder, too. But I dared not speak or strike. That would have precipitated the catastrophe which I somehow had a mad hope of still averting.

" 'It is no joke," Kaluna repeated. 'You are a leper, Lyte Gregory, and you've no right putting your hands on honest men's flesh—on the clean flesh of honest men.'

"Then Gregory flared up.

" 'The joke has gone far enough! Quit it! Quit it, I say, Kaluna, or I'll give you a beating!'

" 'You undergo a bacteriological examination,' Kaluna answered, 'and then you can beat me—to death, if you want to. Why, man, look at yourself there in the glass. You can see it. Anybody can see it. You're developing the lion face. See where the skin is darkened there over your eyes.'

"Lyte peered and peered, and I saw his hands trembling.

" 'I can see nothing,' he said finally, then turned on the *hapa-haole.* 'You have a black heart, Kaluna. And I am not ashamed to say that you have given me a scare that no man has the right to give another. I take you at your word. I am going to settle this thing now. I am going straight to Doc Strowbridge. And when I come back, watch out.'

"He never looked at us, but started for the door.

" 'You wait here, John,' he said, waving me back from accompanying him.

"We stood around like a group of ghosts.

" 'It is the truth,' Kaluna said. 'You could see it for yourselves.'

"They looked at me, and I nodded. Harry Burnley lifted his glass to his lips, but lowered it untasted. He spilled half of it over the bar. His lips were trembling like a child that is about to cry. Ned Austin made a clatter in the ice-chest. He wasn't looking for anything. I don't think he knew what he was doing. Nobody spoke. Harry Burnley's lips were trembling harder than ever. Suddenly, with a most horrible, malignant expression he drove his fist into Kaluna's face. He followed it up. We made no attempt to separate them. We didn't care if he killed the half-caste. It was a terrible beating. We weren't interested. I don't even remember when Burnley ceased and let the poor devil crawl away. We were all too dazed.

"Doc Strowbridge told me about it afterward. He was working late over a report when Lyte came into his office. Lyte had already recovered his optimism, and came swinging in, a trifle angry with Kaluna to be sure, but very certain of himself. 'What could I do?' Doc asked me. 'I knew he had it. I had seen it coming on for months. I couldn't answer him. I couldn't say yes. I don't mind telling you I broke down and cried. He pleaded for the bacteriological test. 'Snip out a piece of skin and make the test.'

"The way Doc Strowbridge cried must have convinced Lyte. The *Claudine* was leaving next morning for Honolulu. We caught him when he was going aboard. You see, he was headed for Honolulu to give himself up to the Board of Health. We could do nothing with him. He had sent too many to Molokai to hang back himself. We argued for Japan. But he wouldn't hear of it. 'I've got to take my medicine, fellows,' was all he would say, and he said it over and over. He was obsessed with the idea.

"He wound up all his affairs from the Receiving Station at Honolulu, and went down to Molokai. He didn't get on well there. The resident physician wrote us that he was a shadow of his old self. You see he was grieving about his wife and the kids. He knew we were taking care of them, but it hurt him just the same. After six months or so I went down to Molokai. I sat on one side a plate-glass window, and he on the other. We looked at each other through the glass, and talked through what might be called a speaking tube. But it was hopeless. He had made up his mind to remain. Four mortal hours I argued. I was exhausted at the end. My steamer was whistling for me, too.

"But we couldn't stand it. Three months later we chartered the schooner *Halcyon.* She was an opium smuggler, and she sailed like a witch. Her master was a squarehead who would do anything for money, and we made a charter to China worth his while. He sailed from San Francisco, and a few days later we took out Landhouse's sloop for a cruise. She was only a five-ton yacht, but we slammed her fifty miles to windward into the northeast trade. Seasick? I never suffered so in my life. Out of sight of land we picked up the *Halcyon,* and Burnley and I went aboard.

"We ran down to Molokai, arriving about eleven at night. The schooner hove to and we landed through the surf in a whale-boat at Kalawao—the place, you know, where Father Damien died. That squarehead was game. With a couple of revolvers strapped on him he came right along. The three of us crossed the peninsula to Kalaupapa, something like two miles. Just imagine hunting in the dead of night for a man in a settlement of over a thousand lepers. You see, if the alarm was given, it was all off with us. It was strange ground, and pitch dark. The lepers' dogs came out and bayed at us, and we stumbled around till we got lost.

"The squarehead solved it. He led the way into the first detached house. We shut the door after us and struck a light. There were six lepers. We routed them up, and I talked in native. What I wanted was a *kokua.* A *kokua* is, literally, a helper, a native who is clean that lives in the settlement and is paid by the Board of Health to nurse the lepers, dress their sores and such things. We stayed in the house to keep track of the inmates, while the squarehead led one of them off to find a *kokua.* He got him, and he brought him along at the point of his revolver. But the *kokua* was all right. While the squarehead guarded the house, Burnley and I were guided by the *kokua* to Lyte's house. He was all alone.

" 'I thought you fellows would come,' Lyte said. 'Don't touch me, John. How's Ned, and Charley, and all the crowd? Never mind, tell me afterward. I am ready to go now. I've had nine months of it. Where's the boat?'

"We started back for the other house to pick up the squarehead. But the alarm had got out. Lights were showing in the houses, and doors were slamming. We had agreed that there was to be no shooting unless absolutely necessary, and when we were halted we went at it with our fists and the butts of our revolvers. I found myself tangled up with a big man. I couldn't keep him off of me, though twice I smashed him fairly in the face with my fist. He grappled with me, and we went down, rolling and scrambling and struggling for grips. He was getting away with me, when someone came running up with a lantern. Then I saw his face. How shall I describe the horror of it! It was not a face—only wasted or wasting features—a living ravage, noseless, lipless, with one ear swollen and distorted, hanging down to the shoulder. I was frantic. In a clinch he hugged me close to him until that ear flapped in my face. Then I guess I went insane. It was too terrible. I began striking him with my revolver. How it happened I don't know, but just as I was getting clear he fastened upon me with his teeth. The whole side of my hand was in that lipless mouth. Then I struck him with the revolver butt squarely between the eyes, and his teeth relaxed."

Cudworth held his hand to me in the moonlight, and I could see the scars. It looked as if it had been mangled by a dog.

"Weren't you afraid?" I asked.

"I was. Seven years I waited. You know, it takes that long for the disease to incubate. Here in Kona I waited, and it did not come. But there was never a day of those seven years, and never a night, that I did not look out on . . . on all this . . ." His voice broke as he swept his eyes from the moon-bathed sea beneath to the snowy summits above. "I could not bear to think of losing it, of never again beholding Kona. Seven years! I stayed clean. But that is why I am single. I was engaged. I could not dare to marry while I was in doubt. She did not understand. She went away to the States, and married. I have never seen her since.

"Just at the moment I got free of the leper policeman there was rush and clatter of hoofs like a cavalry charge. It was the squarehead. He had been afraid of a rumpus and he had improved his time by making those blessed lepers he was guarding saddle up four horses. We were ready for him. Lyte had accounted for three *kokuas,* and between us we untangled Burnley from a couple more. The whole settlement was in an uproar by that time, and as we dashed away somebody opened up on us with a Winchester. It must have been Jack McVeigh, the superintendent of Molokai.

"That was a ride! Leper horses, leper saddles, leper bridles, pitch-black darkness, whistling bullets, and a road none of the best. And the squarehead's horse was a mule, and he didn't know how to ride, either. But we made the whale-boat, and as we shoved off through the surf we could hear the horses coming down the hill from Kalaupapa.

"You're going to Shanghai. You look Lyte Gregory up. He is employed in a German firm there. Take him out to dinner. Open up wine. Give him everything of the best, but don't let him pay for anything. Send the bill to me. His wife and the kids are in Honolulu, and he needs the money for them. I know. He sends most of his salary, and lives like an anchorite. And tell him about Kona. There's where his heart is. Tell him all you can about Kona."

The Chinago

The coral waxes, the palm grows, but man departs.
—Tahitian proverb

Ah Cho did not understand French. He sat in the crowded court room, very weary and bored, listening to the unceasing, explosive French that now one official and now another uttered. It was just so much gabble to Ah Cho, and he marvelled at the stupidity of the Frenchmen who took so long to find out the murderer of Chung Ga, and who did not find him at all. The five hundred coolies on the plantation knew that Ah San had done the killing, and here was Ah San not even arrested. It was true that all the coolies had agreed secretly not to testify against one another; but then, it was so simple, the Frenchmen should have been able to discover that Ah San was the man. They were very stupid, these Frenchmen.

Ah Cho had done nothing of which to be afraid. He had had no hand in the killing. It was true he had been present at it, and Schemmer, the overseer on the plantation, had rushed into the barracks immediately afterward and caught him there, along with four or five others; but what of that? Chung Ga had been stabbed only twice. It stood to reason that five or six men could not inflict two stab wounds. At the most, if a man had struck but once, only two men could have done it.

So it was that Ah Cho reasoned, when he, along with his four companions, had lied and blocked and obfuscated in their statements to the court concerning what had taken place. They had heard the sounds of the killing, and, like Schemmer, they had run to the spot. They had got there before Schemmer—that was all. True, Schemmer had testified that, attracted by the sound of quarrelling as he chanced to pass by, he had stood for at least five minutes outside; that then, when he entered, he found the prisoners already inside; and that they had not entered just before, because he had been standing by the one door to the barracks. But what of that? Ah Cho and his four fellow-prisoners had testified that Schemmer was mistaken. In the end they would be let go. They were all confident of that. Five men could not have their heads cut off for two stab wounds. Besides, no foreign devil had seen the killing. But these Frenchmen were so stupid. In China, as Ah Cho well knew, the magistrate would order all of them to the torture and learn the truth. The truth was very easy to learn under torture. But these Frenchmen did not torture—bigger fools they! Therefore they would never find out who killed Chung Ga.

But Ah Cho did not understand everything. The English Company that owned the plantation had imported into Tahiti, at great expense, the five hundred coolies. The stockholders were clamoring for dividends, and the Company had not yet paid any; wherefore the Company did not want its costly contract laborers to start the practice of killing one another. Also, there were the French, eager and willing to impose upon the Chinagos the virtues and excellences of French law. There was nothing like setting an example once in a while; and, besides, of what use was New Caledonia except to send men to live out their days in misery and pain in payment of the penalty for being frail and human?

Ah Cho did not understand all this. He sat in the court room and waited for the baffled judgment that would set him and his comrades free to go back to the plantation and work out the terms of their contracts. This judgment would soon be rendered. Proceedings were drawing to a close. He could see that. There was no more testifying, no more gabble of tongues. The French devils were tired, too, and evidently waiting for the judgment. And as he waited he remembered back in his life to the time when he had signed the contract and set sail in the ship for Tahiti. Times had been hard in his seacoast village, and when he indentured himself to labor for five years in the South Seas at fifty cents Mexican a day, he had thought himself fortunate. There were men in his village who toiled a whole year for ten dollars Mexican, and there were women who made nets all the year round for five dollars, while in the houses of shopkeepers there were maid-servants who received four dollars for a year of service. And here he was to receive fifty cents a day; for one day, only one day, he was to receive that princely sum! What if the work were hard? At the end of the five years he would return home—that was in the contract—and he would never have to work again. He would be a rich man for life, with a house of his own, a wife, and children growing up to venerate him. Yes, and back of the house he would have a small garden, a place of meditation and repose, with goldfish in a tiny lakelet, and wind bells tinkling in the several trees, and there would be a high wall all around so that his meditation and repose should be undisturbed.

Well, he had worked out three of those five years. He was already a wealthy man (in his own country), through his earnings, and only two years more intervened between the cotton plantation on Tahiti and the meditation and repose that awaited him. But just now he was losing money because of the unfortunate accident of being present at the killing of Chung Ga. He had lain three weeks in prison, and for each day of those three weeks he had lost fifty cents. But now judgment would soon be given, and he would go back to work.

Ah Cho was twenty-two years old. He was happy and good-natured, and it was easy for him to smile. While his body was slim in the Asiatic way, his face was rotund. It was round, like the moon, and it irradiated a gentle complacence and a sweet kindliness of spirit that was unusual among his countrymen. Nor did his looks belie him. He never caused trouble, never took part in wrangling. He did not gamble. His soul was not harsh enough for the soul that must belong to a gambler. He was content with little things and simple pleasures. The hush and quiet in the cool of the day after the blazing toil in the cotton field was to him an infinite satisfaction. He could sit for hours gazing at a solitary flower and philosophizing about the mysteries and riddles of being. A blue heron on a tiny crescent of sandy beach, a silvery splatter of flying fish, or a sunset of pearl and rose across the lagoon, could entrance him to all forgetfulness of the procession of wearisome days and of the heavy lash of Schemmer.

Schemmer, Karl Schemmer, was a brute, a brutish brute. But he earned his salary. He got the last particle of strength out of the five hundred slaves; for slaves they were until their term of years was up. Schemmer worked hard to extract the strength from those five hundred sweating bodies and to transmute it into bales of fluffy cotton ready for export. His dominant, iron-clad, primeval brutishness was what enabled him to effect the transmutation. Also, he was assisted by a thick leather belt, three inches wide and a yard in length, with which he always rode and which, on occasion, could come down on the naked back of a stooping coolie with a report like a pistol-shot. These reports were frequent when Schemmer rode down the furrowed field.

Once, at the beginning of the first year of contract labor, he had killed a coolie with a single blow of his fist. He had not exactly crushed the man's head like an egg-shell, but the blow had been sufficient to addle what was inside, and, after being sick for a week, the man had died. But the Chinese had not complained to the French devils that ruled over Tahiti. It was their own lookout. Schemmer was their problem. They must avoid his wrath as they avoided the venom of the centipedes that lurked in the grass or crept into the sleeping quarters on rainy nights. The Chinagos—such they were called by the indolent, brown-skinned island folk—saw to it that they did not displease Schemmer too greatly. This was equivalent to rendering up to him a full measure of efficient toil. That blow of Schemmer's fist had been worth thousands of dollars to the Company, and no trouble ever came of it to Schemmer.

The French, with no instinct for colonization, futile in their childish playgame of developing the resources of the island, were only too glad to see the English Company succeed. What matter of Schemmer and his redoubtable fist? The Chinago that died? Well, he was only a Chinago. Besides, he died of sunstroke, as the doctor's certificate attested. True, in all the history of Tahiti no one had ever died of sunstroke. But it was that, precisely that, which made the death of this Chinago unique. The doctor said as much in his report. He was very candid. Dividends must be paid, or else one more failure would be added to the long history of failure in Tahiti.

There was no understanding these white devils. Ah Cho pondered their inscrutableness as he sat in the court room waiting the judgment. There was no telling what went on at the back of their minds. He had seen a few of the white devils. They were all alike—the officers and sailors on the ship, the French officials, the several white men on the plantation, including Schemmer. Their minds all moved in mysterious ways there was no getting at. They grew angry without apparent cause, and their anger was always dangerous. They were like wild beasts at such times. They worried about little things, and on occasion could out-toil even a Chinago. They were not temperate as Chinagos were temperate; they were gluttons, eating prodigiously and drinking more prodigiously. A Chinago never knew when an act would please them or arouse a storm of wrath. A Chinago could never tell. What pleased one time, the very next time might provoke an outburst of anger. There was a curtain behind the eyes of the white devils that screened the backs of their minds from the Chinago's gaze. And then, on top of it all, was that terrible efficiency of the white devils, that ability to do things, to make things go, to work results, to bend to their wills all creeping, crawling things, and the powers of the very elements themselves. Yes, the white men were strange and wonderful, and they were devils. Look at Schemmer.

Ah Cho wondered why the judgment was so long in forming. Not a man on trial had laid hand on Chung Ga. Ah San alone had killed him. Ah San had done it, bending Chung Ga's head back with one hand by a grip of his queue, and with the other hand, from behind, reaching over and driving the knife into his body. Twice had he driven it in. There in the court room, with closed eyes, Ah Cho saw the killing acted over again—the squabble, the vile words bandied back and forth, the filth and insult flung upon venerable ancestors, the curses laid upon unbegotten generations, the leap of Ah San, the grip on the queue of Chung Ga, the knife that sank twice into his flesh, the bursting open of the door, the irruption of Schemmer, the dash for the door, the escape of Ah San, the flying belt of Schemmer that drove the rest into the corner, and the firing of the revolver as a signal that brought help to Schemmer. Ah Cho shivered as he lived it over. One blow of the belt had bruised his cheek, taking off some of the skin. Schemmer had pointed to the bruises when, on the witness-stand, he had identified Ah Cho. It was only just now that the marks had become no longer visible. That had been a blow. Half an inch nearer the centre and it would have taken out his eye. Then Ah Cho forgot the whole happening in a vision he caught of the garden of meditation and repose that would be his when he returned to his own land.

He sat with impassive face, while the magistrate rendered the judgment. Likewise were the faces of his four companions impassive. And they remained impassive when the interpreter explained that the five of them had been found guilty of the murder of Chung Ga, and that Ah Chow should have his head cut off, Ah Cho serve twenty years in prison in New Caledonia, Wong Li twelve years and Ah Tong ten years. There was no use in getting excited about it. Even Ah Chow remained expressionless as a mummy, though it was his head that was to be cut off. The magistrate added a few words, and the interpreter explained that Ah Chow's face having been most severely bruised by Schemmer's strap had made his identification so positive that, since one man must die, he might as well be that man. Also, the fact that Ah Cho's face likewise had been severely bruised, conclusively proving his presence at the murder and his undoubted participation, had merited him the twenty years of penal servitude. And down to the ten years of Ah Tong, the proportioned reason for each sentence was explained. Let the Chinagos take the lesson to heart, the Court said finally, for they must learn that the law would be fulfilled in Tahiti though the heavens fell.

The five Chinagos were taken back to jail. They were not shocked nor grieved. The sentences being unexpected was quite what they were accustomed to in their dealings with the white devils. From them a Chinago rarely expected more than the unexpected. The heavy punishment for a crime they had not committed was no stranger than the countless strange things that white devils did. In the weeks that followed, Ah Cho often contemplated Ah Chow with mild curiosity. His head was to be cut off by the guillotine that was being erected on the plantation. For him there would be no declining years, no gardens of tranquility. Ah Cho philosophized and speculated about life and death. As for himself, he was not perturbed. Twenty years were merely twenty years. By that much was his garden removed from him—that was all. He was young, and the patience of Asia was in his bones. He could wait those twenty years, and by that time the heats of his blood would be assuaged and he would be better fitted for that garden of calm delight. He thought of a name for it; he would call it The Garden of the Morning Calm. He was made happy all day by the thought, and he was inspired to devise a moral maxim on the virtue of patience, which maxim proved a great comfort, especially to Wong Li and Ah Tong. Ah Chow, however, did not care for the maxim. His head was to be separated from his body in so short a time that he had no need for patience to wait for that event. He smoked well, ate well, slept well, and did not worry about the slow passage of time.

Cruchot was a gendarme. He had seen twenty years of service in the colonies, from Nigeria and Senegal to the South Seas, and those twenty years had not perceptibly brightened his dull mind. He was as slow-witted and stupid as in his peasant days in the south of France. He knew discipline and fear of authority, and from God down to the sergeant of gendarmes the only difference to him was the measure of slavish obedience which he rendered. In point of fact, the sergeant bulked bigger in his mind than God, except on Sundays when God's mouthpieces had their say. God was usually very remote, while the sergeant was ordinarily very close at hand.

Cruchot it was who received the order from the Chief Justice to the jailer commanding that functionary to deliver over to Cruchot the person of Ah Chow. Now, it happened that the Chief Justice had given a dinner the night before to the captain and officers of the French man-of-war. His hand was shaking when he wrote out the order, and his eyes were aching so dreadfully that he did not read over the order. It was only a Chinago's life he was signing away, anyway. So he did not notice that he had omitted the final letter in Ah Chow's name. The order read "Ah Cho" , and, when Cruchot presented the order, the jailer turned over to him the person of Ah Cho. Cruchot took that person beside him on the seat of a wagon, behind two mules, and drove away.

Ah Cho was glad to be out in the sunshine. He sat beside the gendarme and beamed. He beamed more ardently than ever when he noted the mules headed south toward Atimaono. Undoubtedly Schemmer had sent for him to be brought back. Schemmer wanted him to work. Very well, he would work well. Schemmer would never have cause to complain. It was a hot day. There had been a stoppage of the trades. The mules sweated, Cruchot sweated, and Ah Cho sweated. But it was Ah Cho that bore the heat with the least concern. He had toiled three years under that sun on the plantation. He beamed and beamed with such genial good nature that even Cruchot's heavy mind was stirred to wonderment.

"You are very funny," he said at last.

Ah Cho nodded and beamed more ardently. Unlike the magistrate, Cruchot spoke to him in the Kanaka tongue, and this, like all Chinagos and all foreign devils, Ah Cho understood.

"You laugh too much," Cruchot chided. "One's heart should be full of tears on a day like this."

"I am glad to get out of the jail."

"Is that all?" The gendarme shrugged his shoulders.

"Is it not enough?" was the retort.

"Then you are not glad to have your head cut off?"

Ah Cho looked at him in abrupt perplexity and said:

"Why, I am going back to Atimaono to work on the plantation for Schemmer. Are you not taking me to Atimaono?"

Cruchot stroked his long mustaches reflectively. "Well, well," he said finally, with a flick of the whip at the off mule, "so you don't know?"

"Know what?" Ah Cho was beginning to feel a vague alarm. "Won't Schemmer let me work for him any more?"

"Not after to-day." Cruchot laughed heartily. It was a good joke. "You see, you won't be able to work after to-day. A man with his head off can't work, eh?" He poked the Chinago in the ribs, and chuckled.

Ah Cho maintained silence while the mules trotted a hot mile. Then he spoke: "Is Schemmer going to cut off my head?"

Cruchot grinned as he nodded.

"It is a mistake," said Ah Cho, gravely. "I am not the Chinago that is to have his head cut off. I am Ah Cho. The honorable judge has determined that I am to stop twenty years in New Caledonia."

The gendarme laughed. It was a good joke, this funny Chinago trying to cheat the guillotine. The mules trotted through a coconut grove and for half a mile beside the sparkling sea before Ah Cho spoke again.

"I tell you I am not Ah Chow. The honorable judge did not say that my head was to go off."

"Don't be afraid," said Cruchot, with the philanthropic intention of making it easier for his prisoner. "It is not difficult to die that way." He snapped his fingers. "It is quick—like that. It is not like hanging on the end of a rope and kicking and making faces for five minutes. It is like killing a chicken with a hatchet. You cut its head off, that is all. And it is the same with a man. Pouf!—it is over. It doesn't hurt. You don't even think it hurts. You don't think. Your head is gone, so you cannot think. It is very good. That is the way I want to die—quick, ah, quick. You are lucky to die that way. You might get the leprosy and fall to pieces slowly, a finger at a time, and now and again a thumb, also the toes. I knew a man who was burned by hot water. It took him two days to die. You could hear him yelling a kilometre away. But you? Ah! so easy! Chck!—the knife cuts your neck like that. It is finished. The knife may even tickle. Who can say? Nobody who died that way ever came back to say."

He considered this last an excruciating joke, and permitted himself to be convulsed with laughter for half a minute. Part of his mirth was assumed, but he considered it his humane duty to cheer up the Chinago.

"But I tell you I am Ah Cho," the other persisted. "I don't want my head cut off."

Cruchot scowled. The Chinago was carrying the foolishness too far.

"I am not Ah Chow—" Ah Cho began.

"That will do," the gendarme interrupted. He puffed up his cheeks and strove to appear fierce.

"I tell you I am not—" Ah Cho began again.

"Shut up!" bawled Cruchot.

After that they rode along in silence. It was twenty miles from Papeete to Atimaono, and over half the distance was covered by the time the Chinago again ventured into speech.

"I saw you in the court room, when the honorable judge sought after our guilt," he began. "Very good. And do you remember that Ah Chow, whose head is to be cut off —do you remember that he—Ah Chow—was a tall man? Look at me."

He stood up suddenly, and Cruchot saw that he was a short man. And just as suddenly Cruchot caught a glimpse of a memory picture of Ah Chow, and in that picture Ah Chow was tall. To the gendarme all Chinagos looked alike. One face was like another. But between tallness and shortness he could differentiate, and he knew that he had the wrong man beside him on the seat. He pulled up the mules abruptly, so that the pole shot ahead of them, elevating their collars.

"You see, it was a mistake," said Ah Cho, smiling pleasantly.

But Cruchot was thinking. Already he regretted that he had stopped the wagon. He was unaware of the error of the Chief Justice, and he had no way of working it out; but he did know that he had been given this Chinago to take to Atimaono and that it was his duty to take him to Atimaono. What if he was the wrong man and they cut his head off? It was only a Chinago when all was said, and what was a Chinago, anyway? Besides, it might not be a mistake. He did not know what went on in the minds of his superiors. They knew their business best. Who was he to do their thinking for them? Once, in the long ago, he had attempted to think for them, and the sergeant had said: "Cruchot, you are a fool! The quicker you know that, the better you will get on. You are not to think; you are to obey and leave thinking to your betters." He smarted under the recollection. Also, if he turned back to Papeete, he would delay the execution at Atimaono, and if he were wrong in turning back, he would get a reprimand from the sergeant who was waiting for the prisoner. And, furthermore, he would get a reprimand at Papeete as well.

He touched the mules with the whip and drove on. He looked at his watch. He would be half an hour late as it was, and the sergeant was bound to be angry. He put the mules into a faster trot. The more Ah Cho persisted in explaining the mistake, the more stubborn Cruchot became. The knowledge that he had the wrong man did not make his temper better. The knowledge that it was through no mistake of his confirmed him in the belief that the wrong he was doing was the right. And, rather than incur the displeasure of the sergeant, he would willingly have assisted a dozen wrong Chinagos to their doom.

As for Ah Cho, after the gendarme had struck him over the head with the butt of the whip and commanded him in a loud voice to shut up, there remained nothing for him to do but to shut up. The long ride continued in silence. Ah Cho pondered the strange ways of the foreign devils. There was no explaining them. What they were doing with him was of a piece with everything they did. First they found guilty five innocent men, and next they cut off the head of the man that even they, in their benighted ignorance, had deemed meritorious of no more than twenty years' imprisonment. And there was nothing he could do. He could only sit idly and take what these lords of life measured out to him. Once, he got in a panic, and the sweat upon his body turned cold; but he fought his way out of it. He endeavored to resign himself to his fate by remembering and repeating certain passages from the "Yin Chih Wen" ("The Tract of the Quiet Way"); but, instead, he kept seeing his dream-garden of meditation and repose. This bothered him, until he abandoned himself to the dream and sat in his garden listening to the tinkling of the wind-bells in the several trees. And lo! sitting thus, in the dream, he was able to remember and repeat the passages from "The Tract of the Quiet Way".

So the time passed nicely until Atimaono was reached and the mules trotted up to the foot of the scaffold, in the shade of which stood the impatient sergeant. Ah Cho was hurried up the ladder of the scaffold. Beneath him on one side he saw assembled all the coolies of the plantation. Schemmer had decided that the event would be a good object-lesson, and so had called in the coolies from the fields and compelled them to be present. As they caught sight of Ah Cho they gabbled among themselves in low voices. They saw the mistake; but they kept it to themselves. The inexplicable white devils had doubtlessly changed their minds. Instead of taking the life of one innocent man, they were taking the life of another innocent man. Ah Chow or Ah Cho—what did it matter which? They could never understand the white dogs any more than could the white dogs understand them. Ah Cho was going to have his head cut off, but they, when their two remaining years of servitude were up, were going back to China.

Schemmer had made the guillotine himself. He was a handy man, and though he had never seen a guillotine, the French officials had explained the principle to him. It was on his suggestion that they had ordered the execution to take place at Atimaono instead of at Papeete. The scene of the crime, Schemmer had argued, was the best possible place for the punishment, and, in addition, it would have a salutary influence upon the half-thousand Chinagos on the plantation. Schemmer had also volunteered to act as executioner, and in that capacity he was now on the scaffold, experimenting with the instrument he had made. A banana tree, of the size and consistency of a man's neck, lay under the guillotine. Ah Cho watched with fascinated eyes. The German, turning a small crank, hoisted the blade to the top of the little derrick he had rigged. A jerk on a stout piece of cord loosed the blade and it dropped with a flash, neatly severing the banana trunk.

"How does it work?" The sergeant, coming out on top the scaffold, had asked the question.

"Beautifully," was Schemmer's exultant answer. "Let me show you."

Again he turned the crank that hoisted the blade, jerked the cord, and sent the blade crashing down on the soft tree. But this time it went no more than two-thirds of the way through.

The sergeant scowled. "That will not serve," he said.

Schemmer wiped the sweat from his forehead. "What it needs is more weight," he announced. Walking up to the edge of the scaffold, he called his orders to the blacksmith for a twenty-five-pound piece of iron. As he stooped over to attach the iron to the broad top of the blade, Ah Cho glanced at the sergeant and saw his opportunity.

"The honorable judge said that Ah Chow was to have his head cut off," he began.

The sergeant nodded impatiently. He was thinking of the fifteen-mile ride before him that afternoon, to the windward side of the island, and of Berthe, the pretty half-caste daughter of Lafière, the pearl-trader, who was waiting for him at the end of it.

"Well, I am not Ah Chow. I am Ah Cho. The honorable jailer has made a mistake. Ah Chow is a tall man, and you see I am short."

The sergeant looked at him hastily and saw the mistake. "Schemmer!" he called, imperatively. "Come here."

The German grunted, but remained bent over his task till the chunk of iron was lashed to his satisfaction. "Is your Chinago ready?" he demanded.

"Look at him," was the answer. "Is he the Chinago?"

Schemmer was surprised. He swore tersely for a few seconds, and looked regretfully across at the thing he had made with his own hands and which he was eager to see work. "Look here," he said finally, "we can't postpone this affair. I've lost three hours' work already out of those five hundred Chinagos. I can't afford to lose it all over again for the right man. Let's put the performance through just the same. It is only a Chinago."

The sergeant remembered the long ride before him, and the pearl-trader's daughter, and debated with himself.

"They will blame it on Cruchot—if it is discovered," the German urged. "But there's little chance of its being discovered. Ah Chow won't give it away, at any rate."

"The blame won't lie with Cruchot, anyway," the sergeant said. "It must have been the jailer's mistake."

"Then let's go on with it. They can't blame us. Who can tell one Chinago from another? We can say that we merely carried out instructions with the Chinago that was turned over to us. Besides, I really can't take all those coolies a second time away from their labor."

They spoke in French, and Ah Cho, who did not understand a word of it, nevertheless knew that they were determining his destiny. He knew, also, that the decision rested with the sergeant, and he hung upon that official's lips.

"All right," announced the sergeant. "Go ahead with it. He is only a Chinago."

"I'm going to try it once more, just to make sure." Schemmer moved the banana trunk forward under the knife, which he had hoisted to the top of the derrick.

Ah Cho tried to remember maxims from "The Tract of the Quiet Way" . "Live in concord" , came to him; but it was not applicable. He was not going to live. He was about to die. No, that would not do. "Forgive malice"—yes, but there was no malice to forgive. Schemmer and the rest were doing this thing without malice. It was to them merely a piece of work that had to be done, just as clearing the jungle, ditching the water, and planting cotton were pieces of work that had to be done. Schemmer jerked the cord, and Ah Cho forgot "The Tract of the Quiet Way" . The knife shot down with a thud, making a clean slice of the tree.

"Beautiful!" exclaimed the sergeant, pausing in the act of lighting a cigarette. "Beautiful, my friend."

Schemmer was pleased at the praise.

"Come on, Ah Chow," he said, in the Tahitian tongue.

"But I am not Ah Chow—" Ah Cho began.

"Shut up!" was the answer. "If you open your mouth again, I'll break your head."

The overseer threatened him with a clenched fist, and he remained silent. What was the good of protesting? Those foreign devils always had their way. He allowed himself to be lashed to the vertical board that was the size of his body. Schemmer drew the buckles tight—so tight that the straps cut into his flesh and hurt. But he did not complain. The hurt would not last long. He felt the board tilting over in the air toward the horizontal, and closed his eyes. And in that moment he caught a last glimpse of his garden of meditation and repose. It seemed to him that he sat in the garden. A cool wind was blowing, and the bells in the several trees were tinkling softly. Also, birds were making sleepy noises, and from beyond the high wall came the subdued sound of village life.

Then he was aware that the board had come to rest, and from muscular pressures and tensions he knew that he was lying on his back. He opened his eyes. Straight above him he saw the suspended knife blazing in the sunshine. He saw the weight which had been added, and noted that one of Schemmer's knots had slipped. Then he heard the sergeant's voice in sharp command. Ah Cho closed his eyes hastily. He did not want to see that knife descend. But he felt it—for one great fleeting instant. And in that instant he remembered Cruchot and what Cruchot had said. But Cruchot was wrong. The knife did not tickle. That much he knew before he ceased to know.

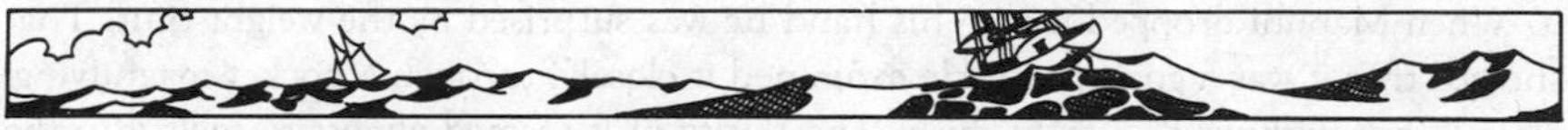

The House of Mapuhi

DESPITE the heavy clumsiness of her lines, the *Aorai* handled easily in the light breeze, and her captain ran her well in before he hove to just outside the suck of the surf. The atoll of Hikueru lay low on the water, a circle of pounded coral sand a hundred yards wide, twenty miles in circumference, and from three to five feet above high-water mark. On the bottom of the huge and glassy lagoon was much pearl shell, and from the deck of the schooner, across the slender ring of the atoll, the divers could be seen at work. But the lagoon had no entrance for even a traditional schooner. With a favoring breeze cutters could win in through the tortuous and shallow channel, but the schooners lay off and on outside and sent in their small boats.

The *Aorai* swung out a boat smartly, into which sprang half a dozen brown-skinned sailors clad only in scarlet loin-cloths. They took the oars, while in the stern-sheets, at the steering sweep, stood a young man garbed in the tropic white that marks the European. But he was not all European. The golden strain of Polynesia betrayed itself in the sun-gilt of his fair skin and cast up golden sheens and lights through the glimmering blue of his eyes. Raoul he was, Alexandré Raoul, youngest son of Marie Raoul, the wealthy quarter-caste, who owned and managed half a dozen trading schooners similar to the *Aorai.* Across an eddy just outside the entrance, and in and through and over a boiling tide-rip, the boat fought its way to the mirrored calm of the lagoon. Young Raoul leaped out upon the white sand and shook hands with a tall native. The man's chest and shoulders were magnificent, but the stump of a right arm, beyond the flesh of which the age-whitened bone projected several inches, attested the encounter with a shark that had put an end to his diving days and made him a fawner and an intriguer for small favors.

"Have you heard, Alec?" were his first words. "Mapuhi has found a pearl—such a pearl. Never was there one like it ever fished up in Hikueru, nor in all the Paumotus, nor in all the world. Buy it from him. He has it now. And remember that I told you first. He is a fool and you can get it cheap. Have you any tobacco?"

Straight up the beach to a shack under a pandanus-tree Raoul headed. He was his mother's supercargo, and his business was to comb all the Paumotus for the wealth of copra, shell and pearls that they yielded up.

He was a young supercargo, it was his second voyage in such capacity, and he suffered much secret worry from his lack of experience in pricing pearls. But when Mapuhi exposed the pearl to his sight he managed to suppress the startle it gave him, and to maintain a careless, commercial expression on his face. For the pearl had struck him a blow. It was large as a pigeon egg, a perfect sphere, of a whiteness that reflected opalescent lights from all colors about it. It was alive. Never had he seen anything like it. When Mapuhi dropped it into his hand he was surprised by the weight of it. That showed that it was a good pearl. He examined it closely, through a pocket magnifying-glass. It was without flaw or blemish. The purity of it seemed almost to melt into the atmosphere out of his hand. In the shade it was softly luminous, gleaming like a tender moon. So translucently white was it, that when he dropped it into a glass of water he had difficulty in finding it. So straight and swiftly had it sunk to the bottom that he knew its weight was excellent.

"Well, what do you want for it?" he asked, with a fine assumption of nonchalance.

"I want—" Mapuhi began, and behind him, framing his own dark face, the dark faces of two women and a girl nodded concurrence in what he wanted. Their heads were bent forward, they were animated by a suppressed eagerness, their eyes flashed avariciously.

"I want a house," Mapuhi went on. "It must have a roof of galvanized iron and an octagon-drop-clock. It must be six fathoms long with a porch all around. A big room must be in the centre, with a round table in the middle of it and the octagon-drop-clock on the wall. There must be four bedrooms, two on each side of the big room, and in each bedroom must be an iron bed, two chairs and a washstand. And back of the house must be a kitchen, a good kitchen, with pots and pans and a stove. And you must build the house on my island, which is Fakarava."

"Is that all?" Raoul asked incredulously.

"There must be a sewing machine," spoke up Tefara, Mapuhi's wife.

"Not forgetting the octagon-drop-clock," added Nauri, Mapuhi's mother.

"Yes, that is all," said Mapuhi.

Young Raoul laughed. He laughed long and heartily. But while he laughed he secretly performed problems in mental arithmetic. He had never built a house in his life, and his notions concerning house building were hazy. While he laughed he calculated the cost of the voyage to Tahiti for materials, of the materials themselves, of the voyage back again to Fakarava, and the cost of landing the materials and of building the house. It would come to four thousand French dollars, allowing a margin for safety—four thousand French dollars were equivalent to twenty thousand francs. It was impossible. How was he to know the value of such a pearl? Twenty thousand francs was a lot of money—and of his mother's money at that.

"Mapuhi," he said, "you are a big fool. Set a money price."

But Mapuhi shook his head, and the three heads behind him shook with his.

"I want the house," he said. "It must be six fathoms long with a porch all around—"

"Yes, yes," Raoul interrupted. "I know all about your house, but it won't do. I'll give you a thousand Chili dollars."

The four heads chorused a silent negative.

"And a hundred Chili dollars in trade."

"I want the house," Mapuhi began.

"What good will the house do you?" Raoul demanded. "The first hurricane that comes along will wash it away. You ought to know. Captain Raffy says it looks like a hurricane right now."

"Not on Fakarava," said Mapuhi. "The land is much higher there. On this island, yes. Any hurricane can sweep Hikueru. I will have the house on Fakarava. It must be six fathoms long with a porch all around—"

And Raoul listened again to the tale of the house. Several hours he spent in the endeavor to hammer the house-obsession out of Mapuhi's mind; but Mapuhi's mother and wife, and Ngakura, Mapuhi's daughter, bolstered him in his resolve for the house. Through the open doorway, while he listened for the twentieth time to the detailed description of the house that was wanted, Raoul saw his schooner's second boat draw up on the beach. The sailors rested on the oars, advertising haste to be gone. The first mate of the *Aorai* sprang ashore, exchanged a word with the one-armed native, then hurried toward Raoul. The day grew suddenly dark, as a squall obscured the face of the sun. Across the lagoon Raoul could see approaching the ominous line of the puff of wind.

"Captain Raffy says you've got to get to hell outa here," was the mate's greeting. "If there's any shell, we've got to run the risk of picking it up later on—so he says. The barometer's dropped to twenty-nine-seventy."

The gust of wind struck the pandanus-tree overhead and tore through the palms beyond, flinging half a dozen ripe coconuts with heavy thuds to the ground. Then came the rain out of the distance, advancing with the roar of a gale of wind and causing the water of the lagoon to smoke in driven windrows. The sharp rattle of the first drops was on the leaves when Raoul sprang to his feet.

"A thousand Chili dollars, cash down, Mapuhi," he said. "And two hundred Chili dollars in trade."

"I want a house—" the other began.

"Mapuhi!" Raoul yelled, in order to make himself heard. "You are a fool!"

He flung out of the house, and, side by side with the mate, fought his way down the beach toward the boat. They could not see the boat. The tropic rain sheeted about them so that they could see only the beach under their feet and the spiteful little waves from the lagoon that snapped and bit at the sand. A figure appeared through the deluge. It was Huru-Huru, the man with the one arm.

"Did you get the pearl?" he yelled in Raoul's ear.

"Mapuhi is a fool!" was the answering yell, and the next moment they were lost to each other in the descending water.

Half an hour later, Huru-Huru, watching from the seaward side of the atoll, saw the two boats hoisted in and the *Aorai* pointing her nose out to sea. And near her, just come in from the sea on the wings of the squall, he saw another schooner hove to and dropping a boat into the water. He knew her. It was the *Orohena*, owned by Toriki, the half-caste trader, who served as his own supercargo and who doubtlessly was even then in the stern-sheets of the boat. Huru-Huru chuckled. He knew that Mapuhi owed Toriki for trade-goods advanced the year before.

The squall had passed. The hot sun was blazing down, and the lagoon was once more a mirror. But the air was sticky like mucilage, and the weight of it seemed to burden the lungs and make breathing difficult.

"Have you heard the news, Toriki?" Huru-Huru asked. "Mapuhi has found a pearl. Never was there a pearl like it ever fished up in Hikueru, nor anywhere in the Paumotus, nor anywhere in all the world. Mapuhi is a fool. Besides, he owes you money. Remember that I told you first. Have you any tobacco?"

And to the grass-shack of Mapuhi went Toriki. He was a masterful man, withal a fairly stupid one. Carelessly he glanced at the wonderful pearl—glanced for a moment only; and carelessly he dropped it into his pocket.

"You are lucky," he said. "It is a nice pearl. I will give you credit on the books."

"I want a house," Mapuhi began, in consternation. "It must be six fathoms—"

"Six fathoms your grandmother!" was the trader's retort. "You want to pay up your debts, that's what you want. You owed me twelve hundred dollars Chili. Very well; you owe them no longer. The amount is squared. Besides, I will give you credit for two hundred Chili. If, when I get to Tahiti, the pearl sells well, I will give you credit for another hundred—that will make three hundred. But mind, only if the pearl sells well. I may even lose money on it."

Mapuhi folded his arms in sorrow and sat with bowed head. He had been robbed of his pearl. In place of his house, he had paid a debt. There was nothing to show for the pearl.

"You are a fool," said Tefara.

"You are a fool," said Nauri, his mother. "Why did you let the pearl into his hand?"

"What was I to do?" Mapuhi protested. "I owed him the money. He knew I had the pearl. You heard him yourself ask to see it. I had not told him. He knew. Somebody else told him. And I owed him the money."

"Mapuhi is a fool," mimicked Ngakura.

She was twelve years old and did not know any better. Mapuhi relieved his feelings by sending her reeling from a box on the ear; while Tefara and Nauri burst into tears and continued to upbraid him after the manner of women.

Huru-Huru, watching on the beach, saw a third schooner that he knew heave to outside the entrance and drop a boat. It was the *Hira*, well named, for she was owned by Levy, the German Jew, the greatest pearl buyer of them all, and, as was well known, Hira was the Tahitian god of fishermen and thieves.

"Have you heard the news?" Huru-Huru asked, as Levy, a fat man with massive asymmetrical features, stepped out upon the beach. "Mapuhi has found a pearl. There was never a pearl like it in Hikueru, in all the Paumotus, in all the world. Mapuhi is a fool. He has sold it to Toriki for fourteen hundred Chili—I listened outside and heard. Toriki is likewise a fool. You can buy it from him cheap. Remember that I told you first. Have you any tobacco?"

"Where is Toriki?"

"In the house of Captain Lynch, drinking absinthe. He has been there an hour."

And while Levy and Toriki drank absinthe and chaffered over the pearl, Huru-Huru listened and heard the stupendous price of twenty-five thousand francs agreed upon.

It was at this time that both the *Orohena* and the *Hira,* running in close to the shore, began firing guns and signalling frantically. The three men stepped outside in time to see the two schooners go hastily about and head off shore, dropping mainsails and flying-jibs on the run in the teeth of the squall that heeled them far over on the whitened water. Then the rain blotted them out.

"They'll be back after it's over," said Toriki. "We'd better be getting out of here."

"I reckon the glass has fallen some more," said Captain Lynch.

He was a white-bearded sea-captain, too old for service, who had learned that the only way to live on comfortable terms with his asthma was on Hikueru. He went inside to look at the barometer.

"Great God!" they heard him exclaim, and rushed in to join him at staring at a dial, which marked twenty-nine-twenty.

Again they came out, this time anxiously to consult sea and sky. The squall had cleared away, but the sky remained overcast. The two schooners, under all sail and joined by a third, could be seen making back. A veer in the wind induced them to slack off sheets, and five minutes afterward a sudden veer from the opposite quarter caught all three schooners aback, and those on shore could see the boom-tackles being slacked away or cast off on the jump. The sound of the surf was loud, hollow, and menacing, and a heavy swell was setting in. A terrible sheet of lightning burst before their eyes, illuminating the dark day, and the thunder rolled wildly about them.

Toriki and Levy broke into a run for their boats, the latter ambling along like a panic-stricken hippopotamus. As their two boats swept out the entrance, they passed the boat of the *Aorai* coming in. In the stern-sheets, encouraging the rowers, was Raoul. Unable to shake the vision of the pearl from his mind, he was returning to accept Mapuhi's price of a house.

He landed on the beach in the midst of a driving thunder squall that was so dense that he collided with Huru-Huru before he saw him.

"Too late," yelled Huru-Huru. "Mapuhi sold it to Toriki for fourteen hundred Chili, and Toriki sold it to Levy for twenty-five thousand francs. And Levy will sell it in France for a hundred thousand francs. Have you any tobacco?"

Raoul felt relieved. His troubles about the pearl were over. He need not worry any more, even if he had not got the pearl. But he did not believe Huru-Huru. Mapuhi might well have sold it for fourteen hundred Chili, but that Levy, who knew pearls, should have paid twenty-five thousand francs was too wide a stretch. Raoul decided to interview Captain Lynch on the subject, but when he arrived at that ancient mariner's house, he found him looking wide-eyed at the barometer.

"What do you read it?" Captain Lynch asked anxiously, rubbing his spectacles and staring again at the instrument.

"Twenty-nine-ten," said Raoul. "I have never seen it so low before."

"I should say not!" snorted the captain. "Fifty years boy and man on all the seas, and I've never seen it go down to that. Listen!"

They stood for a moment, while the surf rumbled and shook the house. Then they went outside. The squall had passed. They could see the *Aorai* lying becalmed a mile away and pitching and tossing madly in the tremendous seas that rolled in stately procession down out of the northeast and flung themselves furiously upon the coral shore. One of the sailors from the boat pointed at the mouth of the passage and shook his head. Raoul looked and saw a white anarchy of foam and surge.

"I guess I'll stay with you to-night, Captain," he said; then turned to the sailor and told him to haul the boat out and to find shelter for himself and fellows.

"Twenty-nine flat," Captain Lynch reported, coming out from another look at the barometer, a chair in his hand.

He sat down and stared at the spectacle of the sea. The sun came out, increasing the sultriness of the day, while the dead calm still held. The seas continued to increase in magnitude.

"What makes that sea is what gets me," Raoul muttered petulantly. "There is no wind, yet look at it, look at that fellow there!"

Miles in length, carrying tens of thousands of tons in weight, its impact shook the frail atoll like an earthquake. Captain Lynch was startled.

"Gracious!" he exclaimed, half-rising from his chair, then sinking back.

"But there is no wind," Raoul persisted. "I could understand it if there was wind along with it."

"You'll get the wind soon enough without worryin' for it," was the grim reply.

The two men sat on in silence. The sweat stood out on their skin in myriads of tiny drops that ran together, forming blotches of moisture, which, in turn, coalesced into rivulets that dripped to the ground. They panted for breath, the old man's efforts being especially painful. A sea swept up the beach, licking around the trunks of the coconuts and subsiding almost at their feet.

" 'Way past high-water mark," Captain Lynch remarked, "and I've been here eleven years." He looked at his watch. "It is three o'clock."

A man and woman, at their heels a motley following of brats and curs, trailed disconsolately by. They came to a halt beyond the house, and, after much irresolution, sat down in the sand. A few minutes later another family trailed in from the opposite direction, the men and women carrying a heterogeneous assortment of possessions. And soon several hundred persons of all ages and sexes were congregated about the captain's dwelling. He called to one new arrival, a woman with a nursing babe in her arms, and in answer received the information that her house had just been swept into the lagoon.

This was the highest spot of land in miles, and already, in many places on either hand, the great seas were making a clean breach of the slender ring of the atoll and surging into the lagoon. Twenty miles around stretched the ring of the atoll, and in no place was it more than fifty fathoms wide. It was the height of the diving season, and from all the islands around, even as far as Tahiti, the natives had gathered.

"There are twelve hundred men, women and children here," said Captain Lynch. "I wonder how many will be here to-morrow morning."

"But why don't it blow?—that's what I want to know," Raoul demanded.

"Don't worry, young man, don't worry; you'll get your troubles fast enough."

Even as Captain Lynch spoke, a great watery mass smote the atoll. The seawater churned about them three inches deep under their chairs. A low wail of fear went up from the many women. The children, with clasped hands, stared at the immense rollers and cried piteously. Chickens and cats, wading perturbedly in the water, as by common consent, with flight and scramble took refuge on the roof of the captain's house. A Paumotan, with a litter of new-born puppies in a basket, climbed into a coconut tree and twenty feet above the ground made the basket fast. The mother floundered about in the water beneath, whining and yelping.

And still the sun shone brightly and the dead calm continued. They sat and watched the seas and the insane pitching of the *Aorai.* Captain Lynch gazed at the huge mountains of water sweeping in until he could gaze no more. He covered his face with his hands to shut out the sight; then went into the house.

"Twenty-eight-sixty," he said quietly when he returned.

In his arm was a coil of small rope. He cut it into two-fathom lengths, giving one to Raoul and, retaining one for himself, distributed the remainder among the women with the advice to pick out a tree and climb.

A light air began to blow out of the northeast, and the fan of it on his cheek seemed to cheer Raoul up. He could see the *Aorai* trimming her sheets and heading off shore, and he regretted that he was not on her. She would get away at any rate, but as for the atoll—A sea breached across, almost sweeping him off his feet, and he selected a tree. Then he remembered the barometer and ran back to the house. He encountered Captain Lynch on the same errand and together they went in.

"Twenty-eight-twenty," said the old mariner. "It's going to be fair hell around here —what was that?"

The air seemed filled with the rush of something. The house quivered and vibrated, and they heard the thrumming of a mighty note of sound. The windows rattled. Two panes crashed; a draught of wind tore in, striking them and making them stagger. The door opposite banged shut, shattering the latch. The white doorknob crumbled in fragments to the floor. The room's walls bulged like a gas balloon in the process of sudden inflation. Then came a new sound like the rattle of musketry, as the spray from a sea struck the wall of the house. Captain Lynch looked at his watch. It was four o'clock. He put on a coat of pilot cloth, unhooked the barometer, and stowed it away in a capacious pocket. Again a sea struck the house, with a heavy thud, and the light building tilted, twisted quarter-around on its foundation, and sank down, its floor at an angle of ten degrees.

Raoul went out first. The wind caught him and whirled him away. He noted that it had hauled around to the east. With a great effort he threw himself on the sand, crouching and holding his own. Captain Lynch, driven like a wisp of straw, sprawled over him. Two of the *Aorai*'s sailors, leaving a coconut tree to which they had been clinging, came to their aid, leaning against the wind at impossible angles and fighting and clawing every inch of the way.

The old man's joints were stiff and he could not climb, so the sailors, by means of short ends of rope tied together, hoisted him up the trunk, a few feet at a time, till they could make him fast, at the top of the tree, fifty feet from the ground. Raoul passed his length of rope around the base of an adjacent tree and stood looking on. The wind was frightful. He had never dreamed it could blow so hard. A sea breached across the atoll, wetting him to the knees ere it subsided into the lagoon. The sun had disappeared, and a lead-colored twilight settled down. A few drops of rain, driving horizontally, struck him. The impact was like that of leaden pellets. A splash of salt spray struck his face. It was like the slap of a man's hand. His cheeks stung, and involuntary tears of pain were in his smarting eyes. Several hundred natives had taken to the trees, and he could have laughed at the bunches of human fruit clustering in the tops. Then, being Tahitian-born, he doubled his body at the waist, clasped the trunk of his tree with his hands, pressed the soles of his feet against the near surface of the trunk, and began to walk up the tree. At the top he found two women, two children and a man. One little girl clasped a house-cat in her arms.

From his eyrie he waved his hand to Captain Lynch, and that doughty patriarch waved back. Raoul was appalled at the sky. It had approached much nearer—in fact, it seemed just over his head; and it had turned from lead to black. Many people were still on the ground grouped about the bases of the trees and holding on. Several such clusters were praying, and in one the Mormon missionary was exhorting. A weird sound, rhythmical, faint as the faintest chirp of a far cricket, enduring but for a moment, but in that moment suggesting to him vaguely the thought of heaven and celestial music, came to his ear. He glanced about him and saw, at the base of another tree, a large cluster of people holding on by ropes and by one another. He could see their faces working and their lips moving in unison. No sound came to him, but he knew that they were singing hymns.

Still the wind continued to blow harder. By no conscious process could he measure it, for it had long since passed beyond all his experience of wind; but he knew somehow, nevertheless, that it was blowing harder. Not far away a tree was uprooted, flinging its load of human beings to the ground. A sea washed across the strip of sand, and they were gone. Things were happening quickly. He saw a brown shoulder and a black head silhouetted against the churning white of the lagoon. The next instant that, too, had vanished. Other trees were going, falling and criss-crossing like matches. He was amazed at the power of the wind. His own tree was swaying perilously, one woman was wailing and clutching the little girl, who in turn still hung on to the cat.

The man, holding the other child, touched Raoul's arm and pointed. He looked and saw the Mormon church careering drunkenly a hundred feet away. It had been torn from its foundations, and wind and sea were heaving and shoving it toward the lagoon. A frightful wall of water caught it, tilted it, and flung it against half a dozen coconut trees. The bunches of human fruit fell like ripe coconuts. The subsiding wave showed them on the ground, some lying motionless, others squirming and writhing. They reminded him strangely of ants. He was not shocked. He had risen above horror. Quite as a matter of course he noted the succeeding wave sweep the sand clean of the human wreckage. A third wave, more colossal than any he had yet seen, hurled the church into the lagoon, where it floated off into the obscurity to leeward, half-submerged, reminding him for all the world of a Noah's ark.

He looked for Captain Lynch's house, and was surprised to find it gone. Things certainly were happening quickly. He noticed that many of the people in the trees that still held had descended to the ground. The wind had yet again increased. His own tree showed that. It no longer swayed or bent over and back. Instead, it remained practically stationary, curved in a rigid angle from the wind and merely vibrating. But the vibration was sickening. It was like that of a tuning-fork or the tongue of a jew's-harp. It was the rapidity of the vibration that made it so bad. Even though its roots held, it could not stand the strain for long. Something would have to break.

Ah, there was one that had gone. He had not seen it go, but there it stood, the remnant, broken off half-way up the trunk. One did not know what happened unless he saw it. The mere crashing of trees and wails of human despair occupied no place in that mighty volume of sound. He chanced to be looking in Captain Lynch's direction when it happened. He saw the trunk of the tree, half-way up, splinter and part without noise. The head of the tree, with three sailors of the *Aorai* and the old captain, sailed off over the lagoon. It did not fall to the ground, but drove through the air like a piece of chaff. For a hundred yards he followed its flight, when it struck the water. He strained his eyes, and was sure that he saw Captain Lynch wave farewell.

Raoul did not wait for anything more. He touched the native and made signs to descend to the ground. The man was willing, but his women were paralyzed from terror, and he elected to remain with them. Raoul passed his rope around the tree and slid down. A rush of salt water went over his head. He held his breath and clung desperately to the rope. The water subsided, and in the shelter of the trunk he breathed once more. He fastened the rope more securely, and then was put under by another sea. One of the women slid down and joined him, the native remaining by the other woman, the two children and the cat.

The supercargo had noticed how the groups clinging at the bases of the other trees continually diminished. Now he saw the process work out alongside him. It required all his strength to hold on, and the woman who had joined him was growing weaker. Each time he emerged from a sea he was surprised to find himself still there, and next, surprised to find the woman still there. At last he emerged to find himself alone. He looked up. The top of the tree had gone as well. At half its original height, a splintered end vibrated. He was safe. The roots still held, while the tree had been shorn of its windage. He began to climb up. He was so weak that he went slowly, and sea after sea caught him before he was above them. Then he tied himself to the trunk and stiffened his soul to face the night and he knew not what.

He felt very lonely in the darkness. At times it seemed to him that it was the end of the world and that he was the last one left alive. Still the wind increased. Hour after hour it increased. By what he calculated was eleven o'clock, the wind had become unbelievable. It was a horrible, monstrous thing, a screaming fury, a wall that smote and passed on but that continued to smite and pass on—a wall without end. It seemed to him that he had become light and ethereal; that it was he that was in motion; that he was being driven with inconceivable velocity through unending solidness. The wind was no longer air in motion. It had become substantial as water or quicksilver. He had a feeling that he could reach into it and tear it out in chunks as one might do with the meat in the carcass of a steer; that he could seize hold of the wind and hang on to it as a man might hang on to the face of a cliff.

The wind strangled him. He could not face it and breathe, for it rushed in through his mouth and nostrils, distending his lungs like bladders. At such moments it seemed to him that his body was being packed and swollen with solid earth. Only by pressing his lips to the trunk of the tree could he breathe. Also, the ceaseless impact of the wind exhausted him. Body and brain became wearied. He no longer observed, no longer thought, and was but semiconscious. One idea constituted his consciousness: *So this was a hurricane.* That one idea persisted irregularly. It was like a feeble flame that flickered occasionally. From a state of stupor he would return to it—*So this was a hurricane.* Then he would go off into another stupor.

The height of the hurricane endured from eleven at night till three in the morning, and it was at eleven that the tree in which clung Mapuhi and his women snapped off. Mapuhi rose to the surface of the lagoon, still clutching his daughter Ngakura. Only a South Sea islander could have lived in such a driving smother. The pandanus-tree, to which he attached himself, turned over and over in the froth and churn; and it was only by holding on at times and waiting, and at other times shifting his grips rapidly, that he was able to get his head and Ngakura's to the surface at intervals sufficiently near together to keep the breath in them. But the air was mostly water, what with flying spray and sheeted rain that poured along at right angles to the perpendicular.

It was ten miles across the lagoon to the farther ring of sand. Here, tossing tree-trunks, timbers, wrecks of cutters, and wreckage of houses, killed nine out of ten of the miserable beings who survived the passage of the lagoon. Half-drowned, exhausted, they were hurled into this mad mortar of the elements and battered into formless flesh. But Mapuhi was fortunate. His chance was the one in ten; it fell to him by the freakage of fate. He emerged upon the sand, bleeding from a score of wounds. Ngakura's left arm was broken; the fingers of her right hand were crushed; and cheek and forehead were laid open to the bone. He clutched a tree that yet stood, and clung on, holding the girl and sobbing for air, while the waters of the lagoon washed by knee-high and at times waist-high.

At three in the morning the backbone of the hurricane broke. By five no more than a stiff breeze was blowing. And by six it was dead calm and the sun was shining. The sea had gone down. On the yet restless edge of the lagoon, Mapuhi saw the broken bodies of those that had failed in the landing. Undoubtedly Tefara and Nauri were among them. He went along the beach examining them, and came upon his wife, lying half in and half out of the water. He sat down and wept, making harsh animal-noises after the manner of primitive grief. Then she stirred uneasily, and groaned. He looked more closely. Not only was she alive, but she was uninjured. She was merely sleeping. Hers also had been the one chance in ten.

Of the twelve hundred alive the night before but three hundred remained. The Mormon missionary and a gendarme made the census. The lagoon was cluttered with corpses. Not a house nor a hut was standing. In the whole atoll not two stones remained one upon another. One in fifty of the coconut palms still stood, and they were wrecks, while on not one of them remained a single nut. There was no fresh water. The shallow wells that caught the surface seepage of the rain were filled with salt. Out of the lagoon a few soaked bags of flour were recovered. The survivors cut the hearts out of the fallen coconut trees and ate them. Here and there they crawled into tiny hutches, made by hollowing out the sand and covering over with fragments of metal roofing. The missionary made a crude still, but he could not distill water for three hundred persons. By the end of the second day, Raoul, taking a bath in the lagoon, discovered that his thirst was somewhat relieved. He cried out the news, and thereupon three hundred men, women, and children could have been seen, standing up to their necks in the lagoon and trying to drink water in through their skins. Their dead floated about them, or were stepped upon where they still lay upon the bottom. On the third day the people buried their dead and sat down to wait for the rescue steamers.

In the meantime, Nauri, torn from her family by the hurricane, had been swept away on an adventure of her own. Clinging to a rough plank that wounded and bruised her and that filled her body with splinters, she was thrown clear over the atoll and carried away to sea. Here, under the amazing buffets of mountains of water, she lost her plank. She was an old woman nearly sixty; but she was Paumotan-born, and she had never been out of sight of the sea in her life. Swimming in the darkness, strangling, suffocating, fighting for air, she was struck a heavy blow on the shoulder by a coconut. On the instant her plan was formed, and she seized the nut. In the next hour she captured seven more. Tied together, they formed a life-buoy that preserved her life while at the same time it threatened to pound her to a jelly. She was a fat woman, and she bruised easily; but she had had experience of hurricanes, and, while she prayed to her shark god for protection from sharks, she waited for the wind to break. But at three o'clock she was in such a stupor that she did not know. Nor did she know at six o'clock when the dead calm settled down. She was shocked into consciousness when she was thrown upon the sand. She dug in with raw and bleeding hands and feet and clawed against the backwash until she was beyond the reach of the waves.

She knew where she was. This land could be no other than the tiny islet of Takokota. It had no lagoon. No one lived upon it. Hikueru was fifteen miles away. She could not see Hikueru, but she knew that it lay to the south. The days went by, and she lived on the coconuts that had kept her afloat. They supplied her with drinking water and with food. But she did not drink all she wanted, nor eat all she wanted. Rescue was problematical. She saw the smoke of the rescue steamers on the horizon, but what steamer could be expected to come to lonely, uninhabited Takokota?

From the first she was tormented by corpses. The sea persisted in flinging them upon her bit of sand, and she persisted, until her strength failed, in thrusting them back into the sea where the sharks tore at them and devoured them. When her strength failed, the bodies festooned her beach with ghastly horror, and she withdrew from them as far as she could, which was not far.

By the tenth day her last coconut was gone, and she was shrivelling from thirst. She dragged herself along the sand, looking for coconuts. It was strange that so many bodies floated up, and no nuts. Surely, there were more coconuts afloat than dead men! She gave up at last, and lay exhausted. The end had come. Nothing remained but to wait for death.

Coming out of a stupor, she became slowly aware that she was gazing at a patch of sandy-red hair on the head of a corpse. The sea flung the body toward her, then drew it back. It turned over, and she saw that it had no face. Yet there was something familiar about that patch of sandy-red hair. An hour passed. She did not exert herself to make the identification. She was waiting to die, and it mattered little to her what man that thing of horror once might have been.

But at the end of the hour she sat up slowly and stared at the corpse. An unusually large wave had thrown it beyond the reach of the lesser waves. Yes, she was right; that patch of red hair could belong to but one man in the Paumotus. It was Levy, the German Jew, the man who had bought the pearl and carried it away on the *Hira.* Well, one thing was evident: the *Hira* had been lost. The pearl-buyer's god of fishermen and thieves had gone back on him.

She crawled down to the dead man. His shirt had been torn away, and she could see the leather money-belt about his waist. She held her breath and tugged at the buckles. They gave easier than she had expected, and she crawled hurriedly away across the sand, dragging the belt after her. Pocket after pocket she unbuckled in the belt and found empty. Where could he have put it? In the last pocket of all she found it, the first and only pearl he had bought on the voyage. She crawled a few feet farther, to escape the pestilence of the belt, and examined the pearl. It was the one Mapuhi had found and been robbed of by Toriki. She weighed it in her hand and rolled it back and forth caressingly. But in it she saw no intrinsic beauty. What she did see was the house Mapuhi and Tefara and she had builded so carefully in their minds. Each time she looked at the pearl she saw the house in all its details, including the octagon-drop-clock on the wall. That was something to live for.

She tore a strip from her *ahu* and tied the pearl securely about her neck. Then she went along the beach, panting and groaning, but resolutely seeking for coconuts. Quickly she found one, and, as she glanced around, a second. She broke one, drinking its water, which was mildewy, and eating the last particle of the meat. A little later she found a shattered dugout. Its outrigger was gone, but she was hopeful, and, before the day was out, she found the outrigger. Every find was an augury. The pearl was a talisman. Late in the afternoon she saw a wooden box floating low in the water. When she dragged it out on the beach its contents rattled, and inside she found ten tins of salmon. She opened one by hammering it on the canoe. When a leak was started, she drained the tin. After that she spent several hours in extracting the salmon, hammering and squeezing it out a morsel at a time.

Eight days longer she waited for rescue. In the meantime she fastened the outrigger back on the canoe, using for lashings all the coconut-fiber she could find, and also what remained of her *ahu.* The canoe was badly cracked, and she could not make it water-tight; but a calabash made from a coconut she stored on board for a bailer. She was hard put for a paddle. With a piece of tin she sawed off all her hair close to the scalp. Out of the hair she braided a cord; and by means of the cord she lashed a three-foot piece of broom-handle to a board from the salmon case. She gnawed wedges with her teeth and with them wedged the lashing.

On the eighteenth day, at midnight, she launched the canoe through the surf and started back for Hikueru. She was an old woman. Hardship had stripped her fat from her till scarcely more than bones and skin and a few stringy muscles remained. The canoe was large and should have been paddled by three strong men. But she did it alone, with a make-shift paddle. Also, the canoe leaked badly, and one-third of her time was devoted to bailing. By clear daylight she looked vainly for Hikueru. Astern, Takokota had sunk beneath the sea-rim. The sun blazed down on her nakedness, compelling her body to surrender its moisture. Two tins of salmon were left, and in the course of the day she battered holes in them and drained the liquid. She had no time to waste in extracting the meat. A current was setting to the westward, she made westing whether she made southing or not.

In the early afternoon, standing upright in the canoe, she sighted Hikueru. Its wealth of coconut palms was gone. Only here and there, at wide intervals, could she see the ragged remnants of trees. The sight cheered her. She was nearer than she had thought. The current was setting her to the westward. She bore up against it and paddled on. The wedges in the paddle-lashing worked loose, and she lost much time, at frequent intervals, in driving them tight. Then there was the bailing. One hour in three she had to cease paddling in order to bail. And all the time she drifted to the westward.

By sunset Hikueru bore southeast from her, three miles away. There was a full moon, and by eight o'clock the land was due east and two miles away. She struggled on for another hour, but the land was as far away as ever. She was in the main grip of the current; the canoe was too large; the paddle was too inadequate; and too much of her time and strength was wasted in bailing. Besides, she was very weak and growing weaker. Despite her efforts, the canoe was drifting off to the westward.

She breathed a prayer to her shark god, slipped over the side, and began to swim. She was actually refreshed by the water, and quickly left the canoe astern. At the end of an hour the land was perceptibly nearer. Then came her fright. Right before her eyes, not twenty feet away, a large fin cut the water. She swam steadily toward it, and slowly it glided away, curving off toward the right and circling around her. She kept her eyes on the fin and swam on. When the fin disappeared, she lay face downward on the water and watched. When the fin reappeared she resumed her swimming. The monster was lazy—she could see that. Without doubt he had been well fed since the hurricane. Had he been very hungry, she knew he would not have hesitated from making a dash for her. He was fifteen feet long, and one bite, she knew, could cut her in half.

But she did not have any time to waste on him. Whether she swam or not, the current drew away from the land just the same. A half-hour went by, and the shark began to grow bolder. Seeing no harm in her he drew closer, in narrowing circles, cocking his eyes at her impudently as he slid past. Sooner or later, she knew well enough, he would get up sufficient courage to dash at her. She resolved to play first. It was a desperate act she meditated. She was an old woman, alone in the sea and weak from starvation and hardship; and yet she, in the face of this sea-tiger, must anticipate his dash by herself dashing at him. She swam on, waiting her chance. At last he passed languidly by, barely eight feet away. She rushed at him suddenly, feigning that she was attacking him. He gave a wild flirt of his tail as he fled away, and his sandpaper hide, striking her, took off her skin from elbow to shoulder. He swam rapidly in a widening circle, and at last disappeared.

In the hole in the sand, covered over by fragments of metal roofing, Mapuhi and Tefara lay disputing.

"If you had done as I said," charged Tefara, for the thousandth time, "and hidden the pearl and told no one, you would have it now."

"But Huru-Huru was with me when I opened the shell—have I not told you so times and times and times without end?"

"And now we shall have no house. Raoul told me to-day that if you had not sold the pearl to Toriki—"

"I did not sell it. Toriki robbed me."

"—that if you had not sold the pearl, he would give you five thousand French dollars, which is ten thousand Chili."

"He has been talking to his mother," Mapuhi explained. "She has an eye for a pearl."

"And now the pearl is lost," Tefara complained.

"It paid my debt with Toriki. That is twelve hundred I have made, anyway."

"Toriki is dead," she cried. "They have heard no word of his schooner. She was lost along with the *Aorai* and the *Hira*. Will Toriki pay you the three hundred credit he promised? No, because Toriki is dead. And had you found no pearl, would you to-day owe Toriki the twelve hundred? No, because Toriki is dead, and you cannot pay dead men."

"But Levy did not pay Toriki," Mapuhi said. "He gave him a piece of paper that was good for the money in Papeete; and now Levy is dead and cannot pay; and Toriki is dead and the paper lost with him, and the pearl is lost with Levy. You are right, Tefara. I have lost the pearl, and got nothing for it. Now let us sleep."

He held up his hand suddenly and listened. From without came a noise, as of one who breathed heavily and with pain. A hand fumbled against the mat that served for a door.

"Who is there?" Mapuhi cried.

"Nauri," came the answer. "Can you tell me where is my son, Mapuhi?"

Tefara screamed and gripped her husband's arm.

"A ghost!" she chattered. "A ghost!"

Mapuhi's face was a ghastly yellow. He clung weakly to his wife.

"Good woman," he said in faltering tones, striving to disguise his voice, "I know your son well. He is living on the east side of the lagoon."

From without came the sound of a sigh. Mapuhi began to feel elated. He had fooled the ghost.

"But where do you come from, old woman?" he asked.

"From the sea," was the dejected answer.

"I knew it! I knew it!" screamed Tefara, rocking to and fro.

"Since when has Tefara bedded in a strange house?" came Nauri's voice through the matting.

Mapuhi looked fear and reproach at his wife. It was her voice that had betrayed them.

"And since when has Mapuhi, my son, denied his old mother?" the voice went on.

"No, no, I have not—Mapuhi has not denied you," he cried. "I am not Mapuhi. He is on the east end of the lagoon, I tell you."

Ngakura sat up in bed and began to cry. The matting started to shake.

"What are you doing?" Mapuhi demanded.

"I am coming in," said the voice of Nauri.

One end of the matting lifted. Tefara tried to dive under the blankets, but Mapuhi held on to her. He had to hold on to something. Together, struggling with each other, with shivering bodies and chattering teeth, they gazed with protruding eyes at the lifting mat. They saw Nauri, dripping with sea-water, without her *ahu,* creep in. They rolled over backward from her and fought for Ngakura's blanket with which to cover their heads.

"You might give your old mother a drink of water," the ghost said plaintively.

"Give her a drink of water," Tefara commanded in a shaking voice.

"Give her a drink of water," Mapuhi passed on the command to Ngakura.

And together they kicked out Ngakura from under the blanket. A minute later, peeping, Mapuhi saw the ghost drinking. When it reached out a shaking hand and laid it on his, he felt the weight of it and was convinced that it was no ghost. Then he emerged, dragging Tefara after him, and in a few minutes all were listening to Nauri's tale. And when she told of Levy, and dropped the pearl into Tefara's hand, even she was reconciled to the reality of her mother-in-law.

"In the morning," said Tefara, "you will sell the pearl to Raoul for five thousand French."

"The house?" objected Nauri.

"He will build the house," Tefara answered. "He says it will cost four thousand French. Also will he give one thousand French in credit, which is two thousand Chili."

"And it will be six fathoms long?" Nauri queried.

"Ay," answered Mapuhi, "six fathoms."

"And in the middle room will be the octagon-drop-clock?"

"Ay, and the round table as well."

"Then give me something to eat, for I am hungry," said Nauri, complacently. "And after that we will sleep, for I am weary. And to-morrow we will have more talk about the house before we sell the pearl. It will be better if we take the thousand French in cash. Money is ever better than credit in buying goods from the traders."

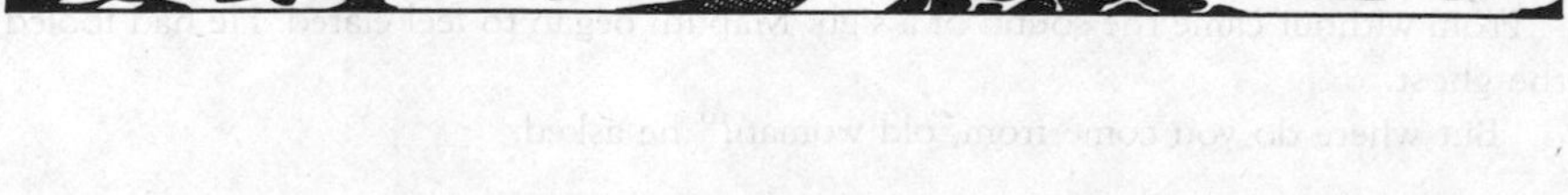

THE SEED OF MCCOY

THE *Pyrenees,* her iron sides pressed low in the water by her cargo of wheat, rolled sluggishly, and made it easy for the man who was climbing aboard from out a tiny outrigger canoe. As his eyes came level with the rail, so that he could see inboard, it seemed to him that he saw a dim, almost indiscernible haze. It was more like an illusion, like a blurring film that had spread abruptly over his eyes. He felt an inclination to brush it away, and the same instant he thought that he was growing old and that it was time to send to San Francisco for a pair of spectacles.

As he came over the rail he cast a glance aloft at the tall masts, and, next, at the pumps. They were not working. There seemed nothing the matter with the big ship, and he wondered why she had hoisted the signal of distress. He thought of his happy islanders, and hoped it was not disease. Perhaps the ship was short of water or provisions. He shook hands with the captain whose gaunt face and care-worn eyes made no secret of the trouble, whatever it was. At the same moment the new-comer was aware of a faint, indefinable smell. It seemed like that of burnt bread, but different.

He glanced curiously about him. Twenty feet away a weary-faced sailor was calking the deck. As his eyes lingered on the man, he saw suddenly arise from under his hands a faint spiral of haze that curled and twisted and was gone. By now he had reached the deck. His bare feet were pervaded by a dull warmth that quickly penetrated the thick calluses. He knew now the nature of the ship's distress. His eyes roved swiftly forward, where the full crew of weary-faced sailors regarded him eagerly. The glance from his liquid brown eyes swept over them like a benediction, soothing them, wrapping them about as in the mantle of a great peace. "How long has she been afire, Captain?" he asked in a voice so gentle and unperturbed that it was as the cooing of a dove.

At first the captain felt the peace and content of it stealing in upon him; then the consciousness of all that he had gone through and was going through smote him, and he was resentful. By what right did this ragged beach-comber, in dungaree trousers and a cotton shirt, suggest such a thing as peace and content to him and his overwrought, exhausted soul? The captain did not reason this; it was the unconscious process of emotion that caused his resentment.

"Fifteen days," he answered shortly. "Who are you?"

"My name is McCoy," came the answer in tones that breathed tenderness and compassion.

"I mean, are you the pilot?"

McCoy passed the benediction of his gaze over the tall, heavy-shouldered man with the haggard, unshaven face who had joined the captain.

"I am as much a pilot as anybody," was McCoy's answer. "We are all pilots here, Captain, and I know every inch of these waters."

But the captain was impatient.

"What I want is some of the authorities. I want to talk with them, and blame quick."

"Then I'll do just as well."

Again that insidious suggestion of peace, and his ship a raging furnace beneath his feet! The captain's eyebrows lifted impatiently and nervously, and his fist clenched as if he were about to strike a blow with it.

"Who in hell are you?" he demanded.

"I am the chief magistrate," was the reply in a voice that was still the softest and gentlest imaginable.

The tall, heavy-shouldered man broke out in a harsh laugh that was partly amusement, but mostly hysterical. Both he and the captain regarded McCoy with incredulity and amazement. That this barefooted beach-comber should possess such high-sounding dignity was inconceivable. His cotton shirt, unbuttoned, exposed a grizzled chest and the fact that there was no undershirt beneath. A worn straw hat failed to hide the ragged gray hair. Halfway down his chest descended an untrimmed patriarchal beard. In any slop-shop, two shillings would have outfitted him complete as he stood before them.

"Any relation to the McCoy of the *Bounty?*" the captain asked.

"He was my great-grandfather."

"Oh," the captain said, then bethought himself. "My name is Davenport, and this is my first mate, Mr Konig."

They shook hands.

"And now to business." The captain spoke quickly, the urgency of a great haste pressing his speech. "We've been on fire for over two weeks. She's ready to break all hell loose any moment. That's why I held for Pitcairn. I want to beach her, or scuttle her, and save the hull."

"Then you made a mistake, Captain," said McCoy. "You should have slacked away for Mangareva. There's a beautiful beach there, in a lagoon where the water is like a mill-pond."

"But we're here, ain't we?" the first mate demanded. "That's the point. We're here, and we've got to do something."

McCoy shook his head kindly.

"You can do nothing here. There is no beach. There isn't even anchorage."

"Gammon!" said the mate. "Gammon!" he repeated loudly, as the captain signalled him to be more soft-spoken. "You can't tell me that sort of stuff. Where d'ye keep your own boats, hey—your schooner, or cutter, or whatever you have? Hey? Answer me that."

McCoy smiled as gently as he spoke. His smile was a caress, an embrace that surrounded the tired mate and sought to draw him into the quietude and rest of McCoy's tranquil soul.

"We have no schooner or cutter," he replied. "And we carry our canoes to the top of the cliff."

"You've got to show me," snorted the mate. "How d'ye get around to the other islands, heh? Tell me that."

"We don't get around. As governor of Pitcairn, I sometimes go. When I was younger, I was away a great deal—sometimes on the trading schooners, but mostly on the missionary brig. But she's gone now, and we depend on passing vessels. Sometimes we have had as high as six calls in one year. At other times, a year, and even longer, has gone by without one passing ship. Yours is the first in seven months."

"And you mean to tell me—" the mate began.

But Captain Davenport interfered.

"Enough of this. We're losing time. What is to be done, Mr McCoy?"

The old man turned his brown eyes, sweet as a woman's, shoreward, and both captain and mate followed his gaze around from the lonely rock of Pitcairn to the crew clustering forward and waiting anxiously for the announcement of a decision. McCoy did not hurry. He thought smoothly and slowly, step by step, with the certitude of a mind that was never vexed or outraged by life.

"The wind is light now," he said finally. "There is a heavy current setting to the westward."

"That's what made us fetch to leeward," the captain interrupted, desiring to vindicate his seamanship.

"Yes, that is what fetched you to leeward," McCoy went on. "Well, you can't work up against this current to-day. And if you did, there is no beach. Your ship will be a total loss."

He paused, and captain and mate looked despair at each other.

"But I will tell you what you can do. The breeze will freshen to-night around midnight—see those tails of clouds and that thickness to windward, beyond the point there? That's where she'll come from, out of the southeast, hard. It is three hundred miles to Mangareva. Square away for it. There is a beautiful bed for your ship there."

The mate shook his head.

"Come in to the cabin, and we'll look at the chart," said the captain.

McCoy found a stifling, poisonous atmosphere in the pent cabin. Stray waftures of invisible gases bit his eyes and made them sting. The deck was hotter, almost unbearably hot to his bare feet. The sweat poured out of his body. He looked almost with apprehension about him. This malignant, internal heat was astounding. It was a marvel that the cabin did not burst into flames. He had a feeling as if of being in a huge bake-oven where the heat might at any moment increase tremendously and shrivel him up like a blade of grass.

As he lifted one foot and rubbed the hot sole against the leg of his trousers, the mate laughed in a savage, snarling fashion.

"The anteroom of hell," he said. "Hell herself is right down there under your feet."

"It's hot!" McCoy cried involuntarily, mopping his face with a bandana handkerchief.

"Here's Mangareva," the captain said, bending over the table and pointing to a black speck in the midst of the white blankness of the chart. "And here, in between, is another island. Why not run for that?"

McCoy did not look at the chart.

"That's Crescent Island," he answered. "It is uninhabited, and it is only two or three feet above water. Lagoon, but no entrance. No, Mangareva is the nearest place for your purpose."

"Mangareva it is, then," said Captain Davenport, interrupting the mate's growling objection. "Call the crew aft, Mr Konig."

The sailors obeyed, shuffling wearily along the deck and painfully endeavoring to make haste. Exhaustion was evident in every movement. The cook came out of his galley to hear, and the cabin-boy hung about near him.

When Captain Davenport had explained the situation and announced his intention of running for Mangareva, an uproar broke out. Against a background of throaty rumbling arose inarticulate cries of rage, with here and there a distinct curse, or word, or phrase. A shrill Cockney voice soared and dominated for a moment, crying: "Gawd! After bein' in 'ell for fifteen days—an' now 'e wants us to sail this floatin' 'ell to sea again!"

The captain could not control them, but McCoy's gentle presence seemed to rebuke and calm them, and the muttering and cursing died away, until the full crew, save here and there an anxious face directed at the captain, yearned dumbly toward the green-clad peaks and beetling coast of Pitcairn.

Soft as a spring zephyr was the voice of McCoy:

"Captain, I thought I heard some of them say they were starving."

"Ay," was the answer, "and so we are. I've had a sea-biscuit and a spoonful of salmon in the last two days. We're on whack. You see, when we discovered the fire, we battened down immediately to suffocate the fire. And then we found how little food there was in the pantry. But it was too late. We didn't dare break out the lazarette. Hungry? I'm just as hungry as they are."

He spoke to the men again, and again the throat-rumbling and cursing arose, their faces convulsed and animal-like with rage. The second and third mates had joined the captain, standing behind him at the break of the poop. Their faces were set and expressionless; they seemed bored, more than anything else, by this mutiny of the crew. Captain Davenport glanced questioningly at his first mate, and that person merely shrugged his shoulders in token of his helplessness.

"You see," the captain said to McCoy, "you can't compel sailors to leave the safe land and go to sea on a burning vessel. She has been their floating coffin for over two weeks now. They are worked out, and starved out, and they've got enough of her. We'll beat up for Pitcairn."

But the wind was light, the *Pyrenees'* bottom was foul, and she could not beat up against the strong westerly current. At the end of two hours she had lost three miles. The sailors worked eagerly, as if by main strength they could compel the *Pyrenees* against the adverse elements. But steadily, port tack and starboard tack, she sagged off the the westward. The captain paced restlessly up and down, pausing occasionally to survey the vagrant smoke-wisps and to trace them back to the portions of the deck from which they sprang. The carpenter was engaged constantly in attempting to locate such places, and, when he succeeded, in calking them tighter and tighter.

"Well, what do you think?" the captain finally asked McCoy, who was watching the carpenter with all a child's interest and curiosity in his eyes.

McCoy looked shoreward, where the land was disappearing in the thickening haze.

"I think it would be better to square away for Mangareva. With that breeze that is coming, you'll be there to-morrow evening."

"But what if the fire breaks out? It is liable to do it any moment."

"Have your boats ready in the falls. The same breeze will carry your boats to Mangareva if the ship burns out from under."

Captain Davenport debated for a moment, and then McCoy heard the question he had not wanted to hear, but which he knew was surely coming.

"I have no chart of Mangareva. On the general chart it is only a fly-speck. I would not know where to look for the entrance into the lagoon. Will you come along and pilot her in for me?"

McCoy's serenity was unbroken.

"Yes, Captain," he said, with the same quiet unconcern with which he would have accepted an invitation to dinner; "I'll go with you to Mangareva."

Again the crew was called aft, and the captain spoke to them from the break of the poop.

"We've tried to work her up, but you see how we've lost ground. She's setting off in a two-knot current. This gentleman is the Honorable McCoy, Chief Magistrate and Governor of Pitcairn Island. He will come along with us to Mangareva. So you see the situation is not so dangerous. He would not make such an offer if he thought he was going to lose his life. Besides, whatever risk there is, if he of his own free will come on board and take it, we can do no less. What do you say for Mangareva?"

This time there was no uproar. McCoy's presence, the surety and calm that seemed to radiate from him, had had its effect. They conferred with one another in low voices. There was little urging. They were virtually unanimous, and they shoved the Cockney out as their spokesman. That worthy was overwhelmed with consciousnes of the heroism of himself and his mates, and with flashing eyes he cried:

"By Gawd! if 'e will, we will!"

The crew mumbled its assent and started forward.

"One moment, Captain," McCoy said, as the other was turning to give orders to the mate. "I must go ashore first."

Mr Konig was thunderstruck, staring at McCoy as if he were a madman.

"Go ashore!" the captain cried. "What for? It will take you three hours to get there in your canoe."

McCoy measured the distance of the land away, and nodded.

"Yes, it is six now. I won't get ashore till nine. The people cannot be assembled earlier than ten. As the breeze freshens up to-night, you can begin to work up against it, and pick me up at daylight to-morrow morning."

"In the name of reason and common-sense," the captain burst forth, "what do you want to assemble the people for? Don't you realize that my ship is burning beneath me?"

McCoy was as placid as a summer sea, and the other's anger produced not the slightest ripple upon it.

"Yes, Captain," he cooed in his dove-like voice, "I do realize that your ship is burning. That is why I am going with you to Mangareva. But I must get permission to go with you. It is our custom. It is an important matter when the governor leaves the island. The people's interests are at stake, and so they have the right to vote their permission or refusal. But they will give it, I know that."

"Are you sure?"

"Quite sure."

"Then if you know they will give it, why bother with getting it? Think of the delay—a whole night."

"It is our custom," was the imperturbable reply. "Also, I am the governor, and I must make arrangements for the conduct of the island during my absence."

"But it is only a twenty-four-hour run to Mangareva," the captain objected. "Suppose it took you six times that long to return to windward; that would bring you back by the end of a week."

McCoy smiled his large, benevolent smile.

"Very few vessels come to Pitcairn, and when they do, they are usually from San Francisco or from around the Horn. I shall be fortunate if I get back in six months. I may be away a year, and I may have to go to San Francisco in order to find a vessel that will bring me back. My father once left Pitcairn to be gone three months, and two years passed before he could get back. Then, too, you are short of food. If you have to take to the boats, and the weather comes up bad, you may be days in reaching land. I can bring off two canoe loads of food in the morning. Dried bananas will be best. As the breeze freshens, you beat up against it. The nearer you are, the bigger loads I can bring off. Goodby."

He held out his hand. The captain shook it, and was reluctant to let go. He seemed to cling to it as a drowning sailor clings to a life-buoy.

"How do I know you will come back in the morning?" he asked.

"Yes, that's it!" cried the mate. "How do we know but what he's skinning out to save his own hide?"

McCoy did not speak. He looked at them sweetly and benignantly, and it seemed to them that they received a message from his tremendous certitude of soul.

The captain released his hand, and, with a last sweeping glance that embraced the crew in its benediction, McCoy went over the rail and descended into his canoe.

The wind freshened, and the *Pyrenees,* despite the foulness of her bottom, won half a dozen miles away from the westerly current. At daylight, with Pitcairn three miles to windward, Captain Davenport made out two canoes coming off to him. Again McCoy clambered up the side and dropped over the rail to the hot deck. He was followed by many packages of dried bananas, each package wrapped in dry leaves.

"Now, Captain," he said, "swing the yards and drive for dear life. You see, I am no navigator," he explained a few minutes later, as he stood by the captain aft, the latter with gaze wandering from aloft to overside as he estimated the *Pyrenees'* speed. "You must fetch her to Mangareva. When you have picked up the land, then I will pilot her in. What do you think she is making?"

"Eleven," Captain Davenport answered, with a final glance at the water rushing past.

"Eleven. Let me see, if she keeps up that gait, we'll sight Mangareva between eight and nine o'clock to-morrow morning. I'll have her on the beach by ten, or by eleven at latest. And then your troubles will be all over."

It almost seemed to the captain that the blissful moment had already arrived, such was the persuasive convincingness of McCoy. Captain Davenport had been under the fearful strain of navigating his burning ship for over two weeks, and he was beginning to feel that he had had enough.

A heavier flaw of wind struck the back of his neck and whistled by his ears. He measured the weight of it, and looked quickly overside.

"The wind is making all the time," he announced. "The old girl's doing nearer twelve than eleven right now. If this keeps up, we'll be shortening down to-night."

All day the *Pyrenees,* carrying her load of living fire, tore across the foaming sea. By nightfall, royals and topgallantsails were in, and she flew on into the darkness, with great, crested seas roaring after her. The auspicious wind had had its effect, and fore and aft a visible brightening was apparent. In the second dog-watch some careless soul started a song, and by eight bells the whole crew was singing.

Captain Davenport had his blankets brought up and spread on top the house.

"I've forgotten what sleep is," he explained to McCoy. "I'm all in. But give me a call at any time you think necessary."

At three in the morning he was aroused by a gentle tugging at his arm. He sat up quickly, bracing himself against the skylight, stupid yet from his heavy sleep. The wind was thrumming its war-song in the rigging, and a wild sea was buffeting the *Pyrenees.* Amidships she was wallowing first one rail under and then the other, flooding the waist more often than not. McCoy was shouting something he could not hear. He reached out, clutched the other by the shoulder, and drew him close so that his own ear was close to the other's lips.

"It's three o'clock," came McCoy's voice, still retaining its dovelike quality, but curiously muffled, as if from a long way off. "We've run two hundred and fifty. Crescent

Island is only thirty miles away, somewhere there dead ahead. There's no lights on it. If we keep running, we'll pile up, and lose ourselves as well as the ship."

"What d' ye think—heave to?"

"Yes; heave to till daylight. It will only put us back four hours."

So the *Pyrenees,* with her cargo of fire, was hove to, bitting the teeth of the gale and fighting and smashing the pounding seas. She was a shell, filled with a conflagration, and on the outside of the shell, clinging precariously, the little motes of men, by pull and haul, helped her in the battle.

"It is most unusual, this gale," McCoy told the captain, in the lee of the cabin. "By rights there should be no gale at this time of the year. But everything about the weather has been unusual. There has been a stoppage of the trades, and now it's howling right out of the trade quarter." He waved his hand into the darkness, as if his vision could dimly penetrate for hundreds of miles. "It is off to the westward. There is something big making off there somewhere—a hurricane or something. We're lucky to be so far to the eastward. But this is only a little blow," he added. "It can't last. I can tell you that much."

By daylight the gale had eased down to normal. But daylight revealed a new danger. It had come on thick. The sea was covered by a fog, or, rather, by a pearly mist that was fog-like in density, in so far as it obstructed vision, but that was no more than a film on the sea, for the sun shot it through and filled it with a glowing radiance.

The deck of the *Pyrenees* was making more smoke than on the preceding day, and the cheerfulness of officers and crew had vanished. In the lee of the galley the cabin-boy could be heard whimpering. It was his first voyage, and the fear of death was at his heart. The captain wandered about like a lost soul, nervously chewing his mustache, scowling, unable to make up his mind what to do.

"What do you think?" he asked, pausing by the side of McCoy, who was making a breakfast off fried bananas and a mug of water.

McCoy finished the last banana, drained the mug, and looked slowly around. In his eyes was a smile of tenderness as he said:

"Well, Captain, we might as well drive as burn. Your decks are not going to hold out forever. They are hotter this morning. You haven't a pair of shoes I can wear? It is getting uncomfortable for my bare feet."

The *Pyrenees* shipped two heavy seas as she was swung off and put once more before it, and the first mate expressed a desire to have all that water down in the hold, if only it could be introduced without taking off the hatches. McCoy ducked his head into the binnacle and watched the course set.

"I'd hold her up some more, Captain," he said. "She's been making drift when hove to."

"I've set it to a point higher already," was the answer. "Isn't that enough?"

"I'd make it two points, Captain. This bit of a blow kicked that westerly current ahead faster than you imagine."

Captain Davenport compromised on a point and a half, and then went aloft, accompanied by McCoy and the first mate, to keep a lookout for land. Sail had been made, so that the *Pyrenees* was doing ten knots. The following sea was dying down rapidly. There was no break in the pearly fog, and by ten o'clock Captain Davenport was growing nervous. All hands were at their stations, ready, at the first warning of land ahead, to spring like fiends to the task of bringing the *Pyrenees* up on the wind. That land ahead, a surf-washed outer reef, would be perilously close when it revealed itself in such a fog.

Another hour passed. The three watchers aloft stared intently into the pearly radiance.

"What if we miss Mangareva?" Captain Davenport asked abruptly.

McCoy, without shifting his gaze, answered softly:

"Why, let her drive, Captain. That is all we can do. All the Paumotus are before us. We can drive for a thousand miles through reefs and atolls. We are bound to fetch up somewhere."

"Then drive it is." Captain Davenport evidenced his intention of descending to the deck. "We've missed Mangareva. God knows where the next land is. I wish I'd held her up that other half-point," he confessed a moment later. "This cursed current plays the devil with a navigator."

"The old navigators called the Paumotus the Dangerous Archipelago," McCoy said, when they had regained the poop. "This very current was partly responsible for that name."

"I was talking with a sailor chap in Sydney, once," said Mr Konig. "He'd been trading in the Paumotus. He told me insurance was eighteen per cent. Is that right?"

McCoy smiled and nodded.

"Except that they don't insure," he explained. "The owners write off twenty per cent of the cost of their schooners each year."

"My God!" Captain Davenport groaned. "That makes the life of a schooner only five years!" He shook his head sadly, murmuring, "Bad waters! bad waters!"

Again they went into the cabin to consult the big general chart; but the poisonous vapors drove them coughing and gasping on deck.

"Here is Moerenhout Island." Captain Davenport pointed it out on the chart, which he had spread on the house. "It can't be more than a hundred miles to leeward."

"A hundred and ten." McCoy shook his head doubtfully. "It might be done, but it is very difficult. I might beach her, and then again I might put her on the reef. A bad place, a very bad place."

"We'll take the chance," was Captain Davenport's decision, as he set about working out the course.

Sail was shortened early in the afternoon, to avoid running past in the night; and in the second dog-watch the crew manifested its regained cheerfulness. Land was so very near, and their troubles would be over in the morning.

But morning broke clear, with a blazing tropic sun. The southeast trade had swung around to the eastward, and was driving the *Pyrenees* through the water at an eight-knot clip. Captain Davenport worked up his dead reckoning, allowing generously for drift, and announced Moerenhout Island to be not more than ten miles off. The *Pyrenees* sailed the ten miles; she sailed ten miles more; and the lookouts at the three mastheads saw naught but the naked, sun-washed sea.

"But the land is there, I tell you," Captain Davenport shouted to them from the poop.

McCoy smiled soothingly, but the captain glared about him like a madman, fetched his sextant, and took a chronometer sight.

"I knew I was right," he almost shouted, when he had worked up the observation. "Twenty-one, fifty-five, south; one-thirty-six, two, west. There you are. We're eight miles to windward yet. What did you make it out, Mr Konig?"

The first mate glanced at his own figures, and said in a low voice:

"Twenty-one, fifty-five all right; but my longitude's one-thirty-six, forty-eight. That puts us considerably to leeward—"

But Captain Davenport ignored his figures with so contemptuous a silence as to make Mr Konig grit his teeth and curse savagely under his breath.

"Keep her off," the captain ordered the man at the wheel. "Three points—steady there, as she goes!"

Then he returned to his figures and worked them over. The sweat poured from his face. He chewed his mustache, his lips, and his pencil, staring at the figures as a man might at a ghost. Suddenly, with a fierce, muscular outburst, he crumpled the scribbled paper in his fist and crushed it under a foot. Mr Konig grinned vindictively and turned away, while Captain Davenport leaned against the cabin and for half an hour spoke no word, contenting himself with gazing to leeward with an expression of musing hopelessness on his face.

"Mr McCoy," he broke silence abruptly. "The chart indicates a group of islands, but not how many, off there to the north'ard, or nor'-nor'westward, about forty miles—the Acteon Islands. What about them?"

"There are four, all low," McCoy answered. "First to the southeast is Matuerui—no people, no entrance to the lagoon. Then comes Tenarunga. There used to be about a dozen people there, but they may be all gone now. Anyway, there is no entrance for a ship—only a boat entrance, with a fathom of water. Vehauga and Teua-raro are the other two. No entrances, no people, very low. There is no bed for the *Pyrenees* in that group. She would be a total wreck."

"Listen to that!" Captain Davenport was frantic. "No people! No entrances! What in the devil are islands good for?

"Well, then," he barked suddenly, like an excited terrier, "the chart gives a whole mess of islands off to the nor'west. What about them? What one has an entrance where I can lay my ship?"

McCoy calmly considered. He did not refer to the chart. All these islands, reefs, shoals, lagoons, entrances and distances were marked on the chart of his memory. He knew them as the city dweller knows his buildings, streets and alleys.

"Papakena and Vanavana are off there to the westward, or west-nor'westward a hundred miles and a bit more," he said. "One is uninhabited, and I heard that the people on the other had gone off to Cadmus Island. Anyway, neither lagoon has an entrance. Ahunui is another hundred miles on to the nor'west. No entrance, no people."

"Well, forty miles beyond them are two islands?" Captain Davenport queried, raising his head from the chart.

McCoy shook his head.

"Paros and Manuhungi—no entrances, no people. Nengo-Nengo is forty miles beyond them, in turn, and it has no people and no entrance. But there is Hao Island. It is just the place. The lagoon is thirty miles long and five miles wide. There are plenty of people. You can usually find water. And any ship in the world can go through the entrance."

He ceased and gazed solicitously at Captain Davenport, who, bending over the chart with a pair of dividers in hand, had just emitted a low groan.

"Is there any lagoon with an entrance anywhere nearer than Hao Island?" he asked.

"No, Captain; that is the nearest."

"Well, it's three hundred and forty miles." Captain Davenport was speaking very slowly, with decision. "I won't risk the responsibility of all these lives. I'll wreck her on the Acteons. And she's a good ship, too," he added regretfully, after altering the course, this time making more allowance than ever for the westerly current.

An hour later the sky was overcast. The southeast trade still held, but the ocean was a checker-board of squalls.

"We'll be there by one o'clock," Captain Davenport announced confidently. "By two o'clock at the outside. McCoy, you put her ashore on the one where the people are."

The sun did not appear again, nor, at one o'clock, was any land to be seen. Captain Davenport looked astern at the *Pyrenees'* canting wake.

"Good Lord!" he cried. "An easterly current! Look at that!"

Mr Konig was incredulous. McCoy was noncommittal, though he said that in the Paumotus there was no reason why it should not be an easterly current. A few minutes later a squall robbed the *Pyrenees* temporarily of all her wind, and she was left rolling heavily in the trough.

"Where's that deep lead? Over with it, you there!" Captain Davenport held the lead-line and watched it sag off to the northeast. "There, look at that! Take hold of it for yourself."

McCoy and the mate tried it, and felt the line thrumming and vibrating savagely to the grip of the tidal stream.

"A four-knot current," said Mr Konig.

"An easterly current instead of a westerly," said Captain Davenport, glaring accusingly at McCoy, as if to cast the blame for it upon him.

"That is one of the reasons, Captain, for insurance being eighteen per cent in these waters," McCoy answered cheerfully. "You never can tell. The currents are always changing. There was a man who wrote books, I forget his name, in the yacht *Casco.* He missed Takaroa by thirty miles and fetched Tikei, all because of the shifting currents. You are up to windward now, and you'd better keep off a few points."

"But how much has this current set me?" the captain demanded irately. "How am I to know how much to keep off?"

"I don't know, Captain," McCoy said with great gentleness.

The wind returned, and the *Pyrenees,* her deck smoking and shimmering in the bright gray light, ran off dead to leeward. Then she worked back, port tack and starboard tack, crisscrossing her track, combing the sea for the Acteon Islands, which the masthead lookouts failed to sight.

Captain Davenport was beside himself. His rage took the form of sullen silence, and he spent the afternoon in pacing the poop or leaning against the weather-shrouds. At nightfall, without even consulting McCoy, he squared away and headed into the northwest. Mr Konig, surreptitiously consulting chart and binnacle, and McCoy, openly and innocently consulting the binnacle, knew that they were running for Hao Island. By midnight the squalls ceased, and the stars came out. Captain Davenport was cheered by the promise of a clear day.

"I'll get an observation in the morning," he told McCoy, "though what my latitude is, is a puzzler. But I'll use the Sumner method, and settle that. Do you know the Sumner line?"

And thereupon he explained it in detail to McCoy.

The day proved clear, the trade blew steadily out of the east, and the *Pyrenees* just as steadily logged her nine knots. Both the captain and mate worked out the position on a Sumner line, and agreed, and at noon agreed again, and verified the morning sights by the noon sights.

"Another twenty-four hours and we'll be there," Captain Davenport assured McCoy. "It's a miracle the way the old girl's decks hold out. But they can't last. They can't last. Look at them smoke, more and more every day. Yet it was a tight deck to begin with, fresh-calked in 'Frisco. I was surprised when the fire first broke out and we battened down. Look at that!"

He broke off to gaze with dropped jaw at a spiral of smoke that coiled and twisted in the lee of the mizzenmast twenty feet above the deck.

"Now, how did that get there?" he demanded indignantly.

Beneath it there was no smoke. Crawling up from the deck, sheltered from the wind by the mast, by some freak it took form and visibility at that height. It writhed away from the mast, and for a moment overhung the captain like some threatening portent. The next moment the wind whisked it away, and the captain's jaw returned to place.

"As I was saying, when we first battened down, I was surprised. It was a tight deck, yet it leaked smoke like a sieve. And we've calked and calked ever since. There must be tremendous pressure underneath to drive so much smoke through."

That afternoon the sky became overcast again, and squally, drizzly weather set in. The wind shifted back and forth between southeast and northeast, and at midnight the *Pyrenees* was caught aback by a sharp squall from the southwest, from which point the wind continued to blow intermittently.

"We won't make Hao until ten or eleven," Captain Davenport complained at seven in the morning, when the fleeting promise of the sun had been erased by hazy cloud masses in the eastern sky. And the next moment he was plaintively demanding, "And what are the currents doing?"

Lookouts at the mastheads could report no land, and the day passed in drizzling calms and violent squalls. By nightfall a heavy sea began to make from the west. The barometer had fallen to 29.50. There was no wind, and still the ominous sea continued to increase. Soon the *Pyrenees* was rolling madly in the huge waves that marched in an unending procession from out of the darkness of the west. Sail was shortened as fast as both watches could work, and, when the tired crew had finished, its grumbling and complaining voices, peculiarly animal-like and manacing, could be heard in the darkness. Once the starboard watch was called aft to lash down and make secure, and the men openly advertised their sullenness and unwillingness. Every slow movement was a protest and a threat. The atmosphere was moist and sticky like mucilage, and in the absence of wind all hands seemed to pant and gasp for air. The sweat stood out on faces and bare arms, and Captain Davenport for one, his face more gaunt and careworn than ever, and his eyes troubled and staring, was oppressed by a feeling of impending calamity.

"It's off to the westward," McCoy said encouragingly. "At worst, we'll be only on the edge of it."

But Captain Davenport refused to be comforted, and by the light of a lantern read up the chapter in his *Epitome* that related to the strategy of shipmasters in cyclonic storms. From somewhere amidships the silence was broken by a low whimpering from the cabin-boy.

"Oh, shut up!" Captain Davenport yelled suddenly and with such force as to startle every man on board and to frighten the offender into a wild wail of terror.

"Mr Konig," the captain said in a voice that trembled with rage and nerves, "will you kindly step for'ard and stop that brat's mouth with a deck mop?"

But it was McCoy who went forward, and in a few minutes had the boy comforted and asleep.

Shortly before daybreak the first breath of air began to move from out the southeast, increasing swiftly to a stiff and stiffer breeze. All hands were on deck waiting for what might be behind it.

"We're all right now, Captain," said McCoy, standing close to his shoulder. "The hurricane is to the west'ard, and we are south of it. This breeze is the in-suck. It won't blow any harder. You can begin to put sail on her."

"But what's the good? Where shall I sail? This is the second day without observations, and we should have sighted Hao Island yesterday morning. Which way does it bear, north, south, east or what? Tell me that, and I'll make sail in a jiffy."

"I am no navigator, Captain," McCoy said in his mild way.

"I used to think I was one," was the retort, "before I got into these Paumotus."

At mid-day the cry of "Breakers ahead!" was heard from the lookout. The *Pyrenees* was kept off, and sail after sail was loosed and sheeted home. The *Pyrenees* was sliding through the water and fighting a current that threatened to set her down upon the breakers. Officers and men were working like mad, cook and cabin-boy, Captain Davenport himself, and McCoy all lending a hand. It was a close shave. It was a low shoal, a bleak and perilous place over which the seas broke unceasingly, where no man could live, and on which not even sea-birds could rest. The *Pyrenees* was swept within a hundred yards of it before the wind carried her clear, and at this moment the panting crew, its work done, burst out in a torrent of curses upon the head of McCoy—of McCoy who had come on board, and proposed the run to Mangareva, and lured them all away from the safety of Pitcairn Island to certain destruction in this baffling and terrible stretch of sea. But McCoy's tranquil soul was undisturbed. He smiled at them with simple and gracious benevolence, and, somehow, the exalted goodness of him seemed to penetrate to their dark and sombre souls, shaming them, and from very shame stilling the curses vibrating in their throats.

"Bad waters! bad waters!" Captain Davenport was murmuring as his ship forged clear; but he broke off abruptly to gaze at the shoal which should have been dead astern, but which was already on the *Pyrenees'* weather-quarter and working up rapidly to windward.

He sat down and buried his face in his hands. And the first mate saw, and McCoy saw, and the crew saw, what he had seen. South of the shoal an easterly current had set them down upon it; north of the shoal an equally swift westerly current had clutched the ship and was sweeping her away.

"I've heard of these Paumotus before," the captain groaned, lifting his blanched face from his hands. "Captain Moyendale told me about them after losing his ship on them. And I laughed at him behind his back. God forgive me, I laughed at him. What shoal is that?" he broke off, to ask McCoy.

"I don't know, Captain."

"Why don't you know?"

"Because I never saw it before, and because I have never heard of it. I do know that it is not charted. These waters have never been thoroughly surveyed."

"Then you don't know where we are?"

"No more than you do," McCoy said gently.

At four in the afternoon coconut-trees were sighted, apparently growing out of the water. A little later the low land of an atoll was raised above the sea.

"I know where we are now, Captain." McCoy lowered the glasses from his eyes. "That's Resolution Island. We are forty miles beyond Hao Island, and the wind is in our teeth."

"Get ready to beach her then. Where's the entrance?"

"There's only a canoe passage. But now that we know where we are, we can run for Barclay de Tolley. It is only one hundred and twenty miles from here, due nor'-nor'west. With this breeze we can be there by nine o'clock to-morrow morning."

Captain Davenport consulted the chart and debated with himself.

"If we wreck her here," McCoy added, "we'd have to make the run to Barclay de Tolley in the boats just the same."

The captain gave his orders, and once more the *Pyrenees* swung off for another run across the inhospitable sea.

And the middle of the next afternoon saw despair and mutiny on her smoking deck. The current had accelerated, the wind had slackened, and the *Pyrenees* had sagged off to the west. The lookout sighted Barclay de Tolley to the eastward, barely visible from the masthead, and vainly and for hours the *Pyrenees* tried to beat up to it. Ever, like a mirage, the coconut-trees hovered on the horizon, visible only from the masthead. From the deck they were hidden by the bulge of the world.

Again Captain Davenport consulted McCoy and the chart. Makemo lay seventy-five miles to the southwest. Its lagoon was thirty miles long, and its entrance was excellent. When Captain Davenport gave his orders, the crew refused duty. They announced that they had had enough of hell-fire under their feet. There was the land. What if the ship could not make it? They could make it in the boats. Let her burn, then. Their lives amounted to something to them. They had served faithfully the ship, now they were going to serve themselves.

They sprang to the boats, brushing the second and third mates out of the way, and proceeded to swing the boats out and to prepare to lower away. Captain Davenport and the first mate, revolvers in hand, were advancing to the break of the poop, when McCoy, who had climbed on top of the cabin, began to speak.

He spoke to the sailors, and at the first sound of his dovelike, cooing voice they paused to hear. He extended to them his own ineffable serenity and peace. His soft voice and simple thoughts flowed out to them in a magic stream, soothing them against their wills. Long forgotten things came back to them, and some remembered lullaby songs of childhood and the content and rest of the mother's arm at the end of the day. There was no more trouble, no more danger, no more irk, in all the world. Everything was as it should be, and it was only a matter of course that they should turn their backs upon the land and put to sea once more with hell-fire hot beneath their feet.

McCoy spoke simply; but it was not what he spoke. It was his personality that spoke more eloquently than any word he could utter. It was an alchemy of soul occultly subtle and profoundly deep—a mysterious emanation of the spirit, seductive, sweetly humble, and terribly imperious. It was illumination in the dark crypts of their souls, a compulsion of purity and gentleness vastly greater than that which resided in the shining, death-spitting revolvers of the officers.

The men wavered reluctantly where they stood, and those who had loosed the turns made them fast again. Then one, and then another, and then all of them, began to sidle awkwardly away.

McCoy's face was beaming with childlike pleasure as he descended from the top of the cabin. There was no trouble. For that matter there had been no trouble averted. There never had been any trouble, for there was no place for such in the blissful world in which he lived.

"You hypnotized 'em," Mr Konig grinned at him, speaking in a low voice.

"Those boys are good," was the answer. "Their hearts are good. They have had a hard time, and they have worked hard, and they will work hard to the end."

Mr Konig had no time to reply. His voice was ringing out orders, the sailors were springing to obey, and the *Pyrenees* was paying slowly off from the wind until her bow should point in the direction of Makemo.

The wind was very light, and after sun-down almost ceased. It was insufferably warm, and fore and aft men sought vainly to sleep. The deck was too hot to lie upon, and poisonous vapors, oozing through the seams, crept like evil spirits over the ship, stealing into the nostrils and windpipes of the unwary and causing fits of sneezing and coughing. The stars blinked lazily in the dim vault overhead; and the full moon, rising in the east, touched with its light the myriads of wisps and threads and spidery films of smoke that intertwined and writhed and twisted along the deck, over the rails, and up the masts and shrouds.

"Tell me," Captain Davenport said, rubbing his smarting eyes, "what happened with that *Bounty* crowd after they reached Pitcairn? The account I read said they burnt the *Bounty*, and that they were not discovered until many years later. But what happened in the meantime? I've always been curious to know. They were men with their necks in the rope. There were some native men, too. And then there were women. That made it look like trouble right from the jump."

"There was trouble," McCoy answered. "They were bad men. They quarreled about the women right away. One of the mutineers, Williams, lost his wife. All the women were Tahitian women. His wife fell from the cliffs when hunting sea-birds. Then he took the wife of one of the native men away from him. All the native men were made very angry by this, and they killed off nearly all the mutineers. Then the mutineers that escaped killed off all the native men. The women helped. And the natives killed each other. Everybody killed everybody. They were terrible men.

"Timiti was killed by two other natives while they were combing his hair in friendship. The white men had sent them to do it. Then the white men killed them. The wife of Tullaloo killed him in a cave because she wanted a white man for husband. They were very wicked. God had hidden His face from them. At the end of two years all the native men were murdered, and all the white men except four. They were Young, John Adams, McCoy, who was my great-grandfather, and Quintal. He was a very bad man, too. Once, just because his wife did not catch enough fish for him, he bit off her ear."

"They were a bad lot!" Mr Konig exclaimed.

"Yes, they were very bad," McCoy agreed and went on serenely cooing of the blood and lust of his iniquitous ancestry. "My great-grandfather escaped murder in order to die by his own hand. He made a still and manufactured alcohol from the roots of the ti-plant. Quintal was his chum, and they got drunk together all the time. At last McCoy got delirium tremens, tied a rock to his neck and jumped into the sea.

"Quintal's wife, the one whose ear he bit off, also got killed by falling from the cliffs. Then Quintal went to Young and demanded his wife, and went to Adams and demanded his wife. Adams and Young were afraid of Quintal. They knew he would kill them. So they killed him, the two of them together, with a hatchet. Then Young died. And that was about all the trouble they had."

"I should say so," Captain Davenport snorted. "There was nobody left to kill."

"You see, God had hidden His face," McCoy said.

By morning no more than a faint air was blowing from the eastward, and, unable to make appreciable southing by it, Captain Davenport hauled up full-and-by on the port tack. He was afraid of that terrible westerly current which had cheated him out of so many ports of refuge. All day the calm continued, and all night, while the sailors, on a short ration of dried banana, were grumbling. Also, they were growing weak and complaining of stomach pains caused by the straight banana diet. All day the current swept the *Pyrenees* to the westward, while there was no wind to bear her south. In the middle of the first dog-watch, coconut-trees were sighted due south, their tufted heads rising above the water and marking the low-lying atoll beneath.

"That is Taenga Island," McCoy said. "We need a breeze to-night, or else we'll miss Makemo."

"What's become of the southeast trade?" the captain demanded. "Why don't it blow? What's the matter?"

"It is the evaporation from the big lagoons—there are so many of them," McCoy explained. "The evaporation upsets the whole system of trades. It even causes the wind to back up and blow gales from the southwest. This is the Dangerous Archipelago, Captain."

Captain Davenport faced the old man, opened his mouth, and was about to curse, but paused and refrained. McCoy's presence was a rebuke to the blasphemies that stirred in his brain and trembled in his larynx. McCoy's influence had been growing during the many days they had been together. Captain Davenport was an autocrat of the sea, fearing no man, never bridling his tongue, and now he found himself unable to curse in the presence of this old man with the feminine brown eyes and the voice of a dove. When he realized this, Captain Davenport experienced a distinct shock. This old man was merely the seed of McCoy, of McCoy of the *Bounty*, the mutineer fleeing from the hemp that waited him in England, the McCoy who was a power for evil in the early days of blood and lust and violent death on Pitcairn Island.

Captain Davenport was not religious, yet in that moment he felt a mad impulse to cast himself at the other's feet—and to say he knew not what. It was an emotion that so deeply stirred him, rather than a coherent thought, and he was aware in some vague way of his own unworthiness and smallness in the presence of this other man who possessed the simplicity of a child and the gentleness of a woman.

Of course he could not so humble himself before the eyes of his officers and men. And yet the anger that had prompted the blasphemy still raged in him. He suddenly smote the cabin with his clenched hand and cried:

"Look here, old man, I won't be beaten. These Paumotus have cheated and tricked me and made a fool of me. I refuse to be beaten. I am going to drive this ship, and drive and drive and drive clear through the Paumotus to China but what I find a bed for her. If every man deserts, I'll stay by her. I'll show the Paumotus. They can't fool me. She's a good girl, and I'll stick by her as long as there's a plank to stand on. You hear me?"

"And I'll stay with you, Captain," McCoy said.

During the night, light, baffling airs blew out of the south, and the frantic captain, with his cargo of fire, watched and measured his westward drift and went off by himself at times to curse softly so that McCoy should not hear.

Daylight showed more palms growing out of the water to the south.

"That's the leeward point of Makemo," McCoy said. "Katiu is only a few miles to the west. We may make that."

But the current, sucking between the two islands, swept them to the northwest, and at one in the afternoon they saw the palms of Katiu rise above the sea and sink back into the sea again.

A few minutes later, just as the captain had discovered that a new current from the northeast had gripped the *Pyrenees,* the masthead lookouts raised coconut palms in the northwest.

"It is Raraka," said McCoy. "We won't make it without wind. The current is drawing us down to the southwest. But we must watch out. A few miles farther on a current flows north and turns in a circle to the northwest. This will sweep us away from Fakarava, and Fakarava is the place for the *Pyrenees* to find her bed."

"They can sweep all they da—all they well please," Captain Davenport remarked with heat. "We'll find a bed for her somewhere just the same."

But the situation on the *Pyrenees* was reaching a culmination. The deck was so hot it seemed an increase of a few degrees would cause it to burst into flames. In many places even the heavy-soled shoes of the men were no protection, and they were compelled to step lively to avoid scorching their feet. The smoke had increased and grown more acrid. Every man on board was suffering from inflamed eyes, and they coughed and strangled like a crew of tuberculosis patients. In the afternoon the boats were swung out and equipped. The last several packages of dried bananas were stored in them, as well as the instruments of the officers. Captain Davenport even put the chronometer into the long-boat, fearing the blowing up of the deck at any moment.

All night this apprehension weighed heavily on all, and in the first morning light, with hollow eyes and ghastly faces, they stared at one another as if in surprise that the *Pyrenees* still held together and that they still were alive.

Walking rapidly at times, and even occasionally breaking into an undignified hop-ski-and-run, Captain Davenport inspected his ship's deck.

"It is a matter of hours now, if not of minutes," he announced on his return to the poop.

The cry of land came down from the masthead. From the deck the land was invisible, and McCoy went aloft, while the captain took advantage of the opportunity to curse some of the bitterness out of his heart. But the cursing was suddenly stopped by a dark line on the water which he sighted to the northeast. It was not a squall, but a regular breeze—the disrupted trade-wind, eight points out of its direction but resuming business once more.

"Hold her up, Captain," McCoy said as soon as he reached the poop. "That's the easterly point of Fakarava, and we'll go in through the passage full-tilt, the wind abeam and every sail drawing."

At the end of an hour, the coconut-trees and the low-lying land were visible from the deck. The feeling that the end of the *Pyrenees'* resistance was imminent weighed heavily on everybody. Captain Davenport had the three boats lowered and dropped short astern, a man in each to keep them apart. The *Pyrenees* closely skirted the shore, the surf-whitened atoll a bare two cable-lengths away.

"Get ready to wear her, Captain," McCoy warned.

And a minute later the land parted, exposing a narrow passage and the lagoon beyond, a great mirror, thirty miles in length and a third as broad.

"Now, Captain."

For the last time the yards of the *Pyrenees* swung around as she obeyed the wheel and headed into the passage. The turns had scarcely been made, and nothing had been coiled down, when the men and mates swept back to the poop in panic terror. Nothing had happened, yet they averred that something was going to happen. They could not tell why. They merely knew that it was about to happen. McCoy started forward to take up his position on the bow in order to con the vessel in; but the captain gripped his arm and whirled him around.

"Do it from here," he said. "That deck's not safe. What's the matter?" he demanded the next instant. "We're standing still."

McCoy smiled.

"You are bucking a seven-knot current, Captain," he said. "That is the way the full ebb runs out of this passage."

At the end of another hour the *Pyrenees* had scarcely gained her length, but the wind freshened and she began to forge ahead.

"Better get into the boats, some of you," Captain Davenport commanded.

His voice was still ringing, and the men were just beginning to move in obedience, when the amidship deck of the *Pyrenees*, in a mass of flame and smoke, was flung upward into the sails and rigging, part of it remaining there and the rest falling into the sea. The wind being abeam, was what had saved the men crowded aft. They made a blind rush to gain the boats, but McCoy's voice, carrying its convincing message of vast calm and endless time, stopped them.

"Take it easy," he was saying. "Everything is all right. Pass that boy down somebody, please."

The man at the wheel had forsaken it in a funk, and Captain Davenport had leaped and caught the spokes in time to prevent the ship from yawing in the current and going ashore.

"Better take charge of the boats," he said to Mr Konig. "Tow one of them short, right under the quarter . . . When I go over, it'll be on the jump."

Mr Konig hesitated, then went over the rail and lowered himself into the boat.

"Keep her off half a point, Captain."

Captain Davenport gave a start. He had thought he had the ship to himself.

"Ay, ay; half a point it is," he answered.

Amidships the *Pyrenees* was an open, flaming furnace, out of which poured an immense volume of smoke which rose high above the masts and completely hid the forward part of the ship. McCoy, in the shelter of the mizzen-shrouds, continued his difficult task of conning the ship through the intricate channel. The fire was working aft along the deck from the seat of explosion, while the soaring tower of canvas on the mainmast went up and vanished in a sheet of flame. Forward, though they could not see them, they knew that the head-sails were still drawing.

"If only she don't burn all her canvas off before she makes inside," the captain groaned.

"She'll make it," McCoy assured him with supreme confidence. "There is plenty of time. She is bound to make it. And once inside, we'll put her before it; that will keep the smoke away from us and hold back the fire from working aft."

A tongue of flame sprang up the mizzen, reached hungrily for the lowest tier of canvas, missed it, and vanished. From aloft a burning shred of rope-stuff fell square on the back of Captain Davenport's neck. He acted with the celerity of one stung by a bee as he reached up and brushed the offending fire from his skin.

"How is she heading, Captain?"

"Nor'west by west."

"Keep her west-nor'west."

Captain Davenport put the wheel up and steadied her.

"West by north, Captain."

"West by north she is."

"And now west."

Slowly, point by point, as she entered the lagoon, the *Pyrenees* described the circle that put her before the wind; and point by point, with all the calm certitude of a thousand years of time to spare, McCoy chanted the changing course.

"Another point, Captain."

"A point it is."

Captain Davenport whirled several spokes over, suddenly reversing and coming back one to check her.

"Steady."

"Steady she is—right on it."

Despite the fact that the wind was now astern, the heat was so intense that Captain Davenport was compelled to steal sidelong glances into the binnacle, letting go the wheel, now with one hand, now with the other, to rub or shield his blistering cheeks. McCoy's beard was crinkling and shrivelling and the smell of it, strong in the other's nostrils, compelled him to look toward McCoy with sudden solicitude. Captain Davenport was letting go the spokes alternately with his hands in order to rub their blistering backs against his trousers. Every sail on the mizzenmast vanished in a rush of flame, compelling the two men to crouch and shield their faces.

"Now," said McCoy, stealing a glance ahead at the low shore, "four points up, Captain, and let her drive."

Shreds and patches of burning rope and canvas were falling about them and upon them. The tarry smoke from a smouldering piece of rope at the captain's feet set him off into a violent coughing fit, during which he still clung to the spokes.

The *Pyrenees* struck, her bow lifted, and she ground ahead gently to a stop. A shower of burning fragments, dislodged by the shock, fell about them. The ship moved ahead again and struck a second time. She crushed the fragile coral under her keel, drove on, and struck a third time.

"Hard over," said McCoy. "Hard over?" he questioned gently, a minute later.

"She won't answer," was the reply.

"All right. She is swinging around." McCoy peered over the side. "Soft, white sand. Couldn't ask better. A beautiful bed."

As the *Pyrenees* swung around her stern away from the wind, a fearful blast of smoke and flame poured aft. Captain Davenport deserted the wheel in blistering agony. He reached the painter of the boat that lay under the quarter, then looked for McCoy, who was standing aside to let him go down.

"You first," the captain cried, gripping him by the shoulder and almost throwing him over the rail. But the flame and smoke were too terrible, and he followed hard after McCoy, both men wriggling on the rope and sliding down into the boat together. A sailor in the bow, without waiting for orders, slashed the painter through with his sheath-knife. The oars, poised in readiness, bit into the water, and the boat shot away.

"A beautiful bed, Captain," McCoy murmured, looking back.

"Ay, a beautiful bed, and all thanks to you," was the answer.

The three boats pulled away for the white beach of pounded coral, beyond which, on the edge of a coconut grove, could be seen a half-dozen grass-houses, and a score or more of excited natives, gazing wide-eyed at the conflagration that had come to land.

The boats grounded and they stepped out on the white beach.

"And now," said McCoy, "I must see about getting back to Pitcairn."

Good-by, Jack

Hawaii is a queer place. Everything socially is what I may call topsy-turvy. Not but what things are correct. They are almost too much so. But still things are sort of upside down. The most ultra-exclusive set there is the "Missionary Crowd" . It comes with rather a shock to learn that in Hawaii the obscure, martyrdom-seeking missionary sits at the head of the table of the moneyed aristocracy. But it is true. The humble New Englanders who came out in the third decade of the nineteenth century, came for the lofty purpose of teaching the kanakas the true religion, the worship of the one only genuine and undeniable God. So well did they succeed in this, and also in civilizing the kanaka, that by the second or third generation he was practically extinct. This being the fruit of the seed of the Gospel, the fruit of the seed of the missionaries (the sons and the grandsons) was the possession of the islands themselves—of the land, the ports, the town sites and the sugar plantations. The missionary who came to give the bread of life remained to gobble up the whole heathen feast.

But that is not the Hawaiian queerness I started out to tell. Only one cannot speak of things Hawaiian without mentioning the missionaries. There is Jack Kersdale, the man I wanted to tell about; he came of missionary stock. That is, on his grandmother's side. His grandfather was old Benjamin Kersdale, a Yankee trader, who got his start for a million in the old days by selling cheap whiskey and square-face gin. There's another queer thing. The old missionaries and old traders were mortal enemies. You see, their interests conflicted. But their children made it up by inter-marrying and dividing the islands between them.

Life in Hawaii is a song. That's the way Stoddard put it in his "Hawaii Noi" :

> *"Thy life is music—Fate the notes prolong!*
> *Each isle a stanza, and the whole a song."*

And he was right. Flesh is golden there. The native women are sun-ripe Junos, the native men bronzed Apollos. They sing, and dance, and all are flower-bejewelled and flower-crowned. And, outside the rigid "Missionary Crowd" , the white men yield to the climate and the sun, and no matter how busy they may be, are prone to dance and sing and wear flowers behind their ears and in their hair. Jack Kersdale was one of these fellows. He was one of the busiest men I ever met. He was a several-times millionaire. He was a sugar king, a coffee planter, a rubber pioneer, a cattle rancher and a promoter of three out of every four new enterprises launched in the islands. He was a society man, a club man, a yachtsman, a bachelor, and withal as handsome a man as was ever doted upon by mamas with marriageable daughters. Incidentally, he had finished his education at Yale, and his head was crammed fuller with vital statistics and scholarly information concerning Hawaii Nei than any other islander I ever encountered. He turned off an immense amount of work, and he sang and danced and put flowers in his hair as immensely as any of the idlers.

He had grit, and had fought two duels—both political—when he was no more than a raw youth essaying his first adventures in politics. In fact, he played a most creditable and courageous part in the last revolution, when the native dynasty was overthrown;

and he could not have been over sixteen at the time. I am pointing out that he was no coward, in order that you may appreciate what happens later on. I've seen him in the breaking yard at the Haleakala Ranch, conquering a four-year-old brute that for two years had defied the pick of Von Tempsky's cowboys. And I must tell of one other thing. It was down in Kona—or up, rather, for the Kona people scorn to live at less than a thousand feet elevation. We were all on the *lanai* of Doctor Goodhue's bungalow. I was talking with Dottie Fairchild when it happened. A big centipede—it was seven inches, for we measured it afterward—fell from the rafters overhead squarely into her coiffure. I confess, the hideousness of it paralyzed me. I couldn't move. My mind refused to work. There, within two feet of me, the ugly venomous devil was writhing in her hair. It threatened at any moment to fall down upon her exposed shoulders—we had just come out from dinner.

"What is it?" she asked, starting to raise her hand to her head.

"Don't!" I cried. "Don't!"

"But what is it?" she insisted, growing frightened by the fright she read in my eyes and on my stammering lips.

My exclamation attracted Kersdale's attention. He glanced our way carelessly, but in that glance took in everything. He came over to us, but without haste.

"Please don't move, Dottie," he said quietly.

He never hesitated, nor did he hurry and make a bungle of it.

"Allow me," he said.

And with one hand he caught her scarf and drew it tightly around her shoulders so that the centipede could not fall inside her bodice. With the other hand—the right—he reached into her hair, caught the repulsive abomination as near as he was able by the nape of the neck, and held it tightly between thumb and forefinger as he withdrew it from her hair. It was as horrible and heroic a sight as man could wish to see. It made my flesh crawl. The centipede, seven inches of squirming legs, writhed and twisted and dashed itself about his hand, the body twining around the fingers and the legs digging into the skin and scratching as the beast endeavored to free itself. It bit him twice—I saw it—though he assured the ladies that he was not harmed as he dropped it upon the walk and stamped it into the gravel. But I saw him in the surgery five minutes afterward, with Doctor Goodhue scarifying the wounds and injecting permanganate of potash. The next morning Kersdale's arm was as big as a barrel, and it was three weeks before the swelling went down.

All of which has nothing to do with my story, but which I could not avoid giving in order to show that Jack Kersdale was anything but a coward. It was the cleanest exhibition of grit I have ever seen. He never turned a hair. The smile never left his lips. And he dived with thumb and forefinger into Dottie Fairchild's hair as gayly as if it had been a box of salted almonds. Yet that was the man I was destined to see stricken with fear a thousand times more hideous even than the fear that was mine when I saw that writhing abomination in Dottie Fairchild's hair, dangling over her eyes and the trap of her bodice.

I was interested in leprosy, and upon that, as upon every other island subject, Kersdale had encyclopedic knowledge. In fact, leprosy was one of his hobbies. He was an ardent defender of the settlement at Molokai, where all the island lepers were segregated. There was much talk and feeling among the natives, fanned by the demagogues, concerning the cruelties of Molokai, where men and women, not alone banished from friends and family, were compelled to live in perpetual imprisonment until they died. There were no reprieves, no commutations of sentances. "Abandon hope" was written over the portal of Molokai.

"I tell you they are happy there," Kersdale insisted. "And they are infinitely better off than their friends and relatives outside who have nothing the matter with them. The horrors of Molokai are all poppycock. I can take you through any hospital or any slum in any of the great cities of the world and show you a thousand times worse horrors. The living death! The creatures that once were men! Bosh! You ought to see those living deaths racing horses on the Fourth of July. Some of them own boats. One has a gasolene launch. They have nothing to do but have a good time. Food, shelter, clothes, medical attendance, everything is theirs. They are the wards of the Territory. They have a much finer climate than Honolulu, and the scenery is magnificent. I shouldn't mind going down there myself for the rest of my days. It is a lovely spot."

So Kersdale on the joyous leper. He was not afraid of leprosy. He said so himself, and that there wasn't one chance in a million for him or any other white man to catch it, though he confessed afterward that one of his school chums, Alfred Starter, had contracted it, gone to Molokai, and there died.

"You know, in the old days," Kersdale explained, "there was no certain test for leprosy. Anything unusual or abnormal was sufficient to send a fellow to Molokai. The result was that dozens were sent there who were no more lepers than you or I. But they don't make that mistake now. The Board of Health tests are infallible. The funny thing is that when the test was discovered they immediately went down to Molokai and applied it, and they found a number who were not lepers. They were immediately deported. Happy to get away? They wailed harder at leaving the settlement than when they left Honolulu to go to it. Some refused to leave, and really had to be forced out. One of them even married a leper woman in the last stages and then wrote pathetic letters to the Board of Health, protesting against his expulsion on the ground that no one was so well able as he to take care of his poor old wife."

"What is this infallible test?" I demanded.

"The bacteriological test. There is no getting away from it. Doctor Hervey—he's our expert, you know—was the first man to apply it here. He is a wizard. He knows more about leprosy than any living man, and if a cure is ever discovered, he'll be that discoverer. As for the test, it is very simple. They have succeeded in isolating the *bacillus deprae* and studying it. They know it now when they see it. All they do is to snip a bit of skin from the suspect and subject it to the bacteriological test. A man without any visible symptoms may be chock full of the leprosy bacilli."

"Then you or I, for all we know," I suggested, "may be full of it now."

Kersdale shrugged his shoulders and laughed.

"Who can say? It takes seven years for it to incubate. If you have any doubts go and see Doctor Hervey. He'll just snip out a piece of your skin and let you know in a jiffy."

Later on he introduced me to Dr Hervey, who loaded me down with Board of Health reports and pamphlets on the subject, and took me out to Kalihi, the Honolulu receiving station, where suspects were examined and confirmed lepers were held for deportation to Molokai. These deportations occurred about once a month, when, the last good-bys said, the lepers were marched on board the little steamer, the *Noeau,* and carried down to the settlement.

One afternoon, writing letters at the club, Jack Kersdale dropped in on me.

"Just the man I want to see," was his greeting. "I'll show you the saddest aspect of the whole situation—the lepers wailing as they depart for Molokai. The *Noeau* will be taking them on board in a few minutes. But let me warn you not to let your feelings be harrowed. Real as their grief is, they'd wail a whole sight harder a year hence if the Board of Health tried to take them away from Molokai. We've just time for a whiskey and soda. I've a carriage outside. It won't take us five minutes to get down to the wharf."

To the wharf we drove. Some forty sad wretches, amid their mats, blankets and luggage of various sorts, were squatting on the stringer piece. The *Noeau* had just arrived and was making fast to a lighter that lay between her and the wharf. A Mr McVeigh, the superintendent of the settlement, was overseeing the embarkation, and to him I was introduced, also to Dr Georges, one of the Board of Health physicians whom I had already met at Kalihi. The lepers were a woebegone lot. The faces of the majority were hideous—too horrible for me to describe. But here and there I noticed fairly good-looking persons, with no apparent signs of the fell disease upon them. One, I noticed, a little white girl, not more than twelve, with blue eyes and golden hair. One cheek, however, showed the leprous bloat. On my remarking upon the sadness of her alien situation among the brown-skinned afflicted ones, Doctor Georges replied:

"Oh, I don't know. It's a happy day in her life. She comes from Kauai. Her father is a brute. And now that she has developed the disease she is going to join her mother at the settlement. Her mother was sent down three years ago—a very bad case."

"You can't always tell from appearances," Mr McVeigh explained. "That man there, that big chap, who looks the pink of condition, with nothing the matter with him, I happen to know has a perforating ulcer in his foot and another in his shoulder blade. Then there are others—there, see that girl's hand, the one who is smoking the cigarette. See her twisted fingers. That's the anaesthetic form. It attacks the nerves. You could cut her fingers off with a dull knife, or rub them off on a nutmeg-grater, and she would not experience the slightest sensation."

"Yes, but that fine-looking woman, there," I persisted; "surely, surely, there can't be anything the matter with her. She is too glorious and gorgeous altogether."

"A sad case," Mr McVeigh answered over his shoulder, already turning away to walk down the wharf with Kersdale.

She was a beautiful woman, and she was pure Polynesian. From my meagre knowledge of the race and its types I could not but conclude that she had descended from old chief stock. She could not have been more than twenty-three or four. Her lines and proportions were magnificent, and she was just beginning to show the amplitude of the women of her race.

"It was a blow to all of us," Dr Georges volunteered. "She gave herself up voluntarily, too. No one suspected. But somehow she had contracted the disease. It broke us all up, I assure you. We've kept it out of the papers, though. Nobody but us and her family knows what has become of her. In fact, if you were to ask any man in Honolulu, he'd tell you it was his impression that she was somewhere in Europe. It was at her request that we've been so quiet about it. Poor girl, she has a lot of pride."

"But who is she?" I asked. "Certainly, from the way you talk about her, she must be somebody."

"Did you ever hear of Lucy Mokunui?" he asked.

"Lucy Mokunui?" I repeated, haunted by some familiar association. I shook my head. "It seems to me I've heard the name, but I've forgotten it."

"Never heard of Lucy Mokunui! The Hawaiian nightingale! I beg your pardon. Of course you are a *malahini,* * and could not be expected to know. Well, Lucy Mokunui was the best beloved of Honolulu—of all Hawaii, for that matter."

"You say was," I interrupted.

"And I mean it. She is finished." He shrugged his shoulders pityingly. "A dozen *haoles*— I beg your pardon, white men—have lost their hearts to her at one time or another. And I'm not counting in the ruck. The dozen I refer to were *haoles* of position and prominence.

"She could have married the son of the Chief Justice if she'd wanted to. You think she's beautiful, eh? But you should hear her sing. Finest native woman singer in Hawaii Nei. Her throat is pure silver and melted sunshine. We adored her. She toured America first with the Royal Hawaiian Band. After that she made two more trips on her own—concert work."

"Oh!" I cried. "I remember now. I heard her two years ago at the Boston Symphony. So that is she. I recognize her now."

I was oppressed by a heavy sadness. Life was a futile thing at best. A short two years and this magnificent creature, at the summit of her magnificent success, was one of the leper squad awaiting deportation to Molokai. Henley's lines came into my mind:

"The poor old tramp explains his poor old ulcers;
Life is, I think, a blunder and a shame."

I recoiled from my own future. If this awful fate fell to Lucy Mokunui, what might not my lot be?—or anybody's lot? I was thoroughly aware that in life we are in the midst of death—but to be in the midst of living death, to die and not be dead, to be one of that draft of creatures that once were men, ay, and women, like Lucy Mokunui, the epitome of all Polynesian charms, an artist as well, and well beloved of men—I am afraid I must have betrayed my perturbation, for Doctor Georges hastened to assure me that they were very happy down in the settlement.

It was all too inconceivably monstrous. I could not bear to look at her. A short distance away, behind a stretched rope guarded by a policeman, were the lepers' relatives and friends. They were not allowed to come near. There were no last embraces, no kisses of farewell. They called back and forth to one another—last messages, last words of love, last reiterated instructions. And those behind the rope looked with terrible intensity. It was the last time they would behold the faces of their loved ones, for they were the living dead, being carted away in the funeral ship to the graveyard of Molokai.

Doctor Georges gave the command, and the unhappy wretches dragged themselves to their feet and under their burdens of luggage began to stagger across the lighter and aboard the steamer. It was the funeral procession. At once the wailing started from those behind the rope. It was blood-curdling; it was heart-rending. I never heard such woe, and I hope never to again. Kersdale and McVeigh were still at the other end of the wharf, talking earnestly—politics, of course, for both were head-over-heels in that particular game. When Lucy Mokunui passed me, I stole a look at her. She *was* beautiful. She was beautiful by our standards as well—one of those rare blossoms that occur but once in generations. And she, of all women, was doomed to Molokai. She walked like a queen, across the lighter, straight on board, and aft on the open deck where the lepers huddled by the rail, wailing, now, to their dear ones on shore.

The lines were cast off, and the *Noeau* began to move away from the wharf. The

* *Malahini*— newcomer.

wailing increased. Such grief and despair! I was just resolving that never again would I be a witness to the sailing of the *Noeau,* when McVeigh and Kersdale returned. The latter's eyes were sparkling, and his lips could not quite hide the smile of delight that was his. Evidently the politics they had talked had been satisfactory. The rope had been flung aside, and the lamenting relatives now crowded the stringer piece on either side of us.

"That's her mother," Doctor Georges whispered, indicating an old woman next to me, who was rocking back and forth and gazing at the steamer rail out of tear-blinded eyes. I noticed that Lucy Mokunui was also wailing. She stopped abruptly and gazed at Kersdale. Then she stretched forth her arms in that adorable, sensuous way that Olga Nethersole has of embracing an audience. And with arms outspread, she cried:

"Good-by, Jack! Good-by!"

He heard the cry, and looked. Never was a man overtaken by more crushing fear. He reeled on the stringer piece, his face went white to the roots of his hair, and he seemed to shrink and wither away inside his clothes. He threw up his hands and groaned, "My God! My God!" Then he controlled himself by a great effort.

"Good-by, Lucy! Good-by!" he called.

And he stood there on the wharf, waving his hands to her till the *Noeau* was clear away and the faces lining her after-rail were vague and indistinct.

"I thought you knew," said McVeigh, who had been regarding him curiously. "You, of all men, should have known. I thought that was why you were here."

"I know now," Kersdale answered with immense gravity. "Where's the carriage?"

He walked rapidly—half-ran—to it. I had to half-run myself to keep up with him.

"Drive to Doctor Hervey's," he told the driver. "Drive as fast as you can."

He sank down in the seat, panting and gasping. The pallor of his face had increased. His lips were compressed and the sweat was standing out on his forehead and upper lip. He seemed in some horrible agony.

"For God's sake, Martin, make those horses go!" he broke out suddenly. "Lay the whip into them!—do you hear?—lay the whip into them!"

"They'll break, sir," the driver remonstrated.

"Let them break," Kersdale answered. "I'll pay your fine and square you with the police. Put it to them. That's right. Faster! Faster!

"And I never knew, I never knew," he muttered, sinking back in the seat and with trembling hands wiping the sweat away.

The carriage was bouncing, swaying and lurching around corners at such a wild pace as to make conversation impossible. Besides, there was nothing to say. But I could hear him muttering over and over, "And I never knew. I never knew."

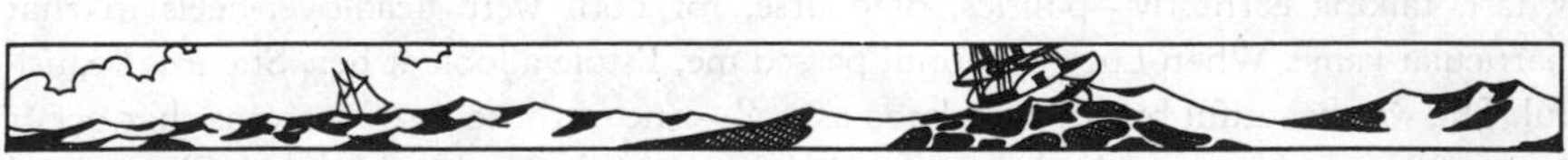

The Bones of Kahekili

From over the lofty Koolau Mountains, vagrant wisps of the trade wind drifted, faintly swaying the great, unwhipped banana leaves, rustling the palms, and fluttering and setting up a whispering among the lace-leaved algaroba trees. Only intermittently did the atmosphere so breathe—for breathing it was, the suspiring of the languid, Hawaiian afternoon. In the intervals between the soft breathings, the air grew heavy and balmy with the perfume of flowers and the exhalations of fat, living soil.

Of humans about the low bungalow-like house, there were many; but one only of them slept. The rest were on the tense tiptoes of silence. At the rear of the house a tiny babe piped up a thin blatting wail that the quickly thrust breast could not appease. The mother, a slender *hapa-haole* (half-white), clad in a loose-flowing *holoku* of white muslin, hastened away swiftly among the banana and papaia trees to remove the babe's noise by distance. Other women, *hapa-haole* and full native, watched her anxiously as she fled.

At the front of the house, on the grass, squatted a score of Hawaiians. Well-muscled, broad-shouldered, they were all strapping men. Brown-skinned, with luminous brown eyes and black, their features large and regular, they showed all the signs of being as good-natured, merry-hearted and soft-tempered as the climate. To all of which a seeming contradiction was given by the ferociousness of their accoutrement. Into the tops of their rough leather leggings were thrust long knives, the handles projecting. On their heels were huge-rowelled Spanish spurs. They had the appearance of banditti, save for the incongruous wreaths of flowers and fragrant *maile* that encircled the crowns of their flopping cowboy hats. One of them, deliciously and roguishly handsome as a faun, with the eyes of a faun, wore a flaming double-hibiscus bloom coquettishly tucked over his ear. Above them, casting a shelter of shade from the sun, grew a wide-spreading canopy of *Ponciana regia,* itself a flame of blossoms, out of each of which sprang pom-poms of feathery stamens. From far off, muffled by distance, came the faint stamping of their tethered horses. The eyes of all were intently fixed upon the solitary sleeper who lay on his back on a *lauhala* mat a hundred feet away under the monkey-pod trees.

Large as were the Hawaiian cowboys, the sleeper was larger. Also, as his snow-white hair and beard attested, he was much older. The thickness of his wrist and the greatness of his fingers made authentic the mighty frame of him hidden under loose dungaree pants and cotton shirt, buttonless, open from midriff to Adam's apple, exposing a chest matted with a thatch of hair as white as that of his head and face. The depth and breadth of that chest, its resilience, and its relaxed and plastic muscles, tokened the knotty strength that still resided in him. Further, no bronze and beat of sun and wind availed to hide the testimony of his skin that he was all *haole*— a white man.

On his back, his great white beard, thrust skyward, untrimmed of barbers, stiffened and subsided with every breath, while with the outblow of every exhalation the white mustache erected perpendicularly like the quills of a porcupine and subsided with each intake. A young girl of fourteen, clad only in a single shift, or *muumuu,* herself a granddaughter of the sleeper, crouched beside him and with a feathered fly-flapper brushed away the flies. In her face were depicted solicitude, and nervousness, and awe, as if she attended on a god.

And truly, Hardman Pool, the sleeping whiskery one, was to her, and to many and sundry, a god—a source of life, a source of food, a fount of wisdom, a giver of law, a smiling beneficence, a blackness of thunder and punishment—in short, a man-master whose record was fourteen living and adult sons and daughters, six great-grandchildren, and more grandchildren than could he in his most lucid moments enumerate.

Fifty-one years before, he had landed from an open boat at Laupahoehoe on the windward coast of Hawaii. The boat was the one surviving one of the whaler *Black Prince* of New Bedford. Himself New Bedford born, twenty years of age, by virtue of his driving strength and ability he had served as second mate on the lost whaleship. Coming to Honolulu and casting about for himself, he had first married Kalama Mamaiopili, next acted as pilot of Honolulu Harbour, after that started a saloon and boarding house, and, finally, on the death of Kalama's father, engaged in cattle ranching on the broad pasture lands she had inherited.

For over half a century he had lived with the Hawaiians, and it was conceded that he knew their language better than did most of them. By marrying Kalama, he had married not merely her land, but her own chief rank, and the fealty owed by the commoners to her by virtue of her genealogy was also accorded him. In addition, he possessed of himself all the natural attributes of chiefship: the gigantic stature, the fearlessness, the pride; and the high hot temper that could brook no impudence nor insult, that could be neither bullied nor awed by any utmost magnificence of power that walked on two legs, and that could compel service of lesser humans, not by any ignoble purchase by bargaining, but by an unspoken but expected condescending of largesse. He knew his Hawaiians from the outside and the in, knew them better than themselves, their Polynesian circumlocutions, faiths, customs and mysteries.

And at seventy-one, after a morning in the saddle over the ranges that began at four o'clock, he lay under the monkey-pods in his customary and sacred siesta that no retainer dared to break, nor would dare permit any equal of the great one to break. Only to the King was such a right accorded, and, as the King had early learned, to break Hardman Pool's siesta was to gain awake a very irritable and grumpy Hardman Pool who would talk straight from the shoulder and say unpleasant but true things that no king would care to hear.

The sun blazed down. The horses stamped remotely. The fading trade-wind wisps sighed and rustled between longer intervals of quiescence. The perfume grew heavier. The woman brought back the babe, quiet again, to the rear of the house. The monkey-pods folded their leaves and swooned to a siesta of their own in the soft air above the sleeper. The girl, breathless as ever from the enormous solemnity of her task, still brushed the flies away; and the score of cowboys still intently and silently watched.

Hardman Pool awoke. The next out-breath, expected of the long rhythm, did not take place. Neither did the white, long mustache rise up. Instead, the cheeks, under the whiskers, puffed; the eyelids lifted, exposing blue eyes, choleric and fully and immediately conscious; the right hand went out to the half-smoked pipe beside him, while the left hand reached the matches.

"Get me my gin and milk," he ordered, in Hawaiian, of the little maid, who had been startled into a tremble by his awakening.

He lighted the pipe, but gave no sign of awareness of the presence of his waiting retainers until the tumbler of gin and milk had been brought and drunk.

"Well?" he demanded abruptly, and in the pause, while twenty faces wreathed in smiles and twenty pairs of dark eyes glowed luminously with well-wishing pleasure, he wiped the lingering drops of gin and milk from his hairy lips. "What are you hanging around for? What do you want? Come over here."

Twenty giants, most of them young, uprose and with a great clanking and jangling of spurs and spur-chains strode over to him. They grouped before him in a semicircle, trying bashfully to wedge their shoulders, one behind another's, their faces a-grin and apologetic, and at the same time expressing a casual and unconscious democraticness. In truth, to them Hardman Pool was more than mere chief. He was elder brother, or father, or patriarch; and to all of them he was related, in one way or another, according to Hawaiian custom, through his wife and through the many marriages of his children and grandchildren. His slightest frown might perturb them, his anger terrify them, his command compel them to certain death; yet, on the other hand, not one of them would have dreamed of addressing him otherwise than intimately by his first name, which name, "Hardman," was transmuted by their tongues into Kanaka Oolea.

At a nod from him, the semicircle seated itself on the *manienie* grass, and with further deprecatory smiles waited his pleasure.

"What do you want?" he demanded, in Hawaiian, with a brusqueness and sternness they knew were put on.

They smiled more broadly, and deliciously squirmed their broad shoulders and great torsos with the appeasingness of so many wriggling puppies. Hardman Pool singled out one of them.

"Well, Iliiopoi, what do *you* want?"

"Ten dollars, Kanaka Oolea."

"Ten dollars!" Pool cried, in apparent shock at mention of so vast a sum. "Does it mean you are going to take a second wife? Remember the missionary teaching. One wife at a time, Iliiopoi; one wife at a time. For he who entertains a plurality of wives will surely go to hell."

Giggles and flashings of laughing eyes from all greeted the joke.

"No, Kanaka Oolea," came the reply. "The devil knows I am hard put to get *kow-kow* for one wife and her several relations."

"*Kow-kow?*" Pool repeated the Chinese-introduced word for food which the Hawaiians had come to substitute for their own *paina.* "Didn't you boys get *kow-kow* here this noon?"

"Yes, Kanaka Oolea," volunteered an old, withered native who had just joined the group from the direction of the house. "All of them had *kow-kow* in the kitchen, and plenty of it. They ate like lost horses brought down from the lava."

"And what do you want, Kumuhana?" Pool diverted to the old one, at the same time motioning to the little maid to flap flies from the other side of him.

"Twelve dollars," said Kumuhana. "I want to buy a jackass and a second-hand saddle and bridle. I am growing too old for my legs to carry me in walking."

"You wait," his *haole* lord commanded. "I will talk with you about the matter, and about other things of importance, when I am finished with the rest and they are gone."

The withered old one nodded and proceeded to light his pipe.

"The *kow-kow* in the kitchen was good," Iliiopoi resumed, licking his lips. "The *poi* was one-finger, the pig fat, the salmon-belly unstinking, the fish of great freshness and plenty, though the *opihis*" (tiny, rock-climbing shell-fish) "had been salted and thereby made tough. Never should the *opihis* be salted. Often have I told you, Kanaka Oolea, the *opihis* should never be salted. I am full of good *kow-kow.* My belly is heavy with it. Yet is my heart not light of it because there is no *kow-kow* in my own house, where is my wife, who is the aunt of your fourth son's second wife, and where is my baby daughter, and my wife's old mother, and my wife's old mother's feeding child that is a cripple, and my wife's sister who lives likewise with us along with her three children, the father being dead of a wicked dropsy—"

"Will five dollars save all of you from funerals for a day or several?" Pool testily cut the tale short.

"Yes, Kanaka Oolea, and as well it will buy my wife a new comb and some tobacco for myself."

From a gold-sack drawn from the hip-pocket of his dungarees, Hardman Pool drew the gold piece and tossed it accurately into the waiting hand.

To a bachelor who wanted six dollars for new leggings, tobacco and spurs, three dollars were given; the same to another who needed a hat; and to a third, who modestly asked for two dollars, four were given with a flowery-worded compliment anent his prowess in roping a recent wild bull from the mountains. They knew, as a rule, that he cut their requisitions in half, therefore they doubled the size of their requisitions. And Hardman Pool knew they doubled, and smiled to himself. It was his way, and, further, it was a very good way with his multitudinous relatives, and did not reduce his stature in their esteem.

"And you, Ahuhu?" he demanded of one whose name meant "poison-wood".

"And the price of a pair of dungarees," Ahuhu concluded his list of needs. "I have ridden much and hard after your cattle, Kanaka Oolea, and where my dungarees have pressed against the seat of the saddle there is no seat to my dungarees. It is not well that it be said that a Kanaka Oolea cowboy, who is also a cousin of Kanaka Oolea's wife's half-sister, should be shamed to be seen out of the saddle save that he walks backward from all that behold him."

"The price of a dozen pairs of dungarees be thine, Ahuhu," Hardman Pool beamed, tossing to him the necessary sum. "I am proud that my family shares my pride. Afterward, Ahuhu, out of the dozen dungarees you will give me one, else shall I be compelled to walk backward, my own and only dungarees being in like manner well worn and shameful."

And in laughter of love at their *haole* chief's final sally, all the sweet-child-minded and physically gorgeous company of them departed to their waiting horses, save the old withered one, Kumuhana, who had been bidden to wait.

For a full five minutes they sat in silence. Then Hardman Pool ordered the little maid to fetch a tumbler of gin and milk, which, when she brought it, he nodded her to hand to Kumuhana. The glass did not leave his lips until it was empty, whereupon he gave a great audible out-breath of "A-a-ah," and smacked his lips.

"Much *awa* have I drunk in my time," he said reflectively. "Yet is the *awa* but a common man's drink, while the *haole* liquor is a drink for chiefs. The *awa* has not the liquor's hot willingness, its spur in the ribs of feeling, its biting alive of oneself that is very pleasant since it is pleasant to be alive."

Hardman Pool smiled, nodded agreement, and old Kumuhana continued.

"There is a warmingness to it. It warms the belly and the soul. It warms the heart. Even the soul and the heart grow cold when one is old."

"You *are* old," Pool conceded. "Almost as old as I."

Kumuhana shook his head and murmured, "Were I no older than you I would be as young as you."

"I am seventy-one," said Pool.

"I do not know ages that way," was the reply. "What happened when you were born?"

"Let me see," Pool calculated. "This is 1880. Subtract seventy-one, and it leaves nine. I was born in 1809, which is the year Keliimakai died, which is the year the Scotchman, Archibald Campbell, lived in Honolulu."

"Then I am truly older than you, Kanaka Oolea. I remember the Scotchman well, for I was playing among the grass houses of Honolulu at the time, and already riding a surfboard in the *wahine*" (woman) "surf at Waikiki. I can take you now to the spot where was the Scotchman's grass house. The Seaman's Mission stands now on the very ground. Yet do I know when I was born. Often my grandmother and my mother told me of it. I was born when Madame Pele" (the Fire Goddess or Volcano Goddess) "became angry with the people of Paiea because they sacrificed no fish to her from their fish-pool, and she sent down a flow of lava from Huulalai and filled up their pond. For ever was the fish-pond of Paiea filled up. That was when I was born."

"That was in 1801, when James Boyd was building ships for Kamehameha at Hilo," Pool cast back through the calendar; "which makes you seventy-nine, or eight years older than I. You are very old."

"Yes, Kanaka Oolea," muttered Kumuhana, pathetically attempting to swell his shrunken chest with pride.

"And you are very wise."

"Yes, Kanaka Oolea."

"And you know many of the secret things that are known only to old men."

"Yes, Kanaka Oolea."

"And then you know—" Hardman Pool broke off, the more effectively to impress and hypnotize the other ancient with the set stare of his pale-washed blue eyes. "They say the bones of Kahekili were taken from their hiding-place and lie to-day in the Royal Mausoleum. I have heard it whispered that you alone of all living men truly know."

"I know," was the proud answer. "I alone know."

"Well, do they lie there? Yes or no?"

"Kahekili was an *alii*" (high chief). "It is from this straight line that your wife Kalama came. She is an *alii.*" The old retainer paused and pursed his lean lips in meditation. "I belong to her, as all my people before me belonged to her people before her. She only can command the great secrets of me. She is wise, too wise ever to command me to speak this secret. To you, O Kanaka Oolea, I do not answer yes, I do not answer no. This is a secret of the *aliis* that even the *aliis* do not know."

"Very good, Kumuhana," Hardman Pool commended. "Yet do you forget that I am an *alii,* and that what my good Kalama does not dare ask, I command to ask. I can send for her, now, and tell her to command your answer. But such would be a foolishness unless you prove yourself doubly foolish. Tell me the secret, and she will never know. A woman's lips must pour out whatever flows in through her ears, being so made. I am a man, and man is differently made. As you well know, my lips suck tight on secrets as a squid sucks to the salty rock. If you will not tell me alone, then will you tell Kalama and me together, and her lips will talk, her lips will talk, so that the latest *malahini* will shortly know what, otherwise, you and I alone will know."

Long time Kumuhana sat on in silence, debating the argument and finding no way to evade the fact-logic of it.

"Great is your *haole* wisdom," he conceded at last.

"Yes? or no?" Hardman Pool drove home the point of his steel.

Kumuhana looked about him first, then slowly let his eyes come to rest on the fly-flapping maid.

"Go," Pool commanded her. "And come not back without you hear a clapping of my hands."

Hardman Pool spoke no further, even after the flapper had disappeared into the house; yet his face adamantly looked: "Yes?—or no?"

Again Kumuhana looked carefully about him, and up into the monkey-pod boughs as if to apprehend a lurking listener. His lips were very dry. With his tongue he moistened them repeatedly. Twice he essayed to speak, but was inarticulately husky. And finally, with bowed head, he whispered, so low and solemnly that Hardman Pool bent his own head to hear: "No."

Pool clapped his hands, and the little maid ran out of the house to him in tremulous, fluttery haste.

"Bring a milk and gin for old Kumuhana, here," Pool commanded; and, to Kumuhana: "Now tell me the whole story."

"Wait," was the answer. "Wait till the little *wahine* has come and gone."

And when the maid was gone, and the gin and milk had traveled the way predestined of gin and milk when mixed together, Hardman Pool waited without further urge for the story. Kumuhana pressed his hand to his chest and coughed hollowly at intervals, bidding for encouragement; but in the end, of himself, spoke out.

"It was a terrible thing in the old days when a great *alii* died. Kahekili was a great *alii.* He might have been king had he lived. Who can tell? I was a young man, not yet married. You know, Kanaka Oolea, when Kahekili died, and you can tell me how old I was. He died when Governor Boki ran the Blonde Hotel here in Honolulu. You have heard?"

"I was still on windward Hawaii," Pool answered. "But I have heard. Boki made a distillery, and leased Manoa lands to grow sugar for it, and Kaahumanu, who was regent, canceled the lease, rooted out the cane, and planted potatoes. And Boki was angry, and prepared to make war, and gathered his fighting men, with a dozen whaleship deserters and five brass six-pounders, out at Waikiki—"

"That was the very time Kahekili died," Kumuhana broke in eagerly. "You are very wise. You know many things of the old days better than we old *kanakas.*"

"It was 1829," Pool continued complacently. "You were twenty-eight years old, and I was twenty, just coming ashore in the open boat after the burning of the *Black Prince.*"

"I was twenty-eight," Kumuhana resumed. "It sounds right. I remember well Boki's brass guns at Waikiki. Kahekili died, too, at the time, at Waikiki. The people to this day believe his bones were taken to the *Hale o Keawe*" (mausoleum) "at Honaunau, in Kona—"

"And long afterward were brought to the Royal Mausoleum here in Honolulu," Pool supplemented.

"Also, Kanaka Oolea, there are some who believe to this day that Queen Alice has them stored with the rest of her ancestral bones in the big jars in her taboo room. All are wrong. I know. The sacred bones of Kahekili are gone and for ever gone. They rest nowhere. They have ceased to be. And many *kona* winds have whitened the surf at Waikiki since the last man looked upon the last of Kahekili. I alone remain alive of those men. I am the last man, and I was not glad to be at the finish.

"For see! I was a young man, and my heart was white-hot lava for Malia, who was in Kahekili's household. So was Anapuni's heart white-hot for her, though the color of his heart was black, as you shall see. We were drinking that night—Anapuni and I—the night that Kahekili died. Anapuni and I were only commoners, as were all of us *kanakas* and *wahines* who were at the drinking with the common sailors and whaleship men from before the mast. We were drinking on the mats by the beach at Waikiki, close to the old *heiau*" (temple) "that is not far from what is now the Wilders' beach place. I learned then and for ever what quantities of drink *haole* sailormen can stand. As for us *kanakas,* our heads were hot and light and rattly as dry gourds with the whiskey and the rum.

"It was past midnight, I remember well, when I saw Malia, whom never had I seen at a drinking, come across the wet-hard sand of the beach. My brain burned like red cinders of hell as I looked upon Anapuni look upon her, he being nearest to her by being across from me in the drinking circle. Oh, I know it was whiskey and rum and youth that made the heat of me; but there, in that moment, the mad mind of me resolved, if she spoke to him and yielded to dance with him first, that I would put both my hands around his throat and throw him down and under the *wahine* surf there beside us, and drown and choke out his life and the obstacle of him that stood between me and her. For know that she had never decided between us, and it was because of him that she was not already and long since mine.

"She was a grand young woman with a body generous as that of a chiefess and more wonderful, as she came upon us, across the wet sand, in the shimmer of the moonlight. Even the *haole* sailormen made pause of silence, and with open mouths stared upon her. Her walk! I have heard you talk, O Kanaka Oolea, of the woman Helen who caused the war of Troy. I say of Malia that more men would have stormed the walls of hell for her than went against that old-time city of which it is your custom to talk over much and long when you have drunk too little milk and too much gin.

"Her walk! In the moonlight there, the soft glow-fire of the jelly-fishes in the surf like the kerosene-lamp footlights I have seen in the new *haole* theatre! It was not the walk of a girl, but a woman. She did not flutter forward like rippling wavelets on a reef-sheltered, placid beach. There was that in her manner of walk that was big and queen-like, like the motion of the forces of nature, like the rhythmic flow of lava down the slopes of Kau to the sea, like the movement of the huge orderly trade-wind seas, like the rise and fall of the four great tides of the year that may be like music in the eternal ear of God, being too slow of occurrence in time to make a tune for ordinary quick-pulsing, brief-living, swift-dying man.

"Anapuni was nearest. But she looked at me. Have you ever heard a call, Kanaka Oolea, that is without sound yet is louder than the conches of God? So called she to me across that circle of the drinking. I half arose, for I was not yet full drunken; but Anapuni's arm caught her and drew her, and I sank back on my elbow and watched and raged. He was for making her sit beside him, and I waited. Did she sit, and, next, dance with him, I knew that ere morning Anapuni would be a dead man, choked and drowned by me in the shallow surf.

"Strange, is it not, Kanaka Oolea, all this heat called 'love'? Yet it is not strange. It must be so in the time of one's youth, else would mankind not go on."

"That is why the desire of woman must be greater than the desire of life," Pool concurred. "Else would there be neither men nor women."

"Yes," said Kumuhana. "But it is many a year now since the last of such heat has gone out of me. I remember it as one remembers an old sunrise—a thing that was. And so one grows old, and cold, and drinks gin, not for madness, but for warmth. And the milk is very nourishing.

"But Malia did not sit beside him. I remember her eyes were wild, her hair down and flying, as she bent over him and whispered in his ear. And her hair covered him about and hid him as she whispered, and the sight of it pounded my heart against my ribs and dizzied my head till scarcely could I half-see. And I willed myself with all the will of me that if, in short minutes, she did not come over to me, I would go across the circle and get her.

"It was one of the things never to be. You remember Chief Konukalani? Himself he strode up to the circle. His face was black with anger. He gripped Malia, not by the arm, but by the hair, and dragged her away behind him and was gone. Of that, even now, can I understand not the half. I, who was for slaying Anapuni because of her, raised neither hand nor voice of protest when Konukalani dragged her away by the hair—nor did Anapuni. Of course, we were common men, and he was a chief. That I know. But why should two common men, mad with desire of woman, with desire of woman stronger in them than desire of life, let any one chief, even the highest in the land, drag the woman away by the hair? Desiring her more than life, why should the two men fear to slay then and immediately the one chief? Here is something stronger than life, stronger than woman, but what is it? and why?"

"I will answer you," said Hardman Pool. "It is so because most men are fools, and therefore must be taken care of by the few men who are wise. Such is the secret of chiefship. In all the world are chiefs over men. In all the world that has been have there ever been chiefs, who must say to the many fool men: 'Do this; do not do that. Work, and work as we tell you, or your bellies will remain empty and you will perish. Obey the laws we set you or you will be beasts and without a place in the world. You would not have been, save for the chiefs before you who ordered and regulated for your fathers. No seed of you will come after you, except that we order and regulate for you now. You must be peace-abiding, and decent, and blow your noses. You must be early to bed of nights, and up early in the morning to work if you would have beds to sleep in and not roost in trees like the silly fowls. This is the season for the yam-planting and you must plant now. We say now, to-day, and not picnicking and hulaing to-day and yam-planting to-morrow or some other day of the many careless days. You must not kill one another, and you must leave your neighbors' wives alone. All this is life for you, because you think but one day at a time, while we, your chiefs, think for you all days and for days ahead.' "

"Like a cloud on the mountain-top that comes down and wraps about you and that you dimly see is a cloud, so is your wisdom to me, Kanaka Oolea," Kumuhana murmured. "Yet is it sad that I should be born a common man and live all my days a common man."

"That is because you were of yourself common," Hardman Pool assured him. "When a man is born common, and is by nature uncommon, he rises up and overthrows the chiefs and makes himself chief over the chiefs. Why do you not run my ranch, with its many thousands of cattle, and shift the pastures by the rainfall, and pick the bulls, and arrange the bargaining and the selling of the meat to the sailing ships and war vessels and the people who live in the Honolulu houses, and fight with lawyers, and help make laws, and even tell the King what is wise for him to do and what is dangerous? Why does not any man do this that I do? Any man of all the men who work for me, feed out of my hand, and let me do their thinking for them—me, who works harder than any of them, who eats no more than any of them, and who can sleep on no more than one *lauhala* mat at a time like any of them?"

"I am out of the cloud, Kanaka Oolea," said Kumuhana, with a visible brightening of countenance. "More clearly do I see. All my long years have the *aliis* I was born under thought for me. Ever, when I was hungry, I came to them for food, as I come to your kitchen now. Many people eat in your kitchen, and the days of feasts when you slay fat steers for all of us are understandable. It is why I come to you this day, an old man whose labor of strength is not worth a shilling a week, and ask of you twelve dollars to buy a jackass and a second-hand saddle and bridle. It is why twice ten fool men of us, under these monkey-pods half an hour ago, asked of you a dollar or two, or four or five, or ten or twelve. We are the careless ones of the careless days who will not plant the yam in season if our *alii* does not compel us, who will not think one day for ourselves, and who, when we age to worthlessness, know that our *alii* will think *kow-kow* into our bellies and a grass thatch over our heads."

Hardman Pool bowed his appreciation, and urged:

"But the bones of Kahekili. The Chief Konukalani had just dragged away Malia by the hair of the head, and you and Anapuni sat on without protest in the circle of drinking. What was it Malia whispered in Anapuni's ear, bending over him, her hair hiding the face of him?"

"That Kahekili was dead. That was what she whispered to Anapuni. That Kahekili was dead, just dead, and that the chiefs, ordering all within the house to remain within, were debating the disposal of the bones and meat of him before word of his death should get abroad. That the high priest Eoppo was deciding them, and that she had overheard no less than Anapuni and me chosen as the sacrifices to go the way of Kahekili and his bones and to care for him afterward and for ever in the shadowy other world."

"The *meopuu*, the human sacrifice," Pool commented. "Yet it was nine years since the coming of the missionaries."

"And it was the year before their coming that the idols were cast down and the taboos broken," Kumuhana added. "But the chiefs still practised the old ways, the custom of *hunakele*, and hid the bones of the *aliis* where no men should find them and make fish-hooks of their jaws or arrow heads of their long bones for the slaying of little mice in sport. Behold, O Kanaka Oolea!"

The old man thrust out his tongue, and, to Pool's amazement, he saw the surface of that sensitive organ, from root to tip, tattooed in intricate designs.

"That was done after the missionaries came, several years afterward, when Keopuolani died. Also, did I knock out four of my front teeth, and half-circles did I burn over my body with blazing bark. And whoever ventured out-of-doors that night was slain by the chiefs. Nor could a light be shown in a house or a whisper of noise be made. Even dogs and hogs that made a noise were slain, nor all that night were the ships' bells of the *haoles* in the harbor allowed to strike. It was a terrible thing in those days when an *alii* died.

"But the night that Kahekili died. We sat on in the drinking circle after Konukalani dragged Malia away by the hair. Some of the *haole* sailors grumbled; but they were few in the land in those days and the *kanakas* many. And never was Malia seen of men again. Konukalani alone knew the manner of her slaying, and he never told. And in after years what common men like Anapuni and me should dare to question him?

"Now she had told Anapuni before she was dragged away. But Anapuni's heart was black. Me he did not tell. Worthy he was of the killing I had intended for him. There was a giant harpooner in the circle, whose singing was like the bellowing of bulls; and, gazing on him in amazement while he roared some song of the sea, when next I looked across the circle to Anapuni, Anapuni was gone. He had fled to the high mountains where he could hide with the bird-catchers a week of moons. This I learned afterward.

"I? I sat on, ashamed of my desire of woman that had not been so strong as my slave-obedience to a chief. And I drowned my shame in large drinks of rum and whiskey, till the world went round and round, inside my head and out, and the Southern Cross danced a *hula* in the sky, and the Koolau Mountains bowed their lofty summits to Waikiki and the surf of Waikiki kissed them on their brows. And the giant harpooner was still roaring, his the last sounds in my ear, as I fell back on the *lauhala* mat, and was to all things for the time as one dead.

"When I awoke was at the faint first beginning of dawn. I was being kicked by a hard naked heel in the ribs. What of the enormousness of the drink I had consumed, the feelings aroused in me by the heel were not pleasant. The *kanakas* and *wahines* of the drinking were gone. I alone remained among the sleeping sailormen, the giant harpooner snoring like a whale, his head upon my feet.

"More heel-kicks, and I sat up and was sick. But the one who kicked was impatient, and demanded to know where was Anapuni. And I did not know, and was kicked, this time from both sides by two impatient men, because I did not know. Nor did I know that Kahekili was dead. Yet did I guess something serious was afoot, for the two men who kicked me were chiefs, and no common men crouched behind them to do their bidding. One was Aimoku, of Kaneche; the other Humuhumu, of Manoa.

"They commanded me to go with them, and they were not kind in their commanding; and as I uprose, the head of the giant harpooner was rolled off my feet, past the edge of the mat, into the sand. He grunted like a pig, his lips opened, and all of his tongue rolled out of his mouth into the sand. Nor did he draw it back. For the first time I knew how long was a man's tongue. The sight of the sand on it made me sick for the second time. It is a terrible thing, the next day after a night of drinking. I was afire, dry afire, all the inside of me like a burnt cinder, like *aa* lava, like the harpooner's tongue dry and gritty with sand. I bent for a half-drunk drinking coconut, but Aimoku kicked it out of my shaking fingers, and Humuhumu smote me with the heel of his hand on my neck.

"They walked before me, side by side, their faces solemn and black, and I walked at their heels. My mouth stank of the drink, and my head was sick with the stale fumes of it, and I would have cut off my right hand for a drink of water, one drink, a mouthful even. And, had I had it, I know it would have sizzled in my belly like water spilled on heated stones for the roasting. It is terrible, the next day after the drinking. All the life-time of many men who died young has passed by me since the last I was able to do such mad drinking of youth when youth knows not capacity and is undeterred.

"But as we went on, I began to know that some *alii* was dead. No *kanakas* lay asleep in the sand, nor stole home from their lovemaking; and no canoes were abroad after the early fish most catchable then inside the reef at the change of the tide. When we came past the *hoiau*" (temple) "to where the Great Kamehameha used to haul out his brigs and schooners, I saw, under the canoe-sheds, that the mat-thatches of Kahekili's great double-canoe had been taken off, and that even then, at low tide, many men were launching it down across the sand into the water. But all these men were chiefs. And though my eyes swam, and the inside of my head went around and around and the inside of my body was a cinder athirst, I guessed that the *alii* who was dead was Kahekili. For he was old, and most likely of the *aliis* to be dead."

"It was his death, as I have heard it, more than the intercession of Kekuanaoa, that spoiled Governor Boki's rebellion," Hardman Pool observed.

"It was Kahekili's death that spoiled it," Kumuhana confirmed. "All commoners, when the word slipped out that night of his death, fled into the shelter of the grass houses, nor lighted fire nor pipes, nor breathed loudly, being therein and thereby taboo from use for sacrifice. And all Governor Boki's commoners of fighting men, as well as the *haole* deserters from ships, so fled, so that the brass guns lay unserved and his handful of chiefs of themselves could do nothing.

"Aimoku and Humuhumu made me sit on the sand to the side from the launching of the great double-canoe. And when it was afloat all the chiefs were athirst, not being used to such toil; and I was told to climb the palms beside the canoe-sheds and throw down drinking coconuts. They drank and were refreshed, but me they refused to let drink.

"Then they bore Kahekili from his house to the canoe in a *haole* coffin, oiled and varnished and new. It had been made by a ship's carpenter, who thought he was making a boat that must not leak. It was very tight, and over where the face of Kahekili lay was nothing but thin glass. The chiefs had not screwed on the outside plank to cover the glass. Maybe they did not know the manner of *haole* coffins; but at any rate I was to be glad they did not know, as you shall see.

" 'There is but one *moepuu,*' said the priest Eoppo, looking at me where I sat on the coffin in the bottom of the canoe. Already the chiefs were paddling out through the reef.

" 'The other has run into hiding," Aimoku answered. 'This one was all we could get.'

"And then I knew. I knew everything. I was to be sacrificed. Anapuni had been planned for the other sacrifice. That was what Malia had whispered to Anapuni at the drinking. And she had been dragged away before she could tell me. And in his blackness of heart he had not told me.

" 'There should be two,' said Eoppo. 'It is the law.'

"Aimoku stopped paddling and looked back shoreward as if to return and get a second sacrifice. But several of the chiefs contended no, saying that all commoners were fled to the mountains or were lying taboo in their houses, and that it might take days before they could catch one. In the end Eoppo gave in, though he grumbled from time to time that the law required two *mocpuus.*

"We paddled on, past Diamond Head and abreast of Koko Head, till we were in the midway of the Molokai Channel. There was quite a sea running, though the trade wind was blowing light. The chiefs rested from their paddles, save for the steersmen who kept the canoes bow-on to the wind and swell. And, ere they proceeded further in the matter, they opened more coconuts and drank.

" 'I do not mind so much being the *moepuu,*' I said to Humuhumu; 'but I should like to have a drink before I am slain.' I got no drink. But I spoke true. I was too sick of the much whiskey and rum to be afraid to die. At least my mouth would stink no more, nor my head ache, nor the inside of me be as dry-hot sand. Almost worst of all, I suffered at the thought of the harpooner's tongue, as last I had seen it lying on the sand and covered with sand. O Kanaka Oolea, what animals young men are with the drink! Not until they have grown old, like you and me, do they control their wantonness of thirst and drink sparingly, like you and me."

"Because we have to," Hardman Pool rejoined. "Old stomachs are worn thin and tender, and we drink sparingly because we dare not drink more. We are wise, but the wisdom is bitter."

"The priest Eoppo sang a long *mele* about Kahekili's mother and his mother's mother, and all their mothers all the way back to the beginning of time," Kumuhana resumed. "And it seemed I must die of my sand-hot dryness ere he was done. And he called upon all the gods of the under world, the middle world and the over world, to care for and cherish the dead *alii* about to be consigned to them, and to carry out the curses—they were terrible curses—he laid upon all living men and men to live after who might tamper with the bones of Kahekili to use them in sport of vermin-slaying.

"Do you know, Kanaka Oolea, the priest talked a language largely different, and I know it was the priest language, the old language. Maui he did not name Maui, but Maui-Tiki-Tiki and Maui-Po-Tiki. And Hina, the goddess-mother of Maui, he named Ina. And Maui's god-father he named sometimes Akalana and sometimes Kanaloa. Strange how one about to die and very thirsty should remember such things! And I remember the priest named Hawaii as Vaii, and Lanai as Ngangai."

"Those were the Maori names," Hardman Pool explained, "and the Samoan and Tongan names, that the priests brought with them in their first voyages from the south in the long ago when they found Hawaii and settled to dwell upon it."

"Great is your wisdom, O Kanaka Oolea," the old man accorded solemnly. "Ku, our Supporter of the Heavens, the priest named Tu, and also Ru; and La, our God of the Sun, he named Ra—"

"And Ra was a sun-god in Egypt in the long ago," Pool interrupted with a sparkle of interest. "Truly, you Polynesians have traveled far in time and space since first you began. A far cry it is from Old Egypt, when Atlantis was still afloat, to Young Hawaii in the North Pacific. But proceed, Kumuhana. Do you remember anything also of what the priest Eoppo sang?"

"At the very end," came the confirming nod, "though I was near dead myself, and nearer to die under the priest's knife, he sang what I have remembered every word of. Listen! It was thus."

And in quavering falsetto, with the customary broken-notes, the old man sang.

"A Maori death-chant unmistakable," Pool exclaimed, "sung by an Hawaiian with a tattooed tongue! Repeat it once again, and I shall say it to you in English."

And when it had been repeated, he spoke it slowly in English:

"But death is nothing new.
Death is and has been ever since old Maui died.
And woke the goblin-god,
Who severed him in two, and shut him in,
So dusk of eve came on."

"And at the last," Kumuhana resumed, "I was not slain. Eoppo, the killing knife in hand and ready to lift for the blow, did not lift. And I? How did I feel and think? Often, Kanaka Oolea, have I since laughed at the memory of it. I felt very thirsty. I did not want to die. I wanted a drink of water. I knew I was going to die, and I kept remembering the thousand waterfalls falling to waste down the *palis*" (precipices) "of the windward Koolau Mountains. I did not think of Anapuni. I was too thirsty. I did not think of Malia. I was too thirsty. But continually, inside my head, I saw the tongue of the harpooner, covered dry with sand, as I had last seen it, lying in the sand. My tongue was like that, too. And in the bottom of the canoe rolled about many drinking nuts. Yet I did not attempt to drink, for these were chiefs and I was a common man.

" 'No,' said Eoppo, commanding the chiefs to throw overboard the coffin. 'There are not two *moepuus,* therefore there shall be none.'

" 'Slay the one,' the chiefs cried.

"But Eoppo shook his head, and said: 'We cannot send Kahekili on his way with only the tops of the taro.'

" 'Half a fish is better than none,' Aimoku said the old saying.

" 'Not at the burying of an *alii,*' was the priest's quick reply. 'It is the law. We cannot be niggard with Kahekili and cut his allotment of sacrifice in half.'

"So, for the moment, while the coffin went overside, I was not slain. And it was strange that I was glad immediately that I was to live. And I began to remember Malia, and to begin to plot a vengeance on Anapuni. And with the blood of life thus freshening in me, my thirst multiplied on itself tenfold, and my tongue and mouth and throat seemed as sanded as the tongue of the harpooner. The coffin being overboard, I was sitting in the bottom of the canoe. A coconut rolled between my legs and I closed them on it. But as I picked it up in my hand, Aimoku smote my hand with the paddle-edge. Behold!"

He held up the hand, showing two fingers crooked from never having been set.

"I had no time to vex over my pain, for worse things were upon me. All the chiefs were crying out in horror. The coffin, head-end up, had not sunk. It bobbed up and down in the sea astern of us. And the canoe, without way on it, bow-on to sea and wind, was drifted down by sea and wind upon the coffin. And the glass of it was to us, so that we could see the face and head of Kahekili through the glass; and he grinned at us through the glass and seemed alive already in the other world and angry with us, and, with other-world power, about to wreak his anger upon us. Up and down he bobbed, and the canoe drifted closer upon him.

" 'Kill him!' 'Bleed him!' 'Thrust to the heart of him!' These things the chiefs were crying out to Eoppo in their fear. 'Over with the taro tops!' 'Let the *alii* have the half of a fish!'

"Eoppo, priest though he was, was likewise afraid, and his reason weakened before the sight of Kahekili in his *haole* coffin that would not sink. He seized me by the hair, drew me to my feet, and lifted the knife to plunge to my heart. And there was no resistance in me. I knew again only that I was very thirsty, and before my swimming eyes, in mid-air and close up, dangled the sanded tongue of the harpooner.

"But before the knife could fall and drive in, the thing happened that saved me. Akai, half-brother to Governor Boki, as you will remember, was steersman of the canoe, and, therefore, in the stern, was nearest to the coffin and its dead that would not sink. He was wild with fear, and he thrust out with the point of his paddle to fend off the coffined *alii* that seemed bent to come on board. The point of the paddle struck the glass. The glass broke—"

"And the coffin immediately sank," Hardman Pool broke in; "the air that floated it escaping through the broken glass."

"The coffin immediately sank, being builded by the ship's carpenter like a boat," Kumuhana confirmed. "And I, who was a *moepuu,* became a man once more. And I lived, though I died a thousand deaths from thirst before we gained back to the beach of Waikiki.

"And so, O Kanaka Oolea, the bones of Kahekili do not lie in the Royal Mausoleum. They are at the bottom of Molokai Channel, if not, long since, they have become floating dust of slime, or, builded into the bodies of the coral creatures dead and gone, are builded into the coral reef itself. Of men I am the one living who saw the bones of Kahekili sink into the Molokai Channel."

In the pause that followed, wherein Hardman Pool was deep sunk in meditation, Kumuhana licked his dry lips many times. At the last he broke silence:

"The twelve dollars, Kanaka Oolea, for the jackass and the second-hand saddle and bridle?"

"The twelve dollars would be thine," Pool responded, passing to the ancient one six dollars and a half, "save that I have in my stable junk the very bridle and saddle for you which I shall give you. These six dollars and a half will buy you the perfectly suitable jackass of the *pake*" (Chinese) "at Kokako who told me only yesterday that such was the price."

They sat on, Pool meditating, conning over and over to himself the Maori death-chant he had heard, and especially the line, "So dusk of eve came on," finding in it an intense satisfaction of beauty; Kumuhana licking his lips and tokening that he waited for something more. At last he broke the silence.

"I have talked long, O Kanaka Oolea. There is not the enduring moistness in my mouth that was when I was young. It seems that afresh upon me is the thirst that was mine when tormented by the visioned tongue of the harpooner. The gin and milk is very good, O Kanaka Oolea, for a tongue that is like the harpooner's."

A shadow of a smile flickered across Pool's face. He clapped his hands, and the little maid came running.

"Bring one glass of gin and milk for old Kumuhana," commanded Hardman Pool.

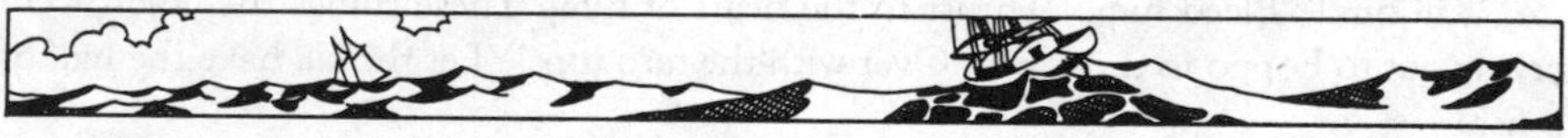

WHEN ALICE TOLD HER SOUL

THIS, of Alice Akana, is an affair of Hawaii, not of this day, but of days recent enough, when Abel Ah Yo preached his famous revival in Honolulu and persuaded Alice Akana to tell her soul. But what Alice told concerned itself with the earlier history of the then surviving generation.

For Alice Akana was fifty years old, had begun life early, and, early and late, lived it spaciously. What she knew went back into the roots and foundations of families, businesses and plantations. She was the one living repository of accurate information that lawyers sought out, whether the information they required related to land-boundaries and land gifts, or to marriages, births, bequests or scandals. Rarely, because of the tight tongue she kept behind her teeth, did she give them what they asked; and when she did was when only equity was served and no one was hurt.

For Alice had lived, from early in her girlhood, a life of flowers, and song, and wine, and dance; and, in her later years, had herself been mistress of these revels by office of mistress of the *hula* house. In such atmosphere, where mandates of God and man and caution are inhibited, and where woozled tongues will wag, she acquired her historical knowledge of things never otherwise whispered and rarely guessed. And her tight tongue had served her well, so that, while the old-timers knew she must know, none ever heard her gossip of the times of Kalakaua's boathouse, nor of the high times of officers of visiting warships, nor of the diplomats and ministers and councils of the countries of the world.

So, at fifty, loaded with historical dynamite sufficient, if it were ever exploded, to shake the social and commercial life of the Islands, still tight of tongue, Alice Akana was mistress of the *hula* house, manageress of the dancing girls who *hula* 'd for royalty, for *luaus* (feasts), house-parties, *poi* suppers and curious tourists. And, at fifty, she was not merely buxom, but short and fat in the Polynesian peasant way, with a constitution and lack of organic weakness that promised incalculable years. But it was at fifty that she strayed, quite by chance of time and curiosity, into Abel Ah Yo's revival meeting.

Now Abel Ah Yo, in his theology and word wizardry, was as much mixed a personage as Billy Sunday. In his genealogy he was much more mixed, for he was compounded of one-fourth Portuguese, one-fourth Scotch, one-fourth Hawaiian and one-fourth Chinese. The Pentecostal fire he flamed forth was hotter and more variegated than could any one of the four races of him alone have flamed forth. For in him were gathered together the cannyness and the cunning, the wit and the wisdom, the subtlety and the rawness, the passion and the philosophy, the agonizing spirit-groping and the legs up to the knees in the dung of reality, of the four radically different breeds that contributed to the sum of him. His, also, was the clever self-deceivement of the entire clever compound.

When it came to word wizardry, he had Billy Sunday, master of slang and argot of one language, skinned by miles. For in Abel Ah Yo were the live verbs, and nouns, and adjectives, and metaphors of four living languages. Intermixed and living promiscuously and vitally together, he possessed in these languages a reservoir of expression in which a myriad Billy Sundays could drown. Of no race, a mongrel *par excellence,* a heterogeneous scrabble, the genius of the admixture was superlatively Abel Ah Yo's. Like a chameleon, he titubated and scintillated grandly between the diverse parts of him, stunning by frontal attack and surprising and confounding by flanking sweeps the mental homogeneity of the more simply constituted souls who came in to his revival to sit under him and flame to his flaming.

Abel Ah Yo believed in himself and his mixedness, as he believed in the mixedness of his weird concept that God looked as much like him as like any man, being no mere tribal god, but a world god that must look equally like all races of all the world, even if it led to piebaldness. And the concept worked. Chinese, Korean, Japanese, Hawaiian, Porto Rican, Russian, English, French—members of all races—knelt without friction, side by side, to his revision of deity.

Himself in his tender youth an apostate to the Church of England, Abel Ah Yo had for years suffered the lively sense of being a Judas sinner. Essentially religious, he had foresworn the Lord. Like Judas therefore he was. Judas was damned. Wherefore he, Abel Ah Yo, was damned; and he did not want to be damned. So, quite after the manner of humans, he squirmed and twisted to escape damnation. The day came when he solved his escape. The doctrine that Judas was damned, he concluded, was a misinterpretation of God, who, above all things, stood for justice. Judas had been God's servant, specially selected to perform a particularly nasty job. Therefore Judas, ever faithful, a betrayer only by divine command, was a saint. Ergo, he, Abel Ah Yo, was a saint by very virtue of his apostasy to a particular sect, and he could have access with clear grace any time to God.

This theory became one of the major tenets of his preaching, and was especially efficacious in cleansing the consciences of the back-sliders from all other faiths who else, in the secrecy of their subconscious selves, were being crushed by the weight of the Judas sin. To Abel Ah Yo, God's plan was as clear as if he, Abel Ah Yo, had planned it himself. All would be saved in the end, although some took longer than others, and would win only to back-seats. Man's place in the ever-fluxing chaos of the world was definite and pre-ordained—if by no other token, then by denial that there was any ever-fluxing chaos. This was a mere bugbear of mankind's addled fancy; and, by stinging audacities of thought and speech, by vivid slang that bit home by sheerest intimacy into his listeners' mental processes, he drove the bugbear from their brains, showed them the loving clarity of God's design, and, thereby, induced in them spiritual serenity and calm.

What chance had Alice Akana, herself pure and homogeneous Hawaiian, against his subtle democratic-tinged, four-race-engendered, slang-munitioned attack? He knew, by contact, almost as much as she about the waywardness of living and sinning—having been singing boy on the passenger-ships between Hawaii and California, and, after that, bar boy, afloat and ashore, from the Barbary Coast to Heinie's Tavern. In point of fact, he had left his job of Number One Bar Boy at the University Club to embark on his great preachment revival.

So, when Alice Akana strayed in to scoff, she remained to pray to Abel Ah Yo's god, who struck her hard-headed mind as the most sensible god of which she had ever heard. She gave money into Abel Ah Yo's collection plate, closed up the *hula* house and dismissed the *hula* dancers to more devious ways of earning a livelihood, shed her bright colors and raiments and flower garlands, and bought a Bible.

It was a time of religious excitement in the purlieus of Honolulu. The thing was a democratic movement of the people toward God. Place and caste were invited, but never came. The stupid lowly, and the humble lowly, only, went down on its knees at the penitent form, admitted its pathological weight and hurt of sin, eliminated and purged all its bafflements, and walked forth again upright under the sun, child-like and pure, upborne by Abel Ah Yo's god's arm around it. In short, Abel Ah Yo's revival was a clearing house for sin and sickness of spirit, wherein sinners were relieved of their burdens and made light and bright and spiritually healthy again.

But Alice was not happy. She had not been cleared. She bought and dispersed Bibles, contributed more money to the plate, contralto'd gloriously in all the hymns, but would not tell her soul. In vain Abel Ah Yo wrestled with her. She would not go down on her knees at the penitent form and voice the things of tarnish within her—the ill things of good friends of the old days. "You cannot serve two masters," Abel Ah Yo told her. "Hell is full of those who have tried. Single of heart and pure of heart must you make your peace with God. Not until you tell your soul to God right out in meeting will you be ready for redemption. In the meantime you will suffer the canker of the sin you carry about within you."

Scientifically, though he did not know it and though he continually jeered at science, Abel Ah Yo was right. Not could she be again as a child and become radiantly clad in God's grace, until she had eliminated from her soul, by telling, all the sophistications that had been hers, including those she shared with others. In the Protestant way, she must bare her soul in public, as in the Catholic way it was done in the privacy of the confessional. The result of such baring would be unity, tranquillity, happiness, cleansing, redemption and immortal life.

"Choose!" Abel Ah Yo thundered. "Loyalty to God, or loyalty to man." And Alice could not choose. Too long had she kept her tongue locked with the honor of man. "I will tell all my soul about myself," she contended. "God knows I am tired of my soul and should like to have it clean and shining once again as when I was a little girl at Kaneohe—"

"But all the corruption of your soul has been with other souls," was Abel Ah Yo's invariable reply. "When you have a burden, lay it down. You cannot bear a burden and be quit of it at the same time."

"I will pray to God each day, and many times each day," she urged. "I will approach God with humility, with sighs and with tears. I will contribute often to the plate, and I will buy Bibles, Bibles, Bibles without end."

"And God will not smile upon you," God's mouthpiece retorted. "And you will remain weary and heavy-laden. For you will not have told all your sin, and not until you have told all will you be rid of any."

"This rebirth is difficult," Alice sighed.

"Rebirth is even more difficult than birth." Abel Ah Yo did anything but comfort her. " 'Not until you become as a little child . . .' "

"If ever I tell my soul, it will be a big telling," she confided.

"The bigger the reason to tell it then."

And so the situation remained at deadlock, Abel Ah Yo demanding absolute allegiance to God, and Alice Akana flirting on the fringes of paradise.

"You bet it will be a big telling, if Alice ever begins," the beachcombing and disreputable *kamaainas* (old-timers) gleefully told one another over their Palm Tree gin.

In the clubs the possibility of her telling was of more moment. The younger generation of men announced that they had applied for front seats at the telling, while many of the older generation of men joked hollowly about the conversion of Alice. Further, Alice found herself abruptly popular with friends who had forgotten her existence for twenty years.

One afternoon, as Alice, Bible in hand, was taking the electric street car at Hotel and Fort, Cyrus Hodge, sugar factor and magnate, ordered his chauffeur to stop beside her. Willy nilly, in excess of friendliness, he had her into his limousine beside him and went three-quarters of an hour out of his way and time personally to conduct her to her destination.

"Good for sore eyes to see you," he burbled. "How the years fly! You're looking fine. The secret of youth is yours."

Alice smiled and complimented in return in the royal Polynesian way of friendliness.

"My, my," Cyrus Hodge reminisced. "I was such a boy in those days!"

"*Some* boy," she laughed acquiescence.

"But knowing no more than the foolishness of a boy in those long-ago days."

"Remember the night your hack-driver got drunk and left you—"

"S-s-sh!" he cautioned. "That Jap driver is a high-school graduate and knows more English than either of us. Also, I think he is a spy for his Government. So why should we tell him anything? Besides, I was so very young. You remember . . ."

"Your cheeks were like the peaches we used to grow before the Mediterranean fruit-fly got into them," Alice agreed. "I don't think you shaved more than once a week then. You were a pretty boy. Don't you remember the *hula* we composed in your honor, the—"

"S-s-sh!" he hushed her. "All that's buried and forgotten. May it remain forgotten."

And she was aware that in his eyes was no longer any of the ingenuousness of youth she remembered. Instead, his eyes were keen and speculative, searching into her for some assurance that she would not resurrect his particular portion of that buried past.

"Religion is a good thing for us as we get along into middle age," another old friend told her. He was building a magnificent house on Pacific Heights, but had recently married a second time, and was even then on his way to the steamer to welcome home his two daughters just graduated from Vassar.

"We need religion in our old age, Alice. It softens, makes us more tolerant and forgiving of the weakness of others—especially the weakness of youth of—of others, when they played high and low and didn't know what they were doing."

He waited anxiously.

"Yes," she said. "We are all born to sin and it is hard to grow out of sin. But I grow, I grow."

"Don't forget, Alice, in those other days I always played square. You and I never had a falling out."

"Not even the night you gave that *luau* when you were twenty-one and insisted on breaking the glassware after every toast. But of course you paid for it."

"Handsomely," he asserted almost pleadingly.

"Handsomely," she agreed. "I replaced more than double the quantity with what you paid me, so that at the next *luau* I catered one hundred and twenty plates without having to rent or borrow a dish or glass. Lord Mainweather gave that *luau*—you remember him."

"I was pig-sticking with him at Mana," the other nodded. "We were at a two weeks' house-party there. But say, Alice, as you know, I think this religion stuff is all right and better than all right. But don't let it carry you off your feet. And don't get to telling your soul on me. What would my daughters think of that broken glassware!"

"I always did have an *aloha*" (warm regard) "for you, Alice," a member of the Senate, fat and bald-headed, assured her.

And another, a lawyer and a grandfather: "We were always friends, Alice. And remember, any legal advice or handling of business you may require, I'll do for you gladly, and without fees, for the sake of our old-time friendship."

Came a banker to her late Christmas Eve, with formidable, legal-looking envelopes in his hand which he presented to her.

"Quite by chance," he explained, "when my people were looking up land-records in Iapio Valley, I found a mortgage of two thousand on your holdings there—that rice land leased to Ah Chin. And my mind drifted back to the past when we were all young together, and wild—a bit wild, to be sure. And my heart warmed with the memory of you, and, so, just as an *aloha,* here's the whole thing cleared off for you."

Nor was Alice forgotten by her own people. Her house became a Mecca for native men and women, usually performing pilgrimage privily after darkness fell, with presents always in their hands—squid fresh from the reef, *opihis* and *limu,* baskets of alligator pears, roasting corn of the earliest from windward Cahu, mangoes and star-apples, taro pink and royal of the finest selection, sucking pigs, banana *poi,* breadfruit and crabs caught the very day from Pearl Harbor. Mary Mendana, wife of the Portuguese Consul, remembered her with a five-dollar box of candy and a mandarin coat that would have fetched three-quarters of a hundred dollars at a fire sale. And Elvira Miyahara Makaena Yin Wap, the wife of Yin Wap the wealthy Chinese importer, brought personally to Alice two entire bolts of *piña* cloth from the Philippines and a dozen pairs of silk stockings.

The time passed, and Abel Ah Yo struggled with Alice for a properly penitent heart, and Alice struggled with herself for her soul, while half of Honolulu wickedly or apprehensively hung on the outcome. Carnival week was over, polo and the races had come and gone, and the celebration of Fourth of July was ripening, ere Abel Ah Yo beat down by brutal psychology the citadel of her reluctance. It was then that he gave his famous exhortation which might be summed up as Abel Ah Yo's definition of eternity. Of course, like Billy Sunday on certain occasions, Abel Ah Yo had cribbed the definition. But no one in the Islands knew it, and his rating as a revivalist uprose a hundred per cent.

So successful was his preaching that night, that he reconverted many of his converts, who fell and moaned about the penitent form and crowded for room amongst scores of new converts burnt by the pentecostal fire, including half a company of negro soldiers from the garrisoned Twenty-Fifth Infantry, a dozen troopers from the Fourth Cavalry on its way to the Philippines, as many drunken man-of-war's men, divers' ladies from Iwilei and half the riff-raff of the beach.

Abel Ah Yo, subtly sympathetic himself by virtue of his racial admixture, knowing human nature like a book and Alice Akana even more so, knew just what he was doing when he arose that memorable night and exposited God, hell and eternity in terms of Alice Akana's comprehension. For, quite by chance, he had discovered her cardinal weakness. First of all, like all Polynesians, an ardent lover of nature, he found that earthquake and volcanic eruption were the things of which Alice lived in terror. She had been, in the past, on the Big Island, through cataclysms that had shaken grass houses down upon her while she slept, and she had beheld Madame Pele (the Fire or Volcano Goddess) fling red-fluxing lava down the long slopes of Mauna Loa, destroying fishponds on the sea-brim and licking up droves of beef cattle, villages and humans on her fiery way.

The night before, a slight earthquake had shaken Honolulu and given Alice Akana insomnia. And the morning papers had stated that Mauna Kea had broken into eruption, while the lava was rising rapidly in the great pit of Kilauea. So, at the meeting, her mind vexed between the terrors of this world and the delights of the eternal world to come, Alice sat down in a front seat in a very definite state of the "jumps".

And Abel Ah Yo arose and put his finger on the sorest part of her soul. Sketching the nature of God in the stereotyped way, but making the stereotyped alive again with his gift of tongues in Pidgin-English and Pidgin-Hawaiian, Abel Ah Yo described the day when the Lord, even His infinite patience at an end, would tell Peter to close his day book and ledgers, command Gabriel to summon all souls to Judgment, and cry out with a voice of thunder: "*Welakahao!*"

This anthropomorphic deity of Abel Ah Yo thundering the modern Hawaiian-English slang of *welakahao* at the end of the world, is a fair sample of the revivalist's speech-tools of discourse. *Welakahao* means literally "hot iron" . It was coined in the Honolulu Ironworks by the hundreds of Hawaiian men there employed, who meant by it "to hustle" , "to get a move on" , the iron being hot meaning that the time had come to strike.

"And the Lord cried '*Welakahao,*' and the Day of Judgment began and was over *wiki-wiki*" (quickly) "just like that; for Peter was a better bookkeeper than any on the Waterhouse Trust Company Limited, and, further, Peter's books were true."

Swiftly Abel Ah Yo divided the sheep from the goats, and hastened the latter down into hell.

"And now," he demanded, perforce his language on these pages being properly Englished, "what is hell like? Oh, my friends, let me describe to you, in a little way, what I have beheld with my own eyes on earth of the possibilities of hell. I was a young man, a boy, and I was at Hilo. Morning began with earthquakes. Throughout the day the mighty land continued to shake and tremble, till strong men became seasick, and women clung to the trees to escape falling, and cattle were thrown down off their feet. I beheld myself a young calf so thrown. A night of terror indescribable followed. The land was in motion like a canoe in a Kona gale. There was an infant crushed to death by its fond mother stepping upon it whilst fleeing her falling house.

"The heavens were on fire above us. We read our Bibles by the light of the heavens, and the print was fine, even for young eyes. Those missionary Bibles were always too small of print. Forty miles away from us, the heart of hell burst from the lofty mountains and gushed red-blood of fire-melted rock toward the sea. With the heavens in vast conflagration and the earth *hulaing* beneath our feet, was a scene too awful and too majestic to be enjoyed. We could think only of the thin bubble-skin of earth between us and the everlasting lake of fire and brimstone, and of God to whom we prayed to save us. There were earnest and devout souls who there and then promised their pastors to give not their shaved tithes, but five-tenths of their all to the church, if only the Lord would let them live to contribute.

"Oh, my friends, God saved us. But first He showed us a foretaste of that hell that will yawn for us on the last day, when he cries '*Welakahao!*' in a voice of thunder. When the iron is hot! Think of it! When the iron is hot for sinners!

"By the third day, things being much quieter, my friend the preacher and I, being calm in the hand of God, journeyed up Mauna Loa and gazed into the awful pit of Kilauea. We gazed down into the fathomless abyss to the lake of fire far below, roaring and dashing its fiery spray into billows and fountaining hundreds of feet into the air like Fourth of July fireworks you have all seen, and all the while we were suffocating and made dizzy by the immense volumes of smoke and brimstone ascending.

"And I say unto you, no pious person could gaze down upon that scene without recognizing fully the Bible picture of the Pit of Hell. Believe me, the writers of the New Testament had nothing on us. As for me, my eyes were fixed upon the exhibition before me, and I stood mute and trembling under a sense never before so fully realized of the power, the majesty, and terror of Almighty God—the resources of His wrath, and the untold horrors of the finally impenitent who do not tell their souls and make their peace with the Creator.*

"But oh, my friends, think you our guides, our native attendants, deep-sunk in heathenism, were affected by such a scene? No. The devil's hand was upon them. Utterly regardless and unimpressed, they were only careful about their supper, chatted about their raw fish, and stretched themselves upon their mats to sleep. Children of the devil they were, insensible to the beauties, the sublimities, and the awful terror of God's works. But you are not heathen I now address. What is a heathen? He is one who betrays a stupid insensibility to every elevated idea and to every elevated emotion. If you wish to awaken his attention, do not bid him to look down into the Pit of Hell. But present him with a calabash of *poi,* a raw fish, or invite him to some low, groveling and sensuous sport. Oh, my friends, how lost are they to all that elevates the immortal soul! But the preacher and I, sad and sick at heart for them, gazed down into hell. Oh, my friends, it *was* hell, the hell of the Scriptures, the hell of eternal torment for the undeserving . . ."

Alice Akana was in an ecstasy or hysteria of terror. She was mumbling incoherently: "O Lord, I will give nine-tenths of my all. I will give all. I will give even the two bolts of *piña* cloth, the mandarin coat and the entire dozen silk stockings . . ."

* See Dibble's *A History of the Sandwich Islands.*

By the time she could lend ear again, Abel Ah Yo was launching out on his famous definition of eternity.

"Eternity is a long time, my friends. God lives, and, therefore, God lives inside eternity. And God is very old. The fires of hell are as old and as everlasting as God. How else could there be everlasting torment for those sinners cast down by God into the Pit on the Last Day to burn for ever and for ever through all eternity? Oh, my friends, your minds are small—too small to grasp eternity. Yet it is given to me, by God's grace, to convey to you an understanding of a tiny bit of eternity.

"The grains of sand on the beach of Waikiki are as many as the stars, and more. No man may count them. Did he have a million lives in which to count them, he would have to ask for more time. Now let us consider a little, dinky, old *minah* bird with one broken wing that cannot fly. At Waikiki the *minah* bird that cannot fly takes one grain of sand in its beak and hops, hops, all day long and for many days, all the day to Pearl Harbor and drops that one grain of sand into the harbor. Then it hops, hops, all day and for many days, all the way back to Waikiki for another grain of sand. And again it hops, hops all the way back to Pearl Harbor. And it continues to do this through the years and centuries, and the thousands and thousands of centuries, until, at last, there remains not one grain of sand at Waikiki and Pearl Harbor is filled up with land and growing coconuts and pine-apples. And then, oh my friends, even then, IT WOULD NOT YET BE SUNRISE IN HELL!"

Here, at the smashing impact of so abrupt a climax, unable to withstand the sheer simplicity and objectivity of such artful measurement of a trifle of eternity, Alice Akana's mind broke down and blew up. She uprose, reeled blindly, and stumbled to her knees at the penitent form. Abel Ah Yo had not finished his preaching, but it was his gift to know crowd psychology, and to feel the heat of the pentecostal conflagration that scorched his audience. He called for a rousing revival hymn from his singers, and stepped down to wade among the hallelujah-shouting negro soldiers to Alice Akana. And, ere the excitement began to ebb, nine-tenths of his congregation and all his converts were down on knees praying and shouting aloud an immensity of contriteness and sin.

Word came, via telephone, almost simultaneously to the Pacific and University Clubs, that at last Alice was telling her soul in meeting; and, by private machine and taxi-cab, for the first time Abel Ah Yo's revival was invaded by those of caste and place. The first comers beheld the curious sight of Hawaiian, Chinese and all variegated racial-mixtures of the smelting-pot of Hawaii, men and women, fading out and slinking away through the exits of Abel Ah Yo's tabernacle. But those who were sneaking out were mostly men, while those who remained were avid-faced as they hung on Alice's utterance.

Never was a more fearful and damning community narrative enunciated in the entire Pacific, north and south, than that enunciated by Alice Akana; the penitent Phryne of Honolulu.

"Huh!" the first comers heard her saying, having already disposed of most of the venial sins of the lesser ones of her memory. "You think this man, Stephen Makekau, is the son of Moses Makekau and Minnie Ah Ling, and has a legal right to the two hundred and eight dollars he draws down each month from Parke Richards Limited, for the lease of the fish-pond to Bill Kong at Amana. Not so. Stephen Makekau is not the son of Moses. He is the son of Aaron Kama and Tillie Naone. He was given as a present, as a feeding child, to Moses and Minnie by Aaron and Tillie. I know. Moses and Minnie and Aaron and Tillie are dead. Yet I know and can prove it. Old Mrs. Poepoe is still alive. I was present when Stephen was born, and in the night-time when he was two months old, I myself carried him as a present to Moses and Minnie, and old Mrs. Poepoe carried the lantern. This secret has been one of my sins. It has kept me from God. Now I am free of it. Young Archie Makekau, who collects bills for the Gas Company and plays baseball in the afternoon, and drinks too much gin, should get that two hundred and eight dollars the first of each month from Parke Richards Limited. He will blow it on gin and a Ford automobile. Stephen is a good man. Archie is no good. Also he is a liar, and he has served two sentences on the reef, and was in reform school before that. Yet God demands the truth, and Archie will get the money and make a bad use of it."

And in such fashion Alice rambled on through the experiences of her long and full-packed life. And women forgot they were in the tabernacle, and men too, and faces darkened with passion as they learned for the first time the long-buried secrets of their other halves.

"The lawyers' offices will be crowded tomorrow morning," MacIlwaine, chief of detectives, paused long enough from storing away useful information to lean and mutter in Colonel Stilton's ear.

Colonel Stilton grinned affirmation, although the chief of detectives could not fail to note the ghastliness of the grin.

"There is a banker in Honolulu. You all know his name. He is 'way up, swell society because of his wife. He owns much stock in General Plantations and Inter-Island."

MacIlwaine recognized the growing portrait and forbore to chuckle.

"His name is Colonel Stilton. Last Christmas Eve he came to my house with big *aloha*" (love) "and gave me mortgages on my land in Iapio Valley, all canceled, for two thousand dollars' worth. Now why did he have such big cash *aloha* for me? I will tell you . . ."

And tell she did, throwing the searchlight on ancient business transactions and political deals which from their inception had lurked in the dark.

"This," Alice concluded the episode, "has long been a sin upon my conscience, and kept my heart from God.

"And Harold Miles was that time President of the Senate, and next week he bought three town lots at Pearl Harbor, and painted his Honolulu house, and paid up his back dues in his clubs. Also the Ramsay home at Honokiki was left by will to the people if the Government would keep it up. But if the Government, after two years, did not begin to keep it up, then would it go to the Ramsay heirs, whom old Ramsay hated like poison. Well, it went to the heirs all right. Their lawyer was Charley Middleton, and he had me help fix it with the Government men. And their names were . . ." Six names, from both branches of the Legislature, Alice recited, and added: "Maybe they all painted their houses after that. For the first time have I spoken. My heart is much lighter and softer. It has been coated with an armor of house-paint against the Lord. And there is Harry Werther. He was in the Senate that time. Everybody said bad things about him, and he was never re-elected. Yet his house was not painted. He was honest. To this day his house is not painted, as everybody knows.

"There is Jim Lokendamper. He has a bad heart. I heard him, only last week, right here before you all, tell his soul. He did not tell all his soul, and he lied to God. I am not lying to God. It is a big telling, but I am telling everything. Now Azalea Akau, sitting right over there, is his wife. But Lizzie Lokendamper is his married wife. A long time ago he had the great *aloha* for Azalea. You think her uncle, who went to California and died, left her by will that two thousand five hundred dollars she got. Her uncle did not. I know. Her uncle died broke in California, and Jim Lokendamper sent eighty dollars to California to bury him. Jim Lokendamper had a piece of land in Kohala he got from his mother's aunt. Lizzie, his married wife, did not know this. So he sold it to the Kohala Ditch Company and gave the twenty-five hundred to Azalea Akau—"

Here, Lizzie, the married wife, upstood like a fury long-thwarted, and, in lieu of her husband, already fled, flung herself tooth and nail on Azalea.

"Wait, Lizzie Lokendamper!" Alice cried out. "I have much weight of you on my heart and some house-paint too . . ."

And when she had finished her disclosure of how Lizzie had painted her house, Azalea was up and raging.

"Wait, Azalea Akau. I shall now lighten my heart about you. And it is not house-paint. Jim always paid that. It is your new bath-tub and modern plumbing that is heavy on me . . ."

Worse, much worse, about many and sundry, did Alice Akana have to say, cutting high in business, financial and social life, as well as low. None was too high nor too low to escape; and not until two in the morning, before an entranced audience that packed the tabernacle to the doors, did she complete her recital of the personal and detailed iniquities she knew of the community in which she had lived intimately all her days. Just as she was finishing, she remembered more.

"Huh!" she sniffed. "I gave last week one lot worth eight hundred dollars cash market price to Abel Ah Yo to pay running expenses and add up in Peter's books in heaven. Where did I get that lot? You all think Mr Fleming Jason is a good man. He is more crooked than the entrance was to Pearl Lochs before the United States Government straightened the channel. He has liver disease now; but his sickness is a judgment of God, and he will die crooked. Mr Fleming Jason gave me that lot twenty-two years ago, when its cash market price was thirty-five dollars. Because his *aloha* for me was big? No. He never had *aloha* inside of him except for dollars.

"You listen. Mr Fleming Jason put a great sin upon me. When Frank Lomiloli was at my house, full of gin, for which gin Mr Fleming Jason paid me in advance five times over, I got Frank Lomiloli to sign his name to the sale paper of his town land for one hundred dollars. It was worth six hundred then. It is worth twenty thousand now. Maybe you want to know where that town land is. I will tell you and remove it off my heart. It is on King Street, where is now the Come Again Saloon, the Japanese Taxicab Company garage, and Smith & Wilson plumbing shop and the Ambrosia Ice Cream Parlors, with the two more stories big Addison Lodging House overhead. And it is all wood, and always has been well painted. Yesterday they started painting it again. But that paint will not stand between me and God. There are no more paint pots between me and my path to heaven."

The morning and evening papers of the day following held an unholy hush on the greatest news story of years; but Honolulu was half a-giggle and half aghast at the whispered reports, not always basely exaggerated, that circulated wherever two Honoluluans chanced to meet.

"Our mistake," said Colonel Stilton, at the club, "was that we did not, at the very first, appoint a committee of safety to keep track of Alice's soul."

Bob Cristy, one of the younger islanders, burst into laughter, so pointed and so loud that the meaning of it was demanded.

"Oh, nothing much," was his reply. "But I heard, on my way here, that old John

Ward had just been run in for drunken and disorderly conduct and for resisting an officer. Now Abel Ah Yo fine-toothcombs the police court. He loves nothing better than soul-snatching a chronic drunkard."

Colonel Stilton looked at Lask Finneston, and both looked at Gary Wilkinson. He returned to them a similar look.

"The old beach-comber!" Lask Finneston cried. "The drunken old reprobate! I'd forgotten he was alive. Wonderful constitution. Never drew a sober breath except when he was shipwrecked, and, when I remember him, into every deviltry afloat. He must be going on eighty."

"He isn't far away from it," Bob Cristy nodded. "Still beachcombs, drinks when he gets the price, and keeps all his senses, though he's not spry and has to use glasses when he reads. And his memory is perfect. Now if Abel Ah Yo catches him . . ."

Gary Wilkinson cleared his throat preliminary to speech.

"Now there's a grand old man," he said. "A left-over from a forgotten age. Few of his type remain. A pioneer. A true *kamaaina*" (old-timer). "Helpless and in the hands of the police in his old age! We should do something for him in recognition of his yeoman work in Hawaii. His old home, I happen to know, is Sag Harbor. He hasn't seen it for over half a century. Now why shouldn't he be surprised to-morrow morning by having his fine paid, and by being presented with return tickets to Sag Harbor, and, say, expenses for a year's trip? I move a committee. I appoint Colonel Chilton, Lask Finneston and . . . and myself. As for chairman, who more appropriate than Lask Finneston, who knew the old gentleman so well in the early days? Since there is no objection, I hereby appoint Lask Finneston chairman of the committee for the purpose of raising and donating money to pay the police-court fine and the expenses of a year's travel for the noble pioneer, John Ward, in recognition of a lifetime of devotion of energy to the upbuilding of Hawaii."

There was no dissent.

"The committee will now go into secret session," said Lask Finneston, arising and indicating the way to the library.

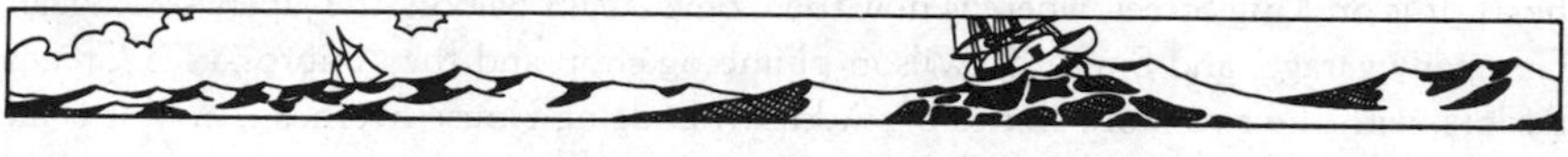

SHIN-BONES

They have gone down to the pit with their weapons of war, and they have laid their swords under their heads.

"IT WAS a sad thing to see the old lady revert."

Prince Akuli shot an apprehensive glance sideward to where, under the shade of a *kukui* tree, an old *wahine* (Hawaiian woman) was just settling herself to begin on some work in hand.

"Yes," he nodded half-sadly to me, "in her last years Hiwilani went back to the old ways, and to the old beliefs—in secret, of course. And *believe* me, she was some collector herself. You should have seen her bones. She had them all about her bedroom, in big jars, and they constituted most all her relatives, except a half-dozen or so that Kanau beat her out of by getting to them first. The way the pair of them used to quarrel about those bones was awe-inspiring. And it gave me the creeps, when I was a boy, to go into that big, for-ever-twilight room of hers, and know that in this jar was all that remained of my maternal grand-aunt, and that in that jar was my great-grandfather, and that in all the jars were the preserved bone-remnants of the shadowy dust of the ancestors whose seed had come down and been incorporated in the living, breathing me. Hiwilani had gone quite native at the last, sleeping on mats on the hard floor—she'd fired out of the room the great, royal, canopied four-poster that had been presented to her grandmother by Lord Byron, who was the cousin of the Don Juán Byron and came here in the frigate *Blonde* in 1825.

"She went back to all native, at the last, and I can see her yet, biting a bite out of the raw fish ere she tossed them to her women to eat. And she made them finish her *poi*, or whatever else she did not finish of herself. She—"

But he broke off abruptly, and by the sensitive dilation of his nostrils and by the expression of his mobile features I saw that he had read in the air and identified the odor that offended him.

"Deuce take it!" he cried to me. "It stinks to heaven. And I shall be doomed to wear it until we're rescued."

There was no mistaking the object of his abhorrence. The ancient crone was making a dearest-loved *lei* (wreath) of the fruit of the *hala* which is the screw-pine or pandanus of the South Pacific. She was cutting the many sections or nut-envelopes of the fruit into fluted bell-shapes preparatory to stringing them on the twisted and tough inner bark of the *hau* tree. It certainly smelled to heaven, but, to me, a *malahini* (new-comer), the smell was wine-woody and fruit-juicy and not unpleasant.

Prince Akuli's limousine had broken an axle a quarter of a mile away, and he and I had sought shelter from the sun in this veritable bowery of a mountain home. Humble and grass-thatched was the house, but it stood in a treasure-garden of begonias that sprayed their delicate blooms a score of feet above our heads, that were like trees, with willowy trunks of trees as thick as a man's arm. Here we refreshed ourselves with drinking-coconuts, while a cowboy rode a dozen miles to the nearest telephone and summoned a machine from town. The town itself we could see, the Lakanaii metropolis of Olokona, a smudge of smoke on the shore-line, as we looked down across the miles of cane-fields, the billow-wreathed reef-lines, and the blue haze of ocean to where the island of Oahu shimmered like a dim opal on the horizon.

Maui is the Valley Isle of Hawaii and Kauai the Garden Isle; but Lakanaii, lying abreast of Oahu, is recognized in the present, and was known of old and always, as the Jewel Isle of the group. Not the largest, nor merely the smallest, Lakanaii is conceded by all to be the wildest, the most wildly beautiful, and, in its size, the richest of all the islands. Its sugar tonnage per acre is the highest, its mountain beef-cattle the fattest, its rainfall the most generous without ever being disastrous. It resembles Kauai in that it is the first-formed and therefore the oldest island, so that it had had time sufficient to break down its lava rock into the richest soil, and to erode the canyons between the ancient craters until they are like Grand Canyons of the Colorado, with numberless waterfalls plunging thousands of feet in the sheer or dissipating into veils of vapor, and evanescing in mid-air to descend softly and invisibly through a mirage of rainbows, like so much dew or gentle shower, upon the abyss-floors.

Yet Lakanaii is easy to describe. But how can one describe Prince Akuli? To know him is to know all Lakanaii most thoroughly. In addition, one must know thoroughly a great deal of the rest of the world. In the first place, Prince Akuli has no recognized nor legal right to be called "Prince." Furthermore, "Akuli" means the "squid" . So that Prince Squid could scarcely be the dignified title of the straight descendant of the oldest and highest *aliis* (high chiefs) of Hawaii—an old and exclusive stock, wherein, in the ancient way of the Egyptian Pharaohs, brothers and sisters had even wed on the throne for the reason that they could not marry beneath rank, that in all their known world there was none of higher rank, and that, at every hazard, the dynasty must be perpetuated.

I have heard Prince Akuli's singing historians (inherited from his father) chanting their interminable genealogies, by which they demonstrated that he was the highest *alii* in all Hawaii. Beginning with Wakea, who is their Adam, and with Papa, their Eve, through as many generations as there are letters in our alphabet they trace down to Nanakaoko, the first ancestor born in Hawaii and whose wife was Kahihiokalani. Later, but always highest, their generations split from the generations of Ua, who was the founder of the two distinct lines of the Kauai and Oahu kings.

In the eleventh century AD, by the Lakanaii historians, at the time brothers and sisters mated because none existed to excel them, their rank received a boost of new blood of rank that was next to heaven's door. One Hoikemaha, steering by the stars and the ancient traditions, arrived in a great double-canoe from Samoa. He married a lesser *alii* of Lakanaii, and when his three sons were grown, returned with them to Samoa to bring back his own youngest brother. But with him he brought back Kumi, the son of Tui Manua, which latter's rank was highest in all Polynesia, and barely second to that of the demigods and gods. So the estimable seed of Kumi, eight centuries before, had entered into the *aliis* of Lakanaii, and been passed down by them in the undeviating line to reposit in Prince Akuli.

Him I first met, talking with an Oxford accent, in the officers' mess of the Black Watch in South Africa. This was just before that famous regiment was cut to pieces at Magersfontein. He had as much right to be in that mess as he had to his accent, for he was Oxford-educated and held the Queen's Commission. With him, as his guest, taking a look at the war, was Prince Cupid, so nicknamed, but the true prince of all Hawaii, including Lakanaii, whose real and legal title was Prince Jonah Kuhio Kalanianaole, and who might have been the living King of Hawaii Nei had it not been for the *haole* (white man) Revolution and Annexation—this, despite the fact that Prince Cupid's *alii* genealogy was lesser to the heaven-boosted genealogy of Prince Akuli. For Prince Akuli might have been King of Lakanaii, and of all Hawaii, perhaps, had not his grandfather been soundly thrashed by the first and greatest of the Kamehamehas.

This had occurred in the year 1810, in the booming days of the sandalwood trade, and in the same year that the King of Kauai came in, and was good, and ate out of Kamehameha's hand. Prince Akuli's grandfather, in that year, had received his trouncing and subjugating because he was "old school" . He had not imaged island empire in terms of gunpowder and *haole* gunners. Kamehameha, farther-visioned, had annexed the service of *haoles*, including such men as Isaac Davis, mate and sole survivor of the massacred crew of the schooner *Fair American*, and John Young, captured boatswain of the snow *Eleanor.* And Isaac Davis, and John Young, and others of their waywardly adventurous ilk, with six-pounder brass carronades from the captured *Iphigenia* and *Fair American,* had destroyed the war canoes and shattered the morale of the King of Lakanaii's land-fighters, receiving duly in return from Kamehameha, according to agreement: Isaac Davis, six hundred mature and fat hogs; John Young, five hundred of the same described pork on the hoof that was split.

And so, out of all incests and lusts of the primitive cultures and beast-man's gropings toward the stature of manhood, out of all red murders, and brute battlings, and matings with the younger brothers of the demigods, world-polished, Oxford-accented, twentieth century to the tick of the second, comes Prince Akuli, Prince Squid, pure-veined Polynesian, a living bridge across the thousand centuries, comrade, friend and fellow-traveler out of his wrecked seven-thousand-dollar limousine, marooned with me in a begonia paradise fourteen hundred feet above the sea, and his island metropolis of Olokona, to tell me of his mother, who reverted in her old age to ancientness of religious concept and ancestor worship, and collected and surrounded herself with the charnel bones of those who had been her forerunners back in the darkness of time.

"King Kalakaua started this collecting fad, over on Oahu," Prince Akuli continued. "And his queen, Kapiolani, caught the fad from him. They collected everything—old *makaloa* mats, old *tapas,* old calabashes, old double-canoes and idols which the priests had saved from the general destruction in 1819. I haven't seen a pearl-shell fish-hook in years, but I swear that Kalakaua accumulated ten thousand of them, to say nothing of human jaw-bone fish-hooks, and feather cloaks, and capes and helmets, and stone adzes, and *poi-* pounders of phallic design. When he and Kapiolani made their royal progresses around the islands, their hosts had to hide away their personal relics. For to the king, in theory, belongs all property of his people; and with Kalakaua, when it came to the old things, theory and practice were one.

"From him my father, Kanau, got the collecting bee in his bonnet, and Hiwilani was likewise infected. But father was modern to his finger-tips. He believed neither in the gods of the *kahunas*" (priests) "nor of the missionaries. He didn't believe in anything except sugar stocks, horse-breeding, and that his grandfather had been a fool in not collecting a few Isaac Davises and John Youngs and brass carronades before he went to war with Kamehameha. So he collected curios in the pure collector's spirit; but my mother took it seriously. That was why she went in for bones. I remember, too, she had an ugly old stone-idol she used to yammer to and crawl around on the floor before. It's in the Deacon Museum now. I sent it there after her death, and her collection of bones to the Royal Mausoleum in Olokona.

"I don't know whether you remember her father was Kaaukuu. Well, he was, and he was a giant. When they built the Mausoleum, his bones, nicely cleaned and preserved, were dug out of their hiding-place, and placed in the Mausoleum. Hiwilani had an old retainer, Ahuna. She stole the key from Kanau one night, and made Ahuna go and steal her father's bones out of the Mausoleum. I know. And he must have been a giant. She kept him in one of her big jars. One day, when I was a tidy size of a lad, and curious to know if Kaaukuu was as big as tradition had him, I fished his intact lower jaw out of the jar, and the wrappings, and tried it on. I stuck my head right through it, and it rested around my neck and on my shoulders like a horse collar. And every tooth was in the jaw, whiter than porcelain, without a cavity, the enamel unstained and unchipped. I got the walloping of my life for that offence, although she had to call old Ahuna in to help give it to me. But the incident served me well. It won her confidence in me that I was not afraid of the bones of the dead ones, and it won for me my Oxford education. As you shall see, if that car doesn't arrive first.

"Old Ahuna was one of the real old ones with the hall-mark on him and branded into him of faithful born-slave service. He knew more about my mother's family, and my father's, than did both of them put together. And he knew, what no living other knew, the burial-place of centuries, where were hid the bones of most of her ancestors and of Kanau's. Kanau couldn't worm it out of the old fellow, who looked upon Kanau as an apostate.

"Hiwilani struggled with the old codger for years. How she ever succeeded is beyond me. Of course, on the face of it, she was faithful to the old religion. This might have persuaded Ahuna to loosen up a little. Or she may have jolted fear into him; for she knew a lot of the line of chatter of the old Huni sorcerers, and she could make a noise like being on terms of utmost intimacy with Uli, who is the chiefest god of sorcery of all the sorcerers. She could skin the ordinary *kahuna lapaau*" (medicine man) "when it came to praying to Lonopuha and Koleamoku; read dreams and visions and signs and omens and indigestions to beat the band; make the practitioners under the medicine god, Maiola, look like thirty cents; pull off a *pule hee* incantation that would make them dizzy; and she claimed to a practice of *kahuna hoenoho,* which is modern spiritism, second to none. I have myself seen her drink the wind, throw a fit, and prophesy. The *aumakuas* were brothers to her when she slipped offerings to them across the altars of the ruined *heiaus*" (temples) "with a line of prayer that was as unintelligible to me as it was hair-raising. And as for old Ahuna, she could make him get down on the floor and yammer and bite himself when she pulled the real mystery dope on him.

"Nevertheless, my private opinion is that it was the *anaana* stuff that got him. She snipped off a lock of his hair one day with a pair of manicure scissors. This lock of hair was what we call the *maunu,* meaning the bait. And she took jolly good care to let him know she had that bit of his hair. Then she tipped it off to him that she had buried it, and was deeply engaged each night in her offerings and incantations to Uli."

"That was the regular praying-to-death?" I queried in the pause of Prince Akuli's lighting his cigarette.

"Sure thing," he nodded. "And Ahuna fell for it. First he tried to locate the hiding-place of the bait of his hair. Failing that, he hired a *pahiuhiu* sorcerer to find it for him. But Hiwilani queered that game by threatening to the sorcerer to practise *apo leo* on him, which is the art of permanently depriving a person of the power of speech without otherwise injuring him.

"Then it was that Ahuna began to pine away and get more like a corpse every day. In desperation he appealed to Kanau. I happened to be present. You have heard what sort of a man my father was.

" 'Pig!' he called Ahuna. 'Swine-brains! Stinking fish! Die and be done with it. You are a fool. It is all nonsense. There is nothing in anything. The drunken *haole*, Howard, can prove the missionaries wrong. Square-face gin proves Howard wrong. The doctors say he won't last six months. Even square-face gin lies. Life is a liar, too. And here are hard times upon us, and a slump in sugar. Glanders has got into my brood mares. I wish I could lie down and sleep for a hundred years, and wake up to find sugar up a hundred points."

"Father was something of a philosopher himself, with a bitter wit and a trick of spitting out staccato epigrams. He clapped his hands. "Bring me a high-ball," he commanded; "no, bring me two high-balls." Then he turned on Ahuna. "Go and let yourself die, old heathen, survival of darkness, blight of the Pit that you are. But don't die on these premises. I desire merriment and laughter, and the sweet tickling of music, and the beauty of youthful motion, not the croaking of sick toads and googly-eyed corpses about me still afoot on their shaky legs. I'll be that way soon enough if I live long enough. And it will be my everlasting regret if I don't live long enough. Why in hell did I sink that last twenty thousand into Curtis's plantation? Howard warned me the slump was coming, but I thought it was the square-face making him lie. And Curtis has blown his brains out, and his head *luna* has run away with his daughter, and the sugar chemist has got typhoid, and everything's going to smash."

"He clapped his hands for his servants, and commanded: "Bring me my singing boys. And the *hula* dancers—plenty of them. And send for old Howard. Somebody's got to pay, and I'll shorten his six months of life by a month. But above all, music. Let there be music. It is stronger than drink, and quicker than opium."

"He with his music druggery! It was his father, the old savage, who was entertained on board a French frigate, and for the first time heard an orchestra. When the little concert was over, the captain, to find which piece he liked best, asked which piece he'd like repeated. Well, when grandfather got done describing, what piece do you think it was?"

I gave up, while the Prince lighted a fresh cigarette.

"Why, it was the first one, of course. Not the real first one, but the tuning up that preceded it."

I nodded, with eyes and face mirthful of appreciation, and Prince Akuli, with another apprehensive glance at the old *wahine* and her half-made *hala lei,* returned to his tale of the bones of his ancestors.

"It was somewhere around this stage of the game that old Ahuna gave in to Hiwilani. He didn't exactly give in. He compromised. That's where I come in. If he would bring her the bones of her mother, and of her grandfather (who was the father of Kaaukuu, and who by tradition was rumored to have been even bigger than his giant son), she would return to Ahuna the bait of his hair she was praying him to death with. He, on the other hand, stipulated that he was not to reveal to her the secret burial-place of all the *alii* of Lakanaii all the way back. Nevertheless, he was too old to dare the adventure alone, must be helped by some one who of necessity would come to know the secret, and I was that one. I was the highest *alii,* beside my father and mother, and they were no higher than I.

"So I came upon the scene, being summoned into the twilight room to confront those two dubious old ones who dealt with the dead. They were a pair—mother fat to despair of helplessness, Ahuna thin as a skeleton and as fragile. Of her one had the impression that if she lay down on her back she could not roll over without the aid of block-and-tackle; of Ahuna one's impression was that the tooth-pickedness of him would shatter to splinters if one bumped into him.

"And when they had broached the matter, there was more *pilikia*" (trouble). "My father's attitude stiffened my resolution. I refused to go on the bone-snatching expedition. I said I didn't care a whoop for the bones of all the *aliis* of my family and race. You see, I had just discovered Jules Verne, loaned me by old Howard, and was reading my head off. Bones? When there were North Poles, and Centres of Earths, and hairy comets to ride across space among the stars! Of course I didn't want to go on any bone-snatching expedition. I said my father was able-bodied, and he could go, splitting equally with her whatever bones he brought back. But she said he was only a blamed collector—or words to that effect, only stronger.

" 'I know him,' she assured me. 'He'd bet his mother's bones on a horse-race or an ace-full.'

"I stood with father when it came to modern scepticism, and I told her the whole thing was rubbish. 'Bones?' I said. 'What are bones? Even field mice, and many rats, and cockroaches have bones, though the roaches wear their bones outside their meat instead of inside. The difference between man and other animals,' I told her, 'is not bones, but brain. Why, a bullock has bigger bones than a man, and more than one fish I've eaten has more bones, while a whale beats creation when it comes to bone.'

"It was frank talk, which is our Hawaiian way, as you have long since learned. In return, equally frank, she regretted she hadn't given me away as a feeding child when I was born. Next she bewailed that she had ever borne me. From that it was only a step to *anaana* me. She threatened me with it, and I did the bravest thing I have ever done. Old Howard had given me a knife of many blades, and corkscrews, and screw-drivers, and all sorts of contrivances, including a tiny pair of scissors. I proceeded to pare my finger-nails.

" 'There,' I said, as I put the parings into her hand. 'Just to show you what I think of it. There's bait and to spare. Go on and *anaana* me if you can.'

"I have said it was brave. It was. I was only fifteen, and I had lived all my days in the thick of the mystery stuff, while my scepticism, very recently acquired, was only skin-deep. I could be a sceptic out in the open in the sunshine. But I was afraid of the dark. And in that twilight room, the bones of the dead all about me in the big jars, why, the old lady had me scared stiff. As we say to-day, she had my goat. Only I was brave and didn't let on. And I put my bluff across, for my mother flung the parings into my face and burst into tears. Tears in an elderly woman weighing three hundred and twenty pounds are scarcely impressive, and I hardened the brassiness of my bluff.

"She shifted her attack, and proceeded to talk with the dead. Nay, more, she summoned them there, and, though I was all ripe to see but couldn't, Ahuna saw the father of Kaaukuu in the corner and lay down on the floor and yammered. Just the same, although I almost saw the old giant, I didn't quite see him.

" 'Let him talk for himself,' I said. But Hiwilani persisted in doing the talking for him, and in laying upon me his solemn injunction that I must go with Ahuna to the burial-place and bring back the bones desired by my mother. But I argued that if the dead ones could be invoked to kill living men by wasting sicknesses, and that if the dead ones could transport themselves from their burial-crypts into the corner of her room, I couldn't see why they shouldn't leave their bones behind them, there in her room and ready to be jarred, when they said good-by and departed for the middle world, the over world, or the under world, or wherever they abided when they weren't paying social calls.

"Whereupon mother let loose on poor old Ahuna, or let loose upon him the ghost of Kaaukuu's father, supposed to be crouching there in the corner, who commanded Ahuna to divulge to her the burial-place. I tried to stiffen him up, telling him to let the old ghost divulge the secret himself, than whom nobody else knew it better, seeing that he had resided there upwards of a century. But Ahuna was old school. He possessed no iota of scepticism. The more Hiwilani frightened him, the more he rolled on the floor and the louder he yammered.

"But when he began to bite himself, I gave in. I felt sorry for him; but, over and beyond that, I began to admire him. He was sterling stuff, even if he was a survival of darkness. Here, with the fear of mystery cruelly upon him, believing Hiwilani's dope implicitly, he was caught between two fidelities. She was his living *alii,* his *alii kapo*" (sacred chiefess). "He must be faithful to her, yet more faithful must he be to all the dead and gone *aliis* of her line who depended solely on him that their bones should not be disturbed.

"I gave in. But I, too, imposed stipulations. Steadfastly had my father, new school, refused to let me go to England for my education. That sugar was slumping was reason sufficient for him. Steadfastly had my mother, old school, refused, her heathen mind too dark to place any value on education, while it was shrewd enough to discern that education led to unbelief in all that was old. I wanted to study, to study science, the arts, philosophy, to study everything old Howard knew, which enabled him, on the edge of the grave, undauntedly to sneer at superstition, and to give me Jules Verne to read. He was an Oxford man before he went wild and wrong, and it was he who had set the Oxford bee buzzing in my noddle.

"In the end Ahuna and I, old school and new school leagued together, won out. Mother promised that she'd make father send me to England, even if she had to pester him into a prolonged drinking that would make his digestion go back on him. Also, Howard was to accompany me, so that I could decently bury him in England. He was a queer one, old Howard, an individual if there ever was one. Let me tell you a little story about him. It was when Kalakaua was starting on his trip around the world. You remember, when Armstrong, and Judd, and the drunken valet of a German baron accompanied him. Kalakaua made the proposition to Howard . . ."

But here the long-apprehended calamity fell upon Prince Akuli. The old *wahine* had finished her *lei hala.* Barefooted, with no adornment of femininity, clad in a shapeless shift of much-washed cotton, with age-withered face and labor-gnarled hands, she cringed before him and crooned a *mele* in his honor, and, still cringing, put the *lei* around his neck. It is true the *hala* smelled most freshly strong, yet was the act beautiful to me, and the old woman herself beautiful to me. My mind leapt into the Prince's narrative so that to Ahuna I could not help likening her.

Oh, truly, to be an *alii* in Hawaii, even in this second decade of the twentieth century, is no light thing. The *alii,* utterly of the new, must be kindly and kingly to those old ones absolutely of the old. Nor did the Prince without a kingdom, his loved island long since annexed by the United States and incorporated into a territory along with the rest of the Hawaiian Islands—nor did the Prince betray his repugnance for the odor of the *hala.* He bowed his head graciously; and his royal condescending words of pure Hawaiian I knew would make the old woman's heart warm until she died with remembrance of the wonderful occasion. The wry grimace he stole to me would not have been made had he felt any uncertainty of its escaping her.

"And so," Prince Akuli resumed, after the *wahine* had tottered away in an ecstasy, "Ahuna and I departed on our grave-robbing adventure. You know the Iron-bound Coast."

I nodded, knowing full well the spectacle of those lava leagues of weather coast, truly iron-bound so far as landing-places or anchorages were concerned, great forbidding cliff-walls thousands of feet in height, their summits wreathed in cloud and rain squall, their knees hammered by the trade-wind billows into spouting, spuming white, the air, from sea to rain-cloud, spanned by a myriad leaping waterfalls, provocative, in day or night, of countless sun and lunar rainbows. Valleys, so called, but fissures rather, slit the cyclopean walls here and there, and led away into a lofty and madly vertical back country, most of it inaccessible to the foot of man and trod only by the wild goat.

"Precious little you know of it," Prince Akuli retorted, in reply to my nod. "You've seen it only from the decks of steamers. There are valleys there, inhabited valleys, out of which there is no exit by land, and perilously accessible by canoe only on the selected days of two months in the year. When I was twenty-eight I was over there in one of them on a hunting trip. Bad weather, in the auspicious period, marooned us for three weeks. Then five of my party and myself swam for it out through the surf. Three of us made the canoes waiting for us. The other two were flung back on the sand, each with a broken arm. Save for us, the entire party remained there until the next year, ten months afterward. And one of them was Wilson, of Wilson & Wall, the Honolulu sugar factors. And he was engaged to be married.

"I've seen a goat, shot above by a hunter above, land at my feet a thousand yards underneath. *Believe* me, that landscape seemed to rain goats and rocks for ten minutes. One of my canoemen fell off the trail between the two little valleys of Aipio and Luno. He hit first fifteen hundred feet beneath us, and fetched up in a ledge three hundred feet farther down. We didn't bury him. We couldn't get to him, and flying machines had not yet been invented. His bones are there now, and barring earthquake and volcano, will be there when the Trumps of Judgment sound.

"Goodness me! Only the other day, when our Promotion Committee, trying to compete with Honolulu for the tourist trade, called in the engineers to estimate what it would cost to build a scenic drive around the Iron-bound Coast, the lowest figures were a quarter of a million dollars a mile!

"And Ahuna and I, an old man and a young boy, started for that stern coast in a canoe paddled by old men! The youngest of them, the steersman, was over sixty, while the rest of them averaged seventy at the very least. There were eight of them, and we started in the night-time, so that none should see us go. Even those old ones, trusted all their lives, knew no more than the fringe of the secret. To the fringe, only, could they take us.

"And the fringe was—I don't mind telling that much—the fringe was Ponuloo Valley. We got there the third afternoon following. The old chaps weren't strong on the paddles. It was a funny expedition, into such wild waters, with now one and now another of our ancient-mariner crew collapsing and even fainting. One of them actually died on the second morning out. We buried him overside. It was positively uncanny, the heathen ceremonies those gray ones pulled off in burying their gray brother. And I was only fifteen, *alii kapo* over them by blood of heathenness and right of hereditary heathen rule, with a penchant for Jules Verne and shortly to sail for England for my education! So one learns. Small wonder my father was a philosopher, in his own lifetime spanning the history of man from human sacrifice and idol worship, through the religions of man's upward striving, to the Medusa of rank atheism at the end of it all. Small wonder that, like old Ecclesiastes, he found vanity in all things and surcease in sugar stocks, singing boys and *hula* dancers."

Prince Akuli debated with his soul for an interval.

"Oh, well," he sighed, "I have done some spanning of time myself." He sniffed disgustedly of the odor of the *hala lei* that stifled him. "It stinks of the ancient," he vouchsafed. "I? I stink of the modern. My father was right. The sweetest of all is sugar up a hundred points, or four aces in a poker game. If the Big War lasts another year, I shall clean up three-quarters of a million over a million. If peace breaks to-morrow, with the consequent slump, I could enumerate a hundred who will lose my direct bounty, and go into the old natives' homes my father and I long since endowed for them."

He clapped his hands, and the old *wahine* tottered toward him in an excitement of haste to serve. She cringed before him, as he drew pad and pencil from his breast pocket.

"Each month, old woman of our old race," he addressed her, "will you receive, by rural free delivery, a piece of written paper that you can exchange with any storekeeper anywhere for ten dollars gold. This shall be so for as long as you live. Behold! I write the record and the remembrance of it, here and now, with this pencil on this paper. And this is because you are of my race and service, and because you have honored me this day with your mats to sit upon and your thrice-blessed and thrice-delicious *lei hala.*"

He turned to me a weary and sceptical eye, saying:

"And if I die to-morrow, not alone will the lawyers contest my disposition of my property, but they will contest my benefactions and my pensions accorded, and the clarity of my mind.

"It was the right weather of the year; but even then, with our old weak ones at the paddles, we did not attempt the landing until we had assembled half the population of Ponuloo Valley down on the steep little beach. Then we counted our waves, selected the best one, and ran in on it. Of course, the canoe was swamped and the outrigger smashed, but the ones on shore dragged us up unharmed beyond the wash.

"Ahuna gave his orders. In the night-time all must remain within their houses, and the dogs be tied up and have their jaws bound so that there should be no barking. And in the night-time Ahuna and I stole out on our journey, no one knowing whether we went to the right or left or up the valley toward its head. We carried jerky, and hard *poi* and dried *aku,* and from the quantity of the food I knew we were to be gone several days. Such a trail! A Jacob's ladder to the sky, truly, for that first *pali*" (precipice), "almost straight up, was three thousand feet above the sea. And we did it in the dark!

"At the top, beyond the sight of the valley we had left, we slept until daylight on the hard rock in a hollow nook Ahuna knew, and that was so small that we were squeezed. And the old fellow, for fear that I might move in the heavy restlessness of lad's sleep, lay on the outside with one arm resting across me. At daybreak, I saw why. Between us and the lip of the cliff scarcely a yard intervened. I crawled to the lip and looked, watching the abyss take on immensity in the growing light and trembling from the fear of height that was upon me. At last I made out the sea, over half a mile straight beneath. And we had done this thing in the dark!

"Down in the next valley, which was a very tiny one, we found evidence of the ancient population, but there were no people. The only way was the crazy foot-paths up and down the dizzy valley walls from valley to valley. But lean and aged as Ahuna was, he seemed untirable. In the second valley dwelt an old leper in hiding. He did not know me, and when Ahuna told him who I was, he groveled at my feet, almost clasping them, and mumbled a *mele* of all my line out of a lipless mouth.

"The next valley proved to be the valley. It was long and so narrow that its floor had caught not sufficient space of soil to grow *taro* for a single person. Also, it had no beach, the stream that threaded it leaping a *pali* of several hundred feet down to the sea. It was a god-forsaken place of naked, eroded lava, to which only rarely could the scant vegetation find root-hold. For miles we followed up that winding fissure through the towering walls, far into the chaos of back country that lies behind the Iron-bound Coast. How far that valley penetrated I do not know, but, from the quantity of water in the stream, I judged it far. We did not go to the valley's head. I could see Ahuna casting glances to all the peaks, and I knew he was taking bearings, known to him alone, from natural objects. When he halted at the last, it was with abrupt certainty. His bearings had crossed. He threw down the portion of food and outfit he had carried, It was the place. I looked on either hand at the hard, implacable walls, naked of vegetation, and could dream of no burial-place possible in such bare adamant.

"We ate, then stripped for work. Only did Ahuna permit me to retain my shoes. He stood beside me at the edge of a deep pool, likewise appareled and prodigiously skinny.

" 'You will dive down into the pool at this spot," he said. 'Search the rock with your hands as you descend, and, about a fathom and a half down, you will find a hole. Enter it, head-first, but going slowly, for the lava rock is sharp and may cut your head and body.'

" 'And then?' I queried. 'You will find the hole growing larger,' was his answer. 'When you have gone all of eight fathoms along the passage, come up slowly, and you will find your head in the air, above water, in the dark. Wait there then for me. The water is very cold.'

"It didn't sound good to me. I was thinking, not of the cold water and the dark, but of the bones. 'You go first,' I said. But he claimed he could not. 'You are my *alii*, my prince,' he said. 'It is impossible that I should go before you into the sacred burial-place of your kingly ancestors.'

"But the prospect did not please. 'Just cut out this prince stuff,' I told him. 'It isn't what it's cracked up to be. You go first, and I'll never tell on you.' 'Not alone the living must we please,' he admonished, 'but, more so, the dead must we please. Nor can we lie to the dead.'

"We argued it out, and for half an hour it was stalemate. I wouldn't, and he simply couldn't. He tried to buck me up by appealing to my pride. He chanted the heroic deeds of my ancestors; and, I remember especially, he sang to me of Mokomoku, my great-grandfather and the gigantic father of the gigantic Kaaukuu, telling how thrice in battle Mokomoku leaped among his foes, seizing by the neck a warrior in either hand and knocking their heads together until they were dead. But this was not what decided me. I really felt sorry for old Ahuna, he was so beside himself for fear the expedition would come to naught. And I was coming to a great admiration for the old fellow, not least among the reasons being the fact of his lying down to sleep between me and the cliff-lip.

"So, with true *alii-* authority of command, saying, 'You will immediately follow after me,' I dived in. Everything he had said was correct. I found the entrance to the subterranean passage, swam carefully through it, cutting my shoulder once on the lava-sharp roof, and emerged in the darkness and air. But before I could count thirty, he broke water beside me, rested his hand on my arm to make sure of me, and directed me to swim ahead of him for the matter of a hundred feet or so. Then we touched bottom and climbed out on the rocks. And still no light, and I remember I was glad that our altitude was too high for centipedes.

"He had brought with him a coconut calabash, tightly stoppered, of whale-oil that must have been landed on Lahaina beach thirty years before. From his mouth he took a water-tight arrangement of a matchbox composed of two empty rifle-cartridges fitted snugly together. He lighted the wicking that floated on the oil, and I looked about, and knew disappointment. No burial-chamber was it, but merely a lava tube such as occurs on all the islands.

"He put the calabash of light into my hands and started me ahead of him on the way, which he assured me was long, but not too long. It was long, at least a mile in my sober judgment, though at the time it seemed five miles; and it ascended sharply. When Ahuna, at the last, stopped me, I knew we were close to our goal. He knelt on his lean old knees on the sharp lava rock, and clasped my knees with his skinny arms. My hand that was free of the calabash lamp he placed on his head. He chanted to me, with his old cracked, quavering voice, the line of my descent and my essential high *alii-* ness. And then he said:

" 'Tell neither Kanau nor Hiwilani aught of what you are about to behold. There is no sacredness in Kanau. His mind is filled with sugar and the breeding of horses. I do know that he sold a feather cloak his grandfather had worn to that English collector for eight thousand dollars, and the money he lost the next day betting on the polo game between Maui and Oahu. Hiwilani, your mother, is filled with sacredness. She is too much filled with sacredness. She grows old, and weak-headed, and she traffics over-much with sorceries.'

" 'No,' I made answer. 'I shall tell no one. If I did, then I would have to return to this place again. And I do not want ever to return to this place. I'll try anything once. This I shall never try twice.'

" 'It is well,' he said, and arose, falling behind so that I should enter first. Also, he said: 'Your mother is old. I shall bring her, as promised, the bones of her mother and of her grandfather. These should content her until she dies; and then, if I die before her, it is you who must see to it that all the bones in her family collection are placed in the Royal Mausoleum.'

"I have given all the Islands" museums the once-over," Prince Akuli lapsed back into slang, "and I must say that the totality of the collections cannot touch what I saw in our Lakanaii burial-cave. Remember, and with reason and history, we trace back the highest and oldest genealogy in the Islands. Everything that I had ever dreamed or heard of, and much more that I had not, was there. The place was wonderful. Ahuna, sepulchrally muttering prayers and *meles*, moved about, lighting various whale-oil lamp-calabashes. They were all there, the Hawaiian race from the beginning of Hawaiian time. Bundles of bones and bundles of bones, all wrapped decently in *tapa*, until for all the world it was like the parcels-post department at a post office.

"And everything! *Kahilis*, which you may know developed out of the fly-flapper into symbols of royalty until they became larger than hearse-plumes with handles a fathom and a half and over two fathoms in length. And such handles! Of the wood of the *kauila*, inlaid with shell and ivory and bone with a cleverness that had died out among our artificers a century before. It was a centuries-old family attic. For the first time I saw things I had only heard of, such as the *pahoas*, fashioned of whale-teeth and suspended by braided human hair, and worn on the breast only by the highest of rank.

"There were *tapas* and mats of the rarest and oldest; capes and *leis* and helmets and cloaks, priceless all, except the too-ancient ones, of the feathers of the *mamo*, and of the *iwi* and the *akakane* and the *o-o*. I saw one of the *mamo* cloaks that was superior to that finest one in the Bishop Museum in Honolulu, and that they value at between half a million and a million dollars. Goodness me, I thought at the time, it was lucky Kanau didn't know about it.

"Such a mess of things! Carved gourds and calabashes, shell-scrapers, nets of *olona* fiber, a junk of *iè-iè* baskets and fish-hooks of every bone and spoon of shell. Musical instruments of the forgotten days—*ukukes* and nose flutes, and *kiokios* which are likewise played with one unstoppered nostril. Taboo *poi* bowls and finger bowls, left-handed adzes of the canoe gods, lava-cup lamps, stone mortars and pestles and *poi*-pounders. And adzes again, a myriad of them, beautiful ones, from an ounce in weight for the finer carving of idols to fifteen pounds for the felling of trees, and all with the sweetest handles I have ever beheld.

"There were the *kaekeekes*— you know, our ancient drums, hollowed sections of the coconut tree, covered one end with shark-skin. The first *kaekeeke* of all Hawaii Ahuna pointed out to me and told me the tale. It was manifestly most ancient. He was afraid to touch it for fear the age-rotted wood of it would crumble to dust, the ragged tatters of the shark-skin head of it still attached. 'This is the very oldest and father of all our *kaekeekes,*' Ahuna told me. 'Kila, the son of Moikeha, brought it back from far Raiatea in the South Pacific. And it was Kila's own son, Kahai, who made that same journey, and was gone ten years, and brought back with him from Tahiti the first breadfruit trees that sprouted and grew on Hawaiian soil.'

"And the bones and bones! The parcel-delivery array of them! Besides the small bundles of the long bones, there were full skeletons, *tapa-* wrapped, lying in one-man, and two- and three-man canoes of precious *koa* wood, with curved outriggers of *wiliwili* wood, and proper paddles to hand with the *io-* projection at the point simulating the continuance of the handle, as if, like a skewer, thrust through the flat length of the blade. And their war weapons were laid away by the sides of the lifeless bones that had wielded them—rusty old horse-pistols, derringers, pepper-boxes, five-barrelled fantastiques, Kentucky long rifles, muskets handled in trade by John Company and Hudson's Bay, shark-tooth swords, wooden stabbing-knives, arrows and spears bone-headed of the fish and the pig and of man, and spears and arrows wooden-headed and fire-hardened.

"Ahuna put a spear in my hand, headed and pointed finely with the long shin-bone of a man, and told me the tale of it. But first he unwrapped the long bones, arms and legs, of two parcels, the bones, under the wrappings, neatly tied like so many faggots. 'This,' said Ahuna, exhibiting the pitiful white contents of one parcel, 'is Laulani. She was the wife of Akaiko, whose bones, now placed in your hands, much larger and male-like as you observe, held up the flesh of a large man, a three hundred pounder seven-footer, three centuries agone. And this spear-head is made of the shin-bone of Keola, a mighty wrestler and runner of their own time and place. And he loved Laulani, and she fled with him. But in a forgotten battle on the sands of Kalini, Akaiko rushed the lines of the enemy, leading the charge that was successful, and seized upon Keola, his wife's lover, and threw him to the ground, and sawed through his neck to the death with a shark-tooth knife. Thus, in the old days as always, did man combat for woman with man. And Laulani was beautiful; that Keola should be made into a spearhead for her! She was formed like a queen, and her body was a long bowl of sweetness, and her fingers *lomi'd'* (massaged) 'to slimness and smallness at her mother's breast. For ten generations have we remembered her beauty. Your father's singing boys to-day sing of her beauty in the *hula* that is named of her. This is Laulani, whom you hold in your hands.'

"And, Ahuna done, I could but gaze, with imagination at the one time sobered and fired. Old drunken Howard had lent me his Tennyson, and I had mooned long and often over the *Idyls of the King.* Here were the three, I thought—Arthur, and Launcelot, and Guinevere. This, then, I pondered, was the end of it all, of life and strife and striving and love, the weary spirits of these long-gone ones to be invoked by fat old women and mangy sorcerers, the bones of them to be esteemed of collectors and betted on horse-races and ace-fulls or to be sold for cash and invested in sugar stocks.

"For me it was illumination. I learned there in the burial-cave the great lesson. And to Ahuna I said: 'The spear headed with the long bone of Keola I shall take for my own. Never shall I sell it. I shall keep it always.'

" 'And for what purpose?' he demanded. And I replied: 'That the contemplation of it may keep my hand sober and my feet on earth with the knowledge that few men are fortunate enough to have as much of a remnant of themselves as will compose a spear-head when they are three centuries dead.'

"And Ahuna bowed his head, and praised my wisdom of judgment. But at that moment the long-rotted *olona-* cord broke and the pitiful woman's bones of Laulani shed from my clasp and clattered on the rocky floor. One shin-bone, in some way deflected, fell under the dark shadow of a canoe-bow, and I made up my mind that it should be mine. So I hastened to help him in the picking up of the bones and the tying, so that he did not notice its absence.

" 'This,' said Ahuna, introducing me to another of my ancestors, 'is your great-grandfather, Mokomoku, the father of Kaaukuu. Behold the size of his bones. He was a giant. I shall carry him, because of the long spear of Keola that will be difficult for you to carry away. And this is Lelemahoa, your grandmother, the mother of your mother, that you shall carry. And day grows short, and we must still swim up through the waters to the sun ere darkness hides the sun from the world.'

"But Ahuna, putting out the various calabashes of light by drowning the wicks in the whale-oil, did not observe me include the shin-bone of Laulani with the bones of my grandmother."

The honk of the automobile, sent up from Olokona to rescue us, broke off the Prince's narrative. We said good-by to the ancient and fresh-pensioned *wahine,* and departed. A half-mile on our way, Prince Akuli resumed.

"So Ahuna and I returned to Hiwilani, and to her happiness, lasting to her death the year following, two more of her ancestors abided about her in the jars of her twilight room. Also, she kept her compact and worried my father into sending me to England. I took old Howard along, and he perked up and confuted the doctors, so that it was three years before I buried him restored to the bosom of his family. Sometimes I think he was the most brilliant man I have ever known. Not until my return from England did Ahuna die, the last custodian of our *alii* secrets. And at his death-bed he pledged me again never to reveal the location in that nameless valley, and never to go back myself.

"Much else I have forgotten to mention did I see there in the cave that one time. There were the bones of Kumi, the near demigod, son of Tui Manua of Samoa, who, in the long before, married into my line and heaven-boosted my genealogy. And the bones of my great-grandmother who had slept in the four-poster presented her by Lord Byron. And Ahuna hinted tradition that there was reason for that presentation, as well as for the historically known lingering of the *Blonde* in Olokona for so long. And I held her poor bones in my hands—bones once fleshed with sensate beauty, informed with sparkle and spirit, instinct with love and love-warmness of arms around and eyes and lips together, that had begat me in the end of the generations unborn. It was a good experience. I am modern, 'tis true. I believe in no mystery stuff of old time nor of the *kahunas.* And yet, I saw in that cave things which I dare not name to you, and which I, since old Ahuna died, alone of the living know. I have no children. With me my long line ceases. This is the twentieth century, and we stink of gasolene. Nevertheless these other and nameless things shall die with me. I shall never revisit the burial-place. Nor in all time to come will any man gaze upon it through living eyes unless the quakes of earth rend the mountains asunder and spew forth the secrets contained in the hearts of the mountains."

Prince Akuli ceased from speech. With welcome relief on his face, he removed the *lei hala* from his neck, and, with a sniff and a sigh, tossed it into concealment in the thick *lantana* by the side of the road.

"But the shin-bone of Laulani?" I queried softly.

He remained silent while a mile of pasture land fled by us and yielded to caneland. "I have it now," he at last said. "And beside it is Keola, slain ere his time and made into a spear-head for love of the woman whose shin-bone abides near to him. To them, those poor pathetic bones, I owe more than to aught else. I became possessed of them in the period of my culminating adolescence. I know they changed the entire course of my life and trend of my mind. They gave to me a modesty and a humility in the world, from which my father's fortune has ever failed to seduce me.

"And often, when woman was nigh to winning to the empery of my mind over me, I sought Laulani's shin-bone. And often, when lusty manhood stung me into feeling overproud and lusty, I consulted the spearhead remnant of Keola, one-time swift runner, and mighty wrestler and lover, and thief of the wife of a king. The contemplation of them has ever been of profound aid to me, and you might well say that I have founded my religion or practice of living upon them."

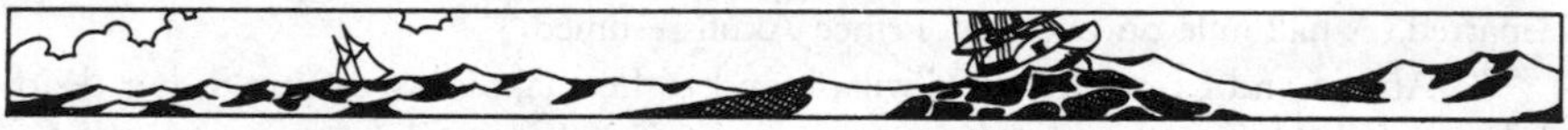

THE WATER BABY

I LENT a weary ear to old Kohokumu's interminable chanting of the deeds and adventures of Maui, the Promethean demi-god of Polynesia who fished up dry land from ocean depths with hooks made fast to heaven, who lifted up the sky whereunder previously men had gone on all fours, not having space to stand erect, and who made the sun with its sixteen snared legs stand still and agree thereafter to traverse the sky more slowly—the sun being evidently a trade-unionist and believing in the six-hour day, while Maui stood for the open shop and the twelve-hour day.

"Now this," said Kohokumu, "is from Queen Lilliuokalani's own family mele:

" 'Maui became restless and fought the sun
With a noose that he laid.
And winter won the sun,
And summer was won by Maui . . .' "

Born in the Islands myself, I know the Hawaiian myths better than this old fisherman, although I possessed not his memorization that enabled him to recite them endless hours.

"And you believe all this?" I demanded in the sweet Hawaiian tongue.

"It was a long time ago," he pondered. "I never saw Maui with my own eyes. But all our old men from all the way back tell us these things, as I, an old man, tell them to my sons and grandsons, who will tell them to their sons and grandsons all the way ahead to come."

"You believe," I persisted, "that whopper of Maui roping the sun like a wild steer, and that other whopper of heaving up the sky from off the earth?"

"I am of little worth, and am not wise, O Lakana," my fisherman made answer. "Yet have I read the Hawaiian Bible the missionaries translated to us, and there have I read that your Big Man of the Beginning made the earth and sky and sun and moon and stars, and all manner of animals from horses to cockroaches and from centipedes and mosquitoes to sea lice and jellyfish, and man and woman and everything, and all in six days. Why, Maui didn't do anything like that much. He didn't *make* anything. He just put things in order, that was all, and it took him a long, long time to make the improvements. And anyway, it is much easier and more reasonable to believe the little whopper than the big whopper."

And what could I reply? He had me on the matter of reasonableness. Besides, my head ached. And the funny thing, as I admitted to myself, was that evolution teaches in no uncertain voice that man did run on all fours ere he came to walk upright, that astronomy states flatly that the speed of the revolution of the earth on its axis has diminished steadily, thus increasing the length of day, and that the seismologists accept that all the islands of Hawaii were elevated from the ocean floor by volcanic action.

Fortunately, I saw a bamboo pole, floating on the surface several hundred feet away, suddenly up-end and start a very devil's dance. This was a diversion from the profitless discussion, and Kohokumu and I dipped our paddles and raced the little outrigger canoe to the dancing pole. Kohokumu caught the line that was fast to the butt of the pole and underhanded it in until a two-foot *ukikiki*, battling fiercely to the end, flashed its wet silver in the sun and began beating a tattoo on the inside bottom of the canoe. Kohokumu picked up a squirming, slimy squid with his teeth, bit a chunk of live bait out of it, attached the bait to the hook, and dropped line and sinker overside. The stick floated flat on the surface of the water, and the canoe drifted slowly away. With a survey of the crescent composed of a score of such sticks all lying flat, Kohokumu wiped his hands on his naked sides and lifted the wearisome and centuries-old chant of Kuali:

" 'Oh, the great fishhook of Maui!
Manai-i-ka-lani—" made fast to the heavens" !
Engulfed from lofty Kauiki!
Its bait the red-billed Alae,
The bird to Hina sacred!
It sinks far down to Hawaii,
Struggling and in pain dying!
Caught is the land beneath the water,
Floated up, up to the surface,
But Hina hid a wing of the bird
And broke the land beneath the water!
Below was the bait snatched away
And eaten at once by the fishes,
The Ulua of the deep muddy places!' "

His aged voice was hoarse and scratchy from the drinking of too much swipes at a funeral the night before, nothing of which contributed to make me less irritable. My head ached. The sun glare on the water made my eyes ache, while I was suffering more than half a touch of *mal de mer* from the antic conduct of the outrigger on the blobby sea. The air was stagnant. In the lee of Waihee, between the white beach and the reef, no whisper of breeze eased the still sultriness. I really think I was too miserable to summon the resolution to give up the fishing and go in to shore.

Lying back with closed eyes, I lost count of time. I even forgot that Kohokumu was chanting till reminded of it by his ceasing. An exclamation made me bare my eyes to the stab of the sun. He was gazing down through the water glass.

"It's a big one," he said, passing me the device and slipping overside feet first into the water.

He went under without splash and ripple, turned over, and swam down. I followed his progress through the water glass, which is merely an oblong box a couple of feet long, open at the top, the bottom sealed water-tight with a sheet of ordinary glass.

Now Kohokumu was a bore, and I was squeamishly out of sorts with him for his volubleness, but I could not help admiring him as I watched him go down. Past seventy years of age, lean as a toothpick and shriveled like a mummy, he was doing what few young athletes of my race would do or could do. It was forty feet to bottom. There, partly exposed, but mostly hidden under the bulge of a coral lump, I could discern his objective. His keen eyes had caught the projecting tentacle of a squid. Even as he swam, the tentacle was lazily withdrawn, so that there was no sign of the creature. But the brief exposure of the portion of one tentacle had advertised its owner as a squid of size.

The pressure at a depth of forty feet is no joke for a young man, yet it did not seem to inconvenience this oldster. I am certain it never crossed his mind to be inconvenienced. Unarmed, bare of body save for a brief *malo* or loin cloth, he was undeterred by the formidable creature that constituted his prey. I saw him steady himself with his right hand on the coral lump, and thrust his left arm into the hole to the shoulder. Half a minute elapsed, during which time he seemed to be groping and rooting around with his left hand. Then tentacle after tentacle, myriad-suckered and wildly waving, emerged. Laying hold of his arm, they writhed and coiled about his flesh like so many snakes. With a heave and a jerk appeared the entire squid, a proper devilfish or octopus.

But the old man was in no hurry for his natural element, the air above the water. There, forty feet beneath, wrapped about by an octopus that measured nine feet across from tentacle tip to tentacle tip and that could well drown the stoutest swimmer, he coolly and casually did the one thing that gave to him his empery over the monster. He shoved his lean, hawklike face into the very center of the slimy, squirming mass, and with his several ancient fangs bit into the heart and life of the matter. This accomplished, he came upward slowly, as a swimmer should who is changing atmospheres from the depths. Alongside the canoe, still in the water and peeling off the grisly clinging thing, the incorrigible old sinner burst into the *pule* of triumph which had been chanted by countless squid-catching generations before him:

" 'O Kanaloa of the taboo nights!
Stand upright on the solid floor!
Stand upon the floor where lies the squid!
Rise up, O Kanaloa!
Stir up! Stir up! Let the squid awake!

Let the squid that lies flat awake!
Let the squid that lies spread out . . .' "

I closed my eyes and ears, not offering to lend him a hand, secure in the knowledge that he could climb back unaided into the unstable craft without the slightest risk of upsetting it.

"A very fine squid," he crooned. "It is a wahine squid. I shall now sing to you the song of the cowrie shell, the red cowrie shell that we used as a bait for the squid—"

"You were disgraceful last night at the funeral," I headed him off. "I heard all about it. You made much noise. You sang till everybody was deaf. You insulted the son of the widow. You drank swipes like a pig. Swipes are not good for your extreme age. Some day you will wake up dead. You ought to be a wreck to-day—"

"Ha!" he chuckled. "And you, who drank no swipes, who was a babe unborn when I was already an old man, who went to bed last night with the sun and the chickens—this day you are a wreck. Explain me that. My ears are as thirsty to listen as was my throat thirsty last night. And here to-day, behold, I am, as that Englishman who came here in his yacht used to say, I am in fine form, in devilish fine form."

"I give you up," I retorted, shrugging my shoulders. "Only one thing is clear, and that is that the devil doesn't want you. Report of your singing has gone before you."

"No," he pondered the idea carefully. "It is not that. The devil will be glad for my coming, for I have some very fine songs for him, and scandals and old gossips of the high aliis that will make him scratch his sides. So let me explain to you the secret of my birth. The Sea is my mother. I was born in a double canoe, during a Kona gale, in the channel of Kahoolawe. From her, the Sea, my mother, I received my strength. Whenever I return to her arms, as for a breast clasp, as I have returned this day, I grow strong again and immediately. She, to me, is the milk giver, the life source—"

"Shades of Antaeus!" thought I.

"Some day," old Kohokumu rambled on, "when I am really old, I shall be reported of men as drowned in the sea. This will be an idle thought of men. In truth, I shall have returned into the arms of my mother, there to rest under the heart of her breast until the second birth of me, when I shall emerge into the sun a flashing youth of splendor like Maui himself when he was golden young."

"A queer religion," I commented.

"When I was younger I muddled my poor head over queerer religions," old Kohokumu retorted. "But listen, O Young Wise One, to my elderly wisdom. This I know: as I grow old I seek less for the truth from without me, and find more of the truth from within me. Why have I thought this thought of my return to my mother and of my rebirth from my mother into the sun? You do not know. I do not know, save that, without whisper of man's voice or printed word, without prompting from otherwhere, this thought has arisen from within me, from the deeps of me that are as deep as the sea. I am not a god. I do not make things. Therefore I have not made this thought. I do not know its father or its mother. It is of old time before me, and therefore it is true. Man does not make truth. Man, if he be not blind, only recognizes truth when he sees it. Is this thought that I have thought a dream?"

"Perhaps it is you that are a dream," I laughed. "And that I and sky and sea and the iron-hard land are dreams, all dreams."

"I have often thought that," he assured me soberly. "It may well be so. Last night I dreamed I was a lark bird, a beautiful singing lark of the sky like the larks on the upland pastures of Haleakala. And I flew up, up toward the sun, singing, singing, as old

Kohokumu never sang. I tell you now that I dreamed I was a lark bird singing in the sky. But may not I, the real I, be the lark bird? And may not the telling of it be the dream that I, the lark bird, am dreaming now? Who are you to tell me ay or no? Dare you tell me I am not a lark bird asleep and dreaming that I am old Kohokumu?"

I shrugged my shoulders, and he continued triumphantly:

"And how do you know but what you are old Maui himself asleep and dreaming that you are John Lakana talking with me in a canoe? And may you not awake, old Maui yourself, and scratch your sides and say that you had a funny dream in which you dreamed you were a haole?"

"I don't know," I admitted. "Besides, you wouldn't believe me."

"There is much more in dreams than we know," he assured me with great solemnity. "Dreams go deep, all the way down, maybe to before the beginning. May not old Maui have only dreamed he pulled Hawaii up from the bottom of the sea? Then would this Hawaii land be a dream, and you and I and the squid there only parts of Maui's dream? And the lark bird, too?"

He sighed and let his head sink on his breast.

"And I worry my old head about the secrets undiscoverable," he resumed, "until I grow tired and want to forget, and so I drink swipes, and go fishing, and sing old songs, and dream I am a lark bird singing in the sky. I like that best of all, and often I dream it when I have drunk much swipes—"

In great dejection of mood he peered down into the lagoon through the water glass.

"There will be no more bites for a while," he announced. "The fish-sharks are prowling around, and we shall have to wait until they are gone. And so that the time shall not be heavy, I will sing you the canoe-hauling song to Lono. You remember:

" 'Give to me the trunk of the tree, O Lono!
Give me the tree's main root, O Lono!
Give me the ear of the tree, O Lono!—' "

"For the love of mercy, don't sing!" I cut him short. "I've got a headache, and your singing hurts. You may be in devilish fine form to-day, but your throat is rotten. I'd rather you talked about dreams, or told me whoppers."

"It is too bad that you are sick, and you so young," he conceded cheerily. "And I shall not sing any more. I shall tell you something you do not know and have never heard; something that is no dream and no whopper, but is what I know to have happened. Not very long ago there lived here, on the beach beside this very lagoon, a young boy whose name was Keikiwai, which, as you know, means Water Baby. He was truly a water baby. His gods were the sea and fish gods, and he was born with knowledge of the language of fishes, which the fishes did not know until the sharks found it out one day when they heard him talk it.

"It happened this way. The word had been brought, and the commands, by swift runners, that the king was making a progress around the island, and that on the next day a luau was to be served him by the dwellers here of Waihee. It was always a hardship, when the king made a progress, for the few dwellers in small places to fill his many stomachs with food. For he came always with his wife and her women, with his priests and sorcerers, his dancers and flute-players and hula singers and fighting men and servants, and his high chiefs with their wives and sorcerers and fighting men and servants.

"Sometimes, in small places like Waihee, the path of his journey was marked afterward by leanness and famine. But a king must be fed, and it is not good to anger a king.

So, like warning in advance of disaster, Waihee heard of his coming, and all food-getters of field and pond and mountain and sea were busied with getting food for the feast. And behold, everything was got, from the choicest of royal taro to sugar-cane joints for the roasting, from opihis to limu, from fowl to wild pig and poi-fed puppies—everything save one thing. The fishermen failed to get lobsters.

"Now be it known that the king's favorite food was lobster. He esteemed it above all *kai-kai* (food), and his runners had made special mention of it. And there were no lobsters, and it is not good to anger a king in the belly of him. Too many sharks had come inside the reef. That was the trouble. A young girl and an old man had been eaten by them. And of the young men who dared dive for lobsters, one was eaten, and one lost an arm, and another lost one hand and one foot.

"But here was Keikiwai, the Water Baby, only eleven years old, but half fish himself and talking the language of fishes. To his father the head men came, begging him to send the Water Baby to get lobsters to fill the king's belly and divert his anger.

"Now this, what happened, was known and observed. For the fishermen and their women, and the taro growers and the bird catchers, and the head men, and all Waihee, came down and stood back from the edge of the rock where the Water Baby stood and looked down at the lobsters far beneath on the bottom.

"And a shark, looking up with its cat's eyes, observed him, and sent out the shark-call of 'fresh meat' to assemble all the sharks in the lagoon. For the sharks work thus together, which is why they are strong. And the sharks answered the call till there were forty of them, long ones and short ones and lean ones and round ones, forty of them by count; and they talked to one another, saying: 'Look at that titbit of a child, that morsel delicious of human-flesh sweetness without the salt of the sea in it, of which salt we have too much, savory and good to eat, melting to delight under our hearts as our bellies embrace it and extract from it its sweet.'

"Much more they said, saying: 'He has come for the lobsters. When he dives in he is for one of us. Not like the old man we ate yesterday, tough to dryness with age, nor like the young men whose members were too hard-muscled, but tender, so tender that he will melt in our gullets ere our bellies receive him. When he dives in, we will all rush for him, and the lucky one of us will get him, and, gulp, he will be gone, one bite and one swallow, into the belly of the luckiest one of us.'

"And Keikiwai, the Water Baby, heard the conspiracy, knowing the shark language; and he addressed a prayer, in the shark language, to the shark god Moku-Halii, and the sharks heard and waved their tails to one another and winked their cat's eyes in token that they understood his talk. And then he said: 'I shall now dive for a lobster for the king. And no hurt shall befall me, because the shark with the shortest tail is my friend and will protect me.'

"And, so saying, he picked up a chunk of lava rock and tossed it into the water, with a big splash, twenty feet to one side. The forty sharks rushed for the splash, while he dived, and by the time they discovered they had missed him, he had gone to the bottom and come back and climbed out, within his hand a fat lobster, a wahine lobster, full of eggs, for the king.

" 'Ha!' said the sharks, very angry. 'There is among us a traitor. The titbit of a child, the morsel of sweetness, has spoken, and has exposed the one among us who has saved him. Let us now measure the length of our tails!'

"Which they did, in a long row, side by side, the shorter-tailed ones cheating and stretching to gain length on themselves, the longer-tailed ones cheating and stretching in order not to be out-cheated and out-stretched. They were very angry with the one with the shortest tail, and him they rushed upon from every side and devoured till nothing was left of him.

"Again they listened while they waited for the Water Baby to dive in. And again the Water Baby made his prayer in the shark language to Moku-Halii, and said: 'The shark with the shortest tail is my friend and will protect me.' And again the Water Baby tossed in a chunk of lava, this time twenty feet away off to the other side. The sharks rushed for the splash, and in their haste ran into one another, and splashed with their tails till the water was all foam and they could see nothing, each thinking some other was swallowing the titbit. And the Water Baby came up and climbed out with another fat lobster for the king.

"And the thirty-nine sharks measured tails, devouring the one with the shortest tail, so that there were only thirty-eight sharks. And the Water Baby continued to do what I have said, and the sharks to do what I have told you, while for each shark that was eaten by his brothers there was another fat lobster laid on the rock for the king. Of course, there was much quarreling and argument among the sharks when it came to measuring tails; but in the end it worked out in rightness and justice, for, when only two sharks were left, they were the two biggest of the original forty.

"And the Water Baby again claimed the shark with the shortest tail was his friend, fooled the two sharks with another lava chunk, and brought up another lobster. The two sharks each claimed the other had the shorter tail, and each fought to eat the other, and the one with the longer tail won—"

"Hold, O Kohokumu!" I interrupted. "Remember that that shark had already—"

"I know just what you are going to say," he snatched his recital back from me. "And you are right. It took him so long to eat the thirty-ninth shark, for inside the thirty-ninth shark were already the nineteen other sharks he had eaten, and inside the fortieth shark were already the nineteen other sharks he had eaten, and he did not have the appetite he had started with. But do not forget he was a very big shark to begin with.

"It took him so long to eat the other shark, and the nineteen sharks inside the other shark, that he was still eating when darkness fell and the people of Waihee went away home with all the lobsters for the king. And didn't they find the last shark on the beach next morning dead and burst wide open with all he had eaten?"

Kohokumu fetched a full stop and held my eyes with his own shrewd ones.

"Hold, O Lakana!" he checked the speech that rushed to my tongue. "I know what next you would say. You would say that with my own eyes I did not see this, and therefore that I do not know what I have been telling you. But I do know, and I can prove it. My father's father knew the grandson of the Water Baby's father's uncle. Also, there, on the rocky point to which I point my finger now, is where the Water Baby stood and dived. I have dived for lobsters there myself. It is a great place for lobsters. Also, and often, have I seen sharks there. And there, on the bottom, as I should know, for I have seen and counted them, are the thirty-nine lava rocks thrown in by the Water Baby as I have described."

"But—" I began.

"Ha!" he baffled me. "Look! While we have talked the fish have begun again to bite."

He pointed to three of the bamboo poles erect and devil-dancing in token that fish were hooked and struggling on the lines beneath. As he bent to his paddle, he muttered, for my benefit:

"Of course I know. The thirty-nine lava rocks are still there. You can count them any day for yourself. Of course I know, and I know for a fact."

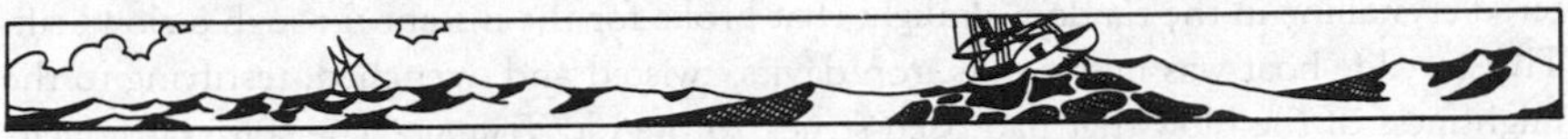

The Sea-Farmer

"THAT wull be the Doctor's launch," said Captain MacElrath.

The pilot grunted, while the skipper swept on with his glass from the launch to the strip of beach and to Kingston beyond, and then slowly across the entrance to Howth Head on the northern side.

"The tide's right, and we'll have you docked in two hours," the pilot vouchsafed, with an effort at cheeriness. "Ring's End Basin, is it?"

This time the skipper grunted.

"A dirty Dublin day."

Again the skipper grunted. He was weary with the night of wind on the Irish Channel behind him, the unbroken hours of which he had spent on the bridge. And he was weary with all the voyage behind him—two years and four months between home port and home port, eight hundred and fifty days by his log.

"Proper wunter weather," he answered, after a silence. "The town is indistinct. Ut wull be rainun' guid an' hearty for the day."

Captain MacElrath was a small man, just comfortably able to peep over the canvas dodger of the bridge. The pilot and third officer loomed above him, as did the man at the wheel, a bulky German, deserted from a warship, whom he had signed on in Rangoon. But his lack of inches made Captain MacElrath a no less able man. At least so the Company reckoned, and so would he have reckoned could he have had access to the carefully and minutely compiled record of him filed away in the office archives. But the Company had never given him a hint of its faith in him. It was not the way of the Company, for the Company went on the principle of never allowing an employee to think himself indispensable or even exceedingly useful; wherefore, while quick to censure, it never praised. What was Captain MacElrath, anyway, save a skipper, one skipper of the eighty-odd skippers that commanded the Company's eighty-odd freighters on all the highways and byways of the sea?

Beneath them, on the main deck, two Chinese stokers were carrying breakfast for'ard across the rusty iron plates that told their own grim story of weight and wash of sea. A sailor was taking down the life-line that stretched from the forecastle, past the hatches and cargo-winches, to the bridge-deck ladder.

"A rough voyage," suggested the pilot.

"Ay, she was fair smokin' ot times, but not thot I minded thot so much as the lossin' of time. I hate like onythun' tull loss time."

So saying, Captain MacElrath turned and glanced aft, aloft and alow, and the pilot, following his gaze, saw the mute but convincing explanation of that loss of time. The smokestack, buff-colored underneath, was white with salt, while the whistle-pipe glittered crystalline in the random sunlight that broke for the instant through a cloud rift. The port life-boat was missing, its iron davits, twisted and wrenched, testifying to the mightiness of the blow that had been struck to the old *Tryapsic.* The starboard davits were also empty. The shattered wreck of the life-boat they had held lay on the fiddley beside the smashed engine-room skylight which was covered by a tarpaulin. Below, to starboard, on the bridge-deck, the pilot saw the crushed mess-room door, roughly bulkheaded against the pounding seas. Abreast of it, on the smokestack guys, and being taken down by the bosun and a sailor, hung the huge square of rope netting which had failed to break those seas of their force.

"Twice afore I mentioned thot door tull the owners," said Captain MacElrath. "But they said ut would do. There was bug seas thot time. They was uncreditable bug. And thot buggest one dud the domage. Ut fair carried away the door an' laid ut flat on the mess table an' smashed out the chief's room. He was a but sore about ut."

"It must 'a' been a big un," the pilot remarked sympathetically.

"Ay, ut was thot. Thungs was lively for a but. Ut finished the mate. He was on the brudge wuth me, an' I told hum tull take a look tull the wedges o' number one hatch. She was takin' watter freely an' I was no sure o' number one. I didna like the look o' ut, an' I was fuggerin' maybe tull heave to tull the marn, when she took ut over abaft the brudge. My word, she was a bug one. We got a but of ut ourselves on the brudge. I dudna miss the mate ot the first, what o' routin' out Chips an' bulkheadun' thot door an' stretchun' the tarpaulin over the skylight. Then he was nowhere to be found. The mon ot the wheel said as he seen hum goin' down the lodder just afore she hut us. We looked for'ard, we looked tull hus room, we looked tull the engine room, an' we looked along aft on the lower deck, and there he was, on both sides the cover to the steam pipe runnun' tull the after-wunches."

The pilot ejaculated an oath of amazement and horror.

"Ay," the skipper went on wearily, "an' on both sides the steam pipe uz well. I tell ye he was in two pieces, splut clean uz a herrin'. The sea must a-caught hum on the upper brudge deck, carried hum clean across the fiddley, an' banged hum head-on tull the pipe cover. It sheered through hum like so much butter, down atween the eyes, an' along the middle of hum, so that one leg an' arm was fast tull the one piece of hum, an' one leg an' arm fast tull the other piece of hum. I tull ye ut was fair grewsome. We putt hum together an' rolled hum in canvas uz we pulled hum out."

The pilot swore again.

"Oh, ut wasna onythun' tull greet about," Captain MacElrath assured him. " 'Twas a guid ruddance. He was no a sailor, thot mate-fellow. He was only fut for a pug-sty, an' a dom puir apology for thot same."

It is said that there are three kinds of Irish—catholic, protestant, and North-of-Ireland—and that the North-of-Ireland Irishman is a transplanted Scotchman. Captain MacElrath was a North-of-Ireland man, and, talking for much of the world like a Scotchman, nothing aroused his ire quicker than being mistaken for a Scotchman.

Irish he stoutly was, and Irish he stoutly abided, though it was with a faint lip-lift of scorn that he mentioned mere South-of-Ireland men, or even Orangemen. Himself he was Presbyterian, while in his own community five men were all that ever mustered at a meeting in the Orange Men's Hall. His community was the Island McGill, where seven thousand of his kind lived in such amity and sobriety that in the whole island there was but one policeman and never a public house at all.

Captain MacElrath did not like the sea, and had never liked it. He wrung his livelihood from it, and that was all the sea was, the place where he worked, as the mill, the shop, and the countinghouse were the places where other men worked. Romance never sang to him her siren song, and Adventure had never shouted in his sluggish blood. He lacked imagination. The wonders of the deep were without significance to him. Tornadoes, hurricanes, water-spouts, and tidal waves were so many obstacles to the way of a ship on the sea and of a master on the bridge—they were that to him, and nothing more. He had seen, and yet not seen, the many marvels and wonders of far lands. Under his eyelids burned the brazen glories of the tropic seas, or ached the bitter gales of the North Atlantic or far South Pacific; but his memory of them was of mess-room doors stove in, of decks awash and hatches threatened, of undue coal consumption, of long passages, and of fresh paint-work spoiled by unexpected squalls of rain.

"I know my buzz'ness," was the way he often put it, and beyond his business was all that he did not know, all that he had seen with the mortal eyes of him and yet that he never dreamed existed. That he knew his business his owners were convinced, or at forty he would not have held command of the *Tryapsic,* three thousand tons net register, with a cargo capacity of nine thousand tons and valued at fifty thousand pounds.

He had taken up seafaring through no love of it, but because it had been his destiny, because he had been the second son of his father instead of the first. Island McGill was only so large, and the land could support but a certain definite proportion of those that dwelt upon it. The balance, and a large balance it was, was driven to the sea to seek its bread. It had been so for generations. The eldest sons took the farms from their fathers; to the other sons remained the sea and its salt-plowing. So it was that Donald MacElrath, farmer's son and farm-boy himself, had shifted from the soil he loved to the sea he hated and which it was his destiny to farm. And farmed it he had, for twenty years, shrewd, cool-headed, sober, industrious and thrifty, rising from ship's boy and forecastle hand to mate and master of sailing-ships and thence into steam, second officer, first and master, from small command to larger, and at last to the bridge of the old *Tryapsic*— old, to be sure, but worth her fifty thousand pounds and still able to bear up in all seas and weather her nine thousand tons of freight.

From the bridge of the *Tryapsic,* the high place he had gained in the competition of men, he stared at Dublin Harbor opening out, at the town obscured by the dark sky of the dreary wind-driven day, and at the tangled tracery of spars and rigging of the harbor shipping. Back from twice around the world he was, and from interminable junketings up and down on far stretches, home-coming to the wife he had not seen in eight and twenty months, and to the child he had never seen and that was already walking and talking. He saw the watch below of stokers and trimmers bobbing out of the forecastle doors like rabbits from a warren and making their way aft over the rusty deck to the mustering of the port doctor. They were Chinese, with expressionless, Sphinx-like faces, and they walked in peculiar shambling fashion, dragging their feet as if the clumsy brogans were too heavy for their lean shanks.

He saw them and he did not see them, as he passed his hand beneath his visored cap and scratched reflectively his mop of sandy hair. For the scene before him was but the background in his brain for the vision of peace that was his—a vision that was his often during long nights on the bridge when the old *Tryapsic* wallowed on the vexed ocean floor, her decks awash, her rigging thrumming in the gale gusts or snow squalls or driving tropic rain. And the vision he saw was of farm and farm-house and straw-thatched outbuildings, of children playing in the sun and the good wife at the door, of lowing kine, and clucking fowls, and the stamp of horses in the stable, of his father's farm next to his, with beyond the woodless, rolling land and the hedged fields, neat and orderly, extending to the crest of the smooth, soft hills. It was his vision and his dream, his Romance and Adventure, the goal of all his effort, the high reward for the salt-plowing and the long, long furrows he ran up and down the whole world around in his farming of the sea.

In simple taste and homely inclination this much-traveled man was more simple and homely than the veriest yokel. Seventy-one years his father was, and had never slept a night out of his own bed in his own house on Island McGill. That was the life ideal, so Captain MacElrath considered, and he was prone to marvel that any man, not under compulsion, should leave a farm to go to sea. To this much-traveled man the whole world was as familiar as the village to the cobbler sitting in his shop. To Captain MacElrath the world was a village. In his mind's eye he saw its streets a thousand leagues long, aye, and longer; turnings that doubled earth's stormiest headlands or were the way to quiet inland ponds; cross-roads, taken one way, that led to flower-lands and summer seas, and that led the other way to bitter, ceaseless gales and the perilous bergs of the great west wind drift. And the cities, bright with lights, were as shops on these long streets—shops where business was transacted, where bunkers were replenished, cargoes taken or shifted, and orders received from the owners in London town to go elsewhere and beyond, ever along the long sea-lanes, seeking new cargoes here, carrying new cargoes there, running freights wherever shillings and pence beckoned and underwriters did not forbid. But it was all a weariness to contemplate, and, save that he wrung from it his bread, it was without profit under the sun.

The last good-by to his wife had been at Cardiff, twenty-eight months before, when he sailed for Valparaiso with coals—nine thousand tons and down to his marks. From Valparaiso he had gone to Australia, light, a matter of six thousand miles on end with a stormy passage and running short of bunker coal. Coals again to Oregon, seven thousand miles, and nigh as many more with general cargo for Japan and China. Thence to Java, loading sugar for Marseilles, and back along the Mediterranean to the Black Sea, and on to Baltimore, down to her marks with crome ore, buffeted by hurricanes, short again of bunker coal and calling at Bermuda to replenish. Then a time charter, Norfolk, Virginia, loading mysterious contraband coal and sailing for South Africa under orders of the mysterious German supercargo put on board by charterers. On to Madagascar, steaming four knots by the supercargo's orders, and the suspicion forming that the Russian fleet might want the coal. Confusion and delays, long waits at sea, international complications, the whole world excited over the old *Tryapsic* and her cargo of contraband, and then on to Japan and the naval port of Sassebo. Back to Australia, another time charter and general merchandise picked up at Sydney, Melbourne and Adelaide, and carried on to Mauritius, Lorenzo Marques, Durban, Algoa Bay and Capetown. To Ceylon for orders, and from Ceylon to Rangoon to load rice for Rio Janeiro. Thence to Buenos Ayres and loading maize for the United Kingdom or the Continent, stopping at St Vincent, to receive orders to proceed to Dublin. Two years and four months, eight hundred and fifty days by the log, steaming up and down the thousand-league-long sea-lanes and back again to Dublin-town. And he was well aweary.

A little tug had laid hold of the *Tryapsic;* and with clang and clatter and shouted command, with engines half-ahead, slow-speed or half-astern, the battered old sea-tramp was nudged and nosed and shouldered through the dock-gates into Ring's End Basin. Lines were flung ashore, fore and aft, and a 'midship spring got out. Already a small group of the happy shore-staying folk had clustered on the dock.

"Ring off," Captain MacElrath commanded in his slow thick voice; and the third officer worked the lever of the engine-room telegraph.

"Gangway out!" called the second officer; and, when this was accomplished, "That will do."

It was the last task of all, gangway out. "That will do" was the dismissal. The voyage was ended, and the crew shambled eagerly forward across the rusty decks to where their sea-bags were packed and ready for the shore. The taste of the land was strong in the men's mouths, and strong it was in the skipper's mouth as he muttered a gruff good day to the departing pilot, and himself went down to his cabin. Up the gangway were trooping the customs officers, the surveyor, the agent's clerk and the stevedores. Quick work disposed of these and cleared his cabin, the agent waiting to take him to the office.

"Dud ye send word tull the wife?" had been his greeting to the clerk.

"Yes, a telegram, as soon as you were reported."

"She'll likely be comin' down on the marnin' train," the skipper had soliloquized, and gone inside to change his clothes and wash.

He took a last glance about the room and at two photographs on the wall, one of the wife, the other of an infant—the child he had never seen. He stepped out into the cabin, with its paneled walls of cedar and maple, and with its long table that seated ten, and at which he had eaten by himself through all the weary time. No laughter and clatter and wordy argument of the mess-room had been his. He had eaten silently, almost morosely, his silence emulated by the noiseless Asiatic who had served him. It came to him suddenly, the overwhelming realization of the loneliness of those two years and more. All his vexations and anxieties had been his own. He had shared them with no one. His two young officers were too young and flighty, the mate too stupid. There was no consulting with them. One tenant had shared the cabin with him, that tenant his responsibility. They had dined and supped together, walked the bridge together and together they had bedded.

"Och!" he muttered to that grim companion, "I'm quit of you, an' wull quit . . . for a wee."

Ashore, he passed the last of the seamen with their bags, and, at the agent's, with the usual delays, put through his ship business. When asked out by them to drink he took milk and soda.

"I am no a teetotaler," he explained; "but for the life o' me I canna bide beer or whusky."

In the early afternoon, when he finished paying off his crew, he hurried to the private office where he had been told his wife was waiting.

His eyes were for her first, though the temptation was great to have more than a hurried glimpse of the child in the chair beside her. He held her off from him after the long embrace, and looked into her face long and steadily, drinking in every feature of it and wondering that he could mark no changes of time. A warm man, his wife thought him, though had the opinion of his officers been asked it would have been: a harsh man and a bitter one.

"Wull, Annie, how is ut wi' ye?" he queried, and drew her to him again.

And again he held her away from him, this wife of ten years and of whom he knew so little. She was almost a stranger—more a stranger than his Chinese steward, and certainly far more a stranger than his own officers whom he had seen every day, day and day, for eight hundred and fifty days. Married ten years, and in that time he had been with her nine weeks—scarcely a honeymoon. Each time home had been a getting acquainted over with her. It was the fate of the men who went out to the salt-plowing. Little they knew of their wives and less of their children. There was his chief engineer—old, near-sighted MacPherson—who told the story of returning home to be locked out of his house by his four-year kiddie that never had laid eyes on him before.

"An' thus 'ull be the loddie," the skipper said, reaching out a hesitant hand to the child's cheek.

But the boy drew away from him, sheltering against the mother's side.

"Och!" she cried, "and he doesna know his own father."

"Nor I hum. Heaven knows I could no a-picked hum out of a crowd, though he'll be havin' your nose I'm thunkun'."

"An' your own eyes, Donald. Look ut them. He's your own father, laddie. Kiss hum like the little mon ye are."

But the child drew closer to her, his expression of fear and distrust growing stronger, and when the father attempted to take him in his arms he threatened to cry.

The skipper straightened up, and to conceal the pang at his heart he drew out his watch and looked at it.

"Ut's time to go, Annie," he said. "Thot train 'ull be startun'."

He was silent on the train at first, divided between watching the wife with the child going to sleep in her arms and looking out of the window at the tilled fields and green unforested hills vague and indistinct in the driving drizzle that had set in. They had the compartment to themselves. When the boy slept she laid him out on the seat and wrapped him warmly. And when the health of relatives and friends had been inquired after, and the gossip of Island McGill narrated, along with the weather and the price of land and crops, there was little left to talk about save themselves, and Captain MacElrath took up the tale brought home for the good wife from all his world's-end wandering. But it was not a tale of marvels he told, nor of beautiful flower-lands nor mysterious Eastern cities.

"What-like is Java?" she asked once.

"Full o' fever. Half the crew down wuth ut an' luttle work. Ut was quinine an' quinine the whole blessed time. Each marnun' 'twas quinine an' gin for all hands on an empty stomach. An' they who was no sick made ut out to be hovun' ut bad uz the rest."

Another time she asked about Newcastle.

"Coals an' coal-dust—thot's all. No a nice sutty. I lost two Chinks there, stokers the both of them. An' the owners paid a fine tull the government of a hundred pounds each for them. 'We regret tull note,' they wrut me—I got the letter tull Oregon—'We regret tull note the loss o' two Chinese members o' yer crew ot Newcastle, an' we recommend greater carefulness un the future.' Greater carefulness! And I could no a-been more careful. The Chinks hod forty-five pounds each comun' tull them in wages, an' I was no a-thunkun' they 'ud run.

"But thot's their way—'we regret tull note', 'we beg tull advise', 'we recommend', 'we canna onderstand'—an' the like o' thot. Domned cargo tank! An' they would thunk I could drive her like a *Lucania*, an' wi'out burnun' coals. There was thot propeller. I was after them a guid while for ut. The old one was iron, thuck on the edges, an' we couldna make our speed. An' the new one was bronze—nine hundred pounds ut cost, an' then wantun' their returns out o' ut, an' me wuth a bod passage an' lossin' time every day. 'We regret tull note your long passage from Voloparaiso tull Sydney wuth an average daily run o' only one hundred an' suxty-seven. We hod expected better results wuth the new propeller. You should a-made an average daily run o' two hundred an' suxteen.'

"An' me on a wunter passage, blowin' a luvin' gale half the time, wuth hurricane force in atweenwhiles, an' hove to sux days, wuth engines stopped an' bunker coal runnun' short, an' me wuth a mate thot stupid he could no pass a shup's light ot night wi'out callun' me tull the brudge. I wrut an' told 'em so. An' then: 'Our nautical advisor suggests you kept too far south,' an' 'We are lookun' for better results from thot propeller.' Nautical advisor!—shore pilot! Ut was the regular latitude for a wunter passage from Voloparaiso tull Sydney.

"An' when I come un tull Auckland, short o' coal, after lettun' her druft sux days wuth the fires out tull save the coal, an' wuth only twenty tons in my bunkers, I was thunkun' o' the lossin' o' time an' the expense, an' tull save the owners I took her un an' out wi'out pilotage. Pilotage was no compulsory. An' un Yokohama, who should I meet but Captun Robinson o' the *Dyapsic.* We got a talkun' about ports an' places down Australia-way, an' first thing he says: 'Speakun' o' Auckland—of course, Captun, you was never un Auckland?' 'Yus,' I says, 'I was un there very recent.' 'Oh, ho,' he says, very angry-like, 'so you was the smart Aleck thot fetcht me thot letter from the owners: "We note item of fufteen pounds for pilotage ot Auckland. A shup o' ours was un tull Auckland recently an' uncurred no such charge. We beg tull advise you thot we conseeder thus pilotage an onnecessary expense which should no be uncurred un the future." '

"But dud they say a word tull me for the fufteen pounds I saved tull them? No a word. They send a letter tull Captun Robinson for no savun' them the fufteen pounds, an' tull me: 'We note item of two guineas doctor's fee at Auckland for crew. Please explain thus onusual expunditure.' Ut was two o' the Chinks. I was thunkun' they hod beri-beri, an' thot was the why o' sendun' for the doctor. I buried the two of them ot sea not a week after. But ut was: 'Please explain thus onusual expunditure,' an' tull Captun Robinson, 'We beg tull advise thot we conseeder thus pilotage an onusual expense.'

"Dudna I cable them from Newcastle, tellun' them the old tank was thot foul she needed drydock? Seven months out o' drydock, an' the West Coast the quickest place for foulun' un the world. But freights was up, an' they hod a charter o' coals for Portland. The *Arrata,* one o' the Woor Line, left port the same day uz us, bound for Portland, an' the old *Tryapsic* makun' sux knots, seven ot the best. An' ut was ot Comox, takun' un bunker coal, I got the letter from the owners. The boss humself hod signed ut, an' ot the bottom he wrut un hus own hond: 'The *Arrata* beat you by four an' a half days. Am dusappointed.' Dusappointed! When I had cabled them from Newcastle. When she drydocked ot Portland, there was whuskers on her a foot long, barnacles the size o' me fust, oysters like young sauce plates. Ut took them two days afterward tull clean the dock o' shells an' muck.

"An' there was the motter o' them fire-bars ot Newcastle. The firm ashore made them heavier than the engineer's speecifications, an' then forgot tull charge for the dufference. Ot the last moment, wuth me ashore gettun' me clearance, they come wuth the bill: 'Tull error on fire-bars, sux pounds.' They'd been tull the ship an' MacPherson hod OK'd ut. I said ut was strange an' would no pay. 'Then you are dootun' the Chief Engineer,' says they. 'I'm no dootun',' says I, 'but I canna see my way tull sign. Come wuth me tull the shup. The launch wull cost ye naught an' ut 'ull brung ye back. An' we wull see what MacPherson says.'

"But they would no come. Ot Portland I got the bill un a letter. I took no notice. Ot Hongkong I got a letter from the owners. The bill hod been sent tull them. I wrut them from Java explainun'. At Marseilles the owners wrut me: 'Tull extra work un engine room, sux pounds. The engineer has OK'd ut, an' you have no OK'd ut. Are you dootun' the engineer's honesty?' I wrut an' told them I was no dootun' his honesty; thot the bill was for extra weight o' fire-bars; an' thot ut was OK. Dud they pay ut? They no dud. They must unvestigate. An' some clerk un the office took sick, an' the bill was lost. An' there was more letters. I got letters from the owners an' the firm—'Tull error on fire-bars, sux pounds'—ot Baltimore, ot Delagoa Bay, ot Moji, ot Rangoon, ot Rio an' ot Montevuddio. Ut uz no settled yut. I tell ye, Annie, the owners are hard tull please."

He communed with himself for a moment, and then muttered indignantly: "Tull error on fire-bars, sux pounds."

"Hov ye heard of Jamie?" his wife asked in the pause.

Captain MacElrath shook his head.

"He was washed off the poop wuth three seamen."

"Whereabouts?"

"Off the Horn. 'Twas on the *Thornsby.*"

"They would be runnun' homeward bound?"

"Ay," she nodded. "We only got the word three days gone. His wife is greetin' like tull die."

"A good lod, Jamie," he commented, "but a stiff one ot carryun' on. I mind me when we was mates together un the *Albion.* An' so Jamie's gone."

Again a pause fell, to be broken by the wife.

"An' ye will no a-heard o' the *Bankshire?* MacDougall lost her in Magellan Straits. 'Twas only yesterday ut was in the paper."

"A cruel place, them Magellan Straits," he said. "Dudna thot domned mate-fellow nigh putt me ashore twice on the one passage through? He was a eediot, a lunatuc. I wouldna have hum on the brudge a munut. Comun' tull Narrow Reach, thuck weather, wuth snow squalls, me un the chart-room, dudna I guv hum the changed course? 'Southeast-by-East,' I told hum. 'South-East-by-East, sir,' says he. Fufteen munuts after I comes on tull the brudge. 'Funny,' says thot mate-fellow, 'I'm no rememberun' ony islands un the mouth o' Narrow Reach.' I took one look ot the islands an' yells, 'Putt your wheel hard-a-starboard,' tull the mon ot the wheel. An' ye should a-seen the old *Tryapsic* turnun' the sharpest circle she ever turned. I waited for the snow tull clear, an' there was Narrow Reach, nice uz ye please, tull the east'ard, an' the islands un the mouth o' False Bay tull the south'ard. 'What course was ye steerun'?' I says tull the mon ot the wheel. 'South-by-East, sir,' says he. I looked tull the mate-fellow. What could I say? I was thot wroth I could a-kult hum. Four points dufference. Five munuts more an' the old *Tryapsic* would a-been funushed.

"An' was ut no the same when we cleared the Straits tull the east'ard? Four hours would a-seen us guid an' clear. I was forty hours then on the brudge. I guv the mate his course, an' the bearun' o' the Askthar Light astern. 'Don't let her bear more tull the north'ard than West-by-North,' I said tull hum, 'an' ye wull be all right.' An' I went below an' turned un. But I couldna sleep for worryun'. After forty hours on the brudge, what was four hours more? I thought. An' for them four hours wull ye be lettun' the mate loss her on ye? 'No,' I says to myself. An' wuth thot I got up, hod a wash an' a cup o' coffee, an' went tull the brudge. I took one look ot the bearun' o' Askthar Light. 'Twas Nor'west-by-West, an' the old *Tryapsic* down on the shoals. He was an eediot, thot mate-fellow. Ye could look overside an' see the duscoloration of the watter. 'Twas a close call for the old *Tryapsic* I'm tellun' ye. Twice un thirty hours he'd a-hod her ashore uf ut hod no been for me."

Captain MacElrath fell to gazing at the sleeping child with mild wonder in his small blue eyes, and his wife sought to divert him from his woes.

"Ye remember Jummy MacCaul?" she asked. "Ye went tull school wuth hus two boys. Old Jummy MacCaul thot hoz the farm beyond Doctor Haythorn's place."

"O, aye, an' what o' hum? Uz he dead?"

"No, but he was after askun' your father, when he sailed last time for Voloparaiso, uf ye'd been there afore. An' when your father says no, then Jummy says, 'An' how wull he be knowun' tull find hus way?' An' with thot your father says: 'Verry sumple ut uz, Jummy. Supposun' you was goin' tull the mainland tull a mon who luved un Belfast. Belfast uz a bug sutty, Jummy, an' how would ye be findun' your way?' 'By way o' me tongue,' says Jummy; 'I'd be askun' the folk I met.' 'I told ye ut was sumple,' says your father. 'Ut's the very same way my Donald finds the road tull Voloparaiso. He asks every shup he meets upon the sea tull ot last he meets wuth a shup thot's been tull Voloparaiso, an' the captun o' thot shup tells hum the way.' An' Jummy scratches hus head an' says he understonds an' thot ut's a very sumple motter after all."

The skipper chuckled at the joke, and his tired blue eyes were merry for the moment.

"He was a thun chap, thot mate-fellow, oz thun oz you an' me putt together," he remarked after a time, a slight twinkle in his eye of appreciation of the bull. But the twinkle quickly disappeared and the blue eyes took on a bleak and wintry look. "What dud he do ot Voloparaiso but land sux hundred fathom o' chain cable an' take never a receipt from the lighter-mon. I was gettun' my clearance ot the time. When we got tull sea, I found he hod no receipt for the cable.

" 'An' ye no took a receipt for ut?' says I.

" 'No,' says he. 'Wasna ut goin' direct tull the agents?'

" 'How long ha' ye been goin' tull sea,' says I, 'not tull be knowin' the mate's duty uz tull deluver no cargo wuthout receipt for same? An' on the West Coast ot thot. What's tull stop the lighter-mon from stealun' a few lengths o' ut?'

"An' ut come out uz I said. Sux hunderd fathom went over the side, but four hunderd an' ninety-five was all the agents received. The lighter-mon swore ut was all he received from the mate—four hundred an' ninety-five fathom. I got a letter from the owners ot Portland. They no blamed the mate for ut, but me, an' me ashore ot the time on shup's buss'ness. I could no be the two places ot the one time. An' the letters from the owners an' the agents uz stull comun' tull me.

"Thot mate-fellow was no a proper sailor, an' no a mon tull work for owners. Dudna he want tull break me wuth the Board o' Trade for bein' below my marks? He said as much tull the bosun. An' he told me tull my face homeward bound thot I'd been half an inch under my marks. 'Twas at Portland, loadun' cargo un fresh watter an' goin' tull Comox tull load bunker coal un salt watter. I tell ye, Annie, ut takes close fuggerin', an' I *was* half an inch under the load-line when the bunker coal was un. But I'm no tellun' any other body but you. An' thot mate-fellow untendun' tull report me tull the Board o' Trade, only for thot he saw fut tull be sliced un two pieces on the steam-pipe cover.

"He was a fool. After loadun' ot Portland I hod tull take on suxty tons o' coal tull last me tull Comox. The charges for lighterun' was heavy, an' no room ot the coal dock. A French bark was lyin' alongside the dock an' I spoke tull the captun, askun' hum what he would charge, when work for the day was done, tull haul clear for a couple o' hours an' let me un. 'Twenty dollars,' said he. Ut was savun' money on lighters tull the owners, an' I gave ut tull hum. An' thot night, after dark, I hauled un an' took on the coal. Then I started tull go out un the stream an' drop anchor—under me own steam, of course.

"We hod tull go out stern-first, an' somethun' went wrong wuth the reversun' gear. Old MacPherson said he could work ut by hond, but very slow ot thot. An' I said all right. We started. The pilot was on board. The tide was ebbun' stuffly, an' right abreast an' a but below was a shup lyin' wuth a lighter on each side. I saw the shup's ridun' lights, but never a light on the lighters. Ut was close quarters to shuft a bug vessel onder steam, wuth MacPherson workun' the reversun' gear by hond. We hod to come close down upon the shup afore I could go ahead an' clear o' the shups on the dock-ends. An' we struck the lighter stern-on, just uz I rung tull MacPherson half ahead.

" 'What was thot?' says the pilot, when we struck the lighter.

" 'I dunna know,' says I, 'an' I'm wonderun'."

"The pilot was no keen, ye see, tull hus job. I went on tull a guid place an' dropped anchor, an' ut would all a-been well but for thot domned eediot mate.

" 'We smashed thot lighter,' says he, comun' up the lodder tull the brudge—an' the pilot stondun' there wuth his ears cocked tull hear.

" 'What lighter?' says I.

" 'Thot lighter alongside the shup,' says the mate.

" 'I dudna see no lighter,' says I, and wuth thot I steps on hus fut guid an' hard.

"After the pilot was gone I says tull the mate: 'Uf you dunna know onythun', old mon, for heaven's sake keep your mouth shut.'

" 'But ye dud smash thot lighter, dudn't ye?' says he.

" 'Uf we did,' says I, 'ut's no your buss'ness tull be tellun' the pilot—though, mind ye, I'm no admuttun' there was ony lighter.'

" 'An' next marnun', just uz I'm after dressun', the steward says, 'A mon tull see ye, sir.' 'Fetch hum un,' says I. An' un he come. 'Sut down,' says I. An' he sot down.

"He was the owner of the lighter, an' when he hod told hus story, I says, 'I dudna see ony lighter.'

" 'What, mon?' says he. 'No see a two-hundred-ton lighter, bug oz a house, alongside thot shup?'

" 'I was goin' by the shup's lights,' says I, 'an' I dudna touch the shup, thot I know.'

" 'But ye dud touch the lighter,' says he. 'Ye smashed her. There's a thousand dollars' domage done, an' I'll see ye pay for ut.'

" 'Look here, Muster,' says I; 'when I'm shuftun' a shup ot night I follow the law, an' the law dustunctly says I must regulate me actions by the lights o' the shuppun'. Your lighter never hod no ridun' light, nor dud I look for any lighter wuthout lights tull show ut.'

" 'The mate says—' he beguns.

" 'Domn the mate,' says I. 'Dud your lighter hov a ridun' light?'

" 'No, ut dud not,' says he, 'but ut was a clear night wuth the moon a-showun".'

" 'Ye seem tull know your buzz'ness,' says I. 'But let me tell ye thot I know my buzz'ness uz well, an' thot I'm no a-lookun' for lighters wuthout lights. Uf ye thunk ye hov a case, go ahead. The steward will show ye out. Guid day.'

"An' thot was the end o' ut. But ut wull show ye what a puir fellow thot mate was. I call ut a blessun' for all masters thot he was sliced un two on thot steam-pipe cover. He hod a pull un the office an' thot was the why he was kept on."

"The Wekley farm wull soon be for sale, so the agents be tellun' me," his wife remarked, slyly watching what effect her announcement would have upon him.

His eyes flashed eagerly on the instant, and he straightened up as might a man about to engage in some agreeable task. It was the farm of his vision, adjoining his father's, and her own people farmed not a mile away.

"We wull be buyun' ut," he said, "though we wull be no tellun' a soul of ut ontull ut's bought an' the money paid down. I'm savun' consuderable these days, though pickun's uz no what they used to be, an' we hov a tidy nest-egg laid by. I wull see the father an' hove the money ready tull hus hond, so uf I'm ot sea he can buy whenever the land offers."

He rubbed the frosted moisture from the inside of the window and peered out at the pouring rain through which he could discern nothing.

"When I was a young mon I used tull be afeard thot the owners would guv me the sack. Stull afeard I am of the sack. But once thot farm is mine I wull no be afeard ony longer. Ut's a puir job thus sea-farmun'. Me managin' un all seas an' weather an' perils o' the deep a shup worth fufty thousand pounds, wuth cargoes ot times worth fufty thousand more—a hunderd thousand pounds, half a million dollars uz the Yankees say, an' me wuth all the responsubility gettun' a screw o' twenty pounds a month. What mon ashore, managin' a buzz'ness worth a hundred thousand pounds wull be gettun' uz small a screw uz twenty pounds? An' wuth such masters uz a captun serves—the owners, the underwriters, an' the Board o' Trade, all pullun' an' wantun' dufferent thungs—the owners wantun' quick passages an' domn the rusk, the underwriters wantun safe passages an' domn the delay, an' the Board o' Trade wantun' cautious passages an' caution always meanun' delay. Three dufferent masters, an' all three able an' wullun' to break ye uf ye don't serve their dufferent wushes."

He felt the train slackening speed, and peered again through the misty window. He stood up, buttoned his overcoat, turned up the collar, and awkwardly gathered the child, still asleep, in his arms.

"I wull see the father," he said, "an' hov the money ready tull his hond so uf I'm ot sea when the land offers he wull no muss the chance tull buy. An' then the owners can guv me the sack uz soon uz they like. Ut will be all night un, an' I wull be wuth you, Annie, an' the sea can go tull hell."

Happiness was in both their faces at the prospect, and for a moment both saw the same vision of peace. Annie leaned toward him, and as the train stopped they kissed each other across the sleeping child.

SAMUEL

MARGARET Henan would have been a striking figure under any circumstances, but never more so than when I first chanced upon her, a sack of grain of fully a hundred-weight on her shoulder, as she walked with sure though tottering stride from the cart-tail to the stable, pausing for an instant to gather strength at the foot of the steep steps that led to the grain-bin. There were four of these steps, and she went up them, a step at a time, slowly, unwaveringly, and with so dogged a certitude that it never entered my mind that her strength could fail her and let that hundred-weight sack fall from the lean and withered frame that well-nigh doubled under it. For she was patently an old woman, and it was her age that made me linger by the cart and watch.

Six times she went between the cart and the stable, each time with a full sack on her back, and beyond passing the time of day with me she took no notice of my presence. Then, the cart empty, she fumbled for matches and lighted a short clay pipe, pressing down the burning surface of the tobacco with a calloused and apparently nerveless thumb. The hands were noteworthy. They were large-knuckled, sinewy and malformed by labor, rimed with callouses, the nails blunt and broken, and with here and there cuts and bruises, healed and healing, such as are common to the hands of hard-working men. On the back were huge, upstanding veins, eloquent of age and toil. Looking at them, it was hard to believe that they were the hands of the woman who had once been the belle of Island McGill. This last, of course, I learned later. At the time I knew neither her history nor her identity.

She wore heavy man's brogans. Her legs were stockingless, and I had noticed when she walked that her bare feet were thrust into the crinkly, iron-like shoes that sloshed about her lean ankles at every step. Her figure, shapeless and waistless, was garbed in a rough man's shirt and in a ragged flannel petticoat that had once been red. But it was her face, wrinkled, withered and weather-beaten, surrounded by an aureole of unkempt and straggling wisps of grayish hair, that caught and held me. Neither drifted hair nor serried wrinkles could hide the splendid dome of a forehead, high and broad without verging in the slightest on the abnormal.

The sunken cheeks and pinched nose told little of the quality of the life that flickered behind those clear blue eyes of hers. Despite the minutiae of wrinkle-work that somehow failed to weazen them, her eyes were clear as a girl's—clear, out-looking, and far-seeing, and with an open and unblinking steadfastness of gaze that was disconcerting. The remarkable thing was the distance between them. It is a lucky man or woman who has the width of an eye between, but with Margaret Henan the width between her eyes was fully that of an eye and a half. Yet so symmetrically molded was her face that this remarkable feature produced no uncanny effect, and, for that matter, would have escaped the casual observer's notice. The mouth, shapeless and toothless, with down-turned corners and lips dry and parchment-like, nevertheless lacked the muscular slackness so usual with age. The lips might have been those of a mummy, save for that impression of rigid firmness they gave. Not that they were atrophied. On the contrary, they seemed tense and set with a muscular and spiritual determination. There, and in the eyes, was the secret of the certitude with which she carried the heavy sacks up the steep steps, with never a false step or over-balance, and emptied them in the grain-bin.

"You are an old woman to be working like this," I ventured.

She looked at me with that strange, unblinking gaze, and she thought and spoke with the slow deliberateness that characterized everything about her, as if well aware of an eternity that was hers and in which there was no need for haste. Again I was impressed by the enormous certitude of her. In this eternity that seemed so indubitably hers, there was time and to spare for safe-footing and stable equilibrium—for certitude, in short. No more in her spiritual life than in carrying the hundred-weights of grain, was there a possibility of a misstep or an overbalancing. The feeling produced in me was uncanny. Here was a human soul that, save for the most glimmering of contacts, was beyond the humanness of me. And the more I learned of Margaret Henan in the weeks that followed the more mysteriously remote she became. She was as alien as a far-journeyer from some other star, and no hint could she nor all the countryside give me of what norms of living, what heats of feeling, or rules of philosophic contemplation actuated her in all that she had been and was.

"I wull be suvunty-two come Guid Friday a fortnight," she said in reply to my question.

"But you are an old woman to be doing this man's work, and a strong man's work at that," I insisted.

Again she seemed to immerse herself in that atmosphere of contemplative eternity, and so strangely did it affect me that I should not have been surprised to have awaked a century or so later and found her just beginning to enunciate her reply:

"The work hoz tull be done, an' I am beholden tull no one."

"But have you no children, no family relations?"

"O, ay, a-plenty o' them, but they no see fut tull be helpun' me."

She drew out her pipe for a moment, then added, with a nod of her head toward the house, "I luv' wuth meself."

I glanced at the house, straw-thatched and commodious, at the large stable, and at the large array of fields I knew must belong with the place.

"It's a big bit of land for you to farm by yourself."

"O, ay, a bug but, suvunty acres. Ut kept me old mon buzzy, along wuth a son an' a hired mon, tull say naught o' extra honds un the harvest an' a maid-servant un the house."

She clambered into the cart, gathered the reins in her hands, and quizzed me with her keen, shrewd eyes.

"Belike ye hail from over the watter—Ameruky, I'm meanun'?"

"Yes, I'm a Yankee," I answered.

"Ye wull no be findun' mony Island McGill folk stoppun' un Ameruky?"

"No; I don't remember ever meeting one in the States."

She nodded her head.

"They are home-lovun' bodies, though I wull no be sayun' they are no fair-traveled. Yet they come home ot the last, them oz are no lost ot sea or kult by fevers an' such-like un foreign parts."

"Then your sons will have gone to sea and come home again?" I queried.

"O, ay, all savun' Samuel oz was drownded."

At the mention of Samuel I could have sworn to a strange light in her eyes, and it seemed to me, as by some telepathic flash, that I divined in her a tremendous wistfulness, an immense yearning. It seemed to me that here was the key to her inscrutableness, the clew that if followed properly would make all her strangeness plain. It came to me that here was a contact and that for the moment I was glimpsing into the soul of her. The question was tickling on my tongue, but she forestalled me.

She *tckh'd* to the horse, and with a "Guid day tull you, sir," drove off.

A simple, homely people, are the folk of Island McGill, and I doubt if a more sober, thrifty, and industrious folk is to be found in all the world. Meeting them abroad—and to meet them abroad one must meet them on the sea, for a hybrid seafaring and farmer breed are they—one would never take them to be Irish. Irish they claim to be, speaking of the North of Ireland with pride and sneering at their Scottish brothers; yet Scotch they undoubtedly are, transplanted Scotch of long ago, it is true, but none the less Scotch, with a thousand traits, to say nothing of their tricks of speech and woolly utterance, which nothing less than their Scotch clannishness could have preserved to this late day.

A narrow loch, scarcely half a mile wide, separates Island McGill from the mainland of Ireland; and, once across this loch, one finds himself in an entirely different country. The Scotch impression is strong, and the people, to commence with, are Presbyterians. When it is considered that there is no public house in all the island and that seven thousand souls dwell therein, some idea may be gained of the temperateness of the community. Wedded to old ways, public opinion and the ministers are powerful influences, while fathers and mothers are revered and obeyed as in few other places in this modern world. Courting lasts never later than ten at night, and no girl walks out with her young man without her parents' knowledge and consent.

The young men go down to the sea and sow their wild oats in the wicked ports, returning periodically, between voyages, to live the old intensive morality, to court till ten o'clock, to sit under the minister each Sunday, and to listen at home to the same stern precepts that the elders preached to them from the time they were laddies. Much they learned of women in the ends of the earth, these seafaring sons, yet a canny wisdom was theirs and they never brought wives home with them. The one solitary exception to this had been the schoolmaster, who had been guilty of bringing a wife from half a mile the other side of the loch. For this he had never been forgiven, and he rested under a cloud for the remainder of his days. At his death the wife went back across the loch to her own people, and the blot on the escutcheon of Island McGill was erased. In the end the sailormen married girls of their own home land and settled down to become exemplars of all the virtues for which the island was noted.

Island McGill was without a history. She boasted none of the events that go to make history. There had never been any wearing of the green, any Fenian conspiracies, any land disturbances. There had been but one eviction, and that purely technical—a test case, and on advice of the tenant's lawyer. So Island McGill was without annals. History had passed her by. She paid her taxes, acknowledged her crowned rulers and left the world alone; all she asked in return was that the world leave her alone. The world was composed of two parts—Island McGill and the rest of it. And whatever was not Island McGill was outlandish and barbarian; and well she knew, for did not her seafaring sons bring home report of that world and its ungodly ways?

It was from the skipper of a Glasgow tramp, as passenger from Colombo to Rangoon, that I had first learned of the existence of Island McGill; and it was from him that I had carried the letter that gave me entrance to the house of Mrs Ross, widow of a master mariner, with a daughter living with her and with two sons, master mariners themselves and out upon the sea. Mrs Ross did not take in boarders, and it was Captain Ross's letter alone that had enabled me to get from her bed and board. In the evening, after my encounter with Margaret Henan, I questioned Mrs Ross, and I knew on the instant that I had in truth stumbled upon mystery.

Like all Island McGill folk, as I was soon to discover, Mrs Ross was at first averse to discussing Margaret Henan at all. Yet it was from her I learned that evening that Margaret Henan had once been one of the island belles. Herself the daughter of a well-to-do farmer, she had married Thomas Henan, equally well-to-do. Beyond the usual housewife's tasks she had never been accustomed to work. Unlike many of the island women, she had never lent a hand in the fields.

"But what of her children?" I asked.

"Two o' the sons, Jamie an' Timothy uz married an' be goun' tull sea. Thot bug house close tull the post-office uz Jamie's. The daughters thot ha' no married be luvun' wuth them as dud marry. An' the rest be dead."

"The Samuels," Clara interpolated, with what I suspected was a giggle.

She was Mrs Ross's daughter, a strapping young woman with handsome features and remarkably handsome black eyes.

" 'Tuz naught tull be smuckerun' ot," her mother reproved her.

"The Samuels?" I intervened. "I don't understand."

"Her four sons thot died."

"And were they all named Samuel?"

"Ay."

"Strange," I commented in the lagging silence.

"Very strange," Mrs Ross affirmed, proceeding stolidly with the knitting of the woollen singlet on her knees—one of the countless undergarments that she interminably knitted for her skipper sons.

"And it was only the Samuels that died?" I queried, in further attempt.

"The others luv'd," was the answer. "A fine fomuly—no finer on the island. No better lods ever sailed out of Island McGill. The munuster held them up oz models tull pottern after. Nor was ever a whusper breathed again' the girls."

"But why is she left alone now in her old age?" I persisted. "Why don't her own flesh and blood look after her? Why does she live alone? Don't they ever go to see her or care for her?"

"Never a one un twenty years an' more now. She fetch't ut on tull herself. She drove them from the house just oz she drove old Tom Henan, thot was her husband, tull hus death."

"Drink?" I ventured.

Mrs Ross shook her head scornfully, as if drink was a weakness beneath the weakest of Island McGill.

A long pause followed, during which Mrs Ross knitted stolidly on, only nodding permission when Clara's young man, mate on one of the Shire Line sailing ships, came to walk out with her. I studied the half-dozen ostrich eggs, hanging in the corner against the wall like a cluster of some monstrous fruit. On each shell was painted precipitous and impossible seas through which full-rigged ships foamed with a lack of perspective only equaled by their sharp technical perfection. On the mantelpiece stood two large pearl shells, obviously a pair, intricately carved by the patient hands of New Caledonian convicts. In the centre of the mantel was a stuffed bird of paradise, while about the room were scattered gorgeous shells from the southern seas, delicate sprays of coral sprouting from barnacled *pi-pi* shells and cased in glass, assegais from South

Africa, stone-axes from New Guinea, huge Alaskan tobacco-pouches beaded with heraldic totem designs, a boomerang from Australia, divers ships in glass bottles, a cannibal *kai-kai* bowl from the Marquesas, and fragile cabinets from China and the Indies all inlaid with mother-of-pearl and precious woods.

I gazed at this varied trove brought home by sailor sons, and pondered the mystery of Margaret Henan, who had driven her husband to his death and been forsaken by all her kin. It was not the drink. Then what was it?—some shocking cruelty? some amazing infidelity? or some fearful, old-world peasant-crime?

I broached my theories, but to all Mrs Ross shook her head.

"Ut was no thot," she said. "Margaret was a guid wife an' a guid mother, an' I doubt she would harm a fly. She brought up her fomuly God-fearin' an' decent-minded. Her trouble was thot she took lunatuc—turned eediot."

Mrs Ross tapped significantly on her forehead to indicate a state of addlement.

"But I talked with her this afternoon," I objected, "and I found her a sensible woman—remarkably bright for one of her years."

"Ay, an' I'm grantun' all thot you say," she went on calmly. "But I am no referrun' tull thot. I am referrun' tull her wucked-headed an' vucious stubbornness. No more stubborn woman ever luv'd than Margaret Henan. Ut was all on account o' Samuel, which was the name o' her eldest an' they do say her favorut brother—hum oz died by hus own hond all through the munuster's mustake un no registerun' the new church ot Dublin. Ut was a lesson thot the name was musfortunate, but she would no take ut, an' there was talk when she called her first child Samuel—hum thot died o' the croup. An' wuth thot what does she do but call the next one Samuel, an' hum only three when he fell un tull the tub o' hot watter an' was plain cooked tull death. Ut all come, I tell you, o' her wucked-headed an' foolush stubbornness. For a Samuel she must hov; an' ut was the death of the four of her sons. After the first, dudna her own mother go down un the dirt tull her feet, a-beggun' an' pleadun' wuth her no tull name her next one Samuel? But she was no tull be turned from her purpose. Margaret Henan was always set un her ways, an' never more so thon on thot name Samuel.

"She was fair lunatuc on Samuel. Dudna her neighbors, an' all kuth an' kun savun' them thot luv'd un the house wuth her, get up an' walk out ot the christenun' of the second—hum thot was cooked? Thot they dud, an' ot the very moment the munuster asked what would the bairn's name be. 'Samuel,' says she; an' wuth thot they got up an' walked out an' left the house. An' ot the door dudna her Aunt Fannie, her mother's suster, turn an' say loud for all tull hear: 'What for wull she be wantun' tull murder the wee thung?' The munuster heard fine, an' dudna like ut, but, oz he told my Larry afterward, what could he do? Ut was the woman's wush, an' there was no law again' a mother callun' her child accordun' tull her wush.

"An' then was there no' the third Samuel? An' when he was lost ot sea off the Cape, dudna she break all laws o' nature tull hov a fourth? She was forty-seven, I'm tellun' ye, an' she hod a child ot forty-seven. Thunk on ut! Ot forty-seven! Ut was fair scand'lous."

From Clara, next morning I got the tale of Margaret Henan's favorite brother; and from here and there, in the week that followed, I pieced together the tragedy of Margaret Henan. Samuel Dundee had been the youngest of Margaret's four brothers, and, as Clara told me, she had well-nigh worshiped him. He was going to sea at the time, skipper of one of the sailing ships of the Bank Line, when he married Agnes Hewitt. She was described as a slender wisp of a girl, delicately featured and with a nervous organization of the supersensitive order. Theirs had been the first marriage in the "new" church, and after a two-weeks' honeymoon Samuel had kissed his bride good-by and sailed in command of the *Loughbank*, a big four-masted bark.

And it was because of the "new" church that the minister's blunder occurred. Nor was it the blunder of the minister alone, as one of the elders later explained; for it was equally the blunder of the whole Presbytery of Coughleen, which included fifteen churches on Island McGill and the mainland. The old church, beyond repair, had been torn down and the new one built on the original foundation. Looking upon the foundation stones as similar to a ship's keel, it never entered the minister's nor the Presbytery's head that the new church was legally any other than the old church.

"An' three couples was married the first week un the new church," Clara said. "First of all, Samuel Dundee an' Agnes Hewitt; the next day Albert Mahan an' Minnie Duncan; an' by the week-end Eddie Troy and Flo Mackintosh—all sailor-men, an' un sux weeks' time the last of them back tull their ships an' awa', an' no one o' them dreamin' of the wuckedness they'd been ot."

The Imp of the Perverse must have chuckled at the situation. All things favored. The marriages had taken place in the first week of May, and it was not till three months later that the minister, as required by law, made his quarterly report to the civil authorities in Dublin. Promptly came back the announcement that his church had no legal existence, not being registered according to the law's demands. This was overcome by prompt registration; but the marriages were not to be so easily remedied. The three sailor-husbands were away, and their wives, in short, were not their wives.

"But the munuster was no for alarmin' the bodies," said Clara. "He kept hus council an' bided hus time, waitin' for the lods tull be back from sea. Oz luck would have ut, he was away across the island tull a christenun' when Albert Mahan arrives home onexpected, hus shup just docked ot Dublin. Ut's nine o'clock ot night when the munuster, un hus sluppers an' dressun' gown, gets the news. Up he jumps an' calls for horse an' saddle, an' awa' he goes like the wund for Albert Mahan's. Albert uz just goun' tull bed an' hoz one shoe off when the munuster arrives.

" 'Come wuth me, the pair o' ye,' says he, breathless-like. 'What for, an' me dead weary an' goun' tull bed?' says Albert. 'Tull be lawful married,' says the munuster. Albert looks black an' says, 'Now munuster ye wull be jokin',' but tull himself, oz I've heard him tell mony a time, he uz wonderun' thot the munuster should a-took tull whuskey ot hus time o' life.

" 'We be no married?' says Minnie. He shook his head. 'An' I om no Mussus Mahan?' 'No,' says he, 'ye are no Mussus Mahan. Ye are plain Muss Duncan.' 'But ye married us yoursel',' says she. 'I dud an' I dudna,' says he. An' wuth thot he tells them the whole upshot, an' Albert puts on hus shoe, an' they go with the munuster an' are married proper an' lawful, an' oz Albert Mahan says afterward mony's the time, "Tus no every mon thot hoz two weddun' nights on Island McGill.' "

Six months later Eddie Troy came home and was promptly remarried. But Samuel Dundee was away on a three-years' voyage and his ship fell overdue. Further to complicate the situation, a baby boy, past two years old, was waiting for him in the arms of his wife. The months passed, and the wife grew thin with worrying. "Ut's no meself I'm thunkun' on," she is reported to have said many times, "but ut's the puir fatherless bairn. Uf aught happened tull Samuel where wull the bairn stond?"

Lloyds posted the *Loughbank* as missing, and the owners ceased the monthly remittance of Samuel's half-pay to his wife. It was the question of the child's legitimacy that preyed on her mind, and, when all hope of Samuel's return was abandoned, she drowned herself and the child in the loch. And here enters the greater tragedy. The *Loughbank* was not lost. By a series of sea disasters and delays too interminable to relate, she had made one of those long, unsighted passages such as occur once or twice in half a century. How the Imp must have held both his sides! Back from the sea came Samuel, and when they broke the news to him something else broke somewhere in his heart or head. Next morning they found him where he had tried to kill himself across the grave of his wife and child. Never in the history of Island McGill was there so fearful a deathbed. He spat in the minister's face and reviled him, and died blaspheming so terribly that those that tended on him did so with averted gaze and trembling hands.

And, in the face of all this, Margaret Henan named her first child Samuel.

How account for the woman's stubbornness? Or was it a morbid obsession that demanded a child of hers should be named Samuel? Her third child was a girl, named after herself, and the fourth was a boy again. Despite the strokes of fate that had already bereft her, and despite the loss of friends and relatives, she persisted in her resolve to name the child after her brother. She was shunned at church by those who had grown up with her. Her mother, after a final appeal, left her house with the warning that if the child were so named she would never speak to her again. And though the old lady lived thirty-odd years longer she kept her word. The minister agreed to christen the child any name but Samuel, and every other minister on Island McGill refused to christen it by the name she had chosen. There was talk on the part of Margaret Henan of going to law at the time, but in the end she carried the child to Belfast and there had it christened Samuel.

And then nothing happened. The whole island was confuted. The boy grew and prospered. The schoolmaster never ceased averring that it was the brightest lad he had ever seen. Samuel had a splendid constitution, a tremendous grip on life. To everybody's amazement he escaped the usual run of childish afflictions. Measles, whooping-cough and mumps knew him not. He was armor-clad against germs, immune to all disease. Headaches and earaches were things unknown. "Never so much oz a boil or a pumple," as one of the old bodies told me, ever marred his healthy skin. He broke school records in scholarship and athletics, and whipped every boy of his size or years on Island McGill.

It was a triumph for Margaret Henan. This paragon was hers, and it bore the cherished name. With the one exception of her mother, friends and relatives drifted back and acknowledged that they had been mistaken; though there were old crones who still abided by their opinion and who shook their heads ominously over their cups of tea. The boy was too wonderful to last. There was no escaping the curse of the name his mother had wickedly laid upon him. The young generation joined Margaret Henan in laughing at them, but the old crones continued to shake their heads.

Other children followed. Margaret Henan's fifth was a boy, whom she called Jamie, and in rapid succession followed three girls, Alice, Sara and Nora, the boy Timothy, and two more girls, Florence and Katie. Katie was the last and eleventh, and Margaret Henan, at thirty-five, ceased from her exertions. She had done well by Island McGill and the Queen. Nine healthy children were hers. All prospered. It seemed her ill luck had shot its bolt with the deaths of her first two. Nine lived, and one of them was named Samuel.

Jamie elected to follow the sea, though it was not so much a matter of election as compulsion, for the eldest sons on Island McGill remained on the land while all other sons went to the salt plowing. Timothy followed Jamie, and by the time the latter had got his first command, a steamer in the Bay trade out of Cardiff, Timothy was mate of a big sailing ship. Samuel, however, did not take kindly to the soil. The farmer's life had no attraction for him. His brothers went to sea, not out of desire, but because it was the only way for them to gain their bread; and he, who had no need to go, envied them when, returned from far voyages, they sat by the kitchen fire and told their bold tales of the wonderlands beyond the sea-rim.

Samuel became a teacher, much to his father's disgust, and even took extra certificates, going to Belfast for his examinations. When the old master retired, Samuel took over his school. Secretly, however, he studied navigation, and it was Margaret's delight when he sat by the kitchen fire, and, despite their master's tickets, tangled up his brothers in the theoretics of their profession. Tom Henan alone was outraged when Samuel, school teacher, gentleman and heir to the Henan farm, shipped to sea before the mast. Margaret had an abiding faith in her son's star, and whatever he did she was sure was for the best. Like everything else connected with his glorious personality, there had never been known so swift a rise as in the case of Samuel. Barely with two years' sea experience before the mast, he was taken from the forecastle and made a provisional second mate. This occurred in a fever port on the West Coast, and the committee of skippers that examined him agreed that he knew more of the science of navigation than they had remembered or forgotten. Two years later he sailed from Liverpool, mate of the *Starry Grace*, with both master's and extra-master's tickets in his possession. And then it happened—the thing the old crones had been shaking their head over for years.

It was told me by Gavin McNab, bosun of the *Starry Grace* at the time, himself an Island McGill man.

"Wull do I remember ut," he said. "We was runnin' our Eastun' down, an' makun' heavy weather of ut. Oz fine a sailor-mon oz ever walked was Samuel Henan. I remember the look of hum wull thot last marnun', a-watchun' them bug seas curlun' up astern, an' a-watchun' the old girl an' seeun' how she took them—the skupper down below an' drunkun' for days. Ut was ot seven thot Henan brought her up on tull the wund, not darun' tull run longer un thot fearful sea. Ot eight, after havun' breakfast, he turns un, an' a half hour after up comes the skupper, bleary-eyed an' shaky an' holdun' on tull the componion. Ut was fair smokun', I om tellun' ye, an' there he stood, blunkun' an' noddun' an' talkun' tull humsel'. 'Keep off,' says he ot last tull the mon ot the wheel. 'My God!' says the second mate, standun' beside hum. The skupper never looks tull hum ot all, but keeps on mutterun' an' jabberun' tull humsel'. All of a suddent-like he straightuns up an' throws hus head back, an' says: 'Put your wheel over, me mon—now, domn ye! Are ye deef thot ye'll no be hearun' me?'

"Ut was a drunken mon's luck, for the *Starry Grace* wore off afore thot God-Almighty gale wuthout shuppun' a bucket o' watter, the second mate shoutun' orders an' the crew jumpun' like mod. An' wuth thot the skupper nods contented-like tull humself an' goes below after more whuskey. Ut was plain murder o' the lives o' all of us, for ut was no the time for the buggest shup afloat tull be runnun'. Run? Never hov I seen the like! Ut was beyond all thunkun', an' me goun' tull sea, boy an' mon, for forty year. I tell you ut was fair awesome.

"The face o' the second mate was white oz death, an' he stood ut alone for half an hour, when ut was too much for hum an' he went below an' called Samuel an' the third. Ay, a fine sailor-mon thot Samuel, but ut was too much for hum. He looked an' studied, and looked an' studied, but he could no see hus way. He durst na heave tull. She would ha' been sweeput o' all honds an' stucks an' everythung afore she could a-fetcht up. There was naught tull do but keep on runnun'. An' uf ut worsened we were lost onyway, for soon or late thot overtakun' sea was sure tull sweep us clear over poop an' all.

"Dud I say ut was a God-Almighty gale? Ut was worse nor thot. The devil himself must ha' hod a hond un the brewun' o' ut, ut was thot fearsome. I ha' looked on some sights, but I om no carun' tull look on the like o' thot again. No mon dared tull be un hus bunk. No, nor no mon on the decks. All honds of us stood on top the house an' held on an' watched. The three mates was on the poop, with two men ot the wheel, an' the only mon below was thot whuskey-blighted captain snorun' drunk.

"An' then I see ut comun', a mile away, risun' above all the waves like an island un the sea—the buggest wave ever I looked upon. The three mates stood tulgether an' watched ut comun', a-prayun' like we thot she would no break un passun' us. But ut was no tull be. Ot the last, when she rose up like a mountain, curlun' above the stern an' blottun' out the sky, the mates scottered, the second an' third runnun' for the mizzen-shrouds an' climbun' up, but the first runnun' tull the wheel tull lend a hond. He was a brave mon, thot Samuel Henan. He run straight un tull the face o' thot father o' all waves, no thunkun' on humself but thunkun' only o' the shup. The two men was lashed tull the wheel, but he would be ready tull hond un the case they was kult. An' then she took ut. We on the house could no see the poop for the thousand tons o' watter thot hod hut ut. Thot wave cleaned them out, took everythung along wuth ut—the two mates, climbun' up the mizzen-ruggun', Samuel Henan runnun' tull the wheel, the two men ot the wheel, ay, an' the wheel utself. We never saw aught o' them, for she broached tull what o' the wheel goun', an' two men o' us was drownded off the house, no tull mention the carpenter thot we pucked up ot the break o' the poop wuth every bone o' hus body broke tull he was like so much jelly."

And here enters the marvel of it, the miraculous wonder of that woman's heroic spirit. Margaret Henan was forty-seven when the news came home of the loss of Samuel; and it was not long after that the unbelievable rumor went around Island McGill. I say unbelievable. Island McGill would not believe. Doctor Hall poohpooh'd it. Everybody laughed at it as a good joke. They traced back the gossip to Sara Dack, servant to the Henans', and who alone lived with Margaret and her husband. But Sara Dack persisted in her assertion and was called a low-mouthed liar. One or two dared question Tom Henan himself, but beyond black looks and curses for their presumption they elicited nothing from him.

The rumor died down, and the island fell to discussing in all its ramifications the loss of the *Grenoble* in the China Seas, with all her officers and half her crew born and married on Island McGill. But the rumor would not stay down. Sara Dack was louder in her assertions, the looks Tom Henan cast about him were blacker than ever, and Dr Hall, after a visit to the Henan house, no longer poohpooh'd. Then Island McGill sat up, and there was a tremendous wagging of tongues. It was unnatural and ungodly. The like had never been heard. And when, as time passed, the truth of Sara Dack's utterances was manifest, the island folk decided, like the bosun of the *Starry Grace,* that only the devil could have had a hand in so untoward a happening. And the infatuated woman, so Sara Dack reported, insisted that it would be a boy. "Eleven bairns ha' I borne," she said; "sux o' them lossies an' five o' them loddies. An' sunce there be balance un all thungs, so wull there be balance wuth me. Sux o' one an' half a dozen o' the other—there uz the balance, an' oz sure oz the sun rises un the marnun', thot sure wull ut be a boy."

And boy it was, and a prodigy. Dr Hall raved about its unblemished perfection and massive strength, and wrote a brochure on it for the Dublin Medical Society as the most interesting case of the sort in his long career. When Sara Dack gave the babe's unbelievable weight, Island McGill refused to believe and once again called her liar. But when Doctor Hall attested that he had himself weighed it and seen it tip that very notch, Island McGill held its breath and accepted whatever report Sara Dack made of the infant's progress or appetite. And once again Margaret Henan carried a babe to Belfast and had it christened Samuel.

"Oz good oz gold ut was," said Sara Dack to me.

Sara, at the time I met her, was a buxom, phlegmatic spinster of sixty, equipped with an experience so tragic and unusual that though her tongue ran on for decades its output would still be of imperishable interest to her cronies.

"Oz good oz gold," said Sara Dack. "Ut never fretted. Sut ut down un the sun by the hour an' never a sound ut would make oz long oz ut was no hungered. An' thot strong! The grup o' uts honds was like a mon's. I mind me, when ut was but hours old, ut grupped me so mighty thot I fetcht a scream I was thot frighted. Ut was the punk o' health. Ut slept an' ate, an' grew. Ut never bothered. Never a night's sleep ut lost tull no one, nor ever a munut's, an' thot wuth cuttin' uts teeth an' all. An' Margaret would dandle ut on her knee an' ask was there ever so fine a loddie un the three Kungdoms.

"The way ut grew! Ut was un keepun' wuth the way ut ate. Ot a year ut was the size o' a bairn of two. Ut was slow tull walk an' talk. Exceptun' for gurgly noises un uts throat an' for creepun' on all fours, ut dudna monage much un the walkun' an' talkun' line. But thot was tull be expected from the way ut grew. Ut all went tull growun' strong an' healthy. An' even old Tom Henan cheered up ot the might of ut an' said was there ever the like o' ut un the three Kungdoms. Ut was Doctor Hall thot first suspicioned, I mind me well, though ut was luttle I dreamt what he was up tull ot the time. I see hum holdun' thungs un front o' luttle Sammy's eyes, an' a-makun' noises, loud an' soft, an' far an' near, un luttle Sammy's ears. An' then I see Doctor Hall go away, wrunklun' hus eyebrows an' shakun' hus head like the bairn was ailun'. But he was no ailun', oz I could swear tull, me a-seeun' hum eat an' grow. But Doctor Hall no said a word tull Margaret an' I was no for guessun' the why he was sore-puzzled.

"I mind me when luttle Sammy first spoke. He was two years old an' the size of a child o' five, though he could no monage the walkun' yet but when around on all-fours, happy an' contented-like an' makun' no trouble oz long oz he was fed promptly, whuch was onusual often. I was hangun' the wash on the line ot the time when out he comes, on all-fours, hus bug head waggun' tull an' fro an' blunkun' un the sun. An' then, suddent, he talked. I was thot took a-back I near died o' fright, an' fine I knew ut then, the shakun' o' Doctor Hall's head. Talked? Never a bairn on Island McGill talked so loud an' tull such purpose. There was no mustakun' ut. I stood there all tremblun' an' shakun'. Little Sammy was brayun'. I tell you, sir, he was brayun' like an ass—just like thot, loud an' long an' cheerful tull ut seemed hus lungs ud crack.

"He was a eediot—a great, awful, monster eediot. Ut was after he talked thot Doctor Hall told Margaret, but she would no believe. Ut would all come right, she said. Ut was growun' too fast for aught else. Guv ut time, said she, an' we would see. But old Tom Henan knew, an' he never held up hus head again. He could no abide the thung, an' would no brung humsel' tull touch ut, though I om no denyun' he was fair fascinated by ut. Mony the time I see hum watchun' of ut aroun' a corner, lookun' ot ut tull hus eyes fair bulged wuth the horror; an' when ut brayed old Tom ud stuck hus fungers tull hus ears an' look thot miserable I could a-puttied hum.

"An' bray ut could! Ut was the only thung ut could do besides eat an' grow. Whenever ut was hungry ut brayed, an' there was no stoppun' ut save wuth food. An' always of a marnun', when first ut crawled tull the kutchen-door an' blunked out ot the sun, ut brayed. An' ut was brayun' that brought about uts end.

"I mind me well. Ut was three years old an' oz bug oz a lod o' ten. Old Tom hed been goun' from bod tull worse, ploughun' up an' down the fields an' talkun' an' mutterun' tull humself. On the marnun' o' the day I mind me, he was suttun' on the bench outside the kutchen, a-futtun' the handle tull a puck-axe. Unbeknown, the monster eediot crawled tull the door an' brayed after hus fashion ot the sun. I see old Tom start up an' look. An' there was the monster eediot, waggun' uts bug head an' blunkun' an' brayun' like the great bug ass ut was. Ut was too much for Tom. Somethin' went wrong wuth hum suddent-like. He jumped tull hus feet an' fetcht the puck-handle down on the monster eediot's head. An' he hut ut again an' again like ut was a mod dog an' hum afeard o' ut. An' he went straight tull the stable an' hung humsel' tull a rafter. An' I was no for stoppun' on after such-like, an' I went tull stay along wuth me suster thot was married tull John Martin an' comfortable-off."

I sat on the bench by the kitchen door and regarded Margaret Henan, while with her callous thumb she pressed down the live fire of her pipe and gazed out across the twilight-sombered fields. It was the very bench Tom Henan had sat upon that last sanguinary day of life. And Margaret sat in the doorway where the monster, blinking at the sun, had so often wagged its head and brayed. We had been talking for an hour, she with that slow certitude of eternity that so befitted her; and, for the life of me, I could lay no finger on the motives that ran through the tangled warp and woof of her. Was she a martyr to Truth? Did she have it in her to worship at so abstract a shrine? Had she conceived Abstract Truth to be the one high goal of human endeavor on that day of long ago when she named her first-born Samuel? Or was hers the stubborn obstinacy of the ox? The fixity of purpose of the balky horse? The stolidity of the self-willed peasant-mind? Was it whim or fancy?—the one streak of lunacy in what was otherwise an eminently rational mind? Or, reverting, was hers the spirit of a Bruno? Was she convinced of the intellectual rightness of the stand she had taken? Was hers a steady, enlightened opposition to superstition? Or—and a subtler thought—was she mastered by some vaster, profounder superstition, a fetish-worship of which the Alpha and the Omega was the cryptic *Samuel?*

"Wull ye be tellun' me," she said, "thot uf the second Samuel hod been named Larry thot he would no hov fell un the hot watter an' drownded? Atween you an' me, sir, an' ye are untellugent-lookun' tull the eye, would the name hov made ut onyways dufferent? Would the washun' no be done thot day uf he hod been Larry or Michael? Would hot watter no be hot, an' would hot watter no burn uf he hod hod ony other name but Samuel?"

I acknowledged the justice of her contention, and she went on.

"Do a wee but of a name change the plans o' God? Do the world run by hut or muss, an' be God a weak, shully-shallyun' creature thot ud alter the fate an' destiny o' thungs because the worm Margaret Henan seen fut tull name her bairn Samuel? There be my son Jamie. He wull no sign a Rooshan-Funn un hus crew because o' believun' thot Rooshan-Funns do be monajun' the wunds an' hov the makun' o' bod weather. Wull you be thunkun' so? Wull you be thunkun' thot God thot makes the wunds tull blow wull bend hus head from on high tull lussen tull the word o' a greasy Rooshan-Funn un some dirty shup's fo'c'sle?"

I said no, certainly not; but she was not to be set aside from pressing home the point of her argument.

"Then wull you be thunkun' thot God thot directs the stars un their courses, an' tull whose mighty foot the world uz but a footstool, wull you be thunkun' thot he wull take a spite again' Margaret Henan an' send a bug wave off the Cape tull wash her son un tull eternity, all because she was for namun' hum Samuel?"

"But why Samuel?" I asked.

"An' thot I dinna know. I wanted ut so."

"But *why* did you want it so?"

"An' uz ut me thot would be answerun' a such-like question? Be there ony mon luvun' or dead thot can answer? Who can tell the *why* o' like? My Jamie was fair daft on buttermilk; he would drunk ut tull, oz he said himself, hus back-teeth was awash. But my Tumothy could no abide buttermilk. I like tull lussen tull the thunder growlun' an' roarun', an' rampajun'. My Katie could no abide the noise of ut, but must scream an' flutter an' go runnun' for the mudmost o' a feather-bed. Never yet hov I heard the answer tull the *why* o' like. God alone hoz thot answer. You an' me be mortal an' we canna know. Enough for us tull know what we like an' what we duslike. *I like*— thot uz the first word an' the last. An' behind thot *like* no mon can go an' find the *why* o' ut. I *like* Samuel, an' I like ut wull. Ut uz a sweet name, an' there be a rollun' wonder un the sound o' ut thot passes onderstandun'."

The twilight deepened, and in the silence I gazed upon that splendid dome of a forehead which time could not mar, at the width between the eyes, and at the eyes themselves—clear, out-looking, and wide-seeing. She rose to her feet with an air of dismissing me, saying:

"Ut wull be a dark walk home, an' there wull be more thon a sprunkle o' wet un the sky."

"Have you any regrets, Margaret Henan?" I asked, suddenly and without forethought.

She studied me a moment.

"Ay, thot I no ha' borne another son."

"And you would . . . ?" I faltered.

"Ay, thot I would," she answered. "Ut would ha' been hus name."

I went down the dark road between the hawthorne hedges puzzling over the why of like, repeating *Samuel* to myself and aloud and listening to the rolling wonder in its sound that had charmed her soul and led her life in tragic places. *Samuel!* There was a rolling wonder in the sound. Ay, there was!

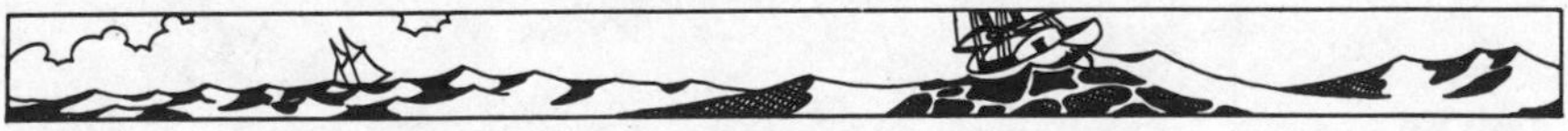

The Sea-Wolf

I

I SCARCELY know where to begin, though I sometimes facetiously place the cause of it all to Charley Furuseth's credit. He kept a summer cottage in Mill Valley, under the shadow of Mount Tamalpais, and never occupied it except when he loafed through the winter months and read Nietzsche and Schopenhauer to rest his brain. When summer came on, he elected to sweat out a hot and dusty existence in the city and to toil incessantly. Had it not been my custom to run up to see him every Saturday afternoon and to stop over till Monday morning, this particular January Monday morning would not have found me afloat on San Francisco Bay.

Not but that I was afloat in a safe craft, for the *Martinez* was a new ferry-steamer, making her fourth or fifth trip on the run between Sausalito and San Francisco. The danger lay in the heavy fog which blanketed the bay, and of which, as a landsman, I had little apprehension. In fact, I remember the placid exaltation with which I took up my position on the forward upper deck, directly beneath the pilot-house, and allowed the mystery of the fog to lay hold of my imagination. A fresh breeze was blowing, and for a time I was alone in the moist obscurity—yet not alone, for I was dimly conscious of the presence of the pilot, and of what I took to be the captain, in the glass house above my head.

I remember thinking how comfortable it was, this division of labor which made it unnecessary for me to study fogs, winds, tides and navigation, in order to visit my friend who lived across an arm of the sea. It was good that men should be specialists, I mused. The peculiar knowledge of the pilot and captain sufficed for many thousands of people who knew no more of the sea and navigation than I knew. On the other hand, instead of having to devote my energy to the learning of a multitude of things, I concentrated it upon a few particular things, such as, for instance, the analysis of Poe's place in American literature—an essay of mine, by the way, in the current *Atlantic*. Coming aboard, as I passed through the cabin, I had noticed with greedy eyes a stout gentleman reading the *Atlantic*, which was open at my very essay. And there it was again, the division of labor, the special knowledge of the pilot and captain which permitted the stout gentleman to read my special knowledge on Poe while they carried him safely from Sausalito to San Francisco.

A red-faced man, slamming the cabin door behind him and stumping out on the deck, interrupted my reflections, though I made a mental note of the topic for use in a projected essay which I had thought of calling "The Necessity for Freedom: A Plea for the Artist." The red-faced man shot a glance up at the pilot-house, gazed around at the fog, stumped across the deck and back (he evidently had artificial legs), and stood still by my side, legs wide apart, and with an expression of keen enjoyment on his face. I was not wrong when I decided that his days had been spent on the sea.

"It's nasty weather like this here that turns heads gray before their time," he said, with a nod toward the pilot-house.

"I had not thought there was any particular strain," I answered. "It seems as simple as A B C. They know the direction by compass, the distance and the speed. I should not call it anything more than mathematical certainty."

"Strain!" he snorted. "Simple as A B C! Mathematical certainty!"

He seemed to brace himself up and lean backward against the air as he stared at me. "How about this here tide that's rushin' out through the Golden Gate?" he demanded, or bellowed, rather. "How fast is she ebbin'? What's the drift, eh? Listen to that, will you? A bell-buoy, and we're a-top of it! See 'em alterin' the course!"

From out of the fog came the mournful tolling of a bell, and I could see the pilot turning the wheel with great rapidity. The bell, which had seemed straight ahead, was now sounding from the side. Our own whistle was blowing hoarsely, and from time to time the sound of other whistles came to us from out of the fog.

"That's a ferry-boat of some sort," the newcomer said, indicating a whistle off to the right. "And there! D'ye hear that? Blown by mouth. Some scow schooner, most likely. Better watch out, Mr Schooner-man. Ah, I thought so. Now hell's a-poppin' for somebody!"

The unseen ferry-boat was blowing blast after blast, and the mouth-blown horn was tooting in terror-stricken fashion.

"And now they're payin' their respects to each other and tryin' to get clear," the red-faced man went on, as the hurried whistling ceased.

His face was shining, his eyes flashing with excitement, as he translated into articulate language the speech of the horns and sirens. "That's a steam siren a-goin' it over there to the left. And you hear that fellow with a frog in his throat—a steam schooner as near as I can judge, crawlin' in from the Heads against the tide."

A shrill little whistle, piping as if gone mad, came from directly ahead and from very near at hand. Gongs sounded on the *Martinez*. Our paddle-wheels stopped, their pulsing beat died away, and then they started again. The shrill little whistle, like the chirping of a cricket amid the cries of great beasts, shot through the fog from more to the side and swiftly grew faint and fainter. I looked to my companion for enlightenment.

"One of them dare-devil launches," he said. "I almost wish we'd sunk him, the little rip! They're the cause of more trouble. And what good are they? Any jackass gets aboard one and runs it from hell to breakfast, blowin' his whistle to beat the band and tellin' the rest of the world to look out for him, because he's comin' and can't look out for himself! Because he's comin'! And you've got to look out, too! Right of way! Common decency! They don't know the meanin' of it!"

I felt quite amused at his unwarranted choler, and while he stumped indignantly up and down I fell to dwelling upon the romance of the fog. And romantic it certainly was—the fog, like the gray shadow of infinite mystery, brooding over the whirling speck of earth; and men, mere motes of light and sparkle, cursed with an insane relish for work, riding their steeds of wood and steel through the heart of the mystery, groping their way blindly through the Unseen, and clamoring and clanging in confident speech the while their hearts are heavy with incertitude and fear.

The voice of my companion brought me back to myself with a laugh. I too had been groping and floundering, the while I thought I rode clear-eyed through the mystery.

"Hello! somebody comin' our way," he was saying. "And d'ye hear that? He's comin' fast. Walking right along. Guess he don't hear us yet. Wind's in wrong direction."

The fresh breeze was blowing right down upon us, and I could hear the whistle plainly, off to one side and a little ahead.

"Ferry-boat?" I asked.

He nodded, then added, "Or he wouldn't be keepin' up such a clip." He gave a short chuckle. "They're gettin' anxious up there."

I glanced up. The captain had thrust his head and shoulders out of the pilot-house, and was staring intently into the fog as though by sheer force of will he could penetrate it. His face was anxious, as was the face of my companion, who had stumped over to the rail and was gazing with a like intentness in the direction of the invisible danger.

Then everything happened, and with inconceivable rapidity. The fog seemed to break away as though split by a wedge, and the bow of a steamboat emerged, trailing fog-wreaths on either side like seaweed on the snout of Leviathan. I could see the pilot-house and a white-bearded man leaning partly out of it, on his elbows. He was clad in a blue uniform, and I remember noting how trim and quiet he was. His quietness, under the circumstances, was terrible. He accepted Destiny, marched hand in hand with it and coolly measured the stroke. As he leaned there, he ran a calm and speculative eye over us, as though to determine the precise point of the collision, and took no notice whatever when our pilot, white with rage, shouted, "Now you've done it!"

On looking back, I realize that the remark was too obvious to make rejoinder necessary.

"Grab hold of something and hang on," the red-faced man said to me. All his bluster had gone, and he seemed to have caught the contagion of preternatural calm. "And listen to the women scream," he said grimly—almost bitterly, I thought, as though he had been through the experience before.

The vessels came together before I could follow his advice. We must have been struck squarely amidships, for I saw nothing, the strange steamboat having passed beyond my line of vision. The *Martinez* heeled over, sharply, and there was a crashing and rending of timber. I was thrown flat on the wet deck, and before I could scramble to my feet I heard the scream of the women. This it was, I am certain—the most indescribable of blood-curdling sounds—that threw me into a panic. I remembered the life-preservers stored in the cabin, but was met at the door and swept backward by a wild rush of men and women. What happened in the next few minutes I do not recollect, though I have a clear remembrance of pulling down life-preservers from the overhead racks, while the red-faced man fastened them about the bodies of an hysterical group of women. This memory is as distinct and sharp as that of any picture I have seen. It is a picture, and I can see it now—the jagged edges of the hole in the side of the cabin, through which the gray fog swirled and eddied; the empty upholstered seats, littered with all the evidences of sudden flight, such as packages, hand satchels, umbrellas, and wraps; the stout gentleman who had been reading my essay, encased in cork and canvas, the magazine still in his hand, and asking me with monotonous insistence if I thought there was any danger; the red-faced man, stumping gallantly around on his artificial legs and buckling life-preservers on all comers; and finally, the screaming bedlam of women.

This it was, the screaming of the women, that most tried my nerves. It must have tried, too, the nerves of the red-faced man, for I have another picture which will never fade from my mind. The stout gentleman is stuffing the magazine into his overcoat pocket and looking on curiously. A tangled mass of women, with drawn, white faces and open mouths, is shrieking like a chorus of lost souls; and the red-faced man, his face now purplish with wrath, and with arms extended overhead as in the act of hurling thunderbolts, is shouting, "Shut up! Oh, shut up!"

I remember the scene impelled me to sudden laughter, and in the next instant I realized I was becoming hysterical myself; for these were women of my own kind, like my mother and sisters, with the fear of death upon them and unwilling to die. And I remember that the sounds they made reminded me of the squealing of pigs under the knife of the butcher, and I was struck with horror at the vividness of the analogy. These women, capable of the most sublime emotions, of the tenderest sympathies, were open-mouthed and screaming. They wanted to live, they were helpless, like rats in a trap, and they screamed.

The horror of it drove me out on deck. I was feeling sick and squeamish, and sat down on a bench. In a hazy way I saw and heard men rushing and shouting as they strove to lower the boats. It was just as I had read descriptions of such scenes in books. The tackles jammed. Nothing worked. One boat lowered away with the plugs out, filled with women and children and then with water, and capsized. Another boat had been lowered by one end, and still hung in the tackle by the other end, where it had been abandoned. Nothing was to be seen of the strange steamboat which had caused the disaster, though I heard men saying that she would undoubtedly send boats to our assistance.

I descended to the lower deck. The *Martinez* was sinking fast, for the water was very near. Numbers of the passengers were leaping overboard. Others, in the water, were clamoring to be taken aboard again. No one heeded them. A cry arose that we were sinking. I was seized by the consequent panic, and went over the side in a surge of bodies. How I went over I do not know, though I did know, and instantly, why those in the water were so desirous of getting back on the steamer. The water was cold—so cold that it was painful. The pang, as I plunged into it, was as quick and sharp as that of fire. It bit to the marrow. It was like the grip of death. I gasped with the anguish and shock of it, filling my lungs before the lifepreserver popped me to the surface. The taste of salt was strong in my mouth, and I was strangling with the acrid stuff in my throat and lungs.

But it was the cold that was most distressing. I felt that I could survive but a few minutes. People were struggling and floundering in the water about me. I could hear them crying out to one another. And I heard, also, the sound of oars. Evidently the strange steamboat had lowered its boats. As the time went by I marvelled that I was still alive. I had no sensation whatever in my lower limbs, while a chilling numbness was wrapping about my heart and creeping into it. Small waves, with spiteful foaming crests, continually broke over me and into my mouth, sending me off into more strangling paroxysms.

The noises grew indistinct, though I heard a final and despairing chorus of screams in the distance, and knew that the *Martinez* had gone down. Later—how much later I have no knowledge—I came to myself with a start of fear. I was alone. I could hear no calls or cries—only the sound of the waves, made weirdly hollow and reverberant by the fog. A panic in a crowd, which partakes of a sort of community of interest, is not so terrible as a panic when one is by oneself; and such a panic I now suffered. Whither was I drifting? The red-faced man had said that the tide was ebbing through the Golden Gate. Was I, then, being carried out to sea? And the lifepreserver in which I floated? Was it not liable to go to pieces at any moment? I had heard of such things being made of paper and hollow rushes which quickly became saturated and lost all buoyancy. And I could not swim a stroke. And I was alone, floating, apparently, in the midst of a gray primordial vastness. I confess that a madness seized me, that I shrieked aloud as the women had shrieked, and beat the water with my numb hands.

How long this lasted I have no conception, for a blankness intervened, of which I remember no more than one remembers of troubled and painful sleep. When I aroused, it was as after centuries of time; and I saw, almost above me and emerging from the fog, the bow of a vessel, and three triangular sails, each shrewdly lapping the other and filled with wind. Where the bow cut the water there was a great foaming and gurgling, and I seemed directly in its path. I tried to cry out, but was too exhausted. The bow plunged down, just missing me and sending a swash of water clear over my head. Then the long, black side of the vessel began slipping past, so near that I could have touched it with my hands. I tried to reach it, in a mad resolve to claw into the wood with my nails, but my arms were heavy and lifeless. Again I strove to call out, but made no sound.

The stern of the vessel shot by, dropping, as it did so, into a hollow between the waves; and I caught a glimpse of a man standing at the wheel, and of another man who seemed to be doing little else than smoke a cigar. I saw the smoke issuing from his lips as he slowly turned his head and glanced out over the water in my direction. It was a careless, unpremeditated glance, one of those haphazard things men do when they have no immediate call to do anything in particular, but act because they are alive and must do something.

But life and death were in that glance. I could see the vessel being swallowed up in the fog; I saw the back of the man at the wheel, and the head of the other man turning, slowly turning, as his gaze struck the water and casually lifted along it toward me. His face wore an absent expression, as of deep thought, and I became afraid that if his eyes did light upon me he would nevertheless not see me. But his eyes did light upon me, and looked squarely into mine; and he did see me, for he sprang to the wheel, thrusting the other man aside, and whirled it round and round, hand over hand, at the same time shouting orders of some sort. The vessel seemed to go off at a tangent to its former course and leapt almost instantly from view into the fog.

I felt myself slipping into unconsciousness, and tried with all the power of my will to fight above the suffocating blankness and darkness that was rising around me. A little later I heard the stroke of oars, growing nearer and nearer, and the calls of a man. When he was very near I heard him crying, in vexed fashion, "Why in hell don't you sing out?" This meant me, I thought, and then the blankness and darkness rose over me.

II

I SEEMED swinging in a mighty rhythm through orbit vastness. Sparkling points of light spluttered and shot past me. They were stars, I knew, and flaring comets, that peopled my flight among the suns. As I reached the limit of my swing and prepared to rush back on the counter swing, a great gong struck and thundered. For an immeasurable period, lapped in the rippling of placid centuries, I enjoyed and pondered my tremendous flight.

But a change came over the face of the dream, for a dream I told myself it must be. My rhythm grew shorter and shorter. I was jerked from swing to counter swing with irritating haste. I could scarcely catch my breath, so fiercely was I impelled through the heavens. The gong thundered more frequently and more furiously. I grew to await it with a nameless dread. Then it seemed as though I were being dragged over rasping sands, white and hot in the sun. This gave place to a sense of intolerable anguish. My skin was scorching in the torment of fire. The gong clanged and knelled. The sparkling points of light flashed past me in an interminable stream, as though the whole sidereal system were dropping into the void. I gasped, caught my breath painfully, and opened my eyes. Two men were kneeling beside me, working over me. My mighty rhythm was the lift and forward plunge of a ship on the sea. The terrific gong was a frying-pan, hanging on the wall, that rattled and clattered with each leap of the ship. The rasping, scorching sands were a man's hard hands chafing my naked chest. I squirmed under the pain of it, and half lifted my head. My chest was raw and red, and I could see tiny blood globules starting through the torn and inflamed cuticle.

"That'll do, Yonson," one of the men said. "Carn't yer see you've bloomin' well rubbed all the gent's skin orf?"

The man addressed as Yonson, a man of the heavy Scandinavian type, ceased chafing me, and arose awkwardly to his feet. The man who had spoken to him was clearly a Cockney, with the clean lines and weakly pretty, almost effeminate, face of the man who has absorbed the sound of Bow Bells with his mother's milk. A draggled muslin cap on his head and a dirty gunny-sack about his slim hips proclaimed him cook of the decidedly dirty ship's galley in which I found myself.

"An' 'ow yer feelin' now, sir?" he asked, with the subservient smirk which comes only of generations of tip-seeking ancestors.

For reply, I twisted weakly into a sitting posture, and was helped by Yonson to my feet. The rattle and bang of the frying-pan was grating horribly on my nerves. I could not collect my thoughts. Clutching the woodwork of the galley for support—and I confess the grease with which it was scummed put my teeth on edge—I reached across a hot cooking-range to the offending utensil, unhooked it, and wedged it securely into the coal-box.

The cook grinned at my exhibition of nerves, and thrust into my hand a steaming mug with an " 'Ere, this'll do yer good." It was a nauseous mess—ship's coffee—but the heat of it was revivifying. Between gulps of the molten stuff I glanced down at my raw and bleeding chest and turned to the Scandinavian.

"Thank you, Mr Yonson," I said; "but don't you think your measures were rather heroic?"

It was because he understood the reproof of my action, rather than of my words, that he held up his palm for inspection. It was remarkably calloused. I passed my hand over the horny projections, and my teeth went on edge once more from the horrible rasping sensation produced.

"My name is Johnson, not Yonson," he said, in very good, though slow, English, with no more than a shade of accent to it.

There was mild protest in his pale blue eyes, and withal a timid frankness and manliness that quite won me to him.

"Thank you, Mr Johnson," I corrected, and reached out my hand for his.

He hesitated, awkward and bashful, shifted his weight from one leg to the other, then blunderingly gripped my hand in a hearty shake.

"Have you any dry clothes I may put on?" I asked the cook.

"Yes, sir," he answered, with cheerful alacrity. "I'll run down an' tyke a look over my kit, if you've no objections, sir, to wearin' my things."

He dived out of the galley door, or glided rather, with a swiftness and smoothness of gait that struck me as being not so much cat-like as oily. In fact, this oiliness, or greasiness, as I was later to learn, was probably the most salient expression of his personality.

"And where am I?" I asked Johnson, whom I took, and rightly, to be one of the sailors. "What vessel is this, and where is she bound?"

"Off the Farallones, heading about sou'west," he answered, slowly and methodically, as though groping for his best English, and rigidly observing the order of my queries. "The schooner *Ghost*, bound seal-hunting to Japan."

"And who is the captain? I must see him as soon as I am dressed."

Johnson looked puzzled and embarrassed. He hesitated while he groped in his vocabulary and framed a complete answer. "The cap'n is Wolf Larsen, or so men call him. I never heard his other name. But you better speak soft with him. He is mad this morning. The mate—"

But he did not finish. The cook had glided in.

"Better sling yer 'ook out of 'ere, Yonson," he said. "The old man'll be wantin' yer on deck, an' this ayn't no d'y to fall foul of 'im."

Johnson turned obediently to the door, at the same time, over the cook's shoulder, favoring me with an amazingly solemn and portentous wink, as though to emphasize his interrupted remark and the need for me to be soft-spoken with the captain.

Hanging over the cook's arm was a loose and crumpled array of evil-looking and sour-smelling garments.

"They was put aw'y wet, sir," he vouchsafed explanation. "But you'll 'ave to make them do till I dry yours out by the fire."

Clinging to the woodwork, staggering with the roll of the ship, and aided by the cook, I managed to slip into a rough woollen undershirt. On the instant my flesh was creeping and crawling from the harsh contact. He noticed my involuntary twitching and grimacing, and smirked:

"I only 'ope yer don't ever 'ave to get used to such as that in this life, 'cos you've got a bloomin' soft skin, that you 'ave, more like a lydy's than any I know of. I was bloomin' well sure you was a gentleman as soon as I set eyes on yer."

I had taken a dislike to him at first, and as he helped to dress me this dislike increased. There was something repulsive about his touch. I shrank from his hand; my flesh revolted. And between this and the smells arising from various pots boiling and bubbling on the galley fire, I was in haste to get out into the fresh air. Further, there was the need of seeing the captain about what arrangements could be made for getting me ashore.

A cheap cotton shirt, with frayed collar and a bosom discolored with what I took to be ancient blood-stains, was put on me amid a running and apologetic fire of comment. A pair of workman's brogans encased my feet, and for trousers I was furnished with a pair of pale blue, washed-out overalls, one leg of which was fully ten inches shorter than the other. The abbreviated leg looked as though the devil had there clutched for the Cockney's soul and missed the shadow for the substance.

"And whom have I to thank for this kindness?" I asked, when I stood completely arrayed, a tiny boy's cap on my head, and for coat a dirty, striped cotton jacket which ended at the small of my back and the sleeves of which reached just below my elbows.

The cook drew himself up in a smugly humble fashion, a deprecating smirk on his face. Out of my experience with stewards on the Atlantic liners at the end of the voyage, I could have sworn he was waiting for his tip. From my fuller knowledge of the creature I now know that the posture was unconscious. An hereditary servility, no doubt, was responsible.

"Mugridge, sir," he fawned, his effeminate features running into a greasy smile. "Thomas Mugridge, sir, an' at yer service."

"All right, Thomas," I said. "I shall not forget you—when my clothes are dry."

A soft light suffused his face and his eyes glistened, as though somewhere in the deeps of his being his ancestors had quickened and stirred with dim memories of tips received in former lives.

"Thank you, sir," he said, very gratefully and very humbly indeed.

Precisely in the way that the door slid back, he slid aside, and I stepped out on deck. I was still weak from my prolonged immersion. A puff of wind caught me, and I staggered across the moving deck to a corner of the cabin, to which I clung for support. The schooner, heeled over far out from the perpendicular, was bowing and plunging into the long Pacific roll. If she were heading southwest as Johnson had said, the wind, then, I calculated, was blowing nearly from the south. The fog was gone, and in its place the sun sparkled crisply on the surface of the water. I turned to the east, where I knew California must lie, but could see nothing save low-lying fogbanks—the same fog, doubtless, that had brought about the disaster to the *Martinez* and placed me in my present situation. To the north, and not far away, a group of naked rocks thrust above the sea, on one of which I could distinguish a lighthouse. In the southwest, and almost in our course, I saw the pyramidal loom of some vessel's sails.

Having completed my survey of the horizon, I turned to my more immediate surroundings. My first thought was that a man who had come through a collision and rubbed shoulders with death merited more attention than I received. Beyond a sailor at the wheel who stared curiously across the top of the cabin, I attracted no notice whatever.

Everybody seemed interested in what was going on amidships. There, on a hatch, a large man was lying on his back. He was fully clothed, though his shirt was ripped open in front. Nothing was to be seen of his chest, however, for it was covered with a mass of black hair, in appearance like the furry coat of a dog. His face and neck were hidden beneath a black beard, intershot with gray, which would have been stiff and bushy had it not been limp and draggled and dripping with water. His eyes were closed, and he was apparently unconscious; but his mouth was wide open, his breast heaving as though from suffocation as he labored noisily for breath. A sailor, from time to time and quite methodically, as a matter of routine, dropped a canvas bucket into the ocean at the end of a rope, hauled it in hand under hand, and sluiced its contents over the prostrate man.

Pacing back and forth the length of the hatchway, and savagely chewing the end of a cigar, was the man whose casual glance had rescued me from the sea. His height was probably five feet ten inches, or ten and a half; but my first impression, or feel of the man, was not of this, but of his strength. And yet, while he was of massive build, with broad shoulders and deep chest, I could not characterize his strength as massive. It was what might be termed a sinewy, knotty strength, of the kind we ascribe to lean and wiry men, but which, in him, because of his heavy build, partook more of the enlarged gorilla order. Not that in appearance he seemed in the least gorilla-like. What I am striving to express is this strength itself, more as a thing apart from his physical semblance. It was a strength we are wont to associate with things primitive, with wild animals, and the creatures we imagine our tree-dwelling prototypes to have been—a strength savage, ferocious, alive in itself, the essence of life in that it is the potency of motion, the elemental stuff itself out of which the many forms of life have been molded; in short, that which writhes in the body of a snake when the head is cut off, and the snake, as a snake, is dead, or which lingers in the shapeless lump of turtle-meat and recoils and quivers from the prod of a finger.

Such was the impression of strength I gathered from this man who paced up and down. He was firmly planted on his legs; his feet struck the deck squarely and with surety; every movement of a muscle, from the heave of the shoulders to the tightening of the lips about the cigar, was decisive, and seemed to come out of a strength that was excessive and overwhelming. In fact, though this strength pervaded every action of his, it seemed but the advertisement of a greater strength that lurked within, that lay dormant and no more than stirred from time to time, but which might arouse, at any moment, terrible and compelling, like the rage of a lion or the wrath of a storm.

The cook stuck his head out of the galley door and grinned encouragingly at me, at the same time jerking his thumb in the direction of the man who paced up and down by the hatchway. Thus I was given to understand that he was the captain, the "Old Man" , in the cook's vernacular, the individual whom I must interview and put to the trouble of somehow getting me ashore. I had half started forward, to get over with what I was certain would be a stormy five minutes, when a more violent suffocating paroxysm seized the unfortunate person who was lying on his back. He wrenched and writhed about convulsively. The chin, with the damp black beard, pointed higher in the air as the back muscles stiffened and the chest swelled in an unconscious and instinctive effort to get more air. Under the whiskers, and all unseen, I knew that the skin was taking on a purplish hue.

The captain, or Wolf Larsen, as men called him, ceased pacing and gazed down at the dying man. So fierce had this final struggle become that the sailor paused in the act of flinging more water over him and stared curiously, the canvas bucket partly tilted and dripping its contents to the deck. The dying man beat a tattoo on the hatch with his heels, straightened out his legs, and stiffened in one great tense effort, and rolled his head from side to side. Then the muscles relaxed, the head stopped rolling and a sigh, as of profound relief, floated upward from his lips. The jaw dropped, the upper lip lifted, and two rows of tobacco-discolored teeth appeared. It seemed as though his features had frozen into a diabolical grin at the world he had left and outwitted.

Then a most surprising thing occurred. The captain broke loose upon the dead man like a thunderclap. Oaths rolled from his lips in a continuous stream. And they were not namby-pamby oaths or mere expressions of indecency. Each word was a blasphemy, and there were many words. They crisped and crackled like electric sparks. I had never heard anything like it in my life, nor could I have conceived it possible. With a turn for literary expression myself, and a penchant for forcible figures and phrases, I appreciated, as no other listener, I dare say, the peculiar vividness and strength and absolute blasphemy of his metaphors. The cause of it all, as near as I could make out, was that the man, who was mate, had gone on a debauch before leaving San Francisco, and then had the poor taste to die at the beginning of the voyage and leave Wolf Larsen short-handed.

It should be unnecessary to state, at least to my friends, that I was shocked. Oaths and vile language of any sort had always been repellent to me. I felt a wilting sensation, a sinking at the heart, and, I might just as well say, a giddiness. To me, death had always been invested with solemnity and dignity. It had been peaceful in its occurrence, sacred in its ceremonial. But death in its more sordid and terrible aspects was a thing with which I had been unacquainted till now. As I say, while I appreciated the power of the terrific denunciation that swept out of Wolf Larsen's mouth, I was inexpressibly shocked. The scorching torrent was enough to wither the face of the corpse. I should not have been surprised if the wet black beard had frizzled and curled and flared up in smoke and flame. But the dead man was unconcerned. He continued to grin with a sardonic humor, with a cynical mockery and defiance. He was master of the situation.

III

Wolf Larsen ceased swearing as suddenly as he had begun. He relighted his cigar and glanced around. His eyes chanced upon the cook.

"Well, Cooky?" he began, with a suaveness that was cold and of the temper of steel.

"Yes, sir," the cook eagerly interpolated, with appeasing and apologetic servility.

"Don't you think you've stretched that neck of yours just about enough? It's unhealthy, you know. The mate's gone, so I can't afford to lose you too. You must be very, very careful of your health, Cooky. Understand?"

His last word, in striking contrast with the smoothness of his previous utterance, snapped like the lash of a whip. The cook quailed under it.

"Yes, sir," was the meek reply, as the offending head disappeared into the galley.

At this sweeping rebuke, which the cook had only pointed, the rest of the crew became uninterested and fell to work at one task or another. A number of men, however, who were lounging about a companionway between the galley and the hatch, and who did not seem to be sailors, continued talking in low tones with one another. These, I afterward learned, were the hunters, the men who shot the seals, and a very superior breed to common sailor-folk.

"Johansen!" Wolf Larsen called out. A sailor stepped forward obediently. "Get your palm and needle and sew the beggar up. You'll find some old canvas in the sail-locker. Make it do."

"What'll I put on his feet, sir?" the man asked, after the customary "Ay, ay, sir."

"We'll see to that," Wolf Larsen answered, and elevated his voice in a call of "Cooky!"

Thomas Mugridge popped out of his galley like a jack-in-the-box.

"Go below and fill a sack with coal."

"Any of you fellows got a Bible or prayer-book?" was the captain's next demand, this time of the hunters lounging about the companionway.

They shook their heads, and someone made a jocular remark which I did not catch, but which raised a general laugh.

Wolf Larsen made the same demand of the sailors. Bibles and prayer-books seemed scarce articles, but one of the men volunteered to pursue the quest amongst the watch below, returning in a minute with the information that there was none.

The captain shrugged his shoulders. "Then we'll drop him over without any palavering, unless our clerical-looking castaway has the burial service at sea by heart."

By this time he had swung fully around and was facing me.

"You're a preacher, aren't you?" he asked.

The hunters—there were six of them—to a man, turned and regarded me. I was painfully aware of my likeness to a scarecrow. A laugh went up at my appearance—a laugh that was not lessened or softened by the dead man stretched and grinning on the deck before us; a laugh that was as rough and harsh and frank as the sea itself; that arose out of coarse feelings and blunted sensibilities, from natures that knew neither courtesy nor gentleness.

Wolf Larsen did not laugh, though his gray eyes lighted with a slight glint of amusement; and in that moment, having stepped forward quite close to him, I received my first impression of the man himself, of the man as apart from his body and from the torrent of blasphemy I had heard him spew forth. The face, with large features and strong lines, of the square order, yet well filled out, was apparently massive at first sight; but again, as with the body, the massiveness seemed to vanish, and a conviction to grow of a tremendous and excessive mental or spiritual strength that lay behind, sleeping in the deeps of his being. The jaw, the chin, the brow rising to a goodly height and swelling heavily above the eyes—these, while strong in themselves, unusually strong, seemed to speak an immense vigor or virility of spirit that lay behind and beyond and out of sight. There was no sounding such a spirit, no measuring, no determining of metes and bounds, nor neatly classifying in some pigeonhole with others of similar type.

The eyes—and it was my destiny to know them well—were large and handsome, wide apart as the true artist's are wide, sheltering under a heavy brow and arched over by thick black eyebrows. The eyes themselves were of that baffling protean gray which is never twice the same; which runs through many shades and colorings like intershot silk in sunshine; which is gray, dark and light, and greenish gray, and sometimes of the clear azure of the deep sea. They were eyes that masked the soul with a thousand guises, and that sometimes opened, at rare moments, and allowed it to rush up as though it were about to fare forth nakedly into the world on some wonderful adventure—eyes that could brood with the hopeless sombreness of leaden skies; that could snap and crackle points of fire like those which sparkle from a whirling sword; that could grow chill as an arctic landscape, and yet again, that could warm and soften and be all a-dance with love-lights, intense and masculine, luring and compelling, which at the same time fascinate and dominate women till they surrender in a gladness of joy and of relief and sacrifice.

But to return. I told him that, unhappily for the burial service, I was not a preacher, when he sharply demanded:

"What do you do for a living?"

I confess I had never had such a question asked me before, nor had I ever canvassed it. I was quite taken aback, and before I could find myself had sillily stammered, "I—I am a gentleman."

His lip curled in a swift sneer.

"I have worked, I do work," I cried impetuously, as though he were my judge and I required vindication, and at the same time very much aware of my arrant idiocy in discussing the subject at all.

"For your living?"

There was something so imperative and masterful about him that I was quite beside myself—"rattled" , as Furuseth would have termed it, like a quaking child before a stern schoolmaster.

"Who feeds you?" was his next question.

"I have an income," I answered stoutly, and could have bitten my tongue the next instant. "All of which, you will pardon my observing, has nothing whatsoever to do with what I wish to see you about."

But he disregarded my protest.

"Who earned it? Eh? I thought so. Your father. You stand on dead men's legs. You've never had any of your own. You couldn't walk alone between two sunrises and hustle the meat for your belly for three meals. Let me see your hand."

His tremendous, dormant strength must have stirred, swiftly and accurately, or I must have slept a moment, for before I knew it he had stepped two paces forward, gripped my right hand in his, and held it up for inspection. I tried to withdraw it, but his fingers tightened, without visible effort, till I thought mine would be crushed. It is hard to maintain one's dignity under such circumstances. I could not squirm or struggle like a schoolboy. Nor could I attack such a creature who had but to twist my arm to break it. Nothing remained but to stand still and accept the indignity. I had time to notice that the pockets of the dead man had been emptied on the deck, and that his body and his grin had been wrapped from view in canvas, the folds of which the sailor, Johansen, was sewing together with coarse white twine, shoving the needle through with a leather contrivance fitted on the palm of his hand.

Wolf Larsen dropped my hand with a flirt of disdain.

"Dead men's hands have kept it soft. Good for little else than dish-washing and scullion work."

"I wish to be put ashore," I said firmly, for I now had myself in control. "I shall pay you whatever you judge your delay and trouble to be worth."

He looked at me curiously. Mockery shone in his eyes.

"I have a counter proposition to make, and for the good of your soul. My mate's gone, and there'll be a lot of promotion. A sailor comes aft to take mate's place, cabin-boy goes for'ard to take sailor's place, and you take the cabin-boy's place, sign the articles for the cruise, twenty dollars per month and found. Now what do you say? And mind you, it's for your own soul's sake. It will be the making of you. You might learn in time to stand on your own legs and perhaps to toddle along a bit."

But I took no notice. The sails of the vessel I had seen off to the southwest had grown larger and plainer. They were of the same schooner-rig as the *Ghost*, though the hull itself, I could see, was smaller. She was a pretty sight, leaping and flying toward us, and evidently bound to pass at close range. The wind had been momentarily increasing, and the sun, after a few angry gleams, had disappeared. The sea had turned a dull leaden gray and grown rougher, and was now tossing foaming whitecaps to the sky. We were travelling faster and heeled farther over. Once, in a gust, the rail dipped under the sea, and the decks on that side were for the moment awash with water that made a couple of the hunters hastily lift their feet.

"That vessel will soon be passing us," I said, after a moment's pause. "As she is going in the opposite direction, she is very probably bound for San Francisco."

"Very probably," was Wolf Larsen's answer, as he turned partly away from me and cried out, "Cooky! Oh, Cooky!"

The Cockney popped out of the galley.

"Where's that boy? Tell him I want him."

"Yes, sir"; and Thomas Mugridge fled swiftly aft and disappeared down another companionway near the wheel. A moment later he emerged, a heavy-set young fellow of eighteen or nineteen, with a glowering, villainous countenance, trailing at his heels.

" 'Ere 'e is, sir," the cook said.

But Wolf Larsen ignored that worthy, turning at once to the cabin-boy.

"What's your name, boy?"

"George Leach, sir," came the sullen answer, and the boy's bearing showed clearly that he divined the reason for which he had been summoned.

"Not an Irish name," the captain snapped sharply. "O'Toole or McCarthy would suit your mug a damn sight better. Unless, very likely, there's an Irishman in your mother's woodpile."

I saw the young fellow's hands clench at the insult, and the blood crawl scarlet up his neck.

"But let that go," Wolf Larsen continued. "You may have very good reasons for forgetting your name, and I'll like you none the worse for it as long as you toe the mark. Telegraph Hill, of course, is your port of entry. It sticks out all over your mug. Tough as they make them and twice as nasty. I know the kind. Well, you can make up your mind to have it taken out of you on this craft. Understand? Who shipped you, anyway?"

"McCready and Swanson."

"Sir!" Wolf Larsen thundered.

"McCready and Swanson, sir," the boy corrected, his eyes burning with a bitter light.

"Who got the advance money?"

"They did, sir."

"I thought as much. And damned glad you were to let them have it. Couldn't make yourself scarce too quick, with several gentlemen you may have heard of looking for you."

The boy metamorphosed into a savage on the instant. His body bunched together as though for a spring, and his face became as an infuriated beast's as he snarled, "It's a—"

"A what?" Wolf Larsen asked, a peculiar softness in his voice, as though he were overwhelmingly curious to hear the unspoken word.

The boy hesitated, then mastered his temper. "Nothin', sir. I take it back."

"And you have shown me I was right." This with a gratified smile. "How old are you?"

"Just turned sixteen, sir."

"A lie. You'll never see eighteen again. Big for your age at that, with muscles like a horse. Pack up your kit and go for'ard into the fo'c'sle. You're a boat-puller now. You're promoted, see?"

Without waiting for the boy's acceptance, the captain turned to the sailor who had just finished the grewsome task of sewing up the corpse. "Johansen, do you know anything about navigation?"

"No, sir."

"Well, never mind; you're mate just the same. Get your traps aft into the mate's berth."

"Ay, ay, sir," was the cheery response, as Johansen started forward.

In the meantime the erstwhile cabin-boy had not moved.

"What are you waiting for?" Wolf Larsen demanded.

"I didn't sign for boat-puller, sir," was the reply. "I signed for cabin-boy. An' I don't want no boat-pullin' in mine."

"Pack up and go for'ard."

This time Wolf Larsen's command was thrillingly imperative. The boy glowered sullenly, but refused to move.

Then came another stirring of Wolf Larsen's tremendous strength. It was utterly unexpected, and it was over and done with between the ticks of two seconds. He had sprung fully six feet across the deck and driven his fist into the other's stomach. At the same moment, as though I had been struck myself, I felt a sickening shock in the pit of my stomach. I instance this to show the sensitiveness of my nervous organization at the time, and how unused I was to spectacles of brutality. The cabin-boy—and he weighed one hundred and sixty-five at the very least—crumpled up. His body wrapped limply about the fist like a wet rag about a stick. He lifted into the air, described a short curve, and struck the deck alongside the corpse on his head and shoulders, where he lay and writhed about in agony.

"Well?" Larsen asked of me. "Have you made up your mind?"

I had glanced occasionally at the approaching schooner, and it was now almost abreast of us and not more than a couple of hundred yards away. It was a very trim and neat little craft. I could see a large, black number on one of its sails, and I had seen pictures of pilot-boats.

"What vessel is that?" I asked.

"The pilot-boat *Lady Mine,*" Wolf Larsen answered grimly. "Got rid of her pilots and running into San Francisco. She'll be there in five or six hours with this wind."

"Will you please signal it, then, so that I may be put ashore."

"Sorry, but I've lost the signal book overboard," he remarked, and the group of hunters grinned.

I debated a moment, looking him squarely in the eyes. I had seen the frightful treatment of the cabin-boy, and knew that I should very probably receive the same, if not worse. As I say, I debated with myself, and then I did what I consider the bravest act of my life. I ran to the side, waving my arms and shouting:

"*Lady Mine* ahoy! Take me ashore! A thousand dollars if you take me ashore!"

I waited, watching two men who stood by the wheel, one of them steering. The other was lifting a megaphone to his lips. I did not turn my head, though I expected every moment a killing blow from the human brute behind me. At last, after what seemed centuries, unable longer to stand the strain, I looked around. He had not moved. He was standing in the same position, swaying easily to the roll of the ship and lighting a fresh cigar.

"What is the matter? Anything wrong?"

This was the cry from the *Lady Mine.*

"Yes!" I shouted, at the top of my lungs. "Life or death! One thousand dollars if you take me ashore!"

"Too much 'Frisco tanglefoot for the health of my crew!" Wolf Larsen shouted after. "This one"—indicating me with his thumb—"fancies sea-serpents and monkeys just now!"

The man on the *Lady Mine* laughed back through the megaphone. The pilot-boat plunged past.

"Give him hell for me!" came a final cry, and the two men waved their arms in farewell.

I leaned despairingly over the rail, watching the trim little schooner swiftly increasing the bleak sweep of ocean between us. And she would probably be in San Francisco in five or six hours! My head seemed bursting. There was an ache in my throat as though my heart were up in it. A curling wave struck the side and splashed salt spray on my lips. The wind puffed strongly, and the *Ghost* heeled far over, burying her lee rail. I could hear the water rushing down upon the deck.

When I turned around, a moment later, I saw the cabin-boy staggering to his feet. His face was ghastly white, twitching with suppressed pain. He looked very sick.

"Well, Leach, are you going for'ard?" Wolf Larsen asked.

"Yes, sir," came the answer of a spirit cowed.

"And you?" I was asked.

"I'll give you a thousand—" I began, but was interrupted.

"Stow that! Are you going to take up your duties as cabin-boy? Or do I have to take you in hand?"

What was I to do? To be brutally beaten, to be killed perhaps, would not help my case. I looked steadily into the cruel gray eyes. They might have been granite for all the light and warmth of a human soul they contained. One may see the soul stir in some men's eyes, but his were bleak, and cold, and gray as the sea itself.

"Well?"

"Yes," I said.

"Say 'yes, sir.' "

"Yes, sir," I corrected.

"What is your name?"

"Van Weyden, sir."

"First name?"

"Humphrey, sir; Humphrey Van Weyden."

"Age?"

"Thirty-five, sir."

"That'll do. Go to the cook and learn your duties."

And thus it was that I passed into a state of involuntary servitude to Wolf Larsen. He was stronger than I, that was all. But it was very unreal at the time. It is no less unreal now that I look back upon it. It will always be to me a monstrous, inconceivable thing, a horrible nightmare.

"Hold on, don't go yet."

I stopped obediently in my walk toward the galley.

"Johansen, call all hands. Now that we've everything cleaned up, we'll have the funeral and get the decks cleared of useless lumber."

While Johansen was summoning the watch below, a couple of sailors, under the captain's direction, laid the canvas-swathed corpse upon a hatch-cover. On either side the deck, against the rail and bottoms up, were lashed a number of small boats. Several men picked up the hatch-cover with its ghastly freight, carried it to the lee side, and rested it on the boats, the feet pointing overboard. To the feet was attached the sack of coal which the cook had fetched.

I had always conceived a burial at sea to be a very solemn and awe-inspiring event, but I was quickly disillusioned, by this burial at any rate. One of the hunters, a little dark-eyed man whom his mates called "Smoke" , was telling stories, liberally intersprinkled with oaths and obscenities; and every minute or so the group of hunters gave mouth to a laughter that sounded to me like a wolf-chorus or the barking of hell-hounds. The sailors trooped noisily aft, some of the watch below rubbing the sleep from their eyes, and talked in low tones together. There was an ominous and worried expression on their faces. It was evident that they did not like the outlook of a voyage under such a captain and begun so inauspiciously. From time to time they stole glances at Wolf Larsen, and I could see that they were apprehensive of the man.

He stepped up to the hatch-cover, and all caps came off. I ran my eyes over them—twenty men all told; twenty-two including the man at the wheel and myself. I was pardonably curious in my survey, for it appeared my fate to be pent up with them on this miniature floating world for I knew not how many weeks or months. The sailors, in the main, were English and Scandinavian, and their faces seemed of the heavy, stolid order. The hunters, on the other hand, had stronger and more diversified faces, with hard lines and the marks of the free play of passions. Strange to say, and I noted it at once, Wolf Larsen's features showed no such evil stamp. There seemed nothing vicious in them. True, there were lines, but they were the lines of decision and firmness. It seemed, rather, a frank and open countenance, which frankness or openness was enhanced by the fact that he was smooth-shaven. I could hardly believe—until the next incident occurred—that it was the face of a man who could behave as he had behaved to the cabin-boy.

At this moment, as he opened his mouth to speak, puff after puff struck the schooner and pressed her side under. The wind shrieked a wild song through the rigging. Some of the hunters glanced anxiously aloft. The lee rail, where the dead man lay, was buried in the sea, and as the schooner lifted and righted the water swept across the deck, wetting us above our shoe-tops. A shower of rain drove down upon us, each drop stinging like a hailstone. As it passed, Wolf Larsen began to speak, the bareheaded men swaying in unison to the heave and lunge of the deck.

"I only remember one part of the service," he said, "and that is, 'And the body shall be cast into the sea.' So cast it in."

He ceased speaking. The men holding the hatch-cover seemed perplexed, puzzled no doubt by the briefness of the ceremony. He burst upon them in a fury.

"Lift up that end there, damn you! What the hell's the matter with you?"

They elevated the end of the hatch-cover with pitiful haste, and, like a dog flung overside, the dead man slid feet first into the sea. The coal at his feet dragged him down. He was gone.

"Johansen," Wolf Larsen said briskly to the new mate, "keep all hands on deck now they're here. Get in the topsails and jibs and make a good job of it. We're in for a sou'easter. Better reef the jib and mainsail too, while you're about it."

In a moment the decks were in commotion, Johansen bellowing orders and the men pulling or letting go ropes of various sorts—all naturally confusing to a landsman such as myself. But it was the heartlessness of it that especially struck me. The dead man was an episode that was past, an incident that was dropped, in a canvas covering with a sack of coal, while the ship sped along and her work went on. Nobody had been affected. The hunters were laughing at a fresh story of Smoke's; the men pulling and hauling, and two of them climbing aloft; Wolf Larsen was studying the clouding sky to windward; and the dead man, dying obscenely, buried sordidly, and sinking down, down—

Then it was that the cruelty of the sea, its relentlessness and awfulness, rushed upon me. Life had become cheap and tawdry, a beastly and inarticulate thing, a soulless stirring of the ooze and slime. I held on to the weather rail, close by the shrouds, and gazed out across the desolate foaming waves to the low-lying fog-banks that hid San Francisco and the California coast. Rain-squalls were driving in between, and I could scarcely see the fog. And this strange vessel, with its terrible men, pressed under by wind and sea and ever leaping up and out, was heading away into the southwest, into the great and lonely Pacific expanse.

IV

WHAT happened to me next on the sealing-schooner *Ghost*, as I strove to fit into my new environment, are matters of humiliation and pain. The cook, who was called "the doctor" by the crew, "Tommy" by the hunters and "Cooky" by Wolf Larsen, was a changed person. The difference worked in my status brought about a corresponding difference in treatment from him. Servile and fawning as he had been before, he was now as domineering and bellicose. In truth, I was no longer the fine gentleman with a skin soft as a "lydy's" , but only an ordinary and very worthless cabin-boy.

He absurdly insisted upon my addressing him as Mr Mugridge, and his behavior and carriage were insufferable as he showed me my duties. Besides my work in the cabin, with its four small staterooms, I was supposed to be his assistant in the galley, and my colossal ignorance concerning such things as peeling potatoes or washing greasy pots was a source of unending and sarcastic wonder to him. He refused to take into consideration what I was, or, rather, what my life and the things I was accustomed to had been. This was part of the attitude he chose to adopt toward me; and I confess, ere the day was done, that I hated him with more lively feelings than I had ever hated anyone in my life before.

This first day was made more difficult for me from the fact that the *Ghost*, under close reefs (terms such as these I did not learn till later), was plunging through what Mr Mugridge called an " 'owlin' sou'easter" . At half-past five, under his directions, I set the table in the cabin, with rough-weather trays in place, and then carried the tea and cooked food down from the galley. In this connection I cannot forbear relating my first experience with a boarding sea.

"Look sharp or you'll get doused," was Mr Mugridge's parting injunction, as I left the galley with a big tea-pot in one hand, and in the hollow of the other arm several loaves of fresh-baked bread. One of the hunters, a tall, loose-jointed chap named Henderson, was going aft at the time from the steerage (the name the hunters facetiously gave their midships sleeping quarters) to the cabin. Wolf Larsen was on the poop, smoking his everlasting cigar.

" 'Ere she comes. Sling yer 'ook!" the cook cried.

I stopped, for I did not know what was coming, and saw the galley door slide shut with a bang. Then I saw Henderson leaping like a madman for the main rigging, up which he shot, on the inside, till he was many feet higher than my head. Also I saw a great wave, curling and foaming, poised far above the rail. I was directly under it. My mind did not work quickly, everything was so new and strange. I grasped that I was in danger, but that was all. I stood still, in trepidation. Then Wolf Larsen shouted from the poop:

"Grab hold something, you—you Hump!"

But it was too late. I sprang toward the rigging, to which I might have clung, and was met by the descending wall of water. What happened after that was very confusing. I was beneath the water, suffocating and drowning. My feet were out from under me, and I was turning over and over and being swept along I knew not where. Several times I collided against hard objects, once striking my right knee a terrible blow. Then the flood seemed suddenly to subside and I was breathing the good air again. I had been swept against the galley and around the steerage companionway from the weather side into the lee scuppers. The pain from my hurt knee was agonizing. I could not put my weight on it, or, at least, I thought I could not put my weight on it; and I felt sure the leg was broken. But the cook was after me, shouting through the lee galley door:

" 'Ere, you! Don't tyke all night about it! Where's the pot? Lost overboard? Serve you bloody well right if yer neck was broke!"

I managed to struggle to my feet. The great tea-pot was still in my hand. I limped to the galley and handed it to him. But he was consumed with indignation, real or feigned.

"Gawd blime me if you ayn't a slob. Wot're you good for anyw'y, I'd like to know? Eh? Wot're you good for anyw'y? Cawn't even carry a bit of tea aft without losin' it. Now I'll 'ave to boil some more.

"An' wot're you snifflin' about?" he burst out at me, with renewed rage. " 'Cos you've 'urt yer pore little leg, pore little mamma's darlin'."

I was not sniffling, though my face might well have been drawn and twitching from the pain. But I called up all my resolution, set my teeth, and hobbled back and forth from galley to cabin and cabin to galley without further mishap. Two things I had acquired by my accident: an injured kneecap that went undressed and from which I suffered for weary months, and the name of "Hump" , which Wolf Larsen had called me from the poop. Thereafter, fore and aft, I was known by no other name, until the term became a part of my thought-processes and I identified it with myself, thought of myself as Hump, as though Hump were I and had always been I.

It was no easy task, waiting on the cabin table, where sat Wolf Larsen, Johansen and the six hunters. The cabin was small, to begin with, and to move around, as I was compelled to, was not made easier by the schooner's violent pitching and wallowing. But what struck me most forcibly was the total lack of sympathy on the part of the men whom I served. I could feel my knee through my clothes, swelling, and swelling, and I was sick and faint from the pain of it. I could catch glimpses of my face, white and ghastly, distorted with pain, in the cabin mirror. All the men must have seen my condition, but not one spoke or took notice of me, till I was almost grateful to Wolf Larsen, later on (I was washing the dishes), when he said:

"Don't let a little thing like that bother you. You'll get used to such things in time. It may cripple you some, but all the same you'll be learning to walk.

"That's what you call a paradox, isn't it?" he added.

He seemed pleased when I nodded my head with the customary "Yes, sir."

"I suppose you know a bit about literary things? Eh? Good. I'll have some talks with you some time."

And then, taking no further account of me, he turned his back and went up on deck.

That night, when I had finished an endless amount of work, I was sent to sleep in the steerage, where I made up a spare bunk. I was glad to get out of the detestable presence of the cook and to be off my feet. To my surprise, my clothes had dried on me and there seemed no indications of catching cold, either from the last soaking or from the prolonged soaking from the foundering of the *Martinez*. Under ordinary circumstances, after all that I had undergone, I should have been fit for bed and a trained nurse.

But my knee was bothering me terribly. As well as I could make out, the kneecap seemed turned up on edge in the midst of the swelling. As I sat in my bunk examining it (the six hunters were all in the steerage, smoking and talking in loud voices), Henderson took a passing glance at it.

"Looks nasty," he commented. "Tie a rag around it and it'll be all right."

That was all; and on the land I would have been lying on the broad of my back, with a surgeon attending on me and with strict injunctions to do nothing but rest. But I must do these men justice. Callous as they were to my suffering, they were equally callous to their own when anything befell them. And this was due, I believe, first, to habit; and second, to the fact that they were less sensitively organized. I really believe that a finely organized, high-strung man would suffer twice and thrice as much as they from a like injury.

Tired as I was—exhausted, in fact—I was prevented from sleeping by the pain in my knee. It was all I could do to keep from groaning aloud. At home I should undoubtedly have given vent to my anguish; but this new and elemental environment seemed to call for a savage repression. Like the savage, the attitude of these men was stoical in great things, childish in little things. I remember, later in the voyage, seeing Kerfoot, another of the hunters, lose a finger by having it smashed to a jelly; and he did not even murmur or change the expression on his face. Yet I have seen the same man, time and again, fly into the most outrageous passion over a trifle.

He was doing it now, vociferating, bellowing, waving his arms and cursing like a fiend, and all because of a disagreement with another hunter as to whether a seal pup knew instinctively how to swim. He held that it did, that it could swim the moment it was born. The other hunter, Latimer, a lean, Yankee-looking fellow with shrewd, narrow-slitted eyes, held otherwise, held that the seal pup was born on the land for no other reason than that it could not swim, that its mother was compelled to teach it to swim as birds were compelled to teach their nestlings how to fly.

For the most part, the remaining four hunters leaned on the table or lay in their bunks and left the discussion to the two antagonists. But they were supremely interested, for every little while they ardently took sides, and sometimes all were talking at once, till their voices surged back and forth in waves of sound like mimic thunderrolls in the confined space. Childish and immaterial as the topic was, the quality of their reasoning was still more childish and immaterial. In truth, there was very little reasoning or none at all. Their method was one of assertion, assumption and denunciation. They proved that a seal pup could swim or not swim at birth by stating the proposition very bellicosely and then following it up with an attack on the opposing man's judgement, common sense, nationality or past history. Rebuttal was precisely similar. I have related this in order to show the mental caliber of the men with whom I was thrown in contact. Intellectually they were children, inhabiting the physical forms of men.

And they smoked, incessantly smoked, using a coarse, cheap and offensive-smelling tobacco. The air was thick and murky with the smoke of it; and this, combined with the violent movement of the ship as she struggled through the storm, would surely have made me seasick had I been a victim to that malady. As it was, it made me quite squeamish, though this nausea might have been due to the pain of my leg and exhaustion.

As I lay there thinking, I naturally dwelt upon myself and my situation. It was unparalleled, undreamed-of, that I, Humphrey Van Weyden, a scholar and a dilettante, if you please, in things artistic and literary, should be lying here on a Bering Sea seal-hunting schooner. Cabin-boy! I had never done any hard manual labor, or scullion labor, in my life. I had lived a placid, uneventful, sedentary existence all my days—the life of a scholar and a recluse on an assured and comfortable income. Violent life and athletic sports had never appealed to me. I had always been a book-worm; so my sisters and father had called me during my childhood. I had gone camping but once in my life, and then I left the party almost at its start and returned to the comforts and conveniences of a roof. And here I was, with dreary and endless vistas before me of table-setting, potato-peeling and dish-washing. And I was not strong. The doctors had always said that I had a remarkable constitution, but I had never developed it or my body through exercise. My muscles were small and soft, like a woman's, or so the doctors had said time and again in the course of their attempts to persuade me to go in for physical-culture fads. But I had preferred to use my head rather than my body; and here I was, in no fit condition for the rough life in prospect.

These are merely a few of the things that went through my mind, and are related for the sake of vindicating myself in advance in the weak and helpless rôle I was destined to play. But I thought, also, of my mother and sisters, and pictured their grief. I was among the missing dead of the *Martinez* disaster, an unrecovered body. I could see the headlines in the papers; the fellows at the University Club and the Bibelot shaking their heads and saying, "Poor chap!" And I could see Charley Furuseth, as I had said good-by to him that morning, lounging in a dressing-gown on the be-pillowed window couch and delivering himself of oracular and pessimistic epigrams.

And all the while, rolling, plunging, climbing the moving mountains and falling and wallowing in the foaming valleys, the schooner *Ghost* was fighting her way farther and farther into the heart of the Pacific—and I was on her. I could hear the wind above. It came to my ears as a muffled roar. Now and again feet stamped overhead. An endless creaking was going on all about me, the woodwork and the fittings groaning and squeaking and complaining in a thousand keys. The hunters were still arguing and roaring like some semi-human amphibious breed. The air was filled with oaths and indecent expressions. I could see their faces, flushed and angry, the brutality distorted and emphasized by the sickly yellow of the sea-lamps which rocked back and forth with the ship. Through the dim smoke-haze the bunks looked like the sleeping dens of animals in a menagerie. Oilskins and sea-boots were hanging from the walls, and here and there rifles and shotguns rested securely in the racks. It was a sea-fitting for the buccaneers and pirates of bygone years. My imagination ran riot, and still I could not sleep. And it was a long, long night, weary and dreary and long.

V

BUT my first night in the hunters' steerage was also my last. Next day Johansen, the new mate, was routed from the cabin by Wolf Larsen, and sent into the steerage to sleep thereafter, while I took possession of the tiny cabin stateroom, which, on the first day of the voyage, had already had two occupants. The reason for this change was quickly learned by the hunters, and became the cause of a deal of grumbling on their part. It seemed that Johansen, in his sleep, lived over each night the events of the day. His incessant talking and shouting and bellowing of orders had been too much for Wolf Larsen, who had accordingly foisted the nuisance upon his hunters.

After a sleepless night, I arose weak and in agony, to hobble through my second day on the *Ghost*. Thomas Mugridge routed me out at half-past five, much in the fashion that Bill Sykes must have routed out his dog; but Mr Mugridge's brutality to me was paid back in kind and with interest. The unnecessary noise he made (I had lain wide-eyed the whole night) must have awakened one of the hunters; for a heavy shoe whizzed through the semi-darkness, and Mr Mugridge, with a sharp howl of pain, humbly begged everybody's pardon. Later on, in the galley, I noticed that his ear was bruised and swollen. It never went entirely back to its normal shape, and was called a "cauliflower ear" by the sailors.

The day was filled with miserable variety. I had taken my dried clothes down from the galley the night before, and the first thing I did was to exchange the cook's garments for them. I looked for my purse. In addition to some small change (and I have a good memory for such things), it had contained one hundred and eighty-five dollars in gold and paper. The purse I found, but its contents, with the exception of the small silver, had been abstracted. I spoke to the cook about it, when I went on deck to take up my duties in the galley, and though I had looked forward to a surly answer, I had not expected the belligerent harangue that I received.

"Look 'ere, 'Ump," he began, a malicious light in his eyes and a snarl in his throat; "d'ye want yer nose punched? If you think I'm a thief, just keep it to yerself, or you'll find 'ow bloody well mistyken you are. Strike me blind if this ayn't gratitude for yer! 'Ere you come, a pore mis'rable specimen of 'uman scum, an' I tykes yer into my galley an' treats yer 'ansom, an' this is wot I get for it. Nex' time you can go to 'ell, say I, an' I've a good mind to give you what-for anyw'y."

So saying, he put up his fists and started for me. To my shame be it, I cowered away from the blow and ran out the galley door. What else was I to do? Force, nothing but force, obtained on this brute-ship. Moral suasion was a thing unknown. Picture it to yourself: a man of ordinary stature, slender of build and with weak, undeveloped muscles, who has lived a peaceful, placid life, and is unused to violence of any sort—what could such a man possibly do? There was no more reason that I should stand and face these human beasts than that I should stand and face an infuriated bull.

So I thought it out at the time, feeling the need for vindication and desiring to be at peace with my conscience. But this vindication did not satisfy. Nor to this day can I permit my manhood to look back upon those events and feel entirely exonerated. The situation was something that really exceeded rational formulas for conduct and demanded more than the cold conclusions of reason. When viewed in the light of formal logic, there is not one thing of which to be ashamed; but nevertheless a shame rises within me at the recollection, and in the pride of my manhood I feel that my manhood has in unaccountable ways been smirched and sullied.

All of which is neither here nor there. The speed with which I ran from the galley caused excruciating pain in my knee, and I sank down helplessly at the break of the poop. But the Cockney had not pursued me.

"Look at 'im run! Look at 'im run!" I could hear him crying. "An' with a gyme leg at that! Come on back, you pore little mamma's darling. I won't 'it yer; no, I won't."

I came back and went on with my work; and here the episode ended for the time, though further developments were yet to take place. I set the breakfast-table in the cabin, and at seven o'clock waited on the hunters and officers. The storm had evidently broken during the night, though a huge sea was still running and a stiff wind blowing. Sail had been made in the early watches, so that the *Ghost* was racing along under everything except the two topsails and the flying jib. These three sails, I gathered from the conversation, were to be set immediately after breakfast. I learned, also, that Wolf Larsen was anxious to make the most of the storm, which was driving him to the southwest into that portion of the sea where he expected to pick up with the northeast trades. It was before this steady wind that he hoped to make the major portion of the run to Japan, curving south into the tropics and north again as he approached the coast of Asia.

After breakfast I had another unenviable experience. When I had finished washing the dishes, I cleaned the cabin stove and carried the ashes up on deck to empty them. Wolf Larsen and Henderson were standing near the wheel, deep in conversation. The sailor, Johnson, was steering. As I started toward the weather side I saw him make a sudden motion with his head, which I mistook for a token of recognition and good morning. In reality, he was attempting to warn me to throw my ashes over the lee side. Unconscious of my blunder, I passed by Wolf Larsen and the hunter and flung the ashes over the side to windward. The wind drove them back, and not only over me, but over Henderson and Wolf Larsen. The next instant the latter kicked me, violently, as a cur is kicked. I had not realized there could be so much pain in a kick. I reeled away from him and leaned against the cabin in a half-fainting condition. Everything was swimming before my eyes, and I turned sick. The nausea overpowered me, and I managed to crawl to the side of the vessel. But Wolf Larsen did not follow me up. Brushing the ashes from his clothes, he had resumed his conversation with Henderson. Johansen, who had seen the affair from the break of the poop, sent a couple of sailors aft to clean up the mess.

Later in the morning I received a surprise of a totally different sort. Following the cook's instructions, I had gone into Wolf Larsen's state-room to put it to rights and make the bed. Against the wall, near the head of the bunk, was a rack filled with books. I glanced over them, noting with astonishment such names as Shakespeare, Tennyson, Poe and De Quincey. There were scientific works, too, among which were represented men such as Tyndall, Proctor and Darwin. Astronomy and physics were represented, and I remarked Bulfinch's *Age of Fable,* Shaw's *History of English and American Literature* and Johnson's *Natural History* in two large volumes. Then there were a number of grammars, such as Metcalf's, and Reed and Kellogg's; and I smiled as I saw a copy of *The Dean's English.*

I could not reconcile these books with the man from what I had seen of him, and I wondered if he could possibly read them. But when I came to make the bed I found, between the blankets, dropped apparently as he had sunk off to sleep, a complete Browning, the Cambridge Edition. It was open at "In a Balcony" , and I noticed, here and there, passages underlined in pencil. Further, letting drop the volume during a lurch of the ship, a sheet of paper fell out. It was scrawled over with geometrical diagrams and calculations of some sort.

It was patent that this terrible man was no ignorant clod, such as one would inevitably suppose him to be from his exhibitions of brutality. At once he became an enigma. One side or the other of his nature was perfectly comprehensible; but both sides together were bewildering. I had already remarked that his language was excellent, marred with an occasional slight inaccuracy. Of course, in common speech with the sailors and hunters, it sometimes fairly bristled with errors, which was due to the vernacular itself; but in the few words he had held with me it had been clear and correct.

This glimpse I had caught of his other side must have emboldened me, for I resolved to speak to him about the money I had lost.

"I have been robbed," I said to him, a little later, when I found him pacing up and down the poop alone.

"Sir," he corrected, not harshly, but sternly.

"I have been robbed, sir," I amended.

"How did it happen?" he asked.

Then I told him the whole circumstance, how my clothes had been left to dry in the galley, and how, later, I was nearly beaten by the cook when I mentioned the matter.

He smiled at my recital. "Pickings," he concluded, "Cooky's pickings. And don't you think your miserable life worth the price? Besides, consider it a lesson. You'll learn in time how to take care of your money for yourself. I suppose, up to now, your lawyer has done it for you, or your business agent."

I could feel the quiet sneer through his words, but demanded, "How can I get it back again?"

"That's your lookout. You haven't any lawyer or business agent now, so you'll have to depend on yourself. When you get a dollar, hang on to it. A man who leaves his money lying around, the way you did, deserves to lose it. Besides, you have sinned. You have no right to put temptation in the way of your fellow-creatures. You tempted Cooky, and he fell. You have placed his immortal soul in jeopardy. By the way, do you believe in the immortal soul?"

His lids lifted lazily as he asked the question, and it seemed that the deeps were opening to me and that I was gazing into his soul. But it was an illusion. Far as it might have seemed, no man has ever seen very far into Wolf Larsen's soul, or seen it at all—of this I am convinced. It was a very lonely soul, I was to learn, that never unmasked, though at rare moments it played at doing so.

"I read immortality in your eyes," I answered, dropping the "sir"—an experiment, for I thought the intimacy of the conversation warranted it.

He took no notice. "By that, I take it, you see something that is alive, but that necessarily does not have to live forever."

"I read more than that," I continued boldly.

"Then you read consciousness. You read the consciousness of life that it is alive; but still no further away, no endlessness of life."

How clearly he thought, and how well he expressed what he thought! From regarding me curiously, he turned his head and glanced out over the leaden sea to windward. A bleakness came into his eyes, and the lines of his mouth grew severe and harsh. He was evidently in a pessimistic mood.

"Then to what end?" he demanded abruptly, turning back to me. "If I am immortal—why?"

I halted. How could I explain my idealism to this man? How could I put into speech a something felt, a something like the strains of music heard in sleep, a something that convinced yet transcended utterance?

"What do you believe, then?" I countered.

"I believe that life is a mess," he answered promptly. "It is like yeast, a ferment, a thing that moves and may move for a minute, an hour, a year, or a hundred years, but that in the end will cease to move. The big eat the little that they may continue to move, the strong eat the weak that they may retain their strength. The lucky eat the most and move the longest, that is all. What do you make of those things?"

He swept his arm in an impatient gesture toward a number of the sailors who were working on some kind of rope stuff amidships.

"They move; so does the jellyfish move. They move in order to eat in order that they may keep moving. There you have it. They live for their belly's sake, and the belly is for their sake. It's a circle; you get nowhere. Neither do they. In the end they come to a standstill. They move no more. They are dead."

"They have dreams," I interrupted, "radiant, flashing dreams—"

"Of grub," he concluded sententiously.

"And of more—"

"Grub. Of a larger appetite and more luck in satisfying it." His voice sounded harsh. There was no levity in it. "For, look you, they dream of making lucky voyages which will bring them more money, of becoming the mates of ships, of finding fortunes—in short, of being in a better position for preying on their fellows, of having all night in, good grub and somebody else to do the dirty work. You and I are just like them. There is no difference, except that we have eaten more and better. I am eating them now, and you too. But in the past you have eaten more than I have. You have slept in soft beds, and worn fine clothes, and eaten good meals. Who made those beds? And those clothes? And those meals? Not you. You never made anything in your own sweat. You live on an income which your father earned. You are like a frigate bird swooping down upon the boobies and robbing them of the fish they have caught. You are one with a crowd of men who have made what they call a government, who are masters of all the other men, and who eat the food the other men get and would like to eat themselves. You wear the warm clothes. They made the clothes, but they shiver in rags and ask you, the lawyer, or business agent who handles your money, for a job."

"But that is beside the matter," I cried.

"Not at all." He was speaking rapidly now, and his eyes were flashing. "It is piggishness, and it is life. Of what use or sense is an immortality of piggishness? What is the end? What is it all about? You have made no food. Yet the food you have eaten or wasted might have saved the lives of a score of wretches who made the food but did not eat it. What immortal end did you serve? Or did they? Consider yourself and me. What does your boasted immortality amount to when your life runs foul of mine? You would like to go back to the land, which is a favorable place for your kind of piggishness. It is a whim of mine to keep you aboard this ship, where my piggishness flourishes. And keep you I will. I may make or break you. You may die to-day, this week or next month. I could kill you now, with a blow of my fist, for you are a miserable weakling. But if we are immortal, what is the reason for this? To be piggish as you and I have been all our lives does not seem to be just the thing for immortals to be doing. Again, what's it all about? Why have I kept you here?—"

"Because you are stronger," I managed to blurt out.

"But why stronger?" he went on at once with his perpetual queries. "Because I am a bigger bit of the ferment than you? Don't you see? Don't you see?"

"But the hopelessness of it," I protested.

"I agree with you," he answered. "Then why move at all, since moving is living? Without moving and being part of the yeast there would be no hopelessness. But—and there it is—we want to live and move, though we have no reason to, because it happens that it is the nature of life to live and move, to want to live and move. If it were not for this, life would be dead. It is because of this life that is in you that you dream of your immortality. The life that is in you is alive and wants to go on being alive forever. Bah! An eternity of piggishness!"

He abruptly turned on his heel and started forward. He stopped at the break of the poop and called me to him.

"By the way, how much was it that Cooky got away with?" he asked.

"One hundred and eighty-five dollars, sir," I answered.

He nodded his head. A moment later, as I started down the companion stairs to lay the table for dinner, I heard him loudly cursing some men amidships.

VI

By the following morning the storm had blown itself quite out and the *Ghost* was rolling slightly on a calm sea without a breath of wind. Occasional light airs were felt, however, and Wolf Larsen patrolled the poop constantly, his eyes ever searching the sea to the north-eastward, from which direction the great trade-wind must blow.

The men were all on deck and busy preparing their various boats for the season's hunting. There are seven boats aboard, the captain's dingey, and the six which the hunters will use. Three, a hunter, a boat-puller and a boat-steerer, compose a boat's crew. On board the schooner the boat-pullers and steerers are the crew. The hunters, too, are supposed to be in command of the watches, subject, always, to the orders of Wolf Larsen.

All this, and more, I have learned. The *Ghost* is considered the fastest schooner in both the San Francisco and Victoria fleets. In fact, she was once a private yacht, and was built for speed. Her lines and fittings—though I know nothing about such things—speak for themselves. Johnson was telling me about her in a short chat I had with him during yesterday's second dog-watch. He spoke enthusiastically, with the love for a fine craft such as some men feel for horses. He is greatly disgusted with the outlook, and I am given to understand that Wolf Larsen bears a very unsavory reputation among the sealing captains. It was the *Ghost* herself that lured Johnson into signing for the voyage, but he is already beginning to repent.

As he told me, the *Ghost* is an eighty-ton schooner of a remarkably fine model. Her beam, or width, is twenty-three feet, and her length a little over ninety feet. A lead keel of fabulous but unknown weight makes her very stable, while she carries an immense spread of canvas. From the deck to the truck of the maintopmast is something over a hundred feet, while the foremast with its topmast is eight or ten feet shorter. I am giving these details so that the size of this little floating world which holds twenty-two men may be appreciated. It is a very little world, a mote, a speck, and I marvel that men should dare to venture the sea on a contrivance so small and fragile.

Wolf Larsen has, also, a reputation for reckless carrying on of sail. I overheard Henderson and another of the hunters, Standish, a Californian, talking about it. Two years ago he dismasted the *Ghost* in a gale on Bering Sea, whereupon the present masts were put in, which are stronger and heavier in every way. He is said to have remarked, when he put them in, that he preferred turning her over to losing the sticks.

Every man aboard, with the exception of Johansen, who is rather overcome by his promotion, seems to have an excuse for having sailed on the *Ghost.* Half the men forward are deep-water sailors, and their excuse is that they did not know anything about her or her captain. And those who do know, whisper that the hunters, while excellent shots, were so notorious for their quarrelsome and rascally proclivities that they could not sign on any decent schooner.

I have made the acquaintance of another one of the crew—Louis he is called, a rotund and jovial-faced Nova Scotia Irishman, and a very sociable fellow, prone to talk as long as he can find a listener. In the afternoon, while the cook was below asleep and I was peeling the everlasting potatoes, Louis dropped into the galley for a "yarn" . His excuse for being aboard was that he was drunk when he signed. He assured me again and again that it was the last thing in the world he would dream of doing in a sober moment. It seems that he has been seal-hunting regularly each season for a dozen years, and is accounted one of the two or three very best boat-steerers in both fleets.

"Ah, my boy," he shook his head ominously at me, " 'tis the worst schooner ye could iv selected, nor were ye drunk at the time as was I. 'Tis sealin' is the sailor's paradise—on other ships than this. The mate was the first, but mark me words, there'll be more dead men before the trip is done with. Hist, now, between you an' meself and the stanchion there, this Wolf Larsen is a regular devil, an' the *Ghost*' ll be a hell-ship like she's always been since he had hold iv her. Don't I know? Don't I know? Don't I remember him in Hakodate two years gone, when he had a row an' shot four iv his men? Wasn't I a-layin' on the *Emma L.,* not three hundred yards away? An' there was a man the same year he killed with a blow iv his fist. Yes, sir, killed 'im dead-oh. His head must iv smashed like an eggshell. An' wasn't there the Governor of Kura Island, an' the Chief iv Police, Japanese gentlemen, sir, an' didn't they come aboard the *Ghost* as his guests, a-bringin' their wives along—wee an' pretty little bits of things like you see 'em painted on fans. An' as he was a-gettin' under way, didn't the fond husbands get left astern-like in their sampan, as it might be by accident? An' wasn't it a week later that the poor little ladies was put ashore on the other side of the island, with nothin' before 'em but to walk home acrost the mountains on their weeny-teeny little straw sandals which wouldn't hang together a mile? Don't I know? 'Tis the beast he is, this Wolf Larsen—the great big beast mentioned iv in Revelation; an' no good end will he ever come to. But I've said nothin' to ye, mind ye. I've whispered never a word; for old fat Louis'll live the voyage out if the last mother's son of yez go to the fishes.

"Wolf Larsen!" he snorted a moment later. "Listen to the word, will ye! Wolf—'tis what he is. He's not black-hearted like some men. 'Tis no heart he has at all. Wolf, just wolf, 'tis what he is. D'ye wonder he's well named?"

"But if he is so well known for what he is," I queried, "how is it that he can get men to ship with him?"

"An' how is it ye can get men to do anything on God's earth an' sea?" Louis demanded with Celtic fire. "How d'ye find me aboard if 'twasn't that I was drunk as a pig when I put me name down? There's them that can't sail with better men, like the hunters, and them that don't know, like the poor devils of wind-jammers for'ard there. But they'll come to it, they'll come to it, an' be sorry the day they was born. I could weep for the poor creatures, did I but forget poor old fat Louis and the troubles before him. But 'tis not a whisper I've dropped, mind ye, not a whisper.

"Them hunters is the wicked boys," he broke forth again, for he suffered from a constitutional plethora of speech. "But wait till they get to cutting up iv jinks and rowin' 'round. He's the boy'll fix 'em. 'Tis him that'll put the fear of God in their rotten black hearts. Look at that hunter iv mine, Horner. 'Jock' Horner they call him, so quiet-like an' easy-goin', soft-spoken as a girl, till ye'd think butter wouldn't melt in the mouth iv him. Didn't he kill his boat-steerer last year? 'Twas called a sad accident, but I met the boat-puller in Yokohama an' the straight iv it was given me. An' there's Smoke, the black little devil—didn't the Roosians have him for three years in the salt mines of Siberia, for poachin' on Copper Island, which is a Roosian preserve? Shackled he was, hand an' foot, with his mate. An' didn't they have words or a ruction of some kind?—for 'twas the other fellow Smoke sent up in the buckets to the top of the mine; an' a piece at a time he went up, a leg to-day, an' to-morrow an arm, the next day the head, an' so on."

"But you can't mean it!" I cried out, overcome with the horror of it.

"Mean what?" he demanded, quick as a flash. " 'Tis nothin' I've said. Deef I am, and dumb, as ye should be for the sake iv your mother; an' never once have I opened me lips but to say fine things iv them an' him, God curse his soul, an' may he rot in purgatory ten thousand years, and then go down to the last an' deepest hell iv all!"

Johnson, the man who had chafed me raw when I first came aboard, seemed the least equivocal of the men forward or aft. In fact, there was nothing equivocal about him. One was struck at once by his straightforwardness and manliness, which, in turn, were tempered by a modesty which might be mistaken for timidity. But timid he was not. He seemed, rather, to have the courage of his convictions, the certainty of his manhood. It was this that made him protest, at the commencement of our acquaintance, against being called Yonson. And upon this, and him, Louis passed judgement and prophecy.

"'Tis a fine chap, that squarehead Johnson we've for'ard with us," he said. "The best sailorman in the fo'c'sle. He's my boat-puller. But it's to trouble he'll come with Wolf Larsen, as the sparks fly upward. It's meself that knows. I can see it brewin' an' comin' up like a storm in the sky. I've talked to him like a brother, but it's little he sees in takin' in his lights or flyin' false signals. He grumbles out when things don't go to suit him, and there'll be always some telltale carryin' word iv it aft to the Wolf. The Wolf is strong, and it's the way of a wolf to hate strength, an' strength it is he'll see in Johnson—no knucklin' under, and a 'Yes, sir, thank ye kindly, sir,' for a curse or a blow. Oh, she's a-comin'! She's a-comin'! An' God knows where I'll get another boat-puller! What does the fool up an' say, when the old man calls him Yonson, but 'Me name is Johnson, sir,' an' then spells it out, letter for letter. Ye should iv seen the old man's face! I thought he'd let drive at him on the spot. He didn't, but he will, an' he'll break that squarehead's heart, or it's little I know iv the ways iv men on the ships iv the sea."

Thomas Mugridge is becoming unendurable. I am compelled to Mister him and to Sir him with every speech. One reason for this is that Wolf Larsen seems to have taken a fancy to him. It is an unprecedented thing, I take it, for a captain to be chummy with the cook; but this is certainly what Wolf Larsen is doing. Two or three times he put his head into the galley and chaffed Mugridge goodnaturedly, and once, this afternoon, he stood by the break of the poop and chatted with him for fully fifteen minutes. When it was over, and Mugridge was back in the galley, he became greasily radiant, and went about his work, humming coster songs in a nerveracking and discordant falsetto.

"I always get along with the officers," he remarked to me in a confidential tone. "I know the w'y, I do, to myke myself uppreciyted. There was my last skipper—w'y I thought nothin' of droppin' down in the cabin for a little chat and a friendly glass. 'Mugridge,' sez 'e to me, 'Mugridge,' sez 'e to me, 'you've missed yer vokytion.' 'An' 'ow's that?' sez I. 'Yer should 'a been born a gentleman, an' never 'ad to work for yer livin'.' God strike me dead, 'Ump, if that ayn't wot 'e sez, an' me a-sittin' there in 'is own cabin, jolly-like an' comfortable, a-smokin' 'is cigars an' drinkin' 'is rum."

This chitter-chatter drove me to distraction. I never heard a voice I hated so. His oily, insinuating tones, his greasy smile and his monstrous self-conceit grated on my nerves till sometimes I was all in a tremble. Positively, he was the most disgusting and loathsome person I have ever met. The filth of his cooking was indescribable; and, as he cooked everything that was eaten aboard, I was compelled to select what I ate with great circumspection, choosing from the least dirty of his concoctions.

My hands bothered me a great deal, unused as they were to work. The nails were discolored and black, while the skin was already grained with dirt which even a scrubbing-brush could not remove. Then blisters came, in a painful and never-ending procession, and I had a great burn on my forearm, acquired by losing my balance in a roll of the ship and pitching against the galley stove. Nor was my knee any better. The swelling had not gone down, and the cap was still up on edge. Hobbling about on it from morning to night was not helping it any. What I needed was rest, if it were ever to get well.

Rest! I never before knew the meaning of the word. I had been resting all my life and did not know it. But now, could I sit still for one half-hour and do nothing, not even think, it would be the most pleasurable thing in the world. But it is a revelation, on the other hand. I shall be able to appreciate the lives of the working people hereafter. I did not dream that work was so terrible a thing. From half-past five in the morning till ten o'clock at night I am everybody's slave, with not one moment to myself, except such as

I can steal near the end of the second dog-watch. Let me pause for a minute to look out over the sea sparkling in the sun, or to gaze at a sailor going aloft to the gaff-topsails, or running out the bowsprit, and I am sure to hear the hateful voice, " 'Ere, you, 'Ump, no sodgerin'. I've got my peepers on yer."

There are signs of rampant bad temper in the steerage, and the gossip is going around that Smoke and Henderson have had a fight. Henderson seems the best of the hunters, a slow-going fellow, and hard to rouse; but roused he must have been, for Smoke had a bruised and discolored eye, and looked particularly vicious when he came into the cabin for supper.

A cruel thing happened just before supper, indicative of the callousness and brutishness of these men. There is one green hand in the crew, Harrison by name, a clumsy-looking country boy, mastered, I imagine, by the spirit of adventure, and making his first voyage. In the light baffling airs the schooner had been tacking about a great deal, at which times the sails pass from one side to the other and a man is sent aloft to shift over the fore-gaff-topsail. In some way, when Harrison was aloft, the sheet jammed in the block through which it runs at the end of the gaff. As I understood it, there were two ways of getting it cleared—first, by lowering the foresail, which was comparatively easy and without danger; and second, by climbing out the peak-halyards to the end of the gaff itself, an exceedingly hazardous performance.

Johansen called out to Harrison to go out the halyards. It was patent to everybody that the boy was afraid. And well he might be, eighty feet above the deck, to trust himself on those thin and jerking ropes. Had there been a steady breeze it would not have been so bad, but the *Ghost* was rolling emptily in a long sea, and with each roll the canvas flapped and boomed and the halyards slacked and jerked taut. They were capable of snapping a man off like a fly from a whip-lash.

Harrison heard the order and understood what was demanded of him, but hesitated. It was probably the first time he had been aloft in his life. Johansen, who had caught the contagion of Wolf Larsen's masterfulness, burst out with a volley of abuse and curses.

"That'll do, Johansen," Wolf Larsen said brusquely. "I'll have you know that I do the swearing on this ship. If I need your assistance, I'll call you in."

"Yes, sir," the mate acknowledged submissively.

In the meantime Harrison had started out on the halyards. I was looking up from the galley door, and I could see him trembling, as with ague, in every limb. He proceeded very slowly and cautiously, an inch at a time. Outlined against the clear blue of the sky, he had the appearance of an enormous spider crawling along the tracery of its web.

It was a slight uphill climb, for the foresail peaked high; and the halyards, running through various blocks on the gaff and mast, gave him separate holds for hands and feet. But the trouble lay in that the wind was not strong enough nor steady enough to keep the sail full. When he was halfway out, the *Ghost* took a long roll to windward and back again into the hollow between two seas. Harrison ceased his progress and held on tightly. Eighty feet beneath, I could see the agonized strain of his muscles as he gripped for very life. The sail emptied and the gaff swung amidships. The halyards slackened, and, though it all happened very quickly, I could see them sag beneath the weight of his body. Then the gaff swung to the side with an abrupt swiftness, the great sail boomed like a cannon, and the three rows of reef-points slatted against the canvas like a volley of rifles. Harrison, clinging on, made the giddy rush through the air. This rush ceased abruptly. The halyards became instantly taut. It was the snap of the whip. His clutch was broken. One hand was torn loose from its hold. The other lingered desperately for a moment, and followed. His body pitched out and down, but in some way he managed to save himself with his legs. He was hanging by them, head downward. A quick effort brought his hands up to the halyards again; but he was a long time regaining his former position, where he hung, a pitiable object.

"I'll bet he has no appetite for supper," I heard Wolf Larsen's voice, which came to me from around the corner of the galley. "Stand from under, you, Johansen! Watch out! Here she comes!"

In truth, Harrison was very sick, as a person is sea-sick; and for a long time he clung to his precarious perch without attempting to move. Johansen, however, continued violently to urge him on to the completion of his task.

"It is a shame," I heard Johnson growling in painfully slow and correct English. He was standing by the main rigging, a few feet away from me. "The boy is willing enough. He will learn if he has a chance. But this is—" He paused awhile, for the word "murder" was his final judgement.

"Hist, will ye!" Louis whispered to him. "For the love iv your mother hold your mouth!"

But Johnson, looking on, still continued his grumbling.

"Look here," the hunter Standish spoke to Wolf Larsen, "that's my boat-puller, and I don't want to lose him."

"That's all right, Standish," was the reply. "He's your boat-puller when you've got him in the boat; but he's my sailor when I have him aboard, and I'll do what I damn well please with him."

"But that's no reason—" Standish began in a torrent of speech.

"That'll do, easy as she goes," Wolf Larsen counselled back. "I've told you what's what, and let it stop at that. The man's mine, and I'll make soup of him and eat it if I want to."

There was an angry gleam in the hunter's eye, but he turned on his heel and entered the steerage companionway, where he remained, looking upward. All hands were on deck now, and all eyes were aloft, where a human life was at grapples with death. The callousness of these men, to whom industrial organization gave control of the lives of other men, was appalling. I, who had lived out of the whirl of the world, had never dreamed that its work was carried on in such fashion. Life had always seemed a peculiarly sacred thing, but here it counted for nothing, was a cipher in the arithmetic of commerce. I must say, however, that the sailors themselves were sympathetic, as instance the case of Johnson; but the masters (the hunters and the captain) were heartlessly indifferent. Even the protest of Standish arose out of the fact that he did not wish to lose his boat-puller. Had it been some other hunter's boat-puller, he, like them, would have been no more than amused.

But to return to Harrison. It took Johansen, insulting and reviling the poor wretch, fully ten minutes to get him started again. A little later he made the end of the gaff, where, astride the spar itself, he had a better chance for holding on. He cleared the sheet, and was free to return, slightly downhill now, along the halyards to the mast. But he had lost his nerve. Unsafe as was his present position, he was loath to forsake it for the more unsafe position on the halyards.

He looked along the airy path he must traverse, and then down to the deck. His eyes were wide and staring, and he was trembling violently. I had never seen fear so strongly stamped upon a human face. Johansen called vainly for him to come down. At any moment he was liable to be snapped off the gaff, but he was helpless with fright. Wolf

Larsen, walking up and down with Smoke and in conversation, took no more notice of him, though he cried sharply, once, to the man at the wheel:

"You're off your course, my man! Be careful, unless you're looking for trouble!"

"Ay, ay, sir," the helmsman responded, putting a couple of spokes down.

He had been guilty of running the *Ghost* several points off her course in order that what little wind there was should fill the foresail and hold it steady. He had striven to help the unfortunate Harrison at the risk of incurring Wolf Larsen's anger.

The time went by, and the suspense, to me, was terrible. Thomas Mugridge, on the other hand, considered it a laughable affair, and was continually bobbing his head out the galley door to make jocose remarks. How I hated him! And how my hatred for him grew and grew, during that fearful time, to cyclopean dimensions. For the first time in my life I experienced the desire to murder—"saw red" , as some of our picturesque writers phrase it. Life in general might still be sacred, but life in the particular case of Thomas Mugridge had become very profane indeed. I was frightened when I became conscious that I was seeing red, and the thought flashed through my mind: was I, too, becoming tainted by the brutality of my environment?—I, who even in the most flagrant crimes had denied the justice and righteousness of capital punishment?

Fully half an hour went by, and then I saw Johnson and Louis in some sort of altercation. It ended with Johnson flinging off Louis's detaining arm and starting forward. He crossed the deck, sprang into the fore rigging, and began to climb. But the quick eye of Wolf Larsen caught him.

"Here, you, what are you up to?" he cried.

Johnson's ascent was arrested. He looked his captain in the eyes and replied slowly: "I am going to get that boy down."

"You'll get down out of that rigging, and damn lively about it! D'ye hear? Get down!"

Johnson hesitated, but the long years of obedience to the masters of ships overpowered him, and he dropped sullenly to the deck and went on forward.

At half after five I went below to set the cabin table, but I hardly knew what I did, for my eyes and brain were filled with the vision of a man, white-faced and trembling, comically like a bug, clinging to the thrashing gaff. At six o'clock, when I served supper, going on deck to get the food from the galley, I saw Harrison, still in the same position. The conversation at the table was of other things. Nobody seemed interested in the wantonly imperilled life. But making an extra trip to the galley a little later, I was gladdened by the sight of Harrison staggering weakly from the rigging to the forecastle scuttle. He had finally summoned the courage to descend.

Before closing this incident, I must give a scrap of conversation I had with Wolf Larsen in the cabin, while I was washing the dishes.

"You were looking squeamish this afternoon," he began. "What was the matter?"

I could see that he knew what had made me possibly as sick as Harrison, that he was trying to draw me, and I answered, "It was because of the brutal treatment of that boy."

He gave a short laugh. "Like sea-sickness, I suppose. Some men are subject to it, and others are not."

"Not so," I objected.

"Just so," he went on. "The earth is as full of brutality as the sea is full of motion. And some men are made sick by the one, and some by the other. That's the only reason."

"But you, who make a mock of human life, don't you place any value upon it whatever?" I demanded.

"Value? What value?" He looked at me, and though his eyes were steady and motionless, there seemed a cynical smile in them. "What kind of value? How do you measure it? Who values it?"

"I do," I made answer.

"Then what is it worth to you? Another man's life, I mean. Come, now, what is it worth?"

The value of life? How could I put a tangible value upon it? Somehow, I, who have always had expression, lacked expression when with Wolf Larsen. I have since determined that a part of it was due to the man's personality, but that the greater part was due to his totally different outlook. Unlike other materialists I had met and with whom I had something in common to start on, I had nothing in common with him. Perhaps, also, it was the elemental simplicity of his mind that baffled me. He drove so directly to the core of the matter, divesting a question always of all superfluous details, and with such an air of finality, that I seemed to find myself struggling in deep water with no footing under me. Value of life? How could I answer the question on the spur of the moment? The sacredness of life I had accepted as axiomatic. That it was intrinsically valuable was a truism I had never questioned. But when he challenged the truism I was speechless.

"We were talking about this yesterday," he said. "I held that life was a ferment, a yeasty something which devoured life that it might live, and that living was merely successful piggishness. Why, if there is anything in supply and demand, life is the cheapest thing in the world. There is only so much water, so much earth, so much air; but the life that is demanding to be born is limitless. Nature is a spendthrift. Look at the fish and their millions of eggs. For that matter, look at you and me. In our loins are the possibilities of millions of lives. Could we but find time and opportunity and utilize the last bit and every bit of the unborn life that is in us, we could become the fathers of nations and populate continents. Life? Bah! It has no value. Of cheap things it is the cheapest. Everywhere it goes begging. Nature spills it out with a lavish hand. Where there is room for one life, she sows a thousand lives, and it's life eats life till the strongest and most piggish life is left."

"You have read Darwin," I said. "But you read him misunderstandingly when you conclude that the struggle for existence sanctions your wanton destruction of life."

He shrugged his shoulders. "You know you only mean that in relation to human life, for of the flesh and the fowl and the fish you destroy as much as I or any other man. And human life is in no wise different, though you feel it is and think that you reason why it is. Why should I be parsimonious with this life which is cheap and without value? There are more sailors than there are ships on the sea for them, more workers than there are factories or machines for them. Why, you who live on the land know that you house your poor people in the slums of cities and loose famine and pestilence upon them, and that there still remain more poor people, dying for want of a crust of bread and a bit of meat (which is life destroyed) than you know what to do with. Have you ever seen the London dockers fighting like wild beasts for a chance to work?"

He started for the companion-stairs, but turned his head for a final word. "Do you know the only value life has is what life puts upon itself? And it is of course overestimated, since it is of necessity prejudiced in its own favor. Take that man I had aloft. He held on as if he were a precious thing, a treasure beyond diamonds or rubies. To you? No. To me? Not at all. To himself? Yes. But I do not accept his estimate. He sadly overrates himself. There is plenty more life demanding to be born. Had he fallen and dripped his brains upon the deck like honey from the comb, there would have been no loss to the world. He was worth nothing to the world. The supply is too large. To himself only was he of value, and to show how fictitious even this value was, being dead he is unconscious that he has lost himself. He alone rated himself beyond diamonds and rubies. Diamonds and rubies are gone, spread out on the deck to be washed away by a bucket of sea-water, and he does not even know that the diamonds and rubies are gone. He does not lose anything, for with the loss of himself he loses the knowledge of loss. Don't you see? And what have you to say?"

"That you are at least consistent," was all I could say, and I went on washing the dishes.

VII

AT last, after three days of variable winds, we have caught the northeast trades. I came on deck, after a good night's rest in spite of my poor knee, to find the *Ghost* foaming along, wing-and-wing, and every sail drawing except the jibs, with a fresh breeze astern. Oh, the wonder of the great trade-wind! All day we sailed, and all night, and the next day, and the next, day after day, the wind always astern and blowing steadily and strong. The schooner sailed herself. There was no pulling and hauling on sheets and tackles, no shifting of topsails, no work at all for the sailors to do except to steer. At night when the sun went down, the sheets were slackened; in the morning, when they yielded up the damp of the dew and relaxed, they were pulled tight again—and that was all.

Ten knots, twelve knots, eleven knots, varying from time to time, is the speed we are making. And ever out of the northeast the brave wind blows, driving us on our course two hundred and fifty miles between the dawns. It saddens me and gladdens me, the gait with which we are leaving San Francisco behind and with which we are foaming down upon the tropics. Each day grows perceptibly warmer. In the second dog-watch the sailors come on deck, stripped, and heave buckets of water upon one another from overside. Flying-fish are beginning to be seen, and during the night the watch above scrambles over the deck in pursuit of those that fall aboard. In the morning, Thomas Mugridge being duly bribed, the galley is pleasantly areek with the odor of their frying; while dolphin meat is served fore and aft on such occasions as Johnson catches the blazing beauties from the bowsprit end.

Johnson seems to spend all his spare time there or aloft at the crosstrees, watching the *Ghost* cleaving the water under press of sail. There is passion, adoration, in his eyes, and he goes about in a sort of trance, gazing in ecstasy at the swelling sails, the foaming wake, and the heave and the run of her over the liquid mountains that are moving with us in stately procession.

The days and nights are "all a wonder and a wild delight" , and though I have little time from my dreary work, I steal odd moments to gaze and gaze at the unending glory of what I never dreamed the world possessed. Above, the sky is stainless blue—blue as the sea itself, which under the forefoot is of the color and sheen of azure satin. All around the horizon are pale, fleecy clouds, never changing, never moving, like a silver setting for the flawless turquoise sky.

I do not forget one night, when I should have been asleep, of lying on the forecastle-head and gazing down at the spectral ripple of foam thrust aside by the *Ghost's* forefoot. It sounded like the gurgling of a brook over mossy stones in some quiet dell, and the crooning song of it lured me away and out of myself till I was no longer Hump the cabin-boy, nor Van Weyden, the man who had dreamed away thirty-five years among books. But a voice behind me, the unmistakable voice of Wolf Larsen, strong with the invincible certitude of the man and mellow with appreciation of the words he was quoting, aroused me.

" 'O the blazing tropic night, when the wake's a welt of light
That holds the hot sky tame,
And the steady forefoot snores through the planet-
powdered floors
Where the scared whale flukes in flame.
Her plates are scarred by the sun, dear lass,
And her ropes are taut with the dew,
For we're booming down on the old trail, our own trail,
the out trail,
We're sagging south on the Long Trail—the trail that is
always new.' "

"Eh, Hump? How's it strike you?" he asked, after the due pause which words and setting demanded.

I looked into his face. It was aglow with light, as the sea itself, and the eyes were flashing in the starshine.

"It strikes me as remarkable, to say the least, that you should show enthusiasm," I answered coldly.

"Why, man, it's living! It's life!" he cried.

"Which is a cheap thing and without value," I flung his words at him.

He laughed, and it was the first time I had heard honest mirth in his voice.

"Ah, I cannot get you to understand, cannot drive it into your head, what a thing this life is. Of course life is valueless, except to itself. And I can tell you that my life is pretty valuable just now—to myself. It is beyond price, which you will acknowledge is a terrific overrating, but which I cannot help, for it is the life that is in me that makes the rating."

He appeared waiting for the words with which to express the thought that was in him, and finally went on.

"Do you know, I am filled with a strange uplift; I feel as if all time were echoing through me, as though all powers were mine. I know truth, divine good from evil, right from wrong. My vision is clear and far. I could almost believe in God. But"—and his voice changed and the light went out of his face—"what is this condition in which I find myself? This joy of living? This exultation of life? This inspiration, I may well call it? It is what comes when there is nothing wrong with one's digestion, when his stomach is in trim and his appetite has an edge, and all goes well. It is the bribe for living, the champagne of the blood, the effervescence of the ferment—that makes some men think holy thoughts, and other men to see God or to create him when they cannot see him. That is all, the drunkenness of life, the stirring and crawling of the yeast, the babbling of the life that is insane with consciousness that it is alive. And—bah! Tomorrow I shall pay for it as the drunkard pays. And I shall know that I must die, at sea most likely, cease crawling of myself to be all a-crawl with the corruption of the sea; to be fed upon, to be carrion, to yield up all the strength and movement of my muscles that it may become strength and movement in fin and scale and the guts of fishes. Bah! And bah! again. The champagne is already flat. The sparkle and bubble has gone out and it is a tasteless drink."

He left me as suddenly as he had come, springing to the deck with the weight and softness of a tiger. The *Ghost* ploughed on her way. I noted the gurgling forefoot was very like a snore, and as I listened to it the effect of Wolf Larsen's swift rush from sublime exultation to despair slowly left me. Then some deep-water sailor, from the waist of the ship, lifted a rich tenor voice in the "Song of the Trade Wind" :

"Oh, I am the wind the seamen love—
I am steady, and strong, and true;
They follow my track by the clouds above,
O'er the fathomless tropic blue.
I keep like a hound on her trail;
I'm strongest at noon, yet under the moon,
I stiffen the bunt of her sail."

VIII

Sometimes I think Wolf Larsen mad, or half-mad at least, what of his strange moods and vagaries. At other times I take him for a great man, a genius who has never arrived. And, finally, I am convinced that he is the perfect type of the primitive man, born a thousand years or generations too late and an anachronism in this culminating century of civilization. He is certainly an individualist of the most pronounced type. Not only that, but he is very lonely. There is no congeniality between him and the rest of the men aboard ship. His tremendous virility and mental strength wall him apart. They are more like children to him, even the hunters, and as children he treats them, descending perforce to their level and playing with them as a man plays with puppies. Or else he probes them with the cruel hand of a vivisectionist, groping about in their mental processes and examining their souls as though to see of what soul-stuff is made.

I have seen him a score of times, at table, insulting this hunter or that, with cool and level eyes and, withal, a certain air of interest, pondering their actions or replies or petty rages with a curiosity almost laughable to me who stood onlooker and who understood. Concerning his own rages, I am convinced that they are not real, that they are sometimes experiments, but that in the main they are the habits of a pose or attitude he has seen fit to take toward his fellow-men. I know, with the possible exception of the incident of the dead mate, that I have not seen him really angry; nor do I wish ever to see him in a genuine rage, when all the force of him is called into play.

While on the question of vagaries, I shall tell what befell Thomas Mugridge in the cabin, and at the same time complete an incident upon which I have already touched once or twice. The twelve o'clock dinner was over, one day, and I had just finished putting the cabin in order, when Wolf Larsen and Thomas Mugridge descended the companion stairs. Though the cook had a cubby-hole of a stateroom opening off from the cabin, in the cabin itself he had never dared to linger or to be seen, and he flitted to and fro, once or twice a day, like a timid spectre.

"So you know how to play 'Nap'," Wolf Larsen was saying in a pleased sort of voice.

"I might have guessed an Englishman would know. I learned it myself in English ships."

Thomas Mugridge was beside himself, a blithering imbecile, so pleased was he at chumming thus with the captain. The little airs he put on and the painful striving to assume the easy carriage of a man born to a dignified place in life would have been sickening had they not been ludicrous. He quite ignored my presence, though I credited him with being simply unable to see me. His pale, wishywashy eyes were swimming like lazy summer seas, though what blissful visions they beheld were beyond my imagination.

"Get the cards, Hump," Wolf Larsen ordered, as they took seats at the table. "And bring out the cigars and the whiskey you'll find in my berth."

I returned with the articles in time to hear the Cockney hinting broadly that there was a mystery about him, that he might be a gentleman's son gone wrong or something or other; also, that he was a remittance man and was paid to keep away from England —"p'yed 'ansomely, sir" , was the way he put it; "p'yed 'ansomely to sling my 'ook an' keep slingin' it."

I had brought the customary liquor glasses, but Wolf Larsen frowned, shook his head, and signalled with his hands for me to bring the tumblers. These he filled two-thirds full with undiluted whiskey—"a gentleman's drink" , quoth Thomas Mugridge —and they clinked their glasses to the glorious game of "Nap" , lighted cigars, and fell to shuffling and dealing the cards.

They played for money. They increased the amounts of the bets. They drank whiskey, they drank it neat, and I fetched more. I do not know whether Wolf Larsen cheated or not—a thing he was thoroughly capable of doing—but he won steadily. The cook made repeated journeys to his bunk for money. Each time he performed the journey with greater swagger, but he never brought more than a few dollars at a time. He grew maudlin, familiar, could hardly see the cards or sit upright. As a preliminary to another journey to his bunk, he hooked Wolf Larsen's buttonhole with a greasy forefinger and vacuously proclaimed and reiterated, "I got money, I got money, I tell yer, an' I'm a gentleman's son."

Wolf Larsen was unaffected by the drink, yet he drank glass for glass, and if anything his glasses were fuller. There was no change in him. He did not appear even amused at the other's antics.

In the end, with loud protestations that he could lose like a gentleman, the cook's last money was staked on the game and lost. Whereupon he leaned his head on his hands and wept. Wolf Larsen looked curiously at him, as though about to probe and vivisect him, then changed his mind, as from the foregone conclusion that there was nothing there to probe.

"Hump," he said to me, elaborately polite, "kindly take Mr Mugridge's arm and help him up on deck. He is not feeling very well.

"And tell Johnson to douse him with a few buckets of salt water," he added, in a lower tone for my ear alone.

I left Mr Mugridge on deck, in the hands of a couple of grinning sailors who had been told off for the purpose. Mr Mugridge was sleepily spluttering that he was a gentleman's son. But as I descended the companion stairs to clear the table I heard him shriek as the first bucket of water struck him.

Wolf Larsen was counting his winnings.

"One hundred and eighty-five dollars even," he said aloud. "Just as I thought. The beggar came aboard without a cent."

"And what you have won is mine, sir," I said boldly.

He favored me with a quizzical smile. "Hump, I have studied some grammar in my time, and I think your tenses are tangled. 'Was mine', you should have said, not 'is mine'."

"It is a question, not of grammar, but of ethics," I answered.

It was possibly a minute before he spoke.

"D'ye know, Hump," he said, with a slow seriousness which had in it an indefinable strain of sadness, "that this is the first time I have heard the word 'ethics' in the mouth of a man. You and I are the only men on this ship who know its meaning."

"At one time in my life," he continued, after another pause, "I dreamed that I might some day talk with men who used such language, that I might lift myself out of the place in life in which I had been born, and hold conversation and mingle with men who talked about just such things as ethics. And this is the first time I have ever heard the word pronounced. Which is all by the way, for you are wrong. It is a question, neither of grammar nor ethics, but of fact."

"I understand," I said. "The fact is that you have the money."

His face brightened. He seemed pleased at my perspicacity.

"But it is avoiding the real question," I continued, "which is one of right."

"Ah," he remarked, with a wry pucker of his mouth, "I see you still believe in such things as right and wrong."

"But don't you?—at all?" I demanded.

"Not the least bit. Might is right, and that is all there is to it. Weakness is wrong. Which is a very poor way of saying that it is good for oneself to be strong, and evil for oneself to be weak—or better yet, it is pleasurable to be strong, because of the profits; painful to be weak, because of the penalties. Just now the possession of this money is a pleasurable thing. It is good for one to possess it. Being able to possess it, I wrong myself and the life that is in me if I give it to you and forgo the pleasure of possessing it."

"But you wrong me by withholding it," I objected.

"Not at all. One man cannot wrong another man. He can only wrong himself. As I see it, I do wrong always when I consider the interests of others. Don't you see? How can two particles of the yeast wrong each other by striving to devour each other? It is their inborn heritage to strive to devour, and to strive not to be devoured. When they depart from this they sin."

"Then you don't believe in altruism?" I asked.

He received the word as if it had a familiar ring, though he pondered it thoughtfully. "Let me see, it means something about cooperation, doesn't it?"

"Well, in a way there has come to be a sort of connection," I answered, unsurprised by this time at such gaps in his vocabulary, which, like his knowledge, was the acquirement of a self-read, self-educated man, whom no one had directed in his studies, and who had thought much and talked little or not at all. "An altruistic act is an act performed for the welfare of others. It is unselfish, as opposed to an act performed for self, which is selfish."

He nodded his head. "Oh, yes, I remember it now. I ran across it in Spencer."

"Spencer!" I cried. "Have you read him?"

"Not very much," was his confession. "I understood quite a good deal of *First Principles*, but his *Biology* took the wind out of my sails, and his *Psychology* left me butting around in the doldrums for many a day. I honestly could not understand what he was driving at. I put it down to mental deficiency on my part, but since then I have decided that it was for want of preparation. I had no proper basis. Only Spencer and myself know how hard I hammered. But I did get something out of his *Data of Ethics*. There's where I ran across 'altruism', and I remember now how it was used."

I wondered what this man could have got from such a work. Spencer I remembered enough to know that altruism was imperative to his ideal of highest conduct. Wolf Larsen, evidently, had sifted the great philosopher's teachings, rejecting and selecting according to his needs and desires.

"What else did you run across?" I asked.

His brows drew in slightly with the mental effort of suitably phrasing thoughts which he had never before put into speech. I felt an elation of spirit. I was groping into his soul-stuff as he made a practice of groping in the soul-stuff of others. I was exploring virgin territory. A strange, a terribly strange, region was unrolling itself before my eyes.

"In as few words as possible," he began, "Spencer puts it something like this: First, a man must act for his own benefit—to do this is to be moral and good. Next, he must act for the benefit of his children. And third, he must act for the benefit of his race."

"And the highest, finest, right conduct," I interjected, "is that act which benefits at the same time the man, his children and his race."

"I wouldn't stand for that," he replied. "Couldn't see the necessity for it, nor the common sense. I cut out the race and the children. I would sacrifice nothing for them. It's just so much slush and sentiment, and you must see it yourself, at least for one who does not believe in eternal life. With immortality before me, altruism would be a paying business proposition. I might elevate my soul to all kinds of altitudes. But with nothing eternal before me but death, given for a brief spell this yeasty crawling and squirming which is called life, why, it would be immoral for me to perform any act that was a sacrifice. Any sacrifice that makes me lose one crawl or squirm is foolish—and not only foolish, for it is a wrong against myself and a wicked thing. I must not lose one crawl or squirm if I am to get the most out of the ferment. Nor will the eternal movelessness that is coming to me be made easier or harder by the sacrifices or selfishnesses of the time when I was yeasty and a-crawl."

"Then you are an individualist, a materialist, and, logically, a hedonist."

"Big words," he smiled. "But what is a hedonist?"

He nodded agreement when I had given the definition.

"And you are also," I continued, "a man one could not trust in the least thing where it was possible for a selfish interest to intervene?"

"Now you're beginning to understand," he said, brightening.

"You are a man utterly without what the world calls morals?"

"That's it."

"A man of whom to be always afraid—"

"That's the way to put it."

"As one is afraid of a snake, or a tiger, or a shark?"

"Now you know me," he said. "And you know me as I am generally known. Other men call me 'Wolf'."

"You are a sort of monster," I added audaciously, "a Caliban who has pondered Setebos, and who acts as you act, in idle moments, by whim and fancy."

His brow clouded at the allusion. He did not understand, and I quickly learned that he did not know the poem.

"I'm just reading Browning," he confessed, "and it's pretty tough. I haven't got very far along, and as it is I've about lost my bearings."

Not to be tiresome, I shall say that I fetched the book from his stateroom and read

"Caliban" aloud. He was delighted. It was a primitive mode of reasoning and of looking at things that he understood thoroughly. He interrupted again and again with comment and criticism. When I finished, he had me read it over a second time, and a third. We fell into discussion—philosophy, science, evolution, religion. He betrayed the inaccuracies of the self-read man, and, it must be granted, the sureness and directness of the primitive mind. The very simplicity of his reasoning was its strength, and his materialism was far more compelling than the subtly complex materialism of Charley Furuseth. Not that I—a confirmed and, as Furuseth phrased it, a temperamental idealist—was to be compelled; but that Wolf Larsen stormed the last strongholds of my faith with a vigor that received respect, while not accorded conviction.

Time passed. Supper was at hand and the table not laid. I became restless and anxious, and when Thomas Mugridge glared down the companionway, sick and angry of countenance, I prepared to go about my duties. But Wolf Larsen cried out to him:

"Cooky, you've got to hustle to-night. I'm busy with Hump, and you'll do the best you can without him."

And again the unprecedented was established. That night I sat at table with the captain and the hunters, while Thomas Mugridge waited on us and washed the dishes afterward—a whim, a Calibanmood of Wolf Larsen's, and one I foresaw would bring me trouble. In the meantime we talked and talked, much to the disgust of the hunters, who could not understand a word.

IX

THREE days of rest, three blessed days of rest, are what I had with Wolf Larsen, eating at the cabin table and doing nothing but discuss life, literature and the universe, the while Thomas Mugridge fumed and raged and did my work as well as his own.

"Watch out for squalls, is all I can say to you," was Louis's warning, given during a spare half-hour on deck while Wolf Larsen was engaged in straightening out a row among the hunters.

"Ye can't tell what'll be happenin'," Louis went on, in response to my query for more definite information. "The man's as contrary as air currents or water currents. You can never guess the ways iv him. 'Tis just as you're thinkin' you know him and are makin' a favorable slant along him, that he whirls around, dead ahead, and comes howlin' down upon you and a-rippin' all iv your fine-weather sails to rags."

So I was not altogether surprised when the squall foretold by Louis smote me. We had been having a heated discussion—upon life, of course—and, grown overbold, I was passing stiff strictures upon Wolf Larsen and the life of Wolf Larsen. In fact, I was vivisecting him and turning over his soul-stuff as keenly and thoroughly as it was his custom to do it to others. It may be a weakness of mine that I have an incisive way of speech; but I threw all restraint to the winds and cut and slashed until the whole man of him was snarling. The dark sun-bronze of his face went black with wrath, his eyes were ablaze. There was no clearness or sanity in them—nothing but the terrific rage of a madman. It was the wolf in him that I saw, and a mad wolf at that.

He sprang for me with a half-roar, gripping my arm. I had steeled myself to brazen it out, though I was trembling inwardly; but the enormous strength of the man was too much for my fortitude. He had gripped me by the biceps with his single hand, and when that grip tightened I wilted and shrieked aloud. My feet went out from under me. I simply could not stand upright and endure the agony. The muscles refused their duty. The pain was too great. My biceps was being crushed to a pulp.

He seemed to recover himself, for a lucid gleam came into his eyes, and he relaxed his hold with a short laugh that was more like a growl. I fell to the floor, feeling very faint, while he sat down, lighted a cigar and watched me as a cat watches a mouse. As I writhed about I could see in his eyes that curiosity I had so often noted, that wonder and perplexity, that questing, that everlasting query of his as to what it was all about.

I finally crawled to my feet and ascended the companion-stairs. Fair weather was over, and there was nothing left but to return to the galley. My left arm was numb, as though paralyzed, and days passed before I could use it, while weeks went by before the last stiffness and pain went out of it. And he had done nothing but put his hand upon my arm and squeeze. There had been no wrenching or jerking. He had just closed his hand with a steady pressure. What he might have done I did not fully realize till next day, when he put his head into the galley, and, as a sign of renewed friendliness, asked me how my arm was getting on.

"It might have been worse," he smiled.

I was peeling potatoes. He picked one up from the pan. It was fair-sized, firm and unpeeled. He closed his hand upon it, squeezed, and the potato squirted out between his fingers in mushy streams. The pulpy remnant he dropped back into the pan and turned away, and I had a sharp vision of how it might have fared with me had the monster put his real strength upon me.

But the three days' rest was good in spite of it all, for it had given my knee the very chance it needed. It felt much better, the swelling had materially decreased, and the cap seemed descending into its proper place. Also, the three days' rest brought the trouble I had foreseen. It was plainly Thomas Mugridge's intention to make me pay for those three days. He treated me vilely, cursed me continually and heaped his own work upon me. He even ventured to raise his fist to me, but I was becoming animal-like myself, and I snarled in his face so terribly that it must have frightened him back. It is no pleasant picture I can conjure up of myself, Humphrey Van Weyden, in that noisome ship's galley, crouched in a corner over my task, my face raised to the face of the creature about to strike me, my lips lifted and snarling like a dog's, my eyes gleaming with fear and helplessness and the courage that comes of fear and helplessness. I do not like the picture. It reminds me too strongly of a rat in a trap. I do not care to think of it; but it was effective, for the threatened blow did not descend.

Thomas Mugridge backed away, glaring as hatefully and viciously as I glared. A pair of beasts is what we were, penned together and showing our teeth. He was a coward, afraid to strike me because I had not quailed sufficiently in advance; so he chose a new way to intimidate me. There was only one galley knife that, as a knife, amounted to anything. This, through many years of service and wear, had acquired a long, lean blade. It was unusually cruel-looking, and at first I had shuddered every time I used it. The cook borrowed a stone from Johansen and proceeded to sharpen the knife. He did it with great ostentation, glancing significantly at me the while. He whetted it up and down all day long. Every odd moment he could find he had the knife and stone out and was whetting away. The steel acquired a razor edge. He tried it with the ball of his thumb or across the nail. He shaved hairs from the back of his hand, glanced along the edge with microscopic acuteness, and found, or feigned that he found, always, a slight inequality in its edge somewhere. Then he would put it on the stone again and whet, whet, whet, till I could have laughed aloud, it was so very ludicrous.

It was also serious, for I learned that he was capable of using it, that under all his cowardice there was a courage of cowardice, like mine, that would impel him to do the very thing his whole nature protested against doing and was afraid of doing. "Cooky's sharpening his knife for Hump," was being whispered about among the sailors, and some of them twitted him about it. This he took in good part, and was really pleased, nodding his head with direful foreknowledge and mystery, until George Leach, the erstwhile cabin-boy, ventured some rough pleasantry on the subject.

Now it happened that Leach was one of the sailors told off to douse Mugridge after his game of cards with the captain. Leach had evidently done his task with a thoroughness that Mugridge had not forgiven, for words followed and evil names involving smirched ancestries. Mugridge menaced with the knife he was sharpening for me. Leach laughed and hurled more of his Telegraph Hill Billingsgate, and before either he or I knew what had happened, his right arm had been ripped open from elbow to wrist by a quick slash of the knife. The cook backed away, a fiendish expression on his face, the knife held before him in a position of defence. But Leach took it quite calmly, though blood was spouting upon the deck as generously as water from a fountain.

"I'm goin' to get you, Cooky," he said, "and I'll get you hard. And I won't be in no hurry about it. You'll be without that knife when I come for you."

So saying, he turned and walked quietly forward. Mugridge's face was livid with fear at what he had done and at what he might expect sooner or later from the man he had stabbed. But his demeanor toward me was more ferocious than ever. In spite of his fear at the reckoning he must expect to pay for what he had done, he could see that it had been an object-lesson to me, and he became more domineering and exultant. Also there was a lust in him, akin to madness, which had come with sight of the blood he had drawn. He was beginning to see red in whatever direction he looked. The psychology of it is sadly tangled, and yet I could read the workings of his mind as clearly as though it were a printed book.

Several days went by, the *Ghost* still foaming down the trades, and I could swear I saw madness growing in Thomas Mugridge's eyes. And I confess that I became afraid, very much afraid. Whet, whet, whet, it went all day long. The look in his eyes as he felt the keen edge and glared at me was positively carnivorous. I was afraid to turn my shoulder to him, and when I left the galley I went out backwards—to the amusement of the sailors and hunters, who made a point of gathering in groups to witness my exit. The strain was too great. I sometimes thought my mind would give way under it—a meet thing on this ship of madmen and brutes. Every hour, every minute of my existence was in jeopardy. I was a human soul in distress, and yet no soul, fore or aft, betrayed sufficient sympathy to come to my aid. At times I thought of throwing myself on the mercy of Wolf Larsen, but the vision of the mocking devil in his eyes that questioned life and sneered at it would come strong upon me and compel me to refrain. At other times I seriously contemplated suicide, and the whole force of my hopeful philosophy was required to keep me from going over the side in the darkness of night.

Several times Wolf Larsen tried to inveigle me into discussion, but I gave him short answers and eluded him. Finally, he commanded me to resume my seat at the cabin table for a time and let the cook do my work. Then I spoke frankly, telling him what I was enduring from Thomas Mugridge because of the three days of favoritism which had been shown me. Wolf Larsen regarded me with smiling eyes.

"So you're afraid, eh?" he sneered.

"Yes," I said defiantly and honestly, "I am afraid."

"That's the way with you fellows," he cried, half angrily, "sentimentalizing about your immortal souls and afraid to die. At sight of a sharp knife and a cowardly Cockney the clinging of life to life overcomes all your fond foolishness. Why, my dear fellow, you will live forever. You are a god, and God cannot be killed. Cooky cannot hurt you. You are sure of your resurrection. What's there to be afraid of?

"You have eternal life before you. You are a millionaire in immortality, and a millionaire whose fortune cannot be lost, whose fortune is less perishable than the stars and as lasting as space or time. It is impossible for you to diminish your principal. Immortality is a thing without beginning or end. Eternity is eternity, and though you die here and now you will go on living somewhere else and hereafter. And it is all very beautiful, this shaking off of the flesh and soaring of the imprisoned spirit. Cooky cannot hurt you. He can only give you a boost on the path you eternally must tread.

"Or, if you do not wish to be boosted just yet, why not boost Cooky? According to your ideas, he, too, must be an immortal millionaire. You cannot bankrupt him. His paper will always circulate at par. You cannot diminish the length of his living by killing him, for he is without beginning or end. He's bound to go on living, somewhere, somehow. Then boost him. Stick a knife in him and let his spirit free. As it is, it's in a nasty prison, and you'll do him only a kindness by breaking down the door. And who knows?—it may be a very beautiful spirit that will go soaring up into the blue from that ugly carcass. Boost him along, and I'll promote you to his place, and he's getting forty-five dollars a month."

It was plain that I could look for no help or mercy from Wolf Larsen. Whatever was to be done I must do for myself; and out of the courage of fear I evolved the plan of fighting Thomas Mugridge with his own weapons. I borrowed a whetstone from Johansen. Louis, the boat-steerer, had already begged me for condensed milk and sugar. The lazarette, where such delicacies were stored, was situated beneath the cabin floor. Watching my chance, I stole five cans of the milk, and that night, when it was Louis's watch on deck, I traded them with him for a dirk as lean and cruel-looking as Thomas Mugridge's vegetable knife. It was rusty and dull, but I turned the grindstone while Louis gave it an edge. I slept more soundly than usual that night.

Next morning, after breakfast, Thomas Mugridge began his whet, whet, whet. I glanced warily at him, for I was on my knees taking the ashes from the stove. When I returned from throwing them overside, he was talking to Harrison, whose honest yokel's face was filled with fascination and wonder.

"Yes," Mugridge was saying, "an' wot does 'is worship do but give me two years in Reading. But blimey if I cared. The other mug was fixed plenty. Should 'a seen 'im. Knife just like this. I stuck it in, like into soft butter, an' the w'y 'e squealed was better 'n a tu-penny gaff." He shot a glance in my direction to see if I was taking it in, and went on. " 'I didn't mean it, Tommy,' 'e was snifflin'; 'so 'elp me Gawd, I didn't mean it!' 'I'll fix yer bloody well right,' I sez, an' kept right after 'im. I cut 'im in ribbons, that's wot I did, an' 'e a-squealin' all the time. Once 'e got 'is 'and on the knife an' tried to 'old it. 'Ad 'is fingers around it, but I pulled it through, cuttin' to the bone. O, 'e was a sight, I can tell yer."

A call from the mate interrupted the gory narrative, and Harrison went aft. Mugridge sat down on the raised threshold to the galley and went on with his knife-sharpening. I put the shovel away and calmly sat down on the coal-box facing him. He favored me with a vicious stare. Still calmly, though my heart was going pitapat, I pulled out Louis's dirk and began to whet it on the stone. I had looked for almost any sort of explosion on the Cockney's part, but to my surprise he did not appear aware of what I was doing. He went on whetting his knife. So did I. And for two hours we sat there, face to face, whet, whet, whet, till the news of it spread abroad and half the ship's company was crowding the galley doors to see the sight.

Encouragement and advice were freely tendered, and Jock Horner, the quiet, self-spoken hunter who looked as though he would not harm a mouse, advised me to leave the ribs alone and to thrust upward for the abdomen, at the same time giving what he called the "Spanish twist" to the blade. Leach, his bandaged arm prominently to the fore, begged me to leave a few remnants of the cook for him; and Wolf Larsen paused once or twice at the break of the poop to glance curiously at what must have been to him a stirring and crawling of the yeasty thing he knew as life.

And I make free to say that for the time being life assumed the same sordid values to me. There was nothing pretty about it, nothing divine—only two cowardly moving things that sat whetting steel upon stone, and a group of other moving things, cowardly and otherwise, that looked on. Half of them, I am sure, were anxious to see us shedding each other's blood. It would have been entertainment. And I do not think there was one who would have interfered had we closed in a death-struggle.

On the other hand, the whole thing was laughable and childish. Whet, whet, whet—Humphrey Van Weyden sharpening his knife in a ship's galley and trying its edge with his thumb! Of all situations this was the most inconceivable. I know that my own kind could not have believed it possible. I had not been called "Sissy" Van Weyden all my days without reason, and that "Sissy" Van Weyden should be capable of doing this thing was a revelation to Humphrey Van Weyden, who knew not whether to be exultant or ashamed.

But nothing happened. At the end of two hours Thomas Mugridge put away knife and stone and held out his hand.

"Wot's the good of mykin' a 'oly show of ourselves for them mugs?" he demanded. "They don't love us, an' bloody well glad they'd be a-seein' us cuttin' our throats. Yer not 'arf bad, 'Ump! You've got spunk, as you Yanks s'y, an' I like yer in a w'y. So come on an' shyke."

Coward that I might be, I was less a coward than he. It was a distinct victory I had gained, and I refused to forgo any of it by shaking his detestable hand.

"All right," he said pridelessly, "tyke it or leave it, I'll like yer none the less for it." And to save his face he turned fiercely upon the onlookers. "Get outa my galley-doors, you bloomin' swabs!"

This command was reinforced by a steaming kettle of water, and at sight of it the sailors scrambled out of the way. This was a sort of victory for Thomas Mugridge, and enabled him to accept more gracefully the defeat I had given him, though, of course, he was too discreet to attempt to drive the hunters away.

"I see Cooky's finish," I heard Smoke say to Horner.

"You bet," was the reply. "Hump runs the galley from now on, and Cooky pulls in his horns."

Mugridge heard and shot a swift glance at me, but I gave no sign that the conversation had reached me. I had not thought my victory was so far-reaching and complete, but I resolved to let go nothing I had gained. As the days went by, Smoke's prophecy was verified. The Cockney became more humble and slavish to me than even to Wolf Larsen. I mistered him and sirred him no longer, washed no more greasy pots and peeled no more potatoes. I did my own work, and my own work only, and when and in what fashion I saw fit. Also I carried the dirk in a sheath at my hip, sailor-fashion, and maintained toward Thomas Mugridge a constant attitude which was composed of equal parts of domineering, insult and contempt.

X

My intimacy with Wolf Larsen increases—if by intimacy may be denoted those relations which exist between master and man, or, better yet, between king and jester. I am to him no more than a toy, and he values me no more than a child values a toy. My function is to amuse, and so long as I amuse all goes well; but let him become bored, or let him have one of his black moods come upon him, and at once I am relegated from cabin table to galley, while, at the same time, I am fortunate to escape with my life and a whole body.

The loneliness of the man is slowly being borne in upon me. There is not a man aboard but hates or fears him, nor is there a man whom he does not despise. He seems consuming with the tremendous power that is in him and that seems never to have found adequate expression in works. He is as Lucifer would be, were that proud spirit banished to a society of soulless, Tomlinsonian ghosts.

This loneliness is bad enough in itself, but, to make it worse, he is oppressed by the primal melancholy of the race. Knowing him, I review the old Scandinavian myths with clearer understanding. The white-skinned, fair-haired savages who created that terrible pantheon were of the same fiber as he. The frivolity of the laughter-loving Latins is no part of him. When he laughs it is from a humor that is nothing else than ferocious. But he laughs rarely; he is too often sad. And it is a sadness as deep-reaching as the roots of the race. It is the race heritage, the sadness which has made the race sober-minded, clean-lived and fanatically moral, and which, in this latter connection, has culminated among the English in the Reformed Church and Mrs Grundy.

In point of fact, the chief vent to this primal melancholy has been religion in its more agonizing forms. But the compensations of such religion are denied Wolf Larsen. His brutal materialism will not permit it. So, when his blue moods come on, nothing remains for him but to be devilish. Were he not so terrible a man, I could sometimes feel sorry for him, as instance three mornings ago, when I went into his stateroom to fill his water-bottle and came unexpectedly upon him. He did not see me. His head was buried in his hands, and his shoulders were heaving convulsively as with sobs. He seemed torn by some mighty grief. As I softly withdrew I could hear him groaning, "God! God! God!" Not that he was calling upon God; it was a mere expletive, but it came from his soul.

At dinner he asked the hunters for a remedy for headache, and by evening, strong man that he was, he was half-blind and reeling about the cabin.

"I've never been sick in my life, Hump," he said, as I guided him to his room. "Nor did I ever have a headache except the time my head was healing after having been laid open for six inches by a capstan-bar."

For three days this blinding headache lasted, and he suffered as wild animals suffer, as it seemed the way on ship to suffer, without plaint, without sympathy, utterly alone.

This morning, however, on entering his stateroom to make the bed and put things in order, I found him well and hard at work. Table and bunk were littered with designs and calculations. On a large transparent sheet, compass and square in hand, he was copying what appeared to be a scale of some sort or other.

"Hello, Hump," he greeted me genially. "I'm just finishing the finishing touches. Want to see it work?"

"But what is it?" I asked.

"A labor-saving device for mariners, navigation reduced to kindergarten simplicity," he answered gayly. "From to-day a child will be able to navigate a ship. No more long-winded calculations. All you need is one star in the sky on a dirty night to know instantly where you are. Look. I place the transparent scale on this star-map, revolving the scale on the North Pole. On the scale I've worked out the circles of altitude and the lines of bearing. All I do is to put it on a star, revolve the scale till it is opposite those figures on the map underneath, and presto! there you are, the ship's precise location!"

There was a ring of triumph in his voice, and his eyes, clear blue this morning as the sea, were sparkling with light.

"You must be well up in mathematics," I said. "Where did you go to school?"

"Never saw the inside of one, worse luck," was the answer. "I had to dig it out for myself.

"And why do you think I have made this thing?" he demanded, abruptly. "Dreaming to leave footprints on the sands of time?" He laughed one of his horrible mocking laughs. "Not at all. To get it patented, to make money from it, to revel in piggishness with all night in while other men do the work. That's my purpose. Also, I have enjoyed working it out."

"The creative joy," I murmured.

"I guess that's what it ought to be called. Which is another way of expressing the joy of life in that it is alive, the triumph of movement over matter, of the quick over the dead, the pride of the yeast because it is yeast and crawls."

I threw up my hands with helpless disapproval of his inveterate materialism and went about making the bed. He continued copying lines and figures upon the transparent scale. It was a task requiring the utmost nicety and precision, and I could not but admire the way he tempered his strength to the fineness and delicacy of the need.

When I had inished the bed, I caught myself looking at him in a fascinated sort of way. He was certainly a handsome man—beautiful in the masculine sense. And again, with never-failing wonder, I remarked the total lack of viciousness, or wickedness, or sinfulness in his face. It was the face, I am convinced, of a man who did no wrong. And by this I do not wish to be misunderstood. What I mean is that it was the face of a man who either did nothing contrary to the dictates of his conscience, or who had no conscience. I am inclined to the latter way of accounting for it. He was a magnificent atavism, a man so purely primitive that he was of the type that came into the world before the development of the moral nature. He was not immoral, but merely unmoral.

As I have said, in the masculine sense his was a beautiful face. Smooth-shaven, every line was distinct, and it was cut as clear and sharp as a cameo; while sea and sun had tanned the naturally fair skin to a dark bronze which bespoke struggle and battle and added both to his savagery and his beauty. The lips were full, yet possessed of the firmness, almost harshness, which is characteristic of thin lips. The set of his mouth, his chin, his jaw, was likewise firm or harsh, with all the fierceness and indomitableness of the male—the nose also. It was the nose of a being born to conquer and command. It just hinted of the eagle beak. It might have been Grecian, it might have been Roman, only it was a shade too massive for the one, a shade too delicate for the other. And while the whole face was the incarnation of fierceness and strength, the primal melancholy from which he suffered seemed to greaten the lines of mouth and eye and brow, seemed to give a largeness and completeness which otherwise the face would have lacked.

And so I caught myself standing idly and studying him. I cannot say how greatly the man had come to interest me. Who was he? What was he? How had he happened to be? All powers seemed his, all potentialities—why, then, was he no more than the obscure master of a seal-hunting schooner with a reputation for frightful brutality amongst the men who hunted seals?

My curiosity burst from me in a flood of speech.

"Why is it that you have not done great things in this world? With the power that is yours you might have risen to any height. Unpossessed of conscience or moral instinct, you might have mastered the world, broken it to your hand. And yet here you are, at the top of your life, where diminishing and dying begin, living an obscure and sordid existence, hunting sea animals for the satisfaction of woman's vanity and love of decoration, revelling in a piggishness, to use your own words, which is anything and everything except splendid. Why, with all that wonderful strength, have you not done something? There was nothing to stop you, nothing that could stop you. What was wrong? Did you lack ambition? Did you fall under temptation? What was the matter? What was the matter?"

He had lifted his eyes to me at the commencement of my outburst, and followed me complacently until I had done and stood before him breathless and dismayed. He waited a moment, as though seeking where to begin, and then said:

"Hump, do you know the parable of the sower who went forth to sow? If you will remember, some of the seed fell upon stony places, where there was not much earth, and forthwith they sprung up because they had no deepness of earth. And when the sun was up they were scorched, and because they had no root they withered away. And some fell among thorns, and the thorns sprung up and choked them."

"Well?" I said.

"Well?" he queried, half petulantly. "It was not well. I was one of those seeds."

He dropped his head to the scale and resumed the copying. I finished my work and had opened the door to leave, when he spoke to me.

"Hump, if you will look on the west coast of the map of Norway you will see an indentation called Romsdal Fiord. I was born within a hundred miles of that stretch of water. But I was not born Norwegian. I am a Dane. My father and mother were Danes, and how they ever came to that bleak bight of land on the west coast I do not know. I never heard. Outside of that there is nothing mysterious. They were poor people and unlettered. They came of generations of poor unlettered people—peasants of the sea who sowed their sons on the waves as has been their custom since time began. There is no more to tell."

"But there is," I objected. "It is still obscure to me."

"What can I tell you?" he demanded, with a recrudescence of fierceness. "Of the meagreness of a child's life? Of fish diet and coarse living? Of going out with the boats from the time I could crawl? Of my brothers, who went away one by one to the deep-sea farming and never came back? Of myself, unable to read or write, cabin-boy at the mature age of ten on the coastwise, old-country ships? Of the rough fare and rougher usage, where kicks and blows were bed and breakfast and took the place of speech, and fear and hatred and pain were my only soul-experiences? I do not care to remember. A madness comes up in my brain even now as I think of it. But there were coastwise skippers I would have returned and killed when a man's strength came to me, only the lines of my life were cast at the time in other places. I did return, not long ago, but unfortunately the skippers were dead, all but one, a mate in the old days, a skipper when I met him, and when I left him a cripple who would never walk again."

"But you who read Spencer and Darwin and have never seen the inside of a school, how did you learn to read and write?" I queried.

"In the English merchant service. Cabin-boy at twelve, ship's boy at fourteen, ordinary seaman at sixteen, able seaman at seventeen, and cock of the fo'c'sle, infinite ambition and infinite loneliness, receiving neither help nor sympathy, I did it all for myself—navigation, mathematics, science, literature, and what not. And of what use has it been? Master and owner of a ship at the top of my life, as you say, when I am beginning to diminish and die. Paltry, isn't it? And when the sun was up I was scorched, and because I had no root I withered away."

"But history tells of slaves who rose to the purple," I chided.

"And history tells of opportunities that came to the slaves who rose to the purple," he answered grimly. "No man makes opportunity. All the great men ever did was to know it when it came to them. The Corsican knew. I have dreamed as greatly as the Corsican. I should have known the opportunity, but it never came. The thorns sprung up and choked me. And, Hump, I can tell you that you know more about me than any living man, except my own brother."

"And what is he? And where is he?"

"Master of the steamship *Macedonia,* seal-hunter," was the answer. "We will meet him most probably on the Japan coast. Men call him 'Death' Larsen."

"Death Larsen!" I involuntarily cried. "Is he like you?"

"Hardly. He is a lump of an animal without any head. He has all my—my—"

"Brutishness," I suggested.

"Yes—thank you for the word—all my brutishness, but he can scarcely read or write."

"And he has never philosophized on life," I added.

"No," Wolf Larsen answered, with an indescribable air of sadness. "And he is all the happier for leaving life alone. He is too busy living it to think about it. My mistake was in ever opening the books."

XI

THE *Ghost* has attained the southernmost point of the arc she is describing across the Pacific, and is already beginning to edge away to the west and north toward some lone island, it is rumored, where she will fill her water-casks before proceeding to the season's hunt along the coast of Japan. The hunters have experimented and practised with their rifles and shotguns till they are satisfied, and the boat-pullers and steerers have made their spritsails, bound the oars and rowlocks in leather and sennit so that they will make no noise when creeping on the seals, and put their boats in apple-pie order—to use Leach's homely phrase.

His arm, by the way, has healed nicely, though the scar will remain all his life. Thomas Mugridge lives in mortal fear of him, and is afraid to venture on deck after dark. There are two or three standing quarrels in the forecastle. Louis tells me that the gossip of the sailors finds its way aft, and that two of the telltales have been badly beaten by their mates. He shakes his head dubiously over the outlook for the man Johnson, who is boat-puller in the same boat with him. Johnson has been guilty of speaking his mind too freely, and has collided two or three times with Wolf Larsen over the pronunciation of his name. Johansen he thrashed on the amidships deck the other night, since which time the mate has called him by his proper name. But of course it is out of the question that Johnson should thrash Wolf Larsen.

Louis has also given me additional information about Death Larsen, which tallies with the captain's brief description. We may expect to meet Death Larsen on the Japan coast. "And look out for squalls," is Louis's prophecy, "for they hate one another like the wolf-whelps they are." Death Larsen is in command of the only sealing-steamer in the fleet, the *Macedonia,* which carries fourteen boats, whereas the rest of the schooners carry only six. There is wild talk of cannon aboard, and of strange raids and expeditions she may make, ranging from opium smuggling into the States and arms smuggling into China, to black-birding and open piracy. Yet I cannot but believe Louis, for I have never yet caught him in a lie, while he has a cyclopaedic knowledge of sealing and the men of the sealing fleets.

As it is forward and in the galley, so it is in the steerage and aft, on this veritable hell-ship. Men fight and struggle ferociously for one another's lives. The hunters are looking for a shooting scrape at any moment between Smoke and Henderson, whose old quarrel has not healed, while Wolf Larsen says positively that he will kill the survivor of the affair, if such affair comes off. He frankly states that the position he takes is based on no moral grounds, that all the hunters could kill and eat one another so far as he is concerned, were it not that he needs them alive for the hunting. If they will only hold their hands until the season is over, he promises them a royal carnival, when all grudges can be settled and the survivors may toss the non-survivors overboard and arrange a story as to how the missing men were lost at sea. I think even the hunters are appalled at his cold-bloodedness. Wicked men though they be, they are certainly very much afraid of him.

Thomas Mugridge is cur-like in his subjection to me, while I go about in secret dread of him. His is the courage of fear—a strange thing I know well of myself—and at any moment it may master the fear and impel him to the taking of my life. My knee is much better, though it often aches for long periods, and the stiffness is gradually leaving the arm which Wolf Larsen squeezed. Otherwise I am in splendid condition, feel that I am in splendid condition. My muscles are growing harder and increasing in size. My hands, however, are a spectacle for grief. They have a parboiled appearance, are afflicted with hang-nails, while the nails are broken and discolored and the edges of the quick seem to be assuming a fungoid sort of growth. Also, I am suffering from boils, due to the diet, most likely, for I was never afflicted in this manner before.

I was amused, a couple of evenings back, by seeing Wolf Larsen reading the Bible, a copy of which, after the futile search for one at the beginning of the voyage, had been found in the dead mate's seachest. I wondered what Wolf Larsen could get from it, and he read aloud to me from Ecclesiastes. I could imagine he was speaking the thoughts of his own mind as he read to me, and his voice, reverberating deeply and mournfully in the confined cabin, charmed and held me. He may be uneducated, but he certainly knows how to express the significance of the written word. I can hear him now, as I shall always hear him, the primal melancholy vibrant in his voice as he read:

> "I gathered me also silver and gold, and the peculiar treasure of kings and of the provinces; I gat me men singers and women singers, and the delights of the sons of men, as musical instruments, and that of all sorts.
>
> "So I was great, and increased more than all that were before me in Jerusalem; also my wisdom returned with me.
>
> "Then I looked on all the works that my hands had wrought and

> on the labor that I had labored to do; and behold, all was vanity and vexation of spirit, and there was no profit under the sun.
>
> "All things come alike to all; there is one event to the righteous and to the wicked; to the good and to the clean, and to the unclean; to him that sacrificeth, and to him that sacrificeth not; as is the good, so is the sinner; and he that sweareth, as he that feareth an oath.
>
> "This is an evil among all things that are done under the sun, that there is one event unto all; yea, also the heart of the sons of men is full of evil, and madness is in their heart while they live, and after that they go to the dead.
>
> "For to him that is joined to all the living there is hope; for a living dog is better than a dead lion.
>
> "For the living know that they shall die; but the dead know not anything, neither have they any more a reward; for the memory of them is forgotten.
>
> "Also their love, and their hatred, and their envy, is now perished; neither have they any more a portion for ever in anything that is done under the sun."

"There you have it, Hump," he said, closing the book upon his finger and looking up at me. "The Preacher who was king over Israel in Jerusalem thought as I think. You call me a pessimist. Is not this pessimism of the blackest?—'All is vanity and vexation of spirit,' 'There is no profit under the sun,' 'There is one event unto all', to the fool and the wise, the clean and the unclean, the sinner and the saint, and that event is death, and an evil thing, he says. For the Preacher loved life, and did not want to die, saying, 'For a living dog is better than a dead lion.' He preferred the vanity and vexation to the silence and unmovableness of the grave. And so I. To crawl is piggish; but to not crawl, to be as the clod and rock, is loathsome to contemplate. It is loathsome to the life that is in me, the very essence of which is movement, the power of movement, and the consciousness of the power of movement. Life itself is unsatisfaction, but to look ahead to death is greater unsatisfaction."

"You are worse off than Omar," I said. "He, at least, after the customary agonizing of youth, found content and made of his materialism a joyous thing."

"Who was Omar?" Wolf Larsen asked, and I did no more work that day, nor the next, nor the next.

In his random reading he had never chanced upon the Rubáiyát, and it was to him like a great find of treasure. Much I remembered, possibly two-thirds of the quatrains, and I managed to piece out the remainder without difficulty. We talked for hours over single stanzas, and I found him reading into them a wail of regret and a rebellion which, for the life of me, I could not discover myself. Possibly I recited with a certain joyous lilt which was my own, for—his memory was good, and at a second rendering, very often the first, he made a quatrain his own—he recited the same lines and invested them with an unrest and passionate revolt that was wellnigh convincing.

I was interested as to which quatrain he would like best, and was not surprised when he hit upon the one born of an instant's irritability, and quite at variance with the Persian's complacent philosophy and genial code of life:

"What, without asking, hither hurried *Whence?*
And, without asking, *Whither* hurried hence!
Oh, many a Cup of this forbidden Wine
Must drown the memory of that insolence!"

"Great!" Wolf Larsen cried. "Great! That's the keynote. Insolence! He could not have used a better word."

In vain I objected and denied. He deluged me, overwhelmed me with argument.

"It's not the nature of life to be otherwise. Life, when it knows that it must cease living, will always rebel. It cannot help itself. The Preacher found life and the works of life all a vanity and vexation, an evil thing; but death, the ceasing to be able to be vain and vexed, he found an eviler thing. Through chapter after chapter he is worried by the one event that cometh to all alike. So Omar, so I, so you, even you, for you rebelled against dying when Cooky sharpened a knife for you. You were afraid to die; the life that was in you, that composes you, that is greater than you, did not want to die. You have talked of the instinct of immortality. I talk of the instinct of life, which is to live, and which, when death looms near and large, masters the instinct, so called, of immortality. It mastered it in you (you cannot deny it), because a crazy Cockney cook sharpened a knife.

"You are afraid of him now. You are afraid of me. You cannot deny it. If I should catch you by the throat, thus"—his hand was about my throat and my breath was shut off—"and began to press the life out of you, thus, and thus, your instinct of immortality will go glimmering, and your instinct of life, which is longing for life, will flutter up, and you will struggle to save yourself. Eh? I see the fear of death in your eyes. You beat the air with your arms. You exert all your puny strength to struggle to live. Your hand is clutching my arm, lightly it feels as a butterfly resting there. Your chest is heaving, your tongue protruding, your skin turning dark, your eyes swimming. 'To live! To live! To live!' you are crying; and you are crying to live here and now, not hereafter. You doubt your immortality, eh? Ha! Ha! You are not sure of it. You won't chance it. This life only you are certain is real. Ah, it is growing dark and darker. It is the darkness of death, the ceasing to be, the ceasing to feel, the ceasing to move, that is gathering about you, descending upon you, rising around you. Your eyes are becoming set. They are glazing. My voice sounds faint and far. You cannot see my face. And still you struggle in my grip. You kick with your legs. Your body draws itself up in knots like a snake's. Your chest heaves and strains. To live! To live! To live—"

I heard no more. Consciousness was blotted out by the darkness he had so graphically described, and when I came to myself I was lying on the floor and he was smoking a cigar and regarding me thoughtfully with that old familiar light of curiosity in his eyes.

"Well, have I convinced you?" he demanded. "Here, take a drink of this. I want to ask you some questions."

I rolled my head negatively on the floor. "Your arguments are too—er—forcible," I managed to articulate, at cost of great pain to my aching throat.

"You'll be all right in half-an-hour," he assured me. "And I promise I won't use any more physical demonstrations. Get up now. You can sit on a chair."

And, toy that I was of this monster, the discussion of Omar and the Preacher was resumed. And half the night we sat up over it.

XII

THE last twenty-four hours have witnessed a carnival of brutality. From cabin to forecastle it seems to have broken out like a contagion. I scarcely know where to begin. Wolf Larsen was really the cause of it. The relations among the men, strained and made tense by feuds, quarrels and grudges, were in a state of unstable equilibrium, and evil passions flared up in flame like prairie-grass.

Thomas Mugridge is a sneak, a spy, an informer. He has been attempting to curry favor and reinstate himself in the good graces of the captain by carrying tales of the men forward. He it was, I know, that carried some of Johnson's hasty talk to Wolf Larsen. Johnson, it seems, bought a suit of oil-skins from the slop-chest and found them to be of greatly inferior quality. Nor was he slow in advertising the fact. The slop-chest is a sort of miniature dry-goods store which is carried by all sealing schooners and which is stocked with articles peculiar to the needs of the sailors. Whatever a sailor purchases is taken from his subsequent earnings on the sealing grounds; for, as it is with the hunters so it is with the boat-pullers and steerers—in the place of wages they receive a 'lay', a rate of so much per skin for every skin captured in their particular boat.

But of Johnson's grumbling at the slop-chest I knew nothing, so that what I witnessed came with the shock of sudden surprise. I had just finished sweeping the cabin, and had been inveigled by Wolf Larsen into a discussion of Hamlet, his favorite Shakespearian character, when Johansen descended the companion stairs followed by Johnson. The latter's cap came off after the custom of the sea, and he stood respectfully in the centre of the cabin, swaying heavily and uneasily to the roll of the schooner and facing the captain.

"Shut the doors and draw the slide," Wolf Larsen said to me.

As I obeyed I noticed an anxious light come into Johnson's eyes, but I did not dream of its cause. I did not dream of what was to occur until it did occur, but he knew from the very first what was coming and awaited it bravely. And in his action I found complete refutation of all Wolf Larsen's materialism. The sailor Johnson was swayed by idea, by principle, and truth, and sincerity. He was right, he knew he was right, and he was unafraid. He would die for the right if needs be, he would be true to himself, sincere with his soul. And in this was portrayed the victory of the spirit over the flesh, the indomitability and moral grandeur of the soul that knows no restriction and rises above time and space and matter with a surety and invincibleness born of nothing else than eternity and immortality.

But to return. I noticed the anxious light in Johnson's eyes, but mistook it for the native shyness and embarrassment of the man. The mate, Johansen, stood away several feet to the side of him, and fully three yards in front of him sat Wolf Larsen on one of the pivotal cabin chairs. An appreciable pause fell after I had closed the doors and drawn the slide, a pause that must have lasted fully a minute. It was broken by Wolf Larsen.

"Yonson," he began.

"My name is Johnson, sir," the sailor boldly corrected.

"Well, Johnson, then, damn you! Can you guess why I have sent for you?"

"Yes, and no, sir," was the slow reply. "My work is done well. The mate knows that, and you know it, sir. So there cannot be any complaint."

"And is that all?" Wolf Larsen queried, his voice soft, and low, and purring.

"I know you have it in for me," Johnson continued with his unalterable and ponderous slowness. "You do not like me. You—you—"

"Go on," Wolf Larsen prompted. "Don't be afraid of my feelings."

"I am not afraid," the sailor retorted, a slight angry flush rising through his sunburn. "If I speak not fast, it is because I have not been from the old country as long as you. You do not like me because I am too much of a man; that is why, sir."

"You are too much of a man for ship discipline, if that is what you mean, and if you know what I mean," was Wolf Larsen's retort.

"I know English, and I know what you mean, sir," Johnson answered, his flush deepening at the slur on his knowledge of the English language.

"Johnson," Wolf Larsen said, with an air of dismissing all that had gone before as introductory to the main business in hand, "I understand you're not quite satisfied with those oil-skins?"

"No, I am not. They are no good, sir."

"And you've been shooting off your mouth about them."

"I say what I think, sir," the sailor answered courageously, not failing at the same time in ship courtesy, which demanded that "sir" be appended to each speech he made.

It was at this moment that I chanced to glance at Johansen. His big fists were clenching and unclenching, and his face was positively fiendish, so malignantly did he look at Johnson. I noticed a black discoloration, still faintly visible under Johansen's eye, a mark of the thrashing he had received a few nights before from the sailor. For the first time I began to divine that something terrible was about to be enacted—what, I could not imagine.

"Do you know what happens to men who say what you've said about my slop-chest and me?" Wolf Larsen was demanding.

"I know, sir," was the answer.

"What?" Wolf Larsen demanded, sharply and imperatively.

"What you and the mate there are going to do to me, sir."

"Look at him, Hump," Wolf Larsen said to me, "look at this bit of animated dust, this aggregation of matter that moves and breathes and defies me and thoroughly believes itself to be compounded of something good; that is impressed with certain human fictions such as righteousness and honesty, and that will live up to them in spite of all personal discomforts and menaces. What do you think of him, Hump? What do you think of him?"

"I think that he is a better man than you are," I answered, impelled, somehow, with a desire to draw upon myself a portion of the wrath I felt was about to break upon his head. "His human fictions, as you choose to call them, make for nobility and manhood. You have no fictions, no dreams, no ideals. You are a pauper."

He nodded his head with a savage pleasantness. "Quite true, Hump, quite true. I have no fictions that make for nobility and manhood. A living dog is better than a dead lion, say I with the Preacher. My only doctrine is the doctrine of expediency, and it makes for surviving. This bit of the ferment we call 'Johnson', when he is no longer a bit of the ferment, only dust and ashes, will have no more nobility than any dust and ashes, while I shall still be alive and roaring.

"Do you know what I am going to do?" he questioned.

I shook my head.

"Well, I am going to exercise my prerogative of roaring and show you how fares nobility. Watch me."

Three yards away from Johnson he was, and sitting down. Nine feet! And yet he left the chair in full leap, without first gaining a standing position. He left the chair, just as he sat in it, squarely, springing from the sitting posture like a wild animal, a tiger, and like a tiger covered the intervening space. It was an avalanche of fury that Johnson strove vainly to fend off. He threw one arm down to protect the stomach, the other arm up to protect the head; but Wolf Larsen's fist drove midway between, on the chest, with a crushing, resounding impact. Johnson's breath, suddenly expelled, shot from his mouth and as suddenly checked, with the forced, audible expiration of a man wielding an axe. He almost fell backward, and swayed from side to side in an effort to recover his balance.

I cannot give the further particulars of the horrible scene that followed. It was too revolting. It turns me sick even now when I think of it. Johnson fought bravely enough, but he was no match for Wolf Larsen, much less for Wolf Larsen and the mate. It was frightful. I had not imagined a human being could endure so much and still live and struggle on. And struggle on Johnson did. Of course there was no hope for him, not the slightest, and he knew it as well as I, but by the manhood that was in him he could not cease from fighting for that manhood.

It was too much for me to witness. I felt that I should lose my mind, and I ran up the companion stairs to open the doors and escape on deck. But Wolf Larsen, leaving his victim for the moment, and with one of his tremendous springs, gained my side and flung me into the far corner of the cabin.

"The phenomena of life, Hump," he girded at me. "Stay and watch it. You may gather data on the immortality of the soul. Besides, you know, we can't hurt Johnson's soul. It's only the fleeting form we may demolish."

It seemed centuries—possibly it was no more than ten minutes that the beating continued. Wolf Larsen and Johansen were all about the poor fellow. They struck him with their fists, kicked him with their heavy shoes, knocked him down, and dragged him to his feet to knock him down again. His eyes were blinded so that he could not see, and the blood running from ears and nose and mouth turned the cabin into a shambles. And when he could no longer rise they still continued to beat and kick him where he lay.

"Easy, Johansen; easy as she goes," Wolf Larsen finally said.

But the beast in the mate was up and rampant, and Wolf Larsen was compelled to brush him away with a backhanded sweep of the arm, gentle enough, apparently, but which hurled Johansen back like a cork, driving his head against the wall with a crash. He fell to the floor, half stunned for the moment, breathing heavily and blinking his eyes in a stupid sort of way.

"Jerk open the doors, Hump," I was commanded.

I obeyed, and the two brutes picked up the senseless man like a sack of rubbish and hove him clear up the companion stairs, through the narrow doorway, and out on deck. The blood from his nose gushed in a scarlet stream over the feet of the helmsman, who was none other than Louis, his boat-mate. But Louis took and gave a spoke and gazed imperturbably into the binnacle.

Not so was the conduct of George Leach, the erstwhile cabin-boy. Fore and aft there was nothing that could have surprised us more than his consequent behavior. He it was that came up on the poop without orders and dragged Johnson forward, where he set about dressing his wounds as well as he could and making him comfortable. Johnson, as Johnson, was unrecognizable; and not only that, for his features, as human features at all, were unrecognizable, so discolored and swollen had they become in the few minutes which had elapsed between the beginning of the beating and the dragging forward of the body.

But of Leach's behavior—By the time I had finished cleansing the cabin he had taken care of Johnson. I had come up on deck for a breath of fresh air and to try to get some repose for my overwrought nerves. Wolf Larsen was smoking a cigar and examining the patent log which the *Ghost* usually towed astern, but which had been hauled in for some purpose. Suddenly Leach's voice came to my ears. It was tense and hoarse with an overmastering rage. I turned and saw him standing just beneath the break of the poop on the port side of the galley. His face was convulsed and white, his eyes were flashing, his clenched fists raised overhead.

"May God damn your soul to hell, Wolf Larsen, only hell's too good for you, you coward, you murderer, you pig!" was his opening salutation.

I was thunderstruck. I looked for his instant annihilation. But it was not Wolf Larsen's whim to annihilate him. He sauntered slowly forward to the break of the poop, and, leaning his elbow on the corner of the cabin, gazed down thoughtfully and curiously at the excited boy.

And the boy indicted Wolf Larsen as he had never been indicted before. The sailors assembled in a fearful group just outside the forecastle scuttle and watched and listened. The hunters piled pellmell out of the steerage, but as Leach's tirade continued I saw that there was no levity in their faces. Even they were frightened, not at the boy's terrible words, but at his terrible audacity. It did not seem possible that any living creature could thus beard Wolf Larsen in his teeth. I know for myself that I was shocked into admiration of the boy, and I saw in him the splendid invincibleness of immortality rising above the flesh and the fears of the flesh, as in the prophets of old, to condemn unrighteousness.

And such condemnation! He haled forth Wolf Larsen's soul naked to the scorn of men. He rained upon it curses from God and High Heaven, and withered it with a heat of invective that savored of a mediaeval excommunication of the Catholic Church. He ran the gamut of denunciation, rising to heights of wrath that were sublime and almost Godlike, and from sheer exhaustion sinking to the vilest and most indecent abuse.

His rage was a madness. His lips were flecked with a soapy froth, and sometimes he choked and gurgled and became inarticulate. And through it all, calm and impassive, leaning on his elbow and gazing down, Wolf Larsen seemed lost in a great curiosity. This wild stirring of yeasty life, this terrific revolt and defiance of matter that moved, perplexed and interested him.

Each moment I looked, and everybody looked, for him to leap upon the boy and destroy him. But it was not his whim. His cigar went out, and he continued to gaze silently and curiously.

Leach had worked himself into an ecstasy of impotent rage.

"Pig! Pig! Pig!" he was reiterating at the top of his lungs. "Why don't you come down and kill me, you murderer? You can do it! I ain't afraid! There's no one to stop you! Damn sight better dead and outa your reach than alive and in your clutches! Come on, you coward! Kill me! Kill me! Kill me!"

It was at this stage that Thomas Mugridge's erratic soul brought him into the scene. He had been listening at the galley door, but he now came out, ostensibly to fling some scraps over the side, but obviously to see the killing he was certain would take place. He smirked greasily up into the face of Wolf Larsen, who seemed not to see him. But the Cockney was unabashed, though mad, stark mad. He turned to Leach saying: "Such langwidge! Shockin'!"

Leach's rage was no longer impotent. Here at last was something ready to hand. And for the first time since the stabbing the Cockney had appeared outside the galley without his knife. The words had barely left his mouth when he was knocked down by Leach. Three times he struggled to his feet, striving to gain the galley, and each time was knocked down.

"Oh, Lord!" he cried. " 'Elp! 'Elp! Tyke 'im aw'y, carn't yer? Tyke 'im aw'y!"

The hunters laughed from sheer relief. Tragedy had dwindled, the farce had begun. The sailors now crowded boldly aft, grinning and shuffling, to watch the pummelling of the hated Cockney. And even I felt a great joy surge up within me. I confess that I delighted in this beating Leach was giving to Thomas Mugridge, though it was as terrible, almost, as the one Mugridge had caused to be given to Johnson. But the expression of Wolf Larsen's face never changed. He did not change his position either, but continued to gaze down with a great curiosity. For all his pragmatic certitude, it seemed as if he watched the play and movement of life in the hope of discovering something more about it, of discerning in its maddest writhings a something which had hitherto escaped him—the key to its mystery, as it were, which would make all clear and plain.

But the beating! It was quite similar to the one I had witnessed in the cabin. The Cockney strove in vain to protect himself from the infuriated boy. And in vain he strove to gain the shelter of the cabin. He rolled toward it, grovelled toward it, fell toward it when he was knocked down. But blow followed blow with bewildering rapidity. He was knocked about like a shuttlecock, until, finally, like Johnson, he was beaten and kicked as he lay helpless on the deck. And no one interfered. Leach could have killed him, but, having evidently filled the measure of his vengeance, he drew away from his prostrate foe, who was whimpering and wailing in a puppyish sort of way, and walked forward.

But these two affairs were only the opening events of the day's programme. In the afternoon Smoke and Henderson fell foul of each other, and a fusillade of shots came up from the steerage, followed by a stampede of the other four hunters for the deck. A column of thick, acrid smoke—the kind always made by black powder—was arising through the open companionway, and down through it leaped Wolf Larsen. The sound of blows and scuffling came to our ears. Both men were wounded, and he was thrashing them both for having disobeyed his orders and crippled themselves in advance of the hunting season. In fact, they were badly wounded, and, having thrashed them, he proceeded to operate upon them in a rough surgical fashion and to dress their wounds. I served as assistant while he probed and cleansed the passages made by the bullets, and I saw the two men endure his crude surgery without anaesthetics and with no more to uphold them than a stiff tumbler of whiskey.

Then, in the first dog-watch, trouble came to a head in the forecastle. It took its rise out of the tittle-tattle and tale-bearing which had been the cause of Johnson's beating, and from the noise we heard, and from the sight of the bruised men next day, it was patent that half the forecastle had soundly drubbed the other half.

The second dog-watch and the day were wound up by a fight between Johansen and the lean, Yankee-looking hunter, Latimer. It was caused by remarks of Latimer's concerning the noises made by the mate in his sleep, and though Johansen was whipped, he kept the steerage awake for the rest of the night while he blissfully slumbered and fought the fight over and over again.

As for myself, I was oppressed with nightmare. The day had been like some horrible dream. Brutality had followed brutality, and flaming passions and cold-blooded cruelty had driven men to seek one another's lives, and to strive to hurt, and maim, and destroy. My nerves were shocked. My mind itself was shocked. All my days had been passed in comparative ignorance of the animality of man. In fact, I had known life only in its intellectual phases. Brutality I had experienced, but it was the brutality of the intellect—the cutting sarcasm of Charley Furuseth, the cruel epigrams and occasional harsh witticisms of the fellows at the Bibelot, and the nasty remarks of some of the professors during my undergraduate days.

That was all. But that men should wreak their anger on others by the bruising of the flesh and the letting of blood was something strangely and fearfully new to me. Not for nothing had I been called "Sissy" Van Weyden, I thought, as I tossed restlessly on my bunk between one nightmare and another. And it seemed to me that my innocence of the realities of life had been complete indeed. I laughed bitterly to myself, and seemed to find in Wolf Larsen's forbidding philosophy a more adequate explanation of life than I found in my own.

And I was frightened when I became conscious of the trend of my thought. The continual brutality around me was degenerative in its effect. It bid fair to destroy for me all that was best and brightest in life. My reason dictated that the beating Thomas Mugridge had received was an ill thing, and yet for the life of me I could not prevent my soul joying in it. And even while I was oppressed by the enormity of my sin—for sin it was—I chuckled with an insane delight. I was no longer Humphrey Van Weyden. I was Hump, cabin-boy on the schooner *Ghost.* Wolf Larsen was my captain, Thomas Mugridge and the rest were my companions, and I was receiving repeated impresses from the die which had stamped them all.

XIII

For three days I did my own work and Thomas Mugridge's too; and I flatter myself that I did his work well. I know that it won Wolf Larsen's approval, while the sailors beamed with satisfaction during the brief time my régime lasted.

"The first clean bite since I come aboard," Harrison said to me at the galley door, as he returned the dinner pots and pans from the forecastle. "Somehow Tommy's grub always tastes of grease, stale grease, and I reckon he ain't changed his shirt since he left 'Frisco."

"I know he hasn't," I answered.

"And I'll bet he sleeps in it," Harrison added.

"And you won't lose," I agreed. "The same shirt, and he hasn't had it off once in all this time."

But three days was all Wolf Larsen allowed him in which to recover from the effects of the beating. On the fourth day, lame and sore, scarcely able to see, so closed were his eyes, he was haled from his bunk by the nape of the neck and set to his duty. He sniffled and wept, but Wolf Larsen was pitiless.

"And see that you serve no more slops," was his parting injunction. "No more grease and dirt, mind, and a clean shirt occasionally, or you'll get a tow over the side. Understand?"

Thomas Mugridge crawled weakly across the galley floor, and a short lurch of the *Ghost* sent him staggering. In attempting to recover himself, he reached for the iron railing which surrounded the stove and kept the pots from sliding off; but he missed the railing, and his hand, with his weight behind it, landed squarely on the hot surface. There was a sizzle and odor of burning flesh, and a sharp cry of pain.

"Oh, Gawd, Gawd, wot 'ave I done?" he wailed, sitting down in the coal-box and nursing his new hurt by rocking back and forth. "W'y 'as all this come on me? It mykes me fair sick, it does, an' I try so 'ard to go through life 'armless an' 'urtin' nobody."

The tears were running down his puffed and discolored cheeks, and his face was drawn with pain. A savage expression flitted across it.

"Oh, 'ow I 'ate 'im! 'Ow I 'ate 'im!" he gritted out.

"Whom?" I asked; but the poor wretch was weeping again over his misfortunes. Less difficult it was to guess whom he hated than whom he did not hate. For I had come to see a malignant devil in him which impelled him to hate all the world. I sometimes thought that he hated even himself, so grotesquely had life dealt with him, and so monstrously. At such moments a great sympathy welled up within me, and I felt shame that I had ever joyed in his discomfiture of pain. Life had been unfair to him. It had played him a scurvy trick when it fashioned him into the thing he was, and it had played him scurvy tricks ever since. What chance had he to be anything else than he was? And as though answering my unspoken thought, he wailed:

"I never 'ad no chance, nor 'arf a chance! 'Oo was there to send me to school, or put tommy in my 'ungry belly, or wipe my bloody nose for me, w'en I was a kiddy? 'Oo ever did anything for me, heh? 'Oo, I s'y?"

"Never mind, Tommy," I said, placing a soothing hand on his shoulder. "Cheer up. It'll all come right in the end. You've long years before you, and you can make anything you please of yourself."

"It's a lie! A bloody lie!" he shouted in my face, flinging off the hand. "It's a lie, and you know it. I'm already myde, an' myde out of leavin's an' scraps. It's all right for you, 'Ump. You was born a gentleman. You never knew wot it was to go 'ungry, to cry yerself asleep with yer little belly gnawin' an' gnawin', like a rat inside yer. It carn't come right. If I was President of the United Stytes tomorrer, 'ow would it fill my belly for one time w'en I was a kiddy and went empty?

" 'Ow could it, I s'y? I was born to sufferin' and sorrer. I've 'ad more cruel sufferin' than any ten men, I 'ave. I've been in orspital arf my bleedin' life. I've 'ad the fever in Aspinwall, in 'Avana, in New Orleans. I near died of the scurvy and was rotten with it six months in Barbadoes. Smallpox in 'Onolulu, two broken legs in Shanghai, pneumonia in Unalaska, three busted ribs an' my insides all twisted in 'Frisco. An' 'ere I am now. Look at me! Look at me! My ribs kicked loose from my back again. I'll be coughin' blood before eyght bells. 'Ow can it be myde up to me, I arsk? 'Oo's goin' to do it? Gawd? 'Ow Gawd must 'ave 'ated me w'en 'e signed me on for a voyage in this bloomin' world of 'is!"

This tirade against destiny went on for an hour or more, and then he buckled to his work, limping and groaning, and in his eyes a great hatred for all created things. His diagnosis was correct, however, for he was seized with occasional sicknesses, during which he vomited blood and suffered great pain. And as he said, it seemed God hated him too much to let him die, for he ultimately grew better and waxed more malignant than ever.

Several days more passed before Johnson crawled on deck and went about his work in a half-hearted way. He was still a sick man, and I more than once observed him creeping painfully aloft to a topsail, or drooping wearily as he stood at the wheel. But, still worse, it seemed that his spirit was broken. He was abject before Wolf Larsen and almost grovelled to Johansen. Not so was the conduct of Leach. He went about the deck like a tiger cub, glaring his hatred openly at Wolf Larsen and Johansen.

"I'll do for you yet, you slab-footed Swede," I heard him say to Johansen one night on deck.

The mate cursed him in the darkness, and the next moment some missile struck the galley a sharp rap. There was more cursing, and a mocking laugh, and when all was quiet I stole outside and found a heavy knife imbedded over an inch in the solid wood. A few minutes later the mate came fumbling about in search of it, but I returned it privily to Leach next day. He grinned when I handed it over, yet it was a grin that contained more sincere thanks than a multitude of the verbosities of speech common to the members of my own class.

Unlike anyone else in the ship's company, I now found myself with no quarrels on my hands and in the good graces of all. The hunters possibly no more than tolerated me, though none of them disliked me; while Smoke and Henderson, convalescent under a deck awning and swinging day and night in their hammocks, assured me that I was better than any hospital nurse, and that they would not forget me at the end of the voyage when they were paid off. (As though I stood in need of their money! I, who could have bought them out, bag and baggage, and the schooner and its equipment, a score of times over!) But upon me had devolved the task of tending their wounds, and pulling them through, and I did my best by them.

Wolf Larsen underwent another bad attack of headache which lasted two days. He must have suffered severely, for he called me in and obeyed my commands like a sick child. But nothing I could do seemed to relieve him. At my suggestion, however, he gave up smoking and drinking; though why such a magnificent animal as he should have headaches at all puzzles me.

" 'Tis the hand of God, I'm tellin' you," is the way Louis sees it. " 'Tis a visitation for his black-hearted deeds, and there's more behind and comin', or else—"

"Or else," I prompted.

"God is noddin' and not doin' his duty, though it's me as shouldn't say it."

I was mistaken when I said that I was in the good graces of all. Not only does Thomas Mugridge continue to hate me, but he has discovered a new reason for hating me. It took me no little while to puzzle it out, but I finally discovered that it was because I was more luckily born than he—"gentleman born" , he put it.

"And still no more dead men," I twitted Louis, when Smoke and Henderson, side by side, in friendly conversation, took their first exercise on deck.

Louis surveyed me with his shrewd gray eyes and shook his head portentously. "She's a-comin', I tell you, and it'll be sheets and halyards, stand by all hands, when she begins to howl. I've had the feel iv it this long time, and I can feel it now as plainly as I feel the rigging iv a dark night. She's close, she's close."

"Who goes first?" I queried.

"Not old fat Louis, I promise you," he laughed. "For 'tis in the bones iv me I know that come this time next year I'll be gazin' in the old mother's eyes, weary with watchin' iv the sea for the five sons she gave to it."

"Wot's 'e been s'yin' to yer?" Thomas Mugridge demanded a moment later.

"That he's going home some day to see his mother," I answered diplomatically.

"I never 'ad none," was the Cockney's comment as he gazed with lustreless, hopeless eyes into mine.

XIV

IT has dawned upon me that I have never placed a proper valuation upon womankind. For that matter, though not amative to any considerable degree so far as I have discovered, I was never outside the atmosphere of women until now. My mother and sisters were always about me, and I was always trying to escape them; for they worried me to distraction with their solicitude for my health and with their periodic inroads on my den, when my orderly confusion, upon which I prided myself, was turned into worse confusion and less order, though it looked neat enough to the eye. I never could find anything when they had departed. But now, alas, how welcome would have been the feel of their presence, the frou-frou and swish-swish of their skirts which I had so cordially detested! I am sure, if I ever get home, that I will never be irritable with them again. They may dose me and doctor me morning, noon and night, and dust and sweep and put my den to rights every minute of the day, and I shall only lean back and survey it all and be thankful in that I am possessed of a mother and some several sisters.

All of which has set me wondering. Where are the mothers of these twenty and odd men on the *Ghost?* It strikes me as unnatural and unhealthful that men should be totally separated from women and herd through the world by themselves. Coarseness and savagery are the inevitable results. These men about me should have wives, and sisters, and daughters; then would they be capable of softness, and tenderness, and sympathy. As it is, not one of them is married. In years and years not one of them has been in contact with a good woman, or within the influence, or redemption, which irresistibly radiates from such a creature. There is no balance in their lives. Their masculinity, which in itself is of the brute, has been overdeveloped. The other and spiritual side of their natures has been dwarfed—atrophied, in fact.

They are a company of celibates, grinding harshly against one another and growing daily more calloused from the grinding. It seems to me impossible sometimes that they ever had mothers. It would appear that they are a half-brute, half-human species, a race apart, wherein there is no such thing as sex; that they are hatched out by the sun like turtle eggs, or receive life in some similar and sordid fashion; and that all their days fester in brutality and viciousness, and in the end die as unlovely as they have lived.

Rendered curious by this new direction of ideas, I talked with Johansen last night—the first superfluous words with which he has favored me since the voyage began. He left Sweden when he was eighteen, is now thirty-eight, and in all the intervening time has not been home once. He had met a townsman, a couple of years before, in some sailor boarding-house in Chile, so that he knew his mother was still alive.

"She must be a pretty old woman now," he said, staring meditatively into the binnacle and then jerking a sharp glance at Harrison, who was steering a point off the course.

"When did you last write her?"

He performed his mental arithmetic aloud. "Eighty-one; no—eighty-two, eh? No—eighty-three? Yes, eighty-three. Ten years ago. For some little port in Madagascar. I was trading.

"You see," he went on, as though addressing his neglected mother across half the girth of the earth, "each year I was going home. So what was the good to write? It was only a year. And each year something happened, and I did not go. But I am mate, now, and when I pay off at 'Frisco, maybe with five hundred dollars, I will ship myself on a wind-jammer round the Horn to Liverpool, which will give me more money; and then I will pay my passage from there home. Then she will not do any more work."

"But does she work now? How old is she?"

"About seventy," he answered. And then, boastingly, "We work from the time we are born until we die, in my country. That's why we live so long. I will live to be a hundred."

I shall never forget this conversation. The words were the last I ever heard him utter. Perhaps they were the last he did utter, too. For, going down into the cabin to turn in, I decided that it was too stuffy to sleep below. It was a calm night. We were out of the Trades, and the *Ghost* was forging ahead barely a knot an hour. So I tucked a blanket and pillow under my arm and went up on deck.

As I passed between Harrison and the binnacle, which was built into the top of the cabin, I noticed that he was this time fully three points off. Thinking that he was asleep, and wishing him to escape reprimand or worse, I spoke to him. But he was not asleep. His eyes were wide and staring. He seemed greatly perturbed, unable to reply to me.

"What's the matter?" I asked. "Are you sick?"

He shook his head, and with a deep sigh, as of awakening, caught his breath.

"You'd better get on your course, then," I chided.

He put a few spokes over, and I watched the compass-card swing slowly to N N W and steady itself with slight oscillations.

I took a fresh hold on my bedclothes and was preparing to start on, when some movement caught my eye and I looked astern to the rail. A sinewy hand, dripping with water, was clutching the rail. A second hand took form in the darkness beside it. I watched, fascinated. What visitant from the gloom of the deep was I to behold? Whatever it was, I knew that it was climbing aboard by the log-line. I saw a head, the hair wet and straight, shape itself, and then the unmistakable eyes and face of Wolf Larsen. His right cheek was red with blood, which flowed from some wound in the head.

He drew himself inboard with a quick effort, and arose to his feet, glancing swiftly, as he did so, at the man at the wheel, as though to assure himself of his identity and that there was nothing to fear from him. The sea-water was streaming from him. It made little audible gurgles which distracted me. As he stepped toward me I shrank back instinctively, for I saw that in his eyes which spelled death.

"All right, Hump," he said in a low voice. "Where's the mate?"

I shook my head.

"Johansen!" he called softly. "Johansen!"

"Where is he?" he demanded of Harrison.

The young fellow seemed to have recovered his composure, for he answered steadily enough, "I don't know, sir. I saw him go for'ard a little while ago."

"So did I go for'ard. But you will observe that I didn't come back the way I went. Can you explain it?"

"You must have been overboard, sir."

"Shall I look for him in the steerage, sir?" I asked.

Wolf Larsen shook his head. "You wouldn't find him, Hump. But you'll do. Come on. Never mind your bedding. Leave it where it is."

I followed at his heels. There was nothing stirring amidships.

"Those cursed hunters," was his comment. "Too damned fat and lazy to stand a four-hour watch."

But on the forecastle-head we found three sailors asleep. He turned them over and looked at their faces. They composed the watch on deck, and it was the ship's custom, in good weather, to let the watch sleep with the exception of the officer, the helmsman, and the look-out.

"Who's look-out?" he demanded.

"Me, sir," answered Holyoak, one of the deep-water sailors, a slight tremor in his voice. "I winked off just this very minute, sir. I'm sorry, sir. It won't happen again."

"Did you hear or see anything on deck?"

"No, sir, I—"

But Wolf Larsen had turned away with a snort of disgust, leaving the sailor rubbing his eyes with surprise at having been let off so easily.

"Softly, now," Wolf Larsen warned me in a whisper, as he doubled his body into the forecastle scuttle and prepared to descend.

I followed with a quaking heart. What was to happen I knew no more than did I know what had happened. But blood had been shed, and it was through no whim of Wolf Larsen that he had gone over the side with his scalp laid open. Besides, Johansen was missing.

It was my first descent into the forecastle, and I shall not soon forget my impression of it, caught as I stood on my feet at the bottom of the ladder. Built directly in the eyes of the schooner, it was of the shape of a triangle, along the three sides of which stood the bunks, in double-tier, twelve of them. It was no larger than a hall bedroom in Grub Street, and yet twelve men were herded into it to eat and sleep and carry on all the functions of living. My bedroom at home was not large, yet it could have contained a dozen similar forecastles, and taking into consideration the height of the ceiling, a score at least.

It smelled sour and musty, and by the dim light of the swinging sea-lamp I saw every bit of available wall-space hung deep with sea-boots, oilskins, and garments, clean and dirty, of various sorts. These swung back and forth with every roll of the vessel, giving rise to a brushing sound, as of trees against a roof or wall. Somewhere a boot thumped loudly and at irregular intervals against the wall; and, though it was a mild night on the sea, there was a continual chorus of the creaking timbers and bulkheads and of abysmal noises beneath the flooring.

The sleepers did not mind. There were eight of them—the two watches below—and the air was thick with the warmth and odor of their breathing, and the ear was filled with the noise of their snoring and of their sighs and half-groans, tokens plain of the rest of the animal-man. But were they sleeping? All of them? Or had they been sleeping? This was evidently Wolf Larsen's quest—to find the men who appeared to be asleep and who were not asleep or who had not been asleep very recently. And he went about it in a way that reminded me of a story out of Boccaccio.

He took the sea-lamp from its swinging frame and handed it to me. He began at the first bunks forward on the starboard side. In the top one lay Oofty-Oofty, a Kanaka and splendid seaman, so named by his mates. He was asleep on his back and breathing as placidly as a woman. One arm was under his head, the other lay on top of the blankets. Wolf Larsen put a thumb and forefinger to the wrist and counted the pulse. In the midst of it the Kanaka roused. He awoke as gently as he slept. There was no movement of the body whatever. The eyes, only, moved. They flashed wide open, big and black, and stared, unblinking, into our faces. Wolf Larsen put his finger to his lips as a sign for silence, and the eyes closed again.

In the lower bunk lay Louis, grossly fat and warm and sweaty, asleep unfeignedly and sleeping laboriously. While Wolf Larsen held his wrist he stirred uneasily, bowing his body so that for a moment it rested on shoulders and heels. His lips moved, and he gave voice to this enigmatic utterance:

"A shilling's worth a quarter; but keep your lamps out for thruppenny bits, or the publicans'll shove 'em on you for sixpence."

Then he rolled over on his side with a heavy, sobbing sigh, saying:

"A sixpence is a tanner, and a shilling a bob; but what a pony is I don't know."

Satisfied with the honesty of his and the Kanaka's sleep, Wolf Larsen passed on to the next two bunks on the starboard side, occupied top and bottom, as we saw in the light of the sea-lamp, by Leach and Johnson.

As Wolf Larsen bent down to the lower bunk to take Johnson's pulse, I, standing erect and holding the lamp, saw Leach's head raise stealthily as he peered over the side of his bunk to see what was going on. He must have divined Wolf Larsen's trick and the sureness of detection, for the light was at once dashed from my hand and the forecastle left in darkness. He must have leaped, also, at the same instant, straight down on Wolf Larsen.

The first sounds were those of a conflict between a bull and a wolf. I heard a great infuriated bellow go up from Wolf Larsen, and from Leach a snarling that was desperate and blood-curdling. Johnson must have joined him immediately, so that his abject and grovelling conduct on deck for the past few days had been no more than planned deception.

I was so terror-stricken by this fight in the dark that I leaned against the ladder, trembling and unable to ascend. And upon me was that old sickness at the pit of the stomach, caused always by the spectacle of physical violence. In this instance I could not see, but I could hear the impact of the blows—the soft crushing sound made by flesh striking forcibly against flesh. Then there was the crashing about of the entwined bodies, the labored breathing, the short quick gasps of sudden pain.

There must have been more men in the conspiracy to murder the captain and mate, for by the sounds I knew that Leach and Johnson had been quickly reinforced by some of their mates.

"Get a knife, somebody!" Leach was shouting.

"Pound him on the head! Mash his brains out!" was Johnson's cry.

But after his first bellow, Wolf Larsen made no noise. He was fighting grimly and silently for life. He was sore beset. Down at the very first, he had been unable to gain his feet, and for all of his tremendous strength I felt that there was no hope for him.

The force with which they struggled was vividly impressed on me; for I was knocked down by their surging bodies and badly bruised. But in the confusion I managed to crawl into an empty lower bunk out of the way.

"All hands! We've got him! We've got him!" I could hear Leach crying.

"Who?" demanded those who had been really asleep, and who had wakened to they knew not what.

"It's the bloody mate!" was Leach's crafty answer, strained from him in a smothered sort of way.

This was greeted with whoops of joy, and from then on Wolf Larsen had seven strong men on top of him, Louis, I believe, taking no part in it. The forecastle was like an angry hive of bees aroused by some marauder.

"What ho! Below there!" I heard Latimer shout down the scuttle, too cautious to descend into the inferno of passion he could hear raging beneath him in the darkness.

"Won't somebody get a knife? Oh, won't somebody get a knife?" Leach pleaded in the first interval of comparative silence.

The number of the assailants was a cause of confusion. They blocked their own efforts, while Wolf Larsen, with but a single purpose, achieved his. This was to fight his way across the floor to the ladder. Though in total darkness, I followed his progress by its sound. No man less than a giant could have done what he did, once he had gained the foot of the ladder. Step by step, by the might of his arms, the whole pack of men striving to drag him back and down, he drew his body up from the floor till he stood erect. And then, step by step, hand and foot, he slowly struggled up the ladder.

The very last of all, I saw. For Latimer, having finally gone for a lantern, held it so that its light shone down the scuttle. Wolf Larsen was nearly to the top, though I could not see him. All that was visible was the mass of men fastened upon him. It squirmed about, like some huge many-legged spider, and swayed back and forth to the regular roll of the vessel. And still, step by step, with long intervals between, the mass ascended. Once it tottered, about to fall back, but the broken hold was regained and it still went up.

"Who is it?" Latimer cried.

In the rays of the lantern I could see his perplexed face peering down.

"Larsen," I heard a muffled voice from within the mass.

Latimer reached down with his free hand. I saw a hand shoot up to clasp his. Latimer pulled, and the next couple of steps were made with a rush. Then Wolf Larsen's other hand reached up and clutched the edge of the scuttle. The mass swung clear of the ladder, the men still clinging to their escaping foe. They began to drop off, to be brushed off against the sharp edge of the scuttle, to be knocked off by the legs which were now kicking powerfully. Leach was the last to go, falling sheer back from the top of the scuttle and striking on head and shoulders upon his sprawling mates beneath. Wolf Larsen and the lantern disappeared, and we were left in darkness.

XV

THERE was a deal of cursing and groaning as the men at the bottom of the ladder crawled to their feet.

"Somebody strike a light, my thumb's out of joint," said one of the men, Parsons, a swarthy, saturnine man, boat-steerer in Standish's boat, in which Harrison was puller.

"You'll find it knockin' about by the bitts," Leach said, sitting down on the edge of the bunk in which I was concealed.

There was a fumbling and a scratching of matches, and the sea-lamp flared up, dim and smoky, and in its weird light bare-legged men moved about, nursing their bruises and caring for their hurts. Oofty-Oofty laid hold of Parsons's thumb, pulling it out stoutly and snapping it back into place. I noticed at the same time that the Kanaka's knuckles were laid open clear across and to the bone. He exhibited them, exposing beautiful white teeth in a grin as he did so and explaining that the wounds had come from striking Wolf Larsen in the mouth.

"So it was you, was it, you black beggar?" belligerently demanded one Kelly, an Irish-American and a longshoreman, making his first trip to sea, and boat-puller for Kerfoot.

As he made the demand he spat out a mouthful of blood and teeth and shoved his pugnacious face close to Oofty-Oofty. The Kanaka leaped backward to his bunk, to return with a second leap, flourishing a long knife.

"Aw, go lay down, you make me tired," Leach interfered. He was evidently, for all of his youth and inexperience, cock of the forecastle. "G'wan, you Kelly. You leave Oofty alone. How the hell did he know it was you in the dark?"

Kelly subsided with some muttering, and the Kanaka flashed his white teeth in a grateful smile. He was a beautiful creature, almost feminine in the pleasing lines of his figure, and there was a softness and dreaminess in his large eyes which seemed to contradict his well-earned reputation for strife and action.

"How did he get away?" Johnson asked.

He was sitting on the side of his bunk, the whole pose of his figure indicating utter dejection and hopelessness. He was still breathing heavily from the exertion he had made. His shirt had been ripped entirely from him in the struggle, and blood from a gash in the cheek was flowing down his naked chest, making a red path across his white thigh and dripping to the floor.

"Because he is the devil, as I told you before," was Leach's answer; and thereat he was on his feet and raging his disappointment with tears in his eyes.

"And not one of you to get a knife!" was his unceasing lament.

But the rest of the hands had a lively fear of consequences to come and gave no heed to him.

"How'll he know which was which?" Kelly asked, and as he went on he looked murderously about him—"unless one of us peaches."

"He'll know as soon as ever he claps eyes on us," Parsons replied. "One look at you'd be enough."

"Tell him the deck flopped up and gouged yer teeth out iv yer jaw," Louis grinned. He was the only man who was not out of his bunk, and he was jubilant in that he possessed no bruises to advertise that he had had a hand in the night's work. "Just wait till he gets a glimpse iv yer mugs to-morrow, the gang iv ye," he chuckled.

"We'll say we thought it was the mate," said one. And another, "I know what I'll say—that I heered a row, jumped out of my bunk, got a jolly good crack on the jaw for my pains and sailed in myself. Couldn't tell who or what it was in the dark and just hit out."

"An' 'twas me you hit, of course," Kelly seconded, his face brightening for the moment.

Leach and Johnson took no part in the discussion, and it was plain to see that their mates looked upon them as men for whom the worst was inevitable, who were beyond hope and already dead. Leach stood their fears and reproaches for some time. Then he broke out:

"You make me tired! A nice lot of gazabas you are! If you talked less with yer mouth and did something with yer hands, he'd a-ben done with by now. Why couldn't one of you, just one of you, get me a knife when I sung out? You make me sick! A-beefin' and bellerin' 'round, as though he'd kill you when he gets you! You know damn well he won't. Can't afford to. No shipping masters or beach combers over here, and he wants yer in his business, and he wants yer bad. Who's to pull or steer or sail ship if he loses yer? It's me and Johnson have to face the music. Get into yer bunks, now, and shut yer faces; I want to get some sleep."

"That's all right," Parsons spoke up. "Mebbe he won't do for us, but mark my words, hell'll be an icebox to this ship from now on."

All the while I had been apprehensive concerning my own predicament. What would happen to me when these men discovered my presence? I could never fight my way out as Wolf Larsen had done. And at this moment Latimer called down the scuttles:

"Hump! The old man wants you!"

"He ain't down here!" Parsons called back.

"Yes, he is," I said, sliding out of the bunk and striving my hardest to keep my voice steady and bold.

The sailors looked at me in consternation. Fear was strong in their faces, and the devilishness which comes of fear.

"I'm coming!" I shouted up to Latimer.

"No you don't!" Kelly cried, stepping between me and the ladder, his right hand shaped into a veritable strangler's clutch. "You damn little sneak! I'll shut yer mouth!"

"Let him go," Leach commanded.

"Not on yer life," was the angry retort.

Leach never changed his position on the edge of the bunk. "Let him go, I say," he repeated; but this time his voice was gritty and metallic.

The Irishman wavered. I made to step by him, and he stood aside. When I had gained the ladder, I turned to the circle of brutal and malignant faces peering at me through the semi-darkness. A sudden and deep sympathy welled up in me. I remembered the Cockney's way of putting it. How God must have hated them that they should be tortured so!

"I have seen and heard nothing, believe me," I said quietly.

"I tell yer, he's all right," I could hear Leach saying as I went up the ladder. "He don't like the old man no more nor you or me."

I found Wolf Larsen in the cabin, stripped and bloody, waiting for me. He greeted me with one of his whimsical smiles.

"Come, get to work, Doctor. The signs are favorable for an extensive practice this voyage. I don't know what the *Ghost* would have been without you, and if I could only cherish such noble sentiments I would tell you her master is deeply grateful."

I knew the run of the simple medicine-chest the *Ghost* carried, and while I was heating water on the cabin stove and getting the things ready for dressing his wounds, he moved about, laughing and chatting, and examining his hurts with a calculating eye. I had never before seen him stripped, and the sight of his body quite took my breath away. It has never been my weakness to exalt the flesh—far from it; but there is enough of the artist in me to appreciate its wonder.

I must say that I was fascinated by the perfect lines of Wolf Larsen's figure, and by what I may term the terrible beauty of it. I had noted the men in the forecastle. Powerfully muscled though some of them were, there had been something wrong with all of them, an insufficient development here, an undue development there, a twist or a crook that destroyed symmetry, legs too short or too long, or too much sinew or bone exposed, or too little. Oofty-Oofty had been the only one whose lines were at all pleasing, while, in so far as they pleased, that far had they been what I should call feminine.

But Wolf Larsen was the man-type, the masculine, and almost a god in his perfectness. As he moved about or raised his arms the great muscles leapt and moved under the satiny skin. I have forgotten to say that the bronze ended with his face. His body, thanks to his Scandinavian stock, was fair as the fairest woman's. I remember his putting his hand up to feel of the wound on his head, and my watching the biceps move like a living thing under its white sheath. It was the biceps that had nearly crushed out my life once, that I had seen strike so many killing blows. I could not take my eyes from him. I stood motionless, a roll of antiseptic cotton in my hand unwinding and spilling itself down to the floor.

He noticed me, and I became conscious that I was staring at him.

"God made you well," I said.

"Did he?" he answered. "I have often thought so myself, and wondered why."

"Purpose—" I began.

"Utility," he interrupted. "This body was made for use. These muscles were made to grip, and tear, and destroy living things that get between me and life. But have you thought of the other living things? They, too, have muscles, of one kind and another, made to grip, and tear, and destroy; and when they come between me and life, I out-grip them, out-tear them, out-destroy them. Purpose does not explain that. Utility does."

"It is not beautiful," I protested.

"Life isn't, you mean," he smiled. "Yet you say I was made well. Do you see this?"

He braced his legs and feet, pressing the cabin floor with his toes in a clutching sort of way. Knots and ridges and mounds of muscles writhed and bunched under the skin.

"Feel them," he commanded.

They were hard as iron. And I observed, also, that his whole body had unconsciously drawn itself together, tense and alert; that muscles were softly crawling and shaping about the hips, along the back, and across the shoulders; that the arms were slightly lifted, their muscles contracting, the fingers crooking till the hands were like talons; and that even the eyes had changed expression and into them were coming watchfulness and measurement and a light none other than of battle.

"Stability, equilibrium," he said, relaxing on the instant and sinking his body back into repose. "Feet with which to clutch the ground, legs to stand on and to help withstand, while with arms and hands, teeth and nails, I struggle to kill and to be not killed. Purpose? Utility is the better word."

I did not argue. I had seen the mechanism of the primitive fighting beast, and I was as strongly impressed as if I had seen the engines of a great battleship or Atlantic liner.

I was surprised, considering the fierce struggle in the forecastle, at the superficiality of his hurts, and I pride myself that I dressed them dexterously. With the exception of several bad wounds, the rest were merely severe bruises and lacerations. The blow which he had received before going overboard had laid his scalp open several inches. This, under his direction, I cleansed and sewed together, having first shaved the edges of the wound. Then the calf of his leg was badly lacerated and looked as though it had been mangled by a bulldog. Some sailor, he told me, had laid hold of it by his teeth, at the beginning of the fight, and hung on and been dragged to the top of the forecastle ladder, when he was kicked loose.

"By the way, Hump, as I have remarked, you are a handy man," Wolf Larsen began, when my work was done. "As you know, we're short a mate. Hereafter you shall stand watches, receive seventy-five dollars per month, and be addressed fore and aft as Mr. Van Weyden."

"I—I don't understand navigation, you know," I gasped.

"Not necessary at all."

"I really do not care to sit in the high places," I objected. "I find life precarious enough in my present humble situation. I have no experience. Mediocrity, you see, has its compensations."

He smiled as though it were all settled.

"I won't be mate on this hell-ship!" I cried defiantly.

I saw his face grow hard and the merciless glitter come into his eyes. He walked to the door of his room, saying:

"And now, Mr. Van Weyden, good night."

"Good night, Mr. Larsen," I answered weakly.

XVI

I CANNOT say that the position of mate carried with it anything more joyful than that there were no more dishes to wash. I was ignorant of the simplest duties of mate, and would have fared badly indeed had the sailors not sympathized with me. I knew nothing of the minutiae of ropes and rigging, of the trimming and setting of sails; but the sailors took pains to put me to rights—Louis proving an especially good teacher—and I had little trouble with those under me.

With the hunters it was otherwise. Familiar in varying degree with the sea, they took me as a sort of joke. In truth, it was a joke to me, that I, the veriest landsman, should be filling the office of mate; but to be taken as a joke by others was a different matter. I made no complaint, but Wolf Larsen demanded the most punctilious sea etiquette in my case—far more than poor Johansen had ever received; and at the expense of several rows, threats and much grumbling, he brought the hunters to time. I was "Mr Van Weyden" fore and aft, and it was only unofficially that Wolf Larsen himself ever addressed me as "Hump" .

It was amusing. Perhaps the wind would haul a few points while we were at dinner, and as I left the table he would say, "Mr Van Weyden, will you kindly put about on the port tack." And I would go on deck, beckon Louis to me, and learn from him what was to be done. Then, a few minutes later, having digested his instructions and thoroughly mastered the manoeuvre, I would proceed to issue my orders. I remember an early instance of this kind, when Wolf Larsen appeared on the scene just as I had begun to give orders. He smoked his cigar and looked on quietly till the thing was accomplished, and then paced aft by my side along the weather poop.

"Hump," he said, "I beg pardon, Mr Van Weyden, I congratulate you. I think you can now fire your father's legs back into the grave to him. You've discovered your own and learned to stand on them. A little rope-work, sail-making and experience with storms and such things, and by the end of the voyage you could ship on any coasting schooner."

It was during this period, between the death of Johansen and the arrival of the sealing grounds, that I passed my pleasantest hours on the *Ghost*. Wolf Larsen was quite considerate, the sailors helped me, and I was no longer in irritating contact with Thomas Mugridge. and I make free to say, as the days went by, that I found I was taking a certain secret pride in myself. Fantastic as the situation was—a landlubber second in command—I was, nevertheless, carrying it off well; and during that brief time I was proud of myself, and I grew to love the heave and roll of the *Ghost* under my feet as she wallowed north and west through the tropic sea to the islet where we filled our water-casks.

But my happiness was not unalloyed. It was comparative, a period of less misery slipped in between a past of great miseries and a future of great miseries. For the *Ghost*, so far as the seamen were concerned, was a hell-ship of the worst description. They never had a moment's rest or peace. Wolf Larsen treasured against them the attempt on his life and the drubbing he had received in the forecastle; and morning, noon and night, and all night as well, he devoted himself to making life unlivable for them.

He knew well the psychology of the little thing, and it was the little things by which he kept the crew worked up to the verge of madness. I have seen Harrison called from his bunk to put properly away a misplaced paint-brush, and the two watches below haled from their tired sleep to accompany him and see him do it. A little thing, truly, but when multiplied by the thousand ingenious devices of such a mind, the mental state of the men in the forecastle may be slightly comprehended.

Of course much grumbling went on, and little outbursts were continually occurring. Blows were struck, and there were always two or three men nursing injuries at the hands of the human beast who was their master. Concerted action was impossible in face of the heavy arsenal of weapons carried in the steerage and cabin. Leach and Johnson were the two particular victims of Wolf Larsen's diabolic temper, and the look of profound melancholy which had settled on Johnson's face and in his eyes made my heart bleed.

With Leach it was different. There was too much of the fighting beast in him. He seemed possessed by an insatiable fury which gave no time for grief. His lips had become distorted into a permanent snarl, which at mere sight of Wolf Larsen broke out in sound, horrible and menacing, and, I do believe, unconsciously. I have seen him follow Wolf Larsen about with his eyes, like an animal its keeper, the while the animal-like snarl sounded deep in his throat and vibrated forth between his teeth.

I remember once, on deck, in bright day, touching him on the shoulder as preliminary to giving an order. His back was toward me, and at the first feel of my hand he leaped upright in the air and away from me, snarling and turning his head as he leaped. He had for the moment mistaken me for the man he hated.

Both he and Johnson would have killed Wolf Larsen at the slightest opportunity, but the opportunity never came. Wolf Larsen was too wise for that, and, besides, they had no adequate weapons. With their fists alone they had no chance whatever. Time and again he fought it out with Leach, who fought back, always, like a wildcat, tooth and nail and fist, until stretched, exhausted or unconscious, on the deck. And he was never averse to another encounter. All the devil that was in him challenged the devil in Wolf Larsen. They had but to appear on deck at the same time, when they would be at it, cursing, snarling, striking; and I have seen Leach fling himself on Wolf Larsen without warning or provocation. Once he threw his heavy sheath-knife, missing Wolf Larsen's throat by an inch. Another time he dropped a steel marlinspike from the mizzen crosstree. It was a difficult cast to make on a rolling ship. But the sharp point of the spike, whistling seventy-five feet through the air, barely missed Wolf Larsen's head as he emerged from the cabin companionway and drove its length two inches and over into the solid deck-planking. Still another time, he stole into the steerage, possessed himself of a loaded shot-gun, and was making a rush for the deck with it when caught by Kerfoot and disarmed.

I often wondered why Wolf Larsen did not kill him and make an end of it. But he only laughed and seemed to enjoy it. There seemed a certain spice about it, such as men must feel who take delight in making pets of ferocious animals.

"It gives a thrill to life," he explained to me, "when life is carried in one's hand. Man is a natural gambler, and life is the biggest stake he can lay. The greater the odds, the greater the thrill. Why should I deny myself the joy of exciting Leach's soul to fever-pitch? For that matter, I do him a kindness. The greatness of sensation is mutual. He is living more royally than any man for'ard, though he does not know it. For he has what they have not—purpose, something to do and be done, an all-absorbing end to strive to attain, the desire to kill me, the hope that he may kill me. Really, Hump, he is living deep and high. I doubt that he has ever lived so swiftly and keenly before, and I honestly envy him, sometimes, when I see him raging at the summit of passion and sensibility."

"Ah, but it is cowardly, cowardly!" I cried. "You have all the advantage."

"Of the two of us, you and I, who is the greater coward?" he asked seriously. "If the situation is unpleasing, you compromise with your conscience when you make yourself a party to it. If you were really great, really true to yourself, you would join forces with Leach and Johnson. But you are afraid, you are afraid. You want to live. The life that is in you cries out that it must live, no matter what the cost; so you live ignominiously, untrue to the best you dream of, sinning against your whole pitiful little code, and, if there were a hell, heading your soul straight for it. Bah! I play the braver part. I do no sin, for I am true to the promptings of the life that is in me. I am sincere with my soul at least, and that is what you are not."

There was a sting in what he said. Perhaps, after all, I was playing a cowardly part. And the more I thought about it the more it appeared that my duty to myself lay in doing what he had advised, lay in joining forces with Johnson and Leach and working for his death. Right here, I think, entered the austere conscience of my Puritan ancestry, impelling me toward lurid deeds and sanctioning even murder as right conduct. I dwelt upon the idea. It would be a most moral act to rid the world of such a monster. Humanity would be better and happier for it, life fairer and sweeter.

I pondered it long, lying sleepless in my bunk and reviewing in endless procession the facts of the situation. I talked with Johnson and Leach, during the night watches when Wolf Larsen was below. Both men had lost hope—Johnson, because of temperamental despondency; Leach, because he had beaten himself out in the vain struggle and was exhausted. But he caught my hand in a passionate grip one night, saying:

"I think yer square, Mr Van Weyden. But stay where you are and keep yer mouth shut. Say nothin' but saw wood. We're dead men, I know it; but all the same you might be able to do us a favor some time when we need it damn bad."

It was only next day, when Wainwright Island loomed to windward, close abeam, that Wolf Larsen opened his mouth in prophecy. He had attacked Johnson, been attacked by Leach and had just finished whipping the pair of them.

"Leach," he said, "you know I'm going to kill you some time or other, don't you?"

A snarl was the answer.

"And as for you, Johnson, you'll get so tired of life before I'm through with you that you'll fling yourself over the side. See if you don't."

"That's a suggestion," he added, in an aside to me. "I'll bet you a month's pay he acts upon it."

I cherished a hope that his victims would find an opportunity to escape while filling our water-barrels, but Wolf Larsen had selected his spot well. The *Ghost* lay half a mile beyond the surf-line of a lonely beach. Here debouched a deep gorge, with precipitous, volcanic walls which no man could scale. And here, under his direct supervision—for he went ashore himself—Leach and Johnson filled the small casks and rolled them down to the beach. They had no chance to make a break for liberty in one of the boats.

Harrison and Kelly, however, made such an attempt. They composed one of the boat's crews, and their task was to ply between the schooner and the shore, carrying a single cask each trip. Just before dinner, starting for the beach with an empty barrel, the altered their course and bore away to the left to round the promontory which jutted into the sea between them and liberty. Beyond its foaming base lay the pretty villages of the Japanese colonists, and smiling valleys which penetrated deep into the interior. Once in the fastnesses they promised, and the two men could defy Wolf Larsen.

I had observed Henderson and Smoke loitering about the deck all morning, and I now learned why they were there. Procuring their rifles, they opened fire in a leisurely manner upon the deserters. It was a cold-blooded exhibition of marksmanship. At first their bullets zipped harmlessly along the surface of the water on either side the boat; but, as the men continued to pull lustily, they struck closer and closer.

"Now watch me take Kelly's right oar," Smoke said, drawing a more careful aim.

I was looking through the glasses, and I saw the oar-blade shatter as he shot. Henderson duplicated it, selecting Harrison's right oar. The boat slewed around. The two remaining oars were quickly broken. The men tried to row with the splinters, and had them shot out of their hands. Kelly ripped up a bottom board and began paddling, but dropped it with a cry of pain as its splinters drove into his hands. Then they gave up, letting the boat drift till a second boat, sent from the shore by Wolf Larsen, took them in tow and brought them aboard.

Late that afternoon we hove up anchor and got away. Nothing was before us but the three or four months' hunting on the sealing grounds. The outlook was black indeed, and I went about my work with a heavy heart. An almost funereal gloom seemed to have descended upon the *Ghost.* Wolf Larsen had taken to his bunk with one of his strange, splitting headaches. Harrison stood listlessly at the wheel, half supporting himself by it, as though wearied by the weight of his flesh. The rest of the men were morose and silent. I came upon Kelly crouching to the lee of the forecastle scuttle, his head on his knees, his arms about his head, in an attitude of unutterable despondency.

Johnson I found lying full length on the forecastle head, staring at the troubled churn of the forefoot, and I remembered with horror the suggestion Wolf Larsen had made. It seemed likely to bear fruit. I tried to break in on the man's morbid thoughts by calling him away, but he smiled sadly at me and refused to obey.

Leach approached me as I returned aft.

"I want to ask a favor, Mr Van Weyden," he said. "If it's yer luck to ever make 'Frisco once more, will you hunt up Matt McCarthy? He's my old man. He lives on the Hill, back of the Mayfair bakery, runnin' a cobbler's shop that everybody knows, and you'll have no trouble. Tell him I lived to be sorry for the trouble I brought him and the things I done, and—and just tell him 'God bless him', for me."

I nodded my head, but said, "We'll all win back to San Francisco, Leach, and you'll be with me when I go to see Matt McCarthy."

"I'd like to believe you," he answered, shaking my hand, "but I can't. Wolf Larsen'll do for me, I know it; and all I can hope is, he'll do it quick."

And as he left me I was aware of the same desire at my heart. Since it was to be done, let it be done with dispatch. The general gloom had gathered me into its folds. The worst appeared inevitable; and as I paced the deck, hour after hour, I found myself afflicted with Wolf Larsen's repulsive ideas. What was it all about? Where was the grandeur of life that it should permit such wanton destruction of human souls? It was a cheap and sordid thing after all, this life, and the sooner over the better. Over and done with! I, too, leaned upon the rail and gazed longingly into the sea, with the certainty that sooner or later I should be sinking down, down, through the cool green depths of its oblivion.

XVII

STRANGE to say, in spite of the general foreboding, nothing of especial moment happened on the *Ghost.* We ran on to the north and west till we raised the coast of Japan and picked up with the great seal herd. Coming from no man knew where in the illimitable Pacific, it was traveling north on its annual migration to the rookeries of Bering Sea. And north we travelled with it, ravaging and destroying, flinging the naked carcasses to the shark and salting down the skins so that they might later adorn the fair shoulders of the women of the cities.

It was wanton slaughter, and all for woman's sake. No man ate the seal meat or the oil. After a good day's killing I have seen our decks covered with hides and bodies, slippery with fat and blood the scuppers running red; masts, ropes and rails spattered with the sanguinary color; and the men, like butchers plying their trade, naked and red of arm and hand, hard at work with ripping and flensing-knives, removing the skins from the pretty sea-creatures they had killed.

It was my task to tally the pelts as they came aboard from the boats, to oversee the skinning and afterward cleansing of the decks and bringing things shipshape again. It was not pleasant work. My soul and my stomach revolted at it; and yet, in a way, this handling and directing of many men was good for me. It developed what little executive ability I possessed, and I was aware of a toughening or hardening which I was undergoing and which could not be anything but wholesome for "Sissy" Van Weyden.

One thing I was beginning to feel, and that was that I could never again be quite the same man I had been. While my hope and faith in human life still survived Wolf Larsen's destructive criticism, he had nevertheless been a cause of change in minor matters. He had opened up for me the world of the real, of which I had known practically nothing and from which I had always shrunk. I had learned to look more closely at life as it was lived, to recognize that there were such things as facts in the world, to emerge from the realm of mind and idea and to place certain values on the concrete and objective phases of existence.

I saw more of Wolf Larsen than ever when we had gained the grounds. For when the weather was fair and we were in the midst of the herd, all hands were away in the boats, and left on board were only he and I, and Thomas Mugridge, who did not count. But there was no play about it. The six boats, spreading out fan-wise from the schooner until the first weather boat and the last lee boat were anywhere from ten to twenty miles apart, cruised along a straight course over the sea till nightfall or bad weather drove them in. It was our duty to sail the *Ghost* well to leeward of the last lee boat, so that all the boats should have fair wind to run for us in case of squalls or threatening weather.

It is no slight matter for two men, particularly when a stiff wind has sprung up, to handle a vessel like the *Ghost,* steering, keeping look-out for the boats, and setting or taking in sail; so it devolved upon me to learn and learn quickly. Steering I picked up easily, but running aloft to the crosstrees and swinging my whole weight by my arms when I left the ratlines and climbed still higher, was more difficult. This, too, I learned, and quickly, for I felt somehow a wild desire to vindicate myself in Wolf Larsen's eyes, to prove my right to live in ways other than of the mind. Nay, the time came when I took joy in the run of the masthead and in the clinging on by my legs at that precarious height while I swept the sea with glasses in search of the boats.

I remember one beautiful day, when the boats left early and the reports of the hunters' guns grew dim and distant and died away as they scattered far and wide over the sea. There was just the faintest wind from the westward; but it breathed its last by the time we managed to get to leeward of the last lee boat. One by one—I was at the masthead and saw—the six boats disappeared over the bulge of the earth as they followed the seal into the west. We lay, scarcely rolling on the placid sea, unable to follow. Wolf Larsen was apprehensive. The barometer was down, and the sky to the east did not please him. He studied it with unceasing vigilance.

"If she comes out of there," he said, "hard and snappy, putting us to windward of the boats, it's likely there'll be empty bunks in steerage and fo'c'sle."

By eleven o'clock the sea had become glass. By midday, though we were well up in the northerly latitudes, the heat was sickening. There was no freshness in the air. It was sultry and oppressive, reminding me of what the old Californians term "earthquake weather" . There was something ominous about it, and in intangible ways one was made to feel that the worst was about to come. Slowly the whole eastern sky filled with clouds that overtowered us like some black sierra of the infernal regions. So clearly could one see canyon, gorge and precipice, and the shadows that lie therein, that one looked unconsciously for the white surf-line and bellowing caverns where the sea charges on the land. And still we rocked gently, and there was no wind.

"It's no squall," Wolf Larsen said. "Old Mother Nature's going to get up on her hind legs and howl for all that's in her, and it'll keep us jumping, Hump, to pull through with half our boats. You'd better run up and loosen the topsails."

"But if it is going to howl, and there are only two of us?" I asked, a note of protest in my voice.

"Why we've got to make the best of the first of it and run down to our boats before our canvas is ripped out of us. After that I don't give a rap what happens. The sticks'll stand it, and you and I will have to, though we've plenty cut out for us."

Still the calm continued. We ate dinner, a hurried and anxious meal for me with eighteen men abroad on the sea and beyond the bulge of the earth, and with that heaven-rolling mountain range of clouds moving slowly down upon us. Wolf Larsen did not seem affected, however; though I noticed, when we returned to the deck, a slight twitching of the nostrils, a perceptible quickness of movement. His face was stern, the lines of it had grown hard, and yet in his eyes—blue, clear blue this day—there was a strange brilliancy, a bright scintillating light. It struck me that he was joyous, in a ferocious sort of way; that he was glad there was an impending struggle; that he was thrilled and upborne with knowledge that one of the great moments of living, when the tide of life surges up in flood, was upon him.

Once, and unwitting that he did so or that I saw, he laughed aloud, mockingly and defiantly, at the advancing storm. I see him yet, standing there like a pigmy out of the *Arabian Nights* before the huge front of some malignant genie. He was daring destiny, and he was unafraid.

He walked to the galley. "Cooky, by the time you've finished pots and pans you'll be wanted on deck. Stand ready for a call."

"Hump," he said, becoming cognizant of the fascinated gaze I bent upon him, "this beats whiskey and is where your Omar misses. I think he only half lived after all."

The western half of the sky had by now grown murky. The sun had dimmed and faded out of sight. It was two in the afternoon, and a ghostly twilight, shot through by wandering purplish lights, had descended upon us. In this purplish light Wolf Larsen's face glowed and glowed, and to my excited fancy he appeared encircled by a halo. We lay in the midst of an unearthly quiet, while all about us were signs and omens of oncoming sound and movement. The sultry heat had become unendurable. The sweat was standing on my forehead, and I could feel it trickling down my nose. I felt as though I should faint, and reached out to the rail for support.

"Cooky," Wolf Larsen called in a low voice. Thomas Mugridge turned a pitiable scared face. "Let go that fore-boom tackle and pass it across, and when she's willing let go the sheet and come in snug with the tackle. And if you make a mess of it, it will be the last you ever make. Understand?

"Mr Van Weyden, stand by to pass the head-sails over. Then jump for the topsails and spread them quick as God'll let you—the quicker you do it the easier you'll find it. As for Cooky, if he isn't lively bat him between the eyes."

I was aware of the compliment and pleased, in that no threat had accompanied my instructions. We were lying head to northwest, and it was his intention to jibe over all with the first puff.

"We'll have the breeze on our quarter," he explained to me. "By the last guns the boats were bearing away slightly to the south'ard."

He turned and walked aft to the wheel. I went forward and took my station at the jibs. Another whisper of wind, and another, passed by. The canvas flapped lazily.

"Thank Gawd she's not comin' all of a bunch, Mr Van Weyden," was the Cockney's fervent ejaculation.

And I was indeed thankful, for I had by this time learned enough to know, with all our canvas spread, what disaster in such event awaited us. The whispers of wind became puffs, the sails filled, the *Ghost* moved. Wolf Larsen put the wheel hard up, to port, and we began to pay off. The wind was now dead astern, muttering and puffing stronger and stronger, and my head-sails were pounding lustily. I did not see what went on elsewhere, though I felt the sudden surge and heel of the schooner as the wind-pressures changed to the jibing of the fore- and main-sails. My hands were full with the flying-jib, jib, and staysail; and by the time this part of my task was accomplished the *Ghost* was leaping into the southwest, the wind on her quarter and all her sheets to starboard. Without pausing for breath, though my heart was beating like a trip-hammer from my exertions, I sprang to the topsails, and before the wind had become too strong we had them fairly set and were coiling down. Then I went aft for orders.

Wolf Larsen nodded approval and relinquished the wheel to me. The wind was strengthening steadily and the sea rising. For an hour I steered, each moment becoming more difficult. I had not the experience to steer at the gait we were going on a quartering course.

"Now take a run up with the glasses and raise some of the boats. We've made at least ten knots, and we're going twelve or thirteen now. The old girl knows how to walk."

I contented myself with the fore-crosstrees, some seventy feet above the deck. As I searched the vacant stretch of water before me, I comprehended thoroughly the need for haste if we were to recover any of our men. Indeed, as I gazed at the heavy sea through which we were running, I doubted that there was a boat afloat. It did not seem possible that such frail craft could survive such stress of wind and water.

I could not feel the full force of the wind, for we were running with it; but from my lofty perch I looked down as though outside the *Ghost* and apart from her, and saw the shape of her outlined sharply against the foaming sea as she tore along instinct with life. Sometimes she would lift and send across some great wave, burying her starboard rail from view, and covering her deck to the hatches with the boiling ocean. At such moments, starting from a windward roll, I would go flying through the air with dizzying swiftness, as though I clung to the end of a huge inverted pendulum, the arc of which, between the greater rolls, must have been seventy feet or more. Once, the terror of this giddy sweep overpowered me, and for a while I clung on, hand and foot, weak and trembling, unable to search the sea for the missing boats or to behold aught of the sea but that which roared beneath and strove to overwhelm the *Ghost.*

But the thought of the men in the midst of it steadied me, and in my quest for them I forgot myself. For an hour I saw nothing but the naked, desolate sea. And then, where a vagrant shaft of sunlight struck the ocean and turned its surface to wrathful silver, I caught a small black speck thrust skyward for an instant and swallowed up. I waited patiently. Again the tiny point of black projected itself through the wrathful blaze a couple of points off our port-bow. I did not attempt to shout, but communicated the news to Wolf Larsen by waving my arm. He changed the course, and I signalled affirmation when the speck showed dead ahead.

It grew larger, and so swiftly that for the first time I fully appreciated the speed of our flight. Wolf Larsen motioned for me to come down, and when I stood beside him at the wheel gave me instructions for heaving to.

"Expect all hell to break loose," he cautioned me, "but don't mind it. Yours is to do your own work and to have Cooky stand by the fore-sheet."

I managed to make my way forward, but there was little choice of sides, for the weather-rail seemed buried as often as the lee. Having instructed Thomas Mugridge as to what he was to do, I clambered into the fore-rigging a few feet. The boat was now very close, and I could make out plainly that it was lying head to wind and sea and dragging on its mast and sail, which had been thrown overboard and made to serve as a sea-anchor. The three men were bailing. Each rolling mountain whelmed them from view, and I would wait with sickening anxiety, fearing that they would never appear again. Then, and with black suddenness, the boat would shoot clear through the foaming crest, bow pointed to the sky, and the whole length of her bottom showing, wet and dark, till she seemed on end. There would be a fleeting glimpse of the three men flinging water in frantic haste, when she would topple over and fall into the yawning valley, bow down and showing her full inside length to the stern upreared almost directly above the bow. Each time that she reappeared was a miracle.

The *Ghost* suddenly changed her course, keeping away, and it came to me with a shock that Wolf Larsen was giving up the rescue as impossible. Then I realized that he was preparing to heave to, and dropped to the deck to be in readiness. We were now dead before the wind, the boat far away and abreast of us. I felt an abrupt easing of the schooner, a loss for the moment of all strain and pressure, coupled with a swift acceleration of speed. She was rushing around on her heel into the wind.

As she arrived at right angles to the sea, the full force of the wind (from which we had hitherto run away) caught us. I was unfortunately and ignorantly facing it. It stood up against me like a wall, filling my lungs with air which I could not expel. And as I choked and strangled, and as the *Ghost* wallowed for an instant, broadside on and rolling straight over and far into the wind, I beheld a huge sea rise far above my head. I turned aside, caught my breath, and looked again. The wave overtopped the *Ghost,* and I gazed sheer up and into it. A shaft of sunlight smote the over-curl, and I caught a glimpse of translucent, rushing green, backed by a milky smother of foam.

Then it descended, pandemonium broke loose, everything happened at once. I was struck a crushing, stunning blow, nowhere in particular and yet everywhere. My hold had been broken loose, I was under water, and the thought passed through my mind that this was the terrible thing of which I had heard, the being swept in the trough of the sea. My body struck and pounded as it was dashed helplessly along and turned over and over, and when I could hold my breath no longer, I breathed the stinging salt water into my lungs. But through it all I clung to the one idea—*I must get the jib backed over to windward.* I had no fear of death. I had no doubt but that I should come through somehow. And as this idea of fulfilling Wolf Larsen's order persisted in my dazed consciousness, I seemed to see him standing at the wheel in the midst of the wild welter, pitting his will against the will of the storm and defying it.

I brought up violently against what I took to be the rail, breathed, and breathed the sweet air again. I tried to rise, but struck my head and was knocked back on hands and knees. By some freak of the waters I had been swept clear under the forecastle-head and into the eyes. As I scrambled out on all fours, I passed over the body of Thomas Mugridge, who lay in a groaning heap. There was no time to investigate. I must get the jib backed over.

When I emerged on deck it seemed that the end of everything had come. On all sides there was a rending and crashing of wood and steel and canvas. The *Ghost* was being wrenched and torn to fragments. The foresail and fore-topsail, emptied of the wind by the manoeuvre, and with no one to bring in the sheet in time, were thundering into ribbons, the heavy boom threshing and splintering from rail to rail. The air was thick with flying wreckage, detached ropes and stays were hissing and coiling like snakes, and down through it all crashed the gaff of the foresail.

The spar could not have missed me by many inches, while it spurred me to action. Perhaps the situation was not hopeless. I remembered Wolf Larsen's caution. He had expected all hell to break loose, and here it was. And where was he? I caught sight of him toiling at the main-sheet, heaving it in and flat with his tremendous muscles, the stern of the schooner lifted high in the air and his body outlined against a white surge of sea sweeping past. All this, and more—a whole world of chaos and wreck—in possibly fifteen seconds I had seen and heard and grasped.

I did not stop to see what had become of the small boat, but sprang to the jib-sheet. The jib itself was beginning to slap, partially filling and emptying with sharp reports; but with a turn of the sheet and the application of my whole strength each time it slapped, I slowly backed it. This I know: I did my best. I pulled till I burst open the ends of all my fingers; and while I pulled, the flying-jib and staysail split their cloths apart and thundered into nothingness.

Still I pulled, holding what I gained each time with a double turn until the next slap gave me more. Then the sheet gave with greater ease, and Wolf Larsen was beside me, heaving in alone while I was busied taking up the slack.

"Make fast!" he shouted. "And come on!"

As I followed him, I noted that in spite of rack and ruin a rough order obtained. The *Ghost* was hove to. She was still in working order, and she was still working. Though the rest of her sails were gone, the jib, backed to windward, and the mainsail hauled down flat, were themselves holding, and holding her bow to the furious sea as well.

I looked for the boat, and, while Wolf Larsen cleared the boat-tackles, saw it lift to leeward on a big sea and not a score of feet away. And, so nicely had he made his calculation, we drifted fairly down upon it, so that nothing remained to do but hook the tackles to either end and hoist it aboard. But this was not done so easily as it is written.

In the bow was Kerfoot, Oofty-Oofty in the stern and Kelly amidships. As we drifted closer, the boat would rise on a wave while we sank in the trough, till almost straight above me I could see the heads of the three men craned overside and looking down. Then, the next moment, we would lift and soar upward while they sank far down beneath us. It seemed incredible that the next surge should not crush the *Ghost* down upon the tiny eggshell.

But, at the right moment, I passed the tackle to the Kanaka, while Wolf Larsen did the same thing forward to Kerfoot. Both tackles were hooked in a trice, and the three men, deftly timing the roll, made a simultaneous leap aboard the schooner. As the *Ghost* rolled her side out of water, the boat was lifted snugly against her, and before the return roll came, we had heaved it in over the side and turned it bottom up on the deck. I noticed blood spouting from Kerfoot's left hand. In some way the third finger had been crushed to a pulp. But he gave no sign of pain, and with his single right hand helped us lash the boat in its place.

"Stand by to let that jib over, you Oofty!" Wolf Larsen commanded, the very second we had finished with the boat. "Kelly, come aft and slack off the main-sheet! You, Kerfoot, go for'ard and see what's become of Cooky! Mr Van Weyden, run aloft again, and cut away any stray stuff on your way!"

And having commanded, he went aft with his peculiar tigerish leaps to the wheel. While I toiled up the fore-shrouds the *Ghost* slowly paid off. This time, as we went into the trough of the sea and were swept, there were no sails to carry away. And, halfway to the crosstrees and flattened against the rigging by the full force of the wind so that it would have been impossible for me to have fallen, the *Ghost* almost on her beam-ends and the masts parallel with the water, I looked, not down, but at almost right angles from the perpendicular, to the deck of the *Ghost.* But I saw, not the deck, but where the deck should have been, for it was buried beneath a wild tumbling of water. Out of this water I could see the two masts rising, and that was all. The *Ghost,* for the moment, was buried beneath the sea. As she squared off more and more, escaping from the side pressure, she righted herself and broke her deck, like a whale's back, through the ocean surface.

Then we raced, and wildly, across the wild sea, the while I hung like a fly in the crosstrees and searched for the other boats. In half-an-hour I sighted the second one, swamped and bottom up, to which were desperately clinging Jock Horner, fat Louis and Johnson. This time I remained aloft, and Wolf Larsen succeeded in heaving to without being swept. As before, we drifted down upon it. Tackles were made fast and lines flung to the men, who scrambled aboard like monkeys. The boat itself was crushed and splintered against the schooner's side as it came inboard; but the wreck was securely lashed, for it could be patched and made whole again.

Once more the *Ghost* bore away before the storm, this time so submerging herself that for some seconds I thought she would never reappear. Even the wheel, quite a deal higher than the waist, was covered and swept again and again. At such moments I felt strangely alone with God, alone with him and watching the chaos of his wrath. And then the wheel would reappear, and Wolf Larsen's broad shoulders, his hands gripping the spokes and holding the schooner to the course of his will, himself an earth-god, dominating the storm, flinging its descending waters from him and riding it to his own ends. And oh, the marvel of it! The marvel of it! That tiny men should live and breathe and work, and drive so frail a contrivance of wood and cloth through so tremendous an elemental strife.

As before, the *Ghost* swung out of the trough, lifting her deck again out of the sea, and dashed before the howling blast. It was now half-past five, and half-an-hour later, when the last of the day lost itself in a dim and furious twilight, I sighted a third boat. It was bottom up, and there was no sign of its crew. Wolf Larsen repeated his manoeuvre, holding off and then rounding up to windward and drifting down upon it. But this time he missed by forty feet, the boat passing astern.

"Number four boat!" Oofty-Oofty cried, his keen eyes reading its number in the one second when it lifted clear of the foam, and upside down.

It was Henderson's boat, and with him had been lost Holyoak and Williams, another of the deep-water crowd. Lost they indubitably were; but the boat remained, and Wolf Larsen made one more reckless effort to recover it. I had come down to the deck, and I saw Horner and Kerfoot vainly protest against the attempt.

"By God, I'll not be robbed of my boat by any storm that ever blew out of hell!" he shouted, and though we four stood with our heads together that we might hear, his voice seemed faint and far, as though removed from us an immense distance.

"Mr Van Weyden!" he cried, and I heard through the tumult as one might hear a whisper. "Stand by that jib with Johnson and Oofty! The rest of you tail aft to the main-sheet! Lively now! Or I'll sail you all into Kingdom Come! Understand?"

And when he put the wheel hard over and the *Ghost*'s bow swung off, there was nothing for the hunters to do but obey and make the best of a risky chance. How great the risk I realized when I was once more buried beneath the pounding seas and clinging for life to the pin-rail at the foot of the foremast. My fingers were torn loose, and I swept across to the side and over the side into the sea. I could not swim, but before I could sink I was swept back again. A strong hand gripped me, and when the *Ghost* finally emerged, I found that I owed my life to Johnson. I saw him looking anxiously about him, and noted that Kelly, who had come forward at the last moment, was missing.

This time, having missed the boat, and not being in the same position as in the previous instances, Wolf Larsen was compelled to resort to a different manoeuvre. Running off before the wind with everything to starboard, he came about and returned close-hauled on the port tack.

"Grand!" Johnson shouted in my ear, as we successfully came through the attendant deluge, and I knew he referred, not to Wolf Larsen's seamanship, but to the performance of the *Ghost* herself.

It was now so dark that there was no sign of the boat; but Wolf Larsen held back through the frightful turmoil as if guided by unerring instinct. This time, though we were continually half-buried, there was no trough in which to be swept, and we drifted squarely down upon the up-turned boat, badly smashing it as it was heaved inboard.

Two hours of terrible work followed, in which all hands of us—two hunters, three sailors, Wolf Larsen and I—reefed, first one and then the other, the jib and mainsail. Hove to under this short canvas, our decks were comparatively free of water, while the *Ghost* bobbed and ducked amongst the combers like a cork.

I had burst open the ends of my fingers at the very first, and during the reefing I had worked with tears of pain running down my cheeks. And when all was done, I gave up like a woman and rolled upon the deck in the agony of exhaustion.

In the meantime Thomas Mugridge, like a drowned rat, was being dragged out from under the forecastle head where he had cravenly ensconced himself. I saw him pulled aft to the cabin and noted with a shock of surprise that the galley had disappeared. A clean space of deck showed where it had stood.

In the cabin I found all hands assembled, sailors as well, and while coffee was being cooked over the small stove we drank whiskey and crunched hard-tack. Never in my life had food been so welcome. And never had hot coffee tasted so good. So violently did the *Ghost* pitch and toss and tumble that it was impossible for even the sailors to move about without holding on, and several times, after a cry of "Now she takes it!" we were heaped upon the wall of the port cabins as though it had been the deck.

"To hell with a look-out," I heard Wolf Larsen say when we had eaten and drunk our fill. "There's nothing can be done on deck. If anything's going to run us down we couldn't get out of its way. Turn in, all hands, and get some sleep."

The sailors slipped forward, setting the side-lights as they went, while the two hunters remained to sleep in the cabin, it not being deemed advisable to open the slide to the steerage companionway. Wolf Larsen and I, between us, cut off Kerfoot's crushed finger and sewed up the stump. Mugridge, who, during all the time he had been compelled to cook and serve coffee and keep the fire going, had complained of internal pains, now swore that he had a broken rib or two. On examination we found that he had three. But his case was deferred to next day, principally for the reason that I did not know anything about broken ribs and would first have to read it up.

"I don't think it was worth it," I said to Wolf Larsen, "a broken boat for Kelly's life."

"But Kelly didn't amount to much," was the reply. "Good night."

After all that had passed, suffering intolerable anguish in my finger-ends, and with three boats missing, to say nothing of the wild capers the *Ghost* was cutting, I should have thought it impossible to sleep. But my eyes must have closed the instant my head touched the pillow, and in utter exhaustion I slept throughout the night, the while the *Ghost*, lonely and undirected, fought her way through the storm.

XVIII

THE next day, while the storm was blowing itself out, Wolf Larsen and I crammed anatomy and surgery and set Mugridge's ribs. Then, when the storm broke, Wolf Larsen cruised back and forth over that portion of the ocean where we had encountered it, and somewhat more to the westward, while the boats were being repaired and new sails made and bent. Sealing schooner after sealing schooner we sighted and boarded, most of which were in search of lost boats, and most of which were carrying boats and crews they had picked up and which did not belong to them. For the thick of the fleet had been to the westward of us, and the boats, scattered far and wide, had headed in mad flight for the nearest refuge.

Two of our boats, with men all safe, we took off the *Cisco,* and, to Wolf Larsen's huge delight and my own grief, he culled Smoke, with Nilson and Leach, from the *San Diego.* So that, at the end of five days, we found ourselves short but four men—Henderson, Holyoak, Williams and Kelly—and were once more hunting on the flanks of the herd.

As we followed it north we began to encounter the dreaded sea-fogs. Day after day the boats lowered and were swallowed up almost ere they touched the water, while we on board pumped the horn at regular intervals and every fifteen minutes fired the bomb gun. Boats were continually being lost and found, it being the custom for a boat to hunt, on lay, with whatever schooner picked it up, until such time it was recovered by its own schooner. But Wolf Larsen, as was to be expected, being a boat short, took possession of the first stray one and compelled its men to hunt with the *Ghost,* not permitting them to return to their own schooner when we sighted it. I remember how he forced the hunter and his two men below, a rifle at their breasts, when their captain passed by at biscuit-toss and hailed us for information.

Thomas Mugridge, so strangely and pertinaciously clinging to life, was soon limping about again and performing his double duties of cook and cabin-boy. Johnson and Leach were bullied and beaten as much as ever, and they looked for their lives to end with the end of the hunting season; while the rest of the crew lived the lives of dogs and were worked like dogs by their pitiless master. As for Wolf Larsen and myself, we got along fairly well; though I could not quite rid myself of the idea that right conduct, for me, lay in killing him. He fascinated me immeasurably, and I feared him immeasurably. And yet, I could not imagine him lying prone in death. There was an endurance, as of perpetual youth, about him, which rose up and forbade the picture. I could see him only as living always, and dominating always, fighting and destroying, himself surviving.

One diversion of his, when we were in the midst of the herd and the sea was too rough to lower the boats, was to lower with two boat-pullers and a steerer and go out himself. He was a good shot, too, and brought many a skin aboard under what the hunters termed impossible hunting conditions. It seemed the breath of his nostrils, this carrying his life in his hands and struggling for it against tremendous odds.

I was learning more and more seamanship; and one clear day—a thing we rarely encountered now—I had the satisfaction of running and handling the *Ghost* and picking up the boats myself. Wolf Larsen had been smitten with one of his headaches, and I stood at the wheel from morning until evening, sailing across the ocean after the last lee boat and heaving to and picking it and the other five up without command or suggestion from him.

Gales we encountered now and again, for it was a raw and stormy region, and, in the middle of June, a typhoon most memorable to me and most important because of the changes wrought through it upon my future. We must have been caught nearly at the centre of this circular storm, and Wolf Larsen ran out of it and to the southward, first under a double-reefed jib, and finally under bare poles. Never had I imagined so great a sea. The seas previously encountered were as ripples compared with these, which ran a half mile from crest to crest and which upreared, I am confident, above our masthead. So great was it that Wolf Larsen himself did not dare heave to, though he was being driven far to the southward and out of the seal herd.

We must have been well in the path of the trans-Pacific steamships when the typhoon moderated, and here, to the surprise of the hunters, we found ourselves in the midst of seals—a second herd, or sort of rear-guard, they declared, and a most unusual thing. But it was "Boats over!" the boom-boom of guns, and the pitiful slaughter through the long day.

It was at this time that I was approached by Leach. I had just finished tallying the skins of the last boat aboard, when he came to my side, in the darkness, and said in a low tone:

"Can you tell me, Mr Van Weyden, how far we are off the coast, and what the bearings of Yokohama are?"

My heart leaped with gladness, for I knew what he had in mind, and I gave him the bearings—west-northwest and five hundred miles away.

"Thank you, sir," was all he said as he slipped back into the darkness.

Next morning No. 3 boat and Johnson and Leach were missing. The water-breakers and grub-boxes from all the other boats were likewise missing, as were the beds and sea bags of the two men. Wolf Larsen was furious. He set sail and bore away into the west-northwest, two hunters constantly at the mastheads and sweeping the sea with glasses, himself pacing the deck like an angry lion. He knew too well my sympathy for the runaways to send me aloft as look-out.

The wind was fair but fitful, and it was like looking for a needle in a haystack to raise that tiny boat out of the blue immensity. But he put the *Ghost* through her best paces so as to get between the deserters and the land. This accomplished he cruised back and forth across what he knew must be their course.

On the morning of the third day, shortly after eight bells, a cry that the boat was sighted came down from Smoke at the masthead. All hands lined the rail. A snappy breeze was blowing from the west with the promise of more wind behind it; and there, to leeward, in the troubled silver of the rising sun, appeared and disappeared a black speck.

We squared away and ran for it. My heart was as lead. I felt myself turning sick in anticipation; and as I looked at the gleam of triumph in Wolf Larsen's eyes, his form swam before me and I felt almost irresistibly impelled to fling myself upon him. So unnerved was I by the thought of impending violence to Leach and Johnson that my reason must have left me. I know that I slipped down into the steerage in a daze, and that I was just beginning the ascent to the deck, a loaded shot-gun in my hands, when I heard the startled cry:

"There's five men in that boat!"

I supported myself in the companionway, weak and trembling, while the observation was being verified by the remarks of the rest of the men. Then my knees gave from under me and I sank down, myself again, but overcome by shock at knowledge of what I had so nearly done. Also, I was very thankful as I put the gun away and slipped back on deck.

No one had remarked my absence. The boat was near enough for us to make out that it was larger than any sealing boat and built on different lines. As we drew closer, the sail was taken in and the mast unstepped. Oars were shipped, and its occupants waited for us to heave to and take them aboard.

Smoke, who had descended to the deck and was now standing by my side, began to chuckle in a significant way. I looked at him inquiringly.

"Talk of a mess!" he giggled.

"What's wrong?" I demanded.

Again he chuckled. "Don't you see there, in the stern-sheets, on the bottom. May I never shoot a seal again if that ain't a woman!"

I looked closely, but was not sure until exclamations broke out on all sides. The boat contained four men, and its fifth occupant was certainly a woman. We were agog with excitement, all except Wolf Larsen, who was too evidently disappointed in that it was not his own boat with the two victims of his malice.

We ran down the flying jib, hauled the jib-sheets to windward and the main-sheet flat, and came up into the wind. The oars struck the water, and with a few strokes the boat was alongside. I now caught my first fair glimpse of the woman. She was wrapped in a long ulster, for the morning was raw; and I could see nothing but her face and a mass of light brown hair escaping from under the seaman's cap on her head. The eyes were large and brown and lustrous, the mouth sweet and sensitive, and the face itself a delicate oval, though sun and exposure to briny wind had burnt the face scarlet.

She seemed to me like a being from another world. I was aware of a hungry outreaching for her, as of a starving man for bread. But then, I had not seen a woman for a very long time. I know that I was lost in a great wonder, almost a stupor—this, then, was a woman?—so that I forgot myself and my mate's duties, and took no part in helping the newcomers aboard. For when one of the sailors lifted her into Wolf Larsen's down-stretched arms, she looked up into our curious faces and smiled amusedly and sweetly, as only a woman can smile, and as I had seen no one smile for so long that I had forgotten such smiles existed.

"Mr Van Weyden!"

Wolf Larsen's voice brought me sharply back to myself.

"Will you take the lady below and see to her comfort? Make up that spare port cabin. Put Cooky to work on it. And see what you can do for that face. It's burned badly."

He turned brusquely away from us and began to question the new men. The boat was cast adrift, though one of them called it a "bloody shame" with Yokohama so near.

I found myself strangely afraid of this woman I was escorting aft. Also I was awkward. It seemed to me that I was realizing for the first time what a delicate, fragile creature a woman is; and as I caught her arm to help her down the companion stairs, I was startled by its smallness and softness. Indeed, she was a slender, delicate woman as women go, but to me she was so ethereally slender and delicate that I was quite prepared for her arm to crumble in my grasp. All this, in frankness, to show my first impression, after long denial, of women in general and of Maud Brewster in particular.

"No need to go to any great trouble for me," she protested, when I had seated her in Wolf Larsen's arm-chair, which I had dragged hastily from his cabin. "The men were looking for land at any moment this morning, and the vessel should be in by night; don't you think so?"

Her simple faith in the immediate future took me aback. How could I explain to her the situation, the strange man who stalked the sea like Destiny, all that it had taken me months to learn? But I answered honestly:

"If it were any other captain except ours I should say you would be ashore in Yokohama to-morrow. But our captain is a strange man, and I beg of you to be prepared for anything—understand?—for anything."

"I—I confess I hardly do understand," she hesitated, a perturbed but not frightened expression in her eyes. "Or is it a misconception of mine that shipwrecked people are always shown every consideration? This is such a little thing, you know. We are so close to land."

"Candidly, I do not know," I strove to reassure her. "I wished merely to prepare you for the worst, if the worst is to come. This man, this captain, is a brute, a demon, and one can never tell what will be his next fantastic act."

I was growing excited, but she interrupted me with an "Oh, I see," and her voice sounded weary. To think was patently an effort. She was clearly on the verge of physical collapse.

She asked no further questions, and I vouchsafed no remarks, devoting myself to Wolf Larsen's command, which was to make her comfortable. I bustled about in quite housewifely fashion, procuring soothing lotions for her sunburn, raiding Wolf Larsen's private stores for a bottle of port I knew to be there, and directing Thomas Mugridge in the preparation of the spare stateroom.

The wind was freshening rapidly, the *Ghost* heeling over more and more, and by the time the stateroom was ready she was dashing through the water at a lively clip. I had quite forgotten the existence of Leach and Johnson, when suddenly, like a thunderclap, "Boat ho!" came down the open companionway. It was Smoke's unmistakable voice, crying from the masthead. I shot a glance at the woman, but she was leaning back in the arm-chair, her eyes closed, unutterably tired. I doubted that she had heard, and I resolved to prevent her seeing the brutality I knew would follow the capture of the deserters. She was tired. Very good. She should sleep.

There were swift commands on deck, a stamping of feet and a slapping of reef-points as the *Ghost* shot into the wind and about on the other tack. As she filled away and heeled, the arm-chair began to slide across the cabin floor, and I sprang for it just in time to prevent the rescued woman from being spilled out.

Her eyes were too heavy to suggest more than a hint of the sleepy surprise that perplexed her as she looked up at me, and she half stumbled, half tottered, as I led her to her cabin. Mugridge grinned insinuatingly in my face as I shoved him out and ordered him back to his galley work; and he won his revenge by spreading glowing reports among the hunters as to what an excellent "lydy's myde" I was proving myself to be.

She leaned heavily against me, and I do believe that she had fallen asleep again between the arm-chair and the stateroom. This I discovered when she nearly fell into the bunk during a sudden lurch of the schooner. She aroused, smiled drowsily, and was off to sleep again; and asleep I left her, under a heavy pair of sailor's blankets, her head resting on a pillow I had appropriated from Wolf Larsen's bunk.

XIX

I CAME on deck to find the *Ghost* heading up close on the port tack and cutting in to windward of a familiar spritsail close-hauled on the same tack ahead of us. All hands were on deck, for they knew that something was to happen when Leach and Johnson were dragged aboard.

It was four bells. Louis came aft to relieve the wheel. There was a dampness in the air, and I noticed he had on his oil-skins.

"What are we going to have?" I asked him.

"A healthy young slip of a gale from the breath iv it, sir," he answered, "with a splatter iv rain just to wet our gills an' no more."

"Too bad we sighted them," I said, as the *Ghost* 's bow was flung off a point by a large sea and the boat leaped for a moment past the jibs and into our line of vision.

Louis gave a spoke and temporized. "They'd never iv made the land, sir, I'm thinkin'."

"Think not?" I queried.

"No, sir. Did you feel that?" (A puff had caught the schooner, and he was forced to put the wheel up rapidly to keep her out of the wind.) " 'Tis no egg-shell'll float on this sea an hour come, an' it's a stroke iv luck for them we're here to pick 'em up."

Wolf Larsen strode aft from amidships, where he had been talking with the rescued men. The catlike springiness in his tread was a little more pronounced than usual, and his eyes were bright and snappy.

"Three oilers and a fourth engineer," was his greeting. "But we'll make sailors out of them, or boat-pullers at any rate. Now, what of the lady?"

I know not why, but I was aware of a twinge or pang, like the cut of a knife when he mentioned her. I thought it a certain silly fastidiousness on my part, but it persisted in spite of me, and I merely shrugged my shoulders in answer.

Wolf Larsen pursed his lips in a long, quizzical whistle.

"What's her name, then?" he demanded.

"I don't know," I replied. "She is asleep. She was very tired. In fact, I am waiting to hear the news from you. What vessel was it?"

"Mail steamer," he answered shortly. "The *City of Tokio,* from 'Frisco, bound for Yokohama. Disabled in that typhoon. Old tub. Opened up top and bottom like a sieve. They were adrift four days. And you don't know who or what she is, eh?—maid, wife or widow? Well, well."

He shook his head in a bantering way, and regarded me with laughing eyes.

"Are you—" I began. It was on the verge of my tongue to ask if he were going to take the castaways in to Yokohama.

"Am I what?" he asked.

"What do you intend doing with Leach and Johnson?"

He shook his head. "Really, Hump, I don't know. You see, with these additions I've about all the crew I want."

"And they've about all the escaping they want," I said. "Why not give them a change of treatment? Take them aboard, and deal gently with them. Whatever they have done they have been hounded into doing."

"By me?"

"By you," I answered steadily. "And I give you warning, Wolf Larsen, that I may forget love of my own life in the desire to kill you if you go too far in maltreating those poor wretches."

"Bravo!" he cried. "You do me proud, Hump! You've found your legs with a vengeance. You're quite an individual. You were unfortunate in having your life cast in easy places, but you're developing, and I like you the better for it."

His voice and expression changed. His face was serious. "Do you believe in promises?" he asked. "Are they sacred things?"

"Of course," I answered.

"Then here's a compact," he went on, consummate actor that he was. "If I promise not to lay my hands upon Leach and Johnson, will you promise, in turn, not to attempt to kill me?"

"Oh, not that I'm afraid of you, not that I'm afraid of you," he hastened to add.

I could hardly believe my ears. What was coming over the man?

"Is it a go?" he asked impatiently.

"A go," I answered.

His hand went out to mine, and as I shook it heartily I could have sworn I saw the mocking devil shine up for a moment in his eyes.

We strolled across the poop to the lee side. The boat was close at hand now, and in desperate plight. Johnson was steering, Leach bailing. We overhauled them about two feet to their one. Wolf Larsen motioned Louis to keep off slightly, and we dashed abreast of the boat, not a score of feet to windward. The *Ghost* blanketed it. The spritsail flapped emptily and the boat righted to an even keel, causing the two men swiftly to change position. The boat lost headway, and, as we lifted on a huge surge, toppled and fell into the trough.

It was at this moment that Leach and Johnson looked up into the faces of their shipmates, who lined the rail amidships. There was no greeting. They were as dead men in their comrades' eyes and between them was the gulf that parts the living and the dead.

The next instant they were opposite the poop, where stood Wolf Larsen and I. We were falling in the trough, they were rising on the surge. Johnson looked at me, and I could see that his face was worn and haggard. I waved my hand to him, and he answered the greeting, but with a wave that was hopeless and despairing. It was as if he were saying farewell. I did not see into the eyes of Leach, for he was looking at Wolf Larsen, the old and implacable snarl of hatred strong as ever on his face.

Then they were gone astern. The spritsail filled with the wind, suddenly, careening the frail open craft till it seemed it would surely capsize. A whitecap foamed above it and broke across in a snow-white smother. Then the boat emerged, half swamped, Leach flinging the water out and Johnson clinging to the steering-oar, his face white and anxious.

Wolf Larsen barked a short laugh in my ear and strode away to the weather side of the poop. I expected him to give orders for the *Ghost* to heave to, but she kept on her course and he made no sign. Louis stood imperturbably at the wheel, but I noticed the grouped sailors forward turning troubled faces in our direction. Still the *Ghost* tore alone, till the boat dwindled to a speck, when Wolf Larsen's voice rang out in command and he went about on the starboard tack.

Back we held, two miles and more to windward of the struggling cockle-shell, when the flying jib was run down and the schooner hove to. The sealing boats are not made for windward work. Their hope lies in keeping a weather position so that they may run before the wind for the schooner when it breezes up. But in all that wild waste there was no refuge for Leach and Johnson save on the *Ghost*, and they resolutely began the windward beat. It was slow work in the heavy sea that was running. At any moment they were liable to be overwhelmed by the hissing combers. Time and again and countless times we watched the boat luff into the big whitecaps, lose headway, and be flung back like a cork.

Johnson was a splendid seaman, and he knew as much about small boats as he did about ships. At the end of an hour and a half he was nearly alongside, standing past our stern on the last leg out, aiming to fetch us on the next leg back.

"So you've changed your mind?" I heard Wolf Larsen mutter, half to himself, half to them as though they could hear. "You want to come aboard, eh? Well, then, just keep a-coming."

"Hard up with that helm!" he commanded Oofty-Oofty, the Kanaka, who had in the meantime relieved Louis at the wheel.

Command followed command. As the schooner paid off, the fore- and main-sheets were slacked away for fair wind. And before the wind we were, and leaping, when Johnson, easing his sheet at imminent peril, cut across our wake a hundred feet away. Again Wolf Larsen laughed, at the same time beckoning them with his arm to follow. It was evidently his intention to play with them—a lesson, I took it, in lieu of a beating, though a dangerous lesson, for the frail craft stood in momentary danger of being overwhelmed.

Johnson squared away promptly and ran after us. There was nothing else for him to do. Death stalked everywhere, and it was only a matter of time when some one of those many huge seas would fall upon the boat, roll over it, and pass on.

" 'Tis the fear iv death at the hearts iv them," Louis muttered in my ear, as I passed forward to see to taking in the flying jib and staysail.

"Oh, he'll heave to in a little while and pick them up," I answered cheerfully. "He's bent upon giving them a lesson, that's all."

Louis looked at me shrewdly. "Think so?" he asked.

"Surely," I answered. "Don't you?"

"I think nothing but iv my own skin, these days," was his answer. "An' 'tis with wonder I'm filled as to the workin' out iv things. A pretty mess that 'Frisco whiskey got me into, an' a prettier mess that woman's got you into aft there. Ah, it's myself that knows ye for a blitherin' fool."

"What do you mean?" I demanded; for, having sped his shaft, he was turning away.

"What do I mean?" he cried. "And it's you that asks me! 'Tis not what I mean, but what the Wolf'll mean. The Wolf, I said, the Wolf!"

"If trouble comes, will you stand by?" I asked impulsively, for he had voiced my own fear.

"Stand by? 'Tis old fat Louis I stand by, an' trouble enough it'll be. We're at the beginnin' iv things, I'm tellin' ye, the bare beginnin' iv things."

"I had not thought you so great a coward," I sneered.

He favored me with a contemptuous stare. "If I raised never a hand for that poor fool"—pointing astern to the tiny sail—"d'ye think I'm hungerin' for a broken head for a woman I never laid me eyes upon before this day?"

I turned scornfully away and went aft.

"Better get in those topsails, Mr Van Weyden," Wolf Larsen said, as I came on the poop.

I felt relief, at least as far as the two men were concerned. It was clear he did not wish to run too far away from them. I picked up hope at the thought and put the order swiftly into execution. I had scarcely opened my mouth to issue the necessary commands, when eager men were springing to halyards and downhauls, and others were racing aloft. This eagerness on their part was noted by Wolf Larsen with a grim smile.

Still we increased our lead, and when the boat had dropped astern several miles we hove to and waited. All eyes watched it coming, even Wolf Larsen's; but he was the only unperturbed man aboard. Louis, gazing fixedly, betrayed a trouble in his face he was not quite able to hide.

The boat drew closer and closer, hurling along through the seething green like a thing alive, lifting and sending and uptossing across the huge-backed breakers, or disappearing behind them only to rush into sight again and shoot skyward. It seemed impossible that it could continue to live, yet with each dizzying sweep it did achieve the impossible. A rain-squall drove past, and out of the flying wet the boat emerged, almost upon us.

"Hard up, there!" Wolf Larsen shouted, himself springing to the wheel and whirling it over.

Again the *Ghost* sprang away and raced before the wind, and for two hours Johnson and Leach pursued us. We hove to and ran away, hove to and ran away, and ever astern the struggling patch of sail tossed skyward and fell into the rushing valleys. It was a quarter of a mile away when a thick squall of rain veiled it from view. It never emerged. The wind blew the air clear again, but no patch of sail broke the troubled surface. I thought I saw, for an instant, the boat's bottom show black in a breaking crest. At the best, that was all. For Johnson and Leach the travail of existence had ceased.

The men remained grouped amidships. No one had gone below, and no one was speaking. Nor were any looks being exchanged. Each man seemed stunned—deeply contemplative, as it were, and, not quite sure, trying to realize just what had taken place. Wolf Larsen gave them little time for thought. He at once put the *Ghost* upon her course—a course which meant the seal herd and not Yokohama harbor. But the men were no longer eager as they pulled and hauled, and I heard curses amongst them, which left their lips smothered and as heavy and lifeless as were they. Not so was it with the hunters. Smoke the irrepressible related a story, and they descended into the steerage, bellowing with laughter.

As I passed to leeward of the galley on my way aft, I was approached by the engineer we had rescued. His face was white, his lips were trembling.

"Good God! sir, what kind of a craft is this?" he cried.

"You have eyes, you have seen," I answered, almost brutally, what of the pain and fear at my own heart.

"Your promise?" I said to Wolf Larsen.

"I was not thinking of taking them aboard when I made that promise," he answered. "And anyway, you'll agree I've not laid my hands upon them.

"Far from it, far from it," he laughed a moment later.

I made no reply. I was incapable of speaking, my mind was too confused. I must have time to think, I knew. This woman, sleeping even now in the spare cabin, was a responsibility which I must consider, and the only rational thought that flickered through my mind was that I must do nothing hastily if I were to be any help to her at all.

XX

THE remainder of the day passed uneventfully. The young slip of a gale, having wetted our gills, proceeded to moderate. The fourth engineer and the three oilers, after a warm interview with Wolf Larsen, were furnished with outfits from the slop-chests, assigned places under the hunters in the various boats and watches on the vessel, and bundled forward into the forecastle. They went protestingly, but their voices were not loud. They were awed by what they had already seen of Wolf Larsen's character, while the tale of woe they speedily heard in the forecastle took the last bit of rebellion out of them.

Miss Brewster—we had learned her name from the engineer—slept on and on. At supper I requested the hunters to lower their voices, so she was not disturbed; and it was not till next morning that she made her appearance. It had been my intention to have her meals served apart, but Wolf Larsen put down his foot. Who was she that she should be too good for cabin table and cabin society? had been his demand.

But her coming to the table had something amusing in it. The hunters fell silent as clams. Jock Horner and Smoke alone were unabashed, stealing stealthy glances at her now and again, and even taking part in the conversation. The other four men glued their eyes on their plates and chewed steadily and with thoughtful precision, their ears moving and wobbling, in time with their jaws, like the ears of so many animals.

Wolf Larsen had little to say at first, doing no more than reply when he was addressed. Not that he was abashed. Far from it. This woman was a new type to him, a different breed from any he had ever known, and he was curious. He studied her, his eyes rarely leaving her face unless to follow the movements of her hands or shoulders. I studied her myself, and though it was I who maintained the conversation, I know that I was a bit shy, not quite self-possessed. His was the perfect poise, the supreme confidence in self, which nothing could shake; and he was no more timid of a woman than he was of storm and battle.

"And when shall we arrive at Yokohama?" she asked, turning to him and looking him squarely in the eyes.

There it was, the question flat. The jaws stopped working, the ears ceased wobbling, and though eyes remained glued on plates, each man listened greedily for the answer.

"In four months, possibly three if the season closes early," Wolf Larsen said.

She caught her breath, and stammered, "I—I thought—I was given to understand that Yokohama was only a day's sail away. It—" Here she paused and looked about the table at the circle of unsympathetic faces staring hard at the plates. "It is not right," she concluded.

"That is a question you must settle with Mr Van Weyden there," he replied, nodding to me with a mischievous twinkle. "Mr Van Weyden is what you may call an authority on such things as rights. Now I, who am only a sailor, would look upon the situation somewhat differently. It may possibly be your misfortune that you have to remain with us, but it is certainly our good fortune."

He regarded her smilingly. Her eyes fell before his gaze, but she lifted them again, and defiantly, to mine. I read the unspoken question there: was it right? But I had decided that the part I was to play must be a neutral one, so I did not answer.

"What do you think?" she demanded.

"That it is unfortunate, especially if you have any engagements falling due in the course of the next several months. But, since you say that you were voyaging to Japan for your health, I can assure you that it will improve no better anywhere than aboard the *Ghost.*"

I saw her eyes flash with indignation, and this time it was I who dropped mine, while I felt my face flushing under her gaze. It was cowardly, but what else could I do?

"Mr Van Weyden speaks with the voice of authority," Wolf Larsen laughed.

I nodded my head, and she, having recovered herself, waited expectantly.

"Not that he is much to speak of now," Wolf Larsen went on, "but he has improved wonderfully. You should have seen him when he came on board. A more scrawny, pitiful specimen of humanity one could hardly conceive. Isn't that so, Kerfoot?"

Kerfoot, thus directly addressed, was startled into dropping his knife on the floor, though he managed to grunt affirmation.

"Developed himself by peeling potatoes and washing dishes. Eh, Kerfoot?"

Again that worthy grunted.

"Look at him now. True, he is not what you would term muscular, but still he has muscles, which is more than he had when he came aboard. Also he has legs to stand on. You would not think so to look at him, but he was quite unable to stand alone at first."

The hunters were snickering, but she looked at me with a sympathy in her eyes which more than compensated for Wolf Larsen's nastiness. In truth, it had been so long since I had received sympathy that I was softened, and I became then, and gladly, her willing slave. But I was angry with Wolf Larsen. He was challenging my manhood with his slurs, challenging the very legs he claimed to be instrumental in getting for me.

"I may have learned to stand on my own legs," I retorted. "But I have yet to stamp upon others with them."

He looked at me insolently. "Your education is only half completed, then," he said dryly, and turned to her.

"We are very hospitable upon the *Ghost.* Mr Van Weyden has discovered that. We do everything to make our guests feel at home, eh, Mr Van Weyden?"

"Even to the peeling of potatoes and the washing of dishes," I answered, "to say nothing to wringing their necks out of very fellowship."

"I beg of you not to receive false impressions of us from Mr Van Weyden," he interposed with mock anxiety. "You will observe, Miss Brewster, that he carries a dirk in his belt, a—ahem—a most unusual thing for a ship's officer to do. While really very estimable, Mr Van Weyden is sometimes—how shall I say?—er—quarrelsome, and harsh measures are necessary. He is quite reasonable and fair in his calm moments, and as he is calm now he will not deny that only yesterday he threatened my life."

I was well-nigh choking, and my eyes were certainly fiery. He drew attention to me.

"Look at him now. He can scarcely control himself in your presence. He is not accustomed to the presence of ladies anyway. I shall have to arm myself before I dare go on deck with him."

He shook his head sadly, murmuring, "Too bad, too bad," while the hunters burst into guffaws of laughter.

The deep-sea voices of these men, rumbling and bellowing in the confined space, produced a wild effect. The whole setting was wild, and for the first time, regarding this strange woman and realizing how incongruous she was in it, I was aware of how much a part of it I was myself. I knew these men and their mental processes, was one of them myself, living the seal-hunting life, eating the seal-hunting fare, thinking, largely, the seal-hunting thoughts. There was for me no strangeness to it, to the rough clothes, the coarse faces, the wild laughter, and the lurching cabin walls and swaying sea-lamps.

As I buttered a piece of bread my eyes chanced to rest upon my hand. The knuckles were skinned and inflamed clear across, the fingers swollen, the nails rimmed with black. I felt the mattress-like growth of beard on my neck, knew that the sleeve of my coat was ripped, that a button was missing from the throat of the blue shirt I wore. The dirk mentioned by Wolf Larsen rested in its sheath on my hip. It was very natural that it should be there—how natural I had not imagined until now, when I looked upon it with her eyes and knew how strange it and all that went with it must appear to her.

But she divined the mockery in Wolf Larsen's words, and again favored me with a sympathetic glance. But there was a look of bewilderment also in her eyes. That it was mockery made the situation more puzzling to her.

"I may be taken off by some passing vessel, perhaps," she suggested.

"There will be no passing vessels, except other sealing schooners," Wolf Larsen made answer.

"I have no clothes, nothing," she objected. "You hardly realize, sir, that I am not a man, or that I am unaccustomed to the vagrant, careless life which you and your men seem to lead."

"The sooner you get accustomed to it, the better," he said.

"I'll furnish you with cloth, needles and thread," he added. "I hope it will not be too dreadful a hardship for you to make yourself a dress or two."

She made a wry pucker with her mouth, as though to advertise her ignorance of dressmaking. That she was frightened and bewildered, and that she was bravely striving to hide it, was quite plain to me.

"I suppose you're like Mr Van Weyden there, accustomed to having things done for you. Well, I think doing a few things for yourself will hardly dislocate any joints. By the way, what do you do for a living?"

She regarded him with amazement unconcealed.

"I mean no offence, believe me. People eat, therefore they must procure the wherewithal. These men here shoot seals in order to live; for the same reason I sail this schooner; and Mr Van Weyden, for the present at any rate, earns his salty grub by assisting me. Now what do you do?"

She shrugged her shoulders.

"Do you feed yourself? Or does someone else feed you?"

"I'm afraid someone else has fed me most of my life," she laughed, trying bravely to enter into the spirit of his quizzing, though I could see a terror dawning and growing in her eyes as she watched Wolf Larsen.

"And I suppose someone else makes your bed for you?"

"I *have* made beds," she replied.

"Very often?"

She shook her head with mock ruefulness.

"Do you know what they do to poor men in the States, who, like you, do not work for their living?"

"I am very ignorant," she pleaded. "What do they do to the poor men who are like me?"

"They send them to jail. The crime of not earning a living, in their case, is called vagrancy. If I were Mr Van Weyden, who harps eternally on questions of right and wrong, I'd ask by what right do you live when you do nothing to deserve living?"

"But as you are not Mr Van Weyden, I don't have to answer, do I?"

She beamed upon him through her terror-filled eyes, and the pathos of it cut me to the heart. I must in some way break in and lead the conversation into other channels.

"Have you ever earned a dollar by your own labor?" he demanded, certain of her answer, a triumphant vindictiveness in his voice.

"Yes, I have," she answered slowly, and I could have laughed aloud at his crestfallen visage. "I remember my father giving me a dollar once, when I was a little girl, for remaining absolutely quiet for five minutes."

He smiled indulgently.

"But that was long ago," she continued. "And you would scarcely demand a little girl of nine to earn her own living."

"At present, however," she said, after another slight pause, "I earn about eighteen hundred dollars a year."

With one accord, all eyes left the plates and settled on her. A woman who earned eighteen hundred dollars a year was worth looking at. Wolf Larsen was undisguised in his admiration.

"Salary or piece-work?" he asked.

"Piece-work," she answered promptly.

"Eighteen hundred," he calculated. "That's a hundred and fifty dollars a month. Well, Miss Brewster, there is nothing small about the *Ghost*. Consider yourself on salary during the time you remain with us."

She made no acknowledgement. She was too unused as yet to the whims of the man to accept them with equanimity.

"I forgot to inquire," he went on suavely, "as to the nature of your occupation. What commodities do you turn out? What tools and materials do you require?"

"Paper and ink," she laughed. "And, oh! also a typewriter."

"You are Maud Brewster," I said slowly and with certainty, almost as though I were charging her with a crime.

Her eyes lifted curiously to mine. "How do you know?"

"Aren't you?" I demanded.

She acknowledged her identity with a nod. It was Wolf Larsen's turn to be puzzled.

The name and its magic signified nothing to him. I was proud that it did mean something to me, and for the first time in a weary while I was convincingly conscious of a superiority over him.

"I remember writing a review of a thin little volume—" I had begun carelessly, when she interrupted me.

"You!" she cried. "You are—"

She was now staring at me in wide-eyed wonder.

I nodded my identity, in turn.

"Humphrey Van Weyden," she concluded; then added with a sigh of relief, and unaware that she had glanced that relief at Wolf Larsen, "I am so glad."

"I remember the review," she went on hastily, becoming aware of the awkwardness of her remark, "that too, too flattering review."

"Not at all," I denied valiantly. "You impeach my sober judgement and make my canons of little worth. Besides, all my brother critics were with me. Didn't Lang include your 'Kiss Endured' among the four supreme sonnets by women in the English language?"

"But you called me the American Mrs Meynell!"

"Was it not true?" I demanded.

"No, not that," she answered. "I was hurt."

"We can measure the unknown only by the known," I replied, in my finest academic manner. "As a critic I was compelled to place you. You have now become a yardstick yourself. Seven of your thin little volumes are on my shelves; and there are two thicker volumes, the essays, which, you will pardon my saying, and I know not which is flattered more, fully equal your verse. The time is not far distant when some unknown will arise in England and the critics will name her the English Maud Brewster."

"You are very kind, I am sure," she murmured; and the very conventionality of her tones and words, with the host of associations it aroused of the old life on the other side of the world, gave me a quick thrill—rich with remembrance but stinging sharp with homesickness.

"And you are Maud Brewster," I said solemnly, gazing across at her.

"And you are Humphrey Van Weyden," she said, gazing back at me with equal solemnity and awe. "How unusual! I don't understand. We surely are not to expect some wildly romantic sea-story from your sober pen?"

"No, I am not gathering material, I assure you," was my answer. "I have neither aptitude nor inclination for fiction."

"Tell me, why have you always buried yourself in California?" she next asked. "It has not been kind of you. We of the East have seen so very little of you—too little, indeed, of the Dean of American Letters, the Second."

I bowed to, and disclaimed, the compliment. "I nearly met you once, in Philadelphia, some Browning affair or other—you were to lecture, you know. My train was four hours late."

And then we quite forgot where we were, leaving Wolf Larsen stranded and silent in the midst of our flood of gossip. The hunters left the table and went on deck, and still we talked. Wolf Larsen alone remained. Suddenly I became aware of him, leaning back from the table and listening curiously to our alien speech of a world he did not know.

I broke short off in the middle of a sentence. The present, with all its perils and anxieties, rushed upon me with stunning force. It smote Miss Brewster likewise, a vague and nameless terror rushing into her eyes as she regarded Wolf Larsen.

He rose to his feet and laughed awkwardly. The sound of it was metallic.

"Oh, don't mind me," he said, with a self-deprecatory wave of his hand. "I don't count. Go on, go on, I pray you."

But the gates of speech were closed, and we, too, rose from the table and laughed awkwardly.

XXI

THE chagrin Wolf Larsen felt from being ignored by Maud Brewster and me in the conversation at table had to express itself in some fashion, and it fell to Thomas Mugridge to be the victim. He had not mended his ways nor his shirt, though the latter he contended he had changed. The garment itself did not bear out the assertion, nor did the accumulations of grease on stove and pot and pan attest a general cleanliness.

"I've given you warning, Cooky," Wolf Larsen said, "and now you've got to take your medicine."

Mugridge's face turned white under its sooty veneer, and when Wolf Larsen called for a rope and a couple of men, the miserable Cockney fled wildly out of the galley and dodged and ducked about the deck with the grinning crew in pursuit. Few things could have been more to their liking than to give him a tow over the side, for to the forecastle he had sent messes and concoctions of the vilest order. Conditions favored the undertaking. The *Ghost* was slipping through the water at no more than three miles an hour, and the sea was fairly calm. But Mugridge had little stomach for a dip in it. Possibly he had seen men towed before. Besides, the water was frightfully cold, and his was anything but a rugged constitution.

As usual, the watches below and the hunters turned out for what promised sport. Mugridge seemed to be in rabid fear of the water, and he exhibited a nimbleness and speed we did not dream he possessed. Cornered in the right-angle of the poop and galley, he sprang like a cat to the top of the cabin and ran aft. But his pursuers forestalling him, he doubled back across the cabin, passed over the galley, and gained the deck by means of the steerage-scuttle. Straight forward he raced, the boat-puller Harrison at his heels and gaining on him. But Mugridge, leaping suddenly, caught the jib-boom-lift. It happened in an instant. Holding his weight by his arms, and in mid-air doubling his body at the hips, he let fly with both feet. The oncoming Harrison caught the kick squarely in the pit of the stomach, groaned involuntarily, and doubled up and sank backward to the deck.

Hand-clapping and roars of laughter from the hunters greeted the exploit, while Mugridge, eluding half of his pursuers at the foremast, ran aft and through the remainder like a runner on the football field. Straight aft he held, to the poop and along the poop to the stern. So great was his speed that as he curved past the corner of the cabin he slipped and fell. Nilson was standing at the wheel, and the Cockney's hurtling body struck his legs. Both went down together, but Mugridge alone arose. By some freak of pressures, his frail body had snapped the strong man's leg like a pipestem.

Parsons took the wheel, and the pursuit continued. Round and round the decks they went, Mugridge sick with fear, the sailors hallooing and shouting directions to one another, and the hunters bellowing encouragement and laughter. Mugridge went down on the fore-hatch under three men; but he emerged from the mass like an eel, bleeding at the mouth, the offending shirt ripped into tatters, and sprang for the main-rigging. Up he went, clear up, beyond the ratlines, to the very masthead.

Half a dozen sailors swarmed to the crosstrees after him, where they clustered and waited while two of their number, Oofty-Oofty and Black (who was Latimer's boat-steerer), continued up the thin steel stays, lifting their bodies higher and higher by means of their arms.

It was a perilous undertaking, for, at a height of over a hundred feet from the deck, holding on by their hands, they were not in the best of positions to protect themselves from Mugridge's feet. And Mugridge kicked savagely, till the Kanaka, hanging on with one hand, seized the Cockney's foot with the other. Black duplicated the performance a moment later with the other foot. Then the three writhed together in a swaying tangle, struggling, sliding, and falling into the arms of their mates on the crosstrees.

The aerial battle was over, and Thomas Mugridge, whining and gibbering, his mouth flecked with bloody foam, was brought down to deck. Wolf Larsen rove a bowline in a piece of rope and slipped it under his shoulders. Then he was carried aft and flung into the sea. Forty—fifty—sixty feet of line ran out, when Wolf Larsen cried "Belay!" Oofty-Oofty took a turn on a bitt, the rope tautened, and the *Ghost,* lunging onward, jerked the cook to the surface.

It was a pitiful spectacle. Though he could not drown, and was nine-lived in addition, he was suffering all the agonies of half-drowning. The *Ghost* was going very slowly, and when her stern lifted on a wave and she slipped forward she pulled the wretch to the surface and gave him a moment in which to breathe; but between each lift the stern fell, and while the bow lazily climbed the next wave the line slacked and he sank beneath.

I had forgotten the existence of Maud Brewster, and I remembered her with a start as she stepped lightly beside me. It was her first time on deck since she had come aboard. A dead silence greeted her appearance.

"What is the cause of the merriment?" she asked.

"Ask Captain Larsen," I answered composedly and coldly, though inwardly my blood was boiling at the thought that she should be witness to such brutality.

She took my advice and was turning to put it into execution, when her eyes lighted on Oofty-Oofty, immediately before her, his body instinct with alertness and grace as he held the turn of the rope.

"Are you fishing?" she asked him.

He made no reply. His eyes, fixed intently on the sea astern, suddenly flashed.

"Shark ho, sir!" he cried.

"Heave in! Lively! All hands tail on!" Wolf Larsen shouted, springing himself to the rope in advance of the quickest.

Mugridge had heard the Kanaka's warning cry and was screaming madly. I could see a black fin cutting the water and making for him with greater swiftness than he was being pulled aboard. It was an even toss whether the shark or we would get him, and it was a matter of moments. When Mugridge was directly beneath us, the stern descended the slope of a passing wave, thus giving the advantage to the shark. The fin disappeared. The belly flashed white in a swift upward rush. Almost equally swift, but not quite, was Wolf Larsen. He threw his strength into one tremendous jerk. The Cockney's body left the water; so did part of the shark's. He drew up his legs, and the man-eater seemed no more than barely to touch one foot, sinking back into the water with a splash. But at the moment of contact Thomas Mugridge cried out. Then he came in like a fresh-caught fish on a line, clearing the rail generously and striking the deck in a heap, on hands and knees, and rolling over.

But a fountain of blood was gushing forth. The right foot was missing, amputated neatly at the ankle. I looked instantly to Maud Brewster. Her face was white, her eyes dilated with horror. She was gazing, not at Thomas Mugridge, but at Wolf Larsen. And he was aware of it, for he said, with one of his short laughs:

"Man-play, Miss Brewster. Somewhat rougher, I warrant, than what you have been used to, but still—man-play. The shark was not in the reckoning. It—"

But at this juncture, Mugridge, who had lifted his head and ascertained the extent of his loss, floundered over on the deck and buried his teeth in Wolf Larsen's leg. Wolf Larsen stooped, coolly, to the Cockney, and pressed with thumb and finger at the rear of the jaws and below the ears. The jaws opened with reluctance, and Wolf Larsen stepped free.

"As I was saying," he went on, as though nothing unwonted had happened, "the shark was not in the reckoning. It was—ahem—shall we say Providence?"

She gave no sign that she had heard, though the expression of her eyes changed to one of inexpressible loathing as she started to turn away. She no more than started, for she swayed and tottered, and reached her hand weakly out to mine. I caught her in time to save her from falling, and helped her to a seat on the cabin. I thought she might faint outright, but she controlled herself.

"Will you get a tourniquet, Mr Van Weyden," Wolf Larsen called to me.

I hesitated. Her lips moved, and though they formed no words, she commanded me with her eyes, plainly as speech, to go to the help of the unfortunate man. "Please," she managed to whisper, and I could but obey.

By now I had developed such skill at surgery that Wolf Larsen, with a few words of advice, left me to my task with a couple of sailors for assistants. For his task he elected a vengeance on the shark. A heavy swivel-hook, baited with fat salt-pork, was dropped overside; and by the time I had compressed the severed veins and arteries, the sailors were singing and heaving in the offending monster. I did not see it myself, but my assistants, first one and then the other, deserted me for a few moments to run amidships and look at what was going on. The shark, a sixteen-footer, was hoisted up against the main-rigging. Its jaws were pried apart to their greatest extension, and a stout stake, sharpened at both ends, was so inserted that when the pries were removed the spread jaws were fixed upon it. This accomplished, the hook was cut out. The shark dropped back into the sea, helpless, yet with its full strength, doomed to lingering starvation—a living death less meet for it than for the man who devised the punishment.

XXII

I KNEW what it was as she came toward me. For ten minutes I had watched her talking earnestly with the engineer, and now, with a sign for silence, I drew her out of earshot of the helmsman. Her face was white and set; her large eyes larger than usual what of the purpose in them, looked penetratingly into mine. I felt rather timid and apprehensive, for she had come to search Humphrey Van Weyden's soul, and Humphrey Van Weyden had nothing of which to be particularly proud since his advent on the *Ghost*.

We walked to the break of the poop, where she turned and faced me. I glanced around to see that no one was within hearing distance.

"What is it?" I asked gently; but the expression of determination on her face did not relax.

"I can readily understand," she began, "that this morning's affair was largely an accident; but I have been talking with Mr Haskins. He tells me that the day we were rescued, even while I was in the cabin, two men were drowned, deliberately drowned—murdered."

There was a query in her voice, and she faced me accusingly, as though I were guilty of the deed, or at least a party to it.

"The information is quite correct," I answered. "The two men were murdered."

"And you permitted it!" she cried.

"I was unable to prevent it, is a better way of phrasing it," I replied, still gently.

"But you tried to prevent it?" There was an emphasis on the "tried" , and a pleading little note in her voice.

"Oh, but you didn't," she hurried on, divining my answer. "But why didn't you?"

I shrugged my shoulders. "You must remember, Miss Brewster, that you are a new inhabitant of this little world, and that you do not yet understand the laws which operate within it. You bring with you certain fine conceptions of humanity, manhood, conduct and such things; but here you will find them misconceptions. I have found it so," I added, with an involuntary sigh.

She shook her head incredulously.

"What would you advise, then?" I asked. "That I should take a knife, or a gun, or an axe, and kill this man?"

She half started back.

"No, not that!"

"Then what should I do? Kill myself?"

"You speak in purely materialistic terms," she objected. "There is such a thing as moral courage, and moral courage is never without effect."

"Ah," I smiled, "you advise me to kill neither him nor myself, but to let him kill me." I held up my hand as she was about to speak. "For moral courage is a worthless asset on this little floating world. Leach, one of the men who were murdered, had moral courage to an unusual degree. So had the other man, Johnson. Not only did it not stand them in good stead, but it destroyed them. And so with me if I should exercise what little moral courage I may possess.

"You must understand, Miss Brewster, and understand clearly, that this man is a monster. He is without conscience. Nothing is sacred to him, nothing is too terrible for him to do. It was due to his whim that I was detained aboard in the first place. It is due to his whim that I am still alive. I do nothing, can do nothing, because I am a slave to this monster, as you are now a slave to him; because I desire to live, as you will desire to live; because I cannot fight and overcome him, just as you will not be able to fight and overcome him."

She waited for me to go on.

"What remains? Mine is the rôle of the weak. I remain silent and suffer ignominy, as you will remain silent and suffer ignominy. And it is well. It is the best we can do if we wish to live. The battle is not always to the strong. We have not the strength with which to fight this man; we must dissimulate, and win, if win we can, by craft. If you will be advised by me, this is what you will do. I know my position is perilous, and I may say frankly that yours is even more perilous. We must stand together, without appearing to do so, in secret alliance. I shall not be able to side with you openly, and, no matter what indignities may be put upon me, you are to remain likewise silent. We must provoke no scenes with this man, nor cross his will. And we must keep smiling faces and be friendly with him no matter how repulsive it may be."

She brushed her hand across her forehead in a puzzled way, saying, "Still I do not understand."

"You must do as I say," I interrupted authoritatively, for I saw Wolf Larsen's gaze wandering toward us from where he paced up and down with Latimer amidships. "Do as I say, and ere long you will find I am right."

"What shall I do, then?" she asked, detecting the anxious glance I had shot at the object of our conversation, and impressed, I flatter myself, with the earnestness of my manner.

"Dispense with all the moral courage you can," I said briskly. "Don't arouse this man's animosity. Be quite friendly with him, talk with him, discuss literature and art with him—he is fond of such things. You will find him an interested listener and no fool. And for your own sake try to avoid witnessing, as much as you can, the brutalities of the ship. It will make it easier for you to act your part."

"I am to lie," she said in steady, rebellious tones, "by speech and action to lie."

Wolf Larsen had separated from Latimer and was coming toward us. I was desperate.

"Please, please understand me," I said hurriedly, lowering my voice. "All your experience of men and things is worthless here. You must begin over again. I know—I can see it—you have, among other ways, been used to managing people with your eyes, letting your moral courage speak out through them, as it were. You have already managed me with your eyes, commanded me with them. But don't try it on Wolf Larsen. You could as easily control a lion, while he would make a mock of you. He would—I have always been proud of the fact that I discovered him," I said, turning the conversation as Wolf Larsen stepped on the poop and joined us. "The editors were afraid of him and the publishers would have none of him. But I knew, and his genius and my judgement were vindicated when he made that magnificent hit with his 'Forge'."

"And it was a newspaper poem," she said glibly.

"It did happen to see the light in a newspaper," I replied, "but not because the magazine editors had been denied a glimpse at it."

"We were talking of Harris," I said to Wolf Larsen.

"Oh, yes," he acknowledged. "I remember the 'Forge'. Filled with pretty sentiments and an almighty faith in human illusions. By the way, Mr Van Weyden, you'd better look in on Cooky. He's complaining and restless."

Thus was I bluntly dismissed from the poop, only to find Mugridge sleeping soundly from the morphine I had given him. I made no haste to return to deck, and when I did I was gratified to see Miss Brewster in animated conversation with Wolf Larsen. As I say, the sight gratified me. She was following my advice. And yet I was conscious of a slight shock or hurt in that she was able to do the thing I had begged her to do and which she had notably disliked.

XXIII

Brave winds, blowing fair, swiftly drove the *Ghost* northward into the seal herd. We encountered it well up to the forty-fourth parallel, in a raw and stormy sea across which the wind harried the fog-banks in eternal flight. For days at a time we could never see the sun nor take an observation; then the wind would sweep the face of the ocean clean, the waves would ripple and flash, and we would learn where we were. A day of clear weather might follow, or three days or four, and then the fog would settle down upon us, seemingly thicker than ever.

The hunting was perilous; yet the boats, lowered day after day, were swallowed up in the gray obscurity, and were seen no more till nightfall, and often not till long after, when they would creep in like sea-wraiths, one by one, out of the gray. Wainwright—the hunter whom Wolf Larsen had stolen with boat and men—took advantage of the veiled sea and escaped. He disappeared one morning in the encircling fog with his two men, and we never saw them again, though it was not many days when we learned that they had passed from schooner to schooner until they finally regained their own.

This was the thing I had set my mind upon doing, but the opportunity never offered. It was not in the mate's province to go out in the boats, and though I manoeuvred cunningly for it, Wolf Larsen never granted me the privilege. Had he done so, I should have managed somehow to carry Miss Brewster away with me. As it was, the situation was approaching a stage which I was afraid to consider. I involuntarily shunned the thought of it, and yet the thought continually arose in my mind like a haunting spectre.

I had read sea-romances in my time, wherein figured, as a matter of course, the lone woman in the midst of a shipload of men; but I learned, now, that I had never comprehended the deeper significance of such a situation—the thing the writers harped upon and exploited so thoroughly. And here it was, now, and I was face to face with it. That it should be as vital as possible, it required no more than that the woman should be Maud Brewster, who now charmed me in person as she had long charmed me through her work.

No one more out of environment could be imagined. She was a delicate, ethereal creature, swaying and willowy, light and graceful of movement. It never seemed to me that she walked, or, at least, walked after the ordinary manner of mortals. Hers was an extreme lithesomeness, and she moved with a certain indefinable airiness, approaching one as down might float or as a bird on noiseless wings.

She was like a bit of Dresden china, and I was continually impressed with what I may call her fragility. As at the time I caught her arm when helping her below, so at any time I was quite prepared, should stress or rough handling befall her, to see her crumble away. I have never seen body and spirit in such perfect accord. Describe her verse, as the critics have described it, as sublimated and spiritual, and you have described her body. It seemed to partake of her soul, to have analogous attributes, and to link it to life with the slenderest of chains. Indeed, she trod the earth lightly, and in her constitution there was little of the robust clay.

She was in striking contrast to Wolf Larsen. Each was nothing that the other was, everything that the other was not. I noted them walking the deck together one morning, and I likened them to the extreme ends of the human ladder of evolution—the one the culmination of all savagery, the other the finished product of the finest civilization. True, Wolf Larsen possessed intellect to an unusual degree, but it was directed solely to the exercise of his savage instincts and made him but the more formidable a savage. He was splendidly muscled, a heavy man, and though he strode with the certitude and directness of the physical man, there was nothing heavy about his stride. The jungle and the wilderness lurked in the uplift and downput of his feet. He was cat-footed, and lithe, and strong, always strong. I likened him to some great tiger, a beast of prowess and prey. He looked it, and the piercing glitter that arose at times in his eyes was the same piercing glitter I had observed in the eyes of caged leopards and other preying creatures of the wild.

But this day, as I noted them pacing up and down, I saw that it was she who terminated the walk. They came up to where I was standing by the entrance to the companionway. Though she betrayed it by no outward sign, I felt, somehow, that she was greatly perturbed. She made some idle remark, looking at me, and laughed lightly enough; but I saw her eyes return to his, involuntarily, as though fascinated; then they fell, but not swiftly enough to veil the rush of terror that filled them.

It was in his eyes that I saw the cause of her perturbation. Ordinarily gray and cold and harsh, they were now warm and soft and golden, and all a-dance with tiny lights that dimmed and faded, or welled up till the full orbs were flooded with a glowing radiance. Perhaps it was to this that the golden color was due; but golden his eyes were, enticing and masterful, at the same time luring and compelling, and speaking a demand and clamor of the blood which no woman, much less Maud Brewster, could misunderstand.

Her own terror rushed upon me, and in that moment of fear—the most terrible fear a man can experience—I knew that in inexpressible ways she was dear to me. The knowledge that I loved her rushed upon me with the terror, and with both emotions gripping at my heart and causing my blood at the same time to chill and to leap riotously, I felt myself drawn by a power without me and beyond me, and found my eyes returning against my will to gaze into the eyes of Wolf Larsen. But he had recovered himself. The golden color and the dancing lights were gone. Cold and gray and glittering they were as he bowed brusquely and turned away.

"I am afraid," she whispered, with a shiver. "I am so afraid."

I, too, was afraid, and what of my discovery of how much she meant to me my mind was in a turmoil; but I succeeded in answering quite calmly:

"All will come right, Miss Brewster. Trust me, it will come right."

She answered with a grateful little smile that sent my heart pounding, and started to descend the companion-stairs.

For a long while I remained standing where she had left me. There was imperative need to adjust myself, to consider the significance of the changed aspect of things. It had come, at last, love had come, when I least expected it and under the most forbidding conditions. Of course, my philosophy had always recognized the inevitableness of the love-call sooner or later; but long years of bookish silence had made me inattentive and unprepared.

And now it had come! Maud Brewster! My memory flashed back to that first thin little volume on my desk, and I saw before me, as though in the concrete, the row of thin little volumes on my library shelf. How I had welcomed each of them! Each year one had come from the press, and to me each was the advent of the year. They had voiced a kindred intellect and spirit, and as such I had received them into a camaraderie of the mind; but now their place was in my heart.

My heart? A revulsion of feeling came over me. I seemed to stand outside myself and to look at myself incredulously. Maud Brewster! Humphrey Van Weyden, the "cold-blooded fish" , the "emotionless monster" , the "analytical demon" , of Charley

Furuseth's christening, in love! And then, without rhyme or reason, all sceptical, my mind flew back to a small biographical note in the red-bound *Who's Who*, and I said to myself, "She was born in Cambridge, and she is twenty-seven years old." And then I said, "Twenty-seven years old and still free and fancy free?" But how did I know she was fancy free? And the pang of new-born jealousy put all incredulity to flight. There was no doubt about it. I was jealous; therefore I loved. And the woman I loved was Maud Brewster.

I, Humphrey Van Weyden, was in love! And again the doubt assailed me. Not that I was afraid of it, however, or reluctant to meet it. On the contrary, idealist that I was to the most pronounced degree, my philosophy had always recognized and guerdoned love as the greatest thing in the world, the aim and the summit of being, the most exquisite pitch of joy and happiness to which life could thrill, the thing of all things to be hailed and welcomed and taken into the heart. But now that it had come I could not believe. I could not be so fortunate. It was too good, too good to be true. Symons's lines came into my head:

"I wandered all these years among
A world of women, seeking you."

And then I had ceased seeking. It was not for me, this greatest thing in the world, I had decided. Furuseth was right; I was abnormal, an "emotionless monster" , a strange bookish creature, capable of pleasuring in sensations only of the mind. And though I had been surrounded by women all my days, my appreciation of them had been aesthetic and nothing more. I had actually, at times, considered myself outside the pale, a monkish fellow denied the eternal or the passing passions I saw and understood so well in others. And now it had come! Undreamed of and unheralded, it had come. In what could have been no less than an ecstasy, I left my post at the head of the companionway and started along the deck, murmuring to myself those beautiful lines of Mrs Browning:

"I lived with visions for my company
Instead of men and women years ago,
And found them gentle mates, nor thought to know
A sweeter music than they played to me."

But the sweeter music was playing in my ears, and I was blind and oblivious to all about me. The sharp voice of Wolf Larsen aroused me.

"What the hell are you up to?" he was demanding.

I had strayed forward where the sailors were painting, and I came to myself to find my advancing foot on the verge of overturning a paint-pot.

"Sleep-walking, sunstroke—what?" he barked.

"No, indigestion," I retorted, and continued my walk as if nothing untoward had occurred.

XXIV

AMONG the most vivid memories of my life are those of the events on the *Ghost* which occurred during the forty hours succeeding the discovery of my love for Maud Brewster. I, who had lived my life in quiet places, only to enter at the age of thirty-five upon a course of the most irrational adventure I could have imagined, never had more incident and excitement crammed into any forty hours of my experience. Nor can I quite close my ears to a small voice of pride which tells me I did not do so badly, all things considered.

To begin with, at the midday dinner, Wolf Larsen informed the hunters that they were to eat thenceforth in the steerage. It was an unprecedented thing on sealing-schooners, where it is the custom for the hunters to rank unofficially as officers. He gave no reason, but his motive was obvious enough. Horner and Smoke had been displaying a gallantry toward Maud Brewster, ludicrous in itself and inoffensive to her, but to him evidently distasteful.

The announcement was received with black silence, though the other four hunters glanced significantly at the two who had been the cause of their banishment. Jock Horner, quiet as was his way, gave no sign; but the blood surged darkly across Smoke's forehead, and he half opened his mouth to speak. Wolf Larsen was watching him, waiting for him, the steely glitter in his eyes; but Smoke closed his mouth again without having said anything.

"Anything to say?" the other demanded aggressively.

It was a challenge, but Smoke refused to accept it.

"About what?" he asked, so innocently that Wolf Larsen was disconcerted, while the others smiled.

"Oh, nothing," Wolf Larsen said lamely. "I just thought you might want to register a kick."

"About what?" asked the imperturbable Smoke.

Smoke's mates were now smiling broadly. His captain could have killed him, and I doubt not that blood would have flowed had not Maud Brewster been present. For that matter, it was her presence which enabled Smoke to act as he did. He was too discreet and cautious a man to incur Wolf Larsen's anger at a time when that anger could be expressed in terms stronger than words. I was in fear that a struggle might take place, but a cry from the helmsman made it easy for the situation to save itself.

"Smoke ho!" the cry came down the open companionway.

"How's it bear?" Wolf Larsen called up.

"Dead astern, sir."

"Maybe it's a Russian," suggested Latimer.

His words brought anxiety into the faces of the other hunters. A Russian could mean but one thing—a cruiser. The hunters, never more than roughly aware of the position of the ship, nevertheless knew that we were close to the boundaries of the forbidden sea, while Wolf Larsen's record as a poacher was notorious. All eyes centred upon him.

"We're dead safe," he assured them with a laugh. "No salt mines this time, Smoke. But I'll tell you what—I'll lay odds of five to one it's the *Macedonia.*"

No one accepted his offer, and he went on. "In which event, I'll lay ten to one there's trouble breezing up."

"No, thank you," Latimer spoke up. "I don't object to losing my money, but I like to get a run for it, anyway. There never was a time when there wasn't trouble when you and that brother of yours got together, and I'll lay twenty to one on that."

A general smile followed, in which Wolf Larsen joined, and the dinner went on smoothly, thanks to me, for he treated me abominably the rest of the meal, sneering at me and patronizing me till I was all a-tremble with suppressed rage. Yet I knew I must control myself for Maud Brewster's sake, and I received my reward when her eyes caught mine for a fleeting second, and they said, as distinctly as if she spoke, "Be brave, be brave."

We left the table to go on deck, for a steamer was a welcome break in the monotony of the sea on which we floated, while the conviction that it was Death Larsen and the *Macedonia* added to the excitement. The stiff breeze and heavy sea which had sprung up the previous afternoon had been moderating all morning, so that it was now possible to lower the boats for an afternoon's hunt. The hunting promised to be profitable. We had sailed since daylight across a sea barren of seals, and were now running into the herd.

The smoke was still miles astern, but overhauling us rapidly, when we lowered our boats. They spread out and struck a northerly course across the ocean. Now and again we saw a sail lower, heard the reports of the shotguns, and saw the sail go up again. The seals were thick, the wind was dying away; everything favored a big catch. As we ran off to get our leeward position of the last lee boat, we found the ocean fairly carpeted with sleeping seals. They were all about us, thicker than I had ever seen them before, in twos and threes and bunches, stretched full length on the surface and sleeping for all the world like so many lazy young dogs.

Under the approaching smoke the hull and upperworks of a steamer were growing larger. It was the *Macedonia.* I read her name through the glasses as she passed by scarcely a mile to starboard. Wolf Larsen looked savagely at the vessel, while Maud Brewster was curious.

"Where is the trouble you were so sure was breezing up, Captain Larsen?" she asked gayly.

He glanced at her, a moment's amusement softening his features.

"What did you expect? That they'd come aboard and cut our throats?"

"Something like that," she confessed. "You understand, seal-hunters are so new and strange to me that I am quite ready to expect anything."

He nodded his head. "Quite right, quite right. Your error is that you failed to expect the worst."

"Why, what can be worse than cutting our throats?" she asked, with pretty naïve surprise.

"Cutting our purses," he answered. "Man is so made these days that his capacity for living is determined by the money he possesses."

" 'Who steals my purse steals trash,' " she quoted.

"Who steals my purse steals my right to live," was the reply, "old saws to the contrary. For he steals my bread and meat and bed, and in so doing imperils my life. There are not enough soup-kitchens and bread-lines to go around, you know, and when men have nothing in their purses they usually die, and die miserably—unless they are able to fill their purses pretty speedily."

"But I fail to see that this steamer has any designs on your purse."

"Wait and you will see," he answered grimly.

We did not have long to wait. Having passed several miles beyond our line of boats, the *Macedonia* proceeded to lower her own. We knew she carried fourteen boats to our five (we were one short through the desertion of Wainwright), and she began dropping them far to leeward of our last boat, continued dropping them athwart our course, and finished dropping them far to windward of our first weather boat. The hunting, for us, was spoiled. There were no seals behind us, and ahead of us the line of fourteen boats, like a huge broom, swept the herd before it.

Our boats hunted across the two or three miles of water between them and the point where the *Macedonia'* s had been dropped, and then headed for home. The wind had fallen to a whisper, the ocean was growing calmer and calmer, and this, coupled with the presence of the great herd, made a perfect hunting day—one of the two or three days to be encountered in the whole of a lucky season. An angry lot of men, boat-pullers and steerers as well as hunters, swarmed over our side. Each man felt that he had been robbed; and the boats were hoisted in amid curses, which, if curses had power, would have settled Death Larsen for all eternity—"Dead and damned for a dozen iv eternities," commented Louis, his eyes twinkling up at me as he rested from hauling taut the lashings of his boat.

"Listen to them, and find if it is hard to discover the most vital thing in their souls," said Wolf Larsen. "Faith? And love? And high ideals? The good? The beautiful? The true?"

"Their innate sense of right has been violated," Maud Brewster said, joining the conversation.

She was standing a dozen feet away, one hand resting on the main-shrouds and her body swaying gently to the slight roll of the ship. She had not raised her voice, and yet I was struck by its clear and bell-like tone. Ah, it was sweet in my ears! I scarcely dared look at her just then, for the fear of betraying myself. A boy's cap was perched on her head, and her hair, light brown and arranged in a loose and fluffy order that caught the sun, seemed an aureole about the delicate oval of her face. She was positively bewitching and, withal, sweetly spirituelle, if not saintly. All my old-time marvel at life returned to me at sight of this splendid incarnation of it, and Wolf Larsen's cold explanation of life and its meaning was truly ridiculous and laughable.

"A sentimentalist," he sneered, "like Mr Van Weyden. Those men are cursing because their desires have been outraged. That is all. What desires? The desires for the good grub and soft beds ashore which a handsome pay-day brings them—the women and the drink, the gorging and the beastliness which so truly expresses them, the best that is in them, their highest aspirations, their ideals, if you please. The exhibition they make of their feelings is not a touching sight, yet it shows how deeply they have been touched, how deeply their purses have been touched; for to lay hands on their purses is to lay hands on their souls."

"You hardly behave as if your purse had been touched," she said, smilingly.

"Then it so happens that I am behaving differently, for my purse and my soul have both been touched. At the current price of skins in the London market, and based on a fair estimate of what the afternoon's catch would have been had not the *Macedonia* hogged it, the *Ghost* has lost about fifteen hundred dollars' worth of skins."

"You speak so calmly—" she began.

"But I do not feel calm; I could kill the man who robbed me," he interrupted. "Yes, yes, I know, and that man my brother—more sentiment! Bah!"

His face underwent a sudden change. His voice was less harsh and wholly sincere as he said:

"You must be happy, you sentimentalists, really and truly happy at dreaming and finding things good, and, because you find some of them good, feeling good yourself. Now, tell me, you two, do you find me good?"

"You are good to look upon—in a way," I qualified.

"There are in you all powers for good," was Maud Brewster's answer.

"There you are!" he cried at her, half angrily. "Your words are empty to me. There is nothing clear and sharp and definite about the thought you have expressed. You cannot pick it up in your two hands and look at it. In point of fact, it is not a thought. It is a feeling, a sentiment, a something based upon illusion and not a product of the intellect at all."

As he went on his voice again grew soft, and a confiding note came into it. "Do you know, I sometimes catch myself wishing that I, too, were blind to the facts of life and only knew its fancies and illusions. They're wrong, all wrong, of course, and contrary to reason; but in the face of them my reason tells me, wrong and most wrong, that to dream and live illusions gives greater delight. And after all, delight is the wage for living. Without delight, living is a worthless act. To labor at living and be unpaid is worse than to be dead. He who delights the most lives the most, and your dreams and unrealities are less disturbing to you and more gratifying than are my facts to me."

He shook his head slowly, pondering.

"I often doubt, I often doubt, the worthwhileness of reason. Dreams must be more substantial and satisfying. Emotional delight is more filling and lasting than intellectual delight; and, besides, you pay for your moments of intellectual delight by having the blues. Emotional delight is followed by no more than jaded senses which speedily recuperate. I envy you, I envy you."

He stopped abruptly, and then on his lips formed one of his strange quizzical smiles, as he added:

"It's from my brain I envy you, take notice, and not from my heart. My reason dictates it. The envy is an intellectual product. I am like a sober man looking upon drunken men, and, greatly weary, wishing he, too, were drunk."

"Or like a wise man looking upon fools and wishing he, too, were a fool," I laughed.

"Quite so," he said. "You are a blessed, bankrupt pair of fools. You have no facts in your pocketbook."

"Yet we spend as freely as you," was Maud Brewster's contribution.

"More freely, because it costs you nothing."

"And because we draw upon eternity," she retorted.

"Whether you do or think you do, it's the same thing. You spend what you haven't got, and in return you get greater value from spending what you haven't got than I get from spending what I have got, and what I have sweated to get."

"Why don't you change the basis of your coinage, then?" she queried teasingly.

He looked at her quickly, half-hopefully, and then said, all regretfully: "Too late. I'd like to, perhaps, but I can't. My pocketbook is stuffed with the old coinage, and it's a stubborn thing. I can never bring myself to recognize anything else as valid."

He ceased speaking, and his gaze wandered absently past her and became lost in the placid sea. The old primal melancholy was strong upon him. He was quivering to it. He had reasoned himself into a spell of the blues, and within few hours one could look for the devil within him to be up and stirring. I remembered Charley Furuseth, and knew this man's sadness as the penalty which the materialist ever pays for his materialism.

XXV

"You've been on deck, Mr Van Weyden," Wolf Larsen said, the following morning at the breakfast table. "How do things look?"

"Clear enough," I answered, glancing at the sunshine which streamed down the open companionway. "Fair westerly breeze, with a promise of stiffening, if Louis predicts correctly."

He nodded his head in a pleased way. "Any signs of fog?"

"Thick banks in the north and northwest."

He nodded his head again, evincing even greater satisfaction than before.

"What of the *Macedonia?*"

"Not sighted," I answered.

I could have sworn his face fell at the intelligence, but why he should be disappointed I could not conceive.

I was soon to learn. "Smoke ho!" came the hail from on deck, and his face brightened.

"Good!" he exclaimed, and left the table at once to go on deck and into the steerage, where the hunters were taking the first breakfast of their exile.

Maud Brewster and I scarcely touched the food before us, gazing, instead, in silent anxiety at each other, and listening to Wolf Larsen's voice, which easily penetrated the cabin through the intervening bulkhead. He spoke at length, and his conclusion was greeted with a wild roar of cheers. The bulkhead was too thick for us to hear what he said; but whatever it was it affected the hunters strongly, for the cheering was followed by loud exclamations and shouts of joy.

From the sounds on deck I knew that the sailors had been routed out and were preparing to lower the boats. Maud Brewster accompanied me on deck, but I left her at the break of the poop, where she might watch the scene and not be in it. The sailors must have learned whatever project was on hand, and the vim and snap they put into their work attested their enthusiasm. The hunters came trooping on deck with shotguns and ammunition-boxes, and, most unusual, their rifles. The latter were rarely taken in the boats, for a seal, shot at long range with a rifle, invariably sank before a boat could reach it. But each hunter this day had his rifle and a large supply of cartridges. I noticed they grinned with satisfaction whenever they looked at the *Macedonia*' s smoke, which was rising higher and higher as she approached from the west.

The five boats went over the side with a rush, spread out like the ribs of a fan, and set a northerly course, as on the preceding afternoon, for us to follow. I watched for some time, curiously, but there seemed nothing extraordinary about their behavior. They lowered sails, shot seals, and hoisted sails again, and continued on their way as I had always seen them do. The *Macedonia* repeated her performance of yesterday, "hogging" the sea by dropping her line of boats in advance of ours and across our course. Fourteen boats require a considerable spread of ocean for comfortable hunting, and when she had completely lapped our line she continued steaming into the northeast, dropping more boats as she went.

"What's up?" I asked Wolf Larsen, unable longer to keep my curiosity in check.

"Never mind what's up," he answered gruffly. "You won't be a thousand years in finding out, and in the meantime just pray for plenty of wind.

"Oh, well, I don't mind telling you," he said the next moment. "I'm going to give that brother of mine a taste of his own medicine. In short, I'm going to play the hog myself, and not for one day, but for the rest of the season—if we're in luck."

"And if we're not?" I queried.

"Not to be considered," he laughed. "We simply must be in luck, or it's all up with us."

He had the wheel at the time, and I went forward to my hospital in the forecastle, where lay the two crippled men, Nilson and Thomas Mugridge. Nilson was as cheerful as could be expected, for his broken leg was knitting nicely; but the Cockney was desperately melancholy, and I was aware of a great sympathy for the unfortunate creature. And the marvel of it was that still he lived and clung to life. The brutal years had reduced his meagre body to splintered wreckage, and yet the spark of life within burned brightly as ever.

"With an artificial foot—and they make excellent ones—you will be stumping ships' galleys to the end of time," I assured him jovially.

But his answer was serious, nay, solemn. "I don't know about wot you s'y, Mr Van Weyden, but I do know I'll never rest 'appy till I see that 'ell-'ound bloody well dead. 'E cawn't live as long as me. 'E's got no right to live, an' as the Good Word puts it, ''E shall shorely die,' an' I s'y, 'Amen, an' damn soon at that.' "

When I returned on deck I found Wolf Larsen steering mainly with one hand, while with the other hand he held the marine glasses and studied the situation of the boats, paying particular attention to the position of the *Macedonia.* The only change noticeable in our boats was that they had hauled close on the wind and were heading several points west of north. Still, I could not see the expediency of the manoeuvre, for the free sea was still intercepted by the *Macedonia* 's five weather boats, which, in turn, had hauled close on the wind. Thus they slowly diverged toward the west, drawing farther away from the remainder of the boats in their line. Our boats were rowing as well as sailing. Even the hunters were pulling, and with three pairs of oars in the water they rapidly overhauled what I may appropriately term the enemy.

The smoke of the *Macedonia* had dwindled to a dim blot on the northeastern horizon. Of the steamer herself nothing was to be seen. We had been loafing along, till now, our sails shaking half the time and spilling the wind; and twice, for short periods, we had been hove to. But there was no more loafing. Sheets were trimmed, and Wolf Larsen proceeded to put the *Ghost* through her paces. We ran past our line of boats and bore down upon the first weather boat of the other line.

"Down that flying jib, Mr Van Weyden," Wolf Larsen commanded. "And stand by to back over the jibs."

I ran forward and had the downhaul of the flying jib all in and fast as we slipped by the boat a hundred feet to leeward. The three men in it gazed at us suspiciously. They had been hogging the sea, and they knew Wolf Larsen, by reputation at any rate. I noted that the hunter, a huge Scandinavian sitting in the bow, held his rifle, ready to hand, across his knees. It should have been in its proper place in the rack. When they came opposite our stern, Wolf Larsen greeted them with a wave of the hand, and cried:

"Come on board and have a 'gam!' "

"To gam," among the sealing-schooners, is a substitute for the verbs "to visit" , "to gossip" . It expresses the garrulity of the sea and is a pleasant break in the monotony of the life.

The *Ghost* swung around into the wind, and I finished my work forward in time to run aft and lend a hand with the main sheet.

"You will please stay on deck, Miss Brewster," Wolf Larsen said, as he started forward to meet his guest. "And you too, Mr Van Weyden."

The boat had lowered its sail and run alongside. The hunter, golden-bearded like a sea-king, came over the rail and dropped on deck. But his hugeness could not quite overcome his apprehensiveness. Doubt and distrust showed strongly in his face. It was a transparent face, for all of its hairy shield, and advertised instant relief when he glanced from Wolf Larsen to me, noted that there was only the pair of us, and then glanced over his own two men who had joined him. Surely he had little reason to be afraid. He towered like a Goliath above Wolf Larsen. He must have measured six feet eight or nine inches in stature, and I subsequently learned his weight—240 pounds. And there was no fat about him. It was all bone and muscle.

A return of apprehension was apparent, when, at the top of the companionway, Wolf Larsen invited him below. But he reassured himself with a glance down at his host —a big man himself but dwarfed by the propinquity of the giant. So all hesitancy vanished, and the pair descended into the cabin. In the meantime, his two men, as was the wont of visiting sailors, had gone forward into the forecastle to do some visiting themselves.

Suddenly, from the cabin came a great, choking bellow, followed by all the sounds of a furious struggle. It was the leopard and the lion, and the lion made all the noise. Wolf Larsen was the leopard.

"You see the sacredness of our hospitality," I said bitterly to Maud Brewster.

She nodded her head that she heard, and I noted in her face the signs of the same sickness at sight or sound of violent struggle from which I had suffered so severely during my first weeks on the *Ghost.*

"Wouldn't it be better if you went forward, say by the steerage companionway, until it is over?" I suggested.

She shook her head and gazed at me pitifully. She was not frightened, but appalled, rather, at the human animality of it.

"You will understand," I took advantage of the opportunity to say, "whatever part I take in what is going on and what is to come, that I am compelled to take it—if you and I are ever to get out of this scrape with our lives.

"It is not nice—for me," I added.

"I understand," she said, in a weak, faraway voice, and her eyes showed me that she did understand.

The sounds from below soon died away. Then Wolf Larsen came alone on deck. There was a slight flush under his bronze, but otherwise he bore no signs of the battle.

"Send those two men aft, Mr Van Weyden," he said.

I obeyed, and a minute or two later they stood before him.

"Hoist in your boat,' he said to them. "Your hunter's decided to stay aboard awhile and doesn't want it pounding alongside.

"Hoist in your boat, I said," he repeated, this time in sharper tones as they hesitated to do his bidding.

"Who knows? You may have to sail with me for a time," he said, quite softly, with a silken threat that belied the softness, as they moved slowly to comply, "and we might as well start with a friendly understanding. Lively now! Death Larsen makes you jump better than that, and you know it!"

Their movements perceptibly quickened under his coaching, and as the boat swung inboard I was sent forward to let go the jibs. Wolf Larsen, at the wheel, directed the *Ghost* after the *Macedonia*'s second weather boat.

Under way, and with nothing for the time being to do, I turned my attention to the situation of the boats. The *Macedonia* 's third weather boat was being attacked by two of ours, the fourth by our remaining three; and the fifth, turn about, was taking a hand in the defence of its nearest mate. The fight had opened at long distance, and the rifles were cracking steadily. A quick, snappy sea was being kicked up by the wind, a condition which prevented fine shooting; and now and again, as we drew closer, we could see the bullets zip-zipping from wave to wave.

The boat we were pursuing had squared away and was running before the wind to escape us, and, in the course of its flight, to take part in repulsing our general boat attack.

Attending to sheets and tacks now left me little time to see what was taking place, but I happened to be on the poop when Wolf Larsen ordered the two strange sailors forward and into the forecastle. They went sullenly, but they went. He next ordered Miss Brewster below, and smiled at the instant horror that leapt into her eyes.

"You'll find nothing grewsome down there," he said, "only an unhurt man securely made fast to the ring-bolts. Bullets are liable to come aboard, and I don't want you killed, you know."

Even as he spoke, a bullet was deflected by a brass-capped spoke of the wheel between his hands and screeched off through the air to windward.

"You see," he said to her; and then to me, "Mr Van Weyden, will you take the wheel?"

Maud Brewster had stepped inside the companionway so that only her head was exposed. Wolf Larsen had procured a rifle and was throwing a cartridge into the barrel. I begged her with my eyes to go below, but she smiled and said:

"We may be feeble land-creatures without legs, but we can show Captain Larsen that we are at least as brave as he."

He gave her a quick look of admiration.

"I like you a hundred per cent better for that," he said. "Books, and brains, and bravery. You are well-rounded, a blue-stocking fit to be the wife of a pirate chief. Ahem, we'll discuss that later," he smiled, as a bullet struck solidly into the cabin wall.

I saw his eyes flash golden as he spoke, and I saw the terror mount in her own.

"We are braver," I hastened to say. "At least, speaking for myself, I know I am braver than Captain Larsen."

It was I who was now favored by a quick look. He was wondering if I were making fun of him. I put three or four spokes over to counteract a sheer toward the wind on the part of the *Ghost,* and then steadied her. Wolf Larsen was still waiting an explanation, and I pointed down to my knees.

"You will observe there," I said, "a slight trembling. It is because I am afraid, the flesh is afraid; and I am afraid in my mind because I do not wish to die. But my spirit masters the trembling flesh and the qualms of the mind. I am more than brave. I am courageous. Your flesh is not afraid. You are not afraid. On the one hand, it costs you nothing to encounter danger; on the other hand, it even gives you delight. You enjoy it. You may be unafraid, Mr Larsen, but you must grant that the bravery is mine."

"You're right," he acknowledged at once. "I never thought of it in that way before. But is the opposite true? If you are braver than I, am I more cowardly than you?"

We both laughed at the absurdity, and he dropped down to the deck and rested his rifle across the rail. The bullets we had received had travelled nearly a mile, but by now we had cut that distance in half. He fired three careful shots. The first struck fifty feet to windward of the boat, the second alongside, and at the third the boat-steerer let loose his steering-oar and crumpled up in the bottom of the boat.

"I guess that'll fix them," Wolf Larsen said, rising to his feet. "I couldn't afford to let the hunter have it, and there is a chance the boat-puller doesn't know how to steer. In which case, the hunter cannot steer and shoot at the same time."

His reasoning was justified, for the boat rushed at once into the wind and the hunter sprang aft to take the boat-steerer's place. There was no more shooting, though the rifles were still cracking merrily from the other boats.

The hunter had managed to get the boat before the wind again, but we ran down upon it, going at least two feet to its one. A hundred yards away, I saw the boat-puller pass a rifle to the hunter. Wolf Larsen went amidships and took the coil of the throat-halyards from its pin. Then he peered over the rail with levelled rifle. Twice I saw the hunter let go the steering-oar with one hand, reach for his rifle, and hesitate. We were now alongside and foaming past.

"Here, you!" Wolf Larsen cried suddenly to the boat-puller. "Take a turn!"

At the same time he flung the coil of rope. It struck fairly, nearly knocking the man over, but he did not obey. Instead, he looked to his hunter for orders. The hunter, in turn, was in a quandary. His rifle was between his knees, but if he let go the steering-oar in order to shoot, the boat would sweep around and collide with the schooner. Also he saw Wolf Larsen's rifle bearing upon him and knew he would be shot ere he could get his rifle into play.

"Take a turn," he said quietly to the man.

The boat-puller obeyed, taking a turn around the little forward thwart and paying the line as it jerked taut. The boat sheered out with a rush, and the hunter steadied it to a parallel course some twenty feet from the side of the *Ghost.*

"Now get that sail down and come alongside!" Wolf Larsen ordered.

He never let go his rifle, even passing down the tackles with one hand. When they were fast, bow and stern, and the two uninjured men prepared to come aboard, the hunter picked up his rifle as if to place it in a secure position.

"Drop it!" Wolf Larsen cried, and the hunter dropped it as though it were hot and had burned him.

Once aboard, the two prisoners hoisted in the boat and under Wolf Larsen's direction carried the wounded boat-steerer down into the forecastle.

"If our five boats do as well as you and I have done, we'll have a pretty full crew," Wolf Larsen said to me.

"The man you shot—he is—I hope?" Maud Brewster quavered.

"In the shoulder," he answered. "Nothing serious. Mr Van Weyden will pull him around as good as ever in three or four weeks.

"But he won't pull those chaps around, from the look of it," he added, pointing at the *Macedonia*'s third boat, for which I had been steering and which was now nearly abreast of us. "That's Horner's and Smoke's work. I told them we wanted live men, not carcasses. But the joy of shooting to hit is a most compelling thing, when once you've learned how to shoot. Ever experienced it, Mr Van Weyden?"

I shook my head and regarded their work. It had indeed been bloody, for they had drawn off and joined our other three boats in the attack on the remaining two of the enemy. The deserted boat was in the trough of the sea, rolling drunkenly across each comber, its loose spritsail out at right angles to it and fluttering and flapping in the wind. The hunter and boat-puller were both lying awkwardly in the bottom, but the boat-steerer lay across the gunwale, half in and half out, his arms trailing in the water and his head rolling from side to side.

"Don't look, Miss Brewster, please don't look," I had begged of her, and I was glad that she had minded me and been spared the sight.

"Head right into the bunch, Mr Van Weyden," was Wolf Larsen's command.

As we drew nearer, the firing ceased, and we saw that the fight was over. The remaining two boats had been captured by our five, and the seven were grouped together, waiting to be picked up.

"Look at that!" I cried involuntarily, pointing to the northeast.

The blot of smoke which indicated the *Macedonia* 's position had reappeared.

"Yes, I've been watching it," was Wolf Larsen's calm reply. He measured the distance away to the fog-bank and for an instant paused to feel the weight of the wind on his cheek. "We'll make it, I think; but you can depend upon it that blessed brother of mine has twigged our little game and is just a-humping for us. Ah, look at that!"

The blot of smoke had suddenly grown larger, and it was very black.

"I'll beat you out, though, brother mine," he chuckled. "I'll beat you out, and I hope you no worse than that you rack your old engines into scrap."

When we hove to, a hasty though orderly confusion reigned. The boats came aboard from every side at once. As fast as the prisoners came over the rail they were marshalled forward into the forecastle by our hunters, while our sailors hoisted in the boats, pell-mell, dropping them anywhere upon the deck and not stopping to lash them. We were already under way, all sails set and drawing, and the sheets being slacked off for a wind abeam, as the last boat lifted clear of the water and swung in the tackles.

There was need for haste. The *Macedonia,* belching the blackest of smoke from her funnel, was charging down upon us from out of the northeast. Neglecting the boats that remained to her, she had altered her course so as to anticipate ours. She was not running straight for us, but ahead of us. Our courses were converging like the sides of an angle, the vertex of which was at the edge of the fog-bank. It was there, or not at all, that the *Macedonia* could hope to catch us. The hope for the *Ghost* lay in that she should pass that point before the *Macedonia* arrived at it.

Wolf Larsen was steering, his eyes glistening and snapping as they dwelt upon and leaped from detail to detail of the chase. Now he studied the sea to windward for signs of the wind slackening or freshening, now the *Macedonia;* and again, his eyes roved over every sail, and he gave commands to slack a sheet here a trifle, to come in on one there a trifle, till he was drawing out of the *Ghost* the last bit of speed she possessed. All feuds and grudges were forgotten, and I was surprised at the alacrity with which the men who had so long endured his brutality sprang to execute his orders. Strange to say, the unfortunate Johnson came into my mind as we lifted and surged and heeled along, and I was aware of a regret that he was not alive and present; he had so loved the *Ghost* and delighted in her sailing powers.

"Better get your rifles, you fellows," Wolf Larsen called to our hunters; and the five men lined the lee rail, guns in hand, and waited.

The *Macedonia* was now but a mile away, the black smoke pouring from her funnel at a right angle, so madly she raced, pounding through the sea at a seventeen-knot gait —" 'Sky-hooting through the brine,' " as Wolf Larsen quoted while gazing at her. We were not making more than nine knots, but the fog-bank was very near.

A puff of smoke broke from the *Macedonia* 's deck, we heard a heavy report, and a round hole took form in the stretched canvas of our mainsail. They were shooting at us with one of the small cannon which rumor had said they carried on board. Our men, clustering amidships, waved their hats and raised a derisive cheer. Again there was a puff of smoke and a loud report, this time the cannon-ball striking not more than twenty feet astern and glancing twice from sea to sea to windward ere it sank.

But there was no rifle-firing for the reason that all their hunters were out in the boats or our prisoners. When the two vessels were half-a-mile apart, a third shot made another hole in our mainsail. Then we entered the fog. It was about us, veiling and hiding us in its dense wet gauze.

The sudden transition was startling. The moment before we had been leaping through the sunshine, the clear sky above us, the sea breaking and rolling wide to the horizon, and a ship, vomiting smoke and fire and iron missiles, rushing madly upon us. And at once, as in an instant's leap, the sun was blotted out, there was no sky, even our mastheads were lost to view, and our horizon was such as tear-blinded eyes may see. The gray mist drove by us like a rain. Every woollen filament of our garments, every hair of our heads and faces, was jewelled with a crystal globule. The shrouds were wet with moisture; it dripped from our rigging overhead; and on the underside of our booms drops of water took shape in long swaying lines, which were detached and flung to the deck in mimic showers at each surge of the schooner. I was aware of a pent, stifled feeling. As the sounds of the ship thrusting herself through the waves were hurled back upon us by the fog, so were one's thoughts. The mind recoiled from contemplation of a world beyond this wet veil which wrapped us around. This was the world, the universe itself, its bounds so near one felt impelled to reach out both arms and push them back. It was impossible that the rest could be beyond these walls of gray. The rest was a dream, no more than the memory of a dream.

It was weird, strangely weird. I looked at Maud Brewster and knew that she was similarly affected. Then I looked at Wolf Larsen, but there was nothing subjective about his state of consciousness. His whole concern was with the immediate, objective present. He still held the wheel, and I felt that he was timing Time, reckoning the passage of the minutes with each forward lunge and leeward roll of the *Ghost.*

"Go for'ard and hard-a-lee without any noise," he said to me in a low voice. "Clew up the topsails first. Set men at all the sheets. Let there be no rattling of blocks, no sound of voices. No noise, understand, no noise."

When all was ready, the word "hard-a-lee" was passed forward to me from man to man; and the *Ghost* heeled about on the port tack with practically no noise at all. And what little there was—the slapping of a few reef-points and the creaking of a sheave in a block or two—was ghostly under the hollow echoing pall in which we were swathed.

We had scarcely filled away, it seemed, when the fog thinned abruptly and we were again in the sunshine, the wide-stretching sea breaking before us to the sky-line. But the ocean was bare. No wrathful *Macedonia* broke its surface nor blackened the sky with her smoke.

Wolf Larsen at once squared away and ran down along the rim of the fog-bank. His trick was obvious. He had entered the fog to windward of the steamer, and while the steamer had blindly driven on into the fog in the chance of catching him, he had come about and out of his shelter and was now running down to re-enter to leeward. Successful in this, the old simile of the needle in the haystack would be mild indeed compared with his brother's chance of finding him.

He did not run long. Jibing the fore- and main-sails and setting the topsails again, we headed back into the bank. As we entered I could have sworn I saw a vague bulk emerging to windward. I looked quickly at Wolf Larsen. Already we were ourselves buried in the fog, but he nodded his head. He, too, had seen it—the *Macedonia,* guessing his manoeuvre and failing by a moment in anticipating it. There was no doubt that we had escaped unseen.

"He can't keep this up," Wolf Larsen said. "He'll have to go back for the rest of his boats. Send a man to the wheel, Mr Van Weyden, keep this course for the present, and you might as well set the watches, for we won't do any lingering to-night.

"I'd give five hundred dollars, though," he added, "just to be aboard the *Macedonia* for five minutes, listening to my brother curse."

"And now, Mr Van Weyden," he said to me when he had been relieved from the wheel, "we must make these newcomers welcome. Serve out plenty of whiskey to the hunters and see that a few bottles slip for'ard. I'll wager every man Jack of them is over the side tomorrow, hunting for Wolf Larsen as contentedly as ever they hunted for Death Larsen."

"But won't they escape as Wainwright did?" I asked.

He laughed shrewdly. "Not as long as our old hunters have anything to say about it. I'm dividing amongst them a dollar a skin for all the skins shot by our new hunters. At least half of their enthusiasm to-day was due to that. Oh, no, there won't be any escaping if they have anything to say about it. And now you'd better get for'ard to your hospital duties. There must be a full ward waiting for you."

XXVI

Wolf Larsen took the distribution of the whiskey off my hands, and the bottles began to make their appearance while I worked over the fresh batch of wounded men in the forecastle. I had seen whiskey drunk, such as whiskey and soda by the men of the clubs, but never as these men drank it, from pannikins and mugs, and from the bottles—great brimming drinks, each one of which was in itself a debauch. But they did not stop at one or two. They drank and drank, and ever the bottles slipped forward and they drank more.

Everybody drank; the wounded drank; Oofty-Oofty, who helped me, drank. Only Louis refrained, no more than cautiously wetting his lips with the liquor, though he joined in the revels with an abandon equal to that of most of them. It was a saturnalia. In loud voices they shouted over the day's fighting, wrangled about details, or waxed affectionate and made friends with the men whom they had fought. Prisoners and captors hiccoughed on one another's shoulders, and swore mighty oaths of respect and esteem. They wept over the miseries of the past and over the miseries yet to come under the iron rule of Wolf Larsen. And all cursed him and told terrible tales of his brutality.

It was a strange and frightful spectacle—the small, bunk-lined space, the floor and walls leaping and lurching, the dim light, the swaying shadows lengthening and foreshortening monstrously, the thick air heavy with smoke and the smell of bodies and iodoform, and the inflamed faces of the men—half-men, I should call them. I noted Oofty-Oofty, holding the end of a bandage and looking upon the scene, his velvety and luminous eyes glistening in the light like a deer's eyes, and yet I knew the barbaric devil that lurked in his breast and belied all the softness and tenderness, almost womanly, of his face and form. And I noticed the boyish face of Harrison—a good face once, but now a demon's—convulsed with passion as he told the newcomers of the hell-ship they were in and shrieked curses upon the head of Wolf Larsen.

Wolf Larsen it was, always Wolf Larsen, enslaver and tormentor of men, a male Circe and these his swine, suffering brutes that grovelled before him and revolted only in drunkenness and in secrecy. And was I, too, one of his swine? I thought. And Maud Brewster? No! I ground my teeth in my anger and determination till the man I was attending winced under my hand and Oofty-Oofty looked at me with curiosity. I felt endowed with a sudden strength. What of my new-found love, I was a giant. I feared nothing. I would work my will through it all, in spite of Wolf Larsen and of my own thirty-five bookish years. All would be well. I would make it well. And so, exalted, upborne by a sense of power, I turned my back on the howling inferno and climbed to the deck, where the fog drifted ghostly through the night and the air was sweet and pure and quiet.

The steerage, where were two wounded hunters, was a repetition of the forecastle, except that Wolf Larsen was not being cursed; and it was with a great relief that I again emerged on deck and went aft to the cabin. Supper was ready, and Wolf Larsen and Maud were waiting for me.

While all his ship was getting drunk as fast as it could, he remained sober. Not a drop of liquor passed his lips. He did not dare it under the circumstances, for he had only Louis and me to depend upon, and Louis was even now at the wheel. We were sailing on through the fog without a look-out and without lights. That Wolf Larsen had turned the liquor loose among his men surprised me, but he evidently knew their psychology and the best method of cementing in cordiality what had begun in bloodshed.

His victory over Death Larsen seemed to have had a remarkable effect upon him. The previous evening he had reasoned himself into the blues, and I had been waiting momentarily for one of his characteristic outbursts. Yet nothing had occurred, and he was now in splendid trim. Possibly his success in capturing so many hunters and boats had counteracted the customary reaction. At any rate, the blues were gone, and the blue devils had not put in an appearance. So I thought at the time; but, ah me, little I knew him or knew that even then, perhaps, he was meditating an outbreak more terrible than any I had seen.

As I say, he discovered himself in splendid trim when I entered the cabin. He had had no headaches for weeks, his eyes were clear blue as the sky, his bronze was beautiful with perfect health; life swelled through his veins in full and magnificent flood. While waiting for me he had engaged Maud in animated discussion. Temptation was the topic they had hit upon, and from the few words I heard I made out that he was contending that temptation was temptation only when a man was seduced by it and fell.

"For look you," he was saying, "as I see it, a man does things because of desire. He has many desires. He may desire to escape pain, or to enjoy pleasure. But whatever he does, he does because he desires to do it."

"But suppose he desires to do two opposite things, neither of which will permit him to do the other?" Maud interrupted.

"The very thing I was coming to," he said.

"And between these two desires is just where the soul of the man is manifest," she went on. "If it is a good soul, it will desire and do the good action, and the contrary if it is a bad soul. It is the soul that decides."

"Bosh and nonsense!" he exclaimed impatiently. "It is the desire that decides. Here is a man who wants to, say, get drunk. Also, he doesn't want to get drunk. What does he do? How does he do it? He is a puppet. He is the creature of his desires, and of the two desires he obeys the strongest one, that is all. His soul hasn't anything to do with it. How can he be tempted to get drunk and refuse to get drunk? If the desire to remain sober prevails, it is because it is the strongest desire. Temptation plays no part, unless—" he paused while grasping the new thought which had come into his mind—"unless he is tempted to remain sober.

"Ha! ha!" he laughed. "What do you think of that, Mr Van Weyden?"

"That both of you are hair-splitting," I said. "The man's soul is his desires. Or, if you will, the sum of his desires is his soul. Therein you are both wrong. You lay the stress upon the desire apart from the soul, Miss Brewster lays the stress on the soul apart from the desire, and in point of fact soul and desire are the same thing.

"However," I continued, "Miss Brewster is right in contending that temptation is temptation whether the man yield or overcome. Fire is fanned by the wind until it leaps up fiercely. So is desire like fire. It is fanned, as by a wind, by sight of the thing desired, or by a new and luring description or comprehension of the thing desired. There lies the temptation. It is the wind that fans the desire until it leaps up to mastery. That's temptation. It may not fan sufficiently to make the desire overmastering, but in so far as it fans at all, that far is it temptation. And, as you say, it may tempt for good as well as for evil."

I felt proud of myself as we sat down to the table. My words had been decisive. At least they had put an end to the discussion.

But Wolf Larsen seemed voluble, prone to speech as I had never seen him before. It was as though he were bursting with pent energy which must find an outlet somehow. Almost immediately he launched into a discussion on love. As usual, his was the sheer materialistic side, and Maud's was the idealistic. For myself, beyond a word or so of suggestion or correction now and again, I took no part.

He was brilliant, but so was Maud, and for some time I lost the thread of the conversation through studying her face as she talked. It was a face that rarely displayed color, but to-night it was flushed and vivacious. Her wit was playing keenly, and she was enjoying the tilt as much as Wolf Larsen, and he was enjoying it hugely. For some reason, though I know not why in the argument, so utterly had I lost it in the contemplation of one stray brown lock of Maud's hair, he quoted from Iseult at Tintagel, where she says:

"Blessed am I beyond women even herein,
That beyond all born women is my sin,
And perfect my transgression."

As he had read pessimism into Omar, so now he read triumph, stinging triumph and exultation, into Swinburne's lines. And he read rightly, and he read well. He had hardly ceased reading when Louis put his head into the companionway and whispered down:

"Be easy, will ye? The fog's lifted, an' 'tis the port light iv a steamer that's crossin' our bow this blessed minute."

Wolf Larsen sprang on deck, and so swiftly that by the time we followed him he had pulled the steerage-slide over the drunken clamor and was on his way forward to close the forecastle-scuttle. The fog, though it remained, had lifted high, where it obscured the stars and made the night quite black. Directly ahead of us I could see a bright red light and a white light, and I could hear the pulsing of a steamer's engines. Beyond a doubt it was the *Macedonia.*

Wolf Larsen had returned to the poop, and we stood in a silent group, watching the lights rapidly cross our bow.

"Lucky for me he doesn't carry a searchlight," Wolf Larsen said.

"What if I should cry out loudly?" I queried in a whisper.

"It would be all up," he answered. "But have you thought upon what would immediately happen?"

Before I had time to express any desire to know, he had me by the throat with his gorilla grip, and by a faint quiver of the muscles—a hint, as it were—he suggested to me the twist that would surely have broken my neck. The next moment he had released me and we were gazing at the *Macedonia* 's lights.

"What if I should cry out?" Maud asked.

"I like you too well to hurt you," he said softly—nay, there was a tenderness and a caress in his voice that made me wince. "But don't do it, just the same, for I'd promptly break Mr Van Weyden's neck."

"Then she has my permission to cry out," I said defiantly.

"I hardly think you'll care to sacrifice the Dean of American Letters the Second," he sneered.

We spoke no more, though we had become too used to one another for the silence to be awkward; and when the red light and the white had disappeared we returned to the cabin to finish the interrupted supper.

Again they fell to quoting, and Maud gave Dowson's "Impenitentia Ultima" . She rendered it beautifully, but I watched not her, but Wolf Larsen. I was fascinated by the fascinated look he bent upon Maud. He was quite out of himself, and I noticed the unconscious movement of his lips as he shaped word for word as fast as she uttered them. He interrupted her when she gave the lines:

> "And her eyes should be my light while the sun went out
> behind me,
> And the viols in her voice be the last sound in my ear."

"There are viols in your voice," he said bluntly, and his eyes flashed their golden light.

I could have shouted with joy at her control. She finished the concluding stanza without faltering and then slowly guided the conversation into less perilous channels. And all the while I sat in a half-daze, the drunken riot of the steerage breaking through the bulkhead, the man I feared and the woman I loved talking on and on. The table was not cleared. The man who had taken Mugridge's place had evidently joined his comrades in the forecastle.

If ever Wolf Larsen attained the summit of living, he attained it then. From time to time I forsook my own thoughts to follow him, and I followed in amaze, mastered for the moment by his remarkable intellect, under the spell of his passion, for he was preaching the passion of revolt. It was inevitable that Milton's Lucifer should be instanced, and the keenness with which Wolf Larsen analyzed and depicted the character was a revelation of his stifled genius. It reminded me of Taine, yet I knew the man had never heard of that brilliant though dangerous thinker.

"He led a lost cause, and he was not afraid of God's thunderbolts," Wolf Larsen was saying. "Hurled in to hell, he was unbeaten. A third of God's angels he had led with him, and straightway he incited man to rebel against God, and gained for himself and hell the major portion of all the generations of man. Why was he beaten out of heaven? Because he was less brave than God? Less proud? Less aspiring? No! A thousand times no! God was more powerful, as he said, Whom thunder hath made greater. But Lucifer was a free spirit. To serve was to suffocate. He preferred suffering in freedom to all the happiness of a comfortable servility. He did not care to serve God. He cared to serve nothing. He was no figurehead. He stood on his own legs. He was an individual."

"The first Anarchist," Maud laughed, rising and preparing to withdraw to her stateroom.

"Then it is good to be an Anarchist!" he cried. He, too, had risen, and he stood facing her, where she had paused at the door of her room, as he went on:

"'Here at least
We shall be free; the Almighty hath not built
Here for his envy; will not drive us hence;
Here we may reign secure; and in my choice
To reign is worth ambition, though in hell:
Better to reign in hell than serve in heaven.'"

It was the defiant cry of a mighty spirit. The cabin still rang with his voice, as he stood there, swaying, his bronzed face shining, his head up and dominant, and his eyes, golden and masculine, intensely masculine and insistently soft, flashing upon Maud at the door.

Again that unnamable and unmistakable terror was in her eyes, and she said, almost in a whisper, "You are Lucifer."

The door closed and she was gone. He stood staring after her for a minute, then returned to himself and to me.

"I'll relieve Louis at the wheel," he said shortly, "and call upon you to relieve at midnight. Better turn in now and get some sleep."

He pulled on a pair of mittens, put on his cap, and ascended the companion-stairs, while I followed his suggestion by going to bed. For some unknown reason, prompted mysteriously, I did not undress, but lay down fully clothed. For a time I listened to the clamor in the steerage and marvelled upon the love which had come to me; but my sleep on the *Ghost* had become most healthful and natural, and soon the songs and cries died away, my eyes closed, and my consciousness sank down into the half-death of slumber.

I knew not what had aroused me, but I found myself out of my bunk, on my feet, wide awake, my soul vibrating to the warning of danger as it might have thrilled to a trumpet call. I threw open the door. The cabin light was burning low. I saw Maud, my Maud, straining and struggling and crushed in the embrace of Wolf Larsen's arms. I could see the vain beat and flutter of her as she strove, pressing her face against his breast, to escape from him. All this I saw on the very instant of seeing and as I sprang forward.

I struck him with my fist, on the face, as he raised his head, but it was a puny blow. He roared in a ferocious, animal-like way, and gave me a shove with his hand. It was only a shove, a flirt of the wrist, yet so tremendous was his strength that I was hurled backward as from a catapult. I struck the door of the state-room which had formerly been Mugridge's, splintering and smashing the panels with the impact of my body. I struggled to my feet, with difficulty dragging myself clear of the wrecked door, unaware of any hurt whatever. I was conscious only of an overmastering rage. I think I, too, cried aloud, as I drew the knife at my hip and sprang forward a second time.

But something had happened. They were reeling apart. I was close upon him, my knife uplifted, but I withheld the blow. I was puzzled by the strangeness of it. Maud was leaning against the wall, one hand out for support; but he was staggering, his left hand pressed against his forehead and covering his eyes, and with the right he was groping about him in a dazed sort of way. It struck against the wall, and his body seemed to express a muscular and physical relief at the contact, as though he had found his bearings, his location in space as well as something against which to lean.

Then I saw red again. All my wrongs and humiliations flashed upon me with a dazzling brightness, all that I had suffered and others had suffered at his hands, all the enormity of the man's very existence. I sprang upon him, blindly, insanely, and drove the knife into his shoulder. I knew, then, that it was no more than a flesh wound—I had felt the steel grate on his shoulder-blade—and I raised the knife to strike at a more vital part.

But Maud had seen my first blow, and she cried, "Don't! Please don't!"

I dropped my arm for a moment, and a moment only. Again the knife was raised, and Wolf Larsen would have surely died had she not stepped between. Her arms were around me, her hair was brushing my face. My pulse rushed up in an unwonted manner, yet my rage mounted with it. She looked me bravely in the eyes.

"For my sake," she begged.

"I would kill him for your sake!" I cried, trying to free my arm without hurting her.

"Hush!" she said, and laid her fingers lightly on my lips. I could have kissed them, had I dared, even then, in my rage, the touch of them was so sweet, so very sweet. "Please, please," she pleaded, and she disarmed me by the words, as I was to discover they would ever disarm me.

I stepped back, separating from her, and replaced the knife in its sheath. I looked at Wolf Larsen. He still pressed his left hand against his forehead. It covered his eyes. His head was bowed. He seemed to have grown limp. His body was sagging at the hips, his great shoulders were drooping and shrinking forward.

"Van Weyden!" he called hoarsely, and with a note of fright in his voice. "Oh, Van Weyden! where are you?"

I looked at Maud. She did not speak, but nodded her head.

"Here I am," I answered, stepping to his side. "What is the matter?"

"Help me to a seat," he said, in the same hoarse, frightened voice.

"I am a sick man, a very sick man, Hump," he said, as he left my sustaining grip and sank into a chair.

His head dropped forward on the table and was buried in his hands. From time to time it rocked back and forward as with pain. Once, when he half raised it, I saw the sweat standing in heavy drops on his forehead about the roots of his hair.

"I am a sick man, a very sick man," he repeated again, and yet once again.

"What is the matter?" I asked, resting my hand on his shoulder. "What can I do for you?"

But he shook my hand off with an irritated movement, and for a long time I stood by his side in silence. Maud was looking on, her face awed and frightened. What had happened to him we could not imagine.

"Hump," he said at last, "I must get into my bunk. Lend me a hand. I'll be all right in a little while. It's those damn headaches, I believe. I was afraid of them. I had a feeling—no, I don't know what I'm talking about. Help me into my bunk."

But when I got him into his bunk he again buried his face in his hands, covering his eyes, and as I turned to go I could hear him murmuring, "I am a sick man, a very sick man."

Maud looked at me inquiringly as I emerged. I shook my head, saying:

"Something has happened to him. What, I don't know. He is helpless, and frightened, I imagine, for the first time in his life. It must have occurred before he received the knife-thrust, which made only a superficial wound. You must have seen what happened."

She shook her head. "I saw nothing. It is just as mysterious to me. He suddenly released me and staggered away. But what shall we do? What shall I do?"

"If you will wait, please, until I come back," I answered.

I went on deck. Louis was at the wheel.

"You may go for'ard and turn in," I said, taking it from him.

He was quick to obey, and I found myself alone on the deck of the *Ghost.* As quietly as was possible, I clewed up the topsails, lowered the flying jib and staysail, backed the jib over, and flattened the mainsail. Then I went below to Maud. I placed my finger on my lips for silence, and entered Wolf Larsen's room. He was in the same position in which I had left him, and his head was rocking—almost writhing—from side to side.

"Anything I can do for you?" I asked.

He made no reply at first, but on my repeating the question he answered, "No, no; I'm all right. Leave me alone till morning."

But as I turned to go I noted that his head had resumed its rocking motion. Maud was waiting patiently for me, and I took notice, with a thrill of joy, of the queenly poise of her head and her glorious, calm eyes. Calm and sure they were as her spirit itself.

"Will you trust yourself to me for a journey of six hundred miles or so?" I asked.

"You mean—?" she asked, and I knew she had guessed aright.

"Yes, I mean just that," I replied. "There is nothing left for us but the open boat."

"For me, you mean," she said. "You are certainly as safe here as you have been."

"No, there is nothing left for us but the open boat," I iterated stoutly. "Will you please dress as warmly as you can, at once, and make into a bundle whatever you wish to bring with you.

"And make all haste," I added, as she turned toward her stateroom.

The lazarette was directly beneath the cabin, and opening the trap-door in the floor and carrying a candle with me, I dropped down and began overhauling the ship's stores. I selected mainly from the canned goods, and by the time I was ready, willing hands were extended from above to receive what I passed up.

We worked in silence. I helped myself also to blankets, mittens, oilskins, caps, and such things, from the slop-chest. It was no light adventure, this trusting ourselves in a small boat to so raw and stormy a sea, and it was imperative that we should guard ourselves against the cold and wet.

We worked feverishly at carrying our plunder on deck and depositing it amidships, so feverishly that Maud, whose strength was hardly a positive quantity, had to give over, exhausted, and sit on the steps at the break of the poop. This did not serve to recover her, and she lay on her back, on the hard deck, arms stretched out and whole body relaxed. It was a trick I remembered of my sister, and I knew she would soon be herself again. I knew, also, that weapons would not come in amiss, and I re-entered Wolf Larsen's stateroom to get his rifle and shotgun. I spoke to him, but he made no answer, though his head was still rocking from side to side and he was not asleep.

"Good-by, Lucifer," I whispered to myself as I softly closed the door.

Next to obtain was a stock of ammunition—an easy matter, though I had to enter the steerage companionway to do it. Here the hunters stored the ammunition boxes they carried in the boats, and here, but a few feet from their noisy revels, I took possession of two boxes.

Next, to lower a boat. Not so simple a task for one man. Having cast off the lashings, I hoisted first on the forward tackle, then on the aft, till the boat cleared the rail, when I lowered away, one tackle and then the other, for a couple of feet, till it hung snugly, above the water, against the schooner's side. I made certain that it contained the proper equipment of oars, rowlocks, and sail. Water was a consideration, and I robbed every boat aboard of its breaker. As there were nine boats all told, it meant that we should have plenty of water, and ballast as well, though there was the chance that the boat would be overloaded, what of the generous supply of other things I was taking.

While Maud was passing me the provisions and I was storing them in the boat, a sailor came on deck from the forecastle. He stood by the weather rail for a time (we were lowering over the lee rail), and then sauntered slowly amidships, where he again paused and stood facing the wind, with his back toward us. I could hear my heart beating as I crouched low in the boat. Maud had sunk down upon the deck and was, I knew, lying motionless, her body in the shadow of the bulwark. But the man never turned, and, after stretching his arms above his head and yawning audibly, he retraced his steps to the forecastle scuttle and disappeared.

A few minutes sufficed to finish the loading, and I lowered the boat into the water. As I helped Maud over the rail and felt her form close to mine, it was all I could do to keep from crying out, "I love you! I love you!" Truly Humphrey Van Weyden was at last in love, I thought, as her fingers clung to mine while I lowered her down to the boat. I held on to the rail with one hand and supported her weight with the other, and I was proud at the moment of the feat. It was a strength I had not possessed a few months before, on the day I said good-by to Charley Furuseth and started for San Francisco on the ill-fated *Martinez.*

As the boat ascended on a sea, her feet touched and I released her hands. I cast off the tackles and leaped after her. I had never rowed in my life, but I put out the oars and at the expense of much effort got the boat clear of the *Ghost.* Then I experimented with the sail. I had seen the boat-steerers and hunters set their spritsails many times, yet this was my first attempt. What took them possibly two minutes took me twenty, but in the end I succeeded in setting and trimming it, and with the steering-oar in my hands hauled on the wind.

"There lies Japan," I remarked, "straight before us."

"Humphrey Van Weyden," she said, "you are a brave man."

"Nay," I answered, "it is you who are a brave woman."

We turned our heads, swayed by a common impulse to see the last of the *Ghost.* Her low hull lifted and rolled to windward on a sea; her canvas loomed darkly in the night; her lashed wheel creaked as the rudder kicked; then sight and sound of her faded away and we were alone on the dark sea.

XXVII

DAY broke, gray and chill. The boat was close-hauled on a fresh breeze and the compass indicated that we were just making the course which would bring us to Japan. Though stoutly mittened, my fingers were cold, and they pained from the grip on the steering-oar. My feet were stinging from the bite of the frost, and I hoped fervently that the sun would shine.

Before me, in the bottom of the boat, lay Maud. She, at least, was warm, for under her and over her were thick blankets. The top one I had drawn over her face to shelter it from the night, so I could see nothing but the vague shape of her, and her light-brown hair, escaped from the covering and jewelled with moisture from the air.

Long I looked at her, dwelling upon that one visible bit of her as only a man would who deemed it the most precious thing in the world. So insistent was my gaze that at last she stirred under the blankets, the top fold was thrown back and she smiled out on me, her eyes yet heavy with sleep.

"Good morning, Mr Van Weyden," she said. "Have you sighted land yet?"

"No," I answered, "but we are approaching it at a rate of six miles an hour."

She made a *moue* of disappointment.

"But that is equivalent to one hundred and forty-four miles in twenty-four hours," I added reassuringly.

Her face brightened. "And how far have we to go?"

"Siberia lies off there," I said, pointing to the west. "But to the southwest, some six hundred miles, is Japan. If this wind should hold, we'll make it in five days."

"And if it storms? The boat could not live?"

She had a way of looking one in the eyes and demanding the truth, and thus she looked at me as she asked the question.

"It would have to storm very hard," I temporized.

"And if it storms very hard?"

I nodded my head. "But we may be picked up any moment by a sealing-schooner. They are plentifully distributed over this part of the ocean."

"Why, you are chilled through!" she cried. "Look! You are shivering. Don't deny it; you are. And here I have been lying warm as toast."

"I don't see that it would help matters if you, too, sat up and were chilled," I laughed.

"It will, though, when I learn to steer, which I certainly shall."

She sat up and began making her simple toilet. She shook down her hair, and it fell about her in a brown cloud, hiding her face and shoulders. Dear, damp brown hair! I wanted to kiss it, to ripple it through my fingers, to bury my face in it. I gazed entranced, till the boat ran into the wind and the flapping sail warned me I was not attending to my duties. Idealist and romanticist that I was and always had been in spite of my analytical nature, yet I had failed till now in grasping much of the physical characteristics of love. The love of man and woman, I had always held, was a sublimated something related to spirit, a spiritual bond that linked and drew their souls together. The bonds of the flesh had little part in my cosmos of love. But I was learning the sweet lesson for myself that the soul transmuted itself, expressed itself, through the flesh; that the sight and sense and touch of the loved one's hair was as much breath and voice and essence of the spirit as the light that shone from the eyes and the thoughts that fell from the lips. After all, pure spirit was unknowable, a thing to be sensed and divined only; nor could it express itself in terms of itself. Jehovah was anthropomorphic because he could address himself to the Jews only in terms of their understanding; so he was conceived as in their own image, as a cloud, a pillar of fire, a tangible, physical something which the mind of the Israelites could grasp.

And so I gazed upon Maud's light-brown hair, and loved it, and learned more of love than all the poets and singers had taught me with all their songs and sonnets. She flung it back with a sudden adroit movement, and her face emerged, smiling.

"Why don't women wear their hair down always?" I asked. "It is so much more beautiful."

"If it didn't tangle so dreadfully," she laughed. "There! I've lost one of my precious hair-pins!"

I neglected the boat and had the sail spilling the wind again and again, such was my delight in following her every movement as she searched through the blankets for the pin. I was surprised, and joyfully, that she was so much the woman, and the display of each trait and mannerism that was characteristically feminine gave me keener joy. For I had been elevating her too highly in my concepts of her, removing her too far from the plane of the human, and too far from me. I had been making of her a creature goddess-like, unapproachable. So I hailed with delight the little traits that proclaimed her only woman after all, such as the toss of the head which flung back the cloud of hair, and the search for the pin. She was woman, my kind, on my plane, and the delightful intimacy of kind, of man and woman, was possible, as well as the reverence and awe in which I knew I should always hold her.

She found the pin with an adorable little cry, and I turned my attention more fully to my steering. I proceeded to experiment, lashing and wedging the steering-oar until the boat held on fairly well by the wind without my assistance. Occasionally it came up too close, or fell off too freely; but it always recovered itself and in the main behaved satisfactorily.

"And now we shall have breakfast," I said. "But first you must be more warmly clad."

I got out a heavy shirt, new from the slop-chest and made from blanket goods. I knew the kind, so thick and so close of texture that it could resist the rain and not be soaked through after hours of wetting. When she had slipped this on over her head, I exchanged the boy's cap she wore for a man's cap, large enough to cover her hair, and, when the flap was turned down, to completely cover her neck and ears. The effect was charming. Her face was of the sort that cannot but look well under all circumstances. Nothing could destroy its exquisite oval, its well-nigh classic lines, its delicately stencilled brows, its large brown eyes, clear-seeing and calm, gloriously calm.

A puff, slightly stronger than usual, struck us just then. The boat was caught as it obliquely crossed the crest of a wave. It went over suddenly, burying its gunwale level with the sea and shipping a bucketful or so of water. I was opening a can of tongue at the moment, and I sprang to the sheet and cast it off just in time. The sail flapped and fluttered, and the boat paid off. A few minutes of regulating sufficed to put it on its course again, when I returned to the preparation of breakfast.

"It does very well, it seems, though I am not versed in things nautical," she said, nodding her head with grave approval at my steering contrivance.

"But it will serve only when we are sailing by the wind," I explained. "When running more freely, with the wind astern, abeam, or on the quarter, it will be necessary for me to steer."

"I must say I don't understand your technicalities," she said, "but I do your conclusion, and I don't like it. You cannot steer night and day and forever. So I shall expect, after breakfast, to receive my first lesson. And then you shall lie down and sleep. We'll stand watches just as they do on ships."

"I don't see how I am to teach you," I made protest. "I am just learning for myself. You little thought when you trusted yourself to me that I had had no experience whatever with small boats. This is the first time I have ever been in one."

"Then we'll learn together, sir. And since you've had a night's start you shall teach me what you have learned. And now, breakfast. My! this air does give one an appetite!"

"No coffee," I said regretfully, passing her buttered sea-biscuits and a slice of canned tongue. "And there will be no tea, no soups, nothing hot, till we have made land somewhere, somehow."

After the simple breakfast, capped with a cup of cold water, Maud took her lesson in steering. In teaching her I learned quite a deal myself, though I was applying the knowledge already acquired by sailing the *Ghost* and by watching the boat-steerers sail the small boats. She was an apt pupil, and soon learned to keep the course, to luff in the puffs and to cast off the sheet in an emergency.

Having grown tired, apparently, of the task, she relinquished the oar to me. I had folded up the blankets, but she now proceeded to spread them out on the bottom. When all was arranged snugly, she said:

"Now, sir, to bed. And you shall sleep until luncheon. Till dinnertime," she corrected, remembering the arrangement on the *Ghost*.

What could I do? She insisted, and said, "Please, please," whereupon I turned the oar over to her and obeyed. I experienced a positive sensuous delight as I crawled into the bed she had made with her hands. The calm and control which were so much a part of her seemed to have been communicated to the blankets, so that I was aware of a soft dreaminess and content, and of an oval face and brown eyes framed in a fisherman's cap and tossing against a background now of gray cloud, now of gray sea, and then I was aware that I had been asleep.

I looked at my watch. It was one o'clock. I had slept seven hours! And she had been steering seven hours! When I took the steering-oar I had first to unbend her cramped fingers. Her modicum of strength had been exhausted, and she was unable even to move from her position. I was compelled to let go the sheet while I helped her to the nest of blankets and chafed her hands and arms.

"I am so tired," she said, with a quick intake of the breath and a sigh, drooping her head wearily.

But she straightened it the next moment. "Now don't scold, don't you dare scold," she cried with mock defiance.

"I hope my face does not appear angry," I answered seriously, "for I assure you I am not in the least angry."

"N—no," she considered. "It looks only reproachful."

"Then it is an honest face, for it looks what I feel. You were not fair to yourself, nor to me. How can I ever trust you again?"

She looked penitent. "I'll be good," she said, as a naughty child might say it. "I promise—"

"To obey as a sailor would obey his captain?"

"Yes," she answered. "It was stupid of me, I know."

"Then you must promise something else," I ventured.

"Readily."

"That you will not say, 'Please, please,' too often; for when you do you are sure to override my authority."

She laughed with amused appreciation. She, too, had noticed the power of the repeated "please".

"It is a good word—" I began.

"But I must not overwork it," she broke in.

But she laughed weakly, and her head drooped again. I left the oar long enough to tuck the blankets about her feet and to pull a single fold across her face. Alas! she was not strong. I looked with misgiving toward the southwest and thought of the six hundred miles of hardship before us—ay, if it were no worse than hardship. On this sea a storm might blow up at any moment and destroy us. And yet I was unafraid. I was without confidence in the future, extremely doubtful, and yet I felt no underlying fear. It must come right, it must come right, I repeated to myself, over and over again.

The wind freshened in the afternoon, raising a stiffer sea and trying the boat and me severely. But the supply of food and the nine breakers of water enabled the boat to stand up to the sea and wind, and I held on as long as I dared. Then I removed the sprit, tightly hauling down the peak of the sail, and we raced along under what sailors call a leg-of-mutton.

Late in the afternoon I sighted a steamer's smoke on the horizon to leeward, and I knew it either for a Russian cruiser, or, more likely, the *Macedonia* still seeking the *Ghost.* The sun had not shone all day, and it had been bitter cold. As night drew on, the clouds darkened and the wind freshened, so that when Maud and I ate supper it was with our mittens on and with me still steering and eating morsels between puffs.

By the time it was dark, wind and sea had become too strong for the boat, and I reluctantly took in the sail and set about making a drag or sea-anchor. I had learned of the device from the talk of the hunters, and it was a simple thing to manufacture. Furling the sail and lashing it securely about the mast, boom, sprit, and two pairs of spare oars, I threw it overboard. A line connected it with the bow, and as it floated low in the water, practically unexposed to the wind, it drifted less rapidly than the boat. In consequence it held the boat bow on to the sea and wind—the safest position in which to escape being swamped when the sea is breaking into whitecaps.

"And now?" Maud asked cheerfully, when the task was accomplished and I pulled on my mittens.

"And now we are no longer travelling toward Japan," I answered. "Our drift is to the southeast, or south-southeast, at the rate of at least two miles an hour."

"That will be only twenty-four miles," she urged, "if the wind remains high all night."

"Yes, and only one hundred and forty miles if it continues for three days and nights."

"But it won't continue," she said, with easy confidence. "It will turn around and blow fair."

"The sea is the great faithless one."

"But the wind!" she retorted. "I have heard you grow eloquent over the brave trade-wind."

"I wish I had thought to bring Wolf Larsen's chronometer and sextant," I said, still gloomily. "Sailing one direction, drifting another direction, to say nothing of the set of the current in some third direction, makes a resultant which dead reckoning can never calculate. Before long we won't know where we are by five hundred miles."

Then I begged her pardon and promised I should not be disheartened any more. At her solicitation I let her take the watch till midnight—it was then nine o'clock, but I wrapped her in blankets and put an oilskin about her before I lay down. I slept only cat-naps. The boat was leaping and pounding as it fell over the crests, I could hear the seas rushing past, and spray was continually being thrown aboard. And still, it was not a bad night, I mused—nothing to the nights I had been through on the *Ghost*; nothing, perhaps, to the nights we should go through in this cockle-shell. Its planking was three-quarters of an inch thick. Between us and the bottom of the sea was less than an inch of wood.

And yet, I aver it, and I aver it again, I was unafraid. The death which Wolf Larsen and even Thomas Mugridge had made me fear, I no longer feared. The coming of Maud Brewster into my life seemed to have transformed me. After all, I thought, it is better and finer to love than to be loved, if it makes something in life so worth while that one is not loath to die for it. I forget my own life in the love of another life; and yet, such is the paradox, I never wanted so much to live as right now when I place the least value upon my own life. I never had so much reason for living, was my concluding thought; and after that, until I dozed, I contented myself with trying to pierce the darkness to where I knew Maud crouched low in the stern-sheets, watchful of the foaming sea and ready to call me on an instant's notice.

XXVIII

THERE is no need of going into an extended recital of our suffering in the small boat during the many days we were driven and drifted, here and there, willy-nilly, across the ocean. The high wind blew from the northwest for twenty-four hours, when it fell calm, and in the night sprang up from the southwest. This was dead in our teeth, but I took in the sea-anchor and set sail, hauling a course on the wind which took us in a south-southeasterly direction. It was an even choice between this and the west-northwesterly course which the wind permitted; but the warm airs of the south fanned my desire for a warmer sea and swayed my decision.

In three hours—it was midnight, I well remember, and as dark as I had ever seen it on the sea—the wind, still blowing out of the southwest, rose furiously, and once again I was compelled to set the sea-anchor.

Day broke and found me wan-eyed and the ocean lashed white, the boat pitching, almost on end, to its drag. We were in imminent danger of being swamped by the whitecaps. As it was, spray and spume came aboard in such quantities that I bailed without cessation. The blankets were soaking. Everything was wet except Maud, and she, in oilskins, rubber boots, and sou'wester, was dry, all but her face and hands and a stray wisp of hair. She relieved me at the bailing-hole from time to time, and bravely she threw out the water and faced the storm. All things are relative. It was no more than a stiff blow, but to us, fighting for life in our frail craft, it was indeed a storm.

Cold and cheerless, the wind beating on our faces, the white seas roaring by, we struggled through the day. Night came, but neither of us slept. Day came, and still the wind beat on our faces and the white seas roared past. By the second night Maud was falling asleep from exhaustion. I covered her with oilskins and a tarpaulin. She was comparatively dry, but she was numb with the cold. I feared greatly that she might die in the night; but day broke, cold and cheerless, with the same clouded sky and beating wind and roaring seas.

I had had no sleep for forty-eight hours. I was wet and chilled to the marrow, till I felt more dead than alive. My body was stiff from exertion as well as from cold, and my aching muscles gave me the severest torture whenever I used them, and I used them continually. And all the time we were being driven off into the northeast, directly away from Japan and toward bleak Bering Sea.

And still we lived, and the boat lived, and the wind blew unabated. In fact, toward nightfall of the third day it increased a trifle and something more. The boat's bow plunged under a crest, and we came through quarter-full of water. I bailed like a madman. The liability of shipping another such sea was enormously increased by the water that weighed the boat down and robbed it of its buoyancy. And another such sea meant the end. When I had the boat empty again I was forced to take away the tarpaulin which covered Maud, in order that I might lash it down across the bow. It was well I did, for it covered the boat fully a third of the way aft, and three times, in the next several hours, it flung off the bulk of the down-rushing water when the bow shoved under the seas.

Maud's condition was pitiable. She sat crouched in the bottom of the boat, her lips blue, her face gray and plainly showing the pain she suffered. But ever her eyes looked bravely at me, and ever her lips uttered brave words.

The worst of the storm must have blown that night, though little I noticed it. I had succumbed and slept where I sat in the stern-sheets. The morning of the fourth day found the wind diminished to a gentle whisper, the sea dying down and the sun shining upon us. Oh, the blessed sun! How we bathed our poor bodies in its delicious warmth, reviving like bugs and crawling things after a storm. We smiled again, said amusing things, and waxed optimistic over our situation. Yet it was, if anything, worse than ever. We were farther from Japan than the night we left the *Ghost.* Nor could I more than roughly guess our latitude and longitude. At a calculation of a two-mile drift per hour, during the seventy and odd hours of the storm, we had been driven at least one hundred and fifty miles to the northeast. But was such calculated drift correct? For all I knew, it might have been four miles per hour instead of two. In which case we were another hundred and fifty miles to the bad.

Where we were I did not know, though there was quite a likelihood that we were in the vicinity of the *Ghost.* There were seals about us, and I was prepared to sight a sealing-schooner at any time. We did sight one, in the afternoon, when the northwest breeze had sprung up freshly once more. But the strange schooner lost itself on the sky-line and we alone occupied the circle of the sea.

Came days of fog, when even Maud's spirit drooped and there were no merry words upon her lips; days of calm, when we floated on the lonely immensity of sea, oppressed by its greatness and yet marvelling at the miracle of tiny life, for we still lived and struggled to live; days of sleet and wind and snow-squalls, when nothing could keep us warm; or days of drizzling rain, when we filled our water-breakers from the drip of the wet sail.

And ever I loved Maud with an increasing love. She was so many-sided, so many-mooded—"protean-mooded" I called her. But I called her this, and other and dearer things, in my thoughts only. Though the declaration of my love urged and trembled on my tongue a thousand times, I knew that it was no time for such a declaration. If for no other reason, it was no time, when one was protecting and trying to save a woman, to ask that woman for her love. Delicate as was the situation, not alone in this but in other ways, I flattered myself that I was able to deal delicately with it; and also I flattered myself that by look or sign I gave no advertisement of the love I felt for her. We were like good comrades, and we grew better comrades as the days went by.

One thing about her which surprised me was her lack of timidity and fear. The terrible sea, the frail boat, the storms, the suffering, the strangeness and isolation of the situation—all that should have frightened a robust woman—seemed to make no impression upon her who had known life in its most sheltered and consummately artificial aspects, and who was herself all fire and dew and mist, sublimated spirit, all that was soft and tender and clinging in woman. And yet I am wrong. She *was* timid and afraid, but she possessed courage. The flesh and the qualms of the flesh she was heir to, but the flesh bore heavily only on the flesh. And she was spirit, first and always spirit, etherealized essence of life, calm as her calm eyes, and sure of permanence in the changing order of the universe.

Came days of storm, days and nights of storm, when the ocean menaced us with its roaring whiteness, and the wind smote our struggling boat with a Titan's buffets. And ever we were flung off, farther and farther, to the northeast. It was in such a storm, and the worst that we had experienced, that I cast a weary glance to leeward, not in quest of anything, but more from the weariness of facing the elemental strife, and in mute appeal, almost, to the wrathful powers to cease and let us be. What I saw I could not at first believe. Days and nights of sleeplessness and anxiety had doubtless turned my head. I looked back at Maud, to identify myself, as it were, in time and space. The sight of her dear wet cheeks, her flying hair, and her brave brown eyes convinced me that my vision was still healthy. Again I turned my face to leeward, and again I saw the jutting promontory, black and high and naked, the raging surf that broke about its base and beat its front high up with spouting fountains, the black and forbidding coastline running toward the southeast and fringed with a tremendous scarf of white.

"Maud," I said. "Maud."

She turned her head and beheld the sight.

"It cannot be Alaska!" she cried.

"Alas, no," I answered, and asked, "Can you swim?"

She shook her head.

"Neither can I," I said. "So we must get ashore without swimming, in some opening between the rocks through which we can drive the boat and clamber out. But we must be quick, most quick—and sure."

I spoke with a confidence she knew I did not feel, for she looked at me with that unfaltering gaze of hers and said:

"I have not thanked you yet for all you have done for me, but—"

She hesitated, as if in doubt how best to word her gratitude.

"Well?" I said, brutally, for I was not quite pleased with her thanking me.

"You might help me," she smiled.

"To acknowledge your obligations before you die? Not at all. We are not going to die. We shall land on that island, and we shall be snug and sheltered before the day is done."

I spoke stoutly, but I did not believe a word. Nor was I prompted to lie through fear. I felt no fear, though I was sure of death in that boiling surge amongst the rocks which was rapidly growing nearer. It was impossible to hoist sail and claw off that shore. The wind would instantly capsize the boat; the seas would swamp it the moment it fell into the trough; and, besides, the sail, lashed to the spare oars, dragged in the sea ahead of us.

As I say, I was not afraid to meet my own death, there, a few hundred yards to leeward; but I was appalled at the thought that Maud must die. My cursed imagination saw her beaten and mangled against the rocks, and it was too terrible. I strove to compel myself to think we would make the landing safely, and so I spoke, not what I believed, but what I preferred to believe.

I recoiled before contemplation of that frightful death, and for a moment I entertained the wild idea of seizing Maud in my arms and leaping overboard. Then I resolved to wait, and at the last moment, when we entered on the final stretch, to take her in my arms and proclaim my love, and, with her in my embrace, to make the desperate struggle and die.

Instinctively we drew closer together in the bottom of the boat. I felt her mittened hand come out to mine. And thus, without speech, we waited the end. We were not far off the line the wind made with the western edge of the promontory, and I watched in the hope that some set of the current or send of the sea would drift us past before we reached the surf.

"We shall go clear," I said, with a confidence which I knew deceived neither of us.

"By God, we *will* go clear!" I cried, five minutes later.

The oath left my lips in my excitement—the first, I do believe, in my life, unless "trouble it" , an expletive of my youth, be accounted an oath.

"I beg your pardon," I said.

"You have convinced me of your sincerity," she said, with a faint smile. "I do know, now, that we shall go clear."

I had seen a distant headland past the extreme edge of the promontory, and as we looked we could see grow the intervening coastline of what was evidently a deep cove. At the same time there broke upon our ears a continuous and mighty bellowing. It partook of the magnitude and volume of distant thunder, and it came to us directly from leeward, rising above the crash of the surf and travelling directly in the teeth of the storm. As we passed the point the whole cove burst upon our view, a half-moon of white sandy beach upon which broke a huge surf, and which was covered with myriads of seals. It was from them that the great bellowing went up.

"A rookery!" I cried. "Now are we indeed saved. There must be men and cruisers to protect them from the seal-hunters. Possibly there is a station ashore."

But as I studied the surf which beat upon the beach, I said, "Still bad, but not so bad. And now, if the gods be truly kind, we shall drift by that next headland and come upon a perfectly sheltered beach, where we may land without wetting our feet."

And the gods were kind. The first and second headlands were directly in line with the southwest wind; but once around the second—and we went perilously near—we picked up the third headland, still in line with the wind and with the other two. But the cove that intervened! It penetrated deep into the land, and the tide, setting in, drifted us under the shelter of the point. Here the sea was calm, save for a heavy but smooth ground-swell, and I took in the sea-anchor and began to row. From the point the shore curved away, more and more to the south and west, until, at last, it disclosed a cove within the cove, a little land-locked harbor, the water level as a pond, broken only by tiny ripples where vagrant breaths and wisps of the storm hurtled down from over the frowning wall of rock that backed the beach a hundred feet inshore.

Here were no seals whatever. The boat's stem touched the hard shingle. I sprang out, extending my hand to Maud. The next moment she was beside me. As my fingers released hers, she clutched for my arm hastily. At the same moment I swayed, as about to fall to the sand. This was the startling effect of the cessation of motion. We had been so long upon the moving, rocking sea that the stable land was a shock to us. We expected the beach to lift up this way and that, and the rocky walls to swing back and forth like the sides of a ship; and when we braced ourselves, automatically, for these various expected movements, their non-occurrence quite overcame our equilibrium.

"I really must sit down," Maud said, with a nervous laugh and a dizzy gesture, and forthwith she sat down on the sand.

I attended to making the boat secure and joined her. Thus we landed on Endeavor Island, as we came to it, land-sick from long custom of the sea.

XXIX

"Fool!" I cried aloud in my vexation.

I had unloaded the boat and carried its contents high up on the beach, where I had set about making a camp. There was driftwood, though not much, on the beach, and the sight of a coffee tin I had taken from the *Ghost*'s larder had given me the idea of a fire.

"Blithering idiot!" I was continuing.

But Maud said, "Tut, tut," in gentle reproval, and then asked why I was a blithering idiot.

"No matches," I groaned. "Not a match did I bring. And now we shall have no hot coffee, soup, tea, or anything!"

"Wasn't it—er—Crusoe who rubbed sticks together?" she drawled.

"But I have read the personal narratives of a score of shipwrecked men who tried, and tried in vain," I answered. "I remember Winters, a newspaper fellow with an Alaskan and Siberian reputation. Met him at the Bibelot once, and he was telling us how he attempted to make a fire with a couple of sticks. It was most amusing. He told it inimitably, but it was the story of a failure. I remember his conclusion, his black eyes flashing as he said, 'Gentlemen, the South Sea Islander may do it, the Malay may do it, but take my word it's beyond the white man.' "

"Oh, well, we've managed so far without it," she said cheerfully. "And there's no reason why we cannot still manage without it."

"But think of the coffee!" I cried. "It's good coffee, too. I know. I took it from Larsen's private stores. And look at that good wood."

I confess, I wanted the coffee badly; and I learned, not long afterward, that the berry was likewise a little weakness of Maud's. Besides, we had been so long on a cold diet that we were numb inside as well as out. Anything warm would have been most gratifying. But I complained no more, and set about making a tent of the sail for Maud.

I had looked upon it as a simple task, what of the oars, mast, boom, and sprit, to say nothing of plenty of lines. But as I was without experience, and as every detail was an experiment and every successful detail an invention, the day was well gone before her shelter was an accomplished fact. And then, that night, it rained, and she was flooded out and driven back into the boat.

The next morning I dug a shallow ditch around the tent, and, an hour later, a sudden gust of wind, whipping over the rocky wall behind us, picked up the tent and smashed it down on the sand thirty yards away.

Maud laughed at my crestfallen expression, and I said, "As soon as the wind abates I intend going in the boat to explore the island. There must be a station somewhere, and men. And ships must visit the station. Some Government must protect all these seals. But I wish to have you comfortable before I start."

"I should like to go with you," was all she said.

"It would be better if you remained. You have had enough of hardship. It is a miracle that you have survived. And it won't be comfortable in the boat, rowing and sailing in this rainy weather. What you need is rest, and I should like you to remain and get it."

Something suspiciously akin to moistness dimmed her beautiful eyes before she dropped them and partly turned away her head.

"I should prefer going with you," she said in a low voice, in which there was just a hint of appeal.

"I might be able to help you a—" her voice broke—"a little. And if anything should happen to you, think of me left here alone."

"Oh, I intend being very careful," I answered. "And I shall not go so far but what I can get back before night. Yes, all said and done, I think it vastly better for you to remain, and sleep, and rest, and do nothing."

She turned and looked me in the eyes. Her gaze was unfaltering, but soft.

"Please, please," she said, oh, so softly.

I stiffened myself to refuse, and shook my head. Still she waited and looked at me. I tried to word my refusal, but wavered. I saw the glad light spring into her eyes and knew that I had lost. It was impossible to say no after that.

The wind died down in the afternoon, and we were prepared to start the following morning. There was no way of penetrating the island from our cove, for the walls rose perpendicularly from the beach, and, on either side of the cove, rose from the deep water.

Morning broke dull and gray, but calm, and I was awake early and had the boat in readiness.

"Fool! Imbecile! Yahoo!" I shouted, when I thought it was meet to arouse Maud; but this time I shouted in merriment as I danced about the beach, bareheaded, in mock despair.

Her head appeared under the flap of the sail.

"What now?" she asked sleepily, and, withal, curiously.

"Coffee!" I cried. "What do you say to a cup of coffee? Hot coffee? Piping hot?"

"My!" she murmured, "you startled me, and you are cruel. Here I have been composing my soul to do without it, and here you are vexing me with your vain suggestions."

"Watch me," I said.

From under clefts among the rocks I gathered a few dry sticks and chips. These I whittled into shavings or split into kindling. From my note-book I tore out a page, and from the ammunition box took a shotgun shell. Removing the wads from the latter with my knife, I emptied the powder on a flat rock. Next I pried the primer, or cap, from the shell, and laid it on the rock in the midst of the scattered powder. All was ready. Maud still watched from the tent. Holding the paper in my left hand, I smashed down upon the cap with a rock held in my right. There was a puff of white smoke, a burst of flame, and the rough edge of the paper was alight.

Maud clapped her hands gleefully. "Prometheus!" she cried.

But I was too occupied to acknowledge her delight. The feeble flame must be cherished tenderly if it were to gather strength and live. I fed it, shaving by shaving, and sliver by sliver, till at last it was snapping and crackling as it laid hold of the smaller chips and sticks. To be cast away on an island had not entered into my calculations, so we were without a kettle or cooking utensils of any sort; but I made shift with the tin used for bailing the boat, and later, as we consumed our supply of canned goods, we accumulated quite an imposing array of cooking vessels.

I boiled the water, but it was Maud who made the coffee. And how good it was! My contribution was canned beef fried with crumbled sea-biscuit and water. The breakfast was a success, and we sat about the fire much longer than enterprising explorers should have done, sipping the hot black coffee and talking over our situation.

I was confident that we should find a station in some one of the coves, for I knew that the rookeries of Bering Sea were thus guarded; but Maud advanced the theory—to prepare me for disappointment, I do believe, if disappointment were to come—that we had discovered an unknown rookery. She was in very good spirits, however, and made quite merry in accepting our plight as a grave one.

"If you are right," I said, "then we must prepare to winter here. Our food will not last, but there are the seals. They go away in the fall, so I must soon begin to lay in a supply of meat. Then there will be huts to build and driftwood to gather. Also, we shall try out seal fat for lighting purposes. Altogether, we'll have our hands full if we find the island uninhabited. Which we shall not, I know."

But she was right. We sailed with a beam wind along the shore, searching the coves with our glasses and landing occasionally, without finding a sign of human life. Yet we learned that we were not the first who had landed on Endeavor Island. High up on the beach of the second cove from ours, we discovered the splintered wreck of a boat—a sealer's boat, for the rowlocks were bound in sennit, a gun-rack was on the starboard side of the bow, and in white letters was faintly visible *Gazelle No. 2.* The boat had lain there for a long time, for it was half filled with sand, and the splintered wood had that weather-worn appearance due to long exposure to the elements. In the sternsheets I found a rusty ten-gauge shotgun and a sailor's sheath-knife broken short across and so rusted as to be almost unrecognizable.

"They got away," I said cheerfully; but I felt a sinking at the heart and seemed to divine the presence of bleached bones somewhere on that beach.

I did not wish Maud's spirits to be dampened by such a find, so I turned seaward again with our boat and skirted the northeastern point of the island. There were no beaches on the southern shore, and by early afternoon we rounded the black promontory and completed the circumnavigation of the island. I estimated its circumference at twenty-five miles, its width as varying from two to five miles; while my most conservative calculation placed on its beaches two hundred thousand seals. The island was highest at its extreme southwestern point, the headlands and backbone diminishing regularly until the northeastern portion was only a few feet above the sea. With the exception of our little cove, the other beaches sloped gently back for a distance of half-a-mile or so, into what I might call rocky meadows, with here and there patches of moss and tundra grass. Here the seals hauled out, and the old bulls guarded their harems, while the young bulls hauled out by themselves.

This brief description is all that Endeavor Island merits. Damp and soggy where it was not sharp and rocky, buffeted by storm winds and lashed by the sea, with the air continually a-tremble with the bellowing of two hundred thousand amphibians, it was a melancholy and miserable sojourning-place. Maud, who had prepared me for disappointment, and who had been sprightly and vivacious all day, broke down as we landed in our own little cove. She strove bravely to hide it from me, but while I was kindling another fire I knew she was stifling her sobs in the blankets under the sail-tent.

It was my turn to be cheerful, and I played the part to the best of my ability, and with such success that I brought the laughter back into her dear eyes and song on her lips; for she sang to me before she went to an early bed. It was the first time I had heard her sing, and I lay by the fire, listening and transported, for she was nothing if not an artist in everything she did, and her voice, though not strong, was wonderfully sweet and expressive.

I still slept in the boat, and I lay awake long that night, gazing up at the first stars I had seen in many nights and pondering the situation. Responsibility of this sort was a new thing to me. Wolf Larsen had been quite right. I had stood on my father's legs. My lawyers and agents had taken care of my money for me. I had had no responsibilities at all. Then, on the *Ghost* I had learned to be responsible for myself. And now, for the first time in my life, I found myself responsible for someone else. And it was required of me that this should be the gravest of responsibilities, for she was the one woman in the world—the one small woman, as I loved to think of her.

XXX

No wonder we called it Endeavor Island. For two weeks we toiled at building a hut. Maud insisted on helping, and I could have wept over her bruised and bleeding hands. And still, I was proud of her because of it. There was something heroic about this gently bred woman enduring our terrible hardship and with her pittance of strength bending to the tasks of a peasant woman. She gathered many of the stones which I built into the walls of the hut; also she turned a deaf ear to my entreaties when I begged her to desist. She compromised, however, by taking upon herself the lighter labors of cooking and gathering driftwood and moss for our winter's supply.

The hut's walls rose without difficulty, and everything went smoothly until the problem of the roof confronted me. Of what use the four walls without a roof? And of what could a roof be made? There were the spare oars, very true. They would serve as roof-beams; but with what was I to cover them? Moss would never do. Tundra grass was impracticable. We needed the sail for the boat, and the tarpaulin had begun to leak.

"Winters used walrus skins on his hut," I said.

"There are the seals," she suggested.

So next day the hunting began. I did not know how to shoot, but I proceeded to learn. And when I had expended some thirty shells for three seals, I decided that the ammunition would be exhausted before I acquired the necessary knowledge. I had used eight shells for lighting fires before I hit upon the device of banking the embers with wet moss, and there remained not over a hundred shells in the box.

"We must club the seals," I announced, when convinced of my poor marksmanship. "I have heard the sealers talk about clubbing them."

"They are so pretty," she objected. "I cannot bear to think of it being done. It is so directly brutal, you know; so different from shooting them."

"That roof must go on," I answered grimly. "Winter is almost here. It is our lives against theirs. It is unfortunate we haven't plenty of ammunition, but I think, anyway, that they suffer less from being clubbed than from being all shot up. Besides, I shall do the clubbing."

"That's just it," she began eagerly, and broke off in sudden confusion.

"Of course," I began, "if you prefer—"

"But what shall I be doing?" she interrupted, with that softness I knew full well to be insistence.

"Gathering firewood and cooking dinner," I answered lightly.

She shook her head. "It is too dangerous for you to attempt alone.

"I know, I know," she waived my protest. "I am only a weak woman, but just my small assistance may enable you to escape disaster."

"But the clubbing?" I suggested.

"Of course, you will do that. I shall probably scream. I'll look away when—"

"The danger is most serious," I laughed.

"I shall use my judgement when to look and when not to look," she replied with a grand air.

The upshot of the affair was that she accompanied me next morning. I rowed into the adjoining cove and up to the edge of the beach. There were seals all about us in the water, and the bellowing thousands on the beach compelled us to shout at each other to make ourselves heard.

"I know men club them," I said, trying to reassure myself and gazing doubtfully at a large bull, not thirty feet away, upreared on his fore-flippers and regarding me intently. "But the question is, How do they club them?"

"Let us gather tundra grass and thatch the roof," Maud said.

She was as frightened as I at the prospect, and we had reason to be, gazing at close range at the gleaming teeth and dog-like mouths.

"I always thought they were afraid of men," I said.

"How do I know they are not afraid?" I queried a moment later, after having rowed a few more strokes along the beach. "Perhaps, if I were to step boldly ashore, they would cut for it, and I could not catch up with one."

And still I hesitated.

"I heard of a man, once, who invaded the nesting grounds of wild geese," Maud said. "They killed him."

"The geese?"

"Yes, the geese. My brother told me about it when I was a little girl."

"But I know men club them," I persisted.

"I think the tundra grass will make just as good a roof," she said.

Far from her intention, her words were maddening me, driving me on. I could not play the coward before her eyes.

"Here goes," I said, backing water with one oar and running the bow ashore.

I stepped out and advanced valiantly upon a long-maned bull in the midst of his wives. I was armed with the regular club with which the boat-pullers killed the wounded seals gaffed aboard by the hunters. It was only a foot and a half long, and in my superb ignorance I never dreamed that the club used ashore when raiding the rookeries measured four to five feet. The cows lumbered out of my way, and the distance between me and the bull decreased. He raised himself on his flippers with an angry movement. We were a dozen feet apart. Still I advanced steadily, looking for him to turn tail at any moment and run.

At six feet the panicky thought rushed into my mind. What if he will not run? Why, then I shall club him, came the answer. In my fear I had forgotten that I was there to get the bull instead of to make him run. And just then he gave a snort and a snarl and rushed to me. His eyes were blazing, his mouth was wide open; the teeth gleamed cruelly white. Without shame, I confess that it was I who turned and footed it. He ran awkwardly, but he ran well. He was but two paces behind when I tumbled into the boat, and as I shoved off with an oar his teeth crunched down upon the blade. The stout wood was crushed like an egg-shell. Maud and I were astounded. A moment later he had dived under the boat, seized the keel in his mouth, and was shaking the boat violently.

"My!" said Maud. "Let's go back."

I shook my head. "I can do what other men have done, and I know that other men have clubbed seals. But I think I'll leave the bulls alone next time."

"I wish you wouldn't," she said.

"Now don't say, 'Please, please,' " I cried, half angrily, I do believe.

She made no reply, and I knew my tone must have hurt her.

"I beg your pardon," I said, or shouted, rather, in order to make myself heard above the roar of the rookery. "If you say so, I'll turn and go back; but honestly, I'd rather stay."

"Now don't say that this is what you get for bringing a woman along," she said. She smiled at me whimsically, gloriously, and I knew there was no need for forgiveness.

I rowed a couple of hundred feet along the beach so as to recover my nerves, and then stepped ashore again.

"Do be cautious," she called after me.

I nodded my head and proceeded to make a flank attack on the nearest harem. All went well until I aimed a blow at an outlying cow's head and fell short. She snorted and tried to scramble away. I ran in close and struck another blow, hitting the shoulder instead of the head.

"Watch out!" I heard Maud scream.

In my excitement I had not been taking notice of other things, and I looked up to see the lord of the harem charging down upon me. Again I fled to the boat, hotly pursued; but this time Maud made no suggestion of turning back.

"It would be better, I imagine, if you let harems alone and devoted your attention to lonely and inoffensive-looking seals," was what she said. "I think I have read something about them. Dr Jordan's book, I believe. They are the young bulls, not old enough to have harems of their own. He called them the holluschickie, or something like that. It seems to me if we find where they haul out—"

"It seems to me that your fighting instinct is aroused," I laughed.

She flushed quickly and prettily. "I'll admit I don't like defeat any more than you do, or any more than I like the idea of killing such pretty, inoffensive creatures."

"Pretty!" I sniffed. "I failed to mark anything pre-eminently pretty about those foamy-mouthed beasts that raced me."

"Your point of view," she laughed. "You lacked perspective. Now if you did not have to get so close to the subject—"

"The very thing!" I cried. "What I need is a longer club. And there's that broken oar ready to hand."

"It just comes to me," she said, "that Captain Larsen was telling me how the men raided the rookeries. They drive the seals, in small herds, a short distance inland before they kill them."

"I don't care to undertake the herding of one of those harems," I objected.

"But there are the holluschickie," she said. "The holluschickie haul out by themselves, and Dr Jordan says that paths are left between the harems, and that as long as the holluschickie keep strictly to the path they are unmolested by the masters of the harem."

"There's one now," I said, pointing to a young bull in the water. "Let's watch him, and follow him if he hauls out."

He swam directly to the beach and clambered out into a small opening between two harems, the masters of which made warning noises but did not attack him. We watched him travel slowly inward, threading about among the harems along what must have been the path.

"Here goes," I said, stepping out; but I confess my heart was in my mouth as I thought of going through the heart of that monstrous herd.

"It would be wise to make the boat fast," Maud said.

She had stepped out beside me, and I regarded her with wonderment.

She nodded her head determinedly. "Yes, I'm going with you, so you may as well secure the boat and arm me with a club."

"Let's go back," I said dejectedly. "I think tundra grass will do, after all."

"You know it won't," was her reply. "Shall I lead?"

With a shrug of the shoulders, but with the warmest admiration and pride at heart for this woman, I equipped her with the broken oar and took another for myself. It was with nervous trepidation that we made the first few rods of the journey. Once Maud screamed in terror as a cow thrust an inquisitive nose toward her foot, and several times I quickened my pace for the same reason. But, beyond warning coughs from either side, there were no signs of hostility. It was a rookery which had never been raided by the hunters, and in consequence the seals were mild-tempered and at the same time unafraid.

In the very heart of the herd the din was terrific. It was almost dizzying in its effect. I paused and smiled reassuringly at Maud, for I had recovered my equanimity sooner than she. I could see that she was still badly frightened. She came close to me and shouted:

"I'm dreadfully afraid!"

And I was not. Though the novelty had not yet worn off, the peaceful comportment of the seals had quieted my alarm. Maud was trembling.

"I'm afraid, and I'm not afraid," she chattered with shaking jaws. "It's my miserable body, not I."

"It's all right, it's all right," I reassured her, my arm passing instinctively and protectingly around her.

I shall never forget, in that moment, how instantly conscious I became of my manhood. The primitive deeps of my nature stirred. I felt myself masculine, the protector of the weak, the fighting male. And, best of all, I felt myself the protector of my loved one. She leaned against me, so light and lily-frail, and as her trembling eased away it seemed as though I became aware of prodigious strength. I felt myself a match for the most ferocious bull in the herd, and I know, had such a bull charged upon me, that I should have met it unflinchingly and quite coolly, and I know that I should have killed it.

"I am all right now," she said, looking up at me gratefully. "Let us go on."

And that the strength in me had quieted her and given her confidence, filled me with an exultant joy. The youth of the race seemed burgeoning in me, over-civilized man that I was, and I lived for myself the old hunting days and forest nights of my remote and forgotten ancestry. I had much for which to thank Wolf Larsen, was my thought as we went along the path between the jostling harems.

A quarter of a mile inland we came upon the holluschickie—sleek young bulls, living out the loneliness of their bachelorhood and gathering strength against the day when they would fight their way into the ranks of the benedicts.

Everything now went smoothly. I seemed to know just what to do and how to do it. Shouting, making threatening gestures with my club, and even prodding the lazy ones, I quickly cut out a score of the young bachelors from their companions. Whenever one made an attempt to break back toward the water, I headed it off. Maud took an active part in the drive, and with her cries and flourishings of the broken oar was of considerable assistance. I noticed, though, that whenever one looked tired and lagged, she let it slip past. But I noticed, also, whenever one, with a show of fight, tried to break past, that her eyes glinted and showed bright, and she rapped it smartly with her club.

"My, it's exciting!" she cried, pausing from sheer weakness. "I think I'll sit down."

I drove the little herd (a dozen strong now, what of the escapes she had permitted) a hundred yards farther on; and by the time she joined me I had finished the slaughter and was beginning to skin. An hour later we went proudly back along the path between the harems. And twice again we came down the path burdened with skins, till I thought we had enough to roof the hut. I set the sail, laid one tack out of the cove, and on the other tack made our own little inner cove.

"It's just like home-coming," Maud said, as I ran the boat ashore.

I heard her words with a responsive thrill, it was all so dearly intimate and natural, and I said:

"It seems as though I have lived this life always. The world of books and bookish folk is very vague, more like a dream memory than an actuality. I surely have hunted and forayed and fought all the days of my life. And you, too, seem a part of it. You are—" I was on the verge of saying, "my woman, my mate" , but glibly changed it to—"standing the hardship well."

But her ear had caught the flaw. She recognized a flight that midmost broke. She gave me a quick look.

"Not that. You were saying—?"

"That the American Mrs Meynell was living the life of a savage and living it quite successfully," I said easily.

"Oh," was all she replied; but I could have sworn there was a note of disappointment in her voice.

But "my woman, my mate" kept ringing in my head for the rest of the day and for many days. Yet never did it ring more loudly than that night, as I watched her draw back the blanket of moss from the coals, blow up the fire, and cook the evening meal. It must have been latent savagery stirring in me, for the old words, so bound up with the roots of the race, to grip me and thrill me. And grip and thrill they did, till I fell asleep, murmuring them to myself over and over again.

XXXI

"It will smell," I said, "but it will keep in the heat and keep out the rain and snow."

We were surveying the completed sealskin roof.

"It is clumsy, but it will serve the purpose, and that is the main thing," I went on, yearning for her praise.

And she clapped her hands and declared that she was hugely pleased.

"But it is dark in here," she said the next moment, her shoulders shrinking with a little involuntary shiver.

"You might have suggested a window when the walls were going up," I said. "It was for you, and you should have seen the need of a window."

"But I never do see the obvious, you know," she laughed back. "And besides, you can knock a hole in the wall at any time."

"Quite true; I had not thought of it," I replied, wagging my head sagely. "But have you thought of ordering the window-glass? Just call up the firm—Red, 4451, I think it is—and tell them what size and kind of glass you wish."

"That means—" she began.

"No window."

It was a dark and evil-appearing thing, that hut, not fit for aught better than swine in a civilized land; but for us, who had known the misery of the open boat, it was a snug little habitation. Following the housewarming, which was accomplished by means of seal-oil and a wick made from cotton calking, came the hunting for our winter's meat and the building of the second hut. It was a simple affair, now, to go forth in the morning and return by noon with a boatload of seals. And then, while I worked at building the hut, Maud tried out the oil from the blubber and kept a slow fire under the frames of meat. I had heard of jerking beef on the plains, and our seal-meat, cut in thin strips and hung in the smoke, cured excellently.

The second hut was easier to erect, for I built it against the first, and only three walls were required. But it was work, hard work, all of it. Maud and I worked from dawn till dark, to the limit of our strength, so that when night came we crawled stiffly to bed and slept the animal-like sleep of exhaustion. And yet Maud declared that she had never felt better or stronger in her life. I knew this was true of myself, but hers was such a lily strength that I feared she would break down. Often and often, her last reserve force gone, I have seen her stretched flat on her back on the sand in the way she had of resting and recuperating. And then she would be up on her feet and toiling hard as ever. Where she obtained this strength was the marvel to me.

"Think of the long rest this winter," was her reply to my remonstrances. "Why, we'll be clamorous for something to do."

We held a housewarming in my hut the night it was roofed. It was the end of the third day of a fierce storm which had swung around the compass from the southeast to the northwest, and which was then blowing directly in upon us. The beaches of the outer cove were thundering with the surf, and even in our land-locked inner cove a respectable sea was breaking. No high backbone of island sheltered us from the wind, and it whistled and bellowed about the hut till at times I feared for the strength of the walls. The skin roof, stretched tightly as a drum-head, I had thought, sagged and bellied with every gust; and innumerable interstices in the walls, not so tightly stuffed with moss as Maud had supposed, disclosed themselves. Yet the seal-oil burned brightly and we were warm and comfortable.

It was a pleasant evening indeed, and we voted that as a social function on Endeavor Island, it had not yet been eclipsed. Our minds were at ease. Not only had we resigned ourselves to the bitter winter, but we were prepared for it. The seals could depart on their mysterious journey into the south at any time now, for all we cared; and the storms held no terror for us. Not only were we sure of being dry and warm and sheltered from the wind, but we had the softest and most luxurious mattresses that could be made from moss. This had been Maud's idea, and she had herself jealously gathered all the moss. This was to be my first night on the mattress, and I knew I should sleep the sweeter because she had made it.

As she rose to go she turned to me with the whimsical way she had, and said:

"Something is going to happen—is happening, for that matter. I feel it. Something is coming here to us. It is coming now. I don't know what, but it is coming."

"Good or bad?" I asked.

She shook her head. "I don't know, but it is there, somewhere."

She pointed in the direction of the sea and wind.

"It's a lee shore," I laughed, "and I am sure I'd rather be here than arriving, a night like this.

"You are not frightened?" I asked, as I stepped to open the door for her.

Her eyes looked bravely into mine.

"And you feel well? Perfectly well?"

"Never better," was her answer.

We talked a little longer before she went.

"Good night, Maud," I said.

"Good night, Humphrey," she said.

This use of our given names had come about quite as a matter of course, and was as unpremeditated as it was natural. In that moment I could have put my arms around her and drawn her to me. I should certainly have done so out in that world to which we belonged. As it was, the situation stopped there in the only way it could; but I was left alone in my little hut, glowing warmly through and through with a pleasant satisfaction; and I knew that a tie, or a tacit something, existed between us which had not existed before.

XXXII

I AWOKE, oppressed by a mysterious sensation. There seemed something missing in my environment. But the mystery and oppressiveness vanished after the first few seconds of waking, when I identified the missing something as the wind. I had fallen asleep in that state of nerve tension with which one meets the continuous shock of sound or movement, and I had awakened, still tense, bracing myself to meet the pressure of something which no longer bore upon me.

It was the first night I had spent under cover in several months, and I lay luxuriously for some minutes under my blankets (for once not wet with fog or spray), analyzing first, the effect produced upon me by the cessation of the wind, and next, the joy which was mine from resting on the mattress made by Maud's hands. When I had dressed and opened the door, I heard the waves still lapping on the beach, garrulously attesting the fury of the night. It was a clear day, and the sun was shining. I had slept late, and I stepped outside with sudden energy, bent upon making up lost time as befitted a dweller on Endeavor Island.

And when outside, I stopped short. I believed my eyes without question, and yet I was for the moment stunned by what they disclosed to me. There, on the beach, not fifty feet away, bow on, dismasted, was a black-hulled vessel. Masts and booms, tangled with shrouds, sheets, and rent canvas, were rubbing gently alongside. I could have rubbed my eyes as I looked. There was the home-made galley we had built, the familiar break of the poop, the low yacht-cabin scarcely rising above the rail. It was the *Ghost.*

What freak of fortune had brought it here—here of all spots? What chance of chances? I looked at the bleak, inaccessible wall at my back and knew the profundity of despair. Escape was hopeless, out of the question. I thought of Maud, asleep there in the hut we had reared; I remembered her "Good night, Humphrey"; "my woman, my mate" , went ringing through my brain, but now, alas, it was a knell that sounded. Then everything went black before my eyes.

Possibly it was the fraction of a second, but I had no knowledge of how long an interval had lapsed before I was myself again. There lay the *Ghost,* bow on to the beach, her splintered bowsprit projecting over the sand, her tangled spars rubbing against her side to the lift of the crooning waves. Something must be done, must be done.

It came upon me suddenly, as strange, that nothing moved aboard. Wearied from the night of struggle and wreck, all hands were yet asleep, I thought. My next thought was that Maud and I might yet escape. If we could take to the boat and make round the point before anyone awoke? I would call her and start. My hand was lifted at her door to knock, when I recollected the smallness of the island. We could never hide ourselves upon it. There was nothing for us but the wide raw ocean. I thought of our snug little huts, our supplies of meat and oil and moss and firewood, and I knew that we could never survive the wintry sea and the great storms which were to come.

So I stood, with hesitant knuckle, without her door. It was impossible, impossible. A wild thought of rushing in and killing her as she slept rose in my mind. And then, in a flash, the better solution came to me. All hands were asleep. Why not creep aboard the *Ghost*— well I knew the way to Wolf Larsen's bunk—and kill him in his sleep? After that—well, we would see. But with him dead there was time and space in which to prepare to do other things; and besides, whatever new situation arose, it could not possibly be worse than the present one.

My knife was at my hip. I returned to my hut for the shotgun, made sure it was loaded, and went down to the *Ghost.* With some difficulty, and at the expense of a wetting to the waist, I climbed aboard. The forecastle scuttle was open. I paused to listen for the breathing of the men, but there was no breathing. I almost gasped as the thought came to me: What if the *Ghost* is deserted? I listened more closely. There was no sound. I cautiously descended the ladder. The place had the empty and musty feel and smell usual to a dwelling no longer inhabited. Everywhere was a thick litter of discarded and ragged garments, old sea-boots, leaky oilskins—all the worthless forecastle dunnage of a long voyage.

Abandoned hastily, was my conclusion, as I ascended to the deck. Hope was alive again in my breast, and I looked about me with greater coolness. I noted that the boats were missing. The steerage told the same tale as the forecastle. The hunters had packed their belongings with similar haste. The *Ghost* was deserted. It was Maud's and mine. I thought of the ship's stores and the lazarette beneath the cabin, and the idea came to me of surprising Maud with something nice for breakfast.

The reaction from my fear, and the knowledge that the terrible deed I had come to do was no longer necessary, made me boyish and eager. I went up the steerage companionway two steps at a time, with nothing distinct in my mind except joy and the hope that Maud would sleep on until the surprise breakfast was quite ready for her. As I rounded the galley, a new satisfaction was mine at the thought of all the splendid cooking utensils inside. I sprang up the break of the poop, and saw—Wolf Larsen. What of my impetus and the stunning surprise, I clattered three or four steps along the deck before I could stop myself. He was standing in the companionway, only his head and shoulders visible, staring straight at me. His arms were resting on the half-open slide. He made no movement whatever—simply stood there, staring at me.

I began to tremble. The old stomach sickness clutched me. I put one hand on the edge of the house to steady myself. My lips seemed suddenly dry and I moistened them against the need of speech. Nor did I for an instant take my eyes off him. Neither of us spoke. There was something ominous in his silence, his immobility. All my old fear of him returned and by new fear was increased an hundred-fold. And still we stood, the pair of us, staring at each other.

I was aware of the demand for action, and, my old helplessness strong upon me, I was waiting for him to take the initiative. Then, as the moments went by, it came to me that the situation was analogous to the one in which I had approached the long-maned bull, my intention of clubbing obscured by fear until it became a desire to make him run. So it was at last impressed upon me that I was there, not to have Wolf Larsen take the initiative, but to take it myself.

I cocked both barrels and levelled the shotgun at him. Had he moved, attempted to drop down the companionway, I know I would have shot him. But he stood motionless and staring as before. And as I faced him, with levelled gun shaking in my hands, I had time to note the worn and haggard appearance of his face. It was as if some strong anxiety had wasted it. The cheeks were sunken, and there was a wearied, puckered expression on the brow. And it seemed to me that his eyes were strange, not only the expression, but the physical seeming, as though the optic nerves and supporting muscles had suffered strain and slightly twisted the eyeballs.

All this I saw, and my brain now working rapidly, I thought a thousand thoughts; and yet I could not pull the triggers. I lowered the gun and stepped to the corner of the cabin, primarily to relieve the tension on my nerves and to make a new start, and incidentally to be closer. Again I raised the gun. He was almost at arm's length. There was no hope for him. I was resolved. There was no possible chance of missing him, no matter how poor my marksmanship. And yet I wrestled with myself and could not pull the triggers.

"Well?" he demanded impatiently.

I strove vainly to force my fingers down on the triggers, and vainly I strove to say something.

"Why don't you shoot?" he asked.

I cleared my throat of a huskiness which prevented speech.

"Hump," he said slowly, "you can't do it. You are not exactly afraid. You are impotent. Your conventional morality is stronger than you. You are the slave to the opinions which have credence among the people you have known and have read about. Their code has been drummed into your head from the time you lisped, and in spite of your philosophy, and of what I have taught you, it won't let you kill an unarmed, unresisting man."

"I know it," I said hoarsely.

"And you know that I would kill an unarmed man as readily as I would smoke a cigar," he went on. "You know me for what I am—my worth in the world by your standard. You have called me snake, tiger, shark, monster and Caliban. And yet, you little rag puppet, you little echoing mechanism, you are unable to kill me as you would a snake or a shark, because I have hands, feet and a body shaped somewhat like yours. Bah! I had hoped better things of you, Hump."

He stepped out of the companionway and came up to me.

"Put down that gun. I want to ask you some questions. I haven't had a chance to look around yet. What place is this? How is the *Ghost* lying? How did you get wet? Where's Maud?—I beg your pardon, Miss Brewster—or should I say, 'Mrs Van Weyden'?"

I had backed away from him, almost weeping at my inability to shoot him, but not fool enough to put down the gun. I hoped, desperately, that he might commit some hostile act, attempt to strike me or choke me; for in such way only I knew I could be stirred to shoot.

"This is Endeavor Island," I said.

"Never heard of it," he broke in.

"At least, that's our name for it," I amended.

"Our?" he queried. "Who's our?"

"Miss Brewster and myself. And the *Ghost* is lying, as you can see for yourself, bow on to the beach."

"There are seals here," he said. "They woke me up with their barking, or I'd be sleeping yet. I heard them when I drove in last night. They were the first warning that I was on a lee shore. It's a rookery, the kind of thing I've hunted for years. Thanks to my brother Death, I've lighted on a fortune. It's a mint. What's its bearings?"

"Haven't the least idea," I said. "But you ought to know quite closely. What were your last observations?"

He smiled inscrutably, but did not answer.

"Well, where's all hands?" I asked. "How does it come that you are alone?"

I was prepared for him again to set aside my question, and was surprised at the readiness of his reply.

"My brother got me inside forty-eight hours, and through no fault of mine. Boarded me in the night with only the watch on deck. Hunters went back on me. He gave them a bigger lay. Heard him offering it. Did it right before me. Of course the crew gave me the go-by. That was to be expected. All hands went over the side, and there I was, marooned on my own vessel. It was Death's turn, and it's all in the family anyway."

"But how did you lose the masts?" I asked.

"Walk over and examine those lanyards," he said, pointing to where the mizzen-rigging should have been.

"They have been cut with a knife!" I exclaimed.

"Not quite," he laughed. "It was a neater job. Look again."

I looked. The lanyards had been almost severed, with just enough left to hold the shrouds till some severe strain should be put upon them.

"Cooky did that," he laughed again. "I know, though I didn't spot him at it. Kind of evened up the score a bit."

"Good for Mugridge!" I cried.

"Yes, that's what I thought when everything went over the side. Only I said it on the other side of my mouth."

"But what were you doing while all this was going on?" I asked.

"My best, you may be sure, which wasn't much under the circumstances."

I turned to re-examine Thomas Mugridge's work.

"I guess I'll sit down and take the sunshine," I heard Wolf Larsen saying.

There was a hint, just a slight hint, of physical feebleness in his voice, and it was so strange that I looked quickly at him. His hand was sweeping nervously across his face, as though he were brushing away cobwebs. I was puzzled. The whole thing was so unlike the Wolf Larsen I had known.

"How are your headaches?" I asked.

"They still trouble me," was his answer. "I think I have one coming on now."

He slipped down from his sitting posture till he lay on the deck. Then he rolled over on his side, his head resting on the biceps of the under arm, the forearm shielding his eyes from the sun. I stood regarding him wonderingly.

"Now's your chance, Hump," he said.

"I don't understand," I lied, for I thoroughly understood.

"Oh, nothing," he added softly, as if he were drowsing, "only you've got me where you want me."

"No, I haven't," I retorted, "for I want you a few thousand miles away from here."

He chuckled, and thereafter spoke no more. He did not stir as I passed by him and went down into the cabin. I lifted the trap in the floor, but for some moments gazed dubiously into the darkness of the lazarette beneath. I hesitated to descend. What if his lying down were a ruse? Pretty, indeed, to be caught there like a rat. I crept softly up the companionway and peeped at him. He was lying as I had left him. Again I went below; but before I dropped into the lazarette I took the precaution of casting down the door in advance. At least there would be no lid to the trap. But it was all needless. I regained the cabin with a store of jams, sea-biscuits, canned meats and such things—all I could carry—and replaced the trap-door.

A peep at Wolf Larsen showed me that he had not moved. A bright thought struck me. I stole into his stateroom and possessed myself of his revolvers. There were no other weapons, though I thoroughly ransacked the three remaining staterooms. To make sure, I returned and went through the steerage and forecastle, and in the galley gathered up all the sharp meat and vegetable knives. Then I bethought me of the great yachtsman's knife he always carried, and I came to him and spoke to him, first softly, then loudly. He did not move. I bent over and took it from his pocket. I breathed more freely. He had no arms with which to attack me from a distance; while I, armed, could always forestall him should he attempt to grapple me with his terrible gorilla arms.

Filling a coffee-pot and frying-pan with part of my plunder, and taking some chinaware from the cabin pantry, I left Wolf Larsen lying in the sun and went ashore.

Maud was still asleep. I blew up the embers (we had not yet arranged a winter kitchen), and quite feverishly cooked the breakfast. Toward the end, I heard her moving about within the hut, making her toilet. Just as all was ready and the coffee poured, the door opened and she came forth.

"It's not fair of you," was her greeting. "You are usurping one of my prerogatives. You know you agreed that the cooking should be mine, and—"

"But just this once," I pleaded.

"If you promise not to do it again," she smiled. "Unless, of course, you have grown tired of my poor efforts."

To my delight she never once looked toward the beach, and I maintained the banter with such success that all unconsciously she sipped coffee from the china cup, ate fried evaporated potatoes and spread marmalade on her biscuit. But it could not last. I saw the surprise that came over her. She had discovered the china plate from which she was eating. She looked over the breakfast, noting detail after detail. Then she looked at me, and her face turned slowly toward the beach.

"Humphrey!" she said.

The old unnamable terror mounted into her eyes.

"Is—he—?" she quavered.

I nodded my head.

XXXIII

WE waited all day for Wolf Larsen to come ashore. It was an intolerable period of anxiety. Each moment one or the other of us cast expectant glances toward the *Ghost*. But he did not come. He did not even appear on deck.

"Perhaps it is his headache," I said. "I left him lying on the poop. He may lie there all night. I think I'll go and see."

Maud looked entreaty at me.

"It is all right," I assured her. "I shall take the revolvers. You know I collected every weapon on board."

"But there are his arms, his hands, his terrible, terrible hands!" she objected. And then she cried, "Oh, Humphrey, I am afraid of him! Don't go—please don't go!"

She rested her hand appealingly on mine, and sent my pulse fluttering. My heart was surely in my eyes for a moment. The dear and lovely woman! And she was so much the woman, clinging and appealing, sunshine and dew to my manhood, rooting it deeper and sending through it the sap of a new strength. I was for putting my arm around her, as when in the midst of the seal herd; but I considered, and refrained.

"I shall not take any risks," I said. "I'll merely peep over the bow and see."

She pressed my hand earnestly and let me go. But the space on deck where I had left him lying was vacant. He had evidently gone below. That night we stood alternate watches, one of us sleeping at a time; for there was no telling what Wolf Larsen might do. He was certainly capable of anything.

The next day we waited, and the next, and still he made no sign.

"These headaches of his, these attacks," Maud said, on the afternoon of the fourth day; "perhaps he is ill, very ill. He may be dead.

"Or dying," was her afterthought, when she had waited some time for me to speak.

"Better so," I answered.

"But think, Humphrey, a fellow-creature in his last lonely hour."

"Perhaps," I suggested.

"Yes, even perhaps," she acknowledged. "But we do not know. It would be terrible if he were. I could never forgive myself. We must do something."

"Perhaps," I suggested again.

I waited, smiling inwardly at the woman of her which compelled a solicitude for Wolf Larsen, of all creatures. Where was her solicitude for me, I thought—for me whom she had been afraid to have merely peep aboard?

She was too subtle not to follow the trend of my silence. And she was as direct as she was subtle.

"You must go aboard, Humphrey, and find out," she said. "And if you want to laugh at me, you have my consent and forgiveness."

I arose obediently and went down the beach.

"Do be careful," she called after me.

I waved my arm from the forecastle head and dropped down to the deck. Aft I walked to the cabin companion, where I contented myself with hailing below. Wolf Larsen answered, and as he started to ascend the stairs I cocked my revolver. I displayed it openly during our conversation, but he took no notice of it. He appeared the same, physically, as when last I saw him, but he was gloomy and silent. In fact, the few words we spoke could hardly be called a conversation. I did not inquire why he had not been ashore, nor did he ask why I had not come aboard. His head was all right again, he said, and so, without further parley, I left him.

Maud received my report with obvious relief, and the sight of smoke which later rose in the galley put her in a more cheerful mood. The next day, and the next, we saw the galley smoke rising, and sometimes we caught glimpses of him on the poop. But that was all. He made no attempt to come ashore. This we knew, for we still maintained our night-watches. We were waiting for him to do something, to show his hand, so to say, and his inaction puzzled and worried us.

A week of this passed by. We had no other interest than Wolf Larsen, and his presence weighed us down with an apprehension which prevented us from doing any of the little things we had planned.

But at the end of the week the smoke ceased rising from the galley, and he no longer showed himself on the poop. I could see Maud's solicitude again growing, though she timidly—and even proudly, I think—forebore a repetition of her request. After all, what censure could be put upon her? She was divinely altruistic, and she was a woman. Besides, I was myself aware of hurt at thought of this man whom I had tried to kill, dying alone with his fellow-creatures so near. He was right. The code of my group was stronger than I. The fact that he had hands, feet and a body shaped somewhat like mine, constituted a claim which I could not ignore.

So I did not wait a second time for Maud to send me. I discovered that we stood in need of condensed milk and marmalade, and announced that I was going aboard. I could see that she wavered. She even went so far as to murmur that they were non-essentials and that my trip after them might be inexpedient. And as she had followed the trend of my silence, she now followed the trend of my speech, and she knew that I was going aboard, not because of condensed milk and marmalade, but because of her and of her anxiety, which she knew she had failed to hide.

I took off my shoes when I gained the forecastle head, and went noiselessly aft in my stocking feet. Nor did I call this time from the top of the companionway. Cautiously descending, I found the cabin deserted. The door to his stateroom was closed. At first I thought of knocking, then I remembered my ostensible errand and resolved to carry it out. Carefully avoiding noise, I lifted the trap-door in the floor and set it to one side. The slop-chest, as well as the provisions, was stored in the lazarette, and I took advantage of the opportunity to lay in a stock of underclothing.

As I emerged from the lazarette, I heard sounds in Wolf Larsen's stateroom. I crouched and listened. The door-knob rattled. Furtively, instinctively, I slunk back behind the table and drew and cocked my revolver. The door swung open and he came forth. Never had I seen so profound a despair as that which I saw on his face—the face of Wolf Larsen the fighter, the strong man, the indomitable one. For all the world like a woman wringing her hands, he raised his clenched fists and groaned. One fist unclosed, and the open palm swept across his eyes as though brushing away cobwebs.

"God! God!" he groaned, and the clenched fists were raised again to the infinite despair with which his throat vibrated.

It was horrible. I was trembling all over, and I could feel the shivers running up and down my spine and the sweat standing out on my forehead. Surely there can be little in this world more awful than the spectacle of a strong man in the moment when he is utterly weak and broken.

But Wolf Larsen regained control of himself by an exertion of his remarkable will. And it was exertion. His whole frame shook with the struggle. He resembled a man on the verge of a fit. His face strove to compose itself, writhing and twisting in the effort till he broke down again. Once more the clenched fists went upward and he groaned. He caught his breath once or twice and sobbed. Then he was successful. I could have thought him the old Wolf Larsen, and yet there was in his movements a vague suggestion of weakness and indecision. He started for the companionway, and stepped forward quite as I had been accustomed to see him do; and yet again, in his very walk, there seemed that suggestion of weakness and indecision.

I was now concerned with fear for myself. The open trap lay directly in his path, and his discovery of it would lead instantly to his discovery of me. I was angry with myself for being caught in so cowardly a position, crouching on the floor. There was yet time.

I rose swiftly to my feet, and, I know, quite unconsciously assumed a defiant attitude. He took no notice of me. Nor did he notice the open trap. Before I could grasp the situation, or act, he had walked right into the trap. One foot was descending into the opening, while the other foot was just on the verge of beginning the uplift. But when the descending foot missed the solid flooring and felt vacancy beneath, it was the old Wolf Larsen and the tiger muscles that made the falling body spring across the opening, even as it fell, so that he struck on his chest and stomach, with arms outstretched, on the floor of the opposite side. The next instant he had drawn up his legs and rolled clear. But he rolled into my marmalade and underclothes and against the trap-door.

The expression on his face was one of complete comprehension. But before I could guess what he had comprehended, he had dropped the trap-door into place, closing the lazarette. Then I understood. He thought he had me inside. Also, he was blind, blind as a bat. I watched him, breathing carefully so that he should not hear me. He stepped quickly to his stateroom. I saw his hand miss the door-knob by an inch, quickly fumble for it, and find it. This was my chance. I tiptoed across the cabin and to the top of the stairs. He came back, dragging a heavy sea-chest, which he deposited on top of the trap. Not content with this, he fetched a second chest and placed it on top of the first. Then he gathered up the marmalade and underclothes and put them on the table. When he started up the companionway, I retreated, silently rolling over on top of the cabin.

He shoved the slide part way back and rested his arms on it, his body still in the companionway. His attitude was of one looking forward the length of the schooner, or staring, rather, for his eyes were fixed and unblinking. I was only five feet away and directly in what should have been his line of vision. It was uncanny. I felt myself a ghost, what of my invisibility. I waved my hand back and forth, of course without effect; but when the moving shadow fell across his face I saw at once that he was susceptible to the impression. His face became more expectant and tense as he tried to analyze and identify the impression. He knew that he had responded to something from without, that his sensibility had been touched by a changing something in his environment; but what it was he could not discover. I ceased waving my hand, so that the shadow remained stationary. He slowly moved his head back and forth under it and turned from side to side, now in the sunshine, now in the shade, feeling the shadow, as it were, testing it by sensation.

I, too, was busy, trying to reason out how he was aware of the existence of so intangible a thing as a shadow. If it were his eyeballs only that were affected, or if his optic nerve were not wholly destroyed, the explanation was simple. If otherwise, then the only conclusion I could reach was that the sensitive skin recognized the difference of temperature between shade and sunshine. Or, perhaps—who can tell?—it was that fabled sixth sense which conveyed to him the loom and feel of an object close at hand.

Giving over his attempt to determine the shadow, he stepped on deck and started forward, walking with a swiftness and confidence which surprised me. And still there was that hint of the feebleness of the blind in his walk. I knew it now for what it was.

To my amused chagrin, he discovered my shoes on the forecastle head and brought them back with him into the galley. I watched him build the fire and set about cooking food for himself; then I stole into the cabin for my marmalade and underclothes, slipped back past the galley, and climbed down to the beach to deliver my barefoot report.

XXXIV

"IT'S too bad the *Ghost* has lost her masts. Why, we could sail away in her. Don't you think we could, Humphrey?"

I sprang excitedly to my feet.

"I wonder, I wonder," I repeated, pacing up and down.

Maud's eyes were shining with anticipation as they followed me. She had such faith in me! And the thought of it was so much added power. I remembered Michelet's "To man, woman is as the earth was to her legendary son; he has but to fall down and kiss her breast and he is strong again." For the first time I knew the wonderful truth of his words. Why, I was living them. Maud was all this to me, an unfailing source of strength and courage. I had but to look at her, or think of her, and be strong again.

"It can be done, it can be done," I was thinking and asserting aloud. "What men have done, I can do; and if they have never done this before, still I can do it."

"What? For goodness sake," Maud demanded. "Do be merciful. What is it you can do?"

"We can do it," I amended. "Why, nothing else than put the masts back into the *Ghost* and sail away."

"Humphrey!" she exclaimed.

And I felt as proud of my conception as if it were already a fact accomplished.

"But how is it possible to be done?" she asked.

"I don't know," was my answer. "I know only that I am capable of doing anything these days."

I smiled proudly at her—too proudly, for she dropped her eyes and was for a moment silent.

"But there is Captain Larsen," she objected.

"Blind and helpless," I answered promptly, waving him aside as a straw.

"But those terrible hands of his! You know how he leaped across the opening of the lazarette."

"And you know also how I crept about and avoided him," I contended gayly.

"And lost your shoes."

"You'd hardly expect them to avoid Wolf Larsen without my feet inside of them."

We both laughed, and then went seriously to work constructing the plan whereby we were to step the masts of the *Ghost* and return to the world. I remembered hazily the physics of my school days, while the last few months had given me practical experience with mechanical purchases. I must say, though, when we walked down to the *Ghost* to inspect more closely the task before us, that the sight of the great masts lying in the water almost disheartened me. Where were we to begin? If there had been one mast standing, something high up to which to fasten blocks and tackles! But there was nothing. It reminded me of the problem of lifting oneself by one's boot-straps. I understood the mechanics of levers; but where was I to get a fulcrum?

There was the mainmast, fifteen inches in diameter at what was now the butt, still sixty-five feet in length, and weighing, I roughly calculated, at least three thousand pounds. And then came the foremast, larger in diameter and weighing surely thirty-five hundred pounds. Where was I to begin? Maud stood silently by my side, while I evolved in my mind the contrivance known among sailors as "shears" . But, though known to sailors, I invented it there on Endeavor Island. By crossing and lashing the ends of two spars, and then elevating them in the air like an inverted "V" , I could get a point above the deck to which to make fast my hoisting tackle. To this hoisting tackle I could, if necessary, attach a second hoisting tackle. And then there was the windlass!

Maud saw that I had achieved a solution, and her eyes warmed sympathetically.

"What are you going to do?" she asked.

"Clear that raffle," I answered, pointing to the tangled wreckage overside.

Ah, the decisiveness, the very sound of the words, was good in my ears. "Clear that raffle!" Imagine so salty a phrase on the lips of the Humphrey Van Weyden of a few months gone!

There must have been a touch of the melodramatic in my pose and voice, for Maud smiled. Her appreciation of the ridiculous was keen, and in all things she unerringly saw and felt, where it existed, the touch of sham, the overshading, the overtone. It was this which had given poise and penetration to her own work and made her of worth to the world. The serious critic, with the sense of humor and the power of expression, must inevitably command the world's ear. And so it was that she had commanded. Her sense of humor was really the artist's instinct for proportion.

"I'm sure I've heard it before, somewhere, in books," she murmured gleefully.

I had an instinct for proportion myself, and I collapsed forthwith, descending from the dominant pose of a master of matter to a state of humble confusion which was, to say the least, very miserable.

Her hand leapt out to mine.

"I'm so sorry," she said.

"No need to be," I gulped. "It does me good. There's too much of the schoolboy in me. All of which is neither here nor there. What we've got to do is actually and literally to clear that raffle. If you'll come with me in the boat, we'll get to work and straighten things out."

" 'When the topmen clear the raffle with their clasp-knives in their teeth,' " she quoted at me; and for the rest of the afternoon we made merry over our labor.

Her task was to hold the boat in position while I worked at the tangle. And such a tangle—halyards, sheets, guys, downhauls, shrouds, stays, all washed about and back and forth and through, and twined and knotted by the sea. I cut no more than was necessary, and what with passing the long ropes under and around the booms and masts, of unreeving the halyards and sheets, of coiling down in the boat and uncoiling in order to pass through another knot in the bight, I was soon wet to the skin.

The sails did require some cutting, and the canvas, heavy with water, tried my strength severely; but I succeeded before nightfall in getting it all spread out on the beach to dry. We were both very tired when we knocked off for supper, and we had done good work, too, though to the eye it appeared insignificant.

Next morning, with Maud as able assistant, I went into the hold of the *Ghost* to clear the steps of the mast-butts. We had no more than begun work when the sound of my knocking and hammering brought Wolf Larsen.

"Hello below!" he cried down the open hatch.

The sound of his voice made Maud quickly draw close to me, as for protection, and she rested one hand on my arm while we parleyed.

"Hello on deck," I replied. "Good morning to you."

"What are you doing down there?" he demanded. "Trying to scuttle my ship for me?"

"Quite the opposite; I'm repairing her," was my answer.

"But what in thunder are you repairing?" There was puzzlement in his voice.

"Why, I'm getting everything ready for re-stepping the masts," I replied easily, as though it were the simplest project imaginable.

"It seems as though you're standing on your own legs at last, Hump," we heard him say; and then for some time he was silent.

"But I say, Hump," he called down, "you can't do it."

"Oh, yes, I can," I retorted. "I'm doing it now."

"But this is my vessel, my particular property. What if I forbid you?"

"You forget," I replied. "You are no longer the biggest bit of the ferment. You were, once, and able to eat me, as you were pleased to phrase it; but there has been a diminishing, and I am now able to eat you. The yeast has grown stale."

He gave a short, disagreeable laugh. "I see you're working my philosophy back on me for all it is worth. But don't make the mistake of underestimating me. For your own good I warn you."

"Since when have you become a philanthropist?" I queried. "Confess now, in warning me for my own good, that you are very inconsistent."

He ignored my sarcasm, saying, "Suppose I clap the hatch on now? You won't fool me as you did in the lazarette."

"Wolf Larsen," I said sternly, for the first time addressing him by this his most familiar name, "I am unable to shoot a helpless, unresisting man. You have proved that to my satisfaction as well as yours. But I warn you now, and not so much for your own good as for mine, that I shall shoot you the moment you attempt a hostile act. I can shoot you now, as I stand here; and if you are so minded, just go ahead and try to clap on the hatch."

"Nevertheless, I forbid you, I distinctly forbid your tampering with my ship."

"But, man!" I expostulated, "you advance the fact that it is your ship as though it were a moral right. You have never considered moral rights in your dealings with others. You surely do not dream that I'll consider them in dealing with you?"

I had stepped underneath the open hatchway so that I could see him. The lack of expression on his face, so different from when I had watched him unseen, was enhanced by the unblinking, staring eyes. It was not a pleasant face to look upon.

"And none so poor, not even Hump, to do him reverence," he sneered.

The sneer was wholly in his voice. His face remained expressionless as ever.

"How do you do, Miss Brewster," he said suddenly, after a pause.

I started. She had made no noise whatever, had not even moved. Could it be that some glimmer of vision remained to him? or that his vision was coming back?

"How do you do, Captain Larsen," she answered. "Pray, how did you know I was here?"

"Heard you breathing, of course. I say, Hump's improving, don't you think so?"

"I don't know," she answered, smiling at me. "I have never seen him otherwise."

"You should have seen him before, then."

"Wolf Larsen, in large doses," I murmured, "before and after taking."

"I want to tell you again, Hump," he said threateningly, "that you'd better leave things alone."

"But don't you care to escape as well as we?" I asked incredulously.

"No," was his answer. "I intend dying here."

"Well, we don't," I concluded defiantly, beginning again my knocking and hammering.

XXXV

NEXT day, the mast-steps clear and everything in readiness, we started to get the two topmasts aboard. The maintopmast was over thirty feet in length, the foretopmast nearly thirty, and it was of these that I intended making the shears. It was puzzling work. Fastening one end of a heavy tackle to the windlass, and with the other end fast to the butt of the foretopmast, I began to heave. Maud held the turn on the windlass and coiled down the slack.

We were astonished at the ease with which the spar was lifted. It was an improved crank windlass, and the purchase it gave was enormous. Of course, what it gave us in power we paid for in distance; as many times as it doubled my strength, that many times was doubled the length of rope I heaved in. The tackle dragged heavily across the rail, increasing its drag as the spar arose more and more out of the water, and the exertion on the windlass grew severe.

But when the butt of the topmast was level with the rail, everything came to a standstill.

"I might have known it," I said impatiently. "Now we have to do it all over again."

"Why not fasten the tackle part way down the mast?" Maud suggested.

"It's what I should have done at first," I answered, hugely disgusted with myself.

Slipping off a turn, I lowered the mast back into the water and fastened the tackle a third of the way down from the butt. In an hour, what of this and of rests between the heaving, I had hoisted it to the point where I could hoist no more. Eight feet of the butt was above the rail, and I was as far away as ever from getting the spar on board. I sat down and pondered the problem. It did not take long. I sprang jubilantly to my feet.

"Now I have it!" I cried. "I ought to make the tackle fast at the point of balance. And what we learn of this will serve us with everything else we have to hoist aboard."

Once again I undid all my work by lowering the mast into the water. But I miscalculated the point of balance, so that when I heaved the top of the mast came up instead of the butt. Maud looked despair, but I laughed and said it would do just as well.

Instructing her how to hold the turn and be ready to slack away at command, I laid hold of the mast with my hands and tried to balance it inboard across the rail. When I thought I had it I cried to her to slack away; but the spar righted, despite my efforts, and dropped back toward the water. Again I heaved it up to its old position, for I had now another idea. I remembered the watch-tackle—a small double and single block affair—and fetched it.

While I was rigging it between the top of the spar and the opposite rail, Wolf Larsen came on the scene. We exchanged nothing more than good mornings, and, though he could not see, he sat on the rail out of the way and followed by the sound all that I did.

Again instructing Maud to slack away at the windlass when I gave the word, I proceeded to heave on the watch-tackle. Slowly the mast swung in until it balanced at right angles across the rail; and then I discovered to my amazement that there was no need for Maud to slack away. In fact, the very opposite was necessary. Making the watch-tackle fast, I hove on the windlass and brought in the mast, inch by inch, till its top tilted down to the deck and finally its whole length lay on the deck.

I looked at my watch. It was twelve o'clock. My back was aching sorely, and I felt extremely tired and hungry. And there on the deck was a single stick of timber to show for a whole morning's work. For the first time I thoroughly realized the extent of the task before us. But I was learning, I was learning. The afternoon would show far more accomplished. And it did; for we returned at one o'clock, rested and strengthened by a hearty dinner.

In less than an hour I had the maintopmast on deck and was constructing the shears. Lashing the two topmasts together, and making allowance for their unequal length, at the point of intersection I attached the double block of the main throat-halyards. This, with the single block and the throat-halyards themselves, gave me a hoisting tackle. To prevent the butts of the masts from slipping on the deck, I nailed down thick cleats. Everything in readiness, I made a line fast to the apex of the shears and carried it directly to the windlass. I was growing to have faith in that windlass, for it gave me power beyond all expectation. As usual, Maud held the turn while I heaved. The shears rose in the air.

Then I discovered I had forgotten guy-ropes. This necessitated my climbing the shears, which I did twice, before I finished guying it fore and aft and to either side. Twilight had set in by the time this was accomplished. Wolf Larsen, who had sat about and listened all afternoon and never opened his mouth, had taken himself off to the galley and started his supper. I felt quite stiff across the small of the back, so much so that I straightened up with an effort and with pain. I looked proudly at my work. It was beginning to show. I was wild with desire, like a child with a new toy, to hoist something with my shears.

"I wish it weren't so late," I said. "I'd like to see how it works."

"Don't be a glutton, Humphrey," Maud chided me. "Remember, to-morrow is coming, and you're so tired now that you can hardly stand."

"And you?" I said, with sudden solicitude. "You must be very tired. You have worked hard and nobly. I am proud of you, Maud."

"Not half so proud as I am of you, nor with half the reason," she answered, looking me straight in the eyes for a moment with an expression in her own and a dancing, tremulous light which I had not seen before and which gave me a pang of quick delight, I know not why, for I did not understand it. Then she dropped her eyes, to lift them again, laughing.

"If our friends could see us now," she said. "Look at us. Have you ever paused for a moment to consider our appearance?"

"Yes, I have considered yours, frequently," I answered, puzzling over what I had seen in her eyes and puzzled by her sudden change of subject.

"Mercy!" she cried. "And what do I look like, pray?"

"A scarecrow, I'm afraid," I replied. "Just glance at your draggled skirts, for instance. Look at those three-cornered tears. And such a waist! It would not require a Sherlock Holmes to deduce that you have been cooking over a camp-fire, to say nothing of trying out seal-blubber. And to cap it all, that cap! And all that is the woman who wrote 'A Kiss Endured'."

She made me an elaborate and stately courtesy, and said, "As for you, sir—"

And yet, through the five minutes of banter which followed, there was a serious something underneath the fun which I could not but relate to the strange and fleeting expression I had caught in her eyes. What was it? Could it be that our eyes were speaking beyond the will of our speech? My eyes had spoken, I knew, until I had found the culprits out and silenced them. This had occurred several times. But had she seen the clamor in them and understood? And had her eyes so spoken to me? What else could that expression have meant—that dancing, tremulous light, and a something more which words could not describe? And yet it could not be. It was impossible.

Besides, I was not skilled in the speech of eyes. I was only Humphrey Van Weyden, a bookish fellow who loved. And to love, and to wait and win love, that surely was glorious enough for me. And thus I thought, even as we chaffed each other's appearance, until we arrived ashore and there were other things to think about.

"It's a shame, after working hard all day, that we cannot have an uninterrupted night's sleep," I complained, after supper.

"But there can be no danger now? From a blind man?" she queried.

"I shall never be able to trust him," I averred, "and far less now that he is blind. The liability is that his part helplessness will make him more malignant than ever. I know what I shall do to-morrow, the first thing—run out a light anchor and kedge the schooner off the beach. And each night when we come ashore in the boat, Mr Wolf Larsen will be left a prisoner on board. So this will be the last night we have to stand watch, and because of that it will go the easier."

We were awake early and just finishing breakfast as daylight came.

"Oh, Humphrey!" I heard Maud cry in dismay and suddenly stop.

I looked at her. She was gazing at the *Ghost.* I followed her gaze, but could see nothing unusual. She looked at me, and I looked inquiry back.

"The shears," she said, and her voice trembled.

I had forgotten their existence. I looked again, but could not see them.

"If he has—" I muttered savagely.

She put her hand sympathetically on mine, and said, "You will have to begin over again."

"Oh, believe me, my anger means nothing; I could not hurt a fly," I smiled back bitterly. "And the worst of it is, he knows it. You are right. If he has destroyed the shears, I shall do nothing except begin over again."

"But I'll stand my watch on board hereafter," I blurted out a moment later. "And if he interferes—"

"But I dare not stay ashore all night alone," Maud was saying when I came back to myself. "It would be so much nicer if he would be friendly with us and help us. We could all live comfortably aboard."

"We will," I asserted, still savagely, for the destruction of my beloved shears had hit me hard. "That is, you and I will live aboard, friendly or not with Wolf Larsen."

"It's childish," I laughed later, "for him to do such things, and for me to grow angry over them, for that matter."

But my heart smote me when we climbed aboard and looked at the havoc he had done. The shears were gone altogether. The guys had been slashed right and left. The throat-halyards which I had rigged were cut across through every part. And he knew I could not splice. A thought struck me. I ran to the windlass. It would not work. He had broken it. We looked at each other in consternation. Then I ran to the side. The masts, booms and gaffs I had cleared were gone. He had found the lines which held them, and cast them adrift.

Tears were in Maud's eyes, and I do believe they were for me. I could have wept myself. Where now was our project of remasting the *Ghost?* He had done his work well. I sat down on the hatch-combing and rested my chin on my hands in black despair.

"He deserves to die," I cried out, "and God forgive me, I am not man enough to be his executioner."

But Maud was by my side, passing her hand soothingly through my hair as though I were a child, and saying, "There, there; it will all come right. We are in the right, and it must come right."

I remembered Michelet and leaned my head against her; and truly I became strong again. The blessed woman was an unfailing fount of power to me. What did it matter? Only a set-back, a delay. The tide could not have carried the masts far to seaward, and there had been no wind. It meant merely more work to find them and tow them back. And besides, it was a lesson. I knew what to expect. He might have waited and destroyed our work more effectually when we had more accomplished.

"Here he comes now," she whispered.

I glanced up. He was strolling leisurely along the poop on the port side.

"Take no notice of him," I whispered. "He's coming to see how we take it. Don't let him know that we know. We can deny him that satisfaction. Take off your shoes—that's right—and carry them in your hand."

And then we played hide-and-seek with the blind man. As he came up the port side we slipped past on the starboard; and from the poop we watched him turn and start aft on our track.

He must have known, somehow, that we were on board, for he said, "Good morning," very confidently, and waited for the greeting to be returned. Then he strolled aft, and we slipped forward.

"Oh, I know you're aboard," he called out, and I could see him listen intently after he had spoken.

It reminded me of the great hoot-owl, listening, after its booming cry, for the stir of its frightened prey. But we did not stir, and we moved only when he moved. And so we dodged about the deck, hand in hand, like a couple of children chased by a wicked ogre, till Wolf Larsen, evidently in disgust, left the deck for the cabin. There was glee in our eyes, and suppressed titters in our mouths, as we put on our shoes and clambered over the side into the boat. And as I looked into Maud's clear brown eyes I forgot the evil he had done, and I knew only that I loved her, and that because of her the strength was mine to win our way back to the world.

XXXVI

For two days Maud and I ranged the sea and explored the beaches in search of the missing masts. But it was not till the third day that we found them, all of them, the shears included, and, of all perilous places, in the pounding surf of the grim southwestern promontory. And how we worked! At the dark end of the first day we returned, exhausted, to our little cove, towing the mainmast behind us. And we had been compelled to row, in a dead calm, practically every inch of the way.

Another day of heart-breaking and dangerous toil saw us in camp with the two topmasts to the good. The day following I was desperate, and I rafted together the foremast, the fore and main booms, and the fore and main gaffs. The wind was favorable, and I had thought to tow them back under sail; but the wind baffled, then died away, and our progress with the oars was a snail's pace. And it was such dispiriting effort. To throw one's whole strength and weight on the oars, and to feel the boat checked in its forward lunge by the heavy drag behind, was not exactly exhilarating.

Night began to fall, and to make matters worse, the wind sprang up ahead. Not only did all forward motion cease, but we began to drift back and out to sea. I struggled at the oars till I was played out. Poor Maud, whom I could never prevent from working to the limit of her strength, lay weakly back in the stern-sheets. I could row no more. My bruised and swollen hands could no longer close on the oar handles. My wrists and arms ached intolerably, and, though I had eaten heartily of a twelve o'clock lunch, I had worked so hard that I was faint from hunger.

I pulled in the oars and bent forward to the line which held the tow. But Maud's hand leaped out restrainingly to mine.

"What are you going to do?" she asked in a strained, tense voice.

"Cast it off," I answered, slipping a turn of the rope.

But her fingers closed on mine.

"Please don't," she begged.

"It is useless," I answered. "Here is night and the wind blowing us off the land."

"But think, Humphrey. If we cannot sail away on the *Ghost*, we may remain for years on the island—for life even. If it has never been discovered all these years, it may never be discovered."

"You forget the boat we found on the beach," I reminded her.

"It was a seal-hunting boat," she replied, "and you know perfectly well that if the men had escaped they would have been back to make their fortunes from the rookery. You know they never escaped."

I remained silent, undecided.

"Besides," she added haltingly, "it's your idea, and I want to see you succeed."

Now I could harden my heart. As soon as she put it on a flattering personal basis, generosity compelled me to deny her.

"Better years on the island than to die to-night, or to-morrow, or the next day, in the open boat. We are not prepared to brave the sea. We have no food, no water, no blankets, nothing. Why, you'd not survive the night without blankets. I know how strong you are. You are shivering now."

"It's only nervousness," she answered. "I am afraid you will cast off the masts in spite of me.

"Oh, please, please, Humphrey, don't!" she burst out, a moment later.

And so it ended, with the phrase she knew had all power over me. We shivered miserably throughout the night. Now and again I fitfully slept, but the pain of the cold always aroused me. How Maud could stand it was beyond me. I was too tired to thrash my arms about and warm myself, but I found strength time and again to chafe her hands and feet to restore the circulation. And still she pleaded with me not to cast off the masts. About three in the morning she was caught by a cold cramp, and after I had rubbed her out of that she became quite numb. I was frightened. I got out the oars and made her row, though she was so weak I thought she would faint at every stroke.

Morning broke, and we looked long in the growing light for our island. At last it showed, small and black, on the horizon, fully fifteen miles away. I scanned the sea with my glasses. Far away in the southwest I could see a dark line on the water, which grew even as I looked at it.

"Fair wind!" I cried in a husky voice I did not recognize as my own.

Maud tried to reply, but could not speak. Her lips were blue with cold, and she was hollow-eyed—but oh, how bravely her brown eyes looked at me! How piteously brave!

Again I fell to chafing her hands, and to moving her arms up and down and about until she could thrash them herself. Then I compelled her to stand up, and though she would have fallen had I not supported her, I forced her to walk back and forth the several steps between the thwart and the stern-sheets, and finally to spring up and down.

"Oh, you brave, brave woman," I said, when I saw the life coming back into her face. "Did you know that you were brave?"

"I never used to be," she answered. "I was never brave till I knew you. It is you who have made me brave."

"Nor I, until I knew you," I answered.

She gave me a quick look, and again I caught that dancing, tremulous light and something more in her eyes. But it was only for the moment. Then she smiled.

"It must have been the conditions," she said; but I knew she was wrong, and I wondered if she likewise knew.

Then the wind came, fair and fresh, and the boat was soon laboring through a heavy sea toward the island. At half-past three in the afternoon we passed the southwestern promontory. Not only were we hungry, but we were now suffering from thirst. Our lips were dry and cracked, nor could we longer moisten them with our tongues. Then the wind slowly died down. By night it was dead calm and I was toiling once more at the oars—but weakly, most weakly. At two in the morning the boat's bow touched the beach of our own inner cove, and I staggered out to make the painter fast. Maud could not stand, nor had I strength to carry her. I fell in the sand with her, and, when I had recovered, contented myself with putting my hands under her shoulders and dragging her up the beach to the hut.

The next day we did no work. In fact, we slept till three in the afternoon, or at least I did, for I awoke to find Maud cooking dinner. Her power of recuperation was wonderful. There was something tenacious about that lily-frail body of hers, a clutch on existence which one could not reconcile with its patent weakness.

"You know I was travelling to Japan for my health," she said, as we lingered at the fire after dinner and delighted in the movelessness of loafing. "I was not very strong. I never was. The doctors recommended a sea voyage, and I chose the longest."

"You little knew what you were choosing," I laughed.

"But I shall be a different woman for the experience, as well as a stronger woman," she answered, "and, I hope, a better woman. At least I shall understand a great deal more of life."

Then, as the short day waned, we fell to discussing Wolf Larsen's blindness. It was inexplicable. And that it was grave, I instanced his statement that he intended to stay and die on Endeavor Island. When he, strong man that he was, loving life as he did, accepted his death, it was plain that he was troubled by something more than mere blindness. There had been his terrific headaches, and we were agreed that it was some sort of brain breakdown, and that in his attacks he endured pain beyond our comprehension.

I noticed, as we talked over his condition, that Maud's sympathy went out to him more and more; yet I could not but love her for it, so sweetly womanly was it. Besides, there was no false sentiment about her feelings. She was agreed that the most rigorous treatment was necessary if we were to escape, though she recoiled at the suggestion that I might some time be compelled to take his life to save my own—"our own," she put it.

In the morning we had breakfast and were at work by daylight. I found a light kedge anchor in the fore-hold, where such things were kept, and with a deal of exertion got it on deck and into the boat. With a long running-line coiled down in the stern, I rowed well out into our little cove and dropped the anchor into the water. There was no wind, the tide was high, and the schooner floated. Casting off the shore lines, I kedged her out by main strength (the windlass being broken), till she rode nearly up and down to the small anchor—too small to hold her in any breeze. So I lowered the big starboard anchor, giving plenty of slack; and by afternoon I was at work on the windlass.

Three days I worked on that windlass. Least of all things was I a mechanic, and in that time I accomplished what an ordinary mechanic would have done in as many hours. I had to learn my tools to begin with, and every simple mechanical principle which such a man would have at his finger ends I had likewise to learn. And at the end of three days I had a windlass which worked clumsily. It never gave the satisfaction the old windlass had given, but it worked and made my work possible.

In half a day I got the two topmasts aboard and the shears rigged and guyed as before. And that night I slept on board and on deck beside my work. Maud, who refused to stay alone ashore, slept in the forecastle. Wolf Larsen had sat about, listening to my repairing the windlass and talking with Maud and me upon indifferent subjects. No reference was made on either side to the destruction of the shears; nor did he say anything further about my leaving his ship alone. But still I had feared him, blind and helpless and listening, always listening, and I never let his strong arms get within reach of me while I worked.

On this night, sleeping under my beloved shears, I was aroused by his footsteps on the deck. It was a starlight night, and I could see the bulk of him dimly as he moved about. I rolled out of my blankets and crept noiselessly after him in my stocking feet. He had armed himself with a draw-knife from the tool locker, and with this he prepared to cut across the throat-halyards I had again rigged to the shears. He felt the halyards with his hands and discovered that I had not made them fast. This would not do for a draw-knife, so he laid hold of the running part, hove taut, and made fast. Then he prepared to saw across with the draw-knife.

"I wouldn't, if I were you," I said quietly.

He heard the click of my pistol and laughed.

"Hello, Hump," he said. "I knew you were here all the time. You can't fool my ears."

"That's a lie, Wolf Larsen," I said, just as quietly as before. "However, I am aching for a chance to kill you, so go ahead and cut."

"You have the chance always," he sneered.

"Go ahead and cut," I threatened ominously.

"I'd rather disappoint you," he laughed, and turned on his heel and went aft.

"Something must be done, Humphrey," Maud said, next morning, when I had told her of the night's occurrence. "If he has liberty, he may do anything. He may sink the vessel, or set fire to it. There is no telling what he may do. We must make him a prisoner."

"But how?" I asked, with a helpless shrug. "I dare not come within reach of his arms, and he knows that so long as his resistance is passive I cannot shoot him."

"There must be some way," she contended. "Let me think."

"There is one way," I said grimly.

She waited.

I picked up a seal-club.

"It won't kill him," I said. "And before he could recover I'd have him bound hard and fast."

She shook her head with a shudder. "No, not that. There must be some less brutal way. Let us wait."

But we did not have to wait long, and the problem solved itself. In the morning, after several trials, I found the point of balance in the foremast and attached my hoisting tackle a few feet above it. Maud held the turn on the windlass and coiled down while I heaved. Had the windlass been in order it would not have been so difficult; as it was, I was compelled to apply all my weight and strength to every inch of the heaving. I had to rest frequently. In truth, my spells of resting were longer than those of working. Maud even contrived, at times when all my efforts could not budge the windlass, to hold the turn with one hand and with the other to throw the weight of her slim body to my assistance.

At the end of an hour the single and double blocks came together at the top of the shears. I could hoist no more. And yet the mast was not swung entirely inboard. The butt rested against the outside of the port rail, while the top of the mast overhung the water far beyond the starboard rail. My shears were too short. All my work had been for nothing. But I no longer despaired in the old way. I was acquiring more confidence in myself and more confidence in the possibilities of windlasses, shears, and hoisting tackles. There was a way in which it could be done, and it remained for me to find that way.

While I was considering the problem, Wolf Larsen came on deck. We noticed something strange about him at once. The indecisiveness, or feebleness, of his movements was more pronounced. His walk was actually tottery as he came down the port side of the cabin. At the break of the poop he reeled, raised one hand to his eyes with the familiar brushing gesture, and fell down the steps—still on his feet—to the main deck, across which he staggered, falling and flinging out his arms for support. He regained his balance by the steerage companionway and stood there dizzily for a space, when he suddenly crumpled up and collapsed, his legs bending under him as he sank to the deck.

"One of his attacks," I whispered to Maud.

She nodded her head; and I could see sympathy warm in her eyes.

We went up to him, but he seemed unconscious, breathing spasmodically. She took charge of him, lifting his head to keep the blood out of it and dispatching me to the cabin for a pillow. I also brought blankets, and we made him comfortable. I took his pulse. It beat steadily and strong, and was quite normal. This puzzled me. I became suspicious.

"What if he should be feigning this?" I asked, still holding his wrist.

Maud shook her head, and there was reproof in her eyes. But just then the wrist I held leaped from my hand, and the hand clasped like a steel trap about my wrist. I cried aloud in awful fear, a wild inarticulate cry; and I caught one glimpse of his face, malignant and triumphant, as his other hand compassed my body and I was drawn down to him in a terrible grip.

My wrist was released, but his other arm, passed around my back, held both my arms so that I could not move. His free hand went to my throat, and in that moment I knew the bitterest foretaste of death earned by one's own idiocy. Why had I trusted myself within reach of those terrible arms? I could feel other hands at my throat. They were Maud's hands, striving vainly to tear loose the hand that was throttling me. She gave it up, and I heard her scream in a way that cut me to the soul, for it was a woman's scream of fear and heart-breaking despair. I had heard it before, during the sinking of the *Martinez.*

My face was against his chest and I could not see, but I heard Maud turn and run swiftly away along the deck. Everything was happening quickly. I had not yet had a glimmering of unconsciousness, and it seemed that an interminable period of time was lapsing before I heard her feet flying back. And just then I felt the whole man sink under me. The breath was leaving his lungs and his chest was collapsing under my weight. Whether it was merely the expelled breath, or his consciousness of his growing impotence, I know not, but his throat vibrated with a deep groan. The hand at my throat relaxed. I breathed. It fluttered and tightened again. But even his tremendous will could not overcome the dissolution that assailed it. That will of his was breaking down. He was fainting.

Maud's footsteps were very near as his hand fluttered for the last time and my throat was released. I rolled off and over to the deck on my back, gasping and blinking in the sunshine. Maud was pale but composed—my eyes had gone instantly to her face—and she was looking at me with mingled alarm and relief. A heavy seal-club in her hand caught my eyes, and at that moment she followed my gaze down to it. The club dropped from her hand as though it had suddenly stung her, and at the same moment my heart surged with a great joy. Truly she was my woman, my mate-woman, fighting with me and for me as the mate of a caveman would have fought, all the primitive in her aroused, forgetful of her culture, hard under the softening civilization of the only life she had ever known.

"Dear woman!" I cried, scrambling to my feet.

The next moment she was in my arms, weeping convulsively on my shoulder while I clasped her close. I looked down at the brown glory of her hair, glinting gems in the sunshine far more precious to me than those in the treasure-chests of kings. And I bent my head and kissed her hair softly, so softly that she did not know.

Then sober thought came to me. After all, she was only a woman, crying her relief, now that the danger was past, in the arms of her protector or of the one who had been endangered. Had I been father or brother, the situation would have been in no wise different. Besides, time and place were not meet, and I wished to earn a better right to declare my love. So once again I softly kissed her hair as I felt her receding from my clasp.

"It was a real attack this time," I said, "another shock like the one that made him blind. He feigned at first, and in doing so brought it on."

Maud was already rearranging his pillow.

"No," I said, "not yet. Now that I have him helpless, helpless he shall remain. From this day we live in the cabin. Wolf Larsen shall live in the steerage."

I caught him under the shoulders and dragged him to the companionway. At my direction Maud fetched a rope. Placing this under his shoulders, I balanced him across the threshold and lowered him down the steps to the floor. I could not lift him directly into a bunk, but with Maud's help I lifted first his shoulders and head, then his body, balanced him across the edge, and rolled him into a lower bunk.

But this was not to be all. I recollected the handcuffs in his stateroom, which he preferred to use on sailors instead of the ancient and clumsy ship irons. So, when we left him, he lay handcuffed hand and foot. For the first time in many days I breathed freely. I felt strangely light as I came on deck, as though a weight had been lifted off my shoulders. I felt, also, that Maud and I had drawn more closely together. And I wondered if she, too, felt it, as we walked along the deck side by side to where the stalled foremast hung in the shears.

XXXVII

At once we moved aboard the *Ghost*, occupying our old staterooms and cooking in the galley. The imprisonment of Wolf Larsen had happened most opportunely, for what must have been the Indian summer of this high latitude was gone and drizzling stormy weather had set in. We were very comfortable, and the inadequate shears, with the foremast suspended from them, gave a businesslike air to the schooner and a promise of departure.

And now that we had Wolf Larsen in irons, how little did we need it! Like his first attack, his second had been accompanied by serious disablement. Maud made the discovery in the afternoon while trying to give him nourishment. He had shown signs of consciousness, and she had spoken to him, eliciting no response. He was lying on his left side at the time, and in evident pain. With a restless movement he rolled his head around, clearing his left ear from the pillow against which it had been pressed. At once he heard and answered her, and at once she came to me.

Pressing the pillow against his left ear, I asked him if he heard me, but he gave no sign. Removing the pillow and repeating the question, he answered promptly that he did.

"Do you know you are deaf in the right ear?" I asked.

"Yes," he answered in a low, strong voice, "and worse than that. My whole right side is affected. It seems asleep. I cannot move arm or leg."

"Feigning again?" I demanded angrily.

He shook his head, his stern mouth shaping the strangest, twisted smile. It was indeed a twisted smile, for it was on the left side only, the facial muscles of the right side moving not at all.

"That was the last play of the Wolf," he said. "I am paralyzed. I shall never walk again. Oh, only on the other side," he added, as though divining the suspicious glance I flung at his left leg, the knee of which had just then drawn up and elevated the blankets.

"It's unfortunate," he continued. "I'd liked to have done for you first, Hump. And I thought I had that much left in me."

"But why?" I asked, partly in horror, partly out of curiosity.

Again his stern mouth framed the twisted smile, as he said:

"Oh, just to be alive, to be living and doing, to be the biggest bit of the ferment to the end, to eat you. But to die this way—"

He shrugged his shoulders, or attempted to shrug them, rather, for the left shoulder alone moved. Like the smile, the shrug was twisted.

"But how can you account for it?" I asked. "Where is the seat of your trouble?"

"The brain," he said at once. "It was those cursed headaches brought it on."

"Symptoms," I said.

He nodded his head. "There is no accounting for it. I was never sick in my life. Something's gone wrong with my brain. A cancer, a tumor or something of that nature —a thing that devours and destroys. It's attacking my nerve-centres, eating them up, bit by bit, cell by cell—from the pain."

"The motor-centres, too," I suggested.

"So it would seem; and the curse of it is that I must lie here, conscious, mentally unimpaired, knowing that the lines are going down, breaking bit by bit communication with the world. I cannot see, hearing and feeling are leaving me, at this rate I shall soon cease to speak; yet all the time I shall be here, alive, active and powerless."

"When you say *you* are here, I'd suggest the likelihood of the soul," I said.

"Bosh!" was his retort. "It simply means that in the attack on my brain the higher psychical centres are untouched. I can remember, I can think and reason. When that goes, I go. I am not. The soul?"

He broke out in mocking laughter, then turned his left ear to the pillow as a sign that he wished no further conversation.

Maud and I went about our work oppressed by the fearful fate which had overtaken him—how fearful we were yet fully to realize. There was the awfulness of retribution about it. Our thoughts were deep and solemn, and we spoke to each other scarcely above whispers.

"You might remove the handcuffs," he said that night, as we stood in consultation over him. "It's dead safe. I'm a paralytic now. The next thing to watch out for is bed sores."

He smiled his twisted smile, and Maud, her eyes wide with horror, was compelled to turn away her head.

"Do you know that your smile is crooked?" I asked him; for I knew that she must attend him, and I wished to save her as much as possible.

"Then I shall smile no more," he said calmly. "I thought something was wrong. My right cheek has been numb all day. Yes, and I've had warnings of this for the last three days; by spells, my right side seemed going to sleep, sometimes arm or hand, sometimes leg or foot.

"So my smile is crooked?" he queried a short while after. "Well, consider henceforth that I smile internally, with my soul, if you please, my soul. Consider that I am smiling now."

And for the space of several minutes he lay there, quiet, indulging his grotesque fancy.

The man of him was not changed. It was the old, indomitable, terrible Wolf Larsen, imprisoned somewhere within that flesh which had once been so invincible and splendid. Now it bound him with insentient fetters, walling his soul in darkness and silence, blocking it from the world which to him had been a riot of action. No more would he conjugate the verb "to do" in every mood and tense. "To be" was all that remained to him—to be, as he had defined death, without movement; to will, but not to execute; to think and reason and in the spirit of him to be as alive as ever, but in the flesh to be dead, quite dead.

And yet, though I even removed the handcuffs, we could not adjust ourselves to his condition. Our minds revolted. To us he was full of potentiality. We knew not what to expect of him next, what fearful thing, rising above the flesh, he might break out and do. Our experience warranted this state of mind, and we went about our work with anxiety always upon us.

I had solved the problem which had arisen through the shortness of the shears. By means of the watch-tackle (I had made a new one), I heaved the butt of the foremast across the rail and then lowered it to the deck. Next, by means of the shears, I hoisted the main boom on board. Its forty feet of length would supply the height necessary properly to swing the mast. By means of a secondary tackle I had attached to the shears, I swung the boom to a nearly perpendicular position, then lowered the butt to the deck, where, to prevent slipping, I spiked great cleats around it. The single block of my original shears-tackle I had attached to the end of the boom. Thus, by carrying this tackle to the windlass, I could raise and lower the end of the boom at will, the butt always remaining stationary, and, by means of guys, I could swing the boom from side to side. To the end of the boom I had likewise rigged a hoisting tackle; and when the whole arrangement was completed I could not but be startled by the power and latitude it gave me.

Of course, two days' work was required for the accomplishment of this part of my task, and it was not till the morning of the third day that I swung the foremast from the deck and proceeded to square its butt to fit the step. Here I was especially awkward. I sawed and chopped and chiselled the weathered wood till it had the appearance of having been gnawed by some gigantic mouse. But it fitted.

"It will work, I know it will work," I cried.

"Do you know Dr Jordan's final test of truth?" Maud asked.

I shook my head and paused in the act of dislodging the shavings which had drifted down my neck.

" 'Can we make it work? Can we trust our lives to it?' is the test."

"He is a favorite of yours," I said.

"When I dismantled my old Pantheon and cast out Napoleon and Caesar and their fellows, I straightway erected a new Pantheon," she answered gravely, "and the first I installed was Dr Jordan."

"A modern hero."

"And a greater because modern," she added. "How can the Old World heroes compare with ours!"

I shook my head. We were too much alike in many things for argument. Our points of view and outlook on life at least were very like.

"For a pair of critics we agree famously," I laughed.

"And as shipwright and able assistant," she laughed back.

But there was little time for laughter in those days, what of our heavy work and of the awfulness of Wolf Larsen's living death.

He had received another stroke. He had lost his voice, or he was losing it. He had only intermittent use of it. As he phrased it, the wires were like the stock market, now up, now down. Occasionally the wires were up and he spoke as well as ever, though slowly and heavily. Then speech would suddenly desert him, in the middle of a sentence perhaps, and for hours, sometimes, we would wait for the connection to be reestablished. He complained of great pain in his head, and it was during this period that he arranged a system of communication against the time when speech should leave him altogether—one pressure of the hand for "yes" , two for "no" . It was well that it was arranged, for by evening his voice had gone from him. By hand pressures, after that, he answered our questions, and when he wished to speak he scrawled his thoughts with his left hand, quite legibly, on a sheet of paper.

The fierce winter had now descended upon us. Gale followed gale, with snow and sleet and rain. The seals had started on their great southern migration, and the rookery was practically deserted. I worked feverishly. In spite of the bad weather, and of the wind which especially hindered me, I was on deck from daylight till dark and making substantial progress.

I profited by my lesson learned through raising the shears and then climbing them to attach the guys. To the top of the foremast, which was just lifted conveniently from the deck, I attached the rigging, stays, and throat and peak halyards. As usual, I had underrated the amount of work involved in this portion of the task, and two long days were necessary to complete it. And there was so much yet to be done—the sails, for instance, which practically had to be made over.

While I toiled at rigging the foremast, Maud sewed on canvas, ready always to drop everything and come to my assistance when more hands than two were required. The canvas was heavy and hard, and she sewed with the regular sailor's palm and three-cornered sail-needle. Her hands were soon sadly blistered, but she struggled bravely on, and in addition doing the cooking and taking care of the sick man.

"A fig for superstition," I said on Friday morning. "That mast goes in to-day."

Everything was ready for the attempt. Carrying the boom-tackle to the windlass, I hoisted the mast nearly clear of the deck. Making this tackle fast, I took to the windlass the shears-tackle (which was connected with the end of the boom), and with a few turns had the mast perpendicular and clear.

Maud clapped her hands the instant she was relieved from holding the turn, crying: "It works! It works! We'll trust our lives to it!"

Then she assumed a rueful expression.

"It's not over the hole," she said. "Will you have to begin all over?"

I smiled in superior fashion, and, slacking off on one of the boom-guys and taking in on the other, swung the mast perfectly in the centre of the deck. Still it was not over the hole. Again the rueful expression came on her face, and again I smiled in a superior way. Slacking away on the boom-tackle and hoisting an equivalent amount on the shears-tackle, I brought the butt of the mast into position directly over the hole in the deck. Then I gave Maud careful instructions for lowering away and went into the hold to the step on the schooner's bottom.

I called to her, and the mast moved easily and accurately. Straight toward the square hole of the step the square butt descended; but as it descended it slowly twisted so that square would not fit into square. But I had not even a moment's indecision. Calling to Maud to cease lowering, I went on deck and made the watch-tackle fast to the mast with a rolling hitch. I left Maud to pull on it while I went below. By the light of the lantern I saw the butt twist slowly around till its sides coincided with the sides of the step. Maud made fast and returned to the windlass. Slowly the butt descended the several intervening inches, at the same time slightly twisting again. Again Maud rectified the twist with the watch-tackle, and again she lowered away from the windlass. Square fitted into square. The mast was stepped.

I raised a shout, and she ran down to see. In the yellow lantern light we peered at what we had accomplished. We looked at each other, and our hands felt their way and clasped. The eyes of both of us, I think, were moist with the joy of success.

"It was done so easily after all," I remarked. "All the work was in the preparation."

"And all the wonder in the completion," Maud added. "I can scarcely bring myself to realize that that great mast is really up and in; that you have lifted it from the water, swung it through the air, and deposited it here where it belongs. It is a Titan's task."

"And they made themselves many inventions," I began merrily, then paused to sniff the air.

I looked hastily at the lantern. It was not smoking. Again I sniffed.

"Something is burning," Maud said, with sudden conviction.

We sprang together for the ladder, but I raced past her to the deck. A dense volume of smoke was pouring out of the steerage companionway.

"The Wolf is not yet dead," I muttered to myself as I sprang down through the smoke.

It was so thick in the confined space that I was compelled to feel my way; and so potent was the spell of Wolf Larsen on my imagination, I was quite prepared for the helpless giant to grip my neck in a strangle hold. I hesitated, the desire to race back and up the steps to the deck almost overpowering me. Then I recollected Maud. The vision of her, as I had last seen her, in the lantern light of the schooner's hold, her brown eyes warm and moist with joy, flashed before me, and I knew that I could not go back.

I was choking and suffocating by the time I reached Wolf Larsen's bunk. I reached my hand and felt for his. He was lying motionless, but moved slightly at the touch of my hand. I felt over and under his blankets. There was no warmth, no sign of fire. Yet that smoke which blinded me and made me cough and gasp must have a source. I lost my head temporarily and dashed frantically about the steerage. A collision with the table partially knocked the wind from my body and brought me to myself. I reasoned that a helpless man could start a fire only near to where he lay.

I returned to Wolf Larsen's bunk. There I encountered Maud. How long she had been there in that suffocating atmosphere I could not guess.

"Go up on deck!" I commanded peremptorily.

"But, Humphrey—" she began to protest in a queer, husky voice.

"Please! please!" I shouted at her harshly.

She drew away obediently, and then I thought, What if she cannot find the steps? I started after her, to stop at the foot of the companionway. Perhaps she had gone up. As I stood there, hesitant, I heard her cry softly:

"Oh, Humphrey, I am lost."

I found her fumbling at the wall of the after bulkhead, and, half leading her, half carrying her, I took her up the companionway. The pure air was like nectar. Maud was only faint and dizzy, and I left her lying on the deck when I took my second plunge below.

The source of the smoke must be very close to Wolf Larsen—my mind was made up to this, and I went straight to his bunk. As I felt about among his blankets, something hot fell on the back of my hand. It burned me, and I jerked my hand away. Then I understood. Through the cracks in the bottom of the upper bunk he had set fire to the mattress. He still retained sufficient use of his left arm to do this. The damp straw of the mattress, fired from beneath and denied air, had been smouldering all the while.

As I dragged the mattress out of the bunk it seemed to disintegrate in mid-air, at the same time bursting into flames. I beat out the burning remnants of straw in the bunk, then made a dash for the deck for fresh air.

Several buckets of water sufficed to put out the burning mattress in the middle of the steerage floor; and ten minutes later, when the smoke had fairly cleared, I allowed Maud to come below. Wolf Larsen was unconscious, but it was a matter of minutes for the fresh air to restore him. We were working over him, however, when he signed for paper and pencil.

"Pray do not interrupt me," he wrote. "I am smiling."

"I am still a bit of the ferment, you see," he wrote a little later.

"I am glad you are as small a bit as you are," I said.

"Thank you," he wrote. "But just think of how much smaller I shall be before I die."

"And yet I am all here, Hump," he wrote with a final flourish. "I can think more clearly than ever in my life before. Nothing to disturb me. Concentration is perfect. I am all here and more than here."

It was like a message from the night of the grave; for this man's body had become his mausoleum. And there, in so strange sepulture, his spirit fluttered and lived. It would flutter and live till the last line of communication was broken, and after that who was to say how much longer it might continue to flutter and live?

XXXVIII

"I THINK my left side is going," Wolf Larsen wrote, the morning after his attempt to fire the ship. "The numbness is growing. I can hardly move my hand. You will have to speak louder. The last lines are going down."

"Are you in pain?" I asked.

I was compelled to repeat my question loudly before he answered.

"Not all the time."

The left hand stumbled slowly and painfully across the paper, and it was with extreme difficulty that we deciphered the scrawl. It was like a "spirit message" , such as are delivered at séances of spiritualists for a dollar admission.

"But I am still here, all here," the hand scrawled more slowly and painfully than ever.

The pencil dropped, and we had to replace it in the hand.

"When there is no pain I have perfect peace and quiet. I have never thought so clearly. I can ponder life and death like a Hindoo sage."

"And immortality?" Maud queried loudly in the ear.

Three times the hand essayed to write but fumbled hopelessly. The pencil fell. In vain we tried to replace it. The fingers could not close on it. Then Maud pressed and held the fingers about the pencil with her own hand, and the hand wrote, in large letters, and so slowly that the minutes ticked off to each letter:

"B—O—S—H."

It was Wolf Larsen's last word, "bosh" , sceptical and invincible to the end. The arm and hand relaxed. The trunk of the body moved slightly. Then there was no movement. Maud released the hand. The fingers spread slightly, falling apart of their own weight, and the pencil rolled away.

"Do you still hear?" I shouted, holding the fingers and waiting for the single pressure which would signify "Yes" . There was no response. The hand was dead.

"I noticed the lips slightly move," Maud said.

I repeated the question. The lips moved. She placed the tips of her fingers on them. Again I repeated the question. "Yes," Maud announced. We looked at each other expectantly.

"What good is it?" I asked. "What can we say now?"

"Oh, ask him—"

She hesitated.

"Ask him something that requires no for an answer," I suggested. "Then we will know for certainty."

"Are you hungry?" she cried.

The lips moved under her fingers, and she answered, "Yes."

"Will you have some beef?" was her next query.

"No," she announced.

"Beef-tea?"

"Yes, he will have some beef-tea," she said quietly, looking up at me. "Until his hearing goes we shall be able to communicate with him. And after that—"

She looked at me queerly. I saw her lips trembling and the tears swimming up in her eyes. She swayed toward me and I caught her in my arms.

"Oh, Humphrey," she sobbed, "when will it all end? I am so tired, so tired."

She buried her head on my shoulder, her frail form shaken with a storm of weeping. She was like a feather in my arms, so slender, so ethereal. "She has broken down at last," I thought. "What can I do without her help?"

But I soothed and comforted her, till she pulled herself bravely together and recuperated mentally as quickly as she was wont to do physically.

"I ought to be ashamed of myself," she said. Then added, with the whimsical smile I adored, "but I am only one small woman."

That phrase, the "one small woman" , startled me like an electric shock. It was my own phrase, my pet, secret phrase, my love phrase for her.

"Where did you get that phrase?" I demanded, with an abruptness that in turn startled her.

"What phrase?" she asked.

"One small woman."

"Is it yours?" she asked.

"Yes," I answered, "mine. I made it."

"Then you must have talked in your sleep," she smiled.

The dancing, tremulous light was in her eyes. Mine, I knew, were speaking beyond the will of my speech. I leaned toward her. Without volition I leaned toward her, as a tree is swayed by the wind. Ah, we were very close together in that moment. But she shook her head, as one might shake off sleep or a dream, saying:

"I have known it all my life. It was my father's name for my mother."

"It is my phrase too," I said stubbornly.

"For your mother?"

"No," I answered, and she questioned no further, though I could have sworn her eyes retained for some time a mocking, teasing expression.

With the foremast in, the work now went on apace. Almost before I knew it, and without one serious hitch, I had the mainmast stepped. A derrick-boom, rigged to the foremast, had accomplished this; and several days more found all stays and shrouds in place, and everything set up taut. Topsails would be a nuisance and a danger for a crew of two, so I heaved the topmasts on deck and lashed them fast.

Several more days were consumed in finishing the sails and putting them on. There were only three—the jib, foresail and mainsail; and, patched, shortened and distorted, they were a ridiculously ill-fitting suit for so trim a craft as the *Ghost.*

"But they'll work!" Maud cried jubilantly. "We'll make them work, and trust our lives to them!"

Certainly, among my many new trades, I shone least as a sail-maker. I could sail them better than make them, and I had no doubt of my power to bring the schooner to some northern port of Japan. In fact, I had crammed navigation from text-books aboard; and besides, there was Wolf Larsen's star-scale, so simple a device that a child could work it.

As for its inventor, beyond an increasing deafness and the movement of the lips growing fainter and fainter, there had been little change in his condition for a week. But on the day we finished bending the schooner's sails, he heard his last, and the last movement of his lips died away—but not before I had asked him, "Are you all there?" and the lips had answered, "Yes."

The last line was down. Somewhere within that tomb of the flesh still dwelt the soul of the man. Walled by the living clay, that fierce intelligence we had known burned on; but it burned on in silence and darkness. And it was disembodied. To that intelligence there could be no objective knowledge of a body. It knew no body. The very world was not. It knew only itself and the vastness and profundity of the quiet and the dark.

XXXIX

THE day came for our departure. There was no longer anything to detain us on Endeavor Island. The *Ghost*'s stumpy masts were in place, her crazy sails bent. All my handiwork was strong, none of it beautiful; but I knew that it would work, and I felt myself a man of power as I looked at it.

"I did it! I did it! With my own hands I did it!" I wanted to cry aloud.

But Maud and I had a way of voicing each other's thoughts, and she said, as we prepared to hoist the mainsail:

"To think, Humphrey, you did it all with your own hands!"

"But there were two other hands," I answered. "Two small hands, and don't say that was a phrase, also, of your father."

She laughed and shook her head, and held her hands up for inspection.

"I can never get them clean again," she wailed, "nor soften the weather-beat."

"Then dirt and weather-beat shall be your guerdon of honor," I said, holding them in mine; and, spite of my resolutions, I would have kissed the two dear hands had she not swiftly withdrawn them.

Our comradeship was becoming tremulous. I had mastered my love long and well, but now it was mastering me. Wilfully had it disobeyed and won my eyes to speech, and now it was winning my tongue—ay, and my lips, for they were mad this moment to kiss the two small hands which had toiled so faithfully and hard. And I, too, was mad. There was a cry in my being like bugles calling me to her. And there was a wind blowing upon me which I could not resist, swaying the very body of me till I leaned toward her, all unconscious that I leaned. And she knew it. She could not but know it as she swiftly drew away her hands, and yet could not forbear one quick searching look before she turned away her eyes.

By means of deck-tackles I had arranged to carry the halyards forward to the windlass; and now I hoisted the mainsail, peak and throat, at the same time. It was a clumsy way, but it did not take long, and soon the foresail as well was up and fluttering.

"We can never get that anchor up in this narrow place, once it has left the bottom," I said. "We should be on the rocks first."

"What can you do?" she asked.

"Slip it," was my answer. "And when I do, you must do your first work on the windlass. I shall have to run at once to the wheel, and at the same time you must be hoisting the jib."

This manoeuvre of getting under way I had studied and worked out a score of times; and, with the jib-halyard to the windlass, I knew Maud was capable of hoisting that most necessary sail. A brisk wind was blowing into the cove, and though the water was calm, rapid work was required to get us safely out.

When I knocked the shackle-bolt loose, the chain roared out through the hawse-hole and into the sea. I raced aft, putting the wheel up. The *Ghost* seemed to start into life as she heeled to the first fill of her sails. The jib was rising. As it filled, the *Ghost* 's bow swung off and I had to put the wheel down a few spokes and steady her.

I had devised an automatic jib-sheet which passed the jib across of itself, so there was no need for Maud to attend to that; but she was still hoisting the jib when I put the wheel hard down. It was a moment of anxiety, for the *Ghost* was rushing directly upon the beach, a stone's throw distant. But she swung obediently on her heel into the wind. There was a great fluttering and flapping of canvas and reef-points, most welcome to my ears, then she filled away on the other tack.

Maud had finished her task and come aft, where she stood beside me, a small cap perched on her wind-blown hair, her cheeks flushed from exertion, her eyes wide and bright with the excitement, her nostrils quivering to the rush and bite of the fresh salt air. Her brown eyes were like a startled deer's. There was a wild, keen look in them I had never seen before, and her lips parted and her breath suspended as the *Ghost*, charging upon the wall of rock at the entrance to the inner cove, swept into the wind and filled away into safe water.

My first mate's berth on the sealing grounds stood me in good stead, and I cleared the inner cove and laid a long tack along the shore of the outer cove. Once again about, and the *Ghost* headed out to open sea. She had now caught the bosom-breathing of the ocean, and was herself a-breath with the rhythm of it as she smoothly mounted and slipped down each broad-backed wave. The day had been dull and overcast, but the sun now burst through the clouds, a welcome omen, and shone upon the curving beach where together we had dared the lords of the harem and slain the holluschickie. All Endeavor Island brightened under the sun. Even the grim southwestern promontory showed less grim, and here and there, where the sea-spray wet its surface, high lights flashed and dazzled in the sun.

"I shall always think of it with pride," I said to Maud.

She threw her head back in a queenly way, but said, "Dear, dear Endeavor Island! I shall always love it."

"And I," I said quickly.

It seemed our eyes must meet in a great understanding, and yet, loath, they struggled away and did not meet.

There was a silence I might almost call awkward, till I broke it, saying:

"See those black clouds to windward. You remember, I told you last night the barometer was falling."

"And the sun is gone," she said, her eyes still fixed upon our island, where we had proved our mastery over matter and attained to the truest comradeship that may fall to man and woman.

"And it's slack off the sheets for Japan!" I cried gayly. "A fair wind and a flowing sheet, you know, or however it goes."

Lashing the wheel, I ran forward, eased the fore and main sheets, took in on the boom-tackles, and trimmed everything for the quartering breeze which was ours. It was a fresh breeze, very fresh, but I resolved to run as long as I dared. Unfortunately, when running free, it is impossible to lash the wheel, so I faced an all-night watch. Maud insisted on relieving me, but proved that she had not the strength to steer in a heavy sea, even if she could have gained the wisdom on such short notice. She appeared quite heartbroken over the discovery, but recovered her spirits by coiling down tackles and halyards and all stray ropes. Then there were meals to be cooked in the galley, beds to make, Wolf Larsen to be attended upon, and she finished the day with a grand house-cleaning attack upon the cabin and steerage.

All night I steered, without relief, the wind slowly and steadily increasing and the sea rising. At five in the morning Maud brought me hot coffee and biscuits she had baked, and at seven a substantial and piping hot breakfast put new life into me.

Throughout the day, and as slowly and steadily as ever, the wind increased. It impressed one with its sullen determination to blow, and blow harder, and keep on blowing. And still the *Ghost* foamed along, racing off the miles till I was certain she was making at least eleven knots. It was too good to lose, but by nightfall I was exhausted. Though in splendid physical trim, a thirty-six-hour trick at the wheel was the limit of my endurance. Besides, Maud begged me to heave to, and I knew, if the wind and sea increased at the same rate during the night, that it would soon be impossible to heave to. So, as twilight deepened, gladly and at the same time reluctantly, I brought the *Ghost* up on the wind.

But I had not reckoned upon the colossal task the reefing of three sails meant for one man. While running away from the wind I had not appreciated its force, but when we ceased to run I learned to my sorrow, and well-nigh to my despair, how fiercely it was really blowing. The wind balked my every effort, ripping the canvas out of my hands and in an instant undoing what I had gained by ten minutes of severest struggle. At eight o'clock I had succeeded only in putting the second reef into the foresail. At eleven o'clock I was no farther along. Blood dripped from every finger end, while the nails were broken to the quick. From pain and sheer exhaustion I wept in the darkness, secretly, so that Maud should not know.

Then, in desperation, I abandoned the attempt to reef the mainsail and resolved to try the experiment of heaving to under the close-reefed foresail. Three hours more were required to gasket the mainsail and jib, and at two in the morning, nearly dead, the life almost buffeted and worked out of me, I had barely sufficient consciousness to know the experiment was a success. The close-reefed foresail worked. The *Ghost* clung on close to the wind and betrayed no inclination to fall off broadside to the trough.

I was famished, but Maud tried vainly to get me to eat. I dozed with my mouth full of food. I would fall asleep in the act of carrying food to my mouth and waken in torment to find the act yet uncompleted. So sleepily helpless was I that she was compelled to hold me in my chair to prevent my being flung to the floor by the violent pitching of the schooner.

Of the passage from the galley to the cabin I knew nothing. It was a sleep-walker Maud guided and supported. In fact, I was aware of nothing till I awoke, how long after I could not imagine, in my bunk with my boots off. It was dark. I was stiff and lame, and cried out with pain when the bed-clothes touched my poor finger-ends.

Morning had evidently not come, so I closed my eyes and went to sleep again. I did not know it, but I had slept the clock around and it was night again.

Once more I woke, troubled because I could sleep no better. I struck a match and looked at my watch. It marked midnight. And I had not left the deck until three! I should have been puzzled had I not guessed the solution. No wonder I was sleeping brokenly. I had slept twenty-one hours. I listened for a while to the behavior of the *Ghost*, to the pounding of the seas and the muffled roar of the wind on deck, and then turned over on my side and slept peacefully until morning.

When I arose at seven I saw no sign of Maud and concluded she was in the galley preparing breakfast. On deck I found the *Ghost* doing splendidly under her patch of canvas. But in the galley, though a fire was burning and water boiling, I found no Maud.

I discovered her in the steerage, by Wolf Larsen's bunk. I looked at him, the man who had been hurled down from the topmost pitch of life to be buried alive and be worse than dead. There seemed a relaxation of his expressionless face which was new. Maud looked at me and I understood.

"His life flickered out in the storm," I said.

"But he still lives," she answered, infinite faith in her voice.

"He had too great strength."

"Yes," she said, "but now it no longer shackles him. He is a free spirit."

"He is a free spirit surely," I answered; and, taking her hand, I led her on deck.

The storm broke that night, which is to say that it diminished as slowly as it had arisen. After breakfast next morning, when I had hoisted Wolf Larsen's body on deck ready for burial, it was still blowing heavily and a large sea was running. The deck was continually awash with the sea which came inboard over the rail and through the scuppers. The wind smote the schooner with a sudden gust, and she heeled over till her lee rail was buried, the roar in her rigging rising in pitch to a shriek. We stood in the water to our knees as I bared my head.

"I remember only one part of the service," I said, "and that is, 'And the body shall be cast into the sea.' "

Maud looked at me, surprised and shocked; but the spirit of something I had seen before was strong upon me, impelling me to give service to Wolf Larsen as Wolf Larsen had once given service to another man. I lifted the end of the hatch cover, and the canvas-shrouded body slipped feet first into the sea. The weight of iron dragged it down. It was gone.

"Good-by, Lucifer, proud spirit," Maud whispered, so low that it was drowned by the shouting of the wind; but I saw the movement of her lips and knew.

As we clung to the lee rail and worked our way aft, I happened to glance to leeward. The *Ghost*, at the moment, was uptossed on a sea, and I caught a clear view of a small steamship two or three miles away, rolling and pitching, head on to the sea, as it steamed toward us. It was painted black, and from the talk of the hunters of their poaching exploits I recognized it as a United States revenue cutter. I pointed it out to Maud and hurriedly led her aft to the safety of the poop.

I started to rush below to the flag-locker, then remembered that in rigging the *Ghost* I had forgotten to make provision for a flag-halyard.

"We need no distress signal," Maud said. "They have only to see us."

"We are saved," I said, soberly and solemnly. And then, in an exuberance of joy, "I hardly know whether to be glad or not."

I looked at her. Our eyes were not loath to meet. We leaned toward each other, and before I knew it my arms were about her.

"Need I?" I asked.

And she answered, "There is no need, though the telling of it would be sweet, so sweet."

Her lips met the press of mine, and, by what strange trick of the imagination I know not, the scene in the cabin of the *Ghost* flashed upon me, when she had pressed her fingers lightly on my lips and said, "Hush, hush."

"My woman, my one small woman," I said, my free hand petting her shoulder in the way all lovers know though never learn in school.

"My man," she said, looking at me for an instant with tremulous lids which fluttered down and veiled her eyes as she snuggled her head against my breast with a happy little sigh.

I looked toward the cutter. It was very close. A boat was being lowered.

"One kiss, dear love," I whispered. "One kiss more before they come."

"And rescue us from ourselves," she completed, with a most adorable smile, whimsical as I had never seen it, for it was whimsical with love.

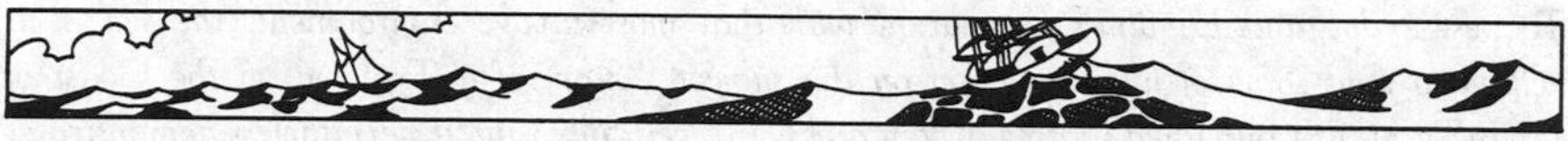

LONDON ON LONDON

To best understand London's fascination with that most savage environment, the sea, it is helpful to read some of his non-fiction on the subject. "Story of a Typhoon off the Coast of Japan" is his first published writing. Often awkward, certainly raw, it nevertheless demonstrates the natural talent and visceral power one associates with all of his work. This power is still evident in the passages from "The Cruise of the Snark," written near the end of his life, but added to this we find some of the wisdom and humor of the mature artist.

STORY OF A TYPHOON OFF THE COAST OF JAPAN

(By John London, age 17. Address, 1321 Twenty-second Avenue, Oakland.)

IT WAS four bells in the morning watch. We had just finished breakfast when the order came forward for the watch on deck to stand by to heave her to and all hands stand by the boats.

"Port! hard a port!" cried our sailing-master. "Clew up the topsails! Let the flying jib run down! Back the jib over to windward and run down the foresail!" And so was our schooner *Sophie Sutherland* hove to off the Japan coast, near Cape Jerimo, on April 10, 1893.

Then came moments of bustle and confusion. There were eighteen men to man the six boats. Some were hooking on the falls, others casting off the lashings; boatsteerers appeared with the boat compasses and water breakers and boat-pullers with the lunch boxes. Hunters were staggering under two or three shotguns, a rifle and heavy ammunition box, all of which were soon stowed away with their oilskins and mittens in the boats.

The sailing-master gave his last orders and away we went pulling the three pairs of oars to gain our positions. We were in the weather boat, and so had a longer pull than the others. The first, second and third lee boats soon had all sails set and were running off to the southward and westward with the wind abeam, while the schooner was running off to leeward of them, so that in case of accident the boats would have fair wind home.

It was a glorious morning, but our boat-steerer shook his head ominously as he glanced at the rising sun and prophetically muttered, "Red sun in the morning, sailor 'take warning.' " The sun had an angry look, and a few light, fleecy "niggerheads" in that quarter seemed abashed and frightened and soon disappeared. Away off to the northwest Cape Jerimo reared its black, forbidding head like some huge monster rising from the deep. The winter's snow, not yet entirely dissipated by the sun, covered it in patches of glistening white, over which the light wind swept on its way out to sea. Huge gunies rose slowly, fluttering their wings in the light breeze and striking their webbed feet on the surface of the water for over half a mile before they could leave it. Hardly had the patter, patter died away when a flock of sea quail rose, and with whistling wings flew away to windward, where members of a large band of whales were disporting themselves, their blowings sounding like the exhaust of steam engines. The harsh, discordant cries of a sea-parrot grated unpleasantly on the ear, and set half a dozen on the alert in a small band of seals that were ahead of us. Away they went, breaching and jumping entirely out of water. A seagull with slow, deliberate flight and long majestic curves, circled round us, and as a reminder of home a little English sparrow perched impudently on the fo'castle head, and cocking his head on one side chirped merrily. The boats were soon among the seals, and the bang! bang! of the guns could be heard from down to leeward.

The wind was slowly rising, and by 3 o'clock as, with a dozen seals in our boat, we were deliberating whether to go on or turn back, the recall flag was run up at the schooner's mizzen—a sure sign that with the rising wind the barometer was falling and that our sailing-master was gettng anxious for the welfare of the boats.

Away we went before the wind with a single reef in our sail. With clenched teeth sat the boat-steerer, grasping the steering oar firmly with both hands, his restless eyes on the alert—a glance at the schooner ahead, as we rose on a sea, another at the main-sheet, and then one astern where the dark ripple of the wind on the water told him of a coming puff or a large white cap that threatened to overwhelm us. The waves were holding high carnival, performing the strangest antics, as with wild glee they danced along in fierce pursuit—now up, now down, here, there and everywhere, until some great sea of liquid green with its milk-white crest of foam rose from the ocean's throbbing bosom and drove the others from view. But only for a moment, for again under new forms they reappeared. In the sun's path they wandered, where every ripple great or small, every little spit or spray looked like molten silver; where the water lost its dark green color and became a dazzling silvery flood, only to vanish and become a wild waste of sullen turbulence, each dark foreboding sea rising and breaking, then rolling on again. The dash, the sparkle, the silvery light soon vanished with the sun, which became obscured by black clouds that were rolling swiftly in from the west-northwest; apt heralds of the coming storm.

We soon reached the schooner and found ourselves the last aboard. In a few minutes the seals were skinned, boats and decks washed, and we were down below by the roaring fo'castle fire, with a wash, change of clothes and a hot, substantial supper before us. Sail had been put on the schooner, as we had a run of seventy-five miles to make to the south'ard before morning, so as to get in the midst of the seals, out of which we had strayed during the last two days' hunting.

We had the first watch, from 8 to midnight. The wind was soon blowing half a gale, and our sailing-master expected little sleep that night as he paced up and down the poop. The topsails were soon clewed up and made fast, then the flying jib run down and furled. Quite a sea was rolling by this time, occasionally breaking over the decks, flooding them and threatening to smash the boats. At six bells we were ordered to turn them over and put on storm-lashings. This occupied us till eight bells, when we were relieved by the midwatch. I was the last to go below, doing so just as the watch on deck was furling the spanker.

Below all were asleep except our green hand, the bricklayer, who was dying of consumption. The wildly dancing movements of the sea lamp cast a pale flickering light through the fo'castle and turned to golden honey the drops of water on the yellow oilskins. In all the corners dark shadows seemed to come and go, while up in the eyes of her, beyond the pall bitts descending from deck to deck, where they seemed to lurk like some dragon at the cavern's mouth, it was dark as Erebus. Now and again the light seemed to penetrate for a moment as the schooner rolled heavier than usual, only to recede, leaving it darker and blacker than before. The roar of the wind whistling through the rigging came to the ear muffled like the distant rumble of a train crossing a trestle or the surf on the beach, while the loud crash of the seas on her weather bow seemed almost to rend the beams and planking asunder as it resounded through the fo'castle. The creaking and groaning of the timbers, stanchions and bulkheads, as the strain the vessel was undergoing was felt, served to drown the groans of the dying man as he tossed uneasily in his bunk. The working of the foremast against the deck beams caused a shower of flaky powder to fall and sent another sound mingling with the tumultuous storm. Small cascades of water streamed from the pall bitts from the fo'castle head above, and, joining issue with the streams from the wet oilskins, ran along the floor and disappeared aft into the main hold.

At two bells in the middle watch—that is, in land parlance 1 o'clock in the morning —the order was roared out on the fo'castle: "All hands on deck and shorten sail!"

Then the sleepy sailors tumbled out of their bunks into their clothes, oilskins and sea boots and up on deck. 'Tis when that order comes on cold, blustering nights that "Jack" grimly mutters: " 'Who would not sell a farm and go to sea?' "

It was on deck that the force of the wind could be fully appreciated, especially after leaving the stifling fo'castle. It seemed to stand up against you like a wall, making it almost impossible to move on the heaving decks or to breathe as the fierce gusts came dashing by. The schooner was hove to under jib, foresail and mainsail. We proceeded to lower the foresail and make it fast. The night was dark, greatly impeding our labor. Still, though not a star or the moon could pierce the black masses of storm clouds that obscured the sky as they swept along before the gale, nature aided us in a measure. A soft light emanated from the movement of the ocean. Each mighty sea, all phosphorescent and glowing with the tiny lights of myriads of animalculae, threatened to overwhelm us with a deluge of fire. Higher and higher, thinner and thinner the crest grew as it began to curve and overtop preparatory to breaking until with a roar it fell over the bulwarks, a mass of soft, glowing light and of tons of water which sent the sailors sprawling in all directions and left in each nook and cranny little specks of light that glowed and trembled till the next sea washed them away depositing new ones in their places. Sometimes several seas following each other with great rapidity and thundering down on our decks filled them full to the bulwarks, but soon they were discharged through the lee scuppers.

To reef the mainsail we were forced to run off before the gale under the single reefed jib. By the time we had finished the wind had forced up such a tremendous sea that it was impossible to heave her to. Away we dashed on the wings of the storm through the muck and flying spray. A wild sheer to starboard, then another to port, as the enormous seas struck the schooner astern and nearly broached her to.

As day broke we took in the jib, leaving not a sail unfurled. Since we had begun scudding she had ceased to take the seas over the bow, but amidships they broke fast and furious. It was a dry storm in the matter of rain, but the force of the wind filled the air with fine spray, which flew as high as the crosstrees and cut the face like a knife, making it impossible to see over a hundred yards ahead. The sea was a dark lead color, as with long, slow majestic roll it was heaped by the wind into liquid mountains of foam. The wild antics of the schooner were sickening as she forged along. She would almost stop as though climbing a mountain, then rapidly rolling to right and left as she gained the summit of a huge sea, she steadied herself and paused for a moment as though affrighted at the yawning precipice before her. Like an avalanche she shot forward and down as the sea astern struck her with the force of a thousand battering rams, burying her bow to the catheads in the milky foam at the bottom that came on deck in all directions—forward, astern, to right and to left, through the hawse pipes and over the rail.

The wind began to drop and by 10 o'clock we were talking of heaving her to. We passed a ship, two schooners and a four-masted barkentine under the smallest of canvas, and at 11 o'clock, running up the spanker and the jib, we hove her to and in another hour we were beating back against the after sea under full sail to regain the sealing grounds away to the westward.

Below a couple of men were sewing "the bricklayer's" body in canvas preparatory to the sea burial. And so with the storm passed away "the bricklayer's" soul.

First Prize—San Francisco *Call*
"Best descriptive article" contest,
November 12, 1893

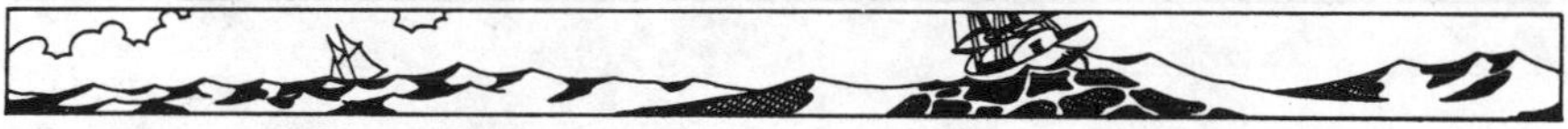

The Run Across

San Francisco—Japan—the "run across"—the southern passage—the tropics. What a wealth of significance such phrases convey! What delightful memories are recalled! What pleasant companionships renewed! What happy hours lived over!

Ah! the very remembrance of the glories of such a voyage is intoxicating, as one recalls those long tropic days, when, with every sail drawing and the northeast trades dead astern, hours slip into hours and days slip into days, and are lost, O so quickly. Days, dreamy and bewitching in their sleepy beauty—days, in which the morn breaks with unrivaled tropic splendor, and the evening shades away almost imperceptibly into night—days, each the counterpart of the other, yet each distinguished by something new, something different—a more glorious sunrise, perhaps, or a more vivid coloring at setting; an unusual display of light and shade on the dancing ocean, or a sky, flecked with the specks of fleecy cloud, golden, crimson and purple, a design more gorgeous than those of previous days.

Time drags not on leaden wings. What of a wheel or a watch! With that steady breeze, ever astern, one almost forgets to steer, so lost is he in contemplation. Each moment new beauties dawn, new glories burst upon him, or new surprises startle and amuse. With dreamy eye, he follows the huge gulls, as, solemn, yet graceful, they sail above the bosom of the deep. Round and round, grandly circling, they ever environ the leaping vessel with their spiral flight. Now the glance is drawn aside by a school of porpoises, or attracted by the silvery flight of flying fish, as they skim from sea to sea, windward, in the path of the sun. The fin of a man-eater, astern, a whale blows to leeward; the horizon is broken by a sail; the wind freshens, and the ocean smiles the merrier; it drops, and the ocean nods and dozes; or a dolphin, harpooned from the jibboom-stays, presents a quivering, ever-changing, and twenty-two miles, sleeping most of the time and getting out at divisions (where the freights always stop for an hour or so) to beg my food. And at the end of the thousand and twenty-two miles I lost that car through a happy incident. I got a "set-down," and the tramp doesn't live who won't miss a train for a set-down any time.

From *The Road*

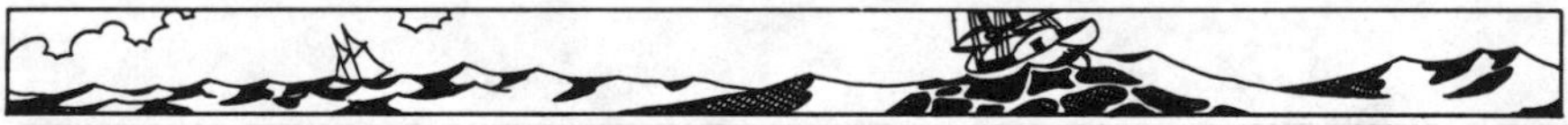

THE INCONCEIVABLE AND MONSTROUS

"SPARE no money," I said to Roscoe. "Let everything on the *Snark* be of the best. And never mind decoration. Plain pine boards is good enough finishing for me. But put the money into the construction. Let the *Snark* be as stanch and strong as any boat afloat. Never mind what it costs to make her stanch and strong; you see that she is made stanch and strong and I'll go on writing and earning the money to pay for it."

And I did . . . . as well as I could; for the *Snark* ate up money faster than I could earn it. In fact, every little while I had to borrow money with which to supplement my earnings. Now I borrowed one thousand dollars, now I borrowed two thousand dollars, and now I borrowed five thousand dollars. And all the time I went on working every day and sinking the earnings in the venture. I worked Sundays, as well, and I took no holidays. But it was worth it. Every time I thought of the *Snark* I knew she was worth it.

For know, gentle reader, the stanchness of the *Snark.* She is forty-five feet long on the water-line. Her garboard strake is three inches thick; her planking two and one-half inches thick; her deck-planking two inches thick; and in all her planking there are no butts. I know, for I ordered that planking especially from Puget Sound. Then the *Snark* has four water-tight compartments, which is to say that her length is broken by three water-tight bulkheads. Thus, no matter how large a leak the Snark may spring, only one compartment can fill with water. The other three compartments will keep her afloat anyway, and, besides, will enable us to mend the leak. There is another virtue in these bulkheads. The last compartment of all, in the very stern, contains six tanks that carry over one thousand gallons of gasolene. Now gasolene is a very dangerous article to carry in bulk on a small craft far out on the wide ocean. But when the six tanks that do not leak are themselves contained in a compartment hermetically sealed off from the rest of the boat, the danger will be seen to be very small indeed.

The *Snark* is a sail-boat. She was built primarily to sail. But, incidentally, as an auxiliary, a seventy-horse-power engine was installed. This is a good, strong engine. I ought to know. I paid for it to come out all the way from New York City. Then, on deck, above the engine, is a windlass. It is a magnificent affair. It weighs several hundred pounds and takes up no end of deck room. You see, it is ridiculous to hoist up anchor by hand-power when there is a seventy-horse-power engine on board. So we installed the windlass, transmitting power to it from the engine by means of a gear and castings specially made in a San Francisco foundry.

The *Snark* was made for comfort, and no expense was spared in this regard. There is the bathroom, for instance, small and compact, it is true, but containing all the conveniences of any bathroom upon land. The bathroom is a beautiful dream of schemes and devices, pumps, and levers, and sea-valves. Why, in the course of its building, I used to lie awake nights thinking about that bathroom. And next to the bathroom come the lifeboat and the launch. They are carried on deck, and they take up what little space might have been left us for exercise. But then, they beat life insurance; and the prudent man, even if he has built as stanch and strong a craft as the *Snark*, will see to it that he has a good lifeboat as well. And ours is a good one. It is a dandy. It was stipulated to cost one hundred and fifty dollars, and when I came to pay the bill, it turned out to be three hundred and ninety-five dollars. That shows how good a lifeboat it is.

I could go on at great length relating the various virtues and excellences of the *Snark*, but I refrain. I have bragged enough as it is, and I have bragged to a purpose, as will be seen before my tale is ended. And please remember its title, "The Inconceivable and Monstrous." It was planned that the *Snark* should sail on October 1, 1906. That she did not so sail was inconceivable and monstrous. There was no valid reason for not sailing except that she was not ready to sail, and there was no conceivable reason why she was not ready. She was promised on November first, on November fifteenth, on December first; and yet she was never ready. On December first Charmian and I left the sweet, clean Sonoma country and came down to live in the stifling city—but not for long, oh, no, only for two weeks, for we would sail on December fifteenth. And I guess we ought to know, for Roscoe said so, and it was on his advice that we came to the city to stop two weeks. Alas, the two weeks went by, four weeks went by, six weeks went by, eight weeks went by, and we were farther away from sailing than ever. Explain it? Who?—me? I can't. It is the one thing in all my life that I have backed down on. There is no explaining it; if there were, I'd do it. I, who am an artisan of speech, confess my inability to explain why the *Snark* was not ready. As I have said, and as I must repeat, it was inconceivable and monstrous.

The eight weeks became sixteen weeks, and then, one day, Roscoe cheered us up by saying:

"If we don't sail before April first, you can use my head for a football."

Two weeks later he said, "I'm getting my head in training for that match."

"Never mind," Charmian and I said to each other; "think of the wonderful boat it is going to be when it is completed."

Whereat we would rehearse for our mutual encouragement the manifold virtues and excellences of the *Snark.* Also, I would borrow more money, and I would get down closer to my desk and write harder, and I refused heroically to take a Sunday off and go out into the hills with my friends. I was building a boat, and by the eternal it was going to be a boat, and a boat spelled out all in capitals—B—O—A—T; and no matter what it cost I didn't care, so long as it was a BOAT.

And, oh, there is one other excellence of the *Snark,* upon which I must brag, namely, her bow. No sea could ever come over it. It laughs at the sea, that bow does; it challenges the sea; it snorts defiance at the sea. And withal it is a beautiful bow; the lines of it are dreamlike; I doubt if ever a boat was blessed with a more beautiful and at the same time a more capable bow. It was made to punch storms. To touch that bow is to rest one's hand on the cosmic nose of things. To look at it is to realize that expense cut no figure where it was concerned. And every time our sailing was delayed, or a new expense was tacked on, we thought of that wonderful bow and were content.

The *Snark* is a small boat. When I figured seven thousand dollars as her generous cost, I was both generous and correct. I have built barns and houses, and I know the peculiar trait such things have of running past their estimated cost. This knowledge was mine, was already mine, when I estimated the probable cost of the building of the *Snark* at seven thousand dollars. Well, she cost thirty thousand. Now don't ask me, please. It is the truth. I signed the checks and I raised the money. Of course there is no explaining it. Inconceivable and monstrous is what it is, as you will agree, I know, ere my tale is done.

Then there was the matter of delay. I dealt with forty-seven different kinds of union men and with one hundred and fifteen different firms. And not one union man and not one firm of all the union men and all the firms ever delivered anything at the time agreed upon, nor ever was on time for anything except pay-day and bill-collection. Men pledged me their immortal souls that they would deliver a certain thing on a certain date; as a rule, after such pledging, they rarely exceeded being three months late in delivery. And so it went, and Charmian and I consoled each other by saying what a splendid boat the *Snark* was, so stanch and strong; also, we would get into the small boat and row around the *Snark,* and gloat over her unbelievably wonderful bow.

"Think," I would say to Charmian, "of a gale off the China coast, and of the *Snark* hove to, that splendid bow of hers driving into the storm. Not a drop will come over the bow. She'll be as dry as a feather, and we'll be all below playing whist while the gale howls."

And Charmian would press my hand enthusiastically and exclaim:

"It's worth every bit of it—the delay—and expense, and worry, and all the rest. Oh, what a truly wonderful boat!"

Whenever I looked at the bow of the *Snark* or thought of her water-tight compartments, I was encouraged. Nobody else, however, was encouraged. My friends began to make bets against the various sailing dates of the *Snark.* Mr. Wiget, who was left behind in charge of our Sonoma ranch, was the first to cash his bet. He collected on New Year's Day, 1907. After that the bets came fast and furious. My friends surrounded me like a gang of harpies, making bets against every sailing date I set. I was rash, and I was stubborn. I bet, and I bet, and I continued to bet; and I paid them all. Why, the womenkind of my friends grew so brave that those among them who never bet before began to bet with me. And I paid them too.

"Never mind," said Charmian to me; "just think of that bow and of being hove to on the China Seas."

"You see," I said to my friends, when I paid the latest bunch of wagers, "neither trouble nor cash is being spared in making the *Snark* the most seaworthy craft that ever sailed out through the Golden Gate—that is what causes all the delay."

In the meantime editors and publishers with whom I had contracts pestered me with demands for explanations. But how could I explain to them, when I was unable to explain to myself, or when there was nobody, not even Roscoe, to explain to me? The newspapers began to laugh at me, and to publish rhymes anent the *Snark's* departure with refrains like, "Not yet but soon." And Charmian cheered me up by reminding me of the bow, and I went to a banker and borrowed five thousand more. There was no recompense for the delay, however. A friend of mine, who happens to be a critic, wrote a roast of me, of all I had done, and of all I ever was going to do; and he planned to have it published after I was out on the ocean. I was still on shore when it came out, and he has been busy explaining ever since.

And the time continued to go by. One thing was becoming apparent, namely, that it was impossible to finish the *Snark* in San Francisco. She had been so long in the building that she was beginning to break down and wear out. In fact, she had reached the stage where she was breaking down faster than she could be repaired. She had become a joke. Nobody took her seriously; least of all the men who worked on her. I said we would sail just as she was and finish building her in Honolulu. Promptly she sprang a leak that had to be attended to before we could sail. I started her for the boat-ways. Before she got to them she was caught between two huge barges and received a vigorous crushing. We got her on the ways, and, part way along, the ways spread and dropped her through, stern-first, into the mud.

It was a pretty tangle, a job for wreckers, not boat-builders. There are two high tides every twenty-four hours, and at every high tide, night and day, for a week, there were two steam tugs pulling and hauling on the *Snark*. There she was, stuck, fallen between the ways and standing on her stern. Next, and while still in that predicament, we started to use the gears and castings made in the local foundry whereby power was conveyed from the engine to the windlass. It was the first time we ever tried to use that windlass. The castings had flaws; the shattered asunder, the gears ground together, and the windlass was out of commission. Following upon that, the seventy-horse-power engine went out of commission. This engine came from New York; so did its bed-plate; there was a flaw in the bed-plate; there were a lot of flaws in the bed-plate; and the seventy-horse-power engine broke away from its shattered foundations, reared up in the air, smashed all connections and fastenings, and fell over on its side. And the *Snark* continued to stick between the spread ways, and the two tugs continued to haul vainly upon her.

"Never mind," said Charmian, "think of what a stanch, strong boat she is."

"Yes," said I, "and of that beautiful bow."

So we took heart and went at it again. The ruined engine was lashed down on its rotten foundation; the smashed castings and cogs of the power transmission were taken down and stored away—all for the purpose of taking them to Honolulu where repairs and new castings could be made. Somewhere in the dim past the *Snark* had received on the outside one coat of white paint. The intention of the color was still evident, however, when one got it in the right light. The *Snark* had never received any paint on the inside. On the contrary, she was coated inches thick with the grease and tobacco-juice of the multitudinous mechanics who had toiled upon her. Never mind, we said; the grease and filth could be planed off, and later, when we fetched Honolulu, the *Snark* could be painted at the same time she was being rebuilt.

By main strength and sweat we dragged the *Snark* off from the wrecked ways and laid her alongside the Oakland City Wharf. The drays brought all the outfit from home, the books and blankets and personal luggage. Along with this, everything else came on board in a torrent of confusion—wood and coal, water and water-tanks, vegetables, provisions, oil, the life-boat and the launch, all our friends, all the friends of our friends and those who claimed to be their friends, to say nothing of some of the friends of the friends of the friends of our crew. Also there were reporters, and photographers, and strangers, and cranks, and finally, and over all, clouds of coal-dust from the wharf.

We were to sail Sunday at eleven, and Saturday afternoon had arrived. The crowd on the wharf and the coal-dust were thicker than ever. In one pocket I carried a check-book, a fountain pen, a dater, and a blotter; in another pocket I carried between one and two thousand dollars in paper money and gold. I was ready for the creditors, cash for the small ones and checks for the large ones, and was waiting only for Roscoe to arrive with the balances of the accounts of the hundred and fifteen firms who had delayed me so many months. And then——

And then the inconceivable and monstrous happened once more. Before Roscoe could arrive there arrived another man. He was a United States marshal. He tacked a notice on the *Snark's* brave mast so that all on the wharf could read that the *Snark* had been libelled for debt. The marshal left a little old man in charge of the *Snark*, and himself went away. I had no longer any control of the *Snark*, nor of her wonderful bow. The little old man was now her lord and master, and I learned that I was paying him three dollars a day for being lord and master. Also, I learned the name of the man who had libelled the *Snark*. It was Sellers; the debt was two hundred and thirty-two dollars; and the deed was no more than was to be expected from the possessor of such a name. Sellers! Ye gods! Sellers!

But who under the sun was Sellers? I looked in my check-book and saw that two weeks before I had made him out a check for five hundred dollars. Other check-books showed me that during the many months of the building of the *Snark* I had paid him several thousand dollars. Then why in the name of common decency hadn't he tried to collect his miserable little balance instead of libelling the *Snark?* I thrust my hands into my pockets, and in one pocket encountered the check-book and the dater and the pen, and in the other pocket the gold money and the paper money. There was the where-withal to settle his pitiful account a few score of times and over—why hadn't he given me a chance? There was no explanation; it was merely the inconceivable and mon-strous.

To make the matter worse, the *Snark* had been libelled late Saturday afternoon; and though I sent lawyers and agents all over Oakland and San Francisco, neither United States judge, nor United States marshal, nor Mr. Sellers, nor Mr. Sellers' attorney, nor anybody could be found. They were all out of town for the week end. And so the *Snark* did not sail Sunday morning at eleven. The little old man was still in charge, and he said no. And Charmian and I walked out on an opposite wharf and took consolation in the *Snark's* wonderful bow and thought of all the gales and typhoons it would proudly punch.

"A bourgeois trick," I said to Charmian, speaking of Mr. Sellers and his libel; "a petty trader's panic. But never mind; our troubles will cease when once we are away from this and out on the wide ocean."

And in the end we sailed away, on Tuesday morning, April 23, 1907. We started rather lame, I confess. We had to hoist anchor by hand, because the power transmission was a wreck. Also, what remained of our seventy-horse-power engine was lashed down for ballast on the bottom of the *Snark.* But what of such things? They could be fixed in Honolulu, and in the meantime think of the magnificent rest of the boat! It is true, the engine in the launch wouldn't run, and the life-boat leaked like a sieve; but then they weren't the *Snark*; they were mere appurtenances. The things that counted were the water-tight bulkheads, the solid planking without butts, the bath-room devices—they were the *Snark.* And then there was, greatest of all, that noble, wind-punching bow.

We sailed out through the Golden Gate and set our course south toward that part of the Pacific where we could hope to pick up with the northeast trades. And right away things began to happen. I had calculated that youth was stuff for a voyage like that of the *Snark,* and I had taken three youths—the engineer, the cook, and the cabin-boy. My calculation was only two-thirds off; I had forgotten to calculate on seasick youth, and I had two of them, the cook and the cabin-boy. They immediately took to their bunks, and that was the end of their usefulness for a week to come. It will be understood, from the foregoing, that we did not have the hot meals we might have had, nor were things kept clean and orderly down below. But it did not matter very much anyway, for we quickly discovered that our box of oranges had at some time been frozen; that our box of apples was mushy and spoiling; that the crate of cabbages, spoiled before it was ever delivered to us, had to go overboard instanter; that kerosene had been spilled on the carrots, and that the turnips were woody and the beets rotten, while the kindling was deadwood that wouldn't burn, and the coal, delivered in rotten potato-sacks, had spilled all over the deck and was washing through the scuppers.

But what did it matter? Such things were mere accessories. There was the boat—she was all right, wasn't she? I strolled along the deck and in one minute counted fourteen butts in the beautiful planking ordered specially from Puget Sound in order that there should be no butts in it. Also, the deck leaked, and it leaked badly. It drowned Roscoe out of his bunk and ruined the tools in the engine-room, to say nothing of the provisions it ruined in the galley. Also, the sides of the *Snark* leaked, and the bottom leaked, and we had to pump her every day to keep her afloat. The floor of the galley is a couple of feet above the inside bottom of the *Snark*; and yet I have stood on the floor of the galley, trying to snatch a cold bite, and been wet to the knees by the water churning around inside four hours after the last pumping.

Then those magnificent water-tight compartments that cost so much time and money—well, they weren't water-tight after all. The water moved free as the air from one compartment to another; furthermore, a strong smell of gasoline from the after compartment leads me to suspect that some one or more of the half-dozen tanks there stored have sprung a leak. The tanks leak, and they are not hermetically sealed in their compartment. Then there was the bathroom with its pumps and levers and sea-valves—it went out of commission inside the first twenty hours. Powerful iron levers broke off short in one's hand when one tried to pump with them. The bathroom was the swiftest wreck of any portion of the *Snark.*

And the iron-work on the *Snark,* no matter what its source, proved to be mush. For instance, the bed-plate of the engine came from New York, and it was mush; so were the castings and gears for the windlass that came from San Francisco. And finally, there was the wrought iron used in the rigging, that carried away in all directions when the first strains were put upon it. Wrought iron, mind you, and it snapped like macaroni.

A gooseneck on the gaff of the mainsail broke short off. We replaced it with the gooseneck from the gaff of the storm trysail, and the second gooseneck broke short off inside fifteen minutes of use, and, mind you, it had been taken from the gaff of the storm trysail, upon which we would have depended in time of storm. At the present moment the *Snark* trails her mainsail like a broken wing, the gooseneck being replaced by a rough lashing. We'll see if we can get honest iron in Honolulu.

Man had betrayed us and sent us to sea in a sieve, but the Lord must have loved us, for we had calm weather in which to learn that we must pump every day in order to keep afloat and that more trust could be placed in a wooden toothpick than in the most massive piece of iron to be found aboard. As the stanchness and the strength of the *Snark* went glimmering, Charmian and I pinned our faith more and more to the *Snark's* wonderful bow. There was nothing else left to pin to. It was all inconceivable and monstrous, we knew, but that bow, at least, was rational. And then, one evening, we started to heave to.

How shall I describe it? First of all, for the benefit of the tyro, let me explain that heaving to is that sea manoeuvre which, by means of short and balanced canvas, compels a vessel to ride bow-on to wind and sea. When the wind is too strong, or the sea is too high, a vessel of the size of the *Snark* can heave to with ease, whereupon there is no more work to do on deck. Nobody needs to steer. The lookout is superfluous. All hands can go below and sleep or play whist.

Well, it was blowing half of a small summer gale, when I told Roscoe we'd heave to. Night was coming on. I had been steering nearly all day, and all hands on deck (Roscoe and Bert and Charmian) were tired, while all hands below were seasick. It happened that we had already put two reefs in the big mainsail. The flying-jib and the jib were taken in, and a reef put in the forestaysail. The mizzen was also taken in. About this time the flying jib-boom buried itself in a sea and broke short off. I started to put the wheel down in order to heave to. The *Snark* at the moment was rolling in the trough. She continued rolling in the trough. I put the spokes down harder and harder. She never budged from the trough. (The trough, gentle reader, is the most dangerous position of all in which to lay a vessel.) I put the wheel hard down, and still the *Snark* rolled in the trough. Eight points was the nearest I could get her to the wind. I had Roscoe and Bert come in on the main-sheet. The *Snark* rolled on in the trough, now putting her rail under on one side and now under on the other side.

Again the inconceivable and monstrous was showing its grizzly head. It was grotesque, impossible. I refused to believe it. Under double-reefed mainsail and single-reefed staysail the *Snark* refused to heave to. We flattened the mainsail down. It did not alter the *Snark's* course a tenth of a degree. We slacked the mainsail off with no more result. We set a storm trysail on the mizzen, and took in the mainsial. No change. The *Snark* rolled on in the trough. That beautiful bow of hers refused to come up and face the wind.

Next we took in the reefed staysail. Thus, the only bit of canvas left on her was the storm trysail on the mizzen. If anything would bring her bow up to the wind that would. Maybe you won't believe me when I say it failed, but I do say it failed. And I say it failed because I saw it fail, and not because I believe it failed. I don't believe it did fail. It is unbelievable, and I am not telling you what I believe; I am telling you what I saw.

Now, gentle reader, what would you do if you were on a small boat, rolling in the trough of the sea, a trysail on that small boat's stern that was unable to swing the bow up into the wind? Get out the sea anchor. It's just what we did. We had a patent one, made to order and warranted not to dive. Imagine a hoop of steel that serves to keep open the mouth of a large, conical cnavas bag, and you have a sea-anchor. Well, we made a line fast to the sea-anchor and to the bow of the *Snark*, and then dropped the sea-anchor overboard. It promptly dived. We had a tripping line on it, so we tripped the sea-anchor and hauled it in. We attached a big timber as a float, and dropped the sea-anchor over again. This time it floated. The line to the bow grew taut. The trysail on the mizzen tended to swing the bow into the wind, but, in spite of this tendency, the *Snark* calmly took that sea-anchor in her teeth, and went on ahead, dragging it after her, still in the trough of the sea. And there you are. We even took in the trysail, hoisted the full mizzen in its place, and hauled the full mizzen down flat, and the *Snark* wallowed in the trough and dragged the sea-anchor behind her. Don't believe me. I don't believe it myself. I'm merely telling you what I saw.

Now, I leave it to you. Who ever heard of a sailing-boat that wouldn't heave to?—that wouldn't heave to with a sea-anchor to help it? Out of my brief experience with boats I know I never did. And I stood on deck and looked on the naked face of the inconceivable and monstrous—the *Snark* that wouldn't heave to. A stormy night with broken moonlight had come on. There was a splash of wet in the air, and up to windward there was a promise of rain-squalls; and then there was the trough of the sea, cold and cruel in the moonlight, in which the *Snark* complacently rolled. And then we took in the sea-anchor and the mizzen, hoisted the reefed staysail, ran the *Snark* off before it, and went below—not to the hot meal that should have awaited us, but to skate across the slush and slime on the cabin floor, where cook and cabin-boy lay like dead men in their bunks, and to lie down in our own bunks, with our clothes on ready for a call, and to listen to the bilge-water spouting knee-high on the galley floor.

In the Bohemian Club of San Francisco there are some crack sailors. I know, because I heard them pass judgment on the *Snark* during the process of her building. They found only one vital thing the matter with her, and on this they were all agreed, namely, that she could not run. She was all right in every particular, they said, except that I'd never be able to run her before it in a stiff wind and sea. "Her lines," they explained enigmatically, "it is the fault of her lines. She simply cannot be made to run, that is all." Well, I wish I'd only had those crack sailors of the Bohemian Club on board the *Snark* the other night for them to see for themselves their one, vital, unanimous judgment absolutely reversed. Run? It is the one thing the *Snark* does to perfection. Run? She ran with a sea-anchor fast for'ard and a full mizzen flattened down aft. Run? At the present moment, as I write this, we are bowling along before it, at a six-knot cilp, in the northeast trades. Quite a tidy bit of sea is running. There is nobody at the wheel, the wheel is not even lashed and is set over a half-spoke weather helm. To be precise, the wind is northeast; the *Snark's* mizzen is furled, her mainsail is over to starboard, her headsheets are hauled flat; and the *Snark's* course is south-southwest. And yet there are men who have sailed the seas for forty years and who hold that no boat can run before it without being steered. They'll call me a liar when they read this; it's what they called Captain Slocum when he said the same of his *Spray*.

As regards the future of the *Snark* I'm all at sea. I don't know. If I had the money or the credit, I'd build another *Snark* that would heave to. But I am at the end of my resources. I've got to put up with the present *Snark* or quit—and I can't quit. So I guess I'll have to try to get along with heaving the *Snark* to stern-first. I am waiting for the next gale to see how it will work. I think it can be done. It all depends on how her stern takes the seas. And who knows but that some wild morning on the China Sea, some gray-beard skipper will stare, rub his incredulous eyes and stare again, at the spectacle of a weird, small craft, very much like the *Snark*, hove to stern-first and riding out the gale?

P.S. On my return to California after the voyage, I learned that the *Snark* was forty-three feet on the water line instead of forty-five. This was due to the fact that the builder was not on speaking terms with the tape-line or two-foot rule.

From *The Cruise of the Snark.*

A PACIFIC TRAVERSE

Sandwich Islands to Tahiti.—There is great difficulty in making this passage across the trades. The whalers and all others speak with great doubt of fetching Tahiti from the Sandwich Islands. Capt. Bruce says that a vessel should keep to the northward until she gets a start of wind before bearing for her destination. In his passage between them in November, 1837, he had no variables near the line in coming south, and never could make easting on either tack, though he endeavored by every means to do so.

SO SAYS the sailing directions for the South Pacific Ocean; and that is all it says. There is not a word more to help the weary voyager in making this long traverse—nor is there any word at all concerning the passage form Hawaii to the Marquesas, which lie some eight hundred miles to the northeast of Tahiti and which are the more difficult to reach by just that much. The reason for the lack of directions is, I imagine, that no voyager is supposed to make himself weary by attempting so impossible a traverse. But the impossible did not deter the *Snark*,—principally because of the fact that we did not read that particular little paragraph in the sailing directions until after we had started. We sailed from Hilo, Hawaii, on October 7, and arrived at Nuka-hiva, in the Marquesas, on December 6. The distance was two thousand miles as the crow flies, while we actually travelled at least four thousand miles to accomplish it, thus proving for once and forever that the shortest distance between two points is not always a straightline. Had we headed directly for the Marquesas, we might have travelled five or six thousand miles.

Upon one thing we were resolved: we would not cross the Line west of 130° west longitude. For here was the problem. To cross the Line to the west of that point, if the southeast trades were well around to the southeast, would throw us so far to leeward of the Marquesas that a head-beat would be maddeningly impossible. Also, we had to remember the equatorial current, which moves west at a rate of anywhere from twelve to seventy-five miles a day. A pretty pickle, indeed, to be to leeward of our destination with such a current in our teeth. No; not a minute, nor a second, west of 130° west longitude would we cross the Line. But since the southeast trades were to be expected five or six degrees north of the Line (which, if they were well around to the southeast or south-southeast, would necessitate our sliding off toward south-southwest), we should have to hold to the eastward, north of the Line, and north of the southeast trades, until we gained at least 128° west longitude.

I have forgotten to mention that the seventy-horse-power gasolene engine, as usual, was not working, and that we could depend upon wind alone. Neither was the launch engine working. And while I am about it, I may as well confess that the five-horse-power, which ran the lights, fans, and pumps, was also on the sick-list. A striking title for a book haunts me, waking and sleeping. I should like to write that book some day and to call it "Around the World with Three Gasolene Engines and a Wife." But I am afraid I shall not write it, for fear of hurting the feelings of some of the young gentlemen of San Francisco, Honolulu, and Hilo, who learned their trades at the expense of the *Snark's* engines.

It looked easy on paper. Here was Hilo and there was our objective, 128° west longitude. With the northeast trade blowing we could travel a straight line between the two points, and even slack our sheets off a goodly bit. But one of the chief troubles with the trades is that one never knows just where he will pick them up and just in what direction they will be blowing. We picked up the northeast trade right outside of Hilo harbor, but the miserable breeze was away around into the east. Then there was the north equatorial current setting westward like a mighty river. Furthermore, a small boat, by the wind and bucking into a big head-sea, does not work to advantage. She jogs up and down and gets nowhere. Her sails are full and straining, every little while she presses her lee-rail under, she flounders, and bumps, and splashes, and that is all. Whenever she begins to gather way, she runs ker-chug into a big mountain of water and is brought to a standstill. So, with the *Snark*, the resultant of her smallness, of the trade around into the east, and of the strong equatorial current, was a long sag south. Oh, she did not go quite south. But the easting she made was distressing. On October 11, she made forty miles easting; October 12 fifteen miles; October 13, no easting; October 14, thirty miles; October 15, twenty-three miles; October 16, eleven miles; and on October 17, she actually went to the westward four miles. Thus, in a week, she made one hundred and fifteen miles easting, which was equivalent to sixteen miles a day. But between the longitude of Hilo and 128° west longitude is a difference of twenty-seven degrees, or, roughly, sixteen hundred miles. At sixteen miles a day, one hundred days would be required to accomplish this distance. And even then, our objective, 128° west longitude, was five degrees north of the Line, while Nukahiva, in the Marquesas, lay nine degrees south of the Line and twelve degrees to the west!

There remained only ont thing to do—to work south out of the trade and into the variables. It is true that Captain Bruce found no variables on his traverse, and that he "never could make easting on either tack." It was the variables or nothing with us, and we prayed for better luck than he had had. The variables constitute the belt of ocean lying between the trades and the doldrums, and are conjectured to be the draughts of heated air which rise in the doldrums, flow high in the air counter to the trades, and gradually sink down till they fan the surface of the ocean where they are found. And they are found . . . where they are found; for they are wedged between the trades and the doldrums, which same shift their territory from day to day and month to month.

We found the variables in 11° north latitude, and 11° north latitude we hugged jealously. To the south lay the doldrums. To the north lay the northeast trade that refused to blow from the northeast. The days came and went, and always they found the *Snark* somewhere near the eleventh parallel. The variables were truly variable. A light head-wind would die away and leave us rolling in a calm for forty-eight hours. Then a light head-wind would spring up, blow for three hours, and leave us rolling in another calm for forty-eight hours. Then—hurrah!—the wind would come out of the west, fresh, beautifully fresh, and send the *Snark* along, wing and wing, her wake bubbling, the log-line straight astern. At the end of half an hour, while we were preparing to set the spinnaker, with a few sickly gasps the wind would die away. And so it went. We wagered optimistically on ever favorable fan of air that lasted over 5 minutes; but it never did any good. The fans faded out just the same.

But there were exceptions. In the variables, if you wait long enough, something is bound to happen, and we were so plentifully stocked with food and water that we could affort to wait. On October 26, we actually made one hundred and three miles of easting, and we talked about it for days afterward. Once we caught a moderate gale from the south, which blew itself out in eight hours, but it helped us to seventy-one miles of easting in that particular twenty-four hours. And the, just as it was expiring, the wind came straight out from the north (the directly opposite quarter), and fanned us along over another degree of easting.

In years and years no sailing vessel has attempted this traverse, and we found ourselves in the midst of one of the loneliest of the Pacific solitudes. In the sixty days we were crossing it we sighted no sail, lifted no steamer's smoke above the horizon. A disabled vessel could drift in this deserted expanse for a dozen generations, and there would be no rescue. The only chance of rescue would be from a vessel like the *Snark*, and the *Snark* happened to be there principally because of the fact that the traverse had been begun before the particular paragraph in the sailing directions had been read. Standing upright on deck, a straight line drawn from the eye to the horizon would measure three miles and a half. Thus, seven miles was the diameter of the circle of the sea in which we had our centre. Since we remained always in the centre, and since we constantly were moving in some direction, we looked upon many circles. But all circles looked alike. No tufted islets, gray headlands, nor glistening patches of white canvas ever marred the symmetry of that unbroken curve. Clouds came and went, rising up over the rim of the circle, flowing across the space of it, and spilling away and down across the opposite rim.

The world faded as the procession of the weeks marched by. The world faded until at last there ceased to be any world except the little world of the *Snark*, freighted with her seven souls and floating on the expanse of the waters. Our memories of the world, the great world, became like dreams of former lives we had lived somewhere before we came to be born on the *Snark*. After we had been out of fresh vegetables for some time, we mentioned such things in much the same way I have heard my father mention the vanished apples of his boyhood. Man is a creature of habit, and we on the *Snark* had got the habit of the *Snark*. Everything about her and aboard her was as a matter of course, and anything different would have been an irritation and an offence.

There was no way by which the great world could intrude. Our bell rang the hours, but no caller ever rang it. There were no guests to dinner, no telegrams, no insistent telephone jangles invading our privacy. We had no engagements to keep, no trains to catch, and there were no morning newspapers over which to waste time in learning what was happening to ur fifteen hundred million other fellow-creatures.

But it was not dull. The affairs of our little world had to be regulated, and, unlike the great world, our world had to be steered in its journey through space. Also, there were cosmic disturbances to be encountered and baffled, such as do not afflict the big earth in its frictionless orbit through the windless void. And we never knew, from moment to moment, what was going to happen next. There was spice and variety enough and to spare. Thus, at four in the morning, I relieve Hermann at the wheel.

"East-northeast," he gives me the course. "She's eight points off, but she ain't steering."

Small wonder. The vessel does not exist that can be steered in so absolute a calm.

"I had a breeze a little while ago—maybe it will come back again," Hermann says hopefully, ere he starts forward to the cabin and his bunk.

The mizzen is in and fast furled. In the night, what of the roll and the absence of wind, it had made life to hideous to be permitted to go on rasping at the mast, smashing at the tackles, and buffeting the empty air into hollow outbursts of sound. But the big mainsail is still on, and the staysail, jib, and flying-jib are snapping and slashing at their sheets with every roll. Every star is out. Just for luck I put the wheel hard over in the opposite direction to which it had been left by Hermann, and I lean back and gaze up at the stars. There is nothing else for me to do. There is nothing to be done with a sailing vessel rolling in a stark calm.

The I feel a fan on my cheek, faint, so faint, that I can just sense it ere it is gone. But another comes, and another, until a real and just perceptible breeze is blowing. How the *Snark*'s sails manage to feel it is beyond me, but feel it they do, as she does as well, for the compass card begins slowly to revolve in the binnacle. In reality, it is not revolving at all. It is held by terrestrial magnetism in one place, and it is the *Snark* that is revolving, pivoted upon that delicate cardboard device that floats in a closed vessel of alcohol.

So the *Snark* comes back on her course. The breath increases to a tiny puff. The *Snark* feels the weight of it and actually heels over a trifle. There is flying scud overhead, and I notice the stars being blotted out. Walls of darnkess close in upon me, so that, when the last star is gone, the darkness is so near that it seems I can reach out and touch it on every side. When I lean toward it, I can feel it loom against my face. Puff follows puff, and I am glad the mizzen is furled. Phew! that was a stiff one! The *Stark* goes over and down until her lee-rail is buried and the whole Pacific Ocean is pouring in. Four or five of these gusts make me wish that the jib and flying-jib were in. The sea is picking up, the gusts are growing stronger and more frequent, and there is a splatter of wet in the air. There is no use in attempting to gaze to windward. The wall of blackness is within arm's length. Yet I cannot help attempting to see and guage the blows that are being struck at the *Snark*. There is something ominous and menacing up there to windward, and I have a feeling that if I look long enough and strong enough, I shall divine it. Futile feeling. Between two gusts I leave the wheel and run forward to the cabin companionway, where I light matches and consult the barometer. "29-90" it reads. That sensitive instrument refuses to take notice of the disturbance which is humming with a deep, throaty voice in the rigging. I get back to the wheel just in time to meet another gust, the strongest yet. Well, anyway, the wind is abeam and the *Snark* is on her course, eating up easting. That at least is well.

The jib and flying-jib bother me, and I wish they were in. She would make easier weather of it, and less risky weather likewise. The wind snorts, and stray raindrops pelt like birdshot. I shall certainly have to call all hands, I conclude; then conclude the next instant to hang on a little longer. Maybe this is the end of it, and I shall have called them for nothing. It is better to let them sleep. I hold the *Snark* down to her task, and from out of the darkness, at right angles, comes a deluge of rain accompanied by shrieking wind. Then everything eases except the blackness, and I rejoice in that I have not called the men.

No sooner does the wind ease than the sea picks up. Teh combers are breaking now, and the boat is tossing like a cork. Then out of the blackness the gusts come harder and faster than before. If only I knew what was up there to windward in the blackness! The *Snark* is making heavy weather of it, and her lee-rail is buried oftener than not. More shrieks and snorts of wind. Now, if ever, is the time to call the men. I *will* call them, I resolve. Then there is a burst of rain, a slackening of the wind, and I do not call. But it is rather lonely, there at the wheel, steering a little world through howling blackness. It is quite a responsibility to be all alone on the surface of a little world in time of stress, doing the thinking for its sleeping inhabitants. I recoil from the responsibility as more gusts begin to strike and as a sea licks along the weather rail and splashes over into the cockpit. The salt water seems strangely warm to my body and is shot through with ghostly nodules of phosphorescent light. I shall surely call al hands to shorten sail. Why should they sleep? I am a fool to have any compunctions in the matter. My intellect is arrayed against my heart. It was my heart that said, "Let them sleep." Yes, but it was my intellect that backed up my heart in that judgment. Let my intellect then reverse the judgment; and, while I am speculating as to what particular entity issued that command to my intellect, the gusts die away. Solicitude for mere bodily comfort has no place in practical seamanship, I conclude sagely; but study the feel of the next series of gusts and do not call the men. After all, it *is* my intellect, behind everything, procrastinating, measuring its knowledge of what the *Snark* can endure against the blows being struck at her, and waiting the call of all hands against the striking of still severer blows.

Daylight, gray and violent, steals through the cloud-pall and shows a foaming sea that flattens under the weight of recurrent and increasing squalls. Then comes the rain, filling the windy valleys of the sea with milky smoke and further flattening the waves, which but wait for the easement of wind and rain to leap more wildly than before. Come the men on deck, their sleep out, and among them Hermann, his face on the broad grin in appreciation of the breeze of wind I have picked up. I turn the wheel over to Warren and start to go below, pausing on the way to rescue the galley stovepipe which has gone adrift. I am barefooted, and my toes have had an excellent education in the art of clinging; but, as the rail buries itself in a green sea, I suddenly sit down on the streaming deck. Hermann good-naturedly elects to question my selection of such a spot. Then comes the next roll, and he sits down, suddenly, and without premeditation. The *Snark* heels over and down, the rail takes it green, and Hermann and I, clutching the precious stovepipe, are swept down into the leescuppers. After that I finish my journey below, and while changing my clothes grin with satisfaction—the *Snark* is making easting.

No, it is not all monotony. When we had worried along our easting to 126° west longitude, we left the variables and headed south through the doldrums, where was much calm weather and where, taking advantage of ever fan of air, we were often glad to make a score of miles in as many hours. And yet, on such a day, we might pass through a dozen squalls and be surrounded by dozens more. And every squall was to be regarded as a bludgeon capable of crushing the *Snark*. We were struck sometimes by the centers and sometimes by the sides of these squalls, and we never knew just where or how we were to be hit. The squall that rose up, covering half the heavens, and swept down upon us, as likely as not split into two squalls which passed us harmlessly on either side; while the tiny, innocent-looking squall that appeared to carry no more than a hogshead of water and a pound of wind, would abruptly assume cyclopean proportions, deluging us with rain and overwhelming us with wind. Then there were trecherous squalls that went boldly astern and sneaked back upon us from a mile to leeward. Again, two squalls would tear along, one on each side of us, and we would get a fillip from each of them. Now a gale certainly grows tiresome after a few hours, but squalls never. The thousandth squall in one's experience is as interesting as the first one, and perhaps a bit more so. It is the tyro who has no apprehension of them. The man of a thousand squalls respects a squall. He knows what they are.

It was in the doldrums that our most exciting event occurred. On November 20, we discovered that through an accident we had lost over one-half of the supply of fresh water that remained to us. Since we were at that time forty-three days out from Hilo, our supply of fresh water was not large. To lose over half of it was a catastrophe. On close allowance, the remnant of water we possessed would last twenty days. But we were in the doldrums; there was no telling where the southeast trades were, nor where we would pick them up.

The handcuffs were promptly put upon the pump, and once a day the water was portioned out. Each of us received a quart for personal use, and eight quarts were given to the cook. Enters now the psychology of the situation. No sooner had the discovery of the water shortage been made than I, for one, was afflicted with a burning thirst. It seemes to me that I had never been so thirsty in my life. My little quart of water I could easily have drunk in one draught, and to refrain from doing so required a severe exertion of will. Nor was I alone in this. All of us talked water, thought water, and dreamed water when we slept. We examined the charts for possible islands to which to run in extremity, but there were no such islands. The Marquesas were the nearest, and they were the other side of the Line, and of the doldrums, too, which made it even worse. We were in 3° north latitude, while the Marquesas were in 9° south latitude—a difference of over a thousand miles. Furthermore, the Marquesas lay some fourteen degrees to the west of our longitude. A pretty pickle for a handful of creatures sweltering on the ocean in the heat of tropic calms.

We rigged lines on either side between the main and mizzen riggings. To these we laced the big deck awning, hoisting it up aft with a sailing pennant so that any rain it might collect would run forward where it could be caught. Here and there squalls passed across the circle of the sea. All day we watched them, now to port or starboard, and again ahead or astern. But never one came near enough to wet us. In the afternoon a big one bore down upon us. It spread out across the ocean as it approached, and we could see it emptying countless thousands of gallons into the salt sea. Extra attention was paid to the awning, and then we waited. Warren, Martin, and Hermann made a vivid picture. Grouped together, holding on to the rigging, swaying to the roll, they were gazing intently at the squall. Strain, anxiety, and yearning were in every posture of their bodies. Beside them was the dry and empty awning. But they seemed to grow limp and to droop as the squall broke in half, one part passing on ahead, the other drawing astern and going to leeward.

But that night came rain. Martin, whose psychological thirst had compelled him to drink a quart of water early, got his mouth down to the lip of the awning and rank the deepest draught I ever have seen drunk. The precious water came down in bucketfuls and tubfuls, and in two hours we caught and stored away in the tanks one hundred and twenty gallons. Strange to say, in all the rest of our voyage to the Marquesas not another drop of rain fell on board. If that squall had missed us, the handcuffs would have remained on the pump, and we would have busied ourselves with utilizing our surplus gasolene for distillation purposes.

Then there was the fishing. One did not have to go in search of it, for it was there at the rail. A three-inch steel hook, on the end of a stout line, with a piece of white rag for bait, was all that was necessary to catch bonitas weighing from ten to twenty-five pounds. Bonitas feed on flying-fish, wherefore they are unaccustomed to nibbling at the hook. They strike as gamely as the gamest fish in the sea, and their first run is something that no man who has ever caught them will forget. Also, bonitas are veriest cannibals. The instant one is hooked he is attacked by his fellows. Often and often we hauled them on board with fresh, clean-bitten holes in them the size of teacups.

One school of bonitas, numbering many thousands, stayed with us day and night for more than three weeks. Aided by the *Snark*, it was great hunting; for they cut a swath of destruction through the ocean half a mile wide and fifteen hundred miles in length. They ranged along abreast of the *Snark* on either side, pouncing upon the flying-fish her forefoot scared up. Since they were continually pursuing astern the flying-fish that survived for several flights, they were always overtaking the *Snark*, and at any time one could glance astern and on the front of a breaking wave see scores of their silvery forms coasting down just under the surface. When they had eaten their fill, it was their delight to get in the shadows of the boat, or of her sails, and a hundred or so were always to be seen lazily sliding along and keeping cool.

But the poor flying-fish! Pursued and eaten alive by the bonitas and dolphins, they sought flight in the air, where the swooping seabirds drove them back into the water. Under heaven there was no refuge for them. Flying-fish do not play when they essay the air. It is a life-and-death affair with them. A thousand times a day we could lift our eyes and see the tragedy played out. The swift, broken circling of a guny might attract one's attention. A glance beneath shows the back of a dolphin breaking the surface in a wild rush. Just in front of its nose a shimmering palpitant streak of silver shoots from the water into the air—a delicate, organic mechanism of flight, endowed with sensation, power of direction, and love of life. The guny swoops for it and misses, and the flying-fish, gaining its altitude by rising, kite-like, against the wind, turns in a half-circle and skims off to leeward, gliding on the bosom of the wind. Beneath it, the wake of the dolphin shows in churning foam. So he follows, gazing upward with large eyes at the flashing breakfast that navigates an element other than his own. He cannot rise to so lofty occasion, but he is a thorough-going empiricist, and he knows, sooner or later, if not gobbled up by the guny, that the flying-fish must return to the water. And then—breakfast. We used to pity the poor winged fish. It was sad to see sordid and bloody slaughter. And then, in the night watches, when a forlorn little flying-fish struck the mainsail and fell gasping and splattering on the deck, we would rush for it just as eagerly, just as greedily, just as voraciously, as the dolphins and bonitas. For know that flying-fish are most toothsome for breakfast. It is always a wonder to me that such dainty meat does not build dainty tissue in the bodies of the devourers. Perhaps the dolphins and bonitas are coarser-fibred because of the high speed at which they drive their bodies in order to catch their prey. But then again, the flying-fish drive their bodies at high speed, too.

Sharks we caught occasionally, on large hooks, with chain-swivels, bent on a length of small rope. And sharks meant pilot-fish, and remoras, and various sorts of parasitic creatures. Regular man-eaters some of the sharks proved, tiger-eyed and with twelve rows of teeth, razor-sharp. By the way, we of the *Snark* are agreed that we have eaten many fish that will not compare with baked shark smothered in tomato dressing. In the calms we occasionally caught a fish called "haké" by the Japanese cook. And once, on a spoon-hook trolling a hundred yards astern, we caught a snakelike fish, over three feet in length and not more than three inches in diameter, with four fangs in his jaws. He proved the most delicious fish—delicious in meat and flavor—that we have ever eaten on board.

The most welcome addition to our larder was a green sea-turble, weighing a full hundred pounds and appearing on the table most appetizingly in steaks, soups, and stews, and finally in a wonderful curry which tempted all hands into eating more rice than was good for them. The turtle was sighted to windward, calmly sleeping on the surface in the midst of a hugh school of curious dolphins. It was a deep-sea turtle of a surety, for the nearest land was a thousand miles away. We put the *Snark* about and went back for him, Hermann driving the granes into his head and neck. When hauled aboard, numerous remora were clinging to his shell, and out of the hollows at the roots of his flippers crawled several large crabs. It did not take the crew of the *Snark* longer than the next meal to reach the unanimous conclusion that it would willingly put the *Snark* about any time for a turtle.

But it is the dolphin that is the king of deep-sea fishes. Never is his color twice quite the same. Swimming in the sea, an ethereal creature of palest azure, he displays in that one guise a miracle of color. But it is nothing compared with the displays of which he is capable. At one time he will appear green—pale green, deep green, phosphorescent green; at another time blue—deep blue, electric, blue, all the spectrum of blue. Catch him on a hook, and he turns to gold, yellow gold, all gold. Haul him on deck, and he excels the spectrum, passing through inconceivable shades of blues, greens, and yellows, and then, suddenly, turning a ghostly white, in the midst of which are bright blue spots, and you suddenly discover that he is speckled like a trout. Then back from white he goes, through all the range of colors, finally turning to a mother-of-pearl.

For those who are devoted to fishing, I can recommend no finer sport than catching dolphin. Of course, it must be done on a thin line with reel and pole. A No. 7 O'Shaughnessy tarpon hook is just the thing, baited with an entire flying-fish. Like the bonita, the dolphin's fare consists of flying-fish, and he strikes like lightning at the bait. The first warning is when the reel screeches and you see the line smoking out at right angles to the boat. Before you have time to entertain anxiety concerning the length of your line, the fish rises into the air in a succession of leaps. Since he is quite certain to be four feet long or over, the sport of landing so gamey a fish can be realized. When hooked, he invariably turns golden. The idea of the series of leaps is to rid himself of the hook, and the man who has made the strike must be of iron or decadent if his heart does not beat with an extra flutter when he beholds such gorgeous fish, glittering in golden mail and shaking itself like a stallion in each mid-air leap. 'Ware slack! If you don't, on one of those leaps the hook will be flung out and twenty feet away. No slack, and away he will go on another run, culminating in another series of leaps. About this time one begins to worry over the line, and to wish that he had had nine hundred feet on the reel originally instead of six hundred. With careful playing the line can be saved, and after an hour of keen excitement the fish can be brought to gaff. One such dolphin I landed on the *Snark* measured four feet and seven inches.

Hermann caught dolphins more prosaically. A hand-line and a chunk of shark-meat was all he needed. His hand-line was very thick, but on more than one occasion it parted and lost the fish. One day a dolphin got away with a lure of Hermann's manufacture, to which were lashed four O'Shaughnessy hooks. Within an hour the same dolphin was landed with the rod, and on dissecting him the four hooks were recovered. The dolphins, which remained with us over a month, deserted us north of the line, and not one was seen during the remainder of the traverse.

So the days passed. There was so much to be done that time never dragged. Had there been little to do, time could not have dragged with such wonderful seascapes and cloudscapes—dawns that were like burning imperial cities under rainbows that arched nearly to the zenith; sunsets that bathed the purple sea in rivers of rose-colored light, flowing from a sun whose diverging, heaven-climbing rays were of the purest blue. Overside, in the heat of the day, the sea was an azure satiny fabric, in the depths of which the sunshine focussed in funnels of light. Astern, deep down, when there was a breeze, bubbled a procession of milky-turquoise ghosts—the foam flung down by the hull of the *Snark* each time she floundered against a sea. At night the wake was phosphorescent fire, where the medusa slime resented our passing bulk, while far down could be observed the unceasing flight of comets, with long, undulating, nebulous tails —caused by the passage of the bonitas through the resentful medusa slime. And now and again, from out of the darkness on either hand, just under the surface, larger phosphorescent organisms flashed up like electric lights, marking collisions with the careless bonitas skurrying ahead to the good hunting just beyond our bowsprit.

We made our easting, worked down through the doldrums, and caught a fresh breeze out of south-by-west. Hauled up by the wind, on such a slant, we would fetch past the Marquesas far away to the westward. But the next day, on Tuesday, November 26, in the thick of a heavy squall, the wind shifted suddenly to the southeast. It was the trade at last. There were no more squalls, naught but fine weather, a fair wind, and a whirling log, with sheets slacked off and with spinnaker and mainsail swaying and bellying on either side. The trade backed more and more, until it blew out of the northeast, while we steered a steady course to the southwest. Ten days of this, and on the morning of December 6, at five o'clock, we sighted land "just where it ought to have been," dead ahead. We passed to leeward of Ua-huka, skirted the southern edge of Nuka-hiva, and that night, in driving squalls and inky darkness, fought our way in to an anchorage in the narrow bay of Taiohae. The anchor rumbled down to the blatting of wild goats on the cliffs, and the air we breathed was heavy with the perfume of flowers. The traverse was accomplished. Sixty days from land to land, across a lonely sea above whose horizons never rise the straining sails of ships.

From *The Cruise of the Snark*

THE *Sophie Sutherland*

It was during the early winter of 1892 that I resolved to go to sea. My Hancock Fire Brigade experience was very little responsible for this. I still drank and frequented saloons—practically lived in saloons. Whisky was dangerous, in my opinion, but not wrong. Whisky was dangerous, like other dangerous things in the natural world. Men died of whisky; but then, too, fishermen were capsized and drowned, hoboes fell under trains and were cut to pieces. To cope with winds and waves, railroad trains, and barrooms, one must use judgment. To get drunk after the manner of men was all right, but one must do it with discretion. No more quarts of whisky for me.

What really decided me to go to sea was that I had caught my first vision of the death-road which John Barleycorn maintains for his devotees. It was not a clear vision, however. . . . It struck me, from watching those with whom I associated, that the life we were living was more destructive than that lived by the average man. . . .

So I considered my situation and knew that I was getting into a bad way of living. It made toward death too quickly to suit my youth and vitality. And there was only one way out of this hazardous manner of living and that was to get out. The sealing-fleet was wintering in San Francisco Bay, and in the saloons I met skippers, mates, hunters, boat-steerers, and boat-pullers. I met the seal-hunter, Pete Holt, and agreed to be his boat-puller and to sign on any schooner he signed on. And I had to have half-a-dozen drinks with Pete Holt there and then to seal our agreement.

And at once awoke all my old unrest that John Barleycorn had put to sleep. I found myself actually bored with the saloon-life of the Oakland water front, and wondered what I had ever found fascinating in it. Also, with this death-road concept in my brain, I began to grow afraid that something would happen to me before sailing day, which was set for some time in January. I lived more circumspectly, drank less deeply, and went home more frequently. When drinking grew too wild, I got out. When Nelson was in his maniacal cups, I managed to get separated from him.

THAT DEAD MEN RISE UP NEVER

The month in which my seventeenth birthday arrived I signed on before the mast on the *Sophie Sutherland,* a three-topmast schooner bound on a seven-months' seal-hunting cruise to the coast of Japan. We sailed from San Francisco, and immediately I found confronting me a problem of no inconsiderable proportions. There were twelve men of us in the forecastle, ten of whom were hardened, tarry-thumbed sailors. Not alone was I a youth and on my first voyage, but I had for shipmates men who had come through the hard school of the merchant service of Europe. As boys, they had had to perform their ship's duty, and, in addition, by immemorial sea custom, they had had to be the slaves of the ordinary and able-bodied seamen. When they became ordinary seamen they were still the slaves of the able-bodied. Thus, in the forecastle, with the watch below, an able seaman, lying in his bunk, will order an ordinary seaman to fetch him his shoes or bring him a drink of water. Now the ordinary seaman may be lying in *his* bunk. He is just as tired as the able seaman. Yet he must get out of his bunk and fetch and carry. If he refuses, he will be beaten. If, perchance, he is so strong that he can whip the able seaman, then all the able seamen, or as many as may be necessary, pitch upon the luckless devil and administer the beating.

My problem now becomes apparent. These hard-bit Scandinavian sailors had come through a hard school. As boys they had served their mates, and as able seamen they looked to be served by other boys. I was a boy—withal with a man's body. I had never been to sea before—withal I was a good sailor and knew my business. It was either a case of holding my own with them or of going under. I had signed on as an equal, and an equal I must maintain myself, or else endure seven months of hell at their hands. And it was this very equality they resented. By what right was I an equal? I had not earned that high privilege. I had not endured the miseries they had endured as maltreated boys or bullied ordinaries. Worse than that, I was a landlubber making his first voyage. And yet, by the injustice of fate, on the ship's articles I was their equal.

My method was deliberate, and simple, and drastic. In the first place, I resolved to do my work, no matter how hard or dangerous it might be, so well that no man would be called upon to do it for me. Further, I put ginger in my muscles. I never malingered when pulling on a rope, for I knew the eagle eyes of my forecastle mates were squinting for just such evidences of my inferiority. I made it a point to be among the first of the watch going on deck, among the last going below, never leaving a sheet or tackle for some one else to coil over a pin. I was always eager for the run aloft for the shifting of topsail sheets and tacks, or for the setting or taking in of topsails; and in these matters I did more than my share.

Furthermore, I was on a hair-trigger of resentment myself. I knew better than to accept any abuse or the slightest patronizing. At the first hint of such, I went off—I exploded. I might be beaten in the subsequent fight, but I left the impression that I was a wild-cat and that I would just as willingly fight again. My intention was to demonstrate that I would tolerate no imposition. I proved that the man who imposed on me must have a fight on his hands. And, doing my work well, the innate justice of the men, assisted by their wholesome dislike for a clawing and rending wild-cat ruction, soon led them to give over their hectoring. After a bit of strife, my attitude was accepted, and it was my pride that I was taken in as an equal in spirit as well as in fact. From then on, everything was beautiful, and the voyage promised to be a happy one.

But there was one other man in the forecastle. Counting the Scandinavians as ten, and myself as the eleventh, this man was the twelfth and last. We never knew his name, contenting ourselves with calling him the "Bricklayer." He was from Missouri—at least he so informed us in the one meagre confidence he was guilty of in the early days of the voyage. Also, at that time, we learned several other things. He was a bricklayer by trade. He had never even seen salt water until the week before he joined us, at which time he had arrived in San Francisco and looked upon San Francisco Bay. Why he, of all men, at forty years of age, should have felt the prod to go to sea, was beyond all of us; for it was our unanimous conviction that no man less fitted for the sea had ever embarked on it. But to sea he had come. After a week's stay in a sailors' boarding-house, he had been shoved aboard of us as an able seaman.

All hands had to do his work for him. Not only did he know nothing, but he proved himself unable to learn anything. Try as they would, they could never teach him to steer. To him the compass must have been a profound and awful whirligig. He never mastered its cardinal points, much less the checking and steadying of the ship on her course. He never did come to know whether ropes should be coiled from left to right or from right to left. It was mentally impossible for him to learn the easy muscular trick of throwing his weight on a rope in pulling and hauling. The simplest knots and turns were beyond his comprehension, while he was mortally afraid of going aloft. Bullied by captain and mate, he was one day forced aloft. He managed to get underneath the crosstrees, and there he froze to the ratlines. Two sailors had to go after him to help him down.

All of which was bad enough had there been no worse. But he was vicious, malignant, dirty, and without common decency. He was a tall, powerful man, and he fought with everybody. And there was no fairness in his fighting. His first fight on board, the first day out, was with me, when he, desiring to cut a plug of chewing tobacco, took my personal table-knife for the purpose, and whereupon, I, on a hair-trigger, promptly exploded. After that he fought with nearly every member of the crew. When his clothing became too filthy to be bearable by the rest of us, we put it to soak and stood over him while he washed it. In short, Bricklayer was one of those horrible monstrous things one must see in order to be convinced that they exist.

I will only say that he was a beast, and that we treated him like a beast. It is only by looking back through the years that I realise how heartless we were to him. He was without sin. He could not, by the very nature of things, have been anything else than he was. He had not made himself, and for his making he was not responsible. Yet we treated him as a free agent and held him personally responsible for all that he was and that he should not have been. As a result, our treatment of him was as terrible as he was himself terrible. Finally we gave him the silent treatment, and for weeks before he died we neither spoke to him nor did he speak to us. And for weeks he moved among us, or lay in his bunk in our crowded house, grinning at us his hatred and malignancy. He was a dying man, and he knew it, and we knew it. And furthermore, he knew that we wanted him to die. He cumbered our life with his presence, and ours was a rough life that made rough men of us. And so he died, in a small space crowded by twelve men and as much alone as if he had died on some desolate mountain peak. No kindly word, no last word, was passed between. He died as he had lived, a beast, and he died hating us and hated by us.

And now I come to the most startling moment of my life. No sooner was he dead than he was flung overboard. He died in a night of wind, drawing his last breath as the men tumbled into their oilskins to the cry of "All hands!" And he was flung overboard, several hours later, on a day of wind. Not even a canvas wrapping graced his mortal remains; nor was he deemed worthy of bars of iron at his feet. We sewed him up in the blankets in which he died and laid him on a hatch-cover for'ard of the main-hatch on the port side. A gunnysack, half-full of galley coal, was fastened to his feet.

It was bitter cold. The weather-side of every rope, spar, and stay was coated with ice, while all the rigging was a harp, singing and shouting under the fierce hand of the wind. The schooner, hove to, lurched and floundered through the sea, rolling her scuppers under and perpetually flooding the deck with icy salt water. We of the forecastle stood in sea-boots and oilskins. Our hands were mittened, but our heads were bared in the presence of the death we did not respect. Our ears stung and numbed and whitened, and we yearned for the body to be gone. But the interminable reading of the burial service went on. The captain had mistaken his place, and while he read on without purpose we froze our ears and resented this final hardship thrust upon us by the helpless cadaver. As from the beginning, so to the end, everything had gone wrong with the Bricklayer. Finally, the captain's son, irritated beyond measure, jerked the book from the palsied fingers of the old man and found the place. Again the quavering voice of the captain arose. Then came the cue: "And the body shall be cast into the sea." We elevated one end of the hatch-cover, and the Bricklayer plunged outboard and was gone.

Back into the forecastle we cleaned house, washing out the dead man's bunk and removing every vestige of him. By sea law and sea custom, we should have gathered his effects together and turned them over to the captain, who, later, would have held an auction in which we should have bid for the various articles. But no man wanted them, so we tossed them up on deck and overboard in the wake of the departed body—the last ill-treatment we could devise to wreak upon the one we had hated so. Oh, it was raw, believe me; but the life we lived was raw, and we were as raw as the life.

The Bricklayer's bunk was better than mine. Less sea water leaked down through the deck into it, and the light was better for lying in bed and reading. Partly for this reason I proceeded to move into his bunk. My other reason was pride. I saw the sailors were superstitious, and by this act I determined to show that I was braver than they. I would cap my proved equality by a deed that would compel their recognition of my superiority. Oh, the arrogance of youth! But let that pass. The sailors were appalled by my intention. One and all, they warned me that in the history of the sea no man had taken a dead man's bunk and lived to the end of the voyage. They instanced case after case in their personal experience. I was obdurate. Then they begged and pleaded with me, and my pride was tickled in that they showed they really liked me and were concerned about me. This but served to confirm me in my madness. I moved in, and, lying in the dead man's bunk, all afternoon and evening listened to dire prophecies of my future. Also were told stories of awful deaths and gruesome ghosts that secretly shivered the hearts of all of us. Saturated with this, yet scoffing at it, I rolled over at the end of the second dog-watch and went to sleep.

At ten minutes to twelve I was called, and at twelve I was dressed and on deck, relieving the man who had called me. On the sealing grounds, when hove to, a watch of only a single man is kept through the night, each man holding the deck for an hour. It was a dark night, though not a black one. The gale was breaking up, and the clouds were thinning. There should have been a moon, and, though invisible, in some way a dim, suffused radiance came from it. I paced back and forth across the deck amidships. My mind was filled with the event of the day and with the horrible tales my shipmates had told, and yet I dare to say, here and now, that I was not afraid. I was a healthy animal, and furthermore, intellectually, I agreed with Swinburne that dead men rise up never. The Bricklayer was dead, and that was the end of it. He would rise up never—at least, never on the deck of the *Sophie Sutherland.* Even then he was in the ocean depths miles to windward of our leeward drift, and the likelihood was that he was already portioned out in the maws of many sharks. Still, my mind pondered on the tales of the ghosts of dead men I had heard, and I speculated on the spirit world. My conclusion was that if the spirits of the dead still roamed the world they carried the goodness or the malignancy of the earth-life with them. Therefore, granting the hypothesis (which I didn't grant at all), the ghost of the Bricklayer was bound to be as hateful and malignant as he in life had been. But there wasn't any Bricklayer's ghost—that I insisted upon.

A few minutes, thinking thus, I paced up and down. Then, glancing casually for'ard, along the port side, I leaped like a startled deer and in a blind madness of terror rushed aft along the poop, heading for the cabin. Gone was all my arrogance of youth and my intellectual calm. I had seen a ghost. There, in the dim light, where we had flung the dead man overboard, I had seen a faint and wavering form. Six feet in length it was, slender, and of substance so attenuated that I had distinctly seen through it the tracery of the fore-rigging.

As for me, I was as panic-stricken as a frightened horse. I, as I, had ceased to exist. Through me were vibrating the fibre-instincts of ten thousand generations of superstitious forebears who had been afraid of the dark and the things of the dark. I was not I. I was, in truth, those ten thousand forebears. I was the race, the whole human race, in its superstitious infancy. Not until part way down the cabin-companionway did my identity return to me. I checked my flight and clung to the steep ladder, suffocating, trembling, and dizzy. Never, before nor since, have I had such a shock. I clung to the ladder and considered. I could not doubt my senses. That I had seen something there was no discussion. But what was it? Either a ghost or a joke. There could be nothing else. If a ghost, the question was: would it appear again? If it did not, and I aroused the ship's officers, I would make myself the laughing stock of all on board. And by the same token, if it were a joke, my position would be still more ridiculous. If I were to retain my hard-won place of equality, it would never do to arouse any one until I ascertained the nature of the thing.

I am a brave man. I dare to say so; for in fear and trembling I crept up the companionway and went back to the spot from which I had first seen the thing. It had vanished. My bravery was qualified, however. Though I could see nothing, I was afraid to go for'ard to the spot where I had seen the thing. I resumed my pacing up and down, and though I cast many an anxious glance toward the dread spot, nothing manifested itself. As my equanimity returned to me, I concluded that the whole affair had been a trick of the imagination and that I had got what I deserved for allowing my mind to dwell on such matters.

Once more my glances for'ard were casual, and not anxious; and then, suddenly, I was a madman, rushing wildly aft. I had seen the thing again, the long, wavering attenuated substance through which could be seen the fore-rigging. This time I had reached only the break of the poop when I checked myself. Again I reasoned over the situation, and it was pride that counselled strongest. I could not afford to make myself a laughing stock. This thing, whatever it was, I must face alone. I must work it out myself. I looked back to the spot where we had tilted the Bricklayer. It was vacant. Nothing moving. And for a third time I resumed my amidships pacing.

In the absence of the thing my fear died away and my intellectual poise returned. Of course it was not a ghost. Dead men did not rise up. It was a joke, a cruel joke. My mates of the forecastle, by some unknown means, were frightening me. Twice already must they have seen me run aft. My cheeks burned with shame. In fancy I could hear the smothered chuckling and laughter even then going on in the forecastle. I began to grow angry. Jokes were all very well, but this was carrying the thing too far. I was the youngest on board, only a youth, and they had no right to play tricks on me of the order that I well knew in the past had made raving maniacs of men and women. I grew angrier and angrier, and resolved to show them that I was made of sterner stuff and at the same time to wreak my resentment upon them. If the thing appeared again, I made my mind up that I would go up to it—furthermore, that I would go up to it knife in hand. When within striking distance, I would strike. If a man, he would get the knife-thrust he deserved. If a ghost, well, it wouldn't hurt the ghost any, while I would have learned that dead men did rise up.

Now I was very angry, and I was quite sure the thing was a trick; but when the thing appeared a third time, in the same spot, long, attenuated, and wavering, fear surged up in me and drove most of my anger away. But I did not run. Nor did I take my eyes from the thing. Both times before, it had vanished while I was running away, so I had not seen the manner of its going. I drew my sheath-knife from my belt and began my advance. Step by step, nearer and nearer, the effort to control myself grew more severe. The struggle was between my will, my identity, my very self, on the one hand, and on the other, the ten thousand ancestors who were twisted into the fibres of me and whose ghostly voices were whispering of the dark and the fear of the dark that had been theirs in the time when the world was dark and full of terror.

I advanced more slowly, and still the thing wavered and flitted with strange eerie lurches. And then, right before my eyes, it vanished. I saw it vanish. Neither to the right nor left did it go, nor backward. Right there, while I gazed upon it, it faded away, ceased to be. I didn't die, but I swear, from what I experienced in those few succeeding moments, that I know full well that men can die of fright. I stood there, knife in hand, swaying automatically to the roll of the ship, paralysed with fear. Had the Bricklayer suddenly seized my throat with corporeal fingers and proceeded to throttle me, it would have been no more than I expected. Dead men did rise up, and that would be the most likely thing the malignant Bricklayer would do.

But he didn't seize my throat. Nothing happened. And, since nature abhors a status, I could not remain there in the one place forever paralysed. I turned and started aft. I did not run. What was the use? What chance had I against the malevolent world of ghosts? Flight, with me, was the swiftness of my legs. But pursuit, with a ghost, was the swiftness of thought. And there were ghosts. I had seen one.

And so, stumbling slowly aft, I discovered the explanation of the seeming. I saw the mizzen-topmast lurching across a faint radiance of cloud behind which was the moon. The idea leaped in my brain. I extended the line between the cloudy radiance and the mizzen-topmast and found that it must strike somewhere near the fore-rigging on the port side. Even as I did this, the radiance vanished. The driving clouds of the breaking gale were alternately thickening and thinning before the face of the moon but never exposing the face of the moon. And when the clouds were at their thinnest, it was a very dim radiance that the moon was able to make. I watched and waited. The next time the clouds thinned I looked for'ard, and there was the shadow of the topmast, long and attenuated, wavering and lurching on the deck and against the rigging.

This was my first ghost. Once again have I seen a ghost. It proved to be a Newfoundland dog, and I don't know which of us was the more frightened, for I hit that Newfoundland a full right-arm swing to the jaw. Regarding the Bricklayer's ghost, I will say that I never mentioned it to a soul on board. Also, I will say that in all my life I never went through more torment and mental suffering than on that lonely night-watch on the *Sophie Sutherland*.

We completed our run across the Pacific, lifted the volcanic peaks, jungle-clad, of the Bonin Islands, sailed in among the reefs to the landlocked harbor, and let our anchor rumble down where lay a score or more of sea-gipsies like ourselves. The scents of strange vegetation blew off the tropic land. Aborigines, in queer outrigger canoes, and Japanese, in queerer sampans, paddled about the bay and came aboard. It was my first foreign land; I had won to the other side of the world, and I would see all I had read in the books come true. I was wild to get ashore.

Victor and Axel, a Swede and a Norwegian, and I planned to keep together. (And so well did we, that for the rest of the cruise we were known as the "Three Sports.") Victor pointed out a pathway that disappeared up a wild canyon, emerged on a steep, bare lava-slope, and thereafter appeared and disappeared, ever climbing, among the palms and flowers. We would go over that path, he said, and we agreed, and we would see beautiful scenery, and strange native villages, and find Heaven alone knew what adventure at the end. And Axel was keen to go fishing. The three of us agreed to that, too. We would get a sampan, and a couple of Japanese fishermen who knew the fishing grounds, and we would have great sport. As for me, I was keen for anything.

And then, our plans made, we rowed ashore over the banks of living coral and pulled our boat up the white beach of coral sand. We walked across the fringe of beach under the cocoanut palms and into the little town, and found several hundred riotous seamen from all the world, drinking prodigiously, singing prodigiously, dancing prodigiously—and all on the main street to the scandal of a helpless handful of Japanese police.

Victor and Axel said we'd have a drink before we started on our long walk. Could I decline to drink with these two chesty shipmates? Drinking together, glass in hand, put the seal on comradeship. It was the way of life. . . .

Queer, fierce, alcoholic stuff it was that we drank. There was no telling where or how it had been manufactured—some native concoction, most likely. But it was hot as fire, pale as water, and quick as death with its kick. It had been filled into empty "square-face" bottles which had once contained Holland gin and which still bore the fitting legend: "Anchor Brand." It certainly anchored us. We never got out of the town. We never went fishing in the sampan. And though we were there ten days, we never trod that wild path along the lava-cliffs and among the flowers.

We met old acquaintances from other schooners, fellows we had met in the saloons of San Francisco before we sailed. And each meeting meant a drink; and there was much to talk about; and more drinks; and songs to be sung; and pranks and antics to be performed; until the maggots of imagination began to crawl, and it all seemed great and wonderful to me, these lusty, hard-bitten sea-rovers, of whom I made one, gathered in wassail on a coral strand. Old lines about knights at table in the great banquet-halls, and of those above the salt and below the salt, and of Vikings feasting fresh from sea and ripe for battle, came to me; and I knew that the old times were not dead and that we belonged to that selfsame ancient breed.

. . . The main street was a madness. Hundreds of sailors rollicked up and down. Because the chief of police with his small force was helpless, the governor of the colony had issued orders to the captains to have all their men on board by sunset.

What! To be treated in such fashion! As the news spread among the schooners, they were emptied. Everybody came ashore. Men who had had no intention of coming ashore, climbed into the boats. The unfortunate governor's *ukase* had precipitated a general debauch for all hands. It was hours after sunset, and the men wanted to see anybody try to put them on board. They went around inviting the authorities to try to put them on board. In front of the governor's house they were gathered thickest, brawling sea-songs, circulating square-faces, and dancing uproarious Virginia reels and old-country dances. The police, including the reserves, stood in little forlorn groups, waiting for the command the governor was too wise to issue. And I thought this saturnalia was great. It was like the old days of the Spanish Main come back. It was license; it was adventure. And I was part of it, a chesty sea-rover along with all these other chesty sea-rovers among the paper houses of Japan.

The governor never issued the order to clear the streets, and Axel and I wandered on from drink to drink. After a time, in some of the antics, getting hazy myself, I lost him. I drifted along, making new acquaintances, downing more drinks, getting hazier and hazier. I remember, somewhere, sitting in a circle with Japanese fishermen, kanaka boat-steerers from our own vessels, and a young Danish sailor fresh from cowboying in the Argentine and with a penchant for native customs and ceremonials. And with due and proper and most intricate Japanese ceremonial, we of the circle drank *sake*, pale, mild, and lukewarm, from tiny porcelain bowls.

And, later, I remember the runaway apprentices—boys of eighteen and twenty, of middle class English families, who had jumped their ships and apprenticeships in various ports of the world and drifted into the forecastles of the sailing schooners. They were healthy, smooth-skinned, clear-eyed, and they were young—youths like me, learning the way of their feet in the world of men. And they *were* men. No mild *sake* for them, but square-faces illicitly refilled with corrosive fire that flamed through their veins and burst into conflagrations in their heads . . . And one last picture I have, standing out very clear and bright in the midst of vagueness before and blackness afterward. We—the apprentices and I—are swaying and clinging to one another under the stars. We are singing a rollicking sea-song, all save one who sits on the ground and weeps; and we are marking the rhythm with waving square-faces. From up and down the street come far choruses of sea-voices similarly singing, and life is great, and beautiful, and romantic, and magnificently mad.

And next, after the blackness, I open my eyes in the early dawn to see a Japanese woman, solicitously anxious, bending over me. She is the port-pilot's wife, and I am lying in her doorway. I am chilled and shivering, sick with the after sickness of debauch. And I feel lightly clad. Those rascals of run-away apprentices! They have acquired the habit of running away. They have run away with my possessions. My watch is gone. My few dollars are gone. My coat is gone. So is my belt. And yes, my shoes.

And the foregoing is a sample of the ten days I spent in the Bonin Islands . . . we never climbed that lava-path among the flowers. The town and the square-faces were all we saw.

North we raced from the Bonin Islands to pick up the seal-herd, and north we hunted it for a hundred days into frosty, wintry weather and into and through vast fogs which hid the sun from us for a week at a time. . . .

The deck was a slaughter-house, week in and week out. There wasn't a malingerer left among us since the Bricklayer slid overside; and we kept up a lively competition to see who would have the biggest number of skins salted down at the close of the season. It was wild, heavy work off the coast of Siberia, with no let-up weeks on end.

Possibly the proudest achievement of my life, my moment of highest living, occurred when . . . we were in a typhoon. All hands had been on deck most of the night. I was called from my bunk at seven in the morning to take the wheel. Not a stitch of canvas was set. We were running before it under bare poles, yet the schooner fairly tore along. The seas were all of an eighth of a mile apart, and the wind snatched the whitecaps from their summits, filling the air so thick with driving spray that it was impossible to see more than two waves at a time. The schooner was almost unmanageable, rolling her rail under to starboard and to port, veering and yawing anywhere between southeast and southwest, and threatening, when the huge sea lifted under her quarter, to broach to. Had she broached to, she would ultimately have been reported lost with all hands and no tidings.

I took the wheel. The sailing-master watched me for a space. He was afraid of my youth, feared that I lacked the strength and the nerve. But when he saw me successfully wrestle the schooner through several bouts, he went below to breakfast. Fore and aft, all hands were below at breakfast. Had she broached to, not one of them would ever have reached the deck. For forty minutes I stood there alone at the wheel, in my grasp the wildly careening schooner and the lives of twenty-two men. Once we were pooped. I saw it coming, and, half-drowned with tons of water crushing me, I checked the schooner's rush to broach to. At the end of the hour, sweating and played out, I was relieved. But I had done it! With my own hands I had done my trick at the wheel and guided a hundred tons of wood and iron through a few million tons of wind and waves.

Jack London

Chronology

1876 January 12. Born in San Francisco, California, to Flora Wellman and "Professor" William Chaney, an astrologer who deserted her during pregnancy. September 7. Flora marries John London, a widower who adopts Jack.

1876–92 Unsuccessful as a farmer and rancher, John London moves family to Oakland. Jack leaves school; works in a cannery. Borrows $300 to buy the "Razzle Dazzle," a small sloop, and becomes an oyster pirate on lower San Francisco Bay; eventually joins the California Fish Patrol. At fifteen he is a regular among sailors and longshoremen in Oakland waterfront saloons.

1893 Signs on board the sealing ship "Sophia Sutherland" for seven months in the Asian Pacific. Although almost completely uneducated, he begins writing.

1894 Travels across U.S. as a hobo; arrested several times for vagrancy; later recounted in "The Road" (1907).

1895 Returns to Oakland, finishes High School; discovers literature.

1896 Attends University of California for one semester. Increasing political awareness leads him to join Socialist Labor Party. Discovers Marx, Nietzsche, Darwin.

1897 Travels to the Yukon during Klondike gold rush. John London dies.

1898 Finds no gold; returns broke. Decides to make his living from his mind, not manual labor. Begins writing seriously.

1899 *Overland Monthly* magazine buys first story, *To The Man on the Trail.* Sells political articles to San Francisco newspapers; becomes known locally as the "Boy Socialist from Oakland."

1900 Marries Bessie Maddern. First national magazine, *Atlantic Monthly,* buys *Odyssey of the North.* Publishes first book, *Son of the Wolf* (stories).

1901 January 15. Daughter Joan born.

1902 Travels to England; spends two months in East London slum, later recounted in *People of the Abyss* (1903). October 20. Daughter Becky born. First novel, *A Daughter of the Snows,* published.

1903 Publishes *Call of the Wild* to instant international acclaim.

1904 Divorce from Bessie makes national headline. Correspondent in Russo-Japanese war for Hearst. Publishes *The Sea Wolf.*

1905 Marries Charmian Kittredge, buys ranch at Glen Ellen, California. Lecture tour across U.S. Publishes Socialist essays, *War of the Classes.*

1906 Covers San Francisco earthquake for *Colliers.* Builds sailboat "Snark."

1907–9 Sails across Pacific on the "Snark." Publishes *The Road* (1907), *The Iron Heel* (1908), *Martin Eden* (1909).

1910 Begins building mansion at Glen Ellen. Publishes *South Sea Tales.*

1913 Writes autobiographical account of his alcoholism in bestselling *John Barleycorn.* Glen Ellen house mysteriously burns down.

1915 *Colliers* correspondent in Mexican Revolution. Health failing.

1916 Resigns from Socialist Party. Dies November 22 from overdose of morphine which had been prescribed for gastrointestinal uremia. It is still debated whether the overdose was an accident or suicide.